The Brothers of Gwynedd

Edith Pargeter

Comprising
Sunrise in the West
The Dragon at Noonday
The Hounds of Sunset
Afterglow and Nightfall

HEADLINE

CONTENTS

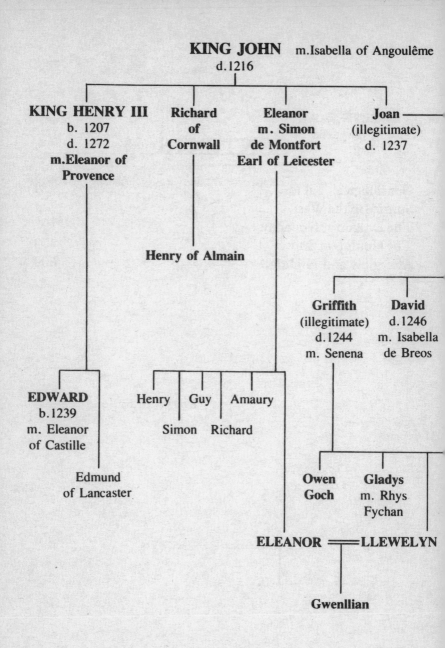

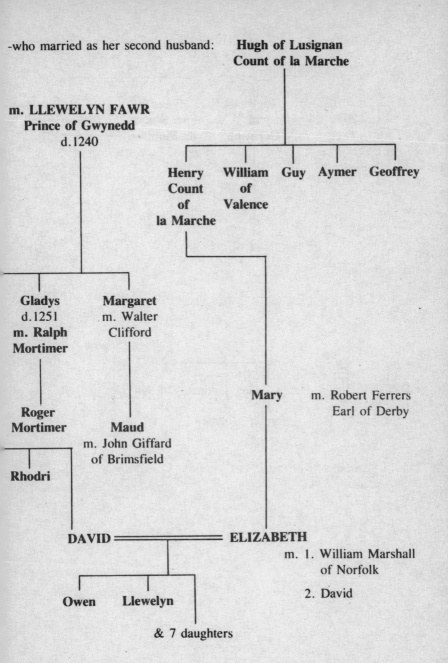

-who married as her second husband: **Hugh of Lusignan Count of la Marche**

m. LLEWELYN FAWR Prince of Gwynedd d.1240

Henry Count of la Marche   **William of Valence**   **Guy**   **Aymer**   **Geoffrey**

Gladys d.1251 m. Ralph Mortimer

Margaret m. Walter Clifford

Mary   m. Robert Ferrers Earl of Derby

Roger Mortimer

Maud m. John Giffard of Brimsfield

Rhodri

DAVID ══════ **ELIZABETH**

      m. 1. William Marshall of Norfolk

        2. David

Owen   **Llewelyn**

& 7 daughters

The chronicle of the Lord Llewelyn, son of Griffith, son of Llewelyn, son of Iorwerth, lord of Gwynedd, the eagle of Snowdon, the shield of Eryri, first and only true Prince of Wales.

CHAPTER 1

My name is Samson. I tell what I know, what I have seen with my own eyes and heard with my own ears. And if it should come to pass that I must tell also what I have not seen, that, too, shall be made plain, and how I came to know it so certainly that I tell it as though I had been present. And I say now that there is no man living has a better right to be my lord's chronicler, for there is none ever knew him better than I, and God He knows there is none, man or woman, ever loved him better.

Now the manner of my begetting was this:

My mother was a waiting-woman in the service of the Lady Senena, wife of the Lord Griffith, who was elder son to Llewelyn the Great, prince of Aberffraw and lord of Snowdon, the supreme chieftain of North Wales, and for all he never took the name, master of all Wales while he lived, and grandsire and namesake to my own lord, whose story I tell. The Lord Griffith was elder son, but with this disability, that he was born out of marriage. His mother was Welsh and noble, but she was not a wife, and this was the issue that cost Wales dear after his father's death. For in Wales a son is a son, to acknowledge him is to endow him with every right of establishment and inheritance, no less than among his brothers born in wedlock, but the English and the Normans think in another fashion, and have this word 'bastard' which we do not know, as though it were shame to a child that he did not call a priest to attend those who engendered him before he saw the light. Howbeit, the great prince, Llewelyn, Welsh though he was and felt to the marrow of his bones, had England to contend with, and so did contend to good purpose all his life long, and knew that only by setting up a claim of absolute legitimacy, by whatever standard, could he hope to ensure his heir a quiet passage into possession of his right, and Wales a self-life secure from the enmity of England. Moreover, he loved his wife, who was King John's daughter, passing well, and her son, who was named David, clung most dearly of all things living about his father's heart, next only after his mother.

Yet it cannot be said that the great prince ever rejected or deprived his elder son, for he set him up in lands rich and broad enough, and made use of his talents both in war and diplomacy. Only he was absolute in reserving to a single heir the principality of Gwynedd, and that heir was the son acceptable and kin to the English king.

But the Lord Griffith being of a haughty and ungovernable spirit, for spite at being denied what he held to be his full right under Welsh law, plundered and abused even what he had, and twice the prince was moved by complaints of mismanagement and injustice to take from him what had been bestowed, and even to make the offender prisoner until he should give pledges of better usage. This did but embitter still further the great bitterness he felt rather towards his brother than his father, and the rivalry between those two was a burden and a threat to Gwynedd continually.

At the time of which I tell, which was Easter of the year of Our Lord twelve hundred and twenty-eight, the Lord Griffith was at liberty and in good favour, and spent the feast on his lands in Lleyn, at Nevin where his court then was. And there came as guests at this festival certain chiefs and lesser princes from other regions of Wales, Rhys Mechyll of Dynevor, and Cynan ap Hywel of Cardigan, and some others whose attachment to the prince and his authority was but slack and not far to be trusted. Moreover, they came in some strength, each with a company of officers and men-at-arms of his bodyguard, though whether in preparation for some planned and concerted action against the good order of Gywnedd, as was afterwards believed, or because they had no great trust in one another, will never be truly known. Thus they spent the Eastertide at Nevin, with much men's talk among the chiefs, in which the Lord Griffith took the lead.

At this time the Lord David had been acknowledged as sole heir to his father's princedom by King Henry of England, his uncle, and also by an assembly of the magnates of Wales; but some, though they raised no voice against, made murmur in private still that this was against the old practice and law of Wales, and spoke for Griffith's right. Therefore it was small wonder that Prince Llewelyn, whose eyes and ears were everywhere, took note of this assembly at Nevin, and at the right moment sent his high steward and his private guard to occupy the court and examine the acts and motives of all those there gathered. David he did not send, for he would have him held clean of whatever measure need be taken against his brother. There was bitterness enough already.

They came, and they took possession. Those chiefs were held to account, questioned closely, made to give hostages every one for his future loyalty, and so dispersed with their followings to their own lands. And until their departures, all their knights and men-at-arms were held close prisoner under lock and key, and the household saw no more of them. As for the Lord Griffith, he was summoned to his father at Aber, to answer for what seemed a dangerous conspiracy, and not being able to satisfy the prince's council, he was again committed to imprisonment in the Castle of Degannwy, where he remained fully six years.

In those few days at Easter, before the prince struck, the Lady Senena conceived her second son. And my mother, the least of her waiting-women, conceived me.

My mother came of a bardic line, was beautiful, and had a certain lightness of hand at needlework and the dressing of hair, but she was never quite as other women are. She was simple and trusting as a child, she spoke little, and then as a child; yet again not quite as a child, for sometimes she spoke prophecy. For awe of her strangeness men fought shy of her, in spite of her beauty, and she was still unmarried at eighteen.

But the unknown officer whose eye fell upon her among the maids that Eastertide had not marriage in mind, and was not afraid of prophecy. She was young and fair, and did not resist him. She spoke of him afterwards with liking and some wonder, as of a strange visitant come to her in a dream. He took her in the rushes under the wall hangings in a corner of the hall. The next day the prince's guard rode in, and he was herded into the stables among the other prisoners until all were dismissed home. She never saw him again, never knew his name, or even whose man he was, and from what country. But he left her a ring by way of remembrance. A ring, and me.

That same night, for all I know that same moment, in the high chamber at Nevin, in the glow of vengeful hope and resolution, the Lord Griffith got his third child and second son upon the Lady Senena. Certain it is that we were born the same day. Nor was the lady more fortunate than her maid. For six years she saw no more of her husband, for he was held fast in the castle of Degannwy, over against Aberconway, and she here in Lleyn, on sufferance and under surveillance, kept his remaining lands as best she could, and waited her time.

At the beginning of the year of Our Lord, twelve hundred and twenty-nine, in January snows, in the deepest frost of a starry night at Griffith's maenol of Neigwl, we were born, my lord and I. The Lady Senena named her son Llewelyn, perhaps in a gesture of conciliation towards his grandsire, for beyond doubt it was in her interests to woo the prince, and she had more hope of winning some favour from him in the absence of her husband's fiery temper and haughty person. Certain it is that she did bring the child early to his grandfather's notice, and the prince took pleasure in him, and had him frequently about him as soon as the boy was of an age to ride and hunt. With children he was boisterous, kind and tolerant, and this namesake of his delighted him by showing, from the first, absolute trust and absolute fearlessness.

As for me, my mother named me after that good Welsh saint who left his hermitage at Severnside to travel oversea to France, to become archbishop of Dol, and the friend and confidant of kings. As I have been told, that befell some five hundred years ago, and more. Perhaps my mother hoped for some sign of his visiting holiness in me, his namesake, for I had great need of a blessing from God, having none from men. I think that at first, when she found her innocent was with child, the Lady Senena made some attempt to discover who had fathered me, that he might be given the opportunity to acknowledge me freely, according to custom, and provide me when grown with a kinship in which I should have a man's place assured. But my mother knew nothing of him but his warmth and the touch of his hands, not even the clear vision of a face, much less a name, for it was no better than deep twilight in the hall where they lay. And those who had visited, that Easter, were so many that it was hopeless to follow and question them all. And the ring, as I know, she never showed. For even to me she never showed it until I left her for the last time.

It may be that had not the prince's raid put an end to all play he would have looked for her again, and not grudged her his name, whether he meant a match or no. But that bold stroke put an end to more things than my mother's brief love, and I was fatherless.

They tell me, and I believe it, that in those first years in Lleyn I was the constant companion of the young Llewelyn, that we played together and slept together, and that sometimes, even, I was the leader and he the follower, and not the other way round, as I should have judged invariable and inevitable. But this part of my life lasted not long, and the memory of it which I retain is of a sunny, disseminated bliss, void of detail. It ended soon. When I was five years old one of the Lady Senena's grooms took a fixed fancy to my mother, and offered marriage, and though she was without any strong wish one way or the other, she did always what her mistress desired, and to the lady this seemed a happy way out of a problem and a burden. Others aforetime had been caught by my mother's beauty, but all had been frightened away by her mute and mysterious strangeness. This man – he was young and strong and good to look upon – wanted her more than he shrank from her. So she was married to him, she acquiescing indifferently in all.

Me, as it proved, he did not want. Before marriage, though he knew of me, I had counted for nothing. But now that he had her, and could in no wise move her to any show of passion, whether of love or hate or fear, or get from her any response but the calm, uncaring submission she showed him always, he began to look round everywhere about her for whatever could touch where he could not, move where he was but suffered, strike a spark where his fire and tinder failed. And he found me.

That year I had with him I do remember still, as one remembers a distant vision of hell. I have been hated, and that most thoroughly. What he could do to avenge himself upon me he did, with every manner of blow and bruise and burn, with every skill of keeping me from the sight of my betters and the company of my prince-playmate. Whatever comforted me he removed, or broke, or soiled and ruined. Whatever I loved he harmed, so that I learned to hide love. And though he never maltreated me before the Lady Senena, he took a delight in letting my mother see my misery. He thought by then that she had not that core of life in her that others have, to make any voluntary action possible, and that she could do nothing to save me.

That he did not know her is not a matter for wonder, for I think none ever did know her, certainly not her son. She was a secret from all men, and she held more possibilities than any man thought for.

When the Lord Griffith had been six years in prison he made an act of submission to his father, and was released, and restored at first to the half of his old lands in Lleyn, and then, when he continued in good odour, to the whole of that cantref. It was the occasion of great joy to his wife and her court, life was set in motion again in the old manner, and it was a time for asking favours. My mother knew the moment to approach her mistress, and did so in my interest, though thereby losing me. For she begged her lady to take me in charge for my protection, and said that she had a great wish to see me lettered, and a priest.

Now the Lady Senena was herself royal, for she was great-granddaughter to Rhodri, lord of Anglesey, and came of a race which had been lavish in gifts both to the old Welsh colleges of lay canons and the new Cistercian abbeys and Franciscan friaries. Therefore she had but to indicate, to whatever community she thought best, her wish that I should be accepted into care and taught, and it was as good as done. She placed me with the lay canons at Aberdaron, in her own Lleyn, and gave a generous sum for my endowment there. And thus I escaped my purgatory and got my schooling at her expense, and her name was shield enough over me, even if the brothers had not been the saints they were.

Nevertheless, I wept when I parted from my mother. But then I thought of her husband, and I did not weep. And Nevin was not so far that she could not visit me now and again, or I her. So I went without more tears, though a little afraid of the strangeness before me. I was then six years old, within a month. It was shortly before the Christmas feast.

Now the clas at Aberdaron was one of the best regarded and richest of all the colleges of North Wales, which were themselves the flower of all the land, unsullied by Norman interference. For it lay on the mainland directly opposite the blessed isle of Enlli, that men begin now to call Bardsey, and there the hermits have kept the old austere order pure to this day, and the very soil is made up of the bones of thousands of saints. Those who would withdraw to Enlli to die in holiness must come by Aberdaron. There they halt and enjoy the hospitality of the canons, and bring with them all the learning and piety and wisdom of mankind to add to the store. There could be no better place for a boy with a great thirst for knowledge. Even one who came with no such thirst could not choose but quicken to the fire of those visitors passing through.

There were twenty lay canons then at Aberdaron, and three priests, besides the abbot: a strong community. Because of the great number of travellers entertained there, the enclosure was large and fine, and there were many officers, among them, besides the scribe, a teacher. Into his hands I was confided. I slept in the doorway of his cell, and later had a cell of my own beside him. I had my share of work about the lands the canons tilled, according to my age, and I took my part in the services of the church, and learned my psalter in Latin by heart. But in the time that was left to me I had never enough of the marvel of studying, and once blessed with the first letters I ever learned, could not rest from adding to them. Finding my appetite was genuine, and not feigned in order to please, my teacher Ciaran took very kindly to me, and came as eagerly as I to the lessons we had together. In opening books to me, he opened the world, and he was good and gentle, and I loved him and was happy. From him I learned to read and write in Welsh and in Latin, and later also in English. And I began to help the steward who kept the books and accounts, for these values and amounts and reckonings were also strong enchantment to me.

Six years I spent thus in the purest peace and serenity, and all this while the world without went on its way, and the news of it came in to us like the distant sound of the waves on the shore, ominous to others, but no threat to our haven. The things that were told to me seemed like stories read in one of Ciaran's books, vivid and alarming, but not real, so that even alarm was pleasure. For the stories of the saints are full of terror and delight, no less than the legends of heroes that the bards recite to the harp.

So I heard that after the return of her lord the Lady Senena, in her joy at the reunion, again conceived, and her third son was born in the spring of the following year. A fourth followed a year later, David, the last of her five children. But whether she named him after his uncle, with that same hope of softening her lord's fortune which had prompted her to give her second son the name Llewelyn, I do not know. There was peace then between them, the prince had enlarged the Lord Griffith's lands greatly, adding to the whole cantref of Lleyn a large portion of the lands of Powys, designing, I think, to leave him with an appanage which should recompense him for the surrender of his wider rights by Welsh law, and reconcile him to becoming a loyal vassal of his brother. But it was not in his nature to see beyond his own wrong to a larger right, and he knew only the title of Gwynedd, and could not envisage Wales, for all he quoted Welsh law. A man is as he is. The Lord Griffith was a fine man, tall and splendid to look upon, fully as tall as his father, and he was of great stature, though gaunt, where Griffith was full of flesh. He was openhanded to a fault where men pleased him, and too quick to lash out where they displeased. He was hasty in suspicion of affront, and merciless in retaliation. He was readily moved by generosity, and lavish in returning it. He never forgot benefit or injury. But he could not see beyond what helped or hurt him and his, and that is a small circle in a vast world, too narrow for greatness.

Doubtless he loved, but never did he understand, his father, that Llewelyn who is rightly named the Great.

This last child of theirs, the boy David, touched my own fortunes nearly. For my mother had at last conceived by her husband, and brought forth a still-born girl three days before her lady bore her boy. And since the Lady Senena was low with a dangerous fever for two weeks after the delivery, and my mother was heavy with milk and yearning, she naturally became wet-nurse to the royal child. I had lost my sister, but I had a breast-brother, a prince of the blood-royal of Gwynedd, seven years and more my junior. This came early in my peace, and moved me deeply. I thought much of this helpless thing drawing its life from my mother, who had given me life also, and of whatever this mysterious thing might be that we two shared. And the bright, resolute, fearless creature who shared the stars of my birth with me, and who had been my fellow before I knew what royalty was, had fallen away from me then, and was almost forgotten.

I had been four years at Aberdaron, and was approaching my tenth birthday, when first we heard from a pilgrim bard that the great prince had been taken with a falling seizure. It was as if the earth had shaken under us. True, the attack was not severe, and had done no more than weaken him in the use of one arm, and draw his mouth a little awry, but we had never thought of him as being subject to age, like lesser men, even though he was now in his sixty-fifth year, for his vigour seemed to reach like a potent essence into the furthest corners of the land, and inspire even those, like me, who had never seen him in the flesh. Truly that flesh was now seen to be mortal. And the shudder of foreboding that shook most of Wales became a tremor of anticipation and hope to those who had sided with Griffith and were biding their time with him. And not only these, for beyond the march in England they surely licked their lips and tasted already the pickings the dogs find after the lion is dead. Him they had let alone now for four years, and would let alone while he lived, with all his conquests rich and fat about him, for they dared not tempt again the force they had ventured too often already to their cost. But with the great prince gone, and an unknown, or untried at least, in his place, then they would close in on all sides to snatch back, if they could, the many lands they had lost to him.

It was the first time that I had ever considered how those who felt as England felt towards us could hardly be anything but enemies to Wales; and it caused me some uneasiness even then, but being so young, I did not apply it too closely to those I had known and served all my life. And soon I forgot the qualm it had cost me, in thinking of other things. For towards the end of this same year – I think it was on the 19th of October, and the place I know was the abbey of Strata Florida, a foundation beloved of the prince and always faithful to his house – there was called a great assembly of all the princes of Wales, and there every man among them took the oath of fealty to David as the next heir. Then indeed we felt that death had moved a gentle step nearer to our lord, and none knew it better than he, or felt less fear of it for himself, or more for Wales. Doubtless he knew better than any how the marcher lords were sharpening their knives, and what a load his son would have to bear.

Now I cannot say whether this ceremony at Strata Florida so inflamed the mind of the Lord Griffith that he took some rash action to assert his rights, or whether the Lord David, armed with so formidable a support, moved against him in expectation of just such a defiance, but certain it is that at the end of this year Griffith was stripped of his lands in Powys, and left with only his cantref of Lleyn, and that by order of his younger brother. By which it was made clear to all that the Lord David had already assumed a part of his royal privilege before his father's death, and that undoubtedly with his father's knowledge and sanction, for no son in his right wits would have reached to take any morsel of power out of those great hands but by their goodwill and grace. And surely the lords along the march, who had lost so much to Gwynedd these last twenty years, were counting days and mustering men already. Prince David had King Henry's word to accept and acknowledge him, and none other, and doubtful though King Henry's troth might be, if it held for any it would hold for his nephew, his sister's son. She, that great lady, her husband's right hand and envoy and counsellor all her days, was dead then more than two years, and buried with all honour and great grief at Llanfaes in Anglesey. She had but one son, though her daughters were married into all the great houses of the march, for better assurance. Yet there remained the Lord Griffith, and he was irreconcilable. And the year following there was sudden bitter blaze between those two brothers, the confiscated lands held hostage being insufficient to keep the elder in check, rather goading him to worse hostility. And before the year was out we heard that David had taken his brother prisoner, and his eldest son Owen with him, and lodged them in the castle of Criccieth under lock and key.

This Owen Goch – 'the Red' by reason of his flaming hair – was the Lady Senena's first child, and being nearly three years older than I, was then approaching thirteen, only a year away from his majority. And I suppose that it seemed a folly to shut up the father and leave in his place a son on the edge of manhood, round whom the same discontents could gather. The girl Gladys came next, a year before Llewelyn. She would not present the same danger, and the younger boys were but children as yet, and could be left with their mother at liberty. Thus for the second time that household was broken apart, and the lady was left to protect her own and manage her family's affairs alone. But she was not molested in her home at Nevin, and the boy Llewelyn, they said, was welcome always at his grandsire's court, and spent more than half of his time there, very gladly, for there was life there, and hunting, and riding, and all the exercise and company a lively boy loves. Nor did his mother hinder, even when she knew that he was much in favour with his uncle David, who was childless by his wife Isabella. The boy was too young, said his mother, to understand, and could not be guilty of disloyalty to his house, and surely it was well to have one child covered by the protection of royal favour, a warranty against the loss of all, if the greatest must be lost. But I think, knowing or unknowing, she was using this boy to go back and forth in innocence and keep her informed of what went forward at Aber, while she waited for the prince to die. For she knew, none better, that there was a well of sympathy for Griffith's case, and that its time for gushing would not come while the lion yet lived. And she had learned how to wait with dignity, and in silence.

Yet I am not sure, even then, how right she was to trust in the innocence of her son Llewelyn. For even without art, news can flow two ways. And at what age art and wisdom begin is a mystery, and at what age those who will some day be men achieve the courage and the clarity to judge and choose and resolve, that is a greater mystery. And this was no ordinary child, with no ordinary grandsire. And they namesakes. There is magic in names.

Howbeit, on the tenth day of April of the year twelve hundred and forty the great Prince Llewelyn, feeling the heavy darkness draw in on him again, and this time believing it an end, had himself conveyed into the abbey of Aberconway, which he loved and had shielded so long, and there took the monastic habit, after the manner of great kings going to their judgment. And wrapped in this blessed cloth he died on the day following, and there his great body lies buried. And doubtless his greater soul has room enough now, even beyond that reach he had in this world. For he was the true friend and patron of the religious, wherever they preserved the purity and austerity of the faith, and whatsoever he did was done with grandeur and largeness of mind, and for Wales, which he loved beyond all things.

*　　*　　*

10

So David ap Llewelyn was Prince of Aberffraw and Lord of Snowdon in his father's room. And in May of that same year he attended King Henry's council at Gloucester, became a knight at the king's hands, after the English fashion, put on the talaith, the gold circlet of his state, and did homage for Gwynedd, pledging himself liegeman of the king of England as overlord, saving only his sovereign right within his own principality. All which had been many times done before, and was no surrender of any part of his due, but his own side of a covenant, of which the reverse was King Henry's sworn acknowledgement of his firm status as prince of North Wales. And the other great magnates of Wales did homage in their turn on the like understanding.

What did not appear was how wide a gulf yawned between the two conceptions of what that status meant. It was not long before all those lords marchers who had lost land to Llewelyn, however long ago, and all those border Welsh who held themselves aggrieved at surrendering to him commotes and castles forfeited for disloyalty, or taken in open battle, began to resort to law and to force, demanding from David the return of losses they would not have dared reclaim from his father. Thus the earl of Pembroke went with an army, in the teeth of the lord of that cantref, to rebuild his lost castle of Cardigan and plant a garrison there, while lawsuits came thick and fast over Mold, and Powys, and the lordship of Builth, which came legally to David as his wife's dower, but not without all possible resistance from her de Breos kin. Any and every disaffected lord, English or Welsh, who could bring a legal plea for the possession of land lost to the father, fairly or unfairly, turned now to rend the son. And King Henry, always maintaining his good faith in recognising his nephew's status, connived at all the activities of those who were bent on plucking his principality to pieces.

Nor was he so rich in solid friends on the borders as his father had been, for the line of Earl Ranulf, Llewelyn's lifelong ally and sympathiser, was extinct in Chester, and that earldom had gone back to the crown, laying bare all the northeast of Gwynedd to the assaults of the enemy.

David in this storm, perhaps not all unexpected but breaking upon him too soon, did his best to delay, after the English fashion, those lawsuits the English brought against him, and as a better instrument to his hand, chose rather than law to submit the impleaded lands to a council of arbitrators nominated from both sides, with the Pope's legate in England at their head. But this measure also he found to be acting against him, and fell back once more upon delay, sending excuses for failure to attend the meetings of a commission he now saw to be no more than a dagger in King Henry's hand. For this whole issue had now been channelled through the king and his council, making a quarrel between two countries rather than between mere men at odds over land. Thus he held off the pack for a year, his envoys, his father's old, able men, going backwards and forwards many times and using every art of persuasion and disruption, but in the end to no purpose. For King Henry saw that he had many allies, so many Welsh princes being either disaffected over land, or aggrieved by Griffith's captivity and disinheritance, and that all

11

that was obstinately being withheld from him by legal means he could acquire by force at little cost, something he dared not attempt beforetime. Having summoned David to appear before the commission at Montford on the Severn in June, and well knowing that he would not come, he made preparations for an attack in arms. And David, though he had word of the martial movements behind the summons, had no way left open to him but to absent himself, and let what must follow, follow.

I tell all this not as I saw it then, being little more than a child, and without understanding of many of the tidings I heard, but as I understood it later, when I had seen more of the world than the clas at Aberdaron. But I was not so young or so ignorant that I could not feel the threat as touching even me, when they spoke of the king of England moving into the marches at the end of July with a great force of men in arms, and setting up his court in Shrewsbury. For what could he be doing there in the borders but preparing the undoing of Gwynedd? Shrewsbury was a great way off, further than I could then imagine, but not so far that the English could not reach even this last corner of Lleyn with fire and sword if war once flared.

Yet I had no notion that events outside our enclosure and our fields and coast could ever touch me as a person, or draw me out of this haven I had grown to love and think of as my lifelong home.

They came for me on the last day of July, two grooms of the Lady Senena's household, bringing a third pony for me.

I was raking the early hay in the field above the shore, about noon, when Ciaran sent one of the brothers to call me in, for I had visitors with the abbot. A clear, bright day I remember it was, with a fresh breeze bringing inland the strong, warm scent of kelp from the beach below me, and the southward sea innocently restless, sparkling with the sun and its own motion. So beautiful a day that I went unwillingly, even believing it would be only for an hour, I who have never seen Aberdaron again.

Abbot Cadfael was waiting for me in the antechamber of the guesthouse within the enclosing walls and with him two men in the Lady Senena's livery. I saw their horses in the stable as I passed, not blown nor sweated, for it was no long ride from Neigwl, where the lady then had her household. The younger of the two riders I did not know. The elder it took me some minutes to know for my step-father. I had not seen him for six years, half my lifetime, and he was changed by double as many summers and winters, for men age by curious lurches and recoveries, now standing still in defiance of time for a dozen years, then sliding downhill by a decade in one season. These years with my mother had been his breaking time, for I think she had won, without fighting, that long battle between them. It was not that she could not love, but that he could not make her love. There was grey in his shaggy dark hair, and his face was hollow and hungry, with deep-sunken eyes. He had been a very comely man. Yet in one thing he was unchanged. I saw by the way his eyes hung upon me in silence that he hated me as of old. But it is one thing I can never forget to him, that as long as he lived he could not cease from loving her. And when I was old enough to understand that purgatory aright, and had myself some knowledge of the pain of love, then I forgave him all, for he was paid over and over for any injury he ever did me.

'Son,' said Abbot Cadfael very gravely, 'there is here a call for you to go out from among us, to another duty.'

At that I was clean knocked out of words and breath, as if one had attempted my life, for Aberdaron was my life, and I had thought it should be so always. I knew by rote already the vows I was to take, and waited for the time without impatience only because I was sure of it. And in one sentence all was taken away from me. I went on my knees to him, and when I could speak I said: 'Father, my heart is to this life and none other. My home is here, and all that I am is yours. How can I go hence, and keep any truth in me?'

He looked at me closely and thoughtfully for a long time, for I think I had not spoken as he had expected of a boy twelve years old. But he said only: 'Truth is everywhere, and your truth will go with you. Child, you were but lent to us a season, and she who lent you requires you of us again. It is not for you to choose, but to accept with humility. I have no right to deny you, nor you to refuse.'

I would have wept, but not with those deep eyes of my mother's husband watching me, for I still hated him then as he hated me. And I knew that the abbot spoke truth, for the Lady Senena had been my provider and protectress all these years, and by rights I belonged to her, and not only could not, but must not refuse her commands. She could cut off my endowment and have me put out of this refuge when she would, but that I knew she would not do. For though she was austere and hard of nature, she was also faithful to whatever she undertook, and would not avenge herself upon an underling. Therefore my debt to her was all the greater, and whatever she asked of me I must do. But to discover, if I might, the magnitude and the duration of my loss – for even losses can be regained after years – I questioned humbly after the cause of my recall.

'That,' said he, 'I cannot tell you. I have received the indication of her wishes, which are that you should return at once with these men, and rejoin your mother at Neigwl. It is your mother's wish also. They have need of you, and to be needed and to fill the need is the greatest privilege in life. Bearing God and his grace in mind always, go and give as you may. There is nothing to regret.'

I asked him, quivering: 'Father, if God will, may I come back?'

He raised his old, weak eyes from me, and looked beyond those men who had come to fetch me, out through the wall of the anteroom, through the high wall of the enclosure, and as far as the inward eye can see. 'Come when you may in good conscience, son,' he said, 'and you will be welcome.' But I knew by the sad calm of his face that he did not expect to see me again.

I asked him for his blessing, and he blessed me. A little he questioned me as to my knowledge, and the skills I had gained to take away with me, and commended me to maintain them all diligently. Then he kissed and dismissed me.

I put together what little I had, my copy of the psalter, a spare shirt, my ink-horn and pens, and the few little brushes I had for illuminating.

And I said my farewell to Ciaran, so barely that the poverty of words hung heavy on me all the way, and I doubted if he knew what I had within me unsaid, but doubt it not now, so long afterwards. Nor doubt that he prayed for me without ceasing, as long as he lived. And then we went. By the upland road we went, turning our backs on that blessed sea that leads outward over the watery brightness to the beauteous isle of Enlli, where the saints are sleeping in bliss. We went towards the rib of Lleyn, that leads into Wales as an arm leads into the body; from rest into turmoil, from peace into conflict, from bliss into anguish. Side by side we rode, my mother's husband and I, and the young groom a few paces behind us. And for three miles of that ride we never said a word for heaviness, however bright was the noonday sky over us.

I had not been on a horse since the day I was brought to Aberdaron, pillion behind a groom, for the brothers of the pure communities abjured not only women, and the eating of flesh, but also riding on horseback. And I was awkward enough, and before we reached Neigwl sore enough, on that broad-backed hill pony, but I kept my seat with some pleasure, and my head high and my back straight with more obstinacy, riding beside this man who hated me, in such mourne silence. I had then no fear of him, and that was surprising to me, though I knew the good reasons for it. He dared not now touch me, if he had been sent to bring me to the Lady Senena. She would expect to see me in good health and good heart, moreover, I was now of an age to speak out volubly against any ill-use. Yet he was double my size, and hate might prove stronger than caution. There was more than wisdom restraining him from laying any hand on me, more even than the witness trotting behind us. He saw now no gain, not even any satisfaction, in killing me. I began to be a little curious about him, and a little in awe of him, as of the tragic and the accursed, from that moment. It is not far from awe to pity, but it was so far then that the end was out of sight, my stature being low, and my vision short.

I asked him, as we breasted one green crest of the hills, and looked upon another valley: 'What does she want with me?'

He said: 'She?' and looked darkly into the sunlit distances and terribly smiled.

'The Lady Senena,' I said, suddenly trembling, because I had not known so clearly until then that for him there was only one she.

'You're wanted,' he said grimly, 'because she will not go without you.' And that was the same she, his, not mine.

'Go where?' I asked. In all these years she had visited me only three times, for to her a journey, even of twenty miles, was a traverse of the world. Yet she had not wished me back, or tried to uproot me out of my green garden of books and vegetables and saints, content to have me content, and still in the same cantref with her. 'Where is it she must go,' I cried out to know, 'with me or without me? How far?'

'Ask the lady,' he said. 'I'm but the messenger. I go where I'm sent, like you. All my task is to bring you.

'But you know,' I said, insistent.

14

'I've heard a name. It might as well be the holy city of Jerusalem. I never was beyond Conway,' he said, 'in my life, what are names to me?'

So I asked him nothing more, for he was as lost as I was. Only after a while I asked for my mother, if she was well, and he said, well, so dourly that I ventured to ask no more as long as we rode together.

There was nothing strange to be seen round the llys at Neigwl, when we came there. In the village and the fields men were working as ever, and there was no more bustle than usual even inside the walls. It was always a lively place. But when we came to stable our ponies I saw that there were more horses within than ever I had seen there in the old days, or even at Nevin, and moreover that there were great bundles and saddle-bags already packed and waiting, covered over with hides and stacked along the wall. If there was no great to-do at this hour, it was because the Lady Senena's plans, whatever they might be, had been made some while since, and now only awaited the right moment for execution.

My mother must have been listening for the sound of hooves, for she looked out from the hall as we clattered across the courtyard, and came hurrying to kiss me. She had a child by the hand, a boy about five years old, who clung to her confidently, and stared up at me with shining curiosity. Very dark he was, with broad cheekbones and wide eyes of a blue like harebells, soft and light, under straight brows as black as his blue-black hair. He was tall for his age, and well-made, and of a bold beauty, and he gazed at me unwaveringly in silence, for so long that I was forced to be the first to turn my eyes away. And I knew this boy for my breast-brother, the youngest of the Lord Griffith's four sons, who bore his detested uncle's name of David.

A second boy, a year or so older, came trailing out from the hall after them to stare at us from a distance before he made up his mind to come close. He approached a little sidelong, hesitant and unwelcoming in his look. This one had something of the colouring of Owen Goch, but as though bleached and faded in the sun, for his hair was of a reddish straw-colour, and his cheeks pale and freckled. When he saw my mother kiss me he came the rest of the way across the dusty court to us in a rush, and laid hold upon her skirt as if to assert his ownership and my strangeness. But in a moment, as she only gave him her free hand without a glance, and continued speaking with me, he lost interest in us both, and looked round for other entertainment, and pulling away his hand again, ran off after one of the maids who passed from the kitchens with her arms full. The youngest stood immovable and watched, saying never a word, and missing nothing, until my mother leaned down to him cajolingly, and turning him after his elder, urged him to go with Rhodri, and Marared would give them some of the honey cakes she was baking. And then he went, at first composedly, and then breaking into a hopping dance of his own, to which he seemed to want and need no audience.

This was the first time that ever I saw the two youngest of the brothers of Gwynedd.

My mother drew me with her into the store-room, I think to be out of sight of her husband when she embraced me, and there she held me

15

against her heart, and said over and over: 'I could not go without you! How could I? I would not go so far and leave you behind.' Then she held me off from her to search my face more earnestly, and asked, almost as if in fear, whether I had been happy at Aberdaron, and whether I was not glad rather to come with her, and travel so far into the world. And I swallowed my regrets, since there was no sense in two of us grieving when only one need, and told her that I was her dutiful son, and I willed to go with her wherever she must go, though God knows I lied, and I hope forgives me the lie. Could I have had my way without hurt to any other, I would have begged a fresh pony, all stiff and sore as I was, and started out on the instant back to my cell and the unfinished haymaking, and my master Ciaran. But since that could not be, for neither she nor I was free, or had any support but in the Lady Senena's service, I comforted her as best I could, myself uncomforted, and asked her where it was we must go, and for how long a time, to make it necessary that I should be recalled. For often enough the court moved between three or four maenols, but none so distant that it implied a parting between us.

'We are going further,' she said, 'very far. She has sent couriers ahead days ago, to have changes of horses ready. And we leave tonight, after dark.'

'But why after dark?' I questioned. 'And where do we go?'

'Eastward,' she said, 'to England. But in secret. No one outside these walls must know.'

'To England?' I said. 'What, all? The children, too?' A foolish question, as I saw, for it was because the children were to be of the party that she, their nurse, must go with them, and would and must take her son with her. And if the lady was thus preparing to remove herself and what family she had about her furtively into England, it could only be into King Henry's care, and there could be but one reason. No wonder the expedition was being mounted by night, and in the expectation of a long exile. How long, the king's army and the Welsh weather must decide. Only dimly did I grasp the meaning of this move, but she did not question it at all. What the lady ordered was her law. 'How many go?' I asked her. 'She and the children, and we – how many more? The steward? And a guard? She'll never ride unprotected.'

'Twenty are gone ahead,' my mother said, 'to make ready and meet us along the way. Three officers ride with us, and ten more men.'

A large party to make so secret and desperate a move. She did not mean to appear before the king of England without some remnants of royal state.

'And Llewelyn?' I said, for I had not seen him yet about the llys. 'Is he in this, too?'

'He is on his way now, he should have been here already. She sent for him yesterday from Carnarvon. And you are to go to her,' she said, 'and she will tell you what your part is to be. Go to her now, she will have heard you are here, she does not like to be kept waiting.'

So I went, for indeed that lady was not one to be trifled with, especially with so grave a business in hand. But as I turned to go on past the hall to the lady's apartments, my mother suddenly called after me, in the

16

child's voice that suited so ill with this learned-by-rote business she had been expounding for me, and with the most hushed and bitter awareness of having somehow offended: 'Child, forgive me – forgive me!'

I went back to her, greatly shaken, and held and reassured her that my only wish was to be with her, that I had no reluctance or regret, while my heart wept in me for longing. There was something deep within my mother that understood more than other men do, while all the shell of her mind was without understanding.

Then verily I went. The Lady Senena was sitting in a great chair in her solar, with a coffer before her, into which she was carefully laying away small packets of valuables, while her steward came and went with certain parchments and consulted with her, discarding some for burning, and adding others to those she would take with her. When I came in she looked up, and I louted to her, and signified that I had come, in duty bound, in answer to her summons.

She was not a tall woman, nor beautiful, but she had a great dignity about her, and was accustomed to being respected and obeyed. She had thick brows that all but met over her nose, and made her seem to frown, and her voice was cool and strong, so that I had always been in some awe of her, and still was, however good she had been to me.

'So you are here,' she said, considering me. 'Have you spoken with your mother?'

I thought it best to know nothing but what the lady herself chose to tell me, so I said: 'Madam, I have, and she sent me here at once to hear what your wishes are.'

She began then to question me closely about my studies, and all I had learned at Aberdaron, and what I told her seemed to content her, for she nodded repeatedly, and twice exchanged glances with her steward and they nodded together. I was indeed more forward in letters than most about her court, and might be of use as a clerk, she said, but in particular I was to earn my place, since her children's nurse would not go without me, as groom and attendant to the young princes. I said I would do my best in whatever work she chose to give me, and go wherever she willed that I should go.

'You do not ask me where,' she said drily.

'Madam, if I am to know, you will tell me.'

And tell me she did, and set me to work then and there, helping the steward to sort out and burn those parchments she did not need, and wished not to leave behind her for others to see. For my eyes were younger and sharper than the old man's, and even in the bright summer the light was dim within the room. So it happened that I was crouched by the hearth-stone, feeding rolls of vellum into a sluggish fire, or laying out those harmless and only once used for cleaning, when there was a rush of loud young footsteps outside, and Llewelyn flung the door wide and came striding in.

I saw him first only as a dark figure in outline against the brilliance of the day outside, and saw him so, in stillness, for a long moment, for he had halted to get his bearings in the dimness of the room, after his ride under that radiant sky. Then he came forward to plump heartily down

17

on his knee and kiss his mother's hand, though so perfunctorily that it was plain he saw no reason for more than ordinary filial respect, and knew nothing as yet of why she had sent for him. And very straightly he went to it and asked, as though, whatever it was, he would see it done, and then be off again to whatever employment she had interrupted.

'I came as soon as I could, mother. What is it you want of me?'

The flames of my small fire, burning up to a brief flare as I forgot to feed it, lit him clearly as he bounded up from his knee. He was then no taller than I, though afterwards he shot up to gain half a head over me. But he was sturdier and squarer than I, and perhaps because of this, perhaps because of that glowing, carefree assurance he had, being born royal, he seemed to me my elder by a year or two, though I knew that to be false. He wore no cloak in this high summer, he had on him only his hose and a short riding-tunic of linen, that left his throat and forearms bare, long-toed riding shoes on his feet, and round his hips a belt ornamented with gold, from which a short dagger hung. And wherever his skin was bared he was burned copper-brown by the sun, so that his thick brown hair seemed only a shade darker. He looked at the coffer his mother had on the table, and at the pieces of jewellery and the documents laid away in it, and his smile of pure pleasure in sun and motion and his own vigour faded a little into wonder and puzzlement.

'What are you doing? What is this?'

'I sent for you,' she said, 'to come home to your duty. Tonight we leave here on a journey. If I have not consulted you before, you must forgive me that, for it was necessary. I could not risk any accidental betrayal, it was best the secret should remain within these walls until all was ready. It is ready now, and we leave here tonight. For Shrewsbury.'

He echoed: 'Shrewsbury?' in an almost silent cry of astonished disbelief. When his brows drew together so, they were almost as formidable as hers, and very like. 'Mother, do you know what you say? King Henry is on his way from Gloucester to Shrewsbury this moment, with all his feudal host. Bent against Gwynedd! Did you not know it? Whatever you could want in Shrewsbury, God knows, I cannot see, but this is no time to stir about it.'

He was slow to understand, though she had told him bluntly enough. And after all, perhaps my experience had made me a year or so older, not younger, than he when it came to probing the political moves of his noble mother. Or he was too near and fond, in the unthinking way proper to his youth, and I, kinless, fatherless, dependent, saw from outside and saw more clearly. Yet when the truth did dawn upon him, he spoke from a vision which I had not, and did not yet comprehend.

His face had sharpened in the unseasonable firelight. I saw all the golden, reflected lines along his bones of cheek and chin quiver and draw fine and clear. He was not smiling at all then. He said: 'Madam, let me understand you! Is that your reason for riding to Shrewsbury? To meet King Henry?'

'I am going,' she said with deliberation, and rising from her chair to be taller than he, 'to confide your father's cause and yours to King Henry's hands, and ask him for justice. Which you well know we have not had and shall not have from any here in Gwynedd. The English in arms will restore us our rights. I am resolved to stake all on this throw. We have been disinherited and insulted long enough. I will have your father and your brother out of prison and restored to their own by the means that offers.'

'You cannot have understood what you are doing,' he said. 'You could not talk so else. The king of England is preparing now, this very minute, to attack our country, our people. You want to make our right in Welsh law one more weapon on the English side, to slaughter Welshmen? Your own kin? You will be siding with the enemy!'

'You talk like a child,' she said sharply, 'and a foolish child! I have waited long enough for Gwynedd to do justice to my lord, your father, and talk of enemies is hollow talk to me. We are disinherited, against all law. I am appealing to an overlaw, and make no doubt but it will hear me, and do right.'

'You cannot do right to my father or any,' he cried, blazing up like a tall flame, 'by doing wrong to Gwynedd! To Wales!'

'You talk of fantasies,' she overbore him, looming against him like a tower, 'while your father rots in Criccieth, a reality, deprived of what is justly his. And you dare talk to me of right! We are going, and tonight. Go, sir, do as you are bidden, go and make ready, and no more words. I did not send for you to teach me my duty, I know it too well.'

Long before this I would gladly have crept away if I could, but I dared not move for fear of reminding them that I was there. And even he, I thought, wavered and blanched a little before her, for in his father's absence she was the law here, and he was still two years short of his manhood, and could not act against her will. Yet I think now he did not give back at all, and even his hesitation was nothing but a hurried searching in his unpractised mind for words which might convince without offending.

'Mother,' he said, low and passionately, 'I do know my father's case, and know he asks but what he feels his right. But I tell you, if I were in his place, rather than get my sovereignty at the hands of King Henry, I would make my full submission to my uncle David as his loyal vassal, and put myself and every man I had into arms to fight for him against England. There should be no factions here when a war threatens, but only one cause, Wales. Do not go! Go rather to Criccieth, and beg my father to remember his own father, and the greatness he gave to Gwynedd, and urge him to offer the oath of fealty to his brother, and come out and fight beside him. Even at his own cost, yes! But I swear it would not cost him so high as you will make it cost him if you go on with this. Do not go, to make traitors of us all!'

She had heard him thus far only for want of breath and words to silence him, and found no argument, for they had no common ground on which to argue. But then she struck him, on the word she could not endure. The clash of her palm against his cheek was loud, and the silence after it louder, until she found a laboured, furious voice to break it.

'Do you dare speak so to me? You have been too long and too often at your uncle's court, it seems! You had better take care how you use the word traitor in this house, for it may well echo back upon your own head. You have been spoiled at Aber! They have bought you, foolish child as you are. Now let me hear no more from you, but go and make ready. You are the eldest son of this house at liberty, and should be doing your duty as its head.'

He stood unmoving, his eyes fixed upon her angry face, and he had grown pale under the sunbrown, so that the marks of her fingers burned clear and red upon his cheek. After a long moment he said, in a voice quiet and even: 'You say truth, and you do well to remind me. I am the eldest son of this house at liberty, and I will do my duty as its head. Have I your leave to go and set about it?'

'That is better,' she said grimly, and dismissed him with no greater mark of forgiveness than that, for she was much disturbed, and still angry. Nor did he ask any. He went out as abruptly as he had come, and the back view of him as he passed from dark to bright in the doorway did not look to me either tamed or penitent.

I saw him again towards dusk, when we brought in the stock. For all must go forward as usual and seem innocent after we were gone. He had chosen a horse for himself with care, and tried its paces about the courtyard, and professing himself but half satisfied, rode it out and round the llys to make certain of his choice. I had been sent out to bring down a flock from the hill grazing, north of Neigwl, and I came out of a fold of the track close to where the road swung away to the north, towards Carnarvon and Aber.

He was walking his horse up the slope over the grass, away from Neigwl and the sea, and when he came to the road he halted a moment and looked back, motionless in the saddle. Thus, his back being turned to me, he did not see me until the first yearling lambs came down into the corner of his vision, and made him look round. He knew then that I was from the llys. Perhaps he did not know whether I was in the secret, or perhaps he did not care. He looked at me calmly, and did not recognise me, but he knew that he was known, and that I, whoever I might be, was reading his mind.

That was a strange moment, I cannot forget it. He sat his horse, solitary and grave, examining me with eyes the colour of peat pools in the sun. He had brought away with him nothing at all but the horse, and a cloak slung loosely over his linen tunic. Whatever else was his he had left behind, to be taken or abandoned as others decided, for valuables are valuables, and we were going where we might soon be either in need or living on English bounty. He wheeled his horse and walked it forward deliberately some few paces along the road northwards, his eyes never leaving mine, and suddenly he was satisfied, for he smiled. And I smiled also at being read and blessed, for his confidence was as open and wide as the sky over us.

He said to me: 'You have seen nothing.' Confirming not ordering.

'Nothing,' I said.

'And I know nothing,' he said. That, too, I understood. The Lady Senena could never be told, nor perhaps would she believe it if any tried to tell her, that the son who would not go with her to England would not send out an alarm after her, either, or betray her intent in any way, having made his own decision yet still allowing her hers. No, it was for me he said it, that I might be satisfied as he was satisfied, and feel no guilt in keeping his secret, as he felt none in keeping hers. And that was no easy way to take, alone, for a boy twelve years old.

He shook the reins, and dug his heels into the horse's flanks, and was away from me at a canter along the track towards the north. He had ridden much, and rode well, erect and easy, as I would have liked to ride. I watched him until he breasted the next rise and vanished into the dip beyond, and then I took the lambs down to Neigwl, and said never a word to any of that meeting.

So when the dusk was low enough, and the hour came for our departure, when the sumpter horses were loaded and sent ahead, and the litters for the lady and her children stood ready, and the horses were being led out saddled from the stables, there was great counting of all the heads, and the word began to go round: 'Where is Prince Llewelyn? Has anyone seen him?' No one had, since he took out his chosen horse to try its paces. We waited for him more than an hour, and men hunted in every possible and impossible place about the maenol, while the Lady Senena's face grew darker and bleaker and angrier with every moment. But he did not come, and he was not found. He was the eldest man of his house at liberty, and he was gone to do his duty as its head, according to his own vision.

Even when she cried out on him at last that he had turned traitor, had abandoned and betrayed his own mother and brothers, I said no word. Unable to understand, she would have been unable to believe that he could go on his own way and not block and prevent hers. She feared pursuit, and therefore every hour became more precious, and she ordered our departure in great haste, and extended our first forced ride as far as Mur y Castell, where her advance guards had fresh horses waiting for us. She would not risk taking the old Roman road across the Berwyns, but had planned a route further south, to give all David's favourite dwellings a wide berth, and our first rest was at Cymer. Thence, with a greatly increased company, we made two easier days of it by way of Meifod to Strata Marcella, and crossed the Severn at a ford below Pool.

And all the way she complained bitterly of her second son's treachery and ingratitude, until she went far to make her daughter Gladys, who was his elder by a year, hate him and decry him even as she did. Being the only daughter, this girl was very dear to her, and much in her confidence. Yet I think there was so much of grief and smart in their blame of him that even hate had another side, and in their softer moments they could not choose but wonder and harrow over old ground, marvelling how he had come to that resolution against all odds, incomprehensible to them, and blameworthy, but surely hard indeed for him, and therefore honest. And this all the more when the journey was nearly over, and no breath of suspicion or pursuit followed us. For if he had not garnered all the favour he could by setting his uncle's huntsmen after us, what was his own welcome likely to be after our flight was discovered? He was known to have been summoned by his mother, and obeyed and returned, the very day of the defection. The revenge that could not reach his mother might fall on him for want of larger prey. And sometimes those two women, a moment after cursing him, wondered with anxiety how he was faring now, and whether he was not flung into Criccieth with his father and his brother.

As for me, I learned painfully to ride, if not well as yet, doggedly and uncomplainingly, I tended the two little boys, I wrote one or two letters of appeal for the Lady Senena to such English lords as she best knew by contact or reputation, urging her cause, and I did whatever clerking there was to be done by the way. But familiar as I became with her argument, I could not forget his. And for which of them was in the right, that I could never determine. For both were honest, and both spoke truth, though they went by opposite ways. Yet being of the party that went one way, I heard now nothing but this side of the case, and matter repeated again and again without opposition grows to fall naturally on the ear. So I doubt I veered with the wind, like other men older than I, and came to be much of the lady's way of thinking before we reached Shrewsbury, which we did, with safe-conducts from the king's council, on the fourth day of August of this year twelve hundred and forty-one.

CHAPTER II

This Shrewsbury is a noble town, formidably walled all round and everywhere moated by the Severn, but for a narrow neck of land open to the north, for the whole town lies within a great coil of that river. It has three gates, two of them governing the bridges that lead, one eastwards deeper into England, one westwards into Wales, and the third gate lies on the tongue of dry land, under the shadow of a great castle. I have seen larger towns since then, though none fairer. But when we came in by the Welsh gate, over that broad sweep of river and beneath the tall tower on the bridge, that August day in the heat, I saw such a town for the first time in my life, and thought it more marvellous than I can tell. For we in Wales had then borrowed very little from this crowding English life that pressed in on our flank, that used coined money, and markets, of which we had scarcely any, and lived in stone houses that could not be abandoned at need, for they were too precious, and grew ordered crops that tied men to one patch of soil. And above all, few of us had ever seen what the English called a city.

The Lady Senena had sent her steward ahead to deal with the bailiffs of the town, being armed already with a recommendation from John Lestrange, who was sheriff of the county. And we were met at the gate, and conducted to a great house near the church of St Alkmund (for this town has four parish churches within its walls) where we were to be lodged. There was fair provision for the lady and her children and officers within, and those of her escort and servants who were married were given the best of what remained, while the young men had reasonably good lying in a barn and storehouse in the courtyard. And it was mark of some respect that our party got so much consideration, for Shrewsbury was crowded to the walls. King Henry and his court and officials had been in the town three days, and many of his barons and lords were installed with him in the guest halls of the abbey of St Peter and St Paul, outside the walls by the English gate. The chief tenants and their knights were quartered in the castle, or wherever they could find room in houses and shops inside the walls, and the main part of the army, a great host, encamped in the fields outside the castle foregate.

But this numbering, vast though it was, was but the half of the stream that had poured into Shrewsbury. There were plenty of clients eager to enlist King Henry's favour, besides the Lady Senena. All those marcher lords who had lost land to Llewelyn the Great, and had been trying through legal pressures to regain it from his son all these past months, had come running to the royal standard, waiting to pick the bones. Roger of Montalt, the seneschal of Chester, who had been kept out of

Mold for many years, Ralph Mortimer, who had trouble with his Welsh neighbours in Kerry, and Griffith ap Gwenwynwyn, who laid claim to most of southern Powys by right of his father, these were the chief litigants. This Griffith ap Gwenwynwyn was a man twenty-seven years old, and had been but an infant when his sire lost all to Llewelyn of Gwynedd. He was married to Hawise, a daughter of the high sheriff, John Lestrange, who had three border counties in his care, and was justiciar of Chester into the bargain, a very powerful ally. The English called this Welsh chief Griffith de la Pole, after the castle of Pool, which was his family's chief seat; and indeed, this young man had been so long among the English that he was more marcher baron than Welsh chief, let alone the influence of his wife, who was a very strong and self-willed lady. But apart from these, there were not a few of the minor Welsh princes here to join the royal standard, some because they felt safer owing fealty to England than to Gwynedd, some with grievances of their own over land, like the lord of Bromfield, some because they upheld the Lord Griffith's right, and had conceived the same hope as had his lady, some in the hope of snatching a crumb or two out of David's ruin for themselves, with or without right. Which was cheering indeed for the Lady Senena, who found herself not without advocates and allies in this foreign town.

But if the outlook was bright for her, it seemed it was black enough for David, with all this great force arrayed against him, and in this summer when the world was turned upside-down. For scarcely ever was there a year when the rivers sank so low, those waters on which Gwynedd counted for half her defence. There had been no rains since the spring, the sun rose bright every morning, and sank cloudless every night, pools dried up, and swamps became dry plains. And all those supporters of the Lord Griffith whetted their swords and watched the skies with joy, waiting for the order to march.

The Lady Senena sent a messenger at once to the abbey, to ask for an audience of the king, and his officers appointed her to come on the twelfth day of August. So we had time enough to wait, and to draw up in detail the petition she intended to present, together with her proposals for an alliance which should be of benefit to both parties. This kept her steward and clerk busy for some days, and I was employed to help in preparing fair copies of the clauses, for I had learned to write a good clear hand. I had also to help my mother take care of the two young princes, for now it was part of my mother's own duties to be waiting-maid to the Lady Gladys, so that I came in for much of the work of minding the little boys. And as they were full of curiosity and wonder at this strange and busy town, I was able to go with them sometimes about the streets, gaping at everything as simply as did the children, for it was as new to me as to them. So many fine buildings, such shops and market stalls, and such a bewildering parade of people I had never imagined. Those four noble churches were of stone, the houses mainly of timber, but large and splendid, the streets so full of life that it seemed the whole business of the kingdom had followed the court here, and London must be empty. And all the while this blue, unpitying sky over all, very beautiful, very ominous.

When the day came, the lady had her daughter, who was growing up very handsome, dressed with great care to adorn her beauty, and the two little boys also made as grand as might be. Rhodri, the elder, was a capricious and uncertain-tempered child, but not ill-looking when he was amiable, and David had always, even then, at five years old, a great sense of occasion, and could light some inward lamp of charm and grace at will, so that he truly shone, and women in especial were drawn to him like moths to flame. I do not know why it was, for I paid him no more attention than I did his brother, but David was much attached to me, and it was because he would have me with him that I was of the party that went before the king.

We went on foot, for it was not far. Only the Lady Senena and her daughter rode in a litter, for it was not fitting for them to arrive at the king's audience on foot. The road was by a fine, curving street that dropped steeply to the bridge on the English side, where there was a double gate, the first a deep tunnel in the town wall, and after it a tower set upon the bridge itself, of which the last span was a draw-bridge. And beyond the bridge, where a brook ran down into the river, the abbey mills stood, and the wall and gatehouse of the great enclosure loomed bright in the unfailing sunshine, with the square tower of the church over all. We went in procession over the bridge and along the broad road to the gateway, and so to the guest-houses where King Henry kept his court. In the anteroom his chamberlain met us, and went in before us to announce the lady.

She took the petition, carefully inscribed and rolled and sealed with the Lord Griffith's private seal, which she kept always about her, and marshalled us in order at her back, and so we went into the glow and brilliance of the royal presence, she first and alone, her daughter after her with my mother in attendance, Rhodri led by the steward, and I with David clinging to my hand. And of all of us he was the least awed and the most at ease.

It was a great room, draped with tapestries and green branches and bright silks, and full of people. The lady halted just within the doorway, and so did we all, and made a deep reverence to the throne. Then, as we moved forward again at the chamberlain's summons, I lifted my eyes, and looked for the first time upon King Henry of England, the third of that name.

He was seated in a high-backed chair at the dais end of the hall, with a great plump of lords and secretaries and officers on either side of him; a man not above medium tall, rather pale of countenance, with light brown hair and beard very carefully curled, and long, fine, clerkly fingers stretched out along the arms of his chair. He was very splendid in cloth of gold, and much jewelled. I saw the glitter before I saw the man, for he was like a pale candle in a heavy golden sconce, and yet he had some attraction about him, too, once I could see past the shell. I suppose he was then about thirty-four years old, and had been king from a child, among courtiers and barons old, experienced, greedy, and cleverer than he, and yet many of them were gone down into disaster, and he was left ever hopeful among the new, who might well prove as ruinous as the old, but also as transient. He had a kind of innocent shrewdness, light and durable. I never knew if it was real or spurious, but it made for survival. He had, as it turned out, other qualities, too, that taught him how to shed others and save himself, as slender trees give with the wind. But that was not in his face, it remained to be learned in hard lessons by those less pliable. That day he smiled on us with great gentleness and grace, and was all comfort and serenity. The only thing that caused me to tremble was a little thing of the body, that he could not help. He had one eyelid that hung a little heavier than the other, drooping over the mild brownness of his eye. It gave me a strange shock of distrust, as though one half of him willed to be blind to what the other half did, and would take no responsibility for it hereafter. But that was an unjust fancy, and I forgot it soon.

He was gracious, he leaned forward and stretched out a hand to the Lady Senena, and she sank to her knees before him, and took it upon her own hand, and kissed it. And that she knew how to do without losing one inch of her stature or one grain of her grandeur, as plain as she was, and the mother of five children, in this court full of the young and beautiful. He would have lifted her at once, but she resisted, retaining his hand in hers. She lifted the roll of her petition, and held it up to him. And whatsoever I have been, and however shaken between conflicting loyalties, I was wholly her man then. And the child clinging to my hand stood the taller with pride, and glowed the more brightly.

'My liege lord,' said the Lady Senena, 'I pray your Grace receive and consider the plea of a wife deprived of her lord by his unjust imprisonment and more disgraceful disinheritance, wholly against law. I commit myself and my children to your Grace's charge, as sureties for my lord's and my good faith and fealty to your Grace. And I ask you for the justice denied elsewhere.'

As he took the roll from her, and as expertly had it removed from his hand by a clerk almost before he touched it, he said: 'Madam, we have heard and commiserated your plight, and are aware of your grievances. You are in safety here, and most welcome to us. You shall be heard without hindrance hereafter.' For there would be no bargaining here, this was a time for measuring and thinking, before the fine script I had put into those clauses came to be examined by older, colder eyes than mine. But he raised her very gallantly, and sat her at his knee on a gilded stool they placed for her. And she, though I swear she had never played such a part before, played it now with so large a spirit that in truth for the first time I loved her. She folded her hands in her gown like a saint, and only by the motion of her head beckoned us forward one by one.

'I present to your Grace my daughter Gladys . . .'

The girl bent her lissome knees and slender neck, very dark and bright in every colouring and movement, and kissed the king's hand, and lifted her long lashes and looked into his face. It was curiosity and not boldness, but I saw him startle, attracted and amused. The young one saw nothing but a man's fair face smiling at her, and smiled in response, marvellously. She hung between woman and child then, the child having the upper hand. And truly she was very comely, more than she knew.

'My son Rhodri. Your Grace is advised already that my eldest son, Owen, is prisoner with his father, in defiance of all honour.'

'I do know it,' said the king. 'Child, you are welcome.' Not a word of Llewelyn, the second son. He could not advance her cause here, he was put out of mind, as though he no longer lived.

'My youngest son, David.'

I loosed his hand, and gave him a gentle push towards the throne, but he did not need it, he knew all that was required of him, and went his own God-given step beyond. He danced, there is no other word, to the step of the throne, and laid his flower of a mouth to the king's hand. He looked up and smiled. I heard all the women there – they were not many, but they were noble and of great influence – breathe out a sound like something between the sighing of the sea and the cooing of doves, for he was indeed a most beautiful and winning child. And the king, amused and charmed, lifted and handed him gently to his mother, and he stood by her unabashed and looked all round him, smiling, aware of approval. I drew back very quietly into the shadows, for I was not needed any more, not until he remembered and wanted me, and that he would not do while his interest was held. He had never been happier, he knew every eye was on him, and every lip smiled on him, even the king's. For Henry left a finger in his clasped hand, and withdrew it only when the hand relaxed of itself, and let the royal prisoner go.

They say he was a fond, indulgent father to his own children, though apt to tire of their company if they were with him long, and to grow petulant if they plagued him. His son and heir was then just past his second birthday, and the queen had a second babe in arms, but these were all left behind in the south, and I suppose it was pleasant to him to play gently for some minutes with a pretty child of whose company he could be rid whenever it grew irksome. For in that audience he spoke as often to the boy as to his mother, and got his answers just as readily. He asked after his adventures on this great journey, and David chattered freely about the ride, and about the wonders he had seen in Shrewsbury. And when he was asked what he would be and do when he was grown, he said boldly that he would be one of the king's knights. His mother gave him a swift, narrow look then, as doubtful as I if that was said in innocence, for clever children, even at five years old, know very well what will please. But since it did give pleasure she said no word of her qualms, then or afterwards. There is no harm in accepting aid where you find it.

So this open audience went very well, and gave promise for the closed conference which was appointed to follow the next day, and the Lady Senena made her withdrawing reverence and led her procession back to its lodging reasonably well content.

And for the hard bargaining that went on at this council at the abbey, the earnest after the show, I was not present, and cannot speak as to what passed. There were present at first only the Lady Senena and her steward on our part, and on the part of the crown King Henry himself for a part of the discussion, and with him his chancellor and his secretary. And after the terms were agreed certain of the marcher barons and the Welsh chiefs were called in to approve and to sign as guarantors. But the terms themselves I do know, for I was set to work making fair copies before ever the agreement was made public, two days later. They seemed to me curious enough, for I knew nothing of money, the minted money they valued, and could not conceive of a man's liberty and rights being reckoned in terms of the round pieces of metal they struck here in this town.

Yet so it was, for money entered into every transaction. After all their conferring, King Henry undertook, in the campaign he intended against the prince of Gwynedd, to bring about the release of the Lord Griffith from imprisonment in consideration of the sum of six hundred marks, and to restore him to his rightful share of the inheritance for three hundred more, one third of the whole sum to be paid in coin, and the remainder in cattle and horses. And a commission of lawful appraisers was to view the stock so rendered in payment, when they were delivered to the sheriff here in Shrewsbury, to make doubly sure that their value was equal to the sum due. To this document many of the marcher lords and Welsh princes also added their signatures as security. And the Lady Senena placed herself and her children under King Henry's protection, and her two youngest sons specifically in his charge, as hostages for her and her husband's future fealty.

Whether she was fully content with this arrangement I do not know, but it was the best she could get, and I think she felt secure that it would be of short term and soon resolved, and the restoration of half Gwynedd to her lord would make payment a light matter. For she listened with great eagerness to all the talk within the town, and paid attention to all the news she could get of the king's preparations, which indeed were impressive. And the season still continued bright without a cloud, and the rivers shrank into mere trickles in the meandering middles of their beds, even the Severn so low that a man could ford it where no fords were at other times. So all men said it was but a matter of marching into Wales, and the elusive warfare the Welsh favoured and excelled at would be impossible, for an army could go in force where normally marsh and mountain stream would prevent. And in a month all would be over. And for once men said truth, for in a month all was over.

We stayed in our lodgings in Shrewsbury, King Henry's pensioners, when the army marched. After they were gone, the town seemed quiet indeed, but with a most ominous quietness, and for some time no news came. They marched to Chester, where the nobles of the north with their knights were ordered to join the muster, and from there advanced westwards into Tegaingl without hindrance, and reached the river Clwyd, which was no let to them, and crossed the great marshes that surround Rhuddlan dry-shod as on a drained field, so rapidly, that Prince David was forced to withdraw or be cut off from his mountains. But even the mountains betrayed him, for they provided him neither rain nor cloud nor mist to cover him. Such a season had never been known in Snowdon. He razed to the rock his castle of Degannwy, on the hither side of Conway, when it was plain that he must abandon it, and he kept his army from the direct clash which must see it shattered. In the

28

end he preferred to sue for peace rather than continue a war which could not be won, but only lost with great bloodshed or with none.

At Gwern Eigron on the river Elwy, the twenty-ninth day of August, the prince of Gwynedd made a complete surrender on terms to the king, and in King Henry's tent at Rhuddlan the pact was confirmed two days later. And a hard and bitter meeting that must have been between these two, uncle and nephew but very much of an age, kinsmen and enemies. And very hard and bitter were the terms of the surrender, though David kept his rank and the remnants of his principality.

Rumour of the end of the fighting came back to us in Shrewsbury early in September, while the army was still at Chester. The Lady Senena sent daily to the sheriff or the bailiffs for news of what most concerned her, her lord's fortunes, and I well remember the day when her steward came back from the castle glowing with the details at last. She was in the hall when he came, and I was taking down for her one more letter of the many with which she had throughout continued to solicit the favour of the powerful, especially those lords who held along the northern march. Therefore I was present when she received the word for which she waited.

'Madam,' said the old man, flushed with joy and importance, for it is always good to be the bearer of news long-desired and wholly welcomed, 'the Lord Griffith is freed, and handed over to his Grace at Chester, and your son with him. They will return here with the king's Grace within the week.'

She clasped her hands and coloured to the brow with delight, like a young girl, and said a fervent thanks to God for this deliverance. And fiercely she questioned him of those other matters, for she was a good hater as well as a loyal lover.

'And the terms? What becomes of all those impleaded lands, Powys, Mold, all those conquests held from their father? Does David give up all? All?'

'All!' he said. 'Everything Llewelyn Fawr took by force of arms goes back to those who claim it. Montalt gets back Mold after forty years. Gwenwynwyn's son will be set up in Powys, and Merioneth returns to Meredith's sons. All the Welsh princes who used to hold directly from the crown are to come back to the crown. Everything he fought for, he has lost!'

A strange thought came into my mind then that I was not listening to a Welsh princess and her officer speaking, but to English voices exulting over a defeated Wales.

'What, all the homages that belonged to King John are to come back to the crown again? A great loss!'

And I thought how the Gwynedd she looked to see divided now by force between the Lord Griffith and his brother was shrunken by all those fealties, and marvelled how she could be glad of it, even for her lord's own sake, for surely he was also a loser, or at best stood to gain only a meagre princedom. But she saw no false reasoning.

'And David will pay!' she said with passion. 'The expenses of this war, also! King Henry will not let that go by default.'

'Madam, he is to give up the whole cantref of Tegaingl, and Ellesmere also, these go to the crown. And there will be a further payment in money, a heavy fine.'

'His justice returns on his own head,' she said. 'And will my lord truly be here within the week, shall I see him again?'

'Madam, he is already with the king, they return together. Your son also.'

'And what provision is made for him? What lands are allotted to my lord?' She shook suddenly to a frightening thought. 'He'll hold them from the king, in chief? Not from David! Say not from David!'

'Direct from the crown, madam. It's agreed that the question shall be determined by his Grace's own court, according to Welsh custom or strict law, as may be decided. Our lord will be there to speak for himself.'

'Then no division is yet made. No,' she said, but with some doubt and reluctance, 'I see there could be no judgment yet. It is a matter for the court, in fairness. Then all will be well. And I did right to come. I tell you,' she said, for her humbly, 'sometimes I have wondered. Am I now justified?'

'Madam,' he said, 'my lord is on his way back to you and to his children, and the Lord Owen with him. What other answer do you need? They are free, and you have freed them.'

She was so abashed, and so glad, that briefly she shed tears, she who never wept. And she called the children, and told them their father was coming in a few days. At which David only stared and pondered with little understanding, for he hardly remembered his father.

I remember also the day that they came. All the citizens of Shrewsbury were out on the streets to see the army return, though the main body of men did not enter the town walls. But the king and his officers and barons rode through from gate to gate, from the castle to the abbey, where they halted again for two nights. The house where we lodged was very close to the street where they passed, and we went down into the crowd to watch, while the Lady Senena and the Lady Gladys had a place in the window of a burgess's house overhanging the route, and took the children with them.

That was a brave show, bright with pennants and surcoats and colours, the horses as fresh and fine as the riders, for there had been no great hardship or exertion in that brief war, no armour was dinted, and no banners coiled. We saw the king go by, a fair horseman, and at his fairest when he rode in triumph, for he swung ever between the rooftops and the mire, higher and lower in his exaltation and abasement than ordinary men, and this was an occasion unblemished by any doubts. I had not yet learned to know the faces and devices of those closest about him, though they all looked formidable enough and splendid enough to me. I saw them as a grand cavalcade of bright colours and proud faces, not as men in the manner that I was a man. Or almost a man, for I had not yet my years. These lived on another level. I knew no parallel for it in Wales, where no man felt himself less a man than another, or bridled his tongue for awe of the great. Great and small surely we had, and every man knew his place in the order, and respected both his own and every other soul's, but not with servility. In this land I felt great wonder and pleasure, but I was never at ease.

I stood with my mother and her husband – for I never thought of him as father to me in any way – among a hot and heaving throng, pressed body hard against body, watching these great ones ride by. And suddenly my mother gave a soft cry, and struggled to free a hand, and as ever, to touch me, not him. And never did this happen but he was aware of it, and I aware of his awareness, as a pain most piercing and hard to sustain. But she never knew it, as though what he felt could in no wise touch her. So she handled me eagerly by the shoulder in his sight, and cried: 'He is there! It is true, he's free!'

I doubt if I should have known the Lord Griffith for myself, for I had not seen him since I was five years old. He rode among a group of lords not far behind the king's own party, on a tall, raw-boned horse, for he was a massive man, full-blooded and well-fleshed, and had lost no bulk in his imprisonment. He towered almost a head over King Henry, and though he was white in the face from being so long shut away from the sun, he looked otherwise none the worse in health, and was now, like his lady, in very good spirits. At whose expense he was provided for this ride, both with clothes and mount, I do but guess, yet take it that as yet all he had came from King Henry. For he was fine in his dress, and his hair and beard, which were reddish fair like Rhodri's colouring, very elegantly trimmed. Close behind him rode a big boy of about fourteen, massively made like his father, but his thick crop of hair, which was uncovered to the sun, was fiery red, almost as red as the poppies in the headlands of the English fields. And that was Owen Goch, the firstborn son.

They passed by us, pale from their prison but bright with joy in their triumph, and people pointed them out for the Welsh princes, and waved hands and kerchiefs. The Lady Senena sat at her upper window motionless and silent, with tears on her cheeks, but her daughter leaned out and shook a silk scarf streaming out on the breeze, and called down to the riders so shrilly and joyfully that the Lord Griffith looked up, and saw his womenfolk weeping and laughing for pleasure at seeing him again live and free and acknowledged joint-heir of Gwynedd. Then the men below waved and threw glances and kisses as long as they were within sight, their chins on their shoulders, until the curve of the Wyle took them away, and the women embraced each other in floods of tears, and hugged the two little boys, and urged them to wave and throw kisses after their father's dwindling figure. For this was but the public presentment, and soon, when King Henry was installed at the abbey, there could be a private reunion even more joyful.

So it went that day. 'There goes one, at least, who has got everything he prayed for,' said my mother's husband, as we struggled back out of the crowd in the street, and drew breath in the courtyard of the house. And so we all agreed, except perhaps my mother, who went in to her mistress very thoughtful and absent, though she said no word.

We waited, and looked for the Lord Griffith to come to us and take up his dwelling in this same house, but instead a page came from the court in the abbey bearing a message from him, desiring his wife to remove herself and the children and all her party, to join him there. And so she did, proudly and in haste, for it seemed that her household was to be of the king's own circle. It was therefore in a guest apartment at the abbey that she at last embraced her lord, and he took his children also into his arms.

I think she had hoped, somewhat against reason, for a quick return to Wales, but she conceded that he spoke good sense when he said that this could not be done overnight. There would be no return until the question of the equitable division of lands had been settled, and that could only be by discussion, and under King Henry's patronage, and would take time and patience. Did it matter, when the end was certain justice? And she owned that indeed they owed everything to the king, and must abide his judgment, as the homage for the lands granted would be due directly to him. And first, said the Lord Griffith confidently, it was fitting and necessary that they should move south to London in the king's train, as was his wish, for thither the defeated David must come the next month, according to the agreement, to appear before a council of the king's magnates and ratify the peace. And at that the Lady Senena was well content, for she longed to see that humiliation visited upon her lord's rival and enemy.

'Let him eat the hard bread he has doled out to others,' she said vengefully. 'And we shall sit among the king's honoured companions, and watch him swallow it.'

So when the king dispersed the middle English part of his muster, and moved on southwards to London, all our party went in his train, just as she had foreseen, and she and her lord and her children were favoured with King Henry's frequent notice and conversation on the journey, and their comfort attended to by his officers wherever we halted by the way. A daily allowance was made for their maintenance, generous enough for all expenses, until the Lord Griffith should be established in his own lands and as the king's vassal. And in due time David ap Llewelyn came, as he had promised, in what state was left to him, to meet with King Henry's council on the twenty-fourth day of October. And if his bearing was proud enough, and his person gallant, yet his humiliation was as deep as even the Lady Senena could have wished, for the king made still new inroads on what remained to him, demanding that Degannwy be handed over to the crown in payment of the expenses of the war, and David had no choice but to submit even to this deprivation. Everything he had pledged he made good. Roger of Montalt got back his castle of Mold, Griffith ap Gwenwynwyn took possession of his father's lands in Powys, the king's lieutenant in the southern march garrisoned Builth, Degannwy passed to the crown, and the king began the building of a new castle at Diserth, near Rhuddlan, for the better containing of his half-ruined neighbour. Everything the Lady Senena had foreseen came to pass, but for one particular.

Neither she nor the Lord Griffith witnessed the despoiling. Very richly and comfortably they were lodged in London, when they reached that city, and their generous allowance continued, enough for all their needs. But their apartment was high in the keep of the Tower of London, that great White Tower, and their privacy well guarded by chosen attendants, though none of their choosing, behind safe lock and key.

It was done so smoothly and plausibly that it took her more than a week to realise that, in spite of all the smiles and promises, she had but rescued her lord from a Welsh prison to fling him into an English one. The king's whole train took up residence in the Tower – for this tower, as they call it, is a city in itself – as soon as we came to London, and there King Henry kept court some days, while the southern part of his host was dispersed again to its own lands. So there was no occasion to wonder that all our party were quartered there, too, the royal children in a small house within the green, with my mother and me in attendance, and my mother's husband as groom and manservant, the Lord Griffith and his lady in a well-furnished apartment in the great keep. The men she had brought with her as escort from Wales were withdrawn to the guardrooms with the garrison, the steward and the clerk had a small lodging in another corner. And thus we were distributed about that great fortress, within easy reach one of another, yet separate. But the whole place being, as it were, one vast household, there was no occasion to wonder, or to question the host's use of his own house and his arrangements for his honoured guests.

For two days no one of us felt any need to look beyond the walls, for we had this new and strange world to examine, and it did not appear until the Lord Griffith made to ride out and take a curious look at London, on the third day, that the gates were impassable to him. The guard turned him back, without explanation but that he had his orders, which it was not for him to question. The Lord Griffith applied forthwith to the officer, with the same result, and then, still in good-humour, for he suspected nothing but a mistake, or some misapprehension as to who he was, to the lieutenant. The lieutenant entreated his patience, but the order did indeed apply to him, for the king was concerned that he should not yet adventure his life in the streets, where he was not known to the citizens, and might be all too well known to some stray Welshman embittered by the recent war, for many such worked and studied in the city, and some who favoured David's cause would certainly be gathering in preparation for his coming. This he accepted as a compliment, that the king should be at such pains to guarantee his safety, however this kindly care limited his movements for a while.

But some few days later he enquired again, growing restive, and on being refused exit without his Grace's own orders to the contrary, requested an audience with the king. But it seemed King Henry had withdrawn for a few days to Westminster, having unfinished business with his council there.

Perhaps he had, for at this time it may be he had not quite made up his mind where his best interests lay. If that be true, in two days more he had come to a decision, for that day the Lord Griffith was stopped not at the outer or the inner gate, but at the door of his own apartments. Two officers, unknown to him, unimpressed by him, perfectly indifferent to his protests, informed him that they had orders to allow the Lady Senena to pass in and out as she pleased, that she might visit her children when she would, take exercise, spend her nights either here with her lord or below in the house where her family was lodged. But that he was to remain within these rooms. They no longer cared to pretend that it was for his own protection. Whatever he needed for his comfort should be provided, the maintenance the king paid him would continue, he should not want for service. But he was not to pass the door of this chamber.

Nor did he, ever again.

It was she who raged, protested, harried every official she could reach with her complaints. He had known captivity before, and recognised its familiar face instantly, and knew his own helplessness. Nor had he the refuge she possessed, for a time at least, in disbelief. If she could get to King Henry, if she could but speak with him in person, all this grotesque error would be quickly set right. She had his promise, somewhat of the price he had asked she had already paid, she would not believe that he knew how her husband was used, or would countenance it for one moment when he did learn of it. So she went valiantly from man to officer, from officer to minister, always put off, always persisting, passed from hand to hand, never getting any answers. As for her husband, he let her do what she would, but he expected nothing.

And as long as she continued resolute, indignant and bold, she never reached King Henry's presence, for he well knew how to protect himself from embarrassment. Still he was at his palace at Westminster, and when she begged to be received by him there, he was unwell, and could see no one. Then she grew cunning, and came mildly with a request for some minor concession to her lord's comfort, and King Henry, receiving these reports of her tamed and pliant, granted her an audience, and talked with her affably of the Lord Griffith's health, promising her the amenities she asked. But when she took heart and spoke of freedom, and of a promise given, the king, still smiling, looked the other way, and the audience was over. Then she, too, knew that she wasted her pains.

She did not go back at once to her husband, for she was too bitter and too deeply shaken. She came to us to shed her grief and rage. For then she believed that she understood what had happened to her and hers.

'They are in conspiracy together,' she said, 'uncle and nephew, the one as false as the other! This was all agreed between them, behind what was written into this peace. David, since he must, would give up what he could not hold, and give it up with the better will since he was promised then, he must have been promised, his brother should never take from him the half of what was left. This is what they have done to him between them!'

There were many, as I know, who thought as she did. But I cannot believe it was so. All defeated as he was, and helpless, what persuasion had David to induce his uncle to prevent Griffith from claiming the half of his shrunken realm? None! There was nothing he had to offer in return, and King Henry gave nothing for nothing. No, I think there was a more private argument that swayed that devious personage. I do believe he had meant to do as he had promised, but after his return to London had considered again, more carefully, what might follow. For if he set up Griffith in the moiety of Gwynedd, thus forcibly removing the worst enmity between these two brothers, and turning them into neighbours of one blood who must both make the best of straitened circumstances, might they not, once the old bitterness had receded by a year or two, come to consider that they had a mutual interest in enlarging that realm to its old borders? And had they not, together, the backing of all the Welsh princes, a solidarity David had never enjoyed? Nor could there soon be such another summer, traitor and vindictive to Wales. Yes, after his fashion I think King Henry reasoned wisely enough. For if he held Griffith in his power, not so vilely used as to alienate him incurably, he could be held for ever over David's head, the strongest weapon against him should he ever take arms again for his lost lands. One move in rebellion, and Griffith could be in Chester with English arms to back him, and hale away half the Welsh princes to his side as before. No, while Griffith lay here in the king's hand, like a drawn sword, David could not stir.

I am the more firmly convinced of this by all that King Henry did in the matter thereafter. On the one hand, he took every precaution to secure his prisoners more impregnably. It soon occurred to him that a vigorous woman like the Lady Senena, who had had the courage and decision to act once for herself and appeal from Wales to England, might have it in her yet, given a suitable focus for her cause, to appeal as fiercely from England to Wales. She could not make use of her husband now, except as a distant symbol, not apt for rousing men to arms, but there was still Owen Goch, his father's image and now, by Welsh custom, a man. Thus with every personal flattery and consideration, but implacably, Owen Goch was removed from our household, upon the pretext of providing more suitably for his father's heir, and made prisoner in a room high in the keep, like the Lord Griffith himself. True, he was allowed exercise within the walls, but with a retinue which was in reality a guard, and armed. The younger boys were thought no threat, and could be let run on a loose rein. And the lady, while her chicks were cooped here – all but one, and that stray was neither heard of from Wales then nor mentioned in England – would not forsake them. Also, all the Welsh men-at-arms were gradually dispersed from the Tower. Some, I know, took service with the king's men, some, I fancy, vanished when David drew the rags of his royalty about him and rode again for home. Only we who cared for the children were left. No doubt we seemed harmless enough. Even the servants who waited on Griffith and his lady were now English. The old steward they let alone until he died in the winter, for he was past sixty years. And the clerk vanished to some new service, I never knew where, for I was considered able enough to shift for us all, should there be need of any drawing of documents in Welsh and English thereafter. Thus we were stripped of the reminders of our own land.

But on the other hand, the king was by no means inclined to alienate us in other ways, once he had us tightly secured. For as soon as he was aware that the Lady Senena had fallen into some state between resignation and despair, and accepted her fate, she was invited very often and as of right into the queen's company, and became a minor figure of this court. And since she could do nothing about her deprivation, she took what she could get and made the best of it, and as I believe, those two strong-willed, resolute women got on well together by reason of their likeness, where had they met on truly equal terms they might have clashed resoundingly for the same reason. But the queen could be generous and warm without condescension to one who was not a rival, and the Lady Senena could take with dignity from one she felt to be at once her creditor and debtor. The Lady Gladys, too, with her budding beauty, became an admired figure among the young women of the queen's retinue, and was much favoured by her, and after some months whispers began to go round that a good match might be made for her. As for the two little boys, they went in and out freely among the other noble children about the court, and being very young, soon took this lavish state for their right, and forgot the more austere customs and habits of Wales. David in particular, with his beauty and his winning ways, was made much of by the noblewomen, and became a favourite even with the king. And surely this imprisonment seemed to them rather an enlargement, for never had they been so indulged and lived so finely.

Thus King Henry hedged his interests every way, keeping his puppets close under his hand, but treating them with every consideration and make-believe honour that should maintain them sharpened and ready for use at need. And their efficacy was made plain, for that year ended with no word of any unrest in Wales, and all through the two years that followed the same heavy quietness held. David of Gwynedd knew only too well the sword that dangled over his head, and he went peacefully, minding his lopped princedom and biding his time, with never a false move.

As for us, what is there to tell? We lived a life unbelievably calm on the surface, but it was a furtive, watchful calm, in which all but the children moved with held breath. Yet no man can live for ever taut like a strung bow, and I remember days when indeed this life of ours seemed pleasant enough, comfortable and well-fed as we were, and like the children we drew perilously near to being content with it.

But not the lady. She closed her lips upon her great grievance, but in her heart she thought of nothing else. I think she hoped at first that David would blaze up again in revolt, and cause her husband to be taken hastily out of his cage and sent with a strong force to draw off Welsh allegiance from him. But as the slow year wore away, and the uneasy peace held fast, she lost hope in this, and fretted after some other way. And she took into her confidence the only Welshman left her, but for myself, still a boy, and that was my mother's husband.

It was fitting that those two should cleave together, for next to her, and doubtless the Lord Griffith himself, whom now we never saw, my mother's husband was the unhappiest among us. For that slothful ease of mind under which the rest of us laboured in this well-furnished prison was impossible to him. There was no taste but wormwood ever in his mouth, and no weather but winter and cold about him, his torment being perpetual, for my mother was ever before his face and by his side, and even in his bed, and at all times submissive and dutiful, and at all times indifferent to him, and by this time he was assured, whether he admitted it or no, that there was nothing he could do, between this and death, to change her or himself. He had her, and he would never have her. Her hate he could have borne, but as she could not love, so she could not hate him. She was now thirty-four years old, and even more beautiful than as a girl, and he could neither live happily with her nor without her.

So it was some relief at least to his restlessness when the Lady Senena began to employ him as news gatherer for her about the Tower. I was not in their confidence, but I saw that he spent much of his time wandering about the fortress, observing at what hours the guard was changed at every gate, and when the wardens made their rounds, and every particular concerning the daily order of this city within a city. To this end he made himself agreeable and useful to the guards, and made himself out, surely truthfully enough, as weary and discontented for lack of work, so that after some weeks he had a few regular familiars among them who were willing to use him as messenger, and would talk freely to him. So patiently was all done that there were some he might truly call his friends. From them he brought in morsels of news from Wales more than were to be heard about the court, where the Lady Senena might pick them up for herself. Also, being very wise with horses, he made himself well accepted in the stables, and was several times among the grooms who went out to buy or to watch at the horse sales at Smithfield on Fridays. And as I know, after the second such occasion the Lady Senena gave him money for some purposes of her own.

It was late in the autumn of the year twelve hundred and forty-three when he came back from the outer world after a trip to buy sumpter ponies, and was closeted a while, as was usual, with the lady. It was as they came out into the hall where I was sitting with my mother and the children that he turned and looked again, and closely, into her face, and said: 'Madam, I have heard mention made of your son Llewelyn.'

It was the first time that name had been uttered openly among us since we had left Shrewsbury, though what she had told her lord in private I do not know. She halted as though she had turned to ice, and in her face I could read nothing, neither hostility nor tenderness.

'What can the horse-traders of London know of my son Llewelyn?' she said, in a voice as impenetrable as her countenance.

'From a Hereford dealer who buys Welsh mountain ponies, and trades as far as Montgomery,' he said. He did not look at her again, and he did not speak until she asked.

'And what does this dealer say of my son?'

'Two drovers came down from Berwyn with ponies. They told him they were bred on their lord's lands in Penllyn. And the name of their lord was Llewelyn ap Griffith. He lives, madam, he is well, he has his manhood, and he is set up on his own lands.'

'Set up by his uncle,' she said, so drily that I could not tell whether there was any bitterness there, or any wonder, or whether she was glad in her heart that he should be living and free, and in some sort a princeling, or whether she grudged him all, and chiefly his freedom. 'So he got his pay,' she said. 'for betraying me, after all. Why else should David give him an appanage, and he with so little left for himself?'

My mother's husband said bluntly, for he had the Welsh openness with those he served: 'Madam, if he had betrayed you we should never have reached the border. Do you think one well-mounted courier could not move faster than we did, with two litters and a gaggle of children? He got his commote for soldier service. These men of his said he was in arms with his uncle at Rhuddlan.'

'There was no blood shed there,' she said sharply, 'and little fighting.' But whether she said it to belittle what he had done or to reassure herself in face of a danger she had not known one of her children was venturing, I could not be sure. And then she said in a muted cry, gripping her hands together: 'He was not yet thirteen years old!'

Then I knew that for all her hard front, and the bitterness that tore her two ways where he was concerned, she still loved him.

That winter came and passed in mild, moist weather, with scarcely any frost but a sprinkling of rime in the mornings, washed away by rain or melted by thin sunshine long before noon. And I noticed that daily the Lady Senena watched the skies and the wind, and bided her time, and was often private with my mother's husband for short whiles. In February, when for the first time the true winter came down, a fair fall of snow and then iron frost to bind it, it seemed to me that their eyes grew intent and bright, as though they had been waiting only for this. And when it held all the last ten days of February, with every day they drew breath more easily and hopefully, and spoke of the weather as though it held more meaning for them than for us, how the word went that the great marshes of Moorfields, outside the north gate of the city, were frozen over hard as rock, but with overmuch deadening snow for good sport, so that the young men who went out there for play were forced to sweep small parts of the ice for their games. And I thought how this way from the city would be the quickest and most secret, once that marsh was past, for the forest came close on that side. But they told me nothing, and I asked nothing.

The last day of February matched all those before. My mother's husband went out from us in the afternoon, and did not come back with the night, but the Lady Senena came in the dusk from visiting her lord, and told us that she would spend the night in the lodging with us, for the Lord Griffith was a little unwell, and she had entreated him to rest, and the guards not to disturb him again until morning.

What she told my mother I do not know, but those two women slept – or at least lay, for I think much of the night they did not sleep at all – in the same bed that night, and I know they talked much, for I heard their voices whenever I stirred from my own slumber. The girl had a little chamber of her own, and the boys slept as children do, wholeheartedly and deeply. I lay in the dark, listening to those two muted voices within, that spoke without distinguishable words, my mother's pitched lower, and now that I heard them thus together, far the calmer and more assured, and the lady's tight, brittle and imploring, like one lost in prayer. I doubt she was not heard.

Towards dawn she slept. When the first light began I was uneasy with the silence, and I got up and pulled on my hose and shirt and cotte, and went stealthily and lifted the latch of the high chamber, to be sure if they breathed and lived. For sleep and silence draw very close to death.

There was a wick burning in a dish of fat, paling now that a little light came in from the sky. My mother lay open-eyed, high on the pillows, her face turned towards me as though she had known before ever I touched the latch that I was coming. She held that great lady cradled asleep on her breast like a child, and over the greying head she motioned to me, quite gently, to go back and close the door. And so I did, and in a few moments she came out to me.

At this time I was already taller than she, but she was so slender and straight that she had a way of towering, not rigidly or proudly, but like a silver birch tree standing alone. She had only a long white shift on her, and her arms were bare, and all her long, fair hair streamed down over her shoulders, and hung to her waist. In this harsh frost, now twelve days old, she seemed to feel no chill. And I have said she was beautiful, and strange.

'Make no sound,' she said in a whisper, 'but let her sleep, she has great need. Samson, I am not easy, I cannot see clear. Somewhere there is a death.'

Daily there is a death waiting for someone, for one who departs and others who remain to mourn. But she looked at me with those eyes that missed what others see and saw what others miss, and I knew that this was very near.

I was afraid, for I understood nothing, though something I did suspect. I asked her: 'Mother, what must I do?'

'Take your cloak,' she said, very low, and peering before her with eyes fixed as it were on a great distance, 'and go and look if there is anyone stirring about the keep, or under Lord Griffith's windows.'

So I wrapped my cloak about me, and crept out shivering into the icy morning, where the light as yet was barely grey, though very clear, and still full of fading stars. It was too early for anyone to be abroad but the watch, and I knew their rounds, even if they kept to them strictly, and on such mornings I had known them none too scrupulous about patrolling every corner, preferring the warmth of the guardrooms. I went softly, keeping under the walls of the houses, and left their shelter only when I must. I could see the great, square hulk of the tower outlined clear but pale against the sky, and beyond it, across the open ground, the tooth-edged summit of the curtain wall, and the ruled line of the guard-walk below its crest. All the grass was thick and creaking with rime, the bushes that stood silent and motionless in the stillness rang like bells when I brushed too close, and shed great fronds of feathery ice on my hose and shoes. I drew closer, circling the rim of the ditch and avoiding the main face where the great doorway was, and the ditch was spanned. There was such a silence and stillness that I should have heard if another foot had stirred in the crisp snow, but there was nothing to hear. I was the only creature abroad.

The Lord Griffith's apartment was very high at the rear part of the keep, with two small windows at the base of one of the corner turrets. I made my way round by the rim of the ditch, which was deep and wide, and for the most part kept clear of briars and bushes. Everything was quiet and nothing strange, until I came under the part where his dwelling was, and looked up at those two round-beaded windows, set deep in the stone. And hanging from the ledge of one of them I saw a dangling line of knotted cloth, no more than two or three yards long, that seemed to end in a fringe of torn threads, light enough to stir in the high air while the coil above hung still. My eyes were young and sharp, and this frayed material I knew for a piece of brocaded tapestry such as might furnish the covering of a bed, or wall-hangings.

Then, halfway to understanding, I looked below, and at first saw nothing stranger than a stony outcrop breaking the level of the ditch's grassy bottom, under the window, for this, too, was covered, thick with rime. But as I looked I knew that it was no stone, but a man, humped heavily upon one shoulder and half-buried in the ground, and about him the rope that had broken and let him fall had made serpentine hollows in the snow and then made shift to heal them with its own new growths of hoar-frost. The pool of darkness under and about him I had taken for a shelf of level shale, for it was so fast frozen and sealed over with rime, but it was his blood. And at first I had thought this body was headless, for he had so fallen that his head was flattened and driven into his shoulders.

The Lord Griffith, ever a big and well-fleshed man, had grown heavier still in his enforced idleness, too heavy for the ancient and treacherous drapings of his bed to sustain him. His hopes and his captivity were alike over. He had escaped out of his prison and out of this world.

CHAPTER III

There was nothing I or any but God could do for him any longer. All I could do was creep back, shivering, to the living, and tell what I had seen. For when the warders of the Tower discovered it there would be such an outcry that we, shocked and stricken as we were, had no choice but to be prepared for it, and ready and able to meet all that might be said and done. Thus, that I might know the better what I was about, I came to hear the rest of it in haste.

The rope she had contrived to take in to him, doubtless coiled about her body, for the warders examined all the gifts she carried to the prisoner, had proved too short at the test, and he had eked it out with the furnishings of his chamber. Unhappy for him that he secured this makeshift part of his line to the upper end. If he had trusted only the last few yards to its rotten and deceitful folds he might have fallen without injury, and made his escape. As it was, my mother's husband, shivering in the cold on the outer side of the curtain wall, had waited in vain until there was no hope left, and he must take thought for his own life, for he could not re-enter the Tower gates without condemning himself, if the plot was discovered. So there would be no shrouded travellers riding out at Moorgate with the first light, across the frozen marsh into the forest. Or at the best, only one . . .

Somehow the thing passed over us, and we endured it. There was no sense in blaming wife or children, or the servants who served them, in face of a grief that could not now be remedied. We watched out the time, owned to nothing, told nothing we knew. And they took him up, that great, shattered man, and gave him a prince's mourning and burial, for King Henry was as anxious as any to be held blameless, well knowing that there would be those who suspected him in the matter of this death. But I know what I saw, and what was after told to me. Moreover, after our lord himself, there was no man lost more by this disaster than the king, for with Griffith dead he had no hold to restrain David, and no fit weapon to use against him. It was the end of his fine plans, as it was of ours. There was nothing he could do but begin over again, and mend his defences as best he could.

My mother's husband did not come back, and though he was quickly missed, and certainly hunted, they did not find him. But for more than a month we waited in anxiety, for fear he should be dragged back, for him they would not have spared, having found the line he had secretly secured from a merlon down the outer face of the curtain wall in a secluded corner, for his lord's escape. It seems to me that all had been very well done, but for that too-short rope, for late though he must have left his own flight, yet he got clean away with both the horses he had provided, for they made

41

enquiry everywhere after good riding horses stabled for pay and abandoned, and none were ever reported. Though truly the coper who had such a beast dropped into his hands masterless and gratis might well hold his peace about it.

Afterwards, when we spoke of this lost venture again, for at first there was a great silence over it, they spoke also before me, being the last man they had. For two husbands were lost, one living and one dead, and they were left with only me, a man according to Welsh law by one year and some months. And freely they said in my hearing the deepest thoughts of their minds and regrets of their hearts, and strange hearing they were. For those two women were changed from that day. The Lady Senena, who had never doubted her own judgment and rightness, was saddened into many misgivings and questionings, and sometimes she said:

'It was I who killed him. Not now, but long ago. I might have prevailed on him to accept a second place, to be content as his brother's vassal, and he might now have been alive and free both, and a man of lands, too. But I was as set as he on absolute justice. Is it now justice God has dealt out to me?'

Now much of this I remembered, as men remember the burden of an old song, familiar but without a name, until it came to me that she echoed the entreaties of Llewelyn, that last day before he left her to go to his duty. But I never reminded her, and I think she did not recall where she first heard this prophecy: 'It would not cost him so high as you will cost him, if you go on with this.' She had cost him life and all, but what profit in telling her so?

And my mother, who all these years had lived with that other man, had lain in his arms, cooked food for him, washed for him, been pliant and submissive to him, and all without letting him set foot over the doorsill of her mind and heart, and often without seeming to know that he lived and breathed beside her, she took to listening with reared head every time the guard passed, or if voices were raised in the courtyards, her eyes wide and her breath held, until she was satisfied that they had not found and hauled him back, bloodied and beaten, to answer for his loyalty with his life. And when this time was past, still she would say suddenly over the fire at night:

'I wonder which way he took, and where he is now?'

I told her he would certainly make for Wales, for his repute was clean there, and he would not want for a lord to take him into service. And I said that he must be safe over the border already, out of the king's reach.

But that was not all that ailed her. For as often as the night was cold she would be wondering if he had a warm cloak about him, and when the spring storms came it was: 'I hope he has a roof over him tonight, and a good fire. He takes cold easily.'

Also, where she had always called him by his name, which was Meilyr, and only now did I begin so to think of him, as a man unique and yet subject to fear and pain and cold like me, now she never spoke a name, but said always: 'he'. 'I wish he took better keep of himself, I doubt he'll be out even in this weather.' 'He never liked leaving Wales. I pray he has comfort there now.' And once she cried out in enlightenment and distress: 'I was not good to him!' And once, in wonder and awe, she said as if to herself: 'He loved me.'

Now when the news of the Lord Griffith's death reached Wales, as news from England did almost as fast as the east wind could blow that way, the manner and suddenness of it, the circumstance that it took place, like a blow aimed at Wales itself, on St David's day, the injustice of the imprisonment which had brought it about, all these combined to make him a hero and martyr, who perhaps had been neither, and also to give to his whole story a fervent Welsh glow that turned every enmity against England, and quite misted over the old dissensions between Griffith and his brother.

Long afterwards I heard an old bard at Cemmaes singing a lament for Griffith, made at his reburial at Aberconway, and hymning the great grief and indignation of the Lord David at this untimely cutting-off. And I was still young enough to make some mock of his singing, for I said that David had had good reason to be glad of the deliverance, for it set him free to strike afresh, and with a united Wales at his back now, for his right. And the old man, though he did not deny it, was undisturbed.

'For,' said he, 'have you room in you for only one view at a time, and do you never look both forward and back together?'

I said that there was something in what he said, but nevertheless such extravagance of grief over a brother he fought with all his life, and whose removal eased his way to glory, was strangely inconsistent.

'When you have half my years,' he said, 'you will have learned that where the human heart is concerned there is nothing strange in inconsistency. Only what is too consistent is strange.'

So it may be that there was truth in the story that David grieved sincerely over the fate of his half-brother, and nothing contradictory in the fiery vigour with which he took advantage of it.

They had only one leader this time, not two, and only one cause, not two. Barely nine weeks after the Lord Griffith died, the Lord David had entered into an alliance with all the Welsh chiefs, but for those very few, like Gwenwynwyn's son in Powys, who were more English marcher barons in their thinking than princes of Wales. And before June began they were in the field, stirring up the spirit of revolt in every corner of the land, raising and training levies, and making rapid raids almost nightly across the border, and into that part of Powys that bordered Eryri, the citadel of Snowdon, the abode of eagles. King Henry's castle of Diserth, built after his bloodless victory of three years before, was in some danger of being cut off from Chester, whence all its supplies and reinforcements must come, and by mid-June the whole of the march was in arms.

But David did more, for he formally repudiated the treaty made under duress with King Henry, and sent an envoy with letters to Pope Innocent stating his case, and appealing for support in maintaining the independent right of Wales. This did not come to light until later in the year, when the king was greatly startled and incensed to receive a writ from the abbots of Cymer and Aberconway, as commissioners for the pope, summoning him to appear at the border church of Caerwys, to answer the charge that he had discarded the promised arbitration in his dispute with David, and resorted wantonly to war, thus procuring by force what should only have been decided, perhaps differently, by discussion and agreement. I spoke with a clerk who had been in council when this writ was delivered, and I vouch for the terms of it on his word. And I have heard it said, though for this I cannot vouch, that the one particular factor which most enraged David, and put it in his mind to resort to the pope, was a rumour reaching him that King Henry, in his casting about for a fresh hold on what he had gained, after the restraint of Griffith was removed, had secretly considered having his elder son Edward, the long-legged four-year old who ran wild about the stables with our young David, declared Prince of Wales. It may be so. If he was not cherishing this intent then, he certainly did so later. And if true, it was justification enough for tearing up the treaty.

Howbeit, the king naturally did not go to Caerwys, but merely made haste to send fresh letters and envoys to Pope Innocent on his own account, putting his own case, no doubt very persuasively. Yet this play filled up the latter months of this year, and caused him to walk warily until he got the answer he wanted, transferring the case once again from Welsh to English law, the English purse being the heavier. So Wales gained half a year in preparing for the battle to come.

At first the defence was left to the wardens of the march, for Henry still preferred to concentrate on compiling his evidence for the pope, and sharpening for use the only subtle weapon he had left. He withdrew Owen Goch from his prison, took him into his own household, and nursed his ambition and ardour until he prevailed upon him to swear allegiance to England in return for the king's support in winning his birthright.

The Lady Senena was no longer so innocent as to believe that she could repose any trust in King Henry's faithfulness, but she had still a shrewd confidence in his self-interest, and indeed it seemed that his need of Owen at this pass was urgent enough to ensure his good behaviour towards him. She therefore made no objection when her son eagerly accepted the king's offer, and willingly swore fealty to him. But in private she advised him to be always on his guard, and in particular to acquiesce until he found out what the king had planned for him. 'For,' said she with a grim smile, 'either Shrewsbury or Chester, at need, is nearer to Wales than the Tower.'

This Owen the Red was then seventeen years old, and with every day more like his father in appearance, very well-grown and already more than six feet tall. He was not ill-looking, but less striking than the Lord Griffith by reason of a certain too-emphatic sharpness in his features, where his sire's for all their impetuosity and pride had been good-humoured. Owen had all his father's rashness and arrogance, but lacked the warmth and generosity with which he could turn back and make amends. His body bade fair to grow as wide, but his mind and nature never would, they closed against other men in suspicion and ready for jealousy.

It may be that his imprisonment, first in Criccieth and then in London, had done something to narrow him, but I think it did not change, but only aggravate, his tendencies. Certainly it had not been arduous here in

England, however he had chafed at it, and it had done nothing to teach him patience or humility. The first offer of sovereignty in Gwynedd had him reaching for it greedily. I think King Henry did not have to exert much persuasion to get him to promise homage for it. And if the fulfilment of his hopes and the wearing of the talaith were delayed, he got something by way of earnest at once, for he was very richly fitted out with clothes at the crown's expense, and provided with a horse and a small retinue to go with him, suitable to a native prince coming home.

The place chosen for his bid was Chester, the nearest strong base to Eryri. And since he must set out squired and escorted almost wholly by English retainers, and with an officer of the king to supervise and direct his efforts, he had need of someone who could write well both in Welsh and English, and Latin, too, if need arose. And there was no one but me. So I became clerk and squire to Owen the Red.

My mother had lost her childlike look since Meilyr fled from London. I know not how it was, but she had grown more comfortable and ordinary, and as though in some way nearer. Much as I had loved her, and she me, being embraced by her, touching her, walking with her had been like touching a picture or a carving, but now she was flesh. And very hard it was for me to leave her, but she willed it so, for she was wholly devoted to the Lady Senena's household, having lived for this family all her days. So I said submissively that I would go.

'And think,' she said, sitting with me that last night, after the children were asleep, 'how close this town of Chester is to the commote of Ial. He was born there, west of the Alun, he may well have gone back there. Surely if he hears that the Lord Owen is in Chester and calling up his men, he will come to him there.'

Hearing her was like another echo in my mind. For she had but one 'he' who needed no naming.

I said: 'He may well.' But did we know whether he was alive or dead?

'It may be,' she said, 'that you will meet him there.'

'And if I should,' I said, 'have you any message to him?'

She sighed, saying: 'It is too late. I shall never see him again.' And I think she was a little sad, but with her it was not easy to know, for there was always a withdrawn sadness about her, and where its roots lay, even now that her feet trod the same earth with the rest of us, I never could fathom.

On that last evening before we rode from London she took out, from the box where she kept her few ornaments, a plain silver ring with an oval seal, a deep-cut pattern of a hand severed at the wrist, holding a rose. I had never seen it before, nor, I think, had any other person among us, except, perhaps, her husband. She put it on my finger, and bade me take it with me, for it was my father's, and who knew? – it might yet bring me in contact with him. And that was the first and last time that she spoke of him to me, at least in all the time I had been of an age to understand and remember. It was long since I had even given a thought to that unknown man-at-arms who had fathered me, and when first she said 'your father' I own I took her to be referring to Meilyr, even though she had never before called him so. But then I knew that of him she would only have felt it needful to say: 'It was *his*!' Yet the first man who took her I do believe she

45

loved, however briefly, and the second, the one to whom she was lawfully given, I doubt she never did, not even then, when his absence was ever-present with her as his presence had never been. For indeed she was always a strange woman.

So I promised her I would wear it, and did so, I confess, with some pride, as though I had acquired with it a place in some legitimate line. And the next day I kissed her, and set out.

It was no easy matter being clerk and personal servant to Owen Goch, for he had grown accustomed to the English ways after his recent heady novitiate at King Henry's court, and required that servants should be servile, while I had still the Welsh habit of speaking my mind freely even to my masters. Familiarity he would not stomach now, but cut it off short, with lashing reproof, or if his mood was ill, with a ready blow, so that I learned to keep my distance in word as well as fact. But once this was accepted, we got on well enough on such terms as he dictated and I endured with an equal mind. It was less wise of him to use somewhat the same tone and manner with the English fighting men who surrounded him, or at least the lower ranks among them, for he knew well enough how to moderate his pride with the knights and their Commander. But Owen, ever over-sanguine, felt himself within grasp of the talaith that should have been his father's, and he would be a prince in every part.

To John de Rohan, who was in fact his guard and keeper rather than the captain of his escort, I am sure he ranked rather as a kind of engine of war on two legs, an expensive but hopefully valuable weapon, somewhat irritating and cumbersome to manipulate about the country, but effective once brought to the proper spot.

I was of an age then to get more profit from adventuring about the world, and in that summer weather I used my eyes and ears to good effect, and found great pleasure in the pageant of man and season and countryside. And often for days, and ever longer as time passed, I forgot my mother and the Lady Senena, and the life we had left behind, and so, I am sure, did Owen Goch. I knew well enough, if he did not, that we were no more free than we had been in the Tower, but it was hard to believe it while we rode in the sunshine thus, and fed well and lay comfortably at every day's end.

We got a ceremonial welcome in Chester, all that Owen could have wished, for they hoped much from him. John Lestrange, the warden of the northern march, received us and saw us installed in a fine lodging, and there was set up the office that was to busy itself about drafting proclamations and appeals to the Welsh, and circulating them throughout the Middle Country as far as Conway, and by means of various agents, even deeper into Eryri. I came into my own there as Owen's best scrivener in the Welsh language, for though he had a fine flow of eloquence like most of his house, he was not lettered beyond the signing of his name. Very fine proclamations we drew up between us, and I was kept busy copying the long pedigree of my young lord, and setting forth his claims and his injuries, King Henry's tender care for him and concern for his just cause, and the peace and benefit that might accrue to Wales if they did right to him, and rallied to his standard against the uncle who shut him out from his inheritance. Throughout all those parts of Wales which were held under the crown these were read and distributed and cried publicly. And where the crown had no sway they were insinuated by whatever agency de Rohan could discover and use.

So the last of the autumn passed, with only one drawback, that we got no result for all our labour. And for myself, I did not see these efforts of mine go out with a single mind or a whole heart, seeing at whose expense and for whose profit this matter was really undertaken. For here was Wales contending against England, and a Welsh prince was seeking to win away as much as he might of Wales to a side which, Owen or no Owen, could only be called England's. And surely there was a part of me that drew relieved breath as every day passed, and still barely a man, and none of substance, took the bait we put out and came to declare himself.

Then Owen, unhappy with this state of affairs, for he had counted on making a strong appeal to all those chiefs who had taken his father's part, at least did something for those few Welsh who were brought in prisoner, for he suggested that they should be offered grace and aid if they would either convert to his banner, or better, go back into Wales as agents for him. But such as accepted this surely took to their heels gladly when they were released to their own country, and did no recruiting for us, and such as elected to join the king's forces did so to save life and limb, and were of little worth, their hearts being elsewhere.

Most of that winter we passed in Chester, but when the hardest of the weather was over we moved out nearer to the salt marshes and sands of the Dee, to the king's manor of Shotwick. I think by then King Henry had given up the idea that Owen could be of much use to him at this stage, but still he required him as a puppet to be produced and give his proceedings a cover of justice when he put an army into the field in earnest, as now he had determined to do. For the Welsh revolt continued vigorous and successful. In February a certain Fitz-Mathew, who was in command of a force of knights controlling the southern march, was ambushed and killed in a hill pass near Margam, and most of his company shattered. And if King Henry could rejoice over one bloody engagement near Montgomery, where, as we heard, three hundred Welshmen were drawn into a net from which they could not escape, and there slaughtered, he was soon grieving again for the loss of Mold, for David stormed and took it at the end of March. That could not pass. With Mold in David's hands again there was no safety for the royal castle at Diserth, it might be cut off from its base of Chester at any time. The king knew then that there was nothing for him to do but call up the whole muster of his knighthood service, and launch a full campaign with the summer, and he began at once to send out orders to his justiciars to collect provisions for his army.

We spent most of that year at Shotwick, for the king would not risk using Owen in the field, though he did entertain and display him at Chester when he came there in August, and halted his army for a week. Then they moved on to the banks of the Conway, and the king began the building of a great new castle on the rock of Degannwy on the east bank, to provide protection from a distance both for Diserth and Chester. They remained in camp there, busy with this building, until the end of October.

Now it chanced that that year the winter came down early and like iron, before autumn was half over, fighting at last for Wales. The whole month of October was bitter and bleak, full of frosts and gales and snow, and in that camp by the Conway they froze and starved, killed and died, with no mercy on either side. The king's army was far too strong to be attacked in pitched battle, which in any case we Welsh never favoured, and it managed to keep open a supply line back to Chester, as well as bringing in supplies by sea from Ireland. But ships are flimsy against such storms as came down that year, and some foundered, and one at least was run aground by a clumsy steersman in the sands on the Aberconway side, and fought over bitterly by both armies, but the Welsh got away with most of its cargo. Their need was at least as great, for the king had landed troops from Ireland in Anglesey and captured or despoiled the late crops there. But King Henry went on doggedly with the building of his new castle, and the work grew rapidly.

One of the few Welsh soldiers who had embraced Owen's cause was our courier back and forth to this camp at Degannwy, and brought us grim accounts of what went forward there, how the English had raided the abbey of Aberconway, across the river, stripped the great church of all its treasures, and fired the barns, how they had given up taking prisoners, and slaughtered even the noblemen who fell into their hands, until David took to repaying the murders upon the English knights he captured. Nightly the Welsh made lightning raids in the darkness, killed and withdrew. And daily the English, after every skirmish, brought back into camp Welsh heads as horrid trophies.

These things he told us, and I could not forbear from watching Owen's face as he listened, for these were the heads of his kinsmen, over whom he desired to rule, and whose support he was wooing. But he was not of such subtlety as to question deeply what he did, and saw no further than the right that had been denied his father and was still denied him.

'And I'll tell you,' said the messenger, steaming beside our comfortable fire, 'one they have killed, though he was brought in prisoner after an honest fight, and that's the youngest of Ednyfed Fychan's sons.' This was the great steward who had served Llewelyn Fawr and now David, in all some forty years of noble, wise dealing, without greed for himself, and with the respect of all. And he was now an old man. 'Hanged him,' said our courier, 'on a bare tree, high for the Welsh to see. And that David will never forgive.'

Sometimes I had wondered, as I did then, about this man, whether he was not carrying news two ways, and not all to the English side of Conway, for he was a bold and fearless creature, as he proved by his many journeys across that torn and tormented country, and would not change his coat simply to buy a little security.

'Yet he cannot hold out long now,' Owen said, wringing hard at the hope that was always uppermost in him. 'Last time he gave in without much blood spilled, and now they tear each other like leopards, and he gives no ground. Surely he must be near surrender. They feel the cold, too. They have lost half their winter store, they must be as hungry as we, they cannot continue thus for long.'

48

I saw then the small spark that lit in the man's eyes when Owen spoke of 'they' and 'we', and I understood him better.

'Last time,' he said, 'the season played false. Now the winter comes early and true as steel. And he has a list of loyal chiefs behind him, as long as your arm, such as he never had before. There's a name high on the list,' he said, eyeing Owen all the while, 'that will be known to you, the name of Llewelyn ap Griffith.'

Owen jerked up his head to glare across the fire. 'He is there? In arms?'

'He is there. In arms. And very apt and ready, too, in the teeth of cold and hunger.'

'You have seen him?'

'I have. Close about his uncle very often, but he is trusted with a command of his own, and they do tolerably well in a night raid. With no son of his own he had good need of such a nephew.'

I felt the sting of every word, though they were not aimed at me. And I leaned back into shadow that I might smile, no matter how bitterly, unnoticed. But I think that man knew. His voice all this while was level, mild and dutiful. And as I have said, Owen was not a subtle person, nor, for that matter, a sensitive listener.

'I can but give you my judgment,' said our courier when he left us. 'There'll be no surrender. Not this year.'

Nor was there. And at the end of October King Henry realised it and made the best of it. He could no longer sustain his exposed position, with such numbers to feed. But he could and did raise Degannwy to a point where it could be garrisoned and supplied, by sea and land, before he ordered withdrawal. It was understood that this campaign was to be resumed and finished, with total victory and Eryri conquered, the following year. But that had been the understanding also this year, and God and his servant, the cold, had disposed.

The king also set up a new justiciar in Cheshire before he went south, one John de Grey, and gave him orders what was to be done by way of strangling Wales indirectly, since he could not do it honestly with his hands. Trade with the land was to cease, totally. In particular there were certain things Wales could not provide herself, as salt, iron, woven cloth, and a sufficiency of corn, and these at least could be denied her.

Then he went south with his army.

An idle winter we passed that year, waiting for the battle-time to come round again, though to my mind fighting is an ill use for the kindly summer. After the early frosts and snows the weather proved less severe, and we had good riding there above the Dee when the salt marshes were hard and firm, and for want of real employment spent much time in the saddle. True, de Rohan's guards were always close, our household was all English, and there were archers among the escort, who could as well bring us down, if we showed a disposition to play King Henry false, as ward off Welsh attack from us. And to tell truth, it irked me that I should have to expect execution from either side at the first free move, as though I had no real place of my own, and no cause, anywhere in this world. But if it irked Owen, he gave no sign. All his impatience was for the seasons to turn, so that the king's unwieldy muster could be on the move again, and hurry to

49

bring him his princedom. He fretted all the winter, gazing westwards.

As for me, I was in two minds. I had been too long in the service of the Lord Griffith's family to feel at ease when my vision showed me black, or even a dubious shade of grey, where they saw white. Yet I was not happy with the letter of the law, and the narrow knife-edge of justice that was slitting so many Welsh throats to uphold a Welsh prince's right. And I had been glad in my heart of the iron winter that had caused the king to withdraw before he suffered worse losses than those already sustained. And I was glad now of every storm-cloud that threatened, and held back the new campaign. Even so, this waiting had to end.

It ended as none of us had expected. On the last day of February a messenger came riding from Degannwy, and turned aside to cross the Dee and come to Shotwick for a fresh horse before hurrying on to Chester. It was pure chance that Owen and I were out in the mews when he came, and so we heard his news before he took it in to de Rohan. For Owen, ever greedy for any word from the west, began to question him at sight, and the rider – he was an Englishman of the garrison, and known to us – saw no reason for denying him.

'My lord, the case is altered with a vengeance,' he said, big with the import of what he carried. 'You've lost a kinsman and an enemy, and what's to come next is guessing, but it's thought in Degannwy we're a great leap nearer getting by luck what we failed to get last year by fighting. We got the word yesterday, and from a sure source: the Lord David's dead!'

'Dead!' cried Owen, and paled and glowed, tossed by a tangle of emotions like a leaf where currents meet. 'My uncle dead? In battle? There's been fighting, then, already?'

The man shook his head, stripping the saddle-cloth from his steaming horse and letting a groom take the bridle from his hand. 'In his bed, at Aber. The sweating sickness did what we failed to do by the Conway. He's dead, and Gwynedd in disarray. They've taken his body into Aberconway, to lie by his father, and the bards are tuning their harps over him. And I must get on to Chester, and let Lestrange know.'

And he went in haste to the house, while the grooms led in his blown mount and began to rub him down and water him sparingly, and saddle a replacement for the ride to Chester, which was no great way. But Owen took me by the arm in mute excitement, and drew me away into the mews, out of earshot.

'Samson,' he said in my ear, quivering, 'saddle up now, for both of us, while they're all taken up with this news. Openly, as always when we ride. Saddle up and lead the horses out, and not a word to anyone. Now, while he's setting their ears alight within!'

I was slow to understand, for he was not wont to be so decisive, and his whims usually made more commotion. I said foolishly: 'What do you mean to do?'

'Slip my collar, now while I may, and ride to Aber. Do you think I'll sit back and let King Henry pluck Wales like a rose from a bush, while she's lost for a leader? If my uncle's dead, childless as he is, Gwynedd is my inheritance. I am going to claim it. Get the horses! Quickly!'

'Thus?' I said, 'without clothes or provisions?'

'If we carried a saddle-bag they'd know, fool!' he said, I own justly.

So I went as he had said, where they were bustling about the courier's beast, and with no concealment or haste, though losing no time, either, I saddled the horses we usually rode, and led them out. The sun was breaking through early mist and cloud at the rise of a fair day, good enough reason for us to change our minds and ride, and unless the grooms thought to come out and watch us depart, how could they know that this time we had no escort riding behind us within easy bow-shot? We had been there among them so long, and seemed so content to leave our future to them, that I think their watch must have been slack enough for some time before this, had we realised it. And within the house they had ears for nothing but the news from Aber.

We mounted and rode, and no one loosed a shout after us. And give him his due, Owen walked his mount down the gentle slope and into the coppice that gave the nearest cover, riding as loose and easy in the saddle as if he meant nothing more than a little lazy exercise over the salt-flats. But when the trees were between us and the manor he set spurs to his horse and steered a course that made good use of ground cover, putting several miles behind us before he uttered a word or drew rein.

'God give us always such luck!' he said then, drawing breath deeply. 'I had not thought it would be so easy. We'll need to cross the Dee above Hawarden, and give Mold a wide berth. Degannwy, too! I won't be rounded up by English or Welsh short of Aber. If they follow, they'll keep to the roads, they'd not be safe else. But we'll do better and move faster. Better than owing any rights of mine to King Henry, now I'll take them for myself, and owe him nothing.'

I thought, as he did, how easy this beginning, at least, had been, and how we might have ventured the attempt, with better preparation, long ago if he had been so minded, and how we had never so much as considered it. The case was changed now, and not only because David was gone, but because Llewelyn remained, already a magnate, acknowledged, followed in war, there on the spot to catch the talaith as it fell, and with it, very logically, the consent and approval of all the chieftains who had followed his uncle into battle. For he was the only prince of his blood there to take up the burden and the privilege. And he the second son! Yes, Owen had good reason for the frantic haste he made on that ride.

We had good going between Dee and Clwyd, and crossed the latter river at Llanelwy, and nowhere did we excite any interest more than other travellers, for Owen was plainly dressed. Beyond Clwyd we took the old, straight road they say the Romans made, keeping well away from the coast and the castles, and prayed that they had not discovered our flight in time to send a fast rider by the direct road to Diserth, to start a hunt after us. But we saw nothing of any pursuit. Once we made a halt and took food at a shepherd's holding in the uplands, and got rest and fodder for our horses, but Owen would finish this ride before night, instead of breaking the journey, so we set out again as soon as the jaded beasts could go, but now in somewhat less haste, for at least we breathed more freely here.

We crossed Conway at Caerhun, and took it gently on the climb beyond, through the pass of Bwlch y Ddeufaen and along the great, bare causeway over the moors. When this track brought us down to sight of the sea we were but a few miles from Aber, and land and sea were growing dark. But the night came clear and bright with stars, and I could still see, across the vast pale stretch of Lavan sands, and the deep water beyond, the long, jutting coast of Anglesey, and the solitary rock of Yyns Lanog, an island of saints as holy as our own Enlli.

We came where the wall of the llys reared beside the track, under the shoulder of the mountains and staring across the sea. I had never before been in Aber, the favourite court of Llewelyn Fawr and his son, the noblest home of this noble line, and I was moved and awed, so grand was the soaring height of the mountains on one hand, and the sweep of the open salt-marshes on the other, melting into the distant glimmer of the sea. It was then so nearly dark that I could not see the timber keep on its high motte towering over the wall, or the roofs of the many buildings within, but the wall ran tall and even beside us until we drew near to the gate, and figures rose out of the dark to halt us. They were calm and made little sound, for they were on their own ground, in the heart of their own homeland, and the court they guarded was in deepest mourning for a chief dead as surely in battle as if he had perished by the Conway red with blood, with his slain heaped around him.

'Where are you bound, friends, by night?' the officer challenged us, and took Owen's horse by the bridle, for we were so nearly foundered by then, or our beasts were, that he knew well enough where we were bound, and turned us in towards the gate without waiting for an answer.

That vexed Owen, weary as he was, for he had forgotten the free ways of Welshmen. He took the man's hand by the wrist and ripped it from his rein and flung it aside. 'Take care whom you handle!' he said. 'I am Owen ap Griffith. Best stand out of my way. I am here to consult with the royal council of Gwynedd and with Ednyfed Fychan, the high steward. Send and let them know that Owen Goch is broken free from imprisonment in England, and come to take up the charge that belongs to him.'

The officer stood back and looked up at him long by the light of the torches his men had brought forth. He was a local man, most likely born in the tref outside the gate of the maenol, and he went bare-legged in the cold and in linen clothing, with only a light leather jerkin on him by way of body-armour, and a coarse cloth cape over his shoulders. He had a great bush of black hair, and another of beard with red in the black, and eyes like arrow-points in the torchlight.

'Ride in, my lord Owen,' he said, when he had mastered the look of us and memorised it. 'But slowly, and my runner will be before you. Follow him to the hall, and ride softly past the lady's apartment, for she's in mourning for her lord and ours, and it's late to trouble her tonight. I'll send word to the Lord Llewelyn that his brother is come, and doubtless he'll be ready to receive you.'

All the household of Aber, the young men of the war-band, the archers and men-at-arms gathered about the great hearth in the hall, the maid-servants, the scriveners, the bards, the children huddled cosily in the skins of the brychans by the wall, fell silent and watched us as we went by. In the vast, blackened roof the wisps of smoke hung lazily circling like the eddies of a sluggish river, and rivulets crept upwards to join it from the pine torches in sconces on the walls. The smell of resin and wood-smoke clung heavy and sweet. I think there had been music before we entered, and a murmur of voices but where we passed there was stillness and silence.

So we were brought into another room, smaller and withdrawn behind hide curtains, where a brazier burned. The walls were hung with tapestries, and skins of bear and wolf were laid on the beaten earth of the floor. The lost imprint of the hand of King John's daughter lay softly on all in that chamber. The torches burned in tall holders of silver, but they were few and dim, only enough to light the way for those passing through, for who had leisure to sit down over wine or warm his feet at a fire in Aber at this time? The young men of the bodyguard, having conveyed their lord with grief and solemnity to Aberconway, might lie down and sleep until they received other orders, but all the solid men of the council must be in almost constant debate over the desert he had left behind, the legal rights of his young widow, the state of readiness of the land for King Henry's next move against Gwynedd, now that its buckler and sword was laid low, with no son to take up the fight after him, not even a daughter to bear princes hereafter.

There was one great chair, higher than the rest on the dais by two tall steps, and carved and gilded. And I had half-expected that Llewelyn would be braced and ready for us there as on a throne already claimed. But the room was empty and silent. We waited some minutes, Owen with mounting impatience and rising gorge, before the curtains swung behind the dais, brusquely and suddenly, and a young man came shouldering through and let the hangings swing to behind him. I have said it was dim within the room, dulling even the red of Owen Goch's hair. The boy came forward a few quick steps before he halted to peer at us, standing there a foot or so lower than he stood. The light of the torches was on him, we saw him better than he could distinguish us.

I knew him to be but two months past seventeen then, for so was I. He had shot up by a head since last I had seen him, and stood a hand's-breadth taller than I, but well short of his brother's, and his shoulders were wide and his limbs long, but he carried little flesh upon him. His face was as I remembered it, all bright, gleaming lines of bone starting in the yellow light of torches and candles, with those fathomless peat-pool eyes reflecting light from the surface of their darkness. And the longer I gazed, the younger did he seem, this boy burned brown with living out of doors in all weathers, so that even in winter, in the long evenings shut within walls, his russet only fined and paled into gold. But what I most remember, beyond the careless plainness of his dress, which was homespun and dun, is the healed scar slashed down the inner side of his left forearm, and its fellow, a small, puckered star under the angle of his jaw on the right side, mementoes of Degannwy in the frost six months ago; and with that, the slight reddening and swelling of his eyelids, that might have marred him if I had not known it for the stigma of private weeping, some two days old.

He said clearly: 'They tell me there is one here claims to be brother to me. Which of you is he?'

I own I thought at first that this was policy, a move to affront and repulse the returned heir, but then I recalled that it was seven years since these two had stood face to face, and those perhaps the most vital seven years of Llewelyn's life, all the time of his enforced growing-up, under angry pressures in which Owen Goch had had no part. I do believe that he was honest. For never have I known him go roundabout of intent, but always straight for his goal. And before Owen could blaze, as he was willing to do, Llewelyn came closer, voluntarily surrendering whatever advantage he had in the height of the dais, and swinging down to look at us intently. I saw his eyes dilate and glow.

'It *is* you!' he said. 'I had thought it was some trick. Well, what's your business with me?' And after a pause, very brief and chill, he said: ' – *brother*!' as though he tried the savour of the word on his tongue, and found it very little to his taste.

'My business is hardly with you,' said Owen, stung and smarting, 'but with the council of Gwynedd. You know me. I *am* your brother, and since you will have me say it, your elder. The prince of Gwynedd is dead, and there is no heir to succeed him. And mine is the next claim.'

'You must forgive my being slow to recognise you,' said Llewelyn. 'I have been so long brotherless here, when I could well have done with a brother. Yes, the prince of Gwynedd is dead. No doubt you came to mourn him, you should have halted at Aberconway for that. As for an heir to succeed him, the council are in some dream that they have one ready to hand.' He drew back a short step, and looked Owen Goch over from head to foot and back again, and his face was bleak, like a man wrung but unwilling to weep. 'Who gnawed through your leash,' he said bitterly, 'you or King Henry?'

At that Owen began to smoulder and to threaten a blaze, and but that he found himself somewhat at a disadvantage, here, there would have been an outburst on the spot. 'What are you daring to charge against me?' he cried. 'If the king's men could have got their hands on me this day, do you think I should not have been dead by now, or on my way back to the Tower? He had no part in my coming.'

'So you say. But you have been his lapdog too long to be easily credited, and it makes good sense that he should toss you in here at this pass to break Gwynedd apart for him, so that he can devour piecemeal what he found too big to swallow whole. Strange chance,' said Llewelyn hardly, 'that offered you a way of escape now, after keeping the doors fast shut on you so long.'

'Well for you,' flamed Owen then, 'who have never been a prisoner! Can you not understand that I have been dogged at every step, never gone from room to room without a shadow on my heels, or ridden out without archers at my back? I broke loose as soon as I could, and I am here, and it is *my* doing – none other's!'

'A year too late,' said Llewelyn. 'Where were you when your masters sacked the church at Aberconway? Where were you when they hanged Edynfed's boy, the child of his old age, high on a tree by the shore of Conway, and stood Welsh heads in a row to freeze along the edge of the tide? Do you think,' he said, 'that we have not your fine proclamations by heart, every word? We know where you were, what you were doing, how you were living princely while we sweated and drowned and died. And we know who paid for it all, the very clothes on your back! And we know what you pledged for it, the future of Gwynedd and of Wales! To hold direct from the king whatever he could get for you!'

The blood had crowded dark and blue into Owen's face. 'You know, none so well,' he said thickly, 'that your mother and mine pledged that for our father, and for me after him, while we were still prisoners in Criccieth. What say did I ever have in it? I was no sooner out of one dungeon than into another.'

'And was it she who repeated the pledge, and signed your name to it, two years ago in Westminster? Oh, we have our intelligencers, too, even in King Henry's court. Who threatened you with rack and rope then? You jumped at it willingly. To get your few commotes of Wales you were ready to help him set fire and sword to the whole.'

'I wanted no such warfare! Was one side to blame for that bitter fighting more than the other? I did nothing but promise natural gratitude and loyalty for the restoration of my right . . .'

'Your right! Your *right*!' said Llewelyn through his teeth. 'Can you see nothing on earth but your right? Has no other man any right, except you? The right to be Welsh, tenant to a Welsh lord, judged by Welsh law, living by Welsh custom? You would have given over your own people to the king's officers to tax and plague and call to war service like the wretched English. Do you expect a welcome for that?'

'Yet it *is* my right,' said Owen, setting his jaw, 'and the council cannot but uphold it. I am the eldest son of our father, and the next direct heir to Gwynedd, and I stand on that right. And if you have complaints against me, so have I against you, and against him that's dead, for he deprived our father of his birthright and his liberty, and you – you turned traitor to your own family and sided with their enemies.'

'I sided with Wales,' said Llewelyn. 'Your grandsire and mine had a vision of Wales that I learned from him. Wales united under one prince and able to stand up to all comers. There's no other way of fending off England for long. I went with my uncle not against our father, but against England, and sorry I was and am that we could not all stand together. Now you come running with the same old ruinous devotion to a right that will dismember Gwynedd, let alone Wales, and feed it to your king, whether you mean it or no, gobbet by gobbet until he has gorged all. And if I can prevent you, I will.'

As Owen had grown redder and angrier, and fallen to plucking at his sleeves with shaking hands, so Llewelyn had grown ever more steady and quiet, as though he took the measure of an enemy who was seen now to be no great threat to him, and in time might even come to lose the complexion of an enemy. He had a way of standing with his feet planted a little apart, very solid and very still, like one set to withstand all winds and pressures from every quarter and remain unmoved. A moment he looked into Owen's congested face, then: 'And I can!' he said with certainty, and turned on his heel to walk back towards the door from which he had come.

To Owen, I think, it seemed that he had said his last word, and that with undisguised contempt, and meant to go away from us without another glance. But I think his intent, having found out all he needed to know in order to determine his future course, was merely to call in his chamberlain, and commit his brother to the care of the servants for board and bed, for even between rivals and enemies hospitality could not be denied or grudged. However it was, he turned his back squarely, without a qualm, as he had turned his face towards us without compromise or evasion. And as he took the first long steps, Owen made a curious small noise in his throat, a moan too venomous for words, and plucking out the dagger he wore at his belt, lunged with all his force after his brother's withdrawing back, aiming under the left shoulder.

I had been standing a little behind him, unwilling to move or make sound or in any way be noticed during this scene, indeed I would gladly have been away from there if I could, for there was no room for a third in that exchange. But now I had good reason to be grateful that there had been no escape for me, for surely, if only for those few moments, Owen meant murder. And even so I was slow to catch the meaning of the sudden rapid motion he made, and snatched at his sleeve only just in time to hold back his arm from delivering the blow with full force. The point of the dagger slid down in a long line, dragged to the right by my retarding weight, cut a shallow slash in the stuff of Llewelyn's tunic, and clashed against the metal links of his belt. Then I got a better hold of Owen's arm and dragged him round towards me, and in the same moment, feeling the rush of our movements behind him even before he felt the shallow prick of the dagger – for there was almost no sound – Llewelyn sprang at once round and away from us, whirling to confront the next blow.

But the next blow was not aimed at him. The opportunity was already lost, Owen turned on me, who had robbed him of it, or saved him from it, I doubt then if he knew which for pure rage. His left hand took me around the throat and flung me backwards, and my hold on his arm was broken, and I went down on my back, winded and shaken, with Owen on top of me.

I saw the blade flash, and tried to roll aside, but the tip tore a ragged gash through my sleeve and down the upper part of my arm, between arm and body. His knee was in my groin, and I could not shake him off. I saw the dagger raised again, and in the convulsion of my dread one of the tall silver candle-holders went over, crashing against a chair, and spattered us with hot wax. I closed my eyes against that scalding shower and the glitter of the steel, and heaved unavailingly at the burden that was crushing me.

The weight was hoisted back from me unexpectedly, and I dragged in breath and looked up to see what had delivered me. Owen was down on one hip, a yard and more aside from me, glaring upwards under the tangle of his hair, and panting as he nursed his right wrist in his left hand. And Llewelyn, with the dagger in his grasp, was stamping out a little trickle of flame that had spurted along the hair of one of the skin rugs, and righting the fallen candlestick.

He was the first to hear the buzz of voices outside the room, and the latch of a door lifting. He flung the dagger behind him into the cushions of one of the chairs, and reached a peremptory hand to Owen's arm.

'Get up! Do you want witnesses? Quickly!'

I had just wit enough to grasp what he wanted, and shift for myself, though lamely, at least quickly enough to be on my feet and well back in the shadows, my arm clamped tight against my side, when they came surging in from two doors. The inner one by which Llewelyn had entered admitted an old, bearded man, once very tall but now bent in the shoulders and moving painfully, and a younger man, perhaps himself as much as fifty, who propped his elder carefully with a hand under his arm. At the outer door the guards looked in from the hall, coming but a pace or so over the threshold, and I saw the maids peering over their shoulders in curiosity and alarm.

Llewelyn stood settling the tall candelabrum carefully on its feet and straightening the leaning candles. He looked round at them all with a penitent smile, and said, looking last and longest at the old man, whom I knew now for that Ednyfed Fychan whose fame almost matched his lord's: 'I am sorry to have roused the house with such a clatter. A mishap. I knocked over the candles. There's no harm done but a smell of burning.'

Whether they entirely believed I could not tell, but they accepted what he wished them to accept, and asked nothing. He kept his face turned steadily towards them, and only I could see the slit in the back of his cotte, and the one bright blossom of blood where the point had pricked him.

'Goronwy,' he said courteously to the old man's son, 'will you take the Lord Owen in charge, and have food and a lodging prepared for him? He has had a long ride, and is weary. And, Meurig, make sure his horses are well cared for.'

The guard drew back obediently into the hall and closed the door. Owen, moving like a man indeed very weary, half-stunned by what he had done and the resolute way it was being buried and denied before his eyes, stepped forward unprotesting, and went where Goronwy ap Ednyfed led him. The old man, standing straighter now that he stood alone, but so frail that I seemed to see death, a good death, looking peaceably over his shoulder, looked at Llewelyn, and briefly at me, and back, without wonder or doubt, at Llewelyn.

'All is well?' he said, in the clear, leaf-thin voice of age.

'All is very well. There is nothing to trouble you here.' He smiled. 'Leave us. You can, with a quiet mind.'

When they were all gone but we two, he made me sit down close to the warmth of the brazier, and himself slipped away for some minutes, very softly, and came back with another cotte on him, and warm water in an ewer, and linen, and helped me to peel the torn sleeve back to the shoulder from my bleeding arm. The gash was shallow but sliced, and had bled down into my waist as I hugged it against me to keep it from being seen. Ashamed to be so waited on by a prince of Gwynedd, I said I could very well bind it myself, and he told me simply and brusquely that I lied, and foolishly. Which I found to be no more than the truth when I obstinately made the assay, and he took back the task from me, tolerantly enough, and made very neat and expert work of it.

When it was done, and I would have risen and withdrawn from him, conceiving in my weariness and confusion of mind that he was done with me now, and wondering sickly what was to become of me, and whether I had not put myself clean beyond the limits of mercy in Owen's household, I who had no kinsmen here in any group to take me in, he bade me sit down again, and himself sat long with his chin in his fists, gazing at me intently. And after a while he said abruptly:

'You could have made your master the master of Gwynedd. Why did you interfere? You came here with him to serve his interests, did you not?'

'Not that way,' I said, and he looked at me sharply, and a little smiled.

'Well, plainly you cannot now return to him. He would either make an end of his unfinished work, and kill you, or else discard you and leave you to fend for yourself.' He leaned a little closer, and moved the torch to cast its light more directly on my face. 'I know you!' he said. 'You are the boy at Neigwl – the boy with the sheep!'

It was the best part of five years gone, and he had not forgotten. I owned it, remembering how he had looked at me then, and found himself content.

'And you never told?' he said.

'No.'

'Neither did I,' he said. 'I knew then you would not. Afterwards, when it came out that my mother had taken the children and fled, my uncle asked me outright if I had known of it beforehand, and I told him the truth. And he said to me that if I could make as solitary a choice as that, well calculated to bring down on me the anger of both sides, then I was a good man for either side to welcome and value, if they had the wit. That is what he was like, at least to me. And he's gone! Fretted away to skin and bone in his bed in seven short days of fever! And my brother comes galloping to pick the bones!'

He got up from his chair suddenly, and turned to walk restlessly between the brocaded wall and the shrouded doorway, to hide the grief and anger of his face, for even if he remembered me with warmth, this was a private passion. To do justice, all the more because it might bring him some shade of comfort, I said what was true: 'He did come of his own will. The king and his officers had no part in it, we took the moment when they were shaken and distracted, and we ran. I don't say it could not have been done earlier. I do say the way offered then, and suddenly, and he jumped at it.'

'I take your words,' said Llewelyn, still pacing. 'I would not take his! Brother or no, it sticks fast in my gullet that he comes running now, when God knows we have troubles enough, even united, and with King Henry ready to prise his sword-point into every chink of disunity we shall crumble away like a clod after frost. But that's none of your doing,' he said, shaking himself clear of the greatest shadow that hung upon him, and turning again to face me and consider me sombrely. 'It seems,' he said, 'that you made a kind of choice of your own, a while ago. Are you willing to abide by it?'

I caught his meaning, and my heart rose in me for pure pleasure. I said: 'My lord, more than willing!'

'If you enter my service there is none here will challenge or offend you, not even Owen. He will learn that he dare not.'

'But, my lord,' I said, much afraid that this unlooked-for offer might yet be snatched away from me, 'he has my pledged fealty.'

'I will ensure that he shall release you. If he values you no more than shows in him, he will not care over- much, and his grudge against you – as I remember him, he bore grudges! – can be bought off. What were you to him? In what service?'

I told him then what I could do, for I think he had taken me simply for manservant and groom; and when he heard that I could read and write in Latin, English and Welsh, was now a fair horseman, and even had some mild practice in arms, though never otherwise than in play and exercise, he was astonished and pleased, and in pleasure he lit up into a child's unshadowed brightness.

'You are what I need,' he said gladly, 'for I do well enough in Welsh, and have some Latin, but in English I go very haltingly. You shall teach me better. And you can also reckon, and have copied documents at law? English law I must learn to know, if I am to understand my enemies.'

'My lord,' I said, still a little afraid of such good fortune, 'I know very well that you must have clerks about you who have served your uncle well and will do as much for you, and I do fear that what you are now offering me is offered out of too much generosity for a very slight service I could not choose but do you. I would not wish to take advantage of a moment when gratitude may seem due, but only to take and hold a post in your service if I deserve and am fit for it. Take me on probation, and discard me if I am not worth my place.'

And at that he laughed at me, frankly and without offence. 'You also make very lofty speeches,' he said, 'and I may yet make good use of your eloquence, but I am not obliged to take your advice. There is the small matter of a life I owe you.' The laughter vanished very suddenly. He said seriously: 'He meant killing.'

'I have good reason to know as much,' I said, shaken by the recollection. 'And to remember that that debt is already paid, and with somewhat over.'

'So much the better, then,' he said, 'that you and I should remain close together, close enough to go on bandying the same small favour about between us the rest of our lives. Yet if you do refuse me, I can but offer you my hospitality here as long as you choose, and a horse to carry you wherever you will thereafter. But I had rather you would not refuse me.'

It was ever his most disarming gift that he had a special humility, the very opposite of his youngest brother, and never took for granted that he should be liked, much less loved. Confident he was of his judgments and decisions, but never of the effect he had on those about him, and I swear he did not know that by then there was nothing within my giving or granting that I could have refused him. So there was eternally renewed pleasure in making him glad. And I said to him: 'With all my heart, if it were for that reason only, I will come to you, and be your man as long as I live. But it is not only for that reason, for there is nowhere in this world I would rather take my stand than here in Aber, and no one under whom I would more gladly serve than you.'

So it was sealed between us. And he put away ceremony, and began to speak of finding me food, and a bed, and fresh clothes to make away with the blood-stained cotte I wore, for we wanted no rumours and curiosity about the llys concerning an ill encounter between the brothers, to add to the load of uncertainty and disquiet the court already bore. And last, as we were about to leave that room, he asked me: 'One thing I have forgotten – I never asked your name.'

I said it was Samson.

At that he gave me one quick, bright look, and began to say: 'I once knew another Samson. . . .' And there he halted abruptly, and looked again at me, very closely and in some wonder, and for a while was not sure of what he thought he saw.

'Not another,' I said. 'The same.'

'You? Was it you? My mother had a tirewoman was left with a child . . . You are Elen's son?' He did not wait for an answer, for now he was all but certain without any word for me. 'Yes, you could well be! But then, if you are my Samson, I saw you here at Neigwl that day, bringing down the sheep, and I did not know you again!'

'You had not seen me,' I said, 'for more than six years, and you saw me then but a moment.'

'Yes, but there's more to it! I never thought of you then, nor dreamed it could be you. They sent you to Aberdaron long before.'

'When your mother fled to England,' I told him, 'my mother would not go without me. They sent to fetch me back that very day that you saw me.'

'And I had thought they would make a canon or a priest of you, and now I get you back thus strangely and simply. I have not forgotten,' he said, the deep brown of his eyes glowing reddish-bright, 'the years we were children together. We had the same birthday, the same stars. We were surely meant to come together again. I missed you when they sent you away. And now you come back with an omen – the dagger that strikes at one of us strikes at both. We are linked, Samson, you and I, we may as well own it and make the best of it.'

To which I said a very fervent amen, for the best of it seemed to me then, and seems to me now and always, the best that ever life did for me, whatever darkness came with the bright.

Thus I became confidential clerk and secretary to the Lord Llewelyn ap Griffith, prince of Gwynedd.

CHAPTER IV

There was never any mention made of what had befallen between Llewelyn and Owen, and that was at Llewelyn's wish and silent order. For the situation of Gwynedd, even though King Henry held back from committing an army to so positive an adventure as the previous year, was weak, exhausted and in disarray, and every additional burden was to be prevented at all costs. So this matter of the rivalry between those two was put away. Llewelyn did it as disposing of a difficulty, and Owen was very glad to do it, since it reflected no credit on him either in the treacherous attack or in its ruthless defeat.

I was present at the meeting of the council, the last but one such meeting Ednyfed Fychan ever attended, there in the hall of Aber. The old man, waxen and frail but with his long and honourable devotion burning in his eyes, presided at the table, his son Goronwy on his right side. The old man had hands that lay on the table before him like withered leaves, and a voice as light and dry as the autumn wind that brings them down, but a spirit like a steady flame. I will not say that there was no high feeling between the brothers at that meeting, for they urged their claims hard after their own fashion, Owen with the more words and the louder voice, since very strongly he felt himself at a disadvantage as the newcomer, and under some suspicion of being King Henry's willing pensioner, Llewelyn in very few words but bluntly and bitterly. But perforce they listened, both of them, to the arguments of the council, for there was no future for any man in claiming the sovereignty over a ruined land. And there was not a man present there, by that time even I, who did not know how grim was the plight of Gwynedd, however defiantly she stood to arms.

'Children,' said Ednyfed, in that voice like the rustling of dried leaves, 'there is no solution here but needs the goodwill of both of you. For past question the Lord Owen is his father's eldest son, nor was he to blame for his imprisonment in England, since it stemmed from imprisonment here in Wales, before he was of age. And he has given us his word that he made his escape when he might, to return here to his own land and take up the defence of Gwynedd. But the Lord Llewelyn, younger though he may be, is known to all here, has never set foot in England, and has fought faithfully for our lord and prince, David, without personal desire for his own enlargement, for never has he asked lands for himself, though lands have rightfully been granted to him. The Lord Llewelyn's wounds speak for him, those who served under him at Degannwy speak for him. He needs no advocate here. And therefore I say to him first, and after to his brother, that the land of Wales has great

61

need of all the sons of Griffith, not as rivals but as brothers, if the land of Wales is to live. Children, be reconciled, divide Gwynedd between you only to unite it in your own union, for unless you fight together you will founder apart.'

This was his matter, if not his words. Indeed, I think he had to use, and repeatedly, many more words to hold this balance. And his son ably backed him, for the minds of these two worked almost as one. Moreover, there was no alternative to what they advocated. Those two, with whatever doubts and misgivings they felt, agreed to divide Gwynedd between them, in order to hold it as one against England.

Among his share, when the division of commotes was arduously worked out, Llewelyn kept his old lands of Penllyn, to which he had become attached as being his first appanage received from David at his majority, and there we spent much of that summer at his court of Bala, though he came several times to Aber to pay visits to his widowed aunt, Isabella, for whom he had some fondness. I saw her several times before she withdrew into England in August, a slender, dark, sad girl, never truly at home in Wales even after sixteen years. She had been but a child when they married her to David, and without him, and lacking children, she had nothing now to bind her to this land, for she was a de Breos by birth, and all her kin were Norman. As a widow she was entitled under Welsh law to a part of the royal stock, and in August these cattle and horses were shod and taken away by drovers to the lands of the earl of Gloucester, and into his protection the lady followed them very shortly after. Her mother had been one of the daughters and heiresses of the Marshal estates, and through her the castle of Haverfordwest came to Isabella, with lands in Glamorgan and Caerleon. So she was provided for amply, and passed out of our lives.

There remained to be decided in this year how Gwynedd should deal with the still outstanding issues between Wales and England, for though the full feudal host was not called out against us this summer, yet we were still in a state of war, and the king's wardens of the march and others were free to make inroads where they could. The council argued for caution and waiting, for the last year's main corn harvest had been lost in Anglesey, and stocks were low for feeding an army in the field. Nor was this a fat year for crops. Better to make the castles secure and provision them well, and be content to hold fast what we held. So we did, and as well for us. At least we lost few men, and no territory, if we gained none.

Yet there was one happening in the late summer that painfully displayed our weakness and helplessness. King Henry had installed one Nicholas de Molis as custos of his castles of Cardigan and Carmarthen, and this was an energetic and ambitious person who had formerly been seneschal in Gascony. During these summer months he launched a successful campaign in South Wales, greatly consolidating the royal holdings there, and then, swollen with this triumph, crossed the Dovey with his army and marched them north through Merioneth and Ardudwy to the Conway valley, and so without hindrance to join the garrison at Degannwy. There was some heat between Owen and Llewelyn once again over how to meet this impudent march clean through the middle lands of Wales, for Owen was ever fierce and rash, and thought every man a coward who was not ready to rush upon a superior host with him. But as for Llewelyn, it was clear to him that this army, in such circumstances, hardly dared delay its passage by essaying much diversion or damage on the way, and that the Welsh forces could be more effectively used where they were finally most needed, in keeping the Conway and ensuring the stronghold of Eryri itself should be held inviolate. He therefore advocated the usual Welsh tactic of withdrawing our people and valuables into the hills, and suffering the intruders to pass, while denying them everything that was movable by way of provisions. And the council sided with him. Thus de Molis reached Degannwy, which in any case was strongly held, but we massed our defences there opposite the castle, and threw back all his attempted raids from that vantage-point. Never once did he get across the river, and of bloodshed that year there was very little.

Howbeit, this unimpeded march, which had crossed lands untroubled by an English army for a century and more, had showed all too clearly how thoroughly King Henry had the more accessible parts of Wales in his power, and how little we could hope to do against him if he decided to put his entire host into the field. And there was very earnest discussion in council as soon as the winter began to close in, and raids and skirmishes ceased. For the drain on the land was remorseless in labour, resources and livestock, and two more such years would be hard to endure.

And that was the last council of all for Ednyfed Fychan, and the last service he did to the land he had served lifelong. Llewelyn spoke his mind, with what reluctance and grief I knew, for we had talked of it beforehand. And he bore to be called timorous by Owen, for whose opinion he cared little, so long as Ednyfed's ancient eyes watched him steadily and did not disapprove.

'There are but two choices before us,' he said, 'and the first is to continue as we are, at war but without fighting, so far as we can avoid it. True, we can hold our losses in bounds by these means, so long as the king also holds back from fielding his host against us, but such a country as ours, barren of grain, wanting salt and a hundred other things that are now denied us, can bleed to death slowly and find that death as mortal as any other. And should King Henry decide to make an end, with such stocks as we have now, and so stripped of allies, fight as well as we might, we could not prevent the quick death from sparing us the slow. And the other alternative – to be blunt – is surrender. I call it so, that we may not imagine its countenance as any more comely than it is. We sue for a truce, and ask for terms of peace, and on the face of it we may reject them if they bite too deep, but to be honest, we cannot afford even to play hard to please. And I am for the second way.'

Owen cried out indignantly that this was abject surrender.

'I have said so,' agreed Llewelyn grimly.

'If you are ready to bow your neck to King Henry's foot, I am not,' protested Owen.

'Times are changed,' flashed back Llewelyn, for he was human, and almost as quick to hit out as his brother, 'since you bowed your neck low enough for his gold chains and his ermine. Not long since, your head was in his bosom, now you have less trust in his mercy – or at least his caution – than I have. Our mother and sister, our brothers, are still in his court and under his protection, and he'll hold back from putting us too openly to shame, for the sake of his own face. Not that the draught will be any the sweeter for that, but there'll be a cloak of decency. He has his pretext – Prince David was his enemy of some years' standing, whom he was sworn to bring to book. We are the innocent inheritors, to be plundered, yes, but not picked clean to the bone or made mock of, provided we behave ourselves seemly. You have nothing to fear.'

Owen flared that it was not he who was fearful, that he was willing to put all to the issue, that there was a time for valour.

'So there will be,' said Llewelyn, with a spark of golden anger in his eyes. 'It is not now. Fortitude, perhaps. And patience. And humility.'

Then Ednyfed spoke. He set before the council all the state of their arms, men and stores, and their nakedness of trustworthy allies, for in Wales then it was every chief for himself, and those who were not demoralised by the too close presence of marcher neighbours, or royal castellans armed with carte blanche to raid and despoil, were quarrelling among themselves, or had been seduced by the king into promising their homage directly to him in return for his protection. Not now, not for many years, could that unity be restored which had almost been perfected under Llewelyn Fawr. And at this present time, he concluded, it was a different service and a different heroism that was required from the grandsons of that great prince.

There was no man there who was happy with the verdict, and some disagreed, and many doubted and feared, but the sum of opinion was that there was no choice but to send at least for a safe-conduct to Chester, and despatch envoys to ask John de Grey for a truce, and a meeting with King Henry to discuss permanent terms of peace.

We came out from the hall, after that council, to a grey and cloudy eve, for it was December, and the dark came early. In the chill air of the courtyard the old steward drew breath deeply, and heaved a great, wavering sigh, and fell like a drifting leaf into his son's arms. They carried him to his bed, and both the princes were with him through the dark hours, and in the first light of dawn he blessed them, and died.

Goronwy, his eldest son, was distain of Gwynedd after him, and Llewelyn's bards made mourning songs for the father, and songs of praise and hope for the son, hymning their noble line as worthy to give birth to great and illustrious kings.

It was Tudor ap Ednyfed, the second son, who went to Chester in the first place, armed with the royal safe-conduct, to negotiate a truce with John de Grey, the justiciar and the king's representative on the border. And later, in mid-April, Owen and Llewelyn received further safe-conducts for themselves and their parties, to meet King Henry at Woodstock. There on the thirtieth day of April a very hard peace was made, too hard for all the civility and ceremony to do much to soften it. And those two, who rubbed each other raw did their sleeves but touch, endured to ride together, to stand together before a curious court, and to keep each his countenance calm and resolute through all, at least in public. I know, for I was of Llewelyn's party, and I witnessed all, and greatly I admired the stern control they kept upon themselves when the need was greatest.

They were forced to give up much, in order to keep at least the heart of their land. All that Middle Country from Clwyd to Conway, the four cantrefs of Rhos, Rhufoniog, Tegaingl and Dyffryn Clwyd, was lost to them, and they renounced all claim to it. Also at last they surrendered Mold. King Henry maintained that the homage of all the minor chiefs of North Wales belonged directly to him, and ensured that any such chiefs who had been adherents of his cause against their own country should be securely established in the lands they claimed. In return for so much sacrificed, Owen and Llewelyn were acknowledged as the lawful princes of all Gwynedd beyond the Conway, but they had to do homage to the king for their lands, and to hold them of him as overlord by military service.

But they got their peace. And it did endure for several years. Trade was delivered from its ban, imports flowed in again. Sad, slow gains to set against such losses, but Wales had been bled into weakness, and needed time to grow whole again.

Thus being received into the king's grace, those two took their places for a few days among the magnates of the court. The queen received them, and among her noblewomen was the Lady Senena. That meeting, being matter for the nobility and not for clerks, I did not see, but as I have heard, she kissed her eldest son with warm affection, and her second son with markedly more reserve, even coldly, for she could never quite forgive him for taking his own way, and still less for being, as she secretly suspected he was, in the right. However, he had made his peace with Owen, she made peace silently with him, and there were never any words either of reproach or reconciliation.

As for me, when I heard that the Lady Senena was in the queen's retinue, I went with an eager heart to make enquiry where she was lodged, for I thought my mother would be there with her. But the lady had left her daughter and her younger sons in London, and my mother was there in attendance on them, so I could not see her. For from Woodstock we rode for the border, and for home.

Those were years of labour and husbandry, and with little to tell, for we had a kind of peace that left us no field for action on any wider front than Gwynedd, and there Llewelyn occupied himself doggedly in raising stock and crops and making his lands as self-sufficient as he could. Owen surely fretted more and did less, for he had his father's lordly impetuosity and restlessness, not made for farming a cantref, nor was he infallible in choosing his officers. But except when the council met in full session we saw little of him, and what I most remember of the remainder of this year of twelve hundred and forty-seven is a steady drawing closer to my lord, until I was hardly ever from his side.

'I had thought,' I said to him once, when we spoke of that first visit to England, 'that the Lady Senena would come home now and bring your sister and brothers with her. Why does the king still detain her?'

'She is still a hostage,' said Llewelyn sombrely, 'though I doubt if she knows it. Hostage for Owen's good behaviour and mine. Not until we've kept his sorry peace another year or two will he let go of my mother. When he's sure we are tamed, then he'll unlock the doors for her. But whether she'll choose to walk out is another matter. For all my father's death, she's grown used to the comfort of an English court now, and to English policies, too. For Owen, if he asked her, she might make the effort to take up her roots again and replant them here. But Owen won't ask her,' he said with a wry smile. 'He wants no elders lecturing him on his duty or telling him how to run his commotes. And for me I think she would not stir.'

There was a one-sided effect of this peace with England, in fact, that continued, though without direct attack, the work of undoing what remained of the unity of Wales. For Gwynedd's submission and the tightening of the royal grasp on the Middle Country made many another small princeling consider that it might be safer to make direct contact and peace with this king, and many did so, settling thankfully under the shelter of his cloak. These he used against those who still continued recalcitrant, and divided and ruled in most of the southern parts of Wales. And by this time there was no one so hot in condemnation of those who voluntarily allied themselves with England as Owen.

Towards the end of the autumn he came riding into Bala, where we were busy making sure of the last of the harvest, for we had there some good fields, and had been at pains to extend them. Owen was full of news, having received letters from England, and fuller still of patriot rage.

'Do you know what she has done? Without a word to us, let alone asking our leave!'

'By the look and the sound of you,' said Llewelyn, watching the gleaners raking the last stubble, 'she would not have got your leave if she had asked it. What else? And what has she done to set you on fire?'

'Why, our mother, of course! Have you heard nothing? She has married our sister, at King Henry's expense and with his goodwill, as if the girl had no male kin to be responsible for her! And to one of the king's Welsh hounds, one of the first of the pack, Rhys Fychan of Dynevor.'

This Rhys Fychan was son to Rhys Mechyll, of the old heart-fortress of Deheubarth, and had come to his inheritance when his father died, three years gone. I suppose at his accession he was about eighteen, which was my lord's age and mine when Owen came with this word, and he had had many difficulties to overcome, an ambitious uncle and a hostile mother not the least of them, so that he had done well to survive and keep his hold on his own, and it was no marvel to Llewelyn or to me that he had made his peace with England and done homage to King Henry a year previously. His was an old and honoured line, going back to the great Lord Rhys, whose last and least descendant was not to be despised as a match. But Owen was Welsh now from the highest hair of his head to his heel, and intolerant of everything tainted with English patronage.

'She might have done worse,' said Llewelyn mildly, and stood for a moment staring back into his childhood, for the Lady Gladys was little more than a year older than he, and came between those two brothers, but he had not so much as seen her for six years. 'She must be turned nineteen,' he said, pondering, 'and he's hardly two years older. And he was there at court last year, paying his respects, and not a bad-looking fellow, either. What would you have? If he took her fancy, and she took his, what could be more natural? I wish them heartily well.'

'The man is a traitor,' said Owen, smarting. 'And she must know it, as our mother surely does! But she grows old, she forgets with what intent she went to England. She has taught our sister to turn with the wind.'

I will not deny there was something in what he said, had it come from one less compromised himself. For whatever human creatures undertake, however purely, with whatever devotion, the ground turns under them and brings them about, facing where they never meant to face, and hard indeed it is to keep a clear eye to the north, and right oneself from such deflecting winds. And the Lady Senena had suffered much, and was weary, so that now I saw what Llewelyn had seen without effort, by pure instinct, how she was lost to us, and lost to her old self, the whole ground having shifted under her.

'Oh, come!' said Llewelyn tolerantly. 'We live among realities. Rhys Fychan is a man caught in their devil's web and doing his best with what he has, just as we are. God knows, there may come a time when we have to treat him as an enemy, but his is no case for hatred. Or overmuch righteousness!' he said, and gave me a smile, knowing Owen would never take the allusion. 'Much less our sister's! If she likes him, God give her joy of him. At least he's her own age, and belike every bit as innocent.'

Owen stamped off to the stables in dudgeon, to see his horse cared for, and left us to follow when the last cart was drawn in. He had no interest in such occupations.

Llewelyn walked beside me with wide eyes fixed upon the bowl of Bala and the mirror of the lake beyond. 'She is my only sister,' he said, marvelling, 'and I do not know her, or she me. Samson, what have we done with our childhood, or what have others done with it, to leave us strangers now?'

The next event of note I remember during these years of slow recovery is the bringing home of the Lord Griffith's body, in the year following the peace of Woodstock. When a year had passed since that treaty, in exemplary quietness and submission on our part, Llewelyn judged that the time might be ripe to advance an intent he had always cherished since his father's death.

'For,' said he, 'King Henry may be satisfied by now, surely, that we have passed our probation, and the granting of a matter so small to him, especially where it touches the church, may appear very good policy.' For his estimate of the king, which proved accurate enough, was that he was an amiable person apart from his crown, and by no means bloodthirsty, but where his royal interests were concerned liable to look all round every concession or request in suspicion of hidden disadvantages, and incapable of any gesture large and generous. And often, in searching so narrowly for the insignificant march that might be stolen on him, he failed to see his best and truest interest when it was large under his nose. 'If he can read any malevolent intent into an act of filial piety,' said Llewelyn, 'let him argue it with ecclesiastics better versed in piety than he is. Or, for that matter, than I am!'

So first it was put to the council, who approved it to a man, Owen most loudly and perhaps with the most surprise and chagrin that it was the unfilial son, the deserter of his family's cause, who put it forward, rather than he, the fellow-sufferer with his sire in Criccieth and in London. And then the formal letters were drawn up, with all ceremony, both to king and archbishop, and committed to the willing and reverent hands of the abbots of Strata Florida and Aberconway, and a splendid escort provided to bring them to Westminster. For with all the abbots of the Cistercian houses Llewelyn was ever on the warmest terms of friendship and regard, like his grandsire before him, and the very echo of that name stood him in good stead.

To these letters, which were sent in the name of both brothers, and to the persuasions of the reverend abbots, King Henry listened, and saw that it could reflect nothing but radiance upon him to accede to the request, while he parted with nothing but the body of a broken tool, and might even a little salve his conscience and silence persistent rumour concerning that death by being gracious now to the remains. He therefore gave his permission and countenanced the removal of the Lord Griffith's corpse from its alien resting-place, and the abbots brought the prince's coffin in slow and solemn procession home to Aberconway, and there interred him with all appropriate rites beside his father and his half-brother. So those two sons of Llewelyn the Great lay together in peace at last.

It was four years more before the Lady Senena came home to Wales. Reassured by so long a period of calm and enforced order in Wales, King Henry declared himself willing to equip the lady and let her take her two remaining children to receive their allotment of land under Welsh law, even the youngest being now of age. It suited very well with the king's designs that even what he had left us of Gwynedd should be parcelled out among as many rival lords as possible, for the more and the more trivial the titles to land there, the less likely was any kind of unity in the future. And it suited well with the Lady Senena's old-fashioned leanings that ancient right should be observed at all costs. She was not yet old, being but five and forty, but experience and care, and especially the long years of being eaten by a sense of bitter grievance, had aged her greatly, and she longed to see all her sons established before she retired into the secluded life which was now increasingly attractive to her. So the agreement was made that Rhodri and David should receive lands of their own, though the supreme rule over Gwynedd remained as before with their two elder brothers. And in the early summer Owen and Llewelyn sent an escort to bring their mother and brothers home.

Doubtless King Henry was also spared a considerable expense once they were gone from his court, and that was some relief to him, for he had difficulties of his own with his council and magnates over his expenditure, and to be able to point to one economy was at least a step in conciliating them. So all in all it suited everyone, though I am sure the Lady Senena felt pain by then in any upheaval in her life, and suffered doubts and depressions of which no one else knew, unless it might be Bishop Richard of Bangor, who accompanied the royal party on their journey, making one of his rare visits to his see.

This Bishop Richard had formerly been a strong supporter of the Lord Griffith's cause against David. After the treaty signed at Woodstock he had forsaken Gwynedd and preferred to make his home in the abbey of St Albans, and came only now and then to visit his flock. But in England he had taken an interest in the fortunes of the Lady Senena and her family, and she had a great respect and reverence for him, though many found him a difficult and thorny priest. Doubtless she was glad to have his support and consolation in setting out on this return journey to her own country, after eleven years of absence.

It was at Carnarvon that the princes received their mother and her retinue, that court being convenient to the commotes the council had agreed to give to Rhodri and David, and also to the bishop's own town of Bangor. Both Owen and Llewelyn rode out a mile or two on the road when they got word that the cavalcade had been sighted, and I went among their companions, for Llewelyn knew that I was eager to get sight of my mother after so long, and bade me leave whatever work I had to do, for it would not spoil with keeping.

It was a slow procession we went to meet, for they had made a fair distance that day, and the horses were tired. The bishop, like the lady, rode in a litter, being already in his elder years, and frail. But a bright spark of blue and white played and darted about the group, now spurring ahead, now whirling to make a circle round them, now dancing along the green verge of the road on one side, now on the other. Restless and eager, this one young horseman fretted a silvery lace of movement about the slow core of the party, hard put to it to restrain himself from outrunning them all and coming first to Carnarvon.

He saw us, and for one moment reined in abruptly, on the crest of a hillock by the roadside. Then he came at a canter, and wheeled broadside before us, his eyes sweeping over us all, eyes the misty blue of harebells, and yet bright, under straight black brows. His head was uncovered and his breast was bare, the linen shirt turned back from his neck, for the June sun was hot. The wind had blown his blue-black hair into a tangle of curls, and stung a bright flush of blood over the cheekbones high and wide like wings.

So I saw my breast-brother again, smiling and eager, no less beautiful than when he charmed the ladies of the court at six years old.

He found Owen easily, and cried his name aloud in a crow of pleasure, and reining very lightly and expertly alongside, flung an arm about his eldest brother and kissed him.

'You I'd know by your hair among a thousand,' he said heartily, 'and glad I am to see you again. But Llewelyn was not red, and it's longer, I might shoot wide.' He laughed with pleasure, for whatever he did he did with all his being. His eyes roved, touched me for an instant and wavered, flashing with a recognition that must wait its time. He walked his horse forward to where Llewelyn waited, smiling but not helping him, for he was too careless of his dress to be known for the prince by his ornaments. 'Yes! Not by your hair, but I know you!' He reached a long brown hand and touched very lightly the star-shaped scar at the angle of Llewelyn's jaw. 'My mother – *our* mother told me, when she came from Woodstock. Did you think she had not noticed? You,' he said, 'among ten thousand!' And he reached both arms, loosing the reins, and Llewelyn embraced him.

When the kiss was given and received, they drew apart, those two, and gazed at each other with something of wonder and curiosity, of which this quick, brotherly liking was but the blunted point. For they had been eleven years apart, and David now was but sixteen. And they said the most ordinary of words, because no others then would have had any meaning, their need of mutual exploration being so great.

'Our mother is well?' said Llewelyn, looking over David's shoulder towards the approaching litters.

'Well, but weary. Bear it in mind, for she'll never admit it, and draw the celebrations short tonight. Give her a day or two, and she'll be arranging all our lives for us,' said David irreverently.

'And Rhodri?'

'He's there, riding beside her litter. We took it by turns, but he has more patience than I. Rhodri is very well, only a little tired of the bishop's supervision. He minds him, I do not. It pleases him better,' said David, 'not to be minded. Where would he find matter for homilies, if we were all like Rhodri? Will you go and meet them?'

So we moved forward again towards the approaching procession, watching the gold-tinted dust eddy upwards, glittering, from the hooves of the horses. And as we went, David laid a hand softly on Llewelyn's arm, and said in his ear, but not so quietly that I did not catch the words: 'Pardon me if I leave you a moment. There's one here I must greet.' And without waiting for a reply he edged his horse very delicately from between his brothers, and brought him sidling and dancing alongside my pony on the edge of the escort.

'Samson . . .? You are Samson, I could not be wrong.' He curbed his horse in such a way that we two fell aside and a little behind, and did it very smoothly, until there was space enough between us and the rest for us to talk openly and alone. And for my life I could not understand this compliment he was paying me, though I felt it pierce to my heart. As he had a way of doing, for good or evil.

'I am indeed Samson,' I said. 'I did not think you would remember me. I am glad from my heart to see you home.'

'I own,' he said, 'we have been apart some years now, and I was not very old or very wise, to remember well. Yet how could I forget *you*? We had one kind nurse, and she was yours, and only lent to me. Oh, Samson, I dearly loved her! How can I say what I need to say? My mother has it in charge to tell you, and I would spare you and her.' He saw how I was straining ahead to try and see into the open litter, from which the curtains were drawn back fully to let in light and air in the radiant June. And he laid his hand on my arm and held me hard. 'Don't look for her!' he said. 'You'll not find her.'

I turned then to look at him fully, and the blue of his eyes was like the pale zenith of the sky over us, almost blanched with pity. Then I understood that I had lost her, that Meilyr, wherever he was and if he still lived, had been robbed of her whom he had never had but in a barren leash of law. And the strangest and best thing then was that this boy beside me, who could laugh, and play, and charm the hearts out of brothers and strangers alike, had tears in his eyes for her and me.

'If we had sent you word,' he said, 'it could have come only a day or two ahead of us, it was better to bring the grief with us, and share it with you. She died three days before we left London, of some fever. God knows what. It made such haste with her, she was gone in a night. My mother labours and frets with it, let me tell her that you know. And if I have done my errand ill, forgive me! She's buried there in London. We did all we could do.'

I told him I had no doubt of it, that I was grateful, that he need not be in any distress, for this was to be his day of reunion. I said I had lived without my mother now for some years, that no man nor woman can be kept for ever by love, that he should reassure his own mother that all was well, that all was very well. Nevertheless, he kept his hand touching my hand upon the bridle until we came up with the litters. And it was a mile and more on the way home to Carnarvon before he was riding again in flying circles about us, and laughing into the wind.

Thus my mother's few poor possessions came back to me at the Lady Senena's hands, and she spoke with regret and affection of the years of service Elen had given to the royal children, and there was no distress between us, the boy having done her office for her. And so unlikely a messenger of mourning never lived, except that birds can sing in cloudy weather as loudly and bravely as in the sun. For he was like a darting kingfisher over a stream, wild with delight in his own energy, youth and brightness, preening himself in the new clothes provided for his homecoming, and inquisitive about everything that had once been familiar, and now had to be learned anew. And once, in the brief time while she was most softened and welcoming to me, the Lady Senena caught my dazzled eyes following his flight, and said to me, half in admiration, it seemed, and half in warning: 'Do not think him as light and shallow as he seems. He is as deep as the sea off Enlli, and as hard to know.'

I thought her partial to Rhodri, as indeed she was, for in his childhood he had suffered occasional illness, and so attached her to himself more anxiously than any of his brothers. Moreover, he was of a somewhat dour temperament not unlike her own, and she understood him better than the youngest and most wayward of her brood, whose alien brilliance reached back to his grandsire.

I watched them often, during those few days spent at Carnarvon, as

71

they sat side by side at the high table in hall, for that was the first and only time that I saw all those four brothers of Gwynedd together, grouped like a family about their mother. And very earnestly I studied all those faces, so like and so unlike, for all had something of both parents in them, but all shaped that essence differently. Owen Goch most resembled his father, being the tallest and heaviest of the four, with florid, russet face and opulent flesh. Only his dark-red, burning hair set him apart. He was very strong, and a good man of his hands, though too ready with them in and out of season, like the Lord Griffith before him, and with the same hot temper. With weapons he was fearless, but too rash and therefore a little clumsy. And for all his ready furies he also, as Llewelyn had once said of him, bore grudges which he never forgot, so that often I had wondered how he contrived to put away the memory of being worsted and having the dagger wrested out of his hand, that night at Aber, and how he could stomach that defeat and work mildly with his brother in court and council. As for me, he had never given me a reminder of it by word or look, hardly met my eyes since that day, and I had kept out of his way to avoid touching, even by the sight of me, a spot that might still be sore. Yet I felt some shame in doing him what I thought must, after all, be an injustice.

Llewelyn, sitting beside him, was well-nigh as broad in the shoulder, and not much shorter, but brown and lean and hard, for he lived a rough outdoor life by choice, as often involved with cattle and fields as with court and council. Eryri is a harsh, stony, untilled land, yet it has fields in some sheltered valleys that can be made to bear beans and pease, if not corn, and he had good reason to remember the winter of hunger after the rape of Anglesey. His brown face, all bone and brow, looked lively and good-humoured in company, and sturdily thoughtful in repose. My lord at this time was twenty-three years old, body and mind formed fully, and both under large and easy control. Often I was aware that he was consciously waiting, and employing his days to the best effect until his time came, for he knew how to wait.

Rhodri was the slenderest of the four, but of resource in getting by device what he could not get by force. His face was fair and freckled, a condition usual with hair of such a light, reddish colour. As a child I remembered him as capable of spite, and capricious in his likes and dislikes as in his interests, blowing all ways in one day, and in and out with everyone about him too quickly to follow his turns. Beside those other three he seemed of light weight, but that weight might be thrown into the scale so wantonly as to upset all. At the manly exercises which showed David at his burning best Rhodri was but mediocre, though he could hold his own with the lump. He was attentive and gentle with his mother, who loved him dearly, and fretted over him constantly.

And David sparkled and shone upon all, the youngest and the most radiant, for to him everything was new and strange, and he was about to enter into the possession of lands of his own, and bright with the excitement of it. He, of them all, knew how to approach all, though his calculations were civil, heartening and kind. And I loved him for the wisdom of which his mother had warned me, for deep he was, as the sea, but better governed, and more sparing of poor men.

Both those young princes were full of the news of the English court, and both talked like men of the world, familiarly naming far places, and great men whose dealings came to us in Wales only as distant legends, though we knew they lived and moved in the same world with us, and could bring about changes that affected our lives, too. The more voluble and loud was Rhodri, the elder, who looked upon David still as little more than a child. But what David had to say was more sharply perceptive, and often critical.

'King Henry has a finger in so many affairs abroad,' Rhodri said, 'I doubt he has no time or attention to give to Wales nowadays. He's very close with Pope Innocent, since he took the cross, two years ago. You knew of that? It eased his situation with Innocent that the old Emperor Frederick died. It was all very well having a sister married to the greatest man in Europe, even if he had had other wives before, and kept hundreds of concubines, as they say, in his court in Sicily. But since the pope has turned against the whole house of Hohenstaufen as the devil's brood, it's well to have Isabella safely widowed, and the whole adventure forgotten.'

'He bids fair to have trouble enough with the sister's husband he still has,' said David, 'and nearer home. There's been the devil to pay ever since Easter, with the Gascons charging the earl of Leicester with God knows what mismanagement in their province, and the earl on his defence, and hard-pressed, too. King Henry hit out at him more like an enemy than a brother – he never could keep his temper when he felt himself measured against a larger man. Earl Simon never raised his voice but once, and then but for a moment.'

'You speak too impudently of his Grace,' said the Lady Senena frowning. 'And what do you know of the matter, a child like you?'

'Everything,' said David, undisturbed. 'I was there in the abbey refectory four days running when the fighting was at its best. I heard them at it.'

'You?' she said indulgently. 'And how would you get admission to a grave court hearing? You are making up vain stories.'

'Edward got me into the room with him. I was curious, and put it into his head. It all ended in a compounded peace,' said David, 'as everybody knows, but Earl Simon had the best of the argument, to my way of thinking. True, he brought it on himself, for from all I hear the man is mad who believes French law and order can be imposed on Gascons. He never understood them, and they would not abide him. In the end the king has imposed a truce, and promised to go himself to Gascony next spring, or to send Edward, and Earl Simon has given up his command voluntarily, on his expenses being paid. They got out of it with everyone's face saved by having Gascony formally handed over to Edward, for he's to have it as part of his appanage in any case. And the earl has gone back to France for the time being, free of his province. He never wanted it in the first place,' said the boy positively. 'He wanted to go on crusade with King Louis, and only gave it up because King Henry begged him to take charge in Gascony. And all it's done is cost him a great deal of money out of his own purse, made him hated in the south, and spilled a whole sea of bad blood between him and the king.'

'You have no right,' said the Lady Senena severely, 'to speak so of either the king or the earl. It would do you more credit if you showed a greater respect for your elders.'

He smiled at her placatingly, but he was unmoved. 'They are men,' he said, 'like other men.'

Now this Earl Simon was a French nobleman of the de Montfort family, who had come into the earldom of Leicester by right of his grandmother Amicia, there being no male heir left in England to the Leicester honour. He was the second son of his father, but his elder brother Amaury held by his French possessions, and surrendered the English right to the next in succession. And this young man had not only come to take up his estates in England, but taken the eye and the heart of King Henry's widowed sister Eleanor, so that she married him, and to that marriage the king was privy. The story caused much scandal, for the lady, who was but sixteen when her first husband died, had rashly taken a vow to remain chaste for life, and for love of Earl Simon she broke that vow, against all pressure upon her from chaplains and archbishops, and wed where her heart was. But all this happened when I was but a child, and I had the story only long afterwards, while we were close to the court in London. King Henry had always geese that were swans, and Earl Simon was high in his regard then, but when he found that the match had brought his own countenance into some disrepute with the clerics the king was affrighted, and though he made no break with his new brother I think he held that embarrassment greatly against him thereafter, and never quite forgave it, so that any new dissension between them had in it the seeds of greater hostility than appeared in the matter itself.

'So Edward's to have Gascony,' said Llewelyn, musing. 'Is it just a way of getting out of the difficulty with no broken heads, do you think, or is the king setting him up already in a court of his own? He's barely turned thirteen.'

Rhodri was confident that it had been but a convenient close to the dangerous dispute with Earl Simon, allowing him to withdraw honourably and gracefully, though doubtless it had been intended that some day young Edward should indeed rule the Gascon possessions. But David shook his head at that, very sure of himself.

'This is but the first move in another game. King Henry has a great many other lands marked down for his heir, and very soon, too. He's being fitted out with a great appanage in readiness for his marriage, though only a handful of people even at court know of the plan. You've heard there's a new king in Castille? This Alfonso has a half-sister, only a child as yet. King Henry is making the first advances to marry Edward to her.'

'And takes you into his confidence before he even sends proctors!' scoffed Rhodri. 'Don't listen to him, he's flying his hawk at the sun!'

'King Henry may not,' said David, unperturbed, 'but Edward does. Where else should I get it?' He looked round with a sudden flashing glance at us all, and said in a lower voice: 'And there's more, and nearer to us. King Henry intends his son shall have all the crown's lands in Wales, into the bargain.'

Curbed and hemmed in as we then were, it sounded no worse than what we had already, and offered promise of something better, for if a separate court and council were set up for the crown's Welsh lands there was a hope, at least, that the administrators might draw upon experience and wisdom from among the better marchers, who knew how to deal with their Welsh neighbours as with men deserving of respect. The Welsh tenants under the present jurisdiction of the justiciar of Chester had complaints enough, that their customs and laws were disregarded, that they were being increasingly squeezed under heavy taxation, and that unjustly administered into the bargain, their lands bled to help supply London, while London turned a deaf ear to their needs. So we heard what David reported thoughtfully, but kept open minds concerning the event.

In the middle days of July, having set up Rhodri already on his portion, we brought David with ceremony home to take possession of his lands in Cymydmaen, in Lleyn, that very commote from which the Lady Senena had set out with her children for Shrewsbury, so long before. The lady went with us, escorted still by Bishop Richard of Bangor, that small, soured, querulous priest, who was desirous of seeing right done to all the brothers before he returned to his see, and thence to his chosen retirement in St Albans.

So we rode back, all together, over the inland roads and the rolling pastures to Neigwl, and came in sight of the sea, pale almost to whiteness in the bright sunlight, with the island of saints gleaming offshore, Enlli, where the holy come to die and be buried in bliss. When we passed by that spot where we had met on the evening of the lady's flight, Llewelyn turned his head and looked at me, smiling, and I knew that he was seeing a boy coming down from the fields with the lambs, as I was seeing a boy on horseback, who turned to look a last time at the home he was forsaking.

But David, who rode between us, reared up tall in his saddle to gaze with bright and hungry eyes down into the walls of the maenol that was now to be his court, the first over which he had ever ruled alone. There were his servants, his councillors, his cattle and horses, and in the hills and trefs around, his tenants, his men in war and peace, owing him service according to Welsh law.

'And all this is mine!' he said, but softly, only for our ears, seeing it was a child's cry of triumph and delight, not fitting the public utterance of the lord of a commote. When we brought him down to the gates, to give his hand to all those who came crowding to attend him, then he was princely and composed enough, and did all with lordly dignity. Nevertheless, that day I think he was utterly fulfilled and content.

So, at some bright peak of their lives, must all men be. The grief is that it lasts not long.

CHAPTER V

King Henry, just as David had said, went in person into Gascony the following year, and there he found it by no means so simple as he had supposed to put right everything he claimed the earl of Leicester had put wrong, for that Count Gaston of Béarn whom he had expected to find a grateful and affectionate kinsman, having championed him in his complaints against the earl, turned out a difficult and rebellious vassal, as obdurate against the king himself as against his viceroy, and there was great to-ing and fro-ing of letters between Bordeaux and England before the king got all into control, the troubles in those distant parts, and the matter of his son's marriage, keeping him absent all the following year.

During this long absence his queen, together with his brother Richard of Cornwall, acted as regents in his room. And it was they who summoned David to court in the first week of July, shortly after the king's departure, to do homage to them as the king's proxies for his commote of Cymydmaen. He had held it then for a year, and I think his pleasure in it was still keen, if he had not received this friendly call back to a wider and more worldly court. Moreover, this was to the queen, with whom he had always found great favour because of her son's attachment to him. He had less fondness for the king, indeed to some degree he showed a certain disdain for that less resolute and dependable personage, though he had been much indulged by him. Certain it is that he received the summons joyfully, almost like one startled out of a comfortable but confining dream to his real waking life. He made great preparation, and provided his party royally for the journey, intent that there should be none about the queen's person more splendid than himself and his retinue. This I bear witness, having visited him on my lord's business shortly before he left for England. I think indeed, however gilded and jewelled, no young man more beautiful graced the court that year, or any year. And so thought many a Welsh lady he left behind him, and I doubt not many an English lady who greeted him.

Who first had his favours I do not profess to know. But by this he was no stranger to women. Nor did any ever complain of him, save perhaps of his absence.

I think the Lady Senena would have liked to travel with him to court on that occasion, but he was not so minded. He was fond of her, but fonder of his own new and heady freedom and dignity, and it must be admitted that she was a managing woman. He persuaded her that his commote of Cymydmaen could not flourish in his absence without a touch as firm as hers, and that there was no one to whom he would so happily confide it, and that sweetened her exclusion from his party. So if he was ruthless in ridding himself of her company, at least he did it in a way that flattered instead of affronting.

Thus he went south from us at the end of June, in great splendour, at least to our eyes. Llewelyn laughed to see how fine he had made himself, and how formally attended, but without unkindness, for the boy was still only seventeen, and in his pride and determination to outshine the nobility of the English court he was making a stand for the good name of Wales, however childishly. Indeed, he laughed at himself, but never relaxing his resolve to show like the sun. And always he had this seeming ability to stand aside from himself and make a mockery of what that self did in all solemnity, either part of him as real and formidable as the other. So he went to his reunion with the queen and the earl of Cornwall, and with Edward, his play-fellow.

He did not come back until the end of July. Most of his escort he sent on ahead to Neigwl, and himself, with only a few attendants, came visiting to us at Carnarvon. He was lively and full of news, but as it were something distracted, as though but half his mind had returned with him, and the remaining half lagged somewhere on the way, reluctant to catch up with him. And he spoke – I noted it, and so, I know, did Llewelyn – of the queen, and Richard of Cornwall, and the two boys Edward and Edmund, and other of that company, very familiarly yet not with any air of boasting his familiarity. Had it been Rhodri we should have seen him plume himself as he spoke. David used their names as simply and naturally as ours, and only from time to time seemed to catch the strange echo of his utterance, and to be startled and shaken by it. For it was that very familiarity that was so strange. And then his eyes would open wider in their blue brilliance, and look round the solar where we sat, at every skin rug and smoky hanging, as though starting out of a dream, or falling headlong into one.

'And this Castillian marriage,' Llewelyn questioned intently, 'that goes forward?'

'So Edward says. At least his proctors are appointed, before the king left England, and they're busy dealing now over terms. If the marriage and the treaty come to fruit, then Alfonso could be the best protector of King Henry's interests in Gascony, where he's in very good odour with even the Béarnais.'

'I'd as soon see King Henry still on thorns, and looking towards Gascony,' Llewelyn said drily, 'as comforted and easy in his mind, and looking my way. The less care he has to lavish on me, the better.'

'Take heart, then,' said David, 'for as fast as he gets out of one morass he's into another. He's barely got clear of the whole dangerous race of the Hohenstaufen, from Barbarossa down, than he swings too far towards the pope in his relief, and finds himself mired to the knees in the opposite swamp. Innocent hates that family and all who are allied to it, and his one desire left in life is to uproot the last of them from the kingdom of Sicily, and set up an emperor more to his taste. Last year he began sounding out candidates for the honour of supplanting him. He began with the earl of Cornwall, but our Richard took very little time to refuse the compliment. As well try to pluck the moon out of heaven, he said, as turn Conrad out of Sicily. King Louis's brother thought a little longer about it, but the answer was the same. And now, it's rumoured, Innocent has mentioned the matter cautiously to King Henry, with young Edmund in mind. The king has not closed with the offer yet, but trust me, he's too deeply tempted and too incurably hopeful to resist, if a firm offer is ever made. It would mean paying off the pope's debts in the enterprise to date – well above a hundred thousand marks, they say – and putting troops into Sicily. If he can so much as land them there! But it might induce Innocent to commute his crusading vow to undertaking this act of cleansing nearer home. All in all, there are those at court who are mightily disturbed about the prospect, for to them it looks like the short road to ruin. Not many are wise to the danger yet, but Richard of Cornwall is, since it was first offered to him, and he had good sense enough to refuse. So you may rely on it, King Henry is more than engrossed in his own plans, and soon will be in his own troubles.'

He said all this without flourishes or hesitation, not afraid to speak as statesmen and councillors do. And while his wits were thus engaged in this enlarged world, peopled by popes and emperors and the paladin brothers of kings, his eyes were brilliant and his cheeks flushed, as though he entered into a kingdom of his own.

'I see,' said Llewelyn, between amusement and wonder, 'you have not wasted your time in England. Is it Edward who discusses these intimate matters with you? Before the king's own council know them?'

'I use my eyes and ears,' said David, and smiled. 'And given a certain sum of knowledge, more follows without questions asked or answered. As, for instance, that if King Henry does indeed want to pursue this latest hope, he can hardly get far with it while he's still at odds with the king of France, and it needs no prophet to judge that sooner or later there'll be an accommodation. Those two will be friends yet, trust me.'

'I had rather they stayed enemies,' Llewelyn owned. 'I breathe more easily so. But you could be right, and I'll bear it well in mind. If my enemy has no enemies elsewhere, how shall I thrive? Go on, tell me what you have heard concerning this Castillian marriage. A great appanage, you said, to set the prince up as a married man. Gascony, that we know of. What else? There'll be equally large endowments nearer home.'

'It's no way certain,' said David, 'what they'll be, for there's no decision made yet, no more than talk. But they say he'll have Ireland. And Chester and its county, and most likely Bristol, too. And Wales, all the crown possessions here. The Middle Country, the castles of Diserth and Degannwy, the lordships of Cardigan, Carmarthen, Montgomery and Builth. Maybe the three castles of Gwent. But nothing's yet certain.'

His face, intent and bright, said that nevertheless it was known to him, as surely as if it had been sealed already. And Llewelyn saw that certainty in him, and sprang upon it.

'But you had this from Edward!'

David acknowledged it, but with reserve, for Edward's father was an ever-hopeful, light and changeable man, and what was not yet made public could be taken back unsaid.

Said Llewelyn: 'I begin to see this boy, this Edward of yours, as a shape that threatens my plans. Chester and Bristol, that's my northern march and the southern one, too. Gwent and the Middle Country, spears into my side. While they stayed with Henry, did they matter quite so much? Henry shifts. This son of his has an immovable sound about him. I would I knew as much of him as you know. God knows I need it, for Edward is the future. And like to live? Yes, surely, you spoke of his rough health, he's for a long life. Talk to me of him,' he ordered, and his voice was urgent and low. 'Tell me all that you know, all that you feel concerning him. Shut your eyes, if you will, and forget I am here. Show me your Edward!'

I know of no one to whom such an order could be easy to obey. It closed David's mouth as though some curse had sealed it, but that was only for a while. He shut his eyes, to me an astonishment, for he rebelled by nature against all such suggestions, and in a little while the tight, bright lines softened in his face, and he did begin to speak of Edward. Softly and haltingly at first, then as if in a dream, with curious happiness and eloquence, so that he seemed to be speaking only to his own heart. He had known this boy, three years younger than himself, for some ten or eleven years, and the king's second son, Edmund, had never made any great mark in their companionship, Edward's bent being always, as it seemed, towards those somewhat his elders. For he was a strong, clever and serious-minded child, able to grapple with those more grown in body and more tutored in mind. And past doubt, as we heard from his own lips, David had been involved in both loving and misliking him, the prince being adventurous and gallant to a degree, willing to match himself against his older comrade, yet able to revert into royalty when outmatched or displeased. A strange child, well aware of his destiny from early years, but proud, too, of his body and its competence, of his mind and its brightness. There was a certain largeness and warmth in him then, that would take a tumble and never grudge it, provided no one laughed. But from what I heard out of David's lips, as he talked blindly from behind closed eyelids, sometimes smiling and sometimes grim, I would not have given much for any who outmatched the prince constantly and innocently, unaware of offence, and trusting to have their own magnanimity reflected in his. For there are those who cannot abide to be any but first, and can afford to throw away one lapse, or two, as largesse, but never more than one or two, for after that the sin is mortal.

When he had talked himself out of breath and words, and into some deep, private place of recollection and discovery, David opened his eyes, and they were wild and a little affrighted, as though only now, with the return of vision, did he realise all that he had revealed. As though the first person he saw was the Edward he had painted for us, his back turned, walking steadily away. For surely he had never before looked inward and examined what he knew and felt of his royal companion, and now that he did so, the very depth and width of his knowledge frightened him, and his having shared it went beyond, and in some way horrified and shamed him.

'What have I done?' he said in a dismayed whisper. 'I have said too much. What right had I to strip him so for you?'

'You did no more than I asked you,' said Llewelyn, smiling at him with astonished affection, 'and did it very well. If I needed a portrait, I have it.'

'But to bind him hand and foot, and stand him in front of you naked!' David cried, twisting and knotting his hands.

At that Llewelyn laughed, and flung an arm rallyingly round his shoulders and shook him. 'I did not see him so! Far from it! Very well and richly clothed in his own abilities you showed him to me, and well worth looking at, too. You're too tender of your loyalties. Faith, I think you've come back to us more an English courtier than a Welsh prince!'

He meant no more than the lightest of touches, and yet it went in like a barb. David shook off the arm that held him and bounded to his feet, white-faced with passion.

'You dare say so to me? You dare? I am as much Griffith's son as you are, and no one, not even a brother, can use such words to me and not be called to account. Is it my fault if I grew up at King Henry's court? You think I've turned my coat for Edward's favour? Every drop of blood in me is Welsh, as Welsh as yours, as royal and as true!'

Llewelyn was too taken aback by this outburst to get his breath for a moment. He stood open-mouthed, the rallying laughter still on his lips, and a great astonishment in his eyes. And before he could retort either with indulgent mockery or blunt and forcible reproof, David had caught himself a little back from us into shadow, as if to hide, turned one wild and angry glance like the sweep of a sword to hold off both of us, and flung out of the room.

'Now what in God's name ailed him,' Llewelyn demanded, gazing after him, 'to take me so desperately in earnest? Does he know so much of his Edward, and so little of me?'

I said no, that he knew well enough, had known even while the words were pulsing hotly out of his throat, that the sting he had felt had never been delivered but in his own mind. But if that was comfort to Llewelyn, it was oddly discomfortable to me. For if, in his unguarded moment, David had been so ready and quick to resent the imagined charge of a divided and shifting allegiance, it was surely because his own heart had already accused him. Llewelyn had touched a wound that was already waiting, open and painful. More, for I had seen the boy's face as he leaped to his feet, and I was sure that if he had not shown his prince to Llewelyn naked and bound, naked and bound he himself had suddenly seen him, and that cry of his: 'What have I done? I have said too much!' was his own recognition of an act of treason on one side, barely a moment before he felt himself assailed by the like accusation from the other.

It seemed to me then that we had none of us given enough thought to the stresses under which those two younger ones laboured, thus translated so late back to their own land, when all their most formative years had been spent in another, and that in innocence, protected and indulged, when they were too young to understand the agonies and wrongs that had brought them there. What they now knew and professed, and even understood, they had never been forced to feel. And Rhodri, perhaps, was centred so shallowly in himself as to be proof against too much thought, but David was subtle, brooding and deep.

Llewelyn had been thinking much as I had, for he said soberly: 'He's newly back, and it comes hard, I daresay. But it will pass. Give him a month or two to settle down at Neigwl, and he'll be too busy and content to look back towards Westminster. All the same, better not make that journey too often, the cost comes too high.'

I asked if I should go after him, for the disquiet and desperation of his face as he left us tormented me, and he was fond of me, and would not bite too viciously if I offended him. But Llewelyn said no.

'Let him alone. He'll come back of his own will, and better so.'

And so he did, before many minutes were past, entering almost as abruptly as he had left us, and taking his stand before Llewelyn, within touch and in the fullest light of the room, with a clear face and wide-open eyes, only a little flushed in the cheeks now after his bitter pallor.

'I ask your pardon,' he said outright and easily, 'for being so ill-humoured. It was foolish to think you meant any evil.'

'Call quits,' said Llewelyn, 'for it was a very feeble joke. That's one subject I shall know better than take lightly again. Faith, it was like putting a torch to tinder!'

'And over as quickly,' said David, with a trace of bitterness, before he hoisted his shoulders and laughed. 'If a real enemy sets light to me you shall find I burn both hot and slow.'

So suddenly and vehemently he made his peace, and they went out together to the mews with David's arm about Llewelyn's neck. But at times he did revert to this flare thereafter, always without warning, and always as one excusing himself, saying how he grudged it that only Llewelyn, of the four brothers, had fought and starved for Wales, while he fattened in comfort as a pampered child at the English court, and how this sense of having been cheated out of his morsel of glory made him sore to touch on that point. So that sometimes I questioned within myself whether it was indeed so soon and safely over, or whether he brooded still in his heart, keeping his trouble to himself. And above all, whether what he revealed of it was the true core, or whether he went about, unknown to himself, to dress it more acceptably for our eyes and his own.

But Llewelyn, who seemed to be most wise in his youngest brother, took him peaceably as he came, and made no to-do, letting him alone with his own good heart and good sense to find his way aright. And when David thus spoke of playing the child in England while Wales bled, and not even chafing at his helplessness for want of understanding, Llewelyn would say bluntly that he need have no regrets, for the true struggle for Wales had not yet even begun, and he had plenty of time in the years ahead to make his name as a paladin.

Once I asked him, when we were alone, if he truly meant this. For we seemed then to be so securely pinned down in our restricted lands, and yet so tolerated and accepted in this limited state, that I could not see how we could again be brought into conflict with England. King Henry was utterly absorbed in his Sicilian plans and his son's marriage, in the business of bringing to an end his long enmity with France, in settling Gascony for Edward and resigning himself to relaxing all hold on

Normandy. His face was set constantly eastward, not westward. It seemed that he had no thought for us, and no intent to trouble us further. And if he had no will to make war, we had no means, or means so slight that the attempt would be madness.

'As yet,' said Llewelyn. 'Yet even now we are not so unready as you may suppose. Still, I grant you there are stones in the way.' He mused for a moment on the greatest and most immovable of these, but went on without naming it. 'It will, it must, come to war in the end, the art will be in choosing the time. For this most marked stress upon Wales, in Prince Edward's appanage, with the earldom of Chester held fast by the crown for him, and Bristol in the south, this is a new threat, whatever its appearance in the documents. His is not meant to be any parchment title. This is a planned move to tighten the royal grip upon Wales. The time will come when we must fight to regain what we have lost, if we are not to find ourselves fighting hard to keep even what they have left us. It cannot stand long as it is. They will take all from us, or we must regain all from them.'

I had learned to have great faith in his judgment, and I knew by his face and his tone that he was in strong earnest. Yet it seemed to me, considering the cautious stillness in which we had lived now such a number of years, that our situation rendered action as impossible to us now as before the peace of Woodstock.

Llewelyn shook his head. 'No! The king's officers are doing our work for us, we need not lift a finger yet, they win friends for us right and left. This la Zuche who holds the Middle Country in his grip, and has sworn to bring it under English control for all time, is worth an army to me. I could not so soon have convinced every knight and lord and tenant in the four cantrefs of his Welsh blood, and his need to remember it, as this man has done. I could not have united all those quarrelling borderers as he has done, in one patriot hate of England and her officers and all her works. He calls recruits for me out of the ground like corn from seed. The time will come when I need only to go and reap the harvest. And a little success there could call back to their allegiance great numbers of those princes elsewhere who offered King Henry their homage out of fear. Success breeds true and fast. Only,' he said, and looked out long over the sea towards Ynys Lanog, for we were riding by the salt-flats of Aber, 'there must also be unity at the top, or we split and fall.'

I was in his close confidence. He spoke with me as with his own soul, and I with him as I had wit, for all my intent was to be of help to him if I might, in whatever enterprise he undertook, whether it was the better draining of a piece of upland bog that might be made to grow food, or the training of the falcons of Snowdon in which he delighted, or the glorious recovery of all the lost lands of Gwynedd, or, yet more wonderful, the reaching forward strongly into his grandsire's dream of a single and splendid Wales under one prince, which I knew to be also his dream. My will was always to see with his eyes, to divine his desire, and to lend whatever might I had to help him achieve it. Therefore I said without conceal: 'The stone in your way is the Lord Owen. God knows I mean no ill against your father, but he had no such vision, and neither has his eldest son. With a great work to be done, he is not the partner you would have chosen.'

In this I was astray, for I believed he had young David in mind. And I think he saw my meaning, for he gave me a long, dark but smiling look, and answered only: 'There are many men in this land I will gladly have as allies and officers, and I hope friends. None I would choose as a partner. The time I have waited for is coming. Slowly, but it is coming. And what I have to do, Samson, can only be done alone.'

'How, then,' I said, willing to follow him into any extremes for that vision, 'will you dispose?'

'In his own good time, and with whatever instrument he chooses, God will dispose,' said Llewelyn.

But the quietness and the waiting continued yet two years, and Llewelyn made no complaint, but went on with his work in orderly fashion.

David visited us but little, busying himself with his lands in Lleyn, though I think with less joy than formerly. For the first lustre was gone from possession, and after his return to his old royal haunts the llys at Neigwl looked poor and rustic to him, and Cymydmaen shrunken and wild. I speak with the wisdom of hindsight, for we knew nothing then of any discontent and unrest in him, and thought it well that he spent so much time on his own lands, believing he cherished and improved, rather than fretting and brooding. Llewelyn had never but once seen the English court, and that was in somewhat diminished state at Woodstock, never at Westminster, and its glories had been as a front opposed to him, never as a warmth enclosing him, such as they had been to David. I, who had seen somewhat of London, though as a servant to my child lords, should have understood better the force of the contrast between David's two estates.

I did not, and the more blame to me.

We took good care, those days, to get regular news of all that went forward about King Henry's court. In February Prince Edward's portion was published, and contained all that David had said: Ireland, but for a few places held in reserve, Chester and its county, Bristol, where his exchequer and offices would be based, all the crown possessions in Wales, the Channel Islands, Gascony entire, with the island of Oléron. A vast endowment. The Welsh grant included even a part of the coast north of Cardigan, so that the powers of England closed their claws on Eryri from every side. And one Geoffrey Langley, a king's officer heretofore best known for his harsh dealings in the law of the forest, was given the Middle Country to milk for his masters, for they held that it could be made to yield a far higher revenue for the prince than it had so far produced. I doubt Langley in the first six months of office did more even than Alan la Zuche had done in several years, to make good Llewelyn's words concerning the raising of an army of embittered Welshmen who waited only for a leader.

We had full reports also, and none so slow in reaching us, either, of the marriage in Burgos. Prince Edward crossed over to Gascony a little before his fifteenth birthday, which fell on the seventeenth day of June of that year, twelve hundred and fifty-four. The queen travelled with him, and also Archbishop Boniface of Canterbury, uncle to the queen, one of those kinsmen of hers from Savoy who were causing so much jealousy and resentment among the English nobility, together with the king's Lusignan half-brothers, his mother's sons by her second husband, who came swarming over from Poitou to make their fortune by rich marriages in England. These foreign kinsmen were one of the chief causes of complaint against King Henry, and brought him into great difficulties in later years, but he valued and favoured them in spite of all blame.

The marriage plans were completed at leisure during the summer months of June and July, and then the prince's party moved on to Burgos, and there King Alfonso knighted him, and towards the end of October the child Eleanor, the king's half-sister, was married to the heir of England with all ceremony in the cathedral of Burgos. Then King Alfonso formally renounced all claims to Gascony, having acquired a close interest in it by another way which suited him well enough, and cost no warfare and no bad blood. For his influence was great with both King Henry and King Henry's son. The prince took his little bride back into Gascony with him, and there they stayed for a full year before coming home to England.

And there was more still to confirm all that David had told us. For King Henry on his way home after the marriage determined to make the first advance towards that composition with France which would set him free to pursue the Sicilian enterprise on his second son's behalf. King Louis was returned at last from his crusading adventures in the east. King Henry sent envoys to him, and solicited a meeting, a personal acquaintance such as could be sealed into friendship. And at Chartres King Louis met him most graciously, and conducted him to Paris, where he was royally entertained, and the queen's Provençal family were brought together in a grand reunion. For this King Louis was more than commonly wise and kind in personal matters, very skilled in turning to pleasure and ease a first meeting that might have been hard and painful. So those two met, and the seed was sown which should bring about a full settlement, a treaty of peace and harmony between their countries, formerly in enmity.

Nevertheless, as Llewelyn had said, a compounding between those two kings boded nothing of benefit to us, for our enemy's rear was thereby secured, and he could turn his attention all the more freely to Wales. Yet such are the chances of the time, it fell out otherwise. For always there is some unforeseen mercy, or unexpected chastening, waiting to be manifested.

The Christmas feast that year was chill and bright and windy. Contrary gales kept King Henry from landing at Dover until the day after St Stephen's, and went driving down the coast of Wales like silver lances, cold as ice. And yet the skies were cloudless and full of stars, most beautiful to see, and there was but a little snow, that dried up in the frost and blew like white dust about the flats. For we kept the feast at Aber, after the old fashion.

We lacked only Rhodri and the Lady Senena at that feast. For Rhodri had at that time a certain lady who took up all his attention, and kept him at home in his own llys, and the Lady Senena, though she made her stay mainly with David at Neigwl, having spent so much of her married life there and having a fondness for the spot, had journeyed in the autumn into the south, to pay a first visit to her daughter Gladys at Dynevor. Between that castle, willing subject to King Henry, and our princedom of Gwynedd, there was no contact, though before the Lady Senena came home to Wales the two princes, at Llewelyn's urging, had offered to Rhys Fychan and his house a compact of mutual aid and support, which remained, unhappily, no more than a parchment pledge, since the members of that house could not even agree among themselves. Yet I know that Llewelyn had blessed his mother's journey, and sent greetings in all kindness to his sister, whose stiff loyalty to her husband he did not any way blame. But no word came back, as he looked for none.

In the brightness of the day the brothers rode much, and by night in hall there was good food and drink in plenty, and good harping, for our bards were famous, and so was Llewelyn's patronage, so that many singers came from other parts to entertain in his hall, and none ever went away empty-handed or discontented with his reward. That Christmas we saw David in uneasy mood, either wildly elated and gay, or withdrawn into a black depression. And often his tongue bit sharply, but both his elders, seeing how deeply he had drunk, bore with him goodnaturedly, and always he sprang back into the light in time to disarm us all. So though it was unusual in him, we thought nothing amiss.

He came to me late in an evening in the little chamber where I kept the rolls, and did my writing and reckoning on Llewelyn's business. I had left the hall early, having some matters waiting for me, and thinking this the best hour to withdraw and see the work done. There were certain complicated cases to be heard in my lord's commote court, two concerning the removal of boundaries, and also a matter of some wreckage cast up by the sea on the edge of the church lands of Bangor, the goods being in dispute between prince and bishop, for Bishop Richard was a contentious and obstinate man. Llewelyn relied on me to have all the needful information tabled and ready to his hand. True, he had also his chaplain and official secretary, but the clerking was left to me at my lord's wish, and it was I who accompanied him when he rode out to preside in all his district courts.

Over this labour David came in to me, alone, and stood by me for a little while reading over my shoulder. He was flushed with wine, but quiet, and very well able to carry what he had drunk with grace, as commonly he did.

'Samson,' he said, after a while of silence, 'you know Welsh law as well as any man here. Tell me, what is the law concerning the succession to a crown?'

'You know it as well as I,' I said, and went on writing, for I had much to do. 'The wise prince names his successor while he's well alive, and sees to it that he's accepted by all.'

'And if the prince is less wise, and never names an edling to follow him?' he persisted in the same low and deliberate voice.

'Then his realm is liable to division among all his sons. But in practice it's far more like to go by consent to the eldest, and see some minor lands given to the others.'

'True,' he said, 'but that's not Welsh law, and you know it, it's a convenience borrowed from the English. Four sons with an equal claim are entitled to fair shares of the inheritance.'

'If they care to stand on their rights, and tear apart what has been laboriously put together,' I said, still paying him little heed, 'they may say so. But with a greedy neighbour waiting to pick off their portions one by one, I would not recommend it.'

'Why, they could still work together and fight and plan together,' he said, 'each for all, could they not? And listen to me, if that is good Welsh law, and English law says the eldest takes all, and gives what he chooses and sees fit to the younger, then by what strange law, neither Welsh nor English, have we apportioned Gwynedd? Samson,' he said reproachfully, seeing I still laboured to round off a word, 'you might at least look at me! Time was when you were kinder.' And he laid one long hand flat over the blank part of my parchment, and prevented me from continuing.

I looked up into his face then, perforce, sighing for my lost time, and he was smiling at me, but darkly, with only the glimmer of mischief in his eyes, for his mouth was petulant and sad.

'Am I your breast-brother, or no?' he demanded, and sat down beside me, leaning against my shoulder.

'You are,' I said, 'and my prince, and at this moment a little drunk, and more than a little perverse. And I have work to do.'

'It will keep an hour. And I am not so far gone in wine as you imagine. Listen, Samson, for I'm in earnest. If law is to be respected, why have we neither gone by the old way, and parted everything fairly among us, nor openly adopted the new way, the English way, and given all to the eldest? By what rule can we claim this settlement was made?'

'There were but two heirs here,' I said, 'when the Lord David your uncle died.' Though truth to tell I might have gone further, and said that there was but one. 'The council recommended them to share equally and rule Gwynedd together, and they consented, and so they have done to this day. All of which you know, so why torment me with such questions when I am busy?'

'If we other two were elsewhere,' he said, 'that was no fault of ours, and should cost us none of our rights. And seeing we were elsewhere, was our fosterage with King Henry so different from any lawful Welsh fostering in the old days, when young princes were put out to grow up with lordly families? When it came to the succession to a crown, do you think every such lord did not back his own fosterling for the honour, and every fosterling make play with his foster-father's power and influence? Supposing I chose to call my royal foster-father to back my claim? And my princely brother, newly made lord of most of the borderlands?'

His voice was wilful, soft and mischievous, and I knew he was but plaguing me. But there was a kind of restless malevolence in such teasing that vexed me, as much for his sake as my own, for it showed all too well he was not happy. So I put down my pen with a sigh, and turned to him.

'Well, I see you must talk out your fill of nonsense, for you mean none of it. Both you and Rhodri were set up with very reasonable portions as soon as you came back to Gwynedd. You hold the lands your father held before you –'

'A part of them,' he said.

'True, then, let us be exact, a part of them. Good land, however, richer than the rocks of Eryri. I thought you were very happy with Cymydmaen,' I said, 'what has made you so restless suddenly with your lot?'

'Oh, Samson,' he said, twisting his shoulders impatiently, 'I am cramped! So narrow and poor a life, how can I settle to it? I could do so much! I know what is in me, and I want my due.'

'Have you spoken of this to your brothers?' I asked him.

'Oh, Samson, do you not see I need your good word there? Llewelyn will listen to you, if you speak for me.'

I still did not believe that this was anything more than a black mood of frustration in him, one of the last echoes of his discontent when he remembered London and the glories of that court. Surely he needed to be rid of it, and as well pour it out upon me as venture a rougher welcome from his elders. But his need would be met when he had cleansed his breast at my expense, and slept off this evening's wine, which, as I knew, he did lightly and vigorously, rising fresh as a lark in the early morning. So I told him simply that I would not be his advocate, because I was not of his party, much as I loved him. I said that neither his plea nor mine would move Llewelyn, for reason enough, because he dreaded and would resist to his last breath the further partition of Gwynedd, which he felt in his heart and blood must be one to survive. I said that the dismemberment of the land, into parcels princed but locally and with no outward eye, would mean nothing but the sly swallowing of each portion in turn by England, until all were devoured. Which could mean nothing but loss and ruin to all. I said that only a single, united Wales could hold its own, in the end, with an England perhaps equally subject to faction, but infinitely stronger, not in courage or grandeur, but in resources of food, materials, weapons and men. I told him, lastly, that Llewelyn had once asserted in practical fashion his own faith in this great, hopeful unity, when it meant that he accepted a lesser part, and surrendered his father's legal right, and his own after it, to fight loyally for the uncle who dispossessed them. And I said that in like manner he, David, might most honourably stand to it as captain of the household guard to Llewelyn now, for the present penteulu was growing elderly, and there was no one on earth I would rather see keeping my lord's head than this, his favourite brother, and my own breast-brother.

By the time I had ended this, and I am ashamed of it when I remember, my right hand was softly reaching again for my pen, and my left was smoothing the parchment and turning it stealthily, ready to continue writing. Which, though he never lowered his great harebell-blue eyes from my face, nevertheless he saw. He had listened unmoving to every word I had said to him, those eyes devouring me, and though I swear he had not so much as quivered, yet he seemed to have drawn back from me

87

very slowly, by some foot or so of charged air, and to have receded into shadow. I remember now his face fronting me, the flush of wine misted over in shade, the broad, high bones of his cheeks and the narrowed, ardent angles of his jaw touched by gleams of light from the torches, and those eyes, like blue lakes, their depths concealed behind the shallow reflection of the sun.

'Well,' he said, 'well! I have listened dutifully, have I not? I see you are his man.' He had ever a very low and beguiling voice, and used it like an instrument of music. 'Well, I do believe you honest towards us all,' he said, 'and I will think of what you have said. But I should never have plagued you so, and I will no more. You may go on with your work now.'

And he got up from his place beside me, and turned to the doorway. And truly I put down my pen, confounded, and would have called him back if I could, though I did not know why. For he went very gently and serenely, as though he had bled out of him all those humours that tortured him and disquieted him. And in the doorway he turned, and smiled back at me with all his youthful sweetness, and said:

'My brother is a lucky man!'

And with that he went out from me. And the next day he rode for Cymydmaen with all his retinue, gaily as ever, and kissed me on departing, very warmly. He said not a word of what had passed between us, and he embraced Llewelyn with particular fervour and affection.

It was past Easter before I saw him again.

In the spring Owen Goch came visiting to Aber twice. On the second occasion, shortly after the Easter feast, David also rode up from Neigwl to join us for some days, in his best and most dutiful humour, full of his activities in his own lands, and willing to ask for advice and listen to it when given. It was not until after he had left us again that the quarrel broke out between Owen and Llewelyn that altered everything in our lives. The boy himself had raised not a word of any grievance, nor seemed to be cherishing any, rather to have put away from him all his regrets for his English glories, and to be bending all his energies to the right running of those lands he held. He was gone, and we were merry enough in hall at the day's end when Owen leaned to my lord, and said suddenly:

'These young brothers of ours – have we done right by them? I tell you, I am not easy in my mind.'

Llewelyn was somewhat surprised to have such a subject launched out of a clear sky, and gave him a long, considering look, though he was smiling. 'Taking things all in all,' he said, untroubled, 'we did exceedingly well by them. We kept, between us, something to bestow on them, at least, and have kept them undisturbed in the possession of it ever since. They might have been still landless and in exile. I am by no means ashamed of my part. You must weigh your own conscience, mine's light as air.'

I am sure he meant no reference to old quarrels and jealousies, but his tone had a certain bite, for he anticipated what was in the wind. But Owen took quick offence, and flamed as red as his hair.

'We have been told before, brother, of your exploits in the October war, while the rest of us sat by good roaring fires eating King Henry's meat. That's old history – or old legend, I doubt! There needs no repetition of that story here. Leave your praise to the bards, who do it with a better grace. I am talking of justice.'

'God's life!' said Llewelyn, laughing. 'I meant no such vaunt, as you should know. You and I between us, I said, have secured them the undisturbed possession of what is theirs, whether by fighting or good husbandry or sound policies, what does it matter? You say, have we done right by them. I say, we have. We – not I!'

'But I think not,' said Owen, jutting his great jaw. 'And it's time we spoke of it now in earnest, for they're no longer boys under tutelage, but young men grown, and will be in need of proper endowment, fitting their rank as princes ready to marry and father families. What's one commote, even the fattest? It belittles their birth to have so poor an establishment.'

'It belittles mine,' said Llewelyn, looking far past his brother, and narrowing his deep eyes upon a distance I could only guess at, 'to sit here squeezed into the narrow measure of Gwynedd beyond Conway. Well, it seems it is not the lot of any son of Griffith to know content. What is it you want of me?'

'Not here,' said Owen Goch, and looked about him with meaning, for I was but two places from my lord's right hand, and Goronwy as near on the other side of them, and chaplain and chamberlain close, and half the household guard and the retainers in the lower part of the hall within earshot. There was noise and talk enough under the smoky timbers of the roof to cover the conversation at the high table, but Owen knew the power of his own voice when his temper was inflamed, and wanted no public dispute yet. Nor, I thought, did he yet intend to draw in the judge of the court, until he had sounded out his brother and had some sort of understanding with him. For if they two agreed, the more open discussion could be decorous and peaceable, and the officers and councillors would listen with respect, even if they demurred. For those two brothers, even the hotter and less governable, had practised this manner of restraint with success now for eight years, though they loved each other no better than the first day. Llewelyn was right, saying that between them they had preserved what could be preserved of Gwynedd, and that was great credit to Owen, for he was the one who took most hurt from containing his passions.

'Not here,' said Owen, 'but in private.'

'Very well,' said Llewelyn, 'we'll withdraw early.'

He waited only for the harper to make an end of his playing, and the wine to circulate freely at the end of the meal, and then made a sign to the silentiary, who struck the pillar of the hall opposite the royal seat with his gavel, and signified that the princes desired to retire. And the hall rose to pay respect to the brothers as they left the high table and withdrew into Llewelyn's private chamber.

'Come with us, Samson,' said my lord, passing by my place. 'Let us have a witness.'

I would as lief he had chosen some other for the honour, but I knew why he did not. There was no other man in that court who knew what I knew about the first meeting of those two at Aber. Things could be said before me, if it came to the worst, that must not be heard, for Gwynedd's sake, by Goronwy or any other. Never unless the times changed for us all, and Gwynedd grew too strong to be torn by any minor dissensions. So I followed into the inner room, and closed the heavy door upon the renewed hubbub of the hall, drawing the curtain over it to shut out even the notes of the harp.

'Now,' said Llewelyn, 'say your say, in as few words as you will.'

There was wine set for them on a table there, and drinking horns, and the candle-bearer had made haste to place lights at their coming. To justify, in some sort, my presence, and signify that I was a servant in formal attendance, I served them with wine, and drew back into shadow from the lighted place where they sat down. There was a small fire of split logs in a brazier, for the April night was chilly, and the kernel of flame and the scented curl of smoke made a barrier between them.

'We are four brothers,' said Owen, 'of whom all have rights in law. When you and I parted Gwynedd between us there was no other here to dispute our rights, but that time is past. We are at peace, and our brothers wait for us to do them justice. I want a fit and proper partition of our common inheritance, fair shares for all.'

'I admire,' said Llewelyn, 'your generosity, but not your wisdom. Are you willing, then, to give away half of what you hold? Or have you in mind that I should surrender all?'

'It would mean each of us surrendering some part of our holding,' said Owen. 'It need scarcely be half. But it is not right or just that David and Rhodri should have only the crumbs, and I say the whole of Gwynedd must be divided afresh.'

'And which of them,' Llewelyn asked shrewdly, 'put you up to be spokesman? And what reward did he propose for you, to compensate for what you will be losing?'

Owen began to fume, and to drink more deeply to feed his fire. 'I need no prompting,' he said haughtily, 'to show me where I am compounding injustice. I know the old law, and so do you, though you may close your eyes against it. I say there must be a proper partition made.'

Llewelyn laid down his drinking-horn with a steady hand. 'And I say this land shall be parcelled out no more. This endless division and redivision is the ruin of Wales and the delight of her enemies, since they can feed fat on one commote after another, while every little princeling shivers and clings to his own maenol, trusting to be spared while he lets his neighbour be dispossessed, and fool enough not to see it will be his turn next. My answer is no. Nor now nor ever at any future time will I be party to dismembering my land.'

'Take care!' flared Owen. 'I can very well take it to the council over your head. I made concessions enough for the sake of peace, I, the eldest son. If it come to a reassessment, I shall not again be so easy.'

'Ah!' said Llewelyn, fiercely smiling. 'Now I begin to see what reward you expect. It is not the rights and wrongs of Rhodri and David you have on your mind, it is the hope of a revision, on new terms, at a council where you can hold me up as the grasping tyrant who will not do right, and end by asserting your seniority, and getting your hands on the lion's share. It would be worth sacrificing something to the young ones, would it not, to be rid of me? Them you might dominate, me you know you never will. What you want of me is not my consent to this idiot proposal, but my refusal, and a court at which you can arraign and dispossess me. If I will not go by the old Welsh way, then you will concede something – oh, very reluctantly! – and agree to what I seem to desire, the practical way of setting up the eldest son as single overlord and keeping Gwynedd one! Out of my own mouth I am to be snared! Go to the council, then, try your influence. You will find they will not sell you Llewelyn so cheaply. Make the assay! I will abide it. You have put your plan and your conscience before me, I have said no. Take it further, and let them declare which of us they value more.'

Owen came to his feet in loud indignation, protesting that he had no such devious thoughts in mind, that he came honestly, prepared to reduce his own state in order to do justice to his brothers, and that there was no man living had the right to cast such accusations in his teeth, far less Llewelyn, whom he had accepted as an equal to his own detriment. Yet I could not help feeling that he made too much noise and fury about his defence, and that he was, in some curious and secret way, not displeased with the way this interview had proceeded.

'What justification can you have,' he said with deep injury, 'for charging me with seeking to be rid of you, when I have worked faithfully with you all these years?'

'The justification,' said Llewelyn, 'of a dagger in my back once! Or have you forgotten, as I have not? Now, it seems, comes the second knife you had concealed about you – but no doubt, not until I turn my back again. Strike, then, what do I care? You will get a very different reception than you expect from the council of Gwynedd.'

Until that moment, I believe, Owen had been satisfied with his answer, and had truly intended what Llewelyn had divined as his purpose. If he was to bring up again the whole matter of sovereignty in Gwynedd, it had to be done in a way which was plausible, such as this scruple over Welsh law and a fair portioning, and also in a way which displayed him in the better and more virtuous light, and placed Llewelyn in the situation of a man accused. It was, in theory, a sound enough plan. But the absolute security of Llewelyn's voice shook him to the heart. For the first time he began to be afraid of putting it to the test, for fear it should react against himself. I saw the tremor of doubt and dread go over his face, and his acted rage break uneasily into a real fury, the only refuge he had when he lost his certainty.

'I will not stay in your house,' he cried, 'to suffer insult upon injury.' And he flung away from us and out at the door in terrible haste. And though he did not gather his retinue and ride that night, in the early hours of daylight next morning he and all his folk were gone.

When we were left alone, Llewelyn said to me, softly and wearily: 'Come and sit down, Samson, and bring the wine with you. God knows I need it. Would you have thought this was brewing? After all this time?'

I said what I believed: 'He'll take it no further.'

'To the council? No, I think not. He is not sure enough of his welcome, though why my confidence should shake his I cannot see. If he was to give up so easily, why and how did he bring himself to begin?'

I said, which was true, that the Lord Owen was not a very subtle or clever man, and did indeed begin things he could not finish. And at that Llewelyn laughed, with real amusement, but the next moment frowned in deep puzzlement. 'That is true. And to do him justice, this assay had a certain devious skill I would not have expected from him. It was more like him to take fright halfway, and let it drop. He'll say no word, to Goronwy or any, not even his own counsellors. We shall hear no more of it.'

In this he was right, for April passed into May, and May into June, and not a word was said more concerning the partition of Gwynedd. It was in a very different way that we heard again of Owen's quarrel.

In early June we were at Bala, in Penllyn, and in the second week of that month a messenger came spurring from the west in great haste, with despatches from Carnarvon for Llewelyn. Goronwy haled him in to the prince at once, for his horse was lathered and his news urgent.

'My lord,' he said, spent for breath as was his beast. 'I come from your castellan at Carnarvon. There's treason afoot in Lleyn! The Lord Owen has gathered all his fighting men in arms, and means to move against you before the month's out. The letter tells all, and how we got the news so soon, I hope soon enough to serve well! And my lord, there's more yet! A shepherd who remembers you from a lad has slipped away from Neigwl to warn us – the Lord David is putting his own household guard into the field along with his brother's men, the two of them have conspired to make war against you.'

Llewelyn uttered a brief, bitter sound between a laugh and a shout of pain, and struck his hands together with the parchment in them, the seal newly broken.

'David, too! He has corrupted the boy, into the bargain. This is his way out of the deadlock, is it? David! This is certain? No possible mistake?'

'None,' said the messenger heavily. 'It was one Peredur brought the word. He said you would know him well, my lord.'

'So I do, and trust him. And he's safe in Carnarvon now?' he asked urgently.

'No, my lord, he went back. He said if he stayed with us it would be known, and they would hasten the attack. He was out in the upland pastures, he trusted to make his way back again without question.'

'I pray he may! Goronwy,' said Llewelyn, unrolling his castellan's scroll between his hands, 'send my penteulu here, and bid him call the muster before he comes. In one hour we'll hold council. I want the captains present, too.' He had a standing guard of a hundred and forty men, and could call up many more at need, and there were good allies on whom he could draw, among his chief tenants. 'See to the messenger,' he said, and dismissed the man with his commendation. 'And have three more ready to ride as soon as we have held council.'

All went forward then according to his will, for his men understood him, and he knew his own mind, which is great comfort to those who follow and serve a prince. So the ordered frenzy of preparation made no great noise or excitement, however strange the event that had launched it. And Llewelyn, in one still moment, leaned for an instant on my shoulder, and drew breath to think, and select, and see his way plain.

'It is not ill done,' he said, catching my eye, and responding with a tight and thoughtful smile. 'It is very well done. There was no way in which I could have dismissed him with a clear mind and a clean heart, however he hampered and vexed me. Now he has written his own dismissal.'

'Yet Owen's forces and David's together,' I said, 'are a formidable army.'

'I am not afraid of the issue,' he said. 'Owen is. He takes up his quarrel with me in the only way he dare. He was afraid to put it to the judgment of the wise, but in avoiding the council he has judged the case himself, and given me best. He may draw his second dagger, but it will be no more effective than his first. Once I overlooked the stroke, for the sake of Gwynedd. Now I will repay it, with a vengeance, for the sake of Wales. Only,' he said, and suddenly his voice ached, and I knew with what pain, for I shared it, 'I wish he had not dragged the boy into it. I wish he had let David alone!

Not until that moment had I thought to look back, and compare those two, Owen with his hot, impetuous, blundering bravery, and his stupidity that undid all his better qualities, and David in his lustrous, secret, restless brilliance, deep as the sea off Enlli, and as hard to know. And I was flooded with a burning doubt and a terrible dismay, recalling now how David had gone from me, that night after the Christmas feast at Aber, closing up his affection from me because I had answered him as Llewelyn's man, I to whom he had come for warmth and counsel in his extremity, for so I now knew it had been. Which of those two minds, I questioned my own heart, was more like to have conceived that circumambient approach, tempting Llewelyn with a proposal to which one of them, at least, knew he would never consent? Which of them was more capable of the snare thus baited, to arraign Llewelyn out of his own mouth before Welsh opinion? Or, when he was unmoved, and showed his strong contempt for the trap, unmanning Owen and frightening him away from the attempted challenge, which of them had the force and boldness to transfer the attack to this clash in arms, a shorter and surer way to the same end? The tongue that could not have seduced Llewelyn would know how to work upon Owen.

Yet I knew nothing, there was nothing certain in this, only within me a hollow place full of doubt, wonder and pain. It could as well be true that David's restlessness and unhappiness had left him easy prey to Owen's dangerous solicitations, and caused him to wish to end his self-torment at all costs, even by this extreme road. I had no evidence to show, no certainty to share. And I held my peace. It was bitter enough to

Llewelyn to know his youngest and dearest brother had been beguiled into turning against him. Why should I twist the knife in him by suggesting that it was David who had done the beguiling?

But if I could not accuse David, neither could I defend him. I said: 'I am coming with you. I can use a sword now as well as some who earn their bread by it. I will not let you go to Lleyn without me.'

'I should like nothing better,' he said, and smiled again, for this grief was also the opportunity of his life, and there was no way he wanted to go but forward. 'We have the same stars,' he remembered, 'you and I. We shall stand or fall together.'

But the manner and tone of his voice was such, that our standing together was assured.

CHAPTER VI

We rode from Bala in the morning early, in the bright June weather, and we rode light, for it was full summer, travel pleasant and fast, and living easy. We had with us the full number of the household guard, one hundred and forty archers and lancers, and some five and twenty knights mustered from the chief nobles, those who habitually followed the court in its progresses, and those tenants who could readily be reached by messenger in so short a time. For it was Llewelyn's intent to move the battlefield, since battlefield there must be, as far westward as possible. Since they could not very long be unaware of our movements, the rapid use of these first two days was invaluable to us, to transfer the field nearer their borders, and select the ground where we might wait for them, rather than letting them, once they knew we had word of their gathering, take their stand on ground of their own selection, and there wait for us to make the onslaught.

We went with all our lances and harness blackened, for the sun would find a blade over miles of country if the enemy had look-outs posted in the right places, though we did not expect such forethought until we drew nearer to their lands. We, for our part, had runners out before us to form a chain as far as the western hill-roads Owen would use to come at us, so that news could be passed along from hand to hand, and keep us informed of all that went on in the camps of Lleyn. Thus we knew when Owen began to move, and knew we had time to spare, for we had been quicker in the launching than he. And having a night to pass, we drew aside to camp near Beddgelert, where Llewelyn and his officers had lodging with the brothers, and heard services in the church.

In the shining dark of the summer night he went out, taking me with him, and made the round of his men encamped within the enclosure, speaking a word here and there of criticism or commendation, and again I saw the good reasons that made him confident of the issue. For all was calm and orderly and eager, and all his men spoke with him as knowing their business very well, and trusting him to know his. Truly all his waiting had not been to no purpose, nor those years wasted or fretted away without profit.

Our second messenger came in before midnight, with word that the household armies of Owen and David had massed at Nevin, and would move up into the plain of Arfon with the dawn. There were some among the cottagers of those parts who had no great reason to love Owen, and were well-disposed towards Llewelyn, and our forward riders had made contact there without danger. So we got some estimate of the numbers the two had mustered, and together they amounted to somewhat more than we had with us.

'No matter,' said Llewelyn, 'we shall need no reinforcements. We are enough to deal.'

He spoke also, as we walked back together in the night, of David, though not naming him.

'He is shamefully misled,' he said. 'Surely I have been traduced to him, and he thinks I grudge him advancement. Owen will have gone to him with some lying version of what was said between us, wanting to make use of him. Faith,' he said ruefully, 'I made the arrows for him to shoot, for indeed I did roughly refuse what was asked, how can I deny it? Yet that was not the way. I would most gladly use the boy, to the full of his powers, when the time offers, and trust him with much. But not that way!'

'When he comes to himself,' I said, 'he will know and understand it.'

'There is a battle between us and that day,' said Llewelyn grimly, 'and I must and will win it, whoever goes down. Yet I pray God David may come out of it whole. I wonder did Owen go also to Rhodri? Though Rhodri is a blab-mouth, and would have let out the secret, besides being no great help in a fight. Maybe he thought it better to leave him out of the reckoning.'

'Or it may be,' I said, 'that Rhodri refused him.'

'Then all would have been out, for he would have betrayed Owen to me as surely as he would betray me to Owen were the matter opposite. Rhodri, given a choice, will keep clear of trouble. Doubtless he would like a larger portion, but not at that risk.'

'Did you ever think,' I asked him as we went in, 'that it would come to this?'

'I waited,' said Llewelyn, 'for God to dispose. And He has disposed. And God forgive me if I boast myself before victory, and bear me witness I will not vaunt myself after it.'

Then he went in and slept. At dawn there was a brief council with his captains, and after it we moved south by Glaslyn water, round the roots of the great mountains, for in that valley no long-sighted look-out could find us, and over the uplands our movements and our few colours might have been visible over miles, even with our steel blackened. Where we left the river and turned west, a third messenger met us, and confirmed that the armies of the two brothers were moving up the easy coastal plain of Arfon, towards the border pass of Bwlch Derwin, where once Trahaearn ap Caradoc defeated Griffith ap Cynan at the battle of Bron yr Erw, and drove him back into Ireland for refuge, before he fought his way home into Gwynedd to avenge the shame by overcoming and killing Trahaearn. But that was long ago, soon after the Normans came. Much was changed at their hands, but the rocks and passes of Eryri were not changed, and by that same road Owen must come.

'By this,' said Llewelyn, 'unless Owen is a bigger fool than I think him, they should know that we are in arms and on our way to meet them.'

'They do know,' said the man, 'but not by which way we come, or how close we are. No question, they'll accept battle wherever we happen to run our foreheads against theirs. And they are in good conceit of themselves, and sure of their fortune.'

Said Llewelyn, but in a manner almost devout: 'So am I.' And indeed all that day he moved and disposed as one bearing consciously, in pride and humility, the burden of his own future, which was the future of Wales.

We who were mounted made a stay near the old place of the Romans by Glan-y-Morfa, to let the foot soldiers overtake us and get an hour of rest. Then we went on towards the great thrusting head of Craig-y-Garn, towering above Dolbenmaen. Here we had the lower, rolling hills of Lleyn on our left hand, and on our right, beyond this sheer crag, the higher peaks and lofty moors stretching away for miles towards the north, bare rock above, heather and bracken and peat-moss below. Here the mountains are not so high as round Snowdon itself, yet high and bare and bleak enough, and in the uplands between the peaks the black marshes fester, and the dark-brown peat-holes reflect the sun from within their circling reeds like long-lashed eyes, the colour of my lord's. The strong, steel-bright bones of his face always called to my mind the rocks of Snowdon, and his eyes those silent lakes between.

Our road avoided the lower ground here, and kept upon the shoulder of the mountain, circling Craig-y-Garn, and crossing brook after brook that came tumbling down from the ridge on our right hand. Thus we climbed towards the watershed, and into the scrub woods that grow in the sheltered places of the pass of Bryn Derwin. And there we took our stand, with our forward look-outs keeping watch down towards Arfon, and the body of our host drawn back in two small cavalry bands flanking the woods, and arrayed where they had the advantage of the slope on either side the way, and passable ground for their advance. The lancers were drawn up in the pass, where it was somewhat sheltered on either hand by low trees and bushes. And the archers climbed in four small groups among the rocks, two to the left, two to the right, and on either side one group higher than the other. There was broken cover there to hide them, and dun as we were, lacking the show of banners and armour, we melted well into that landscape, without even motion to make us visible at any distance.

That was the first time that I had ever worn mail corselet or sword in earnest, though I had some years since taken to exercising at play with Ifor ap Heilyn, who was the best swordsman about the llys at Carnarvon, and he thought fairly well of me for one coming late to the game, and a clerk into the bargain. I was well-grown and strong and had at least a quick and accurate eye, if not the true dexterity of wrist to match it. Nor was I afraid, though I do not know why. Neither in play against my betters, who could bruise if they wished, nor now in the pass of Bryn Derwin was I afraid, but for a corner of my mind that dreaded, against my conviction of blessing, for the issue, and for Llewelyn.

He kept me at his side, with the knights on the right flank, and I was glad. For where he was, was where I willed to be, for good or ill. Nor did he ever send me away from him at any trial or danger, for he read my mind plainly, and held me so in his grace that I might have what most I wanted.

We waited until past noon, before the fore-runners sent back the signal that Owen's army was in sight below the pass. We had not taken the extreme forward position possible to us, commanding the entire downward slope against them. And I think that Llewelyn had avoided this error, and sacrificed its advantages, to prevent their seeing us too soon, assessing the odds too cautiously, and abandoning, with some plausible pretext, the offered combat. For though he had not provoked nor sought this trial, now with all his heart he desired it, and intended it to come to an issue this day, and not to continue hanging over him for more long years, before he was set free to pursue his purpose and his fate.

Then we saw them rise out of the trough beyond, in the gentle bowl of the enclosing hills, first their plumed heads, for they were prouder and more Norman than we, and had exulted in the array of their knighthood, though neither of them was then knight. The long frontal line rose slowly out of the ground, marching in close order, the horsemen first, with that dancing gait horses have on a gradual climb, first their bowing, maned heads coming into view, then the rippling shoulders, and the horsemen sitting erect and swaying to the movement. I have heard music like this motion. And behind the riders we saw the bright heads of the lances splinter in the sunlight, and the faint golden dust like a gilded mist hanging about the foot soldiers.

They saw us, and knew us, across some extended bow-shot of rock, gravel and turf. The long line checked and hung still, staring. Not in surprise, for we might well have cropped up at any point of this onward journey, though perhaps they had not looked to meet us so soon. They stared like hawks fixing before the stoop, measuring mass and distance. And even I saw that they were more in numbers than we, perhaps by thirty to forty men.

Thus these two armies stood confronting each other in the sunlit afternoon, motionless and at gaze, just out of reach one of the other. And Llewelyn said, ranging the line of horsemen ahead for the figures best known to him: 'I will not draw on my brothers without due challenge given. Hold your shots, archers, but cover me close.' And he rode forward some twenty paces before his front rank, and sitting his horse there alone, shouted before him in a great voice:

'You are looking for me, Llewelyn ap Griffith? Who comes here in arms against me, and for what purpose? Peace or war? Speak now, or strike now!'

I saw the light flicker of movement in the still ranks ahead, and cried out a warning he did not need, for he had as good a judgment of the range of the short bow as any man in North Wales. The men of the north were by nature lancers and throwers of the javelin, and our archery as yet felt more at home with the short bow than with the great long-bows the southern men used, drawn to the ear. This arrow loosed at my lord fell a dozen paces short, and struck humming in the turf. He never gave a glance at it, but he laughed, and cried powerfully towards his brother and elder, there in the centre of the foremost rank fronting him:

'I accept your answer, Owen! Come on, then! I am waiting for you!'

He wheeled his horse, turning his back fully on them, and as he moved back to us and to his chosen place, so did they move forward, breaking into the fast and fierce rush the Welsh always used, even against horse-men and fully-armed knights, trusting in agility and speed to strike a first damaging blow, and if forced to draw off in flight, able by reason of their lightness to outdistance pursuit, and find time even to harry it, seizing every chance to turn again and do more devastation. Llewelyn well knew they were hot on his heels, but he had time to order all before they struck, opening his ranks at the impact to take in such as penetrated, and make sure they never drew off again, and signalling the alert to his archers, in cover up the slopes on either side.

Our lancers formed close, butts braced into the ground, the first rank kneeling, the second standing. Owen's horse-men, too ill-disciplined to temper their speed to the footmen's pace – though some clung to their stirrups and were carried with them – struck that wall of lances, and did no more than make its centre shake for a moment. Then the rushing spearmen struck after them, and foot by foot our centre gave slowly back to draw the whole mêlée inward, and it became a hand-to-hand struggle there, edging always a little back towards the east.

We with the two small companies of horsemen remained drawn aside on either hand, a little up the sloping ground, and the rush of the attack was so wild and single that it crashed full into the centre between us like a hammer-blow, leaving us stranded on the flanks. Above us the archers shot a first volley, and a second, into the mass, wounding several horses, and churning the whole into a threshing confusion. Then Llewelyn gave the sign, and we charged down from either side into the shouting, bellowing tangle of horses and men, crushing it between our two matched thrusts.

The battle at Bryn Derwin lasted but one hour in all, from the first clash to the breaking and flight of the remainder of Owen's army. As for me, all I saw of it after the first attack was a turmoil of hand-to-hand fight-ing, almost too close for damage, where I was flung hither and thither by the swaying of the battle, and glimpsed now one enemy fronting me, now another, without, I think, doing harm to any beyond a scratch or two. But I kept close at Llewelyn's quarter, covering his flank as best I might. I know he singled out Owen's plumed helmet as he led our downhill charge, and drove straight at it. His lance struck his brother's raised shield full, almost sweeping Owen out of his saddle, if the shaft had not shivered and left him still force enough to regain his seat. Then they had swords out at each other, but Owen's horse, slashed by a chance blow, and shrieking, reared and wheeled, plunging away from the fight. And other riders came between, loyal to their prince, to fend us off.

This mêlée was brief. The foot soldiers knew defeat first, and drew off as they could, and scattered. Then a few of the horsemen also fled, some were already unhorsed and wounded, some yielded. Only a handful, at the very moment of our downhill charge, had wheeled to meet the attack on the other flank, driving vehemently up the slope to clash with Goronwy's detachment. And these continued fighting tooth and nail when all else was over, even when they knew their fellows had broken and run, and there was nothing to be gained.

So intent was I on this tight whirlpool of motion on the slope opposite that I never saw the moment when Owen Goch was pulled from his horse, half-dazed, and pinned down in the turf under the weight of three or four of our spearmen. Two more led aside and quieted the maddened, trembling horse. But we watched the small, obstinate battle on the hillside, reduced now to two enemy horsemen, of whom one was gradually hedged off from his fellow and surrounded. The other spurred his beast obdurately higher up the slope, clear of immediate reach, and instead of attempting flight, whirled again to drive at us who moved below him. He circled and wove as he came, whirling his sword about him on all sides to fend off attack. Young and tall he was, and slender, but steely, and he drove his horse with hand and spur and knee straight at Llewelyn. And his visor was raised, and I saw that it was David.

His face I could see from eyebrows to mouth, brow and jaw being cased by his helmet. So I saw the smear of blood along one cheek, and the gleam of sweat outlining his bright, lean bones, and the black of his lashes like a soiled frame for two eyes so fixed and pale in their blueness that they looked tranced or mad. Straight at Llewelyn he drove, and leaned in the saddle, and swung a round, mangling stroke at him with his sword.

Llewelyn never reined aside or lifted his own weapon, but stooped under the blow, took David about the body in his left arm as the horse hurtled by, hoisted the boy violently out of saddle and stirrups, with a jerk that spilled one long-toed riding shoe, and flung him down, not gently, into the turf, where he lay sprawled and winded, the sword wrenched out of his hand and lighting far out of reach. There he lay, panting for breath, his chest heaving under the fine chain-mail and the soiled white surcoat, his wide-open eyes reflecting the blanched summer sky.

'Do off his helm,' said Llewelyn, gazing down at him with a hard face and veiled eyes. And when it was done, and the black hair matted with sweat spilled into the grass, he lighted down from his horse and took the boy by the chin, and turned his face roughly up to the light, searching right cheek and left for the gash that bled, and sustaining without acknowledgement the blue, blank stare that clung all the time with wonder and rage upon his own face.

'Are you hurt?' he said, plucking his hand away and standing back a pace or two.

Still heaving at breath, David said: 'No!' He said nothing more, but turned his face haughtily away from being so watched and inspected. And in a moment more he braced his fists into the turf and raised himself, and turning a little lamely on to his knees, thrust himself unsteadily to his feet, and stood with reared head and empty hands before his brother and conqueror. He stood very close. And I, who also had drawn close into my place at my lord's left hand, saw his lips move, and heard the thread of breath through them, as I swear none other there did, except Llewelyn.

'Kill me!' entreated David. 'You were wise!'

His eyes rolled up into their lids, and his knees gave under him. Down he went in a sprawl of long limbs into the grass from which he had prised himself, and lay still, angular and sad, like a fallen and broken bird.

'Take him up,' said Llewelyn to the captain of his guard, 'and have his hurts seen to. Look well to him! Bring him as soon as you may to join us at Beddgelert. But gently! I look to you to deliver him whole and well.'

We took up our wounded, none of them in desperate case, and our dead, of whom there were, God be thanked, but few, and also made disposition for the care of those wounded and killed upon the other part, for from this moment Llewelyn was sole and unquestioned prince of Gwynedd, as he had always meant to be, and ruled alone, and those who had been loyal to his brothers as their lords had but done their true part, and deserved no blame, but rather commendation. They were now his men, and he wanted no waste and no vengeance, but rather that their truth to him should be as it had been to Owen and David. Why harass or maim what in the future you will need to lean on? So all those who were willing to abide the verdict of the day and give their troth to Griffith's son were despatched freely back to their trefs, and sent about their daily business without hindrance or penalty. And doubtless that word went round also to any who had fled and remained in hiding, so that they came back to their homes and took up daily living as before. There was no killing after Bryn Derwin. But at Beddgelert, where the good brothers of the settlement, saints after the old pattern as at Aberdaron, cared for the hurts of the living and said devout offices for the dead, there was a thanksgiving, subdued and solemn. Llewelyn had said truly, there was no vaunting after victory. The matter was too great for that.

I think he spent all that night in the church. For once I was dismissed. There was no man with my lord that night of the twenty-fourth of June. But doubtless God was with him, who had moved a hand and set him up in the estate he had so greatly desired, and not all for his own glory, but for that dream that went with him night and day, of a Wales single and splendid, free upon its own soil, equal with its neighbours, unthreatened and unafraid.

He had always about him this piercing, childlike humility, that walked hand in hand with his vast ambition. For the more he succeeded in exalting the dream, in whose pursuit he was strong, ruthless and resolute, and seemed a demon of pride, the more he marvelled and was grateful within him that he, all fallible and mere man as he was, should be made the instrument of a wonder. And I do know, who was his teacher many years in English and Latin, how eagerly and earnestly he studied to improve, how poorly he thought of his own powers, and how he chafed at his progress, but humbly, expecting no better. And I believe I tell truth, saying that when he came out to me from the church of Beddgelert on the morning after Bryn Derwin his eyes were innocent of sleep, but not of weeping.

After the practical matters had been taken care of, the weapons refurbished, the horses tended, the men rested, then we came to the question of the defeated.

They brought in Owen first and alone before my lord, according to the wish of both of them, for Owen had much to say in his own cause, and Llewelyn was ready to listen. Though I think his mind was already made

101

up, for though some among his own council afterwards blamed him somewhat for his hard usage of Owen upon one offence, they did not know what cause he already had to distrust his elder, and hold him guilty not once, but twice, of the intent of fratricide. Nor did he ever tell that story in his own justification, and since he willed it, neither did I. But when those two spoke together, they understood each other.

Owen came in between his guards, limping and defiant. He had brought away from Bryn Derwin nothing worse than bruises, but his harness was dashed, and his surcoat soiled and torn. He was not bound, but sword and dagger had been taken from him, and even in desperation he could do no harm.

'We were two, somewhat ill-matched I grant you, who had worked in a yoke together many years,' said Llewelyn, looking him steadily in the face, 'and if you have chafed at it often, that I can understand, for so have I. But I did not take up arms, and come against you as against an enemy. Why have you done so to me?'

Owen looked him over from head to foot with a smouldering stare from under his fell of red hair. 'I came to you in good faith,' he said, 'asking for justice for our brothers, and you would not hear me, or join in what I proposed. Truly I bore with you for years, but with our peace undisturbed for so long, and unthreatened now, I thought it a great wrong to hold Gwynedd together thus by force, on the plea of King Henry's enmity. I urged what I thought right, and you refused me. I put it to the issue of arms, wanting another way.'

'There was another way,' Llewelyn said. 'I myself told you that you were heartily welcome to take the matter to our council, and ask them for a judgment. You preferred the judgment of the sword. Have you any complaint of the answer the sword gave you?'

Complaint, perhaps, he had, but his sheer unsuccess he could hardly urge against Llewelyn, and he did not think to blurt out what I had half expected, the direct accusation against David. For such a man as Owen Goch can never perceive, much less admit to others, that his aims and actions have been directed, persuasively and derisively, by another person, and that person his junior, and still looked upon almost as a child. So he was voluble about the unselfishness of his intentions, and his generous indignation against Llewelyn's unreasonable obduracy, but never said: 'It was not my idea, the boy worked on me!'

In the end he began to draw in his horns, and if not to plead, at least to offer a measure of submission.

'I have done nothing of which I am ashamed. Yet any man, the truest of men, may be in error. I don't ask to be readmitted to the old equality. If I was wrong to resort to arms, let me pay for that fault, but in reason. My life may still be of service to you as it is dear to me . . .'

'Your life,' said Llewelyn coldly, 'is as safe with me as mine has been with you. Safer!'

'My liberty, then! You have your victory, keep all the fruits of it. I accept the second place under you. I pledge you my word.'

'I cannot take your word. Nor has any man in Gwynedd a second place from now on, above his fellows. I do not believe you could ever accept that truth, and I do not intend you should ever again be able to disrupt this land. There is nothing I can do with you but hold you prisoner perpetually, out of harm's way and out of mine. I commit you to the charge of my castellan at Dolbadarn, and I set no term to your stay there. It may depend,' he said sombrely, 'on others besides you and me. Take him away!' he ordered, and Owen went out from him stunned and silent, for he had tasted imprisonment already, passing several years of his young life behind bars, and even I, who knew him dangerous and disordered, too erratic to be trusted, felt pity for him.

This castle of Dolbadarn was among the most inaccessible and impregnable in the land, being set on a great rock between two lakes among the mountains of Snowdon, and hard indeed it would be to conceive and execute an escape from it.

'Let David come in,' said Llewelyn then.

They brought him in between them, not a hand being actually laid on him. I do not know how it was that he was always able to emerge from any rough and tumble, any privation, even from being hunted shelterless through the mire, looking a thought more polished and pure than any that came against him. But so it was, his life long. He bore the mark of one shallow wound down the left side of his neck, and was bruised about one cheek, and he moved with a little more care than usual to maintain his presence and grace, for he was stiff with the fall Llewelyn had given him. But what I noted in him at once was that his eyes were quick, live and easy, that had stared up at his brother in the field, in the moment of realisation of what he had done, blanched and stricken. And the voice that had barely found breath enough to husk out its anguished warning then came meekly and mellowly now, again ready to beguile, as he said:

'I am here, and I know my fault. Dispose of me as I deserve.'

It fell upon my ears like a strange echo, as though his intelligence had taken that smothered cry of dismay and prophecy, and translated it into this deceptive submission, asking again for his deserts, but with intent to escape, not to embrace them. Then I was sure of him in my own heart, though proof there was none.

'But I entreat you,' he said, with eyes downcast and voice subdued, 'to show mercy on my brother, and hold him less guilty than I. It was on my behalf he made this stir. I own I did complain that I was starved of my due. I take the blame upon me.'

All this he said with slow, deliberate humility, as though it cost him pain he knew well-earned, and yet so simply and innocently that it gave me no surprise to see that Llewelyn accepted all as the chivalrous gesture of misled youth. It is an art to tell truth in such a way that it cannot be seriously believed.

'You did not complain to me,' said Llewelyn hardly. 'Why not? Do not pretend you went in such awe of me that you dared not make the assay.'

'No,' admitted David, and raised his head and opened wide those clear eyes of his upon his brother. 'You never gave me cause to fear you. Only cause to be ashamed, in your presence, to admit to such a grievance. But to him I could, without shame.'

He said no more. I think he was feeling his way, for he could not know what Owen had said of him. But if that was his difficulty, Llewelyn said then what eased him of his load:

'But why did you listen to him, when he urged war against me?'

'Out of ambition and greed,' said David readily, sure now of his ground. And the hot blood rose in his cheeks, perhaps in the surge of relief that filled him, but it answered well for penitence and shame. 'I have no defence,' he said, and stood in submission. I do not know if he had hoped to be forgiven so lightly as to regain his liberty on the spot, but Llewelyn was not so deluded as that, nor could he afford the gesture.

'Ambition and greed are poor recommendations for a brother,' he said. 'Can you promise you are cured of them by this fall, or must we expect another attempt?'

'To what purpose,' said David steadily, 'if I did promise, promises being so cheap after such an act? At some future time, when I have purged my offence, I trust to *show* you whether I am cured.'

'You will have time enough and leisure enough to consider it well,' said Llewelyn grimly, and forthwith committed him, also, to imprisonment in the castle of Dolbadarn, among the crags of Eryri. And David, as decorously as he had entered, went out between the guards without complaint. I would have wagered he had come to a satisfactory judgment then that it would not be for long. The droop of his head was eloquent of resignation, and that manner of pride that saints have in embracing their trials as just, and not beyond their bearing.

'Let him cool his heels for a year or so,' said Llewelyn when he was gone. 'It will do him no harm. But for him there may well be a use in the future. Did you see how he came at me yesterday? How he stood off half a dozen good men, surrounded as he was? One born fighting-man, at least, our father bred.'

'You have done right,' said Goronwy ap Ednyfed gravely. 'His offence was too gross to be overlooked. And he is not a child, he knows what he does. But yes, I own he is gallant enough. He may do you good service yet, if you can keep him from Owen Goch.'

'We'll take care of that,' said Llewelyn.

I was busy with my lord about all the letters he found needful after this great change, the first and most difficult of them being to the Lady Senena, who was then at Aber, when one of the guards came to say that David, before he was taken away to Dolbadarn, entreated that he might see me for a few moments. Llewelyn hesitated, but then said yes, go to him, for he respected the tie that was between us two on account of my mother Elen, whom David had truly loved. So I went to the cell where he was guarded, and they shut me in with him.

'Don't be afraid,' he said, grinning at the sight of my wary face as I sat down with him, 'I will not ask you to intercede with Llewelyn for me. That's not my purpose. I wanted only to see you, once before I go, since it may be a long while before I have the chance again. And perhaps to discover if you would come – and if he would let you come. And both I know now. I am glad you have not shaken me off as utterly damned.'

'There is only one who can damn you,' I said, 'and that's yourself.'

'And I came near it, did I not?' He caught my doubting eye, and the defiant smile left his face, and he was unwontedly grave. 'You think I am still playing the devil now, I saw it in your face. A speaking face you have, Samson – or I know how to read it. As you read mine, all too clearly. But what would you have? I am nineteen years old, I want my freedom, I want to escape punishment if I can – who but a liar says anything else? Threaten me with pain and punishment, and I will do all I may to avert it. To a point, at least,' he said, frowning over his own words as though finding his way through a labyrinth. 'There may be a place and a time when I cannot escape the doom I've brought down on myself, and when all there is left to do is stand erect and let it fall on me without a cry. But not when it's Llewelyn who threatens. Tell him, if you love him – you do love him, do you not? – tell him not to be too easily appeased, not to melt towards me too soon, not to forgive too recklessly, if he wants to hold me. But tell him – no, do not tell him, only bear with me if I tell *you*! – that he *could* hold me, better than any other, if he can keep the respect I bear him, as well as the love. But if he lose the one, the other is not enough.'

'I am not empowered,' I said, for I still distrusted this seemingly artless bleeding of words, 'to offer you any hope of a short sentence or an early release. Nor am I willing to do what you take such good care not to ask, and plead for you.'

At that he laughed, not quite steadily, and threw his arm about my shoulders and leaned his head against me. 'Fair, sweet Samson, how did you come by so much knowledge of me? And how is it that I still escape you when you have almost grasped me? No, I want my freedom, but not at that price. And with you I play no tricks. Will you believe that? Never, never! Because it would be useless, for Elen gave you her sight. And because I want no such dealings between you and me.'

'In the name of God, boy,' I said, 'I understand you not at all, for nothing can explain to me why you did this thing to both your brothers. Oh, something of what ailed you I do know. You were restless and wretched when you came back from court, all we had here became small and rustic and mean to you, your world too narrow for your energy. All this I know, and it explains nothing. You are far too sound in wit to think doubling your lands would satisfy you, or provide you the kind of field you wanted for your soul to work in. Was it pure mischief only, the will to destroy others because you could not have what you desired? And to destroy which of them? You have made Llewelyn now, and undone Owen, but not even you could have foreseen that end. What was it you intended?'

'Do I know?' said David, ruefully sighing into my shoulder. 'Owen would have come to it in the end, even without me. I bore no more ill-will to him than I did to the sword I drew on Llewelyn. And cared for him as little, I suppose. Do I know what drove me? Yes, I do know! A child's reason! Llewelyn had taken from me something I thought of as mine, and like a child deprived I struck at him.' He shifted his head, and his eyes blazed into my face, and I knew what it was that had been stolen from him. 'Does the child care then whether he has a dagger in his hand?'

I heard again in my mind his voice saying softly: 'I see you are his man!' I remembered his particular affection for me from a child, when I was his slave and familiar. And I knew for how much I, too, had to answer in this matter. He had come to me in his torment of frustration, and I had wanted nothing but to get on with the work I did for his brother. We are all victims one of another. Yet I took comfort in this, that the present trouble had passed with no great damage, rather a hopeful issue, and I was warned now, and could be on guard for both of them. For both I loved. And this being an occasion for speech and not for silence, I told him that his reason, reason enough and forgiven at this moment, was no reason hereafter, for he was my breast-brother, the only one I had, and that was a life-long tie, and dearly welcome to me. That I loved him, and should not cease from loving him. I did not say: 'no matter what folly or what wise wickedness you commit in the future', for it seemed better to assume that this spleen was now ended.

He embraced me, between laughing and weeping, and pressed his smooth forehead against my breast, shaking with this sorrowful mirth. 'Oh, Samson.' he said, quivering, 'always you do me good! Always you leave something unsaid. Must I not promise to amend?'

I told him that love had no right to demand amends.

'You should have been left at Aberdaron,' he said, 'to work out your doom. You would have made a most formidable priest. A little more, and you would have me on my knees, promising an amended life – if I were subject to penitence!'

He had recovered that secret, baffling assurance that set me, like other men, at a distance, and I thought that an ill ending, my time with him being almost spent. Therefore I said what otherwise I would have kept to myself.

'You are as subject to penitence,' I said, 'as I, or any other creature. Why else did you cry out to my lord, whom you had so wronged: Kill me! You were wise!?'

He stiffened in my arms, and his forehead froze against my heart. The words he knew all too well, he did not know until then that I had heard them, for indeed they were but a breath, a thread in the wind. He shrank into himself, drawing by secret, slow degrees away from me, and closing as he went those channels of affection and comfort he had suffered to open between us. When he raised his head from me and sat back, his face was in the chill of a deliberate calm, and he smiled at me with veiled eyes.

'A stunning fall indeed I must have had! Did I verily say so? I thank God my brother did not take me at my word, I have a fancy to go on living many years yet.'

I had overstayed my time already, and the guard was at the door. He was withdrawn from me as never before, and it was I who had driven him.

'I am glad,' he said as they opened the door upon us, 'that my brother has you to read for him where he is unlettered. He will need you!'

The prisoners were gone from us, haled away under escort into the wilds of Snowdon, and we in our turn moved away to our various duties, the chosen castellans into the lands Owen and David had left masterless, my lord and his court back to Bala first, and then, following the letter I had taken down at Llewelyn's dictation, to Aber on the northern coast.

'She will have had time,' said Llewelyn, with somewhat sour good-humour, 'to sharpen her claws.'

The Lady Senena gave us, as he had foreseen, a dour welcome. She had become stout, and was less active than of old, her hair was grey, and at times she spoke of retiring to a hermit's cell, as many other royal women had done in their old age, but I think her energy, however confined now into the activity of the mind, was too great ever to allow of such a withdrawal. Could she have ruled a large household of nuns, that might have provided her what she needed, but the anchorite's life was not for her. She kissed Llewelyn in greeting, but it was as like a blow as a kiss, and when he rose from his knee and relinquished the hand he had saluted with equally perfunctory devotion, she looked him up and down with those deep eyes, under black, locked brows, in so formidable a fashion that he smiled suddenly, remembering another such occasion, when she had thought herself in command of him, as perhaps she thought now.

'What is this you have been doing with my sons?' she said pointblank.

'Which sons, madam?' he said, in a voice patient and equable, for there was neither profit nor pleasure in quarrelling with her, but even less in submitting to her. 'Your second son I have been making into the prince of Gwynedd. That should please you, it was a title you coveted for the father of your sons.'

'And at what a cost!' she said. 'Two of your brothers shamefully used, arraigned like felons and cast into prison. Is that brotherly?'

'Was it brotherly in them to muster an army secretly and come against me in war, without challenge or justification?' he said mildly.

'I want to hear nothing,' she said fiercely. 'You'll tell but one side of the story.'

'You mistake, madam. I will tell neither. I am under no obligation to refer what I see fit to do to you, or to any but my council. Those orders I please to give will be carried out, by you as by others. In courtesy I wrote to you all that you needed to know. If that is not enough for you, enquire of others. Me you will not question.'

All this he said very placidly, but with such authority that she was moved to withdraw into a lengthy silence, while she examined him afresh, and made a more detached assessment of what she saw. Her hands, which were grown knotted and thickened at the joints with the stiffness of middle-age, folded together in her lap, and lay clasped and still.

After a while she said, as if beginning again, and in a voice very little more conciliatory, but still with a new note in it: 'You cannot leave them in Dolbadarn, it is too remote and bleak.'

'Remoteness is its virtue,' he admitted readily. 'That, and the staunchness of the castellan. But they shall be well looked after, I promise you. We cannot, perhaps, provide all the luxuries Owen enjoyed in King Henry's prison, but we'll see to it he's warm and fed.'

'I should prefer,' she said, 'to see as much for myself. I shall visit them in Dolbadarn at once.'

At that he smiled, though grimly. 'No, mother, you will not. Not for six months or more will you be let into Dolbadarn. And even then you will not be left alone with either one of them. I have too sound a respect for your stout heart and sharp wits to allow you even the narrowest chance of letting loose my brothers and enemies on me again so soon. I have work to do before I take the slightest risk of another Bryn Derwin.'

She fumed at this, and said that it was monstrous a brother should not only make captive his brothers, but rob their mother of the very sight of them in their most need and hers. And yet I had the thought in me all the while she scolded him that there was in her voice a note of strange content, almost of pleasure. And he, it may be, felt it in his heart also, if he did not discern it with his ear, for he laughed aloud suddenly, and stooping, caught up her hand again, and kissed her heartily on the cheek, she still glowering but making no demur.

'Oh, mother,' he said, 'if you but knew it, you and I are as like as two peas, and if you rail at me you are but storming at a mirror. Where do you think I got the stubbornness that makes you so angry? Or the force that I need to make Gwynedd great again? Now, make peace with me, for you cannot win if you make war!'

And though for a long time after this she did her best to get concessions from him by trickery, and nagging, and even by seeking to shame him with her portrayal of a poor woman robbed of her children – though tears she could not command, or even feign with any conviction – she never could move him, for always he smiled and refused her, or, if he was preoccupied, failed to notice her, which was worse. But for all that, it seemed to me she liked him better, now that he was her master and she without privilege or influence, than ever she had liked him before, and in their cross-grained way they achieved a cautious, respectful companionship, neither ever admitting it.

For at the end of the six-month delay on which he had insisted, it was he who offered her an escort to take her to Dolbadarn, before she had asked it. And it was she who volunteered him, very gruffly, her troth that, however much she desired and hoped for their release, she would not convey into the castle with her anything that could help the prisoners to escape, or in any way connive at such an attempt. And he took her word without hesitation, and bade her go in freely and alone to her sons, with whatever gifts she pleased, for her bond was enough for him.

A busy year we had of it, we who served Llewelyn, that year of his accession to power. From the autumn he began to send us out with overtures of friendship to all the independent princes and chiefs of middle and southern Wales, to exchange news and views, to collect what reports we could of feeling everywhere, not only towards Gwynedd, but towards England, too. He had even a man in Chester, and very close to the justiciar's household, who sent word of all that went on in the Middle Country and the marches, where discontent and distrust were almost as hot and widespread on the English side of the border as on the Welsh. For the men of the four cantrefs were close to revolt because of the iniquitous exactions of the royal officer, that same Geoffrey Langley once of the forest courts, and his arrogant overriding of Welsh law and customs, while even the marcher lords watched this essay in turning marcher country into tamed English shires, bound by county administrations, with deep suspicion, aware of a threat to their own palatine powers.

'What did I say?' said Llewelyn, watching this seething unrest with satisfaction and hope. 'The man recruits for me better than I could do it myself.'

But when at length the angry Welsh tenants of the Middle Country went so far as to send a delegation to him, inviting his sympathy and advice, and plainly hoping for his leadership, he counselled patience and stillness a while longer, for the time was not yet ripe. Moreover, the autumn was then drawing to a close, and winter coming on, and though he had no objection to undertaking winter campaigning if the need arose, yet he had not stores enough in barn and hold to feed an army in the field this year.

'You have borne it some years now,' he said, 'it is worth waiting a little while longer to take the tide on the flood. What I counsel for this time is that you wait for Prince Edward's first visit to Chester, for as I hear, he's back in England some ten days ago, and has brought home his new young wife to Windsor. Let him at least have time to show whether he has wit enough to listen to Welshmen on Welsh affairs, and respect their manner of life, and put some curb on his officers, who have no such respect. And in the meantime, with another breeding season to come, and another harvest to be sown and reaped, make sure of every grain and every bean you can, and look well to your beasts. And so will I. Then, if he will do nothing to lighten your load, you are in better case to lighten it for yourselves.'

And though they went away disappointed, and were not, perhaps, all provident enough to pay heed to what he said, yet some surely remembered, and thought no harm to be as ready as a man may be, whether for a good or an evil outcome.

This news of Prince Edward's return we had from our man in Chester, who was a smith, and a skilled horse-doctor, often employed by the justiciar himself and the officers of the garrison. Through this man all the news of the court came to us. So we heard that King Alfonso of Castille, King Henry's new ally, had an ambassador at court discussing the next moves to be taken in their treaty of friendship. He was still anxious to secure King Henry's promise to join him in his crusade against the Moors, but the feeling among many of the court officials was that this expedition would never take place, or at least not with Henry's aid, for he was hoping to have his crusading vow further commuted to the pursuance of his Sicilian adventure. Though there was a new pope now, this Alexander would certainly hold him to his bond over Sicily, but if that kingdom could truly be achieved it would count to Henry as a crusade, while absolving him from the expense and inconvenience of sailing for the Holy Land, or even crossing the middle sea to Africa. And the prospect of making good his vow at a profit, instead of a loss, must appeal greatly to Henry, who was always optimistic, and always, in intent, thrifty, though his economies usually cost him dearer than if he had spent freely.

'But he has no hope in the world,' Llewelyn said roundly, 'of ever enjoying the kingdom of Sicily. And he's committed to paying off the papal debts incurred in the war already, under pain of excommunication. It bids fair to cost him more than sending troops to Jerusalem. And Pope Innocent with his own armies had little enough success against the Hohenstaufen, why should King Henry expect to do better?'

'So a great number of the king's magnates are thinking, too,' said Goronwy drily, pondering the smith's despatches. 'It seems there's a deal of unrest over the whole project, it's bringing King Henry's very government into question. His brother had the good sense to decline the honour of pulling the pope's cakes out of the fire for him, only to see Henry fall into the trap in his place, and flounder in deeper and deeper now he begins to show signs of wanting to get out. This whole matter may yet be serviceable to us.'

'Yet it's been the cause of a friendly advance towards King Louis,' Llewelyn said dubiously, 'and that's no benefit to me.'

'That's barely begun yet. It will take years to bring them to terms, if that's what they do intend. And if both keep their eyes fixed upon Naples and Sicily,' Goronwy said reasonably, 'so much the better for us here in the west.'

So we took comfort, but cautiously, in these distant doings of which we began to understand something, at least, during that winter. The old Emperor Frederick, Barbarossa's grandson, dead some years, had left a young son, Conrad, to inherit his crown and his feud with the papacy. Now Conrad also was dead of a fever, some months before Edward's marriage in Burgos, so that throughout that year the project of setting up young Edmund in his place must have seemed reasonably hopeful. But there was another son, of a kind those nations call bastard, one Manfred, who had been named as heir to his brother in the event of the direct line being extinguished, and who had been regent for Conrad in Sicily, and this Manfred was said to be very strongly in possession of the disputed kingdom, and would certainly not be easily displaced.

Very strange these names seemed to me, and much I wondered about those far-off cities and plains where the armies of emperor and pope contended and tore each other, and the still more distant land where that same Frederick, the wonder of the world, had treated with the paynims for the deliverance of the holy places of Christendom. It seemed more than a world away from the rocky pastures of Eryri, and yet the battles and complots of those great men sent echoes even into our mountains, and ripples into the mouths of our rivers.

'I have a crusade of my own,' said Llewelyn, turning his back upon such dreams, 'nearer home.'

And with all his might he pursued it. While the days were favourable he was busy about the better equipping of his fighting men, and in particular the raising of companies of well-mounted and well-armed horsemen, which had never been the custom in Wales, though his grandsire had also made good use of knights in his day. Llewelyn would have as many as he could mount, and procured good horses, able to carry heavily-armed men, wherever he could happen upon them. He encouraged the smiths, also, to make more substantial armour, both mail and some plate, than we were accustomed to, and took great interest in the training of archers and fletchers. And beyond these matters, he studied the making of siege engines, and had workmen build him arblasts, mangons and trebuchets all things foreign to our usual manner of warfare, for the siege was something we rarely attempted in force, preferring to pass by and isolate castles rather than storm them. For the English by custom feared being shut out of walls, and we, when pressed, rather feared to be shut within them.

'My grandsire knew the use of these devices,' he said, 'and profited by them, too. God knows my uncle had little enough chance to use them, he was always the besieged. And in the end we may hardly need them. Effective they may be, but slow to move around the country they surely are. You could lose a battle elsewhere while you shifted these into position about a castle. But let's at least have them. Who knows, there may be a need some day, and we have timber enough.'

And one more thing he would have, and that was a fleet. 'Not again,' he said, 'shall they sail round from the Cinque Ports or put over from Ireland, and burn our corn in Anglesey while we starve.' And he collected skilled men, shipwrights and others, and at his court of Cemais and at Caergybi, in the sheltered waters between Anglesey and the island, he founded boat-yards, and had them lay keels and begin to build him small ships, such as could be put in commission quickly, some masted, for rapid sailing, and a few built for rowers, and sturdy enough to have trebuchets mounted in the middle aisle between the banks of oars. There were coastal fishermen enough to man such craft, men wise in winds and tides. He took delight in this work, and went often to see the progress made.

And in the dark winter nights, when we were shut indoors perforce, we read together in Latin and in English, debated law, and heard music, the great poetry of the bards in hall, and my little crwth in the high chamber when he was weary, for I had learned to play for his pleasure and my own.

So passed the first year of his unchallenged rule in Gwynedd, and the spring and the summer came on again, and we were a long stride nearer to readiness.

During that following spring there came a distant kinsman into Gwynedd as a dispossessed fugitive, who was to prove thereafter a very formidable ally, though at times a wayward and unreliable one. This was that Meredith ap Rhys Gryg who was younger brother to the late lord of Dynevor, Rhys Mechyll, and uncle to Rhys Fychan, who had married the Lady Gladys. There had always been rivalry between uncle and nephew, and as a youth Rhys Fychan had been kept out of his lands for some time by his uncle, who possessed broad lands and many castles in the same region of Wales. And by way of vengeance, now that he was established firmly in the favour of the English, and no longer afraid of his kinsman, Rhys Fychan had enlisted the help of his marcher neighbours and the royal forces in South Wales to oust his uncle from all his lands and drive him into exile. It was a mark of my lord's growing standing and influence among the Welsh chiefs that Meredith should flee into

Gwynedd and make straight for Llewelyn's court, and there both ask for asylum and offer his services in war. And Llewelyn took him in gladly and graciously, not all for policy, for there was much that was likeable about Meredith, and of his courage, daring and ability in battle there was no doubt.

He was a thickset, sturdy, bearded man in his late fifties, loud-voiced and genial, good company at table and a notable singer. As a swordsman he was famous, and for the sake of his lost lands he was a good hater of the English, and an eager conspirator in council when the issue of England came into consideration. I think Llewelyn was in no need of a spur, for all his patience, which some took for timidity, yet Meredith surely confirmed him in all he had in mind to do, and weighed down the balance in favour of action when it might otherwise have hung level. So his coming was an omen, his loud voice among us like a trumpet sounding to battle.

He had, however, one implacable enemy among us, and that was the Lady Senena, who was a whole-hearted champion of her daughter and her daughter's husband, and therefore found only satisfaction in Meredith's expulsion, and was greatly affronted that her son should welcome him into Gwynedd as an ally. For these family relationships with their hates and loves were the trammel and bane of Wales as they were of the marches, and indeed, from all I could ever learn, of England and France and those troubled realms beyond the sea no less. And the more the great laboured to make dynastic marriages, the more they tied their own hands, and put into other hands knives for their own backs. Their history and ours was ever a chronicle of such expulsions and revenges, the tide of fortune flowing now this way, now that, and never safe or still. But the ladies and the waiting-women about the llys at Aber had reason to thank Meredith for some relief, for while he was with us the Lady Senena withdrew in dudgeon to Carnarvon, and her strict and increasingly cantankerous supervision of the household was withdrawn with her.

Doubtless Meredith thought her a harridan, as she thought him a villain, neither being of a temper to acknowledge that there may be some substance even in an opponent's viewpoint, and some justice in his complaint. So it was as well that they should be separated. Surely that lady was destined always to be torn in pieces between those people she loved most, for now she saw her son, the one who had least obeyed or supported her, but also the one who had best fulfilled in his own person the ambitious dreams she had cherished for her line, preparing undoubted rebellion against the English, under whose protection her dear daughter, with her husband and children, enjoyed the peaceful possession of their estates. It may be that she confessed, in her own heart though never to any other, her sad responsibility for these divisions, for if she had stayed in Gwynedd and maintained, in the teeth of all deprivations, the loyalty of her family to Wales, they might now have been all in unity upon one side, if not in total harmony. And it may also be that she had learned somewhat from all these trials, for whatever her own hope in the matter, she kept silence, and gave no warning to any party of what the others intended, but retired into her own helplessness, determined not to do further harm where she doubted her ability to do any good.

So the year went on, with due attention to lambing, and the cultivation of the fields, and the hope of harvest, and the building of boats and fashioning of armour. And in the high summer Prince Edward as earl of Chester paid his first ceremonial visit to that city and shire, and sent out formal proclamations announcing his coming, and appointing times and places where he would receive the homages due to him in the four cantrefs of the Middle Country. He came to Chester on the seventeenth day of July, and towards the end of that month he was conducted by the justiciar and his officers on a tour of his Welsh possessions, making a stay of two or three days at his castle of Diserth, and again at Degannwy, where the chieftains and tenants of the region once Welsh would attend to offer him their fealty.

'Now,' said Llewelyn, reading the smith's despatches with the first spark of excitement in eye and voice, 'we shall see of what he is made.' And when some of the men of Rhos and Rhufoniog sent secretly to ask him whether they should attend or no, he advised without hesitation that they should. 'For,' said he, 'it's well always to see for yourselves whether he means justly by you or not, and whether he has wit and understanding to listen to you, as well as ears to hear you.'

So they went, and we had more than one report thereafter, hopeful and doubtful both. For this was, they said, a very comely and upstanding young man, very tall for his years, which were just seventeen, and in audience gracious and welcoming to all, so that they had been encouraged to open to him their grievances, though with care, and ask hopefully for a more considerate tenderness towards Welsh custom, which was daily flouted. All which he had heard with debonair patience, though whether any of it had sunk in, or whether it was to him the mere tedious business of making a royal appearance, the more cautious among them were not prepared to say. As we heard, there was a great train of young nobles in attendance on him, very gay and frivolous, more interested in the pretty tourneys the prince held in Chester than in the administration of the four cantrefs or the welfare of their inhabitants. There was much money spent on the lavish entertainment and courtly show of those round tables and jousts in Chester, by all accounts, and the prince himself was a very fine lance already, and could hold his own with any who came.

'Before the winter,' Llewelyn prophesied, following this pageantry from a distance with a calculating eye, 'he may well be wishing he had again every mark spent and every lance broken. He will need them.'

The royal party left Chester and rode south on the third day of August. Whether the prince had made any easy promises, or whether the hopeful among his tenants had deceived themselves into believing that he had, I cannot be sure. But for some weeks after his departure there was an expectant quiet, while they waited for the meeting between benevolent lord and dutiful vassals to bear the good fruit it should. Only in September did they begin to give up hope of betterment, for Edward was gone, seemingly, without a glance behind, or a thought to spare for remembering them, and the exactions of the chief bailiff continued as before, and the acts of tyranny in the enforcing of English law, county law, upon

Welsh commotes, without regard for local feeling or respect to tradition.

'Let be,' said Llewelyn, when the young men of the bodyguard grew impatient, and looked to him expectantly, 'a month or two yet, till the corn's all in, and safe stored. If an army's to starve this coming winter, it shall not be mine.'

By the same token he took particular care to see to the late autumn salting of the slaughtered beasts that had not fodder for the winter, for he had been buying in salt as much as he could get. And this last was still in the doing when the unrest in the Middle Country broke out into scattered acts of rebellion, and two of the high men of Rhos crossed the Conway and came riding to Aber to appeal for Llewelyn's aid.

'For,' said they, 'we cannot live longer in this fashion, deprived of our right as free Welsh landholders, our young men forced to give armed service to the English, and our land taxed to keep our own people in chains. Come and make Welsh land Welsh again, for we will die rather than to go on in bond to Langley and his kind. Come and lead us, and we will be your people, in war and peace the same.'

Llewelyn knew his hour then. The season was ripe, the supplies assured, and of winter fighting we Welsh, better prepared and equipped than usual, had no fear. Moreover, we were also better informed on one point than our visitors, for we knew from the smith of Chester that Geoffrey Langley had left that town for Windsor, where Prince Edward kept his court, to render due account to him of all his Welsh lands in the north, believing the Middle Country, if not pacified, securely bound, and helpless to do more than thresh in its chains. And when the prince rose before his council and his guests, very pale with recognition and desire of his destiny, and very bright with the assurance of his own election, we all knew that the waiting was over.

'Go back and tell all those who sent you to me,' he said. 'that I am coming, that I am with them. I, too, have waited for Wales to be Welsh again, and what I can give, and what I can do, towards that end, that I promise you. Go back and tell your people that one week from today I shall cross the Conway and break out of my own bonds, which I have suffered as long as you. And until then, for your sons' sakes, keep the fire damped low, that the blow may fall harder and more suddenly when it comes. When I bring my army across the river, then send me your young fighting men. And by the grace of God I shall make them the instruments of liberty, and bring, God helping me, the most of them safe and free back to you.'

After the Council dispersed, place and time having been appointed and all the needful preparations discussed and put in train, Llewelyn drew me aside with him, and said to me, glowing, for that meeting had been strong wine to him: 'Samson, will you ride with me? There is yet one more thing I must do, to be ready for this day that's coming, and I would have you with me when I do it, for no one has a better right.'

I said gladly that I would go with him wherever he willed, though his intent I had not then divined, nor did I until we turned into the uplands short of Bangor, riding southwards. Then I knew. And he, sensing the moment when the knowledge entered me, turned his head and smiled.

'You do not ask me anything,' he said, inviting question.

'I would not by word or look prompt you to anything, or presume to advise or censure whatever it is in your mind to do,' I said. 'Whatever it may be, the judgment is yours alone. And in your judgment I place my trust.'

'That was one of your loftiest speeches,' he said, mocking me, 'and if you had no personal hopes or fears of what I may be about to do, you would not need such high-flying words. I am going to war. I have room for a good fighting brother who hardly knows what fear is. Provided, of course,' he said grimly, 'he is on my side! I propose to ask him.'

'Him! Not both, then,' I said.

'One, as I remember,' he said, 'did his best to kill me, once.'

'Both, as I remember,' I said, 'have done as much, and with equal ferocity.'

'One to my face, and one behind my back. I see a small difference there,' he answered me mildly. 'There is also a nagging doubt in me concerning the one who rode at me head-on like a mad creature. Was he indeed trying his best to kill? Or to be killed?'

He saw that I was startled, for indeed I had not considered how apt this conclusion might be until this moment. 'Did you think I had not caught what he said to me?' he asked gently. 'I heard it, and so did you. No other. It was as well. There were knots enough to be undone, after that affray, without having to explain David to other men.'

I told him then, honestly, that it had never entered my head to think that David had been seeking to run upon his own death. Nor could I truly believe it now, no matter what he had cried out against himself when he was half-stunned and wholly dazed. And yet Llewelyn had planted a doubt in me that would not be quieted thereafter. He, with his open and magnanimous charity, put the best construction on what David had said and done, able to envisage without too bitter blame a thwarted and restless young man tempted to strike for power even against his brother, and finding no difficulty in the shame and self-hate that caused him to invite retribution afterwards. A simple enough David that would have been. But I was sure in my heart that the David God had visited upon us was in no way simple. Nor had he cried out to his conqueror: *'Kill me, you were justified!'* but: *'Kill me! You were wise!'*

'Well, let it lie,' said Llewelyn, humouring me because he saw me troubled. 'He is young, he called himself ambitious and greedy, but I think it was for glory and action more than for land, and glory and action I can offer him in plenty. We'll make the assay, at least, and hear how he will answer.'

I did not urge him to offer the like opportunity to Owen Goch, for I could not in good conscience make such a suggestion. So when we rode down out of the hills to the neck of land between the two llyns, with the sunset light heavy and bright as fire in the water, and climbed the winding path up the great rock on which Dolbadarn castle stood, he bade his castellan bring forth to us in the high chamber only David.

He came in stepping with soft and wary delicacy, like a cat, and stood blinking for a moment in the full torch-light, for doubtless his own cell, though provided with what comforts were possible, was but poorly lit in the dark hours. He was, as always, very debonair in his apparel, imprisonment could not deface his beauty or his gift of freshness and cleanliness. But he was thinner, and had a hungry look, like a mewed hawk, or a horse starved of exercise. Recognising us, he smiled, even at me, as though we had parted only yesterday, and the best of friends.

'It's long since you honoured me with a visit, brother,' he said. 'And to bring Samson, too, that was kind.'

Llewelyn bade him sit, and he obeyed without comment or thanks. I saw that his face was somewhat haggard, the eyes blue-rimmed like bruises. He had put on a good front, but he was sadly fretted with his confinement, for surely he was one bird never meant to be caged. Llewelyn looked him over closely, and said with compunction: 'I think I have done worse to you than ever you tried to do to me. Do you eat? Do you sleep? Have you had wants that could have been met, and have not asked? What sort of pride is that?'

'Do I look so ill-cared-for?' said David, injured. 'I had thought I made a very fair bid at being what a prisoner should. It takes a while to get into the way of it, but I think I have it now. You may be better pleased with me the next time.'

'If you are in your right wits now,' said Llewelyn directly, 'there need be no next time.'

I saw the small, wary flames of doubt, and desire, and calculation kindle in David's eyes, and from cool burn into vehement heat. Until then he had been on his guard against us and against hope, clenching all his longing and frustration tightly within him lest it should show in voice or face. Now he began to quiver, and with bitter force stayed the trembling, too proud to let us see how desperately he desired his freedom.

'Even in my right wits,' he said carefully, 'I am not good at riddles. If you want me to understand you, you must speak as plainly as to a child.'

'Some time since,' said Llewelyn, 'when for good enough reason I put you here, you declined to promise your loyalty in the future, rightly discounting the force of such a promise, so soon after disloyalty. At some time to come, you said, when you had purged your offence, you trusted to show me by deeds whether you were cured. The time is come now when I need good fighting brothers, when I would gladly have you by my side, and see you put your faith to the proof. If you are so minded.'

'Something has happened,' said David, in a dry whisper, and moistened lips suddenly blanched white. 'Tell me what you mean to do with me.'

He still was not willing to believe that he had any voice in the matter, but as Llewelyn spoke, telling him in simple words exactly what was toward, the colour ebbed and flowed in his throat like a wind-lashed tide, and slowly reached his cheeks, burning over the high bones. His eyes shone bluer than speedwells. I saw him swallow the dry husks of fear that silenced and half-strangled him, and in the piteous hunger and thirst that seized him he looked younger than his twenty years; he who had looked dauntingly critical and knowing at five years old. He did his best to restrain the hope that was devouring him, and not to grasp too soon at the vision of his freedom. But his heart was crying out aloud in him to rise and go, like a falcon clapping its wings.

When it was told, he sat with his arms tightly folded across his breast and hands gripping his shoulders, as if to hold in that frantic bird until the cage was truly opened, and the clear sky before him, while his dark-circled eyes burned upon Llewelyn's face.

'And you will take me with you?' he said, still fearful of believing.

'If you are of our mind, if you will take up this warfare like a man taking the cross, and be faithful to it, yes, then come with us. And most welcome! You need have no fear of that.'

'And I may come forth? Into the light of day again?'

'Into the dusk of a chilly evening, and with a long ride back in the dark,' said Llewelyn smiling, 'if you say yes at once.'

'Tonight? Dear God,' he said, beginning to shake and to shine with the intensity of his joy, 'the midnight will be brighter than anything within here.' And he cast one wild, glittering glance all round the great chamber, and a stony, gaunt cavern of a place it was, for all its rugs and hangings. 'Oh, I would say yes, and yes, and yes, to whatever you please, only to get out of here. Don't tempt me with too much, too suddenly. This, at least, I must not do lightly, nor you, either. There must be something to pay.' He started suddenly forward out of the chair where he sat, and went on his knee in front of Llewelyn, and lifted his hands to him, palm to palm, so that his brother, surprised but indulgent, had little choice but to take them between his own, which he did warmly. 'I make my act of submission to you as my prince and overlord,' said David, in a voice ragged with passion, 'and I do regret with all my heart those follies and treasons I committed against you. From henceforth I am your man, and you are my lord. And that I swear to you –'

'Swear nothing!' said Llewelyn heartily, and clapped a hand over his lips to silence him. 'Your word is enough for me,' he said, and took him strongly under the forearms and plucked him to his feet.

David stood trembling in his brother's hand, half-laughing, yet not far off tears, either, with the excitement and relief of this unexpected deliverance. 'You should have let me bind myself,' he said, 'I thought you had learned better!'

'Fool!' said Llewelyn, shaking him lightly. 'If your word was not bond enough, why should your oath be? Nor do I want you bound. I want you free, and venturesome, and with all your wits about you. And we had best be moving, and take it gently on the road, for you'll find yourself stiff and awkward enough in the saddle after so long without exercise.' Then he leaned and kissed his brother's cheek, and of solemn words there were no more.

So in the onset of the night we took fresh horses, and rode back to Aber under a bright, cold moon, three instead of two.

CHAPTER VII

We mustered at Aber on the last day of October, and on the first of November we crossed the Conway at Caerhun. Llewelyn had mounted as many of his men as possible, amassing great numbers of hill ponies, for speed was at the heart of his plans, and he did not intend the royal castles or the small local offices from which the cantrefs were administered to have any warning of our coming. Beyond the river we split our fastest cavalry into two parts, one to strike directly north-east to the coast, under David, and so sever the Creuddyn peninsula and the castle of Degannwy from all possibility of reinforcement or supply from Chester, while a part of our little fleet kept tight watch over the Conway sands and the sea approaches, to prevent any ship from making in there to the fortress with food or men. The other half of our horsemen, under Llewelyn himself, swept on as fast as possible to the east, to cross the Clwyd at Llanelwy and push ahead to the coast beyond Diserth, thus isolating that castle, too, in lands once again Welsh. Diserth, not having an approach by sea, could more easily be held fast once it was encircled, nor did we have to sit down around it for so much as a day, for by then the young warriors of Rhos and Tegaingl were up in arms and out to join our slower foot soldiers, who followed hard at our heels, and all that was needed was to furnish them with commanders and the core of a disciplined warband, and leave them to hold down what we had repossessed.

It was no part of the prince's plan to waste time and men in attacking the castles, strong as they were, and heavily manned. Nor was there any need, once the garrisons were penned tightly within them and denied any relief. What harm could they do to us? Far better to press onward to the very walls of Chester, and recover all the lost land, thus putting a greater and greater expanse of enemy country between the castles and their base, and securing ever more of our own soil, and ever more firmly. Should it be necessary in the end to reduce the fortresses and raze them, for that there was no haste. No man could now help them without encountering our armies by land or our ships by sea. And though by English measure, and certainly by comparison with the Cinque Ports navy, ours were but poor little boats, yet the mouth of the Conway was better known to our seamen than to the English, and navigable far more easily with our small, shallow craft than with the king's ships.

Of fighting we had some fleeting taste here and there, but disordered and scattered, for the surprise was complete, and even after the first days we moved so fast that hardly a messenger could outride us, and none by more than an hour or two. The garrison at Diserth ventured a sally at us, but mistook our numbers and the nature of their own encirclement, and were glad to withdraw within the walls again with their wounded, leaving a number of dead behind. They came forth no more, but the young men of Tegaingl kept station about the castle and waited hungrily for another clash with them.

Elsewhere, those few places where there was a small force of English stationed made some resistance, but were either overwhelmed and scattered, or drew off and ran for the shelter of Chester. Some minor officers of the royal administration we took prisoners, but most fled, though even some of these, lost in a hostile countryside, were later either taken, or killed by the people of the villages. We had half expected an army to be put into the field from Chester to meet us, and were ready for a pitched battle should it come to that, but nothing stood before us. We had reckoned, too, on some show of retaliation from the lords of the march, however disaffected themselves, when the Welsh broke out in rebellion, but they sat sullen and vengeful in their own castles, and lifted not a finger to hinder us. And that was the greatest surprise of this entire northern campaign, and perhaps made us too optimistic in similar case thereafter. We were not used to being smiled upon by the marcher barons, our uneasy neighbours.

'It seems,' said Llewelyn, astonished, 'that I had even undervalued the dislike and suspicion they feel towards this new order in Chester. God knows how long it may last, but now they hate the spread of royal power in the borders, it appears, more than they hate us.'

And indeed it was clear, by their continuing complacency even after Geoffrey Langley came rushing back into the county from Windsor, that they held us to be fellow-sufferers, who were now busy fighting their battle for them. Hardly a view that would be welcomed by those who lost lands to us, like Robert of Montalt. But those who were not personally at loss looked on our encroachments with no disfavour, seeing the threat of effective royal administration in the marches recede. There was laughter, rather than tears, along the English side of the border when Langley came back into the county just in time to be chased ignominiously into the safety of Chester.

We had halted for a night in Mold to let David and his force catch up with us, having established what was almost siege order round Degannwy. David was in high feather, and in very fair favour with his men, though I think there were a few among the captains who were wary of him as yet, unsure how much truth there was in his new fealty to Llewelyn. But by the time we were patrolling opposite the walls of Chester he had won them all, for he was dashing, intelligent and without fear in battle, and in his own person, eye to eye, he could charm birds out of the trees.

Everywhere we had passed, the chiefs and princes, restored to their free holding, declared themselves as allies of Llewelyn, and placed themselves willingly in fealty to him. Nor did he seek to keep under his own direct hold any part of what he freed, but set up the high men of that country in possession of their own, or where there was no Welsh claimant by reason of the past history of the marches, but either a marcher lord at distance or the crown itself as sole overlord, bestowed the land upon one or another of those allies of his most able to maintain it, thus keeping the full strength of Middle Country loyalty fixed in his own person. And so within one week, no more, we had freed the four cantrefs, and enlarged Gwynedd to its old bounds, and won valuable allies wherever we touched.

And it was but halfway through the month of November, and so much changed, in our fortunes and in our aims. For this rapid and almost bloodless advance could not but open up the possibility of further conquests.

'It is true enough, as the Lord David says,' said Goronwy in council, 'that it would be waste and shame to halt here, but I am for pressing on for another, perhaps a better, reason. To halt now would be to put in danger even what we have already done. It can be secured only by taking it further.'

'I know it,' said Llewelyn. 'All we have done – though I grant you it was done with less risk and less loss than I had dared believe possible – is to take back what was taken from us by the English crown and bestowed upon the prince. But how long can that or any Welsh land be held safe from England, while Welsh chiefs are divided, and can be picked off one by one? I want back not only the Welsh commotes, but even more the Welsh fealties that have been stolen by King Henry. They count for more than land, for they are the only means of protecting the land. Very well, let us learn from our enemies, and pick off the crown's Welsh allies one by one, now, before King Henry can raise the money to come to his son's aid. Let them learn that it is safer to keep their homage at home, as well as more honourable. I wish no ill to any Welshman who has been pressed and daunted into pledging himself to Henry against his own wish. But I think it time to offer such at least a demonstration of the consequence, and if they cannot learn, to set up in their place those who know of what blood they come.'

For the first step he had taken was so great and so vehement that there was no way of keeping his balance now but to go forward and match that step, checking as he went, until he reached a strong and favourable stay. And so said we all.

That was a wet and stormy winter, but for the most part not severe in frost and snow. Such weather always served us Welshmen well, for it fitted our habit of ambuscade, and night raid, and lightning attack and withdrawal, and was very evil for the massed fighting and ordered battles the English preferred. So we felt confident enough to hold our own, even if they should yet put an army into the field against us. But they did not, leaving all to their officers and allies in the threatened commotes. Langley was not a soldier, and though he had a great enough garrison in Chester to hold that town and county, he was afraid to risk an advance to the west against us, lest he should lose half the force he had, and lay even the border towns of England open to attack. So he kept still and mute within the city, and perforce left the forward castles to fend for themselves. As for Prince Edward, I think he had no money in hand to raise a force of mercenaries, as was becoming the English habit, or even to pay the expenses of mustering the feudal host against us. And his father was as poorly furnished at this time, having his own troubles at home with his magnates. The king's brother, Richard of Cornwall, did, as we heard afterwards, provide borrowed money for a campaign, but the weather and the harassments at home, and the speed of our movements, made all null and void, and the money raised was never even spent. Most vital of all, the marcher barons would not lift a finger to aid the administration they themselves feared. So everything Henry attempted came to nought.

As for us, being so close, and having resolved on carrying the assault against those Welsh princes who had voluntarily allied themselves with King Henry aforetime against their own country, and benefited by their desertion, we swept down from Mold into the two Maelors of Griffith ap Madoc, to the very border of England itself. 'For he forsook the old faithfulness of his house to my grandsire,' said Llewelyn, 'and allied himself with England against my uncle when he was worst beset with lawsuits and wranglings, before ever the war began. And he got a pension out of the king's exchequer for his services, too, and is growing fat in the king's favour.'

'He holds fat lands, too,' David reminded us shrewdly, 'and will have had a good harvest. And if they do succeed in fielding an army against us, there's corn enough in his barns and cattle enough in his byres to lighten their load. Shall we leave him all that plenty?'

So we moved down into the softer land of Maelor and Maelor Saesneg, dispersed the fighting men Griffith ap Madoc raised hurriedly against us, and sent him running into Oswestry for shelter. We drove off to the west all the cattle and horses we found that were worth the taking, and much of the stored grain passed into the hands of our allies of Dyffryn Clwyd, and what we could not remove we burned in the barns. Before the end of the month we had secured all the northern march as far as the Tanat, and so stripped it of food supplies that no royal army could well live off that countryside to do us annoy. We made some raids even into England itself, towards Whittington and Ellesmere, to make known the power we had to hold what we had taken. But by then I think they needed no more proof.

'I tell you, Samson,' said David to me in the onset of the last night of November, as we rode back from one such raid, the sky to eastward sullen and smoky with our fires, 'I am sorry for Edward! It was not he who penned us on the further shore of Conway, and it is not he who has driven the men of the Middle Country to this fury. But here is he newly installed in his honour, to have it snatched out of his hands before he has even enjoyed it. And I am sorry,' he added soberly, 'for any of Welsh blood who come in his way if ever he does find himself with men and money to take his revenge. For his nose has been rubbed well into the mire,' he said, 'and that was never a safe thing to do to Edward, boy or man!'

I said it was the fortune of war, and other men had had to bear the like with a good grace, not least David's uncle and namesake. For I well remembered the bearing of Prince David at Westminster, when his fortunes were at their lowest.

'Other men,' said David very gravely, 'are no measure for Edward. Neither for the value he puts on himself, nor for the extremes he will use in exacting his price.'

I said that as far as the north-eastern approaches of Wales were concerned, and for this year at least, we had effectively denied him the means to exact anything, even the more legal of the taxes Langley had been levying for him. And David laughed, and owned it.

'But remember what we have scored up against us,' he said, 'for very surely Edward will remember it, every heifer and every grain.'

We drew off westward then to Bala, to rest briefly and reorganise our forces, which had grown greatly with the accession of allies from all sides, so that it began to seem a live possibility that Wales should indeed be welded into one. Llewelyn had sent also in advance to Aber, and had them bring south some of those engines of war he had been preparing and testing.

'We'll take them with us,' he said, 'or they shall follow after us, south into Cardigan. For we'll go and take back Llanbadarn, if we get no further this year.'

This was that part of the Cardigan coast which had also been given to Prince Edward in his appanage, together with the castles and lordships of Cardigan and Carmarthen, formerly part of the earldom of Gloucester, but held back by King Henry after the death of Earl Gilbert, when the other castles and lands of that great honour were regranted to the heir, Richard. Those two strong castles the crown had long coveted, and so took this means of retaining them. And truly if we had set out to invest or storm them we might have wasted all our substance and our men before making any mark upon them, they were so strongly manned. Such fortresses were better isolated, at little cost, like Diserth and Degannwy, than besieged at the price of long months of bloodshed and tedium together. For us it was ever best to keep on the move. If they could pin us down they might have a hope of dealing with us.

Between us and Cardigan lay the cantref of Merioneth, held by a distant kinsman of Llewelyn, for both were descended from Owen Gwynedd. And this young man was also named Llewelyn, and had but lately come into his inheritance by the early death of his father, who had been an ally of King Henry, and whose loyalty his son, who was not many years past his majority, had assumed along with his lands. We had no great quarrel with him, indeed the prince was loth to harm the boy, but he sat squarely between us and our aim, and moreover, he was himself, however admirably, what we had set out to punish, a willing adherent of England in the teeth of his own birth and breeding, and we could not well spare him and strike at others who were but doing the same as he.

'At least let's send him a herald and offer him the chance to choose Wales,' Llewelyn said, and sent on a messenger to talk with his kinsman. 'Though if he is what I think and hope,' he said to me privately, with some doubt and sadness, 'he'll not change his allegiance now at a breath, when all goes wrong with his master and well for Wales. No, if he comes to us, as he should, it will be later and without leaving a passage open to the enemies of his old lord. It will be of his own choice, and with due warning given, when the scales are not weighted.'

And so it proved, and he was glad and sorry for it. For soon after we had marched across his borders the boy met us in arms, in a narrow valley among the high hills, and for all his forlorn state against so many, would not give place until we broke the formation of his men, and they scattered to save themselves, and in so doing saved their young lord also, for even he had wit to know he could not stop our way alone, and let his friends hustle him away in haste into the mountains. We, for our part, made no haste about pursuing them, and since we pressed on towards the coast, they were forced to withdraw eastward, and I think found refuge in Pool castle after much riding, and there, though still in Wales, were as safe as in the king's court, for Griffith ap Gwenwynwyn was King Henry's man from head to foot, and with him, as yet, we had not meddled. His time was yet to come.

Llewelyn now wrote to appoint a meeting with Meredith ap Owen, to whose rightful holding those lands about Llanbadarn, bestowed by the king upon his son, had formerly belonged. On the way to that meeting, which took place on the sixth day of December of this year of our Lord twelve hundred and fifty-six, some miles south of Llanbadarn, at Morfa Mawr by Llanon, which was a grange of the great abbey of Strata Florida, we conquered without much resistance all that stretch of coast that pertained to Edward, and cast out his officers and garrisons from it. At this same time David, with Meredith ap Rhys Gryg, had made south by a different way, and overrun and possessed the cantref of Builth, while letting alone the town and the castle, which lay on the eastward extreme of the cantref. Thus we all met again at Morfa Mawr, having freed much of mid-Wales. And there came also Meredith ap Owen, true to his time, and greatly moved by so sudden and glorious a change in the fortunes of his country. And there Llewelyn, constant to his policy of securing his allies in their rights, and rewarding their loyalty by making yet greater demands upon it along with great rewards, bestowed upon him the lordship of Llanbadarn and its district, and of the whole cantref of Builth, and Meredith ap Owen gladly received them and acknowledged the prince as his overlord and sovereign.

He was a fine vigorous man, perhaps ten years older than Llewelyn, of grave dark countenance and cool judgment, and as he proved shortly, a formidable fighting man for all his gentle manner, whose allegiance was well worth cherishing.

Thus in somewhat less than six weeks from leaving Aber we had re-possessed and united much of North Wales and mid-Wales, and bound them firmly to Llewelyn as supreme prince, and surely that great man, his grandsire, knew and blessed the achievement. And always the winter weather continued murky, moist and baffling, covering us like a veil from our enemies, and with gales and squalls confounding all that they contemplated against us.

In this two-day stay we made at Morfa Mawr the fletchers and armourers were busy re-flighting arrows and repairing dinted mail, and those engineers who had brought south the siege engines from Llanbadarn caught up with us, having made very good time of it on that journey. We could afford no prolonged rest, for we must make the best use of what remained of this year before the feast of Christmas. And Meredith ap Rhys Gryg, now so near to his own ground and his own castles, fretted even at so short a delay, and looked out always towards the south, where beyond the hills of Pennardd lay the green, rich vale of Towy, and the heart fortresses of Deheubarth. And Llewelyn, seeing him narrow his eyes to gaze so far, and stroke and tug at his bushy beard for want of other occupation for itching hands, laughed and clapped him on the shoulder.

'I have not forgotten,' he said, 'nor am I going back from what I set out to do. Before Christmas you shall be lord in your own lands again. But I have also to remember certain family complications of my own. I have a sister there, and one I would gladly have as a brother if he would come round to our way of thinking. I will not hold back for that, but I want no slaughter if we may avoid it.'

For now we were come to the most vital passage of this war, and one that could not be avoided or postponed. And at night, when we were out alone, walking the outer horse-lines, as he did regularly before sleeping, he said to me, almost in wonder and with some sadness: 'My sister has two boys, and I have never seen them. Fine boys, my mother says. It's a hard thing that I should be a stranger to them, and an enemy.'

But I knew that he would not, for that cause, hold his hand, or let it fall any less heavily on Dynevor, if Rhys Fychan defied him, than on Maelor or Llanbadarn. For he was in no doubt at all where his road lay, and those doubts he had of his own personal actions and intents could not cast any shadow upon the path laid down for him. That he saw always clearly, and pursued it with his might. For there was but one Wales, that must be made truly one if it was to survive. Also he said, more than once on this long and roundabout journey: 'Truly I never knew how various and beautiful was this land of ours!' For like me, he had never before been south so far, never looked out, as we looked now, over Cardigan Bay, or seen the great, rolling, dappled green hills of the south, racing with cloud-shadows like fast ships upon a tranquil sea, so different from the burnished steely crags of Snowdon which were his home. He rode always with wide eyes and a startled smile hovering, between the fighting and the ruling, like a lover discovering ever new and unforeseen beauties in the beloved.

'It may be,' I said, though hardly believing it, 'that Rhys Fychan will be willing to listen to argument, and be reconciled with his uncle.'

'And with his brother?' said Llewelyn, and smiled ruefully. 'I think my sister will not let him, even if he would. But what we did for the boy yonder in Merioneth we'll also do for Rhys, and he must make his own choice.'

Accordingly a herald, went before us, though not too far before, for if Rhys had time, and were ill-disposed, he could send for help to the royal garrison of Carmarthen, which was not far away, and it was no part of my lord's plans to attempt at this stage either Carmarthen or Cardigan castle, both of which were very strongly held, and easily reinforced and supplied from the south, where we had as yet no means of intervening, and no effective allies. We marched, therefore, hard on the herald's heels. And when we had reached Talley abbey with no sign of our man returning, Llewelyn smiled grimly, and said that we surely had our answer. From then on, certain in his own mind that the messenger had been detained in Dynevor to avoid giving us warning of Rhys's intentions, he read them no less plainly, and put out before us well-mounted outriders to keep watch against interception, and particularly against ambush.

The hills declined towards Cwm-du, dipping to cross a brook, and on the slight rise beyond the forest began. We were between the trees, in the dim light of a December afternoon, when we heard the distant sound of a horn from the hanging woods somewhere before us, and knew that Rhys had chosen to come out and fight us in the country he knew, rather than wait for us in Dynevor. He had had time to bring out his muster some five miles from his castle. Doubtless he had been warned of our presence in mid-Wales days since, and made his preparations accordingly, so that when the hour struck he had only to march his men out and take the station he had chosen. And in this tangled woodland, even the ground thinly dappled with snow and baffling to the eye, this could be no planned and ordered battle, but a confused hunt, every man seeking his own adversary, and the advantage with those who knew the ground.

'Not half a mile away,' said Meredith ap Rhys Gryg, rearing his grizzled head to catch the note and distance of the horn. 'Will you take station and let them come to you, or meet them moving? There's an assart just over the crest there that would stead us, cleared and abandoned after. They pasture sheep there in summer.' For he was on his own turf here, no less than his nephew, and knew every fold of the hills, and the way the frost flowed and the winds blew.

'If he chooses to stand,' said Llewelyn, 'he'll maybe have taken that for himself. No, we'll go to him. But gently, and roundabout. Forward softly, and wait until word comes back to us.'

In a little while one of the outriders did come cantering back without haste, through the deep mould of leaves off the track, and reported the fruit of his mission.

'My lord, we saw them from the crest, just as they were leaving the open track. The ground beyond dips, not too deeply, but the slopes are steep enough to keep riders to the track, unless they have good reason to leave it. And thickly treed on both sided. They are moving into cover there on either side, to take us between them as we come. Their numbers we could not guess, so many were already hidden, but by the light reflected here and there they've spread themselves widely. And they have many archers.'

'But can use them only close to the track,' said Meredith. 'The woods grow too thickly to give them any field from above. They'll rely on their first few volleys, and then try to ride us down.'

'They can hardly have known how close we are,' Llewelyn said, considering, 'or they would not have ventured the horn. If they think to enclose us, well, we have time to go a little out of our way and enclose them. Meredith, you know these woods. Take your party up the slope to the right, and work your way above them. You, David, to the left. If you can do it undetected, go forward to the limit of their stand, and when you are there, confirm with each other by a woodpecker's call, and then sound, and close. We shall be at the point of entering their range, if I can judge it aright, and will drive in on them from the track.'

He kept only his mounted men for this party which was to spring the trap, and sent all his archers with the flanking companies. Goronwy he sent with David, and gave the steward the command, to temper David's boldness and audacity with Goronwy's patience and wisdom. And after they had withdrawn into cover and moved well ahead of us, we rode softly on, and having breasted the rise, where there was an open space as Meredith had said, and therefore some limited view ahead, we let ourselves be seen moving down at leisure and sought for the slight shiverings of the bushes that marked where the woods were occupied on either side by more than foxes and deer.

'Two hundred paces, and we're in range,' said Llewelyn to himself, fretting. 'Where is the horn?'

Then we heard the green woodpecker's raucous laugh, far before us, and he uttered a muted cry, and spurred again, to be at the point he desired when the horn sounded, as it did a moment later. And on that he cried the order for which we waited, and our ranks broke apart and plunged to left and right into the trees. The judgment was good, perhaps forty paces or so short, but our impetus was such that we made good that distance, perilously crouched over our horses' necks with swords out, before they well knew what was happening, and spread out among them, choosing each his path and meeting whatever enemy sprang up in his way. The archers were bereft of their targets and helpless from the start. Distantly we heard the clamour and tumult of the two flanking parties, closing in from the slopes. If Rhys had hoped for a surprise, it was he who was taken in his own trap.

The daylight was dim among those trees, but the outlines of powdered snow made it possible to avoid the branches that swept down at us, and preserved a kind of subdued light that was enough to distinguish friend from foe. To do him justice, Rhys fought well, and used his head once he had recovered it, for he drew out such of his horsemen as were able to rally to the horn, and pulled them back to try and block our way, beyond the jaws of the trap now closing about him. But Meredith was swarming down the slope on the one hand, and David on the other, pushing forward as vehemently as Rhys drew back, and being now clear of our confused battle among the trees, their archers could choose their stance and fit and draw without haste or fear, and did great slaughter. Indeed, those on the flanks outran us, and left the way clear behind them for many of Rhys's men, both horse and foot, to get clear away out of the fight by climbing up the slopes and taking to their heels among the trees. But for some time they held their ground bravely enough, and in the twilight and tumult of the woods there was a long and bitter struggle that swayed now back and now forth, without direction, for in such conditions we could but find our marks where they rose at us, and take them one by one. So none of us knew how the others fared, or what carnage was done on either side, until the battle was over.

It was my wish to keep close at Llewelyn's quarter, as always I did, but such was the tangle of men and horses, archers and lancers, among those thickets that I lost him quite. I was busy about the keeping of my own life, where even the shadows swung swords or drew bows at me, and I laboured after him but slowly and without direction. I did not then know what was happening ahead, where David, at his own suggestion but with Goronwy's hearty blessing, had taken the mounted part of their troop far forward under cover of the trees, and occupied the track at Rhys's rear. So when the issue was decided, and the men of Dynevor broke and began to scatter and run from us, and Rhys sought to rally to him all those remaining who could reach his banner, they found David blocking their way back home, and penned between his audacious challenge and the pursuit that massed out of the woods to follow them, they scattered and ran, slipping away singly into the forest, where we hunted them for a while only, and then were recalled by Llewelyn's horn.

Some of those fugitives, breaking away to our right, certainly made their way safely to Carmarthen, where the king's hand was over them. Others, driven eastward instead of west, made for Aberhonddu, and drew off even further, into the security of Gwent. A few managed to get past us in cover, and fled to Dynevor to give the alarm. For Rhys had ventured most of his garrison, and the castle was left defenceless without them.

We rode back, obedient to the call of the horn, in the heavy, late afternoon light, and the ground was crisping under us with frost, the leaves crackling, that had been moist and soft but an hour ago. We mustered to Llewelyn's summons, and salvaged our wounded, who were many, but few in serious case, for that was a battle of wrestling and scratches on our part. Yet there were dead, and not a few. We left them. We could do no other then, for the day was dying above us, and we had a castle to possess. Two, indeed, for David was sent forward to demand the surrender of Carreg Cennen, a few miles beyond Dynevor, while Llewelyn took his main party directly to Rhys's court. And as I know, he had his sister heavy on his mind, she who was but a year older than he, and utterly a stranger and an enemy, and now, for all he knew, widowed and bereaved, her children orphans. For Rhys Fychan was not made prisoner in that affray, nor did we find his body, though we sought for it close about the track until the light was failing. And doubtless many who fled, being hurt and having lost blood, benighted in the forest, died before morning.

Howbeit, we mustered and rode. For however shaken he might be, he was not shaken in his resolve. And before we crossed the last gentle rise and looked down over the broad, gracious valley of Towy it was twilight, and only dimly could we discern, heaving out of the grey-green levels beneath us, the great mound with the river coiling beyond it, a moat to its southern approach, and on the mound the towering shape of Dynevor, the greatest and most sacred of all the castles of the line of Deheubarth.

From that vantage-point it was but a mile. We came with the night, and challenged with horn and voice under the lofty gatehouse, and a trembling castellan, old and surely abandoned to this charge after the active had fled, came out to us from the portal with a flag of truce, and surrendered the castle to Llewelyn.

I remember the hollow sound of the cobbled courtyard under our horses' hooves as we rode in, and the sparse gleam of torches and pine flares in sconces in the walls, and the few frightened domestics who peered out at us from doorways as we passed to the inner court, and drew back hastily into cover if we glanced their way. And the great, empty silence that hung about every tower and every hall like a heavier darkness, so that we knew before we asked that the soul was fled.

The first thing Llewelyn said to the old steward, as he came anxiously to his stirrup to deliver up the keys, was: 'Where is my herald?'

The man had some dignity in his helplessness, though he was greatly afraid. He said that the herald was within, and safe, that the Lord Rhys had meant him no harm, nor discourtesy to his errand, but had ordered his detention until the army should have marched, when there was no longer anything to be gained by riding out, since he could not overtake the host.

And the second thing my lord said to him was: 'Where is your lady? Tell her that her brother is here, and begs her, of her grace, to receive him.'

Some of the womenfolk had crept out from the doorways to gaze at us by then, all in mourne silence and ready for retreat. A few young boys and old men were left to guard them, and stood as wary and irresolute as they, waiting to try the temper of this new master, of whom doubtless they had heard much, most of it blown up out of knowledge, like tales to frighten children.

'My lord,' said the steward, 'the Lady Gladys is gone. There is no one here but myself to deliver the castle to you, as I was charged to do.'

'Gone?' said Llewelyn, shaken and dismayed, for though in a sense he feared this meeting, yet with all his heart he had also hoped for it, and to turn it to better account than conquest and dispossession. 'She is in Carreg Cennen?'

'No, my lord, she was here. When the first wounded man came down from the hills, with the news that the Lord Rhys's war-band was scattered and defeated, she had horses saddled, and left at once with her children, and a small escort.'

'What, now?' cried Llewelyn. 'In the frost, and with night coming on? And to snatch away the children, too! Does she think so ill of me that a death of cold in the forest is better than shelter of my giving?' Whatever else he would have complained in his resentment and hurt he caught back and closed within himself. In a voice dry and calm he asked: 'Which way have they gone?'

'Eastward, towards Brecon. She hopes,' said the old man sturdily, 'to find her lord there, if he lives.'

Llewelyn looked up at the sky, where the stars were sharp and steely with frost, and eastward at the rising hills she must cross. 'Very well,' he said, 'since she will have none of me, there's little I can do to aid her.' He looked down at the offered keys, and turned to reach a hand to Meredith's bridle. 'Here is your lord, make your obeisance to him.' And to Meredith ap Rhys Gryg he said: 'Take possession of your castles and your cantrefs, my friend, and I give you joy of them. Dynevor is yours, and by this time, I doubt not, Carreg Cennen also. Cantref Mawr and Cantref Bychan, the great and the little lands, are yours. Look well to them.'

Thus was Meredith restored to all those lands he had held before, together with the appanage of his nephew, of whom we did not then know whether he was alive or dead. And for his part Meredith acknowledged Llewelyn as his overlord, and undertook to be always his faithful ally and vassal.

Then, the night being upon us wholly, we dismounted and went in, and the grooms who remained, together with our men, saw to the horses. Within Dynevor all was in good living order, but with some sign everywhere of that abrupt departure, a coffer open and clothes unfolded in the high chamber, where the lady had hurriedly put together such warm cloaks and furs as she most needed, and left all else behind, even a ring, forgotten, lying by her mirror. And though Llewelyn did not in any way abate his personal care for all the detail of our living, even seeing to it that the kitchens were manned and the proper order of the hall maintained, yet many times that evening he looked out at the darkness and frowned, and said, as if more to himself than any other: 'To take such young children on such a night ride! And by mountain roads, mile on mile without even a hut for shelter!' And again: 'I would go after her, but to what purpose, if she fears me so much, and wants none of me? I should but frighten her into worse folly.'

In the morning early came a messenger from David, to say that Carreg Cennen was ours, surrendered without resistance, and waited only for Meredith ap Rhys Gryg to choose a castellan and put him in charge there, and upon the arrival of his party to garrison the place, David would rejoin us at Dynevor, or repair wherever his lord and brother pleased to send him.

'I please,' said Llewelyn, 'to send both him and myself home, in time to keep the Christmas feast at Aber, as is fitting when we have so much cause for thanksgiving. What we set out to do here is done.' And though Meredith pressed him to stay longer, he would not, but set all in train for the march northwards. 'We'll go by Builth,' he said, 'where we can move fast and freely, and have another good ally. And it may be we'll give Roger Mortimer something to think on with his Christmas cheer, as we pass through Gwerthrynion.'

But me he drew aside, before the bustle of preparation began, and with an earnest face committed to me a special charge. 'I cannot rest,' he said, 'for thinking of my sister and her boys riding friendless through the hills in such weather, for surely they can have but a feeble escort, and with women and children they'll make but slow speed, and may meet God knows what perils. I cannot go after her, she would only fly me in greater anger, it seems, and I must take my army home. But you – you are not so changed that she will not know you, and you she has no reason to hate or fear. Take ten men, choose whom you will, and take the pick of the horses, for I want you fast and safe, and go and look for her along the roads to Brecon, and offer her safe-conduct wherever she may choose to go. But not like this, running like hunted hares, that I cannot abide. If she will not meet me, see her safe into Brecon, for her word should give you a courier's right to get safe out again. But if she will come, bring her north with you, and reassure her she shall have all possible honour and respect at my court, and her children also. They are princes of my grandsire's and my father's blood, and dearly welcome to me. Bring her if you can. Bring me word of her if you can bring no more. And say that I am sorry we were ever divided.'

I wondered, and then did not wonder, that he chose to send me rather than David, who equally would know and be known to the Lady Gladys. But David was a prince of the royal blood of Gwynedd, and should he venture his head into a castle held by the English, might not get out again so easily as a mere clerk of no importance to them. And Llewelyn, not to speak of the risk to David, would not give them a hold upon anything that could be used in bargaining against him. It was strange that he had so shrewd a grasp of the devious mind of King Henry, whom he had met but once, and under great stress. But without hate or bitterness he had always a very accurate understanding of his opponent. With other opponents, later and of greater malevolence, he was less expert, having no such qualities within himself as those he was required to combat in them, and having to guess at malignant strengths instead of weaknesses, for which latter he had always a humble man's compassion and generosity.

So I said, glad beyond measure to be so trusted by him, that I would do all I could to be of service to the Lady Gladys and to him, and would find her if I could, and if I could, induce her to come home to his court. That phrase pleased him, for he would have liked to believe she might look on it as a home. He had it always in his mind that he might have been the death of her lord, against whom he bore no malice, but whose challenge he could do nothing but accept.

'Do not come back here,' he said, 'for we shall be gone. But make your way northwards to Cwm Hir, for we'll make a halt at the abbey there. And if we're gone from there, they'll furnish you with horses and provisions, and come after us to Llanllugan and Bala on your way to Aber. Somewhere along the road you'll overtake us. For,' he said very sombrely, 'if you do not find her today or tomorrow, I fear she is lost to us both. And when you are certain of that, then come, even without her. For you I cannot spare.'

Then I kissed his hand, which was rare between us, and always at my will, and I went.

CHAPTER VIII

I took with me as guide one of Meredith's drovers, a man named Hywel, who knew that countryside from Dynevor to Brecon and beyond like the lines of his own hand, and we rode hard over the first stages of the journey by the nearest and openest road, for the Lady Gladys had a night's start of us, and to the castle of Brecon it was but a matter of twenty-seven or twenty-eight miles cross-country. My hope was that with the night and the cold coming on, she would have taken the children but a part of the way, to get them safe out of our shadow as she thought, and then sought shelter until daylight in some homestead, for after our Welsh fashion the households there were scattered widely rather than grouped in villages, and hospitality would be given without question to any who came benighted. So I trusted by pushing quickly over the first ten miles either to be ahead of her, and intercept her nearer Brecon, or at worst to overtake her before she withdrew into its walls.

It was barely light when we rode, and the sky was heavy and leaden-grey with the threat of snow, but in the night there had been only sharp frost, and riding was easy. We climbed out of the vale of Towy, up on to the hill ranges where Hywel led us, half heath and half forest, according as the ground folded and the winds swept it. For wherever there was a hollow or a cleft, there the trees grew dark and thick. Twice we encountered shepherds, and twice passed homesteads, and wherever there was creature to ask we asked for any word of our party, and at the third asking, at a hut in an assart of the heathland, we got an answer. They had passed that way indeed, some hours into the darkness, and halted to ask milk for the children, and a warm at the fire. The woman of the house had begged them earnestly to bide the night over, but they would not. She knew her lady, and was in no doubt what visitors she had entertained at her fireside. Nor had she any fear of us, to urge her to silence. They were then, it seemed, some ten hours ahead of us, and had not thought fit to brighten my hopes by halting for the night, at least not so soon. So we pressed on again as hard as we might. And then, with the rising of the sun, though veiled, towards its low winter station, and the change in the frosty air, the threatened snow began to fall.

We left the bare uplands of the Black Mountain on our right hand, and kept to the shoulder track, for much of the way in thick forest. And there we found grim traces of the fight of yesterday, though not, at first, of those we pursued. Among the bushes we came upon a riderless horse, wandering uneasily and cropping, and then stumbled upon the body of his rider, fallen weakened by loss of blood from a great lance-wound in his side, and dead of cold in the night. A second dead man, an archer, a mere hummock in the new-fallen snow, we stumbled over at the end of another mile. These, too, had fled the field and made for the distant shelter of Brecon, only to die upon the journey. We saw in many places the traces of harness flung away to lighten the load as the horses tired.

Then we sighted among the bushes a man who went sidelong and in haste from us, clutching his thigh and hobbling from a lance-thrust in the flesh there, and him we encircled and brought to a stand, and so got word of our quarry again. For he had seen them pass, as he told us readily once he found we meant him no further hurt. He was one more who had fled the field, but he did not know what had become of his lord, for in that falling night every man had made his own way as best he could. He said he had seen and heard a company ride by towards Brecon, briskly but not at a great speed, nearly an hour ago, but had not known who they were, except that there were women among them, and he thought children. We supposed they could be no other but the party we were seeking. The snow being now a fair depth, we might even be able to follow their tracks if we made haste, though the flakes were still falling, and in half an hour or so might obliterate all. They must have rested for the night, as I had hoped, but at some refuge of which we did not know, to be now so close.

We gave the wounded man the masterless horse we had led along with us, and mounted him, and sent him back to the safety of Dynevor, telling him he had nothing to fear if he would serve Meredith ap Rhys Gryg as he had served Rhys Fychan heretofore. And he went very gladly, for lamed as he was, he would have had hard work of it to get forward to Brecon or back to Llandeilo on foot, and one more night of frost might have been his death, as doubtless it was the death of many more who had scattered wounded from Cwm-du. And we hurried on, in high hopes now, and presently spied, in a place where the snow had creamed and drifted, the gashes where several horsemen had driven through the wave. The crude edges they had cut were already softening out again into curving shapes the wind might have blown, but Hywel recognised them still for what they were.

We spurred the more at the sight, and traced the same passage here and there along the forest track. Then, crossing a crest and having an outlook beyond for perhaps half a mile, and in a lull when wind and snow had eased, leaving the air almost clear, we caught one glimpse of them in the distance, as a knot of dark movement upon white, between the dappled darkness of the trees. By the same token, they glimpsed us, and knew they were followed. I suppose they had been casting glances over their shoulders at every stage of that upland journey. They set spurs to their mounts at once, for we saw their speed quicken.

So, too, did ours. Had the snow held off longer, I would have galloped on ahead alone, leaving the rest to follow me more steadily, to show that I came with no ill intent, however urgently. And I think by the time I had drawn clear of my own men and nearer to those who could very easily deal with one lone man if they so pleased, she would have considered, and wondered, and been willing to listen, even before she knew me or I could name myself to her. But I was not many paces ahead of my company when the wind rose again, and drove the renewed snow in white clouds across the forest track, so that we could see but a few feet before us, and must not only ride blind, but check our speed a little or come to grief. Nevertheless we made what haste we dared, and ours was the downhill run, while they would soon be climbing again, and I knew we could overhaul them.

But when next the torn curtains of white parted for an instant, the track before us, an uneven ribbon of white between two belts of black, was empty of them.

'They'll have taken to the forest,' cried Hywel. 'There's a track down through the woods, by the brook-side to the Usk valley. They'll be hoping for a faster and easier ride by that road, now they know we're after them. It's longer by a few miles, but better going once they're in the valley.'

We came to the dip where the brook crossed, coming down from the higher mountains on our right, and a narrow track bore away downhill to the left beside the water, which was no more than a trickle wandering through the icy stones. The snow lay more thinly there, by reason of the overhanging trees, which carried the bulk of the fall, and under the layer of white the leaves and pine needles were thick and springy, dulling the sound of our hooves, so that we hardly wondered at hearing so little from those ahead of us. We halted for a moment and held quite still to strain our ears, and caught the sharp snap of a fallen branch trampled and broken, and then the distant clash of a hoof against stones, where rock broke through the litter of needles for a moment.

'There they go!' said Hywel, satisfied. And there went we after them. The path sloped but gently at first, and was much smoothed out by the silt of years under the trees, making very passable going. And we were somewhat sheltered by the closer stand of firs and bushes from the coldest of the wind and thickest of the snow. Sometimes we caught again the sound of hooves on stones, ahead of us, or plunging dully into earth where the slope grew steep. And once, where the trees fell back, and the torn veils of snow whirled away from us for a moment, I had a glimpse of horse and rider between the trees ahead, and caught my breath in too hopeful relief, seeing the fold of a long skirt swaying beneath the hunched cloak, and above the collar, which I thought to be furred, the drift of a white scarf tied over a woman's head against the rudeness of the wind.

I said, though surely no one heard me, for we had not slackened: 'It is she! She is there ahead!' And I shouted after her against the wind at the pitch of my voice: 'Lady! Wait! Here are only friends!' But I doubt those ahead did not hear. Or if they heard, they did not trust. So we continued this strange pursuit. 'I am Samson,' I bellowed, 'the servant of your house! Wait and speak with us!'

But ahead, the trees had taken the one glimpse I had of her, and now the wind rose, and we could not even hear mark or sign that those we followed still lived and moved before us.

Then I dreaded I did wrong to follow and affright her, since she rode so fearlessly and well on this downhill path, for by her vigour and resolution it was plain that she would endure into Brecon, and I need have no misgivings concerning her. Yet I remembered Llewelyn, and the hurt he felt in being so divided from his only sister, and above all I was his man, as David had once said of me, and wanted no release from that bond. So we followed still, and harder than before, to reach her at last with voice and spur.

'Now I hear nothing,' said Hywel, checking in the middle of the way, with ears pricked and head reared. 'Halt, and listen!' And so we did, holding our breath, but there was not a sound ahead, though the wind had somewhat veered, and blew towards us. 'They must still be ahead,' he said. 'Where else could they go? The going is softer below, they'll have reached the open turf.'

So we went on, to the meadow levels nearer the Usk, where the forests fall back, and the track opened into a valley road, easy to ride. But we saw and heard no more of them.

'They'll have gained,' he said, 'once down here. We'd better ride hard.'

My heart misdoubted then that we had somehow been deceived, but we had no choice but to pursue it to the very walls of Aberhonddu, below Brecon castle, for whether our quarry had shaken us by one route or outrun us by the other, I had to know the end of it. So we galloped, for in caution there was now no gain.

Thus by the valley road we came within sight at last of the bridge over the Usk, across which was our one approach into Brecon. The snow had all but ceased then. We could see the terraces of the hills declining on our right hand towards that same gateway, and we knew that the direct track descended by that ridge. Very plainly, and much ahead of us, we could see the little group of horsemen and horsewomen – for there were several women – galloping down that pathway and on to the approaches of the bridge, where there were other horsemen waiting to receive them and escort them within. There was no longer any sense in haste, we were out-distanced. To go nearer would be only to invite pursuit in our turn.

I drew rein, and so did all those with me, and we watched that reception at the bridge-head, and it was courteous to reverence. Among the several women there I could not distinguish, from the distance where we sat at gaze in the shelter of the trees, the one I had been sent to solicit, but of her welcome into Brecon I could be in no doubt. Whether her lord was there before her was something I could not know. I knew I had lost her. But also that I could at least report her safely in haven with the children.

'In the name of God, then,' said Hywel, staring, for he had seen what I had seen, 'who was that woman we followed down the stream? And was she, God forbid, alone? For in that soft rubble and snow we could have been riding down one horseman or ten.'

I had the same thought in my mind, for it was clear enough how we had been fooled. Under cover of the squalls, and knowing that with the children to carry they must be overtaken before they could reach Brecon, the company had drawn off into the trees on the hillside above the track, while a decoy lured us away down the valley path. And when we had taken the bait and were in full cry towards the Usk, with a glimpse of a woman's cloak to keep us confident, they had returned to the hill track and ridden hard for the town. But if that was true, then one person at least had been abandoned in the forest. And if only one, then a woman. Not one of us, as we agreed, had seen a second figure.

'But more there could well have been,' said Hywel. 'Or if she ventured alone she must have some shelter she knows of in these hills, for I'm sure she's not ahead of us now. She's let us by somewhere on the road.'

I hesitated long what we ought to do. For with our errand thus completed, however lamely, we were committed to riding north to rejoin Llewelyn at Cwm Hir, and our fastest and safest way, considering the weather, would have been to skirt Brecon with care by north or south, and reach the valley of the Wye, and so press on northwards by Builth. True, there were castles on the way that were held by men no friends to Llewelyn's cause, but I had companions with me who knew those ways well, and in the sheltered valley we should do better than over the wild, bleak uplands of Mynydd Eppynt, exposed to every wind. Every other road open to us was a hill road, even if we circled Eppynt by the west. But I thought it preferable, all the same, to make the blizzard an excuse for turning back to spend the night at Dynevor, and making an early start by Llandovery. To this day I do not know how far it was an honest decision, and how far a means of retracing the way by which we had come, and so keeping a watch as we went for the woman who had duped us. For if she was indeed alone and lost in the woods, with the night coming on, and the snow obliterating paths and landmarks, she was in sorry case.

So we turned back and rode along the valley with less haste than when we had come, the leaden afternoon closing upon us. Hywel could find his way in these parts by night or day, and in any weather, we had no fear for ourselves however deep the snow. But I think that when we came to the climbing path we slowed still more, and not all in mercy to our tired horses. Also we spread out into the fringes of the trees, for there she must surely have withdrawn silently when we lost her, and let us pass without a word.

I cannot say that we found her. We had made but a quarter of the climb to the ridge track when she came out of the woods before us, slender and dark against the snow, not avoiding but advancing upon us, with her pale, bright face uplifted. Most strange, she was on foot now, and the furred cloak she had worn was gone from her shoulders. Very small and young and slight she looked, wading through the deep snow with her skirts gathered high in her hands. And as I halted my horse beside her, she said the most unexpected words I could then have heard, the first ever I heard from her:

'Sir, is there any among you is priest or clerk?'

I think we all stared and gaped for a moment, yet her face, which was oval and fierce and fair, with great eyes intent, demanded instant answer, and the questions we had for her fell by the way. I told her we had no priest among us, but I had gone some way in my boyhood towards minor orders, and knew the office. I do not know how it was, but from the moment she appeared before us and spoke so, there was no business we had of any urgency but her business. For in her face, though young and glowing with vigour, there was also, even before she spoke again, the close shadow of death.

'Come with me,' she said. 'There is a man dying.'

I lighted down and offered to lift her into the saddle, for she was soaked to the knees and pinched with cold she seemed not to feel. But she shook her head, saying: 'It is not far,' and turned and plunged again into the trees, and we, picking our way and leading our horses, followed her. Snow shook down upon her and us from the trees, and she shrugged it off and paid no heed.

It was not far. Three hundred paces at the most into the thick and deepening darkness of the trees, invisible from the track, there was a wooden hut, low and leaning, but sound of wall and roof. She led us straight to the doorless opening, and I went in with her.

'He is here,' she said.

It was so dark within that but for the shining whiteness of the snow that had drifted in through the doorway I should not have been able to see him. It gave a kind of light that came from the ground upwards, not from the sky down. The first thing I was aware of was a wave of surprising warmth that met me out of the dark, and the vast, deep sound of breathing that made a part of the warmth, misty and moist on the air. She had left her dying man the great, vigorous body of her horse to warm him, wanting the means to make a fire. More, she had left him the cloak she had worn, and run out into the blizzard without it when she caught the sound of our movements below on the path. I found him by the gleam of the snow that just touched one lax hand with its feathery fringe. He lay on his back, both arms spread at his sides, his eyes wide open, for their glare had a light of its own. He made no sound, but he was not sleeping or dead, or so far gone from the world as to be indifferent to us who came in. He was stiff with agony. I quivered at the very sight of the lines of his body, straight as timber under the cloak she had spread over him.

The woman said, in a whisper for my ear only: 'He crept here when his strength failed. I do not know how he got so far after Cwm-du. He is thrust clean through the bowels, and has a wound in the armpit besides. Take care how you touch him. He cannot last long.'

'You knew of this place?' I said as softly.

'I knew of it. He happened on it. I found him here when I came.'

I said over my shoulder to Hywel: 'Elis has flint and tinder. Get me a torch alight as fast as you can. Then find dead wood for a fire.' And they went, silently. She was quite still there, one step before my left side, her shoulder on a level with my heart, her waist almost between my hands. I said into her ear: 'Has he spoken to you?'

'Not to me! He has said: I have sinned! He is in torment. I would you were a priest,' she said.

Hywel came then at my back, very softly, with a dried branch of pine already sputtering, casting a fitful yellowish light inside that shelter, and peopling it with all its living and dying. He held it before me, stepping over the living body and reaving the torch into the rough boarding of the timber wall. The horse steaming gently into the cold, its neck bowed meekly towards its feet, heaved up its head in mild astonishment, and stared at us with great globes of eyes. And the shape and lineaments of the mortally wounded man sprang into the flickering light, and showed me a face I knew from long since.

I went on my knees beside him on the hard earth floor littered with pine needles, and searched the visage that glared up at me with open and recognising eyes. It was more than twelve years since I had seen him, or he me, but when those great, chill eyelids rolled back he knew me as I knew him. One step from the threshold of death he was still a comely person, my mother's husband, Meilyr.

'Samson?' he said. His voice was thick and harsh from the pain he contained with so much bitter force, but it was clear enough, like the mind that drove it. 'Is it you indeed? Has she sent me her half-priest to make certain I die unshriven and unforgiven?'

Once again, as of old, I saw that for him there was but one she, in this world or another, and his whole being was still cleaving to the memory of her at the edge of death.

'Not so,' I said. 'What was there for her to forgive you but years of love never repaid? Lie still now, and let me see if there is anything man can do for you alive, for of what God in his goodness can do for you after death you need not doubt.'

He said no more for a while, only watched me at every move with those smouldering eyes of grief and rage that I remembered now far better than I could call to mind any of the blows he ever dealt me. I lifted the cloak that covered him, as gently as I might, but the clotted wreckage of his body was past any aid of mine, and the only hope was to let him lie motionless, that the riven flesh, weakening, might slacken its grip of this ceaseless pain. So I covered him again as closely as I dared, and we made a low fire between him and the doorway, so laid that it should not blow smoke over him, but give him its warmth. I took his hand in mine, and it was stiff and cold without response, and yet I knew there was still some force in the hard fingers if he chose to use it. We had wine in a flask, and gave him a little to moisten his mouth, but because of his broken belly I dared not let him drink deep. And when I looked round for the girl, who had said no word and made no sound since we came in, I saw that she was on her knees, and had taken his feet into her lap and wrapped them in the folds of her skirt, and was softly kneading and chafing them at ankle and instep. Her face was quite still and calm, and her eyes were on me. She neither offered nor asked anything, but like the angel of the archives she watched and listened, recording everything for the judgment.

Meilyr lay and suffered this handling, but nothing of him moved except his eyes that followed all we did, and the thin-drawn lips that smiled terribly at our vain endeavours. And once he said: 'You trouble needless. I am a dead man.' And again: 'Elen!' he said, as though to himself. 'She died. The only word I ever had of her, that she was dead.

When I heard the girl had married into Dynevor I came to serve here, thinking I might get word . . . thinking she might even come. Why try to mend me now? To what purpose? I have been a long time dead, ever since the fever took all that beauty out of the world, and my hope with it. If I ever hoped!'

But when we had done what little could be done to ease him at least of the worst of the cold and darkness, there was nothing left for us to do but stay beside him, that he might not die alone. Though if ever man lived alone, from the day that first he set eyes upon Elen's beauty the man was Meilyr. And I had thought that he wronged me, not understanding how direly he was wronged! So I sat beside him, having covered him up from the cold, and held his right hand between my palms. And as Elen had used him, so he now used me, for he neither accepted nor rejected, but was utterly indifferent.

Then remembering what the girl had said of him, that he was in torment and had cried out under the burden of his sins, I asked him if he willed to make an act of contrition and confession, for though I was no priest and could not absolve, yet the voluntary expression of his penitence was the true motion of grace.

Terribly he smiled, his eyes devouring me, and he said: 'I have sinned. Against you. When you were weak and at my mercy, I had no mercy in me. But as I did, so has it been done to me, and more also. She avenged you a thousand times over. Where is the debt now?'

'There is none,' I said. 'It is past and over, and I have forgotten it. So, too, should you.'

'Forgotten,' he said, 'but not forgiven.'

'There was no need, once I understood what trouble divided us. But if you set store upon the word, then yes, forgiven also, long ago.'

'By you,' he said, 'but not by her. When the girl came here to her bridal, she could have sent me her pardon, if she had indeed pardoned me. But never, never a word. Never any, until the word of her death.'

'You do mistake her,' I said, for I was possessed by the awareness of his anguish, and wanted nothing in that hour but to take away the great bitterness of it, if I could not take away the pain. And I began to remember all those things I could tell him truly, of how she had changed after his going, of how, with love or without it, he had become for her the single he in this world who needed no name, as she had always been for him the only woman. So I held fast his hand, and leaned over him that he might see my face by the firelight, and know I was not afraid to have it searched for truth or falsehood. And I began to tell him. Of how she froze in dread for him whenever she heard horsemen riding in, until it was certain that he had got safe away into Wales, or elsewhere, and she need fear no more. Of how she had changed, growing warmer and more like human flesh. Of how, when he was gone from her, she spoke of him constantly, and always with solicitude, troubled and anxious if the weather was stormy, grieving to know if he had a roof and a bed when the nights were cold. Of how he had only become real and close to her when he was lost to her and very far away, and only after they were parted for ever was he constantly at her side. And I said that she was strange, and it was not her fault if she could not love after the fashion of other women, but only in some secret and distant way of her own. Most women's love cries out for presence, and cannot survive without the food of glances and caresses and words. Hers awoke only in absence, and lived and grew without sustenance. I told him, last, how she had cried out like a saint at a vision: 'He loved me!' and lamented like a penitent at confession: 'I was not good to him!'

All this he heard unmoved, except to a dreadful grin of scorn, his lips drawn back from his teeth in agony. He said: 'You lie! In all her life she felt nothing for me, neither love nor hate. What you offer me is out of pity. I need no pity, and no lies. I am too far gone for lies to help me.'

Then I swore to him that all I had said was true, and I would take whatever oath he laid upon me, but still he would not believe, and at my insistence he did but turn his head away, and draw his hand suddenly from between mine, so that the movement troubled his shattered body, and he loosed a great moan. But when he was quiet again he said with certainty: 'If this were true she would have sent me a token. No, I go out of this world damned because of her. What is the mercy of heaven to me if she has none?'

I looked then from his soiled and frost-drawn face, that was growing hollower and greyer before our eyes, to all those, who sat and stood around us, watching in silence, feeding the fire, and listening in dread and awe to every word that passed. And I was greatly afraid for his soul if he departed thus stubborn and mute, and greatly I cared, who once had hated him, or thought I hated him, that after a lifetime of loss in this world he should not suffer eternal loss in the next. And I thought how I had at least time left me before my going to cleanse my bosom, if I sinned now in taking his burden upon me, and how I had the means, if I willed, to try at least one more way to the heart he guarded so bitterly. Until then I had not remembered it.

'I swear to you,' I said earnestly, leaning over him so that he must see me, whether he would or no, 'by my mother's soul that I have not lied to you in any particular. And I will prove it. For she did send you a token, but not by any other, only by me. You know her, when did she ever send letters? But when I left her to go to Chester with the Lord Owen she gave me a thing to bring with me. For you! For, said she, when he hears that Owen is raising his banner, he may come, and you may meet him again. Look, do you know this for hers?'

Since I had my full growth the silver ring was tight and irksome on my finger, and I had taken to carrying it rather on a string round my neck, hidden in my cotte. I drew it out and broke it loose from the cord, and held it before his eyes. And I saw by the sudden bright, incredulous gleam in them that he had seen it among her possessions, and knew it for hers indeed. A great, strange softening came over all the lines of his face, that had been hard and white as bone. His lips fell gently apart, as though he drank and was refreshed. I think I never had seen, and never have seen since, a lie so singularly blessed. I went to take up his hand, to put the ring safely into his palm, and both his hands rose of themselves, carefully cupped as if for a sacrament, to receive it. I kept my own hands close, ready to catch the little thing if it fell out of his cold fingers, but he held it delicately and steadily before his eyes, taking it in like meat and drink both, and of the soul rather than the body.

'It is hers,' he said in a whisper. God be praised, she can never have told him how she came by it, that it was hers was all he knew, and that was enough. 'She sent it to *me?*'

I said quickly: 'You did not come, and I did not know where to find you.' For I was mortally afraid that he would turn on me and ask why I had not discharged my errand to him at once when we found him here, without such long trial before I gave him ease. But for him the act was enough, he cared for nothing more, he had his proof. So easy it was to prove with a lie what he would not believe when I told him truth!

And still he held it before his face, the little severed hand holding the rose, and his lips moved without sound, shaping her name over and over: 'Elen. . . . Elen. . . . Elen. . . .' more blissfully than ever saint offered prayers. And then he said: 'I do repent me of all my hardness of heart, of my doubting, of my greed. . . . Hear me my sins, Samson!'

'In the name of God!' I said. And he spoke, and I listened. With long pauses he spoke, and for pure thankfulness I hardly knew until the close how his voice grew fainter, and laboured ever more arduously and faithfully to reach a fair end, for he was so lost in content that the feebleness of his body passed unnoticed. And greatly I marvelled at the modesty of those sins he spoke of, and at the strange depth of his humility, so long and painfully disguised within the armour of obduracy. For he was as clean as most men, God knows, and cleaner than many. I pray I may have as little on my conscience at the departing as he had, for the greater part of his burden was his own pain, and the greater part of the evil he had done was but the convulsion of resistance against the evil that had been done to him. I was assured, as I heard him out to the end, that if I could be so moved by grief and compassion for him, how much more could God have pity on his creature. And it was in my heart that Meilyr's rest was sure.

I had no power to absolve, but I said for him the prayers due to the dying, and with him the sentences of contrition. And at the end thereof I said: 'Amen!' But my mother's husband, with the ring held up before his eyes, very close because by this he saw but faintly, said: 'Elen!'

After that he spoke not at all, but he folded his hands upon the ring, and held it to his heart, for he could no longer see it, and experienced it rather by the touch of his fingers to the end of his life. With what rapture, the withdrawing exaltation of his face gave witness.

We stayed with him perforce, through the night, keeping the fire fed, and making a bed for the girl with such dry bracken and litter as had been left in the shed, though I think she watched with us most of the time. Some bread and meat we had with us, and with the warmth of the fire and the horses and our own numbers, we did well enough, for all the snow and frost outside.

As for me, I sat all the night through by the only father I had known, and he heretofore an enemy. And in the greyness before the first light of day he died, still clasping the ring I had given him. After death, as happens sometimes, all the lines of his face, that was worn and aging, smoothed out into a marble calm and became by some years younger and fairer. And I began to marvel within myself whether indeed I had lied at all, and whether I needed to confess what I had done as a sin. For more and more clearly I remembered my mother dwelling, at my departure, on how I might well encounter Meilyr in Chester, and how it was too late for her to send any message, for she would never see him again. And how then she gave me the ring, saying with such careful truth that it was my father's, and that – who knew? – it might yet bring me in contact with *him*. I have said she had but one *he*. So two-tongued and two-voiced are words, whoever writes or speaks them takes his life in his hand. And whether I was a liar, or had told truth believing it to be a lie, I no longer knew then, and have not discovered to this day. God sort all!

I looked at my old enemy, and he was dead and in peace, clasping the treasure I purposed never to take back from him. What was that unknown father to me, beside this father I had learned to know all too well for comfort, whether he was mine or no? Let him keep his talisman in the grave, it was of more value to him, misunderstood, than to me who knew its significance.

I got up stiffly, and went out into the forest. There was no new snow, and between the tree-tops the sky was clear and encrusted with stars.

As I came back towards the hut I saw the woman come from among the trees, and strip from her head the scarf and the wimple she wore, letting her hair stream down about her shoulders. Long and dark it was, and fell in heavy waves almost to her waist, and between the swinging curtains of silky black her oval face looked pale but lustrous like a pearl. She had not observed me, and I drew back into the bushes to look long at her without offence, for until now, though I had seen much, I had had no leisure, and no peace of mind, to realise what I saw. First she appeared like a visitant from God to demand our presence where we were needed, and that in a manner to remind us that the time of the birth of Our Lord and the apparition of angels was very close upon us. And then she had withdrawn into silence and watchfulness, unwatched, while Meilyr lived out his last hours in this world. Now at this second coming my mind was as open as my eyes. I saw her in truth for the first time.

I have said of my mother that she was beautiful, and of others have been as certain that they were not so. Of this girl I can never say whether she had beauty or no, for never could I pass beyond seeing into describing. Always there was something to arrest me and put all critical thought out of my reach. She was not tall, only a few inches higher than my shoulder, but very slender, and I thought now, for the first time being in any case to judge, that her age was no more than one or two years past twenty. She had a broad, clear forehead, with straight, thoughtful black brows, and her eyes were of a dark colouring which at a distance I took to be a very dusky blue, but which I found on closer view to be sometimes deep grey and sometimes, according to the light, royal purple, for the black of their lashes caused them to change with the changes of daylight or torchlight wherever she was. The lines of brow and nose and cheek were very pure and spare, with that lustrous sheen that came from the pearly translucence of her skin. And her mouth and chin were shapely, generous and resolute. I could never like the prim, tight, small mouths that were the courtly fashion, so that even those lavish-lipped and open by nature copied the pursed look to be in the mode. She was not so. Wide of mouth she was, and full and passionate of lip, but with such composure about her as to keep all in discipline and balance. But above all, she had a way of doing whatever she did with every particle of her attention and her being, and a way of looking a man in the eyes that both pierced him through and opened her own heart to him, if he had a mind to accept the welcome with reverence. And if he had not, she could do without him. Or if he misunderstood and presumed too far, I doubt not she could close the gates against him too tight for his unlocking.

She neither saw me nor looked round at all to see if she was seen. She stooped to the highest and purest bank of snow under the bushes, filled her hands with it, and washed her face in its coldness, her pearl-whiteness emerging stung into rose. Then she dried herself upon her scarf, and taking a comb from her sleeve, began to comb her long hair, patiently coaxing out the tangles left by her night in the bracken. When she had done, she coiled it up again and pinned it, and covered its darkness with wimple and scarf, until she was as neat as if she had slept in her own bed and made her toilet at leisure in the comfort and safety of Dynevor. And so intent was I that only when all was finished did I think to remember how she had come out here into the frosty dawn without her cloak, for still it lay with mine, covering Meilyr's body.

I went into the hut in haste, and brought out the cloak to her and wrapped it about her shoulders. She turned, holding the folds together at her throat, and looked at me, and for the first time smiled, though briefly and faintly. She shook a little with the cold, as though only now could she feel it, and hugged the fur of the high collar against her cheeks.

'It is not mine,' she said, 'but hers. We exchanged. Someone among you might have known it by sight.'

'As I remember her,' I said, 'though that's some years gone by, you are not even like. The same figure and height, perhaps, and the same bearing and gait. Yes, from behind you could pass. You are one of her ladies?'

'The least of them,' she said. And all the while that we stood close her eyes were searching me through and through.

'Both you and she,' I said, 'mistook my errand, and gave me no chance to reach a better understanding. I was sent after the lady and her party, not to threaten or harry, but to offer her shelter and safe-conduct wherever she would be. In the name of Prince Llewelyn, her brother. But chiefly to entreat her, as he very earnestly desired, that she should place herself in his hands and come with him to Gwynedd, there to use his house as freely as her own, and enter and leave it whenever she pleased. But if she would not give him countenance, then I was to see her safely into Brecon, or wherever else she thought fit, so I could report her safe and well.'

I saw her eyes, that were large enough, God knows, in that young, weary face, dilate and glow into silvery grey within their black nests of lashes. She said, very low: 'Is that why you rode so hard after us?'

'It is. I lost my chance. And since I lost it through your gallantry and wit,' I said, 'I pray you at least to believe what I tell you of my lord's mind and my own.'

She looked at me long, and she said: 'I do believe it, if your lord's mind is as I have seen yours to be.' And after a moment, and ruefully: 'I doubt she would have rejected any advance of his, she's so set against him for her lord's sake. It is a pity!' And again, still pondering: 'It was told us of him, by messengers from Llanbadarn, that he did there no needless violence after victory.'

I understood that she spoke, not of her own lord, but of mine, and that she wondered about him, and in particular about me, being here his envoy. For all night long she had remained silent, only warming the dying man's feet in her lap and cherishing them from movement, but there was nothing had happened in that hut that she had not seen and noted, and made more of than any man could. And I knew this of her not because she was woman, but because she was this woman. 'I see,' she said, 'that I did not at all so well as I intended, by her or by you.'

At that I shook my head. 'By me you did better than well,' I said, 'and by him that's dead within best of all. It is due to you only that he did not die alone and uncomforted, and for that I shall thank you to the day of my own death.'

Her lips moved, but upon so slight a motion of breath that I could not be sure she said: 'And I you!' But thus I think she spoke.

'And now,' I said, 'frost or no, it remains for us to bury him, and that we shall do here, where he died. But your part is done, and nobly, and I would have you safe with your own people. I will give you a reliable escort to bring you into Brecon to join your lady.'

She looked at me steadily, and jutted lip and chin for a long moment, considering. Then with a resolution as final as it was quiet, she said: 'No!'

I was at loss here, not understanding what she meant or what she wanted of me. And I began to say patiently that I could not abandon her here in the forest, or leave her to the mercy of possible unwounded and desperate fugitives from Cwm-du. Leave alone the cold and hunger of winter, her horse being in as great need as herself. And mistaking her reserve, I told her earnestly that she need have no fear of riding with my men, for I would take whatever oath she required that she should be respected in every way among us, by the last and least of our party as surely as by myself. But the dead man I must see decently into the grave here, however temporary his stay, for though he was not blood kin to me, yet in a manner he was closer than blood kin, and I would not move from this place until I had said the office over him for his rest.

She said to me, with the same still and starry face, her eyes never loosing their fixed bold of mine: 'I take your word, for all as for yourself, and I do and will trust myself with you gladly. But will you not extend to me the same choice your lord offered to my lady?'

'You do not wish,' I said, bewildered, 'to go to Brecon?'

She said: 'No!' as forcibly as before. And she said that she would have gone, with all her doubts, but for this chance that had opened for her another way. Duty she owed to her lady, and would have paid, however reluctantly. But God had brought her here to this place, and turned the world and her life about, and by that she would abide, very gladly. For she was Welsh, and of a line from which bards and warriors had sprung, and it was against her grain to flee from the Welsh and take shelter, as if by nature though against her nature, with the English, whose one aim, however they fostered one chieftain against another, was to devour Wales wholemeal.

'Then is it your wish,' I said, 'that we should see you safe back to Carreg Cennan, into the household of Meredith ap Rhys Gryg?'

'Not that, either,' she said. 'I have no father or brother left there to make me welcome, and I think it no wise move to put myself into the protection of a lord like Meredith, with grown sons around him. If I am to beg shelter and refuge, I'll beg it from the highest. If you will take me, I will go with you to your Prince Llewelyn, and if there is a place for me about his court, in service among his womenfolk, I will fill it as well as I may.'

I was taken full aback at this resolution in her, and yet I did not question or advise, hardly knowing then why. It was not long before I knew. For on the face of it this was folly, for her to venture afield into Gwynedd, the one woman among ten men, and for us to burden ourselves with her when our passage might not be without troubles. And this folly I accepted and embraced, never asking a reason of myself or her. I asked her only: 'Do you mean this in earnest? And is there none left here at all who deserves and waits for news of you? Not one person to be in distress for you?'

'To the best of my knowing,' she said steadily, 'not one.'

So then I knew, by reason of the great flood of hope and joy that filled me, why I had no desire to examine or consider all the difficulties that might face us on her account, or the need we had of haste to overtake my lord. And I said to her only: 'Come, then, if that is your wish.' For God he knows it was mine.

We buried Meilyr, my mother's husband, in a deep hollow of the ground among the trees, where the mast and mould of years from the branches had made a loose, crumbling soil that would not harden like the open ground, even in the frost. We broke the soil with our daggers and hands to get deeper, and since we could make no very profound grave without better tools, we prised up rocks from the bed of the brook to pile over him, for fear wolves or foxes should dig him up again. Later we sent word to the canons of Talley, to bring him away and give him better burial. That day there was none but myself to speak the words over him. Yet I think he has not slept less well for that. Could I have laid him with my mother, I would have done it. As it was, I took her ring, when we moved and composed his body, for his hands had loosed their hold of it, and threaded it upon his little finger, that he might not lose it in the earth.

The woman stood with us by that graveside, not heeding the cold or the wind. And when I rose from kneeling beside him, I looked at her, and her eyes were wide and fixed, staring upon the silver band on his finger, where the little engraved hand held the rose. In her face there was nothing to be read, except the rapt solemnity of death's presence, for to be brought face to face with another man's death is to meet one's own death in the way, and this touched her nearly, for she had been the instrument of God in blessing his departure, and I think she grieved and marvelled, as at the loss of something she had not known until then for hers. And that was my case also.

Nor had dead Meilyr yet ended his work with me. But that I did not know when we piled the icy rocks over him, and left him to his rest.

We rode back into Dynevor as the light was beginning to fail, and made a stay overnight for her sake. And in the morning we took fresh horses and set out for the north.

Refreshed and resolute, she rode beside me out of the gatehouse and down the track from the mound. With kilted skirts she rode, astride like a man, and booted, for I think she was determined that she would not be a drag upon our speed, but keep mile for mile with us, untiring. All she had with her was a thin saddle-roll with a few clothes in it, and whatever else women will not leave behind when they leave most of what they possess. And since for the first few miles we faced the east and the dawn, there was a lustre upon her face and a brightness in her eyes, for the sun came up red and splendid across the wasting snow.

It came upon me suddenly that I did not even know her name, for though she must have gathered many of ours from our utterances, there had been no one to speak hers before us, and so positive was her presence that until then I had felt no need to find a talisman for her, as though such a woman could be shut into a charm and held in the hand. But now, realising, I spoke my astonishment aloud, and she looked round at me, and deep into me, as was her way, without a smile.

'Yours I know,' she said. 'They call you Samson. You are the private clerk and close friend of Llewelyn ap Griffith. And well I know I should have told you more of myself than I have, though God knows I have told you true. My name is Cristin, Llywarch's daughter, who was Rhys Mechyll's bard until his death.'

'I have heard him spoken of,' I said, 'many a time.'

She gazed straight before her into the rising sun, and said: 'There is more. Among the men who went out from Dynevor to meet Llewelyn at Cwm-du there was one Godred, a younger son of one of Rhys Mechyll's knights, in Rhys Fychan's service now. Like many another, he has not come back. They have no word of him here at Dynevor, except that one who did come in safely from that fight saw him unhorsed and fallen in the forest, and doubts if he got away with his life. Yet some will make their way alive into Carmarthen, surely, and some into Brecon, and only God knows the names of the spared.'

She turned her head again to look at me, and her eyes in the low, radiant light were burnished silver-grey, and large as moons, but her face was quite calm and still.

'I am Cristin, Godred's wife,' she said. 'Or his widow.'

CHAPTER IX

In the cantref of Gwerthrynion we found the traces of Llewelyn's passage clear, for he had possessed himself of most of that goodly land, ripping away all the western borders of Roger Mortimer's lordship on the march. And only this cantref, out of all he had taken into his power that winter, had he retained for himself, using all the others to bind various of his allies to him, that it might be seen that the deliverance of Wales would be also the enlargement of all those who took part in it. So we passed in peace, with remounts where we needed them, and lodging at request, and came to the Cistercian house at Cwm Hir, always dear to Llewelyn Fawr, and always loyal to his line.

They were gone from there before we came, but only by one day. So we took a night's rest, and went on after them. It was then some five days before the Christmas feast.

Cristin, Godred's wife, rode with us grimly, without complaint or flagging, though often I know she was very weary. At every halt I took care to make provision for her privacy and rest, and at every uprising she came forth fresh and neat, with her youth like armour between her body and any failure or faintheartedness. For she was a very strong-willed lady. And though there was much about her I did not understand, I understood only too well that it might be my irredeemable loss if I questioned her concerning what she had seen fit to tell me, and afterwards had told me no more. And whether she had loved this Godred, and been happy with him, I could not know, for on that subject she had closed both her lips and her heart. But chiefly I told myself that she had cause to believe the word of the soldier who had reported him fallen and wounded, and was sure in her own mind that he was dead, and that being so, she wished to escape from the scene of her loss, being now utterly alone, into some new expectation of life in another country. But whether I believed this because it was the most probable truth, or because I greatly desired it to be so, that I do not know. I do know that daily I prayed earnestly without words that I might be delivered from the sin of praying for his death.

And yet in those days we rode together in such precious comradeship as I had never known with any woman, or ever thought to know. And being forbidden by her silence to speak of her secrets, I found no such prohibition upon my own. In the hospice at Cwm Hir, before I left her to her rest, we sat some while together, and were at peace, and suddenly I desired above all things to tell her all that she must, in her heart, desire to know about the man she had helped to die in blessedness in the foothill forests of the Black Mountains. And I told her all the story of my mother and my mother's husband, and my mother's brief and nameless love, out of which I was born.

'I knew,' said Cristin, 'that it was no simple matter of an errand undertaken, or you would have given him the ring at once, as soon as you knew him, and so discharged it. Then you have sacrificed to his peace of mind all those hopes you had of finding a place for yourself among your father's kin.'

'I sacrificed nothing,' I said. 'I gave him, with good-will, what he valued and needed more than I. As for the hope that I may some day find someone who is kin to me, what have I lost by the gift? I shall not forget the hand and the rose. If I see it again, I shall know it.'

'But you have buried,' she said, 'the only proof you had to give you rights among them, even if you find them. Have you thought of that?'

I had not, for the truth was that long ago I had let go any ambitious idea I had had of establishing myself with my father's house. For now that I had a place in Llewelyn's confidence and an ambition all the dearer and more consuming because it was his, and mine only in reflection from him, I had no need in this world of any other kin.

'Well for you,' she said, watching me with deep gravity, 'if you bury with the ring everything that it signified, and rest content with the present and the future, forgetting the past. What need have you of any man's hand to raise you, when you have a prince as lord and friend? And what of brothers when he uses you as a brother? You have made for yourself a valuable and enduring place which you owe to no man's patronage, and no man's merits but your own. And you tell me you would not change, and have no regrets. Cut off the father you never knew, for he will only eat away a part of your mind that you cannot spare. Better to think rather of sons.'

I said that she was surely right, and to say truth I was shaken and moved that she felt so deeply and spoke so earnestly of my affairs. Indeed there was nothing left in me of feeling towards my lost father, by this time, but a small, disturbing core of curiosity, for from him I had in part the blood that ran in my veins, the impulses that drove me, the wits with which I served my prince, and some share in my face. Desiring knowledge of him was desiring knowledge of myself.

But as for any need to make claim upon his blood and his household, if I did discover it, or to make myself known to any scion of that house, I felt none. The most I wanted of them was to know, not at all to be known. And so I said.

'You are wise,' she said, and I thought she drew breath as though in ease of mind, and let fall a long, soft sigh.

We overtook Llewelyn and the main part of his force at Bala, for there he had halted to disperse for Christmas those of his army companies recruited from Penllyn and Merioneth, before the ranks from the north moved on to their homes. He had kept his word to bring the young men of the four cantrefs back safely, almost to a man, and many of them with booty to show for their campaign. And at Bala, before the chieftains separated, they held council concerning the next moves, for it was certain that the force and impetus we had gained ought not to be allowed to die down again while the winter season again grew wet and wild, with little frost. Even if harder cold should come, we now held the whip hand where food supplies were concerned. By the time my party rode in, the princes had agreed among them how soon they should muster again, the place and the target.

It was my intent to go alone to Llewelyn before I presented Cristin to him, for the sight of a straight and comely young woman entering the hall with me would surely raise his hopes that it was the Lady Gladys I brought to him. But someone had observed us before ever we reached the gate of the llys, and carried him word, and he came out in haste from the high chamber to meet us. He had just come in from riding, and now came from the fireside, unarmed, belting his gown about him, and he was flushed and bright from his exercise. At this time, shortly before his twenty-eighth birthday, he had let his beard grow, being much preoccupied with other matters in the field, and thereafter he kept it so, but close-cropped so that it left his mouth bare, and drew golden-brown lines along his upper lip and round the strong, sharp bones of his jaw, as though some cunning artist had engraved him in bronze. In his eager expectation his eyes also had centres of gold. And even when they lit upon Cristin he was still in hope and in doubt, for he had not set eyes upon his sister for fifteen years and more, and any woman riding in with me then, young and slender and dark, could have passed for the Lady Gladys. Nevertheless, he was quick to perceive that this one was too young.

I lifted Cristin down, and she made a deep reverence to him, but he stopped her quickly, taking her by the hands and raising her, for the courtyard was muddy with melted snow. He said that she was welcome, and turned to embrace me.

'I am glad to have you safe back with us,' he said. 'I feared you might have run your head into more trouble than I bargained for when I sent you out. You've had no losses?'

'None, my lord,' I said. 'Delayed we were, but not by any disaster to ourselves. And though I'm sorry I could not bring you the Lady Gladys, yet she is safe in Brecon with her children. And someone else I have brought, who can give you more news of her than I can, for she has been in your sister's service, and was of her party when she left Dynevor. This is Cristin, daughter of Rhys Mechyll's bard Llywarch. She is left without a protector, and has chosen to be of your party rather than take refuge with the English.'

'This is a story I must hear,' said Llewelyn, 'but out of this cutting wind. Come in to the fire, and I'll have meat and drink brought for you.' And he took her by the hand and led her through the hall of the llys to his own great chamber, where there was warmth, and furs to nest in, and the soft grey smoke of the brazier drifting high in the roof.

'So you have chosen to be wholly Welsh,' he said, when she was seated close to the fire, a horn of wine in her hand and the glow of warmth bringing a mirrored glow into her face, 'when my own sister fled from me. I grant you she might well feel she had good cause. But you, it seems, were not afraid to venture.'

'There is more in it than that, my lord,' she said. 'I fear I have been the cause of your plans going awry, for it was I who drew off Master Samson's pursuit and let my lady get safe into Brecon. As he will tell you. It was well-meant, but I have deprived her of the choice of which I was only too glad to take advantage, and I fear you may think less well of welcoming me when you know all.'

'That,' said Llewelyn, eyeing her steadily, 'I doubt. But if you want Samson to be your advocate, you could hardly do better.'

So I told all that story, how Cristin had played the hart to our hounds, and then gone to earth in the forest, how we had ridden on, in time only to see the Lady Gladys and her company cross the bridge into Brecon, where we could not follow, how we had returned by the same road to look for the woman who had deceived us, and how she had come forth to us out of the woods to lead us to a dying man. There was very little Llewelyn did not know of my grief with Meilyr, and his with me, for in these years of our close companionship we had talked of everything that linked and divided us in the past. He sat listening very intently as I told him of that death and burial.

'Rhys Fychan and I between us,' he said soberly, 'have much to answer for. That was cruel waste at Cwm-du, of Meilyr and many another. Meredith has promised to send me a courier if anything is heard of Rhys himself, whether he lives or is slain. We found some wounded, and a few dead, on our way north again from Dynevor, but of Rhys no sign. For my part I think he was luckier than this man of his, and is with the English now, somewhere in one of those castles they hold along the Towy. I wish he had seen fit to come in with us and own his Welsh blood, and spare so many deaths.'

Cristin looked up with the flush of the wine in her face, holding off sleep now that she was in from the cold, and said doubtfully: 'But as we heard it in Dynevor, you came south to set up Meredith in all his own lands and Rhys's, too. To cast out Rhys as Rhys cast out his uncle.'

'It need not have been so. To set up Meredith again in his own, yes, that I had sworn and have kept. But there was enough there once for both, and could be so again. The tale of their holdings in Cantref Mawr and Cantref Bychan is long enough, and the vale of Towy could very well hold both, if they would but be allies instead of enemies. But a brother who takes the English part when he has a choice I will not endure there. He made his own decision.'

She said: 'I think, none too happily. Between the upper and the nether millstone a man feels his bones turning to powder. I think he chose what he took for safety, thinking the English stronger than you. He may well have other thoughts now.'

'Late,' said Llewelyn, 'for such as Meilyr.'

'Too late,' she questioned persistently, 'for such as Rhys?'

He looked at her with a long, wide-eyed look, taking her in with more attention than before, and slowly he smiled. 'I see that you are a loyal liege-woman to your lord and your lady, as well as a patriot Welshwoman. I cannot answer for what Rhys has done, nor guess what he may do. But I am mortal and fallible enough myself, God knows, to be very ware of damning a man for choosing wrong once out of fear for his life and lands, or shutting my ears to him when he turns and says: I was craven and I own it, and now I have done with it. Closing and locking one's doors may keep many a good man out, and that would be pity.'

For all the cloud of weariness and warmth that was closing her eyes, she was very sharply aware of him, and I knew that he had won her. And that pleased me, having so high a worship for both. She wanted, as I think, to give him pleasure in return for the hope he had freely given her for the prince she had served, for she began to tell him of her lady and her young sons, and to reassure him of their good health and high spirit on the ride to Brecon, the children taking it as a new game. The elder, Rhys Wyndod after his father, was nearly eight years old then, and very like his mother, she said. And the younger, five years of age, was named Griffith for his grandsire.

'And there is more to tell,' she said, 'that a brother may like to know. My lady is again with child. No, you need feel no guilt or fear for her, she was in excellent health when she rode out, and only two months gone. She is strong and takes childbirth easily, and she will do very well, wherever she brings forth her third son. I do but tell you that you may take it into account, in whatever dealings follow. For I am sure Rhys Fychan is not set against you or against Wales, but only vexed for his failure against you, as is only human, and very perplexed as to what is best to do for his life and the good of his line. And if he comes to, she will never be far behind.'

Now this was surprising to me in my lord, whom I believed I knew so well, that he was so much charmed by this news, and asked her so many questions, he who had taken no thought at all for his own succession, and never seemed to see woman unless she spoke out with a voice as profound and shrewd as man. So utterly was he absorbed in his passion for Wales. And surely Wales is also a woman, being in all things both capricious and durable, tyrannous and lovely, harsh and gentle, wayward and faithful. To Cristin, in this first meeting, he spoke as to his match, and me he forgot, and I did not grudge being forgotten, for I greatly desired that she should make safe her place in his court, and be at rest there.

If she had forgotten me, that I might have grudged, but she did not. In all she had to say to him, I was a presence. There was no need to tell me so.

When they were done, for he saw that she was very weary, he said to her: 'Madam, my steward's lady here will make proper provision for your rest. Tomorrow we ride for Aber, and if you are not too tired with your long journey I would have you travel with us, for Goronwy's wife at Aber will welcome you, and I shall be glad to have you keep the feast with us there. If you prefer it, we will provide you a litter. Make your home in my household as long as you please, and use it as your own. And beyond that, is there anything I can do for you, to set your mind at rest?'

She looked up at him out of the cushions and skins that cradled her, and the heavy lids rolled back from her eyes, that were like violets, if violets could be lighted by candles within them. Her face was suddenly so still and so pale that for a moment she ceased to breathe, and all her bones shone white through the skin, as though smitten by frost. One glance she cast at me, and then looked back to him.

'There is something,' she said, 'since you have asked for word from Meredith ap Rhys Gryg of the dead and the living. Of your kindness, will you ask him also for any news of one Godred ap Ivor, a landless knight in Rhys's service? For I am his wife, or his widow, and I would fain know which.'

'That I will do,' he said to her, as gravely and simply as he would have said it to a man. 'God forbid that I should have cost you so high, beyond my repaying. But whatever I can get to hear from Dynevor of Godred ap Ivor, you shall hear the same hour.'

Then he committed her to my care, to see her safely bestowed with the steward's wife, and she and I went out from him together in silence, her arm against mine. I had no word to say. For fear of the wrong answer I could ask nothing. But ever I watched her face as we went, while she looked not at all upon me, but straight before her, and was still white as ice with her own fear, the fellow to mine or its counter-balance, and which I dared not guess. For greatly she had steeled and mastered herself to ask that thing of him, wanting certainty instead of doubt, but there was nothing in her manner to me, then or after, to tell me which certainty it was she dreaded, to hear again of Godred living, or to receive assurance he was dead.

She rode with us next day, fresh as a flower, and now more decorously as a woman should, in a gown I had not seen before, for we were safe in our own country, and there were other women of the party, coming with the court from Bala to Aber to keep the feast. There was no great haste, for messengers had gone before to make preparation for the prince's coming, and we could ride at ease, sparing our horses and ourselves. So it was a pleasant and merry cavalcade that made its way through the mountain roads by Dolwyddelan and on to Bangor, where we halted for the night, and the next morning took the coast road east to Aber.

David had gone on before with the vanguard, to disperse those levies from the parts about Bangor and Carnarvon, and he met us at the crossing of the river Ogwen on that final morning ride, to escort his brother with fitting state to Aber. He had shed his mail, and blossomed in brocades and furs, very handsome and handsomely adorned. And when he had kissed Llewelyn's hand, and been warmly embraced, he fell into our line where it pleased him, exchanging greetings here and there with all those he knew best, and so ranged through the whole length of our procession until he came to me.

'Samson!' he cried, throwing a boisterous arm about me and all but wrestling me out of the saddle. 'I'm glad to see you back with us whole and safe. You were so long, faith, I almost feared we'd lost you. But I hear you had no luck with my sister.'

I owned it, and told him how it had befallen, and when he heard of that last encounter with my mother's husband, and of his death, he was cast into a sadness as true as it was brief, as when he himself had broken to me the news that I should not see my mother again.

'He was a dour fellow,' he said, 'this Meilyr, but never less than patient with me, when, God knows, I was trial enough even to longer-suffering souls than he. It was Meilyr first taught me to ride. I am glad, Samson, that you were brought to him so strangely, and he did not go solitary. Shall we not send word to Meredith to fetch him away to proper burial? For you say the place is marked with stones.'

I said it was already done, for we had sent a messenger from Dynevor to the canons of Talley, with an endowment for his disposal at the abbey. Though doubtless, for all the devout searches they made for others of the fallen, many a man died there in the forests after Cwm-du, and wore away to clean bones undiscovered. And in the justice of God I think their unblessed sleep could not be held against them.

But when I went on to tell him how Cristin had rejected escort into Brecon, and chosen to cast in her lot with a free Wales, David's face lit like a sunrise with startled joy, and he looked round to search among the womenfolk for this new countenance.

'You have brought her here with you? She's among us now? Bring me to speak with this young she-warrior! I did not know my sister had such resolute maidens.'

'She is not a maiden,' I said drily, 'but a wife. Or a widow by now, maybe. Her husband was a knight in Rhys Fychan's bodyguard, and she's had no word of him since Cwm-du.'

'And she is under your protection,' he said, gently mocking me, 'and I am warned to keep my distance, am I?' I was silent, for I had not thought to have given him even so much enlightenment, and I feared to betray myself further. Even so, he grew serious again, and eyed me intently as we rode, not concealing his thoughts, but not plaguing me with them, either. 'I'll never add to her troubles,' he said, 'but you'll not grudge me a word with her, and she so gallant a guest of our house, and so whole-hearted a Welshwoman.' His tone was light and a little mocking still, but his curiosity and his eagerness were real enough, and since there was not a personable young woman in any of the courts of Gwynedd who was not known to him, he could hardly fail to find the new face for himself in very short order. I thought it as well to bring him to her myself, and did so as we rode.

Cristin lifted to him her pearl-clear face, faintly flushed with the sting of the cold air and the exercise of riding, and opened her grey eyes wide upon his beauty. It seemed that she was undisturbed, for her serenity never quivered. It was he who lost the thread of his easy banter for a moment, and let a silence fall like a drift of snow between them. She had that kind of assurance, rooted in a personal pride quite without arrogance, that can endure such silences and feel no need to fill them. It was not often that David found himself at a loss with a woman, and I think the novelty of that experience did not at all displease him. He was much taken, and rode by her the rest of the way to Aber, not exerting himself to charm, for be had never found that there was any need, but rather taking pleasure in being charmed.

I let them alone on that journey, and what they said to each other, he questioning and she replying, I never knew, though I am sure it was formal enough and civil enough, the expected exchanges between princely host and respected guest. When we rode into the maenol at Aber it was David who took her waist between his bands and lifted her down, and did it with little haste and much delicate care, I think partly for pure mischief because I was close, and could not choose but see what pleasure it gave him.

Afterwards he came into my little office and flung his arm about my shoulders in his usual impulsive way, and: 'Find me another such phoenix,' he said, 'since it seems you have the happy gift of plucking them out of the snow. For I won't wrong you by taking yours.'

'She is not mine,' I said patiently. 'She is waiting for news of her husband, and the prince has promised all possible efforts to discover whether he lives or not. With half of Rhys's force gathering alive and angry in Carmarthen and Brecon, there's every chance Godred ap Ivor is somewhere there among them, and waiting for news of her as she is for news of him.'

So I said, though it made my throat stiff and sore to utter such things reasonably, as though I hoped for them, and daily it became harder not to wish her landless knight dead and buried.

'Waiting, perhaps,' agreed David, 'but not greatly exerting himself, surely? Look, this lady was not scattered and lost from a confused fight, as the men were, she rode with my sister's party for Brecon, and left it only to ensure her companions should get safely within. She knew of a hut in the forest, where she could take shelter. Do you suppose Gladys did not know the whole of it, where she would be, where to send for her? You were lucky they left you time for that dawn burial, I dare swear they were not far behind you when you left. If this Godred of hers is in any one of the royal castles along Towy, then long before this he knows what befell her, he'll know what they found in the woods, the ashes of your fire, the staff of your torch, the droppings of your horses. He'll know, or as good as know, since she is not in any of the English fortresses, nor in Dynevor or Carreg Cennen –'

'He may be too notoriously of Rhys's party and in Rhys's former counsels to go asking questions in Meredith's castles now,' I said.

'He would not need to. My sister could and should be doing it for him, under safe-conduct. What's to prevent? So since he must know she is not there, what's left but that she rode north with you, willing or unwilling? He could very well have got Gladys, or Rhys if he lives, to send an envoy here to ask for news of her, who would grudge it? No, either this is a very indifferent husband for such a spirited wife,' he said warmly, 'or else he's dead indeed.'

He stirred out of his serious reasoning suddenly, and looked at me along his shoulder with a sharp and challenging smile. 'Have I comforted you?' he said.

Doggedly I answered him: 'I wish her whatever is for her happiness.

Why should I take comfort in any man's death?' But even that was to say too much, for David was very wise in me. Always he knew my mind earlier and better than I knew it myself, except, perhaps, for what I thought and felt concerning him; and even there I would not be certain he was often deceived.

'I know of several reasons,' he said, still smiling. But he did not think it needful to name them. He got up from sitting beside me, leaving a hand upon my shoulder, and its grip was warm and vital, as though some part of his superabundant life flowed through his sinews into mine. 'Take heart!' he said. 'Your Cristin may yet find herself a free woman.'

'She is a free woman now,' I said obstinately. 'And she is *not mine*.'

He was moving towards the door then. He turned with it open in his hand, and the wintry light spilled over him from outside, glittering and chill, turning his smile to a starry brightness, as pure as ice.

'You think not?' he said, and closed the door softly between us.

Nevertheless, as I know, on the eve of Christmas Eve, after the harpers had played us into a daze in hall, and the wine and the wood-smoke had made us slow and heavy with pleasure and sleep, David did make a certain advance to Cristin, I think without expecting more than a refusal. Perhaps even for the strange, sweet sensation of being refused. I saw him draw up a stool at her shoulder at high table, and lean upon the board beside her, speaking long and persuasively into her ear. And I saw her smiling and calm, no way displeased or tempted, replying to him gently without turning her head. He kept up his siege for a long time, and when he left her at last he took up her hand, that lay easy and empty upon the table, and kissed it with his usual considered and winning grace. Then she did look up at him, with that wide and generous glance of hers that went in deep through a man's flesh to his heart and spirit, and serenely she smiled.

When he had left her, I got up from my own place and went and sat beside her, which I felt to be folly but could not forbear. It was growing very smoky and a little drunken below the fire in the great hall, and there was some singing between the offerings of the bards, and some coupling in the dark corners or where the hangings were ample. Cristin looked round at me, and understood my coming very well.

'Do him justice,' she said, low-voiced and wryly smiling, 'he takes no for an answer. Ah, you need not be anxious for me, not with your foster-brother.'

'He is not used,' I said, 'to being refused.'

'The better for the first to refuse him,' she said. 'But you trouble needless. I am not so beautiful that he need strain against his usual habit to win me, and he has no will to pursue those who are unwilling. Why should he, when he has only to lift a finger to draw nine out of ten after him?'

So much she had learned of him in hardly more than a day, and yet she was the tenth, no, the thousandth, woman, and he moved her only to an open and uncritical liking. But of his complacency I was less sure than she.

154

'You need not trouble about Prince David,' she said, 'while he has his hands full with work that stretches him mind and body, fighting or ruling or hunting or what you will. But when he has not enough work he will turn to playing. And his games could be dangerous. Oh, not to women! The only grief he will ever cause to women is the grief of losing him. But to you, to his brother, to all those nearest and dearest to him, he could do great damage. And to himself. To himself most of all.'

The women were leaving the high table then, and she also rose to go to her bed. I went with her down through the hall, and out into the frosty courtyard, for her lodging, like mine but in another direction, lay in the sheltered dwellings along the curtain wall. It was the eve of the eve of Christmas, as I have said, and sharply cold, and those who left the warmth of the hall to seek their rest crossed the rimy spaces quickly, huddled in their cloaks. But we two slowed and went side by side out into the centre of the courtyard before separating, as though we had both more to say before we could part, and found no right words. There was bright moonlight once we were out of the shadow of the hall, that silvered her from head to foot, like a virgin saint on an altar.

I said, not subtly, for I was in torment: 'And did you truly feel no desire to go with him, as he wished? For all that beauty and vigour and grace of his, no desire at all?'

She halted, and stood still before me, within reach of my hand if I had but stretched it out from my side. With her great eyes dark and clear upon my face she said: 'None.'

'God knows,' I said, 'you need hardly wonder or blush if you had. When he wills, there are few can resist him.'

'You forget,' she said, 'that I am already bespoken.'

'Your heart also?' I asked her, low and hoarsely.

'My heart first, most, and for ever,' she said. And all the while she gazed unwaveringly at me with that mute face and those searching eyes. So then I had my answer.

I lowered my eyes from her, her brightness and stillness gave such pain. I said my goodnight, softly and faithfully, for she did me no wrong, and even to have known and served her was great joy. And I went away from her to my own small chamber, there to pray for continued grace to serve her still as best I might, and to wait with patience and resignation for news of the man who had her heart. For still, if he was dead, for which I must not hope, some day there might be for me the grace of a nearer service. But when I looked back out of the sheltering shadow under the wall she was still standing where I had left her, and looking after me, and only slowly, now that I had vanished, did she also turn away to her own place.

So we kept our Christmas feast with great reverence and gratitude for victories won, hearing service daily in the royal chapel of the llys, and at night we drank deep and heard noble singing to the honour and praise of Llewelyn and David and their allies. And on the last day of the old year came a rider from Meredith ap Rhys Gryg, bringing word that Rhys Fychan was known to be alive and well, and reunited with his wife. The messenger brought also a list of those of his chief tenants, officers and knights to be with him under English protection. But the name of Godred ap Ivor was not among them. Of him nothing was known.

So the hope I would not recognise, since it was the death of her hope, thrust up its head again as often as I ground it underfoot, and grew like a weed.

CHAPTER X

We marched again, one week into the new year of twelve hundred and fifty-seven, and I left her behind at Aber with Goronwy's wife. I say 'I left her' as though she had given me some right to hold myself responsible for her safety and well-being, but indeed she was her own mistress, and I had no more rights in her than any other among us. The only thing I had that was mine alone concerning her was the memory of the journey north together. Not even she could have taken that from me, even had she wished. But she was always my sweet friend, and cherished, I think, those same memories for kindness' sake, if she had no love left to give. So it was well for me, however deep the hurt, that I should leave her for a while.

We mustered at Bala, for this time Llewelyn was bent on settling accounts with Griffith ap Gwenwynwyn of Powys, who in every dissension was unswervingly on the side of England. After the winning of the two Maelors from that other Griffith, Madoc's son, at the beginning of our winter campaign, those mishandled neighbouring lands of Powys Gwenwynwyn stuck sharply into our eastern flank, at once a knife ready to disembowel us and a barrier against our free movement southwards. Moreover, this was the most obstinate and renegade of all our chieftains, a Welsh hater of the Welsh, and his example was a danger to Llewelyn's cause as long as he remained immune.

We struck, therefore, by way of the Tanat valley to the Severn, that great river, and then swept southward, upstream, along the valleys of Severn and Vrnwy both, seizing and settling as we came, until late in the month we reached Griffith's town and castle of Pool. The castle lay between town and river. and escape over the water into England was never difficult for him and his family. We burned the town, but by the time we fought our way into the bailey Griffith was away with his wife and children to the protection of the lady's father, John Lestrange, and appealing also for help to John FitzAlan, who was lord of lands at Clun, and held Montgomery for the king. Though it did him little good, for we pushed on still to the south on our own side the water, and though we did not take the castle of Montgomery itself, for it stands upon a great rock on the English side, in so strong a position that men might waste hours scaling the mound, and attack with mangons and trebuchets is impossible, there being no comparable height convenient to mount them, yet we did sack and lay waste the town below, for a memorial to our visit. All that Lestrange and FitzAlan and Griffith could do between them was to hold the castle itself, for the force they sent out against us we shattered in the fields between Severn and Berriew, and sent them scurrying back up the hill to the shelter of their stone walls.

After this Llewelyn thought it high time to be seen and felt in the south again, for he well knew it would be harder for a prince of Gwynedd to hold together that fragmented region, so strong in marcher castles and so parcelled out among many sons, than to keep a firm hand upon the north, where the sun of his countenance and the shadow of his justice were always close at hand. Before the English had recovered from the shock of Montgomery we were joining forces with Meredith ap Rhys Gryg in Cantref Bychan, and sweeping on towards the sea between Towy and Tawe. Before the end of February we were in Gower, where many of the Welsh tenants of the de Breos lands rose to join us in great joy, and we not only ate away the borders of this Norman barony, but did as much for the power of the king's seneschal in that region, Patrick of Chaworth, the lord of Kidwelly. Not for many years had those two great men been penned within their own fortresses, as they were then, or seen so many of their possessions lopped like branches from the trunk, and been powerless to prevent.

In the month of March we had proof positive of the alarm we had caused in King Henry's court, for a letter came from the king's brother, Earl Richard of Cornwall, requesting Llewelyn to receive a deputation of Dominican friars who would present to him the earl's protestations and proposals for an end to this warfare, and offering him a safe-conduct to meet with them.

'I see,' said Llewelyn, amused but thoughtful, 'that Henry thinks his brother's influence may carry more weight than his own, now Richard has one foot on the steps of the imperial throne.' For this Earl Richard, whose general good sense and steadiness were by no means to be despised even for themselves, was come into a greater title this year, having been elected king of the Romans – that is to say in plainer terms, king of Germany – and emperor-elect, though for all I could see, very little practical gain ever came of it.

'Will you go?' asked David doubtfully. 'Better Richard's good faith than Henry's, I grant you, but I would not stake my life on either.'

But Llewelyn said without hesitation that he would go, and replied courteously to the invitation, accepting the place appointed, and the date. 'For if they are come to the point of being willing to talk,' said he, 'there's a chance at least, if no more, that we may secure everything we have gained. If they'll offer peace on present terms, so much the better. Even a truce would give us time to consolidate.'

David was in some doubt still, for he felt we had not yet gone far enough, and that we should gain more by continuing this impetuous invasion than by halting to strengthen our hold on what we already had. Nevertheless, Llewelyn went to the meeting, for I rode to the earl of Gloucester's castle of Chepstow in his train, as his clerk and secretary, while David, with Meredith ap Rhys Gryg, maintained our proper presence in arms in Gower.

Now on this ride we passed through the whole wide land of Glamorgan, and used our eyes along the way, too, to good effect later in the year. For nothing well learned is ever wasted. But very little else came of the meeting, if nothing was lost.

Earl Richard had sent a long and reasoned letter, very persuasively worded, but its effect was but to appeal to Llewelyn, in the name of the treaty of Woodstock and of right relations between our two countries, to restore the four cantrefs of the Middle Country to Prince Edward's control. And though it was suggested that such a conciliatory move would produce a worthy return, nothing was precisely stated of its substance. Nor did it seem that the Dominican brothers who came as envoys had any authority to bargain beyond what Earl Richard had set out in his own hand, which did not carry us far.

Llewelyn sent by them a long and courtly reply, which we took pleasure in composing, rejecting the argument that he was acting against the interests of his fellow- princes in Wales, for on the contrary, what he had done and was doing had the backing of all of them, with a very few exceptions, and represented the true will of the Welsh people. He said he could not surrender any part of his conquests, for all were Welsh land, though he was prepared to agree that the commotes of Creuddyn and Prestatyn should remain as yet under English control. Which was a mild irony that may have tasted sour to the court, for though these commotes were indeed theoretically dominated by the castles of Diserth and Degannwy, still garrisoned by the English, the garrisons hardly dared put their heads out of door now that they were isolated among free and vengeful Welshmen. And to sum up, Llewelyn would be very willing to discuss a permanent peace on the basis of his present position, but short of that would agree only to a long truce on the same basis. For neither of these courses, it seemed, were the English yet ready. So nothing more came of this visit, and we returned to rejoin David at Carreg Cennen, and went home to Gwynedd for the Easter feast.

There were daffodils in the grass when we came home to Bala, and by the lake the catkins danced in the hazel bushes, for it was a most lovely spring, the renewal of all life. And Cristin was there, for she had ridden down from Aber with Goronwy's wife and children to meet us, and the llys was prepared for the festival with young branches and green reeds and the yellow and blue field flowers, kingcup and violet, and the chapel decked with fresh embroideries.

I had thought on the way, those last miles, that I would avoid her company, for the sweet of that season was so sharp that I could not well bear it. But she was coming down the meadows as we rode in at the gate, with her skirts kilted out of the dewy grass, and her hair down in two loose braids over her shoulders, and her stride was long and lithe, like a boy's, and in her arms, very lightly and easily balanced against her shoulder, she had a new, speckled lamb, still damp and curly from its dam, one of the laggard comers of that spring. One of Tudor's little boys, the youngest, ran and dawdled and ran again behind her, with a wand of willow tufted with yellow catkins in his hand.

Thus at every return she came back into my life, and I was stricken afresh with that extreme quality she had, whether it should be called beauty or by some other name, so that the breath stopped in my throat for pure wonder. So lovely did she seem to me that I knew at last how my mother had appeared to dead Meilyr, and his image rose within me and filled me with that same unendurable pain he had suffered, the chiefest sorrow of the human heart, to love and not be loved in return, to love and know oneself unloved.

I understood then those things he had known, how the sweet and bitter of the beloved's presence are so finely balanced one against the other that the lover can neither live with his darling nor without her, and is forever torn in two by the impossibility of decision, going back again and again to suffer the same anguish, again and again withdrawing only to find the void outside the range of her looks and words a living death. So Meilyr had his full revenge on me at last.

'Bala has a new shepherdess,' said Llewelyn with admiration, reining in beside her. She greeted him only with an inclination of her head, to avoid shifting the weight of the lamb, and said simply: 'The ewe has a second one still coming. Morgan will bring her down with the twin when she's safe delivered. There are hawks hovering. I thought well to get this one into the fold and leave him free. She was very late, he had some trouble with her.'

'You have unexpected skills,' he said, smiling.

'I learned more than needlework,' said Cristin composedly, 'in my father's house. We had sheep, too.' Her eyes were fixed and urgent upon his face, but she would not ask. 'I give you joy, my lord,' she said earnestly, 'of your triumphs won, and wish you all the blessings of this feast.'

'I would I could have brought you joy,' said Llewelyn. 'But of your husband there is still nothing known. I am sorry!'

I saw for a moment that sharp whiteness and tightness of fear in her face until he spoke, and then the softening that was rather of resignation than relief or despair. 'I am grateful for your care of me,' she said steadily. 'I can wait.' And she turned her head a little, and looked at me.

So it was always. Her love I could not have, but her dear trust and companionship I could not forswear, for that would have been a great and undeserved injury to her. And in those bright spring days I learned to keep fast hold of the hope I still had in her friendship, to savour the joy it was to be with her, and to contain the sorrow. For there was promise in her words, and I could wait, too, half a lifetime if need be, to have her mine at last. If she preferred my company, if she confided in me, if she put her trust in me, surely that was immeasurable blessing, even if in the end I gained no more.

Thus I did not avoid her, but made myself ever ready and willing when she sought me out, as often she did. And if there was great pain, there was great bliss, too, such bliss as Meilyr never had from my mother. And we came by a way of living side by side that was gentle and cordial and close, working together in accord, speaking freely of all the daily affairs of the court, but never now of Godred or of ourselves, while we loved and waited, she for him, and I for her.

There was little real fighting in the north that summer, only a reordering of the establishment of those parts of Powys we had taken from Griffith ap Gwenwynwyn, and once in May, to trim straight a position that somewhat irked our forward movement, the taking of one more of his castles, at Bodyddon, which we stormed and razed, not caring to garrison it ourselves, for once emptied of his power it was of no significance to us.

It was elsewhere that the great things were happening, and so suddenly that Llewelyn had no warning, and no time to be upon the scene himself, for the best was over before we even had word of any action in the south.

It was in the evening of the fifth day of June that a courier rode into the llys at Bala, where we still made our headquarters at this time, and made himself known for one of the officers of the war-band of Meredith ap Owen, Llewelyn's ally in Builth and Cardigan. We knew the man, Cadwgan by name, for he had fought with us at Llanbadarn in the autumn, and he was a strong, seasoned man in his fifties, who had served his lord's father before him. He would neither eat nor drink until he had told his tale, though he had ridden since morning without rest or food. We brought him in to Llewelyn in the high chamber, where he was in council with Goronwy and Tudor, and David came running after the rumour of news as eagerly as a boy.

'My lord,' said Cadwgan, when he had bent the knee to Llewelyn and kissed his hand, and hardly waiting to rise again before he began, 'we have won you and Wales a great victory, and dealt King Henry a formidable blow. Three days since, on the Towy, we routed the king's officer and a great host, pricked off their baggage horses, looted their stores, and smashed their army to pieces. What's left has made its way back into Carmarthen, but it's no more than a remnant.'

'They came out after you?' cried Llewelyn, taking fire from this jubilant outcry. 'What possessed them, out of the blue, without fresh offence? I looked for Henry to call out the host against us this year, but here in the north, not on the Towy. Nor has he sent out any such summons, we should have heard of it long before.' Which was true, for his intelligence by now was efficient and swift, and the feudal host ground out to its muster commonly with a month's warning and often more.

'No, my lord, this was a great force, but made up from the garrisons of many castles and from the marcher lordships, and great gain that will be to us, God willing, for this defeat leaves many a good fortress but wretchedly manned, and ripe for taking. But hear me how this fit began, for it concerns your own kinsfolk, and it ends not at all as it began, but with some strange reversals. It's for your lordship to determine how best to use it to your gain.'

Always the first to leap to a hazard, David cried: 'Rhys! I see the hand of Rhys Fychan again in this coil. Who else could have set them on?'

'Hear me the whole story,' said Cadwgan, flushed and grinning, 'and judge. We got word only two days before the end of May that there was great activity about the castle of Carmarthen, and levies coming in from many parts there, so we made our own preparations. My lord, with Meredith ap Rhys Gryg, made all fast at Dynevor, and also placed all their host, a great number, about all the hills around, overlooking the river valley, with all the archers we could muster. But we did not know until they moved that Rhys Fychan was with them, with his own forces, nursed all this while under English protection. We have the truth of it now, past doubt, your lordship will see why. Rhys had talked the king's seneschals in the south into taking up his cause and setting out to restore him to his own. They put their heart into it, too, it was a great host that came along the valley to Dynevor the last day of May, with the king's own officer leading them. Stephen of Bauzan.'

'I know him,' said David. 'The king sets great store by him. He was his governor in Gascony aforetime.'

'He'll be less in the royal favour now,' said Cadwgan heartily, 'for he's lost King Henry a mort of men and great store in horses and goods. They came and took station around Dynevor to storm it, and we let them spread out about the valley meadows that evening as widely as they would, for well it suited us they should feel sure of their ground. We were sure as death of ours. The castle was held well enough to sit out the storm, and we others, the most of us, were all round them in the hills, and had had time enough to choose our cover and our field for shooting. We let them stir in their camps in the dawn of the first of June, and then we opened on them at will with arrows and darts, wherever a man came within range. And from all sides. They could not attack one way without exposing themselves on either flank, and all that day they spent trying to assemble into better positions, and to bring up their engines to break into Dynevor. We knew by then that there were Welsh with them, and they could only be Rhys's men. So then we knew what was afoot.'

'If they set out in such numbers, and so equipped,' said Llewelyn, concerned, 'it could still have been a grim business.'

'So it could, my lord, and we were taking it grimly, I warrant you. Not a man of us thought we should break them as we did, but we trusted stoutly enough we should keep them out and cost them dear. But hear what happened! At earliest dawn on the second day of June our lookouts suddenly cried a marvel, and we looked, and saw a small body of horsemen, who had gathered apart in cover of trees, ride out full gallop straight for the castle gateway, the foremost of them carrying a white surcoat threaded on the point of a lance. And it was Rhys and his Welsh knights, crying to the castellan to open quickly, and let them in, for they were sickened of their servility, and begged to be of our part, free Welshmen like us.'

David uttered a shout then that was half excitement and half derisive laughter. 'And he did it? He opened the gates to such a bare-faced trick? How far were the English behind?'

'My lord, I well understand you,' owned Cadwgan warmly, 'and I would not for my life have been in the castellan's shoes, for he had but a matter of minutes to make up his mind. You say right, the English had the measure of what was happening by then, and they came like devils after. But it was they who turned the trick, for by the very look of them Rhys would not have lived long could they have got their hands on him, and he had good need to batter at the gates and cry to have them opened. It was that, and knowing Rhys well by sight, and some of those with him, too. Whatever settled his mind for him, he opened the gates and they

162

came tumbling and hurtling in and he got the gates to again in time, and loosed every archer he had until the English drew off. But the cream of the jest – and it was a good jest! – is that they had come out only to put Rhys back into Dynevor, and back in Dynevor he was, and the gates made fast behind him, so what were they doing there in the valley, on a fool's errand, and getting picked off by our bowmen as often as they stirred out of cover? I swear to God, if they had taken it the opposite way, and attacked then in a fury, we might have been hard pressed. But the ground had been cut from under them, and they let themselves be confounded. They began a retreat. And that was all we needed. All along the valley they drew off to Carmarthen again, and all along the hills on either side we went with them. First we cut off the heavier and slower, the baggage and the engines, the sumpter horses, and any stragglers who tired. And about noon, at Cymerau, where the Cothi comes down and empties into the Towy, we thought it time to make an end, for fear too many should get back to Carmarthen alive. We were either side of them, and our horsemen had followed lightly along, and were fresh, with the slope in their favour. We made our attack there. It was a slaughter.'

'How many,' asked Llewelyn, glowing, 'got safe away?'

'My lord, if you mean in order, as a body of fighting men, none. As headlong fugitives, running every man for his own life, perhaps one in five who set out from Carmarthen won back to it alive.'

'And de Bauzan?'

'We rode him down. I saw him unhorsed, I thought him wounded, and sorely. They got him away with them. It was the one ordered thing they did. But alive or dead, that we cannot know. They left arms and harness littering the fields. We made a great harvest.'

It was indeed a victory. My eyes were on David's face, and it was torn between delight and outrage, all his bones starting in golden tension, for the summer had gilded him over like precious metal. His eyes, blue and light and stony with rage, grieved helplessly that he had not been there at Cymerau, and I think in some sort blamed all of us for his loss. And I thought then that what Cristin had said of him was wise and true, that unless he was spent recklessly and constantly in action and passion he would turn that same wealth to bitter mischief, to his own hurt most of all.

Llewelyn was other. He could take pleasure in another man's prowess, and never grudge that it was not his own, nor value it the less in the common cause because its credit shone on other men's arms. He sat with his chin on his fists and his eyes wide and thoughtful, and asked questions very much to the point.

'And your losses? Our losses?'

'My lord, a nothing! We were never exposed but in the last onslaught, and then we had the advantage. I count but eleven men dead, no more than twenty-five wounded.'

'Good! And this force was drawn from the castle garrisons in those parts? How far afield?'

'As far as the coast, my lord. There were men there from Laugharne and Llanstephan. What remains of their force is in Carmarthen, and that they did not leave too ill-provided. Being so near us.'

'But the others! Meredith is following up his victory?'

Cadwgan laughed gleefully. 'My lord, by now I think we should hold Llanstephan at least, and some of the others will not be far behind. But Carmarthen we've let alone.'

'It was well done,' said Llewelyn, and thought for a moment in silence. 'And Rhys Fychan and his knights?'

'They sat comfortably in Dynevor,' said David bitterly and scornfully, 'and had no fighting to do. And you, brother, are expected to extend your clemency to this so sudden change of heart.' His voice was like an edge of steel, but more with his own deprived discontent than with any true hatred of Rhys or his sister. He could not endure that there should have been so glorious a turmoil, and he not in the centre of it. I could see with his eyes at that moment, and see the whole of our careful month's work, stiffening the bones of what we had won, drained of any worth or satisfaction for him.

Llewelyn said mildly: 'I asked a question of Cadwgan, lad, not of you,' and looked at the messenger.

'We also have been in great doubt,' said Cadwgan honestly. 'But one thing is certain. This rout would never have taken place but for what Rhys Fychan did. For it wholly overturned the minds of the English, and caused them to act like men defeated before defeat. And that I hold in credit. But what we should think of him, I vow to God, we cannot agree. And we would fain have you come and judge. But as for the present, he and his knights are honourably lodged in Dynevor, and have not been used against the English. Nor,' he said frankly, 'let out of the gates or out of sight.'

'Wisely!' said David. But Llewelyn took no heed of him.

'Nor disarmed? Nor in any way confined, apart from being kept within the gates? And my sister has not been sent for, wherever she may be?'

'Not yet, my lord.'

'That was also wise,' he said with a wry smile. 'We can ill afford to embrace false allies, but still less to discard true ones.'

'True?' cried David, smarting. 'Need you debate concerning Rhys, after all that has passed? There is not a grain of truth in him!'

'There is not a man on earth,' said Llewelyn sharply, 'of whom I would say such a thing. If we are never to write a quittance for things past, which of us will be out of prison?'

He spoke still frowning over his own thoughts, and never so much as glanced at David, and I knew he meant no reference at all to what he had endured and forgiven from his brother. It was David's own heart that wrung the too apt sense out of the prince's words, and cast the hot colour suddenly upward from chin to brow in a burning tide. He was silenced. But Llewelyn was not looking, and noticed no change in him.

'Say to your lord,' said Llewelyn, when he had made up his mind, 'and to Meredith ap Rhys Gryg also, that they should continue to hold Rhys Fychan and his men in honourable liberty within Dynevor, but allow them as yet no part in their campaign. He will know very well he is on probation, you may discover much by his bearing in the meantime. Before midsummer day I'll be with you. Until then he is, let us say, neither ally nor prisoner, but a guest, he and all his. So deal with him. Now take rest and refreshment, and I will write to Meredith.'

Then Cadwgan went away, content, to eat his fill, Goronwy taking charge of him, and Llewelyn sat down with me to write his letters to both Merediths, for he was always aware of the need not to set one before the other of those two kinsmen and neighbours, though indeed they worked in harness singularly well, as Cymerau was the proof. But David lingered, very pale now with intent, and very grave, and came and sat down fronting his brother across the table.

'Hear me a word,' he said. 'In season, this time! I know all too well I often speak out of season. I felt, as I deserved, that sting you gave me, minutes ago. Who am I to deny any man a right to grace?'

'Sting?' said Llewelyn, astonished and gaping at him, half his mind still preoccupied. 'What sting? I know of none. And surely I intended none!'

'You sting best,' said David with a rueful smile, 'in innocence, and in your innocence I do willingly believe. But what you said concerning man's need of forgetfulness and forgiveness both, whether it touched Rhys Fychan or not, touched me shrewdly. I have taken much for granted these past months, God and you did well to remind me.'

Understanding dawning on him then, Llewelyn said in indignant amazement: 'I meant no such nonsense! What devil possessed you to take me so amiss?' And he reached across the table, and cupped a hand round the nape of his brother's neck, and shook him heartily, until the black hair fell down over David's eyes, and though reluctantly, he could not help laughing.

'Fool!' said Llewelyn, releasing him. 'I have *your* past deeds in very good remembrance – seven months of hard campaigning, and never a sour word. You have earned the same right as any other to speak your mind in my counsels, and argue against me wherever you think I am going astray.'

'And so I will,' said David, pushing back his disordered hair from a face wiped clean of laughter, 'though forgetting nothing now. I tell you that you go astray, or may do so, in forgiving too easily, and settling accounts too cheaply. Think about it! I say no more.'

He rose, and turned abruptly towards the door, but there as suddenly he halted and looked back. 'Yes, one more thing, the gravest. I pray you believe and remember that in saying this I do not speak only of Rhys Fychan.'

Then he went quickly away, and left us to our letters.

One week more we spent in making secure those lands in Powys, and then left Goronwy to continue and complete that necessary work, while Llewelyn and David took the greater half of the army south through Builth to Dynevor as he had promised. But before we left we had already received a message from the horse-doctor in Chester, no way surprising in its tidings, but useful in its detail. King Henry, shocked out of his querulous attitude of protest and disbelief by Cymerau – for there had been no such disastrous blow to royal power in South Wales in his lifetime – had sent out his writ to call out the feudal host for a campaign in full array against us. The muster was set for the first day of August, and the meeting-place was Chester.

'There's no justice in the man,' said Llewelyn, reading. 'It seems he's giving me the credit for what the two Merediths have done against him, for it's still at me he aims. They'll be complaining of that, small blame to them.'

In the event, as we learned later, King Henry himself, while knowing well enough by this time who was the head and spirit of Welsh rebellion against him, was torn two ways as to how he might make the best use of his projected muster, and later amended his writ to divert a minor portion of his knight force to the south, though their enterprise there never came to anything.

'We have time,' said Llewelyn, 'to get through a deal of work before the beginning of August.' For he was certain that this time the king would contrive, whether on borrowed money or his own, to mount the great assault he planned, the Welsh situation being now even more desperate for him than in the previous autumn. And even if there were great difficulties surrounding and hampering him, we dared not take the threat lightly. Therefore the prince sat down with Goronwy and his council, before riding south, and worked out most thorough plans for placing Gwynedd in a state of readiness for siege. Our common defence of goods, gear, stock and people was to remove all into the mountains, an operation to which our folk were accustomed, and which could be accomplished in very short order. Other measures were considered this time to frustrate all movement on the enemy's part. Bridges could be broken, tracks and meadows ploughed up, mills and such establishments destroyed, even fords turned into death-traps by excavating great pits in the hitherto safe shallows, which the water would conceal. All these things were planned in detail, together with instructions to those men of the neighbouring trefs who would carry out their execution, but nothing was to be done until shortly before the day fixed for the muster. Events sometimes change even the plans of kings, and we wanted no wasted destruction. Indeed, Llewelyn had encouraged in Wales, after his grandfather's example, the new centralised institutions which must perforce be borrowed from the English in order to resist the English, the use of money and trade, the exaction of feudal dues in return for land, even the founding of a few towns and the award of charters and markets, so that we had more to leave than aforetime in these withdrawals into the hills. But still we could do it at need, and as quickly as before.

Then, having confided this system of defence to Goronwy, and left him to send out the necessary orders in our absence, we rode for Dynevor.

Meredith ap Rhys Gryg came out to meet us as soon as we were heralded, and was close at Llewelyn's side, and voluble, all the last mile of the way. It was no marvel that he was anxious to get in his word first with his overlord, for he was the uncle and rival of Rhys Fychan, and all those good lands in the vale of Towy had been bandied about between those two with equal violence and injustice, each when in power depriving the other, though for Rhys Fychan it had to be said that his uncle had been the first to do unjustly, and for Meredith that he had never yet gone over to the English against his own people.

So Llewelyn was faced with no easy judgment here when he sat in council in the great hall of Dynevor that evening of our coming, with all his allies of the region about him, and their stewards and officers and clerks at their backs to speak in their support. Already there was none in the whole of Wales who disputed his supremacy, but there never was Welshman yet who was not prepared to argue his case endlessly even in the teeth of his lord, and I knew we should have a long and contentious session. Next to David at Llewelyn's right hand sat Meredith ap Owen of Builth and Cardigan, and he was both strong in his prestige from Cymerau, equal to that of Meredith ap Rhys Gryg, and free of those motives of personal greed and personal venom that were likely to unbalance his namesake's opinions. On this able, faithful and incorruptible man Llewelyn greatly relied.

It was, I think, his uncle's doing, since this castle was now in his possession which had been by inheritance the nephew's, that Rhys Fychan was brought into the hall only when the whole council was assembled, as though he had been a prisoner coming in to be judged, which by his bearing he surely felt to be true. Though Llewelyn greeted and seated him courteously, there was no help for it, he knew the business before us set his liberty and possessions at risk, as well as his honour, and it was a very pale, defensive and erect Rhys Fychan who sat down in our circle to weather the storm.

It was the first time I had ever set eyes on the Lady Gladys's husband, and I studied him with much interest while the castellan, who had taken the responsibility of admitting him with his following, set forth the bare facts of his coming. Rhys was some three years older than my lord, which made him at that time thirty-one years of age. He was medium tall, and of a good, upright carriage, his hair and his short beard of a light brown, and his features fair for a Welshman, and well-formed. He looked both proudly and fearfully, which was no marvel in his situation, and the set of his mouth I judged to be at once resolute and resigned, as though, no matter what we made of it, he had taken the step on which he had determined, and was prepared to abide the consequences. He did not therefore have to accept them with any pleasure! And I take it as no reproach to him that he was afraid, and as credit that he gave no expression of his fear. I saw how David watched him, with drawn brows and jutting underlip, and I think his interest was engaged by Rhys's bearing as was mine, and his mind, however doubtful, was open.

When the castellan had ended his brief recital, Llewelyn asked him of himself: 'And you . . . I judge what your opinion was from what you did, for indeed there was heavy responsibility upon you, and yet you did open the gates. Tell me, were you formerly in the service of the Lord Rhys, when he held Dynevor?'

'No, my lord,' said the knight simply. 'I am from Dryslwyn, I came here as the Lord Meredith's man, and his man I have been all my days.'

'Then you took this risk upon the evidence of your own eyes and senses, without prejudice or favour. That I find impressive.'

'My lord, it was plain to me they were in fear, and the English who came after them were in great fury. There was no doubt in my mind the Lord Rhys did what he did without their knowledge and against their interest. I could not let Welshmen be cut down under my walls and never raise a finger to help them.'

'My lord,' said Meredith ap Rhys Gryg roundly, 'there's no dispute over letting them in, and we can take it as true, as my man swears, that this was no plan to bring in his English masters with him. I can think of other motives no more noble, and no better calculated to make us accept him back into our ranks. And the simplest is that he changed his coat because he saw the old looking somewhat threadbare. He was not the only one taken aback by the reception we gave them. De Bauzan liked it no better, but he could hardly run for the gates and demand to be taken in. No, there's no mystery here. Rhys found himself of the losing party, and had no appetite for our archery. He made a leap for safety and the winning side. It's a landmark, I promise you. We've reached the point of being successful enough to draw in the waverers. You'll find he'll not be the last. The fealties that swung slavishly over into King Henry's purse when we were down, will be swinging back, mark me, now we're up again with a vengeance.'

I confess there was something in this, as we found thereafter, not to our surprise. Yet to come back to one's allegiance cautiously, after due approaches and guarantees given, is one thing, and to tear oneself out of the ranks in the field and make that exchange without guarantees of any kind is quite another. And Rhys was not such a fool as to suppose that he would be welcomed with open arms. I expected the prince to ask him at once to speak as to his own motives and in his own defence, but he thought it better to let those who carried grievances and had doubts speak them out now and get relief, before he brought the matter to the issue.

So he called on one and another, and brought them gradually to the point of declaring whether Rhys should be fully accepted into the confederacy or not, though not in such positive terms that they could not veer later if they so wished. And some said one way, and some the other, Meredith ap Rhys Gryg the loudest in opposition. It was not all a matter of the castles he would be required to restore, but also of the long enmity between them, and doubtless some genuine mistrust.

'All we have risked our lives and fortunes,' he said, 'to bring Wales into this ascendant, while he has pledged and maintained his allegiance to England all these years. And are we now to take him into favour, and restore him all that was his? At a gesture, at the first word of repentance, without one act to give it substance? I say no! We cannot throw him back to the English, but we need not therefore embrace him as a brother. What has he done to deserve it?'

Llewelyn looked then at Rhys, who had sat with a face of ice to listen to this, and asked him equably:

'What have you to say in answer?'

168

Rhys opened his lips as though they were indeed stiff and cold, and said: 'That what my uncle says is just. I pledged fealty to King Henry eleven years ago, when I saw no security and no hope anywhere else. If that was a craven act, then we were many craven souls in those days. That I have maintained what I undertook ever since, for that I make no apology. I was taught to abide by my word, and so I have done, until loyalty seemed to me worse than treachery. Now I am doubly a traitor, and not proud of it, and all I want is to change my coat no more. Whether you accept or reject me, I am back among my own. Here I will die.'

Llewelyn looked quickly from him to Meredith ap Owen, that grave, quiet man, and again back to Rhys. 'And in the future,' he said mildly, 'I doubt not you will offer us acts substantial enough, to pay your indemnity?'

'If you accept me,' said Rhys Fychan, 'the event will prove all. All I have to offer is the man I am, and my intent. Take it, or leave it.'

I looked at David then, for this, however effortful, weary and sad, was talking after his own fashion. And I saw that he was moved and hopeful, though he hesitated still.

There passed another such understanding glance between the prince and Meredith ap Owen, and Meredith said, in his great, gentle voice, that was deep as an organ: 'I think I may point to one act already done, which has greatly aided our cause. Rhys has not claimed it, but I make the claim for him, if he is too proud to vaunt his own skills. Ask him, my lord, if he did not make the plan for this great victory we have claimed as ours. Who brought the English to Dynevor in such high hopes, and ensured we should have due warning of their massing at Carmarthen? Who saw them encamped here in the valley at our mercy, and then forsook them and sent them haring back to their castle under our hail of arrows? Ask him, my lord, if we do not owe to him the whole triumph of Cymerau, which we never let him share!'

There was a sharp and wondering silence round the hall at this, while men looked at one another questioning and marvelling, before all eyes turned back to Rhys. And Llewelyn looked at him also, with a veiled smile, and said softly:

'Well? Answer the question! Was this indeed how, and why, you came back to us?'

What colour was left in Rhys's face drained out of it, and left him white as wax. I saw the cold sweat start on his forehead and lip, and for a long moment he struggled with his tongue and his silence, aware that on what he answered depended his whole fate, and feeling in his blood and bones what those about the table wanted from him. For most men see but a little way before their noses. He drew breath very slowly, but his voice was loud and firm as he said: 'No!'

'You have more than that to say,' said Llewelyn when the stone-hard silence grew long. 'Say on!'

'I did not plan this slaughter,' said Rhys, the blood flowing back hot and desperate into his face now that he had cast his die. 'Nor would I, I pray, so use any company that had received me into itself. I asked the English to help me win back what was mine, since I had lost it for their sake. If you think I would so betray any man who put trust in me, then kill me, and be done! Nor did I think Dynevor would escape and triumph, or I would have stood by my own error to the end. No, I believed you were lost, and then I knew you for mine, and I despaired, and willed to be lost with you. My heart sickened, and I could not bear it longer that I was Welsh and traitor. I called up my knights, and we came to die with you. And that is truth, as God sees me! As for your victory, it was yours, none of mine, to my grief. And since I did not wilfully betray my companions,' he said, looking full at Llewelyn, 'as you would have had me do, and since I have given you the wrong but the true answer, do with me whatever you see fit. I have finished!'

He was so blind by the end of this that he could not see that Llewelyn was smiling, that David was glowing like a rose. But there was no silence at all after Rhys made an end, for Llewelyn rose from his place and went round the circle to where Rhys sat, took him by the hands, raised him to his feet, and kissed his cheek. He had to stoop a little, he was the taller.

'You have given me both the true and the right answer,' he said heartily. 'God forbid I should take into my love any man who would sell his friends, however mistakenly cherished, into so fatal a trap. I would you had come to us earlier and more happily, but with all my heart I welcome you, and call you my brother.'

Then David uttered a muted shout of surrender and acclaim, and bounded up from his place to embrace his sister's husband in his turn, and give him the kiss of kinship. And after him, though more soberly still with right goodwill, Meredith ap Owen, for he, too, was of the royal blood of Deheubarth, his father Owen being a first cousin of Rhys's father.

Rhys Fychan himself, thus passed from hand to hand in welcome where he had looked only for rejection and ignominy at the worst, and at the best a long and hard probation, was so stunned and at such a loss that I think he hardly knew what was happening to him, or what the gathering murmur of approbation meant. For though some, no doubt, had reservations, and a few, had they not known themselves so greatly outnumbered, would have refused him countenance, yet when Llewelyn asked if any man had matter to urge against, no voice was raised.

'Never hold it against us,' said Llewelyn then, smiling, 'that we tempted you so grossly, since the issue has shown you are not to be tempted. And now sit down with us in full council, and no more glancing behind, for there are matters arising out of this return which should be settled among us at once.'

But before he would do so, Rhys went on his knees before the prince, and lifted his joined hands, offering homage and fealty after the English fashion, as he had formerly pledged them to King Henry, in token of the severance of all those English ties which had bound him so many years. Publicly and voluntarily he did this, for Llewelyn would not then have asked of him any such gesture. And he did it with a burning face but a bright and steady eye. 'And this,' he said, rising, 'shall be my last allegiance, and this I will never take back.'

Then all present accepted his willing act with acclaim, though it may well be that Meredith ap Rhys Gryg found his assent sour-tasting in his mouth, for he stood to lose by his nephew's gain. And of this Llewelyn needed no reminder.

'Two matters chiefly remain to be dealt with,' he said, resuming his place and his authority, 'now that the main is settled. For this castle of Dynevor, and Carreg Cennen also, were from his father's death the inheritance of the Lord Rhys, and must return to him now. And I have ever in mind the great services of the Lord Meredith ap Rhys Gryg, which must not be slighted. Yet I think there was a time when both lived here, and for both there was room in the two cantrefs, and so there should be again.' Then he went on to show that he knew, by reciting the list of them, how the properties in Ystrad Tywi had been distributed between those two in the days before Rhys expelled his uncle and drove him to take sanctuary in Gwynedd, thus reminding both that if one had grievances from the past, so had the other, and silence and reconciliation might be best.

'It is my hope and counsel,' he said then, 'that you should agree to return to that division, remembering this, that even if you, Meredith, are losing something by Rhys's return, yet you have both not only a common enemy close at hand, but also, together, the means of extending your common estate at the enemy's expense, not at each other's. To cling to a castle and thereby lose an ally with whose help three castles more might be won, is very poor policy. Together you are far stronger and can do far more than the two of you apart could master. And be far more than double the value to the cause of Wales.'

Rhys, who was still dazed and open to emotion with the joy and relief of his reception, offered his hand warmly to his uncle, and promised that for his part he forsook all enmity against him, and begged forgiveness and forgetfulness of his own revenges mercilessly taken when the advantage was with him. And Meredith perforce accepted his hand, though with less enthusiasm, and conceded that the past was past.

'That being so,' said Llewelyn, 'we have here a greater and more effective army by the addition of Rhys and his knights, and an enemy greatly weakened, and fortune waiting only for us to move. You,' he said to the two Merediths, 'have made good use of Cymerau by storming the castles it left empty of men, and it is for you to hold and garrison Laugharne and Llanstephan and Narberth as you see fit. But there's more to be won yet. If they drew on those households, so they will have done on others further afield. What's to prevent us from driving west into Dyfed, and shocking de Valence and Bohun and FitzMartin?'

There was no man there but agreed to that gladly, and as long as he could hold them together with the prospect of action and booty he had them in the hollow of his hand.

'My Lord,' said Rhys Fychan, 'with your leave, we can add to our numbers yet, if two or three days can be spared. There were foot soldiers of mine left to fend for themselves when I was let in here. God he knows they could not be blamed for what I did, but considering what followed, I doubt there were many left by the time they reached Cymerau. They know this country, and by then it was a headlong flight, they could as well slip away into the hills, every man for himself. Give me two days, and I'll get word out to enough of them to reach the rest, and bid them home. If I call, they will come.'

'Well thought of!' said Llewelyn. 'Do so, while we make ready. And one more thing, not the least. Where is my sister? Were you forced to leave her in English care, in Brecon or Carmarthen? It may not be so simple now to get her safely out, but it shall be done.'

'By God's grace,' said Rhys thankfully, 'she is not in any of their castles. Two weeks before we massed at Carmarthen I took her away to a hermitage of women near Hywel, with her maids and the two boys. For she was drawing near her time, and had some women's troubles that frightened her a little, and was not willing to risk bearing her child there in Brecon without me. Thank God the boys would not stay behind, as then I would gladly have had them do. There is a holy woman among the anchoresses at Hywel who is very expert in childbirth, my lady has visited her before, and wanted to be in her care. We can reach them without hindrance, and bring them safe home.'

'Let be until she is delivered,' said Llewelyn, 'if she puts such trust in this holy woman. If need be, we can set a guard about the place, but I think awe of the anchoresses might serve even better to keep her secure until her waiting's over. But then,' he said, 'you have been a long time without news of her, and she of you, that's an ill thing at such a time. Send to her and set her mind at rest, and I hope your own, also.'

And thus it was done. And Rhys Fychan with great joy and fervour went about resuming the control of his own castle, and making lordly provision for his guests.

We reckoned then that we had but three weeks, or four, to spend here in the south, before we must turn homewards to meet King Henry's threatened muster. So after two days we sallied forth again from Dynevor, my lord with his brother, Rhys Fychan and the two Merediths, all at one and in high heart. Rhys's messengers had shaken out the word of restoration and the Welsh alliance through the forests and hills and along the vale of Towy, bidding all who welcomed it pass it on still further, and we had the first-fruits of that sowing already in our ranks when we rode, good lancers and bowmen who had been in hiding since Cymerau, until they should discover which way the wind blew.

We drove west from Cantref Mawr, passing to the north of Carmarthen, and swept into Dyfed, in this summer season a most lovely country, where the clouds ran like new lambs over clean green hills. We ravaged and looted the borders of Cemais, doing great despite to the lands of the lord William de Valence, who was King Henry's half-brother, being one of the sons of the king's mother by her second marriage to the Count of La Marche. This William was lord of Pembroke in right of his wife, and greatly hated in the whole of Dyfed, even by many English barons and marcher lords, so that few tears were shed over what we did to his barns and stock and manors. But our time being limited, we seized a foothold in Cemais by storming the castle of Newport, where Nevern comes down to the sea, and from there made heavy raids southward into Rhos, and came near enough to Haverfordwest to set up a great flutter in Humphrey de Bohun's garrison there. Thus we continued until the first week of July, for the grip of the English marchers was strongest of all in this corner of Wales, and what damage we could do to that stranglehold in so short a time we did. Then we drew off in good order, leaving Newport garrisoned in fair strength, and made our way briskly back to Dynevor.

There was no more bustle than usual about the baileys when we rode in, and we had no warning, except that there was a young woman who came out at the clatter of our arrival to see what was happening, and then clapped her hands and ran into the great hall to carry the news. And we were but dismounting in the inner bailey when another figure appeared in the broad doorway, and came slowly and carefully down the step towards us. She was very richly and gaily dressed, her coiled hair uncovered to the sun, and there was about her an air of joy and solemnity, as though she kept a festival of her own. By the black of that coiled hair, that was almost blue in the sun, like David's, and by the beauty of the face she raised only when she reached the foot of the steps and stood on level ground, I knew her. Those same long lashes and dark eyes she had raised upon King Henry's face, and dazzled him, long ago in the guesthall of Shrewsbury abbey. True, she was not now so slender as then, her body was thickened with maturity, and with the bearing of two children. Of three, rather, for she went with such care upon the steps, and looked up only when she was on level ground, by reason of the infant she carried in her arms. The Lady Gladys had brought her third child home as soon as she was strong enough to bear the journey, impatient for the happy reunion her husband's messengers had promised.

Rhys saw her and gave a cry of triumph and joy, and dropping his rein before the groom could reach him, ran like a deer to embrace his wife and child, which he did, after the impetuosity of his approach, with slow and reverent care. He kissed her above the child's head, tender of its smallness and softness, and then with a timid hand put back the shawl from its face and looked at it in wonder, as though he had not two children already, but this were the first ever to be born, and a miracle.

He looked round then at us, and laid an arm about his wife's shoulders, and brought her to Llewelyn, who stood motionless where Rhys had left him, watching them draw near. At her face he gazed with earnest searching and deep wonder, as Rhys did at the child. He had not seen her for sixteen years, and through most of those years all he had known of her was her implacable enmity towards him. He had everything to learn. Something she had already learned, or so it seemed by her smile, which was faint, mysterious and radiant.

'My lord,' said Rhys, 'I think you have long desired to be better known to your sister, who is my wife. She is here, and hale, and desires as much of you.'

She was the elder by a year, and a woman, and more over, a woman of great assurance, like her mother, yet even she did not know how to begin, for everything that had passed lay between them now, not as a barrier to be stormed, only as a ruinous waste to be clambered over before they could reach each other, and it was hard to find a way through without stumbling. David, who would have clasped and kissed her without a thought, stood back behind my shoulder and let them alone. I felt his hand close upon my arm as he watched them, and I knew that he was smiling. David had many smiles. This one, withdrawn and still, womanishly tender against his will, belonged only to Llewelyn. But it never lasted long.

The child was their salvation. The prince looked down curiously at the tiny head, covered with dark hair, and the crumpled face all new infants wear, and said: 'I am glad to see you so well and happy, and safely delivered. It is another son?'

'It is,' she said.

'And healthy and strong? I grieve that it was I who sent you running from Dynevor with him, when most you needed to be safe at home.'

'He has taken no harm,' she said, 'and neither have I. He is whole and perfect.' And she parted the shawl to show him, and Llewelyn touched the shrunken pink cheek with a large, marvelling finger, and then thrust the same finger delicately into the minute, questing fist that groped in the air. The child's fingers closed on it strongly, and clung. Thus held, he looked at her with innocent pleasure, and asked, as men do over children, valuing symbols: 'What will you call this one?'

'He is already named,' she said. 'And I trust he will grow up as gentle, valiant and magnanimous as his namesake.' She looked up into her brother's face, and said, flushing deeply: 'His name is Llewelyn.'

CHAPTER XI

I came to the Lady Gladys in the evening, when she had withdrawn to the high chamber and left the lords to their wine, and spoke to her of Cristin, for I thought it no blame to Llewelyn if he forgot this one small pledge among all his triumphs and cares of that day. And she was soft and warm and gracious, who had been a proud girl and a prouder woman, for she was much moved by what had passed, and utterly disarmed by all her husband had told her of Llewelyn's dealings with him. She spoke of her brother with wonder and gratitude, and said that she was glad he had by him so loyal and true a friend as I. And she talked of the years of her estrangement as of an ill dream past with the night.

'Had we but met,' she said, 'I could not have held out against him all this time. I must surely have seen him as he is, honest and generous, better than wise. Oh, Samson how strange a childhood we had, that separated us so far and sent us into the world by such different ways. Ways,' she said, 'of which only he chose his own, and against great pressures, as now I see.'

I told her that exactly so he had spoken, grieving that she was his only sister, and he did not even know her. And she smiled, and said: 'That shall be remedied.'

Then I asked her if my lord had thought to question her, or Rhys, as he had not until this visit had opportunity to do, concerning a certain landless knight who had been in Rhys's service at Cwm-du, one Godred ap Ivor. She said that he had not, which was small wonder considering the excitement they had been in, and their total absorption in each other. But even had he so remembered, she said with regret, she could have had nothing to tell him, for though many of Rhys's household army had made their way to one or another of the English-held castles in Ystrad Tywi, and thus the tale of the survivors had gradually been made up, and the warband reformed, yet nothing had been heard again of Godred. True, she said, there were some of the fugitives from Cwm-Du who were thought to have drawn off over the wilds of the Black Mountain, southwards, and placed themselves in the hands of Earl Richard of Gloucester, and possibly some had stayed and entered his service in Glamorgan, but if Godred was among them, that she could not say.

'And surely,' she said, 'if he lived he would have appeared again by now. I knew the young man well, for his wife was one of my women, and dear to me. And to speak truth, I might well say I am glad, if that is not a sin, to think that Godred may be dead, and grateful that I need never meet him face to face and have to answer his questions. For his wife,' she said heavily, 'died in the forest after we fled to Brecon, and I cannot get the load from my heart that her death lies at my door. I should never have let her take so mad a risk for me. It has been heavy on my mind ever since, and will be as long as I live.'

At this I was so stricken with wonder and so moved that I trembled before her and could not speak for a while. For this was one reason I had never thought of, why the lady had not sent after to enquire about Cristin. She had believed from the first that there was no need of questions to which she already knew the answer. Though what had so persuaded and convinced her I was foolish and slow to imagine.

'Madam,' I said, as softly as I might, 'if you can find heart-room for one more joy in this day without surfeiting, I believe I can supply yet one more. With your lord, your possessions, your child all secured, your brother restored, can you yet bear another gift?'

She could not fail to see where I led her, and her dark eyes grew great with incredulous wonder. She said: 'No one ever died of joy. If you mean what you seem to mean, oh, Samson, quickly, tell me so! Is she truly living? Cristin, Llywarch's daughter?'

'Living, and well,' I said, 'and safe under Llewelyn's guardianship in the north. We have been making enquiry after her husband for her sake all this time, but could not reach you in Brecon, to pair our half of the story with yours. And now for my life I do not see how you came to be so sure that Cristin was dead.'

'But they came riding hard after us,' she said, bright and fierce with remembrance, 'through the snow in the early morning. They were gaining on us, we should have been ridden down before ever we could reach the town, and Cristin offered to lead them off by the valley path and leave us free to go forward in safety if the ruse succeeded. She knew of a hut in the woods where she could hide from them and let them by. All this she did for me, and did well. . . .'

'I know it,' I said, 'for I was captain of that company that pursued you, and God knows for no ill purpose.' And I sat down with her and told her all that story, while she sat still and silent, listening. And at the end she said, in a very low voice: 'How strangely we deal with one another! Such horrors as I imagined, and yet they were only ordinary men who rode after, not monsters. If I had known that it was you, I should have been calmed and ready to trust. And yet I had not such trust in *him*. And you know and I know that such things as I imagined have happened, and will happen again, wherever there is warfare. It is not so great a step from man to monster. And what I afterwards believed was not so hard to believe. For you see, she did not come. She said that if the way were clear, and the hunt passed by the hut without pausing, she would return to the upland way and follow us. She knew the country as well as any among us, and she was not afraid to ride alone. But if she had cause to feel it dangerous to come out of hiding, she would bide the night over, if need be, and wait for us to send for her. And in Brecon we waited, but she never came.'

'But in the morning,' I said, 'you did send out for her?'

'We did. And surely you remember what there was for us to find?' She gripped her hands together in her lap and wrung them, remembering, for in grief remembered and changed to rejoicing there is very painful pleasure. 'In the hut, the ashes of a fire, and the trampling of many feet, and

176

blood. But no Cristin. Round the hut the hoof-marks of many horses. And when they hunted further afield round that place, there was the hollow silted with leaves and mould, and in it, covered over with stones, a new grave. . . .'

'You thought it *hers*?' I cried, suddenly pierced through and through with understanding.

'What else could we think? It seemed as clear as day, and as black as night. We thought she had taken shelter there as she intended, only to be discovered by the men she had decoyed away from my trail. Oh, Samson, can you not see how it would have been, if they had been what I supposed? Cheated of their success, with their lord to face after their failure, and this creature in their hands, the girl who had made fools of them and loosed me safe away! We thought they had had their sport with her through the night, and at dawn killed her and buried her. Such things have been and will be again, to all ages. You know it as well as I,' she said.

I owned it, for it was truth. Though by the grace of God there may some day come a time when such things will cease. But in this world? Who knows!

'You did not disturb the grave?' I said. For that also mattered to me.

'We did not. And for two days thereafter there was heavy snow in the hills, and it was a week or more before we could go back there. That time I went with them. The grave had been opened. The stones were laid aside in a cairn, and the hollow was empty. The religious from Talley and Llywel and Llangefelach had been busy collecting and caring for the dead, and this was the work of men of reverence. We did not question any more.'

'He is buried at Talley abbey,' I said, 'Meilyr, my mother's husband. Where I pray he rests in peace, and his soul in bliss, for he had little enough bliss in this world. But Cristin is alive and well in Bala, or perhaps at Aber if Goronwy's family have moved there, and you need not mourn for her any more. If we come safe out of this summer's campaign, and if that is what she wishes, and what you wish, then she shall come back to you.'

And she was so glad, and so moved, that my own resolution to silence was shaken, and I would have told her, I know not how barely and poorly, something of what I felt for Cristin, Llywarch's daughter, as never yet had I told it to anyone, even Llewelyn, who knew the inmost of my heart upon every other matter. But while we were thus rapt into our remembrances and dreams, she most grateful and tender, I most in peril of self-betrayal, Llewelyn came in with his arm about Rhys's shoulders, and after them David with Rhys's second son riding on his back and driving him like a curvetting horse, and Rhys's eldest son, also Rhys, plucking at his brother's ankle and doing his best to bring him down. And there was so much laughter and noise that we were delivered from all solemnity until the children were borne away to bed, very unwillingly. David had always a charm for children, as for their elders. All the more if they were women, but men had no remedy, either.

But afterwards we told this story over again to those three princes. And Llewelyn, counting days, said that we had still time to make some small foray into Glamorgan, not merely to carry the word to any men of Rhys's bodyguard scattered there, that they might return to their allegiance at

Dynevor without fear if they would embrace the Welsh cause with their lord, but also to send a very different message to Earl Richard of Gloucester, who had lived too easy and too undisturbed a life heretofore in his southern lordship. And so it was agreed, though we were drawing near to the middle of July now, and the muster was called for the beginning of August at Chester.

'We made full provision before we came south,' said Llewelyn, unperturbed, 'and Goronwy will have seen all carried forward ready for the day. We have still time for one more fling before we go to stand off King Henry and his host. And though I think it a very slender hope, if by some chance we can recover a lost husband for our shepherdess of Bala, that would be a fitting ending to this campaign, and a goodly gift to take back with us.'

But David was silent, who would commonly have been the first to applaud any such audacity. And his eyes were fixed upon me, as I knew before ever I glanced at him, and they had a chill and rueful blueness, and saw, as always they did, too much, too clearly, and too deep.

Howbeit, we went, leaving Dynevor two days earlier than we should otherwise have done, to the disappointment of the Lady Gladys, who had found great joy in this unlooked-for reunion with her brothers. For there was something in her of David, without his penetration, in that everything she did was done with her might, whether it was loving or hating, and gratitude came as impulsively to her as either of these, so that after his generous and skilful championship of her husband's cause among his peers there was now no one in the world for her like Llewelyn, against whom she had once been implacable.

We went south by Carreg Cennen to Neath, and from there ranged for two days eastward along the fringes of the earl's honour, sacking his manors and levelling his defences, with little resistance. So unprepared for us were they – for I think they had believed us already on our way north again, the king's threat being now so close – that we were able to split our forces into two, and even three, parties, and so range further afield than we could have done with a single army, though not attempting any fortified place while we were so divided. Then we met together again for an attack upon the earl's castle of Llangynwyd, finding it close at hand and in no great state for standing us off, for though well-manned it was in some disrepair.

The garrison put up but a very brief fight. I think a number of them were Welshmen not greatly affected to their lord. Then, when we pressed home our attack, many of them escaped by a postern and fled into the valleys of the small rivers that flanked the castle, where there were woods to give them cover, and so scattered to take refuge in two or three fortified manors belonging to the earl, which could be reached quickly from that place.

Llewelyn was not slow to consider that those who ran might well number among them some of Rhys's men, not yet apprised of the change in their lord's fortunes, and none too happy in the service of the English earl. Therefore he detailed off three small parties of us to beat the woods in the

178

direction of those manors, and take up, if we could, such stragglers as would accept Welsh service in its place, while he and the greater part of our host laid waste the defences of Llangynwyd to make it untenable against us for some time in the future. Of these three parties he gave me one, and we rode due east, down from the highlands where the castle stood, into a river valley well-treed and rich and beautiful. We were but seven men with myself, and we had orders not to adventure against any companies in arms, but to use our Welsh tongues to lure the Welsh, and let the English alone. And so we did, and sent several promising fighting men back to Llangynwyd with tokens from us to ensure them a welcome.

We had reached the limits of our territory, and camped for the night before returning, for the weather was hot and kindly, and we had ample provisions, and good horses if we should need to elude some unexpected attack. Against such possibility we put out two pickets, and took our rest by turns in the grass under the trees. We were not far from one of the small, clear rivers of that country, which covered us by the south approach with a coil of its waters, and at earliest dawn, awaking, I thought with pleasure on that cool stream, and walked down to its banks to bathe. The river-bed being stony and turbulent where the curving channel was worn, I thought there might well be a quiet, spreading pool below, where the ground opened out a little, though still well wooded, and so walked down in that direction, and found it to be as I had supposed. I shed my clothes in the grass among the trees, and was about to cross the open sward to the gently-shelving bank, when I heard a light splash as of a big fish rising, or a diver entering the water, and froze where I was, still within cover. And in a moment I heard someone before me, at no great distance but hidden beyond the silvery alders, begin to sing, by watery snatches as he swam, a light love-song.

A high, pleasant voice it was, and it sang in Welsh. I was in two minds whether to go back and put on my clothes, but here was an evident Welshman, and as evidently alone, for no man sings like that but for his own private pleasure. And if this was one of those scattered souls I was seeking, I could hardly affright him if I came to the bank as I was, or have much to fear in my turn from his nakedness. Then I thought to draw nearer to him, still in cover, for I judged he had entered the water from my side of the river, and somewhere nearby he must have discarded his own clothing. So I went softly between the trees, and found he had left more than shirt and chausses unguarded, for there was a horse grazing on a long halter in the sward, and saddle and leather body-harness and lance propped against the bole of an oak. His sword lay there beside, and a saddle-roll with his cloak strapped to it. This one had not fled from Llangynwyd entirely unprovided!

Coming thus between him and his armaments, I was at advantage over him, and had no need to demonstrate it by any show. I went down through the trees to the bank, which sloped down to a little sickle of gravel.

He was there in midstream, turning and plunging like a gleaming fish, and as I watched he struck out almost silently for the bank opposite, reached two long, muscular arms out of the water, and hauled himself up to turn and sit in the short turf, dangling his feet in the shallows. In the act of turning thus, he saw me and was abruptly still and silent, though for a moment only. It was not surprise or fear, but the wild wariness of woodland animals that gazed across the river at me, measured and weighed me, and was assured of being able to outrun or outwit at need. He laughed and said:

'Goodmorrow to you, Adam! But I had rather it had been Eve who came.' And he drew up one long leg out of the water, and wrapped his arms about his knee and studied me as I was studying him, with his wet hair plastered over his forehead and temples, and the drops running down through the golden-brown curls that matted his chest.

He was younger than I by a few years, and very finely and gracefully made, for a Welshman uncommonly fair. The streaming locks on his brow looked no darker than wheat, even thus full of river water, and when dry showed almost flaxen. He was gilded round the jaw and lips with a short, bright stubble, but clearly he went normally shaven clean like a clerk. Under easy golden brows he gazed at me with round brown eyes, for as yet I had not spoken, and what is there in a naked man to make clear if he is English or Welsh? I had it in my mind that this debonair and gay young man had all those lean, long muscles braced for action, for all his smooth face. But whether he had more reason to fight shy of English or Welsh I could not yet be sure.

'You need not trouble yourself,' I said in his own tongue, and watched his shoulders relax and his smile widen, 'at least I'm no serpent. Your beast and your gear are safe enough for me, but lest you should entertain any thought of meddling with my goods, let me tell you we are seven, and a whistle would fetch the rest running.'

'Also Welsh, like you?' he said.

'Every man.'

He jutted a thoughtful lip at me, and said with certainty: 'But *you* were not at Llangynwyd, that I know!'

'Then your knowledge is at fault, for I was, and so were we all. But of the other party. And be easy, we mean no harm to any man who ran from there, not if he be Welsh. We have a message to you. Where were you meaning to head now? For one of Gloucester's manors?'

He did not answer that at first, but laughed to himself, and slid down into the river again. 'Come in,' he said, making strokes just strong enough to hold him motionless against the current, 'since I take it that's what you came for. There's water enough for two, and on my part no haste.' And he rolled over and plunged out of sight, to reappear on my side of the deeper passage.

So I leaped in and joined him, and we swam a while, and lay in the shallows together after, letting the cool of the flow stream over our shoulders and down our loins. He lowered his head back into it until only the oval of his face broke the surface, and his hair stood wavering out from his temples like yellow weed or pale fern.

'To tell truth,' he said then, 'I was wondering myself what the next move was to be. For I was never much enamoured of Earl Richard's service, and in any manor of his I might find my welcome altogether too warm. For I reckon I was the first out at the postern at Llangynwyd, and with horse and harness that were not mine until yesterday. And though I have a brother who is lord of a manor in Brecknock, I fear I made that sanctuary too hot to hold me some years ago, his wife being young and pretty. And I can hardly go back to my old service at Dynevor, since Rhys Fychan was thrown out of it, for his uncle Meredith is no friend of mine.'

'Then you've not heard the news,' I said. 'For Rhys Fychan is back in Dynevor, and in pledged allegiance to Prince Llewelyn and his confederacy of Wales, and the very message I had for you is that the door's open to any who care to go that road with him. You may ride back when you will, and the gift of one of Gloucester's horses won't come amiss there, either. Or you may go partway with us, for we go back to Llangynwyd, and then northwards for Gwynedd.'

'No!' he cried between delight and disbelief, and rose in a fountain of sparkling drops to stare at me. 'Is that true? Rhys has changed sides, and been well received? How did this come about? I thought that was an irreconcilable enmity on both sides.'

I told him briefly the way of it, and he sank into the water again with a crow of joy. 'I am glad of it!' he said, lying still and straight there like a drowned man. 'I was Rhys's man until Llewelyn broke him, and I'd as lief be his man again, all the more if he's quit his English allegiance. Right joyfully I'll ride with you. You said truly, no serpent but an angelic voice! May I know who it is comes to point me my way? Surely no two friends ever saw more of each other at first meeting!' And he laughed. His was a face very well acquainted with laughter, by the lines of it.

I told him I was Samson, Llewelyn's clerk, and asked his name in return. In utter innocence I asked it, so pleasant and strange was this encounter, with some quality in it of dreaming. Until then, when I awoke.

He said, easy and content, with his eyes closed: 'My name is Godred ap Ivor.'

The bright, bracing chill of the water was suddenly harsh as ice flowing down breast and belly and thigh, the blood so stayed in me at the name. And he lay soothed and smiling and blind beside me, his head tilted back, the large, lace-veined eyelids bland and still.

I rose with infinite care upon my elbow and looked down at him, thus oblivious, never knowing what he had done to me, feeling nothing of the immense loss and grief that weighed upon my heart, filling me slowly like pain poured from a vessel. I looked about us, and there was no man to see and no man to hear, no man to know that I had ever met him in this place. And all I had to do was fill one hand with that floating hair, drag his head down under the water, and roll over upon him to hold him under until he drowned. And no one would know. What would he be but a fugitive knight who had left horse and harness lying, and gone to bathe in a river whose currents he did not know? For months we had written him down as dead. So brief and easy a gesture now to make it true, and Cristin would be free.

That was so terrible a moment of temptation, and came upon me so like a lightning-flash out of a clear sky, that I cannot bear even now to remember it. I do believe with all my heart that there is no man who cannot kill, given the overwhelming need and the occasion. And if I did not, it was not out of any honourable resistance on my part, it was because of Cristin, who did not want him dead, but wanted him living.

And he lay by me in his comely nakedness, the worst offence of all, arrogantly sure of his safety, feeling nothing, fearing nothing.

'Get up, then, Godred ap Ivor,' I said, when I could speak without suffocating or cursing, 'and set about getting dry, while I tell you something that concerns you nearly, and only you. For that name I have known now for many months. I have been looking for you all this time.'

At that he opened his eyes wide, in surprise and interest but without disquiet, and leaping up in a great wave of water, waded ashore to where the risen sun gilded the grass, and for want of cloth or kerchief to dry himself, began to dance and turn about in the sunshine. I followed him ashore more slowly. Even the night had been warm and gentle, and the morning came in quivering heat. It was no labour to dry off in that radiant air.

'I feel,' said Godred, clapping his arms about his shoulders, 'the honour of having had your attention. But how or why is mystery to me. What is it you have to tell?

'You had a wife,' I said, the words coming thick and slow upon my tongue, 'who was in the Lady Gladys's services and fled with her from Dynevor last December.'

'I had,' he said, suddenly still, and looking at me with a reserved face and narrowed eyes.

'Did you never seek to find her, after that flight? It is a long time now, seven months.'

He must have felt some censure in my tone, for his voice was defensive as he said: 'At first I had no chance, for I was two months sick of my wounds after Cwm-du, and knew very little of where I was myself, or what was being done with me. Afterwards, yes, I sent out everywhere message of mine could go. They told me in Brecon she was dead.'

'So they believed in Brecon,' I said.

'You mean she is not?' he said slowly, staring.

'She is alive and well. She is in Gwynedd, living at Llewelyn's court and under Llewelyn's protection.'

He hesitated, frowning, watching me very intently. 'You mean this?' he said. 'She is truly alive? But why should you lie to me!'

'I would not. She lives, and no harm has come to her but the harm of not knowing whether you lived or died.'

'But how?' he cried. 'How did this come about?'

I told him, as barely as it could be told. 'Mercy of God!' he said, like a man rapt in wonder. 'How strangely providence does its work. She mourning me, and I mourning her, and suddenly this return to life! Take me with you to Gwynedd! One more in Llewelyn's army will not be amiss, with the host called out in two weeks' time, and the cause of Wales is the same now north or south. Let me ride with you to fetch Cristin home!'

I said that was our intent, and that he was welcome, I, who had crooked my fingers so short a while before, to drag him under water by the hair and there drown him. That sin was past, and could be confessed and repented.

182

As for the awful sin of wishing I had done so, that would remain with me and be repeated endlessly for many years, if his youth was not cut off by some accident of war to spare me murder.

'And we had better be moving,' I said, to make an end, 'or we shall miss the best of the day.'

He took that for acceptance enough, and went to put on his clothes, and so did I. In a little while he came leading his horse through the trees to me. Clothed, he looked slighter and frailer than I had seen him to be, and younger, for his was a face that would always keep its boyish look. As lightly as he had sung, before ever I set eyes on him, so now he came whistling. He fell in beside me, the horse pacing between us, and began to speak of Cristin, as though her miraculous recovery were the only source of his exultant lightness of heart. Yet constantly I felt that he was ever so by nature. Howbeit, he spoke of her very winningly, having a feeling for words that would have done credit to a bard. His voice, too, was one of his chiefest graces, that pure, high voice for which the men of music love to make songs.

Being still full of a personal and bitter curiosity concerning him, for he had taken away all my present hope and all my peace of mind, and shown me to myself as a murderer by intent, I was observing whatever I could see of him as we walked, and since the led horse was between us I had but glimpses over the swaying neck of his yellow hair crisping into curls as it dried, and paling to the colour of wheat stalks just before ripening, of his face in profile now and then, eager and open, and under his horse's round belly of the lithe, easy stride of his long legs. And after these, I looked upon the left hand that was visible to me, holding his bridle. Brown and strong it was, with broad knuckles and a powerful, flat wrist, good enough for a bowman. And upon the little finger he wore a ring. A plain silver ring with an oval bezel for a seal. This I could see clearly, for it rode close beneath my eyes, so that there could be no mistaking the deeply incised pattern of the seal, a little hand severed at the wrist, holding a rose.

Then I knew what Cristin had known, when she looked upon the ring I gave to Meilyr, and when afterwards, on the ride north together, I told her how I got that ring, and what it meant to me. And I understood at last why she had urged me to put away all thought of the father I had never known, and think no more of the hand and the rose. 'Well for you,' she had said, 'if you bury with the ring everything it signified, and rest content with the present and the future, forgetting the past.'

And I knew at last, too late, hearing her voice in my memory so urgent and passionate, how I had fooled myself and failed her, so grossly mistaking what she meant when she told me I need have no fear of her armour against David, for she was bespoken, heart and all. And yet, she was a wife, and what could she or I do but remember it? Whether we would or no!

But no part of all this coil and tangle of sorrow was his fault, and he, too, had rights, this young man who walked stride for stride beside me, so closely matched, in whom I could not doubt I beheld at last my stranger-father's youngest son. It was not only the ring that told me so, though the ring was the key that unlocked my knowledge. No, for I knew, now, what had been so disturbing to me about that meeting of two naked bathers, facing each other across the river, about that face and its shaping, those eyes, and their arched brows. For though he was fair, and I dark, he well-favoured and I homely, he too light of mind, and I too grave, we were sealed and signed as from the same mintage, mirror-images one of the other, my brother Godred and I.

I told him nothing of my birth, I asked him nothing of his. I brought him back to Llewelyn at Llangynwyd, and presented him as a miraculous mercy, a bountiful act of God. My lord's pleasure in this return of the lost was all the pleasure I expected to get from it. For to him it was indeed not only an unlooked-for grace, but a favourable omen.

'Now I will believe,' he said, greeting Godred, 'that the blessing of God is with our arms, now that this one hopeful aim has been happily achieved, that was not desired for our own glory. Small right we had, after so long, to expect to find you, and you are here. A living encouragement to hope for everything, even the impossible.'

So he saw it, and for him I was glad, for we were going back to Gwynedd, whither David was already gone before us with the vanguard, to face an assault by forces greater in numbers and equipment by far than our own, and it was well that we should go in high heart. And that we did. And I must own that Godred had all the graces and attractions a young man should have, all his bearing, his eagerness now to reach his wife, his gratitude for her restoration, all were right and proper, and moving to behold. All through that journey to the north he spent much time with me, and I could not well forsake or avoid him, to make known to others the contention I felt within myself.

Thus we came again into Gwynedd by the twenty- seventh day of July, and at the fords of the rivers we began to meet with custodians who sprang up out of hiding at our approach to show the safe way across, for the principal fords had already been pitted, and some of the more vulnerable bridges broken. Many of the lowland trefs had been abandoned, the inhabitants with all their gear removing into the mountains. It seemed that Goronwy had done his work thoroughly, and there was little for Llewelyn to do but place his forces where most he wanted them, and have them ready for action.

'They'll come by the north route,' he said, 'near the coast, for he'll want above all to relieve and re-provision Diserth and Degannwy. And that, seeing he cannot stay camped there for ever, or leave his south coast fleet there, either, we'll let him do. It would not be worth good men's lives to stand too stubbornly in his way. Once he's gone we can break again any supply chain he can leave behind him.'

I had expected and dreaded that Cristin would be still at Bala, but all the women of the court had been withdrawn into the castle of Dolwyddelan, high in the mountains of Snowdonia. When we came into those parts Llewelyn, having determined on making his base and headquarters at Aber, whence he could hold the north coast, gave Godred his leave and blessing to ride direct to Dolwyddelan to be reunited with his wife, and either bide with us or take her home to the south with him, according as they chose together. The prince gave him a guide to bring him there the more readily, since he did not know our tracks in the north, and that duty, naturally enough, he assigned to me. In pure goodwill he said that I alone had deserved it. And in my own heart I confessed to God that it was true, and only fitting punishment that I should restore to my dear love the unloved husband of whose death my will was guilty, but not yet my hand.

Then we rode together and alone, and Godred was assiduous in his civil attention to me, and I, in my private bitterness, attributed to him all manner of motives which perhaps never were his: as, that he courted me because he had ambitions in this new service, and had seen that I was close in Llewelyn's confidence, and might advance him; or, that I might, if he did not win my favour, do him harm there; or, that he felt I had some reservations about him, and desired to allay them. But never, which may well have been the truth, that he felt real friendship and gratitude to me, and showed it like any other man.

For I knew that I was unjust to him. I knew I had no grounds for holding against him my resentment or my pain, and yet my ingenuity kept finding me just such grounds. I remembered things about our meeting which had then meant nothing, and in all likelihood meant nothing now, and found them meanings. I recalled the lightness of his mood, as though he had no care in the world, he who had lost Cristin, the treasure I had never possessed, and never now should possess. But he was by nature of a light mind, which is no sin, and had accepted the fact of his loss many months before, was he to weep all day and every day? There was also that thing he had said concerning a brother – my world was now populated with brothers! –who had a manor in Brecknock to which Godred could not go because of some small matter of his brother's young and pretty wife. But whatever that harked back to might have happened before Godred's own marriage to a wife who had more than youth and better than beauty. Indeed, it might never have happened at all, it was such a loose vaunt as gay young men may well use before a stranger, not desiring to give away too much of their true and perhaps anxious selves. It could not seriously be counted against him.

It did not dawn upon me until we were nearing Dolwyddelan that there was some other particular troubling me, with better reason. Something was amiss in his account of his own proceedings since Cwm-du. For he had said in his own defence, when I questioned him about the efforts he had made to find her, that for two months he had lain very sick of his wounds, scarcely alive enough to think of such a quest.

But I had sat naked beside his nakedness in the water, had watched him turn and leap as he swam, and stretch out his arms to the sun as he dried himself. And nowhere on all that fine, athletic body was there mark or scar or pucker of even the smallest wound. Not one blemish in his smooth whiteness.

At the outer ward of Dolwyddelan we were challenged and passed within, over the ditch defences, and up the rocky mound to the inner ward and the hall. The place was seething with activity, and well garrisoned, since so many of the noble women were there for safety in this perilous month.

And now that we were there, Godred fell silent and almost abashed, as near as he could get to that state, and left it to me to go first and order all that passed. Llewelyn's castellan came out to us as we dismounted, recognising me, and I told him our errand was to Cristin, Llywarch's daughter, but not what it was, for I desired with an intolerable, burning desire to know the best and the worst, and that I could learn only from her face, when she came in innocence to see who called for her. And if this was a cruelty I pray it may be excused by the cruel need out of which it sprang.

And by reason of this same desperate need I would not go within, but waited for her in the blanched noon sunlight of the ward, that there might be no shadows to hide from me any quiver of motion and feeling that passed over her muted but eloquent face. If Godred wondered at this, small blame to him. But I think he did not wonder, for in that summer he lived willingly out of doors, and could have been content like a bird, without roof or nest after the brooding of the spring. On other matters perhaps he did wonder, for he watched the doorway as insatiably as did I. If he had not been so blithe and sunlit a creature I would have said he was nervous of his welcome.

The great doorway of the hall showed black like the opening of a cavern, the sun being at an angle that slanted across the opening but fingered only a pace or so within, where it had nothing on which to rest, until she came. Thus she blazed suddenly out of that darkness like a star, so impetuously that her skirts danced as though in a fresh wind, and being dazzled by the flood of light in her face, as abruptly halted and stood stock-still on the upper step until she had her sight again. And having regained it, she looked for me.

There was not left one grain of caution in me to doubt it, for I saw her close and clear, and doubt there was none. So bright she was, there was no bearing her radiance. When she was called forth to a messenger, she knew what face the messenger must wear. She stood smiling in happy expectation, and her gaze swept across the court like a beam of the sun itself, and lit upon me, and was satisfied. She took one flying step to meet me, and her hands came up as if to fill themselves with warmth and light. Then, having found me, she found him beside me.

I cannot say the sun went out, for she was so gilded she could not but be golden. But she was a carven figure, who had been only an instant since a sparkling flame. A second time she was still, and the airy flying of her garments settled about her into carven folds. In her eyes the fire turned to ash. On her mouth the smile was petrified into stone. Yet she kept her countenance. In truth I never knew her to lose it, only to close it like a marble door, as then she did.

It was not with any hate or fear she looked at him, only with the dulled remembrance of old things past, which she, like me, had never thought to see move and breathe again. I would not have said, then, that there was anything amiss with him but that he was not Samson, and that he stood between Cristin and Samson like a great stone wall, long as the world and high as the sky. And God knows, sorry as I was for myself, I was sorrier yet for my secret brother, so comely and so light, quivering here beside me for dread of this meeting after eight months of absence, and not loved as I,

God help me, was loved. Whatever he had been and done, he had not deserved this, nor was he at all armed to resist and conquer it. He did not move until I laid my hand on his shoulder and thrust him towards her. Then he went forward, slowly at first but with a quickening step, his hands held out to her.

And she, too, moved, slowly that woman of golden ice moved and came down the steps to the beaten earth of the courtyard, pale as clay in the rainless midsummer. She did not extend her hands, they were tightly linked under her breast, as if to hold in the heart that cried and fluttered to go free, like a mewed hawk. He went to her and folded his arms about her, and strange it was to find him clumsy about it. And over his leaning shoulder she looked constantly at me, and her eyes were great lamps that had all but gone out, only the last glimmer of a flame alive in them, even while hands stole about his body and lay like delicate, inert carvings under his shoulder-blades, clasping him with resignation to her heart. Even when he stooped his head and kissed her, I swear she never took her eyes from me until his nearness cut me off from sight. And then she closed them.

As for me, the kiss was more than I could endure. I, too, turned my eyes away. I had my bridle rein still in my hand, I span round upon it like a hanged man spinning upon the cord in the convulsion of death, and groped my toes into the stirrup and mounted, and the horse veered under me, feeling my disquiet and despair. I rode through the dark archway from the inner ward, across the ditch and out by the great gatehouse, and never looked back. At a heavy, languid walk we went, for there was no haste to be anywhere, only to be away from that place. But all down the slope to the roadway I could feel the strings of my heart and hers drawn out infinitely fine to breaking with every pace I took away from her. For now indeed I knew the best and the worst of it, and they were one, and in this world, short of murder, which it seemed was not among my skills, there was no remedy.

I rode for Aber by way of the Conway valley. At Llanrwst they told me that the host was already mustering in strength at Chester, according to the king's decree, but Henry had not yet arrived in that city. At Caerhun, before I struck off to the left over the old Roman road across the high moors, I heard it rumoured that the Cinque Ports fleet was on its way coastwise to Anglesey, and that help had been promised from Ireland. Truly a formidable army threatened us, and a fleet far stronger, if not more manageable in our waters, than the small craft Llewelyn had built and gathered together in defence. Where I appeared, there I was known for his right-hand man, and eagerly apprised of all that went forward, and no man saw anything wrong in me, neither in my bearing, nor in the way I received and responded to the news. So does the impetus of habit continue to carry us when the heart has ceased to put forth any power or passion. For I was an empty shell, too numbed as yet to be fully sensible to the pain of my loss.

That came later, and with the suddenness of lightning flash or flight of arrow, when at Aber I left my horse to the grooms, and asked after Llewelyn. They said that he was in his royal chapel, and there I went to seek him.

187

Had I come by daylight he would have known the moment of my entrance by the light entering with me, though the chapel was withdrawn beyond a small ante-chamber. But it was late evening, and the light of the one altar-lamp within, though dim and red, was greater than the last remnant of twilight without, and the door was curtained, and opened silently, and there was no sound to disturb him. Thus I came into the chapel with him, and he did not know he was not alone. And seeing him thus on his knees before the cross and lamp at the altar, I drew aside and stood in the darkness, unwilling to touch with movement or sound so profound a stillness and concentration as I beheld in him.

His eyes were open and his head erect, his hands pressed palms together before his breast. His sword, the one he commonly preferred and carried, was laid upon the altar. I think there was not one tremor of movement in all his braced body and reared head, not even the quiver of a hair. He was always plain in his attire, less from humility than indifference, never feeling any need of trappings or jewels to make him royal, who was royal from head to foot and from the heart within to the hand without. But his blessed plainness kept him man among men as well as a prince among his people. He was twenty- eight years old and in the rising prime of his vigour and power, and I saw his profile drawn in red by the light of the lamp, the spare, cropped beard no more than a heightening of the lean lines of his bones, and saw in that face, in its stillness and unawareness of me, what was not to be seen in the bright mobility of his daily life. There was an ordinary man's solemnity and dread in him, beholding as he did with wide-open eyes the immensity of the burden that lay upon him. And upon him alone, for there was no other being in all his land of Wales who could lift any part of that load from him. He knew it without pride, and accepted it without reluctance, but the weight of what he carried was a fearful and a wonderful thing.

I do not know what prayers he made, for aloud he made none. Whatever was said was said within. I do know that I beheld in him so fierce and purging a flame of resolute love, and so deep a recognition of the perilous nature of his pilgrimage towards the Wales of his desire, that I was suddenly enlarged out of my cramping shell of self, and understood the nature of love, and felt its pain, in such measure that it was hardly to be borne. And all the more, being thus enlarged, did I burn in anguish for Cristin, and for myself, and for Godred whose grief was different but surely no less, and for all poor souls under the skies who bear in silence and fortitude the sorrows of man. For only in beholding something greater did I realise how great was my own scope, the well of passion within me how deep.

I crept into the darkest corner there, and waited out with him the term of his vigil. After a while he stirred and rose from his knees, and lifting his sword from the altar, kissed the cross of its hilt and shot it back into the scabbard. Then he went out, still unaware of me, a shadow among the shadows.

I went forward then and took his place before the altar, for I was no longer an empty shell, but a fountain of feeling and longing, overflowing without restraint, and there was a great need in me of a channel into which I could empty all the passion with which I was charged, for even my pain was power, and pure, and could not be left to run to waste.

What befell me there in the chapel was not so much prayer as a wild disputation with God, before the stream I fed had a bed and banks, and ran with the force of a mountain river. And sometimes the voice that argued against me and for me seemed rather to be the voice of Meilyr, my mother's husband, demanding, for so he had a right to demand, of what I complained, for I loved, which is great blessing, as now he himself knew and acknowledged, and I was loved, which is great blessing also. And who has two such dowers may not cavil because he has not the third, to see his happiness fulfilled in this world. For love is a joy and a force of itself alone, looking for no advantage.

But still rebelliously I complained of my pain, for it was very great, and so clamoured in me that I knew it for a daunting and formidable thing, either for good or evil, and what was I to do with it, to make living still possible, even profitable?

Then that with which I contended said to me that I must offer it to God as an earnest, as a weapon, as the squire proffers his lord a sharp lance in a just cause. And so I did at last, embracing it ungrudgingly and offering it with a whole heart, for such a cause I had, the cause of my lord. This and more I will bear, I said in my soul, and never speak loth word, so my prince speeds well in this coming storm. Let every pain of mine count to him as one step on the hard road to his vision of Wales free and glorious. Transmute my every darkness into a light on his way. For this door closed against me, open to him the door into his heart's fulfilment, and if need be, let my death pay to prolong his life until his work is accomplished.

When I was eased of my too much fervour, I went in to him in the high chamber, where he was closeted with Goronwy and Tudor and a messenger newly in from Chester, from our smith who went in and out as doctor to the garrison horses. Llewelyn rose and embraced me, and was altogether as I always knew him, practical, alert and unassuming. I looked upon him with earnest attention, for I had just accepted him as my reason for being, the one pure purpose and justification I had, having acquiesced in the loss of everything else. And I saw that he was enough, and my life would be filled having nothing more.

He asked me of Godred and Cristin, and I told him, without stumbling, how I had left them embracing. And all must have been well with my voice and face, for he was glad. And in the midst of much perplexity and pain I was glad of his gladness, and even the lie of my content which I offered in his service I commended to God as one grain towards my lord's harvest.

So ended that journey. And so began the campaign of that August and September, for the news from Chester was that King Henry was arrived in the city, and slowly all that ponderous mass of engines, foot-soldiers and cavalry was toppling into motion and rolling westwards like a flood tide to overwhelm us.

CHAPTER XII

The host moved upon us on the nineteenth day of August, crossing into Tegaingl the same day, and upon Welsh soil they lumbered westward like a mountain moving, as heavily and as terribly. We took the field the next day, but divided into raiding parties, not as a massed army, and with orders to hold off from any major engagement, but miss no opportunity of picking off any who strayed unwisely from the host. If we were forced to mass and meet them, we could move far more quickly than they could. But as we had expected, they kept to the northern ways, being bent on relieving Diserth. The ships from the Cinque Ports, for which the muster had been waiting, had by this time made the voyage round to our north coast, and with their cover from the sea the castle was relieved. We thought it no good sense to interfere with this operation, which could be no more than a temporary ease unless the whole of the Middle Country could again be occupied and settled, and this they made little attempt to ensure. So we contented ourselves with penning them securely into these northern lands, and we knew we could isolate Diserth just as effectively a second time as soon as they drew off.

They crossed the Clwyd into Rhos near to Rhuddlan, and among these rivers they lost a considerable number of horses and men, and especially baggage beasts, in our pitted fords. But still we forebore from encountering them in pitched battle, which would have been their desire and gain, their superiority in numbers being so great. So they came, the ships keeping pace with them, along the north coast to Degannwy by the twenty-sixth day of August, and lifted the siege of that castle also, as Llewelyn had foretold they would and allowed them to do. One ship at least they lost for some days, grounded in Conway sands, until a high tide lifted her off, though only at the cost of throwing overboard much of the provision she carried, in order to lighten her. And there at Degannwy King Henry camped ingloriously, and sat inactive day after day until the fourth of September. We could not make out why they should sit there so still and ineffective, but it seemed that they were waiting for their promised reinforcements from Ireland, and these never came. Nor did we see any sign of ships in the offing, our sea patrols off Anglesey keeping constant watch, for we were determined not to lose our harvest in that island granary without a fight. But the need never arose. The weather then was breaking, and on the fifth of September the English struck camp, and began the long withdrawal to Chester, with little accomplished.

For Llewelyn these were ideal conditions, for there is nothing better suited to our Welsh manner of fighting than a retreat in formal order by a larger force. Withdrawal then can easily be turned into rout, measured speed harried into flight, and order broken apart into disorder. But here we attempted not too much, but only hung on their skirts all the way back to Chester, lopping off such as fell behind or ranged too far ahead. And on the hither side of Dee we drew off and let them go.

'He calculates too warily,' said Llewelyn in judgment on the king, without prejudice or malice, 'he begins too late, he gathers way too slowly. In short, he is not a soldier. There are things he does excellently well, but not this.'

Thus ended King Henry's last great expedition into Wales, with little gain and less glory. All those too thorough preparations we had made were needless, though the experience was useful. The mountains of Snowdon remained inviolate, and our women and children and old men came cheerfully back to their villages in the lowlands before the autumn descended. Llewelyn's conduct of this defence, though not gravely tested, had been immaculate, sparing of our men and resources and countryside, and even chivalrous towards the enemy, for we could well have done them far greater damage at little more cost to ourselves. But the prince would not have it so, being more intent on conserving our own forces than destroying theirs.

All this time, as we moved about the Middle Country on the fringes of the English host, I had half-expected Godred to appear among us and offer his lance to add to ours, but he never came. And when the enemy had all crossed the Dee and withdrawn into Chester, there to disperse, and I returned with Llewelyn first to Aber, and then to Dolwyddelan, we heard there from the castellan left in charge that Godred had taken his wife, and ridden south for Dynevor.

'For though the knight would rather have stayed and come to Aber to join you,' he said, 'the lady strongly entreated that he would take her home, and could not wait to be away.'

'It's no marvel,' said Llewelyn. 'She has suffered anxiety and sorrow among us – what could we do against it, until Samson found her husband for her? But surely she'll be glad to be home with him, where she has been happy, and with my sister who values her. And a good lance in the south is as sound value to us as a good lance here in Gwynedd. It is all one.'

As for me, I said not a word.

So was I sealed into my own silence that I wanted for fellows, as though a curtain had been drawn between me and other men, and it was both affront and relief when that one creature came back, some ten days after us, from whom nothing that passed within me was secret, and to whom nothing was sacred. For I had seen little of David while the fighting lasted, he having his own command and I being always with Llewelyn, so that when he rode into Dolwyddelan from Chester he had still all to learn concerning the coming and passing of Godred, and having learned some part of it in easy innocence from Llewelyn himself, kept his mouth shut upon his thoughts, but came flying to me. I was at my work, and had not known of his arrival, but before I could rise to greet him – and indeed I was glad of him – I saw that he was in a great rage with me.

'What's this I hear,' he said, 'of Cristin leaving us? You've let her slip through your fingers, after all this coil? And you – can it be true? – *you* brought the fellow here to fetch her away? Fool, did I not as good as tell you, the first time I set eyes on the pair of you together, that she was yours for the taking? And when you were too deaf and blind to take the drift, did I not *show* you she was steel proof against all others, and would go with you to the world's end if you lifted your finger? When she would not give one thought to me, but followed you into the snow as she had followed you from Brecon to the north? Could you never conceive, in your priestly modesty, that a woman might set her heart on you for her own good reasons, and throw the rest of the world to the winds? One night it took Cristin to make up her mind, and a year was not enough to open your eyes! And now see what you have done to her!'

I was startled and stricken out of all conceal, and told him, as though confessing a sin, that I had had no choice, that even if I had known then what her true desire was – though he had no right to name it for her with so much certainty! –yet it was the will of God that I should chance upon the man, and that finding him alive I could do no other but tell him truth, and render up his wife to him again. But strangely, the pain David gave me, and that without mercy, was like a reviving fire, and to have that spoken of which could not be spoken of with any other was a deliverance like the escape from a dark prison.

'No choice!' said he with furious scorn. 'No *choice*! Had you not a dagger you could have slipped between his ribs there in the forest, and no one the worse or the wiser? Wives can become widows overnight. If you are too nice to do your own work, there are others could do it for you –'

'Never speak so to me!' I said. 'I have been that road, and stopped in time. I will not have you or any other walk it for me.' But I did not tell him, not even David, that Godred was my brother, my father's lawful son.

'Well, as you will! What profit now in harrowing over old ground, what you've done is done. But, man, what you have thrown away! Llewelyn knows nothing, surely, of all this? He seems to take this reunion as a blessing from God! And you have left him in that delusion?'

'I have,' I cried, flaring back at him in my turn, 'and so must you. The prince has great matters on his heart, and a great undertaking one long stage towards its accomplishment, and I will not have even so slight a shadow as my distress cast athwart his brightness, nor one thought of his mind turned aside from the enterprise of Wales to be spent upon me. Is that clear enough?'

At that I saw the flames in his eyes grow tall and pale in the old fashion, and steady like candles in still air as he peered through and through me, half in jealousy, half in impatience, wholly in rage. 'Still his man, I see!' he said. 'As deep committed as ever. What, do you even believe you can buy him a smooth walk through this world by swallowing your own tears? Fool, do you really think God should be grateful to you for flinging his good gifts back in his face? But if you want me silent,

I'm silenced. I'll not overcast my brother's sunrise. And since you're such a chaste and upright fool, I have done. I wash my hands of you!'

And he flung out of the room and left me quivering to the racing of my own blood and the sharp, indignant vigour of my own breath, a man alive again. But in a little while he was back, just as impetuously, to fling his arm about my shoulders and ask my pardon for things said and not meant. And whether in anger or in affection, his was a life-giving warmth.

'God knows,' he said, 'you do exasperate me with your too much virtue and devotion, but who am I to be the measure? If *I* tried to close such a bargain with God, he might well strike me dead for my impudence, but *you*. . . . Who knows, he may have taken you at your word! What would you say if there were signs and omens I could read for you, earnests of heaven's good intent?'

I looked at him speechlessly, and waited for his word, for though his voice was light again and his smile indulgent, he was not in jest.

'Omens come in threes,' he said. 'Two I have brought with me from Mold, one I find coming to birth here. First, Griffith ap Madoc of Maelor has withdrawn his fealty and homage from King Henry, and pledged it henceforth to the confederacy of Wales, like his fathers before him. There is but one Welsh prince now who still denies his blood and clings to England, and that's Griffith ap Gwenwynwyn of Powys, and between my brother and the men of Maelor his chance of holding Powys much longer is lean indeed. Second, King Henry has proposed a truce to last through the winter, and better news to us even than to him, a truce there will surely be. Time to mend all our sheep-folds and sharpen all our swords. And the third – Llewelyn may have opened to you already the scheme he has in mind, of approaching the Scots with a proposal for an alliance?'

I said that he had. For the king of Scots was a boy of fourteen years, and married to King Henry's daughter, a circumstance which had offered a means of placing a great many of Henry's henchmen, both English and Scots, close about the boy's throne, and greatly incensed and alarmed those patriot lords who feared the growth of English power. Two countries threatened by the same encroachment may well make common cause against it.

'Think, then, that if such an approach is to be made, it must be made not for Gwynedd, not for Powys, not for Deheubarth, but for Wales! And all those voices that speak for all those princedoms must be united into one voice, and given utterance through one overlord. I prophesy,' said David, taking my head between his hands and holding me solemnly before him, 'that in the new year the summons will go out throughout this land, to every prince and magnate, to an assembly of Wales, where that one voice will first be heard to speak, and that one overlord will be acknowledged and acclaimed. And his name,' said David, 'I think I need not tell you!'

As he had prophesied, so it befell.

Not many weeks into the new year we rode to that assembly, of all the lords of Wales from north to south, from the marches to the sea. From Gwynedd we came in a great party, David the foremost at his brother's side. Rhodri also came, though Rhodri kept much to his own lands, and had stayed out of trouble and out of the battle-line in the lands of Lleyn while we waited for King Henry's attack, I think not so much out of fear as out of a narrow and suspicious jealousy that he was not prized enough or sufficiently regarded, which kept him usually in a huff against one or other of his brothers, and caused him to refuse such openings as they would have offered him, while complaining that they did not advance him to greater things. As for Owen Goch, he was still prisoner in Dolbadarn, and so continued many years, though with a lightened captivity once his first intransigence ebbed and allowed it. But Llewelyn would never trust him loose again.

Of those others who came, from the south I mention Meredith ap Rhys Gryg of Dryslwyn and Rhys Fychan of Dynevor, from the west Meredith ap Owen of Uwch Aeron, from central Wales Madoc ap Gwenwynwyn of Mawddwy and the three grandsons of Owen Brogynton, Owen ap Bleddyn and the two sons of Iorwerth, Elis and Griffith. From the marches to the east came Griffith ap Madoc of Maelor, with his brother Madoc Fychan, Owen ap Meredith of Cydewain, and the three sons of Llewelyn of Mechain, themselves Llewelyn, Owen and Meredith. In great state they came, and all the noble guest-house of the abbey was filled with their splendour.

There my lord made known his mind concerning the future of Wales and its union under his leadership, and in council there was no dissenting voice. With one accord they accepted him as overlord, on royal terms of protection and justice upon his side, and fealty and service upon theirs, consenting also to the despatch of an envoy, in the name of this new Wales, to compound an alliance with Scotland, for the better guarding of both lands from the encroachments of English power. And Gwion of Bangor was chosen and approved as envoy to the Scottish patriots.

To this day I remember, above all, the burning whiteness of my lord's face when the hands of the last of his vassals were withdrawn from between his hands, and there was a silence, every eye hanging upon him. For he was so pale and bright with desire and resolution and the pride of great humility that he seemed to be as a lamp lit from within. And I remembered that we were born within the same night, perhaps the same hour, and his stars were my stars, and I thought how therefore there might be indeed a logic in this, that whatever I paid in sacrifice might justly weigh to his gain, and it followed that there was nothing for grieving even in my grief.

I will not say that it ever seemed to me that Cristin's coin could justifiably be spent like mine, but Cristin I could neither help nor save. God would surely some day fill up for her the void where she had poured out her love to no avail. As for myself, I thought I was well spent and well lost if I bought one more gleam of lustre for this my prince, who thus spoke to us:

'My grandsire Llewelyn ap Iorwerth took to himself the style and title of prince of Aberffraw and lord of Snowdon, and did great honour to that name. But both these are names of the north, and Gwynedd is but one member in this land, and though I was born there, and of that same line, yet you have laid on me now the right and duty of speaking for north and south alike, for east and west, and of maintaining the rights of all. I think it only fitting that this all should be one. And with your consent I choose to be known henceforth as Llewelyn ap Griffith ap Llewelyn, prince of Wales.'

Every man there, to the last and least of us, caught up the breath from his lips and cried his title back to him with acclaim:

'Llewelyn ap Griffith ap Llewelyn, prince of Wales!'

When we rode from Strata Florida it was a winter dawn, but of sparkling beauty, for there was a clear sky and light frost that silvered the bushes over and rang the branches like bells. For the first mile of this journey of the first true prince of Wales we rode due east, and the sun came up before us into its low zenith vast and glorious, the colour of red gold, as it might have been an orb presented at a coronation.

THE
Dragon
AT
Noonday

CHAPTER I

Still I remember that homecoming we had, when we rode back to Aber from the assembly of all the chieftains of Wales, in the spring of the year of grace, one thousand, two hundred and fifty-eight. We came at the season of the rising of Christ from the dead, when all things rose gloriously with him, the meadow flowers in the grass, the larks soaring from under our horses' feet, the fortunes of Gwynedd, and the star of our prince Llewelyn, no longer prince only of the north, and hemmed in by English power on all sides, but the overlord of many vassals and the entire hope of Wales.

For at that assembly every chieftain of the land but one only had sworn the oath of fealty to my lord and friend, and done homage to him as suzerain, and for this while at least our long-dismembered land was one. Indeed, I think that was the first time in all our history that Wales had been one, no small glory to him who kneaded all those several fragments into a single rock within his hands.

So we came home at that Easter with great elation and lightness of heart, to match the season and the wonder. When we rode between the mountains and the sea into the royal maenol of Aber, the women came out with flowers and singing to meet us. Not the woman I would most gladly have seen, for she was a long ride south out of my ken, and wife to another man. But, even wanting her, I will not deny that I, too, was carried aloft on the wings of that exultation, and the inward grief I had, pierced through and through by her absence, I lifted up in my heart to the glory of God, and as an entreaty for the safe-keeping and blessing of Llewelyn's lordship, and the crowning of his endeavours for my land. For I, Samson, his clerk, the least and the closest of those who loved him, desired most of all things then left in my life his triumph and happiness.

We celebrated the feast as never before, having so much reason for thankfulness. As I remember it, the weather was kind and fair upon the Good Friday, when all we of the prince's company kept the long vigil of grief that the season and our own hearts belied. And after, when the day of the resurrection was come, we were very merry in hall those nights, and very drunken, at least some of us below the fire. For Llewelyn himself never drank deeply, his intoxication coming rather with the draughts of strong mead the bards provided him. They had fuel enough to their fires that spring, and sang his whole life's achievement before him, and all their hopes of him for the future.

'He took up the fallen sword of his royal uncle,
David, to whom he was faithful from his childhood,

And made it more glorious far, a lightning against the invader,
A terror to kings, a rod of justice against treachery.
Who is like him in the field of battle,
And in the council of princes who can match him for wisdom?
In the council of princes the first and greatest,
He took diverse and warring clans into his palms
And fused their fragmented metals into steel with the fire of his
    longing,
A sword of swords to defend Wales, from Montgomery to the sea,
And from Ynys Mon to the farthest reaches of Kidwelly,
No longer many but one, this Wales of his making.
More glorious than his glorious grandsire, whose name he bears,
He has thrust back the English from our borders,
Given us ships and engines of war, taught us the uses of unity,
Held up before us the vision of freedom, never henceforth to be
    forgotten,
And we bereft of it never again content, so bright is its beauty.
He is the lion of Eryri, the bright falcon of Snowdon,
The red-gold dragon in the noonday,
So radiant, the eyes dazzle. . . .'

So sang Rhydderch Hen, the chief of the bards, and Llewelyn listened
with a sceptical smile, though for all his suspicion of flattery it was heady
wine to him.

David, his youngest brother, left his place and came and sat down
beside me, leaning with an arm about my shoulders. And stooping to my
ear he said, in his voice that was tuned clearer than Rhydderch's harp,
and never so sweet as when its matter was bitter: 'As I believe in hot ice
and cold fire, so I believe in Welsh unity.'

'You have seen it,' I said, taking him, as I always took him, warily but
not too gravely. 'New-made and puny, but alive. God forbid we should
ask too much of it at birth, but at least we have seen it born.'

'Into a kindred of litigants and fratricides,' said David no less sweetly,
'where its chances of surviving infancy are slender indeed.'

'God knows,' I said, 'they have seldom brought such a miraculous
child to birth before, what wonder if they make inexpert nurses? Yet you
are newly come from a prodigy, do not turn your back on it yet. They
have all taken the oath of fealty, have they not?'

'All but Griffith de la Pole,' owned David, mocking himself with the
name, for so the English called Griffith ap Gwenwynwyn of Powys, who
alone held out from the Welsh confederacy, and in using the same style
for him David acknowledged that this Welshman born was so drawn
into the Englishry of the marches as to be no longer a true Welshman
at all.

'For Griffith we are not accountable yet. His time will come. Did you
ever know the rest of them at one until now, bound in one oath to one
man?'

I looked along the high table then to see that one man at the height of
his achievement. The smoke of the torches and the candles made a soft

blue mist within the hall, and in that mist the light shot rings of colour and sparks of fire, as sometimes the sun will strike these wonders out of rain. So I saw Llewelyn sit mute and upright within a halo of tinted darts that sparkled like stars, and his face was bright and sharp as crystal, and his eyes looked far. He was not accustomed to waste much thought upon being splendid without, all his intent fixing upon an inward splendour, but this day he had made himself unwontedly fine in honour of the feast, and very fittingly he shone. Not as David, who wore jewels as his right and meed, being so beautiful, but with a strong, brown, warming splendour, full of hope and force and fire. He was twenty-nine years old, at the full of his growth and strength, more than average tall, and broad of bone, but lean and lissome of flesh. Brow and visage, he was brown always, the winter and indoor living doing no more than pale him into gold, a ruddy gold fitting for the dragon of which Rhydderch sang. His hair, too, was but the same brown darkened, and the close-trimmed beard that outlined his bones and left his mouth bare was like a goldsmith's modelling for a coin, such as the English strike of their kings. And that night in hall he wore the golden circlet of his rank, the talaith of Gwynedd that had become the talaith of Wales.

'He would need,' whispered David in my ear, 'to be more than man, to hold those oaths together. We shall see, we shall see, who will be the first to fall away.'

At that I turned sharply, drawing back my head to have him the more clearly in my sight, for he hung upon my shoulder with that half-mocking and half-rueful affection he commonly used towards me. There were always galls to be found somewhere sharpening the sweet of David's converse, and I could not fail to catch an echo here, for it was but three years since he himself had fallen away from his fealty to Llewelyn, and risen against him in arms, in company with Owen Goch, their oldest brother, then partner with Llewelyn in the rule of Gwynedd. For which unjustified assault Owen still lay in close confinement in the castle of Dolbadarn, though David, whom Llewelyn conceived as the victim of his elder's influence and eloquence, was restored to grace and favour, and indeed had earned both in action since. Yet often in this time of his restoration I had known him make allusion of his own wayward will to his default, like one probing with the point of a dagger in idle malice, towards whose heart it was hard to guess, though always he exposed his own. Some such prick, and aimed surely at me, I looked for here. For David knew how to hurt as he knew how to please, and his real and hot affection was a rose with many and long thorns.

'Oh, no, my sweet Samson,' he said in the softest of breaths, 'not I! Not this time! Never again in that fashion, whatever else may follow. Set your loyal, loving, clerkly mind at rest, I stay my brother's man. I do but reason from what we have. A great handful of irreconcilable princes, hungry for land, accustomed to contention, so suddenly assaulted by my brother's vision of a Wales as whole as England, able to stand against England and match as equals. All this they feel and desire, like some epic of the bards. But nothing of it do they understand, and nothing of it can they will, with any charged purpose. Oh, while Llewelyn is there among them to lend them his vision it goes well enough, but as soon as his eye is off them they'll look again at their neighbours and kin, and see them as before, not allies, but rivals, and the manor allotted unfairly to a brother, or the boundary-mark moved by a neighbour, will loom larger to them than the sovereign power of a Wales they've never known.'

He looked up then and caught my eye, no doubt studying him very warily. I would rather he had not, but there was never any way of hiding from him what I was thinking. He laughed, a little hollowly, but without any bitterness or blame. 'You are right,' he said. 'Who should know the way of it better than I, who first began it?'

Nevertheless, as April ran its course in sunshine and sudden squalls of rain, after its fashion on our northern coast, I began to disbelieve in that danger, at least while the oath of alliance was so new, and had brought nothing but good to any of those who joined in it. For it was Llewelyn's power that had set up his liegemen in their own lands, and his influence that held them secure in their tenure, and had even added to their holding newly conquered lands in the march, snatched back from the barons of England. What reason, then, had any to turn away from him?

Yet self-interest need not always be informed by intelligence, and the habit of generations dies very hard.

It was late in April, after we had sent out the last of the prince's deeds of protection and support to his new vassal, that Meurig ap Howel, Llewelyn's best scout from the middle march, came riding into Aber, a little, wrinkled dealer in ponies who traded as far as Oswestry and Montgomery, and regularly brought back to us word of what went on beneath the hangings even in Westminster. For our intelligencers were as wide-ranging and efficient as the king's, if less exalted. King Henry had at least one Welsh prince to be his spy, and that was Griffith ap Gwenwynwyn of Powys, that same man known to his English masters as Griffith de la Pole, from his castle of Pool, by the Severn town of that name. But we made better use of humbler men, Welsh law students and clerks and merchants, and notably our well-established horse-doctor in Chester, who was familiar and respected about the garrison, and on whom we relied for details of the king's muster and plans in his regular summer campaigns against us.

This Meurig was a dried-up little man, well on in years but hardy as a gorse-bush, so grey and so light of weight that he seemed to drift into Aber like a shred of thistledown blown by the silver shower that came in at the gate with him. Goronwy ap Ednyfed, the high steward, brought him in steaming to the brazier in the great chamber, to Llewelyn, for he was bursting with his news.

'You've had no word yet from Ryhs Fychan?' he asked; and being told that we had not: 'I can be no more than a day ahead with it; he'll have a courier on the way to you this moment. My lord, the reconciliation you went to such pains to bring about along the Towy last year is broken. Meredith ap Rhys Gryg has accepted King Henry's peace, and forsworn the oath he took to you barely a month ago!'

At that there was a great rumble of anger and outrage from all those around, and Llewelyn chilled into stone for an instant before blazing into indignation.

'Meredith!' he said. 'He, to be the first traitor! He of all people who owed us the most, who came here a fugitive, ousted from all his lands. And after I set him up again in everything he had lost!'

'I doubted him then,' said David roundly. 'When we took Rhys Fychan in and embraced him, that stuck in Meredith's gullet like a burr. For all he gave him the kiss of kinship like the rest of us, I felt then it had a sour taste to him. He could not stomach that we should accept and approve, and take him into the confederacy on equal terms. But most of all,' he said, 'he could not stomach that his nephew and rival should stand equal with him in your love.'

'And what use,' Llewelyn asked of Meurig, 'has Meredith made of the king's peace? For peace will be the last thing he desires of it.'

'My lord,' said Meurig, 'the very use you expect of him. King Henry has granted him leave to possess himself of Rhys Fychan's lands to add to his own, and has lent him the aid of the seneschal of Carmarthen and the royal garrison there. And they have seized Rhys Fychan's castle of Dynevor and manned it in Meredith's name, while Rhys with his family was at Carreg Cennen. All that you did a year ago between those two is to do again, restoring and reconciling if you can.'

'Not all,' said Llewelyn grimly, 'and not as it was done before. Restore we will, but reconcile? For him to break his oath again as lightly? A pity!' he said. 'I had a great liking for the man.'

And that was not strange, for Meredith ap Rhys Gryg was a great, squat, powerful bear of a fellow, old enough to be the prince's father, a notable drinker, singer and fighter, very good company in hall and on the battlefield, except that it seemed he could change sides faster than most. 'And what of Carreg Cennen?' Llewelyn asked.

'Well held and well victualled, and safe as doomsday,' said Meurig. 'Rhys and his wife and children have nothing to fear inside it.'

This Rhys Fychan of Dynevor was husband to the prince's only sister, the Lady Gladys, a match made by their mother when she and all her children, with the exception of Llewelyn himself, were in the protection (or custody, for so it was, however sweetened) of King Henry of England. A hard struggle Rhys Fychan had had of it to get command of his own inheritance against his ambitious uncle, Meredith, who had kept him out of lands and castles as long as he could. No wonder, then, that when, under the king's protection, Rhys got possession of his own at last, he turned on his uncle and drove him into exile in Gwynedd. Thus those two had taken turns to harry each other, according as the fortunes of the time ran, and it was but chance that when Llewelyn made his bid for the freedom of Wales it should be Meredith ap Rhys Gryg who rode by his side, and Rhys Fychan, the ally of England, against whom he was forced to fight.

In the past summer we had seen the climax of that struggle, for Rhys Fychan had sickened of his subservience to England, and come over at his testing time to the side of Wales. And Llewelyn had been the first to vindicate, accept and welcome him into the alliance, making peace between those two enemies. In that southern part of Wales were many such instances of bad blood between kinsmen, and fratricide and worse were not unknown, chiefly because of the old customary law that all land was divisible, and where there were many sons their portions must be equal, and therefore equally meagre.

In Gwynedd we had some measure of reform from this debilitating system, and out of no princedom but Gwynedd could a prince of Wales have emerged.

'This example,' warned Meurig, 'if it continues unpunished, may sway certain other feeble trees. They say there are some who bend.'

'The wind may blow them to bend the other way before long,' said Llewelyn. And he said to Goronwy, who waited to know his will: 'Send out the writs for two days hence, and have the captains muster in one hour. I stay here. Meurig has yet more to say.'

'There is more,' said Meurig, when Goronwy had gone about his errand. 'This I heard in Shrewsbury, where I ventured without safe-conduct, the garrison wanting horses. There was a royal official lodged at the abbey, on his way between London and Chester, and he had Welsh servants in his train. One was a clerk, in good odour with his master and with other functionaries about Westminster. I was lucky to meet with him. By his tale, my lord, King Henry has been wooing your traitor Meredith ever since last year, when Rhys Fychan repented his servility and turned to Wales. The uncle was a handy way of striking at the nephew. That very month he offered him seisin of all his own lands and all his nephew's for his fealty and homage, and two commotes belonging to his neighbour Meredith ap Owen into the bargain. So easy it is to give away what you have not, if you are a king, my lord!'

'This is sooth?' said Llewelyn. 'Your Welsh clerk has seen this deed?'

'Not that, but he has spoken with one who has. The man he quotes is in the king's own chancellery, and the assault on Dynevor bears him out. Moreover, there is another detail. I believe you will recognise the note! Meredith has held out for safeguards on his own terms. King Henry promises that he will not take into his grace and peace either Rhys Fychan or Meredith ap Owen of Uwch Aeron, without first consulting his new vassal. And for you, my lord – he promises further that he will never receive *you* into that same grace and peace, without the courtesy of getting Meredith's leave first! The traitor fears both you and his kinsmen, he will have the whole protection of the royal writ against you.'

'He has good need to fear me,' said Llewelyn grimly, 'and if he thinks the king's forces along the Towy can stand against mine he has yet something to learn. And you say King Henry has been trailing this lure before him ever since last autumn?'

'The document of grace, remitting all Meredith's past transgressions against either the king or the Lord Edward, is dated the eighteenth of October, and letter patent, at that. And the charter granting him the commotes of Mabwnion and Gwinionydd, in the teeth of their proper lord, bears the same date.'

'He has the devil's own impudence,' said David, with a shout of angry laughter, 'give him that! He has known all these months what he meant to do, and he came to the assembly with the rest and took his oath like a man, and no doubt swallowed it down without gagging. I could almost admire the man his brazen face!'

'He lives in the past,' Llewelyn said, for Meredith was indeed of an older generation, and came of a stormy line. 'Give him the grace of the doubt, he may not have made up his mind when he came to the assembly. Oaths to him are meant at the moment of swearing, but the heat of a quarrel or the smart of being slighted are sanction enough for breaking them a day later. If the offence had been only against me I might have let it pass, but he betrays what he cannot grasp, the common cause of Wales. For that he shall pay. And for the gross offence against my sister's husband, who has kept the peace with him loyally.'

'We march, then?' said David, his face bright at the offer of action, and his eyes alert and glad, for when we took the field, and he had all the fighting his heart craved, that restless energy that festered into mischief when he was curbed had a channel for its flood-tide, and ran violent and clean, sweeping all before it, and he fought and laboured, and gave and took wounds, and went hungry and weary, all with a child's zealous innocence.

Llewelyn looked not at him, but at Meurig, and asked: 'How long have we?'

'King Henry sent out his writs on the fourteenth day of March. The host musters on the seventeenth of June at Chester. "To go against Llewelyn!" '

This we had expected. The brief truce the king had made to tide him over the winter, when campaigning in Wales was too hard and costly, was drawing to its close, and certainly his constant intent against us had not changed. It was a matter of course that he should again attempt a summer war.

'Six weeks is all we need,' said Llewelyn, 'to teach Meredith the meaning of treason. We'll call the fullest muster we may in two days, and go south and make it plain to him that he has no right in Dynevor, that his neighbour's lands are not in King Henry's gift, and that from henceforth any who break their oath to Wales and betray the common cause will pay a heavy price for their treachery.'

'Do we take engines?' asked David, glowing.

'Not this time, we cannot move them fast enough. We must do as much as we may, and be back in time to meet the king's muster. For Dynevor we may hope, but even Dynevor may have to wait a better opportunity if he has it garrisoned too strongly. No, we can do more and more profitable hurt to Meredith by harrying his lands and lopping him of all we can. We'll send to Meredith ap Owen, too, and bring him into the field. He has a score of his own to settle, for those two commotes of his. And now let the captains come in,' he said to Goronwy, 'and, Meurig, we'll talk further when you are rested and fed.'

So we went every man about his particular business in preparation for that campaign, the first stroke of Llewelyn's power as overlord. With the spring so fair, and the land fresh and drying after the passing of the last snow and the early April rains, going would be easy, and at all times we could move so quickly, and needed to carry so little provision with us, that we could pass from north to south and back again, and appear in many places where no man looked for us, all within the space of two or three weeks.

Afterwards, when the council was over, Llewelyn had another hour's talk with Meurig, for he would know more of what the Welsh clerk from Westminster had to tell about affairs at court. For many weeks seething rumours had been reaching us of a growing dissension between King Henry and his magnates.

'It is true enough,' said Meurig, 'the king has troubles at home, and they are growing fast. As I heard it, some of the greatest earls of the land, and some high churchmen, too, have been driven to despair by the chaos the king has made in his rule, bankrupt of money, beset with all the brood of his Poitevin half-brothers, and in particular burdened with this bad bargain he has made with the pope. With the last pope, true, but this one pursues it just as inflexibly.'

I was brought up in the old Celtic tradition of the saints, and I confess the distant actions and arbitrary decrees of popes were always alien to me. Popes drive hard bargains. Of this trouble that plagued King Henry, and yet promised him so much, I knew by rote, yet the image of Pope Alexander, who held out the bait and the trap, remained to me as a strange heraldic beast on a blazon, no kin to my Welsh flesh. The papacy, for reasons but half-known to me, had long hated and desired to be rid of the imperial house of Hohenstaufen, and spent years beating the bushes for a champion to overthrow them and dispossess them of the kingdom of Sicily. And King Henry, when the prize was dangled before him for his younger son, Edmund, could not resist the lure. He had taken the oath, and under pain of excommunication he was pledged to bear the whole vast burden of the debt past popes and present had incurred in this contention, and to carry their banner to victory.

'The king's magnates detest and regret the business of Sicily,' Meurig said, 'but most reluctantly they feel that for his honour, and England's, and their own, they have no choice but to help him out of the pit he has digged for himself. They'll grant him aids, since needs must, to try to win this throne for his boy, and fulfil his obligations under oath, but they want something from him in return, the better ordering of the country's affairs, or why pour their efforts into the void?'

'And what of his parleys with France?' Llewelyn pressed him keenly. 'Whether the pope abates his terms or no, the king cannot get far in this enterprise without making his peace with King Louis.'

'He still desires it, and it becomes ever more urgent. But that, too, may be a long tussle unless fate cuts the knots. At his last council the king had to tell his lords that the pope has refused any change in his demands; the agreement must stand, in full. That means there's interdict hanging over the land and excommunication over the king unless he stirs himself. But desperate ills make desperate remedies, and it may be a dozen earls and barons of England can change the pontiff's mind, if the king cannot. There's no sense in even emperor or pope demanding the impossible.'

'Or prince of Wales, either,' said Llewelyn, and smiled. 'So it stands, then. Not yet resolved on methods or means?'

'So it stood. Like a hanging rock lodged on a mountainside. By now it may be in motion,' said Meurig, blinking his shrewd old eyes. 'Once launched, who can guess where that fall will come to rest?'

'Not in Wales,' said Llewelyn, slowly considering, and increasingly sure of what he said. 'Can he fight that battle, and ours as well? He may get his muster into arms and harness, but can he get them to Chester and into Wales? Not this year!'

'It is not impossible, though I would not say it is *likely*. But when a mountain slides,' said Meurig, twining a finger in his silver beard, 'I have known men felled who thought they walked out of range. And I have known nuggets of gold to be picked up by fortunate souls who kept their wits about them.'

'You say well,' said Llewelyn, and laughed. 'Pray God I keep mine!'

There was then no clarity in our expectations from that landslip that quivered above England. We rode from Aber, in rapid but orderly muster, two days after this visit, still ignorant that the first move had been made in the avalanche. For after the council at Westminster, seven great lords met and conferred, on the Friday after the fortnight after Easter, that is, the twelfth day of April of that year twelve hundred and fifty-eight, and compounded among them a sworn confederacy, every member taking a solemn oath to give aid and support to all the others in the cause of justice and right and good government, saving the troth they owed to king and crown. And then these seven, doubtless, sat down together to define what they desired for England, as we dreamed and argued and fought for what we desired for Wales. And, having defined it, they set out, even as we, to encompass it. For on the last day of April, while we rode south to the avenging of Meredith's treason, those seven led a band of earls, barons and knights, all armed, to confer with King Henry in the palace of Westminster. And disarming at the door, in token of their plighted loyalty, they went in to him and with all reverence but with great firmness set before him the body of their complaints and the sum of their remedies. To take or to leave. And the king, half-reluctantly and half-thankfully, and Prince Edward, his heir, with deeper suspicion and affront, perforce took them.

It was not known to us then who those seven were who set the mountain moving. But soon we knew them, and here I set them down, for fear they should some day be forgotten.

There were among them three earls:

Richard de Clare, earl of Gloucester,
Roger Bigod, earl of Norfolk and earl marshal,
Simon de Montfort, earl of Leicester.

Also to the fore, for he was a man of clear and individual mind, was Peter, Count of Savoy, uncle to Queen Eleanor of Provence, and counsellor to King Henry. And the remaining three:

Hugh Bigod, brother to the earl marshal,

John FitzGeoffrey, of whom I recall little but the name, for he died later the same year,

Peter de Montfort, lord of Beaudesert, no close kin to the earl of Leicester, but head of the English family of that name – for Earl Simon was French, and inherited through his English grandmother, the male line being exhausted.

These seven, hardly knowing themselves what they set in motion, were the beginners of that great ado between crown and baronage that shook the kingdom to the heart for many years, and drew my lord into its whirlpools, to his blessing and his bane.

But as for us, we were about our proper business in the vale of Towy, exacting from Meredith ap Rhys Gryg the full price of treason.

We made south by fast marches, halting but twice on the way, the second time at the abbey of Cwm Hir, and so came over the bare, heathy hills skirting Builth, and struck into the upper valley of the Towy above Llandovery. At that town the castle was securely held for Rhys Fychan, there was no stirring of Meredith's men in those parts, and we were assured our coming was not yet expected. There, too, a body of archers and lancers came east under Meredith ap Owen of Uwch Aeron, the loyal one of our two Merediths, to join us in that enterprise. For though his two commotes were in no great danger, for all King Henry's impudent gift of them and Meredith ap Rhys Gryg's more insolent acceptance, yet the insult from both was sharp, and not to be borne without reprisals. This other Meredith was a quiet, steady, grave man some ten years older than my lord, slow to anger and cautious in council, but staunch to his word and resolute once roused, and Llewelyn set great store by his opinion.

From Llandovery we swept on down the river valley, and did no harm to any holding that was not the seisin of Meredith ap Rhys Gryg, but from what was his we drove off the cattle and burned the barns, and where any holding was fortified we burned that, too, laying his lands open as we passed. All along that green, wide valley we spurred faster than our own report, until we came where the castle of Dynevor, that was Rhys Fychan's principal seat and the heart-castle of his royal line, loomed on its green mound among the flowering meadows, with the river coiling round its southern approaches. There we made a testing assault, but it was plain that the place was very strongly held, for the prestige of conquest no less than for its real worth, and so we made but one night halt there, deploying a small force of archers to occupy the hills around and plague the garrison, so that they would hardly dare venture out of the gates, to test the numbers of those who held them in siege. For this castle, strong though it was, was open to archery from the hills enclosing it, which were well wooded and gave excellent cover. Unlike Rhys Fychan's second castle, which by its very situation was almost impregnable, being built upon a great crag, with sheer cliffs on three sides, and only one ridge by which it could be approached. There in Carreg Cennen the Lady Gladys, with her three little sons and her household, was safely guarded. For which I gave thanks to God, for there was one among her women who drew me by the heart, and whom I dreaded to see as greatly as I longed for it, Cristin, Llywarch's daughter.

But at this time I was not to be put to the torment of looking upon her again, for we had no call to go to Carreg Cennen. Our business was with Meredith ap Rhys Gryg in his fortress of Dryslwyn, a few miles downstream along the Towy valley.

In the night we heard repeated calling of owls across the river, from the woods on the southern side, and knew that Rhys Fychan had brought his own muster from Carreg Cennen to join us. But we made no move as yet, nor did he, beyond sending out a runner who made his way to us safely in the darkness across the open water-meadows below the castle. A little, gnarled, bow-legged knife-man he was, as dark and seasoned as a blackthorn bush, and wise in every track in his native region. We uncovered our turf-damped fire for him, for he had swum the river to come to us, and by night this glimmer would hardly be seen as far as Dynevor for the thick growth of trees between. He said that his lord had left Carreg Cennen well held and his lady in good heart with her children, and, if the lord prince approved, Rhys proposed to join his forces with ours not here, but well downstream, at the easy passage which the messenger would show us, so that the garrison in Dynevor might have no way of judging what numbers we had, or what part of them we had left to contain the defenders within their stolen fortress.

Llewelyn approved him heartily, but said that if Rhys Fychan knew the ford of which he spoke, and knew it passable at this time – for the river was past the highest spring flow, but still fresh and full – there was no need for us to leave cover, and we might await him in the forest. For until now we had run ahead of our legend, and trusted to strike at Dryslwyn before they knew we were anywhere near. The messenger grinned and shook his head.

'My lord, by our advice it's you must cross, not we. Well I know Dryslwyn castle is on this side of Towy, but Meredith ap Rhys Gryg is not in Dryslwyn. He has wind of you. His castellan here in Dynevor got a runner away to him before you closed the ring, and he's in Carmarthen by now, and if you want him it's to Carmarthen you must go. The force that took Dynevor for him is still in arms there, and the king's seneschal has brought a fresh muster in haste from Kidwelly to strengthen Meredith's hand. We had a man there watching when they rode into the town, not two hours before midnight.'

'Then they'll hardly have had time to order their ranks,' said Llewelyn, 'and we had best move fast.' And he questioned the man closely what numbers the seneschal might have with him, for it seemed that King Henry felt obliged to give all possible aid to his first renegade client, as well he might if he wished to attract others.

'If Patrick of Chaworth is leading Meredith's allies in person, and in such force,' said Llewelyn, 'it behoves us to make as notable a demonstration of our own power, or there'll be more waverers. This bids fair to be the feudal host under another name.' For de Chaworth, lord of Kidwelly and king's representative over most of south Wales, did not commit his forces lightly in defence of even a well-disposed Welsh chieftain. Plainly he had his orders from the highest. Meredith ap Rhys Gryg was to stand or fall as a symbol of what King Henry could do for those who came to his peace.

'At what hour,' Llewelyn asked, 'should Rhys Fychan be ready for us beyond the ford?' For it was agreed that the cover was better on that side of Towy if we wished to drive straight at Carmarthen, and though the town lay on this hither side we did not wish to meddle with the town, where we might well be tangled in too long and confused a contest against so strong a garrison. If we could set up an untimely alarm and bring them out over the bridge to us before their order was perfected or their commands properly appointed, we could do them much damage at little cost.

'He is on the move now,' said the man, 'leaving archers to mark Dynevor from the woods. Unless we march within the hour he'll be waiting for us.'

'It suits well,' said Llewelyn. 'I never knew a town yet that liked a dawn alarm. With luck the folk may cause enough confusion to do half our work for us.'

So within the hour we marched, traversing the slopes of the hills among the trees until we were well clear of any eye or ear in Dynevor, and then moving steadily down into the meadows. It was still dark when we crossed the river, the guide going before in a darting, mayfly fashion, for the firm passage was complex, and flanked by deep pools. When he had shown the whole crossing and brought the prince safely over, he stood thigh-deep on a spit in midstream, and guided the rest across. This is a broad valley and green, and even in spring the flow is not dangerously fast. But still I remember the cold of it, and the way my pony quivered and shook her mane as she waded it.

From this on we pressed hard, to be upon them in Carmarthen before they were aware of us, and the meeting with Rhys Fychan's muster, in a clearing among the woods on the southern bank, was accomplished in near-silence and almost on the march. There was little time for greeting of friends or avoiding of enemies when those two war-bands joined. They moved forth from the darkness of the trees, we out of the shrub growth and alders along the river bank. Rhys rode forward and leaned to Llewelyn's kiss, and he was no more than a slender, bearded shape outlined by the gleam of his light mail hauberk in the late moonlight. There was barely four years between those two, Rhys being the elder, and though they had been friends but half a year they had a great understanding each for the other, and needed few minutes and few words to have their plans made. Then we rode, rushing upon Carmarthen as vehemently as we could, for there was already a faint pre-dawn light that made speed possible.

Yet on that ride, though Rhys's lancers were but shapes to me, being helmed and mailed, still I looked about me covertly in constraint and dread to find among them a certain fair and lofty head, and a comely, easy face ever ready for laughter. No friend to me, though he willed to be, and I had no just reason for resisting. And no enemy, either, for he wished me well, and I, if I could not do as much for him, at least prayed earnestly in my heart that I might keep from wishing him ill. For Rhys Fychan's knight, Godred ap Ivor, was my half-brother, though he was not aware of the blood tie as I was. He was lawful son to the father I had never known, and who had known my mother but one night of her life, the night that brought me into being.

God knows that was not to be held against him. Had he come to me otherwise, I might have welcomed a brother. But he had a wife, and his wife was my Cristin, whom I had found in innocence when he was thought dead, and in innocence loved, and in anguish resigned to him when he returned from the dead. God so decreed that it should be I who discovered and restored her her lord. In my life are many ironies, but none greater than that. And three kinds of brothers have I had, and he the only one bound to me by blood, and the only one alien in my heart and mind. For Llewelyn was my star brother, my twin born in the same night, and David was my breast-brother, my mother being his nurse from the day of his birth. And to both my love flowed freely, but to Godred it would not flow. He had but to come within my sight and it froze, and was stilled, proof even against the warmth of hand or breath. For Cristin's sake I could not love him.

In this country I was always aware of him, even as I was of her. On that night ride I looked sidelong at every man who drew abreast of me, and the hairs stood up on my neck like hackles as I peered after the features of faces half-glimpsed under the stars. But he was not there. That was not asked of me, that I should suffer his gladness at sight of me, and bear to ride beside him in the bitterness of fellowship. Surely he was left behind with the garrison in Carreg Cennen.

I gave thanks to God, too soon. And God visited me with another torment, I doubt not well-deserved, seeing how ill I used a harmless, well-intentioned man. It was but nine months since I had turned without a word in the bailey at Dolwyddelan, and left those two together. Just enough time for a child to be conceived and carried and brought into the world! And man and wife reunited after parting and sorrow commonly beget and conceive in the first joy of reunion.

With such piercing thoughts I tore my own heart, well knowing that with her it was not so. For there had been no joy. It was my ultimate grief that I had bestowed on her no blessing, but a curse. For the last glimpse of her face had told me clearly enough where Cristin's joy lay, and where her love was given.

It was ill thinking of these things for which there was no remedy, but I had not long for fretting, there being work to do very soon. For in the haste and turmoil of an alarm at earliest dawn, Meredith ap Rhys Gryg and Patrick of Chaworth brought their armies fumbling and hurtling out of the town of Carmarthen to fend us off, just as we massed and moulded our first charge to shatter them.

The light, everywhere but in the east, was still dove-grey and secret, the eastern sky was a half-circle of palest primrose, with a drop of molten gold at its centre. We came out of the gentle slopes of woodland and over the meadows, driving at the end of the bridge, and across the river from us lights flared and flickered in the town. We saw the half of de Chaworth's host spreading like spilled water from the narrow bottle of the bridge, and galloping wildly into station to hold us off, turgid with haste and confusion, but so many that the heart shrank, beholding them. We saw their numbers multiply, pressing across the bridge. We saw Meredith's banner, and found his thick, hunched body in its leather and fine mail, leaning forward into the thrust of his lance before he so much as spurred to meet us. We struck them while they were no more than half poised, and recoiled, and massed to strike again, before they were well set to stand us off.

That was no very orderly battle, but a violent assault and a rapid withdrawal several times repeated. For a brief while we stripped the bridge-head of its defences, but we had no will to cross, for their numbers, as well as I could estimate, were nearly double ours, and those are odds not acceptable for long to a wise captain. Nor did we want Carmarthen, no doubt rich and profitable to sack, but we had other business, and in this land, where we were welcome to live freely off the tenants, we had no need and no incentive to plunder the townspeople. Many of them might well be of our party, if they had the means to show it. We aimed rather at those persons we most needed to disarm and unman.

For my part, I did my best to keep always in that place I had made my own, at Llewelyn's left quarter, another shield covering his shield. I drove with him against Patrick of Chaworth, whom he singled out from all. And it seemed to me, as I kept station beside him, that he saw in Patrick an image of the king, who was England, and held status as the enemy of Wales. He could better tolerate Meredith, the seduced, than Henry the seducer. It was left for Rhys Fychan, who had the best right, to level his lance at his uncle, and in the shock of their meeting Meredith went dazed over his horse's tail, but his mounted men flowing round him covered him long enough to let him remount, and in the mêlée, which was tight and confused for a while, those two enemies were forced apart. So was I separated from my lord's side, for our two hosts had meshed like interlaced fingers and clung fast, and even at the command of the horn we had some ado to draw off and stand clear to strike again.

It was in this pass, while we heaved and strained with shortened swords and axes at close quarters, that I saw from the corner of my eye Rhys Fychan's livery ripped sidelong from the saddle and crashing to the ground among the stamping hooves, where there was scarcely room to fall. And, wheeling that way, I heard the felled man cry out, clear and shrill in terror even through the clamour that battered our ears, and saw his body, young and lissome, slide down between the heaving flanks, catching at stirrup and saddle and finding no hold. And I saw that the stroke that swept him from his horse had burst the thongs of his helm and torn it from his head, and the hair that spilled out over his face was fair as wheaten straw, or barley-silk in the harvest. So I saw again my half-brother Godred, and terrible it was to me that he should appear to me only at this extreme, for his every danger was my temptation. Once I might have slain him, and no one any the wiser, and I did not. But this time I had only to let him be, and he was a dead man, and my hands unreddened.

So the mind reasons, even in an instant briefer than the splintering of sunlight from a sword. But happily the body also has its ways of thinking, which are all action, too fleet for the mind to turn them back. So I found that I had tugged my pony's head round and urged her with heel and knee, and like the clever mountain mare she was, used to riding tightly with hounds, she straddled Godred and stood over him without trampling so much as one pale hair of his head, while I swung left and right about me to clear a little ground for him to rise, and having won a meagre, trampled space of turf I reached down a hand to him to pull him to his feet.

He rolled from under her belly, heaving at breath, and grasped my hand and clung, leaning heavily on my knee a moment before he lifted his head and knew me. The spark of recognition lit in his round brown eyes in two golden flames. There was time then for nothing more than that, for the mêlée had broken apart, and we made good haste out of the press, he clinging by my stirrup-leather and running beside me, for my pony could not carry the two of us. He was unhurt but for the bruises of his fall, and quick to borrow the first advantage, for when a riderless horse trotted by us close he loosed his hold, clapped me on the thigh by way of farewell, and caught at the trailing bridle. The beast shied from him, but not for long, for by the time I was back at Llewelyn's side and poised for a new assault I saw him come cantering and wheeling smartly into the line. Bareheaded he went into battle with us that time, and so contrived that he rode close to me, and from his place saluted me with raised hand and a flash of his wide eyes as we leaned into the charge.

In that bout we struck them from two sides, sharply but briefly, for there were new reserves still crowding over the bridge to their support. So we drove in vehemently wherever we saw a weak place, to do them what hurt we might while we might. Rhys Fychan sought out Meredith ap Rhys Gryg yet again, and that time I saw the sword cleave through his shoulder harness and into his flesh, and he was down again in the lush grass of the river bank, turning the bright blades red. When we obeyed the prince's signal and quit the field, we turned before dissolving into the cover of the woods, and watched Meredith taken up and carried away in his blood, over the bridge and into the town.

'Not dead nor near it,' said Llewelyn, lingering to see the last of him. 'The old bear will live to fight again many a day.' And I think he was glad. But for this long while Meredith's right arm would strike no blows in battle, and as I knew, having seen him in combat many times, he had but an awkward use of his left, like most men who have not strenuously practised the exercising of that member.

A few dead we left behind us there, but no prisoners, and, though we took some minor wounds away with us, none were grave. We reckoned it, in its measured fashion, a victory, as we rode back towards Dryslwyn from the bridge of Carmarthen. With de Chaworth's hands full, as they surely were, with the salvaging of wounded men and scattered horses, and the shattered order within the town, it was the best time to test out the defences of the castles along the Towy.

Well I knew that I could not escape company on that ride. From the moment we formed and marched, Godred took his captured mount out of the line, and watched our ranks pass until he found me, and then fell in at my side. His yellow head was bared to the early sun falling between the trees, and though his face was bruised, and bore a pattern of shallow scratches over the cheekbone, where the metal of his helm had scored him as it tore free, his youthfulness and brightness were no less than when last I had seen him, the greater part of a year ago. No, they were still more marked because of the lifting of the passing shadow of death. I had heard him cry out against it; I knew he had recognised it as it stooped upon him. I have heard a hare scream so before the hawk struck.

I do not know if he looked sidelong at my face and found in it something that made him approach warily, or whether it came naturally to him at all times to touch lightly and turn gravity to gaiety, even in matters of life and death. For he leaned down first from his taller mount and patted my mare's moist neck, fondling along her mane.

'I owe you as good a fill of oats as ever a pony ate,' he said to her twitching ear. 'Remind me to honour the debt when we halt at Dryslwyn.' And to me he said, no less lightly and agreeably, yet with a note of carefulness, as if he felt some constraint: 'And to you, Samson, I owe a life. When will it please you claim it back from me?'

I could not choose but think then how I had once been tempted to take it from him unlawfully, and how I had now but rendered him in requital what I owed to him, leaving him no debt to me. But I said only, I hope truthfully, that I was thankful indeed to see him none the worse.

'Faith,' said he, 'you come always to be my saving angel. I thought my last hour was come and, I tell you, a good clean lance-thrust would have been welcome, rather than be pounded to pulp among the hooves. Make as little as you will of it, you cannot make it less than a life to me, and I shall follow you round with my gratitude until I can repay you, though I promise to do it without overmuch noise or importunity. I know you have no appetite for being thanked,' he said, watching me along his wide shoulder with a gleaming smile, 'or you would not have ridden away from Dolwyddelan without a word, and left Cristin and me to hunt you in vain, last year when you brought us together again. That was a great grief to her.'

He had a gift for double-edged words. Surely if he had known of my grief he would not have probed my heart with hers. He spoke of things he believed he understood, though he knew no more than the surface. And that was his strength and my weakness, that he could prattle by my side of Cristin, and the time of her loss, and the bliss of her recovery, without one tremor of pain or uneasiness, while every shaft he loosed pierced me to the soul. All his honey, which he poured innocently and assiduously, was gall to me. And in my agitation of mind I began to suffer another disquiet, for now I could not be sure whether I had indeed wheeled my mare astride him on the ground to save or to trample him. Such doubts he never failed to arouse in me, because he sought and praised and affected me, and trusted in my returning his kindness, while to me he was hateful, and his presence a torment. That undoubted guilt tainted all my dealings with him, even those which were clean in intent.

He rode beside me all that day, as good as his word in pursuing me with attentions and thanks which were more than I could bear. Even the work we had to do could not long shake him off from my neck. We circled Dryslwyn castle in cover, hoping the garrison would think us departed and send out some party we could pick off, perhaps with profitable prisoners. If King Henry could persuade Welshmen to his peace, so, perhaps, could Llewelyn recover the fealty of some thus handed over against their will. But the castellan continued very wary, and clearly had no lack of provisions within.

'We should have brought siege engines,' said David, scanning the towers and fretting for an opportunity lost. 'There would have been time.'

'With de Chaworth calling in reinforcements from as far as Pembroke by now?' said Llewelyn. 'Never think he'll hold still in Carmarthen for long. One week, and he'll be moving this way against us. And we have still work to do in Gwynedd before the seventeenth of June. No, let's use our time here on Dynevor, since it may well be short.'

So we marched on, and camped for the night about the uplands that overlooked Dynevor upon the north. Here we could not have used siege engines even had we brought them with us, for Rhys Fychan wanted his castle restored undamaged, if that were possible, and in particular did not wish to risk the life and limb of those of his men now prisoners within. So we gave free rule to the archers, and let them pick off any of Meredith's men who showed themselves too rashly about the walls, and any who ventured out, giving them no rest, and no chance to bring in further supplies for the garrison. By such means a castle may be taken, given time enough, but our time was running out. Whether the king's muster came to fruit or not, it behoved us to be ready to receive the shock.

In the second week of May our scouts sent back word from Carmarthen that reinforcements were moving in from the south in some strength, and it appeared that a massive attempt against us was being prepared. It was high time for us to turn homeward.

'A pity to go with the work half-done,' said David, chafing and burning. 'Leave me here with my own men, and Rhys and I between us will go on with this harrying. With Carreg Cennen to fall back on we can well avoid battle at the worst, and still do Chaworth and Meredith damage enough, and keep them from re-victualling Dynevor. If King Henry gets his muster into motion, you have only to send for me, and I'll be in Gwynedd before him.'

Which was true enough, for the royal army could move but slowly among our forests and mountains, while every hidden path was at our disposal.

'I grieve,' said Llewelyn, frowning upon the distant towers of Dynevor, with Dynevor's lord at his shoulder, 'to leave your castle still in other hands. I promise you it shall not be so long.'

Rhys Fychan, who had sworn fealty to him less than a year ago, pledging it as the last fealty of his life, and never went from it again, made no complaint, but reassured him.

'Lend me David, and between us we will take and hold more land than

Dynevor could buy. For the walls and towers I can wait,' he said.

So David remained, making his headquarters with Rhys Fychan at Carreg Cennen, and entered gleefully on a campaign of pinpricks against the king's seneschal, while Meredith ap Owen, true man name-sake to our traitor, retired to his own country along the Aeron, and we turned back into Gwynedd to receive whatever manner of blow King Henry might launch against us. As for Meredith ap Rhys Gryg, accord-ing to the reports we had he was nursing his wound in Carmarthen still, and was not likely to stir from there for many weeks, so we had no hope of getting him into our hands at this time, and he small hope of meddling with us.

I was not sorry to be turning my back upon that region where I knew my love so near and yet by the width of the world out of my reach. This time of year, with the ripening spring so sparkling and fair, brought me the sharpest reminders of her. Once I saw her coming down the fields at Bala at the Easter feast, with a new-born lamb in her arms. Well for me that I should go back to labour and possible danger, for there was no other remedy to medicine me from my longing after Cristin, excepting only my devotion to Llewelyn.

We made our last night camp in the woods, intending to march before dawn. Rhys Fychan had already withdrawn his foot soldiers on the way to Carreg Cennen, and all that day I had not seen Godred, until towards midnight I sat wakeful by the last fading ashes of our fire, and he came silently through the trees, stepping lightly as a wildcat. I saw the faint glow from the live embers catch the glitter of his eyes, which were always wide and candid to all appearances, like a child's. He smiled on me with his warm, ingratiating smile, that was like a tentative hand laid affectionately on my arm.

'Did you think,' he said in a whisper, for there were sleepers all round us, 'that I would let you go away without a word of farewell?' And he sat down beside me in the grass, and told me the events of his day, how duty had kept him from me until now, as though I had a right to all his company and devotion, and he a need to excuse himself. He said it was a grief to him that the time had not been right for Llewelyn with all his force to visit Carreg Cennen, so that Cristin might have had the joy of seeing me again, and adding her gratitude to his. For they owed me, he said, so much, more now than she yet knew, and her thanks would have had a grace he could not match, and given me a pleasure it was not in his power to give.

So he chattered softly into my ear, and I was chilled and fretted by his nearness so that at first I hardly noted his words, or looked deeper than their surface meaning. Then it was as if a curtain had been drawn from between my understanding and his matter, and I heard clearly the light, insinuating urging of his voice, very cheerful and winning, as though he held out to me certain delights by the gift of which he hoped to win my somewhat morose and difficult favour. And what he was holding out to me, with discreet invitation, was Cristin.

Shallow and easy I had known him from the first, able to live as well without his wife as with her, able to make do with other company wherever it offered, and to make himself comfortable under any roof and at any table. But that he should value her so little as to parade her before me like a pander, and think it an earnest of the great value he set on me into the bargain, this turned my blood so curdled and bitter that I could not abide to sit beside him. And in this same moment I realised at last that to this man, pleasant, well-intentioned, born with only a thistle-down mind and a vagrant heart, I was bound by more, much more, than the blood in our veins. I had plucked him back from death, and I was committed to him, the body of my act for ever hung about my neck. He might escape me, as the receiver of benefits may forget lightly, but I should never escape him, for the giver can never draw back his hand from the gift.

He saw me shiver, or felt it, perhaps, for our gleam of hot ashes was almost dead. He leaned confidently close against my side.

'It grows cold,' he said quickly. 'I am keeping you from your sleep, and tomorrow you march.'

I said yes, that it was time I slept, glad at least of this help he offered me, for the one good gift he had to give was his absence. And I rolled myself in my cloak, to hasten his going. He rose and made his farewells in a whisper, wishing me good fortune and a smooth journey home. And even then he seemed reluctant to go without some last insinuating proffer of goodwill, for as he withdrew into the darkness of the trees he turned to look back at me. I saw the pale rondel of his face, and seemed to see again the winning, intimate smile.

'Can I carry any fair message for you,' he said softly, 'to my wife?'

CHAPTER II

In the last days of May, when we had been home barely a week and were busy about our preparations to meet the king's muster, a young man with one attendant came riding into the llys at Aber, and asked audience of the prince. Very young he was, barely twenty years, shaven clean and with his thick brown hair cut short in the old Norman fashion. There was a Norman look about him altogether, for he had the strong, prominent bones of cheek and chin, and the sturdy build, and the wide way of planting his feet, as though no wind that ever blew could overset the rock that he was. And yet it was the face of a clever and venturous child, and he looked upon Llewelyn, when Tudor brought him into the high chamber, with great eyes of David's own blue, but unveiled, lacking that soft, deceptive haze that shielded David's thoughts at all times.

He spoke, this young man, in declaring his errand, with a largeness, and as it were piety, in his cause which said much for those who had sent him, and the purposes that drove him, and he had a kind of purity very apt to those purposes, possessing it in some natural way, as swans possess whiteness, even among the mire of ponds.

'My lord,' he said, when Llewelyn had greeted and made him welcome, 'I bring you letters from King Henry of England and his council of the reform, and am to take back your reply when you have considered the matter put forward. And I am commanded by king and council to answer whatever questions you may put to me concerning this embassage, so far as is in my power. And that you may know my credentials, my lord, I am the eldest son of the earl of Leicester, and my name is Henry de Montfort.'

So for the first time we looked upon one of that family whose name was to sound so loud, glorious and lamentable a fanfare in the fortunes of England and Wales. But the boy, having delivered the official part of his message, suddenly softened and smiled, abating the severity of his stance like one stepping from a dais or a throne. And a little he blushed, submitting to his own diminished humanity.

Llewelyn looked upon him with some pleasure and much curiosity, for this was not the ambassador he would have expected from King Henry, nor, indeed, had we looked for any communication from him at this time but the ominous news of the first contingents reporting at Chester. He accepted the scroll, thanked the messenger for his errand, and promised him due consideration and an early reply to take back with him. Then he commended him to the chamberlain, to see him well lodged and his man and horses cared for, and desired his company in hall at supper and the pleasure of a long talk with him afterwards. When the door had closed behind him, and only Goronwy and Tudor and I were left in the room with Llewelyn, he broke the seal and unrolled King Henry's letter, and all we watched him read.

When he had done, he let the opened scroll lie spread on his knees for a long moment, while he pondered it still, and then he looked up at us, and smiled.

'Will you hear what King Henry writes to us? The seal is the king's, the style is the king's but the voice speaking has another sound. He writes that he has called a parliament at Oxford on the eleventh day of June, and that he invites me to attend there, or to send proctors in my place with full powers, to discuss the making of a new truce between England and Wales.' He laughed for pleasure at the startled and calculating joy in our faces. 'Meurig was a good prophet, and the rocks have fallen, not upon us. We may put away our plans; there'll be no need to pit the fords or break the bridges this year, and nothing to interfere with the harvest or the stock. England wants truce. Now tell me, does that sound like King Henry speaking?'

'Not to my ears!' said Goronwy. 'There has been some mighty persuasion used upon him, to bring about this change of tone. You might well question the messenger, my lord. It seemed to me he was instructed to be open with you.'

'If that was his meaning,' said Llewelyn, 'we'll get what understanding of it we can. But make use of it we surely will, whether or no. We are offered a truce, we'll take it. More, we'll carry it to the issue of a full peace if we can, and not grudge paying for it, if King Henry wants for funds for his Sicilian venture.'

'You will not go yourself, my lord?' said Tudor doubtfully.

'We'll let the council speak as to that. But I think not. Not at the first summons, as though we had done the suing, or were in haste to get rid of the threat of this June muster. No, we'll choose grave and reverend proctors and do credit to this parliament. Surely one of the most auspicious of King Henry's reign,' said Llewelyn, marvelling, 'at least for us, if not for him.'

So in great elation, though still cautiously, we went about the business of calling the council and preparing letters of accreditation. And at supper in hall young de Montfort sat at the prince's right hand and was pledged from the prince's cup, and his bearing continued open, friendly and serious, though his eyes grew rounder with wonder as he looked about him, and listened to the unfamiliar music of the Welsh tongue, and the singing of the bards. Doubtless that was the first time that he had ever stepped into our country. Now and again, confused by the strangeness of an alien language, he stumbled from English into French, for he spoke both freely. His mother was King Henry's sister, and most of his young life had been spent in England, though his father the earl still had lands in France also.

Afterwards Llewelyn took the boy with him into his own chamber, and kept only me in the room with them, for he wished to talk without formality, and make his own judgment, as yet uncomplicated by any other advice. And that I could be a silent witness he knew, and so had used me many times.

'You know,' he said, 'the content of the letter you brought?'

De Montfort said: 'Yes, my lord, I do know.' And he watched his host's face with his candid eyes and said: 'I hope you will accept the offer made. And I am to tell you that as soon as you have made your mind known, his Grace's council will issue letters of safe-conduct for you or your proctors to come to Oxford, and provide you an escort from the border.'

'His Grace's council are very considerate,' said Llewelyn with mild irony. 'And very anxious to have me quieted and still, at some cost, it seems.'

'I think,' said the boy steadily, 'it suits us both to have truce.'

'I don't deny it,' the prince said. 'Yet it did not suit King Henry last year, upon much the same terms. We do know something of the troubles under which he labours. Now tell me, and I shall trust your account, how do things stand between king, magnates and people at this coming parliament? It is not in my interest to add to England's difficulties, and I covet nothing beyond my own borders. The better I understand, the more likely are we to come to a mutual understanding. What has befallen since the great council of April, to bring about this realisation that war between us is more than either of us can well afford?'

And Henry de Montfort answered him, with confidence and address. How the seven magnates, of whom his father was one, had drawn up and presented to the king their aims and ideas for the reform of the state, with the promise that if he would accept their guidance on these matters, then they would stand by him to the best of their power in the matter of the Sicilian adventure, would raise an aid to help him, and send envoys to persuade the pope to abate the severity of his demands, and withdraw the threat of excommunication if they were not met. And the king and his son, the Lord Edward, and even the Poitevin nobles had agreed to what was rather an offer and appeal than a demand. Twelve councillors chosen from the king's adherents and twelve by the magnates formed the new reform council, which was to meet for the first time in full session at Oxford.

'And what has been done thus far?' Llewelyn asked.

'First, a group of envoys, my father among them, is now accredited to King Louis' court, to negotiate peace between England and France. They make good progress, my lord. Then letters have also been issued for proctors to go to Rome. Besides pleading for an abatement of the heavy terms under which his Grace labours in the Sicilian agreement, they will also ask for a papal legate to come to England, to help and guide us in all the adjustments that have to be made. And thirdly, as my errand proves, we desire a relationship of tolerance, at least, with you, my lord. The greater enterprise is England itself,' said this youth of twenty with noble solemnity. 'It is a duty to extricate the country's honour and the king's from this unhappy affair of Sicily, but also to amend the many things that are wrong in the realm, where we lack a fit system for hearing the pleas of the lesser people, and labour without a justiciar, and with sheriffs irregularly appointed and not easily displaced. I see no reason,' he said, 'to conceal that your forbearance on our borders is necessary to us, if we are to have time to create a just order in England, and a right relationship in Christendom.'

'You speak,' said Llewelyn, a little laughing at him, and a great deal admiring, 'with the tongue of prophecy. Whose is the voice? Your father's? For we have heard, even in Wales, something of the earl of Leicester.'

'The voice is my own,' said the young man, with a fleeting and impish smile. 'My father's is less voluble. But louder!'

'Yet of all voices,' said Llewelyn, 'I think it is not King Henry's.'

The boy leaned to him earnestly, and jutted his rugged Norman chin at him half in offence and half in amiable resolution to convince him, as past question he was himself convinced. He might have practised reserve and recoil very fastidiously, but deceit was not his gift. 'You mistake, my lord,' he said, 'we are all of one mind. King Henry has accepted with relief and gratitude the goodwill and help extended to him. Well I know there have been dissensions enough, but they are put away. One of the greatest of our French noblemen, Peter of Savoy, the queen's uncle, is among the movers of the reform. The magnates, the bishops, are earnest for it. The king, who is always good though not always wise, admits his need of it and embraces it. His Poitevin half-brothers accept it. Oh, my lord, you who have been praised – yes, even in England! –for uniting all the warring clans of Wales, you of all men should be moved by the singular unity of England at this pass. Two unities can rest side by side, to the enrichment of both.'

'If it lies with me,' said Llewelyn, touched and amused, 'they shall.' And he made much of the young man, and talked with him freely of lighter and more personal things until he dismissed him, already yawning, to his lodging. Among other things I remember Henry talked affectionately of his family, of his four younger brothers and his little sister, then five years old, on whom he doted, she being the only girl and the youngest child. Very close and loyal were these de Montforts, thus poised between England and France, and choosing England. No more deliberate choice ever was made, though I think it was made by divination of blood and bowels, and not by conscious will.

After the young man had left us, Llewelyn looked after him for a long moment, thoughtfully frowning, before he asked of me: 'Well, what do you make of him?'

'He is patently honest,' I said, 'and someone has certainly shown him a vision.'

'That I believe,' he agreed. 'But are you telling me King Henry, at his time of life, has taken to seeing such visions, too?'

I owned that was unlikely, but argued, none the less, that what the boy said might well be true, in that the king had known himself in difficulties from which he saw no escape, and might indeed be profoundly glad and grateful if his barons had banded together to attempt his rescue. Without their stern purpose or this boy's fervent exaltation, after his own fashion he might be equally sincere in his adherence to this new-found unity. But whether we should fear it or hope for it was more than I could yet determine. Their mind to us at this moment, it seemed, was clear enough, and we would do well to take what advantage we could of it, while we could.

'So I think, too,' said Llewelyn. 'Though we have seen already how long the unity of Wales remained immaculate, and can England do better, with so many warring interests? A pity if this boy's faith were shattered too soon! I tell you, Samson, I wish it were politic to go myself to Oxford. I should like to see this new council at work with my own eyes, and see what manner of men I have to deal with, if they can mould and master the king's actions as it seems they have done. And I should dearly like,' he said, 'to see the oak that dropped the acorn from which that sapling grew.'

On the day following, the council of Wales met and formally approved acceptance of the invitation to Oxford, and Llewelyn issued his letters of procuration for the parliament, appointing Anian, abbot of Aberconway, and Master Madoc ap Philip, his most trusted lawyer, to attend as his proctors, with full powers to negotiate peace or truce. And Henry de Montfort departed, I think very well pleased with his visit and much interested in all that he had seen at Aber, with the reply to king and council in England. He took leave of Llewelyn with due ceremony, mindful of the dignity of his office, but also with a fresh warmth that was pleasing to see.

I had thought no more of the prince's regrets that he could not be his own envoy and go to observe the procedures of these reforming earls for himself, but after the messenger was gone he came to me with a bright and resolute face.

'Will you go with Madoc and the abbot,' he said, 'as clerk and copier? I shall have as good an account in its way, perhaps, from the two of them, but they will be preoccupied with law and arguments and bargaining, and in any case it will be impossible for a Welsh student or groom to approach them while they are about the court. But while all eyes are on them, you can move among the humbler sort and use your eyes and ears, and you, I know, will be quick to think and feel as I, and settle on the details I should best like to know. Will you do this for me?'

I said I would, and gladly, if I was indeed the best instrument to his purpose.

'You are,' he said. 'You know my mind as you know your own, and your judgment of men I will trust to measure very close to mine. And, see, I have sent word to Meurig in Hereford, concerning that Welsh chancery clerk of his acquaintance, and told him you will be in attendance on my proctors. Besides what you can observe for yourself, he will find some means of coming to you with all he knows of what goes on among the king's officials. If they will abide by this concern with procuring good order at home, then I will keep any truce I make, and pay any indemnity I promise, and take care of my own household. But I greatly need to know.'

So I promised, though with some misgiving, for I had not been in England for twelve years, and had not thought ever to return there. And the memories I had of that time, long overlaid with the business of living here in Wales, were disturbing when they moved in me again, full of reminders of my dead mother and her most unhappy husband, and the imprisonment and death of my lord's father. Old tales, but not so far removed into the past as to be kindly hearing and easy tears. But I fretted vainly, for I was going where I had never been, and into a changed and seething land, frantic with new ideas and hopes, like a pot boiling, and in the event there was nothing to tug me back into the past, and everything to urge me forward towards the future.

On the second day of June the letters of safe-conduct were issued to us from the king's court and some days later were received at Aber. And then we set out, the two proctors with their body-servants, and I as a clerk to them, and crossed into England at Oswestry on the day following. And there we were met by a very gallant company as escort, more nobly led than I had expected, for we were to be accompanied to Oxford by one of those very seven lords who had begun this new enterprise of England.

This name came ever new, like a charm, the name of de Montfort. For our sponsor and escort was none other than Peter de Montfort who was head of the English house, the lord of Beaudesert near Warwick. No close kin to the young man Henry, and of an older generation, I suppose well into his fifties, but almost a neighbour, his Beaudesert being none so far from Earl Simon's Kenilworth, and certainly a loyal adherent and true friend, as after he proved. Thus in all that followed I could not keep from thinking of him as one of that same splendid and fatal family, and so I think of him still.

He was a tall man, of commanding figure but unobtrusive presence, his gestures spare and few, and his voice quiet. His colouring was florid, and his hair and clipped beard a rich russet red, as yet only touched with threads of grey, and he had very grave and considerate eyes which spared, rather than avoided, observing us too closely on that ride together, as also he said no word of the business on which we rode. His courtesy, though doubtless habitual with him, nevertheless underlined for me yet again the importance they set upon this agreement, and I grew ever more certain that our proctors would be able to secure truce at least, if not peace, for a merely nominal sum.

Very pleasant it was, in that warm June weather, riding through the western parts of England, where the gently folded land was softer, the rivers bluer and the water-meadows greener than in our harsh and rocky homeland. Again we rode through Shrewsbury from the Welsh gate to the English bridge, and passed by that great abbey where first I set eyes upon England's king. But after that I was upon unknown ground, as we followed the Severn southwards to Worcester.

Riding behind my masters thus, and having before me the baron of Beaudesert's long, erect back, and his russet head courteously inclined now to his guest upon one side, now on the other, I saw him as greater even than he was, for both our proctors were meagre men to view thus from behind. Face to face was another matter, and I think de Montfort was in no delusion concerning the tough quality of those two with whom his fellows would have to deal.

Abbot Anian was an ascetic of the old, heroic kind, worn to spirit and bone but very durable, and where Llewelyn's interests were at issue, his grey and gentle face was but a weathered scabbard for a steely and resolute mind. For Llewelyn was sometimes at odds with his bishops, whose first loyalty was to the church, and who were in any case more worldly, quarrelsome and litigious men, insistent on rights and privileges which often clashed with those of the prince's under Welsh law, as well as quick to shake the threat of religious sanctions at any who crossed them even on very trivial secular matters. But with all the orders, whether the great

Cistercian houses or the older blessed foundations of the clas and college, and the solitary hermitages of those withdrawn from the world, he was always on terms of love, trust and deep respect, like his grandsire before him. To the bishops the vision of a united Wales was in some degree offensive, even heretical, since they drew their authority from outside Wales. But those who were rooted in the land and had chosen the place of their ministry once for all, whether born Welsh or no, had no such severance within them, and were at one with us.

And for our other proctor, Master Madoc ap Philip, he was elderly and a little crabbed with learning, but equally devoted to Llewelyn's cause, and very well able to chop legal arguments in any court, whether by Welsh, English or marcher law. Out of court he tended to be taciturn, and it surprised me to see him warm almost into loquacity with de Montfort, perhaps because that considerate man never touched upon law, but left it to the lawyers, and instead pointed out along the way whatever was notable, like the noble towers of Worcester cathedral soaring above the waters of Severn, placid and sunny now in their summer flow, or the great Benedictine abbey at Evesham, making a halt purposely for us to see this latter, since we did not intend a stay overnight. And both these I remember now by reason of what befell afterwards, and marvel that I did not then feel my heart either soar or sink in contemplating them, beyond what was due in admiration of pleasure.

Thus briskly but without haste we came to Woodstock, where once Llewelyn had attended King Henry's court and done homage to him for a shrunken princedom, since gloriously restored to its old bounds. Thence in the early evening of a fine day we reached Oxford.

The king's hall lay outside the north gate of the city, a very spacious and noble dwelling, well fitted for large assemblies. But we were accommodated at the Dominican priory, among the backwaters of the Thames. And a very busy and teeming city I found it, this Oxford, crowded as it was with all the king's chief tenants and their knights, for they had come in force and in arms, as though King Henry's intent of moving against Wales still held good. Yet it seemed rather to me, when I had walked among the people in the streets and the retainers in the stables and halls, that every lord came ready in harness and brought his muster with him for fear of needing them in defence of his own head. I would not say they truly felt fear. But they did not intend to be taken by surprise.

Castle, friaries and halls were filled, and one or two of the schools had sent their scholars and masters home, partly in expectation of an air too disturbed for fruitful study while the parliament lasted, partly to make room for those flooding in. But the streets were still full of the schoolmen, of whom, as I was told, there must have been at this time some thirteen to fifteen hundred enrolled there. It was told to me also, though I cannot vouch for its truth, that the king's hall was built outside the gate because St Frideswide, whose tomb in her great church was a place of pilgrimage and still is so, had no wish to be visited by kings, and it was bad fortune for any crowned monarch either to enter her town or approach her grave. Yet in spite of this prohibition I believe King Henry had done so, with proper reverence, and come away none the worse for it.

Peter de Montfort made himself responsible for presenting the Welsh proctors to the king on the third day after our arrival, when all the council and parliament were fully assembled. Then for a few days I was required, for the proper justification of my presence if for no other good reason, to attend the meetings held with the English representatives, at first with King Henry himself present, though that was but a royal gesture, perhaps not even his own, but prompted by his advisers. These meetings were held in a chamber in his great lodging outside the gate, and there I saw, at one time or another, many of those fabled figures who had been until now merely names to me.

King Henry at this time was fifty years old, his face unlined, his features fair, his person very elegant and well tended. He had that willowy youthfulness of pliable people, that kept him somehow from breaking even in tempests, while stronger trees crashed to ground. His image had long faded in my mind, yet when I saw him again it arose fresh as of old, and scarcely changed. He had a certain strangely appealing honesty even in his side-steppings, that disarmed his opponents and expunged his offences. I could well understand that those lords of his old enough to have witnessed his coming to the throne, a child of nine, pretty and trusting, might still feel the old emotion, and the same helpless need to take responsibility for him, and help him out of all the pits he dug for himself by his simple cunning and cunning simplicity. And in spite of all that followed, I do believe that was how this enterprise began, that ended in civil war and tragedy. But not for Henry. In all tempests the willow is a born survivor, and springs erect after the wind has passed, none the worse for a few shed leaves. It is the oaks and cedars that fall for ever.

After the first few meetings, which were concerned with the ceremonies and courtesies, all those learned men tucked up their gowns and set to work on the real tussle, Abbot Anian and Master Madoc bent on procuring not mere truce but, if they could, a permanent peace, and the king's men, as far as I could see, not themselves absolutely opposed to this course, but quite unable to get King Henry's agreement. For like all pliable men, he could also, on occasion, be immovably obstinate. Then everyone was banished from the sessions until there should be a point of agreement ready to be recorded, and I was set free to make my way about the streets and schools and markets of Oxford, and listen and observe.

I was standing just within the gate, one among a crowd of people watching the lords of parliament ride out to the session at the king's hall on the fifteenth day of June, when one standing close at my back said into my ear in good Welsh: 'As fitting a place to meet as any, Master Samson!' And seeing that I stood sturdily and made no start he commended me in English, mentioning Meurig's name freely, for there were Welsh scholars in Oxford as well as English, and we were surrounded by so many other loud conversations, and so little to be distinguished from those about us, that openness was the safest method. He moved forward a little to be at my side, and so for the first time I saw that chancery clerk whom Meurig had encountered at Shrewsbury.

He was younger than I, and very well found, in a good gown, and his hands ringed. It was a sharp, clever, smiling face, shaven smooth as an egg, and lit by wide-open but guarded grey eyes.

'I have been following you,' he said, 'for a day and a half, to make sure no one else was following you. To be honest, I think they are so intent on their own business they have no further interest in ours. At least no one has shown any in you. We may walk together, two clerks with minor business about the court.'

His name was Cynan, and he was in very good repute with his masters. We walked together as he had said, elbowed by the Oxford crowds, among which we were anonymous and invisible, and I told him how far the discussions had progressed, and he told me what went on in parliament itself, for momentous things were happening, there in the king's great hall.

'Behind the scenes,' he said, 'the council of twenty-four, the king's twelve and the barons' twelve, are hard at work on plans for a new establishment to replace their own temporary power. What form it will take I cannot yet tell you, but before you leave it must come to a head. For the present, I can tell you that the envoys are back from Paris, with the terms of the French peace settled and agreed, but for a lot of complicated details, no doubt most concerned with money. It's a family quarrel and a family peace, and that means not one of them is going to part with a grievance or a claim without getting paid for it. But since they all want it, so it will be. You may tell your prince there will be a treaty with France within the year.'

I asked what had been said in parliament concerning the Welsh truce, for I knew it could not be pleasing to those marcher lords who had lost land to us. He hoisted his shoulders and smiled.

'You may say so! There are those who came to this town armed and ready, believing still in the king's writ and pointing their noses towards Chester. Now they find that is a dead issue. If there ever was union in this land, as some truly believed, Wales may be one factor that breaks it apart. Come,' he said, suddenly quickening his stride and drawing me towards the gate, 'I will show you one enemy at least, inveterate and venomous.'

So I went with him, and we joined the gapers about the precinct of the royal hall, watched the lordly arrivals, saw the horses led away by grooms, and the nobles of the land striding into the hall one after another, the rulers of this realm of England.

Cynan said: 'That one, the burly man with the frown and the measured stride and the harassed air – no, he's no enemy to any man, he wills well to all, too well! That is the new justiciar, Hugh Bigod, brother to the earl of Norfolk. Yes, they already have the first thing they demanded, a justiciar. And this one following, this is Gloucester.'

Earl Richard de Clare was a debonair person in his middle thirties, handsome and fair. And I had thought of the earl of Gloucester as a looming thundercloud over the southern march of Wales. Surely men are magnified and diminished by the circumstance into which they are born, and I wonder if they themselves are not malformed and even broken by that accident of birth, being forced into forms for which their hearts and minds have no desire. I looked upon this man and was drawn to him. He had a proud but not a vicious face, rather troubled and open to wounds.

'He is here!' said Cynan in my ear. 'Observe him!'

It was a man of much the same age as de Clare who came stalking into the doorway, dropping his bridle into the groom's hand without a glance, and discarding the retinue of three or four squires and valets who rode behind him. He was of middle height, slender and sudden of movement, with a narrow, fierce, arrogant face, made to look still more elongated by a trimmed and pointed beard and a thin, high-bridged nose, and the sweeping glance of his black eyes was like the circling of a sword, so that I hardly wondered that men made haste to step back out of its range.

'That is William de Valence,' said Cynan, 'the eldest of King Henry's Lusignan half-brothers, and the most dangerous. And the hottest enemy of your prince in this land, if words be any guide. It seems he has been the latest to feel the goad – the men of Cemais have plundered and raided his earldom of Pembroke, that he holds through his wife, and he blames the example and encouragement of the prince of Wales for all his trials. He came here all whetted and ready for the muster and his revenge, to be told the Welsh war is already a dead issue, and a truce in the making. He got up in a fury and told parliament it had no business to be haring off after domestic reforms that could well wait a better day, that its proper work was to march into Wales and avenge his wrongs on Llewelyn. And when he found but lukewarm backing, he turned on the new council and the prime movers of the new order, and denounced them as little better than traitors. That went down badly with many, but it was the earl of Leicester who answered him, and it ended in a burning quarrel. Valence is well hated, by English and Welsh alike.'

'And yet,' I said, 'when they cry out against the foreigners, are they not striking at Earl Simon no less than at Valence?'

He shook his head. 'Never look for logic, at least among crowds, you shall not find it. Aliens, they say, but it means more than being born in France. The earl of Leicester after his fashion is as French as King Louis himself, but when he came here to take up his earldom – and it came to him through an Englishwoman, fairly and honestly – he took up the burden of Englishness without undue self-seeking, and put down roots he meant and means to send deep. Count Peter of Savoy has not even that degree of native blood, but no man rails at him. He puts into this land more than he takes from it, and gives honest counsel to the king. But the Lusignans came to make their fortunes when their house fell into some disfavour in France, they marry land, they accept church office, wherever there's money and advantage, there are they, and all their Poitevin hangers-on come flooding in after them. They see themselves somewhat at risk now, since King Henry feels them to be a liability to him at this pass. But they will cling tooth and nail to what they have, and if they feel it threatened they will not hesitate to break apart this present consent and unity. For what is being said and thought and hoped concerning the earl of Leicester, you may bear it around you.'

And so I did, after we had parted, going about the streets and keeping my ears open. Surely those I heard talking had but a hazy idea yet of what the reform of the realm could mean, or how it was to be brought about, since the makers of the new England were even then only beginning their own consideration of ends and means. But they had suffered for want of a just order, or so they felt, and they had grasped the promise of it now that it was mooted, and their hope was real and urgent and would not be easily satisfied, or easily quenched. Oxford, perhaps, was peculiarly alive to such issues, by reason of the schools, but even in the countryside it impressed me greatly that the simple were following with fierce intelligence the turmoil in the state, and from this troubling of the waters looked for a miraculous cure.

Thus far I had seen many of the great men engaged upon the enterprise, bishops, barons and knights, and those great clerks – for truly some I think were most able men – who served the king. Once I caught a glimpse of Henry de Montfort riding out from the town gate, and with him a younger boy, by the likeness his brother. But I had not yet set eyes on their sire, whose name I heard ever more frequently and ardently on the lips of the people.

It was two days after this first encounter with Cynan that Abbot Anian again took me with him into the final meeting with the English negotiators, for they had secured the best terms they could get, and the agreement was ready to be copied, sealed and exchanged. Peace we could not persuade them to, King Henry stubbornly resisting, but a truce was ours, to run until the first day of August of the following year, thirteen months of grace for Llewelyn to consolidate without hindrance all his gains. And a mere one hundred marks to pay for it! Not one foot of the ground won were we called upon to surrender. The only concession was that the king's officers in Chester should have unhindered access to the Lord Edward's isolated castles of Diserth and Degannwy, to provision and maintain the garrisons, and that we took for granted. For if the truce prohibited us from taking them by storm, then someone had to feed them meantime, and better at the king's expense than at ours. Such were the terms the abbot was taking back to Llewelyn.

King Henry himself appeared for the ceremonious sealing of the agreement, somewhat forcedly gracious, still with one wistful eye on the war of conquest he had intended, as the possibility passed from him. Then the proctors withdrew together, and we clerks were left to gather up all the documents and exchange the needful copies. Master Madoc and the abbot were to stay yet some nine or ten days in Oxford, until all the personal contracts had been prepared, and the letters of guarantee for the payment of the indemnity, and various other details for which their approval was necessary, and that afforded me time to meet again with Cynan, whose account of how things went in parliament would be more exact than what could be gathered in the streets.

I was still in the chamber where the committee had met, copying the last 'datum apud Oxoniam decimo septimo die Junii', when the door opened behind me, and someone came into the room. I took it to be one of the royal clerks returning, for they, too, had left documents lying, and had still work to do. But when the incomer first stood a moment motionless, and then came round between me and the open window-space, then I did look up, and with a start of something like alarm, for this being loomed so large that he cut off the light from me, and the June day was suddenly dark, and my vellum overcast as though clouds had gathered for thunder.

He was a good head taller than any I had seen about the court, head and shoulders above the middle make of man, with broad breast and long arms, and narrow flanks that tapered strongly into long, powerful legs. He stood and looked down at me with a wide, brown stare, unwavering and undisguised by either smile or frown, and the unthinking arrogance of that look said that he had the right to stare so upon any in this land, and ought not to be evaded. His forehead was massive, his features large and regular and handsome, and his dress, short riding tunic and chausses of fine brown cloth stitched with gold, all carelessly royal. But his size alone would have told me that I was looking at the Lord Edward, the heir of England.

I rose and louted to him, and waited his pleasure, since he did not at once lose interest in me and withdraw. And as he looked upon me, so did I upon him, for in many ways he was startling and strange to me. It was thirteen years since I had seen him, and then he had been but six years old, a tow-headed child, already very tall for his age, following our David like his shadow. Now he had hair very darkly brown, almost black, a curious change, and, whatever he might still retain of youthful awkwardness and inexperience, most markedly he was already a man. I made him nineteen, and astonished myself by recalling, out of what hidden place in my memory I cannot tell, that this very day, the seventeenth of June, was his birthday.

It was not until he turned a little, and drew away from the window, and the light fell brightly upon his face, that I saw that this splendid creature was flawed, for as soon as the roundness of his stare was relaxed, his left eyelid drooped over the brown eye with that same dubious heaviness always so noticeable in his father. It gave me a shock of wariness and surprise, for though in the father it seemed fitting after a fashion, in this grand countenance such an ambiguity had no place. It contradicted all that glow of openness and boldness and nobility that he projected about him. It was one more minor shadow after the sudden stormcloud his bulk had cast upon the day.

When he had looked his fill upon me he said, in a voice youthful and light of tone, but measured and assured: 'You are the Welsh clerk the abbot brought with him, are you not?'

And when I owned it: 'I saw you pass with him the other day, and thought that I should know you,' he said. 'If I remember well, your name is Samson. You were David's groom and servant when he was a child in my father's care.'

I said: 'Your memory is better, my lord, than I had any right to expect. I am indeed that Samson. It is kind of you to keep me so long in mind.'

'So you are still in the service of the princes of Gwynedd,' he said. 'I trust all goes well with the Lady Senena? And David – I pray you, when you return, commend me to him. He will remember that we were good friends in childhood.'

'I thank you, my lord, Prince David is well, and so is his mother. He has not forgotten the time spent with you. If he had this opportunity your

Grace has afforded me,' I said, 'on this day of all days, he would wish your Grace all happiness and blessing for your natal day.'

He was surprised and disarmed, and the sudden smile was strange and brief on that monumental countenance. 'I see there is nothing amiss with your own memory,' he said. And he looked at the parchment I had before me, and said, with an unreadable face: 'I trust it may be a day worthy of celebrating for both of us. It should be so, since it is also the day we were appointed to muster at Chester.' And with that, as suddenly as he had come, he withdrew, and left me to finish my work.

Such was the Lord Edward at nineteen, sufficiently gracious to one so insignificant as myself, yet with something ominous about him. I made my way back to the Dominican priory in no very settled mind about him. That he had truly felt affection for David I knew from of old, that the memory of that affection might still warm him I could believe. But always I saw again the left eyelid drooping and veiling the brown eye, and that could not but remind me of King Henry benevolently promising what afterwards he never fulfilled, as though he closed that eye to be blind to his own double-dealing. A small thing of the body, but so slyly apt. In the father, a weak and amiable man by and large, it could be accepted as no more than a timely warning. But if strong men and giants study also to close one eye to their own false intents, then where are ordinary human creatures to look for refuge?

The last meeting that I had with Cynan was on the last day of June, for we stayed the month out in Oxford. And that time we met in the meadows by the river in the cool of the evening, when many scholars and townspeople were strolling there for enjoyment at the end of the working day. Something of what had befallen in the assembly was already common knowledge, criticised and commended in the town. As, that the form of government had been remade in a practical shape, and still by general consent, which was achievement enough. These agreed principles came to be known as the Provisions of Oxford.

After the election of a justiciar, some twenty of the royal castles had been put in the hands of new and trusted castellans. Out of the king's twelve in the council, two had been chosen by the magnates' twelve, and from the magnates' twelve two by the king's men, to elect a new permanent council of fifteen. King and council were to rule together and respect each other. The dates of three parliaments were laid down for every year, though others could be called at need. No one found fault with all this. Since unity had called us there to make truce instead of dispatching the host to Chester to make war, it seemed that for the moment English unity was as great a benefit to us in Wales, and I could be cautiously glad that it continued unbroken.

'No longer,' said Cynan. 'The shell begins to crack, and what will hatch is hard to guess. This reform was never meant to raise the cry "Out with the aliens!" but the winds are blowing it in that direction, whether or no. There's been the devil to pay in the assembly, and the Lusignans have refused the oath that's being required of all the baronage. Those who drafted it added a clause that has frightened away more than the

Lusignans. It was all very well holding men by consent, but it stuck in their gullets to have to add at the end: And he that opposes this is a mortal enemy of the commonweal! All the timid and moderate are taking fright, and some have fallen away besides the Poitevins. But there's another solid reason for their defection – with the king so short of money, the lords of the reform have ordered the return to the crown of certain royal lands and castles he has given away to others, and who holds more of them than his half-brothers? Whatever the cause, they have not only refused the oath, but tried to persuade King Henry to break his, and abandon the new Provisions. I've heard, though God knows yet if it's true, that Aymer of Lusignan, the one that's bishop-elect of Winchester before he's old enough to hold the office, has run off and shut himself in his castle at Wolvesey, and rumour says his three brothers will not be long behind. Now the magnates have no choice but to deal with this dissident brood somehow, and whatever they may do will please neither king nor pope. Aymer is, after all, a bishop-elect. If they try to rid themselves of him, that's hardly likely to endear them to Pope Alexander. And they need his goodwill sorely.'

'But they still intend,' I said, 'to send a delegation to Rome to try to get easier terms for the king? And to ask for a papal legate to come over and help in the settlement?'

'They intend, yes. But the pope has shown no relenting yet, and if Aymer is turned out of his bishopric that won't sweeten him. On the whole,' said Cynan with chilly cynicism, 'the pope has done very well out of holding our poor wriggling king to his bond. If he has not ousted the Hohenstaufen from Sicily, he has got half his crippling debts in the business paid by English tenths and aids. Never trouble about English pockets and English grievances, but leave them to it, take your truce home, and hope to keep it refurbished every year at their expense. What has Wales to do in this dispute but profit from it?'

That was good enough sense, but either I had outgrown my own ideas of the world and the state during this stay in Oxford, or else some disturbing new vision that troubled our content had journeyed to Aber with young Henry de Montfort, and caused both Llewelyn and me to sicken with the same obscure longing. For surely those weighty men who had tried and were still trying to amend the England they lived in had seen a vision that had application even for us in Wales. True, our society was utterly different in its organisation from theirs, yet it could not remain utterly separate. The England we rubbed shoulders with in the marches was an abrasive force, and it mattered to us what manner of England it was. All the more since we must, in a changing world, adapt to it and borrow from it, for no border severs man from man, or one manner of living totally from another.

So I asked what was ever on my mind: 'And the earl of Leicester? What is his stand?'

'His stand is upon the whole reform, and nothing less. He sees an England remade, where all members work together for the common good, guided by a ray of the spirit emanating from the pope, and one in a Christendom made in the same mould of service and selflessness. Never stare

231

so,' said Cynan, smiling somewhat bitterly, for indeed I had turned to examine him narrowly at this unexpected utterance. 'I can recognise a saint when I see one, and a demon, too, and Earl Simon is both – or just falls short of both, and fits together the two halves of him into something unique among men. This is a man who will be cheated of a hundred marks rather than owe one. But also he will exact the last mark owing to him, or, even more strenuously, to his lady, or die still dunning the debtor. He has had saints to his teachers, like Bishop Robert of Lincoln, and both his saint and his demon have drunk deep of them, and been exalted. He is all pride, and all humility. The king dreads him, and Friar Adam Marsh reproves him for his moods and his depressions, and is heeded as reverently as by a raw novice. But what can the common human experience do with a force of nature but take refuge from it? He will stand fast, but in the end he will stand alone.'

I said: 'And I have never seen him!' Almost I added that I had never seen Cynan until now, for he spoke with a tongue not his own, inflamed by the spirit. And I had thought him a clever, loyal, limited exile, holding fast to an ideal of home for his own self-respect. 'I must see this man,' I said, 'before I leave Oxford.'

'You shall,' said Cynan.

He took me – so simple it was – to the great church of St Frideswide, to the chapel where her tomb was, forbidden to kings. That same night we went there, the light already failing, and the lamps about the tomb made a clear reddish radiance. We stood in the darkest corner of the chapel, and there were others going and coming, so that we were in no way significant, and no man marked us.

A man came in from the evening, through the dark of the church into the ruddy light of the lamps, and went without haste to kneel at the tomb. Though he was unattended, there was no need to question if he were noble, and though he was soberly clad, dark-coloured and plain, his plainness had its own splendour. And when he was kneeling, upright and still with linked hands before his face, I had him in profile and saw him clearly. He was no taller than your middling tall man, he had thick shoulders and a powerful body, compact and at peace with itself, at least at this hour. For all his movements, and after, his stillness, were whole and harmonious. When he was not at worship, I could well imagine that same sturdy body knotted into tensions lesser men never know. The linked hands held so still I saw every sinew. They were large, strong and intense, of a braced sensitivity that caused my own hands to clench and quiver. And the head was a bronze head, cropped, naked, marvellous, like a Roman emperor of the nobler sort, with large, bright bone thrusting through flesh and skin and brown, glowing hair, that clung like a beast's rich fell upon the quiet skull. His face was shaven clean like a monk, and it seemed that it could not be otherwise, so pure was the line that framed it, and so fiercely still. He had great, loftily-arched eyelids closed over large eyes, like a prince already carven on a tomb, and a wide, austere, feeling mouth that formed the measured phrases of prayer with fine and private movements, and under this generous mouth a generous jaw graven in gold by the lamps about him.

Cynan said in my ear: 'You have your wish.'

It was not needful to tell me, the print of his legend was deep and clear upon him, and the young Norman vigour I had seen in his son Henry was but the lesser and lighter promise of what I saw now, yet the likeness was marked. Once seen, even at a distance there could never again be any mistaking this man for other than the earl of Leicester.

We watched until he ended his prayer. When he opened his eyes, the great lids rolling back from them into the burnished sockets of bone, they were so large and so straight of gaze that they seemed prominent, though they were deeply set. Their colour could not be determined there in the church; what they had was rather a burning clarity. If, as they said, the king owned he was afraid of him, I think what he meant was rather the holy dread that small, spiral men feel in the presence of the towering and upright. And surely it was the king's saving grace that he could not only feel but confess it. This man might have fears, too, an obligation failed, a principle lowered, a point of honour in doubt, but never of another man.

So we watched him rise from his knees, not with the spring of youth, for he was approaching his fiftieth year, but with a solid, powerful thrust, and pace firmly out of the chapel and out of our sight. And Cynan said: 'Who knows but some day men will make pilgrimages to his tomb? They might get a better hearing from him than from St Frideswide!'

I saw Earl Simon again, the day we rode from Oxford, for he came in courtesy to bid farewell to the envoys. Seen by day, his eyes appeared a deep and luminous grey, more daunting than the blue gaze of his son's innocence, because the father was not innocent, but pure, and that is a more terrible and wonderful thing. Strange to be seen, there followed at his elbow one more accustomed to be followed, and hung attentive on his words and looks at every move. And that was something I had not looked for in the Lord Edward, the heir of England. When it was fixed upon Earl Simon's face, even that veiled left eye opened wide, and the lofty stone face quickened into warmth. Then I understood that the spell the earl had cast upon me by St Frideswide's tomb, and upon Cynan, I know not where, beforetime, was nothing particular to us, but the enchantment he exercised upon most young men, even this royal giant who stood dwarfed beside him. And I thought then that this might be a bond more dangerous to the earl than to the prince, for unless I greatly mistook him the Lord Edward would not take kindly to being spellbound for one moment longer than the reflected magic flattered and enhanced him. And what he had once loved and admired, and then found proof against his possessive affection, he might resent and hate no less fiercely.

Then we rode home with our truce and our thirteen months of grace, and told all that we had seen and heard in Oxford to Llewelyn. And Llewelyn, having put in order all the practical moves the report required of him, brooded long over the shadowy grandeur that hung over the future of England, like a morning too brilliant to promise constancy until nightfall, and ended saying, as I had said: 'I must see this man!'

CHAPTER III

From this time we set to work to make the parchment gain effective, for even when a truce has been agreed by both parties with goodwill, it is no easy matter to guard a long and difficult border from infringement. No prince can be everywhere, or have his officers everywhere, and there are always plenty of roving men of independent mind on both sides of the barrier to make the occasional raid a tempting prospect. There need be no planned offence, either; it is enough if a hunted deer crosses into alien territory.

The order went out to all Llewelyn's allies, castellans and bailiffs immediately the truce was ratified. But there were certain complications in the south, for Meredith ap Rhys Gryg, now healed of the wound he got at Carmarthen bridge, was not fully bound by the truce, being Welsh and not English. Insofar as he was vassal to King Henry he was bound, but in his own lands he had his own rights, and was in no mind to sit quietly after the knock he had taken. But he had David and Rhys Fychan keeping close watch on him from Carreg Cennen, and their power was enough to temper his grievance with caution. And as to Patrick of Chaworth, as the king's seneschal he was obliged to respect the king's truce, and was no longer free, at least openly, to aid his ally. His was a delicate situation, for even when all action between the two sides was halted, it was a matter for exact definition what territory each held, and the need to separate the armed bands was urgent. As long as men have weapons in their hands and an enemy within reach, peace is hard to preserve. But there was nothing to prevent de Chaworth from keeping close company with Meredith, and in force, too, so long as his avowed concern was the procuring of a sensible agreement on boundaries and the disengagement of the armies.

Still, by the time July was past and August well forward, and still the king's seneschal kept the field with a formidable host, it began to seem as if he was more concerned with maintaining a presence in arms than with getting a settlement. Meredith and Patrick were at Cardigan, with a large force drawn from all the marcher lordships, and David and Rhys Fychan were joined by Meredith ap Owen in the cantref of Emlyn, though even so their numbers were much inferior to those Meredith ap Rhys Gryg could field if de Chaworth chose to risk aiding him in a quick assault.

Llewelyn gnawed his knuckles over this threat, and was in two minds about what he should do, for he was unwilling to leave Rhys Fychan exposed to more loss by withdrawing David and his men, and yet a little apprehensive of David's high temper and taste for audacity if he remained on the spot, with the king's men close and ready to provoke him.

Their mother, the Lady Senena, also felt strongly enough about affairs to leave David's maenol at Neigwl, which she controlled in his absence, to the steward's care, and come visiting to Aber, a thing she did less often as time passed. She was well beyond fifty now, and a little slower in her movements and more stooped in her person than of old, and very grey, but her thick black brows were as formidable and her spirit as imperious as ever, and still she gave orders to everyone with the same expectation of being instantly obeyed, except that from Llewelyn she never truly looked for more than the easy tolerance with which he listened and then did as he would. Yet at least he listened, for the Lady Senena, in spite of some past mistakes, had sharp good sense.

'You should fetch the boy away from there,' she said, rapping her stick smartly on the ground for emphasis, 'before he puts your truce in peril, and his own head after it.'

'I have been thinking the same thing myself,' Llewelyn owned, 'though it's rather Meredith I distrust than David, as long as they stand there forehead to forehead like two rams.'

'You should go yourself,' she said roundly, 'and see the peace enforced, and the men brought home.'

'Not for the world!' said Llewelyn. 'I gave him the command, and I would not snatch it back from him. But I may go so far as to send him a mere suggestion, a word of advice. How if we ask Samson to be the courier? No one will know better how to manage David.'

So we went to work and prepared formal copies of the truce, for David to send to both Meredith ap Rhys Gryg and Patrick of Chaworth, as a courtesy to men standing against him in arms when the agreement was made. 'Put it into his head,' Llewelyn said, 'if he has not thought of it for himself, to demand a meeting face to face to settle the details of separation, a meeting with both, mind, for de Chaworth will be a check upon Meredith if he does his proper duty. Since they hold off from the first move, we'll make it for them, and force a response.'

So I was his courier, and rode south alone. It was late in a hot August when I made my way into the commote of Emlyn, and after some enquiry found where the allies were encamped. In that summer weather they had no need to seek a roof at night, or far to go for food; campaigning was a pleasant and even an idle life while everyone held off from battle.

David came out, brown and hard and burning with health, to embrace me heartily, and made no ado about welcoming his brother's counsel. Though Llewelyn did well to move considerately with him, for he could be haughty and quick to take offence when the mood was on him. Nor was it the first time I had been used to make some gesture of guidance acceptable, my privilege with him being curiously strong.

'We are tangled in a net of legal quibbles,' he said, 'and to tell truth I have been looking for a way to bring the thing to a head. But one false move from us, and Meredith may very well cry breach of truce and drag in Chaworth, who by all we have seen is ready and eager for it. Let's try this means! As the king's proxy, Chaworth will be hard put to it to find

235

an excuse for not attending to see fair boundaries drawn, when the parties are the king's vassal and the partner in the king's truce. Let's challenge him! We'll call him in as arbitrator.'

So we sent out those two invitations to conference, with the copies of the royal agreement by way of probe. And David chose to send me as courier to de Chaworth in the castle of Cardigan, to underline by my embassage as Llewelyn's clerk the royal nature of the agreement to which I had been a witness, and the penalties for breaking it. Which I greatly approved in David, in that he was willing in Llewelyn's interest to make use of the personal weight of Llewelyn's name. Every such evidence of the right relationship between the brothers of Gwynedd was sweet to me.

'And a clerk,' said David, sharply teasing me as he sent me forth, 'is half-holy in all circumstances, and may go safely into Cardigan and come again. Still, keep your sword about you. I cannot spare my half-priest.'

I doubt I was more swordsman than priest by that time, having fought so often beside my lord, and never having gone beyond the first stage of seeking orders. But I went as he bade me, and bore myself neutrally and modestly in the halls of Cardigan.

This Patrick the seneschal was a big, fine-looking black-avised man, very gracious but with uneasy eyes. He had got his great lands, like many another of his kind, through marriage to an heiress, his wife Hawise bringing him not only the lordship of Kidwelly, but also the castle of Ogmore, in Glamorgan. These gentry who held through their Welsh or half-Welsh womenfolk kept always a tighter and greedier hold on the soil than those born to it by right, and Patrick was little better liked than William of Valence in Pembroke. Still, he received me into his hall with ceremony, so I gave him back good value in the dignities and styles of those I represented. There were plenty of his officers and knights about him, but no sign of Meredith ap Rhys Gryg. But I had kept my eyes open in the baileys, and I knew Meredith's Welshmen when I saw them, even if they wore English arms.

'My lord,' I said when I had delivered him the scroll of the truce, 'I am commissioned by my lord Llewelyn, prince of Wales, and by his brother Prince David as his lieutenant in these parts, to present you these letters, in token of their acceptance with a whole heart of the contents therof, and their confidence that you, as the seneschal of the king's Grace, will hold to the agreement as faithfully as they undertake to do. It is in the interests of both parties that there should be peace between us here as elsewhere. You know that this is complicated by the position of the lord Meredith ap Rhys. We desire that an impartial judge shall define where the line of demarcation between us is to be drawn, and we hold that there can be no fairer voice than the king's seneschal, in an issue between Welshman and Welshman. In the name of the Prince of Wales, Prince David invites you to preside at a conference to settle all disputed claims and bring about peace between our arms. And he sends, through your courtesy, this same invitation to Meredith ap Rhys Gryg. The time may be as soon as you will, and the place wherever you find just and convenient. If you will, we will move halfway to meet you.'

I could think of nothing I had omitted, to convince him that he had no choice but to accede. And if he accepted, then Meredith had no choice, either, since he was completely dependent upon the English muster to counter the force we could loose against him. It seemed to me that Patrick was relieved at being offered this way out of an uneasy situation, and brightened very thoughtfully as he read and considered. He took the scroll that was superscribed to Meredith, and did not deny that he knew very well where to find him. For all I know, he may have been behind the hangings of the dais that moment, with both ears stretched.

Patrick said what it was incumbent on him to say, paying lip service to the king's will and the sacredness of the king's peace, and after some pondering named Cilgerran as the spot where we should meet, as being between our two stations along the river Teifi, and to that I agreed.

'And as to the day,' he said, 'it is now the last day of August; let it be the fifth of September, then, if that is agreeable to your lord.'

'In his name,' I said, 'I close with that day. At Cilgerran on the fifth of September the conference shall be, and there shall be nothing attempted in arms before that day.'

Thereupon he offered me refreshment while he dictated a letter of acceptance on his own part, and a guarantee that the like would be forthcoming from Meredith ap Rhys Gryg as soon as possible. And before evening I rode back into our camp with the fruit of my embassage, and reported everything to David and his council.

'The castle of Cilgerran is held for the Lord Edward,' said Meredith ap Owen cautiously. For the heir of the Cantilupes, whose stronghold it was, was still only a boy, and Edward was his guardian during his minority.

'That should be a guarantee,' said David. 'Edward may not like the truce, but for his father's sake he will not break it. And surely de Chaworth will never dare misuse a castle Edward holds.' Then he asked me of all I had seen in Cardigan, and I told him as best I could judge what numbers they must have, by the great plump of knights he had about him there, all the more as Meredith ap Rhys Gryg had kept himself and his men well out of sight.

'Double our numbers they may be,' said David, 'but double our worth I doubt. But we'll be first in Cilgerran and choose our ground.'

So we marched in time to make camp on the evening of the third of September, and chose a raised site among trees outside the vil of Cilgerran, with a sweep of the river to cover our right and rear, and good lookout spots from which the approaches from town and castle could be governed. Our forward scouts brought word that de Chaworth himself was not yet in either, though the town was full of his first companies. And early the next day the leaders rode in, for we were now but two or three miles from Cardigan, having gone more than halfway to meet them. A courier came before noon, a middle-aged squire of de Chaworth's household, to appoint our meeting to take place next day in the meadows before the town, where they were setting up tents to give the council shelter at need.

'Patrick has a mature taste in couriers,' said David, frowning after the rider as he departed. 'No sprightly page, but a seasoned man-at-arms, and with his eyes wide open and roving. What need was there for this visit at all but a gesture of courtesy, the prettier the better compliment? The hour was already set in advance.'

Nevertheless he shrugged off this doubt, and we sat out the day with strung patience. When the late dark came down David and Rhys Fychan circled the camp and made sure all was well, and every outpost wide awake. A dark night it was to be, without a moon, but on such summer nights there is always a glimmer of stars. It was very silent and still, the freshening wind of evening already dying, barely a rustle of leaves to be heard.

'My thumbs prick,' said David, straining erect to listen, and shivered, not with fear, rather as a hound quivers, snuffing the wind after quarry. And he sent forward two more men, well beyond the limit of the camp on the road to the town, to lie in cover, and two more in our rear along the river-bank. Nonetheless he let the camp take its rest as though he felt no qualms, only ordering that every man should keep his weapons and harness close to hand while he slept.

Our fires were turfed down to a glimmer, and it was almost fully dark, as dark as it would be that night, when David lay down in his cloak to sleep. It was hard to know if he believed in his own precautions, for he had done off all harness, though he kept it by him, and stretched himself out in comfort to his rest. There had been no call from our outposts, no movement from the town. The first owl I heard calling, called from upstream, well in our rear, and I like a fool took it for a real owl, so hushed and still was all the night about us. But David, who, I swear, had been fast asleep, started up out of his cloak and was on his feet in an instant, stretched and listening, his eyes two pale blue flames, and when the call came again he kicked out at the turfed fire and set it blazing high. Men boiled silently out of the grass and the bushes, reaching out for sword and knife before they were well awake, and David's squire sprang out of the shadows into the glare with his lord's hauberk and sword in his arms. And but for the crackle of the fire the silence had barely trembled as yet. We waited, but facing up-river, away from Cilgerran.

'They cannot be there,' said Rhys Fychan in a whisper.

'They are there,' said David, just above his breath. 'They have spent this whole day making a great circle about us, while we watched them deck their tents for us in the fields. A great circle through the forests on this side the river, to come round on our quarter. And a great circle on the other bank, to cross again upstream from us. The rest will come out from the town to help them finish the work. So they think!'

'Shall I sound?' asked the boy with the horn, quivering.

'Not yet. Between us and them every man knows already. It's only those towards the town may need an alarm, and they are not threatened yet. Let them close in.'

It was long minutes more before they struck the eastward rim of our camp, expecting to fall upon sleeping men, and clashed hand to hand among the scattered trees with men armed and waiting. The first shuddering clang of metals and shrill of cries went through the dark like lightning tearing it, and then David cried: 'Sound!' and the horn pealed higher above the confused din, and we surged forward like leaves blown by its breath, towards the attack, while behind us, back and back to the rim of the open meadows, our comrades started up to keep our circle unbroken. There, at the first advance across the meadows from the town, the archers would have their targets clear. For us it was swords and knives, and every sense sharpened to pick out friend from foe.

They had their night eyes then, as well as we, but we closed our ring to hold them out, and so fought pressing forward rather than giving back, for as long as we could keep our ranks. They were very many, and they came in heavy waves against us, but the shock of surprise was lost. All these who had spent the day closing their trap round us had gone on foot; we were spared the horrid confusion of mangled horses threshing among us and turning our cover into bone-breaking hazards. Man to man is fair odds, night or day, and if they had sent a spy out to view our dispositions, still we had possession of the ground we had chosen, and to take it proved beyond their power.

I kept at David's side as well as I might, as always it was my custom and privilege to keep Llewelyn's left flank when we were in the field together. And hard and hot work it was to keep pace with David, for he was so violent and agile there was no matching him, and in the wildest of the labour I heard him laughing, and a sound like light singing that spilled out of him much as a cat purrs, for pure pleasure, not in the killing itself, though indeed we had not sought it and had no need to feel shame at it, but in his own readiness and skill and prowess, and the mastery of his body. And I also exulted in him, for he was like a living fire in the darkness and din and chaos of the night.

There was then no time to beware of anything beyond arm's-length, the range of a sword or dagger was all the room each man had. But after a while I knew that we had moved forward, while they had made no advance, for we were trampling the dead and wounded, and that frightful floundering, and the cries from under our feet, and the gushing groan of breath as we trod the air unwillingly out of a living man, these were the worst things of that night.

It lasted until the east, towards which we faced, began to grow pearl-grey before the dawn, and then we could see more of what we had done and what had been done to us, and then men began to turn from us and run, slipping away between the trees and plunging into the river. As for the expected attack by mounted knights from the town, we did not know until full daylight whether it had ever been ventured or no, and found it then but a minor part of the battle, for it had been designed only as the final blow, and the archers had dealt with it by starlight before ever it reached our encampment.

So the dawn came, and what was left of the chivalry of de Chaworth and the English lordships of South Wales broke away from us and fled back into Cilgerran to lick its wounds there. And we went somewhat wearily and numbly hunting among the trees for prisoners worth taking, for Welsh worth retrieving and grafting into our own forces if they were so minded, and for our own wounded and dead. As the light brightened we saw that of the enemy the number left here was great, and among them many knights. And it seemed to me that Meredith ap Rhys Gryg, who surely had persuaded de Chaworth to this disastrous madness and treachery, had also let the English bear the brunt of the assault, and kept his own men in reserve. For it was the English who had suffered worst. The tangle of them in the broken and ravaged undergrowth was full of bright devices now smutched and bloodied and buckled, like the flesh beneath the surcoats. We made up the tale of them as well as we could. And combing the soiled grasses low towards the river, David came suddenly to a halt before me, and leaned, gazing long at the ground.

He came, God knows how, always so clean and bright out of every testing, as though the elements that bruised the rest of us had no power over him. In that dawn he should have been streaked with sweat and smoke and blood, if not his own blood, and wearied to stumbling, and here he moved immaculate and light, his black hair only a little damp on his temples, and his eyelids a little heavy over the jewelled blue of his eyes. And close at his feet, where he stared thus ungrieving and unexulting, there was the wreckage of a man, broken and trampled, with a slashed face turned up to the morning light, and a caved breast holding a pool of blackened blood. A tall man once, handsome and dark, with black brows touching, and black beard finely pointed. And very nobly equipped, if so many had not fought over his accoutrements in the dark.

David looked up at me, his eyes like blind blue stones. 'This is he?' he asked. For he had never seen the king's seneschal close before.

I said: 'It is.' I had spoken with him but a few days since; even at this pass I could not mistake him.

So we took up Patrick de Chaworth, persuaded to his death, and had him borne away under flag of truce into Cilgerran.

'A pity!' said David, grim. 'It should have been the one who talked him into this betrayal.'

But though we searched the whole day among the wreckage of that night's work, we found no trace of Meredith ap Rhys Gryg. Could Rhys Fychan have laid hands on his uncle then, I believe he would have killed him, though he was in general a temperate man. But though we found some dead of Meredith's following, the man himself was escaped clean, and the next we heard of him was that he was barricaded into his castle of Dryslwyn with the strongest garrison he could muster, and braced ready for attack, and very unlikely to show his nose out of those walls again until the echoes of Cilgerran had passed away on the wind, men having such short memories.

I think David would have been happy to attempt the storming of Dryslwyn, but Meredith ap Owen and Rhys Fychan said no, and reluctantly he owned that they were right, and there was no credit in breaching the very truce we had just asserted and defended. So he contented himself with sending into Cilgerran, to the dead lord's lieutenant, a formal protest against the breach of faith, and a flat statement, for want of the promised conference, of the demarcation he proposed to observe, and to recommend to the prince of Wales and his chief vassals in the south. And so demoralised were the survivors in the fortress, and so willing to bury the unhappy and unblessed venture, that they accepted David's proposed line hastily, grateful to get out of it so lightly.

David raised his brows and laughed when he read the reply, somewhat startled by his own success. 'So we have come out of it with our own demands met, with limited losses, and with little prospect of further trouble in these parts while the truce lasts,' he said. 'But I wish we could have taken Meredith ap Rhys Gryg back with us in chains, to stand his trial for treason. Small chance of that now. He'll lie still in Dryslwyn like a hare in her form, the rest of the year. We must wait another opportunity.'

Then the canons of Cenarth came and ministered to the dying and buried the dead, doing their merciful office humbly and sadly. And we, declining Rhys Fychan's pressing invitation to linger at Carreg Cennen on our way, made by the shortest route for Gwynedd, keeping company with Meredith ap Owen through his lands along the Aeron, and so coastwise into Merioneth. I think David was sorely tempted to pay the desired visit to his sister, but Carreg Cennen would have taken us too far out of our way, and he wished to render full account to Llewelyn as soon as possible. Therefore he excused himself. And I was mortally glad, for by the grace of God I had been spared Godred's close clinging on this occasion, he being left with the castle garrison, and I had no wish to seek him out when I was delivered from his seeking of me, much less to see him in proud possession of Cristin whom he did not truly value, and had dangled before me, unless love had made me mad with suspicion, like bait to some personal trap in which he essayed to take me. My desire was never to see him again. And truly it should have been, no less, never again to see her, but that I could never quite command.

Howbeit, David would go home, and home we went, to recount to Llewelyn all that had passed. And he, though without any great surprise or expectation of exacting redress, nevertheless made a point of sending a letter of protest to King Henry over his seneschal's faith-breaking, that it might be known what were the rights and wrongs of the matter, and any attempt to put the onus upon the Welsh by a crooked story might be forestalled.

The reply he got was conciliatory, and professed strong disapproval of de Chaworth's unaccountable act, of which neither the king nor any of his officers had had prior knowledge, nor would have countenanced it if they had. The unlucky lord, being dead, could not suffer further from being disowned, yet some of us wondered.

While we were busy in the south, in England, it seemed, the dispute over the oath and the Provisions, so far from being reconciled, had begun to split the ranks of the baronage apart in good earnest. All four of the Lusignan brothers had refused the oath, and being offered in default only a choice between exile for all, or exile for the two who had no land claims or office in England, and safe-custody for William of Valence and the bishop-elect, who had, they had chosen all to leave, and sailed for France along with many other Poitevins. Certainly not to renounce their claims peacefully, to judge by Valence's temper, but rather to recruit sympathy among the powerful in France and from the pope in Rome. While we were fighting the battle of Cilgerran in the first days of

September, Pope Alexander was sitting sourly entrenched against all the exalted arguments of the delegation from England, suspecting their ideas and aims of all manner of treason and heresy, and flatly refusing them countenance, or what they most earnestly asked of him, the despatch of a legate to preside over and regulate the re-making of the realm of England. They came home empty-handed.

Nonetheless, the reformers continued their labours undaunted, and the great council worked tirelessly on the measures of renewal. And one thing at least Earl Simon had procured for the king, and that was the agreement with King Louis. Though the treaty was not yet signed and sealed, the long-awaited peace between England and France stood ready at the door.

Until December I do believe King Henry still piously held to his oath, and meant to go hand in hand with his new council and his magnates, in spite of all the choler of his half-brothers. But in December came the bitter blow that soured his heart ever after against the lords who had forced his hand. Pope Alexander, seeing no hope of getting his way over Sicily with his present candidate, cancelled his grant of the kingdom to young Edmund, withdrew with it the threatening clerical penalties, and began to look round for a more effective claimant. If ever the time came when England could repay the papal debts in full, then Edmund might ask to be restored, but not before. And even so his application could only be made, naturally, if someone else had not been set up in the pretender-ship meantime.

No doubt this came like a blissful release to most of the lords and barons, but it was a desolating shock to King Henry. He had agreed to the proposals of reform only because they were linked with the promise to help him succeed in the Sicilian enterprise. Now he was committed to the reform, but had for ever lost Sicily. Being Henry, and the man he was, this was worse than an irony, it was deceit and treason, for he could never be subjected to humiliation and embarrassment without looking round in fury for a scapegoat, and now he blamed the reformers for his loss, and was convinced they had deliberately wrecked his great project while pretending to assist in it. If he had ever been sincere in accepting the reform, and I think he well may have been, he ceased to be so from that moment, and began to burrow secretly after his freedom and his revenge.

But for us in Wales this period of truce was quiet and prosperous. We tended our country and harvested our resources, and kept our ears pricked for the news from England, and one eye upon Meredith ap Rhys Gryg, still skulking in Dryslwyn, but growing weary now of his own caution. To do him justice, it was never fear that kept him quiet, but only a solid, practical sense that warned him when the stake was not worth the risk. But at last he judged that his part, without doubt the leading part, in the treachery of Cilgerran had drifted far enough down the river to be forgotten, as old grudges easily are where there are always new to be savoured. And he came forth from his seclusion and hunted and raided as was usual with him, leaving the king's new seneschal well out of his plans, and no doubt confident that such private inroads as he could make with his own Welsh forces on territory friendly to Llewelyn would not be at all displeasing to his patron, King Henry, provided the crown could not be implicated in any way.

In early May a rider came into Bala from Rhys Fychan in Carreg Cennen, one of the lancers of his household, grinning so broadly his news could be nothing but a good joke. He was brought to Llewelyn in the mews, where the prince was busy with his hawks, and bent the knee to him very perfunctorily in his haste to get to his message.

'My lord,' he said, 'I bring you brotherly greetings from Rhys Fychan, and sisterly from the Lady Gladys. And I am bidden to ask you where it will please you to take delivery of the person of your traitor, Meredith ap Rhys Gryg, to be tried by his peers?'

There was a general outcry then of astonishment and triumph, and everyone within earshot dropped what he was about and listened without concealment.

'What, has Rhys got the old felon into his hands at last?' said Llewelyn. 'Now how and when did this come about? I thought he had gone to earth for life, and we should have to dig him out with siege engines.'

'My lord,' said the man, broad-smiling with pleasure, 'after the lambing Meredith began raiding our stock, and we lost a few yearlings to him and made no sign. Then a week ago Rhys Fychan pastured some of his best ewes with their lambs not far from Dynevor, where they could be seen from the towers, for we knew Meredith was there, the first visit he's paid there since Cilgerran. There was none but the shepherd with the flock, but we had a good strong company in cover close by.'

'And he took the bait in person?' said Llewelyn, marvelling. 'He has herdsmen and lances enough. You might have got but a poor catch for your trouble.'

'Ah, but, my lord, Meredith's hatred to Rhys is such, he grudges letting even his knights into his feud. Rhys knew him well enough, he came himself to make his choice, he must show his hand in any stroke against his nephew. And he brought a pretty little company in attendance on him, good men, but few. We took them all, with no loss, and no hurt but a few scratches. It was brisk, but we had their measure. And we took Meredith. He is in Carreg Cennen, and he is yours to do with what you will.'

'Come,' said Llewelyn, and helped him away to the hall, 'we must share this with Goronwy and Tudor, and send word out to the rest. This is not my quarrel, but the quarrel of Wales.'

So they debated and made their plans, more gravely once the jest had been enjoyed, and rightly enjoyed, for it was bloodless and just, and there was no killing in any man's mind, as Meredith had brought about all that killing at Cilgerran. There was no doubt but that Llewelyn must move against Meredith as any monarch moves against the traitor, else his claim and style as prince of Wales was of no value. Also the time was approaching when our truce agreement would run out, and we knew that the formal summons to the summer muster against Wales was already issued, and thus far remained in force. We knew, or it came very

243

close to knowing, that this was a matter of form, and the muster would never take place. But for all those who had not our knowledge of the pressures and persuasions in England, the demonstration of genuine power and confidence was essential. So was the right use of Meredith, my lord's first traitor, deep in his debt and absolute in ingratitude. We did not want him slain, we did not want him hurt, we wanted him disciplined, curbed, spared, and brought to submission.

On the twenty-eighth day of May all the great vassals of Wales assembled to sit in judgment. Even Rhodri, the third of the princes of Gwynedd, came from his manor in Lleyn, where commonly he tended to hang aloof between scorn and jealousy, half minding his own lands, half envying the prowess of David, his junior, and wholly resentful of what outdid him, while he spared to attempt rivalry. He read much in Welsh law in those days, privately and secretly, and brooded on Llewelyn's admitted departure from it. But he said never a word.

Before this great assembly Meredith ap Rhys Gryg was brought and charged with treason. And in this matter there was none, not even Rhodri, could charge breach of law against the prince. He presided, but he took no accuser's part, and the verdict was left to the assembly.

Meredith was brought in pinioned, but loosed in the court at Llewelyn's order. He looked in bright, aggressive health and untamed, that square, bearded, loud-mouthed, lusty man, fatally easy to like, and indeed his liking had proved fatal to more than one. He made no submission, and very volubly and fiercely defended himself by accusing all opposed to him. But he could not deny his oath of fealty, for most of those present had witnessed it. Nor could he well deny his breaking of it, which all had seen. The assembly convicted him and, against his obdurate refusal to submit, committed him to imprisonment at his lord's will in the castle of Criccieth.

'Let him stew a while,' said Llewelyn, after he had been taken away, 'and he may come to his senses and his fealty again. I would not let so gross an offence pass, for the sake of Wales, but I cannot altogether forget how he fought at Cymerau. If he returns to his troth it shall not be made hard for him, but securities I must have.'

But for a long time Meredith ap Rhys Gryg maintained his obstinacy in his prison, while his men in the south, led by his sons, held fast to all his castles but otherwise lay very low, not anxious to provoke an attack which the king, in time of truce, could not prevent or censure. Perhaps he hoped that King Henry would refuse to renew the truce now that it was about to lapse, and would come to his vassal's rescue in arms. If so, he was soon disillusioned, for very shortly after he was shut up in Criccieth the expected approach was made on the king's behalf, and Llewelyn sent out letters of safe-conduct for the royal proctors to meet his own envoys at the ford of Montgomery, at the hamlet called Rhyd Chwima, chief of the traditional places of parley on the border. There the truce was extended in the same form for another full year. Once again Llewelyn offered a large indemnity, as high as sixteen thousand marks, for a full peace, but King Henry remained stubborn, and refused the wider agreement.

The king's mind was then on France, rather than Wales, for in the winter of that year he set out for Paris, and there the great treaty between France and England was sealed at last. After, they said, much haggling over family details, just as Cynan had foretold. But signed and sealed it was, and King Henry duly did homage to King Louis for those Gascon possessions he held on the mainland of France, and became a peer of that country.

Now it was while the king was still absent in France, and laid low with a tertian fever at St Omer, that the thing happened which was ever afterwards railed at by the English as a breach of the truce, but which we saw in another light. Truly the truce was broken, but not first by us. And this is how it fell out.

Early in a hard January a messenger came riding into Aber from the cantref of Builth, where the royal castle was held for Prince Edward by Roger Mortimer, the greatest lord of the middle march. Roger, through his mother, who was a daughter of Llewelyn Fawr, was first-cousin to my prince, and there was a free sort of respect and even liking between them, though they seldom met. But inevitably they were also rivals and in a manner enemies, and neither would yield a point of vantage to the other, or to the relationship between them. Indeed it was impossible they should, Mortimer being on his father's side, where his inheritance and his obligations lay, all English, and the king's castellan into the bargain, while Llewelyn was utterly bound by his duty and devotion to Wales. But between them there was no ill-feeling, each acknowledging the other's needs and loyalties. But no quarter, either. An honourable but a difficult bond.

The messenger came in a lather and a great indignation, clamouring that Mortimer had expelled from their holdings the Welsh tenants of Meredith ap Owen, our loyal Meredith, in the cantref of Builth, desiring to have English holders about the castle there. Granted he was responsible for the trust he had taken on, but he had no right to turn out local tenants who had done no wrong.

'Be easy,' said Llewelyn to the envoy from the injured Welshmen, and clapped an arm about his shoulders. 'Go eat, and rest, and follow us at leisure; you shall find your homestead ready to be occupied again.'

'Not so!' said the fellow, burning and happy. 'If you ride, my lord, so do I ride with you.'

And so he did, when we drew in the muster at short notice, left orders to the outlying chieftains to follow, and rode south into Builth in the January snow.

They were never prepared for the speed with which we could move, and that even in the winter. We burst into Builth like the blizzard that followed us, and swept it clear as the north-west gale drove the frozen snow. Those raw English tenants of Mortimer's tucked up their gowns and ran like hares, and the exiled Welsh farmers – for that is land that can be farmed, not like our bleak and beautiful mountains – came flooding back on our heels with knife in one hand and wife in the other and the children not far behind, padding through the drifts with their dogs at heel. In every homestead and holding from which they had been driven, we replaced them, restoring a balance that had been violated in defiance of troth. Where, then, was the breach of truce?

It was not any part of Llewelyn's plan, when we rode out from Aber, to attack the castle of Builth, or to go beyond the violated territories. And thus far we had not set a foot outside our rights, or infringed any part of the agreements to which we were sworn. Whether we were entitled to do so at this point is a delicate question. I know whose hand set this tide in motion, and it was not ours. But to stay it, once launched, was not so simple a matter. Tides must run their course before they turn, and so did ours. Llewelyn swept by Builth on an impetus that could not be stayed, dropped, as it were a calf ripe for birth, a third of his following to encircle the castle, and surged westwards into Dyfed, halting only when the town of Tenby was in flames. Then we withdrew homewards, without haste, consolidating as we passed. But the noose about the castle of Builth remained close and deadly behind us, twined by the men of the cantref, who had their own revenges to take, and drawing ever softly and tenderly tighter as the year wore into spring.

Now, though we did not know it until many weeks later, this action of Llewelyn's, like a fire in the underbrush, ran unseen and broke out in distant places long after we were already satisfied with our expedition and on the way home, intending nothing further against the peace, and believing the flames already put out. As we pieced together the story from Meurig's messages, and from certain word-of-mouth reports gathered from Cynan himself at the ford of Montgomery in August, when in spite of all the truce was again renewed, this was the way of it:

King Henry in his shivering convalescence at St Omer received the news of the Welsh attack upon Builth and Dyfed, doubtless omitting or glossing over the reason for it, and was greatly alarmed. He was obliged by the Provisions, which laid down the dates of the three parliaments, to be back in England for the second day of February, when the Candlemas session should begin, but he was held in France not only by his sickness, but also until he could get from home the money necessary to pay his temporary debts in France. In his fright over Builth he wrote to Hugh Bigod, the justiciar, and ordered him to postpone the Candlemas parliament until he came home, and in the meantime to put aside everything else, and turn all his resources to relieving Builth and guarding the marches. There was to be no parliament without the monarch.

To do him justice, no doubt he expected to delay the proceedings no more than a week or two, but in the end the delay was longer, and its effects more serious. For the earl of Leicester, also on his way home from that prolonged and courtly convocation in Paris, reached England at the end of January, and took fire when he heard of King Henry's order. The dates of the three parliaments were a sacred part of the agreement to which king, prince and nobles had voluntarily set their seals and given their oaths, and here was the king, after his old arbitrary fashion, countermanding parliament on no authority but his own, and trampling his oath underfoot.

It seems a somewhat small infringement, but in truth I think it was not so. For what was dismaying was that the king should feel perfectly at liberty to take back power into his own hands without a word, almost without a thought, never even considering that any man might object, so lightly his oath lay upon him, and always would. And the force of the earl's reaction showed that in his heart, whether known to himself or not, he had never trusted that oath to be heavier than thistledown, and knew that if its breach was passed over now in a little thing, it would be useless to attempt to enforce it later in many great things. At any rate, he took a high and angry line in the meetings of the council, protesting that the king had no right to interfere with the proper calling of parliament, and refusing to countenance the despatch of a money aid to him until it could be done in the proper manner, through parliament.

Thus Henry in St Omer sat and fretted over ever more frightening reports from home, that Dyfed was in flames, that the earl of Leicester was at odds with the count of Savoy and in defiance of the royal orders, and that Edward was much in Earl Simon's company and much under his influence. Which was certainly true, but the king saw in it more than I think was there to be seen. Other and worse rumours haunted him in his convalescence: that ships bearing armed men and barded horses had set sail for England without royal licence, that the Lusignan brothers were collecting mercenaries in Brittany, that Simon himself had sent for foreign troops. Which last was certainly untrue. It seems that Henry's tormented mind went in terror of civil war in England, and was even inclined to believe that his son, under the guidance of the earl of Leicester, was about to make a bid for the throne, and depose his own father. The king was a sick man, and very easily frightened when he felt himself threatened or forsaken.

Forced still to sit biting his nails for want of the money to pay his debts and leave, even when he felt well enough to make the crossing, he wrote to the justiciar again, sending him secret orders to summon a picked force of lords with their armed followings to London by a day late in April. The order came just before Easter, and Cynan said afterwards that the chancery clerks worked day and night to get the writs out in time, all the more desperately because they had to cease all their labours for Good Friday. And what was most marked was that the name of the earl of Leicester was not upon the list of those summoned. Henry had heard by then that Edward was with Earl Simon, and that in protest against the rupture of the parliamentary order they intended to hold a parliament in London in the teeth of Gloucester and the more timorous or orthodox of the council. In a frenzy of suspicion King Henry ordered that the city of London should be closed against his son and his brother-in-law, and strong forces recruited to keep the peace. And the minute he could clear his debts and redeem the jewels he had pledged for money meantime (doubtless he had King Louis' help in that matter) he sailed for home and rushed to Westminster.

As soon as he knew the king was come, Prince Edward hurried to him to pay his respects and make his peace, whether in truly injured innocence or having thought better of a folly I should hesitate to say, but that his associate in the affair was Earl Simon, and of him I could not believe that he nursed any intent against the crown, or would ever have encouraged it in the young man who followed and worshipped him. So I hold Edward innocent of anything more than standing fast on the absolute observance of the Provisions concerning parliament.

But so did not King Henry. They say he refused to see him at first, afraid of weakening out of love once he set eyes on him. Later he relented and, if he did not altogether believe the young man's protestations of loyalty and love, he forebore from saying so, and they were reconciled. But the King, still suspicious, thought best to send his son out of the kingdom for a while, to busy himself in running the affairs of Gascony.

Much of this we did not learn until the middle of the summer, by which time we ourselves had added one more anxiety to the king's troubles. For in July the castle of Builth, round which the men of the cantref were still squatting happily like hounds round an earth, was taken by night, and almost without a blow. There were some among the guards there who hated their overseers far more than they hated the Welsh and, though they gave out that the gate had been stormed by a surprise assault while a foraging party was being let in, the truth is that they opened to our men wilfully, and stood by to see the fortress taken. Rhys Fychan came in haste with his forces from Carreg Cennen, and razed the place to the ground.

Yet in spite of this offence, the royal muster, called as usual about the time of the ending of the truce, was again countermanded, and late in August Bishop Richard of Bangor and Abbot Anian of Aberconway met the English commissioners again at the ford of Montgomery, and this time procured a truce for two years instead of one. If we could not get a full peace, we managed with the next best thing, peace by stages, a year or two gained at a time.

It was while the commissioners were conferring, in a camp in the summer meadows on our side of the ford, that I got the greater part of the true story of that Easter alarm from Cynan, who was there in attendance. On our side the river the ground rises gradually in many folds, on the English side somewhat more steeply into the wooded hills that hide the rock and castle and town of Montgomery, a mile or so distant. There are plenty of quiet thickets there where men may talk privately, as we did.

'I tell you this,' said Cynan, 'the king has a feeling for the shifts of other men's minds, and though he may be too easily hopeful, yet he is often right. This clash has shaken a great many of those who felt themselves touched with suspicion by contagion, and they are busy withdrawing silently, every day another inch or two away from their sworn devotion to the reform. The balance swings gradually King Henry's way. Some were affrighted, a few were truly shocked, none of them want to risk such a tussle again. The king feels the bit between his teeth, and when his confidence is high he can be desperately bold.'

'He swore to the Provisions himself,' I said, 'he cannot say any man forced his hand.'

'He swore in order to get his way over Sicily, and now that he has lost Sicily he feels himself released from his oath. The bargain's broken. It makes no difference that they did their best for him, however reluctantly, even if he believed that, and he does not believe it. Did I tell you he wanted to put the earl of Leicester on trial for acts of treason? But for King Louis he might even have done it, but Louis has far more sense than ever King Henry will have, and sent the archbishop of Rouen over to intervene, of course on some other excuse, but that was the reason for it. So it all passed off into a private clerical enquiry, and they found Earl Simon innocent of any wrong act or intent. Just as well, for he made a strong and calm defence. Strange, that man can take fire at a private quarrel over anything, even money, but when he is under grave public attack he turns quiet, reasonable and patient as any saint. So the quarrel's dropped. By Earl Simon, no doubt, for ever, with no look behind. But the king never forgets. Now he feels himself strong enough to rid himself of this chain of the reform round his neck, soon he'll be bringing back all the Poitevins, elbowing the new sheriffs out of office one by one, and putting back his own men in their places. I'll tell you a thing not everyone even among his own counsellors knows! He has applied to Pope Alexander for formal absolution from his vow to support the Provisions. His best clerk, John Mansel, has gone to Rome on his behalf, to plead for it. And he will get it,' said Cynan.

I said: 'He will still find all the lesser folk of England in the other camp. They have had a taste of getting brisk and impartial justice, through the knights of the shires and the justiciar's perambulations, of seeing malpractices hunted out and punished, even of seeing right done to the lesser man against the greater. Will they give that up easily?'

'It will be done slowly and gently,' he said, 'and by one who believes in his absolute right. But more important, it will be done by a power very well backed in arms.'

'If it rests with the feudal forces of England,' I reasoned, 'they may well be very evenly divided. Supposing, of course, that it ever comes to arms, of which at present I see no sign. Surely this Easter affair was a false alarm bred in the mind of a sick man, and one easily frightened.'

He acknowledged that it was so. Sitting there with me among the bushes, deep in the woods upstream from the ford, he made a strange figure, that smooth, well-combed man in his brushed gown, and yet he was as much at home as in his own office. There was but one change in him, that here, so near to Wales, the rounded softness of his face had sharpened to show the strong Welsh bone beneath the flesh, and his eyes had lengthened their look, and had the narrowed brightness of the mountaineer.

'Keep fast hold of your truce,' he said earnestly. 'Keep fast hold of it and draw it out as long as you can, for it will not always be the feudal host you have to face. The old order grows stiff in the joints, like an old man. The feudal host serves so many days, and goes home, and gladly. Earl Simon may not have brought any French mercenaries into the country, as he was rumoured to have done. *But King Henry did!* And so he will again, Gascons, Poitevins, whatever offers. It is a living, like any other; there are plenty of men who have skills to sell. A paid army does not go home in the winter, or put down its bows and lances to get in the harvest. Times are changing very quickly. So a king who feels he has the pope, and half the nobility, and enough of the paid soldiers of Europe on his side may not greatly care if the common folk of England are against him.' He dropped his white, ringed hands into his lap, and there they knotted suddenly into a grip as still and as hard as stone. 'Or the common folk of Wales!' he said.

All that I had heard from Cynan I related to Llewelyn. We had our truce, we had our peace, so far as it went. Two years is better than one. But the turmoil of England had now become more than our danger or our opportunity, for those ideas that moved men there were surely valid for men everywhere, and moreover, there were not many in the eastern parts of Wales who had not kin upon the other side the border.

Before Christmas, of that year twelve hundred and sixty, Edward was in Gascony. He had been allowed to stay in England until the keeping of the Confessor's feast, the thirteenth day of October, a festival dearly loved by King Henry. There he had knighted a great number of young men, among them the two eldest sons of Earl Simon de Montfort, and then, with several of the new knights in his train, he left for a long jousting tour in France, on his way to his regency in Gascony.

'It is exile!' said David, moved and angry. 'The king is turned idiot, if he conceives that Edward would ever do anything to harm him. Why, even as a child he talked of his father as a gentle simpleton who must be protected. And now he accepts this injustice because it comes from his father. Do you think he would tolerate it from any other?'

'You know him,' said Llewelyn. 'I do not.' And he watched his brother along the table with eyes aloof and attentive, for David had known a life at the English court which was closed to him.

'I do know him,' said David vehemently. 'The best and the worst of him I know, and if you think I am harking back to a childhood affection and seeing him all white, you are greatly mistaken. I never did see him so – nor any other man, for that matter. But of all the things Edward would not do, this is the most impossible. And it is gross injustice to send him away out of the country, like an exiled offender too noble to be put on trial, but too dangerous to be left at large about his father's court.'

'He is going in considerable state,' said Llewelyn, smiling, 'and to a court of his own. And if things go on as they have been threatening in England, you may well see the king beckoning him back to his aid in a hurry before long.'

That proved a true prophecy in the end, except that it took longer to fulfil itself than he had supposed. For the year that we were then about to welcome in saw a deal of change in the situation in England, but all in the king's favour. The shock of the supposed plot had had its effect; Henry had only to play the same strain again and again to keep the greater half of his magnates in more horror of seeming to countenance treason than of continuing to countenance mismanagement and corruption. As for the common people, they were not consulted, or the issue might have been very different. They had tasted a kind of diligent and honest rule that was very much to their liking, and they wanted to keep it, but the process by which it was gradually whittled away was so subtle and oblique that they hardly realised how it was slipping out of their grasp.

It was not further into the year than March, when William de Valence came back, bringing his train of officers and friends with him, and was welcomed at court, for by this time King Henry felt his position so strong that he could boldly set them back in their old position in his favour. Especially did he take courage after the end of May, when John Mansel, his clerk, returned triumphantly from Rome with Pope Alexander's new bull. Cynan had prophesied truly. As the pontiff had refused all countenance or aid to the reform, so now he took his warfare a stage further, for the bull absolved the king from his oath to keep the Provisions, and very shortly afterwards Alexander went further still, releasing not only the king, but all those who had taken the oath, and threatening any who tried to force their constancy, or used any violence against them, with excommunication.

The king made gleeful preparations to announce this decree to his people. He had a large force of foreign mercenaries and levies privately raised at home and, thus fortified, he installed himself in the Tower of London, and thence made public proclamation of the pope's judgments. With the temporal and spiritual power on his side, he was no longer afraid, and when he was no longer afraid he would begin to be vindictive, and also to presume too far on his luck.

The first we heard of this reversal was in late June, when the king wrote to Llewelyn in virtuous jubilation, saying he was now free to consider talks aimed at peace, being firmly established again in his royal authority. As though only the business of the reform had kept him from accepting the prince's offers of peace earlier, though we knew well enough that only the same vexed business had twice, at least, kept him from making war upon us.

'We have nothing to lose by talking,' said Llewelyn warily, and certain exchanges of letters did begin, which if they did nothing else provided us with regular news from England and beyond. And very odd some of those items seemed to me, if any pattern of sense was to be looked for in them. As, for instance, that at the end of May Pope Alexander died, as though the hurling of those two bulls against the reform movement had drained the final energy out of him, and within three months there was a new pope in St Peter's chair, and the parties were at work all over again arguing and angling for his favour as before. Or that King Henry, in the over-exuberance of success, nearly stumbled over into disaster by moving too fast, hunting out of office all the newly-appointed officials he did not like, and replacing them with his own favourites, some so objectionable that even the moderates demurred, and for a while it looked as if the new sheriffs of his appointing would be able to take over the royal castles only by force.

Thus things stood when the autumn began, and we, having made the most of our immunity and a very favourable year, were packing the fruits of our harvest into the barns and thinking ahead to the provisions for winter. Trade being free, we had no lack of salt, the summer having been hot and full of flowers we had honey in plentiful store. And Anglesey had provided a good grain harvest, which we were at pains to house safely. And I thought, I remember, viewing the shorn fields around Bala, when the work was done and the pale gold of stubble shone strangely in the sun, that this was a more blessed life than fighting, and that we were a happy land. If we had few riches, we had few needs. If we lacked power over others, we had a stronghold in ourselves. If we could not command the splendour of popes, we had the small, pure and homely holiness of the saints in their cells, who laid their prayers over us like sheltering hands, instead of hurling bulls of damnation against us. I would not have changed for any land upon earth, so beautiful and particular to me was this land of Gwynedd.

But into this contentment, not mine alone but embracing us all, came the envoy of death, that takes away blessed and banned alike. He came in the person of a squire of Rhys Fychan's galloping into Bala lathered and weary and stained, with the entreaty that we would forward his message also to the Lady Senena and David in Neigwl. For his mistress, the Lady Gladys, Rhys Fychan's beloved wife, was brought to bed prematurely of a dead child, and slowly bleeding to death of that unstaunchable wound, in the castle of Carreg Cennen.

CHAPTER IV

The Lady Senena scorning the slow ease of a litter, mounted a round Welsh cob, astride like a knight and with skirts kilted, and came like a storm-wind from Neigwl with David attentive and patient at her elbow. For though he used her very lightly when times were good, cheating, teasing and cozening her as best suited him, nonetheless he dearly loved her, and at her need reined in hard all his own indulgences. Now in her age she loved and leaned upon his raillery, as old women banter love boldly with young and comely men, in a manner of elegant game kindly and flattering to both. Threatened with bitter loss, his presence beside her reminded her of her remaining treasures. How much she understood of his ways with her, that I do not know. There was nothing he did not understand.

She let herself be lifted down in Llewelyn's arms, and wept upon his breast. Such a condescension she had not vouchsafed to him or any within my knowledge of her, for she was a very masterful lady.

'Mother,' he said, holding her thus, 'we go every one by the same narrow door. One before, and one a little later, does it matter if the way is the same?'

I was standing beside David then, and I felt him grip my arm with his long and steely fingers, and looked aside in time to see the blinding contortion of his face, bitter and brief like a shattered smile, as if he questioned whether the narrow door did not open wider and more generously for some than for others, and whether the way, if not the end, did not bear a variation as extreme as the severance between dark and light. But he never made a sound, and I think he did not know he had clenched his hand upon my arm.

All we set out together to Carreg Cennen, except for Rhodri, who sent word that he was delayed on important business and would follow us and, as ever, came late. For though he was the one who had most attached his mother to him in childhood, perhaps after the Lady Gladys, by his very weakness and a tendency to ill-health, yet he was the one least disposed to family feeling, and most suspicious always that he was being slighted and disparaged. Nor could he bring himself to show as self-centred as he was, as I think Owen Goch the eldest, might have done had he been a free man, but must always do the correct and ceremonious thing, but always grudgingly and with little grace.

We could not wait for him. Llewelyn had already sent forward a courier to have changes of horses waiting for us along the way, and this time the Lady Senena rode pillion behind a lightweight page of the escort, on a big, raw-boned rounsey, well able to carry the double load, for the lady was somewhat shrunken in her elder years, and had never been a big woman. Thus we made forced time, for the time left to the Lady Gladys was measured now in hours, not in days, unless the physicians found some way to stop the slow drain of her blood, which no draughts or potions could replace.

It was near the dusk of a September day when we came into the foothills of the Black Mountain, to that crag that rises above the river Cennen, and climbed the long ridge between the gate-towers, and in the inner bailey Rhys Fychan came out to meet us by the flare of torches. He was drawn and hollow-eyed with lack of sleep, his fair beard untrimmed and his dress untended. He looked at us all as we leaped down at his door, and said only, in a voice cracked with weariness: 'She still lives. Barely lives!' Then he took the Lady Senena in his arm and led her within, and we followed to the antechamber of the room where the Lady Gladys lay.

I did not go in with them, but waited outside the doorway, but the wide door was left open, and what was within I saw clearly, for the bedchamber was small. The evening was warm, and the window-spaces stood uncovered to the afterglow in the west, so that the single lamp by the bedside looked pale and wasted as the face on the pillow. They had raised and propped the foot of the bed, and beneath the sheepskin cover that draped her from the waist down she was swathed and packed with cloths to quench the flow that would not be quenched. She had on a white, loose gown, its sleeves no whiter than the wasted wrists and hands that lay beside her body like withered and discarded flowers. Between the heavy coils of her blue-black hair, as dark as David's, her face was waxen and translucent. It was as though I could see, clear through the delicate, blue-veined eyelids, the dark eyes that once had lifted upon King Henry's face in the hall of Shrewsbury abbey, and charmed him into smiling. For indeed she was, even thus in the awesome pallor of her strange death, a very beautiful lady.

There was a woman sitting on a low stool beside the bed, and when Rhys entered with his visitors she started up and made way for the Lady Senena, drawing back into the shadowy corner of the room. Thus I saw Cristin again in the presence of death, as I had first met her, and as then her influence was a palpable blessing, though she kept silence and stillness, and her calm was unshaken. She watched as the Lady Senena took within her strong hands the pallid hand that lay nearer to her, and nursed and fondled it, and still the face on the pillow lay mute and marble-cold. The mother crooned endearments over her one daughter, and for a long time was not heard, but at length there was a faint convulsion of the large, pale lids, and a flutter of the dark lashes on the ashy cheeks. Rhys Fychan shook even to that omen, but with little hope.

'She has been like this more than a day and a night,' he said, low-voiced, 'growing ever paler. But sometimes she has spoken to me. She may to you. It will be but a thread, you must lean close.'

So they did, the Lady Senena on one side, Llewelyn on his knees on the other. And he also began gently talking to his sister, whether she heard him with the hearing of this world or of the world to come. He told her that all they who were close kin to her would care for her children as their own, and that he would be a heedful lord and a good uncle to Rhys Wyndod and Griffith, and in particular to his godson and namesake, the youngest of her sons. And whether it was the deeper notes of his voice that reached her even through the folds of her sleep, or whether the time had come when she must make her last rally and bid the world farewell, she stirred and opened her lips, and her fragile eyelids lifted from the dimmed darkness of her eyes. One on either side they leaned to her, either holding a hand, though she paid as little heed to their touch as if death had already taken all sense from every part of her but the mind and the spirit.

Something she said, for her lips moved, but sound there was none, and whoever would might interpret her last message to his own liking, and twist it, if he would, into his own name. But I think she was already speaking only with God. For her eyes closed again, and opened no more.

Through most of that night she breathed, though ever more shallowly, and all they watched with her. Rhys's chaplain came again to pray, though he had already ministered to her last wants. And in the hours before the dawn, the time of departures, she departed. I saw the very breath that was but half-drawn, and there halted, leaving her with pale lips severed, as though about to speak, or smile.

It was a calm and quiet going, altogether seemly. It would have been a violation to make any outcry of grief or protest. The Lady Senena with a steady hand drew a kerchief over her daughter's face, and then those two women rose up and sent the men out of the room, closing the door against us, and presently there was running of maidservants with water and cloths, and an ordered and reverent bustle in which we had no part.

And now that his wife was well asleep, Rhys Fychan also consented without murmur to sleep, and Llewelyn saw him to his bed, for he had not closed an eye since the lady miscarried. Like one stunned he fell, and with the semblance of another death he slept.

David came forth with the rest, grave and silent, moving as though he walked in a dream. He drew me away with him to find a corner where we should be in no one's way, and a brychan to stretch out on side by side. He seemed more in wonder and awe than in sorrow, for in truth he had never been so close to death before except in the hot blood and impersonal clashes of battle. He lay on his belly among the furs beside me, his chin in his hands, and stared with wide eyes the way his sister was gone. He was still dusty and soiled from the long ride, and pale in reflection of her pallor, and he looked less than his years then.

'I had not thought,' he said, 'that it could be so gentle. But we have seen only the close, and perhaps even for her it was not all easy and without pain. I have always thought of death as the settlement of a debt – of all the debts in a lifetime. Though truly her account might well be very light and easy to pay. What harm, what wrong, did she ever do to any? Every one by the same narrow door, my brother says.' He smiled. 'I can well see him, when his time comes, riding boldly up and knocking, and the gates will fly open and let him in destrier and all. Me, I doubt not, death will cram piecemeal through the bars of a closed wicket, a long and bloody business.'

I hated to hear him talk so, all the more as this was not said in the black mood that sometimes visited him, but deliberately and with grave thought. And I told him roughly not to be a fool, for he had no more on his conscience than most of us and, moreover, was insistent upon paying his debts as he went, so that he might well find the door open and the record clean when he came. Which would be forty good years yet, I said, to add to his present five-and-twenty.

He looked into me and through me with his dark and lustrous smile, and said: 'You little know what I have in my mind sometimes, and I would never have you know. But God keeps the tally.' And then he said, in the same considering tone, like one earnest to find exact truth in confession, and more concerned with truth than with contrition itself: 'Samson, I am afraid of death.'

And though he said it with an even voice and unblinking eyes, like a man measuring the odds and choosing his ground before a battle, with no intent of giving back or avoiding, yet my heart lurched in me, knowing past doubt that he spoke the truth. So I reached and jerked his palms from under his chin, and pulled him down with me into the hides of the brychan, and he uttered something between a laugh and a sigh, and lay where I had tumbled him, with his forehead in the hollow of my shoulder. And so, presently, he slept.

The castle of Carreg Cennen lay in mourning, and the Lady Gladys, waxen-white like a fine candle and frozen into such distant beauty that nothing of her remained ours, was laid in her coffin. Rhys Fychan arose from his long, deathly sleep refreshed and able to live again, made himself finer than usual in her honour, and took his eldest son by the hand to show him the last of the earthly part of his mother. The boy was twelve years old, in reason somewhat older, being bright and forward of understanding, and he went gravely to the lady's side and kissed her on the forehead in farewell, though the cold of her stung him into fright for a moment, and he clung hard to his father's hand. The younger ones stayed with their nurse, and she told them what all nurses tell their charges when it is certain they will see their mothers no more. But what that is I never enquired.

In this matter of the children David was at his best, for he had kept enough of his own boyhood, when the dark mood was not on him, to make him the most acceptable of us all to such tender creatures, and his play with them was worth a legion to that sorrowful household. So we passed not too painfully through the time of the lady's burial, for which Rhodri arrived just in time, and inclined to feel aggrieved at finding his sister had not waited to take leave of him. We took her to the abbey of Talley, and there she sleeps, we trust, in peace, for she was a good daughter, a loyal and loving wife, a devoted mother, as witness the honour her lord paid to her memory.

Afterwards, when we sat all together in hall in Carreg Cennen, with the whole household below us, and the business of life not so much waiting to be resumed as continuing in indifference to mortal comings and goings, then we took up the duties and anxieties we had laid by for a moment. For the rites of burial are designed less to lay the dead to rest than to set the living in motion again, there being no release from the world short of death.

On the eve of our departure the Lady Senena, who had spent her time mainly with the women and children, and had kept Cristin close about her ever since the two of them had tended the dead together, said to Rhys Fychan at table in the hall:

'There is a request I have to make of you, dear son, that I think you will not refuse me. For my dead daughter's sake, let me have her waiting-woman and take her into my own service. I should like to have by me for the rest of my days one who was so close and kind with Gladys.'

I think Rhys Fychan was not greatly surprised at this. But to me this speech came like lightning out of a clear sky, stopping the breath in my throat for desire and dread. And I looked down to the place where Cristin sat with Godred beside her, and found her looking fixedly upon me, though she was far out of earshot. Our eyes met in that look I had been avoiding hour by hour and moment by moment among the teeming hundreds of the castle, using the very stables and mews, and such places as the women seldom frequented, as shelter from the pain of beholding her. Sombrely and straightly she looked into my face, and it was I who first turned my eyes away.

Rhys said readily: 'I shall be happy to content you, mother, in any-thing within my power. If Cristin is willing to go with you, it might be best for her, for of late years her lady has been like a sister to her, and she will feel her loss sadly. You know what risks she once took for Gladys, and what reason we have for valuing her highly. But there's her husband to be thought of, too.'

'David will find a place for him in his own bodyguard,' said the Lady Senena firmly. 'We have truce now in Wales, but even if you should find a need for armed men, you have only to send to Gwynedd to get both Godred and whatever more you need.'

David, hearing his name, leaned along the table to enquire what was said of him, and she told him, as one taking consent for granted. For one moment he was mute, and his eyes opened a little wider, and flashed one sword-blue glance at me before they looked within, consulting that secret vision he enjoyed, or suffered, in the confines of his mind. A closed world he had there, intricately furnished with good intents that went hand in hand with impulses of malice and mischief, and reckless elations that held up mirrors to forebodings of black intensity.

'Why not?' he said with deliberation, and smiled upon whatever it was he saw within that private room. 'I'll gladly find a place for a good knight, if he says yes to it. And my mother will cherish Cristin. So will we all,' he said, and his smile turned outward towards us, and became human and sweet. But he did not look again at me.

'We'll put it to the pair of them,' said Rhys Fychan, 'and they may choose whether they wish to go or stay.'

So after we left the hall he sent for them to come into the great chamber, where the family sat retired with the cooling embers of their grief on this last evening. And it was David who did the messenger's part and went to bring them.

They came in side by side, but not with linked hands or in any way touching each other. Only once before had I seen them so close, and closer still, when he opened his arms to her in the narrow inner ward of Dolwyddelan castle, and she walked into their embrace with her eyes fixed ever over his shoulder, upon me standing distant and helpless, and never looked away until he stooped his head to kiss her, and then she closed her eyes, to see nothing more. Now they stood before their lord and mine, and waited with mild enquiry to hear what was required of them. He so fair, and agile, and fine, with that smooth and comely face ever ready for smiling, and she so dark and still and erect, seeming taller than she was by reason of her willow-slenderness. She had the bright, white skin that white flowers have, and hair as black as her lady's, but without the blue, steely sheen, and its raven silk was bound up then in a net of silver filigree. A wide, brooding mouth she had, wonderful, dark red as any rose, and eyes like running water over a bed of amethysts, now deep grey, now iris-purple. At this and every face-to-face meeting with her in my life I sought in vain for words to define what she was, and found none exact enough. But still I do not know, after all these years, whether what she had should be called beauty, or whether it bore by rights some other and rarer name.

Rhys Fychan bade them sit, and offered wine. She accepted the stool, but not the cup, and sat with such braced and attentive stillness that I knew she was not privy to this proposition, and did not know what was coming. Godred took what was offered. It would always be his instinct, as bees never say no to open flowers.

Rhys Fychan told them what was proposed. Godred was taken by surprise, but his life was an easy stream of surprises, most of which he welcomed. His brows went up, and his brown eyes rounded. It was not hard to see the wheels of his mind working busily upon the chances. David was brother to the prince of Wales and close to the seat of power, and there was glory and diversity and profit to be had around him. Why not? It was a fair enough estimate, and he had a right to pursue his own interest where no other person's was threatened. I did not blame him.

'I am at my lord's disposal and at my prince's command,' said Godred at his most melodious, 'to serve wherever I best may. But this choice is for my wife to make, since it is her service that is so kindly desired by the lady of Gwynedd. With Cristin's decision I will go.'

'Well, child?' said the Lady Senena, with her knotted, elderly hands quite easy in her lap, never doubting to have her own way. 'Will you come into the north with me? You shall be chief among my women, if you will.'

Cristin sat motionless and silent for a long moment, looking at her with wide eyes and parted lips, while it seemed that she hesitated what to answer. Then in a low, clear voice she said: 'Madam, I rejoice in the honour you do me, and am grateful that you so value whatever service I have been able to do for my lady, who is dead. Such service as I may I will do also for you, lifelong. Yes, I will go with you to Gwynedd.'

'Then I also consent,' said Godred heartily. 'If my lord grants me leave, I will enter the Lord David's service.'

Pleased at gaining her wish, the Lady Senena begged Cristin to put her belongings in order in time to ride with the party the next day, and offered the help of one of her maids to pack those possessions which could follow more slowly. Godred, too, had much to see to, if he was to accompany us, and so they went away to make their preparations. I, who had stood withdrawn all this time, having no part to play in the matter, whatever my longings and fears might be, remained still as they passed me in leaving the high chamber, and willed not to be noticed by word or look. Cristin went by me with a fixed and resolute face, from which even the tremor of surprise and wonder was gone, a marble face. It was Godred who flashed me a jubilant smile and a sidelong gleam, as one confident of an intimate friend who must share his pleasure.

'Good!' said David, when the door had closed after them. 'So that is settled to everyone's satisfaction.' And he looked at me, and slowly smiled his dark, secret smile.

Late in the evening I went about the copying, for Rhys Fychan, of certain small legal agreements of which he required English versions, until I was called away from the work by a page bringing me a mesage from David, who desired me to come to him in the store-room where were the linen-presses and chests belonging to the Lady Gladys. There was no occasion for me to pass through the great hall, where half the household was already sleeping. I went instead by the stone passage, dimly lit by a few smoky torches, and so into the antechamber of the room where the Lady Gladys had died, and by the curtained door into her store-room. Though what David could be doing there, or what he could want with me at this hour, I found hard to guess.

The light there was from two candles in a sconce on the wall, and no brighter than in the passage, yet bright enough to show that the figure bending over an open chest was not David. Nor was there time to withdraw unnoticed, for I had swung the curtain aside without any care to be silent, and as I entered the room she had heard me, and straightened and turned, without alarm, to see who it was who came. She chilled into perfect stillness. The hands a little outspread above the folded gowns in the chest hung motionless, every finger taut. The candles were slightly behind her, and her face was in shadow, yet I felt the burning darkness of her eyes fending me off. So I knew that she had had no part in this, that it was David who had done it to both of us.

It was not my own pain that caused me to draw back from her, it was rather the clear intimation of hers. Time that had done nothing to comfort me had brought her no comfort. In that moment I hated and cursed my breast-brother for his arrogance in meddling with us. And I said, through lips so stiff I could barely speak:

'I ask your pardon! I have been called here mistakenly. I had not meant to intrude on you.' And with that I turned from her, with what an effort I cannot express, and groped my way to the doorway.

I saw her stir out of her marble stillness just as I swung about and grasped at the curtain. Behind me she said sharply: 'Samson!' And when that word halted me with the latch in my hand: 'No, do not go!' she said, in a gentler tone.

I turned about, and she had come a step towards me, and the ice had melted out of her flesh and bones, and it was a live, warm creature who stood gazing at me. 'Come in,' she said, 'and close the door.'

'To what purpose?' I said. 'This was none of my seeking. David sent for me here.' And that was a coward's word if ever there was, but I was angry with him for daring to play God's part with us, and so wrung that I did not know whether it was mistaken affection for us both that moved him, or pure black mischief, to provide himself with entertainment, now that his sport in fighting was taken from him.

But Cristin said: 'David can be very wise. Even very kind. Do you think I do not know you have been avoiding me all these days? All these years! What profit is there in that, since you cannot avoid me for ever? It was time to resolve it. How much of this silence and pretence and avoidance do you think my heart can bear? In the name of God, are we not grown man and woman, able to hold whatever God fills us with? If I am to come north, as I have chosen to do, what future is there for us, if we cannot meet like ordinary human creatures, treat each other with consideration, do our work side by side without constraint?'

In the course of these words all that was ice had become a gradual and glowing fire, and she was as I had known her in the beginning, so gallant and so dear, the heart failed, beholding her. I stood mute in my anguish and my bliss, helpless before her.

She took one more step towards me, since I would not go to her, and now she had but to reach a hand a little before her to flatten it against my heart and feel how it thundered, with what desire and despair. And I but to stretch out my arms and gather her like a sheaf in the harvest, but that her troth and mine lay between us like iron bars. Her face was turned up to me, earnestly searching me. I never knew her to use any wiles upon me or any other. She had her own proud and purposeful chivalry. When she opened her eyes wide, thus, and poured their wit and intelligence and enquiry into me, she also let me in to the deep places of her own nature, and gave me the courage to enter there.

She said: 'Why did you turn away from me at Dolwyddelan, and leave me without a word of farewell, after all we had done and known together? You had no right!'

I said: 'For reason enough. I had no right to stay. You are my brother's wife. You knew it before ever I did. You saw the ring I had from my mother, the fellow to his.'

She moved neither towards me nor away, but held her place. Her eloquent and generous mouth lengthened and quivered, and her eyes darkened into iris-purple. In a slow, hard voice, just above her breath. she said: 'Tell me the truth! Is that all I am?'

By what wisdom of David or mercy of God I do not know, in that moment my heart opened like a flower that has long been bound by frost, as if the sun had come out to warm me, and the rain to water me. I saw her mine and not mine, neither to be taken nor left, by reason of the barrier of duty and faith, by reason of the bond of love and worship. As I was bound not to despoil, so I was bound not to forsake. And I had done ill all this while, in depriving her and myself of what was ours and wronged no man.

I never touched or troubled or enticed her, but stood to face her as she stood to face me, God seeing us. I said, with all my heart and mind and soul: 'You are my love, the first one, the only one, the last one I shall ever know. I have loved you from the first night ever I knew you, before I knew if you were maid or wife. I loved you then without guilt or shame, and so I love you now, and shall lifelong. There will never be any change in me. To the day of my death I shall love you.'

Such ease I got from this utterance, I marvelled how I could have kept from making the avowal long before. Nor was it the ease of surrender and despair, but of release from bondage. And she stood before me so flushed and warmed with the reflection of my release that she was like a clear vessel filled with light.

'Now,' she said, 'you do me justice indeed, and I will do the like for you. Why should you or I go hungry for want of what is ours to feed upon without harming any man or committing any sin? When first I learned to know you, not knowing myself whether I was wife or widow, I loved you for your great gentleness and goodness to a dying man who owned he had used you ill. It may be I did wrong to choose you, but choose you I did, for once lost to me you might never be recovered, and I tell you now, such an election happens only once in any life, and in most lives never. If it was a sin, the sin was mine, and there is no man can blame you. I went with you because it was more to me to have your dear companionship than any other man's love and worship. God he knows I hoped for more, but I have had hopes before that came to grief, and the lot laid on me I could bear. But when you took from me even your dear companionship, in which my heart rested, that I could not bear.'

'I do repent me,' I said, 'that ever I did a thing so weak and so unjust as to abandon you. My love and worship is yours only, and yours lifelong, even if I never speak the words to you again. And my service and loyalty I can offer freely, before all the world. Forgive me, that ever I did you so great a hurt.'

'You have healed me,' she said. 'I give you my pledge for yours. I shall never love any man but you.'

'Yet we are taking from Godred what is rightly his,' I said, though I meant no protest against what was now past changing, but only to make all things clear between us, that we might know what it was we did.

'We are taking from Godred,' she said steadily, 'nothing that he has ever possessed. I was wed to him when I was fourteen years old; I never saw him until the match was made. And we are taking from him, I swear to you, nothing that he values, even if he had once possessed it. I am a dutiful and serviceable wife to Godred, all he has asked of me I have been and done, and will do, and will be. And I have no complaint of him. But my love he never sought, or needed, or regarded. I do him no wrong.'

Behind her the candles guttered, and a thread of tallow ran down from the flame. The curtain swung lightly, for the door behind it was still open. I felt the chill touch of the night wind, as though someone trod close on my heels. But when I stilled to listen for a moment, there was no sound. And such doubt and fear as remained in me I spoke out then, saying it would not be easy, that if she wished to take back her decision

261

and remain in the south I would still be her faithful lover all my days, though apart from her, and such comfort as there was in that knowledge she might have without the heroic pain of nearness and silence. But all she did was to smile at me with that wild radiance making her face glorious, and to ask me: 'Is that your wish?' And there was nothing I could do but say, no! Her peace I desired. My own was safe in her hands. My wish was to see her and to serve her and to be at her call if ever she needed me. But that if it cost her too dear, that I could not endure.

'My mind is as yours,' she said. 'I will not willingly go a month, a week, no, not a day if I had my way, without the sight of you, and the sound of your voice. What you can endure, so can I. If you can make a sacrament out of your sorrow and deprivation, so can I. What I cannot do is to cease from loving you, and I would not if I could. It is the best gift God ever gave me, to love you and be loved in return.'

In these high terms we made our compact, Cristin and I. And then it came upon me that no more must be said, that the time to set the seal on so lofty a purpose was now, when all the words had been uttered that were needed between us, once for all time, and it remained only to prove what we had sworn, and make it binding for ever. And the way to do that was to bid her goodnight and commit her to the blessing of God, and so go from her without so much as the touch of hands, or too lingering an exchange of looks, as if we still had doubts, who had none.

So I did. And she, with as deep an understanding, gave me my goodnight back again, and turned to continue lifting the folded gowns from the chest. From this night on we were to meet before other people, and carry our daily burdens encountering and separating as our duties moved us, demanding nothing, repeating nothing, and even if by chance we met without witnesses, there would be no such exchange again, as none would be needed. Neither would there now be any resentment or any loneliness or any greed, for if we had not that great bliss of love fulfilled in the flesh, yet a manner of fulfilment, stranger and after its own fashion more marvellous, we surely had.

I went out from her like one in an exalted dream, and did not look back, for her image was within me. And I thought myself both blessed and accursed, but if the one was the price of the other, of what then could I complain?

In the inner ward of Carreg Cennen there was a faint silvering of moonlight, and on the wall I could hear the feet of the watch pacing. Out of the shadows near the great hall a man came walking lightly and briskly, and whistled as he came. When he drew near to me he broke off, and haled me cheerfully by name, in the voice of Godred.

'Samson!' said he, as though surprised to find me still among the waking. 'You work late tonight.' And since he halted in friendly fashion, I was obliged to do the same, though I would gladly have avoided him then. 'I am looking for my wife,' he said. 'Surely she cannot still be packing her gowns and bliauts? But you're the last man I should be asking – the prince's own clerk, and a bachelor is hardly likely to be involved with a matter of stuff gowns and linen wimples. I must go and find her.'

Yet he lingered, eyeing me with the intimate smile I had observed in him ever since the turn I had done him at Carmarthen bridge, when he was unhorsed and in danger of trampling.

'I've had no chance to speak with you,' he said, 'since this evening's news, there's been such bustle to be ready to leave tomorrow. But I hope you may think it, as I do, a most happy chance that Cristin and I are to come and serve close to you, in Gwynedd. True, Cristin will be mainly at Neigwl, where the lady makes her home, but it's none so far, and we have peace now to travel and visit. And since David is often in attendance on the prince, I shall hope to be close to you very often during the year. Are you pleased?'

So pointblank a question, and in a tone so warm and trusting, what could I do but own to pleasure? Which I did with the more heart, seeing it had its own enormous truth, out of his knowledge, which yet did him no injury.

'So all things work together for good,' he said. In the light of the moon I could see the fair smoothness of his face, boyish and bright, and the round, candid eyes limpid brown under his tanned forehead and silvery-fair hair. 'I rejoice at being able to serve near to one who has once salvaged my life for me – and once, more precious, my wife! I feel you,' he said, in that high, honeyed voice that made speech into song, 'closer to me than a brother. Forgive me if I presume!' And he linked his hands in most becoming deprecation before his breast, in the full light of the moon, and the fingers of his right hand played modestly with the fingers of his left, turning and turning the ring upon the little finger, a silver seal bearing the image of a tiny hand, severed at the wrist, holding a rose. I had no need to see it more clearly, I knew it well. Once I had worn the fellow to it, my unknown father's solitary gift to my mother. I watched the silver revolving steadily, quite without the spasmodic motion of agitation or strain. 'Closer than a brother!' said Godred, softly and devoutly.

'You make too much,' I said, 'of services that fell to me by pure chance. There is no man among us would not have done as much in the same case.'

'Oh, no, you wrong yourself,' said Godred fervently. 'There are many who would have done less. And perhaps some,' he said, 'who would have done more.' This last in the same honeyed tone, too cloying, as honey itself cloys. 'Now in the north I may be able to repay all. All!' he said, and uttered a soft, shy laugh. 'But I must go find my wife,' he said, and clapped me on the shoulder with the hand that wore the ring, and so passed on, silvered by the moon.

I would have held him back from her then, if I could, to spare her the too sudden and too apt reminder, yet I knew that she was armed and able. It was not that that clouded all my ecstasy as I went slowly to my bed. But I could not help seeing still the slow, measured spinning of that silver ring, white in the moonlight, and hearing the soft insinuation of his voice. And I remembered too well the flickering of the candles in the draught from the door, and the chill of some presence treading hard on my heels. And my own voice saying in its own excuse: 'You are my brother's wife. You knew it before ever I did. You saw the ring . . .'

I prayed hard and slept little. And the next day we rode for Gwynedd.

I said to David, when he brought his tall English horse to pace by my pony on the way: 'Well, are you content with your work?' For still I bore him some ill-will for the trick he had played me, even as I rejoiced, pain and all, at my great gain by it.

Said David, shrewd and shameless: 'Are you?' And he looked at me along his shoulder, smiling. 'You have a look of achievement about you, you and Cristin both. Did you come to a satisfactory understanding?'

'Not as you suppose,' I said sharply, for I was sure in my own mind of what he had intended, and it was galling enough to have one brother soliciting me like a pander, leave alone my breast-brother joining in the game.

'Never be too confident,' said David, 'of what I am either supposing or provoking, you might go far astray. But if you think you could have gone on living in the same world with her and utterly estranged, for God's sake, man, get sense. If *you* could, in your holiness, why should she have to endure the like?'

I own that any smart I felt against him, by that time, was but the reverse of my gratitude, and I admitted to myself that he might well be honest in his concern. But I had to ask him one more thing, for it was on my mind and I could not put it by.

'Tell me this, did you follow me there to see what passed between us?'

'No!' he said, indignant. 'What do you think I am, that I should spy on you?'

So if he had not, another had. But I did not say so to him, for there were already possibilities enough for mischief. 'Closer than a brother!' rang the soft voice in my memory, and still I saw the silver ring revolving with delicate intent about the long finger.

CHAPTER V

Llewelyn moved his court to Aber in the middle of November, as was customary, ready to keep the Christmas feast there, and at the beginning of December Meurig rode into the llys, on his way to his own winter quarters at Caernarvon, for he was thin in the blood, and liked to burrow and hide himself like a hedgehog through the frost and snow. He brought us all the news from England, having come direct from Shrewsbury and, sitting snug by the fire like a little grey cat, talked familiarly of kings and earls and popes, and the building and dismemberment of the grand dream of the Provisions.

'King Henry has gnawed and tunnelled like a rat, and prised gently like frost among the ranks of the reformers, crumbling them apart with his papal bulls and his royal French alliance. He called all his barons to a conference at Kingston at the end of October, feeling himself ready to play the winning stroke. He offered everything possible in reason and magnanimity, amnesty for all who would accept the findings of the meeting. They have given in,' said the old man, scornfully grinning, 'and come to the king's peace, every man of them. He has been gracious and kingly. He has them all in his hand.'

'All?' said Llewelyn sharply.

'All but one,' said Meurig.

'Ah!' said Llewelyn, satisfied, as though his own honour had been vindicated. 'And what had the earl of Leicester to say at Kingston?'

'Never a word, my lord, for he never went there. He and the closest who remained staunch were out in the shires, setting up their own wardens according to the Provisions. I do believe the lesser gentry in the countryside and the common people were ready to stand and fight if need be, but the barons were not. Half they feared what they were doing and what they had already done, and half they craved their old ease again, without too much need for thought, and believed the king's blandishments and swallowed his bait. First Hugh Bigod, that was formerly justiciar, and a good, fair man, too, but over-persuadable, he slipped away and spoke for compromise. Then the earl of Hereford, and then even Gloucester. So in the end they all went to Kingston as they were bidden. All but Earl Simon. And he spoke out on them for a generation of changeable and slippery men he could not abide, when they had sworn every one to do these things and see them done. He has shaken off the dust of England in disgust, and gone away into his French possessions, for he will not touch this mangled remnant they are busy concocting out of the grand design.'

'Then King Henry has won his war,' said Llewelyn, with concern and misgiving, for though the desultory exchanges over peace had continued, they showed no sign of coming to anything, and a king triumphant and vindictive and in full control of his affairs again was less likely, for all his professions of goodwill, to want to conclude a genuine agreement with us.

'I would not say his war has so far even begun,' said Meurig, musing. 'He has brought the great lords of the older sort to heel – all but one – but he has not given any thought yet to the lesser ones, or to those young men who were not consulted when the Provisions were drawn up, and have not been consulted now when they are swept away, but who may very soon find that they have come to like what was begun, and miss it sadly now it's done away with. It's too early to say anything is lost, or anything won.'

So things stood in England that winter. But at least we in Gwynedd received a Christmas gift rather more to our liking, for about the feast of St Nicholas, after Meurig had left us, a messenger rode into the maenol from the castellan of Criccieth, and his news was matter for sober celebration. Meredith ap Rhys Gryg, still kicking his surly old heels in captivity, had at last given in, and indicated his willingness to renew his homage and acknowledge Llewelyn as his overlord.

'True,' said Llewelyn, gratified but undeceived, 'I doubt if his mind towards Rhys Fychan or me has changed much, and once before he swore fealty and did homage, and was forsworn within the month. But at least he shows some sense at last. And we'll see what safeguards we can bind him with this time!'

So they brought Meredith ap Rhys Gryg out of his prison, to a great meeting of the council of Wales at Conssyl. The old bear reappeared before us somewhat fatter and slower for his two years of confinement, but little tamed, though he behaved himself with stolid submission, and contained whatever rage he still felt. The agreement that released him we had drawn up with care, to protect the rights of his neighbours and kinsmen, and he had to give up his prize of Dynevor intact to its rightful owner again, and also surrendered his new castle of Emlyn, with the commote belonging to it. But otherwise he got back all his ancestral lands in return for his homage and fealty, and was received into the prince's grace and peace.

As for the safeguards, they were hard but fair, and no one ever came to hurt through them. Besides the loss of his one castle – for Dynevor never was rightly his – he surrendered his eldest son for a time to live at Llewelyn's court, and was pledged on demand from the prince to render up to him twenty-four sons of his chief tenants, whose families would be sureties for his loyalty should it come into question. And if he broke any of the terms of the compact, he quitclaimed to Llewelyn all his inheritance and rights in Ystrad Tywi, which might be stripped from him without further ado.

To all this he swore, and plumped down on his stiff old knees to do homage. And doubtless much of what he was forced to speak tasted of gall to him, for he was a wild, proud man. Yet by this simple act of submission, which was but returning to what he had freely sworn in the first place, and to one to whom he owed so much, he regained all his own but for the castle and commote of Emlyn, which I think was no harsh dealing. And his son, a grown man and with more sense than his sire, gave his parole cheerfully and had his liberty in Llewelyn's court, and hawked and hunted with the prince to his heart's content while he remained with us.

So this, the prince's first traitor, came to his peace as an example to all others both of firmness and magnanimity. And the only note of regret was struck by Llewelyn himself, saying, after Meredith had departed to his own country, and the news had been sent to Rhys Fychan in Carreg Cennen: 'They will be riding home for Christmas, Rhys and the children. Pity, pity it is that Gladys could not have lived to take her boys back in triumph to Dynevor. It was her favourite home.'

The new year of twelve hundred and sixty-two was barely seven weeks old when the new French pope, imitating his predecessor, issued a bull supporting King Henry in all points. Pope Urban, it seemed, was determined not to allow the king to revive his son's claim on Sicily, for he thought to do much better with another candidate, but because of that he was all the more anxious to satisfy him of his goodwill on all other issues. Earl Simon, though forgetting nothing and abandoning nothing of his ideals, still morosely absented himself in France, and it seemed that everything in England was going tamely King Henry's way.

Thus fortified, he sent out letters to his sheriffs denouncing all those ordinances made in the name of the Provisions. As for those who still feebly contended for a measure of reform, their position had been whittled down stage by stage until they gave way altogether at this blow, and wearily agreed to let the king's brother, Richard of Cornwall, king of the Romans by election, act as arbitrator on such matters as were still at issue. And decent man though Richard was, and sensible, yet he was Henry's brother. It did not take him long to restore the king's right to appoint his own ministers and sheriffs without consulting council or parliament, which was the whole heart of the matter. But at least he strongly urged on his brother the absolute necessity of coming to amicable terms with the earl of Leicester, and warned him to observe good faith in coming to such an agreement, and to adhere to it strictly once it was made.

He was spending wisdom only to see it blown away down the wind. For King Henry, who was always exalted into the clouds or abased into the kennel, was in his glory now, and no way disposed to be lenient to his enemies. In the summer he set off for France, to clear up matters of family business and to employ King Louis' good offices in making the advised overtures to Earl Simon. Louis urged moderation, as Richard had done, and with as little effect. Instead of approaching his sister's husband in conciliatory mood, King Henry dragged out of the past all his old hates and complaints against the earl, and instead of appeasement there was nothing but bitter rancour, which Earl Simon's hot nature could not but reciprocate. So nothing was healed, and nothing satisfied, and the wounds festered.

As for us, we kept our household and minded our own business, to good effect, for without difficulty we procured a renewal of our truce in the month of May, on the same terms as before, and again we gained not one year of grace, but two.

That summer was the time when Richard de Clare, the great earl of Gloucester, died in the month of July, a few weeks short of his fortieth birthday. He left a son turned twenty years, Gilbert, ripe and ready to be an earl, and fretting and furious when, because of the king's absence, he was kept out of his honour month after month, and received no seisin of his right.

David came visiting as soon as he had word of the earl's death, very bright of eye and expectant, for he was restless for action, and weary of the mere daily labour of managing his lands, which, though he could do it very shrewdly if he pleased, he could as well leave to his mother. He had Godred among his retinue, as eager as himself.

'I thought I should have found you in arms,' said David. 'Here's Richard of Clare gone, and no provision made for proper rule in his lands without him, and young Gilbert disparaged and kept waiting. The whole march is in disarray, we could pick off all the Welsh edges of it without trouble or loss, and an occasion for shaking the truce a little is not far to seek; you have only to goad Gilbert into lashing out first. I could do it within the week, and put him wholly in the wrong.'

'You'll do no such thing,' said Llewelyn smartly. 'There's a small matter of my word and seal in the way, even if we had anything to gain by setting the march on fire, and we have not. If I wanted occasions, there have been any amount without goading from me. So far I've had satisfaction by legal means. They meet us, on the whole, fairly enough; the measures of conciliation work.'

'They've worked in the past,' said David, discontented. 'Things are changing in the march, or have you not been informed? There's something in the wind among the young men. There isn't a castle down the border you could not pick like a flower now if you had a mind to.'

'I know it,' said Llewelyn calmly. 'I have been following affairs, as well as you. Old men are vanishing from the scene, and young men take views of their own, and are less happy with King Henry's ascendancy than their elders. Certainly this is an opportunity, if I had no restraints. But I have. A few months ago I pressed the king again to come to a formal peace with Wales. I know he is holding me off, with excuses about Prince Edward's absence and the need to consult him, and I know I could go on taking what I want, while I wait for him to recognise me and all my gains. I choose not to, for more reasons than one. But one is enough. It is barely two months since I set my seal to the new truce.'

David gave him a sidelong glance, and said provocatively: 'The king thanked you in so many words, did he not, for refusing to take advantage of England's household troubles? Are you so anxious to stand well with him?'

'No, with myself,' said Llewelyn, undisturbed. 'Though I believe he has done his best to keep the truce and make amends for infringements.

Take him all in all, he has played reasonably fair with me, and so will I with him. Let Gloucester's lands alone.'

'He is not Gloucester yet,' said David, 'and they're in no hurry to invest him. That's one more disaffected lordling their side the border.'

'And one on mine?' asked Llewelyn, and laughed to see him flush and bite his lip, until suddenly David laughed, too.

'Not so bad as that! But I could be at home in such company, I don't deny it. You know they're ranging about Kent with Roger Leyburn at their head, holding tournaments? And in the marches, too. The justiciar is in a sweat about it, with orders to call in the churchmen wherever they plan a round table, and try to prevent it, but he has his work cut out. There was a great meeting at Gloucester itself – I tell you, I was in two minds about putting on false coat-armour and riding to issue a challenge there, as in the old tales. If you won't find me work to do, why, they might find me very good play, and nearly as rough.'

'Rein in for a little while,' said Llewelyn, 'and there may well be both work and play rough enough even for you.'

This movement of the younger barons had begun in the general uneasiness and discontent after the Provisions were seen to be enfeebled and abandoned, but the spark that set light to the disquiet was a personal one. The Lord Edward had the very able and fiery Roger Leyburn as his steward, and had some cause in his absence, or had been led by his mother to believe he had cause, to suspect his officer of peculation. Roger being of no mind to be made a victim, and stoutly asserting his own good faith, had returned to his estates and drawn round him all the restless young lords like himself, many of them from marcher families. Roger Clifford of Eardisley, John Giffard of Brimpsfield, Hamo Lestrange of the Shropshire family, and Peter de Montfort the younger of the English house, son to that Peter de Montfort who had conducted us to the parliament of Oxford – these were among his allies. Now, according to rumour, Gilbert de Clare was joining the brotherhood, and even the name of Henry of Almain, Richard of Cornwall's son, had been mentioned. There were northerners, too, a de Vesci of Alnwick, a Vipont of Appleby, all young men who had not accepted, as their elders had, the revocation of all the measures of reform. Most had been friends and companions of Edward, many David had known at court, as mere boys. If these young sparks were at violent play in the marches, and David was prevented by truce from working off his energy against them in honest battle, what wonder if he ached to go and join them and spend his fire in their company? Yet their movement was not play, and it had another effect, upon men graver and more earnest than they, for it drew into its current the hopes and longings of the small gentry, the yeomen, the citizens, all of whom had accepted the proclamations of reform with faith and eagerness, and then seen King Henry dash the cup from their lips.

Thus a casual confederacy may become a party almost without its own knowledge, and grow into a cause almost without its own will.

For want of warfare, at least Llewelyn found David some good hunting.

They were often out together late into the evening, and ranged far in the hill forests with the hounds. So it happened that when the weather broke suddenly after a clear day they came home drenched and cold, as often rain brings on great cold after a long settled spell. In hall afterwards Llewelyn ceased to eat, and put his hands to his head, and before we left the table he began to shake with the marsh sickness, and soon fell into a terrible sweat. He was unused to illness, and would not believe or tolerate what was happening to him, until he fell in the drooping fury of helplessness, and had to be carried to his bed.

David sat by him into the night, and so did I, for it took him hard, so that he sank away from us and lost his senses at times, and again returned into shuddering consciousness, turning and tossing, muttering through chattering teeth, and ever soaked in sweat. His face grew hollow and grey, and his eyes sunken. When he opened them it was clear from their burning light that he knew us, but the words that came from his lips were broken and meaningless.

'This is my fault,' said David, distressed and bitter with himself. 'I wish to God I had agreed to turn back earlier, and get home out of the storm. Why should it fall on him, and not on me? There's no justice in it.'

Towards morning he said, as he wiped the sweat from the prince's forehead: 'It is very evil. He may die! I should go for our mother, she will be his best nurse.'

So he spoke with Goronwy, and as soon as it was light he rode, not entrusting the errand to any other. But it was a day before the Lady Senena came, and a grim day for us, for the prince sank even deeper into his wanderings, and the flesh watered away from his bones as fast as ever I saw. I stayed with him all the time, for he had about him at this pass no mother nor brother nor sister, and never had I felt him so solitary and so committed to my care. His physician came and went, but Llewelyn was past swallowing draughts, and we knew there was little to be done but help his strong and resolute body to do its own fighting. So we continued stubbornly replacing his soaked bedding and bathing his tormented face, keeping him wrapped when he was racked with shivering, and cooling his body with distillations of herbs when he burned. When he could not endure the heat of the bed I held him raised against my shoulder, and was nursing him so when for the first time he fell into a shallow but real sleep.

Afraid to stir for fear I disturbed this respite, I held him more than two hours, while his sleep, though troubled at times, yet continued. In the dusk of that day he opened his eyes, that looked at me with recognition, and essayed to smile, saying: 'Samson?' And when I answered, low, that it was I, he whispered: 'Again the same small favour! Harder than parrying a knife!'

Before it was fully dark David returned with the Lady Senena and they came in at once to the bedchamber. And with them, entering silently on her lady's heels, came Cristin. The Lady Senena came to her son's bedside, felt his brow, and turned back the covers from his throat, that was still and ever running with sweat. But I saw by the way her grim face eased, no matter how slightly, that she found him in better case than she had expected, and that she would fight for him with a good heart. I looked beyond her, and found Cristin gazing with a still and serious face upon me, and upon the sick man in my arms. Her eyes smiled. Not her lips. She spoke no word to me, but I knew she was remembering another bedside, in a hut among the snowy woods of the Black Mountain. That patient had been past our saving. This one I knew then would not be lost to us.

'It is not so bad as it might be,' said the Lady Senena, turning back her sleeves. 'He has slept? An honest sleep?'

I said that he had, for two hours, and that he shook now less than before. 'You have done well by him,' she said, 'but now lay him down gently and leave him to us.'

So I did, and myself slept for a while, being sure in my heart by this time that I might do so without fear, for he would live. The attack, which had been rapid and violent in its development, passed no less switfly from him. Within three days he was able to get up out of his bed and walk a little in the sun, gaunt and shaky, but again his own man. When first he arose, uncertainly smiling like one entering in at a doorway to a world unknown, or almost forgotten, he leaned upon David, whose steely, arrogant strength was well able to sustain him. But before he lay down again he called me to him, and asked me to play my crwth, since he was too weak to put his senses to any harder work than listening to music. And so I did, and to my music he slept, which his mother said firmly was the best occupation he could have for some days yet.

So it went until he was stronger, his mother and David and I vying for the frail attention he was able to bestow. Only Cristin fetched and carried, cooked and nursed, without any ambition to take him from us. And she gave orders, too, with authority, to me as readily as to another if I happened to be at hand, as often I was. And that companionship in his service, quite without greed or insistence on personal recognition, was marvellously reassuring to me, and beyond belief rewarding.

But 'it was not long before the prince himself undid the half of our good work. He would ride before he was well fit, for it enraged him that his body should have the mastery over him, and he came back from his ride sweating again and shivering, tried too far too soon. Then there followed an anxious night when the fever racked him again, and at intervals, as before, he wandered, muttering confused words. His mother would have insisted on watching the night through with him, had not Cristin with authority taken her place, and even then she would have a man stand by, for should his state become worse he was too heavy for Cristin to lift and handle alone.

That duty she laid, by custom and without question, upon me, and without question I accepted it. And this befell in hall, before the Lady Senena withdrew to her rest, and all those about the tables above the fire heard it, among them Godred.

His duties being with the guard, and not within doors, I had seen but little of him during those days, yet I knew that when the whole household gathered his eyes were constantly upon me. So they were then, and

271

I saw their knowing brightness. He came to my side as we left the hall, stepping lightly and walking close, and looking at me full with his open, round-eyed smile he said softly:

'I trust you'll have quiet watch tonight. And no occasion to call for other help. No one will dare disturb you uncalled, that's certain, not in Llewelyn's own chamber.'

I understood but would not understand him. And he, as though he talked at random and lightly, following a wanton thought that touched us only by chance, laughed and said: 'That would be a fine romantic scene for a geste – two secret lovers set to such a night-watch together! I wonder how long their continence would last through the night!'

I would not follow him down any of these devious ways he led me, but took my arm from under his hand, and said I had no time or mood for fooleries while the prince was sick, and I must be about my business for him. Godred laughed again, very confidently, and laid the hand I had rejected upon my shoulder for a moment. 'Ah, there'll be time for plenty of changes of mind before morning,' he said in my ear. 'No need to carry your sword for a cross all the hours of darkness, like a new knight at vigil, nor lay it between you and temptation night-long, neither. Life owes you a sweet bed and a warm one now and then. I am expert in your deserts. I owe you so much myself, and you never will give me occasion to repay.' Still softer he said, and giggled: 'Nor her, either! We feel our indebtedness, indeed we feel it!'

And he dug his hard fingers into my shoulder, and so slipped away from me without looking back. And I went to watch by Llewelyn's bed with a chill of misliking about my heart, for there was something changed in Godred and not for the better, something that went even beyond his shameful urging of me towards his wife. That I had heard from him before, but in a fashion somewhat different, lightminded and fulsome at the same time, anxious to have my favour and stand well with me, by whatever means served. All this was present still, but with a bitter after-taste, all the sweetness somehow underlaid with a note of cruelty and spite. Towards her? I could not think so. Towards me, then? He had no occasion more than before, and if he had spied on us at Carreg Cennen he knew it. Nor should he have any occasion this night, or any night to come.

So I put him out of my mind, and went to my duty. And I forgot him in my lord and my love, those two people I most revered in this world. Llewelyn lay uneasily between waking and sleeping, now and then babbling into his pillow and tossing weakly, great beads of sweat gathering and running on brow and lip, but this time he was not turned inward away from us. He knew us, and at moments spoke to us, feebly but with knowledge, even with kindness and humility, begging pardon for the trouble he gave us, and the grief, and thanking us for our care of him. Towards midnight he panted and sweated most, and I lifted him into my arms and held him so, while Cristin bathed his face and neck and shoulders and breast with a cooling infusion of herbs, time after time until his shivering stopped, and he breathed more deeply, and lay more easily in my arms. And so he fell asleep as before, truly asleep, the fever ebbing away. Cristin spread a clean linen pillow under him, and I laid him down, never breaking his sleep.

'It is passing,' she said almost silently over his body. 'Now he will rest.'

In that bedchamber, small and bare enough, there was a little rushlight burning, set back behind his head that it might not trouble his eyes. The hangings on the walls were of woven wool, and we had young branches of pine fastened there, to make the air sweet and spiced. The summer was mild, with little troublesome heat, but the curtained door we left open, to let in air. The window-opening was full of stars. There she and I hung over Llewelyn's sleep together, one on either side of the bed. And by the grace of God we thought not at all of each other, but only of him, until his sleep deepened and eased into a wondrous freshness and grace, and the fever ebbed even out of his bones and left him clean. Then we looked up, our faces but a little way apart, each into the other's eyes.

In the anteroom to the bedchamber, scarcely wider than a passage, there was a brychan drawn close up to the doorway, put there when first Llewelyn began to mend, so that whoever watched with him overnight could get some rest and yet hear any sound from within the sickroom. I said to Cristin in a whisper, rather by signs than by words, that she should go and lie down there, for she was weary, and I would sit up with the prince, and call her if there were any need. But she only smiled at me and shook her head, feeling no need to give any reason, as I felt none to ask for any. I could as well have withdrawn into the outer room myself, for the protection of her good name, even though none but the one person in all the household would ever have dreamed of calling it in question, and there watched out the night at her call, but I did not do it. For such moments as we might have together lawfully were beyond price, and the gift of a night was food for a hungry year to come.

So we trimmed the flame of the rushlight low and clear, and sat with him all night long, his body and bed the sheathed sword between us. Twice he roused a little, not quite awake, and made the wry movements of dry lips that signified his thirst, and then I raised him, and she put honeyed water to his lips, and a fresh, cool cloth to his forehead, and he swallowed and slept again. Such words as we spoke to each other were not of ourselves, but of him, and they were wonderfully few. All night long I never touched her hand. And all night long we were in peace. To be in her presence, unassailed and sinless, was more of bliss than I had believed possible.

In the dead of night the silence was so profound within the llys that every murmur of wind in leaves from without came to us clearly, and towards morning, but long before light, bird-song began in a sudden outburst of confidence and joy, so loud and brave that I marvelled how such fragile instruments could produce such notes without shattering. Then the first pre-dawn pallor appeared in the east, and the first footsteps were heard in the bailey, the creakings and murmurings of men arising unwillingly from rest. And Llewelyn opened his eyes, sunken but clear, and asked for wine.

273

I went to fetch it. If I had not leaped so gladly to answer his wish I should not have seen the curtain of the outer door of the anteroom still quivering from the hand that had just let it fall hurriedly into place, or heard the light, furtive footsteps fleeing, tip-toe, along the stone passage without.

The brychan was drawn close against the open door of the bedchamber, its head shielded by the tapestry hanging. I stooped and felt at the blanket draped upon it, and in the centre it was warm to the touch.

I did not linger then, but did my errand, neither seeing nor expecting to see on my way that person who had kept us company unseen and unheard during the night. For there were many ways out into the bailey and the wards from that passage, and outside in kitchens and stables and byres the household was already stirring. But afterwards, when I came again, and when the Lady Senena had bustled in to take charge, the first ray of sunlight piercing clean through the bedchamber and the open door showed me two more evidences of what I already knew. A tiny mote of sun danced upon the blanket, where all else was still in shadow, for there was a small hole in the tapestry, low towards the head of the brychan. And in passing through that chink, the light irradiated a single shining thread among the dark colours still further darkened by smoke, and I drew out in my fingers a long, curling hair, pale as ripe barley-silk.

I said no word to Cristin or any other. Nor to him, when I met him in the armoury, and he greeted me gaily after his usual fashion, and asked me how the prince did, and if we had had quiet watch. I answered him simply, as though I took him and all his words and acts for honest. Better he should never be sure that I knew anything more of him than the sunlit outer part. Nor could I discern anything in him changed towards me, in voice or face, until I left him there and, leaving him, for some reason looked back. Still he stood smiling after me, all innocent goodwill, with no more of parody in his manner than was usual with him. Only his eyes, so wide and round and brown, and full of speckled golden lights like the shallows of the river where I had first encountered him, were become blind brown stones in his comely face.

After that day the prince mended and this time he paid better heed to advice, and waited for his strength to come back before he tested it too far. By the time September came in, and we were busy with the harvest, he was himself again, a little leaner but as hard and vigorous as ever. And the Lady Senena, satisfied with his progress and his promises, returned to Neigwl and took Cristin with her, and shortly was followed by David and all his retinue. So I was rid of Godred, whom I was farther than ever from understanding, and robbed of Cristin, whom day by day, in presence or in absence, it seemed to me that I knew better, understood more profoundly, and loved more irrevocably.

During the prince's illness, of which rumour had spread far and wide as it always does, the state of lawlessness in the marches had grown worse, and the breaches of truce were many. And still, by Llewelyn's order, his officers held them in check as best they might, and refrained from turning the frequent incidents into major battles. True, the

Welshmen along the border were not saints, either, and from stoutly defending themselves may well have passed, where a tempting opportunity offered, to local revenges, and even to raids of their own. But by now the retinues of the marcher barons had very little to restrain them, and the prince's patience, no more inexhaustible than that of any high-mettled man, soon wore perilously thin.

I think what held him back, where it might well have urged on another man, was the news that came through to us from France of the disaster that had fallen upon King Henry's court there. For in Paris there was a great epidemic of plague, which someone had unhappily carried in among the king's officers. Many died there, and King Henry himself and young Edmund, his son, were also stricken, and lay dangerously ill for some weeks. Rumours that the king was dead, or likely to die, did nothing to restore order in the marches. But late in October we heard that he was out of danger, and allowed to get out of his bed and walk a little.

'Poor wretch!' said Llewelyn. 'I have been in the same case myself. Why should I add to his troubles? As long as he forbears with me, so will I with him.'

But that was before Meurig rode into Aber from Shrewsbury in the early days of November, making for his winter nest earlier than usual because he carried urgent letters that concerned Wales very closely and bitterly.

He did not know what it was he carried, for the roll was sealed; he knew only that it had been brought to him secretly by a Welsh friar, the last of a chain of messengers conveying it not from Westminster, but from King Henry's own court in Paris. Thence it had travelled by the same ship that brought reassurances and orders to the justiciar in London, but in the care of a Welsh seaman. The covering letter was from Cynan, greeting us fresh from a sick-bed which had barely missed being his death-bed, for he was among the royal clerks in attendance on the court, and had been brought down with plague like almost all the rest, though by the grace of God he was mending well when he wrote. There were two enclosures, both copies in Cynan's own hand, though shaky still from his illness, so that Llewelyn frowned over the cramped Latin, and followed a slow finger along the lines.

'He says only his sickness has kept him from sending these earlier, for he could not trust them to any other, or let any other know he possessed copies. The first is not dated. The second, he says, follows it and will date it for us.'

The first letter enclosed was short, and for want of its original seal Cynan had written the name of the sender at the foot, and the name was Griffith ap Gwenwynwyn of Powys. Llewelyn read it through with a frown that changed as he went into a grin of somewhat sour amusement.

'Listen,' he said, 'what Griffith ap Gwenwynwyn writes to his patron King Henry. He greets his lord, and informs him that he has been making enquiries about Llewelyn's health, and it is bad. The prince rallied enough to take exercise, but then twice relapsed into the same sickness, and is said to be very weak, and unlikely to recover. Griffith will send further reports if he should grow worse.' He laughed, disdainfully rather than angrily, for there was nothing unexpected in this. We knew from long since that Griffith was the royal spy on our borders, just as we had Cynan and others in England. Yet there was all the width of the world between a Welsh-born prince slavishly reporting to England on the health of the prince of Wales, and a Welsh clerk in London risking livelihood and life itself in the service of his own country.

'Poor Griffith,' said Llewelyn, 'he has no luck, for all his industry. Here am I alive and dangerous, and the king laid low in his turn. Griffith must be biting his nails now which way to go.'

He unrolled the second scroll, which was longer, and raised his brows at sight of the superscription.

'It is from King Henry himself to his justiciar. The date is the twenty-second of July.'

It was the day he first walked out into the sun again after his relapse. I remembered it, and so did he. He leaned on my arm that day, looking out over the salt flats to the sea.

He read with a darkening face, that struggled with its own betraying thoughts, but mirrored most of them. A long, dour reading it was, and at the end of it he suddenly cursed aloud, and then as abruptly laughed even more loudly, though there was outrage and anger in his laughter.

'His Grace has heard the news of Llewelyn's death! He writes in great haste – he was whole and well himself, then, his turn was still to come! –to make plain his plans for the succession in Wales. Llewelyn is unwived, and without issue, but with a vigorous brother named David ready to pick up the burden he let fall, and that must never be permitted, no, at all costs not David, who would be as single and vehement as his elder. His Grace has an answer to David. Owen Goch is to be freed from his prison and set up in half of what the king proposes to leave of Wales. But he'll gain very little, for Henry means to recover for himself the homages of all the other Welsh princes, leaving Gwynedd at its narrowest to be divided between Owen and David. And how is he to contrive all this? By force of arms! This, while he writes to me piously of peace! The barons of the march are to assemble their arms at Shrewsbury to conquer Wales. He looks for help from certain impressionable princes, not forgetting Meredith ap Rhys Gryg. Well? Those are King Henry's plans for Wales, when he thinks me on my death-bed, or dead already. It is not my word, it is his. Here in plain script. Under his own seal.'

It was as he had said, in every particular. How Cynan ever contrived to get a copy of the letter I could not guess; it may well be that he memorised it complete from another clerk's account, for he was not so close to the crown as to be dealing with such correspondence himself.

'To be fair to him,' said Goronwy, always the most temperate of us, 'this is no proof he was in bad faith in talking of peace with you, or thanking you for your forbearance in his troubles at home. True, he may well have been pursuing that path because he saw no alternative while you lived. It's when he thinks you dead that he feels it a possibility to conquer Wales. After his fashion he is paying you a compliment.'

'A compliment I could well do without,' said Llewelyn, between laughter and rage still. 'How long is it since I heard much the same rumours of him, and held my hand from taking any advantage? When did King Henry ever make the least gesture of generosity towards me and mine? When we were hard-pressed, then he bore harder still on us and took whatever he could. Now I doubt not he would like this letter buried deep, knowing I am well alive. He shall know it even better yet. I tire of my own restraint, seeing he observes none. It is time to show King Henry how exceedingly alive I am!'

What plans the prince would have made, and where his deliberate blow would have fallen, had not others provided occasion, was never made plain. He summoned his host and his allies at leisure, calling David from Neigwl, while he considered the courses open to him, and weighed their advantages. This was the first time that ever he set out of intent not merely to breach the truce but to destroy it.

Occasion, amounting in itself almost to prior breach, was not far to seek, though we did not then know what was toward. The many and increasingly grave raids on the borders had alarmed and enraged others besides the officers of Gwynedd. In particular the Welshmen of Maelienydd, in the central march, uneasy neighbours to Roger Mortimer, were angry and unhappy when they saw that he was thrusting his border forward into their territory and building himself a new castle on the hill of Cefnllys, and thinking it politic not to speak first, but to act, for fear Llewelyn should continue to counsel moderation, raised a force of their own and took the castle by a trick. They had no wish to occupy the site themselves, only to prevent it being used as a base against them, and accordingly they razed the walls and the keep, and so left it. As soon as he heard the fate of his fortress, Roger raised a strong force, helped by his neighbour Humphrey de Bohun, and rushed to Cefnllys to rebuild it. Too weak to attack so powerful a company, the men of Maelienydd did what perhaps they should have done earlier, and hurriedly sent a courier to appeal for aid to Llewelyn.

By a happy irony the messenger arrived on the first day of December, a single day after the arrival of a letter from King Henry himself, still weak and ailing in France, but stirring himself to deal, even from that distance, with the many disorders that plagued his realm, and should, if he had been wise, have kept his mind off meddling with any other prince's territory. Among the many complaints to assail him was one from Mortimer, it seemed, bitterly accusing the Welsh of the assault on his castle, and indicting Llewelyn by name. Which accusation King Henry duly passed on to the prince, requesting explanation for the breach of truce.

'Having got over his disappointment at finding me still alive,' said Llewelyn, 'he's forced back on the old approaches. How gratifying, to be able to write with a clear conscience and deny the impeachment. I have not laid a finger on the truce – yet.'

And he dictated a mild, noncommittal reply, acknowledging the letter, stating that as far as his knowledge went he had not in any way broken his truce with the king, and offering amends for any proven infringements to date, provided the same justice was done to him.

Next day came the man of Maelienydd, in his turn complaining to his prince, defending the action of the Welsh with many and voluble legal arguments, some of them sound, and appealing for help to prevent the reinstatement of Cefnllys.

'We have our occasion,' said Llewelyn, and laughed. 'We even have a case, should we need one. He had no more right to build contrary to the truce than I have to raze what he has built. Maelienydd is a very fair country, and we are courteously invited in; it would be unmannerly to refuse.'

That was the first time that we had meddled so far east, except in our own northern lands, and it says much concerning the situation in those parts, and the fears and hopes of those who lived there, that we were indeed invited, not only by the men of Maelienydd, but after them by those of Brecknock, and welcomed like deliverers when we came.

We made our usual vehement descent, outrunning our own report, with a force greater, as we found, than that Mortimer and de Bohun had furnished for their rebuilding. They were encamped within the broken walls of the castle, and we came so suddenly and unexpectedly that though Cefnllys stands on one end of a lofty ridge, we were able to occupy positions all round it without hindrance, and settled down to hold them under close siege.

It was plain that they had only limited supplies, and that they were advanced so far from Mortimer's base at Wigmore as to be very badly placed for breaking out of our trap, all those miles of hostile Maelienydd separating them from reinforcements. We could starve them into submission in a week or two. But Llewelyn had a better use for those seven days.

'Now let's see,' he said, 'how practical a man Roger can be. For he knows his situation as well as we do, and I think has the good sense to recognise and admit it. I have no great ambition to fight with him, and I would as lief have him out of here and out of my way while I secure Maelienydd.'

He told us what he proposed, and David laughed, and begged to be the ambassador to the besieged. He rode into the enclosure attended by a single squire, and laid before Roger Mortimer, no doubt with a demure and dignified face, the prince's offer. Since it was clear that surrender was only a matter of time, and relief exceedingly improbable, why expend men and resources in postponing the inevitable? Llewelyn had no wish to fight with his cousin. If Mortimer would accept it, he and his army were offered free and unimpeded passage through Llewelyn's lines and across the border, intact to a man, with all their gear.

That was no easy decision to make, but Mortimer was a big enough man, and honest enough with himself, to shrug off what many a younger and rasher captain would have seen as disgrace and dishonour. Indeed, later he was plagued with suggestions in many quarters that he had been in league with the Welsh in this matter, which I can testify was quite false. He could have stayed and fought, and seen many of his men wounded and killed, only to surrender in the end. Instead, he chose to take his whole force home in good order when he was given the chance. For my part, I respected his common-sense, and so, I think, must the wives of his soldiers have done when their men came home unmarked.

We opened our ranks to let them out, and saluted them as they marched by, for we had nothing against them, and the message they were taking back to King Henry was more galling than a bloody defeat would have been.

'I call that good housekeeping,' said Llewelyn, watching their ranks recede towards Knighton. 'We've spent little to gain much, and he's preserved what could be preserved. No fool squandering of men for spite or stubbornness, as your thickheaded heroes would have done. I approve him.'

'I doubt if King Henry will,' said David, grinning. 'Are you sure he'll go tamely home to England?'

'He'll go,' said Llewelyn confidently. 'Not only because he gave his word, but because he's seen how many we are, and how many more we can call out of the ground here. The men of these parts do not love him. And now we're rid of Roger, we'll settle Maelienydd first, and then push on towards Hereford. This border country,' he said, looking across the rolling hills and cushioned valleys with appreciation, 'is very much to my mind. Let's add as much of it as we can to Wales.'

And to that end we laboured, and with much success. The men of the land were with us, our numbers grew by their willing adherence, we had nothing to do but pick off, one by one, the English-held castles that were outposts in this marcher countryside, and that we did briskly and thoroughly. Bleddfa first, and then over the hills into the Teme valley, to take Knucklas, and so sweep down-river into Knighton. The castle there hangs over the town on its steep hillside and, below, the valley opens green and fair. That winter was not hard, there was but a sprinkle of snow before Christmas, and the meadows in that sheltered place were no more than blanched as in the harvest. Thence we moved south to secure Norton and Presteigne, and everywhere the chieftains and tenants came to repudiate their homage to the king and urge it upon Llewelyn, together with their soldier service. Like a ripe apple Maelienydd dropped into the prince's hand, grateful to be gathered so, and overjoyed to be Welsh.

It was at Presteigne we heard, from a merchant who traded wool into Hereford, that King Henry had at last recovered sufficiently to make the sea crossing, and had dragged his still enfeebled body as far as Canterbury, where he meant to spend the Christmas feast, now close upon us.

'Well, since Roger is so quick to call my name in question with him,' said Llewelyn, 'we'll repay the favour in the same terms.' And he sent another letter, politely and formally complaining that Mortimer and de Bohun had occupied with a large force a castle within the seisin of the prince of Wales and, when surrounded and beseiged by the prince's army, had been generously allowed passage through the lines to withdraw to their base, though it would have been easy to compel their surrender. And again he offered amends for any proven breach of truce, provided the barons complained of would guarantee the same. And he ended with a sly reminder that it was wiser to hear both sides of a case before proceeding to judgment.

With this whole region established behind us, we swept on to the south, into the Hereford lowlands as far as Weobley and Eardisley, fat country full of cattle that we rounded up and drove off with us, and barns that we plundered. Very easy farming these lowlanders have, and very well they live. We drew so near to Hereford that the Savoyard bishop, Peter of Aigueblanches, as well hated as any cleric in England, flew into a panic terror and ran for his life into Gloucester, groaning though he was, so they said, with an attack of gout, and from there wrote indignant letters to the king. Henry paid dear in his own convalescence for his glee over Llewelyn's supposed mortal sickness. In that winter the prince was at the peak of his powers, and blazed down that border like a chain of beacon fires.

'He surely knows by now,' said Llewelyn, 'that I am man alive.'

At Hay-on-Wye came messengers from the chieftains of Brecknock, begging him to go into their country and accept their homage and fealty. Never before had we moved thus down the very fringe of the march, eating into those lands claimed and occupied by the marcher lords, where Welsh and English contended always. Surely he added one fourth part to his principality before the Christmas feast of that year.

I think King Henry truly believed at that time that the Welsh intended a great invasion of England itself, but if so, there were few others who took the situation so seriously, and certainly Llewelyn never had any such intention. When the king issued feverish orders to the lords marchers to forget their quarrels and unite against the enemy on their borders, and called them to muster at Ludlow and Hereford in the following February, the exhortation fell on deaf ears. Pitifully King Henry wrote off to Edward in Gascony, reproaching him for his lethargy and indifference in face of Llewelyn's threat, and urging him to come home and lift the burden from his poor old father – as though he himself had not as good as banished the young man into France in disgrace, and ordered him to devote his energies to running his province there, and keep his nose out of English politics.

Nonetheless, we had to pay heed to all threats of mustering the feudal host against us, whether we greatly believed in them or no. So at Christmas we parted company, half of our forces pressing on southwards towards the rich fields of Gwent under Goronwy, with the levies of the southern princes joining him, while Llewelyn with a sufficient company halted long enough to receive the homage of all the princes of Brecknock, and make dispositions to hold what had been gained, and then withdrew at the turn of the year into Gwynedd.

Of how Goronwy fared with his force, that can soon be told, for in the first months of the new year he carried Llewelyn's banner to the very gates of Abergavenny, and only there was the victorious rush to the Severn sea halted, by the stout defence of that same Peter de Montfort who had once conducted us to the parliament of Oxford. He was King Henry's officer in that region, and the only one who held his own against us, until he was joined by John de Grey and a great number of other marcher lords hurriedly massed to his relief. After a skirmish with this army, Goronwy withdrew his men into the hills, where the English were reluctant to follow them, and even the local Welsh tenants, who otherwise would have borne the brunt of the inevitable revenge, took their chattels and made off into cover and into the monasteries, where they had sanctuary. Our thrust went no farther, but turned to consolidation of our great gains already made. And it should be said that in this gathering of the princes of the south once again Meredith ap Rhys Gryg, according to his renewed fealty, brought his levy and fought for Llewelyn and Wales alongside his nephew Rhys Fychan, at which Llewelyn was glad. But whether it was out of duty and good faith, or because the pickings in those parts were fat, I do not venture to judge.

As for us of the prince's party, we returned to Gwynedd in the first days of January, and at Bala we were met by a messenger from Rhodri, who had been left nominally in charge with Tudor in the north.

His news was in his face, for envoys bearing word of sickness and death have a special way of approaching those to whom they are sent. The Lady Senena, who had brought her immediate suite to Aber in the prince's absence, convinced that no one but she could properly oversee the affairs of Gwynedd, had been taken with a falling seizure on the night of Innocents' Day, and though she still lived, she was helpless in her bed, unable to move any part of her left side, foot or hand, and her countenance fixed. She mended not at all, and her time could not be long.

Thus the third sally death made that year, after discarding Llewelyn and King Henry both, was made against the lady. And the third sally was mortal.

CHAPTER VI

They gathered by her bed, those three brothers, as helpless as most men when the hour strikes that cannot be avoided. She lay stiff and still, like a figure already carved on a tomb, though she could move her right arm, and the right side of her face still flushed and paled, and was human flesh to view. It was marvellous to see, now that she lay still who had seldom been still when she stood, how small she was, to have borne all those tall sons. Her grey hair was braided, to save her from irritation where it touched, and she was warmly wrapped against the winter cold in fine wool and under well-cured sheepskins. Her level brows were still black and formidable, and the eyes under them bright and wise. Also bitter, for death she resented, as all her life she had resented what curbed or enforced her will.

Cristin stood at the head of the bed, and she was in command within that room, as if she had received into herself some measure of the lady's mastery to add to her own. 'My lady's mind is clear as it ever was,' she said, 'and she sees plainly, and knows all that passes. She can speak, but it gives her trouble and wearies her. You must listen well.'

Llewelyn went straight to the bedside, and stooped and kissed his mother's forehead. David came more slowly, his eyes great, and I saw the fine beads of sweat stand on his lip, and remembered how he had said, not retreating from it: 'Samson, I am afraid of death!' He also kissed her, on the cheek that still lived. It cost him more. He had not Llewelyn's bold simplicity.

The Lady Senena's eyes followed all their movements until they drew too close, or went beyond her range, and those eyes burned with intelligent purpose still. When she spoke, half her mouth moved freely, the other half resisted, like a log dragged by a strong tide. Her voice was a fine thread, but a clear one. She said: 'Where is Owen?'

Llewelyn said: 'He will come. We'll send for him.' He never flinched or avoided her eye, that was accusing enough.

'Soon!' she said, and it was an order.

'This hour,' said Llewelyn, and smiled at her without shame or dread. 'I leave you,' he said, 'only to do what you wish.' And he turned about and went out of the room on the instant, and sent an escort to bring Owen Goch out of his prison at Dolbadarn to bid farewell to his mother. And then he came back to her, and told her that it was done, and within a day she should have her eldest son with her to close the circle. When he addressed her it was without constraint. Truly I think that while she had her full wit and senses she knew herself nearer to him than to any, for he alone reverenced, loved, challenged and defied her, ever since he was twelve years old, and went his own way without ever grudging her hers.

Owen Goch had been held in Dolbadarn castle then for more than seven years, so long that it was often all too easy to forget that he lived, and his coming to Aber was an event calculated to shatter our peace of mind. Llewelyn had occasionally visited him in captivity, but of late years infrequently, and usually at Owen's own instance, for the prisoner was quite capable of proffering vehement requests and complaints concerning his comfort and well-being. The Lady Senena had visited him regularly, and never ceased to plead his cause, though it was the one thing on which Llewelyn would not be persuaded or softened. Perhaps she was even surprised at his instant acquiescence now, for she was not of a temperament to use her own death-bed to wring concessions out of him. What he denied her, sure of his own justice, when she was hale, she would not find it unreasonable or unfilial in him to deny when she was sick.

However, she accepted his gift without comment, and by mid-morning of the next day Owen rode into the maenol, unbound but strongly guarded. In the years since he rose in civil war against his brother, and so lost his liberty, he had grown soft and fat, being confined for exercise to the castle baileys, no very extensive ground, but he looked in good health, if somewhat pallid in the face, and was princely in his dress, and very well mounted. Like his father before him, he was a heavy, large-boned man, liable to run to flesh, the tallest of the brothers, and his hair and beard were still of the flaming red of poppies, untouched by grey. He had also his father's rash and violent temperament, though without his redeeming openness and generosity, for Owen brooded and bore grudges where the Lord Griffith would have forgotten and forgiven. So even after seven years he would in no wise accept Llewelyn's lordship or agree to any terms, standing obdurately on his total right in Welsh law. Indeed, he had grown more irreconcilable during his imprisonment, and long since ceased to remember that he owed it in large part to his own act.

Llewelyn went down into the courtyard to meet him as he dismounted, approaching him directly, without pretence that their relationship was other than it was, without relenting, without constraint, certainly without any affectation of love. The long ride, on a fine wintry morning with only a touch of frost, must have been most grateful to Owen, and had brought fresh colour to his face. He eyed Llewelyn warily and coldly, but he accepted the wine that was offered on alighting, and asked: 'Our mother still lives?'

'She lives and is waiting for you,' said Llewelyn.

They went to her together, but Llewelyn came out at once, and so did Cristin with him, and left those two alone.

'She cannot last the day out,' said the physician. And before nightfall all those four sons were gathered about her bed, for it was clear she had not long, and her will was the thing about her now most alive, and struggling with bitterness against the compulsion of dying. At that last meeting I was not present, but Cristin was, in constant attendance on her lady, and from her I know what I know of the last hour.

'She could still speak,' said Cristin, 'and be understood, if you attended closely. When the priest had blessed her to God, she blessed them all, one by one, and commended them to behave brotherly to one another, as they hoped for God's mercy. Then she fell into a wandering of the mind for a while, her one good hand straying about the covers, and she talked more clearly then – it might be better if she had not! For she was back in the old days, and they were children to her, and she babbled of David and Edward in the same breath, and so reminded them of the days they spent at court that Llewelyn was like a stranger among them, the only one speaking a different language. She even reproached him, that he forsook his father and his mother, and brothers and sister and all, to go with the uncle that wronged and disparaged them. Is this all true history?'

I said that by the Lady Senena's measure it was, and told her how it befell, and how in my eyes it did him great credit and honour, for he was but a child when he chose and acted like a man.

'And he bore all, and gave no sign,' she said, 'though I know he felt it deeply. For in dying men return to what holds them most, and she was in Westminster with all her brood, excepting only Llewelyn, and he was the outcast, and alone.'

I said that in those days so he was, but it did not turn him from what he meant to do.

'Nor now,' she said, 'right or wrong. For Rhodri was in tears, and David too wrung for any such easy way as tears, but Llewelyn sat by her and watched and listened, and took all as it came, as though he never expected any other. Or perhaps – it may be so – he has an understanding with her that the others have not, on his own terms. His father I never knew, but *I* think he is *her* son, through and through.'

That was truth, and so I told her. The two who most favoured their father were Owen and Rhodri. As for David, God alone knew from what mysterious forbears, from what perilous and resplendent women, he took his being.

'And then,' said Cristin, 'she rallied, and was with us again, out of the past. She left dandling Edward and riding in the queen's retinue, and came back very sharply to this day, and then she looked for Llewelyn, and even moved her good hand towards him, so that he took it up and held it. Her eyes were fierce and bright again, able to match with his. She said: "Son, do justice to your brother!" and he said: "Mother, I will do right to all my brothers, according to my own judgment." And he smiled at her, and I think, however twisted that mouth of hers, that was a smile I saw upon it. It was the last fling of her spirit, and she challenged him, and he stood like a rock and let her take or leave him as he is. And I do believe she took him, all his offences and failings and all, and was glad of him. But what they made and will make of it, God knows. She has shaken them to the roots.'

It was not strange. So forceful a person could not be withdrawn suddenly out of the world without some tearing of the living tissues, and every one of those four, as various as they were, was fonder of her and more deeply twined into her being than he knew.

'She never spoke word again,' said Cristin, 'nor uttered sound. I think there was another such stroke passed through her, for she stiffened, and her hand gripped on his suddenly, and all the flesh of her face seemed to be drawn in like shrivelled leather to the bone. Her eyes rolled up, and she died.'

She was filling her arms with fresh linen from a chest in the great hall when she told me this, and with these sheets and with knotted bunches of dried sweet herbs she went back to the death-chamber to make the Lady Senena decent and comely for her coffin, which the masons were even then cutting. But as she left she said: 'If she had known they would be her last words, would she have spoken them? "Son, do justice to your brother!" Perhaps! She was bred in the old ways, and lived and fought by them, and at the end she clung to them. But what a stone to cast into that pool among those four, at such a time!'

There was but one place then where the royal women of Gwynedd were fittingly laid to rest, and that was in the burial ground of Llanfaes, in Anglesey, that Llewelyn Fawr dedicated to the memory of his great consort, Joan, lady of Wales, and founded beside it the new house of Llanfaes for the Franciscan friars, the closest of all the religious to the old saints of the pure church.

There we bore the Lady Senena on a grey, still January day of the new year, twelve hundred and sixty-three, down from Aber over the salt flats and the wide sands of Lavan, and ferried her across to the Anglesey shore, there to rest after all her triumphs and tragedies. The sea was leaden that day, the tide heavy and slow, and in the stillness of the air the voices of the friars were dulled and distant, as though the world had receded from us as far as from her, though outside this solitude of sand and sea and vast, shadowy sky the tumult of events thundered and shook, waiting to devour us when we returned across the strait, and even followed us there secretly like a smouldering fire in the hearts of those four brothers. For she was gone into the earth, who after her fashion had held them tethered into a loose kind of unity, however they strained at it, and in departing she had turned back to invoke the very spell that severed them.

It began in the hall that night, before all the household, and I think it was David who began it, though the voice that set the note was that of Rhydderch Hen, the oldest of the bards, who played and sang the lady's commemmorative hymn. I may be wrong, the spark may well have come from Rhydderch himself. But David sat so tense and strung that night, and himself spoke so little, that I cannot but wonder. For he knew how to put thoughts in men's minds and actions into their hands that they never fully intended. Moreover, these three days spent again in the company of his eldest brother, brought from prison inevitably to return to prison, had pierced David deep in the conscience softened and rent by his mother's passing, and the words with which she left this world.

Rhydderch began with the praise of the Lady Senena, and the recital of her troubled fortunes in her marriage and her chosen exile with her children, all that old story made gentle and acceptable now even to those who had been torn by contention then. He sang her faithfulness to her sons and her lord, her great strength of mind and will. Then he turned to the subject of filial duty and family loyalty, of the sacredness of a mother's last wish and prayer, and the obligation of a son, prince though he might be, and the greatest of princes, to reverence and observe it. For he sang that even where wrong had been done, brother should forgive brother, as he hoped for forgiveness.

It was not the first time the bards had made known their desire for Owen's release and reinstatement, and that was no great wonder, for they were old men and wedded to the old ways. But this was the first time it had been pressed with such force. Owen Goch himself, who was sitting beside Llewelyn in the centre of the high table – though he knew and we knew his guards were never very far away – began to flush and glow with gratification, and to give forth sparks of hopefulness, but I do not believe he had known beforehand what Rhydderch meant to do. And David burned like a slow and secret fire, and watched Llewelyn's face every moment. But the prince sat unmoved to anything more than a smile of slightly grim tolerance, and thanked and rewarded Rhydderch for his singing.

Soon afterwards Llewelyn, of intent, signalled to the silentiary that he would leave the hall, and withdrew into the high chamber with his brothers, and would have me attend him there. Since Goronwy was still absent in the south, there was no other with us at that meeting, for he foresaw that one or other of them had things to say better said only between themselves. Me he never shut out, since first I came in curious circumstances into his service. I was the silent witness, yet informed enough to make balanced judgments, and I was the recorder if such were needed. So he would say, but I think truly he wanted me because there were moments when he felt himself alone, and I was a brother at one remove, a brother without claims on him, and all the more indissolubly bound to him because there was nothing but my own will to bind me.

The door was barely closed between us and the hall when David said, not aggressively as I had feared, but with a white and quiet passion: 'You have heard our mother's voice, and the voice of the bards echoing it. I know you cannot be indifferent. It was her last wish, her last warning. All of us heard it. Llewelyn, you cannot send Owen back into captivity. You said you would do right to him. Keep your word! Set him free!'

Owen Goch stood gathered up tightly into himself, in that big, lusty body running to fat with such long inaction, and his eyes strayed from brother to brother in uncertainty and watchfulness, reading every tone, every quiver of a face. Doubtless there was a great hope in him, but also a great and obdurate sullenness, at least as far from reconciliation at heart as ever Llewelyn was.

'By what right,' said Llewelyn mildly, and looking only at David, 'do you make yourself our brother's champion, and ask clemency for him? He has made no such claim on his own account.'

'By right of the clemency you showed to me,' said David, and his face was so drawn and shrunken with passion that he looked as one starved. 'Why to me, and not to him? Did not I offend as grossly as he? And yet I am free and indulged, and he is still in ward and landless and solitary, after seven years. You cannot justify it! What has he done that I have not?'

Llewelyn said: 'You have done somewhat that he has not. You offered me, voluntarily, your homage and fealty, and have kept them ever since.'

'You never gave to him,' said David, burning like a tall and bitter flame,

286

'the chance to offer the like. Me you took and him you left. How will you answer for that in the judgment?'

'I will answer for it now,' said Llewelyn. And he turned and faced Owen Goch, who glowered upon him uneasily through the red of his bush of hair and bush of beard, 'I offer it now,' he said. 'The same you chose of your own will to pledge me, David.' But he did not look at David, or speak directly to Owen. At the one he looked, to the other he spoke. 'I say to him,' said Llewelyn, 'that I revere my mother's memory and intent, and I stand in her sight, by God's grace. If Owen will do homage and swear fealty to me as David did, acknowledging me as prince of Wales, if he will quitclaim to me, in return for what lands I assign him, all his claim to sovereignty in Gwynedd or in Wales, then he may go free from this moment, and be established in a fair portion. Fair,' said Llewelyn hardly, 'considering all that has been, and the council shall be the judge.' For the first time he addressed Owen Goch pointblank. 'Will you do so?' he said.

There was a long moment of silence and struggle, as though all those there present held their breath, and fought for air and life. Then Owen Goch heaved himself clear of the hush like a salmon leaping, and said through his teeth: 'No! I have my rights! I keep my rights! You are my younger, and you rob me. I appeal to Welsh law. This land of Gwynedd is partible, every yard of it. I demand my own!'

'You had your own,' said Llewelyn, 'portioned to you by the council of Gwynedd, and fully equal to mine. You were not content with it, you struck for more and lost all. And even if I grant your claim in this land of Gwynedd, where do you stand in this land of Wales? That *I* have won, that *I* have made, that *I* have created with my bare hands? What part have you in that, and what right? None! You are seven years out of date, Wales has outrun you. You may do homage to me and hold lands to the full extent of your claim as my vassal, or you may go back to Dolbadarn and nurse your ancient right in prison. It has no reality anywhere else.'

So he said, forcibly but without any anger or venom, hammering to make all plain, though I think he had little hope that Owen Goch would accept the undoubted grace he was offered. For grace it was. He might then have come to the prince's peace, as many a better and greater had come, and been confirmed in all his holding, and protected under the prince's shadow from all encroachment. But he could not get over the fixed notion that he was the elder, and held equal right, no matter what he had done to imperil it, no matter what Llewelyn had done all this time to assert his better right, by virtue of the efficacy of his rule and the pre-eminence of his arms. For there is no question but Wales, to give it that glorious name, was his creation out of chaos.

'I will see you damned and in hell,' said Owen Goch, through a throat so crammed with hate he could hardly speak, 'before I will do homage to you or pledge you fealty.'

After a moment of bleak silence Llewelyn said evenly: 'I will not hold you to a decision made in heat, that may be regretted when the blood is cooler. Sleep on it overnight, and think what you do.' And he struck his hands together, and called, and the guards came softly in. There was not another word said between them. Owen Goch had enough sense of his own dignity to fend off the affront of being held or enforced. He stalked through the doorway without a look aside, and they closed gently after him and herded him, away to his guarded sleep.

'If either of you has anything to say to me,' said Llewelyn then, with arduous calm, for I knew he was more distressed than he was willing to show, 'say it. I am listening.'

David was silent, but so taut and black of brow that I knew he had much more boiling within him. But Rhodri spoke up with all the loud, indignant righteousness of those who move upon the surface of events, and understand little of what goes on beneath. Nothing of what tormented David was known to him. He had neither betrayed Llewelyn in his warfare for Wales, nor helped him after, as David had. All he saw and felt was the narrow current that moved his own boat. But in the elucidation of that current he had read and brooded over all the law books of the old men, centuries gone.

He went into the assault with such desperate courage that Llewelyn was astonished, and at another time would have been amused, for he never took Rhodri very gravely.

'Owen does right,' Rhodri said vehemently 'to hold strictly to law, and you do wrong to flout it, and have been doing wrong all these years, as you well know. Nor is it any answer to hark back to what is gone, and say that Gwynedd was fairly divided, and Owen sacrificed his rights by acting against you. He did what he did in defence of David's rights and mine, which had never been fairly met, and never have since. It would be honourable to write off what was done then, and begin afresh to do justice to us all. You have the true occasion now to do what should have been done long ago. No one will point the finger at you, or see any weakness in such an act. The bards will approve. It would be fitting, as a memorial to our mother, who made her own will plain before she died.'

He was very pale with passion, so that his reddish freckles stood out darkly over his cheekbones and nose, and his hair, that was a bleached red like ripe wheat-stalks, shook down over his high forehead. Surely he had been brooding for years and preparing what he had to say, and had wanted the courage to begin until the Lady Senena's dying words braced him to the deed. And now that he was launched, he poured out his arguments with such frenzied fluency that it was plain all his reading had been directed to one end, the urging of his own case. For though he was careful to bring in always the matter of Owen's freedom, with much more ferocity did he press the point that all the sons, from eldest to youngest, had equal rights to land, all of which was by law partible.

'Which land?' said Llewelyn with ominous mildness. 'The land of Gwynedd or all the land of Wales? What came to us by inheritance was the shrunken domain of Gwynedd west of Conway. Am I to divide that equally in four and share it with you?'

'The lands of Gwynedd east of Conway have also been recovered,' said Rhodri, well primed with his studies in law, 'and are also partible.'

'Recovered by my hand,' said Llewelyn flatly, 'though I grant to David, with hearty goodwill, that he did his share gallantly there. But where were you? And for the rest of Wales – barring the marcher lordships, and those are matter for action hereafter – there are princes with claims of their own, claims I have been the means of satisfying and guaranteeing, and though they may have done homage and fealty to me, never think they have waived any of their rights in their own commotes, or are likely to look kindly on any claim you may advance on them. No, confine your pleas to Gwynedd west of Conway, where they might – I say *might*! –have some validity.'

Rhodri was thrown somewhat out of his stride, but having begun he could not leave off, for he might never have the force to open the matter again. So he drew furious breath, and went at it with stammering passion, shooting legal quotations like arrows, and so voluble that it seemed he had learned most of the code off by heart. And the longer he went on, the less did he mention Owen's rights, and the more his own, though still he cried out absolutely for Owen's freedom. He needed Owen, if he was to achieve anything, for he was always uneasy at standing alone, and David, though he had begun this, stood by with a dark face and a bitter eye, and said no word now in his support. So Rhodri pressed hard on the theme of his mother's dying wish, and reviled the impiety of rejecting it. And when he was out of breath and words, Llewelyn said:

'Owen still has a choice, if he cares to use it. Don't prejudge what he will do. But I tell you this, if he goes free he goes free as my vassal, owing me homage and fealty, and with the law and the council ready to deal with him if he betrays me. It has been too late to plead the old law of inheritance in Gwynedd ever since our grandfather's day, when by consent it was put aside. You cannot turn time back. I will not give you or any man licence to dismember what I have made into one.'

'You are spurning justice,' flamed Rhodri, made bold by despair, 'and flouting our mother's prayer!'

'In your judgment,' said Llewelyn, 'doubtless I am. Certainly my answer to you is no! No, I will not release Owen as an act of mindless piety, without his submission. No, I will not give you a full fourth share in even the western part of Gwynedd. The lands you hold were apportioned to you by the council, and held to be a fair endowment. You will get no more from me.'

Then Rhodri cried out against him for an unjust tyrant, a spoiler of his brothers, and flung away out of the room in a fury. I thought, then, he was half afraid of what he had already done and said, and wishing to be else-where when Llewelyn's patience broke. But now I think he had another idea and another reason, and made use of his rage as cover for his with-drawal. 'I will not stay in your court,' he cried from the doorway. 'I take my people home tonight.' And so he was gone, and when we heard great hustle and bustle and clatter of hooves in the wards somewhat later, no one wondered at it.

When the door had closed on his going, with a slam that shook a faint drift of dust out of the tapestry curtain, Llewelyn stood somewhat wearily looking after him for a moment, and then said, more to himself than to us: 'God grant that may be the end of it. Who would have thought he had it in him, though! If he could bring half the vigour to the interests of Wales he brings to his own we should have a paladin at our service.' And he poured wine, and drank gratefully, and looked across at David, who remained where he had stood throughout, his eyes burningly intent on his brother's face. 'In the name of God,' he said, 'even if you have more to say, need it be said bolt upright? Or are we still at the bar of a law-court? You, or I?'

'Both, it may be,' said David, darkly smiling, though it was more like a grimace of pain. 'I am sorry, but you have not finished with me. All that I said to you I say again. And neither you nor Owen have answered it.'

'My offer to Owen,' said Llewelyn, 'is still open. Even if he is of the same mind tomorrow, and still rejects it, it will remain open. He has only to submit, and he can have his freedom and his lands again.'

'You know he will not,' said David, and his face was riven suddenly, as though its composure fell apart from some terrible convulsion of pain, until he forcibly reimposed upon it its normal severe and haughty beauty. Only then did I begin to perceive how deeply he was torn by his mother's passing, and the manner of it, and how it had set him at odds with his own heart and mind and conscience. Not often in his life did he turn to do battle with the creature he was, though always he knew its lineaments perfectly, without shame or self-deceit. 'I am not asking you for bargains, or bleating, of justice,' he said, 'I am asking you for a gesture of princeliness at your own risk. If you are not afraid to deny what my mother prayed for, I am. I am, because I am the instrument of his misfortune, and I feel the load upon me like a curse. You can deliver me, as well as Owen, if you will.'

'Fool!' said Llewelyn with affection. 'You wring your own heart for no reason. You have paid off your indebtedness time and time again, you owe nothing to me, and nothing to Owen. Unless he accepts his position as vassal to me, how can I control him, how protect the union I have made? His voluntary submission is vital, not for me, but for Wales, which he could otherwise destroy. Do you think I will imperil that?'

'He will not submit,' said David, with the certainty of despair.

'He will. Though it take him years yet, he will come to his senses. If I can wait, why not you?'

'While I go free,' said David, marvelling, 'and in your trust, and in your bosom!'

'Why should you not? You, whom he enticed into his revolt against me, barely nineteen years old, torn two ways between brothers, and knowing him better than you then knew me? He should have been ashamed,' said Llewelyn hotly, for it was something he had held against Owen from that day, 'so to have seduced you.'

'Sweet Christ!' said David, so low I think Llewelyn did not hear, but I did, for I was closer to him, and much wrung between them, being friends to both. Then he raised his voice, and said harshly: 'You do us both wrong, we were not as you supposed, Owen and I. It was for *my* right he struck, whatever he believed he stood to gain, and it was *I* who put it into his head, and provided him all that argument he broached with you. He was the seduced, and I the seducer! Me you should have loaded with chains, him you should have loosed. What could Owen do against you, with no wits but his own?'

All this he said with such weighted and laborious force that I knew how much it cost him, but to Llewelyn it had, I can well understand how, the sound of argument composed in obstinacy, word by word as he devised it. He looked upon his brother hard and long, between sternness and affection, and said bluntly:

'Those are bold and generous lies, but still lies, and unbecoming between you and me.'

'No lies,' said David, quivering, 'but truth.'

'I do not believe you. If it had been true, you would have spoken up long ago, even if you lacked the courage after Bryn Derwin. It is no way to help Owen by slandering yourself.'

David saw then that he was caught in his own skills as in a net, and could not break through them, but would still have to carry this load of guilt upon his heart. For once before, but then of deliberate intent, he had spoken the truth in such a way that it could not be believed, and now the same fate, unsought, was visited upon him as a requital. He tried, but even for him now words were hard to find, and his persistence in a confession that was taken to be simply a mistaken act of chivalry, a weapon for enforcing his will even at his own sorry cost, at last pricked Llewelyn, who was tired and wrung, into flashing anger at such obstinacy.

'Stop this!' he cried. 'It is unworthy, and I will not witness it. I have said on what conditions Owen goes free, and the reason you know as well as I, and it is not a mere matter of land. There is one cause I care about, and it is Wales, and not for Owen, nor for you, nor for any other will I put Wales in peril after the old fashion. Only a few months since you saw yourself what King Henry intended, if I had been wiped out of the world – to divide and devour, to split up the land and consume it piecemeal, to play brother against brother in the name of Welsh law, which he despises but can still quote for his own purposes! He could not ask for better advocates than I have heard tonight! What does he need with armies if he can get his work done for him by Welshmen without ever unsheathing a sword? And for no pay but promises he need never fulfil!'

'Are you saying,' asked David, whiter than his shirt and stiff as a lance. 'that England has bought me?'

'Not so! There was no need. But if you had been bought, and at a high price, too, you would still be very good value to England. Half your heart,' said Llewelyn unwisely, 'was always in doubt where it belonged, between King Henry and me. I thought that severance had healed. Now I wonder! In the matter of Wales, he who is not for us is against us. It is time to ask where *you* stand!'

If he had not been driven so hard he would not have said it, and it was done to put an end to a colloquy he could no longer bear, but it went in like a sword, all the more because there was, then as always, a degree of truth in it. David stood staring at him for a long, aching time of silence, while he gathered a voice so thick and heavy with outrage and grief that it stuck fast in his throat, and he had to heave the words out of him like gouts of blood. His face was ice, but within he burned, and his eyes were pale blue flames, both fire and ice.

'I stand in the presence of my liege lord,' he said, 'and above the grave of my mother, and confronting the prison that holds my brother, whom I misled and cozened and abandoned. And you expect me to be whole? You understand nothing, you care for nothing, but Wales. Very well, keep your Wales, hold it together with your hands, bind it with your blood, marry Wales, beget Wales, have Wales for brother and mother and all, and cease to be troubled with us mortals. I have done!'

He turned on that word, and flung away out of the room, so violently yet so silently that neither of us had time to say a word more or reach out a hand to him. I heard his footsteps in the stone passage outside the door, and they were swift and hard and steady, as though he knew what he had done, and where he was going, and did not repent of it, however mortal his pain.

'Dear God!' sighed Llewelyn wearily, and passed a hand over his face. 'Was it I did that, or he?'

'Shall I go after him?' I said.

'No. To what end? I am of the same mind still, and so is he, what can we have to say to each other yet? Nor have I any right to call him back. He is a free man. He is gone of his own will, and in time he'll come back of his own will. Have we not seen him stalk away in the same fashion many a time before?' And he looked at me very searchingly, and asked me: '*Was* he lying?'

I said: 'No.' What else was there to say, and what to add?

'The more reason,' said Llewelyn heavily, 'for letting him alone until he pleases to come to. I have been remiss. Too much a prince and too little a brother. Now there's nothing to be done but hope that Owen will think better of his refusal by tomorrow, and save David's countenance and mine.'

For whatever regret he felt, it was not for his decision, and whatever he might take back, it was not the sentence of continued imprisonment. David was right, he was married first to Wales.

David slept at Aber that night, if indeed he did sleep, but in the morning early he collected all his household and rode, himself with a handful of knights going ahead while the rest followed later. The vanguard made no farewells. The rest were ready to march by midday. Rhodri had taken himself off with all his retinue overnight, and Owen, still obdurate, rode with a tight escort for Dolbadarn soon after Prime. For he utterly refused to abate any of his full claims under Welsh law. Aber was emptying fast, and for all it would have happened so even without the quarrel, still that disintegration seemed to me a sad, symbolic thing.

Godred being with David's knights, I was able to speak with Cristin before she left with the main party, and I told her all that had passed. For she was as secret and stout as any man, and had always a steady fondness for David, alone of all women being able to meet him as equals and friends, without illusions and without reservations.

'There are times,' she said, 'when he speaks with me almost as he does with you.' And she flushed, as though by that notice he acknowledged, and she recognised, the bond there was between us. 'If by any means I can help him,' she said, 'I will. For your sake and his.'

Other than that, we said never a word of ourselves. Or of Godred. Above all, never of Godred.

It was towards night when the escort that had taken Owen back to his prison rode again into the maenol at Aber. They came three men short of their number, and several with the bruises of battle. Cadwallon, their captain, sought audience at once of Llewelyn, and made report to him.

'My lord, first I make it plain, the errand you gave us is successfully done. But not without hindrance. When we came down towards the lakeside, where there is cover close about the track, archers in hiding among the trees loosed at us, and then mounted men rode out on us from either side the way. They were more than we, and had the vantage of surprise. Who looks for an ambush about the prince's business in Gwynedd itself? We lost one man killed, and three were wounded, before ever they closed. But we beat them off, none the less. My lord, this was an attempt to take away the Lord Owen Goch out of captivity. No question! They tried to cut him out from among us, but vainly. He is safe in Dolbadarn.' And he said, to be just and make all clear: 'He was not a party to it. Surely he would have gone with them if he could, but I saw his face when it began, and I know he was as much at a loss as we. There was no foreknowledge. It was the other who planned it.'

'The other?' said Llewelyn, as tight as a bow-string, and his voice unnaturally gentle that it might not be unnaturally harsh.

'My lord, pardon the bringer of unwelcome news! We took captive four of the attackers, before the rest broke and fled. Three are lancers of Lleyn. The fourth is the Lord Rhodri, your brother.'

I was by Llewelyn's side then, I saw all the lines of his face and body ease, warming slowly into life. He had expected another answer.

'Rhodri!' he said. 'These were Rhodri's folk, then?' And he drew cautious breath, and his hands upon the arms of his chair slackened, and flushed with blood over the stark bone.

'Yes, my lord, no question. We have taken them into Dolbadarn with the Lord Owen, and there they are in safe hold. Also our wounded we left there to be tended. But for a few scratches the Lord Rhodri is not hurt. And your castellan holds him safe until he receives your orders.'

'He shall have them,' said Llewelyn, 'tomorrow. You did well, and shall not be forgotten. For the man you lost, I am sorry. Bring me his name and estate, and if he has a family, they shall be my charge. It was too much to spend,' he said, more to himself than to us, 'for my failure.' And he dismissed Cadwallon kindly, and sat a long time brooding after he was gone.

'Well,' he said at last, 'I must work with what I am and what I have. Rhodri shall have fair trial, and the law that he so loves, not I, shall say what is to be done with him. And till he has a day appointed him we'll keep him safe, but not in Dolbadarn. Two so like-minded in the one hold might be all too well able to buy a messenger and means. In Dolwyddelan he should be safe enough.'

He got up from his chair and paced a little between tapestried wall and wall, restless and troubled, and looking round at me suddenly he said: 'Here I stand, to all appearances at the zenith, not a Welsh prince against me but one, all the reality mine, nothing remaining but to get England's recognition, and that no longer quite out of reach. Yet it seems, Samson, I have stripped myself of all my kin, mother, brothers and all, in one day. As though a cloud had come over the sun. You remember Rhydderch's red-gold dragon in the noonday? It may be this is God's reminder to me that after the zenith there is no way for the sun to go but down.'

I said stoutly that he made too much of it, for to say the blunt truth, there was but one of his brothers had ever been of much value to him, and he was not at fault here. 'You heard Cadwallon,' I said. 'David was not there.'

'Not in the flesh,' said Llewelyn drily. 'By his own admission and yours he knows how to get others to do his work, even in his absence. Why should he not use Rhodri, if he did not scruple to use Owen?'

Then I understood the heart of his loss, and how it reached out beyond David to touch me in my turn, since I had known all these years, or possessed a conviction so strong as to be almost knowledge, of David's greater guilt at the time of Bryn Derwin, and had never said word to him about it, either in extenuation of Owen's crime or in warning against David. But neither could I speak a word now for myself, while he said none against me. Nor was there any blame or reproach in his face or manner.

I said, and it was true, that it would be simple to send a courier and examine in David's household, without accusing any, at what hour he and his knights had returned, and whether he or any of them could possibly have been in touch with Rhodri's company after they left Aber. For surely this attack had not been planned beforehand, and we knew that Rhodri had ridden away in dudgeon before ever David left the prince's presence. Llewelyn shook his head and smiled.

'No, we'll not send spies to question my brother's grooms and servants against him. We have not come to that. Unless Rhodri accuses him, in my eyes he is clean. Guilt is no simple thing. It may be my own hands are in need of washing as much as any, and that's a salutary thing to have learned. I shall never again be sure – altogether sure – of any man.'

He halted there for a moment, and I thought and dreaded that he was about to add: 'Not even you.' Though my deserts were never more than other men's, yet my need of his trust was extreme. But as I waited he ended, as one accepting, wryly but without grudge, what he saw and recognised: 'Least of all, myself.'

Towards the end of that month of January the council of his peers brought Rhodri to trial for his treason, and committed him to imprisonment at the prince's pleasure until he should purge his offence. He was taken to Dolwyddelan, and there kept in secure hold. As for David, Llewelyn would not pursue him, but waited all the early months of the year for him to return as impulsively and vehemently as he had departed, and take his place among us as before. But even at the Easter feast, which we kept at Bala, we waited and looked for him in vain. David did not come.

CHAPTER VII

About Easter the Lord Edward came hurrying back to England in answer to his father's plea, and was ordered promptly to go and look after his intended heritage of Wales, and he did indeed hasten to Shrewsbury, where he made his headquarters and kept contact with the justiciar of Chester, and tried to enforce the better stewardship of the marcher castles. But all he did in Wales, and that we let him do, was to relieve and reprovision his islanded castles of Diserth and Degannwy. The time of the proposed February muster had gone by unhonoured, for no one stirred to carry out the order. And it was not long before King Henry hastily called his son back to his side, and left us watching from a distance the mad dance of events in England.

At the feast of Pentecost, towards the end of May, a young man rode along the coast road into Aber, watched from a distance as he came. When he drew nearer the watch recognised his arms, and sent word in to the prince. For the second time he welcomed into Aber young Henry de Montfort.

He came unattended, and on urgent business, and Llewelyn received and made him welcome. Goronwy was then not long back from the south, having seen the Welsh gains consolidated as far as the borders of Gwent. I was present with them at that meeting as clerk, as was usual.

'My lord,' said the young man, 'I come to you this time as envoy not from king and council, but from an assembly of those lords, knights and free men who stand firm in support of the Provisions. An assembly most fittingly held at Oxford, where first those principles were set forth and agreed. We are a party believing strongly in that fair and ordered form of government, we desire to uphold it still, according to oath, and to see it established in the realm for the good of all. We have many of the younger nobility with us, and the yeomen of the shires solidly behind us. And that you may know who leads us – my father, the earl of Leicester, is back in England, and presided at this gathering. Those who hold with him begged him to come home and be their leader, and he has again taken up the burden. It is in his name that I come.'

'In his name and in your own,' said Llewelyn, 'you are very welcome. What the earl of Leicester has to say to me I am all goodwill to hear.'

'My lord, when once we spoke of these matters I do believe you were interested and moved. I think we had your sympathy. Do we still hold it?'

'My position,' said Llewelyn, 'is as it was then. As between king and commons I do not presume to intervene. As between ideas I may certainly choose and prefer. But my business remains, as it always was, Wales.'

'Then I am sure you, of all men, know,' said the young man eagerly, 'that the present chaos in the march cannot in the end benefit Wales, whatever short-term gains there may be to be had. Also that King Henry came home at the year's end looking upon you as his arch-enemy, by reason of your campaign in Maelienydd, and bent upon making war upon you, and even now has not abandoned that theme. It is no secret that he is still contemplating calling out the feudal host against you this summer, having failed in February.'

'I have been expecting it,' agreed Llewelyn, smiling. 'And you do not regard me as an enemy?'

'No. Your business is Wales, ours is England. We will not betray ours, but neither will we fail to respect yours. And those who have a common enemy have much to gain by being friends.' He caught the import of what he had said, and blushed, as it seemed he still could, amending with dignity the ill-chosen words. 'It is not the king who is the enemy, it is the old order, and those about the king who seek to fend off all changes. The king is a victim, manipulated by some whose whole concern is to protect their own interests.'

'And how do things stand at this moment,' asked Llewelyn, 'with your own strength?'

De Montfort named names, very lofty names, and strange to note so many of them young. This was no old man's party. There was hardly a man among them of Earl Simon's own generation, except for his faithful friend Peter de Montfort of Beaudesert. The old, those who dug in their heels against change and resented that great lords should be asked to curb their privileges, or common men seek to enlarge theirs, were all with the king. 'The Earl Warenne is with us, Gilbert of Clare, Henry of Almain, Roger Clifford, Leyburn, Giffard of Brimpsfield . . .' The list was long. 'We return absolutely to the Provisions, declaring all who oppose them, but for the king and his family, to be public enemies. And these demands we are sending to the king.'

'He will not agree to them,' said Llewelyn with certainty. 'And what then?'

'I do not accept that his refusal is certain. But we are prepared for it. If need be, we shall move against those who urge the refusal upon him.'

'In arms?' said Llewelyn, eyeing him steadily.

'In arms.'

'And what is it,' Llewelyn asked mildly, after a moment's measuring silence, 'that you want from me?'

'The chief part of our confederacy is in the marches, and from this base we must move. If it comes to war, we must secure the march behind us, with all the passages of the Severn in our hands, before we move east into England. Your presence in arms on the west bank of the river would be worth an army to us.'

Goronwy looked at Llewelyn and smiled, knowing his mind. 'The bridges at Gloucester and Worcester and Bridgnorth would need to be held,' he said, 'and certain fords. It could well be controlled from the west. It is in our interest to keep ward on that border for our own sake, in such troublous times.'

'You shall have what you ask,' said Llewelyn. 'I will take my host and hold station along the border, within your reach whenever you call on me. And in the south Rhys Fychan shall keep ward in the same way. We had best arrange codes and signals I can send out to my allies, we have a long frontage to guard, and you may have need of us in haste, at any point.'

So we were committed, and yet not committed, for out of the confines of Wales he would not pledge more than raiding units of his army, and within Wales he moved upon his own land, and could not be questioned or held to account. But with that the young man was content, it was what he had come to gain. And he dined with us, and was good company when he could call back his mind and spirit from where it habited by choice, somewhere far away in the city of London, in that Tower which I remembered from my boyhood, where that very day, perhaps, Earl Simon's envoys confronted the king with the high demands of the reform.

The council conferred long that night, and when the planning was done those two, Llewelyn and Henry de Montfort, sat privately over their wine even longer, and talked of all manner of things, growing close and eager, for they had much in common, being of that open part of humanity that does not hoard its light, but gives it forth upon other men, sometimes too rashly. And so I heard, for I attended them for a brief while, how they spoke also of that letter King Henry wrote when he believed Llewelyn dead, and the plans he made for supplanting him. And young de Montfort said, after some thought:

'But surely he has put his finger upon your weakness, the only one he could find, saying you are unwived and without issue. With such a princedom as you have to conserve, I do marvel that you have not married and got sons. If I presume, rebuke me but forgive me. For I do know of marriages made, and marriages that could not be made, for reasons of true affection. My father,' he said, with that ardour that possessed him always when he spoke of his parents and kin, 'never thought to aspire to the king's sister, when he came to England, and she in her child-widowhood was pledged to life-long chastity. A wicked folly, I think, to induce a young girl to swear to such a penance, with the whole world before her! But when they met it was a fatal thing, for each desired the other, and no other thing in this world. And she was gallant enough to withstand all the pressures put upon her, and to be forsworn of her oath for his sake. I am their firstborn, and I tell you, whatever the churchmen may say, I think God did not disapprove their love.' So he said, and flushed with pride in those two who begot and bore him. So he well might. They say she was a proud, demanding, difficult lady, this boy's mother, but none ever dared to say that she fell short in her devouring and devoted love to that man she chose and married.

'I would wish to you and to any man that I revere,' said young Henry, 'so proud and single a choice. It may be that you are also waiting for an Eleanor.' And he laughed, softly and hazily, for he was a little in wine, and because of Llewelyn's silence he feared he had trespassed on an unwelcome theme, where indeed I believe the prince was mute only in surprise at his own want of forethought, that he had never before given serious consideration to a matter of such patent importance as his marriage, and the provision of heirs after him. So the boy went on talking to fill a moment's silence and escape into safer pastures.

'My only sister,' he said, 'the youngest of us, is also Eleanor, after my mother. She'll be eleven this year.' And he looked at my lord with a face like a flower wide open to the sun, ardent and vulnerable, and I, for one, considered and marvelled what the sister of such a one might not promise of beauty and gallantry.

Llewelyn had judged rightly, King Henry in the Tower indignantly refused the demands of the reform. He was still so blind to the real enormity of what was happening in his own land that he even persisted in sending out his writs for the muster against Wales at Worcester on the first day of August, but long before that day came, the tide of events had swept on and left the summons awash in its beached pools, like weed cast ashore on Aber sands. For as soon as the word was received of the king's rejection the young marcher confederates struck in arms against their enemies down the border, capturing the bishop of Hereford, shutting him up with all his Savoyard canons in Clifford's castle of Eardisley, and plundering his rich and coveted lands. He was the first and the most hated of the implacable foreign royalists, but after him they turned to others, long since marked out for vengeance.

By then we were on the border as had been promised. Llewelyn sent out his writs to all his vassals and allies on the day that young de Montfort left us, and by the middle of June we marched. Within one week more we had companies deployed from Mold in the north to Glasbury in the south, from which positions we could move easily into action anywhere in the middle march, according as we were needed.

The writ went also, as customary, to David at Neigwl, but because of the extra distance he had to bring his men we did not wait for them, but went ahead and set up our base at Knighton, whence we could very rapidly pierce into England by the Teme valley. The orders sent to David were to follow us to that place with his own muster as quickly as he could. And in the brisk excitement of action it never entered Llewelyn's head or mine to doubt but we should see David within three days, for he could never get into the forward ranks of the battle fast enough to please him. It was shocking to awake suddenly to the truth that five days were gone, and no sign of any detachment from Neigwl, and no message.

'Surely,' said Llewelyn, startled, 'he cannot still be hating me so much that he will not even fight beside me?' But when another day passed, and still no sign, he was displeased in earnest.

'This is not to be borne,' he said. 'He has a right to hold off from his brother as bitterly as he will, but when his prince calls on him for service due he shall meet his obligations like any other vassal, or pay for his neglect as any other would pay.'

I said, though with a doubtful heart, that there might well be some good reason for the delay, and that we should not judge him unheard.

'Nor will I,' he said heavily. 'I am too well aware that I was not without blame in my handling of him.'

It was about that time we were called on, by the signal agreed, to advance into English territory far enough to seal the western bank of the Severn at Bridgnorth, while the young marcher lords closed in and secured the town from the east, and Llewelyn had his men massed to march, and himself would go with them.

'I would not send an officer after him like a bailiff after a defaulter,' said Llewelyn fretting, 'not until I know what occasion I have to treat him so. Samson, do you go! Of all men he'll listen to you, if he will to any. Go as his friend and mine, and bid him come where he is missed and wanted.'

That was a time when I was very loth to leave him, but his need of a better understanding with his brother seemed greater than any need he had of my moderate ability in arms. So I said that I would go, and as soon as his company had ridden, fast and hard along the river valley towards Ludlow, the footmen following at their tireless summer pace, I also rode.

I had his seal, that I might get a fresh mount along the way wherever I needed. Nor did I hurry, for at every mile I hoped to see the dust of David's column bright on the sunny air ahead, and it was my care to keep the way he would be most likely to use with a body of armed men. I found excuses for him very easily, for if he had first been delayed by some accident, and then kept the foot pace, he had a case for his lateness. But I confess what I believed most likely was that he still burned with resentment against his brother, and was bent on absenting himself.

At every place where roads met I made enquiry for him and his men, but nowhere did I hear of their passing. Other news I did pick up along the way, but none of David. At the abbey of Cymer there was a drover halted, returning from England, and he told me that Earl Simon with his army had struck south-east to cut off London from the Channel ports and so from France, so that no more foreign mercenaries could be brought in, and though Richard of Cornwall had hurried to try and intercept him, not in arms but with blandishments, the earl had swerved southwards and left him standing helpless and unregarded, and was now in Kent, where all the knights of the shire had rallied to him joyfully, and all the seamen of the Cinque ports welcomed him with open arms. Three reformer bishops, they said, of London, Lincoln and Coventry, had been sent to the king with a form of peace even while the army was on the march, and since the king was isolated in a London very unfriendly to him, and severed from the aid he had hoped for from France, he would be hard put to it to hold out very long. The speed and force of Earl Simon's movements had won the war before it began.

There was other news to be gleaned when I reached Mur-y-castell, for the seneschal had a daughter married to an armourer in Denbigh, where news from Chester was easily come by, and she had sent him word of what went forward in London, to the great perturbation of the royal garrisons elsewhere, which were helpless to do more than look on from a distance. They said that the Lord Edward, when he saw the drift of events, rushed to the Temple and broke open the royal treasure-chests, and took away all he could to the castle of Windsor, together with a very strong garrison of mercenaries from France, whom he had brought over with him in April, and there he was determined to create a centre of resistance against the reformers. Doubtless he saw them now not as reformers, but as rebels against his father's rights and his own, and there was much to be said, if not for his good sense, at least for his bravery and determination. Certainly he was safer in Windsor than were his parents in the Tower, and the queen had tried to make her escape by water to join her son, only to have her barge attacked by the hostile citizens, and to be forced to take refuge ignominiously in the precincts of St Paul's, to avoid actual violence to her person. Poor lady, she was not accustomed to such usage, and there was indeed a terrifying quality about the affair, so far did it delve into final disorder, shocking to both sides and to us, looking on from afar. The king, they said, had already given way so far as to order Prince Edmund to surrender Dover castle, and it was but a step to his total submission.

After I had crossed the sands of Traeth Bychan and turned into the peninsula of Lleyn I refrained from asking word of David, for this was drawing near to his own lands, and I no longer believed that he had ever set out, or intended to set out, and I would not make public what was amiss, to make it harder to heal. So I came at last down from the hills into Neigwl, to David's llys. It was late afternoon when I entered the gate, and the courtyard seemed its summer self as I remembered it, only a little listless and unpeopled, like a household when its lord is away. The maids looked out, as always they do, to see who came, and before I set foot to ground the castellan was out to greet me. He was an old man, and lame, no longer fit for a war party. He knew me, and knew from whom I came.

I asked for David, and his officer gaped at me in puzzlement. 'Master Samson, the Lord David rode yesterday, with a company of picked men. Have you not met with them along the way?'

I said I had not, and told exactly by which way I had come.

'He said when he left that he meant to make a stay at Criccieth, for he had certain troopers there to add to his company. Did you enquire there? And it may be he had another such halt beyond, before heading for Knighton to join the prince.'

So he said, and clearly Llewelyn's order had been received, and was known to the household here, and it was believed that David had set out to obey it. I do not know, even now, why I did so, but I asked whether news of the Lord Edward's movements and King Henry's humiliations had been brought into the llys after the prince's summons was received. He said yes, that they had heard from Criccieth how the queen was hunted out of her barge, and how Edward had made an unavailing dash across country with his mercenaries from Windsor to Bristol, intending to make a stand there in his own headquarters, but the townsfolk of Bristol had closed the gates and refused him entry, sending him back to Windsor with his tail between his legs, like a scolded hound. And that, said the old man, was no pleasant hearing to one prince, when another was so humiliated, and the Lord David was indignant and disturbed, and short to question or approach.

My heart misgave me then, but I would not make public my doubts until the disaster was proven and irremediable. I asked how many men David had taken with him, and their names, and Godred was among them, at which I breathed more freely, for at least I could speak with Cristin without risking the poisoned attentions of her husband. I asked for her. Since the Lady Senena's death she had stepped into the office of châtelaine here in Neigwl, David being unmarried and having absolute trust in her. It was strange that he, who trusted so few and had no illusions about himself, yet was seldom mistaken in those he did trust.

She came to me in the high chamber, and I told her how matters stood. She was alarmed in the same manner and measure as I, and understood even what I had not had time to say.

'I knew,' she said, 'when he received the prince's writ, that he was in no mood to make any haste, yet he did begin preparations. I thought he would take his own time and keep his own distance, and yet he would go, and be reconciled once he was there. After there was so much talk of Edward being shut out of Bristol, and his mother insulted and abused, then he was blacker in mind than ever I knew him, and withdrew from us all. But still he called his men, and the muster went forward. Only it seemed he reduced their numbers, and chose with care. And the foot soldiers he countermanded.' She looked at me with wide, wild eyes. 'Wait!' she said. 'I have all the keys, of his treasury, too. No, come with me!'

I went with her through David's bedchamber, and into the small room which was his treasury. She unlocked the great chests there, and uncovered the hurriedly discarded hangings and plate and garments that remained, all tossed back at random after the rest was removed. She knew, not I, what should have been there.

'He has taken all that was easily portable,' she said, staring at me wide-eyed across the debris of his flight. 'All the gold and minted money he had, all his ornaments and jewels. And documents! What should he want, carrying his wealth about with him, to join his brother's army at Knighton? It is not to the Severn he's bound with all his best men, it's to the Dee! If you had enquired at Criccieth they could have told you when he was there, and which way he rode from there, since it was not towards Cymer.'

But she knew, and so did I, which way David had ridden. North-eastwards for Llanrwst, Denbigh, Mold and Chester, into the arms of the English garrison. Why else should he take with him all the valuables he possessed, and choose with care those companions who would welcome the change of allegiance and not betray him?

'He must not!' said Cristin. 'It means his ruin, and Llewelyn's bitter grief. He is mad!' And she said, seeing clearly and charitably that part of his act which redeemed it in a fashion: 'No one can say he did it for his gain! His brother's fortunes have never stood so high, King Henry's never been in such disarray. He is gone to an Edward bereft of friends, back to the troth of his childhood. His mother's wanderings have haunted him.' But she said again: 'He must not! He will never forgive himself or be forgiven.'

I took her by the hands a moment, forgetting not to touch in her distress and mine, and oh, the touching even of her fingers was such fiery comfort. I asked her to get me food and wine to take with me, while I got a fresh horse saddled in the stables, and to say no word yet to any of what we knew. Not until there was no help for it.

'There is no help for it now,' she said. 'You cannot overtake him.'

'I may. I doubt if he expects Llewelyn to make the first move, and he has no reason to believe anyone will be sent to enquire after him. If he stopped to add to his company in Criccieth, so he may again at Denbigh or Mold. Let's make the attempt, at least,' I said.

'May God give you wings,' she said, and ran to get me bread and meat, for in this ride there would be no halting but to question and to get a fresh mount. A whole day's start of me was more than enough, he could well be in Chester with all his men, and out of my reach, but since he had no reason to expect pursuit, and every reason to take his best men with him, and make himself as welcome a gift to the English as possible, he might well have moved with deliberation. While there was a hope, I could not relinquish it. I was mounting in the courtyard when Cristin came back with the pack, and I stowed it in my saddle-bag, and touched her hand, and rode. There were others around, not a word was said but the most current of farewells.

At Criccieth I took heart, for on making enquiry I learned that David's company had halted and passed the night there, and left, augmented by three more troopers, with the dawn. If this pattern held good, he might well have stopped again overnight with the same object in view. I had still a long while of daylight left, and no need to spare my horse, having the order that provided me with new on demand. And I rode hard, and got another mount at the settlement of the Knights Hospitallers at Dolgynwal, and went on through the night, over the mountain road to Denbigh. There were other roads he might have taken, but since I could follow only one I chose the most likely, and prayed I might choose aright.

David had an interest in Denbigh, and there was a small timber keep there, and a garrison of his men. And there was also the point that remounts for so many would be harder to come by than my single rounsey; it would be better economy to stay overnight and rest the beasts. So I hoped, and reasoned, and prayed, and came by full daylight to Denbigh. And yes, they told me, the company I sought had spent the night there, and left in the early dawn.

It was now a matter of perhaps two or three hours between us, instead of a day, which was better reckoning, and if they made a stay for a meal, whether innocently in hall at Mold or furtively in the woods by the wayside, I could overtake them yet. I pushed hard towards Mold, through that fine, rolling, forested country that declines into the flats and sands and meadows of the Dee. Once I had fled from Shotwick, on the far side of that river among the salt marshes, with Owen Goch, to confront the boy Llewelyn at Aber, newly bereaved as he was by his uncle's death, and become his servant and friend lifelong. Now I rode that same track, but in the opposite direction, to pluck back, if I could, his best-loved brother from the murderous act of treason.

At Mold they had no word of him. I had to be adroit with my prevarications, not to betray him before the game was played. So now, was I ahead of him, or not? Or had he chosen not to be seen so close to this border, and circled the town in cover, to move towards Chester still ahead of me? In doubt as I was, I pushed on towards England as though I knew what I did, though by this time I was so weary and sore that I reeled in the saddle, and dismounting was great trouble and pain. By God's grace I knew the road here very well, and knew of a place close to the border where it threaded a low but abrupt outcrop of rocks among woods, before the last descent into the levels of Dee began. For this spot I made with all the force and faith I had left. And on the way to it I saw, thin and silver and tall out of the woods on the left of the road, the smoke of a camp-fire going up erect as a larch into the blue morning air.

It was July, the highest of the summer, and still as sleep, hardly a breath of wind. The column of their fire was no more substantial than a hair, but stood braced straight as a plym-line and high as heaven. Then I rode by with a thankful heart to my little defile among the woods, certain that I was between David and England.

I had not long to wait, which was as well, for as soon as I halted and took station in the shade, sleep crowded in on me. I dared not stay in the saddle, or sit down in the grass when I had painfully alighted, but paced stiffly back and forth in cover, at a spot where I could watch the road without myself being observed. A packman went by on his pony, and a local cart, creaking and slow, but there was no other traffic until they came. I heard the broken, soft thudding of many hooves, the mounts of riders going purposefully but at ease. They were close to the border now, they had no reason to hurry or fear, there was no force in these parts, after Mold, that could stand in their way. It was not force that could stop David, even had there been enough men to match his. Either he would turn of his own will, when the time came, or he would not turn at all.

I saw them emerge in loose file from the trees, some way from where I was, David in the lead and alone. He had perhaps some thirty well-mounted and well-armed men in his company, a considerable gift, for I knew what the English court paid for good horses, and what pains they took to import them. And no doubt he had selected his men well, to lend added weight and stature to his own person. And yet he rode, as I saw when they drew nearer, with a face as bleak and dark as midwinter, all his brightness caged and battened within, into a smouldering ferocity. What he did was done with bitter resolution, but quite without happiness. And at that I felt some hope within me.

At the right moment I clambered again into the saddle and rode out, clumsy and dull with weariness as I was, into the middle of the track, and there took station facing them.

He saw me, and his hand gripped and tightened on the rein, and his knees clamped close, every muscle in him stiffening, so that his horse checked and tossed in a shiver of uneasiness. His head was uncovered to sun and breeze, a squire carrying his helm, and he wore only the lightest of hauberks. The wind had ruffled his black hair into curving feathers about cheeks and brow. Though he was burned brown as a nut, all the bones of his face were drawn in golden pallor that chilled into the blue-white of steel or ice as he stared at me. I think he was not surprised at seeing me, only enraged. Beneath the black and level brows his eyes were sharp and mortal as sword-points. And after a moment he shook the rein and edged his horse forward towards me, until we sat almost within touch of each other, but not on a level, for he always liked a very lofty horse, and my rounsey borrowed at Denbigh was sturdy and fast, but not large.

I gave him greeting as I would have given it at any other time, and it was no lie that I was glad to see him, though he had no such feeling then towards me, and pretended none.

'What are you doing here?' he said blackly.

'I am sent to you,' I said, 'with a message from the prince, your brother. He bids me tell you that they have marched on Bridgnorth, and entreats you to come soon where you are missed and wanted.'

I thought the lines of his icy mask blanched still paler, but his look did not change.

'I am going,' he said, 'where many are missed and wanted, and I, perhaps, not at all. But I am going. Where he told me my heart hankered to be, and secretly belonged.'

'You wrong him,' I said, but very low, for I wished to speak only to him, since speak I must. 'You wrong him, and you injure yourself, for he never said so. I heard, as you heard, what he did say, and a part of that was ill-judged from weariness and grief, yet it was not what you make of it. He did not send me to spy or rebuke in his name. He sent me to call you to him as his valued brother. And if you betray him, you betray your own heart. You know it as well as I, it is in your face, in your eyes, in the very bowels that knot and ache in your belly. Turn back now! It is not too late. There is no one knows but Cristin and I, both your true servants and lovers, and both devout in secrecy. You still have your freedom.'

I could no more, for they were too close. I said in a whisper: 'Call them off, send them back a little! At least talk with me!'

They were all eyes and ears at his back, greedy with curiosity. Perhaps some were shaken, and pondered their best interests. Only he, however tortured, was never turned from his chosen path. How great love, envy, reverence and hate there was in him for Llewelyn I never knew until then. There was no other could so drive David to despair, or inflame him to murder. There was no other could so draw him by the heart that in defence of himself he would tear himself and go the opposing way. And also to be reckoned with here was that Edward, with the giant frame and the furtive, drooping eyelid, the companion of his childhood, driven and hunted from Windsor to Bristol and back again, a demigod born, and now harried and derided and witness to his mother's humiliation, such a heroic, outcast figure as might well fire David into partisan action. I do not know the half, even now. Not the half! He was so deep, there was no plumbing him.

He made a gesture of his left hand, without turning his head. He said aloud: 'Go back! Wait on my order!'

I heard the horses stamp and sidle, edging backwards, heard them turned and walked to a distance, doubtless with many a rider's chin on his shoulder. David said: 'It is for you, not for him, I offer this respite. Say what you have to say to me. I am listening.'

So he was in the flesh, but in the spirit not at all, he was fixed and damned, unable to return. Nevertheless, I said what I had to say, with all the urgency I could command, calling him back to us not only in Llewelyn's name, that most wounded and most alienated him, but in mine, and Cristin's, and above all in the name of Wales, the mother of us all. But he said he had had a mother, and knew word for word what she had demanded in dying. Then I prayed his regard for his own fealty, freely given, and his own homage, never forced on him, but forced by him upon Llewelyn, who would have left him free. I cried upon his blood to compel him, and his breeding to make his way clear, and he said that he was bred as English and royal as Edward, and his mother who bore him found no fault in it. Then I was left with nothing to plead but Llewelyn, who meant more to him than Wales, who was the source and stumbling-stone in all this coil of loyalties. And in his eyes Llewelyn had failed and rejected him.

Then I was out of words and arguments, and he was like an unquenchable fire on which I played but a little, helpless sprinkling of rain.

'Are you done?' he said, with that terrible patience that was more malevolent than rage. And since I was mute: 'Then stand out of my way.'

'Never of my own will,' I said, and kept my place and though I was but a symbolic barrier between him and his own irrevocable act, he did not thrust by me and leave me standing. 'I keep my troth, if you do not. I tell you in your teeth, your place is here. Either turn back with me to your duty, or kill me.'

'Stand out of my way!' he said again, even lower and more gently. 'Or I take you at your word.' And he loosened his sword in the scabbard and half drew it out, then as deliberately slid it back again and unslung the thongs that tethered the scabbard to his belt, and hefted sheath and all in his right hand, like one trying the balance of a mace.

'Do what you must,' I said, at the end of my resource. 'As long as I have breath and force I will not take my body from between you and treason.'

He moved so suddenly and violently my eyes never followed what befell, though I know he rose in the stirrups to loom tall as the trees, and the blow itself I saw and did not see, as though a great wind had hurled a broken bough past me too fast for vision. He struck me with all his skill on the left side of the head, and swept me out of the saddle into the dust of the road, and under that thunder-clap mind and eyes darkened. I felt the grit and stones score my cheek. I heard him snap his fingers and call peremptorily to those who waited and watched at a distance: 'March forward!' And doubtless he himself set manner and pace, riding past me without a look behind. I remember there was a kind of distorted light for a few moments, in which I saw the hooves of the horses stamping past my face, before I went wholly into the dark.

When I awoke to the thunder in my head, and the burden of pain that told me plainly enough I was still in the world, it was night, but not darkness, for the nights of midsummer after glowing days are full of a light of their own. I saw trees arching over me, and stars between their leaves, and I was lying in my own cloak on thick, dry grass. There was the smoke of a wood fire in my nostrils, and the glimmer of its flame, bedded low with turfs, nor far from my left side. I heard the soft stamp of hooves in mossy ground, and the lulling sound of a horse grazing at leisure. In the glow of the fire there was a man sitting cross-legged with his chin in his hands, gazing steadily at me, but my eyes were not seeing clearly, and I could not tell who it was, except that it was not David.

He did not observe that I was awake and aware until I tried to lift one hand, heavy as lead, to feel at my head. Then he slid forward to his knees beside me, and put the wandering hand back to ground.

'Let be!' he said. 'He has broke your crown for you, but not past mending. I have cleaned the wound and bound it, and the best you can do for yourself now is sleep the night round, if you can, and let time help you past the smart. Here, drink some wine! There's bread, if you can swallow. If he had struck lower he could have snapped your neck, but he was gracious enough to leave you a throat to drink with.'

He brought a flask and held it to my lips, raising me with a hand indifferent but deft. It was then, when he leaned close to me, that I knew him for Godred. As fair and subtle and smooth as ever, smiling in the firelight, Godred nursed me.

'I see you have your wits and your eyes again,' he said as he laid me down. 'Six hours, after I moved you here into cover, you lay snorting like a bull, so that I feared your skull was broke in good earnest, and then you slid off sidelong into sleep. He never meant to kill, or you'd be a dead man this moment. Never stare so,' he said, grinning at me, 'I'm flesh, and damned to this world, and so are you. No vision, either of heaven or hell.'

In some surprise to hear my own voice clear and firm enough, I said: 'You were with his force, bound for Chester.'

'So I was,' he said, 'and none too happy about it, either. I owe you yet another debt for the reminder how long the prince's arm is. I have thought better of my allegiance. I have read the omens, and made my propitiation accordingly. Here am I, the saviour of Llewelyn's own familiar. I look for a handsome welcome.'

I thought then that he was in some mistake about the state of my faculties, or he would not have talked so airily and bitingly at large in my hearing. He was talking rather to the night and his own reason than to me, breathing out his doubts, his spleen and his pleasure in his own skills aloud, sure that none but a stupefied clod heard him, and safe and satisfied with that audience where he could not have been content with none. And I was unhappy in the role he assigned me, and to appraise him of my, perhaps, too acute attention, I said: 'How did you slip your collar and win back here?'

'Very easily,' said Godred, unabashed, and giggled over the bread and meat he was breaking. 'Every man has his needs. As soon as we were well in cover and the afternoon ebbing, I went aside to attend to mine. By the time any one of them looked round to wonder why I delayed, I was halfway back to where he left you lying. A pity I had not the best of his horses, but the one I have is none so ill, he'll be welcome where we are going, you and I.'

'And I was still where he had left me lying?' I asked.

'Some country kern had moved you to the side of the road and tumbled you there. Not wanting,' said Godred simply, 'to burden himself with some powerful man's discard. Can you blame him? You were bleeding from the scalp like a spring in spate, and all it wanted was a handful of cloth to staunch it. It's clean and drying now.'

'It seems,' I said, 'that I owe you my life.' For such a creature, abandoned in such a case the night over, might well have died for want of staunching, for want of warmth, for want of a draught of water.

'A debt I had to you,' said Godred softly, and his full brown eyes, golden-innocent in the firelight, burned brightly into mine. 'Now it is paid, perhaps. If we need talk of debts and payments, being close as brothers.' He leaned and folded the cloak closer around me, for the small hours of the night brought a pure, silent chill into the air. 'How could I ever have faced Cristin,' he said with measured sweetness, 'if I had let you perish by the roadside?'

Close as brothers we were on that journey we made together, Godred and I. For two days I could ride but for a short time, and we made slow progress down the border, and often were forced to halt for rest. And after his fashion he looked after me well, though for his own practical ends. For having decided his best interest lay in abandoning one master, he fully intended to ingratiate himself as quickly as possible with a new one. As for Cristin, it was plain to me, while all else was a cloud and a dream, that she played no part in his decisions, and counted for nothing in his plans, except where she could be useful to him. For he had left her without a word when he made up his mind to go with David to England, and he made no effort to go back to her or set her mind at rest now that he had changed his purpose. It was I who made shift to write a letter, when we halted at Valle Crucis, and beg the prior to have it sent to her at Neigwl, telling her both Godred and I lived, and were on our way to the prince in Maelienydd. I told her also that David was gone into Chester. There was no help for it, soon it would be common knowledge through Wales, and a national shame.

In those summer nights Godred and I spent together, out of doors, we two alone under the moon, he sat close and watched greedily, either with his shoulder warm against mine, or eye to eye with me across our little fire. There was no escape from him, for I was his key into a new chamber in fortune's house, and he was ever busy with the latest wager and the new-fangled hope. But there was more in Godred's kind and solicitous care than that. For he who never thought to write word or send message to Cristin never ceased to talk of her to me. Of her qualities, of her charms, of his luck in having her to wife. The darker the night, the more his tongue ranged into the intimacies of love.

'They say,' he said, softly marvelling, 'there are wives who have no love for being loved, but only suffer it as a duty. Not so Cristin! Welcoming and warm she is, a true consort. And who sees her only

307

clothed, he cannot know how beautiful!' He leaned so close that his flaxen hair brushed my temple, and sighed his blessedness into my ear. 'Pardon me, if you feel I offend in speaking so of my bliss. I do so only to you, who have rights in her and me both. I could wish you the same happiness I enjoy. Who deserves it more?'

So it went, and ever I put him off with stony indifference, whose heart he pierced and parted and played with as a musician with an instrument. And ever it grew upon me that he tortured not only me, but himself also, and seeing how little he considered or seemed to value her, that was a thing incomprehensible to me. Can men be jealous of what they hold so lightly? I had never thought so. But perhaps when they perceive that another creature treasures what they despise, then the possession held in so slight esteem becomes a jewel to be guarded. But then I was also lost, for no man knew so well as I that he had suffered nothing by my means, for Cristin was as I had first found her, pure as crystal and gold. And it seemed to me that all his intent, increasingly frantic and greedy, was to urge on me the possibility, the desirability, the necessity of possessing and spoiling that purity. Nor did he urge it now by way of wooing my favour, as once he had lightly and pointedly offered her to me, but with the fury and furtiveness of one begging for the only food that might keep him from dying.

I was still too innocent then in the complexities of love, which had been to me as simple and clear as it was mortal, to understand that to such a man as Godred, who had cuckolded many husbands in his time with never a second thought, it might not be a matter of great moment to be cuckolded himself in the same manner. In the flesh! But to be cuckolded in the spirit, to behold his wife loved without sin and loving sinless in return, this was the width of hell beyond forgiveness. Godred desired the lesser offence, to have her his equal and me his fellow.

I think in those days he even ran the risk of growing to the point where he might have become her equal, for I think that never before had any experience of his life been able to enlarge him to contain such suffering. Of his mind and motives I understood nothing. His anguish was an open book to me, the mirror image of mine. And daily and nightly I perceived how like we were to each other, he the bright image and I the dark of the same impress.

Sometimes by our camp fire he sat turning and turning the silver ring on his little finger, until it seemed to me that he and I were bound within just such a circlet, breast to breast, and could never get free one from the other.

But this uncomforted companionship ended, mercifully, earlier than we had expected, for at Strata Marcella, expecting still to have a day's march between us and Llewelyn, we rode into a courtyard full of his men, and a guesthouse peopled with his officers. The first we encountered in the stables told us that all the river crossings were secured, the army of the reform moving methodically eastwards into England, and the prince, at their earnest desire, was pushing north by forced marches to besiege and destroy the long-spared castle of Diserth, to prevent the garrison of Chester from making any move to alleviate the pressure on the royal forces elsewhere.

'He has been asking for you at every halt,' they told me. 'Go to him quickly, he'll be glad of you.'

But not of my news, I thought. And then, as I had not earlier because of my confused brain and the grief of my body and mind, I realised how slow we had been on the way, and knew by their faces that there was very little I had to tell Llewelyn. The news had reached him first not from Wales, but from England, by word from his allies in the march. What I could add might well be some alleviation of what had been done to him. For I knew, better than any other, that it had been done not in self-interest, and utterly without joy.

'Take me in with you,' said Godred eagerly in my ear. 'Speak for me now!'

I said I would speak for him, but not now, that for this moment he had no part. But only very reluctantly did he leave go of my arm, and let me go in without him to the guest-hall of the abbey, where Llewelyn was.

He had left the great chamber, and made use of a small office there, for there were some civil complainants from those parts who prayed audience with him. When I came in he sent the last of them away, and made me sit down before him, for I was still bandaged about the head, and no doubt showed in no very glorious case. He held me pinned to face the light, and eyed me hard, and when he took his hands from my shoulders and turned away from me it was with a rough, abrupt movement, as though in anger.

'There is little you have to tell me of him,' he said, not looking at me. 'I know where he is. The word came into Shrewsbury faster than you could bring it, marked as he has marked you. My bailiffs already administer his lands, and his tenants have pledged me their fealty. Nevertheless, speak, if you have anything to tell me. I am listening.' And again he said, not harshly but with a bleak simplicity that pricked me more deeply: 'The truth, this time. I want no shielding lies.'

I said, with a steadiness at which I myself marvelled, that I had never lied to him but by silence, never even kept from him what was knowledge, only what was misgiving and suspicion.

'Have I no rights even in those?' he said.

It was just, and I was ashamed. For if I was indeed his man, as David said with bitterness, I owed him even my doubts and fears, and his armour was incomplete without them. I said, faintly by reason of my weariness and self-reproach: 'In anything that is mine you have rights, and nothing that is mine will I ever again keep from you, not even my despair.'

'God forbid,' he said, 'that you should suffer any so extreme grief as despair, and not share it with me. Never deprive me, Samson, of what is mine by alliance. You are the closest friend I have, and damage to you is damage to me.'

I said that I accepted that gratefully, but that I had yet somewhat to say to him, in all good faith both to him and to David, as God watched and judged us all. And thereupon I told him, as fully as to my own soul, all that had happened between David and me. What there was to say for him, I said, yet not urging. Llewelyn must take his own stand, but at least upon all the evidence.

He heard me out without question or exclamation, with darkened but quiet brows and attentive eyes. He said: 'You know where we are bound now?'

I said that I did, that we went against Diserth and Degannwy, to destroy them, and to pin down the garrison of Chester from moving south to King Henry's aid. And David was in Chester and a part of that garrison. By the prince's face I knew his mind.

'With the better will,' he said, 'since he is there. I am a bolt loosed at his heart now, for your sake and for mine, and no use to tell me that you forgive him, for I do not forgive. Both those castles I will raze, and drive on to Chester if I can, and if he move on somewhere else I will go after him there. Once he stirred up civil war against me, and I mistakenly held him a misguided tool, who by his own confession was the contriver of all. Now he betrays me and Wales together, and if you think I burn only for Wales, Samson, you do me too much honour, for I am flesh like you. He has not only turned his coat and discarded his fealty, he has preferred Edward before me when it came to the proving. And if he come forth out of Chester in his new cause,' said Llewelyn with soft ferocity, 'and cross my path, I will kill him!'

And truly he believed utterly in what he said. I was the one, not he, who knew that he neither could nor would be the death of his brother. Far more likely, far, that by some fatal, circuitous road David would be the death of him. And since I was pledged now to keep nothing from him, and he to receive and consider whatever I so delivered, I spoke out what was in my mind.

'Have you still in remembrance,' I asked him, 'what he said to you after the field of Bryn Derwin, when he stood unhorsed and bruised and at your mercy? "*Kill me!*" he said. "*You were wise!*" Not defying, not challenging, rather warning and entreating you for your own life, knowing what he had done against you, and might do again. Do you remember?'

He said: 'I remember,' and his eyes burned upon me, their deep brown quickening like fanned embers.

'So much he knew of himself,' I said, 'even then, and so much he valued you and desired your better protection in his own despite. It is all the justification he has, but it is enough. He knows himself and you. Neither you nor I will ever know ourselves as he knows David, or each other as he knows Llewelyn. As often as his right hand launches a blow against you, his left hand will reach to parry it, and his voice will cry you warning: "*Kill me! You were wise!*" '

'You read this,' said Llewelyn darkly, 'as a reason why I should not kill him?'

'Far be that from me!' I said. 'It is fair warning enough of perpetual danger, and the best reason why you should! But it is also the absolute reason why you never will.'

Howbeit, we marched upon Diserth, which the men of the Middle Country were already joyously investing, having leave now to go to extremes. That unlucky garrison had stores for a few weeks, but no more, and their courage was not heightened when they heard how the government of the reform, strongly in command in London, had diverted the king's muster against the Welsh to London itself instead of Chester, to ensure against a defiant stand by the Lord Edward in Windsor, and to enforce the evacuation of all his French mercenaries from England.

That was the most ferocious insult so far offered to the crown, though phrased in the king's name. And Edward, with what bitterness I could imagine, did not wait to be besieged and declared a traitor, but surrendered Windsor and saw his paid soldiers ushered out of the country, and himself stripped naked and helpless. By which time we had taken Diserth, escorted the captive garrison out of it, and razed the walls. Thence we went on to Degannwy, but by September, when we were encamped around that fortress, Earl Simon's party was in complete control in Westminster, King Henry had accepted their demands, and both parties were willing to halt all warlike operations, and spare Degannwy the fate of Diserth.

They urged a brief truce with us. Had it been any other voice that spoke then for England, I doubt if Llewelyn would have heeded or agreed. But though the seal might be King Henry's, the message was Earl Simon's, and the charm of his name and person worked magic wherever it reached. Llewelyn agreed that Degannwy should be revictualled at need, and he would not hinder. But so far was England gone in confusion then that it was never done. We offered passage, but no stores came. By the end of September the starving garrison surrendered, and Edward had not one yard of ground left him in north Wales.

Then there was peace, or at least a great quietness.

And all this time such forces as ventured out from Chester against us were English, every man. They never let David come forth to fight; he ate out his heart within the city. Doubtless at that stage they feared to use him here against the brother he had abandoned, for fear some of those with him might think better of their wager, and turn their coats again. Such was David's fate, that always he sold himself at less than his value, and redeemed himself at more. But what his value was, if every man had justice, that I dare not essay to judge. I leave it to God, who has better scales for weighing, and a more perfect law.

CHAPTER VIII

Now concerning the final months of that year twelve hundred and sixty-three, and what befell then in England, I tell only with the wisdom of hindsight, for to us, patrolling the rim of the march, it seemed then that nothing at all was happening, beyond a confused harrying of individual lands according to the harrier's allegiance – or, all too often, according to his hopes of a quick gain at his neighbour's expense. For Earl Simon's terrible uprightness was no bar to the lawless ambitions of lesser, greedier and more unscrupulous mortals, such as mount in the train of every successful movement merely to share in the pickings. And much injustice was done, some in too hot enthusiasm, some coldly and cynically, to lords who had never turned against the Provisions, but only held back in doubt or timidity from too much zeal in their cause.

After September, when king, bishops and magnates met in St Paul's, and the king's consent to the settlement laid before him was published and approved, it seemed for a time that Earl Simon had truly won, and that the new parliament called to meet in October offered a blessed prospect of repeating the fervour, unity and reconciliation achieved, for however short a time, at Oxford. But aside from the many grievances by that time clamouring for redress, and the many defections and changes of heart caused by them, there were other factors making against the earl, and eating away at the supremacy he seemed to enjoy. For timid and pliable men like King Henry, who cannot be broken, cannot be defeated, either, since they are incapable of despair.

With all his soft, uncrushable obstinacy he clung to hope, and wound about to clutch at every thread that offered. He was tired and in distress, he said, and he desired above all to confer with his dear cousin of France. And to maintain his position he declared, over and over again, publicly and in private, his adherence in principle to the Provisions, the sacred book of the reform. He did so because he had a quick ear for the public pulse, and he knew that the great mass of the people clung to that hope as to holy writ, and if he declared openly against it even that support he enjoyed must dwindle rapidly away. But by affirming piously his own faith in it, and asserting only that it must be subject to discussion and amendment by consent, he was able to show as a harassed and hunted monarch of goodwill, pressed unreasonably hard by men more unbending than himself.

He had his own mild, devious wisdom, for this stand began to work effectively upon many of the older barons close to his throne, who felt affection for him as a man, and some compunction at seeing him hustled and bewildered. So many turned gradually to the king's side again.

312

I think no man knew better what Henry could do in this kind than Earl Simon himself, but he was utterly bound by his own nature and his own inflexible honour. He could not be a tyrant, and he struggled with all his powers against those hard circumstances that were forcing him into tyranny. So though he knew how the king could twist and turn and break his word, he was compelled to take that word as he expected his own to be taken, and he accepted Henry's promise to return faithfully for the October parliament, and let him go to meet King Louis at Boulogne. And he himself with his foremost allies also crossed the Channel to that meeting, believing in Louis' goodwill and influence, and earnestly desirous of coming to a genuine reconciliation under his guidance. For since Earl Simon could not move against the king's person, to take his royal prerogative from him, it was clear that no order could be restored, no progress made, until king and earl could work together in amity.

Such were his hopes and aims, but it fell out very differently. For in France the Savoyard and Poitevin exiles had for months been building up a strong party of royal feeling, and as soon as the emissaries of the reform landed they were arraigned as in a court of criminal justice, and found no goodwill at all to discuss or compromise. I will not say this was done with King Louis' approval, but certainly his efforts at mediation did little to amend it. The Pope also, who had coldly refused the appeal for a papal legate to give spiritual aid and wise counsel some years earlier, now hurriedly appointed Cardinal Gui to that office, and despatched him to the coast, not, I think, as a mediator, but as accuser and judge. And so thought the barons of England, for they made shift by legal delays to deny him entry to the realm, and he never got nearer England than Boulogne, for all his credentials.

In the face of this treatment Earl Simon repudiated all dealings and returned home. And so did King Henry, in time for parliament as he had promised, but he left the queen in France to work with the exiles. Nor did the parliament produce any relenting on either side, but only bitterness. That, and the first revelation of a third power looming large beside those two who already held the eyes of all men. And that was Edward.

It was Earl Simon himself who provided Edward with his first weapon. He was deeply anxious to have a better understanding with the prince, whom he respected and liked. So during that autumn the earl made many approaches through the young men of his party who had been Edward's closest personal friends, Henry of Almain, Roger Leyburn and such, several of them from marcher families. But instead of these persuasions working upon Edward, Edward worked upon them, and to such good effect that he won most of them back to his side. And as I know from Cynan since that time, his best argument in their ears was the threat from Wales. For a shadow they were throwing away the substance, leaving the way open for the constant enemy. So he prevailed and convinced them where their true interest lay, with him and with the crown. Man after man he wooed back to him, in and out of that parliament. And when he was ready, having quietly prepared and provisioned Windsor, he withdrew there and took his father with him, leaving

Richard of Cornwall and certain others, chosen in desperation as mediators, to try to arrive at some compromise that should at least make government possible.

Doubtless Richard tried to be fair, but his judgments came down heavily on Henry's side, yet again restoring to his hands the main offices of state. Thus Henry won the compunction and loyalty of the old, and Edward seduced the affections and ambitions of the young. And from this time forth it was not Henry who ruled and schooled Edward, but Edward who nursed, cherished and governed Henry. So much must be said for him, in extenuation of the deceits and lies he employed without shame later, that he was fighting for his father, and made use of whatever weapons came to his hand.

I remember what David once said of Edward, after we had ravaged the lands bestowed upon him in Wales. 'He has had his nose rubbed well into the mire,' said David, 'and that was never a safe thing to do to Edward, man or boy.' So it was now. All that had been done against him, by the citizens of Bristol who locked him out of his own town, by the order to the host to muster against Windsor if he did not surrender it and disband his French mercenaries, by the London mob that chased his mother into sanctuary in St Paul's, by us who had captured and razed his last two Welsh castles, everything any man had done against him and his he remembered and recorded, and for every act he would have revenge. But all he attributed to Earl Simon, whom once he had followed and admired. And now that he had turned against him there was no limit to his animosity. The measure of his former love was the only even approximate measure of his new and implacable hate, and that measure fell far short.

Safe in Windsor, King Henry issued letters under his privy seal, and took back the chancellery and the exchequer into his own hands, while Earl Simon held the Tower. They say that Henry of Almain, the best of those young men, at least faced the earl and took a personal farewell when he deserted him, pledging himself with earnest grief never to bear arms against his former idol. But Earl Simon was without tolerance for those who looked back, once having set their hands to the plough, and he told him with cold contempt that it was not his prowess in arms for which he had been valued, but the constancy with which he had once been credited, and that he was at liberty to go, and to take his arms with him and use them as he would, for they inspired no terror. So he departed, and went to Edward.

In spite of his protestations and pieties, King Henry showed his hand early in December, when he suddenly made a sally to the south from Windsor, most likely at Edward's urging, to attempt to regain Dover castle, so precious to any monarch hoping to import soldiers from France. But Richard de Grey, who held the fortress, would not hand over his trust, and the king was obliged to retreat again upon London. Earl Simon at this time had retired to his castle of Kenilworth, to leave the mediators free from his shadow, but when he heard of the king's journey he hurriedly came south to London to see what lay behind it. He had the earl of Derby with him, and a limited following, and as they entered London from the north, the king, returning empty-handed, approached from the south.

King Henry conceived that at last he had an opportunity to seize his enemy, and sent in haste to order the citizens of London to close the city against 'the troublemakers'. And certain of the rich men of the town did indeed plot to close London bridge behind the earl, who had entered Southwark, thus leaving his force exposed while the royal army encircled and captured him. But the common people of London, discovering his danger, broke down the gates and brought him safely out of the trap. Virtuously the king denied all ill intent, or any design of bringing in foreign soldiers. But I think it was this adventure that convinced Earl Simon that without reconciliation England was lost to chaos, and he must make all possible sacrifices to obtain a compromise in which all could work together. So he was the first to agree, when the mediators proposed that the final arbitration should be referred to King Louis, and his judgment on all points should be faithfully accepted by both parties.

But he would never, I think, have accepted this but for the king's assurances that the Provisions themselves were not at issue, being generally accepted by all. Less surprising, King Henry also jumped at the proposal, and the road was prepared for a solemn assembly at Amiens in January of the coming year.

As for us, we guarded the march and waited for word, receiving news of all these things after the event, and the fate of England was decided before we knew anything of it. And in singular contrast to that sad confusion beyond the border, the fate of Wales shone steady and bright as a lamp, its unity crowned at last. For about the same time that the men of London were escorting Earl Simon out of the king's net, Llewelyn at Aber received a visitor he had hardly expected, and one who came in state and bearing gifts, with outriders going before him to smooth his entry, for he was a stranger to Llewelyn's court, and bent on ensuring his welcome now that he had made up his mind to come.

His herald came into hall where we were at meat, and made his reverence before the whole household.

'My lord and prince, the Lord Griffith ap Gwenwynwyn, prince of Powys, desires audience and grace at your court, for he comes to speak with you concerning his reception into your peace.'

Llewelyn rose from his place, astonished but wary, and asked: 'How far behind you does the Lord Griffith ride?'

'My lord, in a breath he will be at your gates,' said the herald.

'Then he shall not enter ungreeted,' said Llewelyn, and went out to meet him and bring him within, and there was haste to lay the place for him at the prince's right hand.

I saw him ride in, a big, thickset man in English harness and apparel, with a heavy, handsome face and greying hair and beard, for he was about fifty at that time. He had quick, roving eyes and a wary, calculating mouth, and in all his accoutrements he was very fine, and in all his speeches very smooth and formal, for he came to heal up and swathe into forgetfulness an ancient enmity, having, as I suppose, summed up our situation and that of England, and come to the conclusion that fortune

315

was on our side, and his best interest to make his peace with us. So thought Llewelyn, past doubt, but he willed to make the move as easy as it might be, for Powys was precious, and Wales needed it. Also it was his way to meet every conciliatory gesture with impulsive warmth, for he was by nature generous to a fault, and the first motion of appeal drew him into a response sometimes over-rash, and laid him open to betrayals in spite of all his wit. So while he smiled at himself and Griffith, nevertheless he sprang in person to hold the suppliant's stirrup, and hand him from the saddle.

At that time neither offered the kiss, which was too sacred for policy. But Llewelyn brought him in with his guest's hand upon his shoulder, lodged him, sent him water and wine, and waited upon him at the door of the hall, to bring him to his seat.

After the banquet, that same evening, they came to stark talk in private, Griffith being bent on an early understanding. He was a little uneasy in bargaining, being unsure of his reception, but melted soon, finding himself met with so much candour. It came to hard terms and firm guarantees, and so to an agreement. At a formal meeting two days later, Griffith offered homage and fealty, and received therefore all those lands by heredity his which Llewelyn had occupied. And as for the future, they entered into a compact against the English of the march, based upon the little river of Camlad, by which Griffith was to have all those conquests north of that stream, and Llewelyn all those to the south. For Griffith's chief neighbour and rival, Corbett of Caus, held to the north of the line, and it was not long before he felt the shock of the alliance. There was an old grudge there, that surely had urged Griffith to his submission.

However that was, he had submitted. And the year twelve hundred and sixty-three ended gloriously with Wales truly one, while England was torn in two. So we had our hour.

Whether things might have turned out differently if Earl Simon had been present at the great conference at Amiens is mere conjecture, and lost pains now even to wonder. But he never crossed the sea that winter.

On his way from Kenilworth to embark he turned aside to visit the house of Cistercian nuns at Catesby, where there was a chapel to the blessed St Edmund of Abingdon, and as he departed he was thrown from his horse and broke his leg, so that he was forced to have himself conveyed painfully back to Kenilworth, and there lay crippled and burning while others pleaded his cause in France. But his son Henry was there among the leaders of the baronial party, with Peter de Montfort, and Humphrey de Bohun and others, and no doubt they put their arguments well enough. They had expected a patient process of discussion upon detailed points, and were prepared to give and take. What they got was very different. In a few bare days, and without overmuch consideration, King Louis gave judgment against them upon every point, and declared everyone who was party to the case absolved from all obligation to maintain the Provisions. The pope had already annulled them, King Louis pronounced them void and illegal.

King Henry's voice at Amiens spoke another language from that he had used in England, where he had professed again and again his devotion in principle to the reform. Before Louis he claimed the right to choose his own justiciar – or indeed to dispense with him if he chose – and to nominate his ministers, judges, local officials and castellans without reference to council or parliament. He vowed that acceptance of the Provisions was not consistent with his coronation oath, and insistence upon them violated his barons' oaths of fealty. And king holds with king as against the people, however they may tear each other over territory and conquest.

At the news of that award such a howl of joy went up from all the exiles crowding the French shore that almost we heard it in the march, for now pope and king had declared for them and against the reform, all legality was stripped from it, and what was to hold them back now from mounting an invasion of England with the blessing of state and church, a holy crusade? The pope hurried to reaffirm his agreement with the judgment, and reassert the mortal spiritual danger of all who resisted it. But in England, when the word came like a wave of the sea inland over the shires, the common people and the small gentry, the friars and preachers, the wardens of the peace, all those who had pinned their fervent faith upon the new order, gave vent to a great cry of rage and bitterness, declaring, surely with justice, that King Louis had exceeded the powers granted him, and moreover that they had never been parties to the decision to make him judge, and were not bound by his award. Everywhere they rose to attack those who held against them, and threatened them with the king's displeasure or the pope's ban. They had looked for a judgment that would restore peace, they got a crude blow that could only mean war.

In vain King Henry, upon Louis' advice, hastened to publish his willingness to receive to his peace all those persons who would accept the decision. His peace was not the peace they wanted, and they did not come. They looked towards the sea that alone held off from them the legate's menaces and the exiles' ships and mercenaries, and they began to band themselves together into companies, and exercise in arms, not at all quenched but perilously inflamed.

We in the march soon saw some local flares, for Roger Mortimer, most powerful of the royalist faction in those parts, began to make rapid raids upon certain of Earl Simon's manors in the west, and Llewelyn moved a company of his men to Knighton and another to Presteigne, in the expectation that they might soon be needed. It was not for us to assume the defence of what the earl was quite able to take care of himself, but Roger's lordship of Radnor was open to attack, and offered a way of relieving the pressure upon the baronial position if such a diversion should be needed.

We were at Knighton when a courier brought a letter from the earl. More than one such exchange had passed during that month of January, while Earl Simon seethed and fretted helplessly in Kenilworth. This letter came at the end of that month, and thus it was from the earl's own hand that we heard the news of the award of Amiens. He had but just heard it himself. His sons were newly landed and making for the west to fend off the encroachments of Mortimer, and his request was that Llewelyn would move to meet them, and close in with them upon Radnor. As long as we kept the west, Earl Simon's army in those parts was ensured of supplies, a safe retreat when pressed, and support sufficient to protect it from pursuit.

'There is one more thing the earl of Leicester asks of us,' said Llewelyn in council. 'This combat that now bids fair to burst into the open has shifted its ground, and here are we back at the old game, the Welsh on one side, the marchers on the other, the strongest group King Henry has at his back. It's in the west this war will begin, and we shall have need of a very close understanding if we are to make it prosper. Earl Simon asks that I will accredit to him a trusted officer to represent me at his court, and with him a good messenger who can carry his reports back and forth between us while this stress continues.'

Goronwy and the council agreed that it was a wise move, for our own protection as well as for Earl Simon's, for much might depend upon an instant understanding if the threatening fire burned up in earnest.

'Samson,' said Llewelyn, looking up at me, 'I would have you go. A clerk it should be, to have the safe-conduct of his office, so far as any man is to be safe in such a realm. Will you go?'

I said what he knew, that I would do whatever he asked of me, and serve him wherever he willed. And so it was settled, and he gave me Cadell, a sturdy, reliable young man-at-arms to be my companion, and bade us choose what horses we would, and sent us forth on the journey to Kenilworth, with the earl's courier to guide us and give us cover by his lord's writ. That same day we rode. But before I set out, Llewelyn drew me aside, and very earnestly and hopefully asked me to do more than was in my commission.

'While you are with him,' he said, 'and if you may without offending, for God knows he has his hands full with all the weight of England, study of him these views he holds on kingship and right rule, for I am curious to know more of them.'

So indeed was I, and this charge I undertook most willingly. We were hungry, both, for a deeper comprehension of this great man my lord had not yet even seen. We knew of him that he had been and was the friend and confidant of saints, if not himself a saint, and that he found in kingship an element as purely sacramental as in priesthood. We knew his pride and rigidity, but had heard also of his unexampled humility and patience under reproof. And this was but one pair among the many seeming contradictions in him which I think were no contradictions, any more than the right hand denies the left, but rather the exquisite balances that kept him so whole and so upright. His high and overbearing temper with the strong, and his delicate courtesy to the weak, his unbending insistence on his own rights and devout concentration upon the discharge of his obligations to others. So much we knew of him, and desired to know far more. And I was grateful and bound to him all the more because, the nearer we had drawn to his cause, the less did Llewelyn look hungrily towards Chester, where David was, and the more towards this irresistible heat and brightness that drew men as the sun draws up dew.

One more reason I had to be glad of my mission to Kenilworth, and that was that it freed me for a while of the unrelenting companionship of Godred, who had wormed his way into a secure place among Llewelyn's guard. True it is that he could do whatever was required of him, and do it well enough, and was quick of wit and without fear, but also true that he did no more than was required of him, and necessary to keep him in good favour. And with the rest of his time and energy he frequented me, unswerving and tireless, waiting and watching for I knew not what, for me to die, or succumb to his proffered temptations, or to confide in him and give him power over me – no, I cannot tell. I know only that his absence was to me as a spring of fresh water in a burning day.

By Ludlow and through the forest of Wyre we rode to Kenilworth, such soft and gracious country even the late spite of winter seemed lulled by it, and bit but toothlessly, like a puppy. I never saw such green grass in the first days of February, or such a sun in the heavens, lowly though it lay and briefly though it stayed. And when we came to that great pile that stopped up the roads like a mountain, and fenced itself in with one broad, chill water defence after another, I was struck dumb with wonder, for such a castle I had never seen. I doubted then if it could ever be taken, but by starvation over many months, and later it proved so to the letter. I know no way by which it could ever be stormed or mined, for there was a lake, made by man, that covered three sides of it, and the fourth approach was so menaced by shot and cross-shot that no army could ever draw near enough to do it hurt. Guided and guaranteed by Earl Simon's courier, Cadell and I wound our way through the many guards into the wards of the castle. On all sides its towers soared over us, and the great keep blotted out the noonday. And yet it was a most fair spot, ringed round with softly rolling country like a maze of rich meadows in paradise.

They said to me as soon as I alighted that their lord waited to receive me, and begged my indulgence that he could not come out to me on his two feet, for reasons I knew.

They brought me into a small but rich chamber in one of the minor towers. I remember tapestried hangings that warmed the nakedness of the walls, and a brazier glowing, that gave the most light in that dark apartment, even in the mid-afternoon, before the dusk fell. And a low couch along the wall beneath the hangings, where the great earl sat propped by furs, with his broken leg stretched along the cushions in a bundle of wooden brace and linen bindings, like a weathered log. And I remember how dead that one limb seemed, and how live all else, from the single foot thrust large and vehement against the flags of the floor, to the reared Norman head that turned towards me as I entered, to bring to bear upon me those marvellous deep-set eyes, yet so large and wide and fearless that they seemed to stand out like rounded gems from the sockets. To this day I do not know certainly of what colour they were, they so burned and shone that they had no colour but radiance. I think

319

he was even ill-shaven and somewhat tired when I first saw him in his own house, yet do not know why I should think so, since what I most remember of him is the cleanness, the outline, of all his person, as if he had been chiselled out of some metal too pure to be taken out of the earth.

His voice when he spoke to me was as mild, direct and open as his gaze, pitched rather low, out of the centre of his body, which as I saw him then was but of middle size, sturdy and square but lean. I marvelled, for I had thought him a taller man, what was within him so towered above the flesh and bone.

'I ask your pardon,' he said, 'for not rising to receive you, but you see my condition. Prince Llewelyn's envoy is most welcome to me. I pray you sit down with me.'

In this first of many audiences I had with him, I told him how I had left affairs on the border, and that Llewelyn's force would already be deploying its westward half-circle about Radnor, prepared to close in as soon as the earl's sons had drawn near enough to match the thrust from the east. He asked many and brisk questions concerning the land and the roads, and clearly he was well informed about the watch we already kept upon the fords and bridges over the Severn. In return he told me the latest news of the enemy, though never calling them so. Richard of Cornwall, the regent during the king's absence, was in Worcester by that time, and intended going on to Gloucester, where he meant to keep and hold the bridge if the remaining ones must be sacrificed. I asked after the Lord Edward, whose name, by consent, now took precedence of King Henry's in the tale of our foes.

'He is on the sea at this moment,' said Earl Simon, 'and the king with him. If this wind hold, they must land tomorrow, or very soon. He has sanction to strike now, he will not hold his hand.'

We spoke of where that blow, when it came, was most like to fall, but in speculation upon Edward's actions there was little profit. Yet we were at one in believing that he would try to secure the marches, since he had already lured back to him so many of the young marcher lords, and that he would use the same bogey to bring the rest to heel now.

'The Welsh threat,' I said, 'will be his theme. And Radnor will be his text.'

'No matter,' said the earl, 'so he comes too late to save it.'

I told him then what had already been said through his son, that in my view Llewelyn would never willingly commit his army in out-and-out war against the crown of England, though his sympathies were engaged. Beyond the Severn he would not take them, unless those sympathies swept him away, for his first duty was to Wales, and his first concern to retain the power of bargaining, for her sake, with whatever regime ruled in England. However heartily he might pray the victory of the reform, yet he had to keep open his freedom to deal with whatever England he might find neighbour to him in the future.

'That I understand,' said Earl Simon, 'and respect. He has his cause as I have mine. He is right to pledge to it everything but his honour.'

'And yet,' I said. watching him with intent, 'if you should ask him to take that plunge, and commit his cause to yours, I believe he might do it.'

Earl Simon understood me well, that I was not prompting but appealing. He said: 'Be easy! There are limits to my rights in any man. I shall not ask him.'

Before I rose to leave him on this first occasion, since it seemed all had been done that at this moment could be done, I ventured to speak to him of those principles of kingship of which we had heard, and of which Llewelyn desired a better understanding. At that his eyes shone, and he began to speak with passion of the well-disciplined body in which every member bears its true part, and thence of the body politic, a realm in which the same balance and harmony obtain, where kingship is a sacred trust, and rule not for gain or glory but for the right regulation of the affairs of all men, from the highest to the lowest. And thence again it was but a deeper breath and a stretching out of the being to comprehend a body spiritual in which every realm should be a member performing still its just function, and this should be the true Christendom. And he told me that he had had copied for his own use the tract on kingship and tyranny written by the late, great Bishop Robert Grosseteste of Lincoln, and he would lend it to me to make another copy, if time served, for Llewelyn's study. And so he did, and even marked for me those passages that most engrossed his own thoughts, in case there was too little time for copying the whole. And thereafter he spoke with me, whenever we had leisure from events, of those lofty ideas that so consumed his heart and mind.

As I went out from him the door of his chamber opened before I reached it, and I was face to face with a startled girl on the threshold. Her lips were parted, about to call to him even as she came into the room, and thus on the verge of speech she halted, half-smiling, astonished to be gazing up so closely at a stranger. She was tall for her years, and slender, and bore herself with the simplicity and assurance of her birth, so that it took me some seconds of wonder and admiration to realise that she was hardly past childhood, surely no more than eleven or twelve years old. All that brave candour and innocence that showed so excellent in her brother came to perfection in her. Such warmth and rounded sweetness of line I never saw in any face but hers, such wide, generous shaping of lip, such grand, gallant honesty of eye. She was fairer than her brother, the long braid of her hair a deep, muted gold, and the brow it crowned was ivory-smooth and great with gravity. But the lashes that fringed her clear, gold-flecked eyes were dark almost to blackness.

I stepped back out of her path and made my bow to her, almost too bemused to move or speak, and she, childlike in her courtesies, made me in return the reverence due to older people, however lofty or humble, and looked from me to the earl for guidance. He was smiling upon her, as well he might, if such a jewel was his.

He held out his hand, and she went to him, laying her own small hand in his palm, and looked back gravely at me.

'Be acquainted, Master Samson,' he said, 'with my youngest child and only daughter. This is Eleanor.'

In that teeming household of his, among the thousand souls and more that gathered in hall to meet, knights, squires, lawyers, friars, clerks, men-at-arms, armourers, scholars, gentlewomen and damozels, I learned to know the other members of his family, and knew his imprint even when I met it stripped to the waist in wrestling, or soiled and tousled in leather, whistling over the grooming of a horse in the yard. For the mintage was unmistakable, that face repeating itself with but trivial changes in all that came of his blood. His two eldest sons, Henry whom I knew, and the younger Simon who was as yet unknown to me, were away in the march, and within a few days of my coming they were inside Radnor town, and busy with Llewelyn about the razing of Radnor castle. But three more he had here with him, Guy, already a man grown and in his twentieth year, ready and eager to bear arms, Amaury and Richard still boys of about fifteen and thirteen. The same welcoming and challenging eyes gazed from every one of those Roman heads, yet there were differences between them. Amaury had the sharpest tongue and the most scholarly inclinations, Guy, I think, the most formidable wits and the least governed impulses.

The Countess Eleanor, whom I saw only in hall, and seldom spoke to, was a very handsome woman, as tall as her husband and as fierce and impetuous, but without that deeper part of him that could school even his own fire into humility. All his dreams and lofty aims she shared, but only because they were his, and often without understanding what she nevertheless would have defended to the death. She had a life-long grievance over her dowry, which had never been paid, and doubtless she was extravagant and had good need of plenty of money, but I think it was her right rather than the gold itself that she fought for. And in that she was like Earl Simon, for he would not abate one mark of what was due to him, though he was even more punctilious in paying other men their due. I grew to know and welcome those foibles in him, and those moods of depression and bile, that brought him down to the same earth as ordinary mortals.

To Llewelyn I wrote despatches as often as we had news of movements upon the king's side, and Cadell carried them at speed, with Earl Simon's safe-conduct to shelter him and get him horses in England, and Llewelyn's in Wales. Thus we got word to both English and Welsh forces in Radnor when King Henry and his son landed, and Edward with all the men he could muster rushed westwards, while the king followed more slowly as far as Oxford, where he entrenched himself and gathered all his supporters about him. We were even able to get word to the march when Edward diverted his attack, and instead of charging upon Radnor as we had expected, struck deep into Brecknock, into the lands of young Humphrey de Bohun, one of the few marcher lords who continued on the side of the reform. Earl Simon's sons had therefore to expect his attack upon them, which must follow, from the south instead of the east, and with the importance of the Severn always in mind, they drew back their force towards that river, with Edward in pursuit. They had done what they had set out to do in Radnor, and left Mortimer's lands in disarray; they withdrew out of immediate range of Edward's force, and moved upon Gloucester ahead of him.

Our couriers were in furious activity then, for the whole of the march was in motion, and we were occupied in conveying to every force in the field upon our side the movements of every other, as well as of Edward's army. For Robert Ferrers, the young earl of Derby, one of Earl Simon's most daring and ingenious allies, but also one of the most self-willed and moody, brought his muster sweeping south to storm Worcester, intending to join forces with Henry de Montfort after the fall of Gloucester. This we made known instantly to the de Montfort force, for if the move succeeded we held the vital stretches and crossings of the Severn.

I observe that I have begun to say 'we', though my own lord was now left behind nursing the western rim of the march as before, to afford cover for his friends at need. So closely had I then identified myself with Earl Simon's ends and dreams, yet I felt no divided loyalties within me, as if the two I served were one.

And ever, when chance offered, I bathed my eyes and refreshed my heart in the delight of watching that other Eleanor, artless child and great lady in one fine, fair body. And sometimes I had speech with her, for she had a child's licence to make friends where she would, with a woman's grace to hold the acquaintance in balance. And whether her brother had talked eloquently to her of what he had seen in Wales, or whether her curiosity was native to her by reason of her generous heart, and she desired both to please me and to benefit by the presence of the stranger; however it was, she would know what I could tell her of the ways and customs of Wales, and soon, caught by my decided attachments she asked particularly of our prince. Doubtless I presented him as an object for love, seeing I loved him.

Now this matter of the struggle for Gloucester, which we witnessed helplessly from afar in that month of March, best demonstrates the mood and temper of the Lord Edward from that time forth towards his opponents and all those who held with them and comforted them. For in the first week of the month Henry de Montfort, by a daring trick played by two of his confederate barons, who certainly risked their lives in the frolic, captured the city of Gloucester, but not the castle, which was strongly held for the king. For these two young lords got themselves up as woolmongers, and came up to the west gate with bales on their backs to gain entry, and thereupon dropped their loads and showed their arms, and held the gate while Henry marched his men within. But I will not say that the town of Gloucester, as opposed to the guard, was sorry to be so invaded by the armies of the reform, for the evidence is that they gave in very willingly, and suffered for it thereafter.

But very shortly after this the Lord Edward came with his army, and was privily let into the castle by the garrison, and he had good need to fear when Earl Robert of Derby came scything south from Worcester to join the Montforts. This was when he showed both his wit and his faithlessness. No one knew better than he that Earl Simon's cause was hamstrung by its own goodwill, for the half of its support was bishops and such benevolents, who above all things desired peace and reconciliation, while the other half knew only too well it had no choice but to resist in arms *à l'outrance*. So at this pass Edward sent piously to the bishop of Worcester, that good man, devoted to the Provisions but also to peace, and so prevailed upon him that he went to Henry de Montfort, who held the town securely, and offered in Edward's name, and clearly in good faith, a truce that should lead on – such was promised under oath – to a permanent peace, if Henry would withdraw from the town with his army.

The bishop was honest, no question, he offered what he confided in as in the Host. And as in the Host, young Henry received, revered and believed. Edward's word he took, as he would have expected Edward, with better reason, to take his. And he withdrew from the town.

For his complaisance and gullibility, may God forgive him! For his innocence, honour and purity, may God reward him!

Edward occupied the town, ravaged it to misery and despair for its forbearance to his enemies, fortified and garrisoned it to the utmost, and swept out of it to join his father at Oxford. No more was ever said of truce or peace.

May God also deal so with him according to his judgment. I say no more than that. For we know, every man of us, that there will be a judgment, even for princes.

Young Henry, when he knew how shamefully he had been tricked, left his brother to lead their joint force towards Northampton, where the baronial levies were massing to secure their ground in the midlands, and came hurrying home in person to confess his innocent folly and face his father's anger. He was spared nothing, for the blow was very bitter. In his own defence he said only, with simple truth: 'I took the sworn word of the heir of England. How could I suppose I was dealing with a liar and cheat? Sir, you would also have believed him a man of his word.'

'I should never have considered his terms,' said Earl Simon heavily. 'His truth or falsehood would not have been put to the test. Now you have lost me the west, and sent Ferrers fuming back to his own country in a rage, having wasted his capture of Worcester.'

'I own it,' said Henry, stricken. For the earl of Derby, an insubordinate and wayward man, had withdrawn from his capture and quit the Severn, marching back in a fury to his own country. 'I am at fault, and what I have done cannot be put right now.'

And he submitted without protest to the earl's reproaches, though for my part I could but think how like he was, in his lesser way, to this same proud incorruptible who chastised him, and how justly he could have turned and charged: 'You might well have done the same in my place.' For there is no remedy against the tricks of the devious for those who are themselves men of honour, and at that very time Earl Simon had consented again to one last attempt at conciliation, through a French nobleman who was in England on King Louis' financial business, and as friend to both parties begged to try what he could do to avert war. And what had young Henry done but consent to the promise of just such an attempt? It was not his fault that Edward's faith was rotten. Moreover, Earl Simon later committed even such acts of generous and high-minded folly himself, and lost by them more than his son had lost for him at Gloucester. A man can act only in accordance with his nature, and the weapons of the tricksters outnumber by far the arms of the honourable.

But the boy made no complaint, only bowed his head to the storm and set his jaw at the future.

'I do but scold at my own infirmities,' said the earl at length, sighing as he turned to behold himself in the mirror he had made. 'You did nothing so ill, though ill came of it.' And to me he said: 'It will not be so easy now to keep touch with the prince, since the west is out of our hands, nor is he so likely to be needed and drawn in. I cannot answer for what course this year will take, but it seems we are thrust off into the midlands, and it's there the struggle must come. If your lord would rather that you return to him, I cannot fairly lay claim to you further.'

I wrote therefore to Llewelyn, telling him how matters stood, how the king's host was summoned to Oxford at the end of March, and the earl's forces massing in Northampton, and though the French arbitrator was hard at work trying to bring the parties to discussion with him at Brackley, and both sides had assented to the meeting, there seemed but little chance that anything would come of it. The bishops who spoke for Earl Simon and the reform had offered concessions on all points except the king's right to appoint aliens to his council and offices without reference to the community of the lands but King Henry, though paying lip service to conciliation, would not give way one inch upon this or any other item. I saw no possibility in the end but war, and it seemed that the field of battle had moved into the centre of England, away from the march. Then I sent this despatch by Cadell, and awaited my orders.

I had half expected and half wished to be called home, yet I found I was glad when Llewelyn replied that I should continue with Earl Simon, so far as I judged it safe for me, wherever he might go, and still keep as frequent touch as I might with Wales. By this I knew that even if he would not commit his heritage, his heart was committed.

While the royal army lay at Oxford, the main baronial muster at Northampton, and the hopeful French agent ran back and forth between the two from Brackley, which lies midway along that road, Earl Simon, though still crippled by his injury, which had not knitted well, could rest no longer, but determined to go south to London, which was unswervingly loyal to him. And I went in his retinue, and Cadell along with me, eager and curious at every mile, for he had never been beyond the march until we came to Kenilworth, and London was a marvel to him. The earl could not ride, but he had had a light, four-wheeled chariot made for him, and in that he rode, driven by one of his grooms, or sometimes driving himself. So we made that journey to London, and again I saw that great citadel they call the Tower, that had such long and grim memories for me. There the justiciar had his headquarters, and there Earl Simon took up residence.

325

The whole city had drafted its people into armed bands, under a constable and a marshal, ready to muster whenever the great bell of St Paul's should be rung to call them out. To tell truth, the results were somewhat disorderly, and before Earl Simon arrived there had been some ill-advised local attacks upon royalist lands, notably on Richard of Cornwall's manor of Isleworth, that did nothing to help the cause of conciliation. When a city as great and populous as London seethes with excitement and stands to in unaccustomed arms, even an Earl Simon may find it difficult to control.

But as to what happened next, and who first invoked absolute war, and in what circumstances, I tell truth as we knew it. Certain it is that the Frenchman's negotiations, however barren, had not been broken off. For proof, on the second day of April a safe-conduct was issued to Peter de Montfort as baronial envoy, to meet the royal proctors at Brackley, and this safe-conduct was to remain valid until Palm Sunday, which fell on the thirteenth of that month. Yet on the third day of April King Henry suddenly marched his army out of Oxford, taking with him his war-standard, a dragon with a tongue of fire, worked on red samite, and made straight for Northampton at a forced pace, to lay that town under siege.

The news came to us in the city, and Earl Simon at once set out to relieve the garrison, though we did not fear any disaster, Northampton being so full of trusty levies and so well supplied. The only danger, we thought, was a long siege, which we had the power to break. But we had got no farther than St Albans when we were met by a messenger on a lathered horse, who croaked out his ill news from a dusty throat beside Earl Simon's chariot.

'My lord, Northampton has fallen! Your son's made prisoner, and the lord of Beaudesert and his two sons with him, and many another. All taken! By treachery! The town was entered and stormed in the night. By now I doubt the castle has surrendered. There's rapine and murder in the streets for your sake. Another Gloucester!'

It was so stunning a blow that Earl Simon was knocked out of words and breath, but the greater the disaster that fell upon him, the more quietly and immovably did he rally to resist it; all his furies being spent on things by comparison light. He questioned in few words, and took from the man all that miserable story.

'My lord, at the priory of St Andrew, by the north gate, the prior is a Frenchman, and of the king's party. He had the brothers make a breach in the walls of their house, and by night they broke through the last shell of the town wall, and let the king's men in. In the darkness they made their way by parties all about the town, and struck before dawn. It was so sudden we had no chance. The guards were surprised and overwhelmed first, many of us never had time to lay hands on our weapons. Some companies contrived to fight their way out, and will muster as best they can and come south to join you. But Northampton's lost, and many of your best knights with it, and God help the folk in the town, for Edward is taking revenge on them all.'

Earl Simon made no murmur over his loss of son and allies and arms, fronting what seemed almost a mortal blow to his hopes with a granite face. Quietly he ordered the return to London, and back to the Tower we went, and there he took from those who managed to reach us the full story of the sack of Northampton, and the long list of the prisoners. For several days news came in. The valuable captives were whipped away into the hold of various castles in the marches, to remove them from the immediate hope of rescue. There was now no means of recovering them but by bringing this war to a successful end, for now beyond question this was war.

'It might be worse,' said the earl grimly, when we knew what the king's next moves had been, and Edward's. 'If I have let my chance be wrested from me, he is throwing his away.' For King Henry had moved on to Nottingham, elated by his easy success and neglecting to follow it up energetically, while Edward, though displaying energy enough, was tossing it to the winds by careering north to harry the lands of the earl of Derby.

'He is letting personal hate affect his judgment,' said the earl critically.

While Henry kept Easter in Nottingham, and Edward pursued Robert Ferrers in Derbyshire, Earl Simon turned south. For in France it was certain that the queen and archbishop and the royal clerks were massing soldiers and horses and arms, and sooner or later would try to land them in England. Whoever held the Cinque ports held the narrow seas. And the young earl of Gloucester, Gilbert of Clare, had not been in Northampton, but by reason of the dangerous state of the march was at his Kentish castle at Tonbridge, with a strong force. Between them he and Earl Simon could hope to take the royal castle at Rochester, where was the only substantial royalist force in the south at that time. In the event they took the town, but not the castle keep, and when both Henry and his son came rushing in alarm to raise the siege, Earl Simon pondered briefly whether this was the time and place to stand and fight, and decided against it.

'No, not here,' he said. 'I need to secure London behind me, and keep it safe out of his hands. Let him have such as he can take of the ports, he will not get Dover, nor will he have the goodwill of the seamen or the men of the Weald. We go back to London.'

And back to London we went, leaving Rochester to be re-occupied by the king's army, and even sacrificing Tonbridge, for Gilbert of Clare returned with Earl Simon to the city. Not to sit in the Tower and wait to be attacked, but to re-order and enlarge his army with all the trained bands of London, ready to move again with an impregnable city at his back, before King Henry should have any chance to settle or enjoy his scanty hold upon the coast.

Thus those two armies, at last dressed for battle and no longer postponing, began to move together in the early days of May, the king returning from the coast to the town of Lewes, where Earl Warenne of Surrey had a strong castle, and Earl Simon marching south from London to intercept him. Now no one sought to avoid, but rather each observed, by way of scouts, the course his enemy took, and guided his own force to strike forehead against forehead.

No man can say for certain, but for my part I believe it was Edward who had decreed that attack upon Northampton, while proctors and agents still talked conciliation and issued safe-conducts. It accords well with the tenor of all he did at this time, for his every act shows that he did not consider himself bound by any considerations of honour or good faith in dealing with those he held to be rebels. And I think also that it was Edward who now thirsted to dash against his enemies and destroy them. For Earl Simon had said rightly of him that his hatred unbalanced his judgment. Not that we dared build upon that, for if there was one thing certain about Edward, it was that he could learn. Not that he would therefore hate less, but that he would be better able to control and channel his hate to do the greatest and most terrible harm to those he hated.

It was a temperament Earl Simon did not know, except by rote, for it was out of his scope. Though he used the word freely when he blazed against pettiness and inconstancy, I doubt if he ever hated any man, for in all innocence – no, I do not like that word for him! –in all purity he never found, of his own measure, any that were hateful, but only such as he reverenced, willing to sit at their feet like a scholar guided by his master. But they were legion whom he knew how to despise.

It was the eleventh day of May, and a Sunday, when King Henry's army reached Lewes and camped there. We were at Fletching, ten miles north of that town, in the forest country above the valley of the Ouse, and by our forward scouts we knew when they came, and their numbers, which were certainly greater than ours. It mattered not at all that it was so. The middle of May is not summer, yet in our camp by night there was a warmth upon us like a benediction and, as I think, it arose from a most rare essence, the unity of some thousands of minds at one and at rest.

Three bishops we had with us, of Worcester, London and Chichester, one of them as near a saint as mortal man can reach outside the canon, and he the most intimate and faithful friend of the demon-saint who led us. But that was not our secret. The great calm of ordinary, well-intentioned, reverent and humble blessedness was upon us, of mortal men doing what they devoutly believed to be right and true. There is no other grace needed, for this grace comes of God, without benefit of pope or priest. And I well remember that night, after so long, for the absolute peace of the spirit that lay upon it.

I went out between the camp-fires, muted and turfed by reason of the dry weather and the thick brushwood, up to a little spur of the downs that lifted out of forest into the sky and was roofed over with stars, and there I said my office in the utmost calm, without fear or hope, both impurities, aware only of this blessedness.

In resignation of soul that was pure joy, I made my prayers for my lord, and for my country, and for my love, and from all three I was far distant, and yet I felt them very near. And it seemed to me that I saw them all the more clearly from this small hillock in the far south, as though the starlit air between touched my eyes into clarity beyond mortal, so that my love swelled in me into such grandeur that I could hardly contain it, and it welled into the night and made itself one with the silence and the calm. Then, believing myself alone, I said aloud the first, best prayer. And one in the shadow of the trees behind me said: 'Amen!'

I turned about, and he was there in the darkness of the trees, seated upon a bank of turf that clambered into the knotted roots of an old beach-tree. And so still that I had not marked him when I came, though there he had surely been in his own solitude, apart even from those three holy men who upheld his spirit and blessed his cause. By his voice I knew him, and by the shape of him, like a part, a buttress, of the great tree, or a bastion shielding the wall of a city. He could walk by then, leaning upon a staff, or with a page's shoulder under his hand, but not for too long, and as yet could not sit a horse without pain.

'I ask your pardon,' he said, 'for intruding upon your devotions. I could not move to leave you without disturbing you.'

'My lord,' I said, 'next to God and Llewelyn, there is no creature in heaven or earth I would so willingly trust with my prayers as you. This night I could believe I have been heard as compassionately there as here.'

His voice in the great starry spaces of the night was low and still and utterly assured, for we were all come to this marvellous stay, as upon a rock. Very seldom in a lifetime can men be so sure of what they do, and of their resignation and rightness in undertaking it.

'You know,' he said, 'as every man here knows, that this matter is now come to the issue. There is nowhere further to go, for beyond this point, if he will not bend, we cannot.'

I said that I did know it, and was at peace with it. And I said, in some wonder, that this must be the mark of a holy war, that it brought its soldiers to a high certainty of peace.

'Yet while we have life,' he said, 'and have not clashed forehead against forehead, I must still strive even for the world's peace. Tomorrow I propose to send to the king by Bishop Berksted, and make one more attempt to sever him from those who misuse and delude him. Then if that fail, there is no way to go but forward into battle. Master Samson, I have given some thought to your situation. If we march on Lewes, you will remain in the service of the bishop. I will place you officially in his household, and his hand and your own clerkship will protect you if my fortunes go awry. Very loyal and serviceable you have been to me, and I have been glad of you, but this quarrel is neither yours nor your lord's, and I would have you clear of blame.'

Such was Earl Simon, at the crisis of his greatest obligation still able to give care and thought even to the least. I thanked him for his kindness, but said I could not accept his provision for me.

'Thus far I have come with you,' I said, 'at my lord's will, and the rest of the way I will go with you at my own. Though I began as a clerk, I can take the cross like any other man and, if you will use me, I can use a sword. I could not go back and look Llewelyn in the face again if I forsook you now. He is bound in his own person, but free in mine, and what he cannot do, I can, in his name as well as my own. But for my man

Cadell, if he will accept it, I welcome your good thought. I will write some lines to my prince, and send them tomorrow by Cadell, if you will furnish him a safe-conduct, for by way of London he can still reach Wales safely. And I will have Llewelyn keep him there this time, and not return. After tomorrow,' I said, 'if the news be good, I will carry it back to my lord myself. And if not,' I said, 'I shall be troubled with messages no more, and it will be all one to me who carries him word of my death.'

'Either you are very well prepared for dying,' said the earl drily, 'or your faith in my cause is great. Or it may be both,' he said, musing. 'Who am I to tell?'

'I can think of worse ways to die,' I said, 'than in your cause and your company. And whatever, the outcome, I will not turn my back now.'

I had thought he might be angry at being denied, for he was not used to being crossed, and indeed he had the right to give orders and dispose as he saw fit now that we were in the field. But he did not refuse me. A moment he sat silent, thinking, and then, dark as it was, I saw him smile. He reached out a hand to me, and said:

'Will you lend me your arm back to my tent? The way downhill is harder going than the climb.'

So leaning on me he raised himself, and with my arm under his on the lame side, and his staff helping him on the other, we descended to where the bedded fires loaded the night air with their green earthen scent, and the low murmur of voices and stirring of movement from company to company made a forest quickening, like the awakening of bird and beast before the dawn. Patient beside his tent the young earl of Gloucester waited for him, and took him from my arm to bring him within. But for some long, sweet moments of that night I had heavy and vital upon my heart the greatest man ever I knew, and but for one the best and dearest, and on May nights I feel that weight yet, and am back in the forests of Fletching, in the days before the battle, with the stars above debating secretly my life or death, and the fate of England.

CHAPTER IX

When the morning came, he did as he had said. In council with his barons he composed a letter to the king, assented to by all, and had it sealed with his own seal and Gloucester's. It was a letter altogether devout and courteous, but unyielding, declaring the unswerving loyalty to the king of all those consenting to it, though they were resolved to proceed to the utmost against his enemies and theirs, the evil counsellors who deformed his government and urged him to injustice and unwisdom. This letter was carried by a number of knights and clerks, and the embassage was led by the bishop of Chichester with a party of Franciscan friars. The bishop was entrusted with the matter of argument, and the elaboration of the letter, for the earl was still willing to discuss amendments and adjustments, as he had been all along. Only on the one great thing he was adamant. The Provisions were sacred, for he was bound by oath to them, and could not break his troth. Yet the Provisions themselves could by agreement be modified, and it was his proffer that they should be considered by good and wise men, theologians and canonists, whose recommendations he promised to accept.

This was the mission of the party that set out from Fletching on the twelfth day of May, and rode down the valley of the Ouse to the king's camp at Lewes.

It was middle evening before we saw them returning. The day most of us spent in resting, and refurbishing weapons and harness, and the earl and his captains in their own grave preparations, considering in detail the lie of the ground, and the nice balance between the advantages of surprise and caution, between going to them and waiting for them to come to us. As for me, I wrote my despatch to Llewelyn, thinking to do all words could do to bring him close to me, and acquaint him even with the curious, sweet and ominous calm of my mind at this pass, for greatly I desired to have him share what otherwise I thought, for all his generosity, he might grudge me. But in the end I used less words and balder than was common with me, and set down only the bare bones, and after some struggles with myself and with these intractable letters I let it remain so, trusting him to read on the vellum between the script what had not been written. And I delivered the letter to Cadell, and gave him his orders as though this was a day like any other, and nothing of great moment toward. He was young and of easy condition, and he made no demur, as willing to go as to stay, and of that I was glad.

The earl came out of his tent when they brought him word that the bishop's company was in sight below in the river valley. He had Gilbert of Clare at his elbow, and others of his young men came to gather at his back as he stood and waited. For young they were all, many newly come into their honours, recently knighted or expecting knighthood on this field of battle. His was the party of the future. Only his bishops and officials were of his own generation, and perhaps half of the feudal following of archers and men-at-arms. And even some of those young men who had abandoned him, like Henry of Almain, had done so with rent hearts and deep grief, unable to hold out against Edward.

I think there was not a man among us who expected anything to come of the bishop's embassage, and the sight of his face as he dismounted, grave and very weary, made much clear before he spoke. Behind him the knights also dismounted. They bore two scrolls for the earl's reading. He took them without a word.

'I bring you no comfort,' said Bishop Stephen heavily, 'but the comfort of something worthy at least attempted. The king refuses all further dealings, and rejects what he has been offered. I have done my best, to no avail. They have stopped their ears against reason. To the word that reverend and wise men should arbitrate, they reply with fury and scorn. They are the nobility of England, are they to submit their affairs to the judgment of clerks? They are themselves the experienced and the wise, are they to be charged as evil counsellors, enemies of the crown? The first of the scrolls you hold, my lord, is a challenge to battle, on behalf of all the king's captains, sent to you by Richard, king of the Romans, and the Lord Edward.'

'Who, no doubt,' said Earl Simon with a shadowy smile and a certain resigned sadness, 'was loudest and fiercest in his defiance and rejection.'

'I fear you will not find the terms of his challenge moderate. And had you chosen other words, he would still have found another means of discovering offence in them, for he wills to be offended.'

'I know why,' said the earl, without hatred or blame.

'And the second scroll, my lord, is the king's own reply. The gravest he could make.'

'I know it,' said Earl Simon, and with a strong movement broke the seal. 'I have spent six years staving it off, to no purpose, it is almost welcome to me now. It is the formal act of *diffidatio*. He has renounced our homage and fealty, and withdrawn his overlordship from us. He is no longer our king, and we are no longer his men. But it is his act that severs the tie, not ours.'

He stood before us all, and read it aloud, the denunciation of the solemn obligations of kings towards their vassals, his own excommunication from the body of the realm, along with all the barons who held with him. Even the youngest of those lords, unawed by the spleen of an ageing king for whom they felt mild liking and much impatience and exasperation, grew solemn of face under the banishing stroke of kingship itself.

The earl stretched out his hand to the bishop, and smiled. 'Come within, and take your rest. I have worn you out, body and mind, to no purpose here, but God records the gallantry and the good faith elsewhere. Though I must send to King Henry again tomorrow, and return his courtesy if he will not withdraw it, that I will not do by your hand. I have cost you enough.'

And those two went in together, the lame lord and the gentle and steely bishop, quietly about their remaining business here. And so did we all, knowing now the best and the worst, and those who had not witnessed the return of the envoys, having duties elsewhere, got the word from us who had, and in turn set about making all ready for the morrow. There was little said that evening, but not out of any clouded spirits. Rather every man settled to his own particular task with a single mind, like practical citizens bent on getting the best possible out of tomorrow's market. Armourers went over harness already furbished to its peak, fletchers viewed the reserves of arrows and did their final re-flighting and balancing, lancers sharpened their blades, archers trimmed new shafts and waxed their strings, swordsmen whetted their edges, squires and grooms and boys walked all the horses, and I went to borrow mail and buckler to my size and weight, and to find myself a place, if I could, in Earl Simon's own battle. Not that my prowess or privilege were such as to earn for me an office close to the highest, but only that I desired it, and felt it no sin to bid for it. And Robert de Crevecoeur, a Kentish lord whom King Henry had tried to woo to his side only a few days previously, for the sake of his formidable archers of the weald, accepted me cheerfully into the ranks of his mounted men, and made no question at welcoming a Welshman. He was very young and blithe, and dearly set upon knighthood at the hands of Earl Simon above all men, and on the morrow he got his wish.

So this night went, and we slept without dreams, and waked without fears, however the meaning of the dawn rushed in upon us. For the potent enchantment that held us all enlarged somewhat beyond the bounds of our own flesh and spirit did not break, but carried us still, as long as we had need of it.

When the day was come, Earl Simon also committed to parchment his solemn renunciation of his homage and fealty to his king, in response to the repudiation pronounced against him, and did so in the name of all those King Henry had denounced. But this final severance he gave into the care of the bishops of Worcester and London, to deliver or withhold according to the reception they received from the king. For he would not move without attempting all that could be attempted with honour to avoid out-and-out war, though he knew, barring a miracle from God that he should meet with no response but contumely. And so we all knew. But his dignity, for all his occasional passions flaring like tinder, was not vulnerable by the scorns of littler men. I speak of the soul and the heart, for of the body there were then few men living, as I suppose, so large as the Lord Edward, who most reviled and detested what he had sometime inadequately loved.

So those two bishops rode down the valley to their own ordeal.

They came back in the late afternoon, empty-handed, the renunciation of fealty delivered. For King Henry, buoyed up by the greater numbers he commanded, and the brimstone hatred of those nearest to him, who were sure of victory, would not retract anything he had said or done, but denounced Earl Simon as his felon and traitor, and refused all contact with him. So his great vassal formally withdrew the fealty that was no longer valued or desired, and took back his freedom.

'Get your rest now,' said the earl, 'for we muster at nightfall.' And he issued his orders quietly, and went to his own brief rest. And so did all those young men of his, the buds of the nobility, many of them in arms against fathers and kin, some against elder brothers, all with alliances upon both sides. They did his bidding and copied his example with clear, white faces grave as angels and bright as stars, and after his pattern they composed their lives to passion and prayer, whether to live or die being a lesser thing. And if they knew many more such days in their lives, however long, that I question, and if they did, they were visited by God above other men.

Before the afterglow had faded, the horn summoned us, and to that solemn sound we stood to, and went every man to his place in the ordered companies. Almost in silence we assembled, only those words were spoken that were needful. Earls, barons and knights came forth to join their men half-armed, to be ready for any event and yet go lightly through the night, and they wore on their surcoats the white cross of the crusader. Behind the ranks of fighting men, drawn close in the woods, the sumpter horses gathered with mail, arms and supplies. In the faint remnant of the light the boles of the trees stood ranked like the pillars of a great church, and we were still as pilgrims at their journey's end.

The bishops came forth with Earl Simon. Bishop Walter of Worcester said mass for us all, and gave us solemn absolution, for we had come to this place and this hour with eyes open, and were as men voluntarily dead before our deaths in the quest for the thing we believed in and desired. Then we marched.

There was never such a night's march as that. Some ten miles we had to go, at the speed of the foot soldiers, and before dawn we had to be in possession of the ground Earl Simon had chosen. Therefore the pace was fast and steady, to have time in hand for ordering our ranks at leisure when we reached our stay. And silently we went, except that some of the footmen raised a soft murmur of singing that helped to set the stride. I never made proper reckoning of the numbers we had in all, but estimate that there may have been nearly two hundred knights, as many again of other mounted soldiers, and about four thousand foot soldiers, archers, lancers and swordsmen, including a great number of the trained bands of London. We knew from our outriders that the king had greater strength, notably in knight service. I think it may be said that our scouting was better done than theirs, if, indeed, they did any at all, for in the event our advance passed quite unmarked. They had not expected us to move before day.

But what I chiefly remember is the beauty of that May night, cool and fresh and still, with a few drifting clouds that made shadows in the open spaces even under starlight, after the moon was down, and the green, spring scent of burgeoning bushes and the first may-blossom. And after we came into the track along the river-valley, close to the water-meadows that were brimming from the April rains, the overwhelming fragrance of meadow-sweet.

Earl Simon rode that night, the first time he had tried his ill-knitted bone so hard, and I think not without pain, but to use the chariot here was impossible. For some time the old track along the river ran straight, and the going was smooth, but well before we drew near Lewes we turned aside to the right, into the woods, and climbed up the flank of the downs in a long traverse, in cover all the way. We had the best of guides, for Robert de Crevecoeur and his men of the Weald knew this country-side as they knew their own palms. The only danger was that King Henry or some shrewder soul in his company might belatedly have stationed a brigade on the high ground towards which we made our way. But we heard no rumour of men or movement but our own, and came before full light to the chosen place.

We emerged upon the great, bare shoulder of the downs, and wheel-ing to our left, saw below us in the pearl-grey dawn the town of Lewes, a mile or more distant and deep below us, in the bowl where the river valley opened out into broad fields and soft, marshy hollows. We had made a half-circle about it in cover, and by the position of the sun, not yet risen but turning the sky above it into an aureole of thin, greenish gold, we stood now almost due west of it. For when we looked over the pool of delicate mist that hid all detail in the town, we looked full into the promise of the morning, and that we took in our hearts for an omen.

'In good time!' said Earl Simon, and without pause turned to draw up his array, before the sun rose. He was singularly alone in his leadership, however gallant and devoted those young men who followed him, for without exception they lacked all experience of deploying an army for battle, or making use of the ground afforded. And he was forced to go, with fierce patience, from one end of his station to the other, and place his companies himself, with clear orders. His host he had divided into four sections, brigading a company of foot soldiers and archers with each body of horse. Three of his sections were drawn up as centre and wings, the fourth he held in reserve, to follow at a little distance when we moved down.

When all was ordered and ready, Earl Simon called together those who were not yet knight among his young captains, and himself con-ferred that high order upon them, and girt them with the sword, as was customary before battle, and in particular before so sacred and respon-sible a battle as this. The list of their names was long and proud: two earls among them, Gilbert of Clare and Robert de Vere of Oxford, de Burgh, FitzJohn, Hastings, Crevecoeur, de Lucy, de Munchensey, and many another, all received the accolade at the hand of a man greater than kings.

I was among Crevecoeur's mounted men in the centre battle then, watching the film of mist dissolve from over Lewes town, as though a hand had removed a veil of gauze dropped into the hollow of a green cushion. The towers of Earl Warenne's castle rose on a hillock in the centre of the town, the grey shapes of the priory more to the south, a house of Cluny, and very rich. Though all was still in shadow, being low in that sheltered bowl, the air was clear between, we could see the pattern of a street, and the tower of the church, and the roofs of the houses were honed sharp as daggers. In the hills beyond, the sun showed its rim, and the faint gold flushed into rose. Then the first long ray reached out across the bowl like a burning lance, touched us where we stood, and blazed upon the burnished helm of Earl Simon as he rode back to his own battle.

Out of their dimness below some watchman saw that light, and doubtless cried out and ran to sound the alarm in haste. We heard the first trumpet, shrill and small, then another and another taking up the peal, and all that quiet scene below began to boil and heave, jetting out running men from every part like spurting blood. The barking of dogs we heard, and the rolling of a drum in some high place, perhaps the church tower. Out of the castle men came pouring, and out of the priory, and everywhere about the town there was this festering excitement, as King Henry's host clambered into its harness and tumbled out into the dawn to form its array in furious haste. Whether we on our hilltop, glittering in sunlight while they scurried in shadow, appeared to them as the host of hell or heaven, certain it is the sight of us fell on them like a lightning-stroke.

Yet they had some little time to muster and form, for we were a mile and more distant from them, and must keep our foot pace most of the way, and they lay close and easy about the town, with ample room for movement once the alarm was given. They were more than we, and they had not marched ten miles in the night, but we were awake and aroused, and had the upper ground, through their folly in leaving it unoccupied. We counted the day well begun as Earl Simon gave the signal to march forward, and our three battles began to move steadily down the slope.

We went upon a broad, open spur of ground that kept an even descent aimed at the heart of the town below, but lower down, this ridge narrowed somewhat, and was split into two by the hollow of a little brook, and to keep even ground under them our left wing continued downhill upon the eastern spur, divided from us by the hollow. And as we went it was strange how clearly we saw, and how calmly, those great powers massing against us. The rays of the sun still did not penetrate into the bowl far enough to prick out for us the bright devices of the king's men, yet their colours came to birth gradually in glowing shadow, and many we knew by their coat-armour. And as they watched us descend, so did we watch them as they gathered and took shape in their three battles, and with solemn, ponderous majesty moved forward out of the town to intercept us.

Their right wing was perfect the first, and first to move, forming up under the castle, where they had been lodged. Even before the sun came up fully, and awoke the colours of the banners, I knew by the fashion of the leader who marshalled them what name belonged to him, for I doubt if there was another such giant among the nobility of England. On a raw-boned horse, leaner built and faster than most destriers but huge like his rider, the Lord Edward wheeled his battle into position against our left, on their severed spur. And having excellent eye-sight and a long memory, doubtless he recognised the levies of the city of London, which had sided against his father, several times foiled his own plans, and hunted his mother out of her barge into cowering sanctuary in St Paul's. For grievances, humiliations, grudges, his memory was even longer than for services rendered, as long as life itself.

He spurred his horse, sent his standard forward, had his trumpeter sound, abandoned his foot force to follow as they could, and launched all his mounted strength headlong up the severing hollow and crosswise into the advancing Londoners, driving them eastward across the foot of the ridge, to scatter like spray before his hurricane into the river flats beyond.

It was out of alarm and compassion for his city allies, I think, that Earl Simon loosed his main battle in the charge when he did, for though it served well in the end, for preference he would surely have held his hand a while longer. But loose us he did, to ease the thrust that swept those hapless burgesses sidewise from their ranks, and bring Edward back into the true fight, where he belonged. But Edward had not yet learned, his hatred still ruled his judgment, instead of his judgment honing his hatred into a deadly weapon, as later it did, to all men's bitter peril that ever crossed him, and to the rue of the kin of all such, down to half-grown brothers and unoffending sisters, and the children in their cradles. That day he did but kill and kill whatever he could reach, never stopping to reason how to kill the most of us, or the greatest, only the nearest, and those from London. So we gained and lost by him.

For Earl Simon gave the order to sound, and we set spurs to our horses and drove down the hill into King Henry's central battle, labouring up the first slope towards us. We struck them hard and truly, and swept them back down the hill with us until we hit the first houses of the town. Crushed between us and the adamant walls, they fought back as long as they could, but were gradually shattered into particles that drew back among the buildings as they might, and thus were hunted along streets and alleys, first hotly, then without haste, later even with moderation, seeking to pen rather than to kill or harm. It went not so rapidly as I have made it seem, for so we laboured until near noon, though it passed like a breath, for we were exalted above ourselves, and knew no want nor weariness. I remember marking with astonishment, towards the middle of the day, how hot the sun was, and that the grass was no longer wet with dew.

I think I killed none in that battle, wounded but few, as I got but a scratch or two in return. And truly I was glad it should be so, for there was about our cause some holy reluctance to hurt or hate, even though we could not give ground. The foot soldiers had heavier losses, but few knights died in the onset, the first among them Earl Simon's standard-bearer. The life of such an officer is always at any man's disposal, seeing his devotion is towards that he carries, and no more to his own defence than it is to the slaying of those that come against him. William le Blund died with the standard still aloft over him, and another took it from his dying hand and bore it forward. Thus we drove into Lewes, and gripped and held it.

Then I saw no more of Earl Simon for a while, for he drew back to watch the progress of the battle, and make use of his reserve to the best effect. The morning passed, and Edward still absented himself, hunting his unhappy Londoners about the marsh-land and into the river, and killing as long as he had strength in his arm, or his driven horse could go. We neither saw nor heard of him, and them we could not help. We combed the fringes of Lewes, pricking out at sword-point lord after lords, all those lofty names, Hereford, Arundel, Basset, Mortimer, even names more outlandish to me, for they came from beyond the border of Scotland, vassals out of their own country, Balliol, Comyn and Bruce, the keepers of the northern marches.

King Henry had given his left battle to the king of the Romans and his son, Henry of Almain, and only they, with a handful of their followers, made any headway up the slope of the down, and succeeded in breaking through to its crest, only to find they were cut off from all the rest of their numbers, who were still entangled with the centre and pinned down in the low ground outside the town. Earl Simon's reserve closed the circle about those who had penetrated, and drew in upon them until they were forced to take refuge in a windmill which stood in a high spot there to take the weather. And there, encircled and under threat from the archers if they tried to break out, they at last surrendered and were made prisoner.

Then all was centred around the town, where baron after baron and knight after knight was severed from his support, surrounded and taken. Where we wearied, the reserve came in to relieve us, and Earl Simon used a part of the force, and especially the archers of the Weald, who knew their business and their country, to fling a cordon round Lewes and stop the ways out of it towards the south, for that way lay the easiest escape to the sea, and what was most to be feared was that King Henry might be whisked away, or some of his allies more dangerous than himself might reach France by that route, and add their strength to the invasion force we all knew to be massing there. As indeed a few did break through before the circle closed, and got away by sea from Pevensey, two of the king's half-brothers among them, William of Valence and Guy of Lusignan, together with Hugh Bigod, who had once been a de Montfort man and justiciar of England, and the Earl Warenne, the lord of Lewes himself. For the rest, we made a clean haul of them, all those great lords who parted England among them fell one by one into Earl Simon's hands.

To the north-east of the town he left the approaches open, but with reserves in wait wherever there was cover, for in the early afternoon Edward brought his gorged and sated troops back into the field, and no doubt expected that the day would have gone with his father and uncle as pleasingly as with him. Earl Simon let him in, and the circle closed behind him. Too late he saw the battle-field swept clear of all but puny, scattered clashes, like the last sputtering flames of a dying fire and marked and understood the litter of harness, banners and arms that was left of King Henry's army, and knew that in gratifying his own revenge he had lost his father the battle.

He did not know where the king was, though by then we did, and had a strict watch all round the Cluniac priory, where he had fled to sanctuary. Earl Simon stood between Edward and the same refuge, and even to that angry and embittered mind there was no sense in trying to fight over again, with a handful of tired men on tired horses, the battle already irrevocably lost. Edward turned tail and made for the house of the Franciscan friars, and there took cover with the remnant of his following. As much a prisoner of Earl Simon as if he had surrendered himself into his hands, there he was suffered to stay, and his father among the monks of Cluny, for neither of them could escape.

So ended the battle of Lewes, that many saw as a miracle and the direct judgment of God, so complete was the victory. Yet not without cost. Friars, clerks and monks went about the river flats and meadows and the shoulder of the down after the fight, and reverently took up and buried the dead, to the number of six hundred, and of those it may well be more than half were men of London.

As for us, we secured the castle and made our camps, and gathered the spoils of arms and armour, and set guards, and did all that men must do as scrupulously after a victory as before. We saw to our horse-lines, fed and watered, tended injuries, the smiths repaired dinted armour and ripped mail, and the cooks and sutlers found us meat and bread and ale, and we ate like starving men.

The furnishings of Earl Simon's chapel went with him wherever he went. And most devoutly, that evening, he heard mass and offered thanksgiving with a full heart for the verdict of God, delivered in the blazing light of day before all men, in token that it behoved all men to accept the judgment. For the award of heaven is higher than the award of kings or pontiffs, and even they must bow to it and be reconciled.

CHAPTER X

After the men-at-arms had done their part, and while they slept after their exertions, the clerks and friars began their work, and for them there was no sleep in Lewes that night. Those who were not tending the wounded or burying the dead, ran back and forth all night long between the parties that had been brought to a stand, and must now be brought to a settlement. For complete though the triumph was, it could not do more than determine who now put forth the terms to be met, and since Earl Simon was not and never desired to be a monarch himself, or to displace the monarch that England already had, he was greatly limited, in what he could propose, by his own nature and his conception of duty and right. He aimed always at that which had been his aim from the beginning, an order of government such as had been begun at Oxford, with the consent and co-operation of all the limbs of the state.

By morning they had drawn up a form of peace, and both King Henry and the Lord Edward had given their assent to it, having little choice. It provided for the royal castles to be handed over to new seneschals responsible to council and parliament, for the proclamation of peace in the shires and the strict enforcement of law, so that no partisan upon either side should now molest his neighbour of the other side without penalty, and for the immediate release of young Simon and of the lord of Beaudesert and his two sons, taken at Northampton. The whole immediate purpose of this urgent accord was to ensure the order and safety of the realm, against the uncontrolled malice of faction in the shires, the opportunism of malefactors who thrive on discord, and the threat of invasion from overseas, for everyone realised that the eternal problem of reaching a final amicable settlement still remained, and was as intransigent as ever. And for the sake of law and order, since half the nobility of England was now captive, indeed more than half of the chief persons of authority in the marches, Earl Simon made a gesture no other man could have made, and upon their acceptance of the form already sealed by king and prince, ordered the release to their own lands of all the lords of the march, and also of certain others, the Scot, John Balliol, the sheriff of Northumberland, and a baron of Hampshire who was needed along that coast. They pledged themselves to go home and keep peace and good order, and attend in parliament when called. But bound as he was to accept other men's oaths as his own was acceptable, Earl Simon did not let all the weapons out of his hands, and no blame to him. He named two hostages who should remain in captivity as surety for the observance of all the terms of the peace, and those two were the Lord Edward and his cousin Henry of Almain.

With what bitterness and resentment the Lord Edward accepted his subjection I guess, yet he did give his word. With what weariness, discouragement and timidity King Henry resigned himself to his, that I saw and understood. But I use the wrong word, for resign himself he never did, being unable to despair of his luck. But very piously he subscribed to the terms, his only present advantage lying in assent, and very heartily he wrote to King Louis with a copy of the form of peace, and entreated him to use his good offices with the exiles to persuade them to acceptance, for the safety of the royal hostages, and the preservation of his own precarious rights. All the more since Earl Simon declared himself willing, secure in heaven's verdict for him and the general adherence of the people of England, again to submit matters at dispute to the arbitration of King Louis and his best advisers. Believing as he did in the sacredness of Christendom and the common health of its component lands, no less than in the need for right and just government within each of them, he could do no other.

Thus far I saw matters unfold, with every promise of a good outcome. For shortly after the battle Earl Simon set out to take the king to London, and the young hostages to honourable confinement at Richard of Cornwall's castle of Wallingford, and that being my way also as far as the city, I went with them. But when we came to St Paul's, where lodging was prepared for the king, I sought an audience with Earl Simon, the first time I had been alone with him since the May night under the stars at Fletching.

He walked less lamely by then, but he was not free of pain, and seeing him thus closely, after many days of seeing him in the seat of power, far removed from me and controlling kings and princes with a motion of his sword-hand, I started and checked at seeing him worn away so lean and steely-fine, as though the spirit had fretted away the flesh from his bones. Those bones had been to me a marvel from the first moment I set eyes on him in Oxford, so purely drawn were they, and so taut and polished and private beneath the skin. He had no soft lines that could be manipulated, no pliable mask like King Henry's. What he was he showed to every seeing eye, like mountain, flood and fire, most beautiful and perilous. And still, revealing himself mortal and vulnerable, subject to ills of body and mind, he favoured his new-knitted leg, and eased its weight with a hand when he shifted it. So close and so far he was, and so distanced, and so drawn, I had discovered how to love him.

'I guess your errand,' said Earl Simon, 'and your longing to be home I understand. When you elected to go with me to the judgment, you said you would carry the news to Wales yourself, and so you should. With my blessing and my thanks, to your lord and to you.'

I said then, not with any great foreboding, but knowing that all things were still uncertain, that he might yet need a close liaison with Wales again before long, and that if he desired it and Llewelyn permitted it, I would return to him.

Then he bade me sit down with him, and told me what further moves the council of England had in mind, that Llewelyn might be fully informed without the committal of such vital matters to writing. The

341

first need had been to establish reliable wardens of the peace in all the shires. The second, he said, was to call parliament as quickly as possible, and to ensure that those who attended it truly spoke for the people, and to that end writs had already been sent out. These were the first days of June, and before the month ended parliament must meet and ratify what had been done in the name of the whole realm, or demur and amend it.

'On the lesser people of the shires,' said the earl, 'much has depended, as you have seen, and much will depend on them in the future. I have learned to know them as staunch to their faith, and have leaned upon them hard in contention and battle, and they have not let me fall. Surely their voices should also be heard in peace, and their loyalty remembered. We are calling to this parliament, from every shire, four knights chosen by the shire court to stand spokesmen for their people. With their aid some form of council must be chosen to advise and direct the king's actions, until we can achieve a permanent peace and a proper constitution.'

I asked after the fate of the remaining prisoners of Northampton.

'You touch on a sore and tangled matter,' he owned. 'The marcher lords are being called to parliament and told to bring their prisoners with them, to be exchanged man for man against those we took at Lewes. We cannot leave good men rotting in cells while all the legal arguments are hammered out to the end, but the exchange will certainly be bedevilled by questions of ransom and right. If need be they will have to be released on surety for their price, but we must have them out.' He caught my eye and smiled, reading me well. 'True, before the summer's out I may need every sword and lance I can muster. Neither King Louis nor the cardinal makes any move to call off the pack they have raised against us in France. Well, if we lean only on ourselves, no one can let us fall. Perhaps we should give thanks for threats from without, if they bind us so firmly together within.'

And that was truth, for even before council made any appeal, the men of Kent and Hampshire had risen themselves to patrol the coast and watch for alien sails, and the shipmen of the Cinque ports were prowling the seas on guard. And when later he called, every man answered.

'Yet I will not believe,' he said steadfastly, 'that it need be so. We are an organ of Christendom, how can we live and to what purpose, cut off from the body that nourishes us? No, we must prevail! When God has spoken for us so clearly, surely his vicar on earth cannot for ever shut his ears against the truth.'

When I was with him I shared his faith, so potent it was. Yet I knew, as he knew, that beyond the narrow seas more and more ships and arms were massing even as we spoke, and that the mood of the exiles was most bloodily bent on invasion. At Boulogne Cardinal Gui threatened excommunication and interdict, and although King Henry in his anxiety had written again to Louis, urgently begging for a conciliatory attitude and a helpful spirit, for the sake of the hostages if for no other reason, still the thunderous silence continued. Earl Simon had enemies more than enough, and none of them impressed by the vehemence with which God had stood his friend.

Nevertheless, and whether he willed it or no, this man who sat quietly talking with me was the master of England then, towering above kings.

He gave me his hand when I took my leave of him, and his safe-conduct to get me service and security wherever his writ ran. And so I left him still embattled, since there was only one victory that could satisfy him, and that was denied to him by the obduracy of his enemies. And I rode the same hour, and set out for Wales.

Llewelyn was at Knighton, keeping a close watch on his cousin Mortimer's lands and movements, for it was clear to him that the march was no better resigned to submission than before Lewes, and though he had not yet all the details with which I could provide him, he already foresaw that all those turbulent young men might find their parole easier to give than to keep, even if they had begun in good faith, which was by no means certain in all cases. He welcomed me eagerly, and when I had told him all, as I thought, still found me many questions.

'You have been at the heart of things,' he said, 'while I have been sitting here like a shepherd guarding a fold.' And he took from me again and again the story of Lewes, and said that he envied me.

'But he will need us again,' he said with certainty, 'and soon, and in my country, not in the south. Even his virtues fight against him. He could not leave the march in disorder, for the sake of right and justice, where another would have let right and justice fend for themselves, and the barons of the march lie safe in prison, until all was better secured for his own cause.'

'His cause *is* right and justice,' I said, 'whatever errors he commits on the way. How, then, can he defend them by abandoning them?'

'I know it,' said Llewelyn, 'and he is discovering it. He wills to have all the estates of the realm taking their due part in its governance, and he finds himself forced by the times to take more and more power into his own hands. And I see no remedy. We have already heard how they are standing to in the south, all those sea-coast pirates and fishermen, and the archers of the Weald, expecting the fleet from France, while Louis holds aloof and the cardinal-legate threatens damnation. And I think in his heart the earl of Leicester knows, as I guess, that for all his offers and concessions upon the one part, there will be none on the other. What can he gain by all this to-ing and fro-ing of envoys across the sea, when all they will accept is his surrender or his death?'

'Time,' I said.

'Yes,' granted Llewelyn after a moment's thought, 'that he may. If he can weather the summer, they'll be less likely to put to sea in a winter campaign. And all the coastal castles, those he holds. However great the numbers they gather, they'll find it hard enough to land them. And if paid mercenaries don't run away home for the harvest, they'll take themselves off fast enough when there's no more money to pay them. Yes, every week gained is precious. You say young Henry is keeping Dover for him?'

I said that he was, and the Countess Eleanor was there also, with her two youngest sons and her daughter.

'The other Eleanor,' said Llewelyn to himself, and smiled. 'You have seen this child? Does she resembles her brother?'

I told him, as best I could, what manner of girl she was, of her radiance and simplicity as I had first beheld her, gracious, artless, as blazingly honest as her brother and her sire. He listened with a faint smile, as though half his thoughts were still upon the dangerous game being played along the marches, yet his eyes were intent and rapt. And at the end he said mildly, as if rather to himself than to me:

'And she is not yet betrothed, or promised to any, this lady?'

Before many weeks were out all Llewelyn's forebodings were justified, for in spite of all their oaths the barons of the march did not obey the summons to the parliament in June, or send their prisoners, nor did they surrender such royal castles as they held, Bristol among them. In July, while one more arduous formula of agreement was being hammered out at Canterbury, in the hope of finding favour, however grudging, with King Louis and the legate, Earl Simon was forced to come himself, with the earl of Gloucester, to deal with the troublers of the march, who were raiding and plundering their neighbours and building up their household forces in defiance of law. The earl sent an appeal to Llewelyn to aid him from the west, which he was glad to do upon more counts than one, for the turbulence of the marcher rule threatened us no less than England.

That was a short, brisk campaign, profitable to us and to Earl Simon also, for it added to his strength the castles of Hereford, Hay, Ludlow and Richard's castle, and gave us more land in Maelienydd, bringing Mortimer and Audley and their fellows to surrender at last at Montgomery, and to promise attendance at court with their prisoners. But so they had promised before, and broken their word, and so they could and did again.

Perhaps this time they had truly intended to keep it, if the approaches so patiently made to King Louis and the exiles at Boulogne had met with any acceptance. But though the envoys sailed back and forth tirelessly, still amending, still making concessions on all but the sacred principles, never did legate or king take one small step to meet them. On the contrary, Cardinal Gui reverted to the pope's original denunciation of the Provisions, and ordered the bishops who came as envoys to observe the papal sentence promulgated against the earl and his followers. They as firmly refused, and departed. Late in October the legate formally pronounced sentence of excommunication and interdict against Earl Simon and all who held with him. So the saints fare always in this world.

This utter rejection at Boulogne revived all the vengeful defiance in the march. In that same month of October a band of knights from Edward's castle of Bristol, all intimate friends of his, made a great dash across England to storm Wallingford castle and rescue the prince, intending to carry him back with them to Bristol and gather an army round him. They took the outer ward of the castle by surprise, but the garrison turned their arbalests against them, and even threatened to give them Edward, since they had come for him, by hurling him from a mangonel if the attackers persisted, so that he was glad enough to be brought up on to the walls to beg his friends to give up their mad plan and depart.

The upshot was that Earl Simon, rightly alarmed at so daring an onslaught coming so near success, removed the two hostages into stricter keeping at his own castle of Kenilworth, sent peremptory summonses to all the marchers to attend at Oxford in November with their prisoners, and called up an army of barons and knights to muster there to ensure obedience. But in spite of all their promises, the marchers still did not come. Then the earl was forced to move against them a second time in arms, and sent again to Llewelyn to close in at their rear.

'See how the year has slipped by,' Llewelyn said, when we were in the saddle again, and marching east to match the earl's westward advance, 'and ours the only fighting, after all. If he has done nothing else, he has got England through the summer. They'll not put a fleet to sea now. And next year will be too late, they'll all have gone off to better-paid service.' For December was beginning, and a gusty, wild month it was, though with little frost or snow.

Mortimer, the boldest of the lawless marcher company, made a bid to hold the Severn against the earl, but changed his mind when the chill of Llewelyn's shadow fell on his back. He drew off down the river, but we kept pace with him, and crowded him into Earl Simon's arms for the second time that year, forcing another submission at Worcester.

So near we were then to the earl, and yet those two still did not meet, who were already so drawn to each other, and worked so well together. For time, of which we had enough, was then so wanting to Earl Simon that he was handling two or three desperate problems at the same moment, and we could not hamper his actions. We drew back and stood on guard for him, but he needed us no more then. He had made up his mind that the west could no longer be left to this endless chaos and misrule. All those lands held in the march by the Lord Edward, the palatinate of Chester and the town and castle of Bristol, he determined to take into his own hands, for they were too dangerous to be left to any other. In exchange for them he provided Edward with lands to the same value elsewhere, in less vulnerable counties.

He sent Llewelyn the terms of his settlement with the marchers, for we also were concerned in them. The offenders agreed to withdraw into Ireland for a year and a day, surrendering those royal castles they still held, and releasing at last the unfortunate prisoners of Northampton. Mortimer was allowed to visit Edward with the terms, for the exchange of lands required his consent and charter. And since his release from strict confinement, if not from all surveillance, depended upon his agreement, he had little choice but to agree. At least he might, at the cost of that exchange, be able to see his young wife again, and the infant daughter she had borne him only a few weeks after Lewes.

'Chester!' said Llewelyn, rearing his head suddenly, at gaze into distance, when he heard the terms of the submission. 'If the earl is to have Chester, where does David go?'

There was in his voice and in his eyes a kind of mild astonishment, as though he had remembered something from long ago, once taken grievously to heart, and now recalled as curiously small and distant. He had not thought of David for so long that all the crust of hatred and hurt and resentment that had made his desertion bulk so large had dwindled away, and left only the human form, slighter than his own, of the young brother he had loved and indulged, and by whom he had suffered what now seemed only trivial wounds. Forgetfulness is sometimes easier than forgiveness, and achieves the same end.

'He is still there?' I asked, for I, too, had almost forgotten him. Strange, for he was memorable, if there had been no giants blotting out the light.

'He has been there with Alan la Zuche all the year, holding the town and county for the king. There'll be a new justiciar now, and a new garrison. And he has lost so much, and been left so far out on the fringe of events,' he said, almost with compunction. 'He could never abide to be out of the centre, and here he lies washed up on the rim. And his Edward baulked and prisoner. Poor David!' said Llewelyn, marvelling at the revenges of fate and at himself. 'I could be sorry for him! He is so torn. How could I ever have hated him?'

'I doubt you ever did,' I said in all honesty. 'It is not among your gifts.'

'It could be,' he said with a startled smile, 'if it were not such a waste of time. But with so many things better worth doing, hate is a luxury must wait its turn, and it dies of waiting. I wonder,' he said more sombrely, 'if his is dead, as mine is?'

And for a while I think his mind was again upon his brother, and the wrongs he had suffered of him, and also, perhaps, those he had unwittingly inflicted upon him. But that lasted no long time, for the very reason he had given. The fortunes of Wales were always foremost in his thoughts, and thrust David out of mind. Whatever the force of Llewelyn's sympathies in the long contest between king and barons, and with whatever willingness he took sides, there was no question but he meant Wales to do well out of the conflict, and intended to exploit it to the limit for her sake. And this was the greatest opportunity of all to secure his northern conquests, and make his boundary there inviolable, now that all the former earldom of Chester was being transferred into the hands of his ally, who owed him a share in the benefit.

'We'll turn homeward for the Christmas feast,' he said, 'and we'll see who comes to garrison Chester and rule as justiciar in Earl Simon's name, and what message he has for me.'

He left a moderate force in Maelienydd when we turned northwards, and since it seemed that we were somewhat ahead of the new officials at Chester, we went home to Aber for the Christmas feast, and then repaired to the castle of Mold, to be in close touch with events in the city. The word went round at the turn of the year that all the tenants of the county and honour, as well as the officers of the castle, had received their orders upon Christmas Eve to serve the earl of Leicester as they had been wont to serve the old earls palatine in the former days, before the line of Blundeville died out and the honour reverted to the crown. And Earl

Simon's new justiciar was come, in the person of Luke Tany, and la Zuche, the king's partisan, was about to march out with his men and betake himself elsewhere, perhaps into the lands given to the Lord Edward in exchange. We waited but a day more, and a courier came from Luke Tany, bearing a letter from Earl Simon himself, appointing a day when his envoy would meet with Llewelyn at Hawarden, on the business of the northern march.

Mold is no more than twenty miles or so from Chester, and Hawarden halfway between. We made our way there in advance of the day, and the weather then being fine, with only light frost in the mornings, we had good riding in that pleasant, rolling land. Llewelyn was withdrawn and quiet, but restless and unable to settle, and turned his mount and his gaze towards Chester, and there being no enemy now to hold us at distance, rode as far as the river and lingered there, walking his horse under the very walls of the town, and watching the road that led south from the gate. Then I knew what had drawn him there, and that he had knowledge of it beforehand.

From our place in the rimy meadows we saw the long file of horsemen issuing from the bridge gate, the sun picking out their lance-heads and pennants in a shifting play like little flames. We could even hear the drumming of the hooves across the timbers of the bridge, so clear was the air, and pick out the devices of la Zuche and his knights, Edward's knights, banished to some less vital castle in the south. Llewelyn reared his head to stare upon all those riders, narrowing his eyes to bring them close, and I knew that he was looking for his brother.

So, indeed, was I, but it was Llewelyn who first found him. I knew it by the stillness that fell upon him, and following where he gazed, I saw David riding somewhat aside from the deposed justiciar, but level with him. He was not in mail, but cloaked in fine cloth and fur, and very handsomely mounted and equipped, and though he was but a small figure to us, too far off for his face to be more than an oval mask, by his seat and his carriage in the saddle there was no mistaking him. There was no reason why he should already have observed us, and he would have had to turn and look round over his right shoulder then to do so, since the cortège was moving away from us towards the south. Yet I believe he did know that we were there. Two horsemen motionless in those meadows against the pallid winter turf stood out like trees, and he knew Llewelyn's manner and bearing as Llewelyn knew his. If he was aware of us, he gave no sign. The tilt of his head and easy sway of his shoulders were as always, proud and assured.

They passed, and he dwindled gradually out of our sight, and it was over. Llewelyn wheeled his horse and rode back without a word until we drew near to Hawarden.

'Well,' he burst out then, between self-mockery and a kind of quiet fury, 'I have seen him! Neither sick nor sorry! I need not have troubled!' And he set spurs to his horse, and led the way in a gallop the rest of the journey home.

Earl Simon's envoy rode into Hawarden the next morning, well attended

347

with knights, clerks and lawyers, and we saw with pleasure that the earl had sent us his eldest son to deal in his name. Llewelyn went out to meet him gladly, and embraced him.

'I thought,' he said, 'they had you walled up in Kenilworth as keeper to your cousins since you left Dover. There is no man I would rather see here in your father's place.'

Young Henry was grown and matured since first we had seen him, yet not changed. He had had to deal with many grave matters, and to make decisions even more perilous than the generously wrong decision he had made in trusting Edward at Gloucester, but still he had that straight and confiding eye, and the brightness that grave children have, willing at all times to seek and believe the best, and by reason of their own truth slow to look for lies. And I thought then that such creatures, whatever their gallantry and skill and wit, are at disadvantage in this world, where the current kind are wiser than the children of light. Yet he had learned, and his learning had saddened him.

'If all goes well,' he said, 'my cousins will soon be let loose to the king's care under surveillance, and even if I must still be watchman, I need not be gaoler. At the parliament that's called for later this month we hope to find a form for easing Edward's captivity and mine.'

Llewelyn asked him of this parliament, for the writs sent out for it appeared to be on a wider ground even than in June, and clearly the impulse came from Earl Simon. All the bishops were called, said Henry, more than a hundred heads of the great religious houses, all those barons who were in due obedience and had not flouted previous calls to court, as the marchers had, from every shire two knights respected and trusted, and from a large number of boroughs two burgesses, for the towns had taken active part in the struggle for the Provisions, and willed to continue their aid, as Earl Simon was heartily glad to encourage it. Sandwich and the other southern ports were also sending four men. Though only God knew, said Henry, in the troubled state of many regions, whether all the members would reach the city on time, for the year, in spite of the welcome silence from France, opened in fearful uncertainty, and the marcher lords who should already have withdrawn to their banishment in Ireland were still in their liberties, upon one pretext and another. Nevertheless, a parliament there would be, and upon the writs issued, even if it meant delay.

'The boroughs, too! I see,' said Llewelyn, smiling, 'that your father's body politic grows more, and more agile, limbs with every year.'

'And all function,' said Henry. 'The lowest of men *are* men, of the same affections and infirmities as the highest. I have learned to marvel at what they can do. In the world of the saints and the religious there have been great men raised from the sheep-fold and the plough. I think there is too much waste of many who are wise without learning, and many who are able without power. We have leaned on such at need, in this cause, and they have not failed us. Only the great, established in power, have let us fall.'

That he could not have said, two years ago. He said it now with all his old simplicity, but the matter was new. And since I was come of the lowest, son of a waiting-woman and by-blow of a passing knight, I remembered his saying, and thought upon it often. I have seen dead bodies of the great and the mean stripped naked for tending to burial, and I know there is no way of knowing which is the prince and which the ploughman. Wherefore I think there are princes in all estates, and doubtless in all estates slaves also.

'And I?' said Llewelyn, eyeing his young friend narrowly.

'You have not let us fall,' said Henry, and smiled. 'I say no word of small or great to you. You have another way of ordering your realm, as it were a family, but carried to the ultimate degrees. Who is great or little in a family but by his generation? I think we have something to learn from you.'

'Not if you look for unity,' said Llewelyn fervently, and laughed, and went in with him. And I know they talked much and ardently of those matters at night, after the business was done and the clerks busy copying.

I would not say there was hard bargaining at that conference, for each side had an urgent end to gain, and they so marched together that the outcome was certain. Llewelyn gave what was required of him, and got what he required. What Henry wanted for his father was an absolute and assured peace along the Dee, so that Earl Simon need lose no sleep over his support in that region. And that he had, most willingly. What Llewelyn wanted was recognition for all the conquests he had made in these parts, and renunciation of all English claims upon them, his Saxon neighbour now being the earl himself, an ally instead of an enemy. And that he had.

'For every yard that I have taken back by force in my lifetime,' said Llewelyn, 'was Welsh land from time beyond memory. No part of it English but by seizure.'

'I am empowered,' said Henry, judicial and grave on his father's business, 'to acknowledge that ancient right, and leave in your hands all that you hold along this march.' And so it was sealed and delivered in the agreement.

'And I wish to God,' said young Henry passionately in private, afterwards, 'that the southern march were as securely in your hands, my lord, as the northern, for so we should have quiet minds. If there were no marcher lordships between your power and the Severn in the south, with all my heart I believe we could control the entire border between us. But the marcher hold in the south is so strong, I dread what may go forward there.'

'I see,' said Llewelyn seriously, 'that you rate the vital balance as lying here in the marches. For you as for me.'

'In the name of God!' said young Henry devoutly. 'They are a third country. Except to themselves, they have no loyalties, and except for their own, no law. I am afraid of them. If that is cowardice, I have the wit to be a coward. And the need, bearing as I do this responsibility. United, there is very little they cannot do, to the west as to the east, to you as to me.'

'I will keep the north for you, and the centre,' said Llewelyn. 'I and mine – Rhys Fychan, Meredith ap Owen, all those who hold with me – will do our best in the south. So much I promise you. More I cannot do.'

'More I dare not ask,' said Henry with humility. 'Unless there could be more of *you*! Did you never think, my lord, of getting yourself a noble consort, and a generation of sons?'

'I am thinking of it now,' said Llewelyn.

Earl Simon's great parliament was slow in getting into session, for even at the end of February some of the knights of the shires had not arrived, and those who had, so said Cynan in a message he sent us during that time, were uneasy at the expense of their long stay, and had to be allowed funds from the public purse to maintain them. But in March the debate began, and to all appearances much was achieved. A form of peace was painfully produced, continuing the present provisional rule, re-uniting Henry and the lords he had repudiated at Lewes as king and vassals, and by a clever manipulation of legal forms placing the control of the greatest royal castles in the hands of the council, while not attempting to alienate the king's title to them, or his son's. Dispossession was never in Earl Simon's mind. His hope – a vain hope in this world – was always for final and universal goodwill, so that restraints should wear away naturally and cease to be needed.

As the promised part of this settlement, the Lord Edward was released from captivity, though not from surveillance. He took the oath to maintain the form of government agreed, to refrain from any act against those who had created it, and to forbear from bringing in aliens himself or allowing others to do so, all this on pain of disinheritance if he broke his oath. It seems to me that Earl Simon, even if he never admitted it to himself, knew the worth of Edward's word, and did all he could to bind him.

However that may be, the prince formally accepted all, and acknowledged that the baronage had the right to turn against him and repudiate him if he broke his oath. Then both he and Henry of Almain, his cousin, were released from their prison and given into the king's care. But Henry de Montfort, though no longer their gaoler, as he had said, was to remain Edward's constant companion, and ward on his honesty. And since the king himself was safely in Earl Simon's control, so were the two young men, at one remove.

'I see all manner of dangers crowding in upon him behind this seeming triumph,' said Llewelyn, pondering the outcome with a disturbed and sombre face, 'however bright the surface shines. Again and again it is plain here that he can trust none of them but his own sons and a handful of others, and if his mind does not yet know it, his heart does. Therefore he cannot choose but confide more and more of the needful work to those few, and the rest begin to murmur against his preference for his own, while they themselves are the cause of it. Even his insistence on justice works against him! He has called men of his own party to order, even imprisoned the earl of Derby, for offences against other men's lands, and for that all those who have followed him for gain will turn and hate him, fearing their own turn may come next. He has offended Giffard of Brimpsfield, one of his few supporters in the march, over the misuse of prisoners and ransom, and Giffard is airing his grievance to Gloucester, who sees himself as good a leader as Earl Simon if he had his chance, and may even be in two minds about making his own opportunity. The more Simon stands erect and tries to do absolute right as he sees it – for God knows no man in this world can hope to see it whole every day in the year! –the more the envious will envy and the greedy resent him. And the more certain they are that he will never go back on his word, the more they have him at their mercy. Even his devotion to bishops, the best of their cloth in the land, and their reverence for him, so far from convincing the pope, only turns Simon into Anti-christ and them into heretics, in rebellion against Rome's authority. This is a fight he can win only one way, with the sword, again and again, and that is not the victory he wants. What can this world do with such a man?'

'Or with such bishops,' I said. For no less than nine of them, in full pontificals, had closed that parliament with the solemn excommunication of all those who transgressed against the great charter, the forest charter and the present statutes, the bible of civil liberty.

'Break them,' said Llewelyn bitterly, 'and put smooth noblemen from Savoy and Poitou in their places.'

I said, for I also saw the same stony barrier blunting every attempt at advance: 'He may yet be forced to take the sword again. And with the sword he is their master.'

'If they can force him to hold down England with arms,' cried Llewelyn with sudden passion, 'they will have defeated him, as surely as if they beat him in battle. It is his dilemma. I pray it may not be his tragedy!'

It was as if I argued with my own heart. Every word he said I felt to be true. And greatly I marvelled how he, watching and fretting at a distance, had come by a sharper understanding of Earl Simon than I had gained in the earl's own retinue.

CHAPTER XI

Before the beginning of April we were reminded of all that we had said together, for Meurig came riding into Bala, where Llewelyn's court had removed while the shaky quiet held, with a scrip full of gossip he had collected about the horse-markets of Gwent and Gloucester. Yearly he grew greyer and shaggier and smaller, more like a seeding thistle, but he was wiry and tough as thorn still, and had very sharp ears for all the tunes the wind brought him.

'There's more goes on below the hangings than is known abroad,' he said. 'Gilbert of Clare took himself off from Westminster before parliament ended or the peace was made, and went home to Gloucester with all his men. Some say in displeasure over the earl of Derby's fall, for his own conscience is not altogether clear. Some say for jealousy of the de Montfort sons. There was to have been a grand tournament at Dunstable, a court function, on Shrove Tuesday – did you hear of that? – but they got wind of high feeling between the Clares and the Montforts, and found it easier to call off the occasion on the plea that all good men were needed at court to aid in the Lord Edward's settlement. They put it off until the twentieth of this month at Northampton, hoping the bad blood would need no letting by then. And John Giffard was not long after the earl in quitting London, they say for fear of the law reaching for him as it had reached for Ferrers. He's with Gilbert now, hand in glove. The latest word is that the council called on Gilbert to make good his pledge as guarantor, and see the castle of Bamburgh handed over, and Gilbert has sent a very left-handed answer, pleading that he cannot take any steps because he is fully occupied defending his Gloucester borders. Against *you*, my lord!'

'I have not so much as cast a glance in his direction,' said Llewelyn warmly. 'What can the man be up to?'

'That is what the earl of Leicester is also wondering. Nor is Bamburgh the only castle still detained.'

'I know it,' said Llewelyn drily. 'Shrewsbury, for one.' For we knew by then that David was there, still tethered on his long leash, it seemed, as close as he could get to Gwynedd, as though he had been tied by his heart-strings, as indeed perhaps he was.

'And others,' said Meurig, nodding his silvery head, 'and others! It cannot be overlooked for ever. If Earl Gilbert does not appear at Northampton on the twentieth to run a course among the rest at this tournament, I think the earl of Leicester will be forced to go and smoke him out of Gloucester in person. The young man has been his right hand ever since Lewes; he cannot afford to be at odds with him, or leave him to his sulks. Who would replace him?'

'And they have called another parliament in June,' said Llewelyn, listening and brooding. 'Will it ever meet, I wonder?'

When the prince laid all these considerations before his council, Goronwy put his finger on the heart of the matter.

'There is one man,' he said, 'who could resolve all this if he would, and only one. It is pointless affirming to King Louis and pope and cardinal that England is at one, and King Henry consents to his lot, when it is plain he consents only under duress, however many oaths he swears. But their arguments and their weapons would be blunted if the crown did indeed consent and work with the earl and the council. All that the marchers and their kind are doing is done in the name of the royal liberties and privileges, and all the orders that issue from the chancery under the king's seal are all too clearly Earl Simon's orders, and can be denounced. But it would not be so easy to denounce them if the crown actively linked hands with the earl and repudiated the troublers of the peace. Aloud, voluntarily and credibly. King Henry never will, granted, he has fought every step of the road. But there's one who already carries more weight than King Henry, and shows as a more formidable enemy and a more effective friend. And once he was inclined warmly enough towards the earl and the reform. Surely it is only personal grudges, not ideas, that divide them even now. If the Lord Edward willed to make this government secure, he could call off the marchers, silence King Louis, and disband the invasion fleet, at one stroke. He might even convince the pope. He could certainly disarm him.'

Llewelyn looked to me for answer. 'It is true,' he said, 'I remember, not so long ago, he went so far in support of the earl as to bring himself into suspicion and disgrace for a time. Is there any possibility, do you think, that he may raise himself far enough above his grudges to discover some good in this new order, and give it his countenance, if not his blessing?'

I said: 'None! If he examined it in his own heart and found it perfect in justice and virtue, it would not change him, and he would not relent. Edward can be generous in friendship, even generous from policy, but once he turns to hating his hate is indelible. Edward will not lift a finger to make peace. But he will go to the last extreme to get his revenge.'

When the twentieth of the month came, the earl of Gloucester still absented himself from the tournament at Northampton. According to report, he was encamped with an ominously strong force in the forest of Dean, with John Giffard in his company, and this continued sulking so disquieted Earl Simon that he decided to move to Gloucester himself, and take the king with him, and sent out writs to the baronial forces of the border shires to rally to him at that town. The young earl was headstrong and inexperienced, yet he had shown himself ardent, brave and able, and Earl Simon was grieved at being at odds with him, and very willing to meet him in a conciliatory manner and discuss freely whatever matters rankled with him.

As soon as we heard that the earl had taken his unwieldy court to Gloucester, Llewelyn, restive and uneasy, called up his own levies and moved them down into the central march, to be on the watch for whatever might follow, and ready to act upon it at need. He had a little hunting castle at Aberedw, near Builth, and took up residence there, and he took care to send word to Earl Simon where he could be found.

In the forests and hills round Gloucester, Gilbert of Clare and his fellows camped through the first days of May, and while they received messengers civilly, and even sent replies, they held off from making any closer contact. Earl Simon sent conciliatory envoys to try to arrange a meeting, and Earl Gilbert replied with a long list of bitter complaints, no longer troubling to hide his jealousy, but pouring out all his grievances, over prisoners, ransoms, castles, and the preferment of Earl Simon's sons. This seemed to be some progress, at least, yet all attempts to bring him to the desired meeting were somehow evaded. To us, looking on from Aberedw, it seemed almost that Earl Gilbert was playing for time, while he waited for something to happen.

That whole dolorous court was there with Earl Simon, proof once again that in his heart he trusted none of them. The king, hemmed in with all the officers and ministers who controlled him and spoke in his name, went where he was taken, by then so discouraged and apathetic that I think only his obstinacy kept him alive. And I confess I understand how many who had truly believed in Earl Simon's ideals, but had not his endurance or his responsibility, turned to pitying a tired and ageing man, and felt revulsion at witnessing his plight. Yet I think Earl Simon was as much a victim and a prisoner as he, caught in the same trap, and with even less possibility of escape.

Edward was there, too, accompanied everywhere by his two guardians, Henry de Montfort and Thomas of Clare, Earl Gilbert's brother. No doubt a Clare was added to the warders to try and balance that enmity between Clares and Montforts that was splitting the younger reform party into two, but that must have been an unhappy partnership, damaging to all three. Thomas of Clare slept in Edward's bedchamber. No doubt those two had plenty of time to talk together, while Earl Gilbert was holding off in the forest, and setting the night alight with his camp-fires all round Gloucester.

With all his burdens, Earl Simon did not forget to keep us informed. We heard from him when the bishop of Worcester, eternally hopeful and ardent in the cause of peace-making, undertook to try and bring Gilbert de Clare to a meeting, and felt some relief when news followed, on the fifth day of May, that the young man was softening towards the idea, and had agreed to come down into the city if certain conditions were fulfilled.

'So it may pass over, after all,' said Llewelyn, glad but scornful. 'He's satisfied with the trouble he has caused, and flattered at having great men and reverend bishops running after him, and no doubt he'll enjoy being gracious after the wooing. We were wrong about him, he's lighter than we thought.' For he himself, at twenty, had been joint prince of Gwynedd, tried not only in battle but in the hard discipline of submission for the sake of preserving his constricted birthright, and labouring hard to restore its derelict fortunes. He had no time for tantrums.

So our minds were eased, and Llewelyn hawked and hunted over the uplands that day, without expectation of hearing more until the promised meeting should take place. And we were astonished when another messenger from Earl Simon rode into our narrow bailey the next morning, his horse ridden into a sweat, and his clothes whitened with the dust and pollen of a dry May. He stooped in haste to Llewelyn's hand.

'My lord, Earl Simon sends you word he is gone to Hereford with all his retinue, and begs you will attend him south on your side the border, for he may have good need of you.'

'I will well!' said Llewelyn heartily. 'But why to Hereford, and so suddenly? Is Gloucester at some new trick?'

'No, my lord, this is no contrivance of Gloucester's; he is still in camp, and has not moved a man. But William of Valence has landed from France in his lordship of Pembroke, with the earl of Surrey and a hundred and twenty fighting men. There'll be others following unless we turn back this onslaught at once. The earl is gone to block the roads into England and stay the flood.'

'You go to join him in Hereford?' said Llewelyn. 'You may tell him we shall not be far behind him.' And he sent the man in to get food and rest, while a fresh horse was saddled for his onward journey. When the prince turned upon me, I knew what was in his mind before ever he spoke, for it was in my mind, too.

'Samson,' he said, and his voice was so quiet and so current that it was strange to hear in it what I heard of doubt and entreaty, 'will you go back to Earl Simon with his messenger, and be my voice with him as before? I am not easy among these shifting tides. Go to him, and I'll keep pace with you my side the border. For I cannot go myself!' he said, crying out against what drew and denied him.

I said I would go. What else could I say? I did not say, gladly, there was then no gladness, though there may have been gratitude. I cannot tell. Within the hour I rode for Hereford with Earl Simon's messenger, and with Cadell beside me to be my courier with good tidings and ill.

The king's court was installed in the house of the Black Friars in the city of Hereford, and the strange retinue of officials and army filled the town, from the castle to the enclosure of the Franciscans, and spilled into encampments outside the walls. Something of Earl Simon's rigid discipline of body and mind had bled into the veins of those who served him, and there was order and purpose even then, when the foundations of their brief and splendid world were crumbling.

When they let me in to him, on the morning of the seventh day of May, he greeted me with a faint gleam of pleasure that burned through his black preoccupation for a moment, and warmed both him and me. I saw him greyer than before, the close fell of brown hair, like a beast's rich hide, silvered at the temples and above the great cliff of forehead, and his eyes sunk deeper into his skull than I remembered them.

He said: 'It is barely a year since you left me, after Lewes. I have found that a man may do ten years' living in one year. But you are not changed. I trust your lord is well?'

I said that he was, and of his own will had again sent me to be his envoy and hold the link close between them. And he made me sit down with him, and told me how the matter stood as at that time. As yet there had been no move from the force which had landed in Pembroke, his only information concerning them was that William of Valence and the earl of Surrey had made very correct and peaceable overtures to the religious houses in Dyfed and Gwent, and seemed to be contemplating an appeal through some such go-between towards the restoration of their lands and right of residence in England. Their numbers were not great, and in themselves they were not a great danger, provided entry could be denied to any others hoping to follow them.

I told him that Llewelyn proposed to be ready to match any moves the earl might make, and keep pace with him on the Welsh side of the border, where he could be very quickly reached at any time. But I repeated yet again that his first concern was the unity and stability of Wales, and that he needed and deserved to have his position made regular by formal acknowledgement, which he would not jeopardise by military adventures into England itself. His stand, as one having no covetous designs on any soil that had not been Welsh from time out of mind, could not be abandoned.

Earl Simon smiled. 'I remember,' he said, 'you told me so once before, and warned me that it might be in my power to tempt him from his resolve. Be easy! I will not lure any man from his own crusade to accomplish mine. It is good to have such a man as the prince keeping my back for me. I ask no more.'

In those days of May letters patent and letters close poured out from the city of Hereford, first to the Cinque ports and all the coastal castles, alerting them against the possibility of further attempts at landing troops, then to all the sheriffs of the shires, to hold their forces on the alert to keep the peace, arrest preachers of sedition and rumour-mongers, and insist on the maintenance of the settlement. Then, as stories began to come in of local levies massing in the marches, and brawls and disorder resulting, the sheriffs along the border were ordered to search for and seize those marcher lords who had promised to with-draw for a year of exile to Ireland, but on one excuse or another had contrived to evade keeping their word, and were now openly repudiating it. Rumours were spreading like brush fires along the borders that there was discord and enmity between the earl of Leicester and the earl of Gloucester, and these Earl Simon was intent upon suppressing.

'The man has his grievances, and has said so freely,' he said, 'and I have promised him redress if I am held to have done him any injustice. God knows I am not so infallible that he may not have just complaint against me. But he is a true man to the Provisions and the settlement, and I will not have his faith called in question because he finds fault with me.'

In this he was utterly sincere, for Bishop Walter of Worcester had indeed been successful in bringing de Clare to consent to a conference, but that the landing in Pembroke had caused that matter to be postponed in favour of more urgent business. Yet I could not get it out of my head that Earl Gilbert had been holding off for weeks from such a meeting, as though time, and not a hearing, was what he wanted. Time, perhaps, for the ships from France to put their cargoes ashore in Pembroke? He had not yielded to persuasion until the day before their coming was known, and to him it might have been known before the news came into Gloucester. I said so to young Henry de Montfort, on the one occasion when I saw him in the courtyard of the Dominicans. He bit on the suggestion with some doubt and consternation, as on an aching tooth, but shook his head over it after thought.

'How could he have foreknowledge of it? All the ports are under guard; you see they attempted nothing in the south, but went afield as far as Pembroke. And then, he has not made any move to try and join them, or they to make contact with him. We know he is still encamped where he was, close to Gloucester. I cannot believe he is in conspiracy with the exiles, or in sympathy with them, whatever his differences with my father.'

'Yet Pembroke's lands were in his care,' I said, 'and he should have been prepared to repel any such landing.'

'True,' said Henry, 'and he is certainly guilty of negligence, but surely of nothing more. He has neglected his duty to pursue his own quarrel, but he cannot have abandoned the cause he has fought for like the rest of us.'

So I pressed the matter no more, but I was not easy, for that very aloofness and stillness of Earl Gilbert caused me, as it were, to listen and hold my breath, as though both he and I were still waiting for some future event. However, there was nothing then to bear me out. The general alert continued, and so did the flares and raids in the marches, and the rumours of secret gatherings, but Gloucester made no move, and all the newly-landed exiles did at that time was to send the prior of Monmouth on a mission to the king's court, to plead for the restoration of their lands. A chill reply was sent from the council, saying that justice was open to all in the king's courts, and could be sought there at will.

That was a strange, sad Whitsuntide, in spite of the fair and sunny weather. The king, tired and unresisting, did as he was bid, and hated his own acts, council and ministers; Llewelyn patrolled his own side of the border, round Painscastle and Hay, and passed word back to us regularly, but there was no sign of any move from Pembroke. Earl Simon kept both hands upon the workings of chancery, and began to raise money where he could, from the Hospitallers and any who would loan it, foreseeing an urgent need to come. And Edward went to and fro in a controlled silence that was new in him, taking no part in any of the business of state unless his seal was expressly required upon some document, and then permitting its use with a bland but stony face, all his will and intelligence refraining from what was done with his supposed consent. And for the rest, he read, took exercise, rode, heard mass and music, as though what went forward in England then was nothing to do with him. In some such fashion, I suppose, he justified to himself his oath-breaking and faithlessness, his will and spirit having absented themselves when his tongue uttered all those vows. After all this time I believe I begin to understand even Edward.

On the morning of the Thursday in Whitsun week I saw him ride out of the city to take air and exercise, closely attended, as always, by Henry de Montfort and Thomas de Clare, his keepers, and several grooms, and with a string of lively horses for his testing. They went out in sunshine by the north gate, towards Leominster, and what I noticed as they trotted out from the Dominican friary was that Thomas de Clare leaned to Edward, and said something lightly and gaily into his ear, and that Edward laughed aloud, and rode out laughing. The only grave face among them was Henry's, who did not love his wardship or his ward, and was showing the signs of his unhappiness in that unpleasant duty.

But it was Edward's laughter that lingered in my mind all that morning, for I had not seen him laugh since the days when I had known him as a long-legged four-year-old running wild at our David's heels. And what he should find to laugh about on this particular day, in a situation in which he so dourly maintained a face of grim indifference through all other days, was more than I could fathom.

Before that day ended, all was made plain.

It happened that I was in attendance on Earl Simon in the afternoon, one of several clerks standing by in case he should wish to consult us, for he had matters in hand involving both Wales and England. Bishop Walter of Worcester was at his side, as constantly he was in those days. If the earl found few men constant to his measure, those he did find were worth the keeping. Peter de Montfort of Beaudesert was also among them, and also with us that day. About mid-afternoon there was a flurry of voices in hurried and agitated speech outside the door, and then young Henry came bursting in and confronted his father with a stricken face and staring eyes. His riding clothes were dusty and disordered, and there was a long graze down one cheek, and a smear of blood on his forehead. Earl Simon rose from his chair at the sight of his son, even before the boy gasped out between gulps for breath:

'The Lord Edward – he has escaped us! He is gone, and Thomas of Clare with him. The thing was plotted between them – them and others!'

He had not got so far, when every man there was on his feet. The earl stood stiff and still, gripping the table before him. Yet he did not exclaim, and his voice was low and even as he questioned:

'Where did this happen?'

'About five miles north, climbing up from the Lugg to ride over the commons there. I left a groom at the place. Beyond the ridge there are woods between the river and the old road. I have guards and archers beating the woods now,' he said, but without much hope.

Nevertheless, Earl Simon sent out more searchers before he questioned further: 'How did it chance?'

The young man told the sorry story, grinding his teeth over his own failure, and wiping away the trickle of blood from his cheek with a heedless hand when it vexed him. And the anger and bitterness that had not yet blazed in his father burned fiercely in him.

'He had two spare horses with him, he wanted to try them over the hills there, so he said. He changed to the second, and only when we reached this place to the third. It was the best of the three, and of a creamy-white, a colour to show out well over distance. He tried its paces along the grass away from us, and came back to us again, once, twice, and then loosed it to a canter as far as the ridge, and there checked a third time where he had turned, as if to turn again. And on the top of the next hill, between the trees, a horseman rode out, and I saw him lift his arm and brandish a sword. And at that Edward struck in his spurs and was away headlong, and Thomas, who was close beside me, lashed out with his whip and struck my mare over the face and eyes, and she reared and threw me. When I got up from the ground the Lord Edward had vanished into the woods, and Thomas was over the ridge and climbing the slope, beyond, and my mare was halfway home without me,' he said, writhing with fury. 'I took Edward's horse and went after them. Some of the grooms were ahead of me, and of them I'm sure, they were honest, they had no part in this. But they were not so well mounted, and the start was too great. And there are some of the laggards among them that I doubt whether they were not in the secret. I take the blame upon me,' he said with humble arrogance. 'I have failed in my trust.'

I saw Earl Simon's lips shrink and curve, between a smile and a contortion of pain, but he was not yet ready to comfort his son. There were more urgent matters yet.

'Thomas was in this, then,' he said. 'Surely not his brother, too? But they are gone north, you say.'

'Due north. He could not turn. I have hunters already on all the roads between here and where we lost him. To reach Gloucester, why start north? He could have chosen where he would for his ride.'

'And clean away from Pembroke and de Valence,' said Earl Simon. 'You are right. He is not gone to them. Well, let us improve on this hunt. We have sheriffs in the shires to the north, and a guard on the border.'

And he shook himself like a weathered and experienced hound surging out of the current of a river and questing afresh for scent, and set himself to cover all quarters leading out of Hereford that a fugitive prince might take. When all was done that he could do, he dismissed his attendants. But I did not go. I do not know whence I drew my awareness of privilege, yet I did not feel myself dismissed. I was still there, in the corner of his vision but not absent from his mind, when he sank back at last in his chair, and let his hands lie spread upon the table before him, great, practised, sinewy hands.

It was then I saw that these hands were already old before his face, having experienced and suffered so much, and carried such immense weights. He was then fifty-six years old, and his body a vigorous and powerful instrument that might have belonged to a man of forty. But his hands acknowledged their years.

His son had also remained, motionless and silent in the face of this calm. I believe I learned then how the sons of great men are themselves diminished below their own value, by respect, by fear of failure, by too great love and admiration. This was the best of his sons. Young Simon, the second, was then his father's deputy in Surrey and Sussex, busy watching the sea towards France, and he was bolder, more impetuous, and I think smaller than Henry, but he suffered the same diminution. It is not good nor easy to have a father who is both demon and saint. Had Henry been my son, as then and at other times I felt towards him the bowels of a father, I think he might have been happier, at least if ease is happiness.

He moved with a heavy lameness, tired with his fury of hunting and riding and humiliation, and shaken and bruised by his fall, and came like a child to his father's side, and there fell on his knees and leaned his head against the arm of the earl's chair. I could not see his face, it was in shadow.

'My lord and father,' he said, 'it is I who have failed you. I take the blame upon me.'

Earl Simon did not move his head or look down at his son, but I saw him smile, so marvellously and so mournfully I remember it yet. He took his left hand from the table, and folded it about the young man's head, holding him as in a bronze bowl.

'That you cannot,' he said, 'unless you will to be recreant and forsworn in his place. Child, if a man is not bound by his own oath, believe me, there is no way on earth of binding him.'

He rested a moment, cradling his son, the eldest and dearest, and fashioned so closely after his own pattern. 'Sooner or later we should have lost him,' he said, and suddenly the great, arched eyelids rolled back from his deep eyes, and they were looking full at me, with the last glow of that all-illuminating smile in them.

'If it were not for your presence, Master Samson,' he said, 'I should be saying: Put not your trust in princes! But since you are present, sit down with me, and write in my name to the prince of Wales!'

So began the last correspondence between Llewelyn and Earl Simon, through my hand. What the earl most wanted was reliable information as to where the Lord Edward was gone and who had been the instrument of his escape, beyond the suggestive complicity of Thomas de Clare. And Llewelyn, through his intelligencers in Knighton and Presteigne, might be better placed than we to get news of these matters, since the fugitives had ridden northwards. In the meantime, the earl took steps at once, calling up the entire knight service of England and bidding them travel day and night to come soon to Worcester. But the process of getting all those local levies into motion was always slow, even in emergencies, as the monarchy had acknowledged already by its increasing inclination towards paid soldiers, whose whole business it is to get into action with the least delay, and stay out their term without grudging. By the time the ponderous engine moved, there was a marcher army barring the passage of the Severn at Worcester, and the order to the knights was changed to call them to Gloucester, which the earl had left well garrisoned.

Thus things stood when Cadell rode into Hereford, and delivered us by word of mouth the news Llewelyn had not stayed to have written down.

'My lord, we have found him! The secret was well kept, but this is sure: The Lord Edward, when he fled, was met and escorted to Mortimer's castle of Wigmore, where the lady hid him while the hunt was up, and as soon as the way was clear sent him on to Ludlow. Geoffrey de Genevill is away in Ireland, and may not even know the use made of his castle, but his wife is a de Breose, and they are all kin, and all marchers. And there Roger Mortimer was waiting for him. And there, the next day, Earl Gilbert of Gloucester came to join them. Gloucester was in it from the beginning!'

'Gloucester – hand in glove with Mortimer?' said Earl Simon. 'It cannot be true! The man had agreed to parley with us! For all his waywardness, I trusted him!'

'It is true, my lord,' said Cadell. 'He was never worth your trust, for all these weeks he has been playing his own game and Edward's, holding your eyes and ears upon himself while this plan was laid and hatched. They are in the field now, all their forces joined, and moving down the Severn valley, and if they are not in Worcester by this, as they are certainly between you and that city, it is no more than a day or two before they take it.' And he said, awed by Earl Simon's face, which was still as stone and yet sick with grief, like a carved mourner on a Calvary: 'The Lord Edward himself has taken over the leadership of the army.'

Earl Simon in his own unaltered voice, courteous and low, thanked him for his pains and dismissed him. When there was no other with us in the room he said, as though to himself: 'Gloucester!' and hung upon the name again and again with incredulity and pain, for never had he learned to be prepared for the faithlessness of men. And suddenly he cried out against him, and against Edward, for the cheats, dissemblers and liars they were, and against himself for the trust he had placed in creatures so devious, and swore that Edward had deprived himself of all rights in land or revenue or privilege in England, and deserved to lose his claims to the realm, for he had of his own will taken the oath, under pain of that loss, and he must abide the consequences of his own act. And forthwith he burned into a passionate fury of activity, dictating letters setting out this same theme, and dispatching them to the lords of Ireland, to the men of all the shires, and to the bishops, on whom he urged the solemn duty of renewing the sentence of excommunication against those who had betrayed the cause and shattered the peace. He also redoubled his efforts to build up by loans and other means a reserve of treasure to be laid up at St Frideswide's priory in Oxford, for clearly the greatest strength of his cause was in London and the cities and shires of England, and to reach London and rally all the scattered forces he must take the road through Oxford, which was invincibly friendly to him. The bitterness of his disillusionment never caused him to abandon hope or to give up the fight, even though he found the most of men hardly worth saving, and hardly deserving of the justice and good government he had wanted for them.

But before he moved east into England, as he knew he must do, there were certain things he had in mind to set right, that he might leave no loose threads behind him.

On the nineteenth day of June he sent for me. 'Master Samson,' he said, 'do you know at this moment where to find your lord? I would have you go to him yourself with what I have to say, and present my envoys to him. And they will be not only my envoys, but the envoys of England and of King Henry.'

I said that Llewelyn was no more than twenty miles from us, with the greater part of his force then marshalled along the border. He was encamped at Pipton on the Wye, due west of Hereford by way of Hay, and he had with him there a good half of his council and several of his chief vassals, Rhys Fychan of Dynevor and both the lords of Powys among them.

'So much the better,' said Earl Simon, 'if he is attended in some splendour. This is what I would have you say to him.'

And he taught me such a message as uplifted my heart with joy and eagerness, and had me also write a letter which should further expound his purpose, already in those few words made plain.

That same day I rode, with Peter de Montfort of Beaudesert and certain knights of his train, and also various clerks and chancery lawyers, and we came to Pipton before evening, and to the prince's camp in the rich meadows above the river Wye. In that summer country, with no close enemy, the camp lay spread among green fields and uplands, most princely, and when our party was sighted and reported to him, Llewelyn came out to meet us, glowing with the weeks spent in the sun, and splendidly attended.

When he saw me, and weighed the quality and gravity of those who followed me into his camp, I saw behind his composed and gracious face and warm welcome the wonder and curiosity that filled him, and I rejoiced to be the instrument of his glory and gain. For though he had waited a great while for this day, he did not foresee its coming even now, when it fell ripe into his hands.

We dismounted, and when I had made my obeisance I stood before Llewelyn in all solemnity, as the messenger of another lord to whom he had lent me, and delivered with a swelling heart the embassage with which I was entrusted.

'My lord, Simon de Montfort, earl of Leicester and ancestral steward of England, sends his greetings to the Lord Llewelyn, prince of Wales. By that style and title he addresses you, and he desires that you will receive the mission of these lords from the crown of England with goodwill, to the intent that the king of England and the prince of Wales may compound for a treaty of peace between their two countries.'

The blood so left his face, all his bronze blanched into the palest and clearest of gold, and his eyes burned from deep brown into glowing red with passion and gladness. But the hour was too great and too sudden for elation. Princely he bade them in to lodging, when I had presented them all, and feasted and served them, and sat down with them to bear their business.

Not then did I have leisure to tell him what the earl had said further when he sent me forth, though long afterwards I told him all. How he had said that before leaving Hereford to go to his testing, in the sure knowledge of his own mortality that ensured him here no steadfast stay, he would do right to the prince of Wales, whose loyalty to his word was a gem-stone in this wilderness of falsehood, who had never promised more than he meant to perform, or failed to perform what he did promise. Surely he meant to bind Llewelyn to him even more closely by this act, yet I believe it was not a price offered for future favours, but an acknowledgement of help already given, and more than all, a free act for his own soul's sake, as truly as largesse or prayer.

I think there was never a treaty so momentous made and ratified in so few days, and with so little argument. So I said later to the earl, and he smiled, and said that might well be because it was long overdue, and no one could well object to it as unjust. Yet afterwards there were many who did so object, blaming Earl Simon bitterly for conceding so much in the name of England.

When the lord of Beaudesert had had his say, Llewelyn set out his own terms.

'In the king's name I am promised recognition of my title and right as prince of Wales, with the overlordship of all my fellow-princes, the remission of any illwill the king may still bear to me, the repudiation of all documents that infringe or cast doubts upon my right and title, and the retention of all my present possessions. It is very fairly offered, and I have little more to demand, but that little is important to me. My border is long, and in places vulnerable, lacking the proper protection of castles I can hold as bases. I ask for nothing which has not in old times been Welsh, but I do ask that I may have acknowledged title to such Welsh ground as I may still recover from the king's rebels in the marches. I have in mind such lands as were taken from my grandsire Llewelyn ap Iorwerth, or my uncle David ap Llewelyn. I ask also for certain other castles which are vital for the protection of Wales, namely, Painscastle, Hawarden and Whittington. And in return I am willing to pledge my duty and fealty to the king, and to aid and support,' said Llewelyn with emphasis, 'the present lawful government of England against all its enemies.'

There was some mild demur over these castles he named, and Peter de Montfort said, justly, that these were great concessions, and could not be lightly made. Llewelyn replied as courteously that he well understood that, and they were not lightly asked, for he was prepared to pay a fair indemnity for his gains. The price he offered was thirty thousand marks, to be paid over a period of ten years. It was a great sum, and they opened their eyes respectfully at it, as well they might. It must be said that Llewelyn's housekeeping was exceedingly able and practical; he could and did command large sums when he needed them, and his reputation for prompt payment was high, as the English acknowledged. I suppose no prince ever devised a means of moneying so perfect that it did not lean heavily on someone, but there were few complaints of injustice or misuse in Wales during his rule.

Since every man there desired the treaty, it was very readily made. There were certain elaborating letters written separately, though Llewelyn also stated the gist of them there and then.

'The agreement is with this lawful government, and with King Henry as head of it. If the king should default from his adherence, which God forbid, my obligation to him ceases, until he shall again be in good faith with his magnates. And should the king die, and leave a successor who adheres to the settlement, then I will go on paying the indemnity to him, or, if the lawful community of the realm so desires, I will pay otherwise, but in all events, I will continue to discharge my debts.'

They agreed this was fair, and thereupon the documents were drawn up. We slept overnight in Llewelyn's camp, and when we left with the dawn, for time was short for Earl Simon's business, the prince drew me aside for the only personal exchange we had during that visit.

'Samson,' he said, 'there is one more thing I most earnestly request of the earl of Leicester, and that I would ask of him myself. Say to him that I greatly desire him to meet with me, and ask him to ride the few miles to the abbey of Dore tomorrow, or to appoint me some other place and time, or give me safe-conduct to come to Hereford if need be, for he is pressed, I know. But do not fail me. Unless you send Cadell with other word, I shall go to Dore tomorrow.'

I wondered but did not question, for he asked it as a young man asking favour of someone to whom he owed deference, and that was not his way, and his face had that bright intensity, and his eyes that wonder, that I had seen there whenever he looked within at his vision, as now he was able to see it openly under the sun, without turning his gaze into his own heart. Therefore there was still something secret to him still wanting, and all things else, all that triumph, remained at risk until it was won. So I said that I would press his wish, and was sure it would not be denied.

Nor was it. For when I preferred it to Earl Simon on my return to Hereford, he lifted his head from the letters he was studying, and looked at me with those deep eyes now so large and lambent in their sockets of bone, and said: 'I, too, have long nursed the same wish. Nor will it be time lost, even by the measure of England's need, for I can better plan my movements now with Llewelyn in person than by letter or courier. We go, Samson, south to Gwent as soon as this treaty is made fast, and if Llewelyn will go with me and keep my flank, the rest I will do.'

I was then so close with him, and so concerned for him, and he so acknowledged that bond, that I could and did ask him what plans he had in that southern march.

'To cut off de Valence and his force from crossing to join the rebels,' said Earl Simon, 'and to secure such of Earl Gilbert's castles in Gwent as I can, and cross by Newport into the safety of Bristol, and so to Oxford and London. Plainly I shall be dependent on the prince of Wales for supplies and support during that passage. I have sworn, and I will keep my oath, that he shall not be asked – never by me! –to put his Wales in peril by committing himself out of its bounds. But within those bounds he is an army to me. And I will go to Dore to meet him, with all my heart.'

He bade me ride with him the next day, for he would go otherwise unattended. To that great Cistercian house it was no more than ten miles, for him a breath of freedom in this punishing time. For Llewelyn it was a much longer ride, he must have risen before the sun. We went,

Earl Simon and I, after morning mass from Hereford, but when we came to that glorious rosy-grey house in the blossoming valley, all gilded and green with summer, Llewelyn was there before us.

In the quiet courts of the Cistercian house of Dore, golden indeed that June, under a sky like periwinkle flowers, those two met and joined hands at last.

I watched them come together, I knew the desire that drew them, and the weight of wonder and thought that made their steps so slow and their eyes so wide as they crossed the few paces of earth that parted them. From the moment they set eyes upon each other they looked neither to left nor right, each taking in the other like breath and food and wine. And it seemed to me, when their hands linked and grew together, that there was in them, for all their differences, for they did not look alike at all, some innermost thing that set up a mirror between them, and showed each his own face. Also I saw that Llewelyn had come, like the earl, almost unattended, only one of Goronwy's sons at his back, and that there was a shining splendour upon him, for all this simplicity, that made him unwontedly beautiful and solemn. His dress, that was never planned to impress, was that day most choice in dark and gold. He looked as a prince should look.

'My lord of Leicester,' he said, and stooped to touch with his lips the hand he still held, as fittingly and royally he could, with the awareness of destiny upon him, 'I rejoice that I see you at last, and I thank you for this kindness. I have long desired your acquaintance, and I wish the times better favoured me, for I know I trespass.'

'No,' said Earl Simon, and looked at him long and hungrily, and saw. I think, as I saw, the heart's likeness that surely was there, for still the mirror shone between them. 'No, you refresh me. I have many times had need of you, and need you still. I had believed it was for a cause. I think it was also for my soul's sake. In my desert now there are not many springs.'

He had known deserts in his time, for he had been a crusader.

'My lord,' said Llewelyn, 'I desire all of your company that I may have, but my time is silver, while yours is golden, and I will not hamper your movements, not for my life. So I speak directly. Your son, my lord, I have known and loved some years. You I have loved without knowing you. Until today! My lord Simon, you have also a daughter.'

'I have,' said the earl, enlightened, and smiled, remembering her. 'She is with her mother and my youngest sons in the castle of Dover.'

'And she is not yet affianced? Nor promised to any?' He drew deep breath at the earl's nodded assent, and under his tan he was white to the lips with passion and diffidence, as he said: 'My lord, if it will please you to entertain and favour my suit, I would ask of you your daughter's hand in marriage.'

CHAPTER XII

What he asked, that he had. Earl Simon leaned to him and laid both hands upon his shoulders, and kissed him upon the cheek with the kiss of kinship, for acceptance and blessing.

'My daughter is yet young,' he said, 'not quite thirteen years. But there is no man to whom I would more gladly confide her than the prince of Wales, and none among all those not my sons I would so joyfully welcome as a son. With all my heart I promise her to you, and will record the vow here and now, if you so please.'

So simply was this match made, and so hard afterwards to make, so quickly closed with, and so long awaiting fulfilment. Those two went in together and exchanged their vows in the church of Dore, and from that moment Llewelyn's resolution never wavered.

Until the late afternoon they remained together in the hospice at Dore, and talked together of everything that bound them, first and most urgently of the earl's plans, and the stages by which Llewelyn would match them on his western flank, appointing certain places where messages could readily be exchanged, and further stores delivered for the provisioning of the earl's army. Upon such details they were both brisk and practical, and those few hours were well used. Then they talked also of what hopefully must become family affairs, and of the child Eleanor, on whom Llewelyn had fixed his heart, never having seen her.

'And I confess,' he said ruefully, 'I doubted my right to ask for her, being so much her elder, but I promise you there could no suitor of her own years cherish and care for her as truly as I will, if she also willingly accepts me.'

The earl said, smiling: 'Master Samson, who has been in some degree her friend for a while, can tell you that she has already pursued him with many questions about you and your country. I doubt if she had marriage in mind, then, but you could hardly have had a better advocate to satisfy her curiosity.'

'You have not heard him,' said Llewelyn, 'on the subject of the lady! You do not know how closely I questioned him, or how I have pictured her out of his praises.'

Then her father also talked of her, with love and pleasure, and watching his face soften at the thought of her, I began to understand how great refreshment he found in this day stolen from his immense and crushing cares, all the more because the lady might not many years more have a father to provide and care for her, and it was ease and blessing to him to know that she would have a worthy husband to shield and love her after him. So I came to understand that he entertained ungrudgingly, in that proud, devout and humble mind, the daily possibility of his own death, and took thought for his responsibilities. His wife was the king's sister, and for all her fierce loyalty to the earl could not be allowed to miscarry, for the king's own credit. His sons were men, and could fend for themselves. His daughter was another matter. Lords marry their daughters for many reasons, most of them tied to property and land, and certainly it was no mean thing to be the princess of Wales, but this was no such betrothal for gain, nor was his consent given to persuade Llewelyn to more aid than had been freely tendered. The offer for Eleanor, coming from a man he respected and trusted, was pleasure and release to him. Each of them had come to that meeting bearing a gift of great price.

By the time they parted, late in the afternoon, they had probed each other deep, and reached into those lofty places beyond the art and practice of government, where Earl Simon's visions still shone undimmed after all his disillusionments, half understood with the mind, half sensed with the heart and spirit and blood, no less valid because all men but one fell away from loyalty to them. And I think those two were content with each other, and that there was no falling short.

So we rode back through the early evening to Hereford, and Llewelyn to Pipton. And the next day King Henry set his seal to the treaty, naming Llewelyn prince of Wales, and Peter de Montfort of Beaudesert rode to Pipton and delivered it into the prince's hand.

The day after that we marched, all that great tangle of king, courtiers, officials, clerks, judges, soldiers, south to Monmouth. The last letter patent sent from Hereford was an urgent order to young Simon, in Surrey, to muster all the levies of the shires, and hurry north-west to his father's aid.

If young Simon had indeed been near enough to get his men to the eastern side of Gloucester before the castle fell, and Earl Simon had closed in to meet him from the west, they might well have broken Edward's army between them. But it is a long march from Surrey to the western border, and I doubt if the young man ever truly realised how urgently he was needed, and how much hung upon his coming. Even if he had, it might well have altered nothing, for about the time we moved from Hereford the castle of Gloucester fell, and there was then no crossing of the Severn left to us but by going south.

Only then, I think, did even the earl himself realise how desperate was his situation, thus cut off in the hostile marches from that solid body of support for him that habited in the English cities and shires. With both Worcester and Gloucester closed against him, he hastened his march south, and attacked and took, without much trouble, the earl of Gloucester's castles in the vale of Usk, first possessing Monmouth and establishing a base there, then going on to take Usk, and Newport itself. And all this time Llewelyn with his main force kept pace with us, almost at arm's length, and supplied us all our needs.

As for the earl's first declared objective, to sever the force in Pembroke from all possibility of joining Edward, that hope was lost before ever we reached Usk, for William of Valence was already across the old passage of the estuary of Severn, and had added his strength to Edward's outside Gloucester. That formidable army, most formidably led, came surging south on the opposite bank, and occupied all the English shore.

The old passage of Severn at the opening of the estuary was well known to us, and quick and easy, given proper use of the tides, but it needed boats none the less, and under archery, and facing a landing upon a shore heavily occupied by an enemy, it was impossible. There could only be a massacre. Earl Simon sent out scouts, and accepted their bitter verdict. For him there was no way over into England by that route. Moreover, detachments of Edward's army were moving along the road between Monmouth and Gloucester, and there was no returning to Hereford by that way, either.

There was but one way he could go, and that was deeper into Wales, and that at least was made easy for him by Llewelyn's presence in force in the hills, where he had greatly strengthened his hold on the roadways that threaded the disputed land of Gwent. Cadell rode ahead as courier to inform the prince of our need, and he came down himself into the valley of Usk to meet and accompany the earl to a safe camp already waiting in the hills.

So those two met again, and though Llewelyn in delicacy held aloof from meeting king or officials, and confined his personal encounters to Earl Simon and his son, now his own kinsmen, nevertheless it was strange to see the court of England, sorry and suspect court though it was, guided and guarded and provided food and rest under the wing of the prince of Wales, and so shepherded back by stages in a half-circle towards Hereford. And safe they were under that guardianship, but ineffective. No man could touch them with impunity, but neither could they advance their own cause. No base in Wales could avail the earl to strike effectively at his enemies. No Welsh army, even had all the forces at Llewelyn's disposal been committed to him, could restore him to his severed support in England. The greater the numbers he had to spirit across the Severn, the more inevitable was a premature battle, before they could join hands with young Simon, hurrying north from Oxford.

That was a strange time, that journey through Gwent and Brecknock, like the quiet place at the heart of a great storm. For now the stream of ordinances and letters had ceased, as though all the business of state held its breath, and they were but a great multitude of ordinary men, making their way unhindered and unpressed through a summer country of hills and forests and heathland, camping in the calm and warmth of July nights, and listening, unstartled by rattle of steel or sound of trumpet, to a silence deeper than memory. And sometimes at night, when the wretched tired, apathetic king was sleeping, and the camp settled into stillness, Earl Simon sat with Llewelyn, and the talk they had was not all of wars and treaties and disputes, but of high, rare things that both had glimpsed and both desired to comprehend more fully, if all the ways by which they sought to reach them had not turned about treacherously under their feet, and brought them round in a circle, as now, to the place from which they had set out. For I suppose that this life is but the early part of the pilgrimage, and the search will continue in another place.

In the last days of July we came again to the uplands above Valley Dore, and saw below us, beside the stream in the blanched hay-fields, the rosy grey of the great church where they had first met.

'A month lost,' said Llewelyn ruefully, 'to reach the same place.'

'No month is ever lost,' said Earl Simon. 'Certainly not this. Whatever follows, I may tell you so with truth. But now you must come no further with me. For across the Severn I must go, by some means, however desperate, or there is no future.'

'I am coming with you,' said Llewelyn, 'as far as Hereford, for I have sent some of my men of Elfael, who know these parts and have kin on both sides the border, to spy out the state of the river ahead of you. It's high summer, and little rain now for weeks, there may well be possible fords where no one will think to guard. Our rivers are low, so should Severn be. And I have stores waiting for you below.'

'It could not last,' said Earl Simon with a grim smile. 'In Wales my cause cannot be won, nor yours out of it. And my men tire of your shepherd's table and long for their bread and ale. It is high time to go.'

It was past time, and I think he knew it already. But one last night they conferred together, with young Henry, and Peter of Beaudesert and a few others in attendance, and Llewelyn offered a company of lancers to be added to the earl's foot-soldiery, though without Welsh captains. Thus drafted into the English ranks, they did not commit Wales and its prince. And that reservation the earl understood, and did not blame by word or look. It was Llewelyn who agonised within himself, ashamed and tempted, torn between two duties that could not be reconciled, and no longer sure what was duty and what desire. And the next day his scouts came back with word that Edward was making his chief base at Worcester, expecting that crossing to be attempted, and also on the watch for young Simon's army, which was known to be approaching from the south, and thought to be heading for Kenilworth. At that the earl drew breath cautiously, and approved his son's choice.

'In Kenilworth we could be safe enough, and hold off siege as long as need be. If he makes all secure, and I can get my men across and reach him there, we have time to rally the rest of England. The Severn is the only bar.'

'My lord,' said the messenger, 'I have had speech in Hereford with the steward from the bishop of Worcester's manor on the river at Kempsey. The water is low, he says it might be forded there with care, the country people use it in dry summers. But it is barely four miles from Worcester, you could only attempt it by night.'

'There will be guides,' said Llewelyn, 'to show the way.' For the country people were always, without exception, silently but dourly upon Earl Simon's side.

So the army rested that night, and the next day – it was the last day of July – we left the Welsh forces behind, all but those lancers who were drafted into the earl's foot companies, and with a small party escorted the wandering court of King Henry some way beyond the border, and parted from them only when they were drawing near to Hereford.

They did not halt the march, but Earl Simon laid a hand upon Llewelyn's bridle, and checked and drew aside with him to a knoll above the road, and young Henry and I reined after them, and waited. Henry, being also a kinsman, and I, unasked, because I had here two masters and two roads to go, and was as doubtful as Llewelyn what was right and what wrong. So we sat a few moments watching the knights and troopers riding by, and after them the ranks of the foot soldiers. And I watched Llewelyn's face rather out of compassion than for guidance, and saw how he was torn. His countenance was set and still, but not calm. There was sweat on his forehead.

'Here you must leave us,' said the earl, and again, reining close, offered the kiss, and Llewelyn leaned to it and embraced him. 'For all your aid, and for your company,' said Earl Simon, 'I thank you, and with all my heart I wish you well.'

'In the name of God!' said Llewelyn in anguish, and still held him. 'How can I let you go to this trial without me?'

'You have mapped your own way,' said Earl Simon, 'and I approve you. In your place I would do as you have done. Go back to your own fortune, and bear your own burden. And take this with you,' he said, and shook out from the pocket in his sleeve a small rondel that caught the sun in a delicate flash of painted colours, like an enamelled brooch. 'I had forgotten I had it with me,' he said, 'until last night I made my peace, and destroyed all that I carried of regrets and vain memories. This is not vain. I give it to you as a visible pledge and earnest, against a future too dark to be seen very clearly at this moment. At such times it is well to see one thing clear.'

And he smiled, a sudden brightness as though his soul soared like a bird, and laid the rondel in Llewelyn's palm, and so would have wheeled away from him and spurred after the head of his column, but I reined into his path, for I, too, had rights and duties and desires.

'My lord,' I said, 'if my prince releases me still, I am still in your service, and I have not deserved dismissal.'

He looked from me to Llewelyn, who sat holding the earl's gift in his hand like the relic of a saint, but had not so much as lowered his eyes to it, so captive was he to the giver.

'No!' said Earl Simon. 'Neither have you deserved that I should take you with me where I am going, and you have no protection but mine, all fallible as it may prove. Go back with your lord, Samson, friend, and serve him as before.'

Then I, too, looked at Llewelyn, stricken and torn between us, and I said: 'He is my lord, and it is his bidding I take, and him I shall be serving. And his command I wait, my lord earl, and not yours.'

There was a moment while everything hung like a hawk before the stoop, and I held my breath, feeling my desire and Llewelyn's desire burn utterly into one, as we two shared the same stars at birth. And after a moment he got out of him: 'You have my order. I bid you go with the earl of Leicester, and see him to his triumph in my name!' His voice was sudden and vehement, yet quiet as the flood of a lowland river in spring.

I knew then that he had understood me as I understood him, and in obeying him I took him with me wheresoever I went.

'So I will, my lord,' I said, 'and bring word to you again.'

Once before I had thought that Earl Simon might deny with anger, being so used to obedience, and he had not denied. Even so now he looked back and eyed us mildly, my lord and me, and found no fault. For he so felt the largeness and dignity of his own person that he could not grudge the same to others.

'In the name of God!' he said. 'So, come, and welcome!' Then he looked a moment upon Llewelyn, his head reared and his eyes wide to take in all that hunger and thirst that coveted me my place, and next he shook his rein, and was away after the slow-moving head of his column, and I as dutifully after him.

From the corner of my eye I saw young Henry de Montfort embrace and kiss with Llewelyn, I think without words. He overtook me soon. We fell into our places near the head of the marching column, and the last day of July declined slowly in sunshine and heat.

In the evening and night of the second of August we forded the Severn opposite the manor of Kempsey, making down to the water where there was cover from willows. Some of Bishop Walter's people had been on the watch for us, and stood by to show the best passage. The water was still high enough, but leisurely in its flow, and the bottom firm and smooth, without hazards. A slow business it was, but accomplished before dawn, and at Kempsey we had some rest before the sun rose, for the bishop's household was staunch like its master, and willing to take risks for the earl's cause.

Earl Simon asked urgently after any news of his son's coming with the reinforcements from the south, and the bishop's steward told him what he could.

'All we know,' said he, 'is that the Lord Simon's muster was reported to be nearing Kenilworth two days ago, and that same day the lord Edward left Worcester with a large force and took them eastwards to try and intercept. Since then we have heard nothing, and last night I sent a groom to the city to gather what news he can. He'll set out for home again at first light.'

It is barely four miles from Kempsey to Worcester, and as we were breaking our fast after mass the groom rode in, and was brought to Earl Simon.

'My lord,' he said, 'forgive me if I waste no words to better what is not good. Time is too short. The Lord Edward returned to Worcester with all his force last night. My lord, they brought prisoners with them – noble prisoners!'

'My son?' questioned Earl Simon, low of voice and still of face.

'No, my lord, not he. He escaped them, and is in Kenilworth with the remnant of his following. But I saw the arms of the earl of Oxford, and there were others, barons and knights, all brought into Worcester captive. As I heard it, they surprised your son's force outside the castle, at the priory, where they had lodged overnight, reaching Kenilworth in the early dark, and thinking themselves safe, so near to home.'

'Folly!' said Earl Simon in a harsh cry, and knotted his hands in exasperation. 'To halt outside the walls, with such an enemy as Edward so close! He has lost me good men when I needed them most. How many got into the castle with him? Can you say?'

But there was no way of knowing, or of being certain who was free and who prisoner, nor was there any time to lament longer over losses and opportunities thrown away.

'He has not learned yet to recognise urgency, or to make sure of his intelligence,' said Earl Simon grimly. 'And Edward is already back in Worcester with all his force! I take that to mean he hurried back so soon for my sake. He believes me still on the far side of Severn, and thinks I must attempt to storm the crossing there, as my only way over. I have but one advantage left, that I am already on the English side. But only four miles from him! I could be happier if the four were forty. We are barely through his lines, we must move east as far and as fast as we may, clear of his shadow. In the middle of England I am his match, but here in the marches the power is in his hands.' He thought some moments and said: 'We march in three hours.'

They held brief council, and agreed it was our best policy to move rapidly, before it was realised that we were over the river and through the cordon. Eastwards we must go, and the earl chose to march for Evesham, to put his host on the best and easiest road either northeast from that town by Alcester, to join young Simon and the remnant of his force in Kenilworth, which was as near invulnerable as a castle could well be, or southeast by Woodstock to Oxford and London, for throughout those shires his following was strong and loyal, and there were enough scattered companies of his following to rally to him and make him invincible. Even though I dreaded that his treaty with Llewelyn might have angered some of his noble adherents, their pride being shocked at ceding so much to Wales, yet I knew that the hold he had upon the lesser nobility and the common people would not be shaken. Could he reach Oxford, then his cause was saved.

Nevertheless, we did not march at the third hour, as he had said, for when the time drew near, King Henry was so fast asleep, and so like a worn-out infant in his helplessness, that they had not the heart to awake him. Earl Simon himself went and looked upon him, intending not to spare where he himself and everything he held dear were not spared, but the oblivious face of his king and brother by marriage, stained and loose and exhausted with being dragged up and down the marches, and showing innocent and piteous in sleep, held him at gaze a long time, and turned him away disarmed and resigned. Surely he knew what he risked with every hour lost, but he said: 'Let him have his sleep out!'

Every man among us needed rest, for though we had the better part of this day, little of it was spent in sleep, most in tending our beasts, as jaded as we, making good all that was amiss with arms and equipment, and darkening what little was left bright about us, for the sun was glaring and cloudless, and would be so until well into the evening, and could betray us at a mile or more. We had marched almost ceaselessly since leaving Llewelyn, and this after all those weeks of scouring the borders south and west and north again to find a way back into England. Still we kept order, discipline and pride. No army of Earl Simon's could let go of those. But for the rest, we were by then a dusty, travel-worn, hungry and footsore company. We had few remounts, or none, only the handful of beasts the bishop's grooms could provide us, and many of us went on foot with the archers and men-at-arms by choice, to ease our over-ridden horses.

So we set out in the early hours of the evening, that third day of August, King Henry like a tired child still querulous and complaining, and those around him attentive and courteous but remorseless, for time trod hard on our heels, and we had learned to respect the efficiency of Edward's spies. From Kempsey on the Severn to Evesham on the Avon is roughly fourteen miles of rich, green, smiling country, full of cornfields and orchards, the grain whitening in the sun when we passed that way, and the meadows full of flowers. Laden as we were, we gave thanks when the sun declined and left us the cool of the night, and into the night we still marched, not knowing how far behind us the inevitable pursuit must be. It could not be long before word reached Edward that his enemy was across the river and brushing past his shoulder into freedom.

So we came, halfway through the night, into Evesham, dropping down from the softly rolling upland fields northwest of the town into the wide meadows about the abbey. And there we halted and rested while Earl Simon conferred with his close council in the abbey itself. He knew, none better, how urgent it was to press on, but he was in doubt whether to cross the Avon and strike south-west for Oxford, or turn north towards his own Kenilworth, and in Evesham he hoped to get word whether Edward had yet moved, and in which direction. The best of our horses had gone to his scouts, and they were appointed to meet him again at the abbey. This alone would have caused him some short delay, but indeed many of his commanders urged that, danger or no danger, the men could not go on further without rest and food, and the king was again drooping and weary. When the first of his scouts rode in and reported that Edward had moved from Worcester in fiery haste, but towards Alcester, clearly expecting the earl to attempt to join his forces with those of his son at Kenilworth, Earl Simon accepted the verdict of all, and agreed to a stay of some hours for food and rest before pushing on towards Oxford, the road it seemed he was not expected to take.

Neither he nor any other amongst us had yet experienced the speed and wit and ferocity with which Edward could think and move. It was true that he had made straight for Alcester to cut the road to Kenilworth, but at such a pace that even with this detour he gained ground on us, and hearing reliably that we had not passed through Alcester, immediately turned south and began to close in on Evesham, racing to cut us off also from the road to Oxford and London. We did not know it then, though the storm of his pursuit was in the air, a troubling of the night.

Howbeit, we rested in Evesham, and with the dawn we heard mass and broke our fast. And in the early light the watchman on the tower of the great abbey church sounded the alarm, and cried down to us that the sun on the uplands to the north had caught for a moment a distant glitter of steel. Then we mustered in haste and made ready to move, for the way to Oxford should still be open to us, and every mile that we gained along it would add to our strength.

But before we so much as moved off through the town, a messenger came galloping in wildly from that direction, and cried from the saddle: 'My lord, the road's blocked against us beyond the bridge! A yeoman from Badsey came in by that way not ten minutes since. He has seen them, a great force, moving round from the west to shut us in. He barely got by before they straddled the road. He saw the banner and livery of Mortimer!'

Then we knew that we were taken in a trap from which there was no escape, if Edward was driving down upon us from the north to pen us into the loop of the river that encircles the town, and Mortimer waiting for us on the southern bank. Between the moat of Avon and the ring of marcher armies the noose about us was complete.

I watched Earl Simon's face then, and I saw in it no surprise at all, as though in the inmost places of his soul he had already known this ending beforehand, and learned to contemplate it without lowering his eyes. The grief I saw in him was strong and stable and calm as a rock. And from that moment there was, in a sense, no more urgency. For all that it was now possible to do, we had time enough.

'I had thought to bring you safely to a better stand,' said the earl, 'without committing you to a fight here against the odds. But since there's no other way now for us, let us see what manner of ending we can make. If we have nothing else, we have the choice of ground.'

As deliberately as at some noble exercise he might marshal the lists, so he led his army to the higher ground north of the abbey, to deliver that holy place from his too close presence, and there set out his array, mainly directing his strength against the north, from which Edward must come, but so contriving that we should be able to fight on all sides, for Mortimer surely would not stay out of the battle, though he might come too late to get much glory out of us. Such archers as he had, no great number, the earl placed flanking the lancers, to give what cover they might, for it was certain that Edward had far more knights and heavily armed troopers than we had, and it is ill for light-armed foot soldiers to stand up to cavalry charges. King Henry he set in the midst, with all his own chivalry ringed strongly about him. And when all was ready, he asked absolution for us all from the prior of Evesham, and bade us take what rest we could while we could, for since we could go nowhere, but were arrived at that place to which we had been travelling without our knowledge, there was now no haste to strain beyond, for what was beyond would come to us.

Then there was indeed a calm, however ominous, yet sound and true, and rest they did, on the grass in their stations, while they quietly whetted their edges and strung their bows, and hitched scabbard and quiver ready to hand, and the lancers dug themselves firm grounding for the butts of their lances. Earl Simon took some of his closest companions with him, and went up to the tower of the abbey church to view the approach of the army from the north, and happening to see me among his swordsmen, paused and frowned for a moment, and then called me also to go with them.

The sun was fully risen and high in the sky by that time, and clear in the distance along the dappled fields of the uplands we could see the faint, hanging curtain of glittering dust that moved steadily towards Evesham, and the sparks of colour, still tiny, that flashed through the haze. It was like the steady surge of a long wave on a beach, thrust by the incoming tide, as gentle and as irresistible. As it drew nearer, the colourings and the quarterings grew distinct to the eye, Edward's banners, and Gloucester's, Giffard's, Leyburn's, all those same young men who had banded themselves together in the marches in their hot discontent, and called Earl Simon back from France to lead them, not so long ago.

And yet I think they were not turncoats, nor traitors, though they could not keep the earl's steadfast mind. I do believe they tried to do what they saw as right, however hot blood and inexperience and self-interest and tangled loyalties confused them. And I know that he could find in him no hate or great blame for them as he watched them close about him like a mailed fist to crush him. When they opened their ranks, as they drew nearer, and formed their orderly array on the march, he looked upon them with approval, and smiled, and said: 'I taught them that.' And as if to himself he said, wondering and hopeful: 'If he can learn the discipline of battle, he can learn the discipline of statecraft, too. From his enemies, if need be. But even to a felon a prince should not break his word.' And I knew that he was making his last estimate, both just and critical, of Edward.

Then he shook himself, and turned to us whom he had called to attend him. To the justiciar, Hugh le Despenser, and his kinsman, Ralph Basset, who was warden of the shires in that region, he said seriously that they ought, and he so advised them, to take horse and escape out of this trap, for that was still possible for solitary riders, whom Edward would not break ranks to pursue even if he detected them. He said that they should remove in order to provide a voice for their cause at a better place and in a happier time, so that it should not be utterly silenced. And as one man they smiled, and refused him. He had said what he meant, but he would not urge or persuade. They had their way, and stayed with him.

As we went down again from the tower, leaving a watch behind to signal us from the distance the movements of those approaching, he took me by the arm, and said in my ear: 'Master Samson, this is not your fight nor your lord's fight, and he has a use for you for many years to come. Well I know I can give you no orders, you are not my man, but Llewelyn's and your own. But you are a clerk, and you have a right to sanctuary with the clerks that I have sent into the abbey. Go with them, and stand upon your right, and return whole to your lord. There is nothing better you can do for me.'

But with that fair example before me, out of which I believe he took as much comfort as grief, I also denied him.

'You heard,' I said, 'what Llewelyn said to me when he sent me with you. I am the custodian here of his honour and my own, and more than mere honour, of his love and mine. I will not leave you or separate my fate from yours while we both live. And God willing, I will carry Llewelyn word of your triumph as he bade me.'

'God's will,' said Earl Simon, 'is dark to us, but bright to those who will behold it afterwards. I am content. Do what you must.'

So we went down and took our places, every one. And he took bread and meat in his hands and ate as he stood, his horse gently grazing beside him, looking steadily towards the north.

The tips of the lances and the banners rose out of the crest, the mailed heads after them, all cased up in steel, then the steel-plated heads of the horses, and the turf vibrated and the earth beneath it shook with hooves. The line of horsemen spread and folded in upon us, a hand closing. Earl Simon wheeled his own knights into a fan, and all those braced spearheads went down, levelling as one. And then there was a great shout, and they were upon us.

What can be said about that battle, so unequal and so brief? They came rank after rank out of the ground, growing from the grass like seams of corn. I suppose now that they were not so many as they seemed, yet they outnumbered us twice over, and they could come, and recoil, and come again, and we could but stand, or fall where we stood. Yet I remember clearly that Edward was the spear-head of the first shock, he was the thrust of the lance, and time and again he sprang back only to recover like the gathering wind and sweep forward again. Whatever any man may deny to Edward, I have seen his appalling gallantry, fitter to kill than to spare, more ardent to kill than to live. Nor did his hate run away with him, this time. No, it carried him, like a destrier not subject to wounds or death. He made a method of his hate, for now not only his heart and blood, but also his mind and spirit were in it. And I saw, and I testify, that at the third onset he detached the heaviest-armed of his knights, and hurled them at the vulnerable point where our lancers and archers met, with all their weight fresh and vengeful, and orders to scatter and kill.

That charge, avoiding the earl's mounted men, shattered the Welsh foot, driving in where their spears were not braced, and crumpling them rank by rank, thrusting the long shafts aside and trampling the men. What could they do but break? The archers who gave them their only cover were ridden down, though they took some toll before they fell. The spear-men broke, left without weapons. They were used to fluid hill-fighting, thrust and run, double and strike again, with tree and bush to harbour them. Instead, they were exposed in open ground, ridden down and ridden over, rolled up like soiled rushes, swept aside before the storm-wind. They broke and ran, what else could they do? They scattered like hares over that heath and turf, plunged for shelter into cornfields and gardens, that barely covered them and sheltered them not at all.

But Edward had learned since Lewes. He detached but a minor part of his strength to pursue, the rest he concentrated about our tightening circle, and bit with all his teeth to devour us.

The half our beasts were crippled or dead, more than half our mounted knights left to the sword or mace, having broken their only lances. Those whose horses still could carry them kept a thin outer circle about the centre where the king was, huddled, dazed and shrinking while the fight raged round him. Those barons and knights and other troopers now bereft of horses drew close into an inner circle, and held off the second charge, and the third, with the sword, and the archers who still lived picked off without mercy the mounts of the attackers to bring them down within hand-grip. It was less a battle than a massacre. We had known from the beginning that no retreat was possible. Neither was surrender. Therefore the only end there could be was when all of us were dead, disabled or prisoner, or, for the last few of us, fled the field when everything else was lost. I marvel it took them as long as it did, our broken foot soldiers being scattered and slain, to make an end with the rest of us.

They had remounts, and used them. They had reserves of lances and arrows, and made good, leisurely use of those too, until we were stripped of all but our swords and daggers, and stood among the ramparts of our own dead. And still Edward struck, and circled, and struck again, with fury but without haste, and dimly it came to me, as I wheeled still to face the next thrust, that I should know the arms of the knight who kept so lightly and fiercely at Edward's left flank wherever he turned, and matched his movements like a twin brother. Quartered red and gold, the shield flickered before me here and there, a wandering sun, and was never still, until suddenly they drew off again to look for our weakest place in the circle, and for a moment my eyes were clear of sweat, and I saw on the red and gold the counter-coloured lions of Gwynedd. Then I knew the easy seat and the graceful carriage, though doubtless the harness he wore he had by Edward's grace and favour. Thus for the first time after two years I saw my breast-brother again closer than across the meadows of the Dee.

But that was near the end, and he did not see me, or if he did see me I was so streaked with sweat and dust and blood that he did not know me. Not then. The deaths of so many had levelled us all, man-at-arms and clerk and squire and earl all drew brotherly into the circle and kept one another's flanks faithfully as long as they could stand. Humphrey de Bohun the younger, the only great marcher lord who fought on the earl's side in that battle, went down wounded at my side. Peter de Montfort of Beaudesert, faithful from first to last without wavering, died trampled and hacked under Edward's final charge. So did Hugh le Despenser and Ralph Basset his kinsman, who had both refused to escape the slaughter and live for for a better day.

We were then but the sparse remnants of the circle, drawing in ever closer, and in that last charge they rode us down and crashed into the centre. I was shouldered from my feet and flung some yards aside by the great war-horse of one of Gloucester's knights, and escaped hooves and swords to be stunned against the ground. When I got my wits again and heaved myself up to my knees there was a swaying tangle of men, mounted and afoot, where our ring had been, and I hung winded and dazed at the rim of chaos, witness to the ending I could not prevent.

I saw the blow, but do not know who struck it, that sheered deep into Earl Simon's shoulder and neck, and sent him reeling back with blood drenching his left side. I heard young Henry shriek as his father fell, and saw him leap to intercept the following blow, with only a broken sword in his left hand, and his right arm dangling helpless, and saw the axe-stroke that split his skull and flung him dead over the earl's body. And Guy, the third of those brothers, lying wounded almost within touch of them, vainly stretched out a hand towards his father's empty sword-hand, that lay open and still in the dappled turf.

And I saw, and still I see when the winter is harsh and the night dark and all men show as evil, how two or three of the knights of Edward's army lighted down like eager hunters from their saddles, and reaved off Earl Simon's helmet, stripping the torn mail from his neck, that was already half-severed, and hewing off with random, butcher's strokes that noble head that had conceived, and almost achieved, a vision of order, justice and accord fit for a better world than this.

Then I could look no more, for everything was over.

I got to my feet, leaving my sword where it lay, and turning my back upon that dolorous sight walked aimlessly away, across the field littered with the bodies and arms and cast harness and crippled men. And it was due only to the king that I ever left that field alive. There were some of Edward's men still coursing at large about the fringes of the fight, hunting down fugitives, and one of them might well have dealt with me, but suddenly all their attention was drawn inward to the swaying mass of men I had left behind, for King Henry, buffeted and ridden down unrecognised among the rest, shrieked aloud in terror of his life that he was their king, and no enemy. And someone – they say it was that same Roger Leyburn who led the young men of the marches when they called Earl Simon home – was quick enough to understand and believe, and haled him grazed and frightened out of the press.

Those who had heard rallied eagerly to him. No one had any eyes for me, straying like a sleep-walker between the corpses. And it chanced that the horse of one of those who had leaped down in such haste to the kill was also straying, unhurt, to where there was clean grass to crop. I slid a hand down to gather the rein, and at the touch life leaped again in me like a stopped fountain, and I remembered I still had a lord, and had even a vow on my heart to carry this fatal field back to him, for better or worse to share with him all that burden I had come by at Evesham.

A fine, fresh horse it was, and from the corner of my eye I saw the fringes of thick woodland away to the north, where the Welsh lancers, such of them as survived to get so far, might well have gone to ground. I set my toe in the stirrup and mounted, and crouching low on his neck, drove my heels into his sleek sides and sent him away at a gallop towards the trees. And if any of the many cries that filled the air behind me was an alarm after my flight, it was lost among all the rest, for no man followed me. So I fled from that lamentable place.

*　　*　　*

378

All that night they hunted us, and I did not keep that fine horse, for the roads were watched, where I could have made use of him, and in the forest north of Evesham, where I was forced to go to cover, he was only a means of betrayal to me. I turned him loose at the edge of the wood where no one was in sight, and sent him off with a slash of a branch behind, to be picked up as a stray from the battlefield. And I took to the deep thickets, and put a stream between me and pursuit, in case they brought hounds after us, and there lay up until night, when I trusted the hunt would slacken. For Edward had his king to care for, and urgent matters enough to occupy his mind, and all those he most hated were already dead or captive, all the de Montfort race, all but the children with their mother in Dover, and young Simon agonising with dread and self-blame in Kenilworth, as yet unaware of his bereavement.

There were others of my own race there cowering in the bushes. The first I stumbled on drew a knife on me, and knowing him for what he was I spoke him quickly in Welsh, and he thanked God for me, and put up his weapon. Before nightfall we were seven living men who had thought to be dead. And to make but a short tale of this sorry escape, the hunt we had dreaded reached our station about dusk. We heard hooves on the narrow ride apart from us, and voices high and confident in victory, and the threshing of bushes. We were crouched in thick growth, and lay still as stones, but even so one of those riders checked, and pricked his ears and turned aside towards us. I never traced the moment when he dismounted and slid forward afoot, so lightly and silently he stepped, until a hand thrust through the branches and parted them right before my face, and a face looked down at me between the leaves.

Tall and straight and arrogant he stood, staring down into my face with eyes wide-open and light blue as harebells, fringed with lashes as black as his uncovered hair, for he went unhelmed and light-armed to this cleansing work. Even in the dusk the blue of those eyes shone. He knew me, and I knew him. I got up from my hiding-place and stood fronting him, and I knew he had a drawn sword in his right hand while the left hand held the bushes apart between us.

He never said word to me then, neither smiled nor frowned. His face was as still as marble, and as mute. Only when someone called to him from the ride did he utter a word. He turned his head, and cried back through the trees: 'No, nothing! Go forward, I'm coming!'

He had ears as quick as the fox in the covert, he knew there were more of us, though not, perhaps, how many. He held the screen apart between us a moment more, and as his hand was withdrawn I think the pure, motionless stone of his face shook with the wryest of smiles, before it drew back and vanished.

'Go safely, and give thanks to God!' said David, low-voiced, and was gone like a shadow, the forest hardly quivering after his passage.

CHAPTER XIII

It took us four days to get back into Wales, moving only at night, and we were twenty souls in company by the time we swam the Severn below Stoke, for we dared not go near Kempsey, knowing Bishop Walter must suffer by what had already passed, and could not and must not afford us any comfort now. Nevertheless, we came safely to Presteigne at last, and thence to Knighton. Some wounded we had, but them we sustained in the water between us when we were forced to swim, and nursed among us as we went on land. And often I thought how the news of Evesham must have gone before me, and pierced Llewelyn to the heart, and I not there to perform the duty that was mine. And yet I was bringing him twenty good men back for the price of my delay, and I could not but think that my debts were fairly paid.

As for thinking of what I had left behind me, or of what I had to tell, I thought not at all. I could not. Everything I had seen, and suffered, and done, was live within me, and I so full of it there was no room for thought. I lived and acted, and that was all.

Until I came at last into Llewelyn's presence in the hospice at the abbey of Cwm Hir, and saw his face, that was as ravaged as my own, and his eyes, haunted by what he had seen only within, in the anguish of his own heart, but I in the open light of day. Then indeed I thought on what was done and could not be undone, for the bare fact of it he knew, but it might well be that there was something within my knowledge apt to his need, and not yet known to him.

'I know,' he said heavily. 'They are dead, father and son both, dead and violated. All this land knows it. The heart is gone out of all those who followed and believed in him. It is over. And I let them go to their doom without me! I believed in him as in the Host, but for my own cause I denied his. And now I have destroyed by that denial, since justice there must be, both his cause and mine.'

I had never heard him speak so, or seen that look in his face before, as though he had seen the finger of God write his own doom fiery and plain across the bloody field of Evesham. I said 'God forbid!' and shook like a sick man, for the end of one dream I had seen, and that was bitter enough.

'God forbids,' said Llewelyn, 'that a man should hold his hand and forbear to commit his heart where he believes right and truth to be. How if God offered me that chance as a test, and I have failed it? Had I thrown in all my weight with his, I might have won both his battle and mine. Now it is but just if mine proves to be lost with his.'

All this he said with a fatal calm that chilled me, so far was it from any mood I had ever known in him. And strongly I set myself to compel him out of this darkness, all the more because there was some ground for it, for everything Wales had stood to gain by Earl Simon's friendship and recognition was indeed lost, or to win again. However tamely King Henry had set his seal to the treaty of Pipton, I had no faith in his will to honour his bond now that it was in his power to repudiate it. Yet Llewelyn's justification, if he needed any, was that Earl Simon had been the first to approve him, and so I said.

'Even had you been there with all your host to aid him, you could not have saved him. That was no battle for your people and mine, they could not sustain it. Even for him it was the wrong battle. The time when he lost his fight was when he failed to storm through Gloucester into England as soon as he heard that Edward was gone. He knew it himself when it was too late. Of two visions one may yet be saved. Do you think he would not urge you to the work?'

To that, as yet, he would answer nothing, but he asked me to tell him every detail of what had passed, and so I did, the whole sorrowful history from the moment we left him on the Hereford road. That narration took a great while, and the room darkened about us before it was done. Even so Llewelyn covered his face.

Afterwards he said not a word, at first, of what he had heard, or what he had learned from it, but only asked me to go with him to hear mass in the abbey church, and after it to watch with him for a while, which I did gladly, for there was that working in him that comforted me for his soul and mine. Together we two watched out the greater part of that night, and the grief we shared became a living fire in place of a hellish darkness.

When he came forth his face was clear, pale and bright. Under the stars he said to me: 'Well I know his enemies made use of his dealings with me as a reproach to him, that he gave away England's rights for his own ends, though I asked of him nothing, and he gave nothing, that was not Welsh by right, and lost to England only by force. The guilt I bear in holding back from going with him, when my heart and will desired to go, I cannot measure. That God must do. But if they think to have put him away out of reckoning and out of mind by dismembering his body and befouling his memory, they have everything yet to learn. Others will take up his visions after him, and bring them to veritable birth in England. But I know of two things I can do here to honour him, and those I have sworn to do. I will wrest from King Henry at liberty everything he granted to me under duress. And I will make Earl Simon's daughter princess of Wales.'

The heart and spirit of the reform was broken after Evesham, as well it might be. Castles were surrendered, towns sued to come to the king's peace. Weary and sick and seeing now no man to lead them, even young Simon and the garrison in Kenilworth listened to the first proffers made them, and were ready to deal. But though at first there were hopeful signs for conciliation and moderation, that soon changed.

It was Edward who sent out the first call to all loyal prelates and barons to attend at Winchester in the first week of September, and issued orders to the sheriffs to maintain law, so that no man should despoil his neighbour under the pretext of loyal indignation, ordinances worthy almost of Earl Simon himself. For the king was so low, wounded and weary and dazed, that he was carried away to Gloucester, and thence to Marlborough, to recover from his ills. And only when the gathering at Winchester convinced him that he was again royal, and had real power in his hands, did he begin to feel his own man. Had he continued abased and frightened a little longer, things might have gone more wisely in England. For when Henry was no longer afraid, he would take vengeance on all those who had frightened him, as a braver and stronger man need not have done.

But to us, watching from Wales, the first important act that followed Edward's victory was his prompt march to Chester. Llewelyn smiled sourly at that, and went quietly to Mold to keep a watch on events. But at least it proved that Edward considered us still to be reckoned with, and was in haste to secure his city and county again on our borders, and put his own men back into the seats of power there. At Beeston castle, in mid-August, Luke Tany surrendered Chester to him, and relinquished his office to a new justiciar, James Audley. It was the reversal of the scene we had witnessed less than a year before, in the meadows by the Dee, and as we heard from our ageing friend the garrison horse-doctor, who kept his place through all reversals, David was close at Edward's side when he entered the city, and known to be in the highest favour and intimacy with him.

'I hear he did well at Evesham,' said Llewelyn bitterly. 'And got his pay for it! The king rewarded him with all the lands forfeited by some poor wretch called Boteler. Well, I never doubted his gallantry. And at least he has preserved some kindness for you.'

'Even for Wales,' I said, 'seeing he knew very well there were more of us, and all Welsh. "Go safely," he said, "and give thanks to God!" And a grain of thanks I gave heartily to him, also.'

'I have not forgotten,' said Llewelyn, and almost smiled. 'For that and other reasons, I grudge him to Edward. But this Edward himself – I see qualities in him that speak for David, too. To fight well and to think well is surely a promising beginning.'

In this I think he was right. For it was only at Winchester, where King Henry began to rule again, that the tone of the victors changed, and in place of conciliation there was nothing better than vengeance and spite, and hatred had its way. For there were too many others of smaller quality, like the king, who had felt themselves humiliated and disprized, and yearned to climb back into their own esteem by debasing those who had outmatched them. So tragedy was compounded for two years to come, and a great opportunity lost.

Young Simon in Kenilworth received letters of safe-conduct to go to Winchester, as speaker for all his garrison, and he went with a fair hope, for Edward's first approaches had been generous and large-minded. But at Winchester hatred prevailed, and the terms presented to him were such as he could not tolerate. So he returned unreconciled to his father's castle, and prepared it for a long siege, and so held it in defiance. And I think he achieved his full growth only then, when he was left to uphold that lost cause without hope, but still with dignity.

At Winchester, too, it was concluded, and I do not quarrel with that conclusion, that whatever deeds, acts, grants, charters and other documents King Henry had enacted since Lewes, when he fell captive into Earl Simon's hands, were enacted under duress, and thereby invalid, and all were repudiated. So passed among the rest, as we had foreseen, the treaty made at Pipton.

'More than that I lost at Evesham,' said Llewelyn. 'So be it! Better by far I should bring him to such an act voluntarily. And so I will!'

For us this was the most meaningful of the business at Winchester. Yet we could not be unmoved by the ordinance made on the seventeenth day of September, the triumph of the vengeful, by which all the lands and tenements of all the adherents of Earl Simon were seized into the king's hands. That was the only test, that the defaulter should be ally to the earl, and who was to be the local judge of that adherence? Every man who coveted could cast the accusation. No manner of pure principle was a defence, no clear uprightness of life. All those of one faction were damned, whatever their virtue and goodwill. There was raised at Winchester a great, ghostly company of the dispossessed, by this infamous act of disinherison that was opposed, vainly, by all the wise and humane men on the king's side, Edward, I think, among them. They were outnumbered five to one by men neither wise nor humane, bitter for their former losses, and insatiable for their possible gains.

'Well,' said Llewelyn with grim calm, 'they have Chester secured, their treaty and the royal seal dishonoured and discarded, my ally disposed of and me, as they think, checked and subdued into caution. They think they can turn their backs on me and set about the despoiling of others. I have two ends to serve. Once before King Henry wrote me off his accounts as dead, and found me very much alive. It's time to remind him once again.'

Deliberately he called up the local muster to add to his own guard, enough for his purpose, and rode out from Mold towards Hawarden, that same way we had ridden a year ago to see Edward's garrison march away and give place to Earl Simon's men.

'Hawarden I was promised,' said Llewelyn, 'in his name, and if they deny it now to me, so will I deny it to them. Edward's garrison there threatens my valley.'

In one swift and unexpected assault we took that castle, drove out the household, such as were not worth keeping as prisoners, and stripped roofs and walls low enough to make it uninhabitable. It was done with economy and precision, and it was a hoisting of his standard on his border, as a warning that he had suffered no setback, and had a power that could stand of itself, without confederates.

When it was done, we drew back to Mold, and he called in a reserve force, expecting that some action must soon be taken against him. And in the month of October it came, a very strong army loosed against us from Chester under Hamo Lestrange and Maurice FitzGerald, two marcher lords both experienced and able. But Llewelyn struck hard before they had reached the position they desired, or ordered their array to the best advantage, and broke and scattered them so completely that they fled back into Chester piecemeal, we chasing them to the very gates. They began to talk anxiously of truce with us, and though in the general confusion in England this came to nothing, what we had was as effective as truce, for wherever anything was attempted against us it was quenched at once and without difficulty or loss. So he taught England that Wales had lost no battles, nor been defeated in any wars.

London had submitted to the king before that time, and been fined and penalised and plundered like a conquered city. Disputes and lawsuits over lands seized from the disinherited arose even among the victors, and in many parts of England companies of rebels betook themselves to lonely and difficult places like the eastern fens, and there held out month after month against the king's peace. Worst of all, there was a bitter division between those of the victors who were for mercy and moderation, and those who wanted to crush the defeated utterly and drive them into the wilderness. So the state of England in those days was worse than before Evesham, and though the old cause was hopelessly lost, its surviving adherents had still to put up a rearguard fight for their lives and livelihoods and lands, and some remnant of justice.

During those autumn days Llewelyn kept anxious watch in particular on the distant fortunes of those de Montforts who were left. For the Countess Eleanor, still fiercely loyal to her dead lord, held the castle of Dover, and her daughter was still there with her. Her two youngest sons she had succeeded in shipping away to France, fearing captivity for them if they should be taken. The third son, Guy, wounded at Evesham, lay sick and prisoner at Windsor, and young Simon still defied siege in Kenilworth, though later he slipped away out of that fortress, leaving it well manned and supplied, to join the gathering at Axholme, in the fens.

All this year through we had had no word from Cynan, for we had been nearer to events than he, and moreover, left behind among the minor household clerks in London, at such a time of malice and suspicion, he had been forced to look to his own life and observe absolute caution in his dealings. Now with the monarchy re-established he breathed again, however regretfully at least more easily, and finding a venerable and reliable messenger in a Franciscan of Llanfaes on his way home from pilgrimage to Rome, he sent us in September a full and enlightening account of what went forward in the south.

'They are waiting, it seems,' said Llewelyn, reporting Cynan's news in council, 'the arrival of the new cardinal-legate at Dover. There's no bar to his landing now, he'll be welcomed with open arms. God knows they have need of good and sane counsel to bring order out of the wicked chaos they have made. And this man, since he took over the mission, has at least hurled no more thunderbolts and curses across the sea.' For Cardinal Gui, who had been kept so long in holy wrath at Boulogne, had been called away some months since to become pope under the name of Clement, the fourth so styled, and in his place a new man was appointed, of whom at that time we knew nothing. 'The exiles are on their way home, the queen is expected to make the crossing in the legate's company, and soon. A Genoese, a lawyer, and of good repute,' said Llewelyn, pondering Cynan's usually acute judgment with interest, 'and he comes with wide authority, to preach the crusade, to make peace and reconcile enemies and assuage grudges in all the land of England. And why not in Wales, too? I will gladly use any man of goodwill, and be thankful for him.'

In this manner we first heard of the approach of Cardinal Ottobuono Fieschi, who did indeed enter England with goodwill, and with very good sense, too as we later found, though he had a hard struggle of it. Had the most implacable of the victors paid heed to him, England could have been pacified very quickly. But then he was no more than a name to us.

'Cynan writes further,' Llewelyn said, 'that Edward has left the king resting at Canterbury, and is setting out for Dover himself, not only to meet his mother when she lands, but to try if he can get possession of the castle from Countess Eleanor, first. By persuasion!' But he made a wry face over that word, for something we had seen of Edward's persuasion.

'She is his father's sister,' said Goronwy sensibly. 'He cannot for his good name offer her any offence. But he will not need to. What can she do but make her peace? There is nothing left to defend.'

He spoke truth, there was nothing, except a memory and an ideal, and the integrity of her love. Yet I know that Llewelyn feared for her, and waited in great uneasiness for the next news of her forlorn and solitary stand. There was no possibility as yet of making any approach to her on his own behalf, her situation was so piteous and so difficult that even if there had been a means of sending to her, he would not have done so. She had lost a husband most deeply and passionately loved, and her firstborn son, and was separated from two more sons whose fate she could not aid. It was no time to send proffers to her for her daughter.

'She is very young,' said Llewelyn, steadily looking towards the south-east. 'As yet it could have been only a betrothal. And I can wait. Until her mother is free of this last burden, and has her remaining children back, or at least knows them safe and free. There will be a right time for it!'

So he waited with patience. And in the early days of November Cynan sent another letter. I was at work among the documents of a dry civil case at Mold, when he came into the room with the parchment unsealed in his hand. His face was bleak and still, but his eyes were wide, far-looking and calm. The wound he had received was sharp enough, but short of mortal, because he would not acknowledge it. The first thing he said to me was simply: 'I have lost her!'

I looked up at him in some doubt and wonder, for he had not the look of one admitting loss.

'I have lost her – for a while,' he said. 'Edward is in Dover castle, and the Countess Eleanor is out of it. The prisoners she held there broke out and captured the keep against her, but even if they had not, what could she have done? If she had fought, it would have been the worse for her and for others. And for whom should she hold it, now Earl Simon is dead? Edward has received her into grace, but all she has asked of him is that the gentlemen of her household shall be maintained in all that is theirs, and not held felon for their loyalty, and that he grants. She has accepted his peace, and undertaken to withdraw herself from all activity against him and against the crown and government of England. I doubt if she can love, but she will not oppose him. Poor lady, what is the world, and justice, and the well-being of the realm of England to her, now Simon is gone?'

'It is safely over, then,' I said. 'You would not have had her resist?'

'No, God knows! I dreaded she might,' he said.

Yet I saw that it was she who had dealt him the blow that was twisting his heart so sorely at that very moment, while he kept his will and his countenance. This pain was not all for her. And in truth, deprived though she now was of all her rights, since the king had already bestowed the earldom of Leicester upon his second son, Edmund, and though she stood bereaved of husband and son, solitary in her grief, yet I thought her rich and exalted above all her sisters. Better Earl Simon, dead and abused, the king's felon and the pope's pestilence, the people's hero and the poor men's saint, than all the living and vengeful lords that served in King Henry's retinue and enjoyed his favour.

I said, I doubt not with some taint of blasphemy: ' "Blessed art thou among women . . ." ', and Llewelyn said: 'Truly! But the greater the blessing withdrawn, the deeper is the desolation left behind. She knows little of me, and nothing of this betrothal. He never saw her again. My bride is only a child. I cannot touch or trouble either the one or the other in their sorrow.'

I said that the lady might be glad, for what future was there now for her daughter? And he laughed, rather ruefully than bitterly.

'Glad? She, whose whole peace now depends on the sanction of brother and nephew? She who wants nothing but to turn her back on the world as it is, and remember it in secret only as *he* wanted it? No, she will never be glad of me. But in time – in time, God knows, not now! – she may learn to bear with me. When I am no longer a reminder to Edward of an old alliance that cost him dear, and a marriage with me ceases to be the imagined threat of a new alliance as perilous as the old. No, I can wait! The time will come when she will forget, and he will cease to suspect and fear. But not yet. Even if I could reach her now,' he said in a soft and grievous cry, 'and I cannot!'

I asked him in dread: 'What has she done?'

'She has shaken off the dust of England for a witness against them,' said Llewelyn, 'and set sail for France with her daughter, one day before the queen landed with Cardinal Ottobuono at Dover. They say she did not want to see her brother's detestable wife, and has said she will never set foot in these islands again. She is gone to Earl Simon's sister at the convent of Montargis, and has taken the other Eleanor – *my* Eleanor! – with her!'

When he had thought long, and come to terms with his situation, he said: 'I have two vows in my heart, both debts due to his memory, and if I cannot yet do anything about one of them, let's see how quickly the other may be brought to fruit. One thing at a time!' And he turned his every waking thought to the re-establishment of the settlement he had briefly enjoyed after Pipton, absolutely resolved to compel the recognition of the unity and sanctity of Wales.

Cardinal Ottobuono came to London and set up his office there without delay. On the first day of December he held a clerical council to declare his mission and display his authorities, and to receive oaths of obedience from bishops and abbots, though four of the most saintly bishops of the realm were soon suspended by reason of their devotion to Earl Simon's cause, and so would Bishop Walter of Worcester have been, but that he died, old and tired as he was, before his case ever came to be examined. Howbeit, it did appear that the legate truly intended generosity and mercy, and desired to ensure that justice should not be defiled by malice and self-interest. Llewelyn, encouraged, called his council and proposed, with their approval, to present the Welsh case and his desire for an amicable settlement, without waiting to be invited to do so, the cardinal's brief being all-embracing.

'He'll be beset with petitioners clamouring for their own ends,' he said disdainfully, 'and we'll not press him, but at least we'll let him know that we are here, with both offers and claims to make, civilly waiting for his attention when the time serves.' All which the council heartily endorsed. So he wrote requesting letters of safe-conduct, that envoys from Wales might come to pay his respects, and in the middle of December they were granted.

'If I am to seek a friend at court,' he said, 'it shall be the highest.' And he chose the best and wisest of his lawyers and clerics to go as envoys. Before Christmas they came back to report a very willing hearing, and a degree of interest and sympathy, though the legate's preoccupations at that time were naturally with the most pressing distresses in state and church. 'The more pleasure it must be to him,' said Llewelyn hopefully, 'to hear of one petitioner who has learned how to wait, and who desires peace on present terms, and not the slaughter and ruin of all his enemies. And he shall not forget us, we'll make sure of that!'

In this same month of December young Simon and his company in the fens at last submitted to Edward, who had them securely penned there at a disadvantage, and who, to do him justice, promised, and this time kept his promise, that if they placed themselves in the king's grace they should have no fear for life, limb or liberty. Lands they might and did lose, and they had to find sureties for their submission, and await the king's pleasure, but they fared better than many others later, who still held out in forests and hills.

Having done all that could be done at this time, Llewelyn turned homeward to Aber for the Christmas feast, according to custom, feeling secure enough to remove his forces from the border for the first time in many months. Since my return from Evesham I had scarcely been wenty miles into Wales. Now at last I came at his side along the coast road once more, and under the mountains, gazing across Lavan sands at the shore of Anglesey, with a sprinkling of snow over the salt marshes, and the gulls wheeling and screaming above the tide.

It seemed to me then that I had been away from this place far longer than a year, and had travelled an infinite distance across the world to make my way back to it again. It was even strange to me, like a country seen in a dream, for the soft, rich green and soiled and sorry red of the vale of Evesham filled all the landscape of my mind. I had almost forgotten the faces of people here, and the very echoes were unfamiliar to me. I came as a stranger.

We rode into the gateway of the maenol, and out of every doorway the household came running to welcome us. And the first person I saw, crossing from the mews to the hall with her arms full of fir-branches, and a hood drawn over her black, silken hair, was Cristin.

I was speaking to Llewelyn at that moment, and I broke off mute and stricken in the midst of a word. I know I drew hard on the rein and my horse baulked in offence, marking the break. I had thought she was in Neigwl, safe, distant, delivered from my shadow and delivering me from hers, while I died a little with Earl Simon, and grew a little English in desperate, perverse tribute to him. Last Christmas she had not been here either to trouble or fulfil me. I had not seen her for two whole years. For many months I had not thought of her consciously, but with my blood and bones, she being for ever part of me. The compact we had between us was for all time, and did not waver, but the sudden vision of her was more than my heart could bear of bliss and pain, I was not large enough to contain it. Face and voice failed me. And Llewelyn saw. I knew it then, though he never said a word until later. His mind, also, had ventured into far places among alien people, he was shaken as I was, and he saw with newly-opened eyes.

She was then approaching thirty years of age, but time was of no moment, except that she grew finer, more purely-drawn and to me more beautiful with every year, the whiteness of her skin like sunlit snow under the raven hair, and her eyes iris-grey and clear as light at dawn. So contained and perfect she was within her body, the soul was visible within. Wherever else I had been, whatever else I had done and seen and known, whoever else I had loved after my fashion, for love is an enlargement of the being and lets in other loves, there was no end nor limitation to the love I felt for her. When we were together, brushing arms about our work like other men, I could deal with it and be at peace, but when I saw her newly after so long, and without warning, I doubt it burned in me like a lantern, blinding all those who saw, or all who had eyes to see.

She looked at us and she stayed, her long mouth curling like a bent bow, and her eyes widening and glowing darkly purple. At me she looked, and it was a renewal of vows, and the strong curve of her lips became a smile to be remembered long. Then she went on where she was going, into the hall.

I awoke, and Llewelyn's eyes were on me, waiting courteously and patiently. He had reined in to keep pace with me. I said: 'I did not know she was here. I thought she was still in Neigwl.'

'Last spring,' said Llewelyn, 'after you were away from us, I sent a new castellan to Neigwl, the old man being ill and needing to give over such a charge. The new man had a wife. And Godred being now in my household force here, I thought well to send him to bring his wife to Aber.' So he said, and his voice was level and low and mild, forbearing from wonder or question.

I had not seen Godred, either, since returning from Evesham. Until then I had not remembered him. A strange year, maker or breaker, that had been to me. I said: 'That was right. I am glad to see Cristin here.' And I shook my rein and went forward into the courtyard, and there dismounted, he close beside me.

So we came home to Aber with all our gains and losses, to keep Christmas of the year of our Lord twelve hundred and sixty-five, the year of Evesham.

From the moment I saw her in hall among the household, with Godred at her side, it was as it had been with us beforetime, as close, as calm, as sure, as when we made our compact. We met and spoke each other and passed, with every look and every near approach uplifted and sustained, and the manner of our exchanges when we were alone was not different from the manner of them when Godred was at her elbow. The first speech she had with me was when she entered the hall, the night of our arrival, on Godred's arm, and gave me her hand with open and fearless warmth and bade me welcome from the heart, saying she had prayed for me all the days of my absence. Before all, and proudly and simply, she said it, so that he had not even the twisted satisfaction of conceiving that she feigned reserve and indifference. And when I met her alone in the storeroom, folding away newly-mended hangings, she met me with pleasure and serenity, speaking only of the day's work and the season's festivities, with never one word he could not have heard, had he been crouching behind the door again to listen, as perhaps he was. Not one step towards me nor one step away did she swerve from her path to gratify Godred's perverse longings.

But I think after that Christmas-time there were two who watched us, instead of one, with motives and missions as far apart as darkness and light.

All the following year the struggle in England continued for all Cardinal Ottobuono's patient mediations, as nest after nest of rebels was painfully smoked out of forest and fen, and brought to submission. Young Simon was ordered to leave England, and swear never again to take action against the king or his realms and Edward took him in custody to London to prepare for his departure. But he was warned secretly that he could not trust his captors, and his life might be in danger before ever he embarked. How much truth there was in this warning we cannot know, for no man then trusted his fellows, and even if Edward's intent was honest enough, as for my part I think likely, it was no wonder that those who wished young Simon well were afraid for him.

Whatever the truth, he escaped from the Old Temple and made his way safely to the coast, where the independent men of Winchelsea hid him until they could get him away across the Channel in February. Not many weeks later his younger brother Guy, recovered from his wounds, also made good his escape and followed Simon to France. Some people thought that the escapes had been connived at, as the quickest means of ousting from England the last sons of Earl Simon, but by the alarm that followed I think this was not so. The narrow seas were full of reiving galleys sympathetic to the rebels, and now the fear of invasion was turned about, and King Henry dreaded that the Montforts might raise an army and a fleet to return and fight the war all over again. A vain fear, surely! All that remained was a few forlorn camps of desperate men living wild through that winter and defying the crown. There was no possible hope of a recovery, there was no army, almost there was no cause.

Two men were chiefly responsible for the gradual betterment of this state of disorder, and those two were the cardinal-legate and the Lord Edward. Nor was Edward's part all the fighting and none of the pacification. He did indeed fight, and formidably, and while the fighting endured he was unrelenting. But when he had taken and broken the town of Winchelsea, the most obdurate of the Cinque ports, he did not pillage and burn in revenge, but very quickly turned to offering the merchants good, sensible terms, inviting them to a new age of well-ordered and peaceful trade, and restoring them freely to royal favour and all their privileges. He did so, doubtless, because they were strong and could be either valuable or dangerous to him, and many of his conquered opponents who had not the same power behind them found short shrift and ended on trees. Nevertheless, he showed very shrewd sense, and the ability to rein in his grudges where that was good policy, as King Henry could seldom do.

But it may be that even the better part of Edward's wisdom came from Cardinal Ottobuono, who did truly endeavour for peace, mercy and forgiveness. So when the final siege of Kenilworth was planned in the summer, the legate still tirelessly haunted both parties and battled for a better ending. And in the meantime, there being a limit to one man's energy, ingenuity and time, our affairs in Wales had to wait.

What we chiefly noticed from our side the border was the growing rift between Earl Gilbert de Clare of Gloucester and Roger Mortimer. For Gloucester, though he had been the instrument of Earl Simon's fall, nevertheless was heart and soul for conciliation and did his best to save his old associates from disinherison and utter ruin, while Mortimer, who had been absolute against the Provisions from the beginning, desired the ultimate in vengeance, and encouraged King Henry in his obduracy against all concessions. I think it was as a result of this enmity between neighbours that Mortimer took the step he did in May of that year, meaning to strengthen his own influence, to keep alive the king's resentment, and to remind him that Wales was held to be a continuing danger. For in the middle of the month he suddenly gathered all his men and made a determined drive into Brecon, intending to occupy those lands in the teeth of Llewelyn's lordship.

That was the only time we had to take action all that year. Rhys Fychan moved east from Dynevor to meet the attack, and we drove south through Builth, and between us Mortimer was crushed as in a closing fist, barely escaping with his life back to Wigmore, and leaving behind the greater part of his forces dead or prisoner.

'He chose his time badly,' said Llewelyn grimly. 'I might have been content to drive him off, if I had not to maintain before the legate a position I desire him to recognise. He shall be in no doubt whether I am the master of Wales, or whether I deserve the title to add to the reality. Also,' he said, 'I might have spared him if he had not been among the chief of those who dug Earl Simon's grave. If this display was for King Henry's benefit, I hope he draws the right lesson.'

Then we were again no more than spectators to the turmoil and tragedy of England, for no man raised a hand against us more. The long siege of Kenilworth began that June, and was not ended until December, and even then the castle was never taken. Doubtless the garrison at first believed, as much of England believed, that the earl's sons might yet return with an army from France, but even when that dream was over they did not give in. And all that time, untiring, the cardinal-legate plied between all the parties, procured that parliament convened at Kenilworth, recruited to him all the moderate opinion and goodwill he could find in barons, officials and churchmen, and at last, against long resistance from the king, hammered out a form of settlement by which all who came to the king's grace within forty days should have pardon and indulgence, and those already dispossessed should be able to redeem their lost lands at a fee. Though this form was not all that the legate had hoped for, it was a great gain over anything offered before, and it put an end to retrospective revenges, and made a new beginning possible. Nevertheless, the garrison in Kenilworth fought on until the middle of December, when they gave up hope of aid from abroad, and at last surrendered on these terms. Sick, starving, ragged they marched out of Earl Simon's castle, and on their given word were allowed to depart to their own homes, with their pride and faith unbroken, as a last offering to the earl's memory.

But in the isle of Ely in the fens the rebels still held out, and it seemed that this last bitter sore was to be left festering, perhaps to start a rot within the whole body of the realm, if the earl of Gloucester had not gone beyond exasperation into action. He resolved to go to London in arms, and stop this long persecution, preventing the worst and most violent of the king's advisers from having their way with England. And shrewdly he made known his design to Llewelyn, and asked and received assurance of quiet on his borders while he went to work, and goodwill from beyond the march.

'God forbid,' said Llewelyn, 'that with such a task in hand he should have to look over his shoulder. But who would have thought,' he said, marvelling, 'that the same man who loosed Edward and won the war for the king should now be the man who may save what remains of the reform?'

In the event it worked out not quite as we had supposed, or Earl Gilbert, perhaps, intended. He established himself in London, and some of the rebels from Ely joined him there, while the city itself rose hopefully to him, and again created that commune of London which had so strongly supported Earl Simon. For two months the capital city was a rebel camp, and perhaps that very outburst recalled all the forces in England to their senses, and made them aware with what dangerous fire they played. So in the end it served well enough, for king, prince, officials and rebels all were drawn together under the legate's guidance, and forced to come to terms at last.

Gloucester had come near to being himself a rebel again, yet it was he who put an end to the long-drawn struggle, by showing what was the only alternative, a new war. So he came home unscathed and in due fealty to the king, however suspiciously Edward looked sidewise at him from under his drooping eyelid. And he brought about the final accord that made life supportable and justice at least a possibility in the realm.

'They have been long enough about the affairs of England,' said Llewelyn, drawing satisfied breath, 'now let's see if they are ready to turn to the affairs of Wales.'

Courteously and dutifully he wrote to Cardinal Ottobuono, to remind him that we also waited patiently for his attentions, when he should be free to bestow them, and that we desired, as we always had, a just and lasting treaty of peace with England. His messengers brought back a very favourable and even grateful reply, promising early consideration of the request. King Henry also responded agreeably, declaring himself no less anxious than Llewelyn to have a settled peace. And this was the fruit of the prince's policy of confining his rule and his ambitions to Wales itself, and refraining from exploiting the wounds and dissents of England as otherwise he might have done.

'Perhaps,' he said, when I said so. But his eyes looked far and the shadow of Evesham gathered over them. 'How do I know,' he said, 'how can I ever know, that we could not have won both our battles, if I had had more faith? To the day of my death I shall be in doubt. Only in the judgment shall I come to know the degree of my offence, and whether God sees it through Earl Simon's eyes or mine.'

So I said no more then, for he was resolute in his self-blame, but the more determined to press home to a triumph the cause for which he had sinned, if sin it was. And the day of that triumph was near.

At the end of the month of August King Henry came in great state to the town of Shrewsbury, with Cardinal Ottobuono, the Lord Edward, Henry of Almain, and all the servants and officials of his court, and sent safe-conduct into Wales for Llewelyn's envoys to come there into conference. Llewelyn sent two very experienced men, Einion ap Caradoc and David ap Einion, and since the season was again summer, the golden end of the summer when the evenings draw in but the days are radiant, he took his court into camp in the green valley of Severn in its upper reaches, close to Strata Marcella, and himself lodged in the abbey. And there we stayed through the greater part of September, while messages went to and fro busily, and sometimes we fished, and sometimes we rode, our bodies at leisure and our minds at rest, for time was nothing to us. We had a position that could not be shifted, and we could afford to wait King Henry's yielding, for he needed that peace more than we did.

Nor did we wish him any ill. Llewelyn wanted no more than his own.

The couriers who rode back and forth between Strata Marcella and the town of Shrewsbury, where the king was lodged at the Benedictine abbey outside the walls, brought us the current news as well as the quibbles and counters of argument requiring answer.

'My lord,' they let Llewelyn know, early in September, when the lawyers had barely fleshed their pens, 'your brother, the Lord David, is there in the abbey in the Lord Edward's own retinue. And very well found and attended, and with the prince's arm about his neck as often as not.'

'A passing heavy torque that must be,' said Llewelyn and grimaced. 'Still, I thank you for the warning!'

The conference continued through three weeks of September, while the original proposals from both sides were rejected, amended, amended again, declined again and again rephrased, in the fashion to be expected of so large an enterprise. By that time each side knew what the other would and would not stomach, and the ground between was open to manoeuvre. That was the point when King Henry, never tenacious when it came to fine detail, turned over the whole negotiation to Cardinal Ottobuono.

Then it lasted but four days.

On the twenty-fourth day of September the envoys came with the last draft of the terms. Many items had been agreed already, but a few had been disputed, and some stipulations were only now put forward, though they had clearly been held in reserve until agreement was near.

'King Henry makes one exception,' said Einion ap Caradoc, 'in his willingness to cede to you the homages of all the Welsh princes. He insists on retaining for himself the direct fealty of Meredith ap Rhys Gryg of Dryslwyn.'

'Doubtless at Meredith's urgent entreaty,' said Llewelyn drily, for though the old bear of the vale of Towy had submitted to him after his defection, and kept out of trouble since, he had done as little as he could to aid and support his overlord, and absented himself and his forces from all our recent activities, and it was no secret that he had still not forgiven the reinstatement of his nephew Rhys Fychan, or the prompt punishment of his own treason. 'I said when he came to my peace that he loved me no better than before, and had not changed his mind. This is his first opportunity to slide out of my grasp.' And he thought it over, but briefly, and shrugged the item by. 'It is not worth rejecting the whole for the sake of one Meredith. Let the king keep him, since that is what he wants. But let there be a clause permitting the cession of his homage to me hereafter, if King Henry should ever be so reconciled and reassured as to want to part with it. I would have him if I could, I admit it. A pity to spoil the whole.'

'The king would certainly insist on a further payment for it, in that case,' said Einion, having now had considerable dealings with King Henry.

'He shall have it, if the day ever comes. And let's set it high enough to tempt him,' said Llewelyn, 'since his coffers are empty. I would pay five thousand marks for the homage of Meredith ap Rhys Gryg.'

So that, too, was written into the draft.

'There is another matter,' said Einion, 'which has lain somewhat in the background until now, though I own I have scented it waiting there, and I believe, my lord, so have you. The king requires that suitable provision be made for the Lord David. That you give him again all that he held at the time when he departed from you, or, if reasonable Welshmen now think that portion too small for his needs, that it shall be added to. A committee of Welsh princes, it is suggested, could decide on what is fit for a prince, and your brother.'

I was watching Llewelyn's face as he heard this, and certainly there was no surprise in it for him. He smiled a little, and again was grave, remembering, I think two other brothers he had, both in close ward, as both had offended against him, like David, though these two had no royal patron to take up their cause.

'This he owes to Edward,' he said with certainty.

'It is true, the Lord Edward shows him great favour,' said Einion, 'and he has already been given lands in England. What is better worth thinking about, by this token it must be his own wish to return home.'

'In the teeth of my lordship and at my cost,' said Llewelyn, and laughed aloud without rancour. 'No suing for David! He makes his return, as of right and without penalty, the condition of my recognition. But he comes, if he comes at all, as my vassal. So be it! He surely does not think I will throw this peace away, after eleven years of pressing for it, simply to spite him? He rates himself too high! He has cost me somewhat, but he cannot cost me near so much as that.'

So that, too, was accepted without demur, even without regret. His hot hatred, if it had ever ranked so high, had cooled and vanished long ago. And the terms were written and agreed, and the whole sent back to Shrewsbury, where the next day king, prince and council also accepted it, and Cardinal Ottobuono breathed relief and joy, and blessed the settlement.

That same day King Henry sent back to Llewelyn letters of self-conduct to come to Montgomery on the twenty-ninth of the month, to meet the king and do homage to him at the ford, to be entertained in the castle, and enter into his household as the greatest of his vassals and the closest of his fellow-princes. For though the treaty made him the king's liege man, yet his own principality he held as of independent sovereignty, with its own laws, customs and right entirely free and separate from those of England.

And these were the provisions made in that famous treaty: As to what Llewelyn gained, above all he gained the full recognition by England of his right and title as prince of Wales, to whom were ceded, for himself and his heirs after him, the homages and fealty of all the lesser princes excepting only Meredith ap Rhys Gryg. And of lands, he kept all of what he held, the four cantrefs of the Middle Country, Kerry, Cydewain, Builth, Gwerthrynion and Brecon, even Maelienydd so far as he could establish his present tenure of it, and also the castles of Whittington and Mold, though he agreed to release his prisoner Robert of Montalt, whom he had taken at Hawarden, and to restore that manor to him, but without the right to build a castle there for thirty years to come.

As to what he gave in return, there was the provision for David, his formal homage to King Henry as his accepted overlord, saving the rights of Wales, and a great indemnity to be paid in money, twenty-five thousand marks, though this was five thousand less than he had pledged at Pipton, the remaining five thousand being reserved to compensate for Meredith's homage should it later be granted to him. I doubt if King Henry had that sum, or anything near it, in his coffers at that time, and the treaty made very careful provision for the payment at certain dates of the amounts due, until all had been paid, for certainly in this bargain Llewelyn was helping to restore solvency in an England blighted and poverty-stricken from its long and bitter war.

For eleven years he had striven for this, fending off out-and-out war with truce after truce, paying what he promised, and, saving provocations from others and the occasional outburst of anger, keeping the truce unbroken, always desiring, always requesting, what he now held in his hands by the waters of Severn, peace with recognition, freedom to turn his powers to the arts of government in tranquillity.

In the church of Strata Marcella Llewelyn heard mass, and gave devout thanks to God.

CHAPTER XIV

On the twenty-seventh day of September King Henry removed with his court from Shrewsbury, and took up residence in the castle of Montgomery. Two days later we, being so much nearer, rose and made ready early for the day, and rode in great state to the meeting at Rhyd Chwima, by the ford of Montgomery.

All down the river meadows the grass was seeded and white with ripeness, full of moths, and the late flowers nested in it like larks. The sun shone, and the trees were turning gold, and over us the sky was deep blue without a cloud, and we went gaily caparisoned as for a festival, for that was a ride of no more than ten miles, a pleasure journey along the great river all the way, under Griffith ap Gwenwynwyn's castle of Pool, and so round into the coil of the spreading stream between the willow groves, where the gravel shone clear under the water, and the woods and meadows on the further shore rose into the folded hills that shield Montgomery.

They had pitched a splendid pavilion in the meadow by the water, draped with cloth of gold, and king, legate and court were there to meet us, a great assembly of knights, barons and officers, and two sons of kings. Edward, like his father, had consented fully in the treaty of Montgomery, I believe in good faith and even goodwill. He lost what pretensions he had to the title of prince of Wales, but he was still the heir of England, and his thoughts then, I believe, were fixed elsewhere, for the new settlement had brought him in thankfulness to consider taking upon him, as regards the legate's urging to the crusade, both his father's vow and his own. And he took the assumption of the cross, I grant him that, more gravely than did his father.

Down the blanched and rustling meadows Llewelyn rode, to the spit of sand and turf that ran out into the river, and all we after him. Into the shallow water he splashed, and the silver danced at his horse's heels. When he rode up the green sward on the further shore, towards where King Henry sat before the pavilion on a gilded throne, royal esquires came to take his bridle, and all we who served him dismounted with him and lined the shore. The king's knights kneeled to do off his spurs and ungird the sword-belt from his loins. He wore no mail and no gauntlets, and his head was uncovered, and thus he walked alone up the slope of green turf, his sombre brown made resplendent with scarlet and gold, and kneeled upon the gilded footstool at the king's feet, lifting to him his joined hands and his fierce and joyful face.

King Henry sat in shade, just at the rim of the pavilion's canopy, for the brightness of the sun somewhat troubled his eyes. But Llewelyn kneeled in sunlight, and when he raised his head the sunbeams blazed upon him and touched his sunburned face into minted gold, and the king paled and dwindled into a spectre beside him, like a candle in the noonday.

In a loud, clear voice Llewelyn rehearsed the oath of fealty, saving his own sovereign right within Wales, while the king's thin white hands, a little knotted with increasing age, enclosed his own. And thus he became vassal to King Henry and magnate of England, and also acknowledged prince of Wales, at sworn peace with his neighbour. And as he owed allegiance to the king, so did the king owe the loyal support and protection of his overlordship to Llewelyn, with right and justice in return for this feudal due.

I did not take my eyes from him until it was over, and he rose and stepped back from the throne. As English knights had disarmed him, so Welsh princes, of lineage as long as his own, girded him again with belt and sword, and did on the spurs at his heels, and the lord abbot of Aberconway set upon his head the golden talaith of his estate, as royal a crown as King Henry's. It was then that I drew breath and stirred to look all round that brilliant circle of two courts, and my eyes lit upon David as birds fly home, as though no other in the ring of English faces bore any difference from his neighbour, and only he was marked out from all, the one Welshman upon the wrong side of the throne.

He was close at Edward's side, as they said he was constantly, but he had eyes for no one but his brother. Very wide and blue those eyes were, in a face intent and still, and I could not tell what it was I read in them, whether love or hate, regret for his desertion or resentment that it had achieved so little for him, and that little only at Edward's urging, and lightly granted by Llewelyn out of his own rich plenty.

Too lightly! I saw it then. So lightly that, though he knew as well as I that David must be present here in Edward's train, he had forgotten him utterly, and never looked for him among the bright cavalcade, even when he was riding up the broad track between the rising hills towards Montgomery, at the king's side. Not one thought did he give to him until in the hall of the castle, led by King Henry to the high table between the ranks of his barons and knights, he came face to face with his younger brother, and could not choose but see him.

They were of a height, the two faces eye to eye, and Llewelyn checked for an instant, astonished and reminded, but his flushed and joyful countenance never lost its brightness. I watched David closely then, for he looked as I had seen him look once, years back, before he fell senseless on the field of Bryn Derwin, of which he had been the sole and deliberate cause. Unsparingly he kept his high and arrogant countenance, but behind the defiant stare of his eyes, blue and brilliant as sapphires, it seemed to me that there was another being gazing out from a private prison, and when he said, with the sweet insolence of which he was master: 'My lord, after all I see you do remember me!', what I seemed to hear, in the thread of a voice, warning and entreating, was: '*Kill me! You were wise!*'

I think there were some in the hall who held their breath, expecting a rough exchange and a flare of illwill to besmirch the feast. But Llewelyn clapped a hand upon David's shoulder, and said: 'Very heartily I remember you! Perhaps I can hope now to improve the acquaintance?'

And suddenly he laughed, wildly generous in his triumph, and leaned and kissed the marble cheek that suffered his salute like a blow, and burned where his lips had touched. Then lightly he took his hand from his brother's arm, and passed on to his place of honour beside the king. And David blazed and paled, all the blood forsaking his face, and slowly turning his black, glossy head, watched his brother go to his seat, and never took his eyes from him thereafter all that evening. As I know, for very seldom did I take my eyes from David, smouldering in black and bitter resentment, but to glance for reassurance at Llewelyn, who shone like a golden lantern with his joy and fulfilment.

There was much music that night in Montgomery, the king's music and the music of the bards. And we sat late, after the treaty was sealed and ratified, and as the wine flowed there were calls for this song, and that, and some of us went back and forth ordering the festivities as we were bidden. So I came late in the evening where David had withdrawn below his station and apart, altogether sober still, and from his shadowed place endlessly watching Llewelyn, with such fixed and famished eyes that I was drawn to go to him for pity and dread. Even then he was not aware of me until my shadow fell upon him, and then he shuddered, and his long gaze shifted and shortened to take me in, and was slow to know me, but knew me at last with such recognition as I found hard to fathom. There was compunction in it, and wonder, and a kind of drear self-derision. He said: 'What? Is it you? Now of all times I least need you to set me right.'

I thought, and said, that he well might need me more than he knew. And then he truly looked at me, who had looked through me before, to continue seeing Llewelyn. His face shook. Very strangely minded he was, that night. A little, and I think he would have wept, if there had not been so much anger in him. He said: 'Samson, how is it you haunt me still, seeing I slew you long ago?'

'Slew me and saved me,' I said. 'If you wanted me to remain dead you should have drawn the covert you spared to draw, after Evesham.'

'Dear God!' said David. 'Was it you taught him so to despise me?'

I understood then the ground of his despair and rage. 'Fool,' I said, 'do you not know how much that cost him?'

'It cost him no more than a pat to a hound,' said David bitterly, 'and he lets me back to him good-humouredly, as he would a hound that had gone off on a false scent, coming back shamed with his tail between his legs. He sighs and bears with me, like an experienced breaker with a useless pup. He values me not a pin!'

I began to exclaim against him that he judged well his own desert, but greatly misjudged his brother's largeness of mind and heart. But he cried me down with sudden breathless ferocity.

'Fool, if he had cared a toss for my desertion, do you think he would not have struck me down before all this company, and ordered me out of his sight?' And he spread his arms upon the board before him and sank his head into the crook of them, and shook terribly, like a man in fever, with grief and laughter. 'And I would have let him!' said David, groaning and cursing into his brocaded sleeves. 'And I would have gone!'

Even then, though daunted, I would have stayed with him and made him hear me, but when I laid my hand upon him he started up, very tall and erect, and made his face marble-calm and smiling in a breath, and so turned and stalked away from me towards the high table and his own place, and his gait as he went was long and lissome and soft as a cat's, forbidding all concern or question.

After Montgomery we went back in state to Aber, and David did not go with us, which caused no man wonder, for his offences had been gross, and the requital needed time and a certain ceremony. There were even many, English as well as Welsh, who held that Edward should have kept his favourite out of sight on this occasion. The forms of courtesy have their values and uses. No one took this to be an easy matter, and the delicate legal exchanges concerning his stipulated lands were to go on for more than a year, that being an aid to healing.

Some miles along the great sea-road from Aberconway the men of the royal household of Aber came out to meet us, all the garrison and the bodyguard but for a few duty men, and among them came also Godred, my half-brother, my fair mirror-image, to remind me that my life had still a secret side where there was no victory and no achievement. I was aware that as soon as they met us he looked for me at Llewelyn's left hand, which was ever my place. And since we rode those last miles at joyous ease, keeping no formal order, he made his way to my elbow very soon, and clung there, close to my ear, out of reach of Llewelyn's. And there he spoke with his blithe, serpent voice, and smiled his smooth, guileless smile all the way into Aber.

'Now at last,' he said, 'I trust we may see more of you, now your missions are all done and the peace secured. Once before we hoped for it, and no sooner had we followed you into Gwynedd than you must be for ever wandering out of it. You became such a great traveller, there was no keeping pace with you. Now you and I are in the same service, with time and ease to live close and brotherly.'

I said that David might be returning to his old lands in due time, and would certainly require his old following. This with mild malice, seeing he had deserted David's service for his own advantage, and not at all out of any devotion to Llewelyn. But he laughed openly at that, sure that where the master's treason was wiped out the man's would not be allowed to count against him, especially as it could be represented as loyalty to the higher power.

'That will be a new beginning, for both high and low,' he said, 'with old scores wiped out. I don't know but there's something to be said for living in Lleyn.' And I think he began then, in cold blood, to weigh the advantages, as ready to leave one lord as another. 'I hear there's talk,' he said, 'of the Lord Edward making a rich match for David, now we're all at peace. There's some little kinswoman of his own, left widowed after one of Earl Simon's barons, before she's even properly a wife. They say he has it in mind to give her to David, along with the English knighthood he's already bestowed on him. If he sets up with a noble English wife, she'll need a household of her own. And David thinks highly of Cristin, and would be glad to have her companion to his bride. But it would be shame,' said Godred, wantonly smiling and soft-voiced at my shoulder, 'to take her even so far from you as Neigwl, now *you're* home.'

We were nearing the maenol then, and the women came out to greet us and bring us home in triumph, and I was so intent on looking for her among them that I made him no response, and hardly heeded his baiting. Yet I heard him whisper even more stealthily into my ear, a thread of sound, like a sharp knife slicing through the shouting and singing: 'You know, do you not, that she chose to come north with the old dame only for *your* sake?'

If I had not known it I might have made him some sign then of the depth of that wound, but I did know it, from her own lips, and there was no way he could move me. Moreover, I found her at that moment, a star among her fellows, half-grave, half-bright, wholly beautiful, all the more because she had found me first, and her eyes, like irises wide-open and glowing in sunlight, were waiting to embrace me.

Into that liquid light I fell and drowned, drawn into her being and one with her. How many times have I not died that blessed death! I think I did not halt nor check, nor did my face change, and I do not know how much Godred saw of what we two became before his eyes, or heard of what we spoke to each other in silence. But when I drew back into my body the soul she gently returned to me, and opened my own eyes to those about me, Llewelyn at my right hand rode softly with his chin upon his shoulder, and his gaze wide and deep and reflective upon me, as darkly brown and still as the peat-pools of his own mountains. When he saw me awake and aware he stirred and looked before him, and spoke me freely and cheerily, putting the moment by. But there was nothing he had not seen.

After the feasting and the mirth and the singing of the bards in Aber that night, I went out into the mild darkness of the courtyard, and there was so golden a moon that the sight of it was like a benediction. I walked through the cool stillness to the chapel, and there made my prayers, for that night was to me a home-coming of such power and magic that nothing on earth seemed out of my reach, not even my love, Cristin, Godred's wife. I had only to wait and be still, and everything would be added to me. Yet in humility I consented to forgo what I might not desire, having the inexpressible bliss of what was already granted. For she loved me, and no other. And I prayed passionately grace and mercy for Godred, my brother, who had not that bliss, and only by its bestowal on me had learned to covet and begrudge it.

When I had done, I rose from before the lamp that burned on the altar, and turned towards the darkness, and there was a still and man-shaped shadow in the open doorway, that moved towards me as I moved, as the image advances in a mirror. So used was I to meeting my demon that I halted where I stood, and called him by his name: 'Godred!' Not dreading nor questioning, only in recognition, that he might have peace, if there was the means of peace in him.

'Not Godred,' said the shadow, very low, 'but Llewelyn.'

He came towards the light, and took shape as he came, and within reach of me he stayed. I think he had hardly touched mead or wine all that evening long, the burning within him was the fire of one aim achieved, and one still distantly beckoning.

'I did not follow you,' he said, 'but it was in my mind to send for you. And you were here before me. The dagger that strikes at me strikes also at you, the stars of our birth shone on us both. I have been blinded by my own concerns, but now I see. Forgive me that I did not see from the beginning. I must have cost you dear in your silence many a time.'

I told him what was true, that he had no need to reproach himself or compassionate me, that I had no complaint against man or God that I would not change my fate if I could, that there was but one thing lacking to me, and that was not my love's love, for that I had in fullest measure.

'I know it,' he said. 'I saw her face, also. Did I say we shared one fate? Come here to the light, look on *this* face. I have shown it to no one but you.'

He laid a hand upon my arm, and drew me with him to the small, steady lamp upon the altar, and there he slid from the breast of his gown and laid beneath the light a small silver circlet, the size of a woman's palm, threaded upon a cord that he wore about his neck. The disc was enamelled with soft, bright colours and gleamed like a jewel, and I knew it for the talisman Earl Simon had given him beside the road to Hereford, a year and a half ago.

Some cunning artist had made this tiny image of a great beauty. A little face in profile, pure like a queen on a coin, with one large, confiding eye gazing before, a folded, dreaming mouth, and a braid of dark, gilded hair on her shoulder, the Lady Eleanor de Montfort, twelve years old, looked with a grave, high confidence into her future, towards a bridegroom and an estate fitting her nobility. A wonderful thing it was, but not wonderful enough, for it missed the warmth of her full-face gaze, that stopped the heart with its trust and its challenge.

'You have seen her,' said Llewelyn in awe. 'Is she truly so?'

I said: 'This is but the half. She is more. If this image could turn its head and look you in the eyes, and speak to you, then you would know.'

'And can this face,' he said, rather to himself than to me, and brooding upon the little medallion in fascination and dread, 'ever look upon me as I saw Cristin look upon you?'

It was not my response he wanted, nor even hers, for she was still barely fifteen years old, and a long way off in France, with more than distance, dividing her from him. Rather he longed for a sign from God that he had the right to believe and to hope. And when there was no sign, he took that for a sign in itself, that the duty was laid in his own hands. He took the medallion into his palm and held it before him in the little circle of reddish light, and the face flushed into rose, as if the blood stirred under her pearl-clear skin, and the movement caused the lamp to quiver, so that its light trembled briefly over her folded lips and caused them to smile. He saw it, and smiled in return, in the night of his triumph, with the golden talaith gleaming in his hair.

'There is nothing you or I can do but wait and trust,' he said, 'but that we have learned how to do. I had two vows registered in heaven, to win the acknowledgement of my right, the birthright of her sons, and to lay it at her feet. The first is done. The second, God helping me, I will do, though I wait life-long. You see her, the bud of a royal stem, and the daughter of that tremendous man, better than royal. From such blood, what princes will spring! If they took her away to the end of the world, I would not give her up. Her father pledged her to me, and I have pledged myself to her. The more spears they array between her and me, the more surely will I reach her at last. I have waited but two years for her yet, and she is still hardly out of childhood. For Earl Simon's daughter I will wait as long as I must. Either I will have Eleanor de Montfort, or I will have none.'

So he said, and so he kept. For however Goronwy and Tudor and all his council, thereafter, urged on him his duty to take a wife, and ensure the succession to that throne of Wales which was his own perfected creation, he smiled and passed on unmoved. And however they paraded before him the names and persons of all the noble ladies of Wales, any one of whom he might have had at will, still he never took his eyes from the image of Eleanor, that shone like a private star to him day and night. And still he saw her twelve years old and in profile, waiting, like himself, for the miraculous moment when the bud would blossom, and she would turn her head and look him in the eyes, and reach him her hand upon their marriage day.

THE Hounds OF Sunset

CHAPTER I

In the autumn of the year of Our Lord, twelve hundred and sixty-nine, King Henry of England, third of that name, brought to a triumphant completion his great new church of Westminster, the dream and passion of his life. For such was his devotion to the Confessor that the dearest wish of his heart had always been to create a worthy tomb for the precious relics of that great king and saint, and house it in a splendid church, as a jewel in a casket. And though his long reign – for this was his fifty-third regnal year since his nobles set him on the throne, a child of nine – had been troubled and torn constantly by wars and dissensions and feuds, by entanglements with popes and kings and princes, and though power had slid in and out of his hands, and the winds of other men's wills blown him hither and thither like thistledown, for all these griefs and follies and misfortunes he had never relinquished that purpose and intent, but always returned to it as soon as he was master of his own actions.

As a child he had laid the foundation stone of the new work, when the monks in their ambitious zeal for their saint and their concern for the proper honouring of Our Lady grew dissatisfied with their old church and set out to rebuild, and in particular to add a great Lady Chapel at the eastern end behind the altar. Their plans outgrew their pockets, and devoured all the alms and grants within their reach, and when they despaired and owned their helplessness the king took the work upon himself as an act of piety. Certain follies of his own in the matter of Sicily, certain unattainable ambitions, certain exasperations of his nobles and people tore him away from the work again and again, and counted almost fifty years away before he came at last to this happy consummation. But in this year of his blessed achievement I think he saw all that procession of life and death as but a painted scene of judgment upon a chapel wall, to be contemplated in peace for its colours when its perils were no more than half-remembered dreams.

And we in Wales, who had contended with him life-long until the peace of Montgomery, then two years old, did not grudge him this victory, of all victories. Give him his due, in this passion at least he was not changeable, he who in all things else span with the wind and ebbed and flowed with the tide. He was happier building than fighting, and it showed in the quality of what he built.

It was in July, in the highest summer, when my lord Llewelyn's court was at Rhuddlan, that King Henry's messenger came, bearing a most cordial invitation to the prince of Wales to attend the festivities in

October at Westminster, when the body of the Confessor was to be translated with great splendour and ceremony to the new tomb. It was an earnest of the easy relationship between these royal neighbours that the prince should be among the first to be bidden to the feast, and an even more marked sign of the times that the royal messenger should be that very Welsh clerk of the chancellery who had often served us, in the years of enmity, as our closest intelligencer to the English court. Cynan was not and never had been suspect, but before Montgomery he would never have been sent on the king's errands into Wales, his Welsh blood being reason enough for trusting him only close about the royal offices, and with the lowly work of copying, at that, whatever his ability. Now he came not as clerk and servant but as envoy in his own right, and with a groom to attend to his needs on the way. He did his formal office in hall with a beaming face but an earl's solemnity, but at meat at the high table afterwards he unbuttoned and was a boon companion, proving himself with a good clerkly voice when there was singing. This man I knew well from many meetings in old years upon Llewelyn's business, and to the prince himself Cynan's fine legal hand was familiar enough, but never before had they sat at one table together.

'I see,' said Llewelyn, smiling as he complimented him, 'that we made your fortune at Montgomery as well as our own. You may climb now in the king's favour with a good heart and a single mind.'

Cynan shook his head at that, and said there were no gains without losses, for he grew fat and easy now that his best occupation was gone. And so in truth he did, for he had still that white smoothness about him, but as if somewhat swollen, with the first signs of a paunch under his gown. He had been an old young man, and in time would be a young old man, changing without much change. His brow was by some inches higher, and time was setting about giving him the tonsure I had coveted in my boyhood and never attained.

'I was meant always to be a good doer,' he said, grinning a little wryly at setting himself among the stock we reared, 'but there's no thin living can wear away the flesh like the fret of danger, or keep the neck lissome like the eternal need to be looking over a man's shoulder. Now I rest easy, and turn my victuals into fair, fat meat. Your peace, my lord, may have made my head more secure on my shoulders, but it looks like turning my body into a bladder of lard.'

'God forbid,' said Llewelyn, laughing, 'that I should have to call out my guard again and break this land apart to keep you in hard condition. Are you so discontented with a quiet life? You talk like David. Where there's no mischief there's no sport! Though I think my brother's new little wife has broken him to harness, if her spell holds, and of that we may all be glad.'

So lightly then he spoke of David, whom he had loved best of his three brothers, and who had twice deserted and betrayed him, and twice returned, half-grudging and half-famished, into his too lavish grace.

'And do you carry,' he said, 'the like invitation to David? I take it the Lord Edward would see to that.' For King Henry's heir had grown up, until his thirteenth year, in close companionship with David, then ward at the English court, and that early alliance wrung them both, and had cost us pains enough before our two countries came to so arduous a peace.

'I do,' said Cynan, 'though what part the Lord Edward needed to play is more than I know. The king is happy, he wills less to no man. I think he calls every lord of his acquaintance to share his own blessedness.'

'That I believe,' said Llewelyn, and smiled in some wonder but little bewilderment at the image he had of King Henry, who in happiness would scatter his own substance of mind and body like largesse, and in apprehension or fright would strike out about him with feeble but inexhaustible malice, like a child. In both he was childlike. When he was wounded he would deal out wounds to any who ventured near, when he was in bliss he would spend himself like a fountain of love. But always he must be the centre and spring from which ban and blessing came. 'Tell me,' said Llewelyn, 'of how things go with England.'

This order, tendered in open hall and before the entire household of five hundred and more, Cynan understood as it was intended, and regaled us freely with all the current gossip and news of the court, but not yet with any deeper observation drawn from beneath that surface. The Lord Edward's preparations for his crusade, and the king's for the great celebration in honour of his favourite saint, said Cynan, between them had crowded every other interest out of court. The list of those who had taken the cross and intended to go with Edward to the Holy Land made a resounding catalogue of noble names, among them his brother Edmund, his cousin Henry of Almain, William of Valence, who was King Henry's half-brother, Gilbert de Clare, earl of Gloucester, John de Warenne, earl of Surrey, Roger Leyburn, and many more of the young men who frequented Edward's company.

'And the Lord Edward's wife intends,' said Cynan, 'to go to the east with him. She is as absorbed in this enterprise as he, and he thinks of nothing else.'

'So I have seen,' said Llewelyn, 'when he came to meet me in Montgomery in May, in the matter of the dispute in Glamorgan. Truly I believe he was bent on being fair, and we did get some business done, but while his feet walked the Severn water-meadows, I doubt his head was in Jerusalem.'

'Gloucester has taken the cross, no less than the rest,' said Cynan mildly. But he did not pursue that subject until the prince had withdrawn from hall into the high chamber, and had only a few of his closest with him, Tudor ap Ednyfed, the high steward of Wales – for his elder brother Goronwy, who had held that office before him, was a year dead at that time – the royal chaplain, and myself, his private clerk and servant. Then there was open talk of the dispute my lord had with Gilbert de Clare, earl of Gloucester, the only matter of large significance then troubling the good relations we had with England. Not, indeed, the only source of disputation, for when peace is made after ten years and more of border fighting and civil war, when lands have changed hands ten times over, and large honours been dismembered into a number of lesser holdings, with the best will in the world to word the agreement fairly and honestly, there must still be a hundred plots of land hotly disputed at law, and with reasonably good cases on both sides. The only remedy is in arbitration and give and take, in goodwill on both sides to do justice and keep the peace. But land is land, and ambition is ambition, and all too often goodwill was in short supply when it came to sacrificing an acre or two of meadow or woodland.

The prince had every reason to be highly content with his gains in the treaty of Montgomery, for it had established him as lord of all Wales, and of all the homages of the lesser Welsh chiefs, recognised and honoured in his title and right. And he was bent on fulfilling his part of the agreement loyally, restraining his men from the border raiding to which they had been accustomed as of right all their lives, and paying punctiliously the instalments of the moneys due in fine for his recognition and alliance. If King Henry had such another prompt and cheerful payer, I never heard him named.

By the same token, he willed to abide by the prescribed arbitration in all cases where he held claim to land disputed by others. It was wearisome to wait out the delays, but he bore them with patience and good-humour. There was but this one matter that roused him to the edge of action.

In the south, in the land of Glamorgan, where the earl of Gloucester had a great castellany about Cardiff, he found himself now close neighbour to the prince, and fearing for his hitherto undisputed power, wished to extend northwards into the lands of Senghenydd, and create such another castle and administration there. The lord of Senghenydd was the last of a princely Welsh line, and had held as vassal of the earl, though only perforce, for his heart was with Wales and Llewelyn. And having his own suspicions of this, the earl had seized him and shipped him away to captivity in Ireland, at Kilkenny, and taken over Senghenydd as his own. When he began the building of a great castle at Caerphilly, to hold down the commote he had usurped, Llewelyn at once protested to the king, for this was plain breach of treaty. King Henry did his best to keep the peace between them, and to bring about some form of compromise that would satisfy both, but while the conferences and councils went on and on, so did the building of the earl's castle, and even the prince's patience was not made to last for ever.

Thus this matter stood when Cynan brought the king's invitation. And in the privacy of the high chamber he could offer some reassurance.

'The Lord Edward goes next month to confer with King Louis in France about the order of their sailing, the supplying of their ships, all the business of the crusade. In the summer of next year they intend to sail from Aigues Mortes. Gloucester is pledged, he *must* go. And when he goes, you have time to make your own dispositions, and to bring others, more accommodating, to reason. Two years and more! The king wills well to you, so does the Lord Edward. Oh, I grant you, the earl is already anxious to get out of his obligation, on the plea of his right to defend his border lands, but that goes down very ill with the Lord Edward, who is more than suspicious of the earl's good faith, and bent on forcing him to keep his pledge. It will be hard for him to stand out against his prince, especially when his own young brother is ardent for the crusade, and was among the first to swear. He cannot for shame let himself be displayed as recreant. It would take a brave man to outface Edward.'

'Or a foolhardy one,' said Llewelyn, 'and that he is.'

'So he may work his own undoing. But for my part I think he must resign himself to the crusade, and then you are rid of him.'

Then Llewelyn went on to ask him again of England, and how the days went there, and this time Cynan understood him in the deeper sense, and so answered him, with much thought.

'England,' he said, 'walks very gently and warily, like a sick man only a short while out of his bed, carefully watching every step before, and not looking behind. The wounds of civil war heal slowly, the worst wrongs to those who chose the losing side have been compounded by better sense, and the land is weary, and grateful for this new quietness. It came as something of a shock to them to be taxed, every free man on his belongings, to help to pay for this crusade, and they grumble as usual, but they'll pay, and take it as a mild penance or a thank-offering for peace in the land. The king is safe on his throne again, the succession secure.'

'And that better order that Earl Simon promised and died for?' said Llewelyn sombrely. 'And Earl Simon himself? All forgotten?'

'Nothing is forgotten,' said Cynan as darkly.

'And nothing changed!' said Llewelyn, with remembering bitterness.

Cynan shook his head. 'It is not so. Two things are changed, and for my life I cannot be sure whether for the better in the end, or the worse, or whether the one strikes out the other and leaves the land but a step from where it stood before. The crown came safe out of all that battering because the king was too soft to be crushed. Also the crown is a unity. But the baronage of England has been rent from head to foot, for it went two several ways and tore itself in half, and if it has not bled to death, it lies very sick. There was a balance there between king and baronage on which England depended for her power, and Earl Simon tried to restore it to true when it leaned perilously one way, and even to better the balance struck before. But God was not pleased to give him the victory, and now the scale dips heavily, for where is the force in the nobility to weigh against it? King Henry is old, and has learned a little sense, and moreover he is a weak man who finds it easier now to own his weakness. But when this overweighted power of monarchy is handed down to a powerful heir, then we shall discover the best and the worst of this changed order.'

Llewelyn watched him and said no word, for Cynan spoke as one equally bound to both England and Wales, faithful in giving to us all the benefit of his wisdom and penetration, yet in his own fashion as true to England as Earl Simon de Montfort himself had been when he ripped her apart with the splendour of his vision and the passion of his virtue. King Henry's clerk knew what passed in the mind of his prince, and smiled at him his smooth and rueful smile.

'I take his pay,' he said, 'and while he wills well to Wales, so do I to him, and will not leave him. I, too, grow older. I am not sorry to sleep easy in my bed. But if ever he, or any other in his room, thinks to tear up this treaty and take to the old games, I shall remember my blood. I have not lost my old skills.'

'I will remember it,' said Llewelyn with a shadowed smile. 'Go on. You had more to say. What is this other thing you find changed that may restore the balance of the first?'

'It is that men's ideas need not die with them,' said Cynan, 'any more than scattered seed dies. In the stoniest of places they may root and grow. Even a man's enemies can learn from him. And if King Henry is too old, the Lord Edward is not, and has cold enough reason and shrewd enough judgment to take what he finds good, and make use of it, though he must take it from the hands of a man he has destroyed. Earl Simon will not be the first to turn his enemy into his heir. And England may be the better for it.'

I caught Llewelyn's eye then, and knew that he was recalling, as I was, the last speech ever I had with Earl Simon, on the high tower of the abbey church at Evesham, before the battle, as we watched the Lord Edward's army in a glitter of steel and wavering veil of dust draw in to our destruction, in confident purpose, without haste, forming their strict array on the march. 'I taught them that,' the earl said with critical approval. And after: 'If he can learn the discipline of battle, he can learn the discipline of statecraft, too. From his enemies, if need be.' Those words Llewelyn had never heard but from my lips, I being then his envoy with the earl's army, but I knew he was hearing them now, as I was, in a voice not mine.

'Not England only,' said Llewelyn, with the face of his dead friend and ally still before his eyes, 'but I pray, Wales also.'

'There are signs,' said Cynan. 'Next to the cardinal-legate who made the peace it was Edward who did the most to curb the bloodiest of the victors, and save what could be saved for the disinherited. He leans to the sensible notion that men who pay the tallages and aids should have their own representatives to see they are fairly levied, and men who fight the battles and bear the weight of policy should have a small voice in forming it. And he is all for law. Yes, there are signs.'

'So nothing is utterly lost,' said Llewelyn.

'Nothing lost,' said Cynan, 'and nothing forgotten.'

He stayed with us the night, and Llewelyn wrote a cordial letter to King Henry, accepting his invitation to the feast. And when Cynan left us, it was to ride on across north Wales into Lleyn, to carry the like bidding to David, certainly to be accepted no less heartily. Llewelyn added a message of his own, with the hope that they might ride together in one royal party, to do Wales the greater honour and show a brotherly front. At that time, though David had been settled on his own agreed lands, approved by commission as his due, for over a year, they met but seldom except in formal council, for it needed time to restore without damage the old relationship between them. And that rather to accommodate David, the betrayer, than Llewelyn, the betrayed, who in the hour of his triumph at Montgomery had kissed and forgiven in honour of

Wales and in the vastness of his own content. But it is not so easy to forgive the man you have twice deserted, when his largeness of mind only redoubles your deep discontent with yourself, and David still went stiffly and formally with his brother and over-lord. His homage and fealty cost him dear because he had paid so little for them. I, who knew him better than most, yet never knew him well enough to know whether he would have welcomed the sting, had he been denied grace and countenance and humbled as he deserved, or flamed into open revolt and defiance. I think he himself did not know, for it was never put to the test. The only time he was shaken into complaining to me, it was that he was mislaid and received again with no more heart burning than if he had been a strayed hound, both his defection and his return taken as events too light and trivial for passion or overmuch ceremony. That to Llewelyn he was worth neither a blessing nor a blow. Which was false, though fiercely he believed it. Llewelyn's passion was not as David's, a bitter fire consuming the heart within, but a glowing warmth that shone on the world without. But the one was as hot as the other.

Howbeit, David replied as civilly, and brought his party to join his brother's at Bala, in Penllyn, from which maenol the court set out in state, in good time to enjoy the fine autumn by the way, and reach Westminster a full week before Saint Edward's day.

I looked for their coming with both eagerness and pain, knowing they would come lavishly attended, and that among their retinue would be two closer to me than my own skin, one whom I longed for, one whom I dreaded, and that I could not have the one without the other.

They rode in on a September evening, before sunset. I was down by the lake, in the fields gleaned to a bleached white after the end of the harvest, and sun-gilded in the slanting light, when I heard first the horns sounding merrily in the distance, on the uplands to the north of the maenol, and then the moving murmur that is compounded of the easy thud and rustle of hooves in grass and gravel, and many voices in talk and laughter, the jingle of harness and the chimes of little bridle bells, and the brief, cajoling calls of falconers after their hawks, a far-off music brought near even in its quietness by the stillness of the air. Then there was a high, pure peal of joyous laughter, a child's utterance in sheer delight of heart, and I knew the child unseen from afar, and turned back to the maenol to be beside my lord when he came out to the gate, as come he would, to welcome his guests. The bright procession wound down the bleached track through the deeper upland grass, and brought all its colours and sounds and voices down to the gate where we waited, half the maenol out to do them honour. David showed very splendid in black embroidered with silver, his head uncovered to the freshening breeze, the curving strands of blue-black hair tossed across his forehead, his eyes, that were blue as harebells, just clouding from their journeying innocence into the veiled withdrawal from which he gazed upon his brother. And he on a tall English horse, a red roan, Edward's gift, like the pretty white palfrey that nuzzled at his elbow, and the girl who rode it, astride like a boy, and booted in soft French leather.

David lighted down, and went before us all to bend the knee to

Llewelyn, and kiss the hand that had reached to embrace him. I do not say he did it to offend, rather in stiff insistence on the hard identities of vassal and overlord, but there could have been no surer way of offending. Yet Llewelyn would not resent him, but let him have his way, and only offered him the kiss of kinship when he rose from his knee. They made each other the common offerings of enquiry and acknowledgement, the one in tolerant patience, the other in unsparing duty. Then David turned to his wife, and here we saw another creature, warm and eager, with the veil lifted from his gaze, and his long, arrogant, icy lips molten into a smile. She slipped her feet from the stirrups and reached down her arms to him, and he swung her easily aloft out of the saddle, and held her eye to eye with him and heart to heart a moment, before he set her on her feet and brought her by the hand to Llewelyn.

The kiss that David's stiff cheek had resisted was welcome to her, as was every gesture of friendliness and affection. Llewelyn had to stoop low to her, for she barely reached David's shoulder, and the prince was by the width of three fingers the taller of the two. And seeing her thus accept with impulsive pleasure what he had suffered like a blow or an insult, David, too, flushed and softened a little, though against his will and in his own despite.

She was then no more than twelve years old, and even for her years not tall, but sturdy and well-made. Nor was she beautiful, but for the bloom that all young creatures have. She had great brown eyes like a hind, innocent and wild, and curling hair of the same colour, and a soft, grave mouth given to rare but sudden and whole-hearted laughter. Loud and talkative enough when she was with David, she was quiet and shy in company, though not at all timid. And this was Elizabeth Ferrers, daughter of Robert Ferrers, earl of Derby, and wife to Prince David of Wales.

Child as she was, she was already once wedded and widowed. She was close kin to the king, her mother being his niece, Mary, daughter to the count of La Marche, Henry's eldest half-brother, a royal lady who had been married to Robert Ferrers when she was but seven years old, and her bridegroom only two years older. After the same dynastic custom they had married Elizabeth as a child to one William Marshal of Norfolk, who by his first wife already had sons old enough to be father to this tender creature. But her elderly husband followed the fortunes of Earl Simon, and died in that cause in the year of Evesham. Maid and widow, she had come into the king's wardship when her father, too, was dispossessed of all he had for his part in the civil wars, and since law had allowed her part of her dower lands from the Marshal inheritance, she had brought with her certain manors in Norfolk when King Henry, at the Lord Edward's instance, bestowed her upon David in marriage. A match not to be missed, and David accepted it willingly, lands and lady and all, together with the Lord Edward's patronage and favour. Of all of which, I fancy, he thought he knew the relative values. Yet I saw for myself, now for the third time seeing those two together, a year married after the world's practical fashion, that Elizabeth had had something to teach him, and he had found himself learning without resentment. For every look they exchanged, every touch of their sleeves brushing every intonation of their voices when they talked together, was eloquent beyond words.

I looked among the dismounting company within the courtyard for the face I most desired to see, knowing she would not be far from Elizabeth. For ever since David had brought his bride home, Cristin had been her closest confidante and attendant. David would have no other to care for the child, for in a world where he doubted most men and held most women gently enough but lightly, for Cristin he had and kept always a deep regard and that alone was enough to incline his wife most warmly to her, even if they had not, from the first, been drawn to each other. And I was glad that Cristin should have a fair young creature close to her, to love and guard, she who had no child by her husband, and never would have child by her love. For we were cursed and blessed, she and I, in mutual loving blessed indeed, but cursed in that ours was a love forbidden and impossible of fruit, since she was the wife of my half-brother.

I found her among the first to follow into the maenol, Cristin, Llywarch's daughter, her black hair hidden under a white wimple, and a white mule stepping delicately under her. And as happened always with us at every new meeting when I found her, her eyes were on me, and when mine held them they grew so large and crystal-clear in their purple-grey, the colour of irises, and so drew me into them like the seduction of deep water, that I died in them and was reborn into bliss as a drowning man by the mercy of God and the grace of faith may sink through death into the peace of paradise.

She was within a month or two the same age as David, both being then thirty-three years old. We were long experienced in loving without greed or regret, she and I, and though we never spoke words of love, nor asked any fulfilment but the mutual knowledge we already possessed, neither did we avoid each other, nor any longer dissemble the truth that we had between us such trust and regard as few ever enjoy with man or woman. To what end? Godred knew very well how things stood with us, and knew that we knew, and by all means in his power, having glimpsed a passion of which he was incapable, had sought to drag it down to a level he could first understand, and then befoul. Who knows but it was Godred who kept us resolute in our purity?

So at this meeting, though I knew well that he was there among the company of knights and squires that followed David into the maenol, and needed no telling that he would be looking for me as hungrily as ever I looked for Cristin, I made no ado about going to her directly and with open gladness, and she gave me her hand, and said the same current words that I was saying to her and let me help her down and take the bridle from her. Assignations we never made, but met when we met, and were glad. Surely we had, after our fashion, a compact with God to be endlessly grateful for what had been given us, and not to grasp at more. But we had never undertaken not to hope.

She had barely set foot on the ground, and her hand was still in mine, when he was there between us, clasping an arm of each in his long hands, and deliberately scoring against my wrist the silver ring he wore, the fellow to one I had once worn. His father and mine had long ago given the second ring to the girl he took for one night in the rushes of the hall at Nevin, and she, years afterwards, to her son, the fruit of that union. By that token I had known my half-brother when we met. He had not then known me, nor for some time after, nor had any word ever been said, even now, to make it clear that he knew me for his father's bastard, yet always, when most he willed to remind me how we three were bound together, and how I might, if I willed, draw even closer, make myself his familiar and equal, and enjoy what now I only revered, always he contrived to twist that ring before my eyes, with its little severed hand holding a rose. But he had no power even to make us start, or loose too soon the clasp of our hands. With nothing to hide, why should we hide it?

'Well, Saint Samson?' said Godred, in that high, sweet voice of his, and linking his arm in mine. 'We are to go on pilgrimage together, it seems, to the Confessor's shrine. Three or four weeks of sweet companionship and easy living! I mean to enjoy you to the full, this time.' And with the other arm he encircled Cristin, and so drew us with him towards the hall, leaving the grooms to lead away the horses.

I am swart and plain, and he was lithe and fair and comely, with curling hair the colour of ripe white wheat, and round, gold-brown eyes. Yet she loved me, and not him!

'And Cristin shares my pleasure,' he said, closing his fingers possessively about her shoulder, 'though she is not so quick to utter it as I. We never forget, Samson, that it was you who restored us to each other, when we never thought to meet again. I speak for both – do I not, my love? This once join your voice with mine!'

She looked straight before her, and smiled. 'Samson knows my mind,' she said. 'There is no need to look back so far. He knows I forget nothing. But if you want me to say it, yes, I shall take pleasure in this journey together. Yes, I am happy.'

So he had his answer, but it was not the right answer, though he swallowed it with grace. For it was not what he wanted, it was outrage to him, that she should be happy, when he, though through his own curst nature, was surely among the unhappiest souls on earth.

During the days of our preparations it did happen now and then that I had speech with her alone, while he was busy with his own duties. It was not that at these times we spoke of our own affairs, but there were other things I had to ask of her that needed a degree of privacy, too. David was my breast-brother, my mother's nurseling, my own charge in his childhood, as now Cristin cared for the child he had taken in marriage, and I needed to know the best and the worst concerning him, for no matter how often he offended against Llewelyn and discarded me, yet I could not but love him.

'He is still sore,' said Cristin, 'and still denies with anger that his wounds are self-inflicted. He knows his own sins, but will neither repent them nor accept forgiveness for them. Edward embraced him when he deserted Llewelyn, and he despises Edward in his heart for embracing a traitor. Llewelyn in honour of his triumph tossed David's offences out of mind, and haled him back openly without penalty, never denying he deserved it, and David worships him for it because he could not have done as much himself, and hates him for it because so easy a forgiveness slights both the offence and the offender. They are two creatures made in moulds so different, and yet so linked, they cannot touch without hurt, nor be apart without loss. And yet he does love his brother! Sometimes I doubt he loves Llewelyn more than Llewelyn loves him. He could not so hate him if he did not.'

I asked, for God knows I had good reason to understand the power of personal happiness, what was to be hoped from this marriage Edward had made.

She was standing beside me in the twilight when this passed, having put her lady to bed, for that shy royal creature awoke with the light and tired with the fall of darkness like all children. From the portal of Elizabeth's apartments we could see the silver of the lake like a spilled coin in moonlight. My sleeve was against my love's sleeve, and we were at peace, but for all these souls we loved, and for whom we desired the same peace.

Cristin said: 'She has tamed him. She does not know it – how could she? She is still half a child. There is no one so astonished as David. And how is that possible, since he knows his own beauty? None better! I think he never considered that a wife should look at him and find him beautiful. He took her as a chattel, a means to lands, and to the Lord Edward's continuing favour. I doubt he ever looked at her, until she had looked at him, and gone the way of most women who look at him. Half child she may be, but she is half woman, too. She looked at him, and she loved. Is it so strange? And you know him, he is gentle and playful with children, he awoke only when he found himself clasping a woman he had warmed into life, roused and ready for him.'

'He has bedded her, then?' I said.

'Surely! You have only to look at them. There have an understanding of the flesh.' It was true. There was no mistaking that radiance that shone out of them when they touched each other. She spoke of it with a calm face but a careful voice, regarding without envy but with secret grief what they had and we could never have. 'Her women told her, when they married her the first time, child as she was, what would be expected of her some day as a wife. She was prepared. And did you ever hear of a woman who complained of David's loving? He would have let her alone a year or two yet, I judge, if she had not stirred him. It charmed and moved him that she should love him and show her love.'

'And he,' I said, 'does he also love?'

'He is pleased and disarmed and startled, how can he choose but respond? It's a new delight and a great flattery. Whether it will last, and keep its power, who knows and who can ever know with David? But yes. I think I would call it love. Whatever he does, he will never wilfully hurt her. But without willing it he might destroy her,' said Cristin with great gravity. 'Whoever loves David is in danger.'

And that was truth. And I was all the more glad that this proud, confiding and sensitive child should have Cristin watching over her. The time might come when she would need a friend, and nowhere could she have found another so brave and so loyal.

We rode for London at the end of September, a great party, not only to do credit to the royal house of Wales, but also to pay honour to King Henry, who by and large had played fair with us since the agreement, and who deserved his triumph. We crossed the Berwyns in brisk, bright . weather, and had good hawking there. Llewelyn's falconer had in his charge not only the prince's own birds, but several he had been training as gifts for the king and the Lord Edward, and they made splendid proving flights along the way, and showed their mettle to such good effect that he was in high content with the fruit of his labour. We carried with us also venison for the feasts and for the king's larder.

At Oswestry we crossed into England, with no need of the letters of safe-conduct sent from the court, and that was pleasant indeed. So it should always be, yet men have free passage so seldom, and so briefly. But this autumn was blessed, even to the weather, and the ride into Shrewsbury, where we halted overnight at the abbey, was truly as serene as a pilgrimage, a dream of ease in those lush fields and softly rolling valleys. Yet on this road I had memories, too, for I had ridden it once in Llewelyn's service on the way to the parliament of Oxford, thus far the same road, and there was no evading the reminders of that journey, or the remembered face of the man I had seen at the end of it, kneeling in grand, contained and private prayer at the shrine of St Frideswide. And Llewelyn, too, felt his presence, for I saw how he watched me, and willed not to be seen watching me, and hesitated whether to speak or be silent. Silent he was in the end, for of speech there was no need. He knew and I knew that the image of Earl Simon rode with us all the way.

After Shrewsbury we were on a way new to me, for we took the king's great highway called Watling Street, which they say the Romans made, and which drives by long, straight stretches headlong for London. One night we passed at the priory of Lichfield, and the next at Coventry, no great ride, for we had time and to spare. And when we were private after meat at Coventry, Llewelyn suddenly raised his head and turned to gaze to the south-west, and said, so low that I knew it was for none but himself and me: 'We are very close, are we not, to Kenilworth?'

I said that we were, that if he willed we could linger here a day, and he and I could ride there. If he so willed, alone. His face was fixed and bright, still as a royal head upon a gold coin, and even so coloured, a tissue of fine drawn lines in gilt and umber. Those who thought him moderate and tempered and equable, a man well-set in the cautious craft of state, did not know him as I knew him. He and I were born in the same night, under the same stars, his mother was my mother's patron and mistress, there was no dividing us. And I knew him possessed and inspired, a soul like the flame of a candle on an altar, kindled and unquenchable in dedication to the cause of Wales. Yet in pursuit of that passion he had encountered one perhaps greater than himself, burning with a grander vision, and for a time those two flames had been one. If I forgot nothing, how could I conceive that he should forget?

'No,' said Llewelyn after a long thought, and in a voice so low I strained to hear. 'Not here! Kenilworth is not the place.'

In London we were very honourably lodged, the princes with their immediate households in King Henry's own palace of Westminster, some close officers, of whom I was one, in the guest-halls of the collegiate church of St Peter, the object of our pilgrimage, while the knights of the escort were sent on to that Tower of which I had so many old memories. Thus Cristin, being tirewoman to Elizabeth, remained in the royal island of Westminster close to me, while Godred was removed to the Tower, and both she and I could breathe freely and look each other in the eyes when we met with gladness and calm, untainted by the poison of his misery and malice; which neither of us knew how to cure. And by that blessedness, in part, I remember that great celebration of St Edward's day.

That is a wonder, that city of Westminster, in extent so small, in beauties so great, so teeming then with all the nobility of the land, for there was no earl nor baron nor cleric who did not wish to be present at the translation of the saint. In shape almost square, it is rimmed with water on every side, for on the east lies the Thames with all its ships and barges, while from the west flows in the little river Tyburn, to fill the long ditches that close in the royal enclave from north and south. And all this moated town is filled with the many and splendid buildings of palace and church, colleges and dortoirs and hospices and chapels, the gardens and orchards and cloisters of the monks, the stables and boathouses and offices of the king, and everything needful to life, bakehouse and farm and fisheries, lodgings for good poor men, alms-houses and mews and kitchens. I marvelled at the great press of guests this city could receive and accommodate, and yet at this time it was full to overflowing, and so glowing with ardour and excitement, so full of voices and music, colour and movement, that the dullest heart could not but be stirred.

And there in the midst of this island city rises the long, lofty roof of the great church, visible from every part, from every part commanding and drawing the eye. The marvel within we were not to see until the great day of the translation and the first mass, but the marvel without was enough to hold us at gaze all the days we spent there in waiting. Such noble, springing tracery in stone, such grace of windows and portals, I had never seen. The monks, before their coffers ran dry, had themselves built the Lady Chapel they desired at the eastern end of the old church, and the form of this was fine, but time and the king's passion for his act of piety had outrun it far, and the body of the church which he had now completed, transepts and apse and choir, soared above incomparably tall and fair.

King Henry received Llewelyn and David in audience as soon as we came there, but I did not see him close until the day of the feast, only now and again running about his creation and vanishing again into his palace in transports of excited happiness, his master-mason and clerks and familiars hard on his heels like a swarm of bees. He was then sixty-two years old, and had lived through a long and war-torn reign that had destroyed many a stronger vessel, and though he had ridden out all the tempests he bore the signs upon him. Slender and graceful always, he was now very frail in appearance, his face worn and transparent, his fair, well-tended hair and beard blanched to an ivory-grey, and doubtless he was very weary, but the rapture of his achievement filled him with force and energy. If he had laboured on his kingdom with such devoted concentration of mind he would surely have been the best of kings. But at least, if his talents had not gone into statecraft, they had spent themselves on something lasting, lovely and worthy in the end, and I give him the credit due.

It had been the king's intention that he and his queen should wear their crowns of state upon the saint's feast, and that all things should be ordained in the same fashion as at a coronation, which meant that the customary writs had been sent out to all those who had special ceremonial rights and duties, and for some weeks they had been making great preparations for the occasion. But on the vigil of the feast King Henry made belated proclamation in Westminster Hall that he had had better thoughts in the matter, and deemed it presumptuous to assume the crown a second time, and especially felt it his part rather to be humble and joyful in his service to Saint Edward, than proud in his own estate. So the formal ceremonies were remitted, though all who cared to come to the festival might do so, and after the translation and the mass might remain to share in the banquet.

'That's but half the story,' said Llewelyn, when I attended him in the evening to make preparation for next day. 'It seems he's still beset with civil wars, though minor ones now. The citizens of London had laid out lavishly on plate and robes, since they owe service in the butlery on such state festivals, when the crowns are worn. But then the men of Winchester also laid claim to the butlery. It's a costly business, and no doubt either city would have resisted if it had been exacted from them as a duty, but neither was willing to relinquish it as an honour. There would have been quarrels, at the least, maybe a little blood-letting. He thought wiser to bow out of his crown gracefully and avoid the contention.'

It was too much, I said, to suppose that anything could ever go altogether smoothly and decorously with King Henry. Nothing he touched ever came finally to ruin, but always he walked creaking ice that cracked behind him, and came to land again safely by something a little short of a miracle.

'Ah, he'll ride this little storm,' said Llewelyn, 'at no more cost than the meat and wine he provides them. But he has graver matters on his mind, too, when the light of his shrine is not too brilliant to let him see them. Gloucester has not come to the festival. And tomorrow being the great day, clearly he does not intend to come.'

From our view it was no bad thing that Gilbert de Clare should put himself in ill odour with both king and prince. All the more would they be disposed to listen, in the matter of the rape of Senghenydd and the building of Caerphilly, to the protagonist who did come at the king's invitation, and was prepared, as clearly Gilbert was not, to meet his opponent and consider sensible arbitration. By his intransigence and disobedience we could not fail to gain credence.

'He is mad,' said David, who was with us that evening, and throughout showed a front of unity with his brother, though during the past days he had been much in the Lord Edward's company. 'If he does not come he turns the king into an enemy for the sake of his favourite saint, let alone the matter of the crusade. And Edward is already bitterly angry with him for trying to slide out of his obligations. He took the oath of his own free will, like the rest, and Edward will hold him to it. Gloucester's party should provide one of the strongest companies. Edward is absolute that he cannot fulfill his undertakings to King Louis and to God properly if Gloucester breaks his oath. If he does not come in time for tomorrow, the king will send for him, and he had better pay heed. But my guess is, he'll come. At the last moment, with the worst grace, and insolently, but he'll come.'

But the morrow came, and the whole court and its guests rose with the dawn to make ready, but Gilbert de Clare did not come. Nor, in the end, was this the only vexation King Henry had to contend with on the supreme day of his life, for not only did the citizens of London stand so rigidly on their dignity as to withdraw after the great mass ended, and refuse the feast, while the men of Winchester crowed over them and stayed to eat and drink their fill, but there was also a grander and more bitter contention, which ended with London laid under an interdict for a time, though for all I could see it made little difference to life in the city, and no one fretted overmuch. The trouble arose out of an old rivalry between the two archbishops, for he of York had always insisted that he had the right to have his cross carried before him in the province of Canterbury as at home, and his brother of Canterbury had always resisted it. Now the archbishop of Canterbury at this time, the queen's uncle Boniface of Savoy, was very old, and too frail to be present at the great ceremony, and so his brother of York, Walter Giffard, had his way at the translation, and had his cross paraded before him, to the great offence of all his fellow-bishops, so that they made no move, when the time came, to join him in the procession round the new church, but sat implacably in the stalls of the monks, and let him cense the shrine alone. And old Boniface, when he heard of it, was so resentful that he placed London under interdict, and a month later he said his last mass in England at the coast, before sailing home to his native Savoy, where he died a year afterwards.

But as for the great concourse of worshippers that thronged into the church that day, I think these annoyances fell away from them unnoticed, as motes of dust vanish in a great brightness, or if they are seen at all, show like flying jewels. For truly that was a wonder. I think in this world there could be no building more glorious. The work the king had done – and rightly he can so claim, for though he had the finest masons and jewellers and metal-workers to labour for him, yet he himself had firm views on what he would have, and set it out in detail – comprised the eastern end of the nave, where his own royal chair was,

419

the choir and the north and south transepts, the presbytery and the chapels and ambulatory of the apse, and beyond these to the east a short ambulatory leading to the Lady Chapel, which the monks had built some years before. And behind the high altar, encircled by the chapels, the new shrine of the saint was raised aloft.

Such was the extent of the work. But what can be said of the form, of the great soaring columns of marble that led our eyes upwards as we entered, so high we had to crane backwards to look up into the gilded ribs and bosses of the vault, of the carven shields, the diapered wall-spaces, the filigree windows, the traceries of screen and arcade, of the glorious colours of painted angels and sacred medallions, the grisaille glass studded with armorial shields. The sun shining through them filled all the vault with singing sparks of emerald and ruby and gold.

In this enclosure of splendour, to the chanting of the monks of St Peter and in the presence of all who could crowd anywhere within the walls, the relics of Saint Edward the Confessor were reverently taken in their casket from the old shrine, swathed with rich draperies, and carried on the shoulders of King Henry, his brother Richard of Cornwall, king of the Romans, the king's sons, the Lord Edward and Edmund of Lancaster, and as many more of the great nobles as could get a hand to the bier, to the new, raised shrine aloft behind the altar. Edward's great height so threw things out of balance that he was forced to let the coffin rest in his arm rather than on his shoulder, to accommodate his father, who was a head shorter. Where Edward went, who was not? Many fell short of him by head and shoulders, too.

Those who could not pretend to bearing any part of the blessed burden nevertheless reached a hand on one side or the other, at least to touch, and so walked slowly with the bearers, and among them went Llewelyn and David, one upon either side. Others came to touch but once as the coffin passed. So they carried Saint Edward up the stone stairway into his new chapel, a spacious place floored in red and green porphyry and Purbeck marble, with the great shrine of the same materials in the midst, studded everywhere with semi-precious stones and mosaic work, with a tiered feretory of solid gold at the top. And in this sumptuous tomb they laid him, and heard the first mass of the new church sung in his honour.

It so chanced that I had a place from which there was a clear view of the king's chair, and while mass was said I watched him, for he was so bright and pale that the light seemed almost to shine through him. His seat was raised, and the shrine of the saint was very lofty, and I think he could see, above the high altar, the golden crest of the feretory that marked the holy place. He never took his eyes from it, and for the first time I saw his face free of the single, strange blemish that had always spoiled his comeliness and kingliness, that drooping of one eyelid that cast shadows of doubt over his proffered honesty and gave warning of his twisting ability to deceive, a flaw he had handed on to his son. Edward sat close beside him, his seat lower, but his face on a level with his father's. I had them almost in full-face, the one oval superimposed upon the other, the old upon the young, until the light played tricks and seemed to make the young change places and blot out the old. Henry was grown so fragile and clear, Edward was so large and solid and full of blood and bone, his vigour and violence overwhelmed the king's small, pale flame, but could not extinguish it.

He was then thirty years old, this Lord Edward, a giant just coming to his prime, hardened and experienced in political contention and civil war, a man well-proportioned, long-limbed, moving with confidence and certainty in his body. He had large, heavy, handsome features, a great cliff of a brow, and his hair, which in childhood, as I remembered, had been flaxen, almost silver, was now so dark a brown as to be almost black, and his long, level brows appeared quite black. He affected rich but dark clothing, and little jewellery, having no need of adornment to draw eyes to him, his stature alone making him known wherever he walked. In repose, as I saw it then, his face was severe to grimness, attentive to the mass but not moved, as if his mind was on other business. His left eyelid drooped over the dark brown eye. I thought the flaw in him more marked than when I had seen him previously. Closed up in armour I had seen him last, dealing sharply-judged and unrelenting death at Evesham. But long before that, at Oxford, I had seen him close and spoken with him. He had the heavy lid then, but when he was moved or intent it hardly showed. When he followed Earl Simon and hung on his words it showed not at all. He was not moved now, or else the trick had grown on him unawares. I do believe he was devout, I believe his heart was set on his crusade in absolute and devoted duty, taking upon him both his father's oath and his own. But when I looked again at the king, I saw how far the father had outstripped the son.

He had no such grand abilities, no such stature or prowess in arms, no force such as Edward had, and God knows he had many faults and weaknesses, and had led his own baronage, and us, and all who ever had to do with him, a devious and unkingly dance, as quick to turn and twist as any fox, being a timorous man who used what weapons he had. And yet to the end, and more than all at the end, there was a kind of innocence about him, as of a clean creature soiled by running in fright against obstacles that dirtied his robes but could not corrode his being. Often had I hated him and blamed him, and called him forsworn and devious, and so he had often been, and yet I watched his rapt and dedicated face there in St Peter's church on St Edward's day, and it was washed clean and pure like a child's, and yet deeply sorrowful and humble like a penitent's, and it seemed to me that in his supreme act of devotion he was confessing and repenting all the unworthinesses of his life, and from the heart paying for them as best he could, until God should show him a better and surer way.

I looked at Llewelyn, who was not far away, and saw that he also was contemplating King Henry's face, though I think he had a narrower profile to study than I. His was a countenance I knew far better than my own, broad at the wide-set eyes, that were very straight of gaze and darker and deeper than Edward's, broad at the jutting bones of cheek and jaw, and these bold planes of bone all outlined by the spare curves of clipped golden-brown beard he wore. Not a face to confide too readily, but neither did it evade or conceal. I had seen it once as fixed and devoted as King Henry's was now, when he kept vigil with the sword he had sanctified to the service of a Wales which was then uncreated, as though he set himself to assemble from a scattering of shattered shards a single vessel of gold. And so he had done, and he was acknowledged prince of the nation he had made. It was another kind of achievement, but he knew and respected another man's apotheosis when it shone before his eyes.

So this one passionate devotion looked upon another as single and pure as itself, however different, and recognised and saluted it generously, smiling. And I remember thinking to myself that, if God was of Llewelyn's mind, King Henry was assured of his absolution.

We stayed in Westminster for some days after the festival was over, and Llewelyn had two meetings with the king and the Lord Edward and their closest advisers, to discuss the vexed matter of Senghenydd, and put his own case as to which party was infringing the treaty there. Certain minor disputes concerning the borders were not difficult to resolve, with goodwill on both sides. But though King Henry, two days after the feast-day, had sent letters of safe-conduct to the earl of Gloucester, with the plain intimation that his presence was required as a matter of feudal duty, still Gilbert made no haste to obey. We could not wait his pleasure, but did make natural, though I think fair, use of his absence to emphasise our own case. Then we left for home, taking a very cordial farewell. And this time we went not by the same way we had come, but by Oxford and Worcester, at Llewelyn's wish.

I had no clear idea then of what was in his mind, but when we drew nearer to Evesham, and he took his party for lodging not to that abbey, but to Richard of Cornwall's foundation of Hailes, I did guess at his reason, and when he announced that he meant to spend two nights in that hospitable place I was sure. Not as Llewelyn, prince of Wales, in royal progress of state, would he approach the place of the death and burial of Earl Simon, or make himself known to the monks who had buried his friend. But Evesham is but a little way from Hailes, and with a day in hand he might go there unrecognised and unexalted, like other men. I was ready when he sent for me to him, on the first evening, and shut himself up with me alone.

At the thought of an idle day David had frowned, restless for home once he was away from the court, and asked with his chill formality what he might as freely have declared as his intent, to ride on ahead, with the prince's leave, and be about his proper responsibilities in Lleyn. And I think Llewelyn was glad, for whatever had to do with Earl Simon's memory was tension and disquiet between them, recalling old discords not yet fully forgiven, even upon Llewelyn's side, much less on David's. So we were private, we might go where we would, as humbly as we would, and none to question us, even with his eyes.

'I have a consecration of my own to make,' Llewelyn said. 'Will you ride with me tomorrow, after David has taken his people off? They'll be away early; he's impatient for home now. Unhappy the man with two homes, born Welsh and bred English, and no fault of his own. He tears a string from his heart when he leaves the one, but once that's broken he cannot wait to get to the other, and bind it up again there. And he thinks I do not know!'

Unwilling to speak for or against David where we touched too near the grief he had helped to make, and the warfare in which he had taken the opposing side, I asked him where we rode. At that he smiled, but very gravely.

'You know as well as I, Samson. How could you or I pass so close, and not draw in to pay him honour? And I in particular, who have never yet seen that place. We will go to Evesham, you and I, and go as rustic and plain as any of the country people who frequent his grave. I want no honour, none of the respect given to princes, where he lies, until I have fulfilled both the oaths I made to his memory.'

I said I had somewhat of my own to vow to Earl Simon, and would go with him gladly. And Llewelyn thanked me as though I had done him great courtesy, which was his way.

When I left him, I met with Cristin in the hall of the hospice, coming from her lady's bed-chamber with a blue brocaded gown over her arm, to have some pulled threads of the embroidery stitched back into the pattern. She looked upon me with the radiant stillness that was better than any smile. Her night-black hair was loosed about her shoulders from its day-time braids. Silken and bright and heavy it was always, but absolute black, raven-black, with never a sheen of David's steely blue. It made her brow so white beneath that my eyes dazzled. Cristin went in the sun and the wind freely, and the sun would not burn nor the wind abrade her.

'She is asleep,' she said, seeing me eye Elizabeth's gown. 'She was tired out from the ride today. So much air and such a brisk breeze.'

'Asleep,' I said, 'until he wakes her?'

'He will not wake her,' said Cristin. 'He can be patient and tender to little things; it's with the great he has no forbearance. They tell me,' she said, 'we are to leave you in the morning early.'

'It is true,' I said. 'David wants to get home. And my lord has other needs.'

'At Christmas,' she said, 'doubtless I shall see you.' For those brothers kept the feasts always in strict form, all the more because of the constraint between them, and the tie of kinship was sacred, so that at the Nativity or soon thereafter they must meet.

I said I trusted so, and wished her and her mistress a blessed journey home. And so we parted, as every meeting and every parting went with us, going from each other without a touch of hand or a turn to gaze. Of such small doubts and pleas we had no need. But with her image before my eyes I went out into the late October night, in the hush of the cloister, to breathe the chill and the darkness. Llewelyn, I knew, was gone to make his evening devotions in Richard of Cornwall's great church, for he was as devout as ever was King Henry, though the small, solitary holiness of the Celtic church, so spare and so sweet, haunted his mind and kept him safe from the worldly charm of such foundations as Hailes. God is somewhere within earshot of every altar, but nearer to our hermit-saints than to the lords of the English church. Yet a brave, demanding voice can reach him everywhere. So Llewelyn went alone to make his prayers for the morrow. And I left him to his vigil.

In the morning early David took his people forward for home, and Godred would embrace me fondly before Cristin's eyes, who might not do as much. He took delight in this brotherly close, and was adroit in so handling me, indifferent as I was, as to turn his ring inward upon his finger and leave the imprint of the hand and rose in the flesh of my arm, as though he stamped his ownership upon me with a brand, like a slave, a reminder of how I was tied to him by my bastardy, and she was his possession. But Cristin was not moved, or if she was he could get from her no sign of it. And then they were on their way out from the gates, and I was both delivered and bereft.

Then Llewelyn and I, in plain country brown like any village travellers, took two of the Welsh ponies and rode for Evesham, which lies to the north of Hailes, and about eight miles distant. A pleasant way enough we had, beside a little river, but the day was clouded over, and before we were halfway it began to rain, the soft, warm, wetting rain of the lowlands, and Llewelyn laughed, and said we should be well able to pass for poor, bedraggled pilgrims among the rest. For this tomb to which we were bound was become a place of great holiness and the resort of the common people in their need, as deeply revered as St Thomas's shrine at Canterbury by all the poor and unprivileged who had hoped so much from the living man. And even we knew, as far away as north Wales, that there had been miracles. The nobility of England, weary of discord and anxious to have their old errors put away out of mind, might accept the crown's verdict that Earl Simon had been rebel and felon, Edward might shun the abbey that held that abhorred body as a place unclean – though his avoidance might as well have been from shame as from hatred! – but to the common folk of England this was the resting-place of a saint, and they frequented it for their comfort, and made sad songs and joyful songs about it, publishing Earl Simon's miracles by word of mouth throughout the whole land.

We entered the town by the bridge over the Avon, that same bridge that Mortimer closed against him and brought him to his death. Busy and tranquil we found the place this October morning, and very fair and fat in its loop of river, the ground climbing towards the unmoated side, the north, where the walls of the abbey rose between us and the battle-field. At every step I drew nearer to that unhealed grief, with none of the duties and vexations and pinpricks of everyday to fend off from me the devastation of loss. For I had known Earl Simon, closely and well, all the last months of his life, and left him only when the head was hewn from his shoulders, and he lay dead beside his eldest son on the upland fields of Evesham. His advice and request that I should avail myself of my clerkhood and take refuge in the abbey with his attendant bishops I refused. But my little skill in arms could not weigh the balance in his favour, and what had I out of it but the grief and the grievance of seeing him die? Yes, something more I think I took away with me, a whole memory that did not turn back short of the last extreme, and so could live with the unforgettable talisman of his face, and need not turn its eyes away.

We were within sight of the great abbey gateway when Llewelyn said, in a voice that called me back from my own vindication to consider his thirst: 'Is this town much changed?' For he had never before seen it, except through my eyes.

I said no, not greatly. There were some new houses, as I remembered it, and peace had brought its own increase, and befriended a market surely always rich in goods, but now easy of access for buyer and seller even from far afield. But, no, not greatly changed. It was as I had known it. The abbey, also. A great and generous house, that had not turned its back upon its slaughtered saint.

'True,' he said, 'what need was there for change? They were hospitable to him living and dead.'

There were people enough going and coming about the courts of the abbey, and in and out of the great church. We lighted down from our ponies and left them in hand with a lay brother who came kindly to attend to any who needed him among the visiting folk. Damp from the soft rain, and dun amongst the homespun poor like veritable brothers, we went into the church. Neither he nor I knew where to look for the tomb we sought, but we followed those who went silently before, for all were bound to the same shrine. We who had come from the splendour of St Edward's translation stepped into another holiness, the antithesis perhaps, but not the contradiction, of the first. What can man do more than the best he knows? And if king and rebel – to give him that name he never earned – hold fast that vision, how are they opposed in the eyes of God?

It was in a dark but noble place, Earl Simon's, tomb. Dark, for this was an old and massive church, not lofty like King Henry's building at Westminster, and the thick walls and narrow windows let in little light to the chapel where he lay. But the plain stone tomb was large and spare and grand, like his mind and spirit, a pure flame in an unrelenting austerity. There was a double step before it, each level worn into a deep hollow – dear God, in how short a time, and by how many humble feet! – and a place on the level surface of the gold-grey stone and polished into darkness, and also hollowed, somewhere in the region of that immense heart, but higher than by rights a heart should be, as the hewn stone was shorter than a middling-tall man should be, for there was no man living in England who did not know that the body within that tomb was headless. I know not who was the first who mounted the two steps and used his own judgment to know where to plant that first reverent kiss, but I bless him and envy him, and where his lips rested thousands upon thousands followed him and kissed, and after them, all in good time, Llewelyn and I.

When he had done so, Llewelyn kneeled upon the upper step, and I drew back from him to leave him private. There was a lamp burning at the head of the tomb, and on a narrow wooden prayer-stool there one of the monks kneeled. I suppose that there were two or three who shared this vigil among them, perhaps older brothers with infirmities to be nursed, for the one who kneeled, there when we came was shrivelled and bowed, and bulked no larger than a handful of fragile bones inside his habit. Men and women came and went as I waited, mounted beside the place where Llewelyn prayed, kissed the glossy, mouth-shaped hollow in the slab, and humbly withdrew to pray apart. But when Llewelyn arose from his knees and stepped back, so did the ancient monk who tended the lamp, and turned his head towards my lord, and then I saw his face, which was tiny and old, and worn to bone and spirit, and sweet and calm beyond measure, and his eyes, which were wide open and silver as the moon, whitened over with the veil of age and blindness. Some twenty years, I judge, he had not seen even the light of day, never a shade of difference between dawn and midnight. But he turned his face towards Llewelyn, who moved as silently as a cat, and he smiled with a strange, radiant smile, and came towards him with the careful, accurate gait of the blind who are certain of their ground. He came until he had only to stretch out his hand to touch Llewelyn's breast, and reached out delicately short of touching, and so stayed, his hand spread like a blessing and an entreaty.

'You are the man,' he said, in a voice as thin and small as a bird's chirping. 'My heart turned in me when you entered the chapel. I cannot be deceived. You are of his blood.'

'No,' said Llewelyn, wondering and moved. 'I am only one whom he touched in passing, like all the rest.'

'That cannot be true,' said the old man, shaking his grey tonsure, and drawing down his brows over the blind eyes as if to stare more intently into the face that fronted his own. He advanced his hand yet a little towards Llewelyn's breast, and laid it very lightly over the prince's heart. 'This – this declares you his. I know not of my own knowledge. I am told what is needful. I am told that I touch the son of my saint.'

'Father,' said Llewelyn, shaken, 'I do not lie to you. There is no drop of the earl's blood in me. All his sons are dead or gone out of this land.'

'You have your knowledge,' said the blind monk, faintly smiling, 'and I have mine, and what is mystery and paradox to us is not so to God, who is the maker of truth as of all things. I tell you, I do but as I am instructed, and it is not possible that my knowledge should be deceitful. I say you are the son of my saint, and I bless you in his name, and in God's name.' With the hand that had warmed at Llewelyn's heart, dry and frail on its withered wrist like a dead flower on its stalk, he signed the air between them with a cross before the prince's forehead. 'May the prayers you have made here be answered, and the vows you have renewed come to perfect fruit.'

After a long silence Llewelyn said: 'Amen!' And so in my own mind I said, also, for I knew what pledge had been reaffirmed at Earl Simon's tomb. After I carried back to Wales the full story of the earl's death, Llewelyn made two vows in his memory, the first to extract from King Henry everything Earl Simon had granted him freely, recognition of his right and title to Wales and to the homages of all the Welsh princes. And that he had done. And the second vow was to bring to fruition the marriage he had asked and been granted gladly by the earl, and to make

Simon's only daughter princess of Wales. That yet remained to do. Twice he had sent envoys to reopen the matter with the earl's widow, but the Countess Eleanor would not entertain his plea because of her promise to abstain from all moves that could vex her brother the king, or her nephew the Lord Edward. Withdrawn into France, and living retired at the convent of Montargis, she wanted nothing but to have peace, and dreaded the suspicion with which Edward might look upon any alliance between Earl Simon's friend and ally and Earl Simon's child. And very patiently and obstinately had Llewelyn waited for the passage of time to put that scruple and that fear out of mind, for who could believe, four years after Evesham, that any man or conspiracy of men could again revive a strong baronial party in England? Without Simon it was a dead cause. There was not a lord in the land who wanted the past even remembered. The present tired peace and slow and cautious healing was all they desired. But the countess held to her purpose and would not be moved. Neither would Llewelyn. He would have Eleanor de Montfort or he would have none.

'Amen!' he said again, very softly. 'Father, pray that prayer for me in this place now and again, and how can I fail?'

We went out hushed and thoughtful from the church, and the rain had ceased, and a watery sun peered feebly through the mist and cloud over the valley. In rapt silence we rode back half the distance we had to go, and only then did he say suddenly, in a voice low and diffident and hopeful: 'Samson, I have had a sign from heaven, have I not? A son, he called me!'

'So he did,' I said, 'and held by it. And blessed your intent in Earl Simon's name and in God's name. And surely such old, good men, drawing to their end after a holy life, cannot lie.'

'It must and shall come to pass,' he said, and he was speaking to the dead we had left behind us as surely as to me. 'A son to him I shall be, though not by blood. I shall be his son when I exchange the marriage vows with Eleanor, and take her home to Wales. God willing, his grandsons shall be princes.'

CHAPTER II

It was August of the following year before Edward got his crusaders and their stores aboard his ships, and finally set sail to meet King Louis in the east. He should have joined him and sailed with him from Aigues Mortes, but the dispute with Gloucester and other matters delayed his departure, and he followed more than a month behind the French king's fleet. They never did meet again in this world. When Edward reached the crusader camp at Carthage in November, King Louis was more than two months dead. Not in battle, but of the terrible plague that swept through his army in Tunis, killing in swathes, and lopping off the head and the heart of that great enterprise. The king died only a few days after Edward sailed from Dover. Men remember him as a great and good man, and so I think he tried to be, yet I cannot think of him but with the memory of his judgment at Amiens bitter in my mind, and often I think how much of the anger and grief and violence of the world lies at the door of good men, and how much injustice and wrong they do in their certainty of good intent. Howbeit, he is long dead, and no doubt there is judgment for kings and popes as surely as for poor men, and a judgment not of this world, but with unweighted scales.

As for Earl Gilbert of Gloucester, he fought off all arguments and pleas, and evaded setting out with the rest on this crusade, and Edward sailed without him, and in great anger against him, but in the belief that he had him securely bound to follow with his own force somewhat later. Gilbert, on the other hand, breathed more freely once Edward was on the high seas, and had no intention of quitting his building of his new castle to go hunting Saracens or mamluks in the east. So Llewelyn's vexatious problem of how long to be tolerant and trust to arbitration to hold him, and when to lose patience and take action for want of law, remained acute during that summer. It was galling to be held up as Gilbert's excuse for not being able to quit his border honour, when we had done nothing to accost him, and he did much to affront us. On the other hand, Llewelyn did not wish to be, or even to seem to be, the first to resort to arms, whatever the provocation. So we still held back and waited.

It was barely two weeks after the Lord Edward had left England with his companions that we had an official visitor from King Henry, bearing royal letters, which in courtesy were delivered to Llewelyn in advance of the envoy's arrival, for he came well attended, and was of such importance that the court of Wales would naturally desire to have word of his coming, and be ready to do him honour. The king wrote recalling that by the terms of the peace between England and Wales the crown had retained one, and only one, Welsh homage, that of Meredith ap Rhys Gryg of Dryslwyn, at Meredith's urgent wish, but with the provision that should it ever please the king to cede that homage, also, to Llewelyn, the prince should pay for it the price of five thousand marks. His son Edward, said the king, had often pleaded with him to grant the said homage to Llewelyn, according to the prince's earnest wish, and at Edward's request his brother Edmund, to whom the homage had been given, was willing to cede it again in Llewelyn's favour. The king had therefore yielded to his son's entreaty, and was ready to grant Meredith's fealty to the prince of Wales, if Llewelyn would pay the promised five thousand marks at once, and to Edward, not to the crown, for the king wished the money to be a subsidy for the crusade. And because of the importance of the matter, King Henry was sending Robert Burnell, the lord Edward's most trusted confidential clerk and adviser, to explain in person whatever needed to be explained further. So confident was he not only of acceptance, but of getting the money in full on demand, that he sent with Burnell the necessary charters for the exchange, his own grant of the homage, the Lord Edward's concurrence, and the Lord Edmund's willing cession of the fealty heretofore granted to him, all these to be handed over as soon as the money changed hands.

'So Edward has stood my friend,' said Llewelyn, elated and encouraged at this news. 'He would not have argued for me if he had still entertained any doubts of my good faith.' And I knew that he was seeing this move as one more sign that he might proceed with his design of pursuing the match with Eleanor de Montfort, without fear that her mother's doubts and reservations need be taken seriously. If Edward had no hesitation in trusting and working with the prince, the countess must realise that there was no longer any need for her to stand in the way of the marriage.

David, who happened to be in attendance by reason of council matters when the letter arrived, curled his lip at his brother's innocence. 'Edward has stood Edward's friend, as usual,' he said bluntly. 'He is to have the money for his crusading expense, is he not? He – not Edmund, who surrenders Meredith ap Rhys Gryg to you. He got his twentieth from all free men, or he got at least part of it, and what's yet to come will go into his hands, too, but it's not nearly enough for his needs. He's over head and ears in debt now, when he's barely got his men out of England, and he'll be living on his creditors for years after he comes home. Edward's warm friendship for you is of recent growth, and serves a very useful purpose. Where else could he lay hands on five thousand marks on demand, and get a blessing with it? Oh, take what's offered, by all means, if you want the old bear, and be glad of it – but not grateful! You are paying handsomely for your purchase.'

'I am paying what I undertook to pay, and getting what I have always wanted,' said Llewelyn, not at all moved by David's sour wisdom. 'If he has no cause for complaint, neither have I, each of us is getting what he wants, it's a fair exchange. But I do not believe this is only self-interest on Edward's part. It is not the first instance he has shown me of his goodwill. I would rather deal with him on the borders than with any other of the king's men. He has a better understanding, and longer patience.'

'So he has,' said David readily, but with the same dry tone and disdainful half-smile, 'and both in the service of his own interests, and no others. Take what he offers, if it suits you, but have the wit to realise that you owe him nothing, for it would not be offered if he was not getting full value for it after his own fashion.'

Said Llewelyn, amused and tolerant, but with some chill disapproval, too: 'You have had no cause to sharpen your tongue on him, to my recall. I thought you had great liking for him. There have been times when you have so indicated.'

David's dark and beautiful face did not change, but by the sudden light flush that stained his high cheekbones I knew the mild sting had gone home. It was not so long since David had forsaken Llewelyn in time of war to join Edward, though God knows his motives may not have been near so simple as Llewelyn or any of us supposed. But he said only: 'So I have great liking for him. Too great for my good, perhaps. But not because I see him as big in the soul as in the body. He is a man, faulty like other men, and the more dangerous because born to so much power, and so largely gifted. I take him as he is. And you had better do the same, and enjoy what part of him you can.'

'You have had better opportunity to study him than I,' Llewelyn owned generously, open-minded but unconvinced, 'but my experience is all I can use. Yours is yours, and there's no borrowing. And now there'll be no more studying him for a while; he's bound for the Holy Land, and for my part I wish him good use of my five thousand marks, for he shall have them, and I'll take back my old bear of Dryslwyn.'

'You were a fool else,' said David. 'I never said there was anything wrong with the bargain. But see it as a bargain, for so it is.'

So it was done, with no pretence or reluctance on either side, and the fealty and homage of Meredith ap Rhys Gryg, the old lord of Dryslwyn, the only Welsh prince then out of Llewelyn's jurisdiction, was restored to him.

The consultations that accompanied the transfer were brief and businesslike indeed, since the exchange suited all parties, except, perhaps, the over-persuaded and over-devoted Edmund of Lancaster. And what I chiefly remember of them is the person of this same confidential clerk, Robert Burnell, already of formidable reputation, and to be ever greater thereafter. He arrived without great ceremony, attended well but not ostentatiously. I noted his seat and manner in the saddle before he alighted, for he rode like a merchant or a farmer, that is to say, as one who rides on his own errands, and not to be seen and admired by others, and therefore must ride well, sensibly and durably, to last out long days and hard ways, rather than to dazzle other men and wear out mounts. He had no affectations, but lighted down unaided, himself handed over his bridle to the groom, and eyed the way it was handled, even so, until he was content. So I saw, before ever I truly looked at the man and made note of his stature and visage, that here was one who had mind and eye and heart for every detail, and was not interested in the flowers of his office, however interested he might be – and he was, shrewdly! –in its fruits.

He was above the middle height, and straight as a fir tree. His dark gowns were always of the finest cloth, never of the showiest cut. He was, I suppose, of much the same age as Llewelyn and myself, though I never enquired. If I am right, he was then around forty-one years of age, ten years older than his lord and friend, Edward. He had been in that prince's household since it was formed, when Edward was fifteen years old and being prepared for his marriage to the princess of Castille, and therefore fitted out with an appanage suitable to a married prince and heir to a throne. Burnell was from a small border family of no great importance until he graced it. His abilities were his appanage, and equipped him well enough to found a house and an honour, if he had not been a priest. As it was, there were great horizons open to him in another sphere.

'Old Boniface is dead,' David said to me, coming into my copying-room from the hall, that first evening, flushed and restless with wine, but not drunk. There was a core in him then, I dread of brotherly bitterness, that would not let him get drunk, his wits so raged against surrendering their edge. 'We lack an archbishop of Canterbury, and Edward has made his mind known. Did you not hear of it? Before he took his legions out of England he made a rush to Canterbury, to tell the monks what heavy responsibility they bear, having the election of the high priest in their hands. It was hearing of the old man's death in Savoy that sent him there, with a candidate ready chosen. He told them plainly he wanted Burnell. What could suit him better? Burnell is his man, heart and soul. That's why he's left here, ready and waiting, instead of sailing with the crusaders, as he intended. We shall see, we shall see, what the monks of Canterbury think of Edward's nominee.'

It seemed to me then that the chapter of Canterbury would hardly be likely to flout the wishes of the Lord Edward, but it had to be remembered also that he was now out of the country, and likely to be preoccupied with other high matters for some time to come, so that they had not to confront him face to face if they chose to ignore his orders. Nor was he yet king, at least not in name. In all else I must say his was the ruling will in England, and King Henry was content to have it so, finding his giant son a shield and comfort rather than a tyrant.

Whatever their reasoning, we heard later that the monks of Canterbury in solemn session had elected as candidate for the primacy their prior, a somewhat obscure person hardly known out of their own company, certainly with no great reputation for learning or doctrine. I have forgotten his name, and that in itself says most of what there is to be said about him. I do remember that the election caused anger at the king's court, and was received with cold disapproval in Rome. But the affair hung unresolved for two years after, and England was without an archbishop, because of a long and disputed interregnum in the papacy, and even when a new pope was chosen in the person of Cardinal Tedaldo Visconti, later to be known to Christendom by his chosen name of Gregory X, the new pope-elect was absent crusading in the east with the

Lord Edward, and indeed had already become his close and loyal friend. When he returned to give his attention to his new duties, he examined the prior of Canterbury, and found him wanting in the qualities an archbishop should have, and chose instead the provincial of the Dominicans in England, Robert Kilwardby, a man of learning, purpose and character, who had never looked for the honour, and received it dutifully but with astonishment.

But in this summer of twelve hundred and seventy all this was still to do, and we saw Robert Burnell at work as man of affairs and trustee for Edward his lord. And I think that affairs of state were more his province than matters of faith and doctrine, and as archbishop he would have been wasted. He went straight to the heart of an errand, worded clearly, made decisions firmly and sensibly, was not to be diverted or provoked. By the time all was agreed, the royal charters delivered, and the fee of Meredith's homage paid in full, I found it no wonder that Edward should choose this man as one of the regent-administrators of his affairs and lands in his absence, and in the event of Richard of Cornwall's death, one of the guardians of his children.

He was of powerful build for his height, and moved like one in as firm mastery of his body as of his mind. His colouring was fair, with thick, short hair of a light brown, and eyes as light, flecked with green, and his smooth-shaven face was square and strong, every line sharply drawn. But all this force of decision and judgment he voiced in tones quiet, reasonable and brief. Llewelyn, as I saw, warmed to him, for good reason, being used to grappling with officials whose only intent was to avoid making any clear answer or bringing any doubtful matter to a conclusion. So it was no wonder that he took the opportunity of broaching with Burnell the issue of Senghenydd, and his grievance over the castle building at Caerphilly.

'I know,' said Burnell, 'that both you and the earl of Gloucester have made out strong cases for your rival claims in those parts, both as to the commote itself, and the homage and fealty of its lord, who is now imprisoned in Ireland. You made representations to the king's Grace some time ago, to obtain his release.'

'I did,' said Llewelyn, 'for to my knowledge he has committed no treason against the earl, and it is no fault of his if two overlords both lay claim to him, and he prefers one of them. His Grace replied that it was open to me to bring action on his behalf in the king's courts against Gloucester, since the crown lawyers held that the lord of Senghenydd is of the Englishry. But I cannot bring such action without acknowledging the right of the court and the English dependence of Griffith, and this I do not acknowledge. The man is Welsh, and the land was his by hereditary right. I preferred the arbitration commission, old and good practice, drawn from both sides where disputed rights are concerned. But it moves not as such commissions used to do, but by legal delays and deferments which I find rather English than impartial. And meantime, Earl Gilbert continues to build. It is my contention that building should cease until we have agreement.'

Instead of bandying words to conceal art, Burnell spoke out freely. 'It is truth, you will find the nature of such joint commissions changed. I will not deny it. I do not say it was ever intended, but it is implicit in your lordship's present relationship with the crown. Think how great is that change. Never before has Wales stood in this same interdependence. You are nearer now than you ever were to the crown, and I tell you freely, English officials, by the very nature of your treaty, think of you as reliant upon the royal courts for the maintenance of justice wherever it touches both countries. Law *is* slow. I trust it may also be sure and just, but slow it is, and I well understand how that may gall. I cannot offer you hope of a reversal there. But as to the ban on building until the case is settled, I think there you have a strong argument, and it can be looked into. Can and shall, if I can procure it.'

'I have waited,' said Llewelyn, 'a great while, but to wait until the fortress is complete would be too much to ask of me. The earl claims he is in fear of Welsh incursion, and means only to make his own defence possible. But Senghenydd was never his, though he did impose homage on its lord, and it is not his own he is defending, it is what he had taken unjustly.'

'But you do not claim Senghenydd as yours?' said Burnell with his small, dry smile.

'Senghenydd belongs to Griffith, and should be restored to him, together with his freedom. Ultimately I claim Griffith as my vassal, yes. By treaty I was given acknowledged title to the fealties of *all* the Welsh princes, saving only this Meredith who is now also given to me. But the issue of Griffith's allegiance and Welshness can wait the slow processes of arbitration. What I claim now is that building at Caerphilly should cease. De Clare should not build, nor I destroy. But if he builds,' said Llewelyn bluntly, 'then I shall destroy. I have let the work go too far already.'

And Burnell smiled, and said that he valued the candour of the exchange. He did not say, but it was implicit in his manner, that he himself found Gilbert de Clare a difficult, slippery and insubordinate man, and the Lord Edward would not be gravely vexed to see him curbed.

'Yet I doubt,' said Llewelyn, after the envoy had departed with his strong entourage and his treasure, 'if that gives us free leave to do the curbing. Gilbert is troublesome, but Gilbert is English, a marcher lord, one of their own. It would be folly for us to rely too much on new friendships, when they cross old ones.'

So he waited still for a while, measuring the days until the point should come when for the maintenance of his royal dignities he must act. And as I know, he was well aware that miscalculation might be exceedingly dangerous, whether he moved too soon, and inflamed old animosities, or too late, and encouraged insolent presumption of his weakness. And the danger of hesitation, of threatening action and then not acting, or of acting by derisory half-measures, was the most acute of all.

I believe that Burnell did urge the king to impose a halt to Gloucester's building; he may even have succeeded in getting Henry to make some gesture of prohibition, but if so, it was ignored. And at the beginning of October Llewelyn judged his moment to be upon him, and struck.

We went in force, led by the prince himself, for he would not make this assertion of his rights through any other hand, surrounded Gilbert's great earthwork, and drove the English guards, builders and all, south in haste for their lives, though it was done with such method and deliberation that they recognised the impossibility of preventing us doing what we would, and withdrew without offering battle. Gloucester himself was not there, for parliament was then in session, and he was present in full cry, urging his right to build and the danger that threatened his lands, for once truly, though he did not know it. At the very hour, perhaps, when King Henry was writing urgently to Llewelyn that he had impressed upon Gloucester the necessity for keeping the peace, and that the prince should also observe the like restraint, we were setting fire to Gilbert's timber keep, tearing down his boundary walls, and levelling his earthworks. We destroyed everything, and then, to mark our own reading of restraint, withdrew from the entire commote, making no attempt to occupy it and hold it, as we could have done.

Of course there was great turmoil when the news reached the court, and Gloucester got something out of it in payment for his castle, for there was never any more said about his pledged duty to follow Edward to the Holy Land. Now he could settle vengefully in his marcher lands and purport to be the guardian of the realm as well as of his own claims. Llewelyn was loudly blamed for taking action, but that moved him not at all, and it seemed he had not gravely misjudged his hour, for king and council continued to urge the use of arbitration, and to support the meetings of the commission, though these still tended to talk endlessly and arrive nowhere, as before. However, we had a breathing space, and kept Senghenydd under careful watch, in case of further attempts to build. Gilbert was an incalculable creature, given to bouts of breathtaking audacity, sometimes deservedly successful, sometimes undeservedly, and sometimes disastrous, but also to long periods of unruly and incompetent muddling, arrogantly sure of his rightness and tangling himself and everyone about him in quagmires beyond the capacity of other men. So one never knew what to expect from him. I do not know whether he had breathed in an emulous desire to outbuild King Henry, from his belated and sullen visit to the abbey at Westminster, but this year following found him at a high pitch of excellence rare in him, choosing men ably, appraising their plans modestly and sensibly, and giving ability its head to design such a castle as barons dream of. But until past the end of this year twelve hundred and seventy we had no hint of what went forward, for the site at Caerphilly remained desert.

Christmas we spent at Aber, after the old fashion, for Llewelyn had still a strong attachment to that royal seat by the northern sea. David and Elizabeth came for the feast, in great content with each other. So wild, so tender, so playful was David with this gay girl of his, I saw again my breast-brother, the child who had been in my care years ago, and had me by the heart still, for all I could do. And I saw, I know not how, for her body was not yet changed – perhaps in his constant care for her, and the way he looked upon her mutely as upon a wonder and a dread, but perhaps rather in her large and radiant presence, that warmed the air about her even in the frosts – I saw that Elizabeth was with child.

She was then barely fourteen years old, but more than that in her true being, body, mind and spirit, having loved so early, after being schooled earlier yet to the needs of marriage, at a time when both marriage and love were heathen and distant words to her. Whatever doubts and dreads David had, Elizabeth had none. She was all joy.

'He frets needlessly,' said Cristin, when I found myself some moments alone with her in the night, under a cold moon as we crossed from the buttery and kitchens to the hall. 'She is ripe and ready, and without fear. But who would have thought he would so wear out his heart for her, and wrack himself to a shade with self-blame? What choice had he? She wooed him and won him, almost against his will, all against his conscience. If he seeks you out – he well may! –comfort him, and tell him not to be a fool. She has no need of any pity; she feels herself blessed.'

There was no word said, then or ever, of how her own years were running away in barren blossom from under her feet, of the great longing she had, and I shared, for the generation of the children of our own love, a happiness we could never have, and now saw shining so joyously in this strangely-matched pair. But at night in those feast-days, when Elizabeth with David led the dances, for all his vain wish to shelter and cosset her and force her to rest, then we felt to the full the ache of what we had never possessed, and surely never would in this world. As we valued and were grateful for those blessings we had, which were very great, so we saw clearly the magnitude of the last blessing we were denied. And Cristin's great eyes, iris-dark with longing, followed every movement as Elizabeth danced and sang and shone, and in the midst of her gaiety laid a hand so tenderly upon her girdle, where nothing yet swelled or quickened, caressing in rapture the very mystery of David's seed in her. Cristin watched like one famished, though her face was white and still and tranquil, and her hands folded in calm. Only to me did her eyes betray her, for even so I must have looked, envying David.

Yet my heart smote me suddenly, warning that there was one other who had good cause to know how to read the signs in her face and in mine. And I looked about me in haste and wariness, to find if Godred was there in the hall.

I found him among a group of the troopers of David's retinue, at one of the trestle tables drawn along the walls, easy and at leisure over their wine. He was standing, graceful and slender, with his shoulders braced against one of the timber pillars, and his fair head leaned back against the smoky wood. The large, smooth lids drooped half over his full brown eyes, but I saw the bright gleam of interest and content and malice burning below his light lashes, and his lips were curved in a small, acid-sweet smile. He was staring steadily upon Cristin, but as I watched, as though my attention had drawn his, he turned his head and opened his eyes wide into mine, and his smile broadened into that comradely affection he used upon me, poisoned honey, yet God knows more deadly to him than to me.

I knew then that there was nothing he had not seen and appraised, no part of her longing or mine that he did not recognise, and was not willing to use against us. Slight and light he was, and found no fault with that and made no pretence about it, until he found he could neither tempt nor trick me into wallowing with him in the kennel, nor drag her down to the level of his own loving. He could not endure it that we had between us the one thing he had never valued or wanted, another manner of love, that could even live in abstinence.

Yet even then, when he had discovered jealousy by reason of the value another set on his wife, whom he himself never valued, he seldom resorted to her, or frequented her company, except as a means of tormenting me, or keeping David's goodwill. Other women he had in plenty, and his interest was small indeed in favours he owned by right. It was the one thing in him for which I was devoutly grateful, that his usage of her was civil but indifferent, and she could endure it without distress. It was myself he hated, and lived in the hope of destroying, and as one weapon blunted without effect he was for ever looking about him for another.

I dreaded he might have found one that night.

There was one other who had watched the happiness of David and Elizabeth with open pleasure and private pain, and that was Llewelyn. He carried about his neck the painted image of a girl twelve years old, only a year or two younger than Elizabeth now. It was more than five years since Earl Simon had betrothed her to the prince, by this she was eighteen, and still out of his reach overseas, and the years of his prime were ebbing one by one while he waited for her. And here he saw his youngest brother in joyous wedlock with this eager child, and the fruit of their love, the desired heir, already promised, while he was barren and alone.

He watched them, smiling and tormented, and I saw both the pleasure and the pain clear into resolution, for he had received his third sign.

When I was alone with him in his own chamber, late in the night after the hall was quiet and the household asleep, he told me what I expected to hear, and I was the first he told.

'It is time to put my fortune to the test again,' he said. 'I should be ungrateful if I neglected the clear signs heaven has given me. When Edmund of Lancaster sails with his force, to join the Lord Edward in Tunis, two of the brothers from Aberconway have petitioned to sail under his protection to France. They have missions to Clairvaux and certain other houses there. They can as easily be my envoys to Montargis. Surely by now the countess must be reassured. I mean to renew my suit for her daughter. You and I will prepare gifts and letters, and trust in the word of the blind monk of Evesham. He has promised me success, and I will not believe in failure.'

I was glad for him, for the simple act of determining upon action had warmed and liberated him, and while we made our preparations it was eager anticipation he felt, and the deprivation fell away from him. We drew up letters very courtly and persuasive, recalling how Earl Simon had exchanged vows with Llewelyn at Abbey Dore, and we sent for the countess a mass-book very delicately bound, and illuminated in gold, and for her daughter a rose of enamel and gold-work, with the renewed pledge of Llewelyn's faithfulness to his bond, and desire and prayer for its fulfilment. The brothers of Aberconway were trustworthy and loyal, and so had been always to the royal house of Gwynedd, and above all they could be secret, for clearly he did not wish their errand to be known until he had his answer. It remained only for Edmund to fix a date for his departure, and though he was delayed a few weeks into the year by various vexatious matters and by King Henry's frail health, he got his levies away before the spring came. Then we drew breath and waited for news.

That was a quiet and prosperous spring for us in Wales, troubled only by the word that Gilbert de Clare was again busy building at Caerphilly as soon as the weather was favourable after the early frosts, and this time he had somehow gathered about him masons and planners of quality, and was bent on the erection of a fortress in stone. This at least had the merit, for us, of being a slower enterprise, so that we could afford to sit back and concentrate on formal protests to the court, invoking law and demanding a halt to this new infringement. Though Llewelyn kept tight hold of the borders of Senghenydd none the less, and got word very rapidly, wherever he happened to be, of what went on there.

For the rest, he steadily pursued his policies of settlement, of extending our cultivated fields wherever it was possible, of encouraging the growth of towns, and the founding of markets, and the use of minted money, all measures borrowed from England, truly, and necessarily so, since we had both to compete and cooperate with England. Those years since Montgomery were years of strong development towards a state, not feudal like England, yet learning from feudalism, and most beneficial to all his people. He had an eye, also, to the exact location of his castles, for the best control and protection of the whole land, and it had to be admitted that in the marches there were gaps not yet filled.

So my lord had enough and to spare to occupy his mind, and with the business of local justice he dealt always in person and with great care for detail. And as I remember, we were in session with a difficult family dispute involving the moving of boundaries and the abduction of a girl, in the prince's court at Carnarvon in the first days of April, when a messenger came in from Cynan in London, bringing both letters and a verbal report, he said of great importance. But he waited, none the less, until Llewelyn had the case before him judged and brought to agreement, if not wholly amicably, at least in such a shewd knot that the parties could not break the accord without peril, and the girl restored to her parents undamaged. Then the prince withdrew, with none but myself in attendance, and in his own apartments the messenger came in to him.

He was a groom about the court, Welsh like Cynan who sent him to us, a lusty young man who made his living where he could, but kept one foot fast-rooted on our side of the border. So do all good Welshmen, for this soil is not as other soil, its stony austerity holds all its sons by the heart. Short and thick and dark was this young man, the very pattern of his kind, even to his tongue, which was not short nor thick nor dark, but long and sinuous and silver. But his matter was nothing for our comfort.

'My lord prince,' he said, standing before Llewelyn still dusty from his ride, 'I am the voice of princely events, and lack the art to tell them. My lord, it is no good news, pardon the bearer. Master Cynan's letter will bear out what I have to tell.'

'Speak out,' said Llewelyn. 'You are not the first to be burdened with an ungrateful errand; it shall not be your loss.'

'My lord,' said the groom, taking him at his word, 'on the thirteenth day of March, at a city called Viterbo, in Italy, Guy de Montfort, Earl Simon's third son, fell upon the lord Henry of Almain, the Lord Edward's cousin, as he was hearing mass in the church of San Silvestro, slew him with the sword, and dragged the body out of the church to be mutilated in the square. Master Cynan said you should know of it, for your better advising.'

Cynan could not have known, when he sent that dire message, that Llewelyn's envoys were at Montargis, nor with how fell a sound the news of Guy's catastrophic vengeance came upon our ears. He sent the word to avoid what now was beyond avoiding. We had chosen the worst of times.

Llewelyn said, with a mute and mastered face: 'Tell me all you know. How did this meeting ever come to pass?'

'My lord, the new French king, Philip, was on his way home northwards through Italy with his crusaders, bearing back to France the bodies of his father, King Louis, dead of plague on the crusade, his young wife Isabella of Aragon, who died on the voyage home, his brother, the count of Nevers, and his brother-in-law Theobald of Champagne, the king of Navarre. All these high titles I learned from Master Cynan, who also writes them to you in the letters I brought. And with King Philip was also his brother, Charles of Anjou, whom the popes helped to the throne of Sicily some years past. This Guy de Montfort is now in his service, and his chief officer in Tuscany, so that he came to Viterbo to meet his liege lord. But when he heard that Henry of Almain was in that city with the French king's retinue, he was greatly disturbed, and came the next day to the church where he was, and killed and dragged him out, and so left him lying. My lord, this is all I know. Master Cynan has written more.'

With a mild voice and a shuttered face Llewelyn thanked him for his errand, and dismissed him to be fed and rested and remounted, with his reward in hand. His reward for a blow to the heart. Cynan's letter was indeed fuller.

'God he knows, my lord,' he had written, 'what possessed the man to take his revenge thus, or, indeed, what possessed the Lord Edward to send his cousin with King Philip into Italy, where it was certain the vicar-general in Tuscany of Charles of Anjou must come to welcome his lord. There are those here who say that the Lord Edward sent his cousin, who was most dear to him, and once was a Montfort man, expressly to try to make peace with the Montfort brothers, and bring them to the king's grace, and it may be true. If so, he was sadly amiss in his judgment. Those two brothers, for Simon was in company with Guy when they entered the town, though he was not present at the church, did not know when they came to the meeting that Henry of Almain would be there in the royal retinue. This killing was not planned. They came, and then they heard of his presence. And Guy has sought him out and killed him. I know no more. It may be that you can read this riddle better than I.'

He had added a further writing a day or two later, when more was known:

'The Lord Edward, who has wintered in Sicily as the guest of King Charles, and proposes to sail for Acre very soon, has been informed of his cousin's death. There was talk of his being sent for to come home again, the main crusade being postponed by reason of King Louis' death, and King Henry being in poor health, but now his Grace is better, and it is certain the Lord Edward will hold to his oath and sail for Acre at once. The murderer has been deprived of lands and offices, but is at large, and having strong support from his wife's kin in Tuscany, and they very powerful, will find both refuge and sympathy there. It seems likely little will be done to avenge the crime until the Lord Edward's return, but he will not forget.'

'Indeed he will not,' said Llewelyn, laying the letters by with a steady hand. 'He forgets few favours, but never an injury, and he greatly valued his cousin Henry. Well, it seems the madness of one hour can undo the work of years. Why? *Why* should he do so? What ailed him to throw away, if nothing else were at stake, all the sound work he has done for this new rule in Italy? All the laurels he has won? After six years!'

I remembered then how I had seen this same Guy lying in his blood on the field of Evesham, vainly trying to stretch out a hand towards his sire as he died. 'He saw father and brother killed before his eyes,' I said, 'their cause lost, their friends hounded and disinherited, the very dream in which he grew to manhood hacked to pieces. And he saw on the opposing part all those young men who had once followed and worshipped Earl Simon, and then deserted and brought him to ruin. To come face to face with one of them now, without warning, drove him to remember too much, and too bitterly.'

'But Henry was only one of many, and among the best of them, not the worst. Why single him out for vengeance?'

'He was there,' I said. 'And he was, I think, the most trusted of those who withdrew their allegiance, and the most missed. And close kin, nephew to the earl, cousin to Guy, and sometime dear to both. It is not so hard to understand the impulse to kill, but the act was an indulgence he should have been able to deny himself. Now he has destroyed himself, and set back the hope of reconciliation by years.'

'And with it my hopes,' said Llewelyn, 'or so I dread. We are back where we began. Edward will not forget or forgive this act. It touches neither Eleanor nor me, but will her mother dare to stand upon that view? I doubt it!' The countess was ageing and weary, and sickened with all matters of state and all involvement in the tangled affairs of England, for to say truth, her world had ended at Evesham, and without Earl Simon she was but a shell filled with bitterness. 'Well,' he said grimly, 'until I have an answer I have neither lost nor won. It's still a matter of waiting. At waiting,' he said, ruefully smilling, 'I have had much practice, and am grown expert. A man should enjoy doing what he does well.'

I would not say there was much enjoyment for him in those six weeks we spent waiting for the return of the monks of Aberconway, but at least we were busy enough to help the time to pass, and we made good use of the opening summer. Gilbert de Clare was continuing his building in stone at Caerphilly, and all Llewelyn's formal protests, though they had produced great agitation among the royal officials, and many promises and reassurances, had not caused Gilbert's masons to lay by their tools. This was the season for building, and he was in haste to raise the walls as high as possible before the next winter's frosts called a halt. But between our preoccupation with these weighty matters we had a good spring for lambs, and favourable weather for sowing, also activities not to be despised.

Towards the end of May the brothers of Aberconway returned, having crossed the sea from France in the very ship which brought home under a mourning escort of knights the bones and heart of Henry of Almain, the heart to be enshrined in the king's church at Westminster, the bones to be buried in his father's abbey of Hailes. Since the news of the murder reached him, they said, Richard of Cornwall, king of the Romans, had turned his back upon the world, and was indifferent to the fate of his kingdom, and certainly to his own. It was barely a year before he followed his son out of this world, and was laid beside him in his own foundation. So those two sleep not ten miles from Evesham, where the king's felon and the people's saint takes his rest.

Brother Philip and Brother Iorwerth, the one old and reverend, the other young, both lettered and learned, were received by Llewelyn with all the more serenity and grace for the passion of anxiety he had to suppress, but they knew his mind, and delivered their embassage directly, and I think he was grateful.

'My lord,' said the elder, 'the letter we bring is but the formal acknowledgement of yours, and of your gifts, with the regard and respect of the Countess Eleanor. What further is necessary we were charged to deliver you by word of mouth. My lord, you will know by now that we came there to Montargis after the thing that happened at Viterbo, though we did not then know of it. The countess had already heard that news. She is deeply shocked by her son's senseless and terrible act, and more determined than ever that she cannot and will not countenance any move that will deepen the anger and suspicion that must follow. She pledged her word to do nothing that could touch or harm or disturb the realm of England, and she holds that the match you propose would be an infringement of her word. With the deepest regard for the lord prince's person, acts and motives, she will not attach her daughter to him or to any former ally of Earl Simon, for that would be to incur the displeasure and distrust of her brother the king, and in particular of the Lord Edward. She is adamant.'

Llewelyn said heavily: 'I had expected nothing better, since this death. From my heart I am sorry, but sorry, too, for the lady. Well, you did your errand faithfully. It is no fault of yours that you can bring me no comfort.'

Brother Philip hesitated but a moment before he said: 'My lord, after a fashion I believe I can. It was not possible for me to ask audience of the Lady Eleanor. But I have seen her, walking in the garden with her mother. And I have spoken with such of that household as I might. The lady is now eighteen years old.' He raised his creased old eyes that were experienced in reading men, and looked upon Llewelyn gently, and saw that the prince would not question him concerning Eleanor, and yet longed to know, and to have her spoken of. Deliberately he said, measuring out words: 'She is of great beauty and great nobility. Those who serve her have serene faces and are quick to smile, and talk with her freely and eagerly. I have judged both men and women by this measure, and I know its worth. And this lady is still unaffianced, in a land where her name, her face and her fortune are all magnets.'

'There have been suitors?' Llewelyn asked, burning between his rapture at hearing her praised, and his dread of having her snatched away into a French marriage. His voice was low and level. Too low, too level. Brother Philip understood the use of the voice, and the constraints that can be imposed upon it.

'There have been many such, and of excellent repute.'

'And all rejected?' said Llewelyn. 'Like me?'

'Not like you, my lord, though all rejected. You the countess rejects, for reasons you understand. All others, though with the utmost gentleness, the Lady Eleanor has rejected. Her mother entertains all of good standing who come, but leaves it to the lady, and will not force her choice. And to this day, my lord, she refuses all.'

'She liked none of them?' said Llewelyn, carefully touching hope with aching delicacy, in case it should crumble away in his fingers.

'She gives no reason, my lord. But so consistent is she, it does appear that she may have a reason, to her sufficient. It may well be,' said Brother Philip, 'that she holds herself to have been betrothed by her father in childhood. It may even be that she clings to that bond with heart and will, and is resolved to await its fulfilment.'

CHAPTER III

Though Llewelyn took heart from what the brothers had told him, and held fast by his faith in his own resolution and the divination of the blind monk of Evesham, yet that year ever after seemed a dark and arduous one to us, and, for all the good summer season, brought little joy. It was not only the disaster of Viterbo, which was still spreading its echoes across the whole face of Europe as ripples wash outward from a stone cast into a still pool. It was also marked by a number of other deaths, closer to us, which in an unpractised unity such as Llewelyn had made of Wales, still unstable in its tensions between the old divisive ways and the new nationhood, made for changes and disruptions. Old princes passed, and left young, untried sons to step into their shoes. It was needful to keep a watchful eye and a ready hand upon every commote in the land.

The prince's old and faithful ally in Cardigan, Meredith ap Owen, was already a few years dead, leaving three sons to rule his lands between them. Now there left us also, in the summer of this year twelve hundred and seventy-one, two others who had played a large and turbulent part in Llewelyn's rise to greatness. On the twenty-seventh day of July died the old bear, Meredith ap Rhys Gryg of Dryslwyn, he whose homage had been sold to Llewelyn to help to pay Edward's crusading expenses. He was past seventy years, and had lived through many changes of fortune. He died at his castle on the Tywi, and was buried at the abbey of Whitland, and his son Rhys ruled after him. And less than a month later, at Dynevor, only a few miles distant, died Rhys Fychan, widower of Llewelyn's only sister, and dear to him, the nephew with whom old Meredith had fought and feuded lifelong, as though, for all they could not live in the same country at peace, they could not live without each other, either. Rhys they buried at Talley, beside his beloved wife, and his eldest son, Rhys Wyndod, then turned twenty-one, divided up his lands with his two younger brothers, Griffith and Llewelyn, the last named after his uncle, the prince. All three knew they could rely on the help and support of their kinsman, and of his namesake, the child of the family reconciliation, the prince was particularly fond.

But the death of their father was a shock and a grief to him, for Rhys Fychan was only three years his elder, and had been a loyal friend.

'I am reminded of my own end,' he said with a wry smile. 'I have lived forty-two years, and he was but three years before me. And how if the same hand should fall upon me in my noonday? It well might; it has on many younger. What can any man do but live as if he had a life before him? I know no other way.'

If he had spoken so before the high steward, Tudor would have taken it as a text for the sermon that was always on his mind, how the prince of Wales, more urgently than any his predecessor, having so much more to protect and to bequeath, owed it to himself and his people to marry and get sons to follow after him. For though Tudor knew of the old betrothal to Eleanor de Montfort, he held that marriage to be impossible, even undesirable, and his concern for Wales kept him rightly fretting for the succession. The prince turned a stonily deaf ear to all the advice the council persistently gave, but Tudor did not give up hope of persuading him at last.

Llewelyn read my face, too clearly, and laughed, though somewhat ruefully. 'I know! Rhys Fychan at least left three sturdy sons to take his place, and I stand to leave all at risk. But without faith there is no security, to look for it and loose my hold on what *is* secure would be a sin. I do and will believe that I shall make good all that I have sworn, and if I cannot, I will die still striving. God can provide, and also take away, if he will, what he has provided.'

This I remembered, and so did he, in consternation and sorrow, when later we heard of the saddest of all the deaths of that winnowing year. With father and mother very far off from him in the Holy Land, Edward's heir, John, a child of five years, sickened and died. No doubt he had the best nurses and guardians a child could have, but his mother had torn herself away from him to follow her lord, and a hard choice that must have been, and a hard deprivation for the child, and who knows if he did not die of it? A girl, the eldest, and a little brother were left, but the heir to the throne, after his father, had been taken, and men are quick to read signs and warnings into the bereavements of princes, ever since Pharaoh and his firstborn.

'God knows I am sorry for it,' said Llewelyn, grieving. 'Even in sons there is no security. The quiver can be emptied in less time than it took to fill it. I hold by my own way. What use is there in bargaining with fortune?' And he said, as if to himself: 'Poor Edward! He goes in the love and service of God, and God takes from him what he parted with, even for a while, only sadly and in duty bounden.'

I recall, looking back now at that time, that even as we spoke the Lord Edward's lady was again with child, the daughter Joan that was born in Acre on this pilgrimage. Before ever they reached England again she gave birth also, in Gascony, to another son, for she was fruitful, but her children died too often in infancy, or dwindled after a few years. It seemed that Edward, for all his giant stature and strength, could not breed true.

But there were two in Lleyn who could. In mid-August, at the maenol of Neigwl where both Llewelyn and I were born in one night, Elizabeth gave birth to a daughter, strong, fine and perfect, bringing forth her young, it seemed, as placidly and neatly as any ewe in David's flocks.

'Never a day's sickness and never a complaint,' said Cristin to me after the christening, with the baby in a shawl in her arms, fast asleep with fists doubled under its round chin, and black silken hair short and lustrous like a cat's fell. 'She had danced all the evening, and he in a sweat over her, but not a sign of fear in her. And she went to bed and slept, so peacefully that so did he, and in the night, when she felt the throes beginning, she rose up very softly, not to wake him, and came herself to call me. I put her in my bed in the anteroom, where I slept to be near and ready, and not two hours later I put this creature in her arms, and she laughed for joy, but very softly still, because David was sleeping in the next room. By the time he felt the bustle going on all about him, and came out wild with uneasiness to see what had become of his wife, they were both sleeping, as snug and satisfied as cat and kitten.'

I asked if he had not been disappointed that she gave him a girl and not a son.

'Not a bit of it,' said Cristin, 'nor she, either. She thinks it the easiest thing in the world to bear children, and the finest, and promises him all the sons and all the daughters he can wish for. Besides, he sees his own stamp here, in this black colouring, and the blue eyes – she has his eyes – and that's a very powerful flattery. I thought he might take father-hood lightly, truly I believe he thought so, too, until it happened to him, but we were far out. He has had a revelation – about himself, and Elizabeth and all the world – and it has shaken him to the heart.'

As for Elizabeth herself, there was no need to ask after her health, she bloomed like a rose, and would have no proxy-mothers between herself and her daughter, but shared the child only with Cristin. And this first girl they named Margaret. She was life's answer to a year over-burdened with deaths already known, and the fore-showings of deaths to come.

That autumn Llewelyn took serious thought how to proceed about the new castle at Caerphilly, for so far from halting his building there, Gloucester was pushing hard to raise the walls into a defensible state before the winter, so that the place could be securely held. If we were to move in arms at all, it had to be soon, and in force. Protests and arguments had produced nothing but counter-protests and counter-arguments, until we began to be certain that with the best of wills King Henry, in Edward's absence, was no longer able fully to control the earl's actions, while his council and nobles, who might have commanded for-midable sanctions had they so wished, were some of them firmly on Gloucester's side, and privately anxious to help, rather than hinder, his consolidation of Senghenydd. Safe in Glamorgan, remote from the direct influence of Westminster, Earl Gilbert could do what he chose, in the certainty that his marcher neighbours approved, whether they dared say so openly or no.

So in the end, when October came in, and the building continued, the prince was forced to take action. There had been times when he would have struck upon lesser provocation and without any heart-burning, but now there was so much more to be lost, and so much more due in sober statesmanship to the nation he was creating, that he was deeply reluctant to take any step that might burn up into war, and disturb the loyal peace he desired to preserve with England. But once his mind was made up, he had lost none of his force and fire. He called out his host and took a great company south with him to besiege Caerphilly. Among the rest, David brought his muster gladly from Lleyn, restive for action and more intolerant of delays and irritations than his brother. It was the first time those two had been in arms together since David's defection to England, and that was eight years before. There were dangerous reminders there, but in the pressure of the moment they passed without harm.

I make no doubt we could have taken and destroyed Earl Gilbert's second castle, vastly as it was planned, as easily as we had done the first. But it was never put to the test. As soon as it was known that we had swept south and were encircling the half-built shell, King Henry in a great fright required equally rapid action from his council to bring about a truce before war could flare, and the council sent to Glamorgan the bishops of Coventry and Worcester, requesting a convention with Llewelyn. The prince was glad enough to accommodate them, though if need be he would have pushed his attack to a conclusion. On the second day of November they were brought into his camp and very courteously received. What they had to offer was sensible enough, and could well have been offered earlier if the will had been there. They were commissioned by the king to take Caerphilly into their care, and out of Earl Gilbert's hands. The site should be retained by the crown, and no further building should take place during the truce. But they required also that Llewelyn should withdraw his army from the commote, and be ready to conduct any further negotiations with his Grace's proctors at the ford of Montgomery.

'I am, and have always been, ready and willing to meet his Grace's proctors at any reasonable and fair place he may choose,' said Llewelyn, 'and if you give me the pledge that this site shall remain in crown custody, with that I am content.'

The bishops were careful to add in admonition, as no doubt they had been bidden to do, that King Henry had issued orders to the musters of the march and the border shires to stand ready to aid the earl if the prince of Wales should refuse to withdraw his forces.

'There is no need to tell me so,' said Llewelyn with a curling lip. 'If it is a threat, it does not affright me, and if a warning, it does not influence me. I will withdraw my army for a better reason, because I find the king's offer acceptable, and I take his word for its fulfilment.'

And he removed from Caerphilly at once, dispersed his southern levies, and took the men of Gwynedd home without so much as looking over his shoulder.

'You are trusting,' said David, dubious still.

'Even if I were not – and I do believe him sincere – there's no point in half-doing things,' said Llewelyn good-humouredly. 'It's either form and go, and no second thoughts, or else stay and fight. And if the king fears that would mean outright war, so do I fear it, and neither of us wants it. Whom could it benefit but Gloucester? If I gained a commote, I should have lost two years of solid work and the beginning, at least, of a secure peace. No, I'll keep what I have, and stake Caerphilly on King Henry's word.'

Thus that year ended in truce and the resumption of the wearisome legal arguments, but with nothing lost, and the castle in crown hands. And though the affair took an ill turn in the first weeks of the following year, and in effect Llewelyn lost the game, yet I am still sure that he did right to believe in the king's promise. Both Henry and his bishops acted in good faith, but the truth is that Gloucester was then possibly the most powerful man in the kingdom, and certainly the most lawless, and the old and ailing monarch had no means of mastering him, short of calling out the feudal host to make war on him, and if he had done anything so drastic it is certain they would not have obeyed. Marcher hangs with marcher, baron with baron, and Henry was not the man to overbear his troublesome vassals at the best of times, much less now in his old age.

Exactly how it befell we never did learn, but doubtless the force left to garrison the shell of Caerphilly during that winter was not strong, since Llewelyn had taken his army home, and the march was in any case alerted. However it was, Gloucester got possession of the place again, and manned it with such force that no one cared to try to wrest it from him. He may have raised an alarm of attack as his excuse to seize the castle, or he may have produced some devious point of law. However he contrived it, he was back in Caerphilly in January, and though the prince sent a formal protest to the king, and indeed got back from him, in February, a somewhat lame and apologetic letter attempting explanation and excuse, there was nothing more that could be done about it. David took fire and urged instant action, but Llewelyn would have none of it.

'To repeat what we did in November? To what end? You heard the bishops. Do you think that order has ever been rescinded? No, if I resorted to arms now it would mean the whole border aflame; it would mean war with England. The king could no more prevent it than he could prevent this move Gloucester has made. Caerphilly is not worth it, and I will not do it. I will not do it to Wales nor to England, and I will not do it to King Henry. His brother Richard is dying at Wallingford, and God knows how long after him Henry will be. My business is to conserve what I hold, and make the ground firmer under it. I choose to let Gloucester preen himself on his cleverness and keep his castle. But if he stir out of it to move against me he shall find out how little he has gained.'

And so this matter was left, in a manner satisfactory to none of us, but better than the ruin of war between two countries so recently brought to a peace still fragile. In these years Llewelyn had always a sure sense of how far he might go without wreck, and how much he should endure without outrage, and to this point I do not think he had ever made a mistake. His eyes were always on his ultimate object, which was the firm establishment of the principality of Wales, founded upon rock, and linked by ties of friendship and respect with England. Bound as we were to that powerful and ambitious nation by a border half as long as our frontier with the sea, there was no possibility that we could live and rule ourselves in isolation from our neighbour. But equally, if we surrendered ourselves too lavishly to that alliance we were doomed to be swallowed up. This was both his peril and his opportunity, and between the two there was but a tiny step, to be crossed whenever his balance faltered. To this day I do not know, to my life's end I shall never be sure, when, or if ever, he failed of keeping that balance, or whether from the beginning of the world our doom was written, and with it his, however wise, gallant and devoted. When all is said, this is but the first of worlds, the last is yet to be; and what overturning of emperors and exalting of captives there shall be then, what abasement of victors, what laurels for the vanquished, all this is in the hand of God.

In April of that year of grace, twelve hundred and seventy-two, Richard of Cornwall died, that mild, moderate, sensible man who had tried his best to measure right and wrong and cast his vote with justice, who had had his ambitions and successes, and indulged his pride a little in his kingship over the Romans, that is, of some curious peoples in Germany, whom he visited from time to time, but whom we understood not at all, and he, perhaps, very little. He left but one son, Edmund, to follow him as earl of Cornwall, having lost his heir, Henry of Almain, at the hands of Guy de Montfort in that bloody act at Viterbo. He was, take him for all in all, a good, decent man. He was buried beside his son in his abbey of Hailes. After his death, King Henry saddened and dwindled, for he was a man fond and kind with his kin, and diminished by such departures. And his own sons were far away in the Holy Land, about God's business.

In the same month of April, for us in Wales, arose the business of my lord's next brother, Rhodri, who came between Llewelyn and David.

It was then the ninth year that Rhodri had been in the prince's castle of Dolwyddelan, imprisoned after his attempt to rescue Owen Goch, the eldest of the four brothers, who had been far longer in confinement because of his early attack upon Llewelyn in arms, at a time when they shared the rule in Gwynedd equally between them. Equality was not enough for Owen. He fought for all, and lost all; and at this late time I think there were not many among the ordinary people of this new land of Wales, so much greater than merely Gwynedd, and Llewelyn's unaided creation, who gave a thought to him any longer. But the scholars of the old school, and the ancient lawyers, and the bards, still raised their protests for him from time to time, for they could not get used to the notion of a Welsh state, but still thought of the old law as irrevocable truth and right, and of all Welsh lands as partible between all the sons of the royal house, though they knew as well as the rest of us that a return to the old way would soon tear the country into puny commotes and cantrefs ready to fall at a touch into marcher hands.

By this time I think their complaints were a matter of tradition and sentiment, and they would have been both astonished and confounded if Llewelyn had taken them at their word, and torn his work to pieces again to distribute among his brothers. Of the three of them only David had voluntarily accepted his lesser status as a vassal, and enjoyed his lands upon that ground, and for all his lapses since, had always returned to that stand, even in this last reconciliation that was still chilly and imperfect. Of the other two, Rhodri obstinately held to his ancient rights, though he had never done anything to earn them. And Owen Goch, at the time of Rhodri's attempt on his behalf, had been offered his freedom and a fair establishment if he would accept the same vassal status David held, and had vehemently refused. To be honest, I do not think he had again been asked since that time. Llewelyn had been busy upon the affairs of Wales itself; it was easy to forget the angry, ageing, red-haired man glooming out over the lakes of Snowdon from the hilltop of Dolbadarn.

But now that we were no longer at war, with our eyes for ever fixed upon England, now that four years had passed with only the minor vexations inevitable in any legal settlement, Llewelyn began to consider once again all those other matters which had been shelved in favour of the greatest, especially as their right regulation could only add to the stability of Wales, and help to preserve our good relations with England.

'For there's no blinking the truth,' he said in private to me, 'it's not the best of recommendations to a prince that he has two of his own brothers in his prisons. Though God knows that was no novelty in Wales in the old days, if they did not kill one another outright, driven to murder by this same sacred law of the partible lands our romantics would like to revive.' He was not the first to abandon it, in fact, but had inherited the changed practice from his uncle and grandsire, though it was Llewelyn who came in for the odium from those who hated change. 'Now that I have time to breathe,' he said, 'I confess they are somewhat on my conscience.'

I said there was no need. 'Owen Goch had the half of Gwynedd, and was not content, but snatched at the whole. He deserved to fail, and to pay for it. And since then that first division is long outdated, for all the rest of Wales you have yourself drawn together, he has no rights in it. He had his chance to come to terms and get both lands and liberty at the price of his homage, and he would not do it. What choice had you but to keep him safe where he could do Wales and you no harm?'

We were together in his own high chamber at Aber, late in the evening, as we often sat together, and he looked at me across the glow of the brazier and the dark red of his wine-cup, and laughed at me. 'All the justification in the world will not make my mind quite easy. You are becoming a lawyer like the English, Samson, and faith, so am I, for however much I may want a settlement, it will be on harder terms now than the simple act of homage. I'll take nothing less from Owen or Rhodri than a quitclaim of all their hereditary rights in Wales, engrossed on parchment, sealed and witnessed, something I can produce and they cannot deny. But for that I'd be willing to pay over not only liberty, but money, too, if need be, or land, provided they hold it of me, and not by any other right.'

'You made no such demand on David,' I reminded him.

'David offered his fealty. But I don't say,' agreed Llewelyn with deliberation, 'that I would not ask so much of him, were he now in the same situation. He is not. Whatever he may have done, he has never again raised the cry of his own birthright. And unless he gives me fresh cause, I will not ask anything of him, nor bring up again what has been done in the past. But surely there must be some inducement that could be offered at least to Rhodri, to get him off my hands and my mind. He's the weaker vessel, and the less able to keep his grudges white-hot for years. Let's at least try.'

Rhodri was then thirty-seven years old, and unmarried still, and I remarked, without much thought, that seeing how successful David's marriage bade fair to be, and how it seemed to work most potently upon his tempestuous nature, perhaps a wife could do as much to settle Rhodri. Llewelyn laughed, but then gave me a sharp and thoughtful glance, and said there might well be something in that. The restoration of the lands he had forfeited, upon terms, together with a proper match that would bring him lands elsewhere, might be temptation enough.

So we cast about quietly to find if there were suitable matches available, and made no move meantime, nor as yet did Llewelyn consult his council. There was a certain nobleman whose acquaintance he had made in Westminster, one John le Botillier, who had lands both in England and Ireland, and he had no sons, but only a daughter, Edmunda, who was therefore his heiress, and a very desirable match, and her father had let it be known that he wished to settle her in marriage. There was no haste in the matter, but upon enquiry it was plain that le Botillier was well disposed to the idea of an alliance with a prince of Wales and would be willing to consider any approaches made to him. The lady we had seen in London, at the festival, and she was now turned twenty, and handsome.

'We'll put it to Rhodri,' said Llewelyn, 'before taking it further. If he's compliant, it might do very well. Ride with me, Samson! I'll go myself, and at least deal honestly with him, not leave it to another.' And he said, when we were on our way to Dolwyddelan: 'My mother, before she died, told me to do justice to my brother. Do you remember? And I said I would do right to all my brothers. Easier to say than to do! Sometimes I wonder whether I know where right lies. When the rights of Wales come into collision with Rhodri's, or with Owen's, I see but one claim on me.'

I said, and it was true, that had they been other than they were, they, too, might have set the needs of Wales before their own. But by his tight smile I think he still doubted. Yet even in self-appraisal, and in his rare moods of self-blame and disgust with the shifts to which he was put in his quest, he never took his eyes from his grand aim, the establishment of a Wales solid and secure enough to survive its founder, and in pursuit of that aim he never repented anything he did, whatever its cost to him or another.

In the castle of Dolwyddelan Rhodri had a chamber high in the great keep, but he was allowed the run of the wards for exercise, under guard, and as prisons go, his was by no means of the worst. Sometimes he was even permitted to ride out in the hills, though safely escorted, for the castle stands high on a steep place, and the space within the walls is somewhat cramped. He had been visited, often by myself, once or twice in every year, and his wants and complaints, within reason, were attended to good-humouredly. Owen Goch at Dolbadarn was more closely kept, being a far more formidable person. Rhodri was querulous and critical, but not given to bold or decisive action. The marvel was that he ever brought himself to make that one rash raid, in the attempt to snatch Owen from his escort, though even that he did mainly for his own ends, needing an ally more robust than himself.

Llewelyn had him brought down from his tower apartment into the great chamber, where there was a good fire. Rhodri halted for an instant at the sight of his brother, and then came forward into the room with a wary and suspicious face, looking at us a little sidelong, which was a way he always had, from a child. Sometimes he even walked with a sidewise gait, as though too wary and secretive to approach people straight. He was not greatly changed after his long confinement, by reason of the air and exercise allowed to him. His reddish fair hair had no grey in it as yet, and he looked no older than his years.

'What, in person?' he said, curling his lip. 'I had not looked for such an honour!' He was not feeling as bold as his manner and words suggested, for I saw the rapid, nervous fluttering of his eyelashes, which were of a colour almost rosy. 'You've left me long enough unvisited, there must be some important reason for this visit now.'

'There is,' said Llewelyn bluntly. 'A matter of business. I have a proposal to make to you, and we may as well sit down and be civil together while I make it.' And he sent for wine, and made Rhodri sit beside the fire, close to him.

'I look for no good,' said Rhodri sullenly, 'from any proposal of yours. You have never wished me well, or done me justice, why should I hope for better now? If you had any brotherly feeling for me you would have set me free long ago. What do you want with me more? You have done to me all that is needful, your princedom is safe enough, at my cost, and at Owen's. Go and enjoy it!'

It was David's complaint, though never voiced to Llewelyn, that the prince held him too lightly to care either for his love or his hate, which in his case was never true. But of Rhodri it was true enough. There was no way he could either anger or please my lord, never anything larger than irritation and weariness. So Llewelyn sat back among the fur rugs of the couch, and let his brother's petulant grievances flow over him and pass, like the humming of midges in the high summer. Neither smiling nor frowning, he waited for the feeble shower to spend itself. Then he said mildly:

'Hate me as well as you will, but listen to me, if you want your freedom and a life at large. For you can have it, but at a price. No, let me hear no exclamation, you know only too well there must be a price. We need not go into repetitions of what has been said often enough. Wales is one, and I made it one, and if it cost your life, and Owen's, and mine, I will keep it one. There is no change there; there never will be any change. But short of letting you or any break that unity apart, you wrong me, I do wish you well. I am here to prove it. Will you listen?'

Rhodri was so at loss, and so seeking within his own mind for perils that might still be threatening him, that it took some minutes to awe him into calm, and be sure of his attention. Then Llewelyn told him the entire bargain, bluntly and short, to leave no doubt.

'The father is favourably disposed. The lady is very comely, and a considerable heiress. And I will see that you are set up in a sum fitting to advance this marriage. The price is large. I own it. It is the only price that will buy you this opportunity. I want from you in return a quitclaim of all your hereditary rights in Gwynedd – for in the rest of Wales you have none, and never had any.'

Rhodri gulped, and gazed, and writhed, his breath taken by so unexpected a visitation. I saw how he leaned to the hope of freedom, recoiled from the surrender of his grievance and his claim, and yet could not but realise that the grievance had no hope of being recompensed, the claim no possibility of being acknowledged, whether he took this price or no. There was against him a mind far stronger and larger than his, and a cause not all, not chiefly, selfish, against which his own small struggles were vain. And he was being offered a very fine and comfortable position in the world, a wealthy wife, and his liberty. He leaned and clutched, and started back in dudgeon, and grasped again frantically before the hope escaped him. And Llewelyn let him sway back and forth in anguish as long as he would, without pressing.

'In return for the quitclaim,' he said, 'I will pay you the sum of one thousand marks to acquire this marriage, but the quitclaim I must have.'

'And if I refuse?' said Rhodri, quivering. But to me, at least, it was already clear that he would not refuse.

'Then you remain here as my prisoner, and you have quitclaimed to me all that I require of you, but without any repayment. Let us say,' said Llewelyn, in the gentlest and most reasonable of voices, 'that I stand to gain what I need, whatever your answer may be, but if your answer is yes, and if you make it good, then you also stand to gain a wife, an estate, and a figure in the land. It is not an even choice,' he said, with some distaste, 'but at least it is fairly stated. And you know, for all your grudges, that what I swear to, that I perform.'

And Rhodri did know it, as all men knew it who dealt with Llewelyn, for after he had wrestled with his venom a while, and we had kept silence and borne with him, he said in a strangled voice, and wringing his hands together in rage and relief equally mixed: 'Very well, I agree! I will give you the quittance you want.'

The agreement was drawn up and sealed at Carnarvon on the twelfth day of April, with the approval of the council, though since it was a personal bargain, accepted upon both sides, they had no call to sanction or prohibit. Nevertheless, their blessing, given with great relief at the solution of one long-standing problem and reproach, was worth much, and their witness to the deed far more.

Rhodri was brought down from Dolwyddelan to Carnarvon still under guard, for Llewelyn would not quite loose him out of hold until he had his quitclaim safely sealed. But it was not difficult to see the lavish company that attended him as escort rather than guard on a prisoner, and from the day of his acceptance he had been allowed the services of his own household and clerks, so that there should be nothing underhand about the bargain. By the time they rode into Carnarvon Rhodri was no longer a pressed partner in the deal, having conned over all its advantages to himself at leisure, with no envied and resented brother by to poison the picture for him, and the prospect of an Irish heiress, with a goodly estate in trust for her, and a pretty face to match, had begun to seem far more desirable than a tenuous claim that grew every year more impossible of realisation. So it was no sullen and reluctant prince who brought his retinue into Carnarvon to seal the bond, but a cheerful giver who went about with a small, sidewise, sleek smile, as though he had reached the conclusion that he was not doing at all badly out of the exchange, but had better not reveal as yet that he was aware of it.

In a great conference of council and clergy Rhodri and his clerks delivered the prepared deed, by which he quitclaimed, for himself and his heirs after him, to the prince and the heirs of his body, all his rights and claims by heredity in the lands and possessions of north Wales, and elsewhere throughout the whole principality – though naturally this need not preclude the grant of lands to him to be held of the prince by homage – in consideration of the payment of one thousand marks sterling with which to acquire the marriage of Edmunda, daughter of John le Botillier. The deed also made solemn promise that he would not disturb, or procure others to disturb, the peace of the prince's realm, against his present willing surrender and quitclaim. And to this document he added his seal, together with the seals of the bishops of Bangor and St Asaph, and the abbots of Aberconway, Basingwerk and Enlli, with leave to add also the seals of the archdeacons of the two northern sees. A great number of witnesses, headed by Tudor the high steward of Wales, and including Llewelyn's own law clerks, subscribed to the agreement. Rhodri was at the same moment fast bound, and utterly free. From the time the deed was concluded he was at liberty, and a first payment of fifty marks was made to him at once, to pay his expenses in opening negotiations with le Botillier. Which he set about eagerly, with every prospect in his favour.

And indeed he was not so bad a match for the lady, and not an ill-looking fellow, though vague and colourless beside either Llewelyn's glowing brown or David's raven blackness and brilliance. And in the first exchanges everything went well with his suit, and the father, certainly, was in favour of the marriage, and exactly what befell to break off the arrangement we were never told, for by then the matter had naturally passed completely into Rhodri's hands, and whatever it was, it caused him great chagrin and anger, and he was in no mind to share it. By such grains of gossip as leaked out, it seems that though le Botillier was in favour of accepting Rhodri, his daughter had other ideas, having both a lover and a mind of her own, and contrived to place herself in a situation so delicately compromised that her parents found it wise to let her have her way, and betrothed her to the young man in question. Whether this is true or not, certainly she was married, shortly afterwards, to one Thomas de Muleton.

Now perhaps Rhodri could have borne this rebuff somewhat better if his marriage plans had not been made so publicly and before so great and solemn a concourse, but as it was, the collapse of his hopes could not but be noised abroad just as publicly, and he took it very hard, for though marriage plans are made and unmade in businesslike fashion all the year round with no heart-burning on either side, yet to be the favoured suitor with the parents and to be rejected and outwitted by the girl is less common, and very shaming. From the moment he got the news of the final break Rhodri shut himself up from sight, fearful of covert smiles and castle jokes such as follow the unfortunate, and brooded in the blackest of moods. And within a week he vanished from among us, took his portable treasure and rode away in the night, and the next word we had was that he had entered Chester and confided himself to the justiciar there.

Llewelyn made mild enquiry, not anxious to interfere with his brother's plans, if Rhodri intended to shake off the dust of Wales, only wanting precise news; and I think he would have been willing then to pay a further instalment of the money due, but Rhodri had already ridden south, presumably to London to ask hospitality and service at court, so as we had no further word the prince shrugged, and let him go.

'With goodwill,' he said, sighing, 'if he intends to settle in England, for I am rid of him, and he may do very well there, where he has no claims and no grievances, and no ambitions beyond his reach.'

None the less, it had an unpleasant flavour for us that a prince who found his life soured in Wales should naturally make for King Henry's court, as if fleeing for refuge to the enemy, whereas we had been at peace and in very reasonable friendship for five years.

'It seems we have not yet succeeded in changing men's minds,' said Llewelyn soberly. 'He could have gone openly for me, why should I hinder him?'

'Why, indeed?' said David to me, after hearing this. 'He has what he wanted from him, signed and sealed, with a dozen or so reverend churchmen as sureties, and half the nobility of Wales as witnesses. There's nothing any lawyer, English or Welsh, can do to break that bond, and nothing left to fear from Rhodri. Now he has not even to pay him or feed him. Why hinder his going, indeed!'

He had come to me, as he used to do years before, in my copying-room, where I was busy with some documents concerning cases to be heard in the prince's local court. We were sitting by candle-light, for I had worked so late that even in August the light was gone, but for a violet afterglow over the sea. Elizabeth was not with him on this visit, and without her he was restless and out of humour. The black mood could not endure in her presence, at least not thus early in the charm of their marriage, but now it sat upon his shoulders for want of her, and perhaps in some measure for shadowy regrets and remembrances concerning Rhodri.

'Both you and King Henry,' I said, 'have good cause to know and admit that the prince pays what he pledges. *You* have no call to speak slightingly of his usage, whatever Rhodri may claim. Take care your own debts are paid as punctiliously as his.'

I meant debts not in money, and he so understood me, for he smiled at me darkly across the table, his elbows spread among my parchments and his chin in his cupped hands. His finger-tips pressed deep hollows into his lean cheeks below the rounded and polished cases of bone out of which his eyes shone so wildly pale, clear and bright.

'Ah, now you preach like my true priestly breast-brother,' he said. 'I have heard the note before, I should miss it if ever you gave me up for lost, and cast me out of your prayers. Oh, yes, I have debts still undischarged, have I not, Samson? Twice forgiven, twice restored. I have a great load of amends to make, and gratitude to show, and service to render yet before I shall be clear of my indebtedness. Do you know of a slower and a deadlier poison,' he said, pressing his fingers deeper, so that his long lips were drawn up in an angry smile, 'than having to swallow favour undeserved? Never to be able to find gratitude enough to buy it off, and never to be able to spit it out in rank ingratitude? I'd liefer be treated as an equal and slung into Dolbadarn for twenty years with Owen!'

Knowing him, I said without excitement: 'That is a lie. And you know it.'

He drew exasperated breath, and gnawed his lips for a moment, eyeing me glitteringly from under his long black lashes, and then he laughed.

'Yes, that is a lie! I might wish to prefer such dire payment, but in truth I like my freedom, and my comfort, and my own will, and I suppose if my deserts threatened me again I should again use my wits to cling fast to all those good things, and slip sideways from under the lash. Sweet Samson, I shall come to you no more for confession and absolution. You know me too well. I get no flattery.'

'No penance, either,' I said.

'True, that should bring me still,' he owned, 'seeing what I've just admitted. I wonder if I could ever take to hating *you*, Samson, for letting me off too lightly?'

'As you hate him?' I said, and watched him flinch and frown blackly, and clench his even white teeth hard upon his knuckle, but never for all these writhings take his eyes from mine. Such he was, he could look you in the face as clearly and challengingly as an angel, both while he lied to you and while he told you blazing truth. If he could not come to terms with a man, or a cause, or a world, still he would not turn his face away. Once he told me outright that he was afraid of death, but he never averted his eyes, not even from that enemy.

'You deceive yourself,' I said, 'you do not hate him.'

'Do I not?' said David mildly, still gazing like one interested and willing to learn.

'Think, sometimes, that you have what he lacks and envies you, married happiness, and a child . . .'

'Children!' said David, and let his lips soften into quite another smile, thinking of Elizabeth. 'She is again with child. But no one knows it yet but you, Samson. She says it will a boy this time. She says it as if God had told her. Yes, I have what he may well envy, have I not?' And then he did lower his eyes, but to look within, at this mystery he hoarded within himself, as if he watched the seed burgeon. And more than that, a mystery beyond that mystery. The slow, deepening curl of his lips was triumphant. He enjoyed, he delighted in, his victory over Llewelyn; he prayed it to continue. It was a large and crushing revenge for every real and imagined injury.

'You teach me,' said David, softly and sweetly, 'where gratitude is truly due.' And he rose, the candles quivering faintly in the wind of his movements, and stretched at large, and smiled down at me. 'I will remember it in my prayers,' he said, and turned to the door. 'I'll leave you to your labours now. Good-night!'

454

In the doorway, the soft blue light from the summer sky flowing down all the outlines of his dark figure like moonlit water, he turned and looked back. 'To think,' he said, wondering, 'that he had always this weapon of the quitclaim, if he had cared to use it! They say every man has his price. I wonder what he would have had to offer Owen? Or me, for that matter?'

'He has never asked you,' I said, stung, 'he never will ask you, for such a quitclaim.'

'As well!' said David, soft and muted in the doorway. 'I would not give it to him if he did.'

In October of that year Pope Gregory X, that Cardinal Tedaldo Visconti who was recalled from the crusade to take up his office, and there in the east had become close and faithful friend to the Lord Edward, examined and rejected the prior of Canterbury as candidate for the primacy of England, looked warily but briefly at Edward's choice, Robert Burnell, that formidable cleric of affairs, and passed carefully over him to choose Robert Kilwardby, the Dominican. So the national province had an archbishop again after two years, a man of scholarship, piety and intellect.

And one month later, in his palace of Westminster, King Henry died as he had lived, among the turbulent outcries of a populace preoccupied with a minor quarrel over the mayor of London. His death was hastened, as many believed, because of his hurried pilgrimage to calm another local disorder in Norwich, which otherwise flickered out without great damage. All his life he was haunted and hunted by such annoyances, yet he had reigned for fifty-six years, and survived everything life and England could do against him. He lived to see his dearest dream take shape in this world, in his church at Westminster, and few men have that joy. And he died, for all the turmoils he had provoked and suffered, better regarded than in his youth, and the mourning for him was not feigned nor formal, though muted by the natural erosions of time, for he was old, and had had his span fairly.

Since the deaths and burials even of kings give but very brief warning, Henry was in his tomb before ever we heard of his departure. The official word from the regents and the royal council did not reach us until the twenty-sixth day of November, being sent out along with the formal letters in the new king's name to all his sheriffs and officers in the land. But we had fuller information three days before that, for Cynan sent his lively Welsh groom to bring us the news, his master's letter supplementing his own account.

'His Grace was buried,' Cynan wrote, 'in his abbey church four days after his death, and they have laid him according to his wish, in the tomb from which the relics of Saint Edward were translated three years ago. By one means or another he will make his way into heaven. The Lord Edward being absent, the council and his own proctors have taken charge, and for four days England had no king, though there was never any question of his peaceful succession or his welcome. After the funeral mass, before the tomb was closed, all the bishops and barons and others present went up to the high altar, and took the oath of fealty to King Edward. A new seal has been made for him, and King Henry's seal was broken by the archbishop of York after the oath had been sworn by all. The first to swear was Gloucester, who was sent for to the king on the day he died, and has pledged himself to forgo all old grudges against Edward, and guard the kingdom for him until he comes, and all the signs are that he means it and will do his best. They have written to Edward to let him know of his father's death, and urged him to return quickly. By this time his term in the east is over, and he must be on his way back, but as far as is known it was his intention to winter with Charles of Anjou in Sicily, as he did on his journey east. Now he may change his plans, but equally he may not, for he made good certain of his arrangements before sailing, and has absolute trust in his proctors to act now as his regents.'

These proctors were the archbishop of York, Robert Burnell, and my lord's cousin, Roger Mortimer, his troublesome and aggressive kinsman, neighbour and enemy in the middle march. Those two had an old rivalry that was also, after its fashion, a friendship. So we knew with whom we should have to deal in any disputes or agreements that might arise.

'So the old man is gone,' said Llewelyn, pondering his own regret with some surprise. 'I have fought him most of my life, and never thought I might grieve for his death. But we had grown used to each other, and there was a certain security in that. Now we begin afresh. And not with Edward, not yet.'

The old man was gone, and the new man not yet come, and there could be no homage rendered until he did arrive in person in his kingdom. The oath of fealty, that the baronage had taken at the high altar after the burial, could indeed be sworn in the king's absence, but the meeting of hands was impossible, and it was somewhat unusual, though not unknown, for the two acts to be separated after this fashion. So we expected only to continue our dealings with England as before, until Edward's arrival, and were prepared to be as accommodating with his regents as we had tried to be with his father.

At this time Llewelyn still had a number of matters at issue with England, and had listed his complaints after the normal fashion, and we were in process of arranging a meeting of the commission at the ford of Montgomery, the usual place of parley. When, therefore, he received a letter from the regents, he expected that it should be appointing a date for this arbitration. It was indeed a summons to the ford of Montgomery for an official meeting, but not of such a neighbourly kind as we had looked for. The regents sent a writ to order him to attend in person at the ford on the twentieth day of January of the coming year, to take the oath of fealty to King Edward in absence, in the persons of those who would be sent to represent the crown.

This writ came to us in December, and bore the date of the twenty-ninth of November, and there was about this indecent haste an ominous note of incivility which both stung and amused Llewelyn. King Henry had been dead just two weeks when they called the prince, with less ceremony than would have been used to an earl. Surely they were pressed with business then, a great burden of legal adjustments necessary after the passing of one king and the succession of another, and they sent out all their official writs and documents in great haste, and made little distinction between persons. And yet this pricked and clung like a burr, even in my skin, and I am sure in Llewelyn's. But he also was a busy man, and wasted little indignation on the summons.

'The dogs bark as loudly as they can when they are barking for a lion,' he said good-humouredly. 'Where's the haste, when I cannot do homage until Edward is here to close his hands on mine? Why should I swear my fealty to the king's shadow? I'll wait for Edward.' And he went on with the business of his commote court, which was then occupying him, and for all I could see, forgot the whole matter.

Now this is of importance, for some have thought that even at this time he had it in mind to avoid repeating to the son the homage he had rendered to the father, seeing this change in the monarchy as his opportunity to hold fast what he had gained and achieve a completely independent status for Wales, in alliance, certainly, but an alliance equal on both sides, without hint of vassalage of any kind. But this is false, and even the suggestion has arisen only of late. He had no such move in mind. He said as he meant, for in all border disputes he had relied more upon Edward than upon any other, and had very solid trust in him. But for some of his officials he felt no such kindness, and to affront them, I confess, was not unpleasant to him. They had caused him trouble enough. But to avoid his homage, no, he never entertained such a thought. By treaty he had pledged himself not only to King Henry but to his heirs, and as he had pledged, so he kept. But he did not think it of any importance to make a ceremony of vowing fealty while homage was impossible.

He was more displeased, I believe, shortly after, when he received a curt reminder that there was one sum of the indemnity to England in arrears, and another instalment due at the Christmas feast. Which was true enough, though he had already despatched the arrears about the time of the king's death, and it was receipted later, and reminders in advance had never been customary or necessary, for there was no man in the treasury who did not know that the prince of Wales was not only the promptest payer the crown had, but in fact the only prompt payer. The monarchy was eternally in debt, Llewelyn almost never, and never for long.

'This is insolent,' he said, tossing the letter aside to me. 'When they appoint me a day to put right the wrongs done to me in the borders, as I have asked and asked, then I'll pay them the next money due, and not before. And the earlier Edward comes home, the better pleased shall I be. I thought Burnell, at least, had a finer understanding.'

I said that I read in the tone of this demand, rather, the loud and arrogant voice of his cousin Mortimer. And at that he laughed, and said I might well be right, for Roger was a bull who made head-down for his adversary. And back he went to his work, and let the crude demand lie. I know on what terms we had dealt with England, and I say, and say again, that in this attitude he was justified, and I, who loved and lived for him, never thought then that there was any need to advise or persuade him to any other tone. Those who say the change was in him, they lie. He changed only when all changed. And had he remained constant when all changed, what would it have availed him? Nothing!

At the Christmas festival at Aber, according to custom, David came visiting, to preserve the proper form, but without his Elizabeth, for she was near her time, and therefore, to my grief, without Cristin, who was never parted from her, and to my ease, without Godred, either, for he resisted being parted from Cristin. This I put down, though not quite easily, to a desire to look like a good husband, for of real and loving care for his wife he had none, but a man must keep his status and his face. It was a snowy Christmas, as I recall, white across the salt flats and crusted with frost along the edge of the sea. The mountains hid in sparkling mist well into the new year, and we in the maenol under the cleft of the hills had a snug, smoky Christmas, no way troubled, unless it was by David's fretting for his beloved girl. We told him again and again she had the best of care, which he acknowledged, and that she had borne her first daughter in joy, within three hours, and laughing, which also he owned and vaunted. Even so, he grudged every moment away from her.

Consequently he did not stay long with us after the new year began, but was in haste to get back to Lleyn, though he knew that Cristin would have had a messenger on the road hot-foot to him if there had been any need for his return. But he waited for a meeting of the council which was held in the first week of January, being still insistent upon his duty, even when his mind was elsewhere and he contributed little. He did, however, prick up his ears and look very thoughtful when he heard of the arbitrary letter from the regents, though Llewelyn mentioned the matter but currently in passing, with reference to the need to hold something in reserve to force amends for border infringements. For there is no doubt that these had increased since King Henry's death, not in any drastic fashion, but by local raids, and some interference with merchants and the passage of goods. I do not think this was in any sense official policy, or that the regents countenanced it or knew much about it. It was rather that with one king dead and another not yet come, those who lived a lawless life by choice in the marches, remote from the seat of power, and in the tenancy or service of almost equally lawless lords, felt themselves freed from any strong surveillance, and indulged their normal sport to the full. By the time law could get to them, they were again dispersed and about their innocent business. This was the case generally in the march, but in the centre and the south, especially where we were neighbour to the vast and powerful honours of Gilbert de Clare of Gloucester and Humphrey de Bohun of Hereford, it was not merely the lesser people who plundered as opportunists, but there were also some planned and methodical incursions by the lords themselves into land manifestly Welsh. The regents were able and hard-working men, but carried a great load, and were held by the sheer weight of their documentary business to London, where the needful offices were. The prospect of their coming in person to examine and suppress the raiding in the borders did not terrify the marchers at all. They might deal out verbal penalties from Westminster, but distance was blessed, and they were not Edward. So the borderers made hay while the good weather lasted, and the only means we had of preventing was in arms, and that we were anxious to limit to what was clearly fair defence, short of actual retaliation.

'I have never been long in default with the money I am pledged to pay,' Llewelyn said, 'and I do not blink the fact that it is due by treaty. If I withhold it or delay it, it can be said that I am failing to fulfill my terms, and that goes against my grain. But it is truth that these pinpricks along the border have become dagger-wounds, and to my mind the terms of the treaty are already being broken from their side. I have lodged my complaints so often that I grow weary. The only direct weapon I have to my hand is this money. Perhaps I have been too prompt up to now. They write me into their accounts a month ahead of time, and have spent half what they get from me before they get it. It may cause them to read my letters more carefully and keep their own bond more exactly if I hold back what is now due. Let them perform their part, and I'll perform mine.'

Tudor approved, though cautiously. Some of the council were prepared to go further, having border troubles in their own commotes, and all shrugged aside the summons to the ford as of little importance, which was certainly Llewelyn's own opinion. He preferred direct dealings with Edward always, and had found them by far the best way of getting grievances attended to and wrongs righted.

'When the king comes home,' he said confidently, 'we shall have no more trouble and misunderstanding, even if there's no lasting cure for a contentious border as long as men are men. I rely on Edward's goodwill and good sense. It is these officials who offend.'

So with general approval we held back the payment due that Christmas, though it was his habit to have the amount ready and waiting, so far as that was possible, whenever it fell due. And with that the council dispersed. But David, frowning and thoughtful, sought out Llewelyn before he gathered his people and rode for home.

'Take care,' he said seriously, 'how you deal with these regents. Never take them too lightly; they are not light men.'

'Did you disapprove?' said Llewelyn, surprised. 'Why did you not say so?'

'No, it's well enough to stand upon the treaty, and insist they do their part. But don't take it too far, if you'd be wise. These officials *are* Edward. Make no mistake. Edward will not uphold you or any against them; they represent his name and right – however they conduct themselves. They may do in his absence things he would rather they had not done, but if they are done in his name they will be law and binding, and he will maintain them, and oppose all those who challenge them. Even you!'

All this he said earnestly but coolly, as he performed all his vassal duties, not as a brother warning his brother of unwisdom. And I, who was watching his face and guessing at the mind behind it, judged from the distant spark in his eyes that more than half of him was already away with Elizabeth, and in a vision he held in his arms the son she had promised him, the first of a line, the founder of a dynasty. For all the controlled austerity of his face, there was triumph in his eyes. It was the first time I had ever seen him look upon Llewelyn with something near to pity. Punctiliously he warned him of possible danger. Once I had said to my lord that as often as David's right hand struck at his brother, his left would reach to parry the blow.

I went down with him to the stables, and walked beside him as far as the gate when he rode, swathed in furs against the cold. I asked him to give my greetings and service to Elizabeth, and to Cristin, and when he said he would, his voice was quick and warm, and he laid a hand upon my shoulder. There was little he did not know concerning Cristin and me, though I think Godred remained to him a bright, shallow mystery.

'I would you had my happiness!' he said, and meant it.

'Do you wish as much to him?' I said.

David shook his shoulders impatiently. 'It is his own choice to be barren and alone. It is not yours.'

'He will not always be so,' I said, and prayed that my heart might be as certain of it as my voice sounded.

'You think not?' said David.

'Surely not! God forbid I should look forward hopefully to any death, but the Countess Eleanor cannot live for ever, even if she continues adamant all her life, and nothing else stands in the way. After all this time, who can raise any objection?'

'The Countess Eleanor is no more than a dozen years or so older than he is,' said David, and his voice was slow, considering and cool. 'No man can tell when his time will come. He may yet go before her. And here is this heritage without an heir, and he values it so little! A kingdom, and he will not give it a prince!'

It was the same text to which Tudor spoke frequently and at length, though less often to Llewelyn these days, knowing it would be vain. But Tudor said these things with anxiety and exasperation and sorrow. In David's voice was none of these; it kept its soft, speculative level and the calm of its music unshaken by any indignation. A very beautiful voice he had, but as I knew from my own long alliance with him, it could fret and scald and slash with passion enough when he so pleased.

'While I,' he said, so softly and drily that he seemed to be speaking to himself rather than to me, though I knew it was meant for my ears, and meant to disquiet a little, 'I have heirs – perhaps a prince by now! –but no kingdom. Thus is this world arranged at cross-purposes, Samson. Have you never wished to move the pieces into a better pattern? Or do you still believe God knows best, and should not have his elbow jogged?'

'Go home,' I said, 'and take your mischief with you, and forbear from plaguing your wife as you delight in plaguing me.'

And at that he laughed aloud, and stooped low from the saddle to embrace me about the shoulders, and rode out of the gate with a plunge of his heel and swirl of his cloak, keeping the rimy edges of grass along the coast road to avoid the glassy ice. And after him his retinue, well-mounted, rich and bright with colours, equipped and harnessed most princely, a king's retinue.

CHAPTER IV

A small judgment awaited David and Elizabeth that January for their too much pride and delight in their fruitfulness, for the expected son was a second daughter, as fine and dark and bold as the first, but not so beautiful, taking after her mother rather than her sire but for the black hair. She came as sweetly and readily as the other, for this lady was gifted for bearing as few women are, and all her children lived and flourished, and she, meantime, remained so young and vigorous that after some years of tending her girls she appeared rather as their elder sister than their mother.

This girl they named Gladys, after David's only sister, many years dead in her bloom. And I think that the check to their exultation was but mild and brief, for they both loved their children, and took great pleasure in enjoying them. Moreover, Elizabeth had proved her gift of giving birth, and he his generosity in engendering, and as for the sons, it was but a matter of time. So the little one was never made to feel she must pay for her error in not being a boy, but was cherished and worshipped from her birth. And as love is a rare virtue, and surely prized in heaven, so I count the family blessedness of those two perilous and hapless creatures as their justification and their crown. By this time David so loved, as she deserved and exulted in his love. He was a creature hard to trap, but she had him in the snare of her own immeasurable worship. He never swerved from her, never again looked at any other woman, he who had ensnared all the beauties of England and Wales before Edward cast this innocent child-widow in his path, brown as a mouse, mild as rain, plain as a little sister.

'Is he happy?' asked Llewelyn, in some doubt, when we got word of the child's birth. 'He wanted, he expected, a boy.' Of his voice I knew even those tones that were lost in the quietness of his speech. He suffered what David never knew, all his bowels cramped with longing, for he was all a man, and obstinately celibate for his love. A passing strange thing is love, outside the regulation of the flesh, entering into the spirit. I have seen his face so translated by desire, he passed beyond David's recognition.

'He is happy,' I said. 'You need not fret for David.' But for Llewelyn my heart turned and curdled in me, remembering David's grievance and David's vaunt, crying aloud that he had a prince without a kingdom, or would have soon, while Llewelyn had a kingdom without an heir. With all the goodwill in the world on Llewelyn's part, and, for all his stiff-necked insistence on his vassal status, a great deal of obdurate and hurtful love left on David's, yet this division of their personal fortunes was no way helpful to the restoration of the old trust and affection between them.

In the early spring of that year twelve hundred and seventy-three we had news from Cynan at court that disquieted Llewelyn more than he would confess. King Edward on his slow way home from the Holy Land had sent his wife into Spain, both to visit her brother the king of Castille, and also to conduct certain minor matters of business on his behalf in those parts, while he went into Italy, to Orvieto, to renew his friendship with Pope Gregory the crusader. The queen was then carrying another child, and had with her her baby daughter Joan, born at Acre. Doubtless she was glad to rest awhile in her native country, before she went on into Gascony to meet Edward there. He had written to his council that he would make haste to get home, but kings never have quiet from affairs, and there were some restive lordlings in Gascony who were still prepared to outface even Edward, so that his presence was needed there. In the end he delayed a whole year.

But as at this time of which Cynan wrote, he was with Pope Gregory at Orvieto. And there he learned that Guy de Montfort, the murderer of Henry of Almain, was still at large, sheltered and safe in the territories of the people of Siena, having his father-in-law, the Red Count of Pitigliano, as a most powerful ally. Edward in great fury demanded aid from the Sienese to hunt down the assassin, and though they refused him, they did so in fear and trembling, and Siena and Florence and other cities of Tuscany begged the king not to resort to war. So, doubtless, did his friend the pope, and Edward could not well go against him, but he did use every possible legal threat to induce Guy to submit himself to the church's condemnation and penance. His unremitting hatred and rage appalled all who witnessed them, not that Guy had not earned it, but that its intensity and deadliness were more and less than human, giant like his body, but not subject to any curbs or temperings of time, or resignation, or magnanimity, as human rages should be.

'In the end,' wrote Cynan, 'he has failed to get his enemy into his hands, but has done the best he could to destroy him, inducing the pope to issue against him the most frightful bull of excommunication possible. He is left no human rights, he can hold no lands, own no property, take shelter nowhere without imperilling those who shelter him. With that the king has had to be content, and has now left Orvieto on his way to the pass of Mont Cenis. But from all I hear, feeling in Italy is not near so unfavourable to Guy, and as soon as the king's back is turned there will be ambassadors enough willing to try to bring the man to submission and absolution. More ominous is the revelation of King Edward's mind towards those who incur his displeasure.'

'As well,' said Llewelyn wryly, reading this dolorous account of the turbulent fortunes of Earl Simon's third son, 'that I am making no move at this time, and can make none, in the face of the countess's absolute rejection. At waiting, I believe, I am the most accomplished of princes, certainly the most experienced. I can wait yet a year or two. Even King Edward's animosity must wear itself out sooner or later. At least I can take good care of Wales, while I wait for the day when I can lay it at Eleanor's feet.'

At this time he was concerned to repair certain gaps in the main border defences, which he wished to ensure by means of a string of castles, as the

English did. From the north, by Chester, he had Mold, and Whittington in Salop, and safe support at Dinas Bran, but in the middle march, over against Montgomery, his position was less well established, and for some time he had been planning to place a new castle, a strong building in stone, somewhere in that region, and preferably in conjunction with a town and a market. He chose the crest of a great ridge overhanging the valley of the upper Severn, just where the lesser river Mule flows into it, in the cantref of Cydewain, perhaps four miles from the ford where our conventions met, and five from the royal castle of Montgomery. From the summit of that hill, where the rock breaks through the turf, there is a glorious view over all that grand valley, for many miles to the south, and less widely to the north, while across the river valley the folded hills rise again, hiding Montgomery, but revealing all the river crossings between. It seemed a most defensible site, and the river junction below a very profitable place for a township, access being both good from all directions, and controllable from the castle. As soon as the weather was favourable for the moving and cutting of stone and laying of foundations, building began, with a great army of workmen and masons.

This place the people of Cydewain called Dolforwyn, the 'Angels' Meadow', and the township Llewelyn founded beneath it, where the rivers joined, we called Abermule.

About the twenty-fourth day of June, when the building was forward and in good heart, and Llewelyn in the summer weather, after some weeks encamped below the hill to supervise the work, had withdrawn with his entourage to Dinorben, he was astonished to receive a visitor in the person of the reverend prior of Wenlock, which is a Cluniac abbey in Salop, not too far distant from those parts of the border, bearing a letter from King Edward's regents, issued through the royal chancellery. The prince received the reverend father with all courtesy, and such soldierly hospitality as we could offer him in a summer camp, and contained his curiosity about the message until we were out of the presence of the messenger. For the prior was old and gentle and very benign, and knew no more than we did what he carried, being charged only to deliver it, and to bring back the prince's answer.

'I have a premonition,' said Llewelyn, hesitating to break the seal, 'that these lieutenants of the king use the most innocent and well-willing to carry their worst crudities. It is one way of disarming offence.' But he would not give it to me to open and read to him, being, I rejoice to remember partly at my instruction, fluent in Latin as in Welsh, and almost as good in English, if his French, like mine, was something wanting. He read slowly, burning visibly into pure, silent anger, his burnished summer brown flushing into copper-red, but all in stillness. When he looked up at me, the skin of his face was drawn tight over starting bones, his eyes, which were normally peaceable in their deep, rich peat-brown, had red flames tall and bright in their depths.

'This is not to be borne,' he said, smouldering but quiet, torn between indignation and disdain. 'They have run mad with the glory of being deputies to greatness. Do you know what they dare to write to me, Samson? They straitly forbid me to continue with my plans to build a castle at Dolforwyn, or to found a market town at Abermule, to the hurt of his Grace's crown rights and neighbouring markets. They forbid me! In my own Welsh lands! What market rights has England on this side of Severn to be infringed? None! And what right has one sovereignty to forbid another to build or found within its own territories? None! I am not even appropriating a site from a vassal of my own. I am the one person who has the right to build there without asking leave of any man living.'

And this was true, for Griffith ap Gwenwynwyn of Powys, the greatest of his vassals and the last to come to his fealty, held only a part of Cydewain. Nevertheless, I fancied then that Griffith was not best pleased by the founding of the castle, having an eye to his own trade rights and privileges at his castle and town of Pool, though that was a matter of eight miles distant from Abermule, and it could hardly be said that the prince was encroaching, trade with England in those parts being brisk, and the border not as turbulent as further south. But Griffith was jealous of his power, and grudging of his homage even when he came to it finally of his own free will and for his own ends.

'This outdoes their order to rush to swear my oath of fealty to a couple of abbots, almost before Henry was in his tomb,' said Llewelyn, and suddenly laughed, though angrily, remembering how little sleep he had lost over that. For having chosen, and stated his choice firmly, to wait for Edward in person, I think he had quite forgotten the matter of the summons to the ford of Montgomery, assuming that his decision would be accepted, and the matter dropped until the king came home. Whereas, as we afterwards learned, on the January day appointed in the original order, the abbots of Dore and Haughmond, escorted by a company from Montgomery, duly attended at the ford of the river, and waited until well into the afternoon for Llewelyn to come to the meeting. And since that was a bitter winter month, and the ford a bleak enough place in such weather, no doubt they had hard things to say in private about the prince's contumacy. Nevertheless, the regents must have shrugged off their too zealous attempt and recognised Llewelyn's right to prefer a direct meeting, for from that day nothing more was ever heard of persuading him to the oath until the king's arrival.

'But this shall not pass so simply,' he said warmly. 'Insolence and presumption towards me I can repulse without aid, but when they presume grossly against the laws that unite and separate England and Wales, they injure more than me, and do no service to their own lord, and he shall know it.'

'Will you send an answer by the prior?' I asked, thinking he might prefer rather to send a formal protest to Westminster by Welsh clerks at law, or even by one of Tudor's sons, who often did such errands for him where ceremony was advisable.

'As well by the prior as by any,' said Llewelyn, 'since he will respect the seal, and be witness to whom it was superscribed if others show less respect.' And he asked: 'Where, according to Cynan's last despatch, is the king arrived now?'

Then I caught his drift, and approved, and so did Tudor when he heard, and those few of the council who were then with us. For according to Cynan, who was well informed about all the news from Edward's wandering court, they were now on their way to Paris, after delaying a while among the queen-mother's relatives in Savoy, and by the end of July they should be guests of King Philip in the French capital. Moreover, the king intended to take to himself a great part of the business of England, now that he was so close to home as France, and a steady stream of messengers, envoys, clerks, clerics and barons was already crossing and recrossing the Channel on his affairs.

'Good!' said Llewelyn. 'Then they will have no excuse for detaining in their own hands any letter expressly addressed to the king.' And he dictated to me the following letter:

'We have received the letter written in your Grace's name, and dated at Westminster on the twentieth day of June, forbidding us to build a castle on our own land near Abermule, or to found there a town and establish a market. We are certain that the said letter was not sent with your Grace's knowledge, and that if you were present in your kingdom, as we would you were, no such mandate would ever have been issued from your royal chancery. For your Grace knows well that the rights of our principality are entirely separate from the rights of your realm, notwithstanding that we hold our principality under your Grace's royal power. You have heard, and to some degree have seen for yourself that we and our ancestors have always had power within our boundaries to build castles and fortresses, and to set up markets, without prohibition by any man, or any announcement of such work in advance. We pray your Grace not to give ear to the malicious suggestions of those people whose desire it is to exasperate your mind against us. Dated at Dinorben, on the feast of St Benedict, the eleventh day of July.'

Thus with clarity, force and dignity did he reply to the unjustified and illegal demand made upon him, and with absolute confidence exempted Edward from any part in the insult. And in this I think he was right. Even now I think so. And the letter was sealed and clearly superscribed to the king in person, and the prior's attention called to this when he undertook to carry it, as I am sure he did faithfully. But it had to pass through other hands than his before ever it could be delivered to the one man for whom it was intended.

'And the building,' said Llewelyn shortly, 'goes on.' And so it did, in the face of the garrison of Montgomery, so that its progress could hardly have been overlooked.

Now in the matter of this letter, which plainly is of great importance, I must set down here that we never heard word more of it, nor, indeed, of any objections to the founding of Abermule, or any attempts to prevent the raising of the castle on the hill above. I do not know what happened to the letter. It may be that it was duly sent on to King Edward, that he entirely agreed with what Llewelyn had written, and instructed his regents to cease interfering with the prince's actions. I say it *may* be so. But in that case I should have expected the king to write personally to Llewelyn in acknowledgement and reassurance, for he was punctilious in correspondence and courtesy in the normality of business. And no such reply ever came. Or it may be, and for my part this is what I believe, that the regents, in spite of the personal nature of the letter, arrogantly considered it within their mandate to open and use it freely, and retain it in their own hands instead of forwarding it to the king. Its content may well have persuaded them that they had better not attempt to press a demand which could be so firmly resisted at law, let alone in practice, and therefore they took no further action, and perhaps were very glad to let the attempt go by default. In either case, the effect upon the building of Dolforwyn was the same, but the effect upon the future relations of Wales and England was by no means the same, for if the letter remained in the chancery records, then Edward can never have been made aware of his lieutenants' overbearing and illegal demand or Llewelyn's justified resentment of it, and he cannot have seen and known what absolute faith Llewelyn had in the king's goodwill and intent to do right, and how little in his officers. If, therefore, that letter was detained and suppressed in Westminster, then I say that whoever took that act upon him took also a heavy burden of guilt upon his soul.

Nor had he any excuse, for by the end of July a great number of the nobility were flocking to France, some to greet Edward, clear some point with him, and return, some to accompany him and work with him in his duchy of Gascony, whither he departed late in August to rejoin his queen. There were messengers enough and to spare, sailing weekly from Dover. Even though affairs kept him in Gascony so long, from this time the reins of government were in Edward's hands, though the regents still held great power at home, and I could not but remember David's warning that Edward would support his officers against all men as though they partook of his sovereignty.

However, there was still a year to run before Edward came home. This delay was not at first expected, for in August, about the time the king left Paris for Gascony, Llewelyn received a letter from the justiciar of Chester, Reginald de Grey, informing him that the king had fixed on the octave of Easter of the next year for his coronation, and cordially inviting the prince to be present. It is true that in the same letter he reminded Llewelyn of the amount of the indemnity still owing, and requested payment, but that hard touch of business was softened by a more friendly request that Wales would supply venison for the king's larder on the occasion, as Llewelyn had sometimes done before when a feast was toward.

The prince replied as warmly, acknowledging the invitation, guaranteeing to provide the venison by the date required, and diplomatically evading the question of the money, since he had only David and one or two other of his counsellors with him at that time, but promising a proper answer to the regents at Michaelmas. For as he had complaints to those officers still unredressed, he chose to conduct any correspondence about the money also with them, pointedly making the two issues one. A course which had not yet produced for us much in the way of amends or compensation, and for them nothing in sterling, but he persevered, and hoped for Edward's coming.

Later, because of the many matters occupying the king in Gascony, this date was changed to the nineteenth of August, by which time many things had also changed.

*　　*　　*

466

As I remember, it must have been after the building of Dolforwyn began that Griffith ap Gwenwynwyn's eldest son, Owen, began to frequent David with open admiration, and to spend much time in his company. This Owen was a man about twenty-seven years old, a good-looking young fellow enough, not over-tall, and not burly like his father, but rather taking after his English mother, Hawise Lestrange, who was the daughter of a former sheriff of Salop. Slender and well-proportioned like her, and of rather fair colouring, Owen had followed his father's example, no doubt due to her influence, and adopted the English manner of dress, harness and all besides, being to all appearances a marcher lordling rather than a Welsh prince. Indeed, the English called these men of Powys by the name of de la Pole, after their castle of Pool, and often in the past, before he came to the prince's peace, Griffith had taken part with the English of Shrewsbury against Wales. But at this time they had been ten years in fealty to Llewelyn, by no means to their loss, for in the treaty of Montgomery they, too, had gained and kept some lands won with the prince's aid.

Griffith ap Gwenwynwyn was the greatest vassal the prince had, and he valued him accordingly, and also respected his hardihood in battle and his forceful qualities in peace. The community of Wales would have been maimed without Powys. But their relationship had been always a matter of shrewd business, not a close friendship, such as the prince had had with his brother-in-law Rhys Fychan, or Meredith ap Owen of Cardigan, both now dead. To come down to stony truth, they did not love each other. Griffith grudged the prince's ascendancy, even while he subscribed to it for his own gain, for he was a proud and envious man, whose narrowed eyes measured every vantage, and his tongue complained of every slight, real or imagined. Llewelyn disdained such jealous and calculating minds – Griffith would have said he could afford to, being supreme – but made what accommodation his warm nature could manage, to make the alliance work harmoniously. And so it had, whatever the difficulties and reserves, for ten years.

'I'm glad Griffith's boy has fallen under David's spell,' said Llewelyn once when we rode from Dolforwyn, late that autumn. 'I have been prepared for some coldness in that quarter, knowing our friend's temper, though God knows Pool is far enough away to hold its own in trade, and my castle is no threat to him. But if his heir is cultivating my brother, the sire can hardly be nursing too great a grudge. That one has his family well in hand. All but his wife!' he added honestly, and laughed, for that lady, elegant and fragile as she appeared, was known all along the march for her iron will and quiet but steely tongue, and the thin white hand she extended for kissing was rumoured to have a firm and regal grip on her husband and all her children.

Dolforwyn was then rising against the sky in a great rectangular enclosure of walls and wards, without corner turrets, for the height of the ridge was such that it commanded a view all around and a well-manned curtain wall would be its main defence. The keep was first planned upon a square base, but in the building the masons changed to a round tower, for what reasons I now forget, but the shell rose sheer and strong, almost ready to be filled with household and garrison. It was a noble, solitary, sunlit place, the river like a silver serpent below.

'By next year, say Easter, we'll have a garrison and a castellan within,' said Llewelyn, 'and take good care that Griffith and his lady shall be among the first guests, and very honourably received. Whatever I can to reassure him, that I'll do.'

In such a mood, contented but cautious, did we approach that Christmas season. And as was the custom still, we repaired to Aber for the keeping of that feast.

David came from Lleyn with all his household, and a retinue of knights and troopers somewhat larger than usual. He was in great finery and very wild spirits, and constantly Elizabeth watched and worshipped him, herself seeming the quieter for his exhilaration, as though he dazzled her into stillness. There was nothing to be observed about her body yet to make me wonder, she was slim as a willow, but that quality of brightness about her caused me to look for enlightenment to Cristin, who was close at her side with the year-old Gladys in her arms. Cristin understood the look, and smiled her slow and radiant smile. When it was possible to have speech together she told me it was as I supposed.

'She is again with child. But not a word yet. There's hardly a soul knows but David, and now we two. She wants a son for him, she will have a son. She so prays, heaven can hardly deny her. But she dreads some stroke of fate if she lets it be known too soon.'

'And David?' I asked, watching the arched security of her arm under the child, and the easy way her body leaned to balance the weight, and all the natural accomplishment of motherhood that came by grace to one deprived of all hope of bearing children. I marvelled that she, so deeply aware of loss, should yet be so little saddened, for she had genuine joy in these daughters not her own.

'This time David is sure. This time it will not fail. He is as you see him, exalted as high as the mountains. But he has his moments of doubt, too, and then there's no going near him. I never knew him so lofty when up, and so black and brittle when down. And he has six months or more to wait in this perilous state yet! You would think his fate was in the balance this very December.'

During that Christmas festival we saw far more of his ups than his downs, the stimulus of company, music, wine and feasting naturally turning him towards the light. He drank more than was usual with him, he danced, and sang, and rode, and hunted while the weather was bright, and was never still for a moment but when he slept. Sometimes, indeed, his gaiety seemed too feverish and too strung, designed to fill his days to the exclusion of all thought. And what I noted most was that never once that December did he seek me out, as often in the old days he used to, in the late evening when he tired of the music and smoke and ceremony in the hall. He spoke me blithely in passing, among other people, but never did I encounter him alone. For my part, I would have done so gladly. For his, as I came to understand, he wanted no close companionship with me, for I knew him too well.

Llewelyn beheld his brother's elation with pleasure, seeing him drop at last the formal deference he had for so long preserved in his dealings with his prince. 'If he is coming out of his sulks with me at last,' he said to me privately, 'so much the better for us both. It has been hard to know how to have him without offending, he is thornier than a holly-bush.'

So when David proposed, if he might, to stay on through January with all his people, and prolong this family party, Llewelyn was glad, and said so heartily, forgetting the extreme caution of his recent handling to throw an arm about David's shoulders and hug him boisterously.

'You could do nothing to please me so much. Stay as long as you will, and most welcome. You bring life into the court with you.'

So he said, and in the circle of his arm David stood stiff and still, like a man of ice, for his face had blanched into a blue, burning whiteness, and his eyes, as I have seen them do at other times, had closed their shutters against the world and were staring within, in fascination and grief and horror, as though he saw every evil thought or act of his life graven into his own mirrored face. So he was for an instant only, and then his ice melted, and the dark, smiling grace came back to his countenance, that was turned, large-eyed, upon Llewelyn. Something brief and graceful he said, and escaped out of the embrace, and Llewelyn let him go without another thought. And all that light-hearted company stayed, all through January and into February, though now I cannot think that one heart among them was very light.

At the new year it was fine and cold, but towards the end of January the sun removed, heavy cloud came down and swallowed the mountains, mist closed in and devoured the sea. Aber was an island in blank greyness, and the sky drooped ever lower and heavier upon us. Then the snows began, great, drifting snows that blocked all roads. Deprived of riding, the court settled down equably to pass the time at home in the maenol, and sit out this bad weather. Stores were ample; we had no need to worry. Only David, restless and uneasy, prowled the wards like a caged beast, and eyed the sky a hundred times a day for a break that did not come.

I say, only David, yet there was a manner of echo from his disquiet that ran also through the men of his retinue, and had them edging along the walls from stable to hall, and hall to armoury, as though waiting for something of which they were half afraid.

'Would not you tread warily,' said Godred, grinning and holding me affectionately by the elbow, as we watched David lunge through the outer ward, 'if you were groom or page of his? But there's nothing ails him that a quick thaw won't cure. He hates to be cramped.' All which was true, and there was no need to say it to me, nor could I imagine what there was in his words to keep him quietly giggling to himself, though he was given to such secret communings meant to be heard but not understood, and in the course of them he laughed a great deal. 'Hates to be cramped in his acts or in his ambitions,' sighed Godred, 'and if you shut him in he'll break out. A nice, quick thaw, say in the next week or so, would suit him royally.'

But the thaw, when it came, suited no man, for at the month's end the snow turned to torrential rain, that went on day and night, with gales that ripped the mists away and drove the black clouds headlong across our sky, but never tore a chink between us and the sun. The little river that ambles down to the salt flats through Aber became a rushing flood, all the lower meadows stood under shivering water, and all the streams burst their banks throughout the whole of north Wales. From the hills the snow dislodged in half-melted floes, swelling the floods. There had never been such a season. Cramped we were indeed, for there was no sense in stirring out of the gates. And David's fever burned clear white like the hottest of flames, but the fiercer he burned, the more silent he became.

All that second day of February he walked apart when he could, and his eyes looked within, as though he had shut himself into an even narrower prison than the maenol of Aber. That was the day that the clouds first thinned and broke, and the rain ceased, when first we saw the mountains again, and the shore, and even the distant silver line of the island of saints across the sands of Lavan. So far from releasing David into his former buoyancy, this change turned him mute, distant and still, with an air of listening to something, or for something, that we could not hear. He watched the sky, and looked out over the subsiding waters as the brook sank slowly towards its proper bed, and his face was as still and inexpressive as stone. In the evening, when the meal was over, and the hall smoky and red with torches, Elizabeth missed him from her side, and when he did not return in a little while, sent me to find him. She was anxious about him by then, for though he showed to her a face more like his own, and for her could smile and speak reassurance, yet she knew there was something amiss with him, and feared he was ill.

In the wards the snow was melting raggedly, drawing crooked white edges under every wall. There was someone standing just within the shadow of the great doorway, and as I drew close I saw that it was Cristin. She laid a hand upon my arm, and that was a rare thing, for us to touch each other.

'He is in the chapel,' she said, knowing my errand without need of telling. 'He has been there alone all this while.'

'She has missed him,' I said, 'and is uneasy. He will not want that.'

'No,' she said, 'not at any cost.' And she took her hand slowly from my arm, and I crossed the wet, dark ward and went in to him.

He was not kneeling, but standing close to the altar, and the only light within being the altar lamp, its red glow shone upward into his face, and I say it for a moment fixed and drawn in fire, like the mask of a man in hell. Or like the face of a man wrestling with terrible and blasphemous prayers. But when he heard me enter, and swung round to face me, then the half-lit face I saw was quite calm and resolute, and the blue eyes mildly veiled.

'Samson?' he said. 'Is it you?' I was in darkness, but he knew. 'Always my careful shepherd! Am I not free to take my thirst to the spring like any other man?' His voice was light and mocking, but a tone higher than I knew it.

Being in no mind to try to take from him what he was plainly unwilling to share, I told him flatly that I was sent by his lady to find him, for she was afraid he sickened. And at that he uttered something neither sigh nor laugh.

'So I do sicken,' he said. 'I sicken God, man and myself, but it is not a sickness of the body that makes me loathsome.' And the next moment he said lightly: 'Say a prayer for a fine night, before you follow me in, for if the roads are passable I'll be on my way to my own tomorrow.' And he went past me with a large, easy step, and made his way back to the hall and his wife, and kept his countenance and his tranquillity the rest of the evening.

But in the night I could not rest, I hardly know why. It was not simply the recollection of words and actions so strange and yet so small, it was rather something in the air after that long isolation of the floods and the rains, a fearful stillness that hung on the night now that the endless streaming, whispering, rippling noises of the waters were hushed. When the whole maenol was asleep, the silence was as tall and wide as the night, and charged with uneasiness. I lay listening for any sound to make the void again populated, and how many imaginary footsteps I heard I do not know, but one I heard that was not imaginary. It passed by my tower chamber towards the stair, and halted for a brief moment outside Llewelyn's own sleeping apartment, which was close, for I had always a corner very near him, and if ever he needed anything in the night, it was me he called to him. When those quiet feet paused, I rose up silently from my brychan and girded my gown about me, for who would thus stand motionless in the dark outside my lord's door? But in a moment the footsteps resumed, slipping away until they ceased, the stairway swallowing them up.

I needed no light to find my way anywhere I pleased about Aber, and it seemed that this restless one after midnight needed none, either. He knew this place as I knew it. I let myself out and went to open Llewelyn's door, very softly. In the darkness within his long, peaceful breathing measured the depth and tranquillity of his sleep. Whoever had ill dreams in Aber that night, the prince had none. I closed the door again upon his rest, and eased the latch silently into place, and for a while I stood guard outside his room, waiting and listening. But there was no more movement, and after a time I went back to my bed, and there lay waiting in vague disquiet without understandable cause, until I fell asleep.

It was but a shallow and wary sleep, for what awoke me next was the first faint change in the darkness, hardly a lightening, rather a softening in the texture of the night. Dawn was still more than an hour away, but for early February it was a clear night and with stars, and by our northern reckoning rather warm, a heavy, moist air. I had lain no more than ten minutes drowsing and wondering, when of a sudden my door was opened and someone came in. There was almost no sound in her coming, all in a moment she was there, barefoot in her nightgown with a shawl round her shoulders, and over the shawl the spilled marvel of her black, silken hair, stirring round her like living darkness, and curtained within that marvel her pale, bright face, with huge eyes limpid and iris-coloured like the first promise of morning that came in with her, and its first freshness that breathed in her breath. Thus for the first time came Cristin to my bed, and departed again as virgin as she came. For what had Godred's occasional marital demands to do with her virginity?

I started up naked in the skins of the brychan, and could not arise before her because of that nakedness. And for want of better words – for of such there are none – I said her name: 'Cristin!'

In a whisper she said: 'David is gone! He never went in to her. His pillow is unpressed. Samson, I dread for her. She was asleep too soon to wait for him. She does not yet know. But if she awakes and misses him, God knows what may befall her. There is nothing else can cause his son to burst her womb untimely, but if she fears for David she may miscarry. Samson, find him!'

I clutched the furs about me, and watched the vision that was my Cristin, a light that dazzled my eyes, though but half-seen in darkness. I said: 'Go back and stay with her, and tell her, if she wakes, that all's well, he rose for sheer wakefulness, and I am with him. She knows he has his moods, she may believe it. And I'll find him.'

She said, in that clear thread of a voice, under her breath and barely audible, as she herself was a phantom faintly shining in the absence of light: 'God bless you, my dear love!' Not a word more. And she was gone as she had come, and I was alone.

I rose up hastily and did on my clothes, and went out, down the stair and through the silent passages and rooms, through the hall where all the sleepers stirred and snored. Everywhere I passed like a shadow, stretching my ears after any sound or movement to betray another wakeful presence, but there was none. Nor did I believe he would be anywhere there among other men. The place for which I made with the most confidence was the chapel, where once already to my knowledge he had taken some struggle or distress of his own, only to be called away without an answer. But he was not there, either. And the first pre-dawn light was beginning to soften the black of the east into dove-grey, and I dreaded that Elizabeth would awake and come forth herself to search for him, before I could make good what I had promised her, that I should be with him.

There was no possibility that he would be in any of the guest lodgings in the wards, only those public places remained, the stables and mews and store-houses, and what should he want with them? The watch on the main gate was awake and aware, and had had an undisturbed night, and seen no one stirring.

It was almost by chance I found him, as I stood in the inner ward, turning about to look if anything moved anywhere around me, or any shape broke the merloned line of the wall. And he was there, he or someone, a tall blackness swathed in a cloak, motionless against the sky above the postern gate. He neither saw nor heard me. His back was turned, for he gazed steadily out over the wall to the south-east.

I mounted the wooden staircase to the guard-walk, in the corner close to where he stood, and went to him without any great care to conceal my approach, but without any deliberate utterance, either, for it was so strange to see him standing like a carven man, black and still and cold in the February dawn. I knew by the infinitely faint bracing of his shoulders the moment when he knew he was no longer alone, and by the want of any larger movement that he knew very well who it was who came. His face was tight and pinched with the cold, as if he had stood out the night there, but it was quite still and calm, a dead calm, as if something had ended, something the passing of which was not yet recognisable as either to be mourned or welcomed. His eyes never shifted their gaze from the hills, but it was a drained, exhausted gaze, no longer urgent. He said not a word, but when I touched him he turned and went with me, and at the head of the stairway he withdrew out of my hand, and went before me down into the ward. And there was Elizabeth coming out from the tower door in a flutter of blue, dressed and cloaked and anxious, with Cristin at her shoulder.

There was light enough then to recognise us by manner and gait and stature across the ward, and we came as a relief to them, walking towards them as we did in the most commonplace way in the world. They could not see the frozen blankness of his face. Elizabeth cried out his name, at once glad and reproachful, and flew to take him by the shoulders, and suddenly he heaved himself out of his torpor with a shudder and a moan, and recoiled from her, evading the innocent embrace.

'Don't touch me!' he said in a soft, wild cry. 'You'll soil your hands!'

The look of astonished hurt and disbelief on her face, in that first moment of doubt and uncertainty she had ever suffered from him, struck him clean out of the trance that had held him bound, and he realised what he had done. He flung up both hands and shut his palms hard on his cheeks, and shook out of him, like gouts of blood: 'A bad dream – I have had a bad dream!' And before she had time to question or to weep, he leaned and caught her up passionately and tenderly into his arms. 'Lisbet, it's over now! It's gone! All's well now – all's very well!'

The fright went out of her face readily. She laid her arms about his neck and caressed him, lamenting with the serenity of past and mistaken pain: 'Where have you been? Why did you go away from me?'

He carried her away into the tower, back to the bed-chamber he had deserted, and certain am I they lay and loved like starving creatures until they fell asleep in each other's arms.

We two were left in the ward, between the dwindling banks of snow under the walls, looking after them with still faces. Until Cristin said: 'I do not know what it is we have seen. But I know it is well that only you and I have seen it. And I hope that you and I have seen the last of it here. I think I should not like the echoes, if there were to be echoes.' And she gave me her hand, as we went slowly back together into the hall, for the chill that was upon us needed some unlooked-for grace to warm it out of our bones.

And when David and Elizabeth appeared again among us, he was himself, alert, calm and rational, only perhaps a little quieter and more chastened than usual, like a convalescent out of danger and grateful for it. There was no more listening and prowling, no extremes of elation and depression, rather two or three days of harmony and reason. And as soon as the roads were reported passable, he took leave of Llewelyn, and his whole party left for home.

So for some time we believed, Cristin and I, that we had indeed seen the last of that night's alarm. Nevertheless, there were to be echoes. And she was right. When they came we did not like them.

473

CHAPTER V

On the sixth day of that same February the king's regents sent one William de Plumpton to Chester, to take delivery, or so they hoped or professed to hope, of the instalment of money under treaty which had not yet been paid, and which Llewelyn was withholding as a means of enforcing settlement of grievances. It was hardly a reasonable expectation that the envoy should get anything to take back with him, in any case, seeing the floods were still out wherever there was river or stream flowing, and the marshes round Rhuddlan remained a lake, so that it would have been almost impossible to reach Chester by the day of his visit. I do not say Llewelyn would have complied even had the season been favourable, but at that time it was pointless even to try.

By the end of February, when the court was at Criccieth, travel was normal again, and the regents sent to complain of non-delivery of the money. Llewelyn replied, as he did consistently in these exchanges, to the king personally, though whether his letters ever left England is doubtful. He wrote freely acknowledging that he was bound to pay the amount due, and informing King Edward that the sum was ready and waiting to be paid to the king's attorneys, provided the king fulfilled faithfully what was equally due from him under the treaty. In particular he asked that the earls of Gloucester and Hereford, and after them the marchers in general, should be ordered to surrender those lands they had illegally occupied and were as illegally detaining. Whereupon payment should be made immediately.

Whether this letter ever went overseas or no, it did bring a measure of response, for the king, or the regents in his name, ordered a commission to be sent in May to Montgomery, to arbitrate on the mutual charges of breaches of the peace, and to try to bring about a treaty with the earl of Hereford. I see in this the hand of the king himself, or else of Burnell, the most reasonable of the regents and the closest to his master's mind, whose chief difficulty in border matters was to curb the impetuosity of his colleague Roger Mortimer. Marchers make very poor arbitrators on marcher affairs, as judges do of their own cases.

We were again at Aber, towards the middle of March, when a messenger came riding in from Llewelyn's master-mason at Dolforwyn, which was almost ready to be garrisoned, though much work remained to be done as soon as the new building season made conditions possible. A small guard had camped in some discomfort through the winter, and it was Llewelyn's intention to visit the castle and give his mind to the siting of the new town as soon as he could. The message he received hastened that day, though not as we would have wished.

'My lord,' said the envoy, a trooper of the guard, 'I am bidden to tell you of suspected treason. At the end of January the prior of Strata Marcella sent to us to say that one of the brothers, on an errand into Pool, had seen unusual activity about the castle, and great numbers of armed men, it seemed to him in preparation for some foray, for he saw how they were busy about the stables and armoury, furbishing weapons and fletching arrows, and both the Lord Griffith and his son Owen – Owen especially – directing all, as if for some great move. He promised to send word again if this company set out with intent, but we had no further word from him until he sent to say that they must have left secretly, by night, for certainly they were gone from the castle, which was about its business as always, and no more men within than usual. My lord, you recall those days of heavy rain and great floods. The prior set watch, and the brother appointed saw a strong company come riding home into Pool, also by night, and in sad order, half-drowned and without any booty or prizes. We judge the floods turned them back. But we do not know from where, for the prior's watch was on the castle gates, and the castle is the end of all roads at that place.'

'I know it,' said Llewelyn, braced and intent. 'It is all but in the river. It must have been no more than an island and a causeway then. True, they could have come from any point. And we do not know when they set forth?'

'No, my lord, only when they crept home again like drowned rats. And that was the night of the third of February. We have the prior's word.'

'His word I take,' said Llewelyn truly, for there was not a single Cistercian house in north Wales that was not his loyal ally. 'But your captain and the master of my works have their own opinion, I think. Speak out what they have to say.'

'My lord,' said the man warmly, 'I speak out my own thoughts as well as theirs. Ever since you began the building of Dolforwyn, we have had word again and again how Griffith ap Gwenwynwyn resented your presence there. It was the common gossip of Pool that he feared for his market, and also kept close touch with Sprenghose in Montgomery, and made good certain the king's men there feared the same prejudice to their gains. I do not say the English have any part in what he planned. I do say he is ready to lean on them if he brings down judgment on his own head by his own actions, and has sought to prepare their minds to come to his support. We think Griffith planned to attack your castle of Dolforwyn by stealth, perhaps intending to blame the English, since they have shown concern about the foundation, and meant to accomplish this raid now, before you have a full garrison there to defend it. We think he meant to destroy what you have built, and your guard that holds it for you, but the winter barred his way. My lord, the upper Severn has been out of its banks more than three weeks, high over the water-meadows and into the rock of the hillside. Close as we lie, I believe they had no means of reaching us.' And he said, watching the prince's face: 'I do not think the lord prince is any way surprised.'

'No,' said Llewelyn, 'no way surprised.' He did not love this house of de la Pole, and was not loved by them, and only advantage had ever drawn or held Griffith to him, and only advantage would hold him now, and yet Powys could hardly be spared. He sat back in his chair, and thought, and there was no pleasure in it. For the sake of Wales he would not cut off Powys, not for his own life, if he might retain it by any decent means. But for the sake of Wales, just as surely, he could not let any treason pass unpublished and unpunished. He shut his eyes for some minutes, to look beyond the hour.

When he opened them again, he was resolved. 'I will deal,' he said. 'I am grateful beyond words to your master, to the prior and his brethren, and to you for your honest embassage. Now I will deal accordingly.'

It was late in March when Llewelyn set forth with his high steward and his immediate court to inspect and approve the work done at Dolforwyn, and there we kept the Easter of that year. It had been his intention to do so in any case, and his going there in state provoked no suspicion and gave no forewarning, nor did it occasion any surprise that while he was in the neighbourhood he should send for his greatest vassal to attend him, and bring his eldest son Owen with him. They came with disarming smiles, attentive and dutiful, the father a big, powerfully-made, greying man with strong features and a keen sense of his own dignity and state, the son almost as tall but lightly made and graceful. Both of them, I thought, were a little too effusive in their compliments, and their eyes a little too wary, but the relations between the princes, however profitable to both, had never been personally warm.

In the hall of Dolforwyn, still largely a shell, half-furnished for living, and before Tudor and most of the members of his council, his clerks and personal household, Llewelyn stood up before those two, and himself told them that they were under suspicion of deceit and disloyalty, against their sworn fealty to him and to Wales.

They started back from him open-mouthed, in utter dismay, I am sure not feigned, for they had thought their abortive moves had passed unknown, and been devoutly thankful for it. They cried out their innocence of any such offences, and their unswerving loyalty to the lord prince and their own fealty.

'At least, my lord,' cried Griffith, 'let us know our accusers. Whoever they may be, let them meet us face to face, and make their charges here, where we can refute them.'

'There shall be proper opportunity at law for you to refute the charges,' said Llewelyn, 'and for this time, if you seek an accuser, I accuse you. The council are here to see that justice is done to you, according to Welsh law.' And this he said with emphasis, knowing that Griffith had a way of preferring English law if he could get it, and also that the causes at issue between England and Wales, formerly always judged by an arbitration commission, had of late slipped nearer and nearer to becoming suits in the royal courts, which was by no means what he understood by the terms of the treaty, and posed perilous pitfalls for Wales in just such cases. He did not intend that Griffith should be allowed to inveigle this cause into a king's court.

'I do not know who can have poisoned your mind against us,' protested Griffith vehemently, 'but I swear there is no truth in what they have told you. And if I am to be able to defend myself, at least I must know of what I am accused. Can I prove every moment of my loyalty, and my son's loyalty? Let me know what acts are alleged against me, at what times and places, that I may be able to bring evidence to the contrary. And time – I must be allowed time to bring my witnesses.'

'You shall have time enough,' said Llewelyn. 'We intend to set up here today a bench of judges to hear and examine both your evidence and mine, and take whatever witness they please in this neighbourhood. You shall have a day assigned, and a place, to answer. And the charge I think you should know, as you have said. It is known that at the end of the month of January you gathered in your castle of Pool a large company of armed men, with horses and supplies, and that they rode out secretly by night upon some as yet unproved errand, I say treasonous. Thanks to God who sent the floods, they never achieved whatever their purpose was. They were seen re-entering Pool, also in darkness, on the night of the third of February. And you, my lord Owen, were seen to be their leader.'

'It is false!' cried Owen, paler than his shirt, and his voice cracking. 'Whoever says so, lies!'

'When you come to hear the sworn evidence,' said Llewelyn drily, 'I think you will wish to take back that word.'

The young man drew in his horns at that, doubtless wondering desperately with whom he might be confronted, and how much the observer could know. But still they argued sturdily, why should they do so, what cause had they ever given to be thought disloyal, and what advantage could there possibly be to them in raiding and pillaging in the depths of the winter, if that was what was suspected? Against what manor or maenol or settlement, to be worth so secret an enterprise?

'Against this very castle and settlement, which you never liked,' said Llewelyn, 'and which you have spoken against more than once. It does not deprive your own market, nor infringe your rights, I am building on my own lands, but as I have heard, you would not have been sorry to see this place razed – all the more, perhaps, if it could be put down to some lawless action by the Englishry, who have also been casting ominous eyes at it for the sake of Montgomery. In the end *you* may tell *me* where you rode. I would advise it. If this matter is cleared fully, there shall still be access to my peace.'

After he had said this I saw those two, father and son, exchange one rapid and stealthy glance, and look away again, and I wondered if Llewelyn with his customary bluntness had not given away more of his case than was altogether wise, though I knew why he did it. It was his wish to show them at once that their best policy was to make a clean breast of the affair and accept whatever penalty was imposed, with the implicit assurance that it would not be extreme. He did not want out-and-out hostility, for fear Wales should be maimed of one of its vital provinces. Nor, indeed, was his ever a mind for extremes, which produce counter-extremes in the recoil. What he had now suggested seemed rather to calm than to alarm them. They continued to protest total innocence, and absolute confidence, but they accepted a day some ten days ahead, the seventeenth of April, for the hearing, and the place was fixed at Llewelyn's manor of Bach-yr-Anneleu in Cydewain, which was handy for both parties.

'Very well,' said Llewelyn, 'name your arbitrators.' And he himself for his part chose Tudor, with one of his brothers, and Anian ap Caradoc, who was one of his chief law clerks. Griffith named one of his own officers of Powys, and his justiciar, and one other whose name I have forgotten. It is a long time since I saw those documents. Then they chose and agreed on the prior of Pool, as a just man bound to neither side, to fill the seventh place. And those two withdrew from Dolforwyn to set about preparing their defence. They went wary, anxious and wincing, but not desperate, and I think their heads were together even on the ride home.

The seven judges in the meantime were at liberty to examine and take statements around Pool and Dolforwyn, but I think Griffith had taken good care to get out of the castle any of those men who knew what had been planned, and little fresh information was gleaned, except the curious fact that the company of armed men, clearly a war-band, had left Pool castle not merely one night before their re-entry, but four. The poacher who had been out in the woods that night was none too anxious to tell what he had seen, but did so honestly, and the justices turned a blind eye to what else he had been about. It was a puzzling detail. In such weather, what could Owen have been doing with his men for those four days? Apart from that we got rumours and little more.

On the seventeenth of April the judges sat at Llewelyn's manor, and Griffith ap Gwenwynwyn and his son came before them. But it fell out somewhat differently from what we had expected, for as soon as the court was convened Griffith and Owen asked leave to speak, and said outright that they pleaded guilty to the offence with which they were accused, that they had indeed plotted treason against the lord prince, in despite of the fealty they owed him. They desired to confess their fault and throw themselves upon the prince's mercy.

Llewelyn did question a little concerning those four full days lost.

'My lord,' said Owen, who had led the unlucky expedition, 'when we found the valley road impassable, rather than abandon the enterprise we tried to make a circle through the hills and come at Dolforwyn from the north side, and though we made a part of the journey, we crossed between the brooks that drain into the Bechan, and then we could go no further, nor get back with safety, and it took us two days to make our sorry way home to Pool. My lord, now in more blessed condition I thank God there was no harm but to us who invoked it.' He was a smooth young man, and bent on salving his threatened prospects if he could by any means do it.

'Well,' said Llewelyn, 'I have done. You are confided to your judges.'

Then those seven justices conferred, and with no voice dissenting – bear in mind always that Griffith's own justiciar was one of the seven – they accepted that plea of guilty, and gave their verdict that in view of the absolute confession of treason, the two accused were placed, as to their bodies, lands and possessions, at the disposal of the lord prince, to do with them and all things theirs whatsoever he would. Thus everything Griffith owned passed into Llewelyn's hands, to give back or retain, as he pleased. And what he pleased he had already considered, weighed and measured, to balance enforcement with remission, and penalty with clemency. He was as pale and grave as his traitors when he made his mind known. And they – I say it, who saw them then, and know what plaintive play they made thereafter with their wrongs – they were immeasurably happy with the outcome, having expected worse, even with their careful precautions.

'The most of your lands and possessions,' said Llewelyn, 'I am moved to grant back to you. There are certain exceptions.' He named them, all territories which had traditionally been in dispute between Gwynedd and Powys. They lopped Powys perhaps of one-quarter of its ground. 'You may make your petition for the remainder,' he said, 'upon conditions.' And those conditions also he set out in full. Griffith and Owen had every opportunity to protest against them, had they so wished. They were main glad not to make any such protest. I think they were astonished and gratified at the modesty of their loss.

Nevertheless, I own it was not easy for Griffith to swallow the indignity, when he was forced to go on his sixty-year-old knees before the prince, and ask humbly for the restoration of the remainder of his lands, for him and his heirs, pruned of those small parts beyond the Dovey, in Cyfeiliog, and of thirteen vils near the river Lugg, and most of Arwystli. To the conditions attached he assented, not gladly, but that was not to be expected, and I do not think they were unjust or excessive. First, Owen was taken into Llewelyn's keeping as hostage for his and his father's loyalty. Then also twenty-five of the chieftains of the lands regranted to Griffith were to give their fealty instead to the prince, and swear a solemn oath to be faithful to the prince as against Griffith if he again offended. And last, all the parties had to agree that if Griffith or his heirs again attempted treason against Llewelyn, then the prince should have the right to take possession again of all the lands in the traitor's hold, and keep and enjoy them for ever. The compact was not complete until Griffith, with what grace he could, authorised this seizure in the event of his own default.

On the following day he and his son executed a deed likewise rendering all their possessions forfeit to the prince if Owen should attempt to escape from Llewelyn's custody, and be lawfully convicted of such an attempt. His parole was thought hardly a strong enough guarantee and since it was far less trouble, and more agreeable for him, if he could be out of close ward and merely an enforced guest at court, a sanction of such severity might hold him as effectively as bars.

We remained in Cydewain until the time came for the May meeting at the ford, where Edward's commissioners duly came, and some of the mutual complaints were dealt with by sensible give and take, though others proved more intractable, and there was little but parchment progress with the envoys of the Earl of Hereford. But something of interest we learned there, for it came out that Rhodri, who had shaken off the dust of Wales in chagrin after his marriage plans foundered, was now in London, in the service of the queen-mother, and moreover, had found a more complacent bride, and one just as profitable, for he was married to a lady who was an heiress in Gloucestershire.

'Who would have thought it?' said Llewelyn, relieved and amused, as well as heartily glad for him. 'Without benefit of my thousand marks, all but fifty, he has done as well for himself, after all. That's one load off my mind. Beatrice, she is called, it seems, and they say a pleasant lady. Who knows, he may have run at the right time for his own fortunes.'

There had never been any further mention of that debt owed to Rhodri, and there was little point in pursuing him with it, even had we known until then where to find him. And shortly thereafter he went abroad to France in the queen-mother's retinue. Llewelyn shrugged aside the commitment for the time being, since there had been no claim laid upon it. But for his brother, though the least to be remarked of all his brothers, he was pleased and assuaged. The old law of lands partible equally between brethren, though he stood out against it all his days for the sake of Wales, Wales as a people, a tongue and a nation, hung heavy upon his heart. Such a curse it can be, to be one of four brothers, in a land that keeps such customs. How much easier was Edward's lot, by all men acknowledged as the sole heir to monarchy, and even the lot of his brother, accustomed to accept and illuminate his lesser but glorious place, having its own rights and not encroaching upon the greater.

'I have even heard,' said Llewelyn, 'that this lady is with child. Rhodri is from good stock. Who knows but my grandsire may repeat himself out of Rhodri's loins as well as any other? There may be greatness yet from what I fear I reckoned too small. Let's, at all costs, wish him well!'

So we went home cheered rather than burdened, satisfied that the evil of Griffith ap Gwenwynwyn was curbed and frustrated, and that what ill effects remained from that collision could be softened and soothed away by our usage of Owen, while he remained with us. I know that Llewelyn had in mind a fairly early release, and reassuring patronage in the meantime. The young man went with us dutifully, nervous, attentive, almost obsequious in his determination to wipe out the past, and Llewelyn took care to pay him some civil attention in return, though they had little in common. Such relationships are not easy upon either side.

On our way back into Gwynedd we halted overnight at Corwen, in the vale of Edeyrnion. Some of the solid men of those parts came to the prince with various pleas and petitions, and among them was a miller, a stout man and enterprising, who had his mill a few miles up the river from that place, and since there were often people wishing to cross the Dee by his boat and save themselves a league or two on foot, he came to ask licence to provide a ferry and man it at that spot. It was a reasonable request, and quickly granted, and I went to write him the needful licence and get it sealed, and afterwards walked up with him some way along the riverside, to take the evening air, for it was a fine night after a stormy day.

It so happened that the river was running fairly high, and is always rough water there. I remarked that he would need a sturdy ferryman if his service was to operate on any but summer days, and he allowed that there were times when he would not ask any man to risk his life on that crossing, though most of the year he knew it himself well enough to master it, and he could find men at least as good to do the work for him. I said, eyeing the broken water, which was storm-brown, that I would not care to tackle it myself even now, in late May. And he laughed, and said this was nothing, this would not hinder him.

'You should have seen it in those winter floods we had. Man and beast, we were up in the roof of the mill, though we stand high, and we had to wade to get out. I mind one night when it was at its worst, there came a company riding downstream and wanting to cross. What they were doing out in such numbers God knows, forty of them if there was one! But they came shouting, was there not a ford a little higher, for they must get over. And I laughed in their faces, asking after a ford, when a man had to ford his own fields, let alone a torrent like the Dee. Then they would have me take them across in my boat, but I would not have attempted one trip, let alone the four or five I should have had to make. And with horses? Not for the world! I think they would have taken the boat by force, they were so urgent, but that they were afraid to handle it themselves when it came to it. They were even mad enough to think of trying to swim the beasts across. But not mad enough to do it!' he said, and laughed.

All this I heard at first but currently, as of mild interest between two companions passing the time, but before he was halfway through his story I was sharply intent, and hearing echoes in every word, for could there have been two such parties out in such weather, and on such urgent business that only God could turn them back with his storms? I asked of him: 'What night was this? Can you recall?'

'That I can,' said the miller confidently, 'for the next day was the first break in the clouds, and by evening the rain stopped, though it was ten days before the Dee was back in its bed. It was the first night of February.'

Two days out from their muster at Pool, and two days before their draggled return. It was too apt to be untrue. The company that Owen had led out of the castle stealthily by night had ridden, not up the Severn or through the hills to the raiding of Dolforwyn, but hard towards the north-east, only to be turned back by the Dee in flood. And if that was true, then upon some blacker business than Dolforwyn, or why should they compound so willingly with that story and throw themselves gratefully on Llewelyn's mercy? If they had not had worse to fear by letting the case be pursued further they would have fought it out in the court and denied everything but some local brawl not threatening their fealty.

'But I tell you this,' said the miller with certainty, 'though they rode on downstream to try elsewhere, I'm sure they never got across Dee that night, nor that sen-night, either.'

No, thought I, they never did. And I asked him, with no too great show of interest: 'What could they have wanted so desperately on the way north, in such weather? Was there anything to be noted about them out of the ordinary?'

'Out of the ordinary enough, come to think of it,' said the miller, 'when we have such order as the prince has made in the land. They were armed, every man, with bows or steel.'

After I had left the miller I took that singular story back to Llewelyn, and repeated it for his ear alone.

'Have up young Owen,' said Llewelyn at once, 'and let's see what he has to say to this. But first ask Tudor to come to me. No one else.'

I took my time about finding and bidding in Owen ap Griffith, that the prince and Tudor might have time for consultation. For beyond question the boy would deny, and cling fast to his own story, but more depended on the manner of his denial. He went in with me very quiet and wary, but in his situation so he well might, and we did not hold that against him as proving or disproving anything. He saluted the prince very respectfully, and sat but gingerly and stiffly when he was bidden, eyeing Llewelyn with apprehensive eyes.

'Tell me again,' said Llewelyn amiably, 'for I wish to be informed in every detail, all the course of that wild ride you made in the floods to try to reach Dolforwyn. We had but the outline before. Now fill in the colours.'

'I fear,' said Owen, licking his lips, 'the lord prince wishes only to remind me of an iniquity I already regret, and would wish out of mind. But I have deserved it.' Which was no bad beginning, considering all things, and as I have said, there was more of his secret and guileful mother in him than his overbearing father. And he drew breath and described, with increasing confidence, in the end almost with relish, every mile of the way, which brooks they had crossed, where they camped miserably overnight, where they found themselves perilously bogged between rivers in flooded heath, never too stable even in better weather. A good story it was, all the more as he cannot then have expected to have to produce it, and must have been improvising.

'That is comprehensive enough,' said Llewelyn at the end, 'and leaves not an hour unaccounted for of all those you wasted in this quest. So the miller from upstream here is wrong, is he, if he says you were ranging with this same band along the Dee on the first night of February, seeking a crossing, when by rights you say you should have been somewhere in the peat-bogs north-west of Dolforwyn? If he says that *you*, leading this migrant company, tried every means to get him to ferry you over? Mistaken, do you think? Or lying? Or dreaming, perhaps?'

Owen turned a yellowish white like old parchment, and shrank where he sat, but he kept his countenance better than I would have thought was in him. Twice he swallowed hard – we watched every move – and tried to find a voice to answer, but I think he was giving himself a little time, all he dared, for thought. They came in the night, they were many, cloaked. Could the miller know any man of them again? It was Owen's only weapon, and he clung to it.

In a dry and laboured whisper he said: 'My lord, I will not claim any man lies, when I do not even know him. I must answer only what I do know, that I was not there, nor any men of mine. I have told you where my men were that night. To my shame! Is not that enough?'

'Shall I send to the mill,' asked Tudor, 'and have the miller come in person to testify?' And Llewelyn said: 'It would be well,' and still watched Owen. But the young man had played it off in the only possible way, desperate wager though it was, and had no option now but to sit out whatever came, and still steadily deny.

'Then there were two companies of men out in arms for no good purpose,' said Llewelyn, 'in two separate parts of my realm, were there? Some forty in number in each? And both at the same most fortuitous time? It is asking a lot to ask me to believe it.'

'My lord, how can I answer for other men? I have told you the truth, and I am paying the price asked of me. What more can I do?'

So he said, and clung to it through all questioning, even when Tudor and Llewelyn from both sides pressed him hard and fast, and with whatever traps they could devise. Later, the next day, the miller was brought, and Owen was confronted with him, but so straitly that the man was told not to show recognition or nonrecognition or say a word in the young man's presence, the more to agonise him with doubt of the outcome, that if he feared enough he might prefer to confess and be done with it. But he feared confession more, knowing what he had to confess, than continued obduracy.

'My lord,' he said, sweating, 'let me know if this fellow claims he saw me that night and knows me again. For if he says so, then indeed he lies, though he may have seen armed men, and may say so in all good faith.'

'He does not claim to know you again,' said the prince honestly. 'In the dark, among so many, it would be a very long chance. And your livery and any marks of your household I'm sure were well hidden. No, *he* is not the liar. But I bid you now, think well what you are about, for it's you I hold, and on you it depends how I hold you. I want the truth of this strange business, and however you deny, I tell you to your face I believe it was you and yours trying to cross the Dee that night. You had much better cleanse your breast now, for in the end I shall find out all.'

From the green pallor of Owen's face I fancy he was even then equally sure of it, but he could not do other than persist in his denial, and so he did, against all pressures. Thus he came into a stricter keeping, and from a guest became a prisoner. But nothing could we get out of him. Nor now could we let it rest, for doubt of what lay behind it. All through June and into July Llewelyn had his clerks and agents questioning about the Dee and also in Cydewain, for north of the Dee we never heard word more of this armed band, thus confirming that they never got across the river. But in Pool by this time everything was so dissembled and dispersed that there was nothing to be learned there. And it was not until well into July that the prince received at Rhuddlan a letter from Cynan, brought by that same Welsh groom of his.

'The bearer,' wrote Cynan, 'has recently been in the king's castle of Montgomery with me, on some minor business, and having better access to the gossip of the stables than I, learned somewhat more of the matter of your troubles with the lord of Powys. I do not take gossip for proof, but it is worth noting. You may not know, but the garrison at

483

Montgomery are very well aware, that one very close to you paid a visit to the castle of Pool in November of last year, and was a guest there more than a week, and that without any ceremony, but rather softly and with few attendants, which is not his habit, and without his wife, which is even more strange. There are some in the neighbourhood who whisper that he may not be quite innocent of taint in the treason to which Griffith and his son have confessed. If I trespass, hold me excused. The precedents you know better than I. I speak of your brother, the Lord David.'

Llewelyn sat long, after he had read this, withdrawn into himself, before he roused himself with a great effort to question the groom, who said out freely what he had heard, and knew the difference, too, between common castle gossip and the grain of hard but ambivalent truth within it. Then with thanks and a reward, and in his normal calm manner, the prince dismissed him.

'Dear God!' said Llewelyn then, to himself rather than to Tudor and me. 'It must not be true.' But he did not say that it could not be. And I, for my part, was so stunned that at first I could not bring my mind to connect and examine as it should have done, and make sense of what I knew but he did not, those night hours in February when David deserted his bedchamber and his wife to stand out the cold of the night on the wall like a sentinel, while the distant mischief he might well have had a share in brewing either succeeded or failed. As soon as I remembered his face, in the chapel as on the guard-walk, I knew that he had known. Something, if not all. But what he could have had to gain, by some furtive raid on Dolforwyn or any other of the prince's garrisons, was mystery to me. The torment was, that in his love there was so much hate, jealousy and resentment that he was capable, in the last anguish, of acts unfathomably senseless, so long as they were sufficiently hurtful.

So little was I enlightened at that point, that my dismay and my understanding stopped there, when I had so much more knowledge, had I been able to arrange the pieces in their true pattern. If, indeed, to this day I know the true pattern. Perhaps only God knows it, and just as well. In his hands justice is assured, and mercy possible.

'Griffith's son has been paying court to him a year and more,' said Llewelyn, vainly fending off what he knew he must do. 'Why should he not pay a visit to Pool, since he was welcome there? There's nothing in that.'

'Softly, and almost unattended?' said Tudor. 'Without his wife and children?'

'It is not like him, no. But what is like him? He changes like the sky. I will not believe he has taken part in anything aimed against me.'

'Would it be the first time?' said Tudor harshly.

I said, and it was labour to say it: 'I have somewhat to tell you that perhaps should have been told earlier. But I thought it was over and done, and no grief to any man. Hold me excused, for I did not deliberately keep it from you, but only let it lie as something finished, something I had no cause to remember. I have cause now!'

Llewelyn turned his head and looked at me curiously, all troubled and saddened as he was, and a little smiled, seeing me as lost and daunted as he was himself. 'Tell me now,' he said.

I told him everything I recalled about that night, even to what David had cried out to Elizabeth when she ran to clasp him, how she should not, for she might soil her hands. And I reminded him how, after that night, David had been gentle and calm and almost humble, like a man grateful for deliverance out of danger. 'For so it always was with him,' I said, 'that as often as his right hand struck a blow at you, his left hand would reach to parry it.'

'It was God parried it this time,' said Llewelyn grimly, 'with snows and rains.'

I said: 'David prayed.'

'For better weather to prosper his design?' said Llewelyn.

'So he bade me pray,' I said. 'But what his own prayer was at the chapel in Aber before I came, only God knows, and David.'

'I have not judged him,' said Llewelyn heavily. 'Not yet. I shall not be his judge.' And he laid aside Cynan's letter with a steady hand, and said to Tudor: 'Call a council, and let them deal. I am the complainant, they must advise me what to do.'

And so in due course they did, with one voice ordering that David should be summoned to appear before a court at Rhuddlan on a date in the middle of July, to answer to a charge of implication in treason. As I remember, he sent back word, as it were with raised brows and a disdainful smile, that in view of the tone of the summons, which was to him incomprehensible, he must refuse to appear except under safe-conduct. Llewelyn without comment issued the required letters. But his face, when he thought himself unobserved, was so full of grief that it was hard to bear.

And just at this most unhappy time came the news that Edward was again in Paris on his way home, and that his coronation had been fixed for the nineteenth day of August. All England was waiting for its king, and we hung upon David's word from Lleyn, David's word which was always and endlessly fatal for us, as if he had been created to destroy what his brother built, whether he would or no. For if he was fatal to us, how much more fatal was he to himself.

'In the name of God,' said Llewelyn, wrung, 'how can I go to Westminster for this crowning? What, and leave this dangerous riddle still unsolved behind me? Unless I can get to the bottom of it and resolve all, I will not go to England. I'll send and excuse myself from attending, and by all means send venison for Edward's feast, but I'll not leave Wales in such a tangle of treachery and secrets. He will have to hold me excused for the sake of my own realm, and there's none should understand that better.'

As he had said, so he did. For indeed there was great danger to Wales in the eruption of such a case at law between the prince and his own brother, worse than the more understandable clash with the lord of Powys, and it was vital that Llewelyn should be seen and known to be present in his principality, and in full control of its destinies. The stability of Wales was too new and fragile to withstand any shocks. Moreover, David accepted the letters of safe-conduct, and condescended to set out to face the council at Rhuddlan in the middle of July. At that time Edward was on his way from Paris to Montreuil, and thence, after concluding a sound trading pact with the countess of Flanders, he soon embarked for Dover.

Now I know that afterwards there were many men willing to swear that even at this time the prince had resolved, in his own mind, not to attend King Edward's coronation, and to reserve his fealty and homage if by any means he could, having turned against the king on the suspicion that he had some part in, or at least approved, the border infringements that constantly plagued us, and even the affair of Griffith ap Gwenwynwyn. But I know that this is not true, that his mind towards Edward was as it had always been, and he had not then even considered the possibility of enmity or ill design on Edward's part. I know, for I wrote the letter at his command, that was sent to Reginald de Grey in Chester as late as the twenty-sixth of March of that year, pointing out that he had not yet been informed of the king's intended date of arrival in his kingdom, or the new arrangements for his coronation, and asking to know as soon as possible. And this letter was sent from Aber just before we set out for Dolforwyn, which was *after* the first news reached us of the treachery of Griffith ap Gwenwynwyn. It never entered his head, until much later, to suspect Edward of anything, or to seek to evade the fealty and homage due to him. He would have attended the coronation in due state, and certainly in friendship, if it had not been for this far more grave matter of David's implication, and the dangers it threatened to the unity of Wales.

Thus David came with a small retinue of knights to Rhuddlan in the latter days of July, when Edward was already preparing to embark for England. Elizabeth he left at home in Lleyn, not only because of the grave nature of this visit, but for good reason enough, which he told court and council with proud and ceremonious intent upon entering the hall. He looked as always immaculate and graceful, stepping clean through all the foulness he engendered at his worst, and spurning those impulsive human virtues he showed at his best. Alone he came before the assembled council in hall, leaving his train outside and wearing no weapon, and he stood well back from us all, to be single and beautiful as he well knew how, and said in a clear voice:

'My lord prince and brother, you must excuse me some small delay in obeying your summons. Family affairs kept me. If you can forget for a moment the cause for which I am called here, and be glad with me, I pray of you that goodness and grace. In the morning of the day before yesterday my lady bore me a son.'

Thus very becomingly he announced his news, but his face was not as his voice, but arrogant and bright, his eyes blindingly blue with triumph, and upon Llewelyn he suddenly smiled, and his smile was sweet, cruel and vindictive, as he avenged himself in advance for whatever could be said of him or done to him. But it was his mistake, for though he never looked at me, it was then he struck all the pieces of that puzzle

486

together in my mind, and I remembered his voice saying, in wilful mischief then not wholly serious, but now, perhaps, gone beyond mischief: 'A kingdom, and he will not give it a prince! While I have heirs – perhaps a prince by now – but no kingdom!' And truly now he had his prince, while Llewelyn was still barren and alone.

If his intent was to pierce to the heart, as I think, then it fell blunted. For Llewelyn was large of mind and generous, and could not, for all his own longing, grudge blessing to another, even his suspect brother. Indeed, in another way David's shaft did him good service, for it disarmed the prince's judicial sternness to such purpose that I think he began almost to doubt what his own ears had heard, even to feel a little ashamed of suspecting his brother. He gave him joy openly and warmly, and enquired after Elizabeth. And even David, I believe, was shaken into some small burning of shame at being so rewarded for his venom, for he flushed as he made answer:

'My lady is well, and the child well, I thank you. He is whole and strong and perfect, and we have called him Owen.'

Judge how difficult it was, after such an exchange, to bring the affair back into the shape of an impeachment. But Tudor was not and never had been dazzled by David, and reminded the assembly drily that it would be well to proceed to business.

'You say well,' said David as roundly. 'I am here to listen to certain charges against me, as I understand, and to answer them as best I can, or to be appointed a day later to answer them. It is fitting that my own affairs should be left out of it. I am at the prince's and the council's disposal.' But always he kept in his eyes that blue, exulting, affronting brightness, and still he smiled upon Llewelyn.

Then Tudor spoke out what he knew, and what we suspected, and told him strongly: 'You stand impeached of conspiracy and treason. If you can show that these facts mean something other than they seem to mean, and that you are clear of all offence against the prince and his realm, we are ready to hear your answer.'

'My answer,' said David, aloof and cool, even scornful, 'is to deny that ever I entertained, since those my offences that are all too well known, any wrong intent against the prince, or committed any traitorous act, or joined in any dark conspiracy against his power or his possession. I say that I am guiltless of what you allege against me. That part of your story that is true I accept, that is, that I did visit Owen ap Griffith at Pool, at the time you mention. Why should I not? I went there for no ill purpose, but because I was invited. If there was any plotting done in that place, I knew nothing of it and saw and heard nothing of it, and if there was any action taken, as you say and as Owen now says, by the men of Pool against your head, my lord, then it comes as news to me as to you, for I had no part in it. I deny all your charges. And since I hear them now for the first time, I ask leave to examine them at more leisure before I refute them all, as be sure I shall.'

'It is within your power,' said Llewelyn, 'to refute them now, or at least to make fuller answer than a mere denial. That every man accused can make, guilty or innocent. Will you not satisfy us now, and set suspicion at rest?'

'These are serious charges,' said David, 'and to me particularly serious, since I am your brother, and owe you closer allegiance than any.' So proudly, and with such lofty injury he said it, I swear Llewelyn for an instant felt himself the one accused. 'This I promise you, you shall be satisfied, with a full and final answer, but that requires other witness and other proofs than mine, and I need the help of my own clerks to muster evidence. Either accept my word, and discharge me now from all blame, or appoint a day for me to come to trial, and give me fair time to make ready my defence.'

'So be it,' said Llewelyn heavily, for he had hoped to be rid of that load without a further delay. 'It is your right.' And the council conferred, and at the prince's urging set the date for the hearing later than otherwise they would have wished, in October, at Llanfor in Penllyn. And David, on his word to appear there, was dismissed, and left Rhuddlan without waiting to exchange a word in private with his brother, that being the only smart he had left to administer, like a blow in parting.

After he was gone I was torn two ways, whether or no to speak out to Llewelyn what was in my mind. But I could not deny him what might well be strength to his case, and I knew I could trust him not to let it prejudice David's. For the whole torment of this matter was that even in our suspicions we could well be wrong. The men of Pool had confessed their treachery, but David denied all, and for all the weight of circumstance, his visit to Pool, his strange behaviour at Aber in February, there might be no more in his guilt than the harbouring of a partial knowledge, even a suspicion, which he did not reveal. Of so much, in my heart, I knew him guilty, but his guilt might go no further than that.

In the end I told the prince all, all those things David had said concerning his children, and in particular the son of whose coming he was so sure, and who was now newly arrived in this world.

'I dread,' I said, 'that since becoming father to children he has found his lands growing too cramped for him, and for his ambitions for them, and has turned yet again to his old complaint, that all Welsh land is partible, and he has never received his due. For himself he accepted his lesser estate, but for them? It is his aim to leave a dynasty well endowed, and to send his son out into the world like a prince.'

'That I can understand,' said Llewelyn wearily, 'though even so I could not countenance or condone it. Wales is not truly mine, or only mine as everything I am or have belongs to Wales, all but the soul. What is not mine I cannot give away, even if I would. Yet I do understand his impatience with me, who live alone and sleep cold, and nurse, as he says, a kingdom without an heir. And I had thought he had wit enough to see, and knew me well enough to be sure, that I am *not* without an heir, though I have none yet of my body. If I die unwed, David *is* my heir, and his son after him,' But in a moment he said sharply: 'No! He *was* my heir! If he proves guilty now, does he think I will let Wales go to one who turned traitor to Wales?'

So David had had everything to lose, and nothing to gain, and that was always his fate, to spend all his energy and wit to waste, and only in moments unguarded, and very lightly valued, to give out those small acts and impulses of warmth that endeared him to so many men. I do remember how once he broke to me the news of my mother's death, with such skilful sweetness, and a touch so gentle, and tears in his own eyes, for she had been his nurse. But not even his affection was a safe gift, though precious, and worth the risk.

'But the mystery remains,' I said,'for what would it profit his purpose to muster an armed band from Powys, and seek to enlarge his lands by force? No, it will not do. He would do better asking you for more, and he could have made a good case, with his first son in his arms. And you would have listened. He should have known it!'

'I am as lost as you,' said Llewelyn. 'This matter is very dark, and I will use all the men I have to seek out and find some light upon it. I pray David will show sense and speak out whatever he knows, but I cannot rely upon it. Our own hunt must continue.'

And so it did, both in Powys and along the Dee, and to some extent in David's own Lleyn, for if he had plotted, then some of his own people must be in the plot. Nor was this the only anxiety we had then, for word had come from Maelienydd that Roger Mortimer was building a fine new castle at Cefnllys, a stone fortress, whereas the treaty gave him leave only to repair the old one and put it in good order. A wooden enclosure and keep is a sensible means of defence on a border, but a stone castle with ditches and fortifications is a base from which to move outward, and we knew enough of my lord's cousin Mortimer to know that he would not scruple to use that base illegally if he saw the opportunity, and would hang on tooth and nail and with all the resources of law to what he got without benefit of law. Only a day after David had left us, in the castle of Mold, which he had set out to inspect, Llewelyn wrote a letter of protest to King Edward about the building, with a sting in it for Mortimer above the open reproach, for he was one of King Edward's regents, and should have been foremost in maintaining his law and treaty obligations. But Roger was always a headlong creature, and would not brook restraint.

A miserable August we had of it, while the summer weather invited to joy, and the harvest began in very good heart. For with the whole burdened business of a principality there was now overladen this distress and suspicion between brothers. And still Owen ap Griffith in my lord's prison clutched at his wellknown story and would not part from it, though fright ate at his innards, and sturdily he swore that there had never been collusion between him and David, but he felt simple admiration and worship for David, and his only act had been against Dalforwyn, for dread and envy of its influence on the market and township of Pool.

And while we in Gwynedd agonised, and sifted, and probed after the truth of a complex matter, King Edward of England landed at Dover on the second day of August with his queen, and his daughter Joan of Acre, and the baby son Alfonso, born in Gascony, two foreign fruits brought back from the crusade. After the voyage, though undertaken in the best time of year, doubtless they were all glad to break their journey and rest as guests of Earl Gilbert of Clare at Tonbridge, and the Earl Warenne at

Reigate, before they made their state entry into a London cleaned and festively arrayed for their reception, on the eighteenth of the month. At Westminster all the space within the island enclosure was filled with bright pavilions, and all the halls painted and furbished for the occasion. And on the day following, being a Sunday, Edward and his queen were crowned in the abbey, and for fifteen days thereafter all London feasted and made merry. But without the prince of Wales.

And to record a small act of restitution or revenge, according as you view it, from the ceremony in the abbey the archbishop of York was firmly shut out by his superior of Canterbury, because he insisted on his right to have his cross carried before him. So his former victory at the translation of Saint Edward was fully requited at the coronation of King Edward.

As for Llewelyn's absence, there was never any sign that the king took it amiss, or failed to accept his excuses. Whatever men may have said afterwards in late wisdom, there was no ill-feeling then begun, no slight intended, and none suspected.

The time for David's appearance at Llanfor drew near, and Llewelyn removed the court to Bala, and there waited for the day of the hearing in depression and agitation of mind, but resolute to have out the truth and deal full justice. For the sake of his own pride and position he could do no less, but even more for the sake of Wales.

On the day appointed the council sat, and the bench of judges were prepared, and everyone waited for the accused to appear. But all that day passed, and the dark came down, and until full midnight we waited, that it might not be said we made him defaulter before his due day was ended. For there are delays and accidents on the road, and a man may be forgiven a lamed horse or a detour to ford a stream. But midnight passed, and David did not come. And then we knew he would not came.

Llewelyn had sat out the death of the day grave and silent and with a motionless face, like a stone man in his chair. When it was dead past question, he turned his head towards Tudor, and said:

'Take a guard of twenty men, and fetch him. Bring him in chains.'

CHAPTER VI

That I was sent with that party was an afterthought on his part, and a concession. Not only had I almost a confessor's privilege with David, however he used me in despite of it, but also I was the person who knew the truth concerning that night at Aber, and I, better than any other, might relate to those events whatever David might do or say now at bay. We had great need of all the evidence we could glean. So when Tudor rode with his armed guard, I went with them into Lleyn, to the taking of David.

I think Tudor already had it in mind that we should not find him. I know I had. Once before I had ridden to Neigwl to recall David to his duty, and found him flown, and that with less reason than now. So we asked at Criccieth if anything had been seen of him, but the answer was, nothing. Certainly he had not ridden through that town or halted at that castle. The castellan said that to the best of his knowledge David's court was at Nevin, and thither we went, but Tudor detached two men to ride northwards of our course, for if he had indeed run, and not by way of Criccieth, he must have gone by the pass of Bryn Derwin, where once in his turbulent youth he had stirred up Owen Goch to make war on Llewelyn for the whole of Gwynedd, and been unhorsed and made prisoner. The first of his three betrayals, forgiven in a year. I was sure in my heart then that this third would never be forgiven.

We came down to the outer sea at Nevin in the blue autumn afternoon, the sun faintly overcast, the sky and the sea melting one into the other without division. Above the outer fence of the maenol there was smoke drifting languidly, but thin and rare, as from only one or two low fires. And there was a guard at the gate, but only two men, and they lethargic and dispirited, and at sight of us approaching in some fear and more resignation. About the yards a few maids moved, in the stables there were only two or three work horses, but the stock grazed in the outer meadows, cattle and sheep. The castellan, a man of the local tref, came out from the hall and stood before us, blank-faced but erect, for he had his orders from his lord, and he was still in his lord's service until another took possession.

'In the prince's name,' said Tudor, sure now what to expect, 'where is the Lord David?'

'He is not here,' said the castellan. 'He bade me say to the prince, or to the prince's messenger, that they are welcome to what remains in Nevin and in Lleyn, since he cannot take it with him where he is gone.'

'He is a defaulter and recreant,' said Tudor, 'and we need no permission of his to take possession of all his lands and goods. He has failed of his day and of his sworn word. You had better look to your duty to the prince now, for you are without any other master.'

'I know it,' said the man, with a wooden face. 'Now I have done his last behest, and I am free of him. Ask me what you need to know.'

'Where is he gone? When, and by what road? Is there still time to overtake him?'

'I doubt it,' said the castellan. 'He left, with the most of his armed men and his family and attendants, in the night, four days ago.' That was a well-judged time, not so soon as to be still under close watch, since if he went about his business confidently and calmly to within four days of his hearing it might seem to all men that he was sure of the outcome, and in no fear of facing it. And not so late that he could not, by night, get his party across Wales either to Chester or Shrewsbury before he was hunted. 'The road he took he did not confide to me, there were none in the secret but his guard, not even the lady. But I know they set off by Bryn Derwin, and it's my belief they'll make for Shrewsbury by Cymer, and pass well south of Bala.'

'They'll have circled round us the night before we sat waiting for him,' said Tudor, 'and gained two miles for every mile we rode westward. Still, we'll make the attempt.' And he sent two riders with fresh horses and orders to get remounts by the way, on the fastest route eastward, to enquire at all halts and alert all garrisons, and two more back to Llewelyn to carry word and get his orders.

'And now,' said Tudor grimly, 'let's see what he has taken, besides a wife hardly recovered yet after his son's birth, and that same son, and two small girls. With that burden we may take him yet.'

I knew already who else was gone, I knew it by the strings of my heart stretched out to breaking. God knows how he had accounted to Elizabeth for that night flight, though she would have followed him wherever he led. But I am sure he never let any word of it out to Cristin until they mounted and rode, for though she was in his service, or in his wife's service, she would not have let him go without a fight, for his own sake no less than for Llewelyn's. But when she was faced with the decision, and no time for argument or prevention, she would go with Elizabeth and the children. What else could she do? Unwilling, unhappy, loyal, knowing to what risk and sorrow he was dragging his defenceless lady, Cristin could not desert her. She was gone, and I might never see her again. Gone with Godred, for certainly Godred knew all, while I was left here without even the sweet anguish of seeing her face, and knowing that she loved me.

We went through the maenol, the castellan attending. David had taken his gold, his jewellery, all his portable treasure, and by the emptiness of the stables, some thirty knights and troopers, no doubt carefully chosen, together with his wife and children, with Cristin and perhaps one other maidservant to care for them. Nevin was an empty shell, deserted by its lord.

As soon as Tudor's messenger reached him, Llewelyn sent out riders to all his garrisons along the border, and they scoured the Welsh side of the march, but in vain. David was already through the net and gone to earth in England, and for some weeks we heard of him no more. And still we did not know what lay behind all this coil of conspiracy and treachery, and had no way now of probing to the final truth.

'Yes, one way, perhaps,' said Llewelyn. 'We know him guilty now, and do not know of what, and I cannot leave it there. Let's see what someone else can make of this flight, someone who does know what the crime was, and is still in my hands to dread paying in full for it. Let Owen ap Griffith in his prison know that David is fled. And if he so receives the news as to think we know more than we do, so much the better, he'll sweat the more.'

So it was done. And sweat he did, being left now to bear the whole burden of the prince's revenge, and the more it delayed, the more did he fear it. All in all, I think he did well to sit out the rest of that month without blabbing, for as he was left to carry all, so he had the option of speaking out without contradiction, and piling the whole crime, or the lion's share of it, upon David.

I remember that November of Edward's first regnal year as a fatal month, the time when an opportunity for accord and understanding was not so much neglected or missed, as snatched away wantonly by chance, never to be repeated. It may well be that the fortunes of Wales turned about purely because of this mishap, and if that is true, then no man was to blame for it, and all the wisdom on earth could not have prevented it.

This is what befell: As soon as his coronation was well over, and he had looked about him and secured control of all those matters outstanding in Westminster – and I repeat, with no sign of dissatisfaction or reproach at Llewelyn's absence from his crowning – King Edward turned to an accommodation with Wales, such as his father had achieved before him, and with every expectation of a peaceful continuance. He sent to the prince, early in November, to ask him to send envoys to meet him at Northampton, to make arrangements for receiving Llewelyn's fealty and homage in person, as the prince had desired, at a place and time agreeable to both. And Llewelyn gladly sent his proctors as requested, for it was no advantage to him to have this matter hanging unresolved, any more than to Edward. The messengers came back satisfied with their reception, and reported that they had agreed to the date the king had suggested, which was the twenty-fifth day of this same month, and the place, which was Shrewsbury. It was a sensible and proper arrangement, and Llewelyn had no fault to find with it.

But in the days immediately following the return of the envoys, came also the hoped-for message from Owen ap Griffith's custodian. Terror for himself had overcome Owen's obstinate silence. He begged that he might have audience of the bishop of Bangor, or some other reverend man, and cleanse his bosom by confession.

'Now we may learn the truth at last,' said Llewelyn, relieved, and as glad as it was well possible to be, with David so heavy on his heart. 'Whatever it may be, I shall be grateful to have it out in the open. I had best not make him face me on the occasion. We'll hale him out to Bangor, and confront him with bishop, dean, chapter and all, if it will make his tongue wag more freely. But, Samson, be present for me. I would have you stay unseen, and take down what he has to say.'

Relations between Llewelyn and the bishop of Bangor at this time were most cordial, and so they were with all the abbots of all the Cistercian houses of Wales. In St Asaph, in Anion II, he had a most difficult and contentious prelate, so jealous for the privileges of his see that he resented others having any rights at all, and was endlessly embroiled in lawsuits of all kinds. Anion had even complained of the prince to king and pope as hostile to the church, by which he meant hostile to Anion, or at least a match for Anion, and all the Cistercian priors of Wales had combined to send an indignant letter of rebuttal to the pope against this slur on a most just and devout prince. But Einion of Bangor was loyal, humane and reasonable, and with deep concern accepted the task of taking confession from Owen ap Griffith. In the chapter-house of his cathedral this meeting took place, in the middle of November, and I, who recorded it, remember it still, word for word as it unfolded.

They brought in Owen from his prison, greyish-pale from close confinement, and fretted and thin with his long companionship with fear. He had not been ill-used or starved, and his modish cotte and chausses were still elegant, and his light brown hair and short beard well-trimmed, and yet he looked both wretched and neglected, so eaten up with fear was he. He looked from face to face round the circle of reverend men, with uneasy eyes, all in one rapid glance, and came and kneeled at the bishop's feet, and kissed Einion's hand with obsequious fervour.

'There is something you wish to say to us,' said the bishop, 'for the relief of your soul. You may speak out without fear. Confession will be health to you.'

It was rather for the best advantage of his body, to my mind, that Owen had made up his mind to speak, sure that everything was bound to come out, and thinking it wiser it should come from him, and he get whatever remittance was possible out of it. He joined his hands in entreaty, and cast down his eyes nervously, and made his confession on his knees. I had thought he might even then be exercising some devious discretion as to what he told and what he omitted, and rearranging truth to his own best showing, but no, it was a straightforward tale he told, now that his mind was made up. If he revealed all, then nothing more could emerge to damn him.

'My lord, to my shame I have not only offended against the prince's grace, but in fear I have lied to cover my worse guilt. I desire to make full confession now, in the hope of your lordship's intercession and the lord prince's mercy. But I am in your hands and in his, to dispose of as he pleases. I acknowledge it, and whatever he does with me, I make no complaint. I have deserved his anger. But I would have this burden of secrecy and sin off my heart at all costs.'

Not all, perhaps, but it was worth a bold cast to try to salvage something out of the wreck. The bishop bade him speak, and promised to do for him, body and soul, what could be done.

'Do you make this statement of your own free will, or has any threatened or forced you, or put the words into your mouth?'

'My lord, no one has prompted me, I speak of my own free will, being sound in mind, and knowing what I do. I am come now to a better condition, I would make such restitution as I can.'

'Then speak,' said the bishop, 'and put away doubts and fears.' Which in Owen's situation was easier to say than to do, but he judged the fear upon that side to threaten him less than elsewhere, and plunged into his story.

'My lord, you know already that the lord prince got wind, early in the year, of my father's disaffection and mine, and how we had put into the field a war party with evil intent against him, and how he believed that we had attempted the destruction of his castle of Dolforwyn, out of jealousy and despite because of our rights and privileges close by at Pool. And when he impeached us of this offence, seeing that it was useless to deny, we confessed our guilt, and let it be thought that the rivalry of Dolforwyn was all the matter of contention, and that we had indeed intended its razing, and nothing more. My lord, we lied. The enterprise was larger, and the sin, too. And it touches also, most deeply, the Lord David, who is now fled into England. I was set to win him into our plan, and so I did. In everything we did, he was a willing partner.'

'And who,' asked the bishop, 'so set you on to seduce him? Was it your father?'

For the first time the young man faltered even in his desire to have this ordeal finished. 'No,' he said, very low, and writhed, and in a moment got out, even lower: 'My mother!'

'Then your father took no part? Did he know of your plotting?'

'He did know. He did take part. But not the leading part. Do not ask me further to accuse her! I was guilty, let that be enough.' And indeed he had said enough already to be understood by any who had ever known that slender, steely lady of Pool, Hawise Lestrange the marcher's daughter. Into whatever plan she conceived, she could drive both husband and son, and that without ever raising her voice.

'Go on,' said the bishop.

'My part was to win over David, and I did it. He has often shown discontent with his lands, and he is bold and able. He entered into a bond with us to enlarge both his estate and ours. He promised his eldest daughter to me in marriage, and he promised my father, and me after him, both Kerry and Cydewain to be added to Powys, in return for the armed aid we pledged him to accomplish what he most desired. I was to lead a strong company in secret to the lord prince's maenol at Aber, and that we sought to do, but the floods turned us back at the Dee and prevented our evil.'

'You say it was to Aber you were bound?' said the bishop, still astray and in great amazement. 'In the name of God, with what intent? What could you hope to do there, in the very heart of the lord prince's power?'

'What God in his wisdom prevented,' said Owen, and knotted his hands in dread of his own words, and wrung out frantic tears. 'We conspired to murder the prince in his bedchamber, and make the Lord David prince of Wales in his place.'

In the blank hush that came upon us all I heard not even a breath, and then the long, faint sigh of every man present, so soft that it might have been the sound of the sudden, bleak November sunlight creeping across the flagged floor. The bishop sat chilled to stone. My pen had stabbed deep into the parchment and splayed its point, blotting the leaf. God knows what we had expected to hear, but it was not this, never quite this. Bishop Einion drew back a little from being touched by Owen's shaking hands, and himself shook with anger and disbelief.

'Wretch, do you know what you say? Are you lying still for some purpose of your own? If this was what you intended, the Lord David surely cannot have known it was meant to go so far.'

'I do know!' said Owen, shaking and weeping. 'As God sees me, I am telling the truth. The proofs are written and sealed, my mother keeps all the agreements we made in a coffer at Pool, you may send for them. David's seal is there. He did know! He knew all! On the second night of February we were appointed to reach Aber in the darkness, and he was to let us in.'

Then there was no more mystery for me in all the curious detail of that night in Aber, David's face in the red glow of the altar lamp in the chapel, tormented and ravaged between exultation and loathing. David's restless prowling as he watched the weather, his words, his frozen vigil above the postern gate, that was barred but not guarded. Llewelyn was never as careful of his personal safety as he should have been, and who knew it better than David? Who could better lead a party of armed raiders to the prince's bedchamber in the dark, and in silence? But God had prevented, and saved him from the act. No one could save him from the intent. And perhaps only God, not even David, knew the content of those desperate prayers of his that night, whether they were for clearing skies and hardy fellow-conspirators and a princely heritage for his son, or that God would tear the skies open and send down the torrents of judgment to make an impassable moat about Aber. For as often as David's right hand launched a blow at Llewelyn – David who never repented his evil against any other – his left hand would reach to parry it.

'He gave me to know,' said Owen, bleeding words freely now that the worst was said, 'that if he had no son of his body, by marriage with his first daughter I should be his heir.'

David must have laughed at that, knowing already what they did not know, that his Elizabeth was again with child, and certain in his own mind that this time she could not fail of providing him a son. And so she had, and the grand inheritance David had earned for him was a shameful exile in England, bereft of all lands and honours. So far had he over-reached himself.

'He was to let us in by the landward gate, and lead us to the lord prince's room. And when Llewelyn was dead, then David's men and mine would take possession of the maenol and name him prince in his brother's place. And to this we all swore, and set our seals, if you doubt my word. But the floods turned us back, and the day passed without that terrible sin.'

'I thank God!' said Bishop Einion.

496

'And we thought it was over! That we had done no more than sinned in intent, and wasted our labour and time, as we deserved, that we were safe, and it had all passed without effect and without detection. But time and vengeance have pursued us ever since, thus slowly and surely, without any haste.'

'God's time is endless, and his patience without limit,' said the bishop. 'Never think that he has forgotten, or failed to see.' And he said heavily: 'Have you done? Or is there yet more to tell?'

'I have done,' said the poor wretch, grovelling.

'I cannot yet give you absolution, there is more required of you than confession. Do you empower me freely to say to the lord prince all that you have said to me?'

'Oh, my lord, with all my heart I entreat you to, and to lift this burden from me. I want to make what amend I can.'

'I will speak for you,' said the bishop, 'but with a heavy heart. Yet if you mean that truly, there is grace to be had.' And he sent for those guards who had brought the prisoner, and committed him again to their charge, to be returned to his prison. And I wrote to the end all that I had to write, and took it with me to await the prince's bidding, after the bishop should have spoken with him. But all that while that I waited – for it was no short telling – I could not cease from seeing David's face, after the night was passed and he had lain lost in his wife's arms until late in the morning, a face so weary and so at peace, as though after his own confession. I remembered its wondering humility and gratitude, washed clean of all greed and desire, even if that state of chastened bliss lasted not long. That was when he had thought, like Owen but with how much more intensity, that it was over, that his mischief had been prevented and his better prayers heard, that he was delivered from evil. While at every step the shadow of his act, which was itself now only a shadow, trod hard on his heels and waited its due time to lay a hand upon his shoulder.

'Once I have heard it,' said Llewelyn when I went in to him, 'now let me hear it again as you took it down from his own lips.' And I read to him, he sitting perfectly quiet and alert and calm, all that deposition of Owen ap Griffith, how the prince's death was to be brought about by the conniv-ance of his own best-loved brother, and that brother exalted to his vacant sovereignty over the principality he alone had made, single-handed, out of chaos. By the time it was done the last daylight was dying, for the days were short then, and I got up to go and trim the candles, but he put out a hand with a sharp, pained gesture to halt me, and: 'Let be!' he said. 'There is light enough left for me to see where I am going.' So I sat down with him again, and waited.

'Once,' he said, musing, 'he rode at me headlong on the field of Bryn Derwin, mad-set to kill or be killed, but that was in open combat, face to face. I had not thought he hated me enough to conspire with so small a creature to spit me to my bed while I slept. Explain him to me, Samson, if you can, for I am lost.'

But I said never a word, for there never was any creature living under the sun could truly explain David, least of all David. He knew himself, and even his lies were never disguises from his own self-knowledge, but knowledge is not understanding.

'Though it is but a step,' Llewelyn said out of the gathering dark, 'from seeing Wales as his inheritance after me, since I am celibate, to growing impatient at the waiting. He is not the first to want to hasten the succession. The same impatience has been the death of more than one Welsh father, since time was. Strange that I never saw it as having any influence between him and me. And now, Samson, tell me, how often am I to turn the other cheek?'

'No more!' I said. 'Now you must think only of yourself. He has made himself the enemy, it is none of your doing.'

'No,' said Llewelyn, 'there's more at stake. Bear with me an hour or so, Samson, while I think for Wales.'

In all that he said and did then, it was for Wales he was thinking, and for that cause he was able to suppress his own desolation and grief and anger, and forgo his own revenge.

'I am walking a ridge between two abysms,' he said after he had been some time silent. 'The two most powerful men in Wales, after me, have made common cause again me, and what I do now against them every princeling in Wales will be watching, and what I do must be seen to be justice, that they may accept it and take warning, but it must not be seen to be tyranny or cruelty, or others will be antagonised. I stand to lose allegiance whether I am too harsh or too merciful. If they conclude they may lightly break my peace, and not be crushed, some will do it, as they did it lightly in the past when Wales was not one, but many. If they think the measures I take too extreme, they will fall away out of indignation. If only I had had this land twenty years longer, even ten years, without interruption! It would have withstood all forces bent on breaking it apart. But this is a perilous time. We are not yet what some day we may be, God willing. We are not a state, not even a people. We are a loose bonding of little lands and tribes and families, of men who see no further forward, as yet, than tomorrow, and for a small, snatched advantage today will throw even tomorrow away. There is no man but Llewelyn can hold Wales together. If,' he said, very sombrely, but with resolution rather than misgiving, 'if Llewelyn can.'

I waited and was still, for he needed no word from me. For a while he, too, was silent, and then he resumed: 'I may not take revenges like other men. I may only bring offences to justice. Did you ever consider, Samson, what a cruel deprivation that may be, that afflicts kings and princes, not to be permitted to hate and resent, and feel outrage like other men?'

I said, only too truly, that it was not a deprivation from which all kings suffered. In the darkness he laughed, but somewhat hollowly.

'But by their own deed, duly sealed,' I said, 'all Griffith ap Gwenwynwyn's lands are forfeit to you.'

'No,' said Llewelyn. 'Only if they offended again, and that I cannot charge, for this, however magnified now, is the past offence. So much justification I have for being patient and lenient. Not for their sakes, God knows, though I would rather have them as allies than enemies, but for the sake of Wales. Owen I hold, and will hold. He is safe enough.

David I have lost for the time being, and he must wait. But Griffith is there in Pool, and thinks this whole matter over and finished, for his part in it, for he knows nothing yet of his son's confession. I do not want Griffith dispossessed, I do not want him prisoner, I want him bound to me, with all Powys – for Powys I cannot spare. I want him shaken and chastened, but not broken or humiliated further, so that he shall be glad to hold fast to me and keep his own. And if I can bring him to a manner of reconciliation and renewed fealty, I will do it. I must preserve the wholeness of Wales as best I may, and at whose cost I may, liefer my own than break this land apart.'

'News travels fast, even when few seem to know it,' I said. 'Griffith knows of David's flight before now. He may draw the same conclusion from it as his son drew. There is need of haste.'

'There is,' said Llewelyn sombrely, 'but of care, too. And I have not forgotten that there are only a few days left before I must set out for Shrewsbury, to meet King Edward. I am bound to him by treaty, and I agreed to the twenty-fifth day of this month, and go I must, though I would rather far that I had this matter of Griffith and Powys safely behind me, and could come to my first formal meeting with Edward as master of all Wales past question, with no dissentient. My fealty and homage would be paid on so much sounder a stand, and I could press my demands over the borders with so much stronger a voice. But there is no time. Until I come back from Shrewsbury, the less that gets out about Owen's tale, the better. We'll not alarm Griffith too soon if we can avoid it. And it may be that the next move will come better from a prince already safely installed in fealty and alliance with the new king of England, and invested with his overlord's authority in the marches as well as his own.'

'And David?' I asked.

'There is nothing I can do about David at this time,' said Llewelyn heavily out of the mourne darkness. 'Neither embrace him nor kill him. As well! I might be tempted to kill rather than to embrace. When next I meet with David we may finish, one way or the other, what was begun at Bryn Derwin.'

On the twenty-second day of November, therefore, the prince, with a large escort and in noble state, set forth on the journey to Shrewsbury to meet with King Edward there, and to swear the oath of fealty and perform the act of homage to the sovereign in person, as he had always intended and considered himself bound to do, for though he had maintained his position that the treaty had been frequently infringed, he did not hold those infringements as being grave enough to cancel his duty under it. As he was pledged, so he meant to do.

Had those two met at Shrewsbury that day, my story and my prince's story and my country's story might have been altogether different, blessedly different. And this is the lost moment for which, I see, no man can be blamed, but only some malevolent chance as wanton as lightning stroke. For at Shrewsbury we were met, on what should have been the eve of that encounter, by a messenger bearing a letter from the king, written at Cliff, which was a hunting-lodge he had in Northamptonshire, on the very day Llewelyn set out from home. Edward had got so far, when he was taken ill with the sudden and violent bursting of an abscess, and was so much weakened that he could not continue his journey. He wrote regretting that illness prevented him from keeping his engagement, for he could not ride, but said that he would try to arrange another mutually agreeable date and place as soon as his health permitted. He did not fail to add a reminder that there were arrears of the money due under treaty still outstanding, and requested that they be paid, for even on a sick-bed Edward was a man of business. But having stated his reasons for withholding those sums many times, and also his willingness and ability to pay them as soon as he got satisfaction on his part, Llewelyn did not then pay much attention to that part of the letter. For since his first priority was thus frustrated, he was able to turn his mind and attention, with relief, to the second.

'We go home, then,' he said at once, roused and fierce, 'and set about the business of Griffith ap Gwenwynwyn.'

He wrote in reply to Edward's letter, also regretting that the meeting was prevented, and by such an unwelcome cause, and wishing his Grace a speedy recovery. And then we turned our backs on Shrewsbury and rode hard for home.

Our best hope, unrecognised, we left lying broken behind us.

Of those five nobles and clerks that Llewelyn chose to go as his ambassadors to Pool, led by Cynfric ap Ednyfed, Tudor's brother, I was one. Always he relied upon me to render an account faithful to the last detail, and I think found in me a mind tuned like his own, so that what I distrusted he took care to examine carefully, and where I found matter for sympathy he was at least willing to examine and withhold judgment. Whatever his reason, I was among those chosen. We had our orders, strict and precise, for his will was to win back Griffith and Powys with a whole heart, and he was prepared to go far to ensure success. Our task was to present ourselves formally at Pool as representatives of the prince of Wales, and to inform Griffith honestly of the content of his son's confession, without prejudice to his reply. For we were to invite him, and by all possible means persuade him, to return with us of his own accord to the prince, not as a prisoner but honourably as our companion, to make his answer to what his son Owen alleged, either to clear himself freely of the charges therein made, or, if he pleaded guilty to them, as the occasion was already past and had accomplished no evil, to confess to them and throw himself upon the prince's mercy, which he was assured should not be denied.

This, I swear, is what Llewelyn charged us with when he sent us forth. Do you know of another prince, so threatened and so abused, who would send his envoys with such large terms to his enemy?

On the last day of November, in a cloudy and melancholy afternoon light, we five rode into the town of Pool, and down to the river meadows where the castle was raised. We bore no arms, and went unattended, in token of the openness and honesty of our intent, and at the castle gates asked audience of Griffith in the name of the prince of Wales, his overlord, on matters of state. Peaceable as our aspect was, it aroused a great deal of fluttering within, until Griffith sent word in haste to admit us at once, and himself came hurrying out in his furred gown to meet us on the steps of his great hall. His heavy-featured face wore a fixed and somewhat ungainly smile, with little true welcome in it, but a great effort at appearing welcoming. He bore himself as though nothing had happened since April, when he had confessed to disloyalty and resigned himself to the loss of some part of his lands and the enforced absence of his eldest son. Having cleared that account in full, his manner seemed to say, there can be nothing in this visit now to trouble my conscience, and nothing to fear. But his eyes looked sidelong and were not quite easy. Whether any word had reached him of Owen's confession or no, certainly he knew of David's flight.

Our part was to be grave, detached and impartial, for it was possible, if hardly probable, that Griffith had not been admitted to the fullest extent of his lady's and his son's design. Princes can be dispossessed and their lands usurped without going so far as murder. But I grant you it was not likely he should be innocent, and our errand was to make it clear to him, even so, that he need not dread extremes if he returned willingly to his fealty. When he brought us into his high chamber and dismissed all other attendance, Cynfric as spokesman delivered our embassage.

'You know, my lord, as all this land knows, that the Lord David has fled to England, instead of standing his trial on suspicion of plotting against the sovereignty of the lord prince. The prince sends you word by us that since that flight your son Owen has voluntarily made a full confession of conspiracy to treason and murder. He charges that you are also implicated, on these heads.' He recited them, with date, place and time. Griffith sat stiff and erect in his chair, his countenance motionless, only his eyes flickering now and then from face to face round the circle of us. 'The prince urges you,' said Cynfric, 'to return with us to his court, and to make your answer to his face concerning these charges, either to clear yourself and satisfy him, if you are innocent, or to repledge your fealty and ask for and obtain his clemency by confession if you are guilty. The event is past, and for what was then known of it you have already made reparation. If you will accept the prince's grace and return to your troth you need not fear that mercy will not be forthcoming.'

Griffith asked, in natural anxiety, after his son.

'Your son is in close hold,' said Cynfric, 'but safe and well. No harm has come to him, no harm will come. His offence is purged. If the same honest peace can be made with you, the matter is over.'

Griffith sat for a while in glum thought, and then roused himself to play host worthily in his own castle, shaking off the heaviness of uncertainty.

'You must give me time to speak with my wife,' he said, 'and consider what I do. Stay overnight, and give me the privilege of feasting the prince's ambassadors, and after dinner I will give you my answer.'

And that we did, accepting it as a good sign, for surely he was visibly resigning himself to the inevitable agreement, having so much to lose by enmity and so much to keep and conserve by humility and good sense. He presented us to his lady, who kept a calm, unsmiling face, ceremonious but not gracious, and sat among us at the high table as stately as a queen, and jewelled. Hawise Lestrange was as tall as her lord, but slim as a willow, with long, elegant hands and long, elegant face. Without the slightest friendliness she took excellent care of our entertainment that night, and very lavish it was. In particular we were pressed to drink our fill, but in Griffith's house, and on our errand, we did not care to deplete his stores more than we need. He had not yet given us an answer, or we might have been more disposed to carouse with him. But after dinner he excused himself and left us to take counsel with his wife, and came again with a calmed and resolved face.

'I thank you for your errand. It shall not be vain. Tomorrow I promise I will ride with you to where the lord prince is, and I will satisfy him of my troth.'

Well content, we went at length to the chambers prepared for us, two small tower rooms upon different floors reached by a stone stairway in the wall, Cynfric and I in the upper room, our three colleagues below. From this sleeping-place all the noise and bustle of the hall was so distant as not to be heard. I marvelled how soon the whole castle fell silent, and since we had ridden much of the day, and sat content and well-fed in smoky hall all the evening, I fell asleep and slept deeply.

Too deeply! Even when the sounds of nocturnal activity did draw near, they failed to rouse me. Not until the sudden weight of hands bearing down out of darkness pinned me to the brychan, and a great palm gripped my mouth, did I start out of sleep, and try to spring up in alarm, but by then it was too late to do more than struggle fruitlessly under the heavy body that held me down. I heard the threshing of Cynfric on the other side of the room, and someone cursed him horribly, and then two bodies fell crashing to the stone floor, and all the time there was a muted grunting as of a man gagged with cloth, or a smothering sleeve. How many there were of them it was hard to tell, but enough, six at least to deal with the two of us. Griffith took no chances. They had brought no lights into the room with them, they knew where to find us without benefit of torches.

It took them some time to subdue Cynfric, and they were not gentle, for he had awakened more readily than I, and done some small damage to one or two of them, even with no weapon but his hands. But they had us both pinioned at last, and muted, and hobbled our feet, too, before they dragged us out to the stairway. There were two or three others waiting there with torches, men of Griffith's guard, and all of them as blown and exercised as those who had fallen upon us. The door of the room below was standing open. We had little doubt that our companions had been overpowered first, and that we were being hauled away to join them in captivity. And I remember thinking even then that Griffith was mad to toss away so viciously his own best hope, one he was lucky to be offered.

Pool castle was strange to me, I knew only the hall and those tower chambers, and we were dragged down so many staircases and along so many stony passages that I was lost. But I knew we were down beneath the level of the hall, and it needed very little guessing to expect some lightless prison below ground, without window, where too curious visitors could be tossed for security, and have no notion what went on in their absence, or why they were so disposed of. Killing I did not look for. He had little to gain that I could see even by throwing us into his dungeon, but nothing at all by killing us. Nor, in fact, did our captors do us any great hurt, however unpleasant the hole into which they finally thrust us.

A narrow door opened on a steep flight of steps, down which we were rolled hastily when they had unbound us, and we fell among other bodies in darkness. Hands reached to prop and steady us, and voices hailed us by name, challenging and anxious, for they had feared worse for us. We in our turn, ridding ourselves of the cloth that gagged us, told over all their names. We were five sorry ambassadors, and five very angry prisoners, but prisoners we were, and there was nothing to be done about it, against a garrison of hundreds, and without even a dagger among us.

'The more fools we,' said I, smarting, 'to put any trust in any promise or oath of Griffith ap Gwenwynwyn. We should have known he had some lying trick up his sleeve.'

'If we are fools,' Cynfric said, groping for a wall for his back in the stony darkness, and stretching out his legs resignedly before him, 'Griffith is a worse fool. He has tricked himself out of Powys now. He could have kept all he had at the price of renewing his oath and leaving his son a while longer as hostage for him. Now he has beggared himself and abandoned his son. Grace will not be so easily come by after this.'

Seven days we spent in that stinking hole, but at least after the first day they gave us some light, and regularly they fed us, even if they did thrust our meat in to us like feeding hounds. The dungeon folded into three cells opening one from another, which at least, when we could dimly see, gave us a measure of decency. There was but the one way out, and as often as they opened the door at the stairhead they set it bristling with long lances to fend us off. But to say truth, we saw no profit in compelling them to complete Griffith's work by killing us, whether in desperation or by accident, when we were as certain of Llewelyn's eventual coming as we were of dawn, though neither could we see. And after we had once tried questioning the guards who brought us food, and found them charged not to answer, and afraid to ignore that charge, we ceased from questioning, and sat down doggedly to wait. The misuse of ambassadors was something Llewelyn would not endure, that we knew. And as he had shown great patience, so he could show equally great vehemence and vigour at need.

We counted the days by the meals they brought us, and by our count it was the seventh day of December when the narrow door above us opened without three or four lance-heads immediately bristling through it like the spines of a hedgehog, and opened wide to the wall instead of gingerly by a hand's-breadth, and further, remained open. The guards we had begun to know did no more than peer in and then draw back respectfully out of the light. A head we knew far better leaned in and narrowed its eyes into our stinking darkness.

'Cynfric?' said Tudor's voice dubiously. 'Are you all safe below there? Come forth and be seen!'

'Here!' said Cynfric, mounting towards his brother as the first of our line. 'What kept you so long? We feared we might have to keep Christmas without you.'

They embraced, for all the stench we brought up with us. There were other known faces crowding in behind Tudor, first reaching to touch us and be sure we were whole and well, then laughing at us, for we must have been a forlorn sight, unshaven, unwashed, draggle-tailed and cold. They brought us triumphantly into the inner ward of the castle where Llewelyn was posting his men, not for the garrisoning of Pool, but for its destruction. They were already bundling faggots to his orders, laying logs and brushwood under the walls, and marshalling the garrison and the fragments of the household to be despatched into the world for refuge.

For no good reason, except that I was just emerged from darkness, I looked up into the December sky, chill and distant with frost, and very still, and against that pallid grey I saw at the top of the tower Griffith's war-banners fluttering limply down to wither over the merlons of the wall. He had not stayed to lend his own defiance to that barren gesture, I knew it then. Once we were underground, and the castellan and his men ordered to stand to for siege, Griffith had taken his leave in haste, and there was but one way he could have gone. As often as I hear of the power and prowess of this lord of Powys, I remember how he ordered up the flag of war, bade his seneschal stand fast and defy the world, and then took to his heels into England with all his family, and all he could carry of his wealth. I have the measure of Griffith, having known him. Whatever the dominant, Griffith would find a means of ingratiating himself with it. Whatever the climate, Griffith would grasp a place in the sun. Even if he mistook the hour and missed his hold, Griffith would find a means, and quickly, to amend his standing. Whoever died, for personal passion or for a cause larger than personality, Griffith would survive.

Llewelyn came leaping down from the guard-walk on the wall, in leather hauberk and booted to the thighs, to reassure himself that we were all sound and whole. He was alight like a flame, very bright and steady-burning in the December gloom, but it was an angry brightness, and until he had spent it in action he would have no inner peace. Too much patience and forbearance had eaten him from within, and now his indignation at least had room to range.

'I delayed too long,' he said, smouldering, 'and bore too much, and at your cost. I thank God you have come to no harm. When ambassadors are so used, there's an end of tolerance. I should have struck the moment the word reached me. I marvel I did not. I'm grown so used to holding back, I delayed yet again, and sent the abbot and prior of Cymer to hunt out Griffith in his new lair and offer him a last chance to return to his fealty and renew the unity of Wales, with the promise of mercy still. I began to dread,' he said, and shivered, 'that I had lost the power to strike hard. Now I feel like a man restored.'

'Regret nothing,' said Tudor firmly. 'You did right to make even that last bid for his allegiance, if only to let the world see where the right is, and how far you have gone to reconcile him. Now, if he has eyes, King Edward must know these are obdurate traitors who have gone to earth in his borders. Time and time again they have been offered the chance of return, and still refused.'

'Well,' said Llewelyn, heaving up his shoulders largely, 'whether I did well or ill, it's done. Now we have other things to do. Since Griffith refuses to restore the unity of Wales, I will, without leave or aid from him. Now everything he has is doubly forfeit, for this offence is worse than the other.'

We asked if they had had fighting, for in our prison no sound from without reached us.

'Very little, and halfhearted at that,' said Llewelyn. 'Griffith's castellan had no great appetite for the defence, small blame to him, when his lord had none! He surrendered at the first assault. The place was well manned and provisioned, too, and the outer buildings cleared and burned for action – that's part of our work done for us. Take your ease, for we'll bide the night here before we send the castle after its barns.'

So all we who had come out of the dark went to cleanse ourselves and find or borrow fresh clothing, to stretch our cramped limbs and take exercise, or rest in better comfort bones bruised and stiff from stone. And that seemed to us a delectable day, not only because we were alive and free, but because the sovereignty of Wales was also at large, justifiably and manifestly, and the happier for it. For action can be happiness, whether it turn out in the end to be ill-judged or well, after long and frustrating abstinence.

That night after we had eaten in hall the prince held a field council, having with him more than half of his own council of Gwynedd, though not of the other lands of Wales. And there he told us what was in his mind to do, which was to proceed through all the lands and tenements of Powys, if possible peacefully, if necessary with the sword, to take over all manors and strongholds of those lands, and set his own officers over them, annexing Powys to his own inheritance. Legally he had every justification in the deed executed by Griffith and Owen at Bach-yr-Anneleu in April, by which they ceded everything to him if they again offended against their troth. Morally he had every right even without that deed, since Griffith had himself needlessly abandoned both his oath and his lands, piling fraud on fraud and felony upon felony. And during that month of December it pleased me to see Llewelyn forget, in the flush and purposeful haste of conquest, the bitter inward sadness and desolation of David's treachery. I knew that ease could not outlast action, but at least it renewed him for a while.

The following day we packed and marched, having first seen Griffith's garrison out of the castle, to be distributed among certain of the maenols under the control of officers of our own. And the castle of Pool, once empty, we fired behind us, and left a party in the town to complete the destruction after the fire died and cooled.

We went like an east wind through Llanerch Hudol and Caerinion and Griffith's remaining portion of Cyfeiliog, proclaiming the prince's lordship everywhere, installing his officers, planting his garrisons wherever they were needed. There was little resistance, no more than a scuffle here and there, and no bloodshed. Yet so deep is the sense of hereditary possession in Wales that this procedure, however justified and however sound in law, seemed to the bishops shockingly drastic, and they wrote to the prince in mid-December urging moderation. Though plainly, since the lord of Powys had deserted his lands and refused the generous offer of freedom to return to them, his forfeiture was a matter of practical management as well as of law, for someone had to administer Powys. Griffith had swept away into exile with him his wife, his second son Lewis and his younger children, and an estate without a head can very rapidly rot into disorder. We had annexed the whole of Powys by then, making a circle northward through the cantrefs of Mochnant and Mechain, and withdrawing gradually into Gwynedd, leaving the land firmly settled.

At Rhydcastell, which is a grange of Aberconway, we drew breath on the twentieth day of December, and Llewelyn chose to pass the Christmas festival there. From that place he replied to the bishops, pointing out that their appeal for an accommodation and peace between the parties had much better be addressed to Griffith and David, who had both resisted the prince's efforts to achieve just such a consummation, and obdurately refused to return to their sworn fealty. It was not he who had prevented a reconciliation, nor he who first caused the breach by plotting murder.

In the stillness after action he was suddenly at loss, brought face to face again with the reality of betrayal, which he had done nothing to deserve. He was always hard put to it to comprehend the curious, secret, complex jealousies and hatreds and motives of those whose natures were not open like his own. Where he saw reason to complain, he complained at once and forthrightly, where he had a grievance he blazed it out of him, and then it was done. Also he listened to the complaints of others, not always with understanding, but always willingly. I never can discover in my own mind how he and David came from the same seed and the same womb, or how they came to love so much, and claw each other so deep.

Rhydcastell was a pleasant enough manor, sheltered and close to the rich, wooded valleys of Conway and its tributaries, but I cannot say the Christmas we spent there was a happy one. It had a certain sense of achievement to celebrate, not without satisfaction, but quite without joy. There were too many reminders of the disaster which had begun, unrecognised, a year ago, and of the false serenity we had felt then, and the brightness of Elizabeth and her children making the court at Aber gay. Now they were somewhere in England, in an exile that could please no one, and dependent on patronage for their maintenance. Such an inheritance had David laid up for his new-born son by snatching at the future too soon.

But until the beginning of the new year we had no certain knowledge of where they were. Then on the second day of January came a friar of Llanfaes, who had been on pilgrimage to other Franciscan houses, and halted some days at Westminster, and he brought a letter from Cynan.

'They are in Shrewsbury,' said Llewelyn, when he had read. 'David and Griffith both, with all their households. And their heads are together as before, and their men are still in arms. So says Cynan. More, he says it is known that they have sworn a new oath of mutual support against whom, we hardly need ask. Once they had burned their boats, there was little left for them to do but turn on me and make me pay for all – that I understand. But listen what Cynan has to say further! This is the meat of the matter! This is what caused him to write, for the rest I could have learned by other means very shortly. "The king has issued a mandate, *not made patent*, to the sheriff of Salop, instructing him to allow the fugitive Griffith ap Gwenwynwyn, with all his household, to dwell in peace in the town of Shrewsbury until he should receive any contrary order. And your brother, the Lord David, who is in Griffith's company there, has certainly written to the king appealing for aid and maintenance for himself and his family. The families of these two lords are large, and include, as you know, many well-armed men They may not be the easiest of neighbours to your borders." '

So blunt and open a warning, sent from the court by one of Edward's own chancery clerks, I had not expected, even though the bearer was also a good Welshman. It seemed to me that Cynan was not far from the moment of choice, and it was clear, when that breakage came, what his choice would be.

'I take the point,' said Llewelyn grimly, 'and I will secure my borders in the middle march, and be ready. From David, from Griffith, I look for nothing but growing hatred and despite now. Since they have refused return, and there's never any standing still, they have no way left to go but deeper into their own venom. But that Edward should give them protection and countenance! You see what Cynan says – "*not made patent*"! With good reason, for by that sign he must know he does vilely to harbour traitors. I would not have believed he could bear to signify approval to treason.'

'Don't judge too hastily,' said Tudor. 'Do we know what gilded story the king has been told? Would David go to him with the truth? No, he'll have made it a very different tale, with himself the wronged and persecuted brother driven out of his lands into exile. You know him, how fatally plausible he is. The king is his only hope of advancement now, he'll play on him with every device and charm he has.'

And so I said, too, and his charms and devices were many and seductive, and from childhood he had kept some hold and claim on Edward. And yet I was not satisfied, for all the story of that conspiracy to kill, unearthed by painful stages over a year of searching, was by then notorious through the whole of Wales, and could not have failed to penetrate into England and reach the court, since they had their agents everywhere, just as we had. It was hard to believe that Edward did not know where the truth lay. But it could still be believed that he withheld judgment until he had heard all sides of the matter, and the order to let the felons live openly in Shrewsbury might be only a temporary measure. So I said, and Llewelyn heard me with a dark and doubting face.

'There is more in it than that. Fugitives is the word Cynan uses, surely of intent. It was Edward's word to the sheriff. He might well keep his mandate close! The treaty made at Montgomery forbids either

England or Wales to receive and harbour the fugitives of the other. He knows he is breaking treaty. He cannot choose but know. Never tell me there's a line of any document concerning his rights that Edward does not know by heart.'

One of his law clerks present, who had been an envoy at the drawing up of that treaty, looked a little uneasy at this, and frowned like a man searching his memory, and said that as to the wording, the lord prince was slightly in error, for the word 'fugitive' did not occur in the king's responsibilities towards Wales, though it did in Llewelyn's undertakings towards England.

'The phrase, as I recall, is that King Henry promised, for himself and his heirs, "inimicum vel adversarium principis vel heredum suorum non manutenebunt contra principem vel iuvabunt." '

'Is that not to vary without differing?' said Llewelyn impatiently. 'Are not David and Griffith my enemies and adversaries, and is not Edward now maintaining and aiding them against me? If the word "fugitivum" had been added, what difference would it have made?'

To him there was indeed no difference, because he did not play with words like cards in a game, but held fast to conceptions of duty, undertaking and honour. What use was it to tell him, even if we had then grasped the rules of the game, that Edward could claim the exiles he entertained had not yet, from his land, attempted any move against the prince, to come within the terms of the treaty? Or that Edward's lawyers would have a thousand arguments, even if the exiles did continue their treasons from without, to prove the treaty was not infringed, and Edward not obliged to take any restraining action?

'He knows,' said Llewelyn quite positively, to himself rather than to us. 'He knows what he is doing! I have not evaded my obligations under treaty, there is no personal matter at issue between us. *He* has made the first move towards enmity. Take note of it!'

And so I did, in great trouble of mind, yet not quite recognising what I saw. For this was the moment when Llewelyn's belief in Edward's good faith was first, and fatally, shaken. Thereafter there was no return to the old, easy, honourable enmity, played out fairly and with honest men's regard and respect for an honest opponent. Never, until they came to blows. The battle-ground was the only ground where they could meet.

At night, when Llewelyn called me to him to play the crwth before he slept, he said, softly but abruptly after long silence: 'I have not yet pledged him fealty or done him homage. It is the only weapon I have, if he takes arms of his own choosing against me.' And he looked up at me and smiled, seeing my uneasiness. 'No, I have no hope of withholding any homage for ever. I owned it due, and I shall pay it. But, oh, Samson, if I could with honour, how gladly I would! To have Wales entirely separate, entirely free, a state equal with England!' And he closed his eyes upon the vision, for he was very weary. But in a moment he opened them again, and said wryly, quoting an old Welsh proverb: 'Truth is better than law! But how shall we prove it, against the tide, if Edward maintains that law is better than truth?'

CHAPTER VII

There is no man can say that Llewelyn acted rashly or in haste during that spring season after Griffith's flight, or took his own way without consulting his council. He was more than usually careful to sound out the opinions of the elders, and to weigh the consequences of what he did before taking action. He made no complaint to the king, and no sign of knowing where his enemies were lodged, much less of being aware that they stayed there with the king's sanction and approval, and virtually under his protection, until they themselves took action and showed all too plainly that they were based on Shrewsbury, and moreover were freely allowed to make armed sallies from that town, against the terms of the treaty. This forbearance on his part was primarily to protect Cynan, or any other royal servant of Welsh birth, who might come under suspicion of sending us secret information, but also to demonstrate to the whole world that the offence came first from Griffith's men, and Edward could no longer plead that they were not conducting themselves as 'enemies and adversaries of the prince, contrary to treaty'.

The first raid into Cydewain came late in February, a rapid strike from Shrewsbury into the lands south of Pool, and a quick retreat, driving off several head of cattle and burning barns full of grain. One villager was killed in that fight, and a number of families left homeless. Llewelyn, when he heard of it, sent for one of the chief men of that part, and took a detailed statement from him, as an eye-witness, that no one might be able to challenge his story. Then he wrote formally to Edward, setting forth the truth of the matter, whence the onslaught was launched, what booty had been taken, and by whose men, naming names, and making it clear that no intelligent man could fail to note how the king's officers, though they had not taken any part themselves, certainly had done nothing to prevent or restrain the attack, as undoubtedly they could have done. Nothing on such a scale was begun from Shrewsbury but the bailiffs of the town and the sheriff of the shire knew about it. But they had not banned the raid, nor taken any steps to punish the offenders since.

Soon afterwards there were two more such raids, briefer but also hurtful, into the commotes of Deuddwr and Ystrad Marchell. The Welsh there defended themselves stoutly, but could not pursue the retreating enemy into England. Each time Llewelyn wrote again, always fully, and in March King Edward finally sent a reply, in very correct but distant form, saying he had received the prince's letters complaining of various trespasses along his borders, partly following the reception of the prince's enemies into the march, partly from other causes, but not having with him those advisers he would wish to consult in the matter, he thought it better to leave dealing until his proposed Easter parliament in London, when all his counsellors would be present. And he asked that Llewelyn would send to that parliament legal envoys fully instructed in the matters at issue, and promised to do whatever was right according to treaty.

It was a very civil letter, and promised fairly enough, but there were things about it that troubled me, as though I saw again between the lines the heavy droop of the eyelid over the wide brown eye, hiding half the king's thoughts. Why, for instance, did he lump together these specific complaints concerning the traitors and rebels with the ordinary infringements to which we had grown almost accustomed along the border? They belonged in a category very different, and Llewelyn had most markedly distinguished between them. And where was the need of consulting all his parliament and council, nobles and clerics, some three months after he himself, consulting no one, had issued orders that the fugitives should be free to live as they pleased in Shrewsbury? The time to take counsel would have been before he opened his arms to traitors.

'He is playing the delaying game with me,' said Llewelyn, and the suspicions he nursed against the king grew larger and blacker. Nevertheless, he did send envoys, expert in law and fully briefed concerning the facts, to the king's Easter parliament, and of talk there was plenty, but still all of promises without action. King Edward wrote, early in May, that he had heard the complaints of the envoys, and had instructed the sheriff of Salop to fix a day for meeting according to custom, to discuss such complaints from both sides, and to make mutual amends for any injuries done. The present ambassadors, he claimed, were not fully empowered, and therefore no judgment could be arrived at in Westminster concerning the trespasses alleged to have been committed against the prince by the king's magnates.

This, after Llewelyn had named them! '*His* magnates!' he said angrily. 'The two greatest are *my* magnates, and my traitors, and he dares lay claim to them? What is he about? Is he so preoccupied with other business that he has not realised how great is this offence and this danger? Or is he welcoming it after his own fashion, and looking for profit from it, all in good time?'

Nor was he the first of us to begin to suspect as much, for Tudor had already voiced to me a similar dread. Moreover, before long the king's attitude hardened, and he no longer empowered de Knovill, the sheriff of Salop, to meet with our envoys and make amends in the old way, but ordered him to make none, nor accept any from us, until Llewelyn should have regularised his position by performing his homage to Edward, though up to that time no further arrangements had been made, nor any further demand, for that formality, and it was Edward's own illness that had prevented it before. We did not know of this prohibition until later, but we saw for ourselves that no meeting ever took place, and no redress was made. Moreover, the depredations of Griffith and David from Shrewsbury grew bolder, and were carried out by such formidable numbers that we suspected – it may be wrongly –

that their own forces were augmented by some of the king's men, perhaps not officially ordered, but willingly serving as auxiliaries, and sure that de Knovill would turn a blind eye.

Llewelyn complained once again, in terms stronger and more direct than before.

'Write to King Edward,' he said, 'that since my envoys returned from parliament there have been no less than six further raids made on my territories by the men of Griffith ap Gwenwynwyn, who are maintained and protected in the county of Salop, and their crimes publicly defended there. Of the booty they took on these six raids, from all the border commotes of my realm in this region, part has been sold openly in the markets of Shrewsbury and Montgomery, which can hardly be done without the knowledge of the authorities responsible for those towns. Four horses belonging to me have been taken from the groom travelling with them, and my man publicly beheaded. The peace can hardly be maintained if such felonies are permitted. Though the king's own men are not directly to blame, yet their maintaining and protecting of the criminals is as great a peril to peace as if they themselves had committed the offences. I therefore pray your Grace to do justice, and order your sheriff to arrest the felons, whose names, should they be still unknown to your Grace, I can and will supply. I expect justice and fair amends from you, and the prevention of such disorders in the future, and I beg for an answer to this letter by the bearer.'

This was sent on the twenty-second of May, from Aberyddon, and could hardly have been more explicit.

'But not wholly true, I doubt,' said Llewelyn bitterly, 'for I tell you, I am no longer sure that I expect from Edward any measure of justice or any amends.'

This was also the mood of most of us who had followed this exchange of letters. Looking back now, I am not sure how far we were just in our turn to Edward, who had all the complex business of state upon his mind, of which this affair of the Welsh traitors may have seemed to him only a minor part. Yet I am not satisfied with this, because of small, perilous points, like his insistence on treating David and Griffith and the complaints against them in just the same way as he treated Llewelyn's legal wrangles with de Bohun over disputed lands farther south, as though all these men were his own barons. This he knew was not the case, and his continued refusal to differentiate cannot have been anything but deliberate. At this time the only grievance he can possibly have had against the prince was the withholding of the money due under treaty, and again and again Llewelyn had stressed that it was ready and waiting to be paid if the king would also perform what was due from him under treaty, that is, to curb and compensate for the border infringements of which we had cause to complain. But Edward was a proud and domineering man, and a single grievance was enough, even if he had not chosen, in that month of June, to provide himself with a second and greater.

On the twenty-fourth day of the month he issued a summons to the prince of Wales to present himself at Chester on the twenty-second of

August, to take the oath of fealty and perform his homage as a vassal. True, he offered letters of safe-conduct for the journey into the town, but it was not yet forgotten, in Wales or in England, what the worth of Edward's word had been to Henry de Montfort at Gloucester, and to many another whom he chose to consider as rebels and obdurate, or his parole and solemn oath when he was hostage to Earl Simon, and turned recreant without a qualm.

The messenger who brought the summon was a young clerk we did not know, and therefore Llewelyn merely thanked him for his errand and offered him entertainment overnight, making no show of what he felt concerning the matter of the message. But the young man smiled, and said: 'I am entrusted also with another piece of news, I will not say all welcome, since it concerns a death, but perhaps not all unwelcome. And I am bidden to mention to you the name of Master Cynan, who taught me the message. For I am his sister's son, and I owe my place at court to him.'

'Then you are doubly welcome,' said Llewelyn heartily, 'and I look forward to hearing all your uncle's news over dinner. Speak out his message now, whatever it may be.'

'My uncle bids me tell you,' said the boy, 'that the king has received word, only a week ago, of the death of his aunt, the Countess Eleanor de Montfort, at the convent of Montargis, where she has lived since she left England. Her daughter, the Lady Eleanor, is now in the guardianship of her brother Amaury, still unwed, still unaffianced. To the best of my uncle's belief, it is she herself who has resisted all offers made for her. If you are still of the same mind, my lord, your way lies open.'

Late in the evening I looked for him and could not find him, though he had presided at the high table as always, with a calm face and a commanding eye, and been gracious to the young man, Cynan's nephew, who had brought him two such momentous and perilous messages. Not a word had he yet said to us of either, gone beyond indecision, beyond exultation or despair, forgetful of the king in the sudden sense he had of being near to Eleanor, as though the miles of air between had shrunk, so that he could all but stretch out his hand and touch her cheek. I should have known from old experience where to find him, and there he was, when I thought on the certainty at last, alone in his chapel before the small altar light, not on his knees but standing erect, his eyes upon the little silver glimmer that flowed reflected down the cross, and in his cupped hands before him the painted and enamelled medallion that Earl Simon had given to him long ago, the image of a child's grave and marvellous face in profile, with the heavy braid of dark-gold hair coiled upon her shoulder. Twelve years old she was when that portrait was made, hardly older when her father betrothed her to the prince, and now she was a woman grown, twenty-two years old, and I had not seen her for those ten years, and except in this image, Llewelyn had never seen her.

'God forgive me,' he said, very low, for he knew who came in to him without looking round, 'God forgive me that I can be glad, when she has lost a mother she surely loved. But if she has waited, as I have – oh,

Samson, if she has indeed waited for me with a single heart, as I for her – then even she may be glad at the heart of her sorrow. And when I see her face to face, and take her hand, it shall be my life's work to make her glad, and fend off from her every sorrow and every doubt. At Evesham I was promised I should be his son. The blind man blessed me, in Earl Simon's name and in God's name, and wished me fulfilment. It cannot fail!'

I wondered then if there had ever been times when he had doubted of winning her, for he was human like other men, and could not be always constant in faith. But it is all one, for I believe, whatever the exaltations and despairs of his spirit, he had never contemplated giving up the fight, and to die still pursuing an ideal is not defeat, but victory. Now it was so near that his extended hands touched the hem of her garment.

'I must not take her consent for granted,' he said, 'nor her brother's approval, either. She has never seen me, I am only a name to her, remembered for the sake of her father. But now at least I may send and offer for her in good faith, and she may say yes or no to me, and at no other person's leave but hers will I take her. There is a wine-ship of St Malo lying in Caergybi now, and ready to leave. My envoy and notaries shall sail with her, and with good weather they may be in France within the week. This Montargis is south of Paris, is it not?'

'Twenty leagues or so,' I said, 'perhaps twenty-five.'

'And Montfort l'Amaury, from which her family came?'

'Closer still, very close to the city.'

I had never been over the sea, but often, in the days when I was Llewelyn's envoy in Earl Simon's retinue, I had talked with his son Henry, and sometimes with the earl himself, about the lands in France which they had left to put down deep and powerful roots in England. As for Eleanor, I think she had never seen France until her mother took her away after Earl Simon's death at Evesham. She was born in Kenilworth, the youngest of her line, and the only daughter after five sons, three of them now dead, one just absolved from excommunication but still rightless and landless, one, the last, a scholar of Padua and a papal chaplain. To his care she was now committed, and with his goodwill, in no way bound by promises made to Edward, as her mother's had been, she could be married.

'In a month,' said Llewelyn, his eyes steady and bright upon the flicker of silver light on the altar, 'I may get her answer. I would to God I could go myself, if she consents, and bring her home, but I dare not turn my back here. It is her dower, and her son's inheritance, I am nursing now, and I must hold it safe for them. But, Samson, if she consents – you knew her, she will not have forgotten! –I would have you go as my proxy, and speak the words for me at our first wedding.'

Not until the wine-ship had sailed, and with it Cynfric and the prince's best notaries, with his proposals and gifts, did Llewelyn turn his attention to King Edward's summons to Chester. But when he did, it was clear that a part of his mind had been busy with it in secret. For things had changed greatly since he set forth to meet the king at Shrewsbury on the same errand, and illness prevented. He had then had no complaints or grievances against the king, and no suspicions of his motives and intentions. Now he had all these, and to a grave degree.

'Since we have some weeks of grace,' he said, 'this shall be done in proper form, and not I, but the council of the princes of all Wales, shall make the decision.' And he called such a council to assemble in the next month. All the magnates of his realm received his writs, and all attended.

Llewelyn read out to the assembly the king's summons, and laid it on the table before them.

'Less than a year ago,' he said, 'I received such a summons to Shrewsbury, and set out to obey it and keep that appointment. But then it was at a place and date agreed between us, and I had nothing to argue against it. I will not keep secret from you that I would gladly see Wales free of all obligation to any other monarch, if I might do so upon terms of peace with our neighbours, and without breaking faith. But that I cannot do, as yet. I made a treaty with King Henry, and I am bound by it still, and do not wish to repudiate the bond. Provided the king, as the other party to the agreement, keeps its terms and performs his own obligations, I have promised him homage and fealty and I shall pay it. But a treaty requires the keeping of faith by both sides. As to my own part, I have not until this time, as I see it, defaulted in any point. I have held back the recent moneys due under treaty, but I have said repeatedly that it is ready to be paid as soon as reparation is made for violations of my borders and acts of aggression against my men. Until a year ago I would have said, also, that King Edward has kept to terms, and respects the treaty. Now I am less certain. Hear my reasons, and tell me honestly if I am making much of little, and finding malice where none is.

'As to the infringements of our borders, they began before the king returned to England, and in part I know they are to be expected, and cannot be charged against him. Nor dare I claim my own men are invariably guiltless. But see how these troubles have increased during this year since he came home, when I expected them to be strongly taken in hand. I have written letter after letter, detailing every violence, every offence; he cannot say he is not informed. There has been offered no remedy.

'Again, and still closer to the mark, those traitors who conspired against my life fled at once, when charged, to England, and that in David's case when he had every opportunity to defend himself in court, and in Griffith's case even after his son's confession, and after clemency had been twice offered to him if he would come to my peace. They were sure of their welcome, or why make such a choice? Do all princes welcome their neighbours' traitors with open arms? Princes of goodwill, with no evil intent? Even if they shelter and maintain and tolerate them, do they leave them at large on the borders of the land they have offended, and allow them to raid across those borders at will? I think not. Yet this is what King Edward has done. He cannot say he was not told the full truth about their conspiracy, he cannot say he has not been told of their depredations from Shrewsbury. Still there has been no remedy, and no change.

'I have been long in looking beyond this point, but I am come to it now. In all that Edward now does, and all that he deliberately refrains from doing, I see the gradual erosion of the treaty of Montgomery. I am driven to believe that he means, when he has weakened it enough, to repudiate it, and be free to conduct the old enmity against Wales, in the hope of conquest, and that he will use my brother, and Griffith ap Gwenwynwyn, and any other such powerful tools as may fall into his hands, to that end.

'Now consider, and tell me, in the light of all this, how am I to reply to this summons to Chester?'

They hesitated long, pondering, all watching him with doubt and anxiety, his young nephews of Dynevor most earnestly. The elders among them, I think, had reached the same suspicion long before Llewelyn opened his mind to it. But it was Tudor who took up the argument, and very gravely.

'I have gone this road,' said he, 'a stage further even than the lord prince. This murder was planned for February of last year, while King Edward was still away from his kingdom – true enough. But how far away? In Gascony, and then on the road to Montreuil and Calais. For a good year before he came home there were couriers running back and forth to him across the sea, and half the business of England was in his hands, and half the court of England overseas in his company. Was it so hard for those who planned our lord's death to send their messages back and forth among the rest? How if the assassins were sure of their welcome in England because it was promised in advance?'

I was watching Llewelyn's face when this was said to him, and I knew then past doubt that such a thought had never so far entered his mind, being so alien to his own nature, which he was all too apt to attribute as candidly to his enemies. I knew, too, that now, at Tudor's instance, the notion struck deep as a sword-thrust, and would not be easily dislodged, however he contended against belief.

He sat roused and startled. 'Are you saying,' he asked with care, 'that the king may have been a party to the plot to kill me?'

'I am saying more. I am saying that the king may have instigated it,' said Tudor stoutly.

'I cannot believe it,' said Llewelyn. 'He may be willing to go far in his lust for conquest, but he could not stoop so low as to suborn murder. It is impossible!'

'How so, my lord? Only in the sense that this king regularly performs the impossible. It was impossible a noble prince should pledge his good faith time and time again in Earl Simon's war, and time and time again break it, but he did it. It was impossible he should give his parole, with the most solemn oaths, and callously discard it, but he did that also. Consider the circumstances! Has he not all his life been close to your brother? Has not David once before deserted Wales for England, and served Edward, even in arms, to the best of his power? Who was it wrote into the treaty the provisions for David, that he should be re-established in at least the equal of what he had before? Did Edward scruple to make use of a traitor then? To reward a traitor? You know he did not! Strange, indeed, if such an attempt on the lord prince's life were timed so carefully to herald the king's home-coming without implicating him, and he unaware of it, who had the most to gain. Stranger still, when it failed, that those who did the work should fly so directly into his arms, unless he owed them protection for their services. It would suit King Edward very well to have David installed in your place. David is his creature. You belong to yourself and to Wales.'

'You make too strong a case,' said Llewelyn, very pale, 'though I won't deny a certain logic. It may not be as you say, but only that circumstances give it colour.'

'True,' said Tudor, 'that it *may* not be as I have said, but not true that I make too strong a case. I make the case we must make, and must consider fully, before we can know what it is wise to do now. For the end of it is, that it very well *may* be as I have said. And that is more than enough. Has he behaved all this year as if intending justice, or has he nursed the murderers, given them aid and protection, allowed them to run riot over his borders with impunity, against your rights and your lands? You know the answer better than any!'

Then Madoc ap Griffith of Maelor spoke up. So many of the older princes had passed from the world in those last few years that Llewelyn's council showed as a circle of young men, with only a few of Tudor's generation to add experience to their ardour, and Madoc, who was the eldest of four brothers, ranked almost as an elder of Wales among these glowing boys. He was shrewd, reasonable and provident, a good man in council.

'There is one further point to be made,' he said. 'The king summons the lord prince into Chester to do his homage, and while Chester is a border town, it is also a royal garrison town, and to enter it is one thing, to leave it may be quite another. I have in mind the precedent of the lord prince's father, who accepted a king's word and went into the Tower as his guest, but never left that place again alive.'

'The king has offered safe-conduct,' said Llewelyn fairly.

'So he may, and he may even be honest in offering it. At the best, let us say he is. Even so, he puts no restraints upon your traitors and would-be assassins in Shrewsbury. We know he allows the Lord David access to his own court and person, what reason have we to suppose the king will curb his freedom if he attend him to Chester? A murderer can just as well strike in Chester as in Aber, once he is sure of the king's indulgence. And that's to put the best construction upon it. At the worst, if the king set them on once, or sanctioned what they suggested, so he can set them on again, and still, in public, wash his own hands.'

'Madoc is right,' said Tudor. 'It is not safe for the prince to go into any royal town where his enemies may move about at will, and in arms. It should not be asked of him. It was always the custom to meet in the open at the border, either at the ford of Montgomery or some similar spot, as the dukes of Normandy used to meet the kings of France on the Epte. If the king is sincere in wishing to continue the treaty and keep its terms, he should be willing to ensure that homage may be performed in a safe place. It is my view that the lord prince should take that stand, give his reasons, and decline to go into Chester.'

516

Then several of the others present also spoke, some doubting if the king could be planning expansion by murder, but all wary of allowing Llewelyn to go into an English city, where, if treachery was indeed contemplated, he would have no means of extricating himself. Llewelyn sat and listened to all, himself adding nothing more, and it was clear to me that he was greatly shocked by what had been suggested, but almost as much by his own slowness to recognise the full extent of his danger as by the danger itself. Had not David, even, in his devious way, constantly warned him against putting any trust in Edward, or taking his intelligent self-interest for goodwill?

'Give me your counsel, then, man by man,' he said when they had all done, 'am I to go to Chester or no.' And one by one they spoke out, from the eldest to the youngest, and every man said no. By the measure of the threat to the treaty, our one safeguard against England's greed, by the measure of the distrust all felt towards Edward, not one was in favour of compliance with the royal summons. It came to the youngest present, Llewelyn's nephew and namesake, not yet eighteen. The boy flushed red with passion as he said: 'No, do not go! For the sake of Wales, do not put yourself at risk.'

'I am at risk whether I go or refuse to go,' said Llewelyn, and smiled at the young man, who was dark and bright and beautiful, like his mother before him, 'I am at risk every day of my life, waking or sleeping. So are we all. It is a good thing to remember it, sometimes. But Wales I will risk as little as I may, God and you guiding me. I shall do as you have advised. I will write and set down yet once more those injuries I feel should be amended before I swear fealty, and the reasons why I will not come to Chester. I will make reasonable request for a safer place, and declare my own intent to keep honourably to terms if Edward will do the same.'

'It might also be well,' said Madoc, pondering, 'to prepare such a statement as may be offered to another authority, if the king is not minded to be accommodating.'

'I had thought of it,' said Llewelyn. 'Pope Gregory is a wise and just man, and easy of approach, as I have heard. I'll give my mind to it. If we are to look for friends in need, we'll go to the highest.'

Thus armed with the approval of all his magnates, the prince answered Edward's summons as he had said, courteously but decidedly, declaring his willingness to assume all the duties implied or stated in the treaty, provided Edward would do the same, and in particular charging him to end his illegal support for those who unquestionably had been and still were acting against the prince. This was the chief stumbling-block, being by far the most serious breach of treaty. If that was set right, and a safe and proper place agreed for their meeting, Llewelyn would take the oath and do homage as was due.

Edward, so we heard, was very angry when he received this letter. In the first place, whatever some men may have said, wise long after the event, concerning the previous considerable delay in regularising Llewelyn's position as vassal of the English king, there never had been any prior refusal or even avoidance, for only once before had the prince

517

been summoned to the meeting, and then he had set out without any resistance or reluctance to keep the engagement, and only Edward's illness had prevented the matter from being completed. Consequently this firm and reasoned refusal now came as a shock to the king, who could never bear to be denied. Whatever his own motives, he had certainly expected unquestioning compliance on Llewelyn's part. Then also, he had made the journey to Chester, certainly not only for the prince's sake, but publishing the fact that the homage was to take place there, and an offence against Edward's dignity and face was mortal. He could be generous to those who threw themselves at his feet in total submission – if that may be called generosity, for rather was it that when they so satisfied his desire to dominate he ceased to care about them – but firm and steady resistance drove him to ever-mounting ferocity. He at once issued another summons, ignoring everything Llewelyn had written to him concerning the place and the terms, to come to him at Westminster, three weeks after Michaelmas. Chester had been declined, he flung Westminster itself, the very centre of his power, in the prince's face.

'I have taken my stand,' said Llewelyn grimly, laying this new summons aside, 'and I shall not depart from it. I cannot go back. If his aim is to convince me he has designs on my life, he makes progress. From Westminster to the Tower is not so far, as my father discovered, but from the Tower to Westminster is a lifetime's journey. This I'll answer, but not until answer is due. Let him wait until the day he himself has appointed, and he shall have all the answer he deserves, and as civilly as before. But he is mad if he thinks I will come to Westminster at his bidding.' And he turned again, quite calmly, to the composition of his manifesto to Pope Gregory, who was Edward's friend and fellow-crusader, and yet was honest enough to be trusted by those who held Edward to be their enemy. We were well advanced with it by then, and it was a lengthy document, first outlining again, as a reminder, the main terms of the treaty of Montgomery, negotiated and blessed by a papal legate, which should by law and right govern the relations between Wales and England, then detailing the main counts on which England was now breaking those terms.

By then we knew that the crown was paying money to keep David and his household. The entire plot against the prince's life we set down for Pope Gregory to read, with all the raids mounted since that time from Shrewsbury, and winked at, or worse, by de Knovill, the king's sheriff, at the king's orders. And lastly we complained of the king's persistent citing of the prince to places unsafe for him, where his felons and traitors were free to move about him at will.

So grave a document was drawn up with the counsel and participation of all the chief law officers and elders of the prince's realm. Whoever says he acted of his own might, and arbitrarily, he lies. Whatever was wisest and most earnest in Wales took part in this appeal to the chief arbiter of Christendom. When it was drawn, we were as men drained and fulfilled, who could do no more, having done their best.

On the day that we had it ready, Cynfric and the notaries came back from Montfort l'Amaury with letters and messages from Amaury de Montfort and his sister, the Lady Eleanor.

So strange a day it was, hot and long and dusty with harvest, the sky a pallid blue clear as crystal, and never a cloud in all its bowl. And we were newly come to the full understanding of danger, and had accepted it and made our dispositions because there was no alternative, and yet that day was so full of the bright solemnity of joy that there was no room in it for any other passion or repining. From the moment Cynfric rose from his knee before Llewelyn, and showed him a beaming face, and held him out letters, there was no looking back.

'These,' said Cynfric, 'from Amaury de Montfort, on behalf of his sister and his house. And this from the Lady Eleanor, who speaks for herself, to the same effect, and to your comfort and worship.'

So he conveyed at once the purport of what was afterwards read and re-read many times for its savour, as slowly and lovingly as the finest wine satisfied a great thirst.

To the match, so long delayed but never abandoned, her kinsmen consented, in the terms of the settlement there was no dispute nor demur. But what best pleased Llewelyn was her own letter, written with her own hand. I know, for to me he showed it that night, in the summer twilight, after we had heard mass.

'For you knew her,' he said, 'and you will know the very voice in which she speaks these words to me, and I think it must resemble his voice, as surely her mind resembles his mind.'

She had written to him, at once with noble formality and so blazing and direct an intimacy that it was as if she walked towards us in the fields with outstretched hands:

'To the most noble and puissant Llewelyn, prince of Wales, greetings and reverence. My dear lord, though I have never seen you but through other eyes, yet I have known you from my childhood, and what my father did not live to tell me concerning his pledging of my hand to you, my mother did tell me, though only in regret when she also told me why she felt herself bound. But having been promised the impossible, I have chosen not to lower my eyes to anything less. The pledge made at my father's will I have kept at my own. That we may join our hands very soon, and see each other face to face, and that God may keep you safe and glorious until that day comes, is the prayer of your affianced wife, Eleanor de Montfort.'

I said: 'Yes, this is Eleanor. The very note of her voice, and the large, straight look of her eyes. She is his daughter, no question.'

'Now we have a double errand overseas,' he said, glowing. 'The envoys to the pope shall sail with you, they for Rome, you for Montargis, and with as little ceremony as possible and as little delay, for it may well turn the scale for us if we get our case into the pope's hands first. Edward will not be far behind, once he gets wind of it. Tudor has the ship in hand – there's a merchantman with a Winchelsea master loading timber and wool from the Aberconway granges, and he goes next to Calais for cloth of Flanders. Go to her, Samson, stand in my place with her and speak the vows for me, and come back in her household when she comes home to Wales. There is no man but you I want for my proxy.'

It needed no saying that I would do for him whatever he asked of me, and to do this I was glad from the heart, and yet it was a time when I was loth to leave him. Only when it came to such a separation did I truly see how the clouds had gathered over him black and heavy, and all in the course of a year, when he had done nothing to dare the thunder. To this day I do not know what to believe concerning the possibility that Edward procured or encouraged the conspiracy against Llewelyn's life. I do not know whether he actually was guilty, nor do I know whether I believe in his guilt. I do know, from what came later, that he was quite capable of it, but as at that time I doubt if he had considered such a course or recognised what use he could make of it. Rather the assassins first fell into his hands with their armed men, as apt tools for provocation without committing himself, and then he saw what use could be made of them, and once launched, how far the matter could be taken. If that be true, then David was guilty not only of Llewelyn's wrongs and dangers, but also of the temptation and corruption of Edward.

'I wish I left you in more settled case,' I said, 'with this business of homage and fealty safely over.'

'Or put clean out of the reckoning,' he said, and laughed. 'If I could refuse it outright without myself breaking treaty, I would do it. But if he comes to terms and does his part, it is due and I must pay it. Should I hope for him to continue immovable, and give me my bid for freedom?' And he shrugged off the tempting dream, for he did not believe it would go to that length, and knew the dangers if it did. 'God gives with one hand and takes with the other,' he said. 'If my secure peace is the price to be paid for Eleanor, I'll pay it without grudging.'

Of that journey, the first and last ever I made out of these islands, my telling must be brief. The ship from the Cinque ports took us up off Carnarvon from one of Llewelyn's own coastal boats, the abbot of Cymer, his chaplain, and the notary Philip ap Ivor, the prince's envoys to the papal court in Rome, and I, alone, sailing to join the household of Eleanor de Montfort at Montargis. It was then September, but a very pleasant autumn, blue-skied and breezy, excellent for sea-going, though I am not gifted in that kind, and even a brisk wind and some feathering of the waves were enough to make me queasy. The master of the ship was a great, thick-set man shaped like one of his own wine-casks, and of the independent and masterful mind of all the Cinque ports men. He owned his ship; and it was to him the same as owning a kingdom. Even Edward, after the civil wars, in which the south-coast sailors had favoured Earl Simon's cause, had found it expedient to make peace with them on generous terms, and turn their minds to the future and the promise of good trading conditions and royal patronage, rather than trying to take revenge for their siding against him. He was not always so reasonable with those who wielded no sort of power to make his revenges cost him dear.

This master, who had been one of the last to abandon the piratical harrying of the royal ships at the end of those wars, and had held out until it was clear not only that he could do no further good, but also that he had his chance of coming to the king's peace without penalty, talked freely of those days and his own exploits, and spoke the name of Earl Simon boldly and simply as one revered and remembered, as saint and legend. Also he knew many ballads and songs about the earl and his heroic deeds, and his miracles, and could sing them very well, and when he found that I was interested he repeated them over to me that I might take them down and learn them. That was enough to seal him my friend, and he put himself out, the weather down the coast being easy and brisk, to show me something of the governance of a ship, the use of the steering oar, and how the great sail might be manipulated to suit the wind. But I did not tell him that I had known that great man who was his idol, nor that I was bound to the dwelling of the earl's only daughter, to speak the marriage words with her in my prince's name.

He was a good man, stout and fearless, and both able and daring in his use of his ship. I would we had had him on the return journey, it might have turned out very differently. What he could not run from he might very well have rammed.

All down the coast of Wales we had favourable winds and clear skies, and I saw the long, beautiful shore of my land as I had never yet seen it. But after the passage of the headlands of Dyfed the winds grew stronger and the sea rougher across the open water, and round the toe of England the crests of the waves were white and high. I was grown used to it by then, and could walk the deck securely even as we leaned and creaked in the swell, and I began to take pleasure in the voyage for its own sake, which had been to me, until then, only a mild hardship between me and the fulfilment of my errand. I marvelled no longer at our master's sense that his own element, which he rode and ruled and endured more than half the time he spent living, was the true and manifest reality and freedom, and the land was a kind of prison full of limits and bars, where he felt himself cramped and diminished. Once in the mid-sea there was no man was his master, neither king nor pope, though he respected both as he required to be respected.

It was a long journey across the south parts of England, so drawn out that I learned somewhat of the ground of English power, which habits mainly in this southern land. Here are those parts fronting France, which is a very great country and in peace and alliance with England, hence the power is redoubled as long as this amity continues. We of Wales habit but a part of the western fringes, and have no such access to the wider world of Christendom. Popes and kings listen to us as best they can, but we are a voice from very far away, and out of a strange land. England lies between us and all those ears that otherwise might hear our complaint.

In sudden cloud and mild rain we came to our master's home port of Winchelsea, and put ashore part of our cargo, all the timber and half, perhaps, of the wool. Then we made across to Calais, in the last week of September, and there disembarked, the abbot and his colleagues to take

521

the long road to Rome, I with them as far as Paris, for under the abbot's holy shadow travel was safer and more respected by the sheriffs. And at Paris we separated.

I had but a short way to ride from the capital city, to the castle of Montfort l'Amaury, from which place Earl Simon's family took their being and their name, and where Eleanor's cousins of the French branch made their principal home. For a party from that place was to ride with me to Montargis. I had very gay company, therefore, for the rest of the journey, those twenty or so leagues to the convent founded by Earl Simon's sister Amicia. Round this family foundation there lay rich estates and a fair town, and all the guest apartments of the convent, and the houses of grace to which the Countess Eleanor had retired with her household after Evesham, were full of the relatives and knights and friars attendant on Eleanor, her daughter. She was niece and cousin to kings, and provided already with the household of a princess.

We came there in the late afternoon, in time to show me those fair fields about the convent in the slanting light before sunset, all golden. It was then past the middle of October, but still serene and mild. Amaury de Montfort came to me in my lodging to conduct me to his sister.

He was then about twenty-seven or twenty-eight years old, cleric, scholar and wit, a papal chaplain and a man to be reckoned with in Christendom. I had not seen him since he was fifteen, in the old days at Kenilworth, and I doubt if I should have known him again, for he had grown somewhat away from the family build and the family face, hair and complexion darkening with time, his countenance lengthened and narrowed instead of keeping the massive, bony grandeur of the earl's imperial head. His cheeks were olive and lean, his eyes very dark and deep set, and intensely brilliant. They say he had a sharp and biting tongue that made him many enemies, but that I had no occasion to experience, for to me he was open and gracious after the manner of all his house.

He had not known, until my coming, who would be sent from Wales to be Llewelyn's proxy, and but for my name I am sure he would not have known me, as there was no reason he should after so long. But the name Samson touched some old memory. He looked at me with fixed attention, and then unlocked his thin dark brows and said: 'Yes, now I remember you! You were the prince's man with my father, at Kenilworth before Lewes.'

'I was,' I said, 'but there was no reason why I should stay in your mind for so many years on that account.'

'But on another account, perhaps,' he said. 'My brother Guy, when he escaped from England and the king's prison after Evesham, told us the whole story of that battle. You were bidden to leave my father's battle-line and go with the bishops, and you refused to leave him.'

'So did others,' I said. 'Earl Simon was not an easy man to leave, once drawn to him.'

'Some did not find it hard,' said Amaury, suddenly grim, and I knew he was thinking of all those young men who had made the earl their idol for a while, but fallen away when the road grew steep and dark. And in particular of Henry of Almain, the best of them and the most bitterly resented. Amaury had never reconciled himself to the loss of his family's English possessions or his own clerical prebends in England, and continued from France and Italy to wage legal war against all who now held them. I might even have considered him far more likely than Guy to have committed that murder at Viterbo, had it not been known and proved that he was in Padua at the time, and had not spoken with his brothers for some time previously.

I asked after Guy, as we walked together through the courts of the convent and into the cloister garden from which Eleanor's apartments opened. For Pope Gregory had ordered his incarceration in one of the fortresses in papal territory, after his submission, and all we knew since then was that he had been absolved from excommunication, but not from any of the other bans imposed upon him.

'He is still a prisoner in Lecco,' said Amaury. 'It is not the most rigorous of custodies, it might well be possible to slip out of it, and our cousin John would be willing to set him up in some sort of command if he could, but it's impossible anywhere in papal lands. And all this is due to Edward!' It needed no great penetration to see that there was no love lost between these two cousins, however well-disposed the cousins of Montfort l'Amaury might be. We had reached the green enclosure outside Eleanor's rooms then, and suddenly Amaury looked up straightly at me, and said seriously:

'You realise how ill Edward may take this marriage?'

I was surprised, and said what seemed to me obvious, that no one in his right wits could possibly attribute any share in Guy's guilt to his innocent young sister, who had never taken any part in the dissensions of the past.

Amaury smiled again, but darkly. 'How well do you know Edward?' he said, but not as one requiring or expecting an answer. And I thought no more of it then, for we had stepped into the cool stone doorway, and entered a long, low-ceilinged room, lit by two candelabra branching from the walls. At the far end of the room, where long windows still let in the sunset light, three women were sitting in tapestried chairs about a table, two of them stitching at the same piece of sewing, a blue, brocaded gown spread across the board to let them take each a sleeve. The third, who sat with her back to the sunset, with her book lifted before her to receive the light, was reading to them in a full, clear, childlike voice, low-pitched and moving. I did not know the poem she was reading, but it was a love-poem. When she heard our steps on the stone she laid by her book, and rose and came round the table to meet us, and so stepped from the sunset light that made an aureole about her, as round a virgin on an altar, to the light of the candles that fell full upon her face and breast, and caused the hieratic image to flower suddenly into a woman sculptured in dark gold and ivory.

At twelve years old she had been tall for her age. At twenty-two she was only a little above the middle height, but so erect and slender that she seemed taller than she was, and the coil of braided hair above her great ivory brow, still honestly wide and plaintively rounded like a child's, caused her to move with a marvellous, upright grace, as if she balanced a heavy crown on her head. She wore a gown of a colour hardly darker than parchment, but its silken texture and the candle-light turned it to the same muted gold as her hair. And she gazed at me, between long lashes almost black, with those wide-open, wide-set, translucent, green-golden eyes I remembered, so huge and clear that only honesty and goodness dared look straight into them, for fear of their mirroring magic.

I looked at her, and I saw again the young, ardent, grave face of her best brother, Henry, dead with his father at Evesham, and the noble, austere head of Earl Simon himself, as first I saw it in the church at Oxford, with great eyelids closed, and deliberate lips silently forming the measured words of his prayers. She was all the nobility of her house in one flower, and all the beauty. Those English chroniclers who afterwards wrote of her in superlatives, as most beautiful and most elegant, did not lie.

She stood with the soft candle-light flowing down the folds of her gold and reflecting from her whiteness, with a half-smile on that mouth of hers, that folded together firmly and purely as the leaves of a rose, and gazed upon me for a moment with the sweet, courteous grace she showed to all strangers. But as I stepped before her into the same charged space of light, and she saw me clearly, her eyes burned brighter gold, and her lips parted in joy.

'Master Samson!' she said, and held out her hands to me.

I clasped and kissed them, moved beyond measure that she should remember and recognise me after so long. Behind me Amaury said drily: 'I see you need no office of mine here, you are old friends.' And he went away quietly and left us together. The two ladies went on serenely with their sewing. And I sat down with Eleanor de Montfort, and talked of Llewelyn. And it was as it had been at Kenilworth, when she was a child, and questioned me of Wales, and of the prince I served, and learned of me that he was a man to be loved, since I so plainly loved him.

On the eve of the marriage, in the cloister garden by the fountain, she said to me: 'You were the voice that first sang him for me, in such clear tones that I could not but be drawn. And you were the brush that first drew and painted him before my eyes, in such radiant colours that my child's heart fixed and elected him. And then my brother Henry also talked of him much, with affection and admiration. I never saw my father again, after he had finally met with Llewelyn, but when my mother told me that he had accepted the prince's proffer for me, it was as though a choice I had made in my own heart was confirmed and vindicated and approved, as well by heaven as by my father. For to me he had always been as the pillar of a church, quite upright and incorruptible, and his will, which had never been other than gentle and loving to me, was heaven's will. What use was it, then, for her to tell me in the same breath that what had been promised could never be? I understood her reasons, but I knew she was wrong, that it could be and would be, and all I had to do was wait.'

'And if he had been less captured, and less constant?' I said. For marriages are made and unmade for many noble children, with old bridegrooms who die, with distant bridegrooms who are cut off by war or by changes of alliance, with opportunist bridegrooms who happen on a better match before the first can be completed. Few such arrangements, however sworn, would have survived the years and the disputes that had threatened theirs.

'That was not how you had shown him to me,' she said serenely, and smiled. 'It was he who asked for me, at a time when others might well have been thinking better of the idea, had they toyed with it, for it was the last summer, and Edward was already loose, and the shadows gathering, and all those who looked first to their own security were drawing off and changing sides. If he pledged himself to me then, and was as I had seen him through your eyes, then he would not lightly turn from what he had sworn.'

We were sitting together on the stone rim of the fountain, before the evening came down, and she put out her hands and cupped them in the sparkling fall of the water, letting it fill her palms and spill over in silver. She gazed into the quivering pool as into a crystal, with a face grave, assured and tranquil.

'But even if he had changed,' she said, without sorrow or blame or wonder, 'that could be no reason for me to change. A woman should have her own truth and troth, as well as a man. If I could not marry according to my father's will and my own, then there is room enough for me at Montargis, within the rule as without.'

'And did you never have any doubts of the ending?' I asked.

'No,' said Eleanor, and smiled, opening her fingers and letting the mirror of silver dissolve through them into the stone bowl below. 'None. Never.'

The next day, in the church of Montargis, in the presence of a great company of her kinsmen and knights, she was married in absence, and made her vows to Llewelyn, prince of Wales. And mine was the hand that clasped her hand, and the voice that spoke the proxy words for my lord, after so long of waiting.

Before that celebrant company, with those vows in my ears, and that woman beside me, a woman like a lamp of alabaster shedding radiance, I caught my breath once on the words given me to say, and Eleanor's beauty pierced me through suddenly like a sword of flame, and for that one moment it was no golden girl of twenty-two years hand-in-hand with me, but a slender woman approaching forty, raven-haired and iris-eyed, and it was to Cristin, no less than to Eleanor, that I spoke the sacred vows of love, not knowing then if I should ever see her again, but knowing that I must never hope for more than the bliss and pain of beholding her face and standing ready to serve her, even if time turned back and restored her to Wales and me.

So sudden and so keen was that visitation that I turned my head to look her in the eyes, those deep eyes that changed colour with the light from clear grey to royal purple. There never was a time that we two met, and I looked for her among many, but when I found her her eyes were already fixed and unwavering upon me, drawing me down into her being. But here I came to myself, beholding a different vision, the face beside me younger and lovelier, and not turned to me, but gazing straight before her towards the altar. A pure face in profile, clear as a queen on a coin, one large, confiding eye open wide to confront whatever came, a folded, dreaming mouth, Eleanor as Llewelyn had viewed her for ten long years of waiting, in the medallion her father had given him, looking with a grave, high confidence into her future, towards a bridegroom and an estate fitting her nobility. She, too, had waited, she who had never swerved from her certainty, and admitted no doubts. None! Never!

She had me by the hand, and her clasp was warm and vital and sure. And I, too, believed. I was ashamed to disbelieve, having her silent faith like a pillar of flame beside me. So I completed with all my heart the words that justified her, and renewed and registered my own vows in heaven.

CHAPTER VIII

There was a week or more of preparation and packing after the marriage, for it is no light matter to get such a large household moving, with all the treasure and plate and clothing belonging to its members, and such a number of officers and servants in attendance, not to mention several horses belonging to some of Eleanor's knights, who had favoured and valuable beasts and would not leave them behind. There was also some discussion about the best way to proceed, for the distance to St Malo from Montargis was much the same as to Calais, but to embark at St Malo would shorten the sea route by several days. Amaury pointed out that to go by St Malo it would be necessary to enter Brittany, and the duke of Brittany was close ally of England, and his son married to King Edward's sister Beatrice. He did not expect any interference with our passage, but had pricking thumbs about the advisability of letting any word of his sister's marriage reach Edward until we were all safely in Wales, and the whole matter an accomplished fact. But as against any risk from that quarter, we could save a number of days on the journey, and be in Wales the sooner. In the end it was agreed to send an agent ahead to charter two ships at St Malo, while the slow cortege followed at leisure and halted at Avranches until all was ready. And that we did.

Winter travel is no light undertaking, and that promised to be a hard and capricious winter, but Eleanor's party rode in very good spirits, and everything then seemed hopeful and bright. We were delayed at Avranches for most of November and into December, first by the need to find two good ships, and then by very contrary winds which kept us from embarking for some while longer. But before Christmas everything was ready, and the prospect of keeping the festival at sea did not in any way discourage Eleanor. All the lading was done before her own party rode from Avranches, and on the eve of Christmas Eve we put to sea.

Eleanor would have me stay in the leading ship with her immediate household and officers, her brother, her two ladies, and some of her knights, the remainder with most of the friars and the minor officers and the horses being in the second ship. These ships of France were built somewhat higher out of the water than the Winchelsea ship in which I had made the passage over, and I thought were less manoeuvrable to the winds, and less speedy and stable, but they had more comfort for the ladies, the stern-castle having a very neat and solid cabin built within it, and the fore-castle the like, though smaller. We had good winds to take us out from the Channel westwards, the seas were not rough, indeed the master complained rather of lack of wind than of too much, and altogether, even in cramped quarters, Christmas passed in simple but devout good cheer. For Eleanor was happy, and her happiness made a glow all about her that exorcised all fears and doubts. There was never any lady so ready and careful as she – but it was not care, for it came to her by nature – to see to the comfort and content of all those who served her, and the more joy she had, the more did she wish to see every soul about her joyful.

In those days, while we were making well out to sea to clear the toe of England, she would be always out in the weather, cold though it might be, with a cloak wrapped about her and a scarf over her hair, narrowing those eyes that never else were narrowed, to peer as far ahead as vision could carry her, towards Llewelyn and Wales. She walked unconcerned along the planking when the ship swayed, and balanced on the fore-castle like a willow, yielding and recovering, leaning her long fingers on whatever sailorly arm offered, and smiling towards her lord.

'What is that land?' she said, pointing where a low blue line, heaving just clear of the long level of the waves, and barely darker and more stable than their flow, showed ahead of us. 'Is that England? Cornwall, it would be here?'

The master said no, not England, but the first glimpse of the nearest of the Isles of Scilly. 'We'll round them, and keep well clear. You may not so much as see England, but only your granite cliffs of Dyfed, and the coast of Wales.'

'Soon, soon, I pray!' she said. But he said it might be several days yet, for the winds grew slack and capricious, and he could but do what was possible. And then she said, with that immense sweetness she had, that she was in his hands, and so rested, and would not for the world press either him or God, but was grateful to both.

Such she was, this princess of Wales. And of such there are few. But shortly we learned even more of her, and she it may be, of herself. For we grow by conflict, and whatever challenges us calls forth what is within, and often we have guests dwelling with us we did not know until fate knocked at their door.

It must have been about the turn of the year, though my memory here is at fault and I cannot pin down the exact day, while we were circling round those blue-green islands in the ocean, leaving England well away on our right hand and out of sight, that the look-out called down from his chilly nest above the mast to warn of two sail bearing south towards us, one upon either hand. It was no way strange that they should be here, in this stretch of sea, since the islands were furnished from Cornwall, but the separate courses of these two seemed to him to be curiously matched, as though they trimmed sail to keep abreast but apart. They looked like ordinary merchantmen, and he gave warning of them only for the steersman's information, lest he should be surprised by the apparition of one or the other on his flank.

The steersman shouted back to him, and as the two shapes emerged a little larger and clearer out of the faint sea-mist, he shifted his course by a point to pass between and give them both a wide berth. It seemed to us, watching them grow from mere bobbing gulls to looming barques, lower-built than our ship but larger and faster, that they closed in slightly towards us as they came. And from the nearest of the islands, as I looked astern towards our sister ship, I saw a long, dark shape suddenly surge out from the hazy blue of the shore, like a sped arrow, one of those low, snake-like rowed boats such as the Norse raiders or stray pirates from Scotland and the northern islands used. The look-out noted it at the same moment, and sang out its discovery.

'I do not like this,' said Amaury, watching the three, and noting how they ringed us. 'Surely the sea-ways are cleared of piracy since the peace?'

'Never cleared,' grunted the master, brooding, 'but in more than four years I've met with none. This looks too planned to be honest.'

'Can we run between them and get clear? If they have to come about to chase us we may gain time enough to outrun them.'

'We can try,' said the master, and try he did, with a rigged sail and a relay of rowers, but those two ships coming to meet us had gauged their own powers and ours, and had time and seaway enough to close in before we could slip between them. By this time, when we were forced to ease to avoid ramming or being rammed, or closing within their reach, we could see the men moving on board both of them, assured and intent, too plainly giving all their attention to us. They seemed well crewed, but showed no arms, and thus far no disposition to attack. Their tonnage, though, appeared to be considerably greater than ours, and very well tended and maintained, no beggarly keels such as prey on the lonelier sea-routes for a murderous living.

There was a big fellow in a frieze cloak on the fore- castle of the ship closing slowly in on us from the left. I caught the gleam of mail when the wind ripped back the folds of the frieze, and saw that he wore sword and dagger. Eleanor's knights were all out on the deck with us, quiet and watchful, and more than one was already buckling on his own harness. Eleanor stood in the doorway of her cabin, her two ladies peering anxiously over her shoulders. She said not a word so far, she simply listened to what those said who knew the seas better than she, and watched the approach of those two unknown barques with measuring eyes, waiting for enlightenment.

A long, echoing hail came to us across the water. The cloaked man cupped his hands into a trumpet about his mouth and bellowed down the wind: 'Heave to! I have a message to you!'

'Send it from there!' roared the master back to him in French for his English, and still we crept forward. They risked damage to themselves if they tried to lay alongside us too suddenly, without crippling us first, and now we were fully abreast of the pair, in between them, and even drawing past by inches. Amaury saw it, and hissed at the captain: 'Now, break for it and row, we may clear them yet!'

The captain bellowed an order, the rowers heaved mightily, the ship leaped under us, and indeed we might have got clear away, if we had not been so absorbed in the two large ships as to forget the long-boat from the islands. It had circled our sister ship, which was slower than we, and lain off at a small distance, watching and listening. It seemed harmless to us, formidably though it was manned, for it was so low that boarding us from that serpent-shape would have been impossible. But that was not its purpose. As our rowers bent into their oars, so, with a sudden shout, did theirs. The boat sheered forward through the water like a dart, over-hauling us at speed. Its raised, iron-shod prow sliced through our steering-oar, severing it with a violent shock and flinging the steersman across the deck to lie stunned under the gunwale, then plunged on, hardly checked, to tear all the oars on our steerboard side to flinders. The ship was brought up shuddering, and heeled about round its crippled side, splinters of wood flying. In the island boat, as it sailed past us and drew clear in a flurry of spume, the crew shipped their oars and stooped their heads low for protection, letting their razor-sharp prow do the work of destruction for them.

We were flung about the deck like leaves in a gale, and clung by what-ever came to hand until our helpless ship partially righted herself in the water. By that time the larger of the two pirates had closed in on our other flank, until with a creaking and tearing of timbers she ground our remain-ing oars to pulp, and dragged groaningly alongside us. Then suddenly great numbers of men came surging up from where they had lain hidden, all along her side, dragged us close with grapples, and came swarming over the gunwale, with weapons naked in their hands, twice, thrice the number we had on board.

The tall man in the cloak, red-bearded and armoured, advanced upon us at their head. We closed in a half-circle about the women, and drew in our turn.

'Put up,' said the stranger, halting ready, 'and come to no harm, or fight, if you see fit, and take the consequences. You would be ill-advised.'

It hardly needed saying. We were a handful, and he had a small army. Nevertheless, Amaury in his rage, and perhaps seeing before the rest of us what lay behind this interception, launched himself forward and lunged at the man with all his might, but the other merely stepped back from him, not accepting single combat, and three or four of his henchmen closed as one on Amaury and bore him down by sheer weight, wrenching the sword out of his hand and clubbing him to the deck with the hilt of it. He lay stunned, with a trickle of blood flowing from his scalp, and then all his fellows leaned hand to hilt and would have flung themselves upon a like fate, if Eleanor had not caught two of them, the nearest, by the sleeve, and cried sharply: 'No!'

It drew all eyes to her. Until then she had been clinging unnoticed in the doorway of the cabin, shaken by the heaving and shuddering of the ship, and in deep shadow behind our ranks. But at her voice everyone fell still, and when she stepped forward we opened a passage for her, though watch-fully, and keeping close on either side.

'No,' she said, 'no more of that! I want no killing, and no violence.' And she went to her brother, and so did the two Franciscans of her company, and raised him gently, dazed and bleeding. 'Take him and tend him,' she begged them. 'I must speak with this man.' There was no fear in her voice or her face. I think I never saw her afraid for herself. And the friars helped Amaury away to a pallet in the fore-castle, and she remained, facing her captor squarely, slender and straight and gallant, without pride or pre-tence. He looked at her beauty, and was struck dumb for a moment.

'If you have business here,' she said calmly and courteously, 'your business is with me. All here are my people, I take responsibility for them. What is it you want with us?' And she added, in the same serene tone: 'You do not look like a pirate, and I had not thought that pirates would be so well-found as you seem to be, or need so many men to crush so few. We are two unarmed ships on a lawful journey. Of rights you have none. Of demands clearly you have. Let me hear them.'

'I am armed,' said the bearded man, 'with authority enough, and have a commission to perform, and I intend to perform it. There is no intent to offer either offence or violence to you, madam, nor to any who serve you if they obey my orders.'

'Whose orders?' said Eleanor. 'Let me know your name and title. Are you a knight?'

'Madam, I am. But my name and rank are very little to the purpose. The orders I give, I have also been given.'

She smiled a little, not unkindly, as if she did not wonder that he preferred to keep his name out of the affair, but she did not press him. 'Given,' she said, 'by whom?'

'By the king's Grace, Edward of England.'

'Ah,' said Eleanor, unsurprised, 'I had begun to understand as much. I have never heard that my cousin had a trading interest in piracy, so I imagine his interest is in my person rather than in any ransom I could pay.'

Her opponent could have been in little doubt then with whom he spoke, but there were two other women standing there in the background, wide-eyed and pale, and he wished to be certain. 'You are,' he questioned, 'the Lady Eleanor de Montfort?'

'No,' said Eleanor, looking up at him within hand's touch, with those wide, gold-flecked eyes that showed him the mirror image of his own diminution before her. 'I am Eleanor de Montfort, princess of Wales.'

He was struck out of words, for this was not within his orders, but he could not disbelieve her, confronted with those eyes. 'And what does a king of England require of the princess of Wales,' she asked patiently, 'that has to be extracted by these extravagant means?'

'These ships,' he said, recovering himself in some suppressed fury, 'and all in them are taken into custody at the king's orders. You and your ladies shall not be molested, but the men of your household will be kept under guard until the king's pleasure is known.'

She frowned over that, and said carefully, no longer baiting him but bargaining seriously: 'These ships are under charter to me, but their masters and crews have no responsibility in this matter. All Master Derenne has done is to hire to me his ships, his men and his skills, and the king has no right or need to exact any penalty for that, whatever he means to do with me and mine. Have I your word that as soon as we are on land I shall be allowed the use of my own treasury to pay what I owe, and that ships and crew will be permitted at once to return to France? It would be unjust to detain them.'

'I cannot give you such a guarantee,' he said, uneasy, 'it is not within my competence. It does not rest with me.'

'Be so good, then, as to make known to the king that I make that request for them. That at least, I suppose, you can do?'

'I can and will,' he said.

'And may I keep my friars with me? They will attempt nothing to trouble you.' She did not ask for her brother, for she knew by then that whoever was allowed to go unbound, he would not be. There was a heavy load upon her, and she had to think for all her people. The friars were allowed her. 'Where are you taking us?' she asked.

'Into Bristol, madam.'

'Very well,' said Eleanor, and turned to leave him, as though that ended her need to endure his presence. But she looked back to add, thinking of the shattered oars and the broken steer-board: 'They have good repair yards in Bristol, I understand. I hope the king will bear the cost of putting Master Derenne's ships in order.' And she went away without a glance behind, to where the friars were cleansing and binding up Amaury's broken head.

They put an armed crew aboard either of our ships, and rigged a makeshift steering-oar to get us into port. Our sister ship was not damaged, having been boarded without bloodshed in the consternation when we were crippled. All of us men aboard they disarmed, and transferred us to their own vessels, though Amaury bitterly complained of being forced to leave his sister in the hands of such fellows, and with only her servants and friars to guard her. I doubt if he truly feared any affront to her, for she was the king's cousin and the king's captive, and Edward would have required account of any injury done to her, however he himself injured her. It was rather a way of being insulting to our captors, since Amaury could do them no other harm, and a means of ridding his heart of some of the venom and frustration he suffered. For indeed our happy expedition had turned into disaster, and we had no way of getting word to anyone who might help us, Llewelyn least of all.

In the larger of the Bristol ships they let us take exercise on deck under close guard at times, and that was the only glimpse we had, for the rest of that voyage, of Eleanor, the distant flutter of a scarf or the gold of her hair unbraided to the wind, on the stern-castle of Master Derenne's ship in line before us. She, I think, complained not at all. It would have altered nothing, as Amaury's ferocity altered nothing, and she was more concerned with ways of dealing that might, perhaps, lighten the burden for some of us, and better our sorry circumstances. She thought much, and was wary of both resentment and despair, neither of which could be profitable. Before we reached Bristol she had made slaves of most of those seamen who had been sent to capture her, and friends of more than one, though the knight who had planned the capture and been in charge of it she avoided and treated with cold civility.

Concerning this man I have since learned something, though not much, and after we were landed in Bristol I never saw him again. It is possible that Edward, though willing to hire and pay for such dubious services, did not particularly desire to be reminded of them afterwards. The man's name was Thomas Archdeacon, and Cynan later kept close watch on the rolls, and discovered that in May of the year then beginning, twelve hundred and seventy-six, the sheriff of Cornwall was empowered to pay to a man of that name the sum of twenty pounds, to cover his expenses in carrying out some unspecified mission on the king's behalf off that coast. There cannot be much doubt what that commission was. I would not say he was very well paid for his trouble.

The year was already in its first weeks when they put us ashore at Bristol, and we were hurried away into close confinement in Bristol castle, to await the king's orders as to our disposal. There, as I learned later but guessed even then, Eleanor exercised her reasoning, her firmness and her masterly good sense to support the power of her beauty, and so worked upon the governor of the castle that we were well used, as far as leniency could be taken without risking our escape, for none of us had given any parole, and it would have been worth the castellan's office if he had let us get away from him. She also procured the release of the ships, and saw to it that their expenses were paid at her cost. Truly she was Earl Simon's daughter, feeling and generous to the least, as to the greatest, who served her, perhaps more punctilious to the least because of their greater need. Nor would she owe a penny, nor rest until the last owing was paid.

At the end of January we knew, from the activity about us, that King Edward had made clear his pleasure concerning us. Eleanor with her personal household was to be conducted to honourable captivity – such is the phrase of those who lose all honour by enforcing it – at Windsor. Her brother and her knights were bound for imprisonment in Corfe castle until it should please Edward to release them. Helpless to protect Amaury and his fellows, Eleanor turned her mind to enlarging her permitted household to contain as many of us as she could. She fought for the friars, with good hope, since the orders command a degree of reverence, and most men prefer not even to seem to be oppressing the church. And she fought also for me, insisting that I was her clerk, and she could not be adequately looked after without me. Edward might still have known me at sight, and left me to rot. But the governor of Bristol did not know me, and my Latin and French being adequate to convince him, he accepted her plea and added me to her company.

The day I was restored, which was the eve of our departure under strong guard for Windsor, she talked with me very gravely and intently. It seemed to me that she had lived a year's experience in one month, and grown taller, more serene and of greater authority, all the lines of her glorious face drawn finer and clearer as though challenge made her doubly alive.

'Samson,' she said, 'help me to understand, for I must know what is expected of me in order to be able to confound it, and what is believed of me if I am to refute it. Why has my cousin done this cruel and indefensible thing to me? He knows he has no right, law has no part in it. What does he hope to gain by imprisoning me? Or to prevent?'

I told her then what Amaury believed to be true, and what he had hinted to me when I came to Montargis. 'You realise how ill Edward may take this marriage?' In our crowded cells in Bristol he had elaborated on that theme with bitter venom.

'Your betrothal to Llewelyn was made by Earl Simon when those two were allies with the barons of the Provisions against the king's power. It was a very potent alliance, though it failed in the end for other reasons. Amaury believes Edward sees the accomplishment of the marriage now as a deliberate step towards reviving a baronial party, again allied to Wales, against the crown. That he sees you as the focal point of a dangerous rebellion aimed at his sovereignty and his life.'

She thought that over for some minutes in silence, and then shook her head with decision. 'I do not believe any sane man could entertain such a fear. It is ten years since the party of the barons was broken. What signs of life has it shown since? After the first disordered years of revenge, everything has been at peace, and everyone has been glad of it. If you raised the cry of de Montfort now, not one magnate would rally to it. Not one! If I know it so clearly, Edward would have to be a little mad not to know it. He has nothing to fear from that quarter.'

'Amaury would say,' I told her, 'that on that subject Edward *is* a little mad. Especially since the death of Henry of Almain.'

'Yes,' she owned sadly, 'for that indeed he may hate us, but it surely gives him no cause to fear us. I could believe that he might strike against me for his revenge, if I was the nearest de Montfort. But out of genuine fear of some conspiracy against him . . .? Amaury believes this,' she said, considering. 'Do *you* believe it?'

'No. Edward is as shrewd a judge of possibilities as most men, he knows he is as firmly seated on his throne as any man who ever occupied that seat. He knows the old baronial cause is dead, he cannot be genuinely afraid of its revival. But he may very well use that as his pretext for what he wants to do.'

'And that is?'

'To break Llewelyn,' I said. 'To force him to concede everything, to swear fealty and do homage without guarantee of any recompense, any reaffirmation of the treaty, any correction of the present abuses. He has tried already with threats and demands, but he lacked a weapon terrible enough. Now he believes he has one.'

'So I am to be the means of bringing my husband to his knees in total submission, am I?' said Eleanor, opening her gold-flecked eyes wide. 'My cousin may even expect me to add my own pleas to his open threat. Does he know how long we have waited already, without being broken by worse threats than his? A year or two in Edward's prison I can bear. I could not bear it if Llewelyn so mistook me as to think I valued my freedom above his honour and dignity. If we had some means of getting word to him!'

I said that with patience and care, so we might have, once we were in Windsor, for the court must come there now and again, and even in the king's retinue there were quiet Welshmen like Cynan and his nephew, who had not forgotten their origins.

'If only I could send you back to him,' she said, 'I would, but I dread there'll be no chance of that. We shall be well guarded. I must deal as best I can. I could be angry, but anger is waste of time and passion, when it changes nothing.' And by some steely magic of her own she did abjure anger, she who was Earl Simon's daughter, and had inherited his scornful intolerance of the devious and unjust. She steered her solitary course with resolution and method, winning over one by one those persons who came into close contact with her, and who, from castellan down to turnkeys, had surely expected very different usage from her. As at Bristol, so at Windsor, when they brought us there, Eleanor conducted herself as would a state guest, gracious and gentle to all, with never complaint or mention of her wrongs, as though they fell beneath her notice. Nor was this course one merely of policy, for as she said, these simple people who brought her food, tended her fire and guarded the enclosed courtyard where her apartments were, were none of them blameworthy, but forced into this confinement as she was, and they deserved of her, and received always, the great sweetness of address and courteous consideration which were natural to her. It was not long before they began to love her.

Within the suite of rooms in that closed yard, the princess's household moved about freely, for it was a corner walled in every way, with but one gate in and out, and that strongly guarded. Escape was as good as impossible, unless someone among the guard should turn traitor, and there was no hope of that. There was a little patch of grass, wintry and bleached in that January weather, and a shrubbery and garden. Some care had been taken to ensure her comparative comfort while keeping a very fast hold of her. The comfort she acknowledged with grace, the precautions for her safe-keeping she never seemed to see. When she asked for a lute, they brought it, and also at her request, a rebec for me, since I had told her I could play the crwth, which is not so different. If she wanted books, they brought those, also. For freedom she did not ask, or appear to notice her deprivation. There was only one person to whom she would prefer that request.

She had her own chapel there, and was provided a chaplain, though she preferred the company and service of her own Franciscans. There she lived a confined and tedious life with her two ladies, and waited for Edward to acknowledge by his appearance in person the deed he had countenanced, and to demonstrate by his approach that he was not ashamed of it. I know that she wanted him to come, that even in such circumstances – in particular in such circumstances! –it was a discourtesy that he did not visit and face her after what he had done.

'He *must* come,' she said, reassuring herself when she doubted, 'he is too proud to shun the ordeal for ever and leave me to his underlings. He will get no peace until he has faced me. Neither shall I. I want to make plain to him, to his face, what I took care to tell his jackal the moment he seized me, that I am already a wife. Whatever Edward can alter, and spoil, and frustrate by keeping me caged here, he cannot undo my marriage.'

But it was two months and more before the court came to Windsor. We had no news all that time, we lived in a bubble cut off from the world, like all prisoners, and for us, seeing in what situation I had left Llewelyn in the autumn of the previous year, it was an anxious matter to have this sinister silence veiling all. Unknown to us, his envoys were still at the papal court, but Edward's ambassadors had followed them there hot-foot with a long *ex parte* account of the worsening relations between England and Wales, including the statement that the summons to Chester had been at Llewelyn's request and to suit Llewelyn's convenience, which I knew to be untrue, for it came quite unexpectedly, without consultation, and Edward had already broken off in advance all his pretences at making amends in the borders. Pope Gregory took the Welsh complaints seriously, and did intervene with Edward, advising further arbitration and deprecating any hasty action. But that was a year of misfortune in Rome, and in the first few months the pope fell ill, and died, and the resulting interregnum left Wales without a protector at the highest court in Christendom.

We were likewise ignorant that the king had again cited Llewelyn to go to Winchester to do his homage, late in January, at that very time when Master Derenne's crippled ship was limping into Bristol. Again the prince had replied that it was not customary to demand that he should go into England, that it was not safe for him, and that his council would not permit it. He had not then heard of the fate that had befallen Eleanor.

Edward's response was to summon the prince again at once, to appear three weeks after Easter, at Westminster, for which season and place a parliament had been called. Llewelyn as steadily repeated his conditions, and his refusal until they were met. But this time he did know of the gross offence offered to Eleanor, and wrote denouncing it, and demanding that she should be released and sent safely to him. If Edward had counted on forcing his submission by this means, he had judged very badly. It was impossible, after that monstrous illegality, for the prince to give way by one inch, or have any dealings with the author of such a crime but upon arrogantly equal terms of armed enmity, or finally with the sword in the field.

But none of this did we then know. And when, in mid-March, the bustle of great preparations and the coming and going of many officers about the castle of Windsor made itself heard even in our fastness, we stretched our ears and gathered what we could from the servants who attended Eleanor, and guessed that King Edward was bringing his queen and his court to spend Easter there before parliament sat at Westminster.

'Now,' said Eleanor, 'he cannot slight me further by leaving me unvisited, as though he had had no part in bringing me here. He *must* come!'

Never until then had I known her to let her hunger and grief sound in her voice, and even then it was for no more than a moment, and she was almost ashamed of it, and flushed as she shook the weakness away from her. But I knew that her sorrow and longing were very great, as great as the acknowledgement she allowed them was small, and the crisis of meeting Edward face to face and maintaining her position was to her the first great step towards her ultimate victory, in which she never ceased to have faith.

From beyond our walls we heard bustle and haste, fanfares and music and commotion all that day, and in the evening the merry-making in the royal halls sent its echoes to us in waves on the wind, but no one came visiting to our island.

Not until the third evening did he come. She was pale with waiting then, and wanted to fill up the moments that brought no arrivals with whatever came to hand, for fear of their echoing emptiness. We were making music, she and I, and the girls with their sweet, light voices, playing and singing a French tune they knew well, I following by ear on the rebec, when the door of her parlour opened, and the doorway was filled with a man's giant shape. There had been so little noise, and we, perhaps, were making so much, that for some minutes we did not mark his entry, but went on with the song, and though that was honest, and not designed, yet it fitted very neatly with Eleanor's needs. Her head was bent with love over the lute, and her hands on the neck and strings were fleet, devoted and beautiful, when doubtless she should have been instantly at the king's feet with her mouth full of entreaties. By the time one of the girls observed him, and fell mute, we were close to the end of the refrain, and we three who were left finished it neatly, and looked up at one another, smiling, before we understood that we were observed, and by whom.

That was an ample enough room, though small as palaces go, and its doorway just large enough to let in giants. His thick brown hair scarred the stone of the arch above him, and his great shoulders filled the opening from side to side. That night he was all sombre brown and heavy gold, with a thin gold coronal in his curls because it was a festival, and he presiding in state. In these years of his maturity his features were large, heavy, smooth and handsome, with a monumental stillness when he was not in anger. Of grace he had none, but he had a grand, practised command over every part of his vast body that caused him to move majestically, and passed for grace. His drooping eyelid was very clear then, and shocking in its furtive meanness. I understand that I do him injustice, but I do so in the truth of what I saw. So did nature do but dubiously by him, marking him with this flaw. And perhaps she knew her business!

I never was so aware of the grand, wide honesty of Eleanor's eyes as when she laid aside her lute, that evening, and rose to meet him. Never so aware, and never so proud and glad. She barely came up to his breast, and she overmatched him with those great, golden eyes that mirrored to him, without any design of hers, his inescapable imperfection, where she was perfect.

God knows what he had expected, but whatever the expectation, she would always come as an astonishment. She made him the deep reverence due, as did we all, but he had eyes for nobody but Eleanor.

'I am glad,' she said, 'your Grace has the charity to visit your prisoners, since it is at your pleasure we are here. Your Grace's invitation to England would have been more appreciated if it had been rather more formally phrased.'

'Madam,' said the king, in some constraint, as well he might be, considering the sting of her words and the sweetness of her voice. 'I much regret the necessity for putting you to this inconvenience.'

'So do I,' said Eleanor, 'and I have no possibility of amending it, but your Grace has that option, if you care to use it. It would be a much simpler matter to unlock the doors and lend me an escort and horses, than to commission Bristol pirates to seize me in mid-ocean. And I think it would be more likely to win you whatever it may be you want of me and mine.' Her voice was both brisk and serene. I would even say there was a faint, rueful smile in it.

'I did not come,' said the king, goodhumouredly enough, 'to ask your advice on policy, madam. I am sorry that you should be the victim in a matter in which you have been no more than the innocent tool, but I need you here as hostage for others less harmless than you, and here, I regret, you must reconcile yourself to staying until I can safely release you. I came, rather, to see for myself that you are in good health and spirits, and have everything you need for your comfort and maintenance.'

'I have not,' she said with emphasis.

'You have only to ask,' he said, and bethought him in time, and added with the surprising echo of her wry smile: ' – within reason!'

'Mine is a request eminently reasonable,' said Eleanor, 'in a new-made wife. Nothing can ensure my comfort until you restore me to my husband. No!' she said in a sharp cry, seeing him open his lips to refuse her out of hand. 'Do not so simply dismiss what I am saying! This once let us talk like sensible cousins at odds about a matter which is subject to reason, and try to find where we can meet, and how we can dispose of those misunderstandings that divide us. You *are* my cousin. You used to call me so. You would not deny that I have never done you any wrong, nor wished you any. Whatever you may have against my house, do not make me the scapegoat, nor, above all, read into my marriage any sinister designs that have no existence but in your thoughts. Sit down with me, cousin, and pay me the compliment of listening to me, for it is my life you are playing policy with now, and you have no right to use me as a chessman, no right to make or unmake my marriage, no right to tell me whom I shall love. You have might, and that is all. It would be better to use it sparingly, and let reason have its say, too. Then, if you withstand me, having heard my arguments, you need never hear them again, for I will never again ask of you what I am asking most gravely now.'

'I have nothing against you,' he said, reluctant but dazzled. 'I have said so. But I will not countenance this marriage until the prince of Wales has regularised his position, and done homage as my vassal.'

'You are not asked to countenance it,' she said calmly. 'God has already done that. You realise, do you not, that I *am* his wife?'

'The marriage is not yet consummated,' he said bluntly, 'and can be annulled. Indeed, cousin, you might even thank me some day for giving you the opportunity to think again. With your person, and your lineage . . .'

She smiled then into his face, with a spark of real amusement. 'So might many a good Christian count or baron have whispered into the ear of *your* Eleanor, through all those five years or more she lived with you virgin as a child. Would you have liked that any better than I like your suggestion now? No, believe me, this marriage will never be undone by anything short of death. I promise you that. Come, now that you are here, give me twenty minutes of your time, drink wine with me, and listen. Then, if you are not moved, I am done.'

He gave in to her then, though with a guarded face and wary eyes. And certainly he did listen, and certainly he watched her steadily, and with both eyes wide open, too, which meant that he was shaken out of his common granite assurance, though there was no telling what the result would be. And she, making her one great bid, the first and the last, to bring Edward to terms which should make a common future possible, used her marvellously pure and honest face and her lovely voice to charm and convince him, and wore out the very fibres of her heart in the effort. Even then I was curiously aware, without understanding fully, that she was fighting as much for Edward as for herself and Llewelyn. And, oh, if she could have triumphed then, she could have changed the world.

She told him exactly what her marriage meant, what it was and what it was not, how she had clung to her betrothed as a matter of faith pledged, how constantly Llewelyn, too, had sought to renew and complete the contract, not suddenly now, as a gesture of defiance against England or an attempt to revive a rebel faction, but year after year throughout, before ever Edward came to the throne, when Welsh relations with King Henry were at their best and most cordial, and it would have been lunatic folly to attempt or desire disruption. She showed him, beyond all rational doubt, that it was a match made out of mutual love and desire, and contained within it no dark designs to trouble the peace of any man, but concerned only two people in the world, and further, that to attribute to it such unworthy aspects was mortal insult to those two people, besmirching what was to them sacred, and multiplying for the future all the possibilities of misunderstanding and ill will. She told him what damage he had already done by his act of piracy and abduction. And then she showed him how by releasing her he could more than make amends, for she, of all people who might attempt it, was best equipped to undo the present wrong without revenges, and more, to interpret him to Llewelyn as now she was interpreting Llewelyn to him, with every hope of convincing each of the other's integrity, and bringing about a better-grounded future.

She had the eloquence of angels, and their immense, compelling gravity. I saw her father looking through her face. But she was talking to a monarch, not a man.

When she had done, and it could not have been better done, she was so drained that her face was whiter than snowdrops. He sat gazing at her still, and he said: 'That you are saying what you believe, that I grant. I never held you to blame for the use others might make of you. But I cannot accept your truth as justifying those behind you. You have lived a cloistered life, you know nothing of this rough world, or what men are capable of. I will say of Llewelyn that he could not have a better advocate. But I'll keep the weapon I have. I am sorry that you should be the sufferer. I will do what can be done to make your stay less irksome. If there is anything that can give you pleasure, ask for it.' He was rising as he said it.

'I have asked,' she said, 'and you have refused. I shall not ask again. There is nothing else you can offer me to compensate.'

He looked about the room as he crossed it, marking the lights, the furnishings, to see if anything was missing. 'You could have the freedom of Windsor,' he said unexpectedly, 'if you would give me your parole.'

Out of her languor and weariness she smiled. 'You are paying me half a compliment. Did you realise that?' It was true. When in his life before, or perhaps after, did Edward ever offer to accept a woman's parole? Or so much as realise that she might possess honour, as surely as a man? 'But only half,' she said, 'or you would know what my answer is. No, I will give you no parole. If I can escape you, I shall. But be easy, I shall use no murder, nor piracy, nor violence as the means.'

He did not wince at that. He was never ashamed of anything he did. But he did pause at the door to look at her again, with a kind of grudging wonder. 'Very well!' he said. 'Then I regret you must stay in close ward. A pity! You could have made your own lot so much easier.'

'Well, if you dare not let me out,' said Eleanor, 'you may let others in. I can be visited, if you trust your castellan to use discretion. It would pass the time for me, and we may as well put on some show of civility. I do not intend to make my visitors listen to my grievances, your queen and her ladies need not fear, if they are so kind as to come and see me.'

'You shall not be neglected,' he said, 'while we are here.'

'And something else I can and will beg of you,' she said, 'and that is mercy for my people. Their only crime has been to follow me. If you will not release my knights, at least ease their captivity. And my brother . . .'

He cut in upon her there with a darkened face. 'Ask nothing for your brother! Keep to your own distaff, and leave the men of your house to me.' And he turned and went out from her without another word.

She sat for a long time tired and sunk deep in thought after he was gone. 'Strange!' she said. 'He *does* believe it! He is still afraid of us. He still hates us. He can credit the impossible, provided it discredits a Montfort. I fear I have done my lord a very ill favour by linking him in marriage with a woman of the house of Ganelon.'

Nevertheless, after that day she was visited, for the queen herself set the pattern, and it was certain that the queen did nothing without the king's leave and approval, more likely at his orders. Eleanor took the opportunities she was given, and set herself to win the good opinion of all those ladies who came to see her, and presently, having the management of her own household within her constricted quarters, herself began to invite and to entertain, to cast a cloak of normality about her unhappy position. Having her nature, it was hard indeed not to be liked. Before the Easter parliament was over, at which Llewelyn certainly sent by his envoys the same adamant reply, the same terms for his homage, and the same indignant demand for his wife's release, Eleanor had won over most of the women who frequented the queen's society, and made the queen herself a half-unwilling friend.

'If he cannot love us,' she said, 'at least let's see if I can make it harder for him to hate us.'

She kept her word, and never, to any of her visitors, said one word of complaint, or anything that could embarrass those who were free while she was captive. And Edward could not choose but know how gallantly and gently she bore herself, and with what arduous patience. But while I was there he did not come again.

Late in April, after the day Edward had appointed for Llewelyn's homage at Westminster was come and gone, as vainly as its predecessors, we had two other visitors, however, even less expected than Edward. There was a spell of mild, fair weather about that time, and as the little courtyard and garden were well sheltered but admitted the southern sun, we had carried out benches for the women to the grassy patch, and they were sitting there with the sweet spring light upon their embroidery, while Eleanor tried out softly upon the lute a tune she was making to a French love-song. Her two ladies bore captivity more lightly than she, living much as they would have lived anywhere. But she had lost flesh in her waiting, for all her gallantry, and the sweet, vivid face was closer every day to that glorious mask of bone and intellect I had first seen solitary among many, in prayer at St Frideswide's tomb in Oxford. Nor was her ordeal yet near its end.

The single gateway that admitted to our court clashed open while she was fingering out, with a private frown, a difficult vocal line, and marking its notation on a leaf beside her. She did not immediately notice, but I did, and looked round. Eleanor's chamberlain, old in the service of her mother, came trotting across to her from the portal, and stooped to her ear. She looked up, turning her head towards the gate, and she was smiling, and a little surprised. She laid the lute aside, and got up to meet her visitors. Under the stone archway David walked, stooping his head where the roof leaned low, and holding Elizabeth by the hand.

I never was more confounded, even knowing him as I knew him, which was to know that no man on earth could ever know him and be secure of what he knew. He had envied his brother, grown impatient with waiting for the succession, let himself be seduced into a dream of murder – I say a dream, for I do not know if ever he truly contemplated the reality – fled his brother's judgment, and from the shelter of Edward's shadow done his worst and bitterest to stamp out of existence any remnants of their feeling as brothers, avenging himself on David no less than on Llewelyn. And now he came visiting to his brother's wife, wronged and captive as she was, bringing his own most innocent, loving and bewildered child-wife as unwitting advocate for him in the approach. He came with a white, taut face, deep-eyed, solemn and brittle, most delicately groomed and dressed, David inviolate in his beauty, so clean after all his flounderings in and out of the mire, and so vividly coloured, the blue-black hair curving in blown sickles round his cheeks, and the raven lashes curling back widely from his harebell-blue eyes. He was near forty, and still he kept his wild, vulnerable face of a clever boy, and not one of his scars showed in him. Never, life-long.

And Elizabeth, herself immaculate in valiant innocence, went bravely with him wherever he led her, and never knew she was his armour against all threats, and namely the threats from his own nature and his own memories. While he clasped her hand, he could believe in himself as she believed in him, whether she understood or no. The sweet brown mouse with the shrill, child's laughter was grown into a woman now, a little thicker in the body, a little rounder in the face, mother of four children, still giving birth as neatly and smugly as a cat, and every bit as ready and protective of all her brood, including her spouse.

I never asked and cannot claim to know why he came, whether in pure curiosity to see what manner of woman his brother had chosen, or to preserve a position of his own in balance between the courts of England and Wales, or whether in truth he felt compunction towards this girl who had never wronged him, and had no part in the tangled fury he felt towards Llewelyn, and desired at least to touch hands with her and exchange some human words, even if he could not avow his guilt and ask her forgiveness. I did not linger to hear, though I think it was a very formal and restrained visit, in which Elizabeth played the chief part. But what did flash into my mind at the first sight of them approaching was the use that I might make of them, and I stooped in haste to Eleanor's ear, and said to her:

'If she speaks of her children – and she will – ask her to come again and bring them to see you!'

Then I went away out of earshot, out of sight of them, for fear David should call too much attention to me, since so far I had escaped Edward's recognition, and passed simply for Eleanor's Welsh clerk. If Elizabeth came again with her children, in all likelihood so must Cristin come as their nurse, and so I should not only gain a spring of cool water for my eternal thirst, but with God's help get some word of what went on outside the walls, and send a message to Cynan.

I kept out of sight until they were gone, and then went to Eleanor, who sat looking after them very thoughtfully. 'So that is David,' she said slowly. 'Now was it at his wish they came here, or did she compel him to it out of the simple kindness of her heart? She was happy when I asked if I might see her children. She likes to give pleasure. And she will bring them. Now what is it you hope for from that?' And when I told her I hoped for a chance to send word out to be carried to Llewelyn in Wales, she quivered as a high-bred hound quivers, waiting for its release. 'Oh, if I could but tell him that I stand with him, that I have no regrets, that I ask nothing of him but to maintain his truth and his right, as I will mine here. Yes, it would be worth anything. Better yet if I could send you safely back to him, you who know my mind better than any.'

I said I should be loth to leave her, but most vehemently she urged that he had the greater need of me, for hers here was but the passive part, and all she had to do was to refuse to be moved, while he had to sustain his country and his cause, even to the edge of war if need be. For to give way once to Edward was to be condemned to give way eternally. And she made me promise that if ever the chance offered, I would take it, as in duty bound to rejoin my lord.

After two days Elizabeth came again. The good weather still held, and Eleanor with her ladies was again in the garden, which began to seem very cramped and poor in that blossoming spring. The guard at our gate opened for Elizabeth without question. Clearly David was well installed in his old place at Edward's side, and Edward's bounty was paying for David's household. But he did not appear with his wife this time. She came in flushed and proud and glowing, with her two little girls dancing beside her, one clinging by either hand. The elder was then approaching five years old, the second turned three, and both as active and bright as butterflies. And behind this trio came in my Cristin, in a loose grey gown, bearing in her arms David's son and heir, Owen, then within two months of his second birthday. There was a third daughter left behind at home with the younger nurse, for she was only five months old, born in Shrewsbury.

Our eyes met the moment Cristin came in. It was always so. But I was aghast at what I saw, in spite of the radiance of her look, that told me there was no change within, for without she was so direly changed. She carried the little boy as lightly on her arm as once I had seen her carry a new lamb down from the hills of Bala, but her step was heavier and slower, and her face was fallen hollow and white, her eyes sunk deep within her head and the eyelids faintly puffy and soft, her lips also a little swollen. I could not move nor speak for dread that she was fallen gravely ill, and she so cut off from me and from all who knew her best, all but this child-woman Elizabeth, who lived only for her children, and did not seem to see the change in their nurse.

Eleanor and Elizabeth sat down together in the sun, and the two ladies-in-waiting came in haste to enjoy the novelty of the children, and began an animated game with them on the grass. Elizabeth held out her arms for her son, and Cristin gave him to her. I had my freedom and opportunity, for she could very well hold this little group together and happy.

Cristin drew back from them gently, and turned and walked with me, away beyond the shrubs and bushes, into the cool of the ante-room. I watched her poor, fallen face and ached for her. Even when we sat down together, we who for years had so seldom been alone with our love, for a while I could not speak. Then I got out in dread:

'What is it with you? Are you ill?'

'No,' she said, and smiled, and even her smile was pain. 'No, not ill. Listen, Samson, for we may not have long. I am charged with a message to you. You have friends here, others besides me. They have a plan to bring you safely away out of this place, and home to Wales. If you will go? Will you go? We dare not attempt more. Her they will never let out of these walls, nor out of their sight. You they may.'

I told her then what had been in my own mind, to get word to Cynan that might be sent on to Llewelyn, in reassurance at least that his wife was heart and soul with him in his stand, and desired him to make no concessions for her. But I knew, even without Eleanor's urging, that if the chance offered to get back to him I must take it, all the more as the clouds gathered more ominously.

'One will come to the governor, while the court is still here in Windsor,' said Cristin, 'with the request to borrow you, as being fluent in Welsh and versed in Welsh law, to copy some documents for David. Oh, never fear, David's seal will be available, and David is so close to Edward, no one will question it. There will be horses waiting for you at a safe place.'

'And leave some poor soul to answer for stealing or copying David's seal?' I said, doubtful. 'Or bring David himself into suspicion?'

'No need,' she said. 'Your guide is coming with you. He also is Welsh, and if there is to be fighting, he wills to be home and fighting beside his own people. No one else will come into suspicion.'

'No one but you,' I said. 'You could suffer for me. Who else could have brought me this message?'

'No,' she said, shaking her head. 'You need not fear for me. I am strongly protected, no one will point at me. I wish to God I could ride with you, Samson, as once we rode together to Llewelyn, but I can no more go and leave her now than I could when he brought us to the border, all in innocence, and only then let me see where we were bound. Now we go armed, David and I, enemies bound by a truce. But whatever evil he may have done, he will not let any harm come to me. I am the cross that dangles before his conscience, I am the voice saying: Repent! He cannot do without me, he would be lost.'

Her voice was soft and wild, and her low laughter very bitter. I asked her: 'Was it he who warned Edward, and had him send pirates to seize our ships at sea? Is that also to his account?'

'No,' she said, 'that was not David. That word came from Brittany, while you waited for the good winds. Hard to keep secret the passage of such a party, and Edward has his spies everywhere. Do not put down to David more than his due, his load is heavy enough. He can see no end now but destruction for himself or Llewelyn, he feels himself far past forgiveness. Now he wants to bring on the ruin he foresees, to pull down the house over himself or wipe his brother out of the world and try to forget him. Since there's no going back, he is frantic to complete what he has begun. If I left him, there would be no one who knows the truth, no face that has only to appear before him to remind him of the judgement. David needs me even more than she does. It would be hard for me to leave him.'

I said again, for her voice was so slow and grievous, and her face so burning with white despair: 'Cristin, something has happened to you! You are ill!'

'No,' she said, 'I am quite well. Will you go, Samson? Promise, for my sake! I want you free, and far away from here.'

I promised, for she clung so to my hand, and her hollow eyes devoured my face with such longing. 'Yes, I will go. Whatever you wish I will do, but don't ask me to go from you gladly. And you so changed, so pale and strange! If it is not sickness, it is worse. For God's sake, do not keep it from me! Something terrible has befallen you . . .'

She heaved a great, shuddering sigh, and clasped her hands under her breasts. 'Yes, something has befallen me indeed. I did not want to own it, I did not want you to know, but it is written in my face, and you'll get no rest now for thinking and dreading. He has found a way at last of avenging himself on you and on me! So simple it was, and yet he never thought of it before! He, who fell into bed beside me and snored the night away dreaming of all his other women, suddenly he grasped what would most surely destroy me, and strike you to the heart. Since we came to England he has never let me alone, night after night after night with his hate and glee and pride in his cleverness.'

She stood up abruptly beside me, and spread her arms wide, to show how her girdle was tied high under her bosom, and her body gently swollen under the grey woollen gown.

'Do you not see what God and Godred between them have done to me? I am four months gone with child!'

CHAPTER IX

In this desolate situation I was forced to leave Windsor – my lord threatened, my lady captive, my love pregnant with Godred's monstrous progeny, a dagger, not a child, begotten in hate and despite. Ever since he married her, for policy and establishment like most marriages, he had slighted and misprized her, now he persecuted her with his attentions only to poison and kill both her and me. She said to me before she left me, with a calm more terrible than her desperation: 'I will never bear any child but yours!' But I knew, and so did she, that she could not harm the life within her, however she shrank from it in horror. She would bear it and she would care for it, and Godred would gloat as he watched her wither, and the incubus devour her, and savour the thought of me eaten alive in Wales by the same disease. Above all, what cruelty to the child, to create it out of hatred and cherish it out of malice, making it a death before ever it lived, when she could so deeply have loved a child engendered in kindness. And even worse if he came, in his own way, to love and value it for the damage it had done on his behalf.

So judge in what anguish I went to my duty.

I told no one. I was tempted for a while to entrust Eleanor with that whole story, and pray her to stand friend to Cristin if by any means she might, for her heart was great enough to find room for the miseries of others, even when it might well have been full of her own. But I did not do it. There was no possibility of confiding Cristin's secrets, her darkness and her need, to any other soul, so passionately were they hers. So I was compelled to let her carry that burden alone.

Duly they came for me, early in one of the first evenings of May, a young servant in David's livery, bearing a written request with David's seal, begging leave to borrow the services of the Welsh clerk, for some intricate copying that required knowledge of both Welsh and English law, since he had only his immediate household with him on this visit, and had left his own law-men in Shrewsbury. Clearly David's demand, thus proffered, was almost as good as Edward's order, it being assumed without question that he had Edward's sanction and approval for everything he did. And a clerk is no great matter, and hardly likely to risk breaking loose on his own when he can sit comfortably enough, even in a virtual prison, under the protection of his lady's name. So nobody made any bones about asking Eleanor's leave, which she graciously gave, and for the first time since entering Windsor, I passed that iron gate that sealed off the princess's prison.

The last look I had from her, shining and private like a blessing, went with me down through the town beside my guide, and across the river to the house where David was lodged.

There was nothing difficult in our escape, because no one was hunting us. We simply rode out of Windsor towards the north-west, briskly and confidently as though we were on approved business, and were never questioned until we reached Wales, though we pressed hard at first, and rode well into the night, lodging having been prepared for us at a grange near Oxford. There we slept out the rest of the dark hours, and went on with fresh mounts in the dawn.

'We can be easy enough,' said my companion contentedly. 'No one will have missed you, not yet. The castellan will think you are detained overnight on David's business, and I take it your lady will make no mistakes, know nothing and say nothing?'

I said he might rely on that. He was from Lleyn, and had been home-sick, he said, ever since he had been fool enough to cross the English border in David's train, and was main glad now to be going home, where he belonged. If there was to be fighting, as everyone seemed to expect, it was not for Edward of England he wanted to fight.

I asked after Cynan, and whether he had made proper preparation to defend his own innocence if suspicion should fall his way. But my companion did not even know the name, and was surprised at the question. Then who, I asked, were his fellows in my rescue, and who had arranged access, in any case, to David's seal, since that could hardly be Cynan's work.

He looked at me along his shoulder. and considered how much to tell me. 'His orders were that you were not to know, but I thought you must have guessed it. The Lord David's seal will have been mislaid some-where about his household, where anyone – meaning your servant here! – might have got hold of it, and in due time it will be found again, no doubt very convincingly. He wants none of his people implicated, you need not fear. I am the scapegoat, once I'm safe in Wales, and I shall have no objection to that! But as to how it was planned – why, the simplest way possible. Who do you think affixed David's seal to the request for you, if not David?'

It was not the surprise it might have been, once I accepted it. It fitted still with that image I had of him, for ever torn, so that in England, when he had cast in his lot there, half at least of his heart fought for Wales, and in Wales a hundred ties of almost equal potency drew him back towards England, and never, never could he be content anywhere, and never could he be faithful, because faith to one land was treason to the other.

'Then all this is his work? The relay of horses, the night's lodging, all?' I thought of Cristin, who had wanted me away from her, very far away where I could not see her anguish or be a tormented witness of the birth she dreaded, and I could believe that David had had her, too, in mind. For there were some for whom he had always a kindness, and to them, after his fashion, he was faithful.

'All his,' said the young man. 'Playing one hand against the other for plain wantonness, or wishing himself back where he can never go again – who knows? But if that was it, he'd grudge it to us – and it was he offered me the chance, and only smiled on the wrong side of his face when I jumped at it. He's snug enough there at the king's elbow, and has picked the stronger side, on the face of it. But it's my belief he'd change with you and me if he could.'

God knows he may have been right. Certain it is that David had deliberately extracted me from Edward's grip and restored me to Llewelyn, to the old land and the old loyalty, into which he was certain he himself could never enter again.

Llewelyn was at Rhydcastell when we came there after that journey, late in May. We were barely dismounting and leading our jaded horses into the tableyard, when someone must have run to him with the news, where he was newly in himself from riding, and stripped to shirt and chausses, for it was an early summer, and hot there between the hills. He came out in haste, his bared breast russet-brown. and the small lines of thought and frowning graven into his brow in ivory against the sunburned gold, which the bleached brown of his clipped beard did no more than outline in a single shade darker. The marks of the summer were on him, but the marks of the winter, too. Not all Edward's harassment, not all the border malice of the marchers, operating with their master's tacit approval, could have honed down the lines of that bold, bright face to this fine-drawn carving, or put the first traces of grey in his hair, either side the brow. He was fretted for Eleanor, as she for him. Those two had never yet seen each other in the flesh, and they were pared away to spirit and longing for love.

He cried: 'Samson!' in a shout of joy, and came to embrace me, and of his gladness I was so glad as to be shaken almost to tears. 'I thought I had sent you to your death,' he said. 'You are whole and free, thank God, you at least! Come in with me and tell me all you have to tell, let me know the best and the worst, for I am starved. No man of mine could get any true word or any comfort in Westminster. I have begged in vain, and thundered in vain, they would tell us nothing but that he has her, and all her company. You, too, Samson! And now you are here! If I can accept a first miracle, so I can believe in a second!'

I told him in a breath what seemed to matter most. 'She is well, and unshaken, and sends her true mind by me. I am here with her blessing and at her wish.'

He laid his arm about my shoulders, and turned suddenly in revulsion from going within, and haled me away instead into the fields, to a high, grassy knoll that looked down upon the valley, and there we lay in the rich green grass together, in the scent of the little spicy pink flowers of pimpernel and centaury, and the sweet air of freedom. And I was grateful to him for this blessing, that we had no walls about us, no listeners, no echoes. Under that sky it was possible to believe in the victory of truth, and the reunion of divided lovers.

There I told him all that melancholy and angry history, from first to last, dredging up for him out of my memory every look and every word of Eleanor's, and indeed not one was ever forgotten. And it was like the sudden bliss of steady and gentle rain upon a great drought, slaking the thirsty soil, setting the sap flowing in new life, filling the world with a young, green sweetness in which all the flowers of hope burst into bud. He lay with his chin in his hands, and listened, sometimes asking a quick question, perhaps only to imagine again her voice repeating its calm and queenly defiance.

'Whatever he may hold against me,' he said, not angrily but heavily, 'whatever suspicions he may have of me, it was vile to make her the victim, and viler to try to use her as a weapon. And I tell you, Samson, when first I got word of it, I was in two minds, and if I had been a free man I should have massed all my power in one great thrust, hopeless or not, as much to destroy him as to deliver her. But I am not free to be senselessly brave and throw my life and all away. I hold Wales in my hands, this land I have half-made into a nation, and cannot abandon now. It is hers as well as mine, but most of all it is the hope of the future, of my sons by her, and of other men's sons, every soul who speaks the Welsh tongue has rights in it. I have not had long enough!' he said, drumming his fist tormentedly against the thick grass. 'It is not made, but only making! If I had had ten years more, if King Henry had lived ten years longer, this danger need never have been. But I have not had long enough! Not long enough to wipe out all those centuries of disruption.'

'You could not have delivered her,' I said, 'you could only have fallen helpless into Edward's hands, which is what he wants, for if you fall, Wales falls.'

'I know it!' said Llewelyn. 'It would have been folly to abandon the way of law for the way of war. My envoys are still at the papal court, waiting for a new appointment now Gregory is dead. God rest him, he did his best for us. I have sent further letters. The new pontiff will know from the first of Edward's crime. I had complaints enough before, now this becomes my chief and first complaint, and manifestly just. No, it would have been mad to rush to arms, I should have destroyed my own case, for I take my stand on the treaty, which he wants broken and discarded. If he could goad me into being the one to shatter it, he would have won. But, oh, it was hard not to fight for her!'

I said: 'She is of your mind. You cannot yield now, not by a single point. The terms you stand on are just, and you have offered homage according to treaty and custom.'

'I have done more,' said Llewelyn, half enraged with himself even for that. 'I have offered to take the oath of fealty to his envoys, if he will send them to me, to satisfy him until we can agree on a safe place to meet for homage. He has refused. He stands absolutely on my total submission, and my consent to attend wherever he summons me. I stand absolutely on seeing the treaty honoured and reaffirmed, its breaches repaired, and my wife sent to join me, before I will take the oath or lay my hands in his. It is deadlock. This one concession I offered, to break it, and he refuses. I shall make no more. I shall not offer that again.'

'She above all,' I said, 'understands the necessity for standing fast against him. "I could not bear it," she said to me, "if Llewelyn so mistook me as to think I valued my freedom above his honour and dignity. I ask nothing of him," she said, "but to maintain his truth and his right." If you once give back an inch, he will press you back again and again, toe to toe, and give you nothing in return.'

'I confess,' said Llewelyn, brooding, 'I still do not understand him. He was not always so with me. Why this stony enmity now?'

'It is the first touch of resistance,' I said, 'that turns Edward mad. What does not move at his thrust, even if it mattered nothing to him when first he laid hand on it, becomes to him the total enemy, and he cannot rest until he has hurled it out of his path and ground it to powder under his feet.'

'He should sooner have practised on Snowdon,' said Llewelyn grimly, 'than on Eleanor and me.'

Afterwards I told him, when what most mattered was done, what I had until then withheld, and he pointedly had not asked, who it was had won me out of Windsor.

'So I supposed,' said Llewelyn drily. 'He had always a kindness for you, in spite of all the times he used you ill. It is the one thing that still does him honour. As for me, I have been through this to-and-fro of his once too often. David is dead to me.'

But concerning Cristin I did not tell him anything, not because I grudged him the half of my load as I would have given him the half of my joy, but for a simpler reason that confounded me more. For when I opened my lips to speak of her, my throat closed, and I had no voice. So I accepted the judgment of God, and held my peace.

In the months that followed Llewelyn manned his borders, fended off the offences that grew with every week, and steadily sent complaints, with details, times, witnesses, in every case that came to his notice. To Rome he sent again to remind the new pope, whose election we awaited with hope and anxiety, of the utterly illegal detention of Eleanor, and all the other, lesser wrongs which defaced the treaty relationship between the two countries. And at the beginning of July we heard, with great joy, which of the candidate cardinals had been elected. He had taken the name of Adrian, as he had been the cardinal of St Adrian, but we knew him by another name.

'They have chosen Ottobuono,' cried Llewelyn, understandably elated, 'Ottobuono Fieschi. The very man who made this treaty, and took pride in it. He was our friend then, and laboured honestly for us. Praise God, we have a friend there who knows every article of the document he himself fashioned. He will not let it be repudiated.'

We rejoiced indeed, with what seemed to us good reason, knowing this to be a man of incorruptible good-will, and knowing that he understood as well as we did the importance of the treaty he had worked out of the end of the barons' war. We rejoiced too soon. He was all we believed him, but he was also old and frail. That was a year of deaths. Before August was out, when he had been pope but one month, Adrian the Fifth died.

Wales was again left friendless. There came in a Spanish pope, with a great reputation for learning, and having a progressive and forceful mind, or so we heard, but one that knew nothing of us, and had never set foot in these islands, much less played any part in bringing them to an arduous and equitable peace. I do believe Pope John listened, and did his best to hold a balance, but it was Edward who first got his ear, and Edward, crusader, vassal of France, king of England, duke of Gascony, was universally known, and carried weight in every court of Europe and the east. It would have needed a voice more peremptory than the thunder of God to shout him down.

I do not see what Llewelyn could have done in that year that he did not do, to make known the true state of the case. In April, while I was still captive in Windsor, the dean and chapter of Bangor had written to the archbishop of Canterbury, repeating the full facts of the conspiracy of David and Griffith against the prince's life, as Owen had confessed them, so that Archbishop Robert should not be able to plead ignorance of the crime and criminals that Edward was harbouring, and the seriousness of the breach of treaty that that protection constituted. In June Llewelyn himself also wrote to the primate, who had urged him to keep the peace in the march, pointing out how frequent were the disturbances of that peace caused by English attacks, now so constant and apparently so organised as to amount to a state of war. In July, again, he sent a complaint that his men, going on their lawful business to the fairs and markets of Montgomery and Leominster, had been robbed of their goods, and some hundred or more imprisoned, and one at least killed, and that the marchers made no secret of their intent to continue such seizures, in defiance of the treaty.

'Even if we cannot get justice now,' he said, 'at least we'll make sure the truth is on record, for other and less prejudiced minds to judge. For I'm sure Edward never writes one word of cherishing my traitors and assassins, or seizing my wife, but only and always that he has summoned me to do homage and I have refused him. And not even that is true.'

Long afterwards Cynan told me of the letter Edward wrote to Pope John in September of that crisis year, when I am certain he had already not merely made up his mind to resort to war, but actually set the machines of war secretly in motion, before ever he got his desired condemnation of Llewelyn from his parliament. What Llewelyn had guessed at was accurate enough. There was not one word of any offences on the king's side. David and Griffith might not have existed. He wrote only of the homage refused, and then charged all the border clashes to the prince's account. You would not have known from those despatches, said Cynan, that there was in the world, much less in Edward's prison at Windsor, a lady who was princess of Wales by right.

Llewelyn made one more reasoned attempt to forestall fate, but reason had little say left in this dissension, except the cold reason of Edward's resolution on conquest. The prince again sent envoys to the Michaelmas parliament, bearing letters offering fealty and homage on the terms due by treaty, and not otherwise. What Edward claimed he most wanted, Edward was offered, upon terms which did no violence to justice or to his rights, as he was doing violence to the rights of others. But this was not absolute submission, and that was the only answer he would consider.

He took the last step, and took it deliberately and coldly. He called a full council of his chief prelates and magnates, and demanded and obtained from them the unanimous judgment that the prince's petition should not be heard, but that the king should go against him as a rebel and a disturber of the peace. The marches were to be put into a state of immediate defence – defence, being, of course, Edward's word – and the feudal host was summoned to muster on the day of St John the Baptist of the following summer, at Worcester.

These formal orders, being promulgated during that parliament, were common knowledge, and our envoys brought the news back with them. What lay behind we had to estimate for ourselves, for certainly Edward would not sit still through the winter.

'This is no threat of war to come when the host gathers,' said Llewelyn. 'It is war now, and I fear we shall soon learn it. If he times his muster thus for midsummer, half a year away, he means to have a good part of his work done for him before ever he takes on that expense. This will be every marcher lord for himself with a free hand to raise what forces he can and take what land he can. And we with a long and uneasy border, laced with the lands of small chiefs who may well fear to be squeezed between two rocks, and rush to take cover behind the greater. We have seen it so often before!'

In council and in camp, travelling the length of his land before the worst of the winter set in, he was resolute, cheerful and practical, improving wherever possible on the dispositions he had already made. But I know, who was always beside him, how his heart was eaten with foreboding and grief over those two springs of his life, Eleanor and Wales.

'We'll still keep plying him with approaches,' he said grimly, 'as long as it's safe for bishop or clerk to travel into England, and as long as he'll issue safe-conducts. He shall not be able to say it was I who broke off all contact. I have never sought to avoid my obligations to him, but only when he performs his part will I perform mine. That I'll keep repeating as long as I can get an envoy within earshot of him. Whether he'll listen is another matter. I think his ears have been stopped all this year, if truth were told.'

I thought so, too, but if continued diplomatic missions could postpone action even for a few weeks more, we should have our ally, winter, on the doorstep, and frost and snow might hold back what Edward certainly would not curb willingly. And all the council agreed with the prince's consistent messages, patiently repeating that this was was not to the purpose, that right should be done on both sides, and could not be one-sided. But Llewelyn had long ceased to believe in any success from reasoning.

'If I am to pay now,' he said to me once, as we looked out from the walls of Dolforwyn across the Severn towards Montgomery, 'for what I failed to do for Earl Simon, God grant I may not be asked to pay it through his daughter!'

As for me, at this time I was torn so many ways that there was no rest for me night or day, for not only was I racked with all the cares that oppressed my lord, and troubled deep by the recollection of what Eleanor's distress must be, on his behalf rather than her own, but also I could not get out of my mind, waking or sleeping, the thought that the tale of Cristin's months was come to an end, and somewhere far from me, perhaps in Chester, where we heard David had taken his men to join the garrison, the time of her labour was come upon her, and she already turned forty years old, and bearing her first child, in peril of her life and of her peace, in hatred and despite, in fear and loathing, poisoning what should have been a youthful joy. And she was mine, heart and soul mine, and I would have died for her, and I could do nothing to help her.

We kept Christmas but poorly and on the move that year, for the most part at Dolforwyn and in the marches of Salop, where Llewelyn thought well to draw in from certain outlying lands to shorten his line, rather than lose men to the forces from Montgomery and Oswestry, which were already skirmishing along the river valley. Before we left that castle we received a rider who had made his way through the English patrols and swum the river with his horse to get to us, and came weary, draggled and muddy into Dolforwyn, but vigorous and grinning still. And that was the young clerk Morgan, Cynan's nephew.

'You must forgive me, my lord,' he said, when we had fed him and given him dry clothes, and brought him to Llewelyn, 'that I bring no letters. What I bring you I carry in my head this time, and it's my head I risked to bring it. My good uncle has taught me a long list of what the king has in hand for Wales. Will you hear it?'

And he delivered it word for word as he had learned it. How Edward had set up three commands along the march, the first at Chester, where the earl of Warwick was commander, with David as his lieutenant, the second here opposing us in the middle march, under Roger Mortimer, and the third in the south, where Pain de Chaworth commanded from Carmarthen. The king's own standing corps of knights and troopers was divided between the central and southern commands, and the commission of all three commanders was to collect supplies, recruit foot-soldiers wherever they offered, and above all, to receive local Welsh princes to the king's peace, offering them protection in the future for their defection, should England and Wales again come to terms. And protection meant that once they had pledged their fealty to Edward, out of natural fear, that fealty should be retained in any agreement afterwards.

'They are issuing proclamations inviting all the small men along the march to get out of the line of battle,' said Morgan very earnestly, 'and some are wavering, and may well fall. This is the king's first weapon, he will use it to the full, and even spend to make it effective. When the lion roars, even well-bred hounds, of good gallantry, take to the bushes.'

'Small blame to them,' said Llewelyn ruefully, 'when they have no better training yet. I have seen it coming, friend, I know what I face.'

'And further, my lord, my uncle bids me tell you that the king has sent overseas for war-horses, he is buying more than a hundred in France. He has sent to Gascony for crossbowmen, and approached the king of France to allow the shipping of men and horses from Wissant to England. In December he sent out writs for the feudal levy, for the first day of July, at Worcester. As to the bowmen from Gascony, this is but the beginning. He will get more. And he is furbishing all the ships of the Cinque ports fleet for sea service.'

He drew breath, after so much talking of matters learned by heart, a ruddy, well-made young man, bringing with a good heart news that might be bad or good to us, according as we made use of it. 'I am finished, my lord, I know no more.'

'We're bound to you for your trouble,' said Llewelyn, smiling at him, 'and something troubled because we are bound. You did very well by us in getting here. But how can we ensure that you get back as safely?'

'Never fret for that, my lord,' said Morgan cheerfully. 'I am not going back. My uncle does not expect me. I am a Welshman, and I can use sword or lance, as you please to employ me. I have come to add one more, for what he's worth, to the forces of Wales.'

With a full heart the prince made it clear to him that his worth was as great as his welcome was warm, and prayed that Cynan, who remained behind to bear the possible vengeance for his nephew's defection, had made provision for his own safety.

'It was he who bade me go freely,' said Morgan, 'and he can very well take care of himself, he is not answerable for my follies, and has my leave to disown me as hard as he will. He said he might yet be of service where he is, now that he has made his choice, and of messengers God will provide at need.'

Such crumbs of honest comfort and gladness we had, and not a few. But those who thus came to join us at the risk of their lives were the poor and landless, who had nothing but their lives to lose. With those minor chieftains, especially those who inherited but little by reason of having many brothers, it was another story, and we knew from the beginning that it must be so, The smaller their patrimony, the less possible was it for them to raise men enough to defend it by force, and Wales was but a word still, there was hardly one among them who was prepared to let go of a commote in the borders in order to help his neighbours inland to preserve the heart of a country.

Before the year ended, Mortimer had raised so great a force at the king's pay at Montgomery, and had so many added companies from Lestrange and Clifford and Corbet, all with lands there to enlarge, that we were pressed back in a number of skirmishes from the borders of Salop, and soon they were encroaching into Powys. Griffith ap Gwenwynwyn had naturally remained sitting hungrily there on the fringes of his own lost lands when David went to join the earl of Warwick at Chester, and was more eager even than the king's own men to recruit and mass supplies, and push the advance into southern Powys, to get back his own, however justly forfeit. And before the first month of that year twelve hundred and seventy-seven was over, the earl of Lincoln had brought a strong force to join Mortimer's command, and they were rolling us back far into Powys, and setting up Griffith again in his lordship of Pool, though as a vassal holding from the king, a mere baron of England.

Wherever Llewelyn himself fought, the fortunes of the conflict were stayed, at least for a time, the magic of his presence was such, but he could not be everywhere, and when his back was turned the faint-hearted began to count their chances after the old manner.

'It begins,' said Llewelyn grimly, when we heard of the first defector in Maelor, and he left the middle march as well held and supplied as he might, and went north to try to secure other waverers in the parts near Chester. He also sent his last embassage to Edward, who still graciously gave safe-conduct, to preserve his own appearance of patience, though with no intention of listening, to present once again his offers of terms to avert out-and-out war. The only response was Archbishop Kilwardby's commission to his brother of York, certainly at Edward's direct order, to pronounce sentence of excommunication against the prince, and this was done. It meant little in practical terms to us in Wales, but it did express Edward's final and absolute refusal to listen to any terms but abject surrender, or consider himself longer to have any human obligations to the rival he desired to overthrow.

As for the progress of this war that was not yet officially a war, the king's strategy during the period of preparation was clear. He reserved his use of the feudal host for the final blow, and spent the months between in such a campaign of recruitment and reinforcement as had never been used against us before. His officers built up, chiefly at Chester, but also at Montgomery and Carmarthen, great reserves of food, arms and horses, and provisions of all kinds, and also took on large numbers of men at royal pay both as workmen and soldiers. Thus while no war had begun, from three bases, widely spaced, three considerable armies were gnawing away, as opportunity offered, great pieces of Welsh land, and either turning them over to marcher barons to be held and garrisoned, or fortifying them for the crown. At the same time crown officers were busy proclaiming, as Morgan had foretold, Edward's willingness to receive Welsh chiefs to his peace upon favourable terms.

Now this may seem to be invitation only to cowards and traitors, but indeed it is not necessarily so, and Llewelyn never quite condemned those who succumbed. Consider the position of such a one as Madoc of Bromfield, one of four brothers, whose lands south of Chester jutted perilously into English territory, being surrounded more or less on three sides, and situated between two very strong English bases. Such a promontory of Welsh ground he could not defend against the crown forces alone, nor could the support of his overlord long maintain it. He had a choice between fighting for it until he was driven back out of it or killed in the fighting, abandoning it and withdrawing with all his forces to join Llewelyn and make a stand further west, or else accepting the king's offer and transferring his allegiance in order to keep his lands. He need not thereupon promise also to fight on Edward's side – though some did – it was enough if he ceased to fight against him. And to make his choice in this dire situation such a young man had only the guidance of a long past of holding and preserving a man's own small principality, a tradition barely changed as yet by Llewelyn's proffered vision of a Welsh nation. It was no great wonder that so many, in the most dangerous and exposed positions, gave way and made their peace. What was wonder was that so many stood out, and refused the bait.

Thus in the month of January both Madoc and his brother of the region south of Dee sued to Chester that they might retain and enjoy their lands unmolested if they came to the king's peace, and David and the earl of Warwick received them into fealty.

Further south, in Brecknock, the earl of Hereford, who had for so long been preferring claims to certain lands held, and acknowledged as being held, by Llewelyn, raised a large force on his own account, and turned the war to his own advantage by possessing himself of those lands before he began at leisure to make his preparations to join the king's muster. It was because of the strong pressure just to his north, from Mortimer and the earl of Lincoln, that he was able to manage this with so little effort, for we were fully occupied on the Severn. And still further south, along the Towy, the royal forces from Carmarthen under Pain de Chaworth began a great drive up the river. And here they were assured in advance of one willing ally. Rhys, the son of Meredith ap Rhys Gryg, Llewelyn's sometime ally and later unrelenting enemy and unwilling vassal, held the castle of Dryslwyn and the lands about that part of the river, and he had been very quiet and careful up to this time, islanded as he was among the sons of Rhys Fychan, the prince's nephews, who were fiercely loyal. But when Pain drew near with a considerable force, Rhys ap Meredith very pliantly bargained for terms, was promised he should hold his lands as before once the war was over, if he would but swear fealty to the king and allow them to be used as a royal base while fighting lasted, and closed very happily with that offer. He was, I think, of all those many who deserted Wales, the only one who deserted gladly, having inherited his surly old father's quarrel.

With Dryslwyn secured, the command in the south could take its time about subduing the other princes along the Towy. Llewelyn had no opportunity to go to their aid, for he was fully occupied in the north, making fast his line against the threat from Chester.

We had left the castle of Dolforwyn well garrisoned and provisioned, and its position was strongly defensible, but one thing we could not ensure for them. By fatal chance that was an early spring almost without rain or snow, a circumstance that not only negated many of our defences by marsh and river, but also dried up the well at Dolforwyn. Llewelyn said bitterly that the error was his, that he should have made better trial of the water supply before he placed a castle there, but the season was unusually dry, and once the combined forces of Mortimer and Lincoln had moved up the Severn valley to the siege, the castle could not long hold out, nor could we come to their relief. Early in April the garrison surrendered. So brief a history this castle had, and so tragic, full of contention, deceit, warfare and loss.

At no time during this winter and spring did the royal forces strike any direct blow at Gwynedd itself, the heartland of Llewelyn's power. No, their efforts were all directed at gnawing away the edges of his outlying lands, and lopping away from him one by one the lesser princes who supported him, thus denying him, when the time came, both men and bases outside his own principality. But in other and more devious ways they struck close to home. In May an indignant page-boy, who had overheard talk not meant for his ears, came rushing to Tudor with what he had gleaned. Rhys ap Griffith ap Ednyfed, who was a nephew of the high steward and a trusted bailiff of the prince, had sent a petition to the king from Llewelyn's very court, seeking the royal peace for himself and his brother, and what the boy had overheard was their agreement on flight, they had actually received Edward's safe-conduct, and were making ready to use it. Tudor, in shame and anger, had them both seized and securely held before he broke this bitter news to Llewelyn. Instead of riding into Chester with the king's letter, they were thrown into the prince's prison, and kicked their heels there in discontent for the rest of the year. So close did treason come.

It was then drawing near the day of the king's muster, his various companies already beginning to gather at Worcester. But as the term of feudal service is short, and he would have to revert afterwards to paid levies – though we had reason to believe that he preferred them – Llewelyn estimated that he would move north in arms from Worcester as quickly as possible, and make Chester his base, to strike at once at the prince's main stronghold. We were at Ruthin, with outriders stationed at intervals along the border to bring us early news of any movements, when a company of men rode in from the south, having travelled by way of Cymer and Bala, and the two young men who led them were brought in to where Llewelyn sat with Tudor and his captains in council. At sight of them he rose with an astonished cry, quicker to recognise them than were the rest of us, for they were stained and dusty and unkempt with hard and hasty riding. The younger flung himself first into the prince's arms, and then at his feet, and clung to his hands and kissed them. And then we saw that it was the youngest of the prince's nephews, his namesake and godson, Llewelyn ap Rhys Fychan, and the other was his brother Griffith.

'My lord,' blurted the boy, half in tears, and still with his face pressed against Llewelyn's hands, 'we are come to join you, to fight beside you. We have brought you all the best we could gather. There's no other home or place for us, now. The south's lost – Dynevor, Carreg Cennen, Llandovery – all lost! The king's officers have taken them to make another Carmarthen, a crown stronghold. And our brother – our brother . . .' He was choked with tears and swallowed fiercely to clear his throat of the grief that strangled him, but for some moments could not get out a word more.

Llewelyn freed his hands and took the boy by the forearms and strongly raised him. 'Not dead?' he demanded in alarm. 'Rhys is not killed?' He held the young man in his arms, the dark head buried in his shoulder, and looked across him at Griffith, who was fair, slender and quiet after his father's fashion, and slow to anger or outcry. 'What has happened to him?'

'He is alive and well,' said Griffith. 'No harm has come to him.'

'He has submitted!' cried the young Llewelyn, muffled by his uncle's clasp but loud in accusation. 'He has surrendered his castles and gone with the king's men to Worcester, to make his submission to Edward! So have Griffith and Cynan ap Meredith of Cardigan, for themselves and their nephew. There is no one left of Deheubarth to keep faith with you, only we two.' And he wept aloud for anger and shame. He was young, only twenty years old, and his uncle's worshipper from childhood.

Still Llewelyn eyed the older brother. 'They have all sued for grace,' said Griffith honestly but without excitement, 'and promised homage. We wanted no part of it. We are here. Those who would follow us we have brought with us.'

'And most welcome,' said Llewelyn, 'with or without your following.' He lifted the disconsolate boy away from him, and shook him gently between his hands. 'Never take it so hard, he is pressed in a way you cannot yet know, and he does but go after his kind. It is you who have learned something new. Though he has chosen a different way, that does not make your brother a villain.'

The boy lifted his head and blazed at his uncle with great, dark-blue eyes. 'He is not my brother,' he said with passionate bitterness. 'I have renounced him! I am done with him!'

Llewelyn's smile, though to my eyes somewhat grim and dread, nevertheless respected such rage and grief, and would not mock the boy's vehemence. He clapped him lightly on the shoulder, and laid an arm about him to bring him to a seat among the council.

'Don't write him out of your life too soon,' he said. 'Time will teach you – not too roughly, I pray God! –that brothers are not so easily done with!'

Thus we came to the beginning of July, with our powers drawn in upon themselves and shrunk to half the ground we had formerly held, with most of the south already occupied, and much of the border territory hacked away, leaving the king's approach to Gwynedd open but for our arms. It had been our invariable custom in the past to avoid great loss by withdrawal into our difficult mountain country, to keep our forces intact and deny all our resources to the enemy, while doing him all the injury we could, and then, when he was at length forced by pressure of time and weather and want of funds to recoil and break off the engagement, to follow at every step, regaining the lost lands and harrying the retreating foe. Our speed of movement and our knowledge of the ground was our strength. And thus it had seemed right and wise to do yet again, rather than crash into pitched battle with immensely larger numbers than our own. Never before had we had cause to doubt these tactics, again and again they had served us well. Yet now, as I know, Llewelyn had moments of grave disquiet and self-searching, even self-blame, before he was shown cause.

'God forgive me,' he said to me once, as we rode along the river near

Rhuddlan, and looked out broodingly towards Chester, in the summer calm that mocked our anxieties, 'God forgive me if I have misread the signs, and let him deceive me. How if this time it goes not as we are used to? If he has some new design? We have relinquished so much with hardly a fight. I know it has paid us time and again, but how if this time it was a mistake? Samson, year after year I have thought over the time before Evesham, and been shamed that I did not then have the courage to throw myself and all I had into Earl Simon's fight. Now it is on my heart that I may have made the same error again – that I should never have surrendered so much ground, but struck hard and risked all to break their concentrations as they formed, and keep them from ever moving far into Welsh ground.'

'You could not have done it,' I said. 'You could not have held together all those little chieftains in the south, kept fast hold of Bromfield, and fended off three armies, by your own strength alone. You were right, it is time that threatens us, the years you have not been granted to change men's minds and hearts.'

'Well,' he said, and set his jaw, 'we must work with what we have, fallible chieftains, a flawed prince, and brave but mortal men. I doubt it is not only poor Rhys Wyndod and his like who have erred in harking back to the past. I fear I may be just as guilty. Have I not loosed my hold of much of Wales to make Gwynedd into a fortress?'

In its way this was true, but also true that it was by far the soundest policy for us, for of all Wales the most unconquerable land was our sheer, silvered mountain country of Snowdon, and if half was to be sacrificed for a time to ensure an impregnable base from which all could be recovered, then that base could only be Gwynedd.

Upon this fortress of steely rock King Edward, in the first weeks of July, began his expected advance.

CHAPTER X

It is a strange thing that Welshmen should undo Wales, but so it was. We were a society so inward and tribal, so little disposed to look to a wider state, that as the chieftains in all the lands but Gwynedd fell away when threatened, and made their peace one by one, hardly one considering an association with his neighbours for a common resistance, so the ordinary men of those disputed and ceded lands listened with interest when the king's men came recruiting among them, and cheerfully contracted to fight for the side that was able to arm and pay them. Fighting was their business, and this was work and wages offered, and it mattered nothing to them that they were asked to fight against Wales. Wales was a word still, and no more. They belonged to a village and a commote, not to a nation, which was itself a conception out of their knowledge. So great numbers of men born Welsh, speaking the Welsh tongue, took Edward's pay and went to war for him against Llewelyn.

The prince was right. He had not had long enough to reach hearts and minds, to teach a new generation how the very air that nourished Wales was changed. It was his grief that the hour came upon him so much too soon. It was his glory that even in the short time he had, he had won so many voices and minds, even if not enough. His young namesake from Dynevor raged and ate out his heart when he knew how many south Welsh archers had accepted Edward's pay. But Llewelyn himself never cursed them.

So far as I can recount King Edward's movements in that campaign, he must have left Worcester about the tenth day of July, with some eight to nine hundred cavalry, and of foot soldiers, lancers, knifemen, archers and swordsmen, perhaps nearly two thousand five hundred, to be added to those already recruited in the three commands. He moved, for such a company, very rapidly, through Shrewsbury to Chester, where he came on the fifteenth day of the month, and there he had also the men of the earl of Warwick, and David's two hundred and twenty troopers of his bodyguard, all in Edward's pay. Of archers and spearmen here, in the retinue of the various lords of those parts, there were perhaps two thousand, with large numbers of crossbowmen among them. The archers of Macclesfield were famous, and the muster included one hundred of them. It was no light army, and not lightly supported and provisioned. I tell you, we had never encountered so calculated and organised a force aimed at us. It was not easy to make the adjustment and see them coldly and truly.

About the same time that the host was moving up from Shrewsbury to Chester, we had word from our patrol boats, keeping watch off

Anglesey, of the ships of the Cinque Ports navy being sighted rounding the island, holding well off from the land, and clearly sailing to rendezvous with Edward and lie at his orders in the estuary of the Dee. Gradually their numbers were reported, as they were sighted, to the number then of eighteen ships. Somewhat later others followed them, bringing the tally to twenty-seven, and one of them at least was French. The masters and sailors owed the king fifteen days of service without pay, from the day they came into effective action, and from the beginning of August he must have taken them into full pay, and very dear they would cost him. Our scouts also reported great numbers of men assembled at Chester who appeared to bear no arms, but to be workmen massed for some prodigious task, as though Edward intended extensive building, or something equally unusual in such a campaign. We began to see the full, daunting extent of his preparations, the like of which had never been used against Wales before, and I confess it chilled us.

'He is willing to beggar himself,' said Llewelyn, 'to break me.'

We had our line of outposts, the first defence, along the forest land above the Dee, and the mass of our northern forces well in cover inland, ready to act upon whatever word we received. The forest there was of great extent and very thick, a sturdy protection to us because we knew it well, and could penetrate it where we would with small, fast-moving raiding parties, while the royal army could not hope to operate well in such country, or bring us to open battle. It was our design to harry their every move by raids, and draw them as far into the forest as we could, where we could pick off any stragglers very easily, and hamper all their movements, especially since we expected them to be laden with all their baggage and supplies once they moved from Chester. And this was the first miscalculation, for they had now a large and powerful fleet lying in the estuary, and when they marched from Chester they marched almost as light as we, the ships carrying their supplies and keeping pace with them along the coast. Nor did Edward advance deep into the forest at all. He moved with method along the coast, his ships alongside, and all that great army of knights, troopers, archers and labourers went with him, north-westward towards the abbey of Basingwerk.

We in the forest moved with them, too, picking off any unwary enough to stray, and by night local knifemen silently stalked and killed such as they could of the sentries guarding the camps. But soon we saw how different this war was to be from any we had known. Edward's burdening himself with all those labourers was explained within two days, for they were felling trees ahead of the host, strongly guarded as they worked, and opening up a great swathe to make a road which an army could use. Unless we could prevent, we should be robbed of one of our greatest advantages, the difficulty the English always had in bringing up their supplies. Now they had the ships on one hand, and were tearing apart our forest to make a highroad on the other.

By day and by night we harried and raided them, and took heavy toll, but with our cover stripped in this wide swathe between us and them, and their picked companies of archers, more than three hundred of them, constantly on guard while the labourers worked, we had lost much of our sting. We tried every means of luring them into the thicker woods, but plainly Edward's plans were absolute and his orders were obeyed, and there were very few rash sallies, and only when we pressed them hard at some risk to ourselves. In ten days they had cut their way to within a few miles of the abbey of Basingwerk, where there was a great level plane of rock jutting out into the estuary, and there the main army made a strong camp, cleared about on every side so that we had no cover to approach them undetected. And there they stayed, so arraying their forces that it was clear they meant to fortify and hold that spot as a base. This rock we called the Flint.

An advance guard, strong in archers, still pushed on along the coastal edge of the forest with the woodsmen, who continued their felling, digging and levelling, and burned the underbrush as they went. Our scouts brought back word that the king had taken up residence at Basingwerk, and seemed prepared to stay some time, and that there was great activity at the main camp at the Flint. Several of his Cinque Ports ships were observed going back and forth to Chester, and bringing up and unloading cargoes of timber, while other materials, cords, wooden planking, lime, were already being carted along the new road in an endless chain of wagons. Within a few days we heard what was toward, though we had guessed it before. Edward's labourers were building there a very large and strong base post, which would surely be well garrisoned even when the main army moved on.

This was the first time that Llewelyn turned to tactics the Welsh seldom used, and made one attack in force against the half-built stronghold. We did not then know it, but at that time Edward was not with his army, but had taken ship and crossed the estuary to return to Chester, partly to ensure that his transport lines in Cheshire were working properly, partly to meet his queen at a spot where he had decided to build a great abbey, to be called Vale Royal. This was the time he chose to see the foundations of that church laid, so confident and resolute was he, and such deserved trust did he place in his captains in the field, Warwick, Montalt, de Knovill, the warden of the Cinque Ports, who commanded the fleet, and many more. Yes, and David, too, for David was always close about his person and first among the defenders wherever we attacked. Thus it happened that in Edward's absence David with his own guard and other troops was in command of the defences of Flint the day the prince made his strongest bid to destroy the fences and walls they had raised. It was to be then or never, before too much work had been done, and too much ground cleared about it.

It was all timber, and might be fired if the wind was right. A wind driving up the estuary was what we wanted, for our best approach was from seaward, where the road was still in the making and less open, and with good fortune we might even fire any ships that happened then to be lying alongside, and destroy their landing-stage.

It was early in August that we got what we wanted, and in the early evening made our attack. Llewelyn had sent a company of archers ahead along the half-made road to make a feint at attacking the workmen there, and draw the guards to defend them, and by this means though at some loss, for they never relaxed their watchfulness altogether, we did break through them and get across the road close to Flint, and drove down upon the palisades in strength. We had bowmen placed in cover as near as we dared, who loosed fire-arrows before us into the camp, and there was a good blaze within and a stir of wild activity before we reached the walls.

That fight was short and very fierce, and there were men killed on both sides, but they had such numbers that we never broke through to the ships. Surely we left much damage behind us when we withdrew, but not as great as we had hoped, for the traitor wind dropped with the gathering evening, instead of freshening as we had expected, and the blaze merely opened a large gap in the outer defences, and destroyed some supplies within. But what I chiefly remember of the clash is David marshalling the guard as they mounted in haste to meet and break our charge.

He was but lightly armed, and his face uncovered, and I saw him before he had discovered Llewelyn, and realised who led the attack. David's movements in action were always as sharp and cutting as lightning-stroke, but cold, if a kind of keen happiness can exist hand in hand with coldness. He was a born fighter, and could scent battle like a hound, but it was informed delight, not passion, that dictated what he did in battle. So he began this defence, very briskly and practically deploying his men and holding station with his line as they rode at us. Then he saw his brother. His face so changed, it might have been another man. Every line of his fine bones sharpened and burned deadly white, and the blue of his eyes dilated into a steely blaze, and from keeping his purposeful pace he suddenly spurred forth from the line, wrenching out his sword, leaned forward in the saddle and drove at the prince like a madman. So I had seen him do once before, very long before, on the field of Bryn Derwin, the field of his first treason. Now, as then, I saw in his blanched face and desperate eyes a terrible anguish of hate and love, and the more terrible hope of an end to it. Towards that end he drove with all his might, and he might have achieved it, if the young Llewelyn ap Rhys Fychan, his nephew, had not deliberately wheeled in between them, with a defiant scream of anger, and confronted David with the younger, purer mirror-image of his own face, spitting generous rage.

I think he could have killed the boy very easily, and perhaps would have done, almost without thinking, but for that likeness between them, as if God had flung the fresh, sweet remembrance of his own youth in his face. He let his sword-arm fall, and checked so violently that his horse reared and swerved aside. And then his own ranks had overtaken his rush, and the two lines clashed and intermingled in a close, confined melee, in which the brothers were swept apart.

Twice thereafter, in the press, I caught glimpses of David's ice-pale face, straining towards Llewelyn, but the other Llewelyn kept always jealously close at his uncle's flank, and in any case, that fight was nearly over. Something we had done, as yet at little loss. But if we did not draw off soon our losses would be great, for the camp was pouring out against us great numbers of reserves, and all surprise was over. Llewelyn signalled the withdrawal, and we massed and drew off in good order, gaining enough ground to wheel and storm across the road at speed, and so gain the shelter of the trees, where the advantage was ours. We put a mile or more between us and the borders of the Flint before we checked, but they did not pursue us into cover. They never did. Edward's will had decreed it, and they did his will with a confidence we could not but admire.

We left the stockade burning, but alas, it did not burn long. We also left a number of dead behind us, and took several wounded away, including the boy Llewelyn, who had a long gash in his forearm, of which he was proud, for he was exalted with the air of battle, and still enraged for his adored uncle.

'I hate traitors!' he said, quivering still when we bound him up in camp, and made him comfortable.

'So do we all, child,' said the prince sombrely, 'though not so sorely, perhaps, as they hate themselves. You had no call to fling this body of yours in between, very prettily as you did it, and much as I'm beholden to you for the thought. I could have satisfied him.'

And he praised and teased and soothed the excited young man into charmed quietness, and left him with the one brother he still acknowledged.

'We are beset by brothers, every one of us,' he said, when he came out to me by the campfire in our clearing, in the onset of the August night. 'It is the whole story of Wales, this blessing and curse of brotherhood, the spring of loyalty, of jealousy, of murder, of all the heroisms and the villainies of our history.' And he lay down on his belly in the rough grass, and gnawed on a spray of sorrel, with its hot, spicy taste, and pondered long on what we had both seen. 'In God's name,' he said, 'what is it he wants? To kill, or to be killed?'

I said: 'Either. He wants an end, it hardly matters which. He wants to offer you the chance you would not take at Bryn Derwin, or else to make an end of you, and so cut the knot that binds him. But he cannot do it, and you will not. I doubt his end is ordained otherwise.'

'And mine?' said Llewelyn, and smiled.

We never managed to destroy the base camp at Flint. They spent three weeks and more making it into a fortress. Edward came back from his pious labours at Vale Royal in mid-August, and by then the second part of his military road was extended well forward, for here the forest was less thick, and in parts they had only to fell and clear scattered trees, to open the field of fire for their defending archers. As soon as Edward came, the main army moved on. By the twentieth day of August it had reached Rhuddlan, from which our garrison withdrew into the hills, for Rhuddlan is among marshes on the right bank of the Clwyd, not far inland from the coast, a place tenable, perhaps, by an encroaching army moving in from the low land, but not by us who had to rely on the mountains for our heart-fortress. We did not forsake it gladly, for it covers two advances, one along the coast to Conway, one inland up the

Clwyd towards Ruthin and Denbigh. But the dry season, not for the first time in our history, had laid it open to direct assault, instead of being inviolable behind marsh after marsh, and the truth is, we could not hold it.

We made Edward pay a high price both in men and money to get there. But we could not keep him out of it.

For the feudal host had been but the beginning of Edward's resources. By this time in August he had paid reinforcements coming in, in such numbers as we had never known, we reckoned nearly sixteen thousand foot at this time, and probably three hundred lances. Where he got the money to pay such numbers, and how deep he sank into debt, I cannot guess, but we cost him a great sum, that I know. The number of the crossbow quarrels that his arbalestiers loosed on us was beyond our reckoning, and must alone have cost a fortune.

Meantime, we also had a few strange reinforcements, deserters from Edward's army, a handful of foot soldiers and archers, but far more of his labourers on the roads. They grew weary of such hard work and peril of their lives, and fled into the woods, where we gathered and questioned them. Some wanted only to slip away and go home, being pressed men, some were Welsh, and desired to change sides, and we took them in gladly. God knows there were enough Welsh by that time shamelessly in Edward's pay. Welsh friendlies, the English called them. We had another name for them.

Still the military road unrolled mile by mile through the forest ahead of Edward's main host, while Reginald de Grey commanded the base camp at Flint, and a second such strong garrison was established at Rhuddlan, thus protecting the king's rear and his supply lines. The detail that most surely opened our eyes to the gravity of our situation at that point was that the ships began to bring stone and other building materials as soon as the wooden fortifications were secure enough, and the workmen within the camp-sites began to dig foundations, both at Flint and Rhuddlan. This we beheld with deep disquiet. Neither the wide, cleared forest road nor this determined building accorded with our past experiences.

'This I do not like at all,' said Llewelyn. 'He would not go to so much trouble and expense if he meant to use these bases only for a season and then withdraw from them. Surely he cannot mean to man them through the winter? I do not believe he has the money or the supplies to feed two such garrisons and fight a winter war.'

A campaign continued through the winter was something we had never had to contend with before, for with long lines of communication and many mouths to feed it was impracticable in the mountains. But given two strong bases open to the sea, and a fleet of ships well able to cope with coastwise sailing even in wintry conditions, it began to look like a daunting possibility.

'Certainly,' said the prince, gnawing his lip over the threat, 'he seems to have plans for staying, even if he breaks off the fighting till the spring. No man cuts such a road or ships such loads of stone but to make a permanent stay.' And that meant this time we might be hard put to it to regain any part of what we had yielded. Either we must storm their camps and utterly destroy them, a terrible undertaking, or else they would hold what they had gained, and renew the advance when season and weather made it possible.

There was no sign of any slackening in their pressure on us, the road rolled on towards the Conway, clearly the king's objective, and moved with terrible speed. Nine days it took them to move their advanced base from Rhuddlan to Degannwy, and short of hurling ourselves at them in pitched battle there was nothing we could do to prevent. We could and did make them pay heavily in men and supplies for every mile, but we could not stop the march of that road. All we could do was fall back before it, and withdraw beyond the Conway, on the granite heart of our land.

From Aberconway we could not so easily be shifted, having the great heights of Penmaenmawr at our backs, and all the complexities of Snowdon close at hand to shelter and hide us at need. So things stood at the end of August, Edward on the eastern side of the estuary, we on the western, and the ebb and flow of the tides between. But Edward had his ships, far too formidable for our smaller boats to tackle, and who has the mastery of the sea can cut off mainland from island, and draw a tight noose about such a prize as Anglesey.

It may be that we should have foreseen it, but even if we had I doubt if we could have prevented, for we had no such fleet to move an army across the strait, nor dared we detach half our force, and so weaken the garrison of our beleaguered Snowdonia. But Edward had the numbers, even though he had dismissed many of the Welsh levies at this time, and kept a smaller army to feed, but all of picked men, both the cavalry and the foot, and notably all the expert archers. At the beginning of September, very shortly after he reached Degannwy, he shipped a strong division across to the island, where the corn harvest was still standing. Fighting there must have been, but the companies we had there could not withstand such an army. On the heels of this invasion force Edward shipped also a large number of scythemen and reapers, and gathered our harvest, the chief grain supply of all north Wales, for the use of his own men. Those two weeks of September were the most desolate blow he dealt us, and the most irresistible. When the news reached us, we knew our case was desperate.

Llewelyn called a council in the mountains above Aber. We looked down from our crags to that best-loved court, and across Lavan sands to the island we had lost. A sombre gathering that was. There were some among his captains who were all for fighting to the end, but more who were not afraid to say what they saw, and what they saw, if we pushed this to the last, was the loss of all.

'At least we are not come to that yet,' said Tudor. 'But for Anglesey we hold all Gwynedd west of Conway, as we always did, and I cannot believe that Edward, however determined he may be, looks forward with any very high stomach to assaulting this eagles' nest in winter. It is possible it may suit him as well as us to talk terms for another ending.'

'It is true,' said Griffith ap Rhys Fychan, the elder of the two nephews, though with a very reluctant face. 'The lord prince still has enough bargaining power to be worth listening to. And the autumn begins to close in.'

His brother showed by the wryness of his face how bitter the thought of suing for terms was to him, but to do him justice, he kept his eyes fixed upon his uncle's face, and bit back whatever his passionate heart might have longed to say.

Llewelyn said with deliberation: 'We have contended on the wrong terms, yet I do not see what else we could have done. The one time when we might have upset the king's plans was at the beginning, by a total stroke against him before he could get his armies and his workmen into movement. But then we could not foresee so strange a war. No one has ever proceeded against Wales in this fashion. He has planned a march not merely to reach Degannwy, but to make a way which can be maintained and used again and again, and he has refused to be drawn into the hills and the forests after us, where we might have the advantage. He has left garrisons at all his bases, and patrols on the roads between, to ensure his lines, and he has taken our winter supplies from us, and added them to his own. And we had best realise that he has done more than snatch our granary from us in taking Anglesey. His next step, if we force him to continue, will be to put a fresh army ashore from Anglesey across the strait, and take us in a tightening cord from the west, and to send reinforcements up the Clwyd from Rhuddlan, and draw the noose about Snowdon from the east. But gradually and methodically as he does everything, because he may find it more practical to starve us out than attempt us by storm. I begin to see that it could be done. I would not have believed the day would come when one man could turn Snowdon into a single great castle under siege, to be starved into surrender.'

That was stark talking, and the more shocking because he weighed these considerations without rage, and without shutting his eyes to a single aspect of the grim truth. They looked at one another bleakly, and in their turn weighed his words.

'It comes to this,' he said, no less calmly. 'If we fight on, we may cost him very dear to take, but if he proceeds as heretofore, my judgment is that he can take us, and he will. If we ask for terms, we can stand fast on keeping everything we now hold, and what we still hold is the heart and source from which everything else has been won. And may be won again, some day, when time favours us, and we have learned how to make better use of our wits and our resources. It is not a matter of abject surrender. We know we are not come to that, and be sure Edward knows it every bit as well. If I am wide awake to our situation, so is he to his. I do not think he wants to drag this warfare on into the winter. I do think he may be very glad if we offer him the chance to avoid that labour and pain. And I think it may be wise to do so, for if we force him, he will certainly strike back, and strike hard. I begin to know him.'

I heard then in his voice, harsh and grim as it was, the note of something beyond knowledge. He liked what he knew. This is truth, that those two were on their best terms of respect and regard when they were at each other's throats in honourable battle. I would swear that those worse suspicions they had cherished, each of the other, had died and been burned to ash in the fire of that summer war. Neither of them any longer believed that the other had coldly planned murder or treason. They were two strong creatures who had crashed forehead to forehead like rams or rutting deer, and could not by their very natures yield ground once the horns were locked. There was a huge respect in their enmity that neither of them had been able to appreciate while they angled and argued, but only when they clashed in thunder.

'If we are to ask for truce and talk terms,' said Tudor with certainty, 'it must be at once, while we are still whole, and before he can even suppose that we are weakened by loss of the harvest. If the worst befalls, and we can get no honourable terms, we shall have lost nothing and committed ourselves to nothing, and gained time for the winter to close in on him as well as on us. We can still fight to the death if we must.'

'True,' said Llewelyn, 'but I will not even enter into negotiations but in good faith.' And when he had heard all that they had to say, he said: 'I will give myself this one night. Tomorrow I shall have decided.'

He took horse and rode out that night alone over the uplands of Moel Wnion, looking over the sea, and I went after him, unseen, to the rim of the camp and beyond, and sat on a hillock in the bleached autumn grass and watched him from far off. He walked the horse gently, riding slack and easy, in solitary thought, alone with the lofty rocks and immense skies of his Gwynedd, which he stood to keep or lose, according as he played this game aright. A bitter choice it was he had to make, but one many a good man had had to make before him, in conditions even more galling and grievous, though this was sorrow enough. I think the few scudding clouds above the sea spoke with him, and the wheeling falcons that hovered like black stars against the sunset, and the folds of the uplands under their long, seeding grasses, the colour of the stubble Edward's reapers had left on Anglesey. For if the south had crumbled and fallen away from him, and the marches shattered as soon as English hands tore at them, this pure rock of Gwynedd remained, and was still inviolate. It never yet had belonged to any but its own princes. And when it came to the last allegiance, Llewelyn was not only prince of Wales, but prince of Gwynedd, too, and prince of Gwynedd first, and if all else deserted him, Gwynedd would not, and he must not desert or imperil Gwynedd. So I think his decision was made before ever he came trotting gently home again into camp. He was never one to cast the load of choice, where it hung so heavy and hard to bear, upon other men.

But had there still been doubt, as I think there was none, it would not long have survived that return. For by then we had received into our camp one more deserter from among Edward's labourers, a forester from Hoyland, one of three hundred pressed men who had stubbornly sought their freedom throughout, so persistently that a force of cavalry was drafted to guard them at work. Edward's pressed labour, though well enough paid, was not popular, especially with married men who were forced to leave their wives and families. This man wanted nothing more than to get home, but his only means of evasion at this stage was to take to the Welsh hills, and in expectation of probable questioning he had armed himself with all the information he could gather, as fair pay for our helping him on his way by a safe route.

When Llewelyn came back we were waiting to bring this man to him, and willingly he repeated what he had already told us.

'My lord, I've kept my eyes and ears open, and this was no secret about Degannwy. They say the king issued it in open letter. If he destroyed you, my lord, if you were killed or dispossessed, he promised to divide a half of Snowdon and Anglesey and Penllyn between your two brothers, the Lord David and the Lord Owen – or the whole of Snowdon and Penllyn if he made up his mind to keep all Anglesey.'

'Did he so!' said Llewelyn, drawing in breath hard. 'Half to himself, and the other half between those two! When was this agreement made?'

'A good three weeks ago, my lords, when the king came back from Vale Royal.'

'And published, you say? Made letter patent?'

'So I heard it.'

'And upon what terms,' asked the prince quite gently, 'were my brothers to hold this land of mine?'

'Why, from the king, my lord. And to do him the service all his barons owe, and attend his parliament if he calls them.'

'So I supposed,' he said, as if to himself. 'Barons like any other barons, holding of the king in chief. And Gwynedd parted into a crown province and two diminished honours at Edward's good grace! No, there is no humiliation could be visited on me so bitter as that. Even if he had lavished all on David, and left it whole, that would have been more bearable. But it is the old story, divide, and divide again, and part into fragments, the better to swallow all piecemeal.' He roused himself from his deep and grievous dream, and courteously thanked and rewarded the forester, and we gave the man shelter for the night, and fed him, and next morning set him safely on his way.

Llewelyn called his council that same night, for his mind was made up.

'You have heard,' he said, 'what Edward intends for Wales, to hack even its heart into two pieces, to take one for himself and again part the other between two lords. Never again would Gwynedd have any power to draw the fragmented princedoms of Wales into one. No, they shall not have it! I would rather go on my knees to Edward and offer him fealty and homage on his terms than let this thing happen. But we are not yet come to that. There is but one way to prevent the king from dealing as he has promised with Owen and David, and that is to force him still to deal with me. If I submit, he is at least robbed of his excuse for destroying me and turning this land into a mere appendage of his English shires. I can still bargain. If he asks too much, I can still fight, but that shall be my last resort, since it is the frailest hope. Tomorrow we'll send a flag of truce across the estuary to Degannwy, and ask the king to receive envoys and talk terms for peace.'

In mourne silence they accepted his decision. Only his young nephew and worshipper, mastering his quivering face and resolutely swallowing his tears, protested at the injustice, that his uncle should be forced to submit to indignity and humiliation in defence of what was his by right, for he feared King Edward's vengeful mind.

'It is what I do,' said the prince harshly, 'not what is done to me, that shows to my credit or my shame. There is only one man born who can humiliate me, and his name is Llewelyn ap Griffith. And I will see to it that he shall not.'

Before we slept he sent for me, and told me that if the king agreed to negotiate, and received his envoys, he wished me to go with them as one of their clerks, and be their messenger back and forth to him.

'For these will not be brief or easy bargainings,' he said, 'and though I know I must lose much of my state, I am resolved not to lose my honour. There are things I will not do, and things I will not forgo, and the chief of them I would rather not have written into any agreement or discussed as a bargaining counter publicly. It is enough if there is an understanding about it between Edward and me.'

I knew then of whom he was thinking, and I knew he chose me to be his voice because I already understood his mind. But I will not pretend I thought it an easy thing, or greatly to be desired, to approach Edward in my lord's name.

'Tudor's business,' said Llewelyn wryly, seeing my dutiful but dubious face, 'will be with the king's officers. Yours with the king. I will give you my personal letter to him and my small seal for a token. I do not think he will refuse to see you. I think it may even appease him if I advance a plea of my own, apart from the hard terms he may seek to impose. In view of the whip hand he holds, my condition – for it is a condition, and I stand fast on it – may seem light and easily granted now. It cannot threaten him any longer, or even seem to threaten.'

I said I would go to him, and do whatever was required of me.

'You know it already,' he said. 'I want his promise that my wife shall be restored to me. On every other point I will listen to him and meet him. But unless I have his word that Eleanor shall be released, there are no terms he can offer me that I will accept.'

In the morning following, Llewelyn with his court and his chief command returned to Aberconway, and the prince sent a boat with a herald across the estuary under flag of truce to Degannwy, and before the morning was over the herald returned with letters of safe-conduct from the king. We drew no hopeful conclusion from this promptness, for we had no proof yet that he felt any relief or satisfaction in being approached. But no sensible man turns aside what may well be the offer of what he wants, with less trouble, cost and loss to him than taking it by force. And his expenses to that point were extreme, though how much we had cost him we did not find out until much later, and would hardly have believed if anyone had told us the sum then.

The king, as soon and as decisively as he had replied to our approach, at once retired to Rhuddlan, shortening his lines while leaving a working guard behind him, and took the opportunity to dismiss a great part of his foot soldiers, though he kept reasonable forces in Anglesey and at Rhuddlan, while Reginald de Grey continued as warden and commander at Flint. The fleet he kept with him until the end of the month. We knew it could easily be recalled, but his sending it home was a sign that he took the negotiations seriously and had cautious hopes of them.

Tudor was the prince's chief envoy, as was right and proper, and the high steward had with him a young lawyer and clerk who was then coming into prominence in Llewelyn's service, Goronwy ap Heilyn of Rhos, while on the king's side they had to deal with Brother William of Southampton, the prior provincial of the Dominicans in England, Robert Tybetot, who had been on crusade with Edward and was his close friend, and the king's clerk, Anthony Bek. All these were closeted together with their advisers for long and arduous hours of argument and bargaining at Aberconway, breaking off at intervals while messengers went back and forth, from mid-September to early November, and long before the end we were assured that an agreement would be hammered out, however bitterly, for it suited both parties, and neither was willing to break off and resume fighting but for the most grave and desperate reasons, which accordingly neither provided. Indeed, it grew clearer as we went that those two opponents, though they fought each other over every point as stoutly as in the field, and the fight was just as much in earnest, understood each other very well upon these terms of honourable enmity, and felt no remaining rancour, as though the encounter in battle had been an absolution.

As for me, I rode to Rhuddlan and sought an audience of the king on the second day, by which time he had surely been told that the envoys appeared to be sincere, and were not attempting delays for mere reasons of policy. I presented my letter to his chamberlain, and showed the prince's seal, and after an hour of waiting in the anteroom I was summoned to Edward's presence. It no longer mattered that he might remember me, indeed the likelihood was but small, for it was a long time since last he had spoken to me at the parliament of Oxford, far longer still since I had been attendant on David when they were children together. And at Windsor, in Eleanor's retinue, he had never noticed me.

Nevertheless, when I went in to him and made my obeisance he looked at me hard and long, as though some corner of his memory retained a picture of which I was a faint reminder. But he did not pursue it. He was alone in the room when I entered. Possibly Llewelyn's letter had requested that the audience might be private, for he summoned no one while I was with him, and no one entered to trouble him with any other business. It seemed to me that even his giant body and great strength showed signs of wear and weariness. The droop of his eyelid was marked, but beneath it the brown eye glittered. He spoke to me very civilly but coldly, saying he was informed that I bore a private request from the prince of Wales, to be considered apart from the negotiations proceeding elsewhere, and giving me permission to expound the matter freely.

'It concerns,' I said, 'the lady who is close kinswoman to your Grace, and closer still to my prince. The princess of Wales is detained at your Grace's pleasure. The lord prince has no desire now to revive any complaint or ill-feeling upon that score, the time for such considerations being long past. But he bids me tell you that while he means and intends to come to terms of peace with you, and will do everything to that end, his wife's freedom and her right to join him are matters on which he cannot bargain, and should not be allowed to influence those issues which others are now debating. It is more fitting that her two kinsmen should behave with grace and consideration towards her, and towards each other. He asks, and I ask for him, that your Grace will promise that she shall be restored to her husband, when these talks have borne fruit and the peace is made.'

'I have yet to see,' said the king abruptly, 'how sincere the prince is in his wish to make and keep peace.'

'That,' I said, 'your Grace will see in due time. But I know it now. He is not asking that you shall make any concession until you are satisfied of his good faith. He is asking that this one most dear and most vital wish shall be granted as soon as you are satisfied.'

'And if I refuse to give him that assurance?' he asked, not angrily or arrogantly, rather as truthfully wishing to know.

'Then there will be no agreement. There are no other graces nor clemencies that can make any peace acceptable to him, if this is denied. Your Grace can say yes or no to peace and war in this one answer. Everything else is debatable. This is not.'

He accepted this from me as if Llewelyn had spoken it in person, gravely, even dourly, but quite without offence. He thought for a while, darkly and heavily, watching me but not seeing me. Then he said:

'And he wants, you say, only my word?'

'Yes. Your Grace's word is all.'

'And he will take my word? Unwritten, unsealed, without witness?'

'As he expects you to take his,' I said.

'The satisfaction I require,' said Edward, 'may not be short or easy. I have had good reason to withhold my countenance from this marriage, and I shall not be in haste to believe better of it. But if the lord prince makes treaty with me on terms acceptable, and shows by his keeping those terms faithfully that I no longer have reason to doubt him, then I give my word, the Lady Eleanor shall be delivered to him in marriage. The burden of proof lies upon him.'

'Your Grace will have your proof,' I said.

And that word I took back across the estuary to Llewelyn in Aberconway. And when I had delivered all, I asked him, for truly I was in need of being sure: 'And do you verily trust in his word? For so I swore to him, and for my life I do not know if I could swear the same upon my own account. I am not in two minds about him, I am in ten. He is a man I cannot reach, but the fault may well lie in me. He has given his promise. Not easily, not immediately, not warmly, not kindly, but he has given it. Do you trust in that word?'

Llewelyn was silent for some time before he answered me, but I could detect in his silence no disquiet at all, only a kind of probing wonder, as if he peered into his own mind as well as Edward's.

'Yes,' he said softly, like one reaching a hand delicately to touch an image in his mind that was still a source of astonishment to him, 'yes, I trust in that word.'

When, therefore, they clawed out from laborious hours of contention the terms of the treaty of Aberconway, one week into the month of November, Llewelyn at Aberconway considered them dispassionately, with an equable mind, endured what was injurious to his person and state, weighed what was hopeful for Wales, and rested content in Edward's word for the consummation of his love. On the ninth day of November he accepted the text agreed. On the following day, at Rhuddlan, King Edward did the same. Guardedly, and with mutual reservations, I think both were glad, and both, perhaps, with reason.

These were the main items of this agreement:

Item: The Prince submitted himself to the will and mercy of King Edward. Though stated as an absolute, it was well understood by both sides that this clause hung together with all the detailed conditions that followed, and was effective only when all were effective. The formula was necessary to Edward's position in relationship to his own barons, and he was careful to insist upon it. As fine for the insurrection and damage done by himself and all his people, Llewelyn was required to pay to the king fifty thousand pounds sterling. But the understanding concerning Eleanor was not the only clause not stated in the text, for it was agreed beforehand that this great fine was merely a gesture to be recorded, and payment would be immediately remitted, as indeed it was. Edward was well in need of money – there never was a time when he was not – but even he knew he could not get it in that quantity from a prince he had just deprived of half his lands and a year's harvest.

Item: Llewelyn ceded to the king, for himself and his heirs, the whole of the Middle Country, those four cantrefs which once had nominally belonged to Edward as prince, with all the rights pertaining, and also conceded into his hands all those lands the royal forces had taken by conquest during the war, and now in fact held. But if any lands had been captured from the prince by others than the crown, and retained, then the king would entertain the prince's claims at law to those lands, and do him justice according to the laws and customs of those parts where they lay.

Item: The prince was to be absolved from his excommunication, and his lands freed from interdict, and when that was done he was to go to Rhuddlan in state to take the oath of fealty to the king, who would then appoint him a day to visit Westminster and do homage there formally.

Item: The prince was to release his eldest brother, Owen Goch, who had been many years his prisoner. But here Edward was careful and punctilious towards Llewelyn's honour and rights, for he did accept that Owen's imprisonment had begun when he rose treacherously against his brother, with whom he then shared the rule in Gwynedd, and sought to take all for himself. Therefore his release was hedged about with conditions. He was to be delivered to the king's commissioners, and would then have the choice between coming to definite terms of peace and settlement with Llewelyn by agreement, such agreement to be approved by the king, or else, if he stood on his birthright still, he could remain in royal custody until he had been tried for his insurrection by Welsh law, in the lands where the offence was committed. Then, if the judges found him blameless, he might pursue his claim to equal rights in Gwynedd, and the king would see that the legal process treated him fairly. In this matter I think the king did Llewelyn a good service, for the grievances of Owen Goch had troubled his peace for many years, and this was as good a way of disposing of the incubus as any, and bore the stamp of crown law as well as Welsh law.

Item: Other prisoners held because of their defection were to be released unconditionally, and many restored to their lands, such as Rhys ap Griffith ap Ednyfed, the high steward's nephew. This was natural practice after a peace. A victorious king could not well leave his adherents in captivity. Among those thus let out of prison was Owen ap Griffith ap Gwenwynwyn, none the worse for Llewelyn's usage, and soon hand in glove with his father in gloating over the prince's diminution, and doing everything possible in law to vex and harass him.

Item: The names of those Welsh princes, outside Gwynedd, whose homage was to be retained by Llewelyn were stated, and they were but five, Rhys ap Rhys ap Maelgwn of northern Cardigan, and four others, all kinsmen, in Edeyrnion, in Powys. Thus all the other chiefs of Powys and of the south became vassals holding their lands from the crown. And even these five were to be vassals of the prince of Wales only for Llewelyn's lifetime, afterwards reverting to the crown. And yet, though this reduction of his nominal state was very bitter, Llewelyn was left with vassals, and was given in the treaty, most markedly, the title of prince of Wales. Surely Tudor and Goronwy ap Heilyn stood firmly upon this point of courtesy, yet I think it was not at all displeasing to Edward to agree to it. I was and am in ten minds about him.

Item: All lands which had been occupied during the war because their lords had defected to the king were to be restored to them.

Item: The king gave over freely to Llewelyn all the lands David owned by hereditary right in Gwynedd, and would compensate David with equal lands elsewhere. But on the death of David or Llewelyn those lands were to revert to the crown. This, I think, was less at David's plea than at Edward's discretion, for he felt it easier and more prudent to keep those two brothers apart, and the simplest way was to remove David's interests and holdings completely from Gwynedd. Though in fact he was less wise when it came to allotting the lands concerned, for he gave him the two inland cantrefs of the Middle Country, and thus placed this divided creature, torn in two between England and Wales, in the marches between the two, where the dissension within could most desperately rend him.

Item: The king granted to the prince the whole of Anglesey, which was to be handed back to him by the royal army then in possession. Nominally he was to pay an annual rent for the island of a thousand marks, payable at Michaelmas, but this, again, was remitted. The clause was put in to assert formally the king's acquired right there.

Item: The holders of land in the Middle Country, and the other territories formerly Llewelyn's and now taken over by the king, were to continue undisturbed in their possessions, and enjoy their liberties and customs as before, except for any among them who were regarded by Edward as malefactors, and refused such grace.

Item: Any legal contentions arising between the prince and any other person were to be determined and decided according to marcher law if they arose in the marches, and by Welsh law if they arose in Wales. So simple-sounding a clause ought not to give rise to complications and entanglements, but indeed matters of law and land are never simple, and here in these few lines endless troubles lay waiting to be hatched.

Item: Such lords as happened to hold lands both in those portions held by the king and those remaining with Llewelyn should do homage for the first to the king, for the second to the prince.

Item: The king confirmed to Llewelyn all the lands which the prince then held, without prejudice or threat, and to his heirs after him, except for Anglesey, which was confirmed to Llewelyn for life and afterwards only to the heirs of his body, no others.

Then followed the guarantees to ensure the keeping of the treaty. The prince was to hand over as hostages for his good faith ten of his noblemen, who would be honourably treated and need fear no penalties. The king promised an early release of these hostages if all went well, and he kept his word. Further, in every cantref held by the prince, twenty good men were to be guarantors annually of his good faith, and withdraw their fealty from him if he defaulted.

No question but this was a grievous constriction upon the prince's greatness, and bound him hand and foot to his dependence henceforth upon Edward, yet it still left him prince of Wales, not shorn of his right and title, not holding his land from Edward, but only, as before, under the power of the king of England. Had David been set up in his place, he would have held his lands directly from the king, and been a prince only by Edward's courtesy. Llewelyn was prince by right, and acknowledged right, that held good on both sides the borders. And though the terms and the safeguards were iron-hard, and meant to be, yet there was in all Edward's conduct of this submission a kind of harsh, unbending tenderness that spared to hurt or abase while he made all fast.

'I am back where I began,' said Llewelyn, facing the truth stonily. 'Well, I was not ashamed to be prince of half Gwynedd-beyond-Conway once, and now I am prince of the whole of it, and why should I be ashamed?'

For him there was no repining. He set himself to fill the place he had accepted open-eyed, and to maintain it, and for all his losses it was still a place any earl of England would have envied him.

Immediately on the sealing of the treaty he set to work to execute all the necessary deeds to put all its clauses into effect, and on the day of the ratification, the tenth day of November, Llewelyn rode in state to Rhuddlan to meet the king and take the oath of fealty. The king's plenipotentiaries, Robert Tybetot and Anthony Bek, with others of the king's council and the bishop of St Asaph, escorted him to within three miles of Rhuddlan, and there he was met by Edward's chancellor, that same Robert Burnell who had once brought the prince the homage of Meredith ap Rhys Gryg at Edward's request, and now came with all ceremony and honour to lead a prince to a king, rather than a vanquished man to the victor. With him came the earl of Lincoln, Henry de Lacy, who was as close a friend to the king as was Tybetot. And this noble escort was to be in attendance on the guest in Rhuddlan, and accompany him safely back to his own country afterwards.

Resolute and practical as he was, I knew well that not even Llewelyn could swallow so bitter a draught as this treaty without pain. To have half his lands hacked away from him, to lose all but five of his vassal princes and all his present hope for the Wales of his vision, was to be lopped of half his heart and drained of half his blood. The hurt of this coming ordeal might have been terrible indeed, had Edward been in a mood for vengeance. Instead, nothing could have been done that he did not do, to make it endurable. Whatever happened afterwards, whatever he did to others, I remember the Edward of that day with gratitude, for he was tender of Llewelyn's face as of his own, and paid him all the honour and deference due to an equal. Set it to the balance of his account in the judgment. To the end of my life I shall always be in more than one mind about Edward.

The king's hall at Rhuddlan was a great structure of timber then, but the stone foundations of his new castle were already in, and the walls beginning to rise. Edward's knights were gathered to welcome the prince's party, squires came to hold his stirrup and take his bridle. The earl of Lincoln and Bishop Burnell – for he was bishop of Bath and Wells as well as chancellor – ushered Llewelyn into the hall and into Edward's presence, and the glitter of that military court, spare and deprived of the grace of women, made a fitting setting for the meeting of those two men. War was the business that had brought them together, war lost and won, and soldiers know the fickleness of victory and defeat, and the narrowness of the gap between them. A man does not mock what may be his own fate tomorrow, or a year hence, at least, no wise man.

The king was seated in state, with his officers about him, when Llewelyn entered the hall. Edward was in rich, dark colours as always, very properly and carefully royal, and wearing a thin gold coronet, and at all points prepared to dominate, if not to daunt. His heavy-featured face, never given to smiling, remained aloof and stern throughout. Yet when Llewelyn advanced up the hall to him with his long, straight stride, weathered and brown and sombre, Edward suddenly rose from his seat and came to meet him those few paces that counted as a golden gift in my eyes, and astonished the prince into smiling. They stood a charmed moment face to face, quite still, each of them held. Edward was the taller by a head, but so he was among all those who surrounded and served him. And it disquieted Llewelyn not a whit that he must tilt back his head to look up at him, any more than it awes a noble child, who must do as much for the meanest grown man.

'The lord prince is very welcome to our court,' said Edward, and gave him his hand, and Llewelyn bent the knee to him briefly, and kissed the hand. 'I hope this day,' said Edward, 'instead of an ending, may be counted as a new beginning between us.'

'That is my intent,' said Llewelyn. 'I have accepted these dues, and I shall pay them. The proof shall not be in words, but the first earnest well may.'

In due form before that assembled court he rehearsed the oath of fealty, in a loud, clear voice, and with wide-open, deep eyes upon Edward's face. And after that they sat down together, and went forward with the business of the day with due ceremony but briskly. There the king formally remitted the great fine, and the annual rent for Anglesey in perpetuity, and Llewelyn was left to pay only the residue of the old debt under the treaty of Montgomery, the money he had been withholding as a means of getting his grievances set right. Edward promised release for the hostages within half a year, which showed that he was relieved and reassured thus far in his meeting with his defeated enemy. And Llewelyn, seeing that the king, whatever his successes and prospects, was direly in need of ready money, paid two thousand marks of the money due from him on the spot, to the keeper of the royal wardrobe.

In such mutual considerations and such a strange but true accord did this half-dreaded meeting pass. Those two had met several times in old days, at conferences on the border, but briefly and upon precise business, and since Edward became king they had never met at all, and that was a strange metamorphosis, creating a new Edward. Now they came face to face, sat elbow to elbow at the board, and the enemies they had hated and confronted at distance were only illusions and dreams. At Rhuddlan they were new-born, each to the other. The business of the treaty, though heavy and grave and blotting out everything else until it was done, seemed but the veil that waited to be withdrawn from between them.

Afterwards they feasted the prince, and he was set at Edward's right hand at the high table, and they came to the open, easy talk of host and guest together. From my place lower in the hall I watched them, and marvelled, and yet did not marvel, for the world is full of exaltations and basements, but men are men, and each is the man he is, and neither height nor depth changes the soul of a steadfast man. And what they said to each other I never knew, but for some few utterances that carried in a quietness.

'I never yet got a fair fall from a better lance,' said Llewelyn clearly, 'that I was not able to rise up, bruises and all, and give him credit for his skill. I might curse my own ill-judgment, but I should never grudge him his glory.'

The king turned to look at him with close attention, reserved of feature still, but with no droop to that tell-tale eyelid of his. And though I missed whatever he replied, it seemed to me that this forthright declaration gave him both satisfaction and thought.

I was seated at one of the side-tables, no great distance from them, but withdrawn into shadow near the curtained passage by which the squires and servers went in and out. I had not heard anyone enter and halt at my back, until a low voice said in my ear: 'If you are thinking, Samson, that his Grace the king could say as much, put it out of your head. He never took a fall from any man but it poisoned his life until he had paid it back with a vengeance.'

I knew who was there, before I turned my head to see David leaning at my shoulder, with the small, devilish smile on his lips, and the hungry, mocking blue brightness in his eyes. He had a cloak slung on his shoulder, with a fine shimmer of rain upon it.

I said drily that the king had looked his approval, and should know his own mind.

'He does approve,' said David. 'He approves such chivalrous usage in every other man breathing, but it does not apply to Edward. Others may fall, and rise again without malice and without disgrace. Edward must not be felled, ever. Bear it in mind for my brother's sake. The price would be too high for paying.'

He drew up a stool at my elbow and leaned in the old familiar way upon my shoulder, and smiled to see me search his face in mortal doubt and distrust. 'And never think it was Edward who had the delicacy to find me duties to keep me out of sight at this feast. No, that was my doing. Doubtless we shall have to meet, before my brother goes back to Aberconway, but for tonight at least I can spare him the sight of me.' He said it as one quite without shame, merely making sensible dispositions to avoid embarrassment on either part. 'Well, we are both losers, are we not? He is back within the palisade of his mountains, and I am exiled.'

'Self-exiled,' I said, 'and to a fat barony.'

'Ah, but it was not a barony I wanted for my son! It was a kingdom. Will you teach me, Samson, how to take a fair fall as ungrudgingly as *he* does it?'

I said he had no choice but to be content, and resign himself to a lesser estate. And once begun I said much more, how it was he who had made this war, how he was his brother's curse and demon, undoing all that Llewelyn did, unmaking wantonly the Wales that Llewelyn had made, bringing down all that splendour into the dust, so that the work was all to do again, if not by Llewelyn by his son or his son's son, when an honourable way opened. For now the prince was bound by his word and faith, and the dues he had acknowledged he would pay in full. Very softly I said it, so that no other ear should hear, and truly there was nothing to be gained now by anger or denunciation. And he leaned upon my shoulder and listened to all without resentment or defence, and though I could not bear to look at him then, I felt that all that time he was watching Llewelyn, and with what passion there was no guessing, but the ache of it was fierce and deep, and passed from his flesh into mine through the hand laid about my neck.

'Sweet my confessor,' he said, when I had done, in that soft voice that was music even in its malice, 'never labour to find me a penance extreme enough to pay all my score. I have already done that. A kingdom is not all I have lost!' And in a moment he said, lower yet: 'Do you hate me?'

'No,' I said, despairing. 'I would, but it is not in my power. As often as I come near to it, I meet you again, and though all is changed, nothing is changed.'

'Does *he*?' said David.

'God knows! He believes he does.'

'It would be something,' said David ruefully, 'even to be hated as is my due.' He gathered his cloak over his shoulder with a sigh, and drew back his stool, rising to return to his watch, or whatever duty it was he had appropriated to himself. 'I must be about my work. It was only to see you that I came.'

I knew better than that. It was to look at Llewelyn from afar, himself unseen, and to steel his heart before the ordeal of meeting face to face. Nor could I let him go like this, for my heart also had its needs. I caught at his arm and held him, before he could leave me. I said in entreaty: 'But one word more! For God's sake give me some news of Cristin! How is it with her now – with her and the child?' The word so stuck in my throat, it was no more than a croak, but it reached him. He was still in my grasp, eye to eye with me, shaken out of all pretences.

'The child!' he said, his lips forming the word without sound. 'Oh, Samson, I had forgotten,' he said with sharp compunction, 'how much you must have seen in Windsor – and how little news of her can have reached you since .. .'

'It must be a year old by now,' I said, labouring against the leaden weight on my heart. 'Is she well? Was it hard for her?'

'Cristin is well,' said David, with the swift, warm kindness I remembered in him from long ago, when he brought me the news of my mother's death, as now he sprang to ward off any dread of another death as dear. 'Safe and well with my wife in Chester, you need not fear for her. Neither Elizabeth nor I will ever willingly let harm come to her. But the child . . . She miscarried, Samson. The child was born dead.'

CHAPTER XI

There was enough to be done, in that last month of the year, to keep us all from fretting over losses and deprivations. Llewelyn had a great deal of business with the royal officers concerning the release of both Welsh and English prisoners, the handing over of Anglesey, and other such matters, as well as the necessary adjustment of his own administration to his new and straitened boundaries and circumstances. There was no time for repining, for at Edward's invitation – he might have made it an order, and it was understood to have the force of one, but he used the more gracious term – the prince was to make his state visit to spend Christmas with the court at Westminster, and there perform his homage to Edward with all due ceremony, and before that visit it was expedient that he should be rid of his prisoners, have the matter of Owen Goch settled, and be ready to make a fresh start.

As for me, I had at least the peace David had granted me. I knew that Cristin was alive and well, and by a strange grief and a stranger grace delivered from her incubus, and that no guilt lay upon her, for the fault was not hers, only the peril and the suffering. And in London, God willing, I might see her and speak with her again. Of Godred I thought not at all, for there was no profit in it. I dreaded to think of him still pursuing her with his hatred, and trying to get her with child yet again, since this one poor imp had escaped him. I feared to consider the possibility that even Godred suffered, and could love a child of his own body, even one got for devilish purposes. In remembrance of my half-brother there was no comfort and no rest, nothing to benefit him or me, much less Cristin. My comfort was that she was dear to David, and David's loyalty, where it existed, was immutable. His own brother was not safe with David, but Cristin was safe. So I gave my mind and heart to helping Llewelyn in all that he had to do, to satisfy the terms of the treaty.

'At least,' he said, when he had sent for Owen Goch to be delivered out of Dolbadarn, 'perhaps I shall get peace from all my brothers now. David is a baron of England, and what small adjustments need to be made to him for the land rights he's quitting in Gwynedd can be made and sealed by the king, and let him quarrel with that arbitrator if he dare. The matter of Rhodri's quitclaim and its price is in Edward's hands, too, and Rhodri has a wealthy wife in England, and employment in the queen-mother's service, where he's surely more use than ever he was to me or to Edward in war. Now let's lean on Edward for help with Owen! Why not? I shall have some good out of the evil, after all. It is not I who must confront Owen with the choice before him.'

And that was truth, for as soon as Owen Goch was brought out of

Dolbadarn and provided with a new wardrobe and household, he was handed over to the king's commissioners, in whose care he must have felt himself safe enough. So the choice put before him was not weighted either way, for it was the English who posed it. He could either be provided with a landed establishment agreed with Llewelyn and approved by the king, or else stand his trial for old treason by Welsh law, and bid for his whole birthright if he was acquitted. He chose to make peace with his brother, and let the law rest. It was no great wonder. Owen Goch was then fifty years old, and almost half his life had been spent in captivity. It is true that he could have gained his release long since, if he had been willing to accept the vassal status he was thankfully closing with now, but he had been more stubborn and unbending then, and would not consider any such concession. He was growing more lethargic now, and less combative. He came out of Dolbadarn morose but subdued, after his fashion still a fine-looking man, large and in good health but for his corpulence, but pallid from confinement and indolence, and with his fiery-red hair and beard laced with grey. He was insistent on good attendance, quick to regain the imperious temper of a prince within his own household, but he no longer desired to challenge his brother at the risk of being adjudged traitor. I think Llewelyn heaved a great sigh of deliverance when Owen made his choice for a land settlement, and then to be let alone on his lands.

Llewelyn offered the whole cantref of Lleyn. Considering his own narrowed borders, I think it was generous, but he, also, was buying a measure of peace of mind. Owen jumped at the offer, astonished to be priced so high, after so many years. The king's commissioners solemnly considered and discussed, and came to the same decision. Owen was settled in Lleyn before the year ended, with Edward's officers to help him administer and rule while he was stiff from confinement still.

The night after this was achieved, and very shortly before we prepared for the departure to England, Llewelyn sent for me to his own chamber before he slept, and had me play to him for an hour or more. He lay in his bed and listened, and breathed long and deep. All the burden of his royal line and his royal struggle, unblessed by Welsh law, borne virtually alone, lay so heavy on his breast that he heaved sigh after deep sigh against it, and could not heave it off his heart.

When his breathing grew long and slow I ceased playing, thinking that he slept. But when I rose silently to steal out from him without disturbing his slumber, he made some small, involuntary movement among the furs of the brychan, and I stilled to listen, and knowing him awake, asked if I should leave the candles for his chamberlain to snuff.

'No, quench them,' he said. And when I had snuffed out the last, and the dark closed on us, I heard the faintest thread of his voice breathe, I think to God rather than to me, and with such resignation and pleading: 'I am tired!' It was the saddest thing ever I heard from him, and the most solitary.

I went out from him as softly as I might, and drew to the door.

The next morning he arose refreshed and vigorous, and never again did I hear him utter word or sound to express the depth and desolation of his loss, or complain of the half-lifetime he had spent in building what was now razed almost to its foundations. He took up the simple daily burdens. bought in corn to replace the part of the harvest that had been consumed by the king's army or carried away, set trade moving again across the borders to bring in salt and cloth, and enable the monks of Aberconway to sell their wool. The king aided willingly in re-opening the channels of commerce and making it possible for Welsh goods to reach English border markets, for trade was of value to both sides. If there were any local raids and fights on these occasions, or any ill-usage of Welshmen venturing into Montgomery or Shrewsbury or Leominster at this time, it was the result of hot blood and high feeling so soon after the end of hostilities, and no fault of Edward's, and he gave strict orders to his officers to curb such offences and make amends where due.

Then we set out for London to keep Christmas with the king.

A great and glittering party that was, for we went more carefully splendid than usual, having a princely dignity to uphold in conditions possibly more difficult than at Rhuddlan. And I will say for him that Edward did his full part to make the visit outwardly royal, however hard the control he exercised behind the curtain. He sent a noble escort to meet the prince and conduct him to Westminster. Bishop Burnell led the party, and with him came the treasurer, who was the prior of the Hospital of St John of Jerusalem, Henry de Lacy, earl of Lincoln, and two of the greatest of the marcher lords, Roger Clifford and the prince's cousin Mortimer. Short of sending his own brother, the king could not have done the prince of Wales greater honour. Thus gloriously attended, we entered that island city of Westminster once again, on the eve of Christmas Eve, and were courteously received and splendidly lodged, Edward offering audience at once in greeting. And on Christmas Day in full court, before all the assembled nobility of England, Llewelyn was conducted ceremoniously into the king's presence, and did homage to him.

There were young lords there, and new officials, and many ladies, who saw the prince of Wales for the first time, though the chief officers of state knew him, even those who had never had direct dealings with him, from his visit at the translation of St Edward the Confessor. Thus many awaited their first glimpse of him as a defeated man, out-thought and out-fought and brought now to an act of submission he was held to have resisted for five years. And for once he had given some thought to his appearance in this hard role, for his pride could be stung by scorn, mockery or pity like any other man's, and he had the dignity of Wales in his hands, as well as his own. Yet he, who had never denied his defeat, or called it anything but what it was, would not stoop to arm himself with compensatory finery. He wore his best, and he wore jewellery, the polished mountain stones of his own Snowdon, but only as he would have decked himself at any feast to do honour to his host and the season. He chose to be dark, plain and without weapons, putting off even the ornamental dagger that would have passed muster well enough at his belt.

'Homage is homage,' he said, 'and I have incurred it and am bound by it. Unarmed is unarmed. There shall not be so much as a brooch on me that could prick his hand or my honour.'

But the talaith, the gold circlet of his rank, that he wore. For Wales, though shrunken to the bounds of Gwynedd-beyond-Conway was still a distinct and separate princedom, not held from Edward, not subject to him. Thus the prince made plain his own reading of the relationship between them.

When the earl of Lincoln brought him into the king's great hall, every head craned to see him, and every eye fixed upon him, and that is a heavy ordeal when the necks stretch only from curiosity, not ardour, and the eyes are the eyes only of enemies or of those indifferent. The good opinions of individual men among them he had still to win, and did win, in the two weeks and more he was to be a guest in London. But he looked only at Edward, huge and grave and splendid in crown and state, and kept his eyes steadfast on the king's face as he walked the length of that great room to the steps of the throne.

Two of his brothers were among the crowd of lords and officers flanking the throne on either side, David close to Edward's shoulder, Rhodri withdrawn among the lesser men. The eldest was lording it happily in his new freedom on his lands in Lleyn. At his testing time, Llewelyn was brotherless. He had no one to lean on, and there was no one to let him fall. And better so.

He needed no one, he was prepared for this moment long before, and he was able to put away from him the circumstances in which it was required of him, and to perform it as directly and simply as if that first meeting planned at Shrewsbury had truly taken place. It was not he who paled and stiffened as he went on his knees on the steps of Edward's throne and lifted up his hands to the king, joined palm to palm, large, brown, able hands. Not he whose brows drew sharply together as in a spasm of pain, when Edward leaned and enclosed the prince's hands in his.

I was watching Llewelyn, but I was aware of David. Very handsome and fine he was in black and gold, and very confident and graceful at the king's side. Elizabeth among the queen's ladies might well glow with pride in him. But with every step that Llewelyn took towards his homage, those high, winged cheekbones of David's tightened and burned slowly into points of blazing white, and fine lines of pallor drew themselves along his jaw, until it seemed the bones would start through the gleaming skin. White as bone and smooth as bone, like an ivory carving of a face, he watched his brother kneel and lift up his hands. There was no contortion, no movement of that face, until the sharp, brief convulsion of his brows. Only his eyes were so desperate a blue that they looked like lapis lazuli inlaid under the high-arched lids. And I could not choose but wonder if he had suffered such pain when he paid his own homage for Rhufoniog and Duffryn Clwyd. I think not. Then he would have been graceful, easy and inwardly scornful, for he had shown Edward already, by his usage of this same brother, how lightly he held his troth, and it was Edward's fault if he paid no heed. But Llewelyn's troth was not light. A heavy load it was, and a tight shackle upon his freedom, yet he could bear it, and go his own way without discarding it. It was David, of all people in that great concourse, David, who found this joining of hands hard to bear.

There was a moment when it came into my mind that I might be seeing this the wrong way round, that it was Edward he grudged to Llewelyn, and not Llewelyn to Edward. And that was when the king very graciously clasped the hands he had been enclosing, and himself raised the prince to his feet, spoke some words of sudden, smiling condescension to him, and warmed from stone into human flesh. Until I looked again at David, and saw the blood flowing back easily into his cheeks, and his cool, bright eyes attentively studying Edward's face, flushed into content and benevolence at having got what he wanted at last, by force or fraud or no matter how. It hardly needed the slow curl of David's lip, aloof and disdainful, to set me right. It was not every man, Welsh or English, who had the hardihood to feel scorn for Edward.

The feast that Christmas night in Westminster was long, rich and splendid, and the prince of Wales was its guest of honour. No question but Edward was elated with his prize, and at his board and about his palace did everything to display him and show him favour. And gradually I began to understand the curl of David's lip as he beheld the first token of that favour. For I was present at many of those business meetings that took place during the last days of December, and the first two weeks of the new year twelve hundred and seventy-eight. Publicly in hall, feasting, dancing, out and about the city and on London river, wherever the queen and her ladies were, Edward showed his most friendly and beneficent face to the prince of Wales. But privately in conference, over the complex details of the treaty arrangements, his hold was tight and arbitrary, and his voice dry and commanding. The first great thing he had wanted, that he had got, and that was Llewelyn's fealty and homage. Everything else he sat down to exact in the same manner.

'For God's sake, what should we expect?' said Llewelyn, shrugging. 'He asks but what is due. He has not stepped one pace beyond what the treaty gives him.'

'Nor drawn one pace back,' said Goronwy ap Heilyn.

'Why should he? You and I, my friend,' said Llewelyn with good humour, 'both agreed to the terms as written. How can we complain now? He has not been ungenerous. He has put back a fair number of dispossessed young men into their lands, my nephews among them.'

'As vassals of the crown,' said Tudor sadly.

'According to treaty. And we know it, every man of us.'

It was true. Rhys Fychan's two young sons were installed once again as lords of Iscennen, along the Towy, as their elder brother had been allowed home again earlier, though not repossessed of his castle of Dynevor, which the crown intended to keep. Similarly several of Llewelyn's former tenants in the Middle Country were restored to their lands, but holding them from the crown. It pleased and comforted Llewelyn that these unfortunate young men should have protection still when he could not protect them. He had lost them, but they had not lost everything.

But though he was jealously aware of his duty to watch the interests even of the vassals who had been taken from him, since they were most of them loyal Welshmen, as deprived and repressed as he, the first thing he had sought on his own account was news of Eleanor, grace to meet her at last, and a firm promise that his proxy marriage with her would be allowed to be blessed finally in a more formal ceremony. It did not gall him to bend the knee and do homage to Edward, but it chafed him bitterly to have to ask grace of another to be allowed to visit his own wife. Nor was he spared the pain of waiting and watching at the Christmas feast, to allow Edward, if he so planned, to make the generous gesture of bringing her from Windsor of his own accord. He did not do it. Llewelyn was forced to make the approach. Nor was his request granted at once. Edward first desired to examine for himself the arrangements made, the nature and location of the dower lands the prince proposed to settle on his bride. The lady was the king's cousin, and in his care, and it was his duty to approve the proposals made for her future establishment, and to ensure that provision for her was adequate to her rank and needs.

I could not but remember, when this was said, that Amaury was also the king's cousin, and Amaury was still prisoner in Corfe castle, for no crime, however much Edward might dislike him, and still close – kept though two popes in succession had requested, urged and demanded his release. Some half-dozen of Eleanor's knights and officers were likewise in captivity, in spite of her pleas for them, for I was sure she had never ceased to protest at their detention, and to affirm that they had done nothing but their simple duty in serving and accompanying her.

Yet the manner in which Edward countered and delayed in the matter of Eleanor was not unfriendly, only cautious and austere, as though he still distrusted, and yet was disposed to give his blessing to the match. At the beginning of January he indicated to Llewelyn that he might send his proctors to Windsor to talk with the princess about her dower and her marriage settlement, and the constable would be instructed to allow the party free access, and leave to confer with her in private or with witnesses, according as they might desire. It was the first concession, and on the fourth day of January Goronwy ap Heilyn, with two others, paid that visit, and came back so deep in slavery to the lady that his face spoke for him. Llewelyn, starving, stooped to beg for what had not been offered. I think it was the one thing for which he came near hating Edward, that he had to ask what even a tyrant should have given freely. And strangely, Edward hovered half a day on the edge of refusal, though avoiding rather than speaking plainly, and then veered about and resolved to grant, and that with every mark of favour and approval, as if the idea had stemmed from him in the first place. He allowed the visit, he would himself accompany and present the prince to his bride.

They rode for Windsor handsomely escorted, but by none of Llewelyn's people, only a gay company of Edward's knights and squires. Either the king still did not quite trust in his hold over the prince, and wanted this meeting under his own eye to observe every word that passed, or else he was truly making an effort to convince us of his goodwill, and meant his patronage as an honour, an earnest of favour and familiarity to come if Llewelyn behaved well towards him and kept to terms. Llewelyn himself, though he would far rather have had the freedom of riding alone, took the king's attention at its open value, and was encouraged and reassured by it.

'I know well I am on probation,' he said to me, somewhat grimly, before they rode. 'Was there not some worthy in the Bible who served fourteen years for his chosen bride? I am like to run him close for mine.'

Being free of all duties while they were gone, on a fine wintry day without frost, I went out alone beyond the great church to the west gate, and so into the palace court, and crossed to the alley of St Stephen's, for David was lodged in one of the houses of the canonry with his family and his body-servants, the men of his following being at the Tower. All these days in Westminster I had half-hoped and half-dreaded to catch a glimpse of my dear in attendance on Elizabeth, but when that lady was in the queen's company Cristin was never with her, being left, as I guessed, to take care of the children. There were five of them now, as I had heard, and their mother placed absolute trust only in Cristin. So many of us, God knows, had learned to do that, too many leaned upon her. I was famished for the sight of her face and the sound of her voice, even if I might hope for no more, and this day I was resolved at least to walk by the house, and touch the walls within which she moved and breathed.

David himself had been sparing of his appearances, attending on the king only when he was summoned, and then remaining, as far as possible, apart from the Welsh guests. Not shame, but some manner of dire struggle with himself held him off. Edward, no doubt, thought he had only to issue his order, and himself behave as though no strains and stresses existed, and all men would fall into the pattern. But it is not so easy to take up and knit again threads torn from the heart, and truly Llewelyn had said, and meant, that he had been through David's to-and-fro once too often, and David was dead to him.

In the royal hall they had met and passed without words several times, but among so many who was to take particular note of how Llewelyn looked through his brother, as though he had not been there? They were not the only enemies of recent months now forced into proximity, and compelled to contain whatever hatred and enmity they still felt. They were only the two greatest of many like them.

The house where David's family was lodged was towards the further end of the alley, its upper windows looking over the Long Ditch where it flows down into the Thames. It had a garden and a courtyard, and its own stable, and when I drew near it I heard the voices of children shrilling in the yard, and my heart leaped, for if they were there, loosed out to play in the winter sunshine, then Cristin would be there, too, watching over them.

I could not forbear, I pushed open the narrow wicket in the yard-gate, and stepped through. Two little girls and a sturdy round boy were tossing a ball to one another round the courtyard, and a third girl-child. perhaps just turned two years old, was staggering in reckless runs between them to catch vainly at the flying toy as it soared well above her head. And on a stone bench against the stable wall Cristin sat wrapped in a blue cloak, holding in her lap the last-comer, still a month or two short of a year, a bright brown boy, with thick hair the colour of bracken, and large, bold, fearless eyes that lit on me as hers did, by that secret magic she had, the instant I passed the wicket, as though both she and the child had been waiting only for me.

Her hair, still raven-black and smooth, was down in a long braid over her shoulder, and her head was uncovered, for the hood of her blue cloak had slipped back and lay in folds at the nape of her neck. With her clear white face, oval and pure as pearl, framed in that deep blue, and the little boy thrusting his strong feet against her knees and raising himself in the circle of her arm, she brought to mind all the fairest paintings in manuscripts or stained glass of the mother of God holding her child, and she had in her eyes all the foreshowing and foreknowledge of sorrow beyond the brief experience of joy. But there was none of that sick despair and grievous loneliness I had seen in her at Windsor, only a white and stoic calm, and a resigned, unquenchable gentleness. She looked like one who has touched hands with death, and on the very threshold felt the hand disengage, and has turned back without complaint or question to take what pleasure she may in the living, and in quietness, and abandoning all self-seeking, finds there more pleasure than she thought for.

I stood unmoving to gaze at her, for she was beautiful as never before, finer drawn in every line, her lips, that smiled at sight of me, had regained their long, firm shaping, the white, arched lids of her eyes were smooth and clear. Thinner and older she was, worn away to pure spirit by that nine-months penance and the birth-death that ended it, but she was my Cristin in all her gallantry and force, unbroken.

She saw me look from her to the child on her knee, and her smile deepened. There was no shadow in her eyes and no constraint in her voice, as she said: 'Not mine! Only borrowed.'

'David told me,' I said, 'in Rhuddlan.' I could not say that I was sorry. Now that I saw her healed I could not be sorry, my heart in me was crying out defiant joy. 'Is this one David's?' I asked her.

'He is.' She knew already what was in my mind, and why I so stared at him. Beholding those big, fearless eyes, darker than peat water in the mountains but full of the sun, and that rich brown colouring, if only my lord's proxy marriage in Montargis had been a marriage completed I should never have thought to ask whose boy this was. He harked back three generations to his great-grandsire.

'This face he had from birth,' said Cristin, 'and this colouring. And the name his father has given him,' she said, 'is Llewelyn.'

I sat with her on the yard bench in the fair winter day, watching the children play, we two together like well-blessed parents taking pleasure in our young, we who had nothing but our love, and that doomed never to bear fruit in this world, or never earthly fruit. I told all that had befallen me since she came to bring me word of deliverance in Windsor, and begged me to leave her for her sake. And she told me of how it was in Chester, with David active in war and frantic always to be of every party that ventured an advanced guard, or planned a perilous raid, all the more if it would take him face to face with his brother in arms, and how he took always a high and arrogant line with the king's officers, and would have a prince's rights among them, yielding to none but Edward himself. And how no word was ever spoken between them concerning what he had done and what he had tried to do, but never anything Edward could offer, no concession in taking all his men into royal pay, no promise of dominance in Wales after victory, no permission to retain what booty he took, nothing ever was enough for him, so high did he set the price of his treason. And that I understood, for the world was not enough to repay it. Only his death or Llewelyn's could have satisfied him, and they both lived on. And still there was not room in the world for both, never short of a miracle, to cast them back once for all into each other's arms.

Thus we talked of those two brothers, and of the prodigies of creation and destruction they had wrought between them. We sat, as it were, in the shell of a noble castle not utterly ruined, but slighted by a passing enemy, with years of labour to be spent on it before ever it could be defensible again. But so have many castles been, time after time on the same site, and yet risen again, and again become seats of majesty.

But not one word did she say of her suffering, and her miscarriage, not one word of Godred. Of him we never spoke in the old days, but since Windsor I was afraid for her, and I needed to know.

'You have told me nothing,' I said, 'about yourself.'

'What should I say of myself?' said Cristin gently. 'You see me, you touch me, I am here beside you. There is nothing you need to know of me that you do not know.'

'There is,' I said. 'I need to know that you are safe from harm. That he no longer persecutes you.'

'I am free from him here,' said Cristin, measuring out words with care. 'He is at the Tower with David's officers and troopers. I have not seen him for nine days and more. But you need have no fear for me. There'll be no more such births and deaths, even when we are under the same roof again. Since I lost him his son he pesters me no more. If he comes to my bed at all, he lies far off from me. He holds it against me that the child died. He will always hold it against me.'

'He may try to harm you, then, in some other way,' I said, tormented, 'if he has turned so against you.'

'No,' she said, 'you need not fear it. He speaks to me as he would to a servant keeping his house, civilly but coldly. He shows no anger and no hatred, he never touches me. I have peace from him. Since his son died, I also am dead for him, being useless. I shall never conceive again.'

Her voice was low and meditative and tranquil, and her face serene and plaintive. My heart ached for her, because of the little ones still tossing their ball about the yard, and the baby boy half-asleep and crooning merrily to himself in her arm. But her heart was at rest.

'Never grieve for me,' she said. 'I do not grieve. I have what I prayed for. If it was a sin to pray for such a dark deliverance, I have sinned, and I will pay for it. But if ever I did Godred any wrong, it was in some way I could not help, not with my will, and it is not for me to apportion penance, only to bear it. It would have been a worse sin to bring his son into the world, when he wanted it only as the instrument of evil, against you, against me, against the innocent who is dead. True, he came to think of it with love before the end, and surely he would have loved it as well as he can love, but I think his love is a heavier curse than his hate. And now I am free of both, and so is the child.'

I said, trembling at this calm that passed so far beyond intensity: 'It sounds but a drear world for you. I wish to God I had the means to fill it with brightness and joy.'

'So you do!' said Cristin, her voice burning into sweet, warm passion, and she turned fully to me, with her great eyes glowing purple as irises under the high white brow, and laid her hand over mine. 'So you do, and will lifelong, from the night I first met you in the snow to the day of my death. Oh, I have other joys,' she said, smiling. 'I have children, even if I must borrow them. I have friends. But above all I have this, that I love you and you love me, beyond change, and safe, utterly safe, from any betrayal. I would not change with any woman on earth.'

I folded both my hands about hers and held it, and it was warm and firm and steady. And I said to her all those things we had never said to each other but once, when we made our compact, and it was such strange bliss to get the words out of my heart and string them like pearls for her to wear.

As I reckoned the time of day afterwards, about this same hour that I sat clasping the hand of my love, so did Llewelyn at Windsor first see the face and touch the hand of Eleanor de Montfort.

We were still sitting thus, hand in hand, when the yard gate was flung open, and David rode in, flushed and vivid on a grey horse. The children heard, and dropped their ball to run and meet him, and the elder boy, approaching four years old then, reached up fearlessly to his father's stirrup. David leaned down and took the boy under the armpits, and hoisted him to the saddle before him, and walked the horse gently into the stable with the three little girls clamouring after him. When he came out to cross to the house he had a girl by either hand, and the six-year-old Margaret trotting at his heels, but the boy had stayed to see the horse rubbed down and groomed. With all these blossoming creatures clinging about him, and himself glowing with exercise, David was like a fine tree bearing at the same time flowers and fruit.

He said a word in the ear of the eldest girl, and put the hands of both her sisters in hers, and sent them dancing before him into the house, and then he turned and came to us.

'My conscience and my confessor with their heads together!' he said. 'I tremble for the fate of my poor soul.' And smiling, he stooped and held out his arms for his younger son, and the boy crowed and went to him eagerly from Cristin's lap. 'Come away in with him, Cristin,' said David. 'You'll take cold sitting here so long, and I dare say Samson will condescend to accept a place by my fire and a seat at my table, now we've all made peace. Without prejudice to your loyalties,' he said to me, and filled a careless fist with my hair before he clapped me on the shoulder and walked away into the house, dancing his delighted son on his arm.

So we arose and followed them in, David who had plotted Llewelyn's death, and the boy who bore Llewelyn's face, and at David's wish had been given Llewelyn's name.

'Who is evil?' said Cristin, watching them. 'Who is good? It is too hard for me. All I can do is love where love is drawn from me. That cannot be wrong.'

*   *   *

So all that day I stayed with my dear, and it was the most I had ever had of her since our first journey together. But before I went back to await the prince's return, David prayed me to come and speak with him privately. He asked me of Llewelyn, for since he avoided a direct meeting he was in want of reliable news, and he was right in saying that there was no placing any trust in the rumours of the court. I told him of the visit to Windsor, and of our cautious hopes that this was an indication of some unbending on Edward's part.

'I had heard of it,' said David, frowning and gnawing his lip. 'He was in two minds about it, so it seems. Some days ago he was bent on holding her in reserve, in case my brother needed a touch of the whip. Now he's graciously bringing them together. Well, it's another way of using his weapons.'

I said truthfully that though the king had taken good care of his own interests, and exacted what he could out of the peace, yet he had not been ungenerous, and Llewelyn well understood that he was still being tested, took Edward's suspicions and precautions with good grace, and appreciated his magnanimity in showing so much favour.

At that word David's smile turned very sour. 'Edward's favour is never magnanimity. For God's sake get that into my brother's head if you can. He spends favours to get his own ends, and he expects value for all. If he has graciously led Llewelyn to his wife, it means he has decided to take them over, both, to move them where he wants them, as he moves his other dolls, to place them under an unescapable obligation to him for life. Others give to give, Edward gives to get. It is a new kind of villeinage. Warn my brother so!'

I protested at this that the king had never attached any conditions to those concessions he had made previously, and none were attached to this.

'They are understood,' said David grimly. 'By Edward at least, and they had better be understood by all those he takes under his wing. If he does not get value for his money he will take it, and with interest. It is better not to be in his favour. But if a man must, let him learn to fend for himself, and see to it that he sells nothing of himself in the process. Take what's given, by all means – since he makes no conditions, force him to stand to that. But never think he'll be outbargained easily. It is Edward who makes the rules. We break them at our peril.'

'And you?' I said, for this was a man deep in Edward's debt now speaking, at least in the world's eyes and Edward's.

He smiled at me without resentment, though somewhat sombrely. 'I have not broken the rules – yet! If ever I do, it *will* be at my peril. All I have done as yet is to make my own rules in return, and stick to them. If he lavishes favours on me, I put up my price still higher. If he bestows a rich bride on me, and thinks to own the pair of us, we join hands and form a league of our own. He has bought neither of us. He has not enough resources to afford us.'

'Neither could he ever come near the price of Llewelyn or Eleanor,' I said with certainty. 'They are neither of them for sale. When they give, it is a gift, not a price. They expect the same dealing from him.'

'You know that, I know that,' said David readily, 'but Edward does not know it. By all means keep them in innocence and him in delusion, but watch over them, Samson.' He saw how I looked at him, and flinched, and as suddenly laughed, rising to herd me to the door with an arm about my shoulders. 'For God's sake go back where you belong. I do not know if I threaten your peace, but God knows you are perilous to mine. Go see as deep into Edward as you do into me, and Llewelyn may be safe, if there's any safety.'

At the doorway Cristin was waiting, and for her sake he relinquished me, clapped me loudly on the cheek by way of farewell, and left us together. We went without a word said. At the gate I took her hand and kissed it. 'God go with you, and God bring you back,' she said, and with that blessing I went from her.

Llewelyn came home with the onset of dark, but went away again to the king's table, and I had no speech with him then. His face was bright but distant, like the face of a man who has seen the Sangrail of all legend, though he moved and spoke as briskly as ever, and went to the royal board as in duty bound. I thought then of all David had said, and wondered how true it was that in Edward's mind every motion of hospitality, every cup filled at that board, every gesture of friendliness, was scored as a debt, a link in a chain binding a slave.

To a Welshman the guest is holy, all that is in the house is his, he must not be questioned or prompted, when he leaves is his own concern. Blood feud, as of right, follows any violation of the sacred relationship. The home is not a spider's web, spinning gummy threads to bind and confine, but a hearth and a board open to guests and God.

When he came back from the meal in hall it was late, but he asked me to attend him for a while before he slept. It was the hour when we talked together most freely, and I think he wanted with all his heart then to talk of her, but he was so full of her that his wonder and gratitude and joy found no words fitting, and his voice would cease in the middle of speaking, and his mind go away from me silently, back to the chamber in Windsor castle, and the woman rising to come to meet him.

'I have lost and won,' he said. 'By God's goodness I see my gain outweigh my loss. Oh Samson, I only half-believe this grace is meant for me.'

He told, though haltingly, how the king brought him in to her, and when they were formally made known to each other, left them together. It might be true that Edward, having decided to permit the marriage, had also decided to take possession of it and make it his own festival, but it was not true that he used no discretion or consideration in so arranging matters. I said nothing to the prince of what David had said to me, for mention of the very name would have darkened the brightness of that healing evening. I resolved rather to watch how this thing developed, and speak out only if I must.

'He will not be in any haste to give her to me,' said Llewelyn, wryly smiling. 'I know I must prove my good faith, he takes no man's on trust. But now I am sure that in the end all will be well. No, all is well now! I have seen her, I have looked into her eyes, and seen Earl Simon's eyes looking through them, the same nobility, the same truth, and accepting me as generously as he did. She was glad, Samson! It was with her as it was with me. Now I have seen her look at me as sometimes I have seen Cristin look at you, and beyond that no man can go. Such a spirit, and in a vessel of so much beauty!'

Then in his rapture of humility and exaltation, so moved by his joy in her that he felt a saint's tenderness towards all things living, he bethought him of what he had said, and caught impulsively at my hand, reproaching himself for having so little regard for the deprivation I suffered, when he was promised such blessedness.

'God knows,' he said, 'I wish I could share with you, whose waiting has been longer even than mine, the happiness that is held out to me. If I could lay Cristin's hand in yours, by any means in my power, I would do it. I am learning how much the happy owe their fellows.'

'You need not grieve for me,' I said. 'We were born in the same night and under the same sky. All the while that you have been with Eleanor at Windsor, I have been with Cristin. I have seen her, and held her hand in mine. In the same hour! Our stars have not betrayed us.'

For all this hopeful beginning, and every indication on his part that the ending would be favourable, Edward made no haste, and offered no more such glimpses during that visit. Rather he concentrated on the stern business of preparing the administration of the Welsh lands he had taken into his own care, and though he expected Llewelyn to take part in all the conferences, and consulted him freely, it was Edward's will that carried all before it. The lands being now taken out of his hands, the prince could but advise, and intercede where he thought not enough weight was being given to Welsh custom and feeling, pleading the cause of his lost vassals even when he could no longer affect their fate. Edward showed every sign of listening with care, and wishing to retain their peaceful adherence by treating them fairly, but what he and his officers best understood was their own system of shires and sheriffs, and they tended to believe it must necessarily be best even for the Welsh.

The prince, with Tudor, and Goronwy ap Heilyn and others, worked loyally with the king's men, and did what they could to ensure justice and peace. There were two judicial commissions set up during that month of January, to deal with all legal claims and cases in that part of Wales which was outside the principality, and therefore under the king's administration. One was to work in the eastern parts, the other in Cardigan and the west, and in both a balance was kept between English and Welsh members, for Edward declared his intent of appointing many men of Welsh birth to office in his new territories. Then there was also a third commission to be formed, to see to all the agreed restitution of lands and freeing of prisoners, to take the oaths of Llewelyn's guarantors, and receive his hostages, and even to view the lands he wished to bestow on Eleanor as her dower. With all this business the first two weeks of January passed very quickly, and the prince with his household prepared to set out for home.

Certainly everything seemed to be moving very fairly, according to the treaty, and Llewelyn received so much reassurance from the king's actions concerning the judicial commissions that any doubts he might still have felt were quieted.

'He is dealing honestly,' he said, 'and if his trust in me is slower to grow than mine in him, well, we are two men. It is for me to show him what he will not quite believe for the telling.' And he set himself to act steadfastly and honourably within his truncated state, and wait for his reward with patience.

I made occasion to seek out Cynan before we left for home, to let him know that his nephew was alive and well, and safe with us in Gwynedd.

'I begin to wish I had run with him,' said Cynan, sighing. 'And yet if ever sound Welshmen were needed here, it's from this on. Every man trusted enough to get office under the king has a duty now to take his pay and stand between him and the englishing of Wales, for with all the good-will in the world it will come to that. There are those who have turned their backs on the old country already, and are busy doing the king's work for him before he knows he wants it done. Tell your lord to keep a close eye on Griffith ap Gwenwynwyn, and get used to thinking of him now as Griffith de la Pole, for that's the style he demands henceforth, and every-thing he does goes with it. And being a convert, he'll be more a marcher baron than Mortimer or Bohun, and lean harder on his Welsh neighbours to show his zeal. He's got a family settlement on the English plan already – the eldest son gets all.'

I said that Griffith had tended towards the marcher ways for many years, moving by short steps towards becoming an English baron.

'No short steps now,' said Cynan. 'Full tilt! De la Poles they'll be from now on, and even begin to believe in their Norman blood. And keep close watch when Griffith gets near the judicial commission, for he's bent on getting his revenge for the way the prince has always bested him. I judge he's already listing all the pleas he can bring for recovery of land, and in law there's endless mischief to be made.'

I took due note of it, for the possibilities ahead, in all the claims and counter-claims the turmoil of war leaves in its tracks, were already worrying our lawyers.

'Who knows?' said Cynan before I left, patting his growing paunch and stroking his grizzled dark hair. 'I may come and leave my bones in Wales, yet!'

I also went, in the twilight alone, to walk past the house in the canonry, and say farewell to Cristin. But it seemed that David also was contempla-ting a move from London, for the courtyard was full of a bustle of maidservants and grooms and knights, and through the open wicket I saw Godred among them, marshalling loads in readiness for the sumpter horses. He was as he had always been, fair and healthy and confident, as though time and even the long poison of jealousy and malice had no power over him. So I first thought, but when I looked longer and more narrowly I saw that all that comeliness and brightness of his seemed to have been clouded over with dust, as when a fair tree first shows the signs of drought. I waited a while, unseen, but he did not move into stable or house, and I was loth to go in and meet him, to goad either his anger or his misery. So I said my farewell unseen and unheard in the dimness of the winter eve-ning, and went away.

The fair warning Cynan had given us soon began to show fruit. We had been home in Gwynedd no more than two weeks when at the very first sitting of the judicial commission for east Wales, at Oswestry on the ninth day of February, Griffith ap Gwenwynwyn entered several pleas for damages to his lands and castle at Pool against Llewelyn, and in particular entered a claim to those districts of Powys which Llewelyn had retained after the conspiracy against his life, when he returned the rest of Griffith's lands into his keeping.

Much of this land had come back into Griffith's hands during the war, but not all, and he sought to regain the rest, and to establish his title to all. Now it must be said of the parts in question, notably Arwystli, that they had belonged in old times to Gwynedd, not to Powys, and only during the last three generations had they been in dispute, sometimes held by Powys, sometimes by Gwynedd, which was the reason the prince had kept them in his own hands when the chance offered. Though Arwystli was almost surrounded by the cantrefs of Powys, it belonged by tradition to the mountain lands of Snowdon, and though ringed on all sides by portions of the sees of St David's and St Asaph's, itself it belonged to the see of Bangor. Thus a case could be made upon both sides, but the prince's case rested upon longer history, and he felt strongly about this portion of his hereditary lands, as a matter of pride and principle. He resented in particular that it should go to the insolent renegade Griffith, who had turned his back upon his own people.

The prince had no intention of appearing in any court to the plea of Griffith, and therefore at a later sitting of the commission, in this same month of February, he had his attorneys take out a writ and proceed with a claim in his name to the whole of Arwystli. The head of the commission then was a certain Master Ralph Fremingham, but shortly afterwards he was removed, upon some suspicion of his own probity, which hardly promised well for his judgments. However, this first lodging of Llewelyn's writ was under Fremingham, and took place at Montgomery, to which place he considered he ought not to have been cited, Montgomery being a royal town, whereas the lands impleaded were wholly Welsh, and the treaty was precise in stating that pleas concerning Welsh land should be tried according to Welsh law, and that meant in the lands concerned, as well as by Welsh process. Llewelyn's case throughout rested on this, and he insisted on Welsh law, as was only right. However, in order to initiate his case at once, he allowed his attorneys to produce his writ at Montgomery, but also made a formal protest to the king against being cited there to a court in England.

King Edward replied reasonably that in cases concerning two magnates holding in chief of the crown it had always been usual, even where Welsh law was concerned, to hear them at fixed dates and places, appointed by the justices. There were already some differences in their reading of the treaty. Llewelyn held that the phrase 'according to the custom of those parts' was crystal clear, meaning Welsh law for Welsh lands, but the king was beginning to hedge it about with other phrases of his own choosing, such as 'as ought to be done of right, and according to the custom of those parts', or 'as was usual and accustomed in the times of his predecessors', as if what mattered was to adhere to the previous usage of King Henry and others before him in dealing with matters either Welsh or English.

'And who,' I said once to Tudor, 'is to be the judge of what ought to be done of right? Edward?' For if so, clearly that phrase might on occasion cancel out the treaty phrase, if he chose to consider that what Welsh law decreed did not fulfil his own notion of right.

However, the prince continued in his arduous but resolute patience and good humour, and therefore when the king himself appointed a day for the commission to hear the Arwystli plea at Oswestry, on the twenty-second day of July, the prince sent his attorneys, fully briefed, to present his formal claim against Griffith for the whole cantref of Arwystli.

Griffith ap Gwenwynwyn was a litigious person at all times, and well versed in all the tricks of delay, annoyance and obstruction. The commission was now headed by one Walter de Hopton, and the remaining three justices were all Welsh, and one of them our own Goronwy ap Heilyn, which on the face of it certainly argued that Edward's intent was to avoid bias and do right as well to Wales as to England. But the other two were Rhys ap Griffith ap Ednyfed, renegade from the prince's own trusted household, and another defector, from the Welsh cause, Howel ap Meurig, both of them now in the king's service. Both were experienced justices, but their reputation was hardly calculated to give us confidence in their impartiality in such a cause. And in fact, with all the goodwill in the world, the commission, like its plaintiffs, was tied hand and foot by the difficulties of its task, for to disentangle Welsh, marcher and English interests and laws was then work for heroes or madmen.

Griffith began by challenging the credentials of the prince's attorneys. They produced Llewelyn's letter accrediting them, and firmly stating that the cause must be heard according to Welsh law. Griffith still refused to admit their authority, upon every technical point he could dredge out of his litigious memory, and on his plea the case was adjourned to the next sitting in September. Yet two days later, when Griffith brought up his own claim against the prince, and Llewelyn did not appear, as he had determined from the beginning, the court, seeing his attorneys present though silent, gave them instructions to notify him of the date he should appear in September, thus acknowledging that they were indeed his accredited representatives, though two days earlier they had allowed Griffith's objection to their status to cause the prince's case to be adjourned.

These are tedious matters, but they can ruin, madden and even kill, can undo good men and lay waste noble countries.

Letters and messengers went to and fro between the king and the prince, civil, dutiful but persistent on the prince's part, voluble and legalistic on the king's. Sometimes he used so many words, and they revolved clause within clause so artfully, that it was difficult to be sure of his real meaning, but always his professed meaning was to do even-handed justice, and that as rapidly as he could without risk to the rights of either party. He was then conducting cautious advances towards settling the details of the prince's marriage, but was in no hurry about it. Llewelyn shrugged, conceded the genuineness of the king's doubts, however vain they might be, and endured stubbornly, assured of the ending. And he was encouraged when Edward appointed a court session at Rhuddlan in September, over which he would preside in person, and hear both the Arwystli plea and also the case of Rhodri's final settlement, which was still pending, and had been committed to the king by both brothers.

That was a strange hearing, as it concerned Arwystli. Llewelyn had high hopes of it, for now he had Edward himself to deal with, and in our experience Edward was decisive and swift once he had facts before him. The attorneys put forward the claim, asked and were granted Welsh law, as was only right for lands deep in the heart of Wales, and produced their proofs. Griffith ap Gwenwynwyn appeared in rebuttal, and made his answer. By Welsh law the status of the land was clear, and no law but Welsh had ever run in that land. By Welsh law, all the formalities having been observed, and each party having had its say, it should not even have been possible to put off a judgment. Yet Edward, pondering long and attentively, in the presence of the lawful Welsh judges of Rhuddlan, who had been brought in to hear and pronounce, of his own will and on his own responsibility adjourned the case, putting it back into the competence of the Hopton commission.

'He was all too sure what the judges would decide,' said Tudor angrily, that evening, when we debated this setback. A very severe shock it had been to Llewelyn, but he would not do less than justice to Edward.

'No,' he said, 'he is honest. I am sure of it. He has honest doubts about these procedures of ours, and whether they produce truth or not. He finds himself at sea in Welsh law as I do in English. He wants to examine further. It is galling, but we should not complain unless we have something to hide, and I have nothing.'

So he accepted what desperately disappointed him, and made no ado. And the next day, in some measure, he had his reward. For that was the day when Rhodri appeared against him with a formal claim on his purparty of all the lands of Gwynedd. This cause went forward readily enough, and with mutual consideration. Rhodri made his claim through his attorneys. Llewelyn through his produced in court Rhodri's quitclaim for those same rights, in consideration of the payment of a thousand marks. Rhodri acknowledged the quitclaim but said he had not received the money payment. Llewelyn said and showed that he had made a first payment of fifty marks, and in his turn acknowledged that the balance was still due. Thus they came without dispute to a fair settlement. Rhodri agreed to renew his quitclaim and Llewelyn acknowledged a debt to him of nine hundred and fifty marks, and not having the money ready to be paid immediately into the court, agreed to a date for its delivery, and that it should be distrained by the king's officers on his lands and chattels if he defaulted.

There were some among us who had doubts of this procedure, and thought it a dangerous precedent, for if once such an interference with his right was allowed in his own lands, it might be used against him in other causes. But he was positive that he could do no less, the debt being acknowledged, and further was disdainfully certain that he was risking nothing, since by meeting the obligation before the date assigned he could and would prevent a precedent from being created.

Then came the first check, and though it was delivered so reasonably and simply that Llewelyn himself attached no importance to it, and found in it no sting, yet I did, and so did at least one other. The king looked up mildly from under his drooping eyelid, and said: 'The sum being so great, I require another surety.'

Whatever the prince might have replied to that demand, through his attorneys, it was never needed or delivered. At the back of the hall there was a sudden movement, light and swift, as someone leaned and plucked at a sleeve before him, and I caught the blue-black sheen of David's hair. During all those sessions of the court he had of necessity been present in Edward's train, but he had kept out of sight, and refrained from troubling his brother even by appearing before him. Now he stooped his head to whisper in his law-clerk's ear, and in a moment the man stepped out free of the public ranks, and addressed the king.

'Your Grace, a further surety is forthcoming. The Lord David ap Griffith desires to be partner in the acknowledgement, and grants that the money shall also be levied on his lands and chattels in England or elsewhere.'

A stir went round the court at that. Llewelyn's eyes opened wide in astonished wonder, and he turned his head quickly to look for his brother, the first time, I swear, he had done so since David fled to England. Edward jerked up his head and sought him no less sharply. I will not say he was displeased, but he was startled, and whatever caused him surprise, or did not in every way behave as he expected, was in some degree offensive to him. However, he had no choice but to accept the proffer, which he did without comment, and had it enrolled in the records.

While the clerk was entering it, I saw Llewelyn's urgent gaze roving the ranks from which the attorney had stepped, and knew the moment when his eyes lit upon David, withdrawn as far as he could into the corner of the hall. The colour rose into David's face in a great wave, but knowing himself discovered he stood his ground, and looked back steadily at the prince, without by smile or frown or movement of any kind acknowledging how the meeting of eyes pierced and shook him. As for Llewelyn, he was lost in amazement, and stared as though by the very constancy of his regard he might penetrate this last of David's mysteries. But the width of the hall was between them, and there was no more he could do, until the king declared the case settled, the deed of quitclaim was delivered once again, and the court rose for that day.

Then, as soon as Edward made to withdraw,, and all his magnates gathered about him, Llewelyn turned his back upon them, and thrust his way through the press towards the corner where David had stood. But David also had turned, as soon as he might with propriety, and stalked away towards the nearest door, and the tides of movement within the hall parting and crossing every way, we saw only the lofty flash of the light on his blue-black crest in the doorway, and then no more of him.

CHAPTER XII

Whatever Edward's intended stab, whatever David's impulsive generosity and resentment, in that session at Rhuddlan, both passed by without great significance, for Llewelyn paid his debt to Rhodri long before the day appointed, as was his habit, and that was the end of all Rhodri's claims in Gwynedd. Nor did Llewelyn pursue David to seek any explanation, but let him go his own way, and said no word of what had passed, even to me. In a little while it was as if it had never passed at all. David had made his gesture, which had cost him nothing, and which he had known, since he knew his brother, would cost him nothing. Nothing, that is, in money or goods. Edward had made his, drawing in the rein sharply to remind a spirited horse who was master, and Llewelyn, by reason of his free Welsh acceptance that he had no more privilege at law than any other man, had never even noticed the curb. And the irony was that Edward took that princely and proud humility for submission to himself, and was appeased and gratified by it, when no part of it belonged to him or did him any homage. And Llewelyn took the king's resultant benevolence for true and voluntary goodwill, and liked him the better for it. So they were both encouraged.

Within ten days after he left Rhuddlan, King Edward set free the hostages delivered to him under the treaty, and wrote appointing the day and the place of the marriage of his beloved kinswoman Eleanor de Montfort to his noble and well-loved vassal, Llewelyn, prince of Wales.

The day assigned was itself an omen, as was the king's appropriation of the right to assign it, and to order as his own pageant the marriage he had gone to such lengths to prevent. He had chosen to give his cousin in marriage with his own hand, upon the thirteenth day of October, the day of St Edward the Confessor, the special patron of his father and himself, and the place, appropriately, was the border town of Worcester, where Welsh and English could fitly meet, and where there was a noble cathedral. For the whole court was to remove there to grace the marriage day. And clearly the royal patron of the feast also intended to bear the whole expense himself.

'At least,' said Llewelyn, 'when he is at last satisfied that I approach treaties in good faith, he makes handsome acknowledgement, not grudgingly or by halves. He is doing me all the honour he can, and making a measure of amends to Eleanor. It would be churlish to resent even heavy-handed patronage, when it springs from goodwill and a wish for reconciliation all round.'

But for my part, though I understood his acceptance and pleasure, and his assumption that Edward's kindness meant what it purported to mean,

597

I could not help remembering David's warning, and seeing the very choice of St Edward's day as the king's way of setting his seal upon bride and bridegroom alike, and marking them for his, and all the lavish gifts and giving as the price he was willing to pay to purchase them, a price for which he expected full value, and would exact it if he failed to get it. Try as I would, I could not get this view of the king's proceedings out of my mind, but neither could I reject Llewelyn's view. It seemed to me that both might be true. Edward would not be the first nor the last to assert possession and manipulate people like dolls, as David had said, without himself fully realising what his true purpose was. It did not necessarily mean that his professed friendship was false, or his motives all unworthy.

Llewelyn took the generous view because of his own generosity, that knew no tethered giving, and scorned to buy and sell favours. But David, who could not rule his own life or find his own way, yet saw deeper into other men than did his brother.

It is true that there were other causes for disquiet concerning Edward's attitudes. He still had Amaury de Montfort in close imprisonment, together with several of the gentlemen of Eleanor's household, even now, when he was giving his blessing to the marriage which was the sole cause of their captivity. How could he justify himself? Llewelyn thought and said, and it may be truly, that Edward surely nursed some lingering suspicion that Amaury, even though he was not present, had contributed to the lasting hatred that brought about the death of Henry of Almain, and that was the cause of his lasting vindictiveness towards him. But what had those others done, knights and servants of Eleanor, and far removed from the crime at Viterbo? It was still some years before they all regained their liberty, after many, many prayers on their behalf.

'Take what's offered,' David had said, 'and since he makes no conditions, force him to stand to that.'

Llewelyn said: 'Let us take what he gives – all the more for fear it may be withdrawn – and then bid for what has not been offered us.'

In this they seemed not so far apart. Yet David spoke of putting up his own price, Llewelyn of pressing for the deliverance of others. There was not the meanest in Eleanor's service that he did not feel for as for his own. But the first consideration was the deliverance of Eleanor.

We rode for Worcester, by way of the border crossing at Oswestry, on the ninth day of October, the prince in full and careful state, with all his chief officers and councillors and an imposing retinue of noblemen and knights of the household. The autumn was fine and still, with a veiled sunlight most of the way, and every mile we rode brought back to me memories both sad and splendid. Here at the border crossing the Welsh envoys to Earl Simon's parliament at Oxford had been met by that other de Montfort, Peter of Beaudesert, unshakeably loyal from beginning to end, and dead at Evesham like his lord and friend. And when we approached the Welsh gate of Shrewsbury, and passed through that fair town to the English bridge and the abbey beyond, I beheld again the hall where I had first set eyes on King Henry of England, when this King Edward was but two years old.

As though he had been following the pilgrimage within my mind, Llewelyn beside me said: 'We have been a great journey, you and I, Samson, since first you came into Aber with Owen Goch, to ward off his dagger from my back.' We were riding a little ahead of his retinue, or he would not have spoken of that attempt. He had never said word of it to any but me. 'But I doubt we have but ridden a great circle,' he said, 'to come back to where we began.'

I said no. For he was still prince of Wales, still had vassals, still enjoyed the recognition of his right within his own land by the crown of England, none of which was true when we began. And then we journeyed with our faces set towards a battle, but now towards a wedding-feast.

'It is true,' he said, his face kindling. 'I have been taking too much upon myself. There is also a future, and a new generation comes with it. It may be my part will have been done, and my discharge honourably earned, when my son is born, out of the line of Gwynedd and out of that blood of hers, better than royal. Why should we try to rob those who come after us of their struggle and their glory? If I can hold what I still have, and hand it on to him undiminished for the ground of his own endeavour, that will be enough for me.'

In Worcester, which is a very gracious town on the bank of the Severn, and blessed with many noble houses, the king's court was established in the bishop's palace, and the attendants of his guard in the castle, while the prince was lodged in the guest-houses of the monastic college. As soon as we were installed there, Llewelyn went to attend the king, and I to see if by any chance I could get word whether David and his family were also come to grace the wedding-day. I thought it most likely that Edward would expect his attendance, and certainly frown upon his absence, for if it was the royal policy to pacify and reconcile Wales with England and brother with brother, he would not tolerate the frustration of his plans by one he considered so deep in his debt. The retort at Rhuddlan may have been a little too sharp, but at least it had accorded well enough with what Edward now seemed to intend. Too blatant a recoil in the other direction would not be so coolly accepted.

I went out into the court of the college, and sought for anyone I might know, going or coming about the palace, and walking in the cloister, a little fatter and a little greyer but always as smooth and neat as of old, I met Cynan.

There was seldom anything to be asked about the movements of the court and courtiers that Cynan could not answer. We went out into the garth, where there was some sunshine and little wind, and sat for a while together, while he told me all the gossip of the palace.

'Surely he's here,' he said, when I asked him of David. 'Who is not here? The prince will have enough noble witnesses. Not only Edward and his queen, but the king of Scots into the bargain, as well as all the officers of the realm. King Alexander is being wooed and urged to renew the homage he made to the English crown long ago. And doubtless he will, but only by way of putting himself under the roof of Edward's power, though his Grace would like more, and has a way of speaking of the act of homage as "for the kingdom of Scotland", as though Alexander held it from him and was his vassal-in-chief like any other magnate. At least he has not ventured to attempt so much against the prince of Wales. Not yet! But bear it in mind, bear it in mind! Appetite grows with tasty food, and the larger the man, the more food he requires.'

I said even he might have some trouble swallowing the crags of Snowdon, but that, to do him justice, he seemed to have no ambitions now in that direction. His intentions had never seemed more reasonable and friendly.

'True,' said Cynan, spreading his palms over his firm round belly, 'but I have known more convincing doves. Still, speak as we find! He has other things on his mind to keep him busy. Archbishop Kilwardby was called to be cardinal-bishop of Porto in the summer, the king seized his opportunity to press Bishop Burnell's claims again, and this time the monks of Canterbury took good heed in what waters their best fish would be caught, and voted as he wanted them to vote, and he has sent a strong mission to Rome to urge his chancellor's case, but it seems that Pope Nicholas is in no hurry to commit himself. I judge the pontiff thinks they make a formidable enough team as they are, and all he has to enforce his own views here is this appointment to Canterbury. He'd be a fool to throw away his one weapon. Edward won't get his way.'

I asked if Burnell himself wanted the primacy, for able though he was, well capable of filling that post to good effect, he might find himself less free to act, and more directly responsible to Rome, than in his profitable double calling.

'Better hope for him to stay where he is,' said Cynan. 'If any man has influence on the king, he has, and he's well-disposed and shrewd, he could be a useful friend yet. But you were asking about David. He's lodged in the town with his lady, at St Wulstan's hospice, though himself he's usually about the king's presence. It's not far, down hill from the gate and you'll find it.'

'He has the children with him?' I asked.

'The whole brood. He gets beautiful, vigorous children,' said Cynan appreciatively. 'Strange how these things go! The king with all his health and strength fathers puny little creatures who sicken from birth. The girls survive, but the boys dwindle and die. He's lost two, and his third is a poor little wretch more often ill than well. And David's progeny come bursting into the world as pretty as flowers and as lusty as hound pups, and never look back.'

I left him still musing fatly in the cloister garth over the curious workings of providence, and went out into the town as he had directed me, to the old house Bishop Wulstan founded as a hospice for travellers. There were apartments there for many guests, and the courtyard and stables were full of comings and goings, and busy as a fair. Beyond, there was a small kitchen garden, and an enclosed court, and there I saw the three eldest of those same beautiful and lusty children playing with a half-grown cat belonging to the house, rolling a woollen ball for her to chase. But Cristin was not there, only a little nursemaid of sixteen years sat on the stone rim of the well sewing, and watching over the children.

I asked her if Cristin was within, but she said that she was gone with the Lady Elizabeth to hear vespers, and afterwards to make some small alterations in the veil of the head-dress the queen had purchased in the town as a gift to the princess of Wales. For the people of Worcester were known for the making of fine fabrics and stuffs, and the quality of their brocades, and so was Cristin for the delicacy of her needlework.

So I was disappointed, and yet I took heart even at knowing that she was well and valued, and close in Elizabeth's confidence as always. I turned back through the stable-yard to the gate, resigned to waiting until the morrow for a glimpse of her.

Llewelyn came from the king's audience, ate but very little and drank less and went in deep solemnity of mind to hear compline, and to spend some time in prayer afterwards in the church. Now that he was come to the very eve of the apotheosis of his life, so strangely linked with the fall of his worldly fortunes, that balance hung in his mind like the consummation of a long pilgrimage, at once chastening and testing, and blissful reward. As he was without personal vanity, though he had a hot and devoted pride in his state and his land, so he accepted discipline and loss as a part of his human due, and probably earned, like the next man's. And as he possessed the true and assured humility of those who respect themselves and others, and ask no special favours, so the near approach of great happiness astonished and awed him, as being beyond his deserts, and demanding of him the utmost in generous effort by way of acknowledgement.

He came back to his apartments silent, grave, immense of eye, as though he had seen a great light, but was not dazzled. And when all the remaining business in preparation for the morrow was done, and all his people dismissed, he kept me with him in his own chamber, and I knew there was something he wanted, though still pondering the wisdom of proceeding with it, but still more the impossibility of being at rest without it. Half I knew in my heart what it was, even before he turned to me, all graven in gold and bronze against sudden blanched white; for the blood left his face, and the dark pools of his eyes, withdrawn deeper now, in his middle years, into the pure, stark caverns of bone, burned from within with a fierce, fixed light.

'Samson,' he said, 'my brother is here in this town, is he not?'

At this depth he had, and always had had, but one brother.

I said: 'Yes, he is here.'

'And you know where to find him?' he said, never taking those deep eyes from me.

I said yes, I knew.

'Go to him, Samson,' said Llewelyn, not ordering but entreating, 'and ask him, of his grace, to come to me.' He saw how I gazed, pondering the meaning of such a plea, when he was able to command if he would. 'I have a great need in me,' he said, low-voiced, 'to be reconciled with all men, but most with one I have loved most, and smarted against most fiercely. The deeper the wrongs between us, whether mine or his, the more need I have of mutual forgiveness. If I am to go to her tomorrow with a quiet mind, I must have peace and absolution all about me. There is no other way of approaching perfection. I cannot touch her hand while I still have an ill thought in me. Once in a life comes this moment, I will not let it be defaced.'

I was more than willing, but I thought of David burning in defiance of his own chivalry and striding away out of the court at Rhuddlan, and I dreaded his obduracy. I said: 'What if he will not come?'

'I cannot call him on his fealty,' said Llewelyn, 'he no longer owes me any, he has given his fealty elsewhere. I am not his lord, and he is not my vassal. So much the better. I can only ask him, out of old kindness. The rest lies with him.' And in a moment, when I was already at the door, he said, quite softly and certainly: 'But he will come.'

I went down through the town to St Wulstan's hospice, and it was clear dark, and all the sky above me was a moony stillness, hushed and windless. I had barely reached the doorway of the guest-hall when I met Godred in the passage, and at sight of me he stood squarely in my path, and made to halt me with the presence of his particular love and friendship, which still he kept up as of old, though every last vestige of goodwill in it was long since turned to gall. I saw then, in the torchlight, that the flaxen gold of his hair was dusted over, as it were with ash, and his comeliness dried and withered with malice, but still he liked his comfort and his finery, and took good care of his body, which was youthful still.

'Samson!' he cried in high, glad tones of welcome. 'They tell me you were here earlier in the day, looking for Cristin. A pity you should miss her! But why did you not come and spend an hour or two with me, brotherly as in the old days? We could have passed the time very pleasantly, you and I, talking of old friends. We all grow older year by year – even Cristin! You know we lost our child? And that she'll have no more?'

Once he would have been handling me before this, but now he did not come within touch, only stood blocking my path with his smiling face like a mask, and his eyes gazing from far within his skull, like fine, furtive beasts peering out of ambush. He no longer cared even to trick or trap me into Cristin's arms, no longer grudged us the anguished triumph of our virtuous love, or lusted after the victory of dragging us down to his level, where we could be despised and forgotten, perhaps even forgiven. He had gone beyond that, into pure and perfect hatred of us both, but now that she had lost him his son, the child of his revenge, she had become as it were both holy and an abomination to him, and could not be touched, and all that immense hatred turned towards me.

All this was in his face, like the growing shadow of deadly sickness. And him I could not hate. He was his own torment, and his own poison. I was sorry for him.

'Not now!' I said. 'I am here on the prince's business. Stand out of my way, or, better, bring me to your lord.'

'Endlessly dutiful, and never time for dalliance,' said Godred, sighing, and turned and led me to the room where David was. 'Some day,' he said to me, with his hand at the door and his glance sliding along his shoulder to my face, 'you and I will reach that quiet hour or two together that time has never given us, with no one else by to come between – not even Cristin.' And he went away and left me to go in to David.

Cristin and Elizabeth were sitting at a small inlaid board playing at tables. David was watching them moodily over his wine, his face in repose but not at ease, the black, winged brows drawn down into a tight line above half-closed eyes. They all looked up when I entered, surprised and enquiring, for the hour was getting late.

'My lord,' I said, 'your brother sends me to ask you, of your grace, to come to him.' It was my whole message, I saw no need to add one word.

'Now?' said David, and drew his feet in under him and sat sharply forward in his chair, astonished. 'Of my grace?' he said, and the contortion of a smile came and went on his lips in an instant, like a flash of stormy light.

'Now?' said Elizabeth, echoing him, startled and distrustful, and reaching, as always, to stand between David and anything that might shape into a threat. 'So late? Can it not wait until tomorrow?'

'Hush, love!' said David, with quite another smile. 'Who knows whether tomorrow comes for him? And think how full tomorrow is to be. It may well be tonight or never.' And he looked at me, and through me, and very far beyond, perhaps back, perhaps forward, I could not tell. 'My brother!' he said. 'Not the prince?'

'Your brother. Not the prince.'

'I will come,' said David.

We went uphill through the streets with two of his attendants to light us with torches, and I brought him into the room where Llewelyn sat alone. The prince rose as soon as the door opened, but did not come to meet us, and when I would have stepped back and left them together, David laid a hand quickly and imperiously upon my arm. With his eyes on his brother's face he said: 'Stay with me! God knows I may need my confessor.'

'Stay with us,' said Llewelyn, echoing and amending. 'We may both need a witness, we could not have a better. What is there you do not know already about us both?'

So I remained in the room with them, standing apart, and what passed that night I know, and none other knows it now in this world.

'You sent for me,' said David as the silence grew long. 'I am come.'

'That was kind, and I am grateful,' said Llewelyn. 'David, of all the needs I have now, the greatest is to be at peace with you. I am going to a new beginning and a great happiness, and I cannot go without an act of purification, and the peace of absolution. While I am in enmity with you I am not whole. For my part, I ask pardon for all I have done amiss towards you, for too much preoccupation with other things and too little regard to your wants, for failures of understanding and of kindness. I ask your forgiveness. Will you take my hand, and be my brother again?'

The candles were low and dim in the room, the twilight kind to those two, but even so I watched the colour drain away out of David's face until he burned whiter than the puny flames, and the blue of his eyes was both bright and blind, as though he looked equally at Llewelyn and deep into his own being. But his voice was even and low as he said: 'It is generous in you to make the first move, but beware of being too hasty.'

'I have not made the first move,' said Llewelyn, and smiled. 'You did

603

that, at Rhuddlan, when you would not let me seem, even for an instant, to be without a guarantor.'

The first ease of blood returning came faintly into David's face. 'I dislike insolence,' he said, 'in underlings, but hate it in kings. You would be justified in believing that was done against Edward rather than for you.'

'So I might,' said Llewelyn, 'if you had not fled me so resolutely when I came looking for you. I am ashamed that I did not do then what I am doing now, and pursue you until I had you safe in hold. Well? May I have an answer?'

'Not yet!' said David, recoiling. 'There is much I have to say before I let you take me back into your favour. Forgive me if I rehearse again what you already know, but if you will not call it to mind, I must. Have you forgotten Bryn Derwin? The first time I played you false? It was I who stirred up Owen to play my game for me, I who put the arguments into his mouth, and when that came to nothing, the sword into his hand and the treason into his mind. I told you then you would do well to kill me, while you could, before I did worse to you, but you would not do it. Within the year you took me back into your grace, mistaking me for the innocent tool. You gave me land and office, and trusted me, and I took and took from you all that you offered. But I had warned you! Why would you not be warned?'

'This is foolish,' said Llewelyn gently. 'I have not asked you for any promises or any recantations. There are no conditions. Let the past alone, we have all been at fault.'

'No!' said David. 'Let me speak. If you have needs, before you can go clean and whole to Eleanor's love, so have I before I re-enter into yours. I have not finished yet. There was a second time – do you remember? When you went to keep the border for Earl Simon, and called me on my fealty, and because of some high words between us, and because of my will to take them in the worst meaning possible, I withdrew myself and my best men from you, and went over to the king's side. Have you forgotten that? Samson will not have forgotten! He tried to bring me back to my duty, and I all but slew him and left him lying. The second treason! No, wait!' he said in a sharp, wrung cry when Llewelyn would again have hushed him. 'I have not finished yet. There was a third betrayal, the worst. I cannot claim I hatched that plot myself, it took a woman to do that. But when Owen ap Griffith came to me with the bait, I swallowed it. There was I with children, and you barren and unwed, and Wales to be won for the son I was sure of getting. We planned your death! Have you forgotten so soon? But for the floods we should have accomplished it.'

All this he said without any visible pride or shame, without any expression of regret or plea for pardon, without one word of excuse or explanation, without dwelling on or hastening past loathsome details. For him the healing was in uttering these things and laying them open without conceal. But even then I could not be certain, nor, I think, could he, whether he would ever have let it come to the proof, that night in the February storms, whether it was success or failure he prayed for in the chapel at Aber.

'Leave this!' said Llewelyn. 'It is too grievous. And I have not asked you anything of all this, and feel no need to hear it.'

'But I need to say it, and to be sure that you have it well in mind. I am what I am! I make no pretence to show better or worse. I *know* what I am. And if you want to make peace with me, it must be with open eyes, without any promises or pledges of amendment. God may amend me! I doubt if I can.'

'One question, then, I will ask, and only one,' said Llewelyn. 'Do you not want to be reconciled with me?'

Very mildly and simply he said it, and David writhed, and tried three times to answer, and each time withdrew and swallowed the words, unable to get out the severing lie, unwilling to pour out the aching truth, because if once he showed his longing he knew it would be supplied out of hand. Shamelessly he had taken from both Llewelyn and Edward whatever was offered, as I think despising Edward for welcoming and making use of a traitor, and even in some degree disdaining Llewelyn for so rashly forgiving and harbouring one to his own danger. Shamelessly he had taken, and acknowledged no debt in return, but this one thing, and on this one night, he could not accept without feeling himself bound for its full price. The sweat stood on his forehead and lip, and he was mute. And Llewelyn read him rightly for once, and smiled.

'There have been others,' he said mildly, 'have betrayed three times, and yet in the end died for the cause they betrayed.'

'But, by your leave,' said David, wrestling with his devils, 'you are not yet the son of God, only of Griffith, like me. And it will be some while yet to cock-crow. True,' he said, with a tormented grin that was like a contortion of pain, 'I am come by night and with torches to salute you – worse than Saint Peter! Would you not do well, even yet, to avoid and denounce while you may? After the kiss it will be too late!'

For answer, Llewelyn took three long strides across the room, certain now of his victory, gripped his brother by the shoulders, and kissed him, first on the right cheek, then on the left. In his grasp David shook terribly, like a beast in a fever. But at the second touch he heaved a great groan out of him, and caught Llewelyn fiercely into his arms, and returned the kiss with passion.

A moment they clung thus, supporting each other. Then David slid from between the steadying hands, crumpling like an empty gown at his brother's feet, and with long palms clasping the prince's knees, broke into a storm of desperate and blissful weeping.

I went out with him when he left us, an hour later, flushed with assuaged grief, hushed with weariness and wonder, for a brief while purged of all ills, and docile and biddable as a child. A long while they had sat and talked together after that third peace was made, not of any great things, not disposing of old grudges or making more of penitence, but very simply, as memories stirred or thoughts blew them, like severed friends discovering each other afresh after long absence. In the autumn night the moon was still high, whiter and better than his servants' torches. and silvered his face in such daunting purity, as if he had just been born into a man's prime without sin.

'No, come no further,' he said, when I had brought him out as far as the gate. 'I am confessed and shriven clean, I need my confessor no more tonight. Only pray for me, that I have heart for my penance, for this time it will be a life-long penance. I never shall quit him again, Samson. For what I am worth, he has won me. I only pray I may not do him worse injury with my love and loyalty than ever I did with my treason. I am two-edged, Samson! I dread I need not even turn in a man's hand to cut him to the heart.'

So he said, and the moonlight that blanched him was overcast for a moment by a drift of cloud, and shadow passed across his face. But when it was gone, and the light came again, he was tranquil as before, and if he moved like a man exhausted, it was the exhaustion of happiness.

'Go and get your rest,' I said, 'if you mean to attend him in his glory at the church door tomorrow.' The prince had not asked it, nor thought of it, but I knew it would make him glad, and it kindled David's eyes into pale blue flames, as though I had lighted a lamp.

'Well thought of!' he said. 'So I will, and be splendid enough to do him credit, too. I shall be the one gift of his marriage day that Edward cannot claim to have given him.'

And he laughed, with devilry in his laughter again, and by way of sealing the ceremonies of the night kissed me, too, in parting, and went away down through the town, to his bed and his Elizabeth.

The next day, therefore, when Llewelyn's groomsmen assembled before the hour at the great door of Worcester cathedral, one among them came unexpectedly, and he the finest and most glittering of all. And if some among the younger princes, notably Llewelyn ap Rhys Fychan of Iscennen, received him with dubious and offended faces and unflattering astonishment, Tudor and the elders were quick to grasp the meaning of his presence, and be thankful for it. One enmity the less, and one so close and damaging, was wedding gift enough. And when Llewelyn himself came to take his stand before them at the door, and the look those two exchanged made their reconciliation and their joy in it plain to be seen, even the young nephews, jealous for the prince's rights and burning with resentment of his wrongs, melted in the warmth of his high contentment, and were tamed.

A fresh, bright day it was, after that clear night, with mild sunlight and a breeze blowing, and a fair scene that was, above the green meadows and the winding river. Before the great porch of the church the knot of glittering gallants waited, with Llewelyn standing alone at their head. That day he was all russet and gold and burning red, and on his hair the gold talaith, the crown of Wales, for he still had a principality to bring to his bride, and held it not from Edward but of hereditary right, and so would assert, for her sake even more than for his own, but most of all for the sake of his sons unborn, whose inalienable heritage it was. David glowed and smiled when he saw it, approving.

Then came the court guests, a very splendid company, led by the queen and her noblewomen. This Spanish Eleanor was a slender lady, tall and fair, and in her manner very gentle, quiet and gracious, not beautiful or of assertive character, but in her own fashion steadfast and brave, as they say she had proved herself again and again in the crusade. After her party came the great officials of state, Robert Burnell, bishop and chancellor, the justiciar of Chester, the wardens of the marches, Mortimer, Clifford, Bohun, even William of Valence, the king's uncle and lord of Pembroke, and Gilbert de Clare of Gloucester. King Alexander of Scotland also came, a widower at that time after the death of King Edward's sister, Margaret. A fine man in the prime of life he was, and handsome. All the nobility of the land flocked into the cathedral of Worcester to do honour to the prince of Wales, and after them the lesser people of the court, and the attendants, until the vast church was full of colour and light and brilliance.

I saw Elizabeth go by in the queen's train, and saw the look she exchanged with David as she passed, so full of pride and delight in him, and he of tenderness towards her, that their love was plain for all to see. And I thought again of the warning David had expressed only to me, and would not cast as a shadow, however slight, upon Llewelyn's day of happiness. These two Edward had joined in marriage, and though they seemed to move as free of him as the birds in the sky, how if he had never yet needed to collect the debt he conceived they owed him? And what if some day he did call in the bond they did not acknowledge, and demand payment in full for all his outlay?

I was thinking of it still when the king came crossing the green from the palace, with Earl Simon's daughter on his arm.

Beside his huge figure she looked tiny, fragile and delicate, for the crown on her head came well short of his shoulder, and she had to reach up to lay her hand upon his arm. Beside his magnificence of black and scarlet and ermine she walked like a pale candle-flame carried very steadily, for she was all ivory and gold from head to foot. Those who had not seen her before, for she had been kept in virtual retirement still, drew breath deep and long as they set their eyes on her, for the beauty she always had, which was indeed excelling, was doubled in this deliverance, and made of her a blinding light that dazzled the eyes. To watch them come, at distance, you would have said she was an exquisite image he had bought, and could have been carried aloft on the palm of his hand. But to look closely into her face, as she fixed her eyes upon Llewelyn and advanced towards him, looking neither right nor left, as to a lodestar, was to see her larger than Edward's grandeur, and more durable than his majesty, and to know that he had not money nor jewels enough in his treasury, nor lands enough in all his dominions, to buy the jewel that she was.

They mounted the steps towards us, and came to Llewelyn. And there before the doorway the king laid Eleanor's hand in Llewelyn's hand, and I wondered if he saw as he did it that neither the one nor the other gave ever an eye to him, or was any longer aware of his great shadow falling across their joined hands. They had eyes only for each other, the prince's deep and dark and full of secret light, and Eleanor's wide and clear in gold-flecked green, like sunlight in spring forests. Their faces were pale and serene, the one as rapt as the other, and they did not cease to gaze upon each other thus in wonder and bliss as they turned together, and went hand in hand into the cool dimness of the church, to their second marriage.

That was not the end of the king's favours. At the steps of the altar, before they were blessed, he laid his own personal gift upon the open pages of Llewelyn's prayer book, a bookmark of woven gold and silk, intricately made. And over their marriage-feast, that night in the bishop's palace, he himself presided, in vast good humour, and bore the expense of all. And I saw the small curl of David's lip, and knew that he was reckoning how lavish the sum laid out to buy what could not be bought, and saw, too, the stern, straight line of his black brows over aloof and critical eyes, and knew he resented the very suggestion of such a purchase, where for himself he had merely shrugged and despised, taken all and conceded nothing. But Llewelyn, I am sure, saw nothing but somewhat possessive kindness, and a desire to seal the peace with promise of a friendly future, and for the sake of Wales that was a good omen.

When the long evening ended, they brought bride and groom in procession to the prince's apartment, where the bedchamber was decked for them, and the candles lighted. And there the bridal pair said their thanks and their goodnight, with that same rapt composure that had possessed them ever since their hands touched, but with such authority that even the king accepted it as dismissal, and drew off his retinue and left those two together.

When the door was closed upon them and all was quiet, I went out into the cloister and walked in the cool of the night, and saw the last candle go out in their chamber, and thought of Cristin, who had been left behind with the children. All that day I had not seen her, but now my heart was the lighter because David was reunited with his brother, and would surely join his household with Llewelyn's on the morrow, and ride to Oswestry in the wedding company.

So my lord came at once to an ending and a beginning, and the loss he had sustained was compensated with as great a gain. And, I, too, sat alone in the night, weary but cautiously content, measuring my own losses and gains, and found a good hope in the omens of that day.

But the best and strangest omen was yet to come. For when I had been alone there in the silence a great while, and was about to rise and go in from the chill of the air, suddenly I heard from the window above me the paired murmur of two voices, in words too soft to be distinguished, and needing no interpreter, two threads of sound that interwove and caressed like the strands of a song. And then the deeper voice pealed out in a cascade of exultant bronze laughter, and over it the other soared like a silver fountain of sparkling drops. And I sat lost in amazement and giving thanks to God, as I listened to the sweetest sound ever I heard, the prince and princess of Wales laughing aloud together for joy, and in each other's arms at last.

Afterglow AND Nightfall

CHAPTER I

I, Samson, clerk, servant and friend life-long to Prince Llewelyn, born under the same roof and in the same night as my lord, have told how he laboured steadfastly to make of Wales a noble sovereign state, peer to England and in peace with her, how for a few years that aim was achieved, when after the treaty of Montgomery he lived side by side in amity with King Henry the Third until that monarch's death, and how thereafter, with the succession of King Edward, all things changed, and England and Wales were again driven to war.

Of that year of struggle I have told, when the lesser Welsh princes, not yet ready for the vision of nationhood and clutching each at his own local right, fell away before the king's lance, and a hard-fought war ended perforce in a hard-fought peace. By that treaty, drawn at Aberconway, my lord was forced to relinquish half his realm, won with his own hand, in order to keep inviolate his hereditary stronghold of Gwynedd-west-of-Conway, the mountain fastness of Snowdon. And having accepted with fortitude this grievous diminution, he did homage and swore fealty to Edward, accepting also the bond of his pledged word.

Yet in this great loss there was also great gain, for in sacrificing the labour of many years he achieved also the desire of many years, his promised wife, Eleanor de Montfort, the great earl's daughter and the king's own cousin, whom Edward had not scrupled to seize by piracy at sea and hold prisoner as his cruellest weapon of war, but whom now, appeased by victory, he brought forth to her bridal.

And one more thing, to him of great value, my lord regained on his wedding eve, the love and allegiance of his youngest, best-loved and most perilous brother, David, three times traitor and three times forgiven.

I tell now of what befell after the peace was a year old, of how that marriage and that reconciliation fared, and how the war continued by other means, with words for swords, and courts of justice for battle-fields.

From the marriage at Worcester we rode home to Gwynedd in the soft, moist October weather, all that great company of us, Llewelyn's household and David's together in amity, Llewelyn and David side by side, after so long of estrangement, and all the leisurely string of us, their retainers, drawn out after their heels like a bright ribbon trailed across the green fields of England, to the border at Oswestry.

Thus far, to mark his patronage and favour to the very rim of his English lands, King Edward paid the expenses of his cousin's travel and baggage, having already borne the cost of the wedding-banquet, and bestowed the bride on her bridegroom with his own hand. The same huge and heavy hand that had turned the key upon her to prevent that very marriage, until it could be celebrated on his terms and under his auspices. But Edward's shadow lengthened and dwindled behind us when we reached Welsh soil, and pressed the upland turf of our dismembered homeland above Glyn Ceiriog.

In vast content we rode, bringing Eleanor home at last to her own place. But ours was a contentment muted and still, no loud and easy happiness. We were like men spent after great endeavour, having both won and lost, and once having valued and acknowledged our losses, the more grateful for our gains and the more aware of them. With falconry and music we passed the gentle time on the journey, but our hawking was subdued and languid, and our music pensive and soft, like the autumn country through which we made our homeward way. At morning the sun was veiled and coloured like gold, and the dew feathered from our horses' hooves, and over the slopes of the hills the warm purple flush of heather burned slowly into the sombre fire of bracken. The skies over us were pale and lofty, and the birds flew high, and even their songs had a rueful sound, as though they, too, owned their losses while they hymned their gains. For it is great gain to be alive, and have heart to sing, but great loss, even in the beauty of autumn, to feel and dread that the golden summer is over.

Eleanor rode at her husband's side every mile of that journey. There was no need for any man to wonder what measure of happiness those two had in being matched at last, for though they spoke but little, and looked more often upon the fair, loved land than upon each other, feeling no need to gaze or to touch, they so shone that their radiance kindled the very air into gold about them, no midday dazzle, but the mellow and tender gold of the sun drifting towards its bed, after the long climb to the zenith.

They were autumn thoughts I had, those days, and there is no autumn without regret, however kindly the air, and bright the leaves, and rich the harvest. And I could not choose but remember that I, like my lord and friend, was forty-nine years old, drawing close to fifty when the year turned, and he had waited thirteen years for his love before he won her, and I longer still for mine, and fruitlessly still. Yet whenever I rode beside the horse-litters in which David's wife and children were carried, my heart was comforted, beholding Cristin among the cushions with Elizabeth's youngest girl in her lap, and the two elder sisters nestled one on either side of her, as confidingly as if she had been their mother instead of their nurse, and a happy and prolific wife instead of a misused and barren one. And then, as surely as the love and worship rose in me cool and fresh as spring water filling a dried well, Cristin would raise her head and turn her iris-grey eyes to meet mine, and there I saw another manner of radiance, not fecund and joyous like Elizabeth's, not fulfilled and crowned like Eleanor's, yet radiance for all that, and knew that it belonged to me, and to no other man in all this dear world. For there are many kinds of harvest, and the bevy of vigorous, blossoming children that surrounded David and Elizabeth furnished but one make of precious fruit. There are others, invisible, unweighed, uncounted, not to be assessed by the world's values, vouchsafed sometimes even to those who find their loves too late.

But this was the bride's festival, and the bride's triumph. She looked about her at a fair, wild, melancholy world that changed with every mile, and up into a sky alive with birds and feathered with sailing clouds, and was filled with wonder and delight.

'No, this is not England! It is another earth,' she said, 'and another air.'

At David's entreaty we halted for one week of November at his castle of Denbigh, though Llewelyn would rather have gone home at once to Gwynedd-beyond-Conway, which was now his whole principality. But the reunion of those two brothers required a visible sacrament, therefore he accepted with good will the invitation extended, and while Tudor ap Ednyfed, the high steward of Wales, went ahead into Gwynedd with all but the prince's immediate household, we who were closest lingered and hunted in Denbigh, and were entertained lavishly until it was time to move on to Aber and prepare for the Christmas feast.

That stay at Denbigh came strangely to me and to many. David had held his two inland cantrefs of the Middle Country but a year, having been granted them by King Edward after the war that snatched them out of Llewelyn's hands. David was Edward's vassal now, like any baron of England, and owed no fealty to his brother, whose undoing he had surely been, second only to Edward. Yet here, so soon afterwards, he was playing host to the brother and lord he had deserted and betrayed. It was not easy for good Welshmen to stomach, and there was no man knew it better than David. On the night before we left, at the high table in hall, he chose to get the matter into the open.

'I take it as a great grace,' he said in a clear voice, looking Llewelyn in the face, 'that you have consented to break bread and be a guest in my house, and a royal favour that your lady honours my hall with her presence. Since it's known to all men how we have been estranged, so I would have all men know that we are reunited. Concerning desert or blame we two have said no word. For my part, I'm content to be thankful for peace between us, and to pledge my good faith to keep it.'

Llewelyn understood his need, and readily went to meet him. 'There's no profit,' he said heartily, 'in looking back. We begin from where we stand, and no complaints. A few weeks, and we go together into a new year, and what we had or had not, and did or did not do, three years ago is no help and no harm to us now. Let's live with what is.' And seeing that they had at that moment, as David had intended, the silent attention of all that teeming household in hall, he added: 'And since we're at peace, and travelling is safe and easy again, I pray you'll come as before, and share Christmas with us at Aber, with your lady and the children.'

David grew pale at that, remembering the Christmas feast at Aber four years earlier, when he had plotted against the life of this brother who now publicly opened that life to him again. Out of that treachery arose all Llewelyn's losses, and all the grief and damage of the war, and the restrictions of the hard peace. But they eyed each other steadily and were content.

'With all my heart,' said David.

So they made plain to all men that whatever had happened between them, and however they were now divided by fortune, Llewelyn prince of a shrunken Wales, but its prince still, David a baron holding from King Edward and owing feudal allegiance only to him, they were by their own deliberate choice brothers once again.

Certainly there must have been many who still doubted. Three times treacherous, who was David to pledge his good faith now and be trusted? Three times magnanimous and each time the loser by it, was not Llewelyn incurably his own enemy and his brother's dupe? Even Cristin, when I spoke out this misgiving to her, said only: 'God knows! But as they could never live together, so they cannot live separated. The prince is right, they must manage with what they have, and handle it as best they can.' Even as we, though that she did not say.

While we remained in Denbigh I had at least the opportunity of speaking with her now and then as we went about our work. Every word and look of hers was bread and life to me, I was rich while we were within the same walls, and for that reason the accord between Llewelyn and David was all the more precious to me.

'Elizabeth is satisfied,' said Cristin. 'She would be friends with everyone, and have contentment all about her. Where David goes, she will go, and whatever David undertakes, she will plunge her hands into it with him, to the shoulder, to the heart. But she was not happy when he left Llewelyn. She felt him broken in two, and is certain now that he is healed. Should we question her knowledge, because it is a child's knowledge? Children are guided by God. I am willing to trust where she trusts.'

And I where Cristin trusted, though I did not say that, either. So I went from her comforted, since I loved both Llewelyn and David, the one with every reason, the other against almost all reason. Are we not all in some measure children? And should we question what we know as children know?

Godred ap Ivor was in the stables when we went to saddle up for departure. I had seen little of him while we were in Denbigh, which suited me well, and yet to some degree made me uneasy, so far was it from his old usage of me. True, his pursuit of me had passed through many changes, from his youthful calculation that my privilege with Llewelyn might be made to advance his career, and his shameless dangling of Cristin before me as bait to that end, through his malice and offence at finding us able and resolute to love in abstinence where he found it easy to gorge without love, to his realisation that he had a better and sharper weapon, and his persecution of her, so long a wife neglected and misprized, with an unsparing lust now loathsome to her, until he got her with child not for love, but in my despite. But it was common to all these phases that where I was, there he would follow me if he could, with his fondling fingers and insinuating voice, dropping poisoned honey. Now, unless chance threw us in each other's way, he let me alone, only watching narrowly from a distance. Since his wife miscarried and his son was born dead, the small pinpricks of his venom, though he used them still, afforded him no relief. His long hatred had corroded his being so deep there was no fit expression for it within his scope, and he was waiting for his hour of tremendous revenge.

But if he did not haunt me now, neither did he avoid me. He turned from the pony he was saddling, and his flaxen hair against the dappled shoulder showed in ashen pallor, more grey than fair. I could never look him in the face without being reminded how like we were in our differentness, though he was taller, and still comely, and had been bright and debonair in his youth, and I was swart and dark and plain. As two carvers may copy the same model, and produce two alien stone images, yet each true to the original, so we both mirrored the father we shared, of whom he was the true mintage, and I the bastard.

'You're away then,' he said, and showed his even teeth in a narrow smile. 'There'll be changed times about the court from now on, now he's got his princess at last. Your nose will be out of joint.' And when I made him only a brief greeting in reply, he watched me over the pony's neck with light, malignant eyes, and grinned without mirth. 'After so many years so close in his confidence and favour, you'll feel the cold. He's got himself a closer confidante now, and has better than music in his bed-chamber.'

There was never any profit in answering him, he kept his tongue always just short of public offence, though always insinuating foulness. So I merely said something empty about having no fears for my employment as long as the promising spate of lawsuits cast up by the war continued, and went about my own saddling.

'But I'm forgetting,' he said softly at my back, 'you're in favour with the princess, too. A double assurance is good! I tell you, Samson, my friend, they've set you an example. Have I not been holding up marriage to you for years as the only estate for a sensible man? If my wedded happiness could not convince you,' he said, grinning like a famished wolf, 'the prince's should win you over. Find yourself a wife, Samson – a beautiful gentle wife like my Cristin. Only not barren,' he said, suddenly in a breathy whisper from a shut throat. 'Get one able to carry your son full-time, and bring him into the world alive . . .' He strangled on the end, and turning, flung away silently among the bustle in the stable-yard, and left me stricken to stone.

I could not go from Denbigh and leave things so. I sought out Cristin, where she was busy with the little girls, dressing the younger ones for the day, and braiding Margaret's long hair.

'You need not fret,' said Cristin calmly, when she understood what was on my mind. 'Godred is not mad, he intends me no harm. If you have no other warranty of that, you have his own self-interest. He has a good office and some influence here in David's service, and I am the privileged companion of David's wife. How long would he keep his place and his easy living if he did me any hurt? Or his life and liberty, for that matter?'

'With such a load of hatred in him,' I said, 'he may some day forget even his own interests for the pleasure of sating it, and you here within his reach, and I far away.'

'No,' she said with certainty, 'not Godred! Never! That is one thing he never forgets. Hatred can wait its turn, if it threatens his comfortable bed and fat table, and the money in his pouch. Besides, it is not me he hates the worst. He has ceased even to use his tongue on me. I do not matter enough to him now to be persecuted. Godred has done with me, except as his body-servant, the mender of his clothes and fetcher and carrier of his wants. I wish I could be as sure he will never attempt anything against *you*! *You* matter to him altogether too much. You are the shadow on his self-esteem, the spot on his skin that he scrubs and gouges at, and cannot scrub away. Guard yourself, Samson, wherever he is. No, I know you are not afraid of him, but I am in earnest. Do not be with him but among people. Never alone!'

'He never seeks me out now,' I said, 'as he used to. Perhaps I am making too much of a moment of spleen.'

'He has had little chance lately,' said Cristin. 'In England it was my one consolation that you were out of his reach. And even after the peace was made, there was no visiting between the prince's household and ours. But now they're reconciled there'll be the old easy in-and-out between them, David's people and Llewelyn's rubbing shoulders freely every few weeks. Within a month we're to come to the prince at Aber.'

She was gazing at me very earnestly as she said it, frowning at the risk she saw in this free mingling, but then she drew breath softly, and so did I, seeing the sweet reverse of that danger. She said again: 'You need not fret. My bed is with the children, close to Elizabeth's chamber. There he never has any call to come. With five of them to care for, I'm seldom anywhere else, and even if Nest takes my place, and I sleep in my own chamber, he never troubles me. He has plenty of other beds, as he always had, mine only chills him to the bone. You need not fear for me. You can go in peace.'

'Before the new year,' I said, 'you will come after us to Aber. It is only a very short while. God be praised!' I said, very low, and 'God be praised!' said Cristin in her turn almost silently, and smiled.

We came over the high, rolling hills of Rhos towards evening, but before the sun was low, and so to the crossing on the Conway at Caerhun. A mellow afternoon it was, the westward sky all soft and misty gold, and the colours of the forests like fading flames, as we emerged upon a grassy crest, and saw the silver coil of the river below us, coming from the south and widening before our eyes into tidal water. Thus, from above, we could see the pale tints of the sand under the silver, and the deep blue-green of the channels where the salt sea mingled, and beyond the valley the high mountains soared, fold upon fold and peak behind peak, all gilded with that molten western light that dropped out of the sky like tears from the eye of a veiled but splendid sun. They were like a great army drawn up in battle array, with no break in the wall of their lances, or like a giant castle of bronze and steel, impregnable, without gates. To us they were home. We knew the ways in, where no way showed, and had the password that opened the invisible portals. To her, born in Kenilworth in the rich lowlands of England, raised in the cloister of Montargis in the green, civilised pastures of France, God knows what they were, but it was wonderful. She was the first to rein in, and sit and gaze, and all we drew aside and left those two together, waiting, as he waited, and with the same agony and rapture, for her to speak.

She looked down at the serpent of river that marked the harsh limit of the lands left to her lord, and her face was bright and still and aware, and her eyes, wide-set under a lofty ivory brow, immense and attentive, golden-hazel, green-flecked, the colours of a radiant autumn in her early summer face. Eleanor's eyes were always mirrors through which God gazed. Those who looked into them saw themselves there, and all but the best turned their own eyes away, and dissembled. They mirrored and matched what she saw. The mountains of Wales did not bow their heads nor quench their golden light before her, and neither did Eleanor lower her eyes. Once she had lifted her head to behold their summits, there she was held. I saw the reflected gold colour her cheeks, and the parting of her lips widen into the promise of a smile.

When she had looked her fill, she turned her head the little way she needed to look into Llewelyn's eyes, and he was gazing at her with a face withdrawn and almost grim, but as for her, she never ceased to reflect unshadowed splendour. Once she glanced down again at the spilt ribbon of the Conway, before she spoke.

'All that lies beyond,' she said, 'is yours?'

'And that is all,' he said, 'that is mine. It is not what I had thought to bring you, when I plighted my troth to you. Nor am I the man I meant to offer you.'

His voice was low and equable, for he had been resolute from the first in accepting his diminished state and making the best of it, as he had made the best of his remaining bargaining power to exact from Edward better terms of peace than many had thought possible. But the grief of loss, and especially the thwarting of his lifelong ambition for Wales, was none the less bitter for that, and all the more desolating now that he had brought his wife at last to behold for herself, on this journey through the ravished Middle Country, the magnitude of his deprivation, which was also hers. And for all he would not suffer his pain to appear in his face or shake the firmness of his voice, he could not be so wrung and she not know.

A moment she was silent, her eyes still upon the distant peaks, and the flush of the west reflected in her face. Then she said: 'As to the lands, they may be narrower than once they were, but they are loftier than anything my cousin has in his realm, and there is room enough there for me. As to the man,' she said, and turned and looked at him with burning certainty, 'he has never been greater than he is now. My heart could hold no more.'

'God willing,' he said very quietly, 'there shall be more, some day, when the time favours us and we have paid all our dues. If not for us, for those who come after. I will never cease from hoping to give back to you in honour all that I have failed to keep safe for you now. And there will be room in your heart for all.'

'I need nothing more,' said Eleanor. 'I want for nothing. I have what I wanted.'

Such a way she had with words, enlarging and glorifying them so that the briefest and simplest utterance spoke more than gilded phrases. A moment they sat eye to eye, caught away from us and we forgotten. Then he reached a hand to her bridle, and they led the way down together out of the hills to the Conway shore opposite Caerhun, and there we crossed the silver barrier into Gwynedd, and Eleanor had come home.

That evening we rode only as far as Aberconway, along the river-bank, and there at the abbey we spent the night, and the following day took the coastal road to Aber. The weather was changing then, there was a wintry wind, and the touch of frost before the dawn. There was beauty still in the colours melting and changing over Lavan sands, under the vast steel-blue shoulder of Penmaenmawr, and mystery in the distant grey thread that was the coastline of Anglesey drawn along the horizon. Eleanor looked about her with wide, grave eyes of joy, at the sword-edges of the cliffs on her left hand, at the white curl of foam hissing along the sand on her right, at the far-off point of Ynys Lanog of the saints across the grey waters, at the tumbled, screaming flight of gulls all about the clouded sky. The grandeur of our land did not daunt her, rather it fulfilled her own greatness of heart and mind. She had said well, there was room enough for her in the mountains of Gwynedd. She was not made for the cloistered life, nor for a small, confined sphere of action, she with Earl Simon's blood in her veins.

Thus we brought her in great but sober happiness to Aber, and there made ready for the Christmas feast. And whatever loss Llewelyn still suffered, in her he knew nothing but gain.

David brought his family and a princely retinue to share the festival with us, as he had promised, and things were almost as in the old days. But he brought with him also a fine, Davidish fury over his usage at the hands of the justiciar of Chester, and would hold council with his brother and demand his sympathy. And that, too, was like old times, and did them both good rather than harm. David without a passion to occupy him had always been David looking for mischief, and if he could not have battle in the field, he would as soon have it in the justiciar's court as anywhere.

'You have already had sour experience of law under the treaty,' he said. 'What do you say to this? There's a claim out against me for lands I've held barely a year and a half, and had openly from the king's own hand. William Venables has taken out a writ of entry against me for possession of Hope and Estyn!'

It came as a true astonishment to Llewelyn, as his startled face bore witness. For whatever the prince's tangles at law might be, David had come out of the recent treaty as an ally of the king, and a favourite into the bargain, set up in life with two of the four cantrefs of the Middle Country, and granted the lands of Hope and Estyn, on the borders, to provide him with a second castle in addition to Denbigh. For any man to come forward and lay claim to those lands, in the teeth of that grant, was surely an instance of the litigious madness that was driving so many lords and tenants into follies that would prove both ineffective and costly. There were enough recent and genuine grievances to be set right, after a year of turmoil during which lands had changed hands three or four times, and the treaty of peace made provision for any man who felt himself to have legitimate claims to put them forward in whatever court was appropriate. But others had caught the acquisitive fever, and were digging up tenuous claims traced back to a grandsire who had once held a manor under very different circumstances, or an ancestor who had married a minor heiress and never succeeded in getting hold of her dower lands. The whole country on both sides the march seethed with lawsuits. But it was something new for one of the king's recent gifts to be challenged.

'Venables?' said Llewelyn, frowning. 'On what grounds can he possibly put forward any such claim?' The Venables family was old and of importance in Cheshire, and as Mold had bounced in and out of Montalt hands a dozen times within a century, so at some distant point a Venables might have had a precarious hold on Hope.

'Do I know,' said David impatiently, 'until he opens his plea? Whatever his line may be, I'm ready to answer it. How can there be a better claim than mine? That is not the issue! Venables has sworn out his writ in the justiciar's shire-court at Chester, and the justiciar has accepted it and summoned me there to answer it. Into England! Into Chester! He cannot do it, and he knows it. It's plainly stated in the treaty that causes concerning land shall be tried according to the custom of those parts where the land lies, whether it be Wales or march land. Chester is an English shire-court, and Hope and Estyn are in Wales, and I will not appear to any plea concerning them in the justiciar's court. I blame Venables for the attempt, but Badlesmere more for abetting it.'

'You and I, it seems,' said Llewelyn with a wry smile, 'are contending against the same monster. My case was exactly as yours when I opened my claim to Arwystli. Like you I was cited to Montgomery, a royal town, when the impleaded land is wholly Welsh.'

'And you accepted it!' said David, between reproach and sympathy. 'It was your mistake. You put yourself in their hands once you acknowledged such a court.'

'I made a proxy appearance to present my writ, and that was all. And I wrote at the same time to the king, and made the very point you are making, that I should not have been cited there, and did not accept that it was proper procedure. You'll find, as I found, that he has a legal answer to that. He'll tell you, if you challenge him, what he told me. He'll agree with you as to the clause in the treaty, but point out that in cases between two barons or magnates holding in chief of the crown it has always been customary, even where Welsh law is concerned, to hear them at fixed dates and places, appointed by the justices. He'll tell you you must not resent falling in with this procedure – just as he told me.'

'I've not forgotten!' said David, glowering. 'He himself appointed you a day at Oswestry, and you conceded the place but not the process of law. And little enough it got you! Only a reference back to the king himself, and a hearing before him at Rhuddlan.'

'Under Welsh law,' said Llewelyn.

'Granted! And he presided over a hearing by Welsh law, with the proper Welsh judges in court to hear the pleas, and by rights you should have got your verdict then and there. Edward had an answer even then! He adjourned the court, arbitrarily, on his own responsibility, without allowing the judges to pronounce a verdict. Did you not feel, then, that there would always be a legal answer, if your case showed signs of coming to a successful conclusion? Oh, I've followed the Arwystli case from the beginning,' he said, 'and learned by it. I can also devise answers – even to Edward's answers!'

'Granting they're in the wrong over this business of Hope,' said Llewelyn reasonably, 'you can hardly blame the king for that before you've informed him of it. You may well be wasting all this rage, he may take his officer's action as ill as you do. He gave you the lands, he'll surely do you justice if you do but apply to him.'

'That I shall do, and profit by your example. But I'll deal with Badlesmere, too,' he promised, gnawing his lip vengefully. For this Guncelin de Badlesmere, then justiciar of Chester, was no friend of his, and they had had high words before over other matters, David's lands lying so closely neighbour to the county of Chester. 'I have not yet had any satisfaction out of him,' said David, brooding, 'for his thinning out my forests, as if they were on English land, and cutting great roads through them across the border. Half the cantref is up in arms about it. Those are our hunting coverts, and our pig-pastures, yes, and our protection, too. What right have they to destroy them?'

'You are not the only one,' said Llewelyn drily, 'to be breathing fire over that ordinance. The same thing is happening in our cousin Mortimer's lands in the middle march, and by the clamour he's making over it, it's no more pleasing to a marcher baron than it is to a Welsh prince. The king has a reasonable plea enough. You know yourself it's true that the forests are the best haunts of robbers and masterless men, and safe roads through will be to the benefit of trade on both sides.'

'Well for you!' said David fiercely. 'Your forests they cannot touch, yours is still a principality, and sovereign, if it is smaller than once. But even you would do well to keep a close watch on these new roads . . .' There he bit off whatever had been skipping so vehemently from his tongue, and prowled the room for some minutes in silence, to begin again abruptly upon another course. 'You have been given another day to proceed with your plea on Arwystli, have you not?'

'The fourteenth day of January,' said the prince, 'at Oswestry.'

'And will you go? And concede the place?'

'I shall send my attorneys,' said the prince, 'and bear with the king's ruling that causes in chief are heard where the justices appoint. I shall make no other concession. The plea must be heard by Welsh law, and no other.'

This matter of Arwystli was becoming increasingly important to him by reason of the delays and prevarications he felt he had encountered in pursuing it. Most of that cantref, which lies in the very heart of Wales, remained in the hands of his arch-enemy and traitor, Griffith ap Gwenwynwyn of Powys, who had plotted against the prince's life in peace and taken the opposing side against him in war, and like most gross offenders, could never forgive the man against whom he had offended, but now from the safety of King Edward's overlordship and favour pursued every possible means of pestering and wounding him. Arwystli had had a troubled history, sometimes held by Gwynedd, sometimes by Powys, but in ancient times it had been considered unquestionably as belonging to Gwynedd, and Llewelyn grudged it bitterly to a renegade Welsh lord who now aped and flattered the English and did all possible offence to his own Welsh neighbours, besides his spite against the prince himself. So there was far more at stake in this matter than the worth of the land in question.

'And you?' said Llewelyn, watching his brother with wary affection. 'What will you do? There's this to be thought of, neither you nor I can wish to seem obdurate against the authority of the king, and even when his officials are at fault, the summons comes in his name. To enter a formal protest is fair, even necessary. To make an equally formal appearance in answer to the summons, while rejecting the *court's* authority, might be wise.'

'I had thought of it,' said David. 'That I might even enjoy,' he said, with a dark and mischievous smile.

'By your attorneys, I would advise,' said Llewelyn hastily, foreseeing David's enjoyment dropping into the smooth surface of Badlesmere's shire-court like a stone into still waters. But he smiled.

'In person,' said David, 'or where's the sport? Oh, never fear, I can be discreet where my own good's involved. But I'll make Badlesmere sweat!'

'Whatever the case,' said Llewelyn mildly, 'you need not fear the result. What plea can Venables possibly put up, to compare with your right, when the king himself gave you the lands, and so recently? The man's a fool to waste his time in the attempt.'

At that David looked at him long, and seemed to debate within himself whether to say what was on his mind, or leave well alone. In the end he did not speak, but shrugged off the matter for the time being, and returned to his wine and his Elizabeth, who was as fierce in the cause of Hope and Estyn as he was, and eternally confident of his wisdom and rightness in all he did. As for Eleanor, she listened with a thoughtful face but a silent tongue, and left them to dispose of their legal problems as they saw fit. Out of deference for her, I think, David had somewhat curbed what otherwise he might have said outright against Edward, for not only he, but half the lords and chief tenants of the Middle Country were seething with resentment at the arbitrary ways of the king's bailiffs, and their encroachments on ancient Welsh rights which had never before been threatened. In a single year the administration had made malcontents of those who had gladly sheltered under its shadow when war loomed, and enemies of those who had fallen away from Llewelyn to serve the king and save themselves. There was a kind of rough justice in it, that they had rushed to embrace English protection, leaving Wales to its fate, only to find out, and so soon, that they did not all like the governance they had invoked, and were already looking round for someone to rescue them from it. In vain, if they looked to Llewelyn. He had set his seal to a treaty, and his word was his bond. The men of the Middle Country lay in beds they themselves had made, and found them beds of thorns.

I met David again later that evening in the inner ward of the maenol, taking a breath of the night air before he went to his rest. He was standing under the stars, gazing up with a still face at the guardwalk above the postern gate, where once he had kept vigil by night, waiting for the men of Powys to ride in silently to the work of murder, and set him up as prince in his brother's place. As soon as he was aware of me, I knew he was remembering that time, and he knew as much of me. I never had asked him, I never was to ask him, anything concerning that night. When Llewelyn called him back to him, asking nothing, and he came in desperate and rebellious love, making no confession and expressing no penitence, all question was for ever put out of my power. But when David was alone, he remembered, and so did I.

I would have passed by and let him be, but he spoke me softly and calmly: 'Samson!' and I stayed. 'Samson,' he said, laying his arm in the old way about my shoulders, 'after that hearing at Rhuddlan, when Edward adjourned my brother's plea so strangely, that same month he set up a commission to enquire into how barons of Wales had been accustomed to plead in land disputes. I remember they sat at Oswestry towards the end of the month. Reginald de Grey had the commission, and one of the king's clerks with him – Hamilton, that's the man. William Hamilton. Edward claimed it was set up to make doubly sure of proceeding justly. But I have it in mind, Samson, that it was for exactly the opposite reason. Tell me this, since the commission sat two full months ago, and reported its findings immediately, can you think of a reason why those findings have never been made known? Did anything ever come of them? Nothing! Yet the record of that inquisition is lying somewhere in the king's treasury, very quietly. It is on my mind, Samson, that it will never be heard of again, at least, never in Wales. For good reason! It must have found absolutely for Llewelyn's claim, that Welsh land is ruled by Welsh law, and no other.'

I said, and meant it, that while I did not cherish any blind confidence in the king's disinterestedness, neither did I think this judgment on him as yet in any way justified, and we should await the outcome of the January hearing at Oswestry. It was common knowledge that English law was always tedious in its delays and prevarications by comparison with the clear simplicity and promptness of our own laws of Howel the Good, and further, that Edward was so in love with its complexities as to be a little mad on the subject.

'Edward's madness,' said David with a hollow laugh, 'like Edward's generosity, exists only in the service of Edward's interests. I advise you, for my brother's sake, keep a careful watch on everything the king says or does, and in particular everything he writes. When he becomes most voluble and obscure, then watch him most carefully. And if the Oswestry session proves me wrong, I'll do penance gladly, and you, my beloved confessor, shall set it for me, as sharply as you will.'

I said that the prince's men of law were inevitably in expectation of trickery to begin with, that being the nature of law-men everywhere. And then I said, to lighten his sombre mood, that in any event his own case was different, since he held what he held by the king's own wish.

'We shall see!' said David. 'You heard Llewelyn say that Venables is a fool to challenge the king's grant? To the best of my knowledge, Venables is no fool at all, but very shrewd, and with an eye to his own good. Who's to say that someone – oh, not Edward! – has not whispered in his ear where his best interests lie, and how far he may go with impunity? My demon prompts me that this is the king's way of recovering what he already regrets having given. And that, too, will be seen, all in good time.'

We walked back to the tower together, and he took his arm from about me, and yawned, and turned towards the stairway. But there he paused and looked back, and in the dim light from a single torch I saw his face sharply and sombrely outlined.

'One more thing, Samson! Should you ever be in those parts where they are, look for yourself at Edward's new trade roads through the forests. Granted a clear way, where officers can patrol freely, may be good for trade. But ask yourself whether any merchant, with pack-horses and a few stout journeymen, needs that breadth of open land. Then remember how we moved up from Chester to Flint, from Flint to Rhuddlan, how many thousands strong, in that last war, with the foresters felling and the labourers carting ahead of us. Oh, speak out on me!' he said, seeing how I watched him without a word. 'Do you think I have forgotten on which side I fought then? Curse me, if you will. But after that, listen to me!'

'I shall never curse you,' I said, 'until he does. And he never will. And I am listening.'

'Samson, I cannot get it out of my head or my heart, or wherever it so lodges and oppresses me,' said David, 'that after all the arguments at law are exhausted, those roads are Edward's last argument.'

I was present in court when the bench of judges under Walter de Hopton sat at Oswestry, that Hilary session, to hear the prince's plea on Arwystli, for I went as a clerk to Llewelyn's attorneys. Therefore I know all that passed in that courtroom, and I set it down here that it may not be lost or forgotten. For this was the first time that ever the two opponents joined battle fully over this plea, almost a year having been drained away in delays and adjournments.

We were well primed before ever we left Gwynedd, and the prince's stand was unshakable. He acceded to the king's ruling that such important cases between lords must be heard at places and times fixed by the judges, surrendering the exact position stated in the treaty, that a cause should be heard in the lands where it arose. But not one point more would he yield. Arwystli was Welsh, had always been Welsh, lay in the

623

very heart of Welsh land, and could not be, and never had been, subject to English common law. On that we stood absolutely.

The hall where the bench sat was full, for the meeting of those two implacable enemies, even by proxy, drew men from all the country round to watch, and especially lawyers, eager to observe the conduct of such important pleas. Griffith ap Gwenwynwyn came in person, with a bevy of law-men about him, and kept close to their sleeves during the hearing, ready to pluck and whisper and prompt, for he was certainly as skilled in prevarication as any of his advisers, though he preferred to work through them. His big frame had run somewhat to fat since I had last seen him, his thick brown beard and hair were laced with grey, and his walk slower and more ponderous than of old. He was then in his middle sixties, strong as a bull, but growing clumsy, and his English finery of furred gown and ample surcoat made him look bulkier than he was. He settled himself solidly in his place behind the line of his lawyers, and swept the court with sharp, narrowed eyes, dwelling longest upon the prince's attorneys, seated opposite. Most of Arwystli was in his hands, he would not let it go without a long and bitter struggle.

We had three justices on the bench before us, two Welsh and one English, but there was not a man in court who did not know that the judgment rested with the presiding judge, and the others were there merely to supply a fair balance and a knowledge of Welsh customs and traditions. One of them was Goronwy ap Heilyn, a good friend to us and sometime among Llewelyn's own lawyers, who had accepted office under the king in this commission with the true intent to maintain and protect justice for his fellow-countrymen, for he was a man of Rhos, and knew and loved the north. The other was Howel ap Meurig, no friend to us, which at least made the bench appear impartial. He was an englishified Welshman who had abandoned his own country for royal service more than fifteen years earlier, and done very well out of it, with a knighthood and a coat of arms to show, but he was no more on an equal footing with Walter de Hopton than was Goronwy.

I had seen this Hopton before, but never so close. He came from a border family that held land both in Hereford and Salop, and he was in middle life, perhaps fifty then, but looked younger, being very neat and smooth, with well-shaven chin and pale, plump cheeks, and very quick, cool eyes that he kept half-hidden under large white eyelids. He was himself no mean litigant, as a great many men had already learned to their cost.

As soon as the judges were seated and the court in session, Hopton signified to the prince's chief attorney that he might proceed. Master William rose, and at once demanded that Griffith ap Gwenwynwyn, as the opposing party, should attach himself by producing hostages, according to Welsh law, after which formality the prince would willingly prosecute his right in the matter according to *cyfraith*, the Welsh code of Howel the Good. This on two grounds, that the land in question was wholly Welsh, lay within the borders of Wales, and both the parties claiming it were themselves of Welsh blood and estate; and further, that the treaty obtaining between England and Wales laid it down that claims of land within the boundaries of Wales should be conducted according to Welsh law. Both tradition and custom, and the letter of the treaty, demanded that the cause be tried by Welsh law and no other.

Griffith's lawyer got up to counter, prodded briskly by his lord.

'The Lord Griffith,' said the attorney, 'is a baron of the king's Grace, a marcher lord holding the land of Arwystli by barony of the king, as he does all his other lands. He is ready to proceed and defend his holding according to the common law, as is his right.'

'Though the Lord Griffith is a baron of the king, and a marcher,' said Master William, 'that cannot affect the land of Arwystli, which cannot possibly be called march land. March land is that which is close adjacent to Welsh land. This cannot be said of Arwystli. It lies in the central parts of Wales, and within the boundaries of the principality, and is purely Welsh. There is no way in which it can be considered as march land. Moreover, the Lord Griffith and all his forebears are of Welsh condition, as can well be proved according to Welsh law, if the bench require such proof. I ask again that this cause be conducted according to Welsh law.'

Hopton looked under his pale eyelids at Griffith and his covey of lawyers, but did not have to prompt them for an answer. The second in rank rose from his place, and leaned for a moment to his lord, who was whispering in his ear some last admonition.

'If it please the court,' said the man, smoothing his sleeves, 'there are any number of lords marchers who hold lands not merely adjacent to the border, but as deep into the heart of Wales as is Arwystli, but nevertheless hold them by barony from the king, as they do their other lands. I instance Maelienydd and Gwerthrynion, which are held by Roger Mortimer, but lie in the distant parts of Wales. A case was brought against him for possession of certain of these lands, and he was impleaded not by Welsh law, but *coram rege*, in the king's court at Windsor, and that case was concluded in Shrewsbury, under the king's justices. I can cite other such cases, all concerning lands deep in Wales, but pleaded by common law. Should the court require that these be proven here, I am willing to prove them. His Grace King Edward is in seisin of all pleas arising between his barons of the march and of Wales, to be heard before him in his court, according to common law. Should such a case be prosecuted otherwise, the lord king's prerogative is prejudiced, and the crown deprived and affronted.'

There was heard the true voice of Griffith himself, who knew only too well how to turn what sounded like a plea at law into a sly reminder how vulnerable was the position of special commissioners appointed by the king. As they had been set up, so they could as quickly be put down. As a plea the peroration might sound strong, but was in fact very weak, for how could the king's prerogative be infringed by strict observance of the terms of a treaty the king himself had argued out, agreed to and sealed hardly more than a year previously? Not even precedent should be able to upset a clearly stated ruling so recently laid down. For quite apart from the general principle stated in the treaty of Aberconway, that cases should be tried in those parts where the disputed lands lay, and by the kind of law there applying, there was also a special clause particularly laying down this rule in cases brought by the prince of Wales. There it was set down in so many words that if Llewelyn wished to claim right in any lands taken and held by others than the crown – excepting only the Middle Country, which was ceded in full – the king would show him justice according to the laws and customs of those parts where the impleaded lands lay. I remember even now how the Latin ran – *secundum leges et consuetudines partium illarum in quibus terre ille consistunt.* There could not be a clearer undertaking. Nor was Griffith's parade of precedents much to the point, since it could not wipe out that clause, and further, the prince of Wales was not a baron either of Wales or of the march, but a sovereign prince, and again, could not be used as were those barons. The procedure in the treaty had been devised and agreed particularly to define his position and the treatment to which he was entitled.

Legally, then, this was pleading high in sound but low in relevance, and the real purport was at the end, in what was rather a warning, even a threat. 'Beware,' said Griffith's attorney, shrewdly eyeing Hopton in particular, but the two Welsh assessors also, 'how you take even the least risk of infringing the king's prerogative, whatever sanction of treaty and seal you may have for the act that incurs his displeasure. Wise men, if they are not sure of their ground, defer.'

I wondered then, and was ashamed of the thought and put it from me, whether King Edward's own men of law had not conferred with Griffith and put this pointed pleading into his mouth. But it seemed too base a procedure, and I told myself I was falling into David's too suspicious frame of mind before we had tested out the king's honesty and goodwill. Whereas from Griffith this was just what might have been expected. So I absolved the king from complicity. Since then I have wondered, many times.

'You wish to make a counter-plea to this?' asked Hopton, looking at Master William and keeping his bland face inexpressive.

'With the court's permission.' And the old man took up all those points which Griffith's plea had merely covered over without touching. That he had made no mention of the special provision made in the treaty for this very purpose, and approved, indeed laid down, by the king. That as tenure by marcher barony was not the same as tenure by English barony, so the status of the prince of Wales conformed to neither, for which reason the provision before-mentioned had been devised. So far merely in refutation, but then he went further.

'The lord king, as all men know, is lord of many lands and provinces, and each of these lands under his dominion has its own laws and customs according to the traditions and usages of that part where it lies. Gascony, Scotland, Ireland, England, each has its own ways and laws, and that greatly to the enlargement of the crown's privileges, and not at all to their derogation. The prince of Wales seeks only the same right for his person and his principality, that he should also have his own law, the law of Wales, and proceed according to that law, and not otherwise. And especially he invokes those clauses in the treaty of peace between himself and the lord king, by which the king himself, of his own will, granted Welsh law to the prince and people of Wales. I say that this is his entitlement by common right, as those other nations gathered under the king's lordship have their laws and customs, and their language. But also by a particular right, laid down by the king in treaty, he seeks to enjoy the privilege so markedly granted him under the royal seal.'

Adam, his clerk, who sat beside me in court, was glowing and grinning by then, for the old man's blood was up, and he had never spoken to better purpose. I had thought Griffith might attempt no further in that line, having to all appearances the worst of the argument, but he did pluck at his man's sleeves and send him into the lists again, somewhat less confidently but volubly still.

'With the court's leave, it must be observed that all those several nations, however they may do in other causes, in the king's court are governed by a single common law, and not by varying and opposing laws in one and the same court. The king's Grace is in seisin of pleas in his court between his barons, whether Welsh or marcher, and therefore in that court and by common law this plea should proceed. According to that law the Lord Griffith is ready and willing to answer all claims, but not by the *cyfraith* of Howel Dda.'

'And my prince,' said Master William, 'lays claim to the Welsh law expressly granted to him by the king in the treaty, and is ready to pursue his right to judgment, and to answer any and all claims, by that law and no other. For if he abandoned that right, it would be a concession without precedent, and greatly to his diminution.'

On these opposing declarations the parties stood, and neither would give way. It was open to the bench to weigh and decide between the two claims, indeed that was held to be the reason why this commission had been set up, and not at all to adjourn and defer and commit all perilous decisions to another court, but I knew then that that was what they would do. Not only because Goronwy, and I believe rightly, would come down on the side of the treaty and of Welsh law, while Howel ap Meurig as surely would incline to Griffith's side and find plausible reasons for it, which would leave Hopton in the position of having to cast the final vote himself. That would in any case have been reason enough, for he was too cautious ever to let himself be placed in so vulnerable a position. But I believe he had another and more absolute reason for avoiding. Those reasons he gave were sound enough, but I do not believe he ever had to do more than seem to consider. It was never intended that the prince's claim should come to any conclusion that day. Apart from the record, all those pleadings and counter-pleadings had been breath wasted.

'You are absolute in maintaining these positions?' said Hopton mildly, turning his half-hidden eyes from one attorney to the other. They said firmly that they were, and neither could nor would move from them.

'This matter is of such importance,' he said then, 'the parties provided on both sides with such weighty arguments, that it seems rather to have been lifted out of our competence. Both make direct appeal to royal privilege and claim royal sanction, the one by treaty, the other by baronage, and there is substance in both, and both touch the crown prerogative closely. I must confer with my colleagues.' And he did so, with great earnestness and in low voices, while his clerks wrote away busily for some ten minutes, but we knew what the end of it would be. I could not blame the bench too much for taking the easy way out of their trap.

The clerk rapped for silence at length, and Hopton delivered his judgment. 'We are agreed that we cannot of our own power interpret the clauses of a treaty drawn by the king, except in his presence and with his guidance. Nor could we take any decision affecting the prerogative of the crown without the sanction of the crown. We are therefore agreed that this case must be adjourned *coram rege*, and we appoint both parties a day for that hearing in the king's court, one month after Easter, on the last day of April, so that his Grace can decide the questions of law here involved, and make his will known.'

And on that the bench rose, and Griffith ap Gwenwynwyn rose after, with a swirl of his furred gown, and stamped gleefully out of court with his rookery of lawyers on his heels. And we went away irritated and disappointed, but not really astonished. It was ill news to take back to Llewelyn, though I did not think it would come as any great surprise to him, either, however arduously he had reserved his judgment. One thing I was sure of, and that was that he would not attend on the day appointed in April, for there was no course open to him but to stand on his Welsh right. If he once surrendered it, they had a precedent for ever after, and to use against other men. Or if he did send proxies, it would be only to state his position and stand immovably upon it, as he had done in Oswestry.

Llewelyn and Eleanor were in Ardudwy at that time, and there we returned and reported what had passed. But we found David there before us, without his family on this occasion, for he had ridden west in haste and excitement, in the fresh flush of battle, to compare his own fortunes in litigation with his brother's and was half furious, half perversely gratified, to find his worst prophecies confirmed. I heard his voice uplifted in the high chamber before I entered the hall, and his law clerk, Alan of Denbigh, met me in the stables and gave me the whole story.

'Oh, he made his appearance there in Badlesmere's court, as summoned, to the day and the hour, but not by his attorneys. He went in person, and took no one with him but me, and that only to have a witness both while he stayed and after he left, for he never had any idea of acknowledging the competence of the court, and he had no trust in them for what they might get up to behind his back. And right he was! He waited until the case was called and Venables put in his writ, and then he stalked out into the centre of the room alone, where no one could fail to see and hear him. You know him! He made a figure, there's none can do it better!' And he grinned, remembering, and so did I, imagining David bestriding the floor in his arrogance of beauty and disdain, to the eclipse of Badlesmere and all his assessors.

'He said that he was there only out of reverence for the king's Grace, and to make plain that he did not own the competence of the court and was not bound to answer for his lands there, for they were a part of the true soil of Wales, and belonged in no way to Cheshire, where alone Badlesmere's writ runs. And then he pronounced his summoning there as illegal, and cried aloud like a trumpet that he committed the lands in question to the peace of God and the king. And stalked out, and left a dead silence behind him for a long while, till they got their breath back, and what was left of their legal dignity. Man, it was a massacre! But they'll make him pay for it! No royal officer likes to be outshone and outfaced in his own court, and if Badlesmere is no strong man, there's one strong enough and to spare behind him.'

'And after he left?' I asked.

'It was pitiful law, they were hardly themselves, but it was very pointed spite. They let Venables proceed with his plea, as though nothing had happened, and brought in that David had refused to plead, though he'd made no formal appearance at all, only repudiated the competence of the court. It made him angrier than ever when I followed him with the news. Lucky I was there to see! There was only one assessor there who had the honesty to speak out against the judgment and refuse his agreement, and that was the earl of Lincoln's steward. He opposed them from beginning to end, and has had his opposition enrolled. That's one good man we can call to witness for us.'

We had fared no better, and so I told him. It behoved the princes to work together in these matters, and see that their efforts fortified each other.

'They'll have their heads together now,' said Alan. 'The lord prince may allow himself a few days for thought, but my lord will certainly be drafting his letter to the king in his mind this minute, and it will be a strong one.'

Over the wording of that letter David haled me, too, into service. It was written that same evening after supper, in Llewelyn's high chamber, the prince sitting quietly by and forbearing from urging prudence or changing the fiery words David dictated.

The facts of the hearing at Chester David recounted to the king briefly and truly, and with the same force demanded, rather than requested, a just remedy. It was a prince's letter, courteous enough but worded to an equal, who owed him fair treatment and could be called to account if he did less than justice.

'Write,' said David, staring before him across the glow of the brazier to where Alan sat at the table with his parchment and his pens, 'write that in view of the illegality of the process, I beg his Grace to have the plea, the judgment and the persons of the doomsmen who gave that judgment, brought to his own presence. Further, I request that the pursuit of this plea in the shire-court of Chester be suspended.'

'You are taking a high line,' said Llewelyn, but without disapproval.

'If I fail in that now, how can I begin after? Wait still, Alan, I have more to say. If this matter is to move at all, and not be deferred and delayed and lost by creeping inch upon inch, I must find the answer to what Edward's answer will be, and spare at least one letter. Write this, Alan! "Since your Grace, by the ordinance of God, is king of many countries, speaking varying tongues and administered according to varying laws, which your Grace has seen no cause to change, let the laws of Wales, also, if it please your Grace, remain unchanged and respected as are those of the other nations under your crown." '

I saw Llewelyn's eyes open wide and dark under his deep brow, and a faint and private smile touch his lips and vanish again. For David had wrested out of his own heart the very principle, almost the very words, Master William had advanced in court, and yet no one had recounted to David in detail, at that time, what had passed in Oswestry. The outcome he knew, but certainly not all the arguments. He had come to the same lofty place of his own passion, and seen the same vision, he who had exchanged his rights in Gwynedd for lands of the king's gift, and fought for the king against his own people. True, this high flight was in defence of his own possessions, yet the cry he uttered was not only for himself.

And he had said more even than he knew. It was Llewelyn who had heard and marked the true meaning. In a moment naked and unguarded David, three times renegade, had cried out for the rights of Wales, and cried from the heart, with all the patriot authority of the prince his brother.

CHAPTER II

Now as to the progress of these two lawsuits, so fatal in themselves, and so ominous as they represented hundreds of others, that plagued and maddened lesser men throughout all those lands no longer in Llewelyn's principality, what happened to both during the remainder of that year can be easily told, for though many letters passed, and many men sat and deliberated, or seemed to deliberate, the sum total of what befell is, nothing!

David sent his letter, and I will not claim that nothing at all came of that, for King Edward instructed the justiciar of Chester to hold an inquisition among the men of the lands neighbour to Hope and Estyn, to determine whether those impleaded manors were in Wales or England. That inquisition was duly taken, and the men of the neighbouring parts confirmed with one voice that the lands were Welsh, and no law but Welsh had ever applied to them. But David's vengeful joy was curbed by sour disbelief, and wisely so, for in spite of this judgment, taken at the king's wish and published openly, Venables continued his plea in the Chester court as though nothing had changed, and was allowed to do so. Soon David was writing another peremptory letter to Edward calling attention to the anomaly, and demanding a remedy. Thus he persisted in his part as a spokesman for Welsh rights, and saw no illogic in it, and no bad faith, as indeed there was none. He had a party at his back by then, all those in the Middle Country who smarted under the same whip, and saw in him the champion who burned all their inarticulate complaints into one fiery utterance, loud enough to be heard even in Westminster.

As for the prince, he proceeded with less noise, and more forbearance, feeling himself tied as David was not. He did not wait for the date Hopton had appointed *coram rege*, but wrote well in advance to Edward, setting out his own view of the process to date, and why he would not and could not, pending a decision about the process of law to be followed, obey the summons to appear on the last day of April. He asked the king to receive an envoy to explain personally all that was involved. Edward replied courteously and willingly, inviting the approach. And the prince sent Brother William de Merton, the warden of the Franciscan friary at Llanfaes, to be his advocate at court.

Friar William was elderly and austere, well versed in law and of honest and forthright mind, though he knew how to furnish his severities with a courtly dress. He was also devoted to the prince and his house, and undertook the office with goodwill. But when he reached London, in the first days of April, it was to find the king making ready in haste to go to France, where he had business with King Philip, and also

631

other matters concerning his many and quarrelsome relatives in those parts, and all Friar William was able to bring back with him was the king's verbal acknowledgement that he had done his errand well and prudently, that the matter was understood, but was too complex to be dealt with summarily, and must await his return, when he would give it his full attention. So when the day appointed by the Hopton bench came, the suit was not pursued, and the prince sent no attorneys, though Griffith ap Gwenwynwyn, as I heard, did put in a formal appearance to keep the issue alive, and the official record favourable to him.

'No help for it,' said Llewelyn, sighing. 'Not even King Edward can be everywhere and deal with everything at the same time.'

Friar William had brought personal letters for Eleanor with all the news from court. The queen's mother was recently dead, and the county of Ponthieu, in the north of France, which she had held, now came to her daughter. 'Which is to say, to Edward,' said Eleanor, 'and though he has indeed business with King Philip, trying to keep the peace between him and King Alfonso of Castile, yet I think my cousin will be spending half the time of his visit making sure of his hold on Ponthieu.'

'Compared with which,' Llewelyn owned honestly, 'Arwystli may seem a very small manor, and my claim of little consequence. But justice is not a small thing, nor of little consequence.'

'And we are not the only people suffering from his passion for order in all things,' said Eleanor, still pondering the news from London. 'It seems he has set in motion a great inquest into the tenements and liberties of all his shires, and drafted panels of commissioners to do the probing. There'll be indignation enough in England, without looking westward into Wales. Every man who holds land to the value of twenty pounds a year is to be distrained by the sheriffs to accept knighthood, whether he wants the honour or not. That will set them by the ears! It's more burden than honour, these days. A strange man,' she said, frowning, 'my cousin Edward!'

'I do believe,' said Llewelyn, 'that you feel some affection for him, even after all that has happened.'

'I *know*,' she said, smiling, 'that *you* do! Of myself I'm never quite so sure. I am not as crystal-clear as you, and not as generous. I do not forget, because he showed us such marked honour and such lavish entertainment at Worcester, that we both suffered for it over and over beforehand, against all right, and that paying a blood-debt, though it goes some way to repair a wrong, does not bring back to life what was killed. Three years of my life with you Edward stole from me, and from you those three years and more. It is over now,' she said, 'and I am too happy by far to bear any grudges or want any revenges, but I remember, and I have learned. I can look at Edward as he is, and find much to like, and still keep my distance and stay on my guard.'

I was there in the high chamber with them, that summer night at Llanfaes, at a desk in the corner of the room, copying music for Eleanor, for she not only played two or three stringed instruments herself, but also took a great interest in the music of the prince's chapel, and eagerly sent for new compositions when chance offered.

'Samson knows,' she said, appealing to me, 'for he was with me then, how Edward first came to me in Windsor, when I was his prisoner. No way ashamed, and yet he was not easy. I had not seen him since I was a small child, and beneath his notice.'

She had not been beneath his notice in Windsor, but every way a match for him and more, for she had nothing to be ashamed of, and much to accuse him of, had she so chosen.

'Well, it is past,' she said. 'I could get nothing from him, but neither could he from me. Once we had made certain of that, and set our jaws to face it out, we got on very well together. Like two enemies who respect each other, brought together in the prison of a common enemy, and making truce between them in order to make life more possible. I got to know him very well, my cousin Edward, the best of him and the worst. The strength and the weakness. He is very strong. And very weak,' she said.

'There are not many would say that of him,' said Llewelyn, amused, 'who have fought against him, as I have. Or watched, even from a distance, his handling of men and events. Whatever else he may be, I see him as a giant.'

'You have not done the fighting over a chess-board, brow to brow,' said Eleanor, 'as I have. At such close quarters you hear the hard breathing, not the fanfares, and see the sweat and not the banners.'

'And were you victorious?' he asked, laughing, but marking her words very attentively for all that.

'I wish I could say so! I would have given every mark I had to be able to beat him,' she owned, reflecting his laughter, 'but I am not good enough. But once I came very near it, and brought him up short in stalemate at the end. For half an hour he dreaded I might defeat him. If you had seen him then, stiff to the finger-ends, and his jaw set like a man-trap, you would know Edward as I know him. If he could laugh at himself or bear that others should, if he saw any other human creature as having quite the same rights as he has, if he could take a fair fall and give fair credit ungrudging, then he would be great indeed. But he cannot and he does not. A giant he is, his ability is towering. But inside the giant there's a dwarf, fearful of being uncovered, and if ever his armour is pierced, to him hatred would come easy. I do not fear the giant,' said Eleanor, suddenly grave and vehement, 'but of the dwarf I could be very much afraid.'

The king remained in France until the middle of June, making himself known to the officials of Ponthieu, and staying some time in his fine new city of Abbeville, but two weeks after his return home he wrote to the prince concerning the discussions he had had with Friar William de Merton, regretting, very graciously, that the exigencies of his business in France had kept him from dealing with the matters discussed at once. But he promised that he would do so in his Michaelmas parliament, and assigned a date for the hearing, the thirteenth day of October, which he said he had also appointed to Griffith ap Gwenwynwyn, in order that the business in hand might be settled in his own court. To that end, he desired Llewelyn to send to Westminster some of his trusted and discreet men, informed about the case in hand and versed in the law of Howel the Good, and in the customs pertaining to the lands concerned. Then the king would hear the case and do such justice that the prince should be well satisfied.

Llewelyn heaved great vindicated breaths at this reasonable response to his approaches. 'I felt in my bones,' he said, cheered and glad, 'that it was the old trouble – so many officials and bailiffs between us, we cannot get to grips, and as soon as I am face to face with Edward the fog clears. Could he have spoken more directly than this? I am to send attorneys skilled in Welsh law – you see, he grants me my Welsh law! –and the rest lies with him. Even the day is a good omen,' he said. For the thirteenth of October was the first anniversary of his wedding day, the day of St Edward the Confessor, so sacred to King Edward and to his father before him.

I remember still every word of that letter, and I tell you, it could not in any interpretation be made to mean anything but what it clearly said, and had Llewelyn been far readier to detect trickery than ever he was, he must have come to the same conclusion, that no man could commit himself so fully, and then draw back or move aside.

So that summer passed in good hope, and in caring for a principality still prosperous in its ancient customs, and still growing in markets and towns, so far as its mountainous lands permitted. For the prince never lost sight of his aim, even now that he was curbed into half his former territory. There was still much to be done by good husbandry, and even within the limits of Snowdonia growth was possible. He had, moreover, the delight of taking his wife with him about this lovely, stony, glittering land of his, and watching his own love reflected in her face. There was in her a splendour that had waited, unaware of its hunger, for this wild, forbidding land, and found in it nothing daunting, but only liberty. She had a bardic strain in her, she brought the trouvère music of northern France to our western wilds, and found meaning echoes in our songs, and after a while she began to make her own songs, marrying those two in melodies to melt the heart.

When we both had leisure from other matters, she would have me teach her something of the Welsh language, and studied earnestly and quickly, asking me at every lesson for ingenious words of endearment and love in her new tongue, to be used, surely, for Llewelyn's ears only, when they lay in each other's arms. In all things, great or small, she found by grace fresh means of giving him astonishment and delight.

When the autumn drew on, and the appointed time for parliament was nearing, the prince wrote from Aberyddon to the king, repeating as a reminder almost the very terms Edward had used in bidding his envoys to the session, 'in order,' he said pointedly, 'to pursue my claim to Arwystli in your Grace's presence, according to the law of Howel the Good, which is Welsh law.' And he went on to beg the king to do justice without further delay, since the prince had already brought up the matter before both the king and the king's justices, and it had cost him high to send so many envoys all over England, and so far quite vainly.

He did not know, he said, at whose instigation his cause at law had been thus obstructed.

'You are severe with him,' said Eleanor, cautiously approving.

'That was not my intent. I put the case plainly, so that there can be no misunderstanding. I have quoted him his own bidding word for word, so that *he* shall know he has not been misunderstood. Or if he claims he has, and his instructions do not mean what I have read them as meaning, he has time to say so before the case is heard.'

So this letter was sent ahead of the envoys, and brought no protestations in answer, which was reassuring. Llewelyn began to be confident of the result, for it seemed certain at last that his claim to have Welsh law over Welsh land was conceded without further argument. The prince therefore sent another letter over another matter, punctiliously thanking the king for declining to entertain in his court a plea that manifestly belonged in the prince's jurisdiction. This was but one among hundreds of cases then embittering the whole air of the borders. The widowed lady of Bromfield had for some time been suing her brother-in-law of Ial for certain lands which he held of the prince, but being a troublesome and mischievous woman she had sued first in the Welsh courts, then in the English, putting the unlucky lord of Ial in danger of offending both overlords, since if he answered in the king's court for lands he held of the prince, that would be insult to the prince, but if he failed to answer a summons to the royal court, that would certainly blacken his face with the king. Both he and Llewelyn had appealed for a ruling, and Edward firmly remitted the case to the prince's court, and that with very pleasing promptitude. Possibly he found the lady of Bromfield more trouble than she was worth, and was not sorry to get rid of her.

'Well, let's at least give thanks where they're due,' said Llewelyn, and wrote a warm acknowledgement. And this case also we took as encouragement, and began to believe that all was going smoothly at last.

Llewelyn felt a particular responsibility in his dealings with this Margaret of Bromfield and her family, for her husband had been his ally and friend until the pressures of war broke him, for his lands were very exposed to English attack. He had left two young sons, still children, for whom Llewelyn felt a guardian's concern, and he took care to watch how their lands were administered during their infancy, and to intervene when he thought they were being abused. These lands were no longer a part of his principality, but fell under the king, and the prince could exercise only a friendly influence, but the king had been gracious and accommodating in the matter, and Llewelyn did not fail to send thanks for his consideration.

'Everything I have incurred,' he said, 'I will discharge, whether it be the payment of the money due, the deference owing from vassal to overlord, or the simple acknowledgement of favour or kindness. If his pride is to exact all, mine is to render all. As I stand on my own rights, so I'll do full justice to his.'

This he said, and made good, and his annual payments of the money due under treaty were indeed made regularly, promptly and in full, and often allocated by Edward to this need or that in his kingdom, or to discharge one of his debts, long before they were due, so certain was he of getting them to the last penny.

By the same messenger who carried Llewelyn's letters, Eleanor also wrote to the king, in response to some point he had raised concerning her mother's will. Scarcely a letter went from her without some courteous but insistent reminder about her brother Amaury, who was still a prisoner in Corfe castle at the king's pleasure, but all her pleas had so far failed to move Edward. Some of the servants of her former household were likewise prisoners, for no crime but that of accompanying their mistress when she sailed from France to join Llewelyn, already her husband by proxy, in Wales. Popes and bishops had interceded for Amaury, for he was a papal chaplain, but King Edward, for all his piety, was proof against popes, and ceded no grain of his rights to archbishops, and turned a deaf ear to all. It was the one sorrow Eleanor had, that all her efforts could not deliver her own men from their chains.

But at that time, in the bright autumn at Aberyddon, we had high hopes that things were moving in a better direction, and soon we might be able to secure justice at law, and clemency for the captives.

About the twentieth day of October David came riding in, in better spirits than we had seen him lately, for the rubbing of the royal officials in the Middle Country increasingly chafed him, but now he was glittering and full of news.

'I'm tossed out of Hope to go and amuse myself elsewhere,' he said. 'Cristin tells me to get from under her feet, for the love of God, for she has her hands full without me.' He flung an arm about my shoulders at the mention of her, for he had always known how things were with us, 'She's very well, and very happy, with a child in either arm, and Elizabeth purring like a cat. Not one daughter this time, but two! And pretty as flowers, and loud as blackbirds!'

'So they always are,' said Llewelyn, hugging him heartily. 'There's not one of yours but comes dancing into the world. I give you joy! And Elizabeth? All's well with them all three?'

'Would I stir,' said David, 'until I was sure of it? Twin girls, and made in her image! There cannot be too many Elizabeths in the world. I speak who know best. Five daughters she's given me, and think of all those happy husbands, when the years have rolled round!'

I do, I think of them now, remembering that prophecy. All those little girls of his, so vastly and indiscriminately loved, for David was gifted for fatherhood, go dancing before my eyes to their fate, and all the husbands who might well have exulted in them, as he did in their mother, are pale and void as mist, sucked empty of promised joy. But that belongs not here. Doubtless God has the whole account recorded.

'One babe, and the women are still just sufferable,' said David. 'Two, and there's no holding them. I am not even allowed to choose names, they're already chosen – Eleanor and Elizabeth.' He looked at the princess and smiled. 'What else?'

'I am proud!' said Eleanor, and leaned and kissed his cheek. It was the first time she had so touched him, for truly she did not commit herself easily, as Llewelyn was prone to do, though never did she shut out any who approached her with entreaty. And it seemed to me that by that salute David had gained a kind of credit, considered and bestowed with open eyes, as when a seal is appended to a document until then invalid. He had, I believe, had some doubts of his standing with her, not without reason. She was not bound to him by blood, as Llewelyn was, in the inescapable tie that fetters love hand and foot. And she was wise from the heart and mind together, the best wisdom in this world. I think David had feared her. Her eyes were mirrors of truth, and he knew what his truth was, and leaned aside and avoided. But where she sealed with her own ungrudging seal, I trusted, and was glad.

David had then almost forgotten his grievance over Hope and Estyn in his family joy. Also his second protest to the king had secured, if not a suspension of the Venables plea in the Chester shire-court, at least an indefinite delay, for the case had been adjourned *sine die*, pending a decision by Edward, as to the findings of his own commission. So when we showed David the king's letter, clearly asking for envoys versed in Welsh law, even he, after reading and re-reading the lines with close care, could find no flaw, no way by which any man of honour, much less a king, could extricate himself from what was there set down.

It turned out very differently when Master William and his companions came back from Westminster in the last days of October, and made their way to Aberyddon. As soon as they rode into the bailey, wearied and dusty from the journey, our thumbs pricked, and when they came in to Llewelyn all of us present there knew from their faces and the discouraged sag of their shoulders that they had nothing good to tell.

'So we have not sped!' said Llewelyn heavily. 'Well, speak freely, it's best to know how we stand, and there's no man doubts you have done your part well and ably.'

'My lord,' said the old man, 'I had rather you learned the king's mind from the king's own mouth than from mine. Here is his letter. What words he has used to you I do not know. All too many he has used to me, and with all possible patience and consideration, but I am as far off from knowing his intent as I was before. I can guess at it many ways, and fear it one way in particular, but determine and be sure of it I cannot.'

'Yes, this is familiar!' said David bitterly. 'This is Edward! Yet how *could* he get out of what he wrote to you? – even he? Or was it some unpractised clerk who wrote that last letter, and forgot to leave the boltholes open? He said it in so many words – "the law of Howel the Good" – no "buts", no "ors", no "unless" . . . Some honest fellow in the chancellery will be in trouble for that.'

'Do you tell me,' said Llewelyn, breaking the seal of the scroll with a sharp pluck, 'that Edward does not read over and ponder before he sends? I think not!' And he unrolled the parchment and read, with set face and darkening brows, but without outcry, once in silence, then aloud to us all.

' "We have listened attentively in our present parliament to all that the lord prince's attorneys have put forward on his behalf in the cause between him and Griffith ap Gwenwynwyn, concerning Arwystli and certain other lands. We find that the lord prince's attorneys had not been given full powers to act for him in the case, and though we might, therefore, have ruled this as a default and proceeded to judgment in our court, and indeed perhaps ought to have done so, we have instead adjourned the case to our next parliament at Westminster, to a date three weeks after next Easter. Since the peace between us declares that disputes in the march must be decided according to march law, and such as arise in Wales according to the laws and customs of Wales, we order the prince of Wales to appear before us, either in person or by his lawyers, fully empowered by him and well versed in that law which the prince desires, or in the law which the aforementioned Griffith prefers, that justice may be done as God and right decree, and our council approve, and there may no further delays.

' "Dated at Westminster, the twenty-fifth day of October, in the seventh year of our reign." '

He looked up over the scroll. 'Not given full powers! How can he say it? He knows you were fully empowered, and fulfilled every condition he laid down. Now he demands you shall come with authority to deal in *either* law, where before he spoke only of Welsh law. "That law which the prince desires, *or* in the law which Griffith prefers . . ." He is not asking simply for men *versed* in both laws, and able to dispute over which applies – no, he is saying I am to authorise you to go to him prepared to plead by whichever law *he* claims applies! To submit in advance to having my case tried however *he* decrees, when he knows and I know that Arwystli is Welsh to the bedrock, and never has been subject to any law but Welsh.'

'It is a means of delaying for another half-year,' said David, smouldering, 'and after that he'll find yet another means, and always paying lip-service to justice and law. Still professing he wants no more delays, as if you were the one to blame, and still luring you on to hope, with his virtuous testimony that march law applies to the marches and Welsh law to Wales, as though he were not standing in the way of that very principle. No fox could twist and turn better. Whatever words he uses will always serve his purpose, for he will always reserve to himself the sole right to expound what they mean, in the teeth of language, in the face of truth.'

Llewelyn looked at Master William, whose weary old face was as grim as his own. 'Did you gather anything, from all he had to say in court, to give us a better opinion of what he is about? I myself could put a dozen different interpretations upon this letter, and doubtless I have put the worst. Let me know your mind.'

'In my view,' said the old man, 'his Grace uses words not to expound, but to conceal his meaning. The conclusion I could draw from one sentence he refutes in the next. But one thing was clear. His Grace did not intend to permit the case to begin at this session, whatever pretext might be needed to halt it. No, still one more thing is certain – Griffith ap Gwenwynwyn was in no fear or concern at all, from the first.'

'No, for he had his assurance in advance,' said David sourly. 'He was contending in a match he knows he will not be allowed to lose.'

'Yet he himself has pleaded Welsh law when it suited him,' said Master William. 'Last year the men of Montgomery brought suit against him that his fair and market at Pool were to the damage and loss of the king's market at Montgomery, and he retorted with a plea that he need not answer for anything concerning Pool in the king's court, for the town lay in Wales, and every lord having a town in Wales could hold market and fair in his own lands without hindrance. It's true he lost his case then, for it was the king's profit at stake, but nonetheless he stood fast on his Welsh status, not a word then of pleading as a baron holding from the king. This case I cited before his Grace, but I was silenced by the ruling that I was not properly empowered. I was not allowed to proceed.'

'You could not have done more,' said Llewelyn consolingly. 'Where ears are shut, your eloquence and knowledge are wasted. Never fret for that, it's no fault of yours. So have others pleaded Welsh law,' he said, laying the letter by, 'and been allowed it. My cousin, Mortimer, for one. It seems the same privilege is not to be allowed to me, unless I fight hard for it. As I will!'

'What do you mean to do?' asked David, quivering. 'Fight, you say! With what weapons?'

'Law,' said Llewelyn emphatically, divining his flight and plucking him to earth. 'However it may be loaded against me, I have no other permissible weapon, and I shall use none. But whatever the unbalance, I'll contend as long as I have breath, in whatever court Edward may sanction, and by one law and one law only, and we shall see who has the longer endurance. I'll wait his half-year, and send my envoys, empowered to argue to the death in both laws, but not to proceed with my plea in any law but Welsh. And whatever the next shift may be to silence me and sicken me into withdrawal, I will never withdraw. There's more at stake than Arwystli, and for more Welshmen than Llewelyn.'

It was from that day that the prince's faith in King Edward's honesty was first shaken. If he fought on, as he was determined to do, in the name of Welsh rights rather than for any gain he could expect in the matter of Arwystli, it was in the conviction that the scales were weighted against him. But in a sense this was still a legal game, which might be won even against unfair odds. It was not a life and death matter.

It became so, I believe, that same December, just after we kept St Nicholas' day. There was a session of the Hopton commission held at Montgomery on the ninth, and Master William's clerk Adam attended, in the case of a Welsh tenant of Mortimer who had a grievance there. He came back in great excitement and indignation, and would see Llewelyn at once.

'My lord,' he said, 'I was in court when Griffith ap Gwenwynwyn brought in a plea against the crown for certain lands that were taken from him when he was your vassal, and after the war held by the king. Griffith claimed hereditary right to them, and Mortimer and the bailiff of Montgomery appeared against him for the king, and pleaded Welsh law.'

'So may every man, Welsh, marcher or English, it seems, even the king,' said Llewelyn with a wry smile. 'Every man, but me. And what had they to urge by Welsh law?'

'Why, my lord, that a man who claims hereditary right to any land, and fails to prosecute his right for a year and a day, he has forfeited his right. And then Griffith ap Gwenwynwyn rose up in person, and said outright that Welsh law, this so-called law of Howel the Good, ought not to have any force against him, for the king's Grace had it in mind to annul it wholly.'

Llewelyn was still as stone for a moment. Then he said, and his voice was quiet and mild: 'Did he indeed say so? Loud as ever?'

'Loud, my lord, and certain, and without shame. As one having official knowledge. Wherever the king's writ now runs, he said, law is to be the king's law. And then the justices were horribly disturbed and out of countenance and Hopton spoke up in a great hurry, and said they did not believe, for their part, that the king wished to annul the law *in toto*, but only to correct certain parts of it which were not wholly in accordance with right, and to remove some which were no way acceptable, and manifestly ought to be removed.'

'Yes,' said Llewelyn, with the dry rustle of a laugh, 'doubtless Griffith has spoken too soon. It is his way.' He was silent for a moment, deep in black and brooding thought, and then he roused himself to thank Adam and dismiss him. 'You have done me good service,' he said, 'and it shall not be forgotten. Let Master William know what you have heard.'

When we were alone he said ruefully: 'Out of the mouths of infants and fools truth drops at the wrong moment. I should be grateful to Griffith for letting me know the worst.'

I said, though without certainty, that I would not take Griffith's word, thus used in court argument concerning his own interests, for what was in King Edward's mind.

'Neither would I,' said Llewelyn, 'if Hopton had not rushed so hastily to put a better gloss on it. He tried to sweeten it liberally, but note, he did not deny it. There must be truth in it! He means to bring all Wales, all that he holds, all that is not my principality and safe from him, into the jurisdiction of English law, as well as into his shire order and under his bailiffs. And yet he promised to all Welshmen, as he promised to me, our own law unviolated. It is written into the treaty, and it should bind him, as God knows it does bind me. And I still cannot believe,' he said, fretting at old memories and doubts, 'that all the time that treaty was making, clause by clause, he was in deliberate bad faith. I cannot believe it! It never showed in him or in his envoys. There was hard bargaining to hold what we held, and when it was ceded, I believe that was done as honestly as it was grudgingly. Had it been light to give, he would have given it lightly.'

And I, too, remembered every day of that month-long negotiation, and it was fought fiercely, but I believe cleanly. But my mind misgave me that we were dealing with one who entered into undertakings in good faith enough, and yet when they began to irk him could find the most just and virtuous reasons for qualifying or discarding them, who could re-examine his own given word, and convince himself that it meant something quite other than it said, and that he would be false and recreant if he did not follow the newly-discovered spirit and repudiate the letter. Studied from under that drooping eyelid of his, that alone marred his grandeur as it had marred his father's grace, doubtless words slid obliquely from their original sense to spell out what Edward desired them to mean.

'His own law naturally seems to him the best, for us as for the English,' said Llewelyn, 'that I can understand. And ours, being alien, may seem to him distasteful and disordered. But he has promised to observe it faithfully, and let him twist and recant as he will, and with all the power in his hands, if I must fight him to the end of my life to pin him to his word, I will do it. If he prevails against me, what hope will any other Welshman have of justice? I am bound by the treaty, there is no weapon allowed me but law, and even that, it seems, even that I must wield with my hands manacled.'

This matter of the Arwystli suit, which had now become a touchstone to determine the king's sincerity or duplicity, and affected every man of Welsh blood who had a grievance at law and hoped to right it by the code he knew and trusted, was not the only cause of vexation to the prince at this time, though it was the gravest. There were many other suits entangling him, some of them malicious and brought only to plague him, some collusive, to afford Griffith ap Gwenwynwyn legal cover, and assist him to manipulate the irritating delays in which he took such pleasure.

There was also another matter which had dragged on for some years, and was causing great annoyance and loss. Before the recent war a certain merchant ship had come to wreck in rough weather off our coast, and the men of Gwynedd had fished ashore such of the crew as survived, and salvaged all the goods the ship was carrying, which then legally belonged to the prince, who held right of wreck in all his lands. But after the peace was made, and the rush to law began, the owner of the vessel, one Robert of Leicester and a rich man, went to the king with the tale that his ship had not been lost by wreck, and the prince had no right to the goods she carried, and so he had obtained royal letters enabling him to bring suit for recovery of his merchandise or its value in the Chester shire-court, where naturally he had no difficulty in getting judgment in his favour.

Now this was in any case wrong in law, for the suit, if he wished to press his claim, should have been brought in the land where the loss complained of occurred, that is, in Llewelyn's own court in Wales, and therefore its process in Chester was an affront and infringement of the prince's sovereign right. In addition to this, the justice of Chester from then on proceeded to distrain on whatever property of Llewelyn fell into his hands, and as we relied on Chester for much of our buying of necessities, we suddenly found it unsafe to send there to buy in supplies, for as fast as they were paid for they were seized for their value against the sum claimed by Robert of Leicester. The prince suffered diminution of his right by the slight of his court, a challenge to his right of wreck which could never have arisen by Welsh law, and the repeated loss of his purchases, together with danger to his messengers if they attempted to keep them, for the justiciar's men were not gentle.

There were also, of course, those clashes along the border which wise chiefs discouraged, but also took for granted, and paid out the compensation due when just complaints were made against their men. This had always been done on an even footing, each side in conference with the other either admitting or disputing the charges made, until sensible agreement was reached, and each paid its score fairly. But at this time such encroachments were greatly aggravated along the marches of Salop, led by Griffith ap Gwenwynwyn and his sons, and willingly aided by many of the local men, and when Tudor went to the border to meet the sheriff of Salop and make mutual amends for all trespasses then charged, notwithstanding that most of the Welsh offences had already been paid for and the steward was willing to amend those remaining, the sheriff refused to make any such amends on his part unless he should receive direct orders from the king to do so. This again was not only an unjust imbalance, but a breach of treaty, though Llewelyn did not therefore charge it against Edward himself, for we knew only too well that the king's officials were arrogant and exacting beyond their master, and he could not know everything that was going on in all parts of his kingdom.

Thus all these vexed matters stood in the early spring of that year twelve hundred and eighty. In February the prince wrote to the king informing him of the distraints at Chester and the dispute on the Salop border, mindful that after Easter parliament would again assemble at Westminster, and determined to ensure that all his complaints were documented before his envoys must again appear in Edward's court. The king replied in the matter of the goods from the wreck, disclaiming all previous knowledge of the affair, which we could hardly accept, seeing Robert of Leicester had taken out royal letters before ever he could bring suit at Chester. At the coming parliament, said Edward, the prince's attorneys should be able and ready to inform him fully about the case, and he would do right, as was always his will and intent.

'Very heartily,' said Llewelyn, 'we'll do our part, if he'll do his. He shall not be able to say he was not fully informed.' And once again he asked Brother William de Merton to be his special envoy and take all these affairs in his care when parliament met, and armed him with his best legal advisers, and with all manner of attestations from the clergy and friars of Gwynedd to show that the prince's right to have Welsh law in the Arwystli case was irrefutable.

Now it chanced that at this time John Peckham, the new archbishop of Canterbury, who had held office just a year and was full of zeal for the wellbeing of his whole flock, in Wales as in England, was in correspondence with Llewelyn concerning a long-standing dispute between the prince and the bishop of Bangor, which Archbishop Peckham greatly desired to bring to a happier composition. This again was but one of the fruits of the recent war, like so many of our vexations, for by and large the prince had always a warm and affectionate relationship with this Bishop Einion. But the lot of such a bishop, subject to his prince and greatly dependent on his goodwill and protection, but equally subject to Canterbury and the papacy, and through his archbishop very much exposed to the grace or enmity of the king of England, too, was not easy in time of war, and kindly and pious though Einion was, I would not say he was cast in any heroic mould. When he received his archbishop's letters ordering him to promulgate the excommunication of Llewelyn as a rebel against Edward, he had small choice, short of heroism, but to obey and pronounce, and so he did, and thereafter was so uneasy for his safety, I think needlessly, for the prince gave very little thought to him then, that he fled into England until the peace was made. Afterwards he came back to his see, but we found him more than usually prickly and difficult and doubtless there was some stiffness also on the prince's side, after all that had passed. But I think it was the soreness of his conscience that kept the bishop so long estranged, and made him pick upon every real or imagined slight, or trespass upon the Church's rights, to prop up his self-esteem. Certainly Archbishop Peckham understood the tribulations and abrasions of trying to balance the privileges of prince and primate, and was well qualified to make peace between the two in Wales, and being an ardent, busy person, was pressing his services upon Llewelyn to that end.

'And indeed I should be glad to be friends with my bishop again,' said Llewelyn. 'He was never so thorny until now, and he has been a good friend in the past. Since the archbishop is well-disposed, why should we not make use of his good offices? I'll write and bid him here into Wales. Who knows but he may help us more ways than one!'

'Don't embroil him in law,' said Eleanor. 'Poor John Peckham has had enough of meddling with my cousin's prerogative there.'

The new primate had indeed suffered a sharp lesson at Edward's hands, for he had come into his high post bursting with reforming zeal as a champion of the Church's pure rights and privileges, and felt strongly that the king was all too rapidly consolidating the crown's hold in fields formerly held to belong to the clergy. In particular, with his frenzy for law, he was infringing, or so Peckham felt, the jurisdiction of the clerical courts. The new archbishop set out to issue a stern warning, with a number of sweeping sentences of excommunication against certain kinds of people who seemed to him to be offending not against morality, but against the supreme rights of the Church. As, for instance, all those who procured letters from lay courts to impede trials he held to belong to courts ecclesiastical, or any officer who flouted the writ requiring him to arrest an excommunicated person. The king had a quick eye for such impertinence, and within two weeks the archbishop was summoned to appear before king and council in parliament, and made to withdraw three of these general sentences on sharp legal grounds, a humiliation he was not likely to forget easily.

'Oh, I'll not drag him into my lawsuits,' the prince promised, laughing. 'But he's been taking a friendly interest in Amaury's case, as well he may, being the Holy Father's deputy in England. If we can get him here in person, then we can solicit his help for your brother without fear of being misinterpreted.'

She embraced the idea with delight, for Amaury was the one cloud upon her happiness. 'Yes, oh, yes, for Amaury we can entreat his help without trespassing, he is very much the archbishop's business. If he can win what I've begged for so often without grace,' she said with ardour, 'I won't grudge it to him that I've been so long denied. Even if he could prevail on Edward to allow a visitor, that would be something!'

'That we may ask for at once, and of the king himself,' said Llewelyn. 'At the worst he can but refuse, and if he is surprised into giving his consent, so much the better. And the archbishop we'll reserve until you can work on him yourself, for if he can refuse you, love, then no other need try. When Brother William de Merton goes with my lawyers to attend this Easter parliament, Samson shall go with them and carry my invitation to the archbishop, and ask permission of the king to visit Amaury in Corfe. If the request is made publicly and without warning, it may be harder to refuse it. And if it is refused, then we'll enlist the archbishop's help and try yet again.'

So Eleanor joyfully put together a few books which she thought might be approved without suspicion, and certain personal gifts for her brother, and also a purse of money for his use, for Edward was not celebrated for making generous living allowances to his prisoners, or paying for much in the way of service for them. And I learned many messages from her and from Llewelyn, some concerned with Amaury's own properties and business abroad, more with her affection and anxiety for him, and the efforts she had made and would continue to make on his behalf. And when Master William and his companions set out for London, I rode with them.

Further south than Westminster I had never been but once, and that was with Earl Simon's army in the days of his glory, when he won his battle at Lewes and gathered England into his hands. Now I rode to his youngest son, four years a prisoner for no crime but being a de Montfort, and drawing to himself, as the only man of his house within reach, all the hatred Edward felt for that whole detested race, all the more black and bitter because once he had worshipped the great earl, more truly than ever in his life he had worshipped any other but himself, or ever in his life was to worship any thereafter.

We arrived in Westminster more than a week before parliament was due to meet, and went in a body to an audience of the king, to present our credentials, and there before a large company of his officers and counsellors I made my request on the prince's behalf. It sounded mild and innocent enough, and came unexpectedly, and I had thought that Edward might give his consent as a matter of policy, since there were several of his lords spiritual present, who knew very well that the pope had expressed impatience and displeasure at Amaury's long detention. But Edward was never to be trapped into making a hasty answer that he might soon regret. He sat erect in his great chair, dark-gowned and sombre and huge, and looked at me impassively across the table, his face austere and still his left eyelid markedly drooping over the large brown eye.

'We take due note of the lord prince's petition,' he said in the most

644

deliberate and reasonable of voices, 'but it should not be addressed to us, and we must be held excused if we cannot answer it. The Lord Amaury de Montfort is not in our keeping, but in that of the lord archbishop of Canterbury.'

And that was all! So simple it was to deny without denying. We were dismissed graciously, and he had done us and our lord no wrong. Yet in some degree, I considered when I thought it over in quietness, he had committed himself to a statement, and before witnesses enough, and could not withdraw it. He had not said such a visit could not take place nor that such a request should not have been made, but only that it should not have been made to him, for he was the wrong authority. Well, if I was turned away from one court of appeal, I could spare the time and the effort to seek out another. I went straightway, and made enquiry for Archbishop Peckham, but here I met with another check, for they told me that he was not in London at that time, but on a tour of the middle shires, making his pastoral visitations, and had last written from Trentham, in Staffordshire, a week ago.

I was crossing by the infirmary gardens to the stables, determined not to give up so easily, when I saw among the people emerging from the gateway of the farmery a large, bulky, comfortable figure in a black, clerkly gown, pacing with an easy gait I thought I should know. Indeed, he was sure of me before I could be sure of him, and came up to me bountifully and broadly smiling.

'Well, well! Samson it is! I thought I should know that thrusting walk. What brings you to Westminster again? It's long since we saw you here.'

'The prince's business, as always,' I said, 'and as always, you may be very useful to me in carrying it out.'

'I'll walk with you,' said Cynan, 'wherever you're bound, for it seems you're in more haste than I am.' But he shook his head when he saw I was leading him towards the stables. 'Not leaving us again so soon, and I've but just found you?'

He was not greatly changed in the last few years, except that he had put on yet more flesh, and his forehead had grown taller as his black hair receded. Always he was neat and well-brushed, never a speck of dust on his gown, and his smooth, pale hands ringed and placidly folded, Cynan was accomplished and discreet, and had been many years about the court, but he had never forgotten his Welsh blood. He was comfortable where he was, and little tempted to throw away his comforts, and after his own fashion he had played fair with his English masters and given them zealous service while they played fair with Wales. But where he considered they were breaking faith and dealing unfairly, he had felt himself free to inform the prince accordingly, whether in peace or war. Many times his own head might have paid for its dual loyalties if luck, as well as skill, had not been on his side.

I told him what my business was in Westminster, and how it was thwarted, and what I had learned concerning the movements of the archbishop. At Peckham's name Cynan grinned hugely at some private glee.

'About his pastoral visitations!' he said fatly. 'So he is, the good, stubborn man. And so he did write a letter to the king just eight days ago, and I saw the look on the royal face after he had read it, and kept well out of his way the rest of the day. Those two are like oil and water, my friend! Peckham writes lovely letters – I know more of them than I should, but I'm in the chancellery now, and moderately close to Burnell's confidence, and there's no great love lost there, either. This is the way of it! The king had forbidden Peckham to include in his visitations the royal free chapels, and Peckham is absolute for his right to visit, and doling out excommunications freely if any try to prevent. Except his Grace, of course! This last letter was a fair example of their exchange. Peckham deprecates his own unworthiness, but insists on the church's rights, and *will* visit, with God as his warrant. They've put every obstacle in his way, even armed men, but go he will. In the last line but one he tells his Grace that God will take vengeance for the wrong done against the Church by his Grace's order. In the last, he prays the blessing of God on his Grace and all those who loyally love him.'

'Do you tell me this,' I asked curiously, 'to warn me off from pursuing this obstinate archbishop into the midlands?'

'Far be it from me!' said Cynan devoutly. 'Rather to assure you of an interested listener, and one with a strong motive for sanctioning what you ask. Did not his Grace himself say it rested with Peckham? So be it, and his Grace must stand by his word. At least try it. And, I tell you what, put it into his mind that should there be any question of your integrity, it may be guaranteed by having a trusted chancellery clerk travel with you. I spoil for exercise here, I grow fat. A few days of country air would do me good.'

So he was always, with his smooth, innocent hands turning men the way he would have them go, and usually laughing, though often behind a demure, unlaughing face.

'After Trentham,' he said, considering, 'he was heading for Lichfield and Stafford. Somewhere there you will find him. Go safely! If I cannot be sowing the seed until you return, at least I'll be cultivating the ground.'

And with that he left me, ambling away in his bland, benevolent fashion through the stable-yard and the gardens towards the southern reach of the Long Ditch, and the outflow into the Thames. And I went to claim my horse, rested and fed and ready for the road, and set out northwards for those midland shires where the archbishop doggedly pursued his right even against arms. And I tell you, my regard for him and my hopes of him were rising together.

I made for Stafford, as Cynan had advised, and was much interested along the road, for I had never seen so much of England alone. At Stafford they directed me on to Eccleshall, where the bishop of Lichfield had a castle, and there at last I found Archbishop Peckham in residence, on Palm Sunday. Between the services of the church I asked for an audience, by no means the only one thus asking, and late in the afternoon I was admitted to his presence.

He was sitting in a round-backed chair at a table in a small, dim room, a man barely of the middle height, and round of body, though not fat.

They said he practised great austerity, and recommended it to others, though he did not impose it, and therefore his rotundity must have been by nature, and not at all the fruit of indulgence. I never doubted that if he bore the reputation of abstinence, it was deserved. That man's sins were not of hypocrisy. His face, too, was round and ruddy and candid, shaven very smooth, with an effect of great friendliness and infinite curiosity towards all men, though then he looked tired and vexed and discouraged, as well he might. He measured me, and pondered. His eyes were kindly but harried.

I made my reverence, and first presented him the prince's letter of invitation, telling him how I had enquired for him in London in vain, and therefore made bold to follow him to this place. He thanked me for my errand, and did not then immediately unseal the letter, having other unfinished business, but said that if I would wait he would send for me again in the evening. And at that I begged his indulgence a few minutes longer, and made my prayer for Amaury, telling him as in innocence what the king's answer had been.

'You speak,' he said, 'as one not altogether unmoved by the thought of this prisoner. Perhaps not simply a messenger?'

Feeling myself safest as well as happiest in speaking full truth to this man, I said: 'I have known the prisoner from a boy. I care for him, having so known him, and for the princess, his sister, more, knowing her as a loyal servant may. There is here no design but to comfort all those who grieve apart. Your lordship knows better than I what such severance can mean.'

'I commend your loyalty,' he said. His voice was warm and brisk and very firm, the voice of a kindly, choleric man. 'His Grace did not forbid,' he said thoughtfully.

'No, my lord,' I said. 'He said only that the Lord Amaury is in your charge, not in his, and therefore he could not presume to give or to deny.'

'And you are willing to submit all that you carry to scrutiny by the king's castellan at Corfe?'

'Most willing,' I said. 'And further, my lord, if it be thought wise, I would welcome a witness to the interview, who could report all I may have to say or to hear when I speak with the Lord Amaury. It may be that the chancellery would wish to have such a report, for the sake of us all.'

I saw his eyes gleam at that, and knew that he had taken the point at vantage, for such a presence would not only protect him from possible blame, but involve the chancellor Burnell in the decision, Edward's most trusted officer. According to Cynan, who missed nothing that went on about the court and its offices, the relations between Peckham and Burnell were civil, but watchful and armed, and I think not as a matter of jealousy – for Burnell had been Edward's candidate for the vacant primacy, and warmly urged, and Peckham appointed by the pope in the king's despite – but because those two were of such opposed natures that they could not get on together. Indeed, as it proved later, a great many men, saints among them, found it very hard to live in amity with Peckham, even though the man at his best could get halfway to being a saint himself.

'You deserve,' said the archbishop, 'that your prayer should prosper. You carry no letter of authorisation from your prince?'

I had no such letter of credence, for we had not thought it necessary, but I had my own seal which carried the prince's sanction, and I said that the princess's gifts to her brother were open to inspection if he should require. He said, very kindly, that he himself was perfectly satisfied, but that for the sake of complete openness my suggestion that a clerk should accompany me might be a good one. Then he asked me to wait upon him again in two hours, when he would give me a letter to carry to Corfe, and also whatever was needed in reply to the prince's message. And so I left him.

When he sent for me again it was to present me not one letter but three. He was as instant in appreciation and acknowledgement as he was in complaint and reproof where he thought it due, and it was plain that the prince's invitation, indicating his desire to be reconciled with his bishop, had given the primate pleasure.

'This,' he said, 'I can despatch directly to the lord prince, if you are likely to be absent from him for long. Though I dare say there is no great haste, for the visit cannot take place for a few weeks.'

I said that I would gladly be the bearer, and intended a return to the Welsh court as soon as my errand to Corfe was done.

'Very well,' he said, 'I entrust my answer to you. This second letter you will take to the chancellery on your way through London, and wait to know if the chancellor wishes to send a witness with you, as I have suggested to him. And this third you will deliver to John de Somerset, who keeps Corfe castle for his Grace. I have recommended the bearer to him, and myself given approval to the visit, but he is still the person responsible for the prisoner's safe-keeping, and you will observe any conditions he imposes, and accept his veto should he feel unable to admit you.' But his manner said that, however his recommendation was worded, it would hardly be for the castellan of Corfe to overturn the arrangements Archbishop Peckham had approved. And very devoutly I thanked him, made all my precious missives secure in my saddle-bags, and set off on the long ride south again to Westminster.

I presented my letter at the chancellery as soon as I arrived, and was not surprised at being told to come back next day. No doubt the matter would have to be referred to Burnell himself, but I did not see him on this occasion. He was a busy man at all times, and the preparations for parliament kept him occupied. When I returned to the same small, dark office next day, the official who had my business in hand was writing busily, and gave me but the edge of his attention.

'Ah, yes!' he said. 'You are the envoy who wishes to speak with the Lord Amaury. The chancellor has agreed to the provisions suggested by the archbishop, and you already have his letter to de Somerset.' He rang the handbell he had on his table, and in a few minutes Cynan came in, large and dignified and demure, and stood eyeing me steadily while he waited for his orders, like one measuring a new acquaintance with whom he is to spend a few days of his time. 'Master Cynan will accompany you,' said the officer, returning to his writing. 'I see you understand English well enough, but should you need it, he speaks Welsh. If your errand is honest, he'll be of assistance to you.'

'Unquestionably he will,' said Cynan, as we went together out of the chancellery. 'No need to look over your shoulder on this journey, no one will be following or watching you, that is my business. No need even to guard your tongue. I've had long experience in rendering reports acceptable from very unpromising first drafts.'

I asked how he had contrived the matter as he wanted it, and how, indeed, he came to be advanced so far into Burnell's confidence as to be in a position to know of all that went on.

'Oh, it's policy to select Welshmen for advancement now,' he said, 'wherever it can be done with safety. See how many of us the king is employing about his private business, and into Welsh lands especially. The best of his advisers have told him plainly that it takes a Welshman to rule Welshmen, and if suitable Welshmen run short, a seasoned, hard-headed marcher is to be preferred to some imported baron from Essex or Kent. There's good sense in that, if his Welsh bailiffs were not compelled to enforce English law, and answerable to English masters. Oh, Edward means to hold on to what he has gained, and tie it down by every manner of chain he can devise, but he would like to keep a measure of goodwill where he can.'

I said that from what I could hear he was having very little success, for the Middle Country was seething with complaints against his officers and their arbitrary ways. In choosing his Welshmen he was all too given to preferring renegades to the honest men.

'True,' said Cynan, 'and doubly foolish, for the honest men resent them for turning their coats, and the renegades set out to be doubly zealous, to prove their new loyalty to the king, and make themselves even worse hated. I will say for the chancellor that he knows how to pick his men – and I should know, being one of them. But kings are expected to reward service, and the renegades look to be paid their price. How did I get my way? It was no great trick, I took care to put myself markedly into Burnell's notice yesterday, when you brought the archbishop's letter, and hinted that knowledge of Welsh might be an asset, from every view. I think he would be glad to have de Montfort freed and sent back to Rome, for his part. The young man is a stumbling-block to bishops.'

The next day we rode together from London, with a pale, bright sun rising, and had very pleasant travel on our way south to Guildford and Winchester, and so southward and westward still into the high heath of the Purbeck hills, where in a cleft of the downs Corfe castle rises on its high mound, a very formidable stronghold. We had much to talk about on the way, for he would know how his young nephew Morgan did, who had come to lend one more right arm when we were at war, forsaking his service under the crown, and was now well established in Llewelyn's body-guard. And I was greedy for all he could tell me of those manipulations of law which plagued us, and how far they were honest, if infuriating to us, and how far calculated to serve some darker purpose. Cynan owned he was himself in doubt. Of the king's zeal for codifying and reforming there could be no question, but where a passion for order ended and a lively and unscrupulous self-interest began was a matter hard to determine.

'His father,' said Cynan thoughtfully, 'had a gift for turning everything to his own account in conscious virtue, and convincing himself into the bargain, and there's more of his father in Edward than most men think for. I would not say but his law may prove every bit as pliable as his use of words.' And he stroked his full, smooth chops, and pondered. 'I tell you this,' he said, 'the more it may seem to your prince that his Grace is pushing him to the limit of his endurance, the more stubbornly he should endure. For whether it has yet entered Edward's head to *drive* him to revolt or not, very surely it would occur to him to make the utmost use of the first act of rebellion. I will not say he wants it, seeing he's hard to read, but I will say if it came he would welcome it. It's all he needs by way of excuse and opportunity, to finish what he could but half-do last time.'

I said he need have no fear where Llewelyn was concerned for he was well aware of the danger of allowing himself to be provoked, and was resolved to fight only with the legitimate weapons of law, which were not forbidden to him. This in addition to what bound him more than caution, his seal upon the treaty of Conway.

'I know, I know,' said Cynan, sighing. 'God knows no man has the right to question the prince's patience. But every man has his breaking-point. Bear it in mind, at least. Bear it in mind!'

At Corfe we wound our way up to the castle gatehouse, and I presented my letter for John de Somerset. The castellan kept us waiting some while for his decision, but the archbishop's consent and the chancellor's vicarious presence, to say nothing of Cynan's impressive person in itself, made up his mind for him at last. Once admittance was gained, Cynan improved the occasion and his own image by laying claim to more than the hour's visit at first ordained, and hinting plainly that no other attendance was required, since he alone bore the chancellor's charge to hear what passed and render account of it. So after some delay we were brought into the tower room where Amaury spent his solitary days, and there shut in with him.

A very lofty room it was, far too high for hope of escape, even if ropes would have brought the captive down to better ground than the inmost ward, with many more walls between him and freedom. He was immured here almost within sight of the sea, with the soaring air of the Purbeck hills, open and heather-tinted, and cloud-shadowed, for ever outspread to view from his narrow window, and for ever out of reach. That added a dimension to his grievance, as though hell had been lifted and propped on high above paradise, to refine the torments of the damned with the constant vision of bliss. But for the rest, once the eyes could leave that outer radiance and look round within, he was lodged in decent comfort, and with many refinements, though of little worth to him, no doubt, after four years.

It was a square stone room, not great, but with hangings on the walls and rugs on the floor, and a small brazier burning red in the centre over a great flat stone. There was a round table and two cushioned chairs, and a high-built bed against one wall, and a chest for his linen and gowns, better provision than many had in Edward's hold, but no fair price for the wrong done him. And as soon as he rose from his chair and dropped his quill beside his half-written parchment, turning to face us, I saw that he had not changed at all, nor ceased to keep due account of all his wrongs, and his father's wrongs, and the wrongs of his brothers dead and his one brother living, and the wrongs of his sister, whom he loved, alone of all human creatures, almost as well as he loved Amaury de Montfort.

This youngest son of Earl Simon was not greatly like his brothers, had not their broad, brown nobility, the eyes wide-open and wide-set, the large, candid gaze. The great forehead, that he had, and the mind within was a match for any, but he was made in a leaner, hungrier mould, and darker-coloured, his face gaunt, his eyes deep-set, black and brilliant, quick to anger and to scorn. Unjust confinement had made him burn still blacker and more bitterly, but taught him to contain his rage and wait for the hour when it could be loosed to better effect. He looked at us without welcome, as though we had interrupted him in the composition of important work. Then he knew me, and for an instant bright golden sparks flared in his eyes. I saw him cast one glance at Cynan, and douse the betraying flames. Cynan saw it, too, and smiled.

'They told me,' said Amaury, 'that I had a permitted visit. I appreciate the courtesy to a prisoner, but you must forgive me if I am slow to understand. They told me nothing more.'

'Be easy,' said Cynan comfortably, 'for Samson knows me as well as you know him, and there's no need here for discretion. Keep your voices low, if you will, though I think there's nothing to be feared.' His own voice was soft but serene. He plucked up the stool that stood by the bed, and set it down against the door, and there he took his seat, his ear inclined to the latch. 'What enters my left ear, within here, goes out at my right,' he said, 'but never a word unchecked from my mouth, I promise you. And whatever my right ear picks up from without, you shall hear of.'

'You are Peckham's man?' said Amaury curiously, for he had expected no such usage. 'You are not likely to hear me slander him, he has been kind after his fashion. And I have learned to save my curses, they are wasted in this solitude.'

'Burnell owns my time and labour,' said Cynan, hoisting the collar of his gown against the draught from the door, 'but he has not bought my blood, nor tried to, to do him justice. You may forget I am here, unless some over-zealous warder creeps about the passage outside.' He closed his eyes. 'Use your time,' he said.

So Amaury and I sat down together, he still silent and wary for a while, but coming gradually to life, and finding the tongue that had been stilled for want of company through most of his days and all his nights. 'Samson!' he said, tasting a known name, and drew long breaths. 'This is better than I looked for. Afterwards I shall miss it more. For God's sake, talk to me of my sister. I am starved of news and of voices. You may croak, and you will still be music to me.'

I delivered him the gown and the gifts she had sent him, and the purse, the books being detained for examination before he could be allowed them, and he took and handled all slowly and long, for pleasure that they came from her. 'I have little need of this,' he said fingering the purse, 'for I am not stinted, at least, nor cold, nor threadbare as yet, but I take it gladly for her sake, and will use it when I may. Has my cousin relented towards me so far? It has taken long enough. It must be at her entreaty. I could loathe him less if I could believe he has a real kindness for her.'

I told him we had to thank Archbishop Peckham, though Eleanor had asked and asked times without number, and still continued her entreaties whenever she could get a hearing. And I told him how the archbishop was to visit Wales after the present parliament, and there was hope, at least, of persuading him to use his influence still further, for which reason this visit must pass without arousing the least regret or suspicion in the king's mind.

'Oh, report me tamed, submissive and resigned!' said Amaury, with a short, hard laugh that proved him none of these things, but was nevertheless live laughter, however sour its note. There was colour burning his lean cheekbones, and a spark in his eyes. I doubted I had sounded too hopeful, and led him to a peak from which he must fall with some pain, and yet he was not the man to believe easily in any good fortune, after all this while. 'Say I pray constantly for Edward's Grace – so I do, that he may meet his favourite, Justice, brow to brow, and get his deserts in full. Your witness beholds me, meek as a lamb and obedient to the king's will. It will give him pleasure to believe that even a de Montfort may be chastened.'

There was so much bitterness in him that it filled the veins of his spirit like blood. But at least prison had not dulled his brain, nor rotted his body, nor in any way unfitted him to bear a masterly part among other men, if ever he could get free. His person was princely rather than clerical, and he was but thirty-two years old, with a life before him. Only Edward stood in his way. And what could I promise him, but that Eleanor and the prince would never cease their efforts for him until he was set at liberty?

'That I never doubted,' he said, 'of her at least. She was always loyal, and never could rest while any of her acquaintances were abused or cheated. I doubt if I deserved her fondness, but that I came from the same sire. He had but one daughter after his five sons, but she is his best imprint and his nearest match.'

Whatever else this difficult man failed and fell short in, for his sister he had a deep and constant reverence and affection, and for that alone, even if I had not felt and sometime shared his manifest wrongs, I keep for him a kindness owing nothing to his merit or mine.

So I spoke of her, seeing it was the best gift I could give him, who could not give him any assurance of liberty. I told him how she lived among us prized and worshipped, what delight she took in her new country, and how it fitted with her spirit and welcomed her into its heart, and how his injuries were the only thing that marred her immense happiness. For in Gwynedd nothing fell short of her hopes, but rather exceeded them, and her married joy was excelling.

'She will bear him princes,' said Amaury, and in his tone I read all his thirsty hopes that her sons would take back from Edward all that Edward had taken from their father, all that Edward had taken from their grandfather, who had been Edward's paragon and then Edward's antichrist. I said that was also Llewelyn's hope, for which he would die gladly if he could not achieve it living, and that both Eleanor and Llewelyn waited without impatience upon God's will and God's time to grant them children.

'You comfort me!' said Amaury, and I knew he was foreseeing, whether he fully believed in it or not, rather Edward's loss and chagrin than Llewelyn's triumph. For he had never met this brother on whom so much depended for his fitting vengeance. But Edward he knew, and with all his being hated. 'I would I could have met him face to face, my Welsh kinsman,' he said, and when I would have protested that so he surely would, he met my eyes and laughed and I was mute. 'Oh, no,' said Amaury, 'if ever Edward find it expedient to let me out of his cage, it will be to hurry me overseas, not to turn me loose to roam in Wales. He will never feel safe while there's a male of my race at liberty in his realm.'

It was no more than truth, however hard to believe that a monarch so unshakably fixed on his throne should still fear the very name of de Montfort, fifteen years after the threat of its power had passed from England, and even in the person of a young cleric who had been only a child when the old conflict ended.

'Though I grant him his grudge against Guy,' said Amaury ruefully, and asked after news of his one remaining elder brother, that unfortunate and misguided Guy de Montfort who had murdered the king's cousin, Henry of Almain, at Viterbo, and kindled again a hatred that might have died naturally but for his act. He had paid heavily for a deed done in bitter passion, being shut up in an Italian prison, excommunicate, deprived of all lands and offices and even the common human rights other men enjoyed for many years, notwithstanding there were many influential men about Europe, kinsmen and friends, who felt sympathy for him, and from time to time tried to procure some relief for him. At this time he was already absolved from excommunication, but landless and rightless still, but there were rumours in Paris, so we had heard, that he had escaped from his prison in Lecco and was in hiding somewhere, probably under the unacknowledged protection of his former lord, the king of Sicily, who had every reason to hope that a most able general and governor might some day be reinstated in the Church's grace, and could be used again in office. The French de Montforts, for all their high favour with King Philip and the pope, had pleaded in vain for his restoration.

'Who knows?' said Amaury with a sour smile. 'Guy may be a free man again before I am, and I have slaughtered nobody. Though I will not say I have never thought of it, nor that it might not have been a satisfaction.' And he plied me with many more questions about his family, and charged me with many commissions to Eleanor, who was concerned about his lands and affairs while he was captive, and supplied me with a list of matters on which she wished to know his will. His replies I committed to memory. It seemed that the very act of recalling his lands and offices and asserting his will concerning them was refreshment to him, as exercise is to the body. So in the end we left him cheered and revived when our time ran out.

Cynan signed to us when he heard footsteps in the stone passage, and the heavy jangle of keys at the lock. He rose and put the stool back in its place, and was standing at my elbow when the king's castellan came in to tell us that the visit must end. Before these witnesses Amaury arose with me, darkly composed and again bitterly grave, and took leave of me with his thanks, and his loving greetings to those who had sent me.

The last thing he said to me, as we left him, was: 'Say to my little sister that my prayers and my blessings are always with her. For I do not think I shall see her again in this world.'

And though I knew that he meant only, as he had before said, that Edward would never release him but to hustle him out of Britain, yet the words stayed with me long after the door closed between us, and hung heavy on my heart all the way back to London, as though he had prophesied a death.

CHAPTER III

By the time we came back to Westminster I had somewhat put by the chill of Amaury's farewell, and on the whole was fairly content with my own errand, for the prisoner surely could not be held for ever, when pope after pope had complained of his detention, and many friends whose loyalty Edward could not doubt had advised and urged his release. When we reached London I was anxious, rather, to hear how the delegation to parliament had fared, and made haste, as soon as I had parted from Cynan, who had his own report to render to the chancellor, to hunt out Master William's clerk, Adam, and hear what he had to say.

'Whatever else it may be,' he said, 'it is certainly delay, and no period put to it this time. There was a very full session yesterday, after Brother William de Merton had had several interviews with the king in council, and all the attestations we brought with us had been studied, or at least handled and looked at, for hang me if I know whether any man paid attention to them, or whether the answer we got was already determined on long since. All the written word we have to take back with us is a brief letter to the effect that his Grace has presided in parliament to consider the Welsh articles, that a decision was reached with general agreement, and we are to report it fully to the prince by word of mouth. Not a word more, except, no doubt, a pious ending about his Grace's tireless endeavours to do the prince all possible justice! And the devil of it is, it may still be true! A more earnest and benevolent face you never saw. But his eyelid was more than usually heavy, over the eye he sometimes chooses to blindfold from spying on his own proceedings.'

'But what was it he had to say?' I asked, for Adam was apt to run on when he was aggrieved, and there was enough of the lawyer in him to come to the point only after many circlings. 'What is this decision reached with general agreement?'

'Why, the king began with an avowal that his intent is to observe the treaty in all points – as far as the royal majesty and duty allow. Mark that, it's the text and no mere rider. For he went on to say that not by that nor by any other treaty could he, even if he wished, surrender any prerogative or liberty handed down to him by his forebear kings of England as free custom in time of peace. So his treaty clause becomes: "according to the laws and customs of those parts in which the disputed lands lie, *and according to the manner of procedure observed by his forebear kings in similar case*". It says but the half of that, but according to the king it means the whole. Oh, he quite accepts, he says, that the Welsh should have their own laws – such as are just and reasonable and don't infringe the rights of the crown. Such he'll keep faithfully. But he has no right and no power to do anything that derogates the rights of the crown or the kingdom of England, for these belong not merely to him, but to the kings who'll come after him. A sacred trust! So if any Welsh laws and customs seem to him unjust or bad or senseless, then his regal dignity will not allow him to countenance them, for he took a solemn coronation oath to root out all such from his kingdom, and no later oath or agreement can possibly relieve him of that sacred vow. But all our Welsh ways that don't offend, those he'll keep faithfully – so far as they're in harmony with justice. Make what you can of so many words, what I make of them is that he alone is to be the judge of what is good and what is bad, and can bless or discard Welsh law exactly as it suits him, without appeal. And holding up his coronation vow as a shield! The words of the treaty are all subject to an unwritten saving clause – "saving always my royal interests".'

It might have been David speaking, but that David would have been in a piercing, princely rage, and Adam worded with the sour humour lawyers acquire from long experience of justice and injustice dressed alike and indistinguishable.

'At the end of it all,' I said, 'he must have declared *some* intent. What follows now?'

'Why, he intends to send a commission into the Welsh lands and the marches, to enquire into exactly what are the laws and customs of those regions, by taking evidence on the spot. And also to cause the rolls of his own reign and the reigns of his predecessors to be searched for precedents that may be applied to this case. Though God knows they'll find none, for there are none. And when he has all the evidence from both enquiries before him, then he'll accept their findings and do justice!'

'And when,' I said, 'is this commission to begin its work?' Though I knew already that this detail had been omitted. For I was becoming by degrees as black a cynic as Adam or David.

'Ah, that is not yet stated! From parliament to parliament can be half a year. From the announcement of intent to the sittings of this enquiry can be stretched as far as Edward pleases!' said Adam. 'And that is all we have to take back with us to the prince. But I tell you this,' said Adam, suddenly both graver and brighter than throughout this exposition, 'if he has not yet found a legal way of flatly refusing us Welsh law, but only delaying it, in my eyes that's a sign that in the end he has no way out but delay, for he knows he cannot, without showing as rogue and contemptible, declare Arwystli to be English or march land. If he could find against us he would have done it long ago. All he can do, with any appearance of decency, is fend us off with pious pretexts. And all we have to do, to win in the end or force his hand to plain roguery, is outlast him in patience.'

It was a good, sound legal thought, and went with me gratefully all that day. But also it put it into my mind that there had already been one such enquiry, taken in the year of Llewelyn's marriage, that inquisition of which David had spoken, held by Reginald de Grey and the king's clerk, William Hamilton. Its findings had never been made public. Because, said David, they must have proved simply that to Welsh lands Welsh law applied, and no other did or ever had.

So I sought out Cynan again before we rode, the next morning, and asked him, if he might without risk to himself, to probe into the treasury records and discover what Grey's commission had reported, and send me word in simple code whether the verdict they gave was white, that being Welsh, or black, or some shade of grey between. It could neither hasten nor influence this new inquisition, but it could provide us with good armaments, if David's suspicion proved true, against any slanted verdict Edward might produce from his latest device.

'Grey is a solid English baron, and true to Edward as any man in England,' said Cynan, 'but an honest man for all that, no liar. Hamilton – well, he's a crown clerk, a king's man. But if this enquiry was taken when you say, then he had no cause to believe his brief was other than it seemed. The treaty was new, the sides had not hardened, the arguments were legal, not partisan. None of the manipulators had yet got his bearings. I suspect people told truth, and truth was written down. Yes, I will get you these findings, these crossbow quarrels, if I can. But be careful,' said Cynan, 'how you shoot them! There may be fat, comfortable, cowardly men like me between you and your target!'

I had hoped that we might return to Wales by way of Denbigh, but it did not happen so, for Llewelyn had sent word that we should join him in Carnarvon, and thither we rode by the nearest and most convenient way, and for that while I had neither sight of Cristin nor speech with David, to tell him what I had asked of Cynan.

Brother William de Merton reported to the prince all that had been said and done in Westminster, and more sourly, what had been said over and over while nothing was done. And I, more happily, gave him the archbishop's letter, heartily accepting his invitation and promising to come to Wales in June, and went on to render a full account of the conditions under which Amaury was held at Corfe, and all the messages he had sent by me, and the wishes he had expressed with regard to his lands and benefices, and his cousins in France.

Eleanor took great comfort from all I had to tell, and found pleasure in writing his greetings and his commissions to John de Montfort in Montfort l'Amaury, happy to have something positive to do for her brother, and encouraged to believe that with Archbishop Peckham's help more might yet be achieved.

I told them, also, of the undertaking Cynan had given me, to try to discover what report had been lodged and carefully forgotten in the treasury, after Grey's commission of two years earlier.

'That was well thought of,' said Llewelyn. 'Provided he does not expose himself to suspicion with his probing! Even to have those parchments in my hands, I would not put Cynan's life in danger.'

He had swallowed Brother William's faithful recital of Edward's declaration in parliament with a wry face and a burst of exasperated anger, but certainly without much surprise.

'He'll run out of the means of delay in the end,' he said, grimly recovering himself, 'and however he may wish to keep me penned into my present bounds, and have Arwystli held by a time-server deep in his debt, I fail to see how he can possibly deny me Welsh law in the end. He winds about the clear words of the treaty with so many more, and so obscure and devious, as to hide their meaning utterly, but he cannot change what he agreed, and I still do not believe he is prepared to go so far as to break his oath and dishonour his seal, when all his subterfuges are exhausted. I have only to counter every move he tries, and wait out every delay. I am skilled at waiting. I have studied the art for years.'

Sometimes the princess came to my little copying-room to try over music with me, for that was one of the ways she had of making unexpected gifts to Llewelyn, all the more if he was weary, or vexed. And then she would talk freely, as once when I was in her captive household at Windsor, and the only servant she had there who knew the land to which her heart inclined, and the lord she longed to reach. So I had entered once and for all into her confidence, and that lady was gifted for friendship as she was for love.

Thus she came to me on a June night, shortly before Archbishop Peckham was expected among us, and after we had tried over the song she was perfecting, she with voice and lute, I with the crwth, she sat considering our performance and nursing her instrument like a loved child, and then she smiled, and said: 'I have become a maker of love-songs. That is his doing.' A moment she was silent, then she said: 'Samson, if my cousin held an enquiry only two years ago into the manner of pleading for barons of Wales in Welsh and marcher-land cases, why does he need to set up another one now?'

I said honestly: 'Not for anything it can uncover, only for the time it will take enquiring.'

'So I thought you would say,' said Eleanor, and smiled. 'And so says Llewelyn, and can even laugh, and own that sometimes he has not been above prevarication himself, when an immediate reply was inconvenient. But whether it is that I have an uncommonly black view of humankind, or whether I know my cousin too well for comfort, I see more in this new move than a simple means to delay. I think he needs a new commission because the first one did not provide him the answers he wanted, and this time he must and will take all the necessary steps to ensure that this one shall. There'll be a carefully selected bench, well-chosen witnesses, sessions will be held in the places most likely to be favourable to the king's wants, and the questions asked will be drafted to draw the right responses. I think, Samson, we should be well advised to be thinking out, and drawing up, a schedule of questions of our own, to supplement Edward's. Will his judges, for instance, ask whether there are in Arwystli duly appointed Welsh judges, properly authorised to administer Welsh law there, and exercising those duties regularly? I doubt it! But there are, and if Welsh law did not apply there, those judges would never have been placed in office, they would not be needed, and they would have no authority. I think,' she said, stroking the strings of her lute with a small, wry smile, 'we could be of the greatest assistance to his Grace in the matter of drafting apt and useful interrogatories. We might put them in as a petition from the prince, out of pure goodwill to be helpful.'

Enlightened and astonished, I said that she was like to prove the best lawyer we had among us, and that it should be done – out of pure goodwill!

'In the meantime,' she said ruefully, 'we have not even a date for the commencement, and be sure he will give his men as long as possible before they must report their findings. Let's use the time to enlist Archbishop Peckham's good offices. We'll both urge his help for Amaury, and if Llewelyn is too proud to plead his own cause, well I am too proud not to.'

So quietly we made ready those pertinent matters that could with best effect be forced upon the commission's notice, and waited for the archbishop to come. It was the second week in June when he rode into Carnarvon, sparsely attended, and for such a prelate with very moderate ceremony, so that at first we thought him personally modest and austere, while in fact he was neither, except in his appetites. Pride he had, and proper respect he would exact to the last grain, but it was not expressed in haughtiness on his part, or demanded as servility from others.

Friendly and inquisitive I had thought him, and so he was, and well-intentioned towards everyone, but for all that his kindly, sharp eyes could be steely and censorious if any resisted or differed from him, and his smiling, benevolent mouth was tight and obstinate in repose. The most diverse opinions were held of him. Some said he was a true saint, doing his best to follow his Saviour's commandments and tireless in his efforts for those who appealed to him in distress. Others that he would give and serve lavishly such as flattered and grovelled to him, and as readily out with bell, book and candle against all who dared to contradict him. Some revered him as a strong and able administrator and defender of clerical rights, others called him a meddlesome busybody who could not keep his fingers out of anybody's business. Some averred his compassion and sympathy were wide enough to encompass all who came, others said he was prone to favourites, and so narrow that his maledictions were more frequent than his blessings. Some thought he had a gift of delicate understanding which the ungodly could not appreciate, others said wrathfully that the man trampled in heavy-footed where angels themselves would have walked softly. And it can be said of Archbishop Peckham that almost everything ever said of him was true.

He was of limitless energy, quick and agile in movement, and blew through the corridors of Carnarvon like a brisk wind. In the saddle he looked like a sack of Aberconway wool, but he rode fast and daringly for all that, enjoyed hunting, when he had leisure for it, and here he was removed from his pastoral cares for a while, and Llewelyn saw to it that he had good sport. At the high table in hall he was inclined to turn the talk into one long, benevolent homily, but benevolent it was, and we took it as it was meant. Indeed he made a very good impression, and if his well-meant interference in all manner of things not directly his province was sometimes maladroit, yet everyone accepted it with good humour for its evident kindliness. I have heard that others found him harder to bear, and he was always shocked and hurt at the resentment he could arouse at his worst, hurt as children are hurt when they have made an innocent advance and been rebuffed. We took care not to ruffle him, and not all because we had hopes of his aid. Both prince and princess liked him well.

In his handling of Bishop Einion he must have been more adroit than usual, and doubtless it was flattering to have the archbishop of Canterbury busily trotting back and forth with soothing words. Also I think Einion in his heart wanted to be reconciled, and was glad to have the excuse of his clear pastoral duty to heed his primate's counsel. For though it took several visits to bring him to terms, he did gradually yield to persuasion, and agreed to compromise on some of the thorny issues that most vexed him, where the rights of church and crown clashed. Llewelyn in turn took conciliatory steps to meet him, and the archbishop, delighted with his success, brought them to sit down together in peace before he left us, and gave his blessing to the accommodation he had helped them to reach.

He was much interested, while he stayed with us, in Llewelyn's hounds, a strain which the prince himself bred and trained, and as Llewelyn then had a litter of three couple almost ready for the chase, he promised to send them as a gift to the archbishop as soon as their training should be complete. And in the most friendly fashion the primate parted from us, and was escorted by most of the court for the first few miles of his journey home.

'He has promised to continue his efforts for Amaury,' said Eleanor, after he was gone, 'and I am sure he will not fail of his promise, for he says the case is to come up in the October parliament. I shall write to Edward and add my own plea. And he seems truly to have some feeling for Llewelyn's cause, and some understanding of his complaints. *My* complaints,' she said, and smiled, 'for the prince made none to his guest, but I was not so delicate. The archbishop says he will speak up for us with Edward, and I believe him.'

So, too, did I believe him. For with all the things that were said and were all of them true concerning Archbishop Peckham, one thing I never heard any man say of him. Obstinate, bigoted, crass, often misguided he might be, but he did not lie, and he was never false.

Llewelyn had not, until then, made any reply to Edward's declaration in parliament. Now he did so, with biting gentleness setting down his pleasure that king and council in assembly had emphasised their wish to keep the treaty of Aberconway in every particular, and to do him right. Then drily he had me list all the particulars in which they did him wrong.

'Surely three years,' he wrote, 'should be long enough to settle one simple article, which the very wording of the treaty shows can and should be settled without delay or difficulty, given the will. Unless, by any chance, I have enemies whose interest and design it is to prevent such a consummation?'

The affair of Robert of Leicester he also appended, for though the king had assured Brother William de Merton that he would order the justiciar of Chester to cease all distraints on Robert's behalf against the prince's goods, nevertheless a further seizure had been made. At which the prince professed a surprise he hardly felt, though he avowed his inability to believe that the current distraint was made with the king's knowledge, and prayed him to reinforce his order to let be.

'I grow as fluent a liar as Edward,' he said, grimacing at the end of this letter. 'We are so far apart,' he said, suddenly grieving, 'and I have a principality to guard and cherish as well as he, and how can I go hunting after him where he goes, to pluck him by the arm and make him face me man to man? When I was in his company, for all his hardness I understood him, and for all his might, I was his peer and we spoke as peers. Now at this distance I have lost him, and I feel that loss.'

The letters flew back and forth that summer, for Llewelyn had many things to complain of, and Edward seemed to feel some guilty need to justify himself. But the first letter that came, soon after the foregoing was despatched to London, was from Archbishop Peckham, sending hearty thanks for his hounds, and for his entertainment in Wales, and that was cheering and helped to balance Edward's long and verbose epistle from Langley, which arrived a week later, again earnestly avowing his good intent to keep the terms of the treaty, but insisting that those terms were not completely clear, and that he must preserve his royal prerogative and do, in this matter, whatever had been customary in similar case in the days of his predecessors. Together with much piety concerning his duty to consult the prelates and magnates of his realm, a course to which Llewelyn should not take exception, since no one could suppose such grave and wise men would give their lord bad advice.

'Since he will have given them the advice first,' said Llewelyn, between amusement and despair, 'from his point of view that may very well be true.'

In other matters the king was more accommodating, and said that he had ordered the justiciar of Chester to restore the goods recently seized, and to instruct Robert of Leicester to take his case, if he wished to pursue it, to the prince's court, where it belonged, and not to trouble the royal courts again unless he alleged he was denied justice at the prince's.

'I am heartily tired of law,' said Llewelyn in a great sigh. 'I was not cut out for a litigant.'

And still the king had not so much as appointed the members of his commission. Llewelyn could not even hasten to discharge the labours that disgusted him, and be rid of them. Still he must wait, and even the stoutest heart can be eaten hollow by too much waiting.

In middle August came another letter from the archbishop, long and circumstantial. The prince opened it with curiosity, for he had expected none just then, but read it with disbelief and consternation. Then he called in Master William to view its terms with him, for every sentence rang like an echo of Edward's utterance in parliament. But here that pious apologia was underlined and reinforced by even stronger reservations. In one respect only it showed finer than its example, it spoke in far plainer terms.

Almost word for word the archbishop repeated that the phrase in the treaty to which we attached so much importance, 'according to the laws and customs of those parts where the lands lie', could not be understood otherwise than as meaning the laws and customs by which kings of England had been used to rule those parts in the past, and determine causes arising there. Its sanction could apply only to such laws and customs as were just and reasonable, since the king by his coronation oath was bound to banish from his realm all that were unjust and unreasonable. And here the archbishop went even further than Edward had gone, for he launched out into a long denunciation of certain of our Welsh laws as being against right and against religion. Cases of homicide, which we distinguished from murder, were dealt with in Wales by enforced arbitration to bring the parties to peace, and make reparation for the wrong done, instead of proceeding to summary judgment. God knows we thought this better and more Christian than ploughing ahead to still more killing, but plainly Peckham felt otherwise. However, his main theme was that the king's coronation oath was inviolable, and no subsequent oath such as the sealing of a treaty could make it void. And he made a great virtue of having interceded for us as he had promised, and procured for him the concession – compromise, I believe, was the word used – that such Welsh laws as were just and reasonable should be maintained, to which plea the king had graciously assented. Thus the archbishop laboured to obtain justice for us!

'This,' said Llewelyn, stunned, 'this we must look upon as a concession? Do words no longer mean anything but what Edward decrees they shall mean? And am I to believe that this man shut his eyes and ears while he was here with us, and understood nothing? Or has Edward so worked on him since, that he is no more than an echo of his master? No, for he goes beyond Edward! He is prompting Edward to tighten the noose! If it rests with him the laws of Howel the Good will be wiped out wherever the royal writ runs. Thank God it does not yet run in Gwynedd!'

Both Master William and Tudor spoke out in even stronger terms about this juggling with words, which was as little convincing when it came from Peckham by letter as when Edward pronounced it solemnly in parliament. Either the words 'according to the laws and customs of those parts where the lands lie' meant what they said, or no words could be held, with any certainty, to mean anything at all, for all were subject to manipulation at the king's will. Nor did the portion of law to which they applied come within any possible body of jurisprudence offensive to even the most censorious mind. Peckham might object to certain points in our criminal procedure as much as he would, but this was a straightforward matter of rival claims to land, and of the formula by which those claims should be judged. At best the archbishop's partisan declaration was irrelevant. At worst it must be dishonest.

'No!' said Eleanor. 'I cannot think he ever set out to deceive. Even if he did not truly abhor falsity, as I believe he does, he is too sure of his own rightness, too confident all men must agree with him, to be able to dissemble. Too vain, if you will! No, he meant what he said here among us, he has tried to speak up for our case, and believes he has done us service. And he means what he has written now. He has gone back full of zeal to study this law of Wales, and found too many points where it offends his religious rigour.'

'Helped, no doubt, by Edward and all his men of law,' said Llewelyn grimly. 'I remember very well the terms in which the king spoke at his Easter parliament, as Brother William reported them. You hear the echoes here! Word for word the same, until he goes beyond even Edward.'

'Yes,' she said, 'I don't deny it. But nowhere has he said that the Welsh way offends where land is disputed. No, truly I believe this is an honest man. He may set his face against Welsh law on certain points, but he will not stand by and see you wronged and deprived where he finds no fault with Welsh law. Even if we must feel that we have an enemy in him, I believe it will be an honourable enemy.'

'I should find it easier to think so,' said the prince, 'if he had not taken up so wholeheartedly the most specious plea of all – that these few words to which Edward voluntarily set his seal may not mean what they plainly say, because Edward's coronation oath *may* not be compatible with them. Had he quite forgotten the words of his coronation oath when he set his seal to the treaty? Should it not have been clear to him then whether there might ever be conflict? Whether he ought not to put in some saving clause to cover his duty to his realm? Can you believe that Edward ever worded anything without weighing every letter before he passed and sealed it?'

'I did not say,' she said ruefully, 'that Edward need always be an honourable enemy. I spoke only of the archbishop.'

'I am not sure, love,' said Llewelyn, reluctantly laughing, 'that you are paying Archbishop Peckham much of a compliment. If he is no rogue, then he has swallowed the king's twisted arguments whole, and taken them for honest, and I doubt that makes him a fool. I am not sure which I would rather deal with. Certainly if this is an earnest of his friendship, as he preens himself, it might be better to have him for an enemy.'

'All we can do,' she said stoutly, 'is to go on putting him to the test. Judge him by his fruits!'

'So we will,' said Llewelyn, and smiled at her. 'So we must.'

And at that it stayed, though even she was more saddened than ever she owned. But she would not either lose faith and let hope go by default, nor condemn a man before his deceit was proved beyond doubt.

It was not until the fourth day of December of that year, when we were once again preparing for the Christmas feast, that Edward at last appointed his three commissioners, the bishop of St David's, who was keeper of the king's wardrobe, Reginald de Grey, and Walter de Hopton, safe king's men every one, though that was not to say they might not also be just men, however little likely to command much trust within Wales. Their business was to enquire and report, so said the commission itself, by what laws and customs the king's forebears had been wont to rule and judge a prince of Wales or a Welsh baron of Wales in any disputes arising. For this task they were allowed half a year, for their report was not required to be delivered until the fourth day of May of the year following. The places where they were to enquire were appointed in advance, and by whom but Edward? And even had their

663

fourteen questions been drawn up by an unbiased arbitrator – which I doubt – the juries before which they would be used, the witnesses to be called, depended absolutely on the will of the commissioners.

David did not bring his household to spend Christmas with us that year, for once again Elizabeth was within a month of her time. He came instead for a brief visit in the new year, alone and in no festive mood, for his own affairs proceeded no more favourably than his brother's. He came to me in my copying-room, the evening before he left again for home, and leaned at my shoulder over the parchment I was working on, as many years ago he had leaned, with his blue-black head against my cheek.

'We all of us posture and dance to Edward's tune like slaves,' he said morosely. 'Wales is become a prison, where lords and commons alike struggle to maintain their rights against a load of chains. Venables still pursues his case against me for Hope, and in spite of all Edward's pieties, in spite of all the declarations that Hope is Welsh, he's still allowed to pursue it in the Chester shire-court. Llewelyn is still denied Welsh justice over Arwystli, on one pretext after another. In the west de Knoville refuses to meet on the border for mutual reparations, as was always done, but summons Llewelyn's bailiffs to him wherever he chooses, out of their own land.'

'Howbeit,' I said, 'they do not go!'

'Not yet, but how long before Edward's nagging wears my brother down? He cannot bear this constant haggling and meanness, it is not in his nature. Either he will break, and give in, send his men like servants wherever the king's seneschal calls them – oh, not out of fear or weakness, unless disgust is weakness! –or else he must burst out in revolt, and drive the royal bailiffs out of Wales.'

'He will do neither the one nor the other,' I said. 'He has only one course open to him, and that is to outlast the king at every turn, in patience, in stubbornness, to hold fast what he has, and go on contending to his life's end for what more he ought to have, and for every point of his right and prerogative. But not in arms.'

'You think not?' said David, and eyed me consideringly along his shoulder. 'Not if all the chiefs of Wales outside his own principality, all those who suffer now worse than he does, our nephews in the south, the princes of Maelor and Cardigan – not if all these banded together to complain to him of their wrongs, and begged him to deliver them again, as he did once before? Would he not move even then?'

'He would not,' I said, 'even if he were free to do it. He would not, because it would be playing into Edward's hands. But it does not arise. He is not free. He set his seal to a treaty, he swore fealty to the king, saving his sovereign right in his own land. Whether Edward has broken treaty by his curious games with words, is for Edward's conscience to answer. But nothing that has happened yet serves to set Llewelyn free from his oath and the sanctity of his seal. Why ask me foolish questions? You know him as well as I do.'

'Yes,' he owned with a sigh, 'I know him.' And he was silent for a long time, darkly regarding his own linked hands. Then he said softly and mildly: 'Yet time may force his hand. What we do cannot always depend only on our own will. We find ourselves doing things we never meant to do, in spite of all our struggles, in spite of our own natures. I never thought I should return to my brother's grace, even if he opened his arms to me a third time, but when the hour came he called me, and I had no choice. No choice at all! And you – do you remember once, Samson, how I raged at you for bringing Cristin's husband back to her, when she could as well have gone on believing him dead, and been happy with you? Could you not, I said, have slipped your dagger into his ribs then, when you alone knew he lived, and left him unmourned in the south? And if you were too nice to do your own rough work, I said, there were those could do it for you. But you would neither go that way yourself nor let me. How long ago can it be? Dear God, it must be more than twenty years! Have you forgotten?'

I had not forgotten then, I have not forgotten now. I said: 'Cristin has been your friend as well as mine, you know her as I know her. Do you think I could ever have approached her over her husband's body?'

He lifted his head and looked at me steadily, with his eyes the soft blue of summer distances, Snowdon's colour in clear, settled weather. 'No,' he said, 'on the face of it, impossible. Impossible, since she is the woman she is, and you the man you are. No, I saw you would not thank me for it if I set you free, much less put your hand to the work yourself. Not for your life! And poor wretch, is it Godred's fault he stands in the way? He's been no bad servant to me. And yet,' he said, 'I foresee even your hand may be forced, some day. In the end you may have to kill him. And when you come red-handed from the deed, I think she may very well be waiting for you, and not turn away.'

But I would not answer him a word, for that way I refused to look, and in this mood I found in him nothing but dismay. And after a while he went away to drink himself below the level of remembrance, and I was left to my disordered thoughts.

So passed that Christmas.

The king's commission began their sessions at Chester early in the new year, and then their procedures became plain to see, and though we let them alone there, where they could manage things much as they liked, we had our own questions ready to present as a petition at their next sitting, which was at Rhuddlan. I think Master William's appearance there, as soon as the bench sat, came as a shock to the commissioners, but before a full hall and assembled witnesses they could not decline to receive the prince's petition and enroll its contents before any evidence was taken, and so they did. Master William took care to pronounce in court what was there set down: that the prince requested that his own interrogatories should be added to those drawn up by the royal officials, since the purpose of the enquiry was to determine the truth. In particular he asked the commission to enquire of witnesses whether in those disputed lands there were duly accredited Welsh judges, whose duty it was to administer Welsh law there, for clearly if Welsh law did not apply there would be no need for such judges to be appointed and sworn to serve. And in case any difficulty was experienced in getting answers to this question from other witnesses, the prince here provided the information himself. The sons of Kenyr ap Cadogan were duly appointed judges of Welsh law in Arwystli, and Iorwerth Fychan held the same office in the lands between Dovey and Dulas.

Having ensured that this testimony was enrolled, the old man withdrew and left them to hear their witnesses, and then we had certainty that, whatever happened, the existence and the names of those judges could not be omitted from the rolls.

It was not long after this small victory for Eleanor's scepticism was recorded, that her determined faith also had its reward. For though parliament's discussion of Amaury's case had concluded without any apparent change or decision, nonetheless the princess's appeal and the archbishop's intercessions must have had their effect, for early in that year twelve hundred and eighty-one the king suddenly released Amaury, not from all restrictions upon his liberty, but from close confinement, and removed him from his tower in Corfe castle to the safe-keeping of Archbishop Peckham, who lodged him comfortably at Sherbourne and greatly eased his conditions. That was blessing and relief enough, more than he had yet expected, and greatly enhanced by Peckham's personal kindness to him, in which we found it easy to believe. For nothing would so dispose that good prelate to further benevolence, as the sense of benefits already conferred, and the conscious glow of good deeds done.

We began to credit that a better understanding all round was not an impossibility. To believe in it was to labour for it, and to look for every happening or utterance that could be regarded as evidence for its approach.

In the January of this year Griffith ap Gwenwynwyn took up again that case of the thirteen vils in Cydewain which he had formerly claimed against the king, but this time he took out his writ for them against Roger Mortimer, to whom the king had granted that cantref, and therefore the disputed vils among the rest.

'Roger claimed Welsh law last time, when he appeared on Edward's behalf,' said Llewelyn, interested. 'Now let's see how he will proceed on his own. We have need of good precedents.' And he sent a clerk to observe how the pleading went at Montgomery when the case came up. Griffith pleaded that Mortimer had formerly defaulted of putting in an appearance and claimed judgment against him, but Roger by his attorneys at once replied that by his attendance he had now amended any default, for by Welsh law, which applied to the disputed land, a defendant could make up to three defaults, but could not therefore have judgment pronounced against him and lose his seisin of the land unless he defaulted a fourth time. Naturally Griffith hotly contested Mortimer's right to demand Welsh law, upon the old plea that both were barons of the king and ought to plead by common law, while Mortimer stood firm on the fact that Cydewain was Welsh, and only Welsh law could apply to it.

It was so like his own first encounter with Griffith that Llewelyn could not but hang eagerly on the outcome, for the sake of the unsettled fate of Arwystli. The justices, as before, considered the two pleas so strong and so contradictory that they needed further guidance to decide between them, and postponed the case until April, and then once more into June. This brought us to the time when Edward's inquisition must already have made its report, due in May, and we were all waiting in anxious expectation for the king to make public what it had to say.

Llewelyn was then in frequent correspondence with his cousin Mortimer, chiefly by reason of their shared resentment against Griffith, for Mortimer was as enraged by the legal war waged against him as was the prince, and bore it with much less patience, being a hot-blooded and forthright man. He had strong feelings about the folly of forcing English law upon Welshmen, and was uneasy about what he could not but hold to be infringements of the treaty. His loyalty to the king was far past question, but he was wise in the special marcher wisdom, and knew how to deal sensibly with Welsh tenants no less than with English, and certainly was not without sympathy for them. He, too, had been forced to gouge out new roads through his forests, which displeased him as if he had been wholly Welsh himself, instead of but the half. Those two cousins, though they had often fought on opposing sides, and even in peace had contended many a time over other issues, never in life bore any malice or dislike each to the other, but always a hearty respect, and a degree of wary affection, and now, stung over and over by the same gadfly, they exchanged rueful and angry sympathy, and ended closer than for many years.

It so happened that at the end of May one of the brothers of Llanfaes, who had been to London on Brother William de Merton's business to the Franciscans there, came back bearing a message which he said was for me. In his dealings with a small matter involving the chancellery he had encountered Robert Burnell's clerk, Cynan, and had been charged to give me word, he said, of the colour of a certain healing herb, shy of growth and hard to find out, of which that same Cynan had spoken with me when last I was in Westminster. I knew then what this embassage meant, and my heart leaped, and I waited for Cynan's verdict with held breath.

'He bade me tell you,' said the friar, 'that this rare herb bears a flower as white as snow.' And he folded his hands and smiled, incurious about what this mystery could mean, but aware that it filled me with joy, and therefore himself pleased.

I took the word to Llewelyn at once, and he seized on it as gladly as I. 'Well, now we know, and the knowing is all. Grey and Hamilton got true answers, and reported that Welsh land is, always has been, and always ought to be, subject only to Welsh law. We can never say that we already know what they found, for Cynan's sake. But if it come to the worst we can recall that this inquisition was held, and ask to know its findings. Now let's wait for what Grey and his fellows will answer this time. Edward must declare himself soon.'

And some days into the month of June, so he did, if what he wrote to the prince could be called a declaration, for it was as mysterious as Cynan's white-blossomed herb, and even harder to interpret. The tone of his letter was serene, friendly and gracious, all encouragement, but its meaning was as cloudy as the summit of Snowdon in rainy weather. Somewhat thus it went:

The king desired to inform the prince of Wales that he now had before him the findings of the inquisition on the laws and customs which had been followed in Wales and the marches of Wales in the time of the king's father and his predecessors, and also the result of the search into the official rolls, and that the findings in both cases agreed. The king had therefore caused it to be proclaimed that those same approved laws and customs should be observed now as before, and by this letter he signified to the prince that he might proceed with his cause, for the king had instructed his justices of the courts concerned to respect and observe the findings of inquisition and inspection, and to show Llewelyn speedy justice in accordance with them.

'So much talk of findings,' said Llewelyn in blazing exasperation, 'and not a word of what those findings are! All I am told is that I may proceed, and I shall have justice – speedy! he dare use the word, after four years – in accordance with what he has discovered. But what that is, I am not to know. Only one thing is made *almost* clear, that if I pursue my claim it must be before the king's justices, in the place they choose. Well, I conceded so much before, I may do so again. It is the only thing I will concede.' And he delivered me the parchment, and asked me: 'What do you make of it? See if you can read between the lines better than I. Need he be so guarded if he had found, or brought, or made evidence for denying me Welsh law?'

I read it over, recalling how absolute had been the result of the first such enquiry, and it did seem to me that the king was taking care to sound reasonable and conciliatory, as though making ready to yield a step or two with the appearance of grace. Just so he would certainly have written if, in spite of all his precautions, the evidence ran all against him, too clearly for him to manipulate it further, and he found himself faced with the necessity for allowing the case to proceed by Welsh law, and still keeping his own countenance. His way, when he could no longer resist an event, was to take it over and direct it, as though it had been his own conception from the beginning. Not that I did not realise that he might have many other delays to deploy, but it did seem to me that he was on the point of surrendering this one.

So I said, and Llewelyn considered it with me, and felt as I did. However cautiously, we should accept this proffer, and bring the claim for Arwystli once again before the Hopton bench.

'And now I remember,' he said, burning up eagerly, 'that Roger has the fifteenth of this month appointed him to answer Griffith ap Gwenwynwyn over the vils in Cydewain. We shall see what comes of that. Arwystli is as Welsh as Cydewain, the situation is exactly the same. If Roger wins his plea for Welsh law, the message becomes clear.'

He therefore sent me to Montgomery to watch the process of his cousin's case, a pleasant enough jaunt in the June weather, with long days and fair skies, and a kind of hope in our hearts that all might yet be well, that Edward, when his stratagems were done, would not thwart justice to the end, that misunderstandings could be eased away from between two princes who still had, in spite of all, a high respect and regard for each other.

I sat well back in the court at Montgomery, and watched Griffith, fierce and gaudy and loud as a turkey-cock among his rookery of black-gowned lawyers, come sweeping into the room armed for battle, and take his place centrally behind his spokesmen, ready to prod and prompt as always. The court was full, but Mortimer himself did not attend, being by no means so in love with litigation as his opponent.

It was not a long hearing, since the bench sat mainly to deliver judgment held over from two previous sessions. But Griffith's lawyers stated in formal terms his claim to the lands, and to have them by common law, both parties being the king's barons. Roger's attorneys replied with his claim that the lands were undeniably Welsh, and entitled him to Welsh law, and by Welsh law he was not in default, as Griffith had previously claimed. Then it was for the bench to give judgment.

There was no reluctance in the presiding judge this time to weigh claims equably and deliver a verdict he had withheld from Llewelyn. His face was placid and assured as he spoke out the considered view of his bench, undoubtedly approved in advance in higher quarters, or why those two adjournments? He found that the land claimed was Welsh, and should be impleaded by Welsh law, by which three defaults could be made without loss of seisin, therefore Mortimer was not in default, and Griffith's writ by common law brought him nothing. Mortimer was left without day, in possession of his lands, and Griffith was subjected to a fine and lost his claim.

And this despite the undoubted fact that here was a plea between two parties both marcher barons of the crown. Welsh law was upheld, and judgment given by it. And past question, if Cydewain was Welsh, so was Arwystli, and so must be impleaded and judged. It was in all points the complete justification of the stand Llewelyn had taken from the beginning, and I was so elated, I hardly had time to enjoy the spectacle of Griffith ap Gwenwynwyn glooming and storming out of court with lowered head and baleful brow, like an angry bull, all his train of lawyers scurrying after him with gowns flying, a thunder-cloud about a lightning-flash. Once, at least, that master-litigant met his match, though he did not therefore give up all hope, but clung by the edges of his claim, hungrily and vengefully, waiting for a new hold on his lost vils, such as might arise, for instance, if Roger, the immediate incumbent, died. Into the interstice between the lord's death and the heir's grant of seisin Griffith was willing and eager to crawl, like the worm that is drawn to the dead.

But I rode home happier than I had been for many a day, because I could again believe there was justice to be found somewhere entangled in Edward's network of law. And I told my lord and my lady, we three privately together, all that had passed.

'God be thanked!' said Llewelyn, heaving a great breath that eased him of a year of struggle and despondency. 'At last we have Edward's cypher put into plain speech. Welsh land may have Welsh law, even where the dispute is between two barons of the King. Edward can hardly reverse his own decision now this is made public. The cases are exactly similar, and no less is due to a prince of Wales than to a baron of the king. Now I can go forward with my suit with a good heart. The way is open at last!'

He resolved to prosecute his case at Montgomery in the October session of the Hopton bench, and at once wrote to Roger Mortimer and gave him joy of his victory, all the more heartily, as he freely owned, because it afforded the perfect precedent for what we hoped would soon be ours. Mortimer replied with a cordial invitation to the prince to visit him at Radnor while the lawyers argued the case at Montgomery. Thus he might be close at hand to watch events, and also Mortimer had certain matters to put to him that might be to the advantage of both cousins.

That was a happy and hopeful time with us, a family alliance shaping with the strongest baron in the middle march, and every prospect of winning Arwystli, and with it a better promise of a just relationship with England. The treaty, our one protection, began to appear safer than for some years.

Late in September we set out for the marches, and Llewelyn had but one disappointment, that Eleanor thought best not to come with us. 'You will be altogether occupied,' she said, 'with men's business, both at Radnor and Montgomery, and though I should be very glad to meet with your cousin Mortimer, for this time I think I would rather not ride so far. You will not be long away. I'll come slowly south as far as Bala, and wait for you there.'

He was concerned at once, for she had always been so constant at his side. And though she smiled at him with clear eyes and open face, he held her by the hands and looked at her earnestly, and was uneasy.

'You are paler than usual. It is not like you to sit at home. You are not ill, love?'

'No,' she said, and laughed, and I thought her glow was even brighter than of old, pale though indeed she was. 'No, I am very well. All is as it should be with me. But this once I will to stay behind, and when you come back as far as Bala you shall find me there to greet you.'

So he let her have her way, though not quite easy about her. But she shone so bright in those last days before we left that he was cheered and reassured. Whatever she wanted he would do, even if it severed him from her for as long as ten or fifteen days. As for me, I wondered, for it needed a powerful motive to cause her to leave his side, however little he, in his humility, questioned her ability to live without him so long. And perhaps I watched her even more devoutly than usual in those days, and noted that she kept her own apartment until well into the morning, upon various pretexts. But on the morning that we rode for Radnor she came down early to speed us on our way, and I saw her at the turn of the stairway pause and hold by the wall a moment, and marvelled at her look, for her cheeks were pale and her eyes heavy, and yet her lips so smiling, and her eyes so glad and hopeful when she believed no man was watching her.

And as I gazed, she laid her hand upon her body under the heart, and that was so tender and protective a caress that my heart opened and swelled with knowledge, and I stood so lost in enlightenment that I forgot to take myself out of her sight, but was still standing like a man in a dream when she came on down the stair.

Seeing me, she checked only for an instant, startled, and then smiled in content, and came on more slowly. And as she came she opened her eyes wide and wonderfully to let me into her mind, and laid a finger to her lips. So I understood what she felt no need to say, that she was not yet sure, that by the time he returned to her in Bala she would be sure, and then her news would crown his joy if he came triumphant, and be the blessed consolation for all losses if fate and Edward still denied him justice.

Thus she passed by me silently, and went out into the inner ward to kiss Llewelyn and speed him on his way. And I, as she had entreated me, held my peace and followed after like a biddable child.

At Radnor we had a hospitable welcome from Roger Mortimer and his lady, who was a de Breos, marcher through and through, like her husband. This cousin of my lord's, his elder by some years, was a gaunt, dark, fiery person, loud-voiced and impetuous, but large of mind, too, with true feeling for his lands and his people, who lay between Wales and England, torn both ways when there was dispute, and never utterly at home in either camp. There were two sons of the house, Edmund the heir, and Roger the younger, able, unchancy young men, like so many marcher sons not yet possessed of their own lands, and therefore full of all the enterprise and daring necessary to their kind, without the responsibility their father carried. They featured rather their mother, being fairer in colouring and slighter in build, while the lord of Wigmore and Radnor himself showed a strong resemblance to his Welsh grandsire, Llewelyn Fawr, in the shaping of his bold, thrusting bones and the taut flesh that covered them, in his hawk-nose, and the deep, bright caverns of his eyes. He was the blacker of the two, and the leaner, but when he sat beside Llewelyn at the high table the mark of their great forebear was clear in them both, and they might almost have been brothers.

What the lord of Radnor had to propose to his cousin we did not at first learn, though clearly he was blazingly scornful and bitterly resentful of Griffith ap Gwenwynwyn's overweening presumption, and the liberties that highly successful renegade took even with chancellor and king. But Roger's approaches were held in check until we who were bound to appear at Montgomery on the sixth of October had set out for that royal town. We went in high hopes, not because we were too easily elated and too trusting of Edward's honesty, but because we had that invaluable precedent of Mortimer's successful defence by Welsh law to prop us, and were willing to whip it out and flourish it before Hopton or any other royal justice if he barred our way. It was so recent that it could hardly be outweighed by any other precedent. We felt we had a shield that could not be penetrated even by Edward's arrows.

In this high mood we rode, I but a private observer for my lord, up the winding hill through the town of Montgomery, and out on to the high rock where the castle stands, and into the wards, and thence, having committed our mounts to the grooms, into the great hall.

There was no knowing from Hopton's bland face whether he had his orders in advance, as we thought probable, or even if he had, what they were, and we held our breath when Master William got up to make his formal claim on Llewelyn's behalf to the whole land of Arwystli, and the land between the Dovey and the Dulas, and that by Welsh law, as was implied from the opening of the cause, now nearly four years past.

When he sat down, that was the moment for Griffith to make his protest and claim the common law, so setting the old cycle revolving helplessly once again for four years more, or for the bench to demur that the rival claims of the two systems had never yet been settled. We waited, and Hopton sat mute, courteously waiting for the defendant to reply, either in person or by his attorney. The pause was long, I think now intentionally long, and we drew cautious breath and knew that one peril had passed. The Mortimer precedent was too recent and too famous to be denied, every man in the court knew of it. We felt safe then. No one was going to deny us Welsh law, and invite the obvious rejoinder. Yet I wondered, even before a word was said, why Griffith, hunched and hugging himself behind his sombre troop, had a small tight grin on his face, as though he enjoyed a joke very private and sharply sweet of taste.

For my part, I was shaken when he got up himself to make his counter-plea, instead of leaving it to his attorney. He hitched his furred gown about him at leisure, and ran a sharp glance along the line of us where we sat, and I dreaded then that after all he had something still hidden in that wide sleeve of his, but could not guess what it would be.

'If it please the court,' he said, all reason and sweetness, 'I am willing and ready to answer to the plea, in the proper form, and will not dispute the manner of procedure but in one point. Since the prince of Wales and I myself are both barons of the king, I ought not to answer unless the lord prince brings a writ to court.'

We did not at first understand why he should be in such secret glee at having this defence in hand, for it sounded feeble enough and Master William rose to answer it, I think, in as great innocence as we.

'The prince's writ,' he said, 'was duly taken out and delivered into this court when this plea was begun. The date was the seventeenth day of February of the king's sixth regnal year. I myself delivered it.'

Hopton pondered the date, or affected to, and said: 'That was not, I think, before the present bench? I was not then in office.'

'It was before Master Ralph de Fremingham,' said the old man, still confident. That was the first presiding justice of this commission for east Wales, who held office but a few months, and was removed in somewhat dubious circumstances.

'We have no record of this writ,' said Hopton smoothly, 'and since the defendant pleads that as a baron he should not answer without a writ, it seems that we cannot proceed at this sitting, but must make enquiry further to try and recover it.'

Now the pattern of deceit began to appear all too clearly, for courts surely keep records, and those records should be complete, and even if the clerking of the Hopton commission proved inefficient, the writ must have been listed in the chancery rolls. It should have been a simple matter enough to refer to chancery and prove the issue, though it was a reflection upon Hopton himself that such a reference should have been necessary. But he made no mention of chancery, and no apology for his inability to prove the writ by the archives of his own court.

'My colleagues,' said Master William, 'will bear witness that I brought and handed over the prince's writ at the first hearing. It must be in existence, and it should not be impossible to find it. I must protest against any further delay.'

'It is regrettable,' said Hopton magisterially, as though it reflected not at all upon him, 'but since we have not the writ, and cannot proceed without it, there is no other course open to the bench but to adjourn until it can be recovered.' And he ordered that word should be sent to Ralph de Fremingham, to enquire if he held the writ and the opening of the process, and bid him send them into court the eighth day of December, by which date he trusted to be able to proceed with the case. And on that, with Griffith grinning like a gargoyle on a tower, Hopton adjourned the plea until December.

As for us, we went out dashed into a new kind of despair, not because the pretext in this case was itself so grave a matter, for writs can be taken out a second time if need arise, but because it came as a plain indication that however many obstacles we overcame in this cause, there would always be others raised to baulk us. The plain truth was, that Edward had served notice upon the prince that whatever happened, he should never have Arwystli.

'In the name of God,' said Adam, as we went dispiritedly to the stables for our horses, 'why should Fremingham have that or any other writ, or any part of the records? Is that how they run their courts, and Edward so proud of his gift for law? In Wales we should be ashamed of such wretched clerking.'

'He will not and cannot have it,' said Master William bleakly. 'He may very well recollect that it was brought, and say so, but of course he'll say he has kept none of the records in his hands, and why should he? And he at least will be telling the truth. The prince's original writ will never be seen again. Nor, I warrant, will the entry of that first hearing survive long in the roll of the court after this, even if it has not already been removed. No, it is not a mere delay of two months they've secured by this stratagem, it is the time it takes to swear out a new writ from chancery and begin the process at law all over again. If,' he said heavily, 'the prince's heart can stand so grievous a mockery and humiliation. He has been bled slowly of his heart's-blood for years. Somewhere there is an end to what even the saints themselves can bear.'

CHAPTER IV

That lamentable news we took back to Llewelyn at Radnor with very heavy hearts. He knew from our faces not only that his just hopes, were dashed yet again, but that they would always be dashed, for the hands that held supreme power had themselves set up an impassable barrier against them, in Edward's interest and Edward's will.

He heard us in silence to the end, and then with an equable voice and a face chilled and stony said some words of reassurance and comfort to the old man, whose voice trembled in the telling, and who ended nearly in tears. Then he commended him for his courage and pertinacity in a very unrewarding cause, and dismissed him gently, and his colleagues with him. But he asked me to stay. We had found him closeted with Mortimer when we came, and there was then no other left in the room but we three and Roger's chaplain and secretary. The silence hung heavy upon us all for a while, and Mortimer leaned his elbows upon the table and watched his cousin's face doubtfully, as Llewelyn sat straight and still in his chair, following with fixed eyes the departure of an old regard.

Remembering, I find it astonishing how often his respect and liking for Edward received wounds that might well have been mortal, and yet revived to live again. Even after this, I know he had some illusions left, and still believed there were things to which Edward would not stoop. It took another and a stranger stroke, perhaps the only one Edward ever struck at him in innocence, to give his lingering liking the *coup de grâce*.

When the prince had thus sat still and alone among us some while, Mortimer reached out a lean hand and grasped him by the shoulder. 'You are used very shabbily,' he said bluntly, 'and I am sorry for it. I tell you openly, if you had beaten Griffith at his own game, and whipped Arwystli from under his nose, I should have been as happy about it even as you. The man is insufferable to me and to many.'

Llewelyn stirred into life again, the dark colour flooding back into his face. 'Unhappily not so to the king,' he said harshly.

'He has been useful,' said Mortimer, and shrugged.

'In helping to contain and discipline me,' said Llewelyn remorselessly, 'and is still being used to the same end.'

'His plea will stand,' warned Mortimer with compunction. 'The law will uphold him, he has a right to demur at answering without a writ. I don't presume to guess who was obliging enough to make away with it for him, since he could hardly get at it himself. As to the king's Grace, he is my liege, and I'll say no word of him. But what will you do now? Will you send your men to court in December?'

'To be subjected again to what they have suffered so often on my behalf? No! I'll rather write yet again to the king, and deal directly with him, though in my heart I know it will be fruitless. At least he shall know that if I am cheated, I know it, and despise the act and the cheat.'

Mortimer got up abruptly and began to pace the room, making two or three rapid prowls about the table, until he halted as suddenly behind Llewelyn's chair, and dropped both hands upon his shoulders. 'I take it,' said he, 'that we are in confidence here?'

'You may trust Samson as you trust me,' said Llewelyn.

'And that I do,' he said heartily, 'for though we've fought often enough and hard enough, I should be a fool indeed if I thought you could ever fight unfairly, with eyes in your head like yours. I am more likely to do a little conniving and insinuating myself, and I'm no great hand at it, either. I've been long in coming at what I had to say to you, chiefly by reason of this cause of yours. I waited to see what tricks Griffith would shake out of his sleeve this time, and whether you and I were as close in enmity to him as I thought. It seems you have even better reason than I to man your defences against him. But make no mistake, he has not done with me, either, he is only waiting for another chance. There's no end to his effrontery, and none to his greed. I am in fealty to the king, and I am his man, and there's an end of it, whether all his acts seem good to me or whether they do not. But as to Griffith ap Gwenwynwyn, he is a very different matter. You and I have a common enemy, and a common use for reliable allies. Why should not we two enter into a treaty of alliance? To support and aid each other in all matters whatsoever, saving only our fealty to Edward? Old foes or not, we've dealt honestly with each other, and we come of the same blood, and I'm no happier when you fall victim to an overweening trickster than when the same snake comes striking at my heels. What do you say?'

'I say,' said Llewelyn, flushed with surprise, for he had not guessed at this, and it had a warmth and candour about it that came very gratefully to him then, 'that there's never an Englishman with whom I would rather be on good terms, and never one I'd rather have to keep my back against a false world. I have an oath of fealty to keep, like you, but you of all men are never likely to lead me into imperilling that. Yes! I say yes, such a pact I'll gladly make with you. As solemnly as you will.'

'I mean it solemnly,' said Mortimer. 'I have a soul to stake, and I'm willing to take that load upon me, if you are.'

'In time of peace?' said Llewelyn. 'On what terms?'

'Peace and war and all,' said Mortimer hardly. 'Why not? Saving our vows to Edward, that goes without saying.'

Llewelyn considered, and saw in his mind an embattled neighbour to Arwystli, and neighbour to him if ever he won Arwystli, a strong line of defence deep into mid-Wales, a way into the south. All the prohibitions against enlargement he knew, and all the dangers barring his way, and yet the offer was honest and greatly to be desired, and the ally, impetuous and ungovernable as he was, honest to the backbone. And that was pure delight to him, after so much dishonesty. He said: 'Saving our vows, yours and mine both, yes! I am your man, if you are mine!'

*   *   *

It was but three days later that they drew up between them, and sealed with the most solemn sanctions, their treaty of mutual assistance and perpetual peace and accord against all enemies, saving only their obligations to King Edward, and in Roger's case also to the Lord Edmund, the king's brother, under pain of excommunication if they failed of their promises. The bishops of Hereford and St Asaph took cognisance of their vows, which bound them, as in peace, so in war, the one to the other.

Thus those cousins, one half-English, half-Welsh, the other wholly Welsh, were brought together by their mutual hostility to Griffith ap Gwenwynwyn, and their common detestation of greed, malice and falsity. And fortified with this pledge, and embittered and stiffened by the duplicity of Edward's court at Montgomery, we turned homeward in mid-October, to meet with Eleanor at Bala.

She came out to the gate of the maenol to meet us when we rode in, having caused the watch on the wall to notify her as soon as the prince's banners were seen in the distance. She was bravely adorned, and so beautiful with joy that the heart ached, beholding her. She walked like a queen, erect and ceremonious, her head raised and her gaze high and bright, as though she had been a crystal cup full to the brim of magical wine, and must not shake one drop from the rim.

When he set eyes on her he trembled and checked his horse, knowing that something miraculous had befallen her, but not knowing what it could be, and so dazzled that he had no heart to question or wonder. I was close at his side, and I saw the severity and sadness and dour resolution cast out of him in a moment, as though a fresh wind had blown drifts of cobweb and mist away, and left him, too, bright as the sun with the reflection of her certainty.

He lighted down to her like a man in a dream, and took her face between his hands and held her so, gazing at her face for a long time before he kissed. And she wound her arms about his body and strongly embraced him, and neither of them had a word to say, not then nor all the while they walked together, hand in hand, back into the maenol. On that occasion she did not welcome him home in words, for there was no need when her every look and movement and every thread of her vestments was a prince's welcome. Nor did he feel any wish to ask how she did, and how she had done those days without him, for that, too, was in her face. And if she had seen in his distant countenance, before he was transfigured, how his affairs had sped at Montgomery, she spared to ask and remind him, for she had other plans.

Afterwards, in hall among the whole household, everything went as it always went, yet with a kind of secret and ceremonious wonder, as if we played a pageant of our own daily life, with redder torches, richer laughter, sweeter music and stronger wine than ever graced meal in hall on working days. Until the prince and princess, surely at her instance, withdrew early to their own chamber. And there, I think, in his bed, in his arms, on his heart, there she told him.

It was he himself who told me, and never knew that I needed no telling. I think he was in great need to open his heart to someone, for he was so full of joy that he could not contain it alone, and as in older days the stars of our shared birth drew him to me. I had still a small room close to theirs, and I lay long awake, for their sake exultant and fearful and grateful, taking to myself a morsel of his burden and his blessing even before he offered it. And I was in no way astonished when my door opened, and in the light of my tiny lamp I saw him come silently within, and shut out the world behind him. He had a woollen gown wrapped about his nakedness, and above its high collar his face looked strangely young and in great awe. Fine, abrupt bones he had, that took the light and caused him to shine in outlines of gold, and the close-clipped traces of beard he wore only drew those lines in softer, broader strokes and mellowed their sharpness. His eyes, which were always the soul of his face, shone huge and dark, with a profound brilliance under their brown depths. He was fifty-two years old, and I had good reason to know it, being day for day the same age, and I would have sworn this man was new to the burning maturity of thirty years, and the blessed burdens of marriage and fatherhood. Such illusions the night commands, and the little lamps of night light up for us.

'Are you waking, like me?' he said in a whisper, and came to my bedside, as I rose among the covers, and stood looking down at me with that rapt smile I saw on his lips once before, on his marriage-day. 'I am too full to lie still. I have left her sleeping,' he said, seeing how I gazed at him. 'She will not miss me. She has company, the nearest and dearest wife could have or desire. Our child sleeps with her. Oh, Samson, Eleanor is with child!'

With all my heart I gave him joy, and made room for him on the edge of the brychan beside me. He had little need of words from me, so many welled up from within him to his wonder and her praise.

'All that beauty and bravery and generosity,' he said, 'will be repeated to the world's gain. Oh, Samson, I feel myself enhanced and diminished both, diminished and comforted. Why should I dare hope to do all things, alone, to make a nation in one lifetime? I am only man, and fallible, it is time I admitted it, and now I may, for there will be a future, and it belongs to another generation, and will be shaped by other hands. It does not matter if my hands grow feeble. I will cede my rights and my burdens into my son's hands without reluctance, and never grudge him his battles and his triumphs. What I have failed of achieving, he will achieve, or his son after him.'

I said, and truly, that now he was more than ever justified in standing by the treaty that was the best protection Wales had, and all his arduous patience and faithfulness under provocation was vindicated.

'I know it,' he said. 'There was never any other way possible, and not only for my sworn word and honour, but for the preservation of what is left to us. I am bound, but God grant that before my boy is grown, he need not be bound. He has pledged no fealty, sealed no treaty. He will take his own way, and in as far as I can prepare the ground for him, I will do it. I will serve as long and as humbly as I must, and stand down when I should, ungrudging, if I can see a better man to come. The great-grandson of Llewelyn ap Iorwerth, the grandson of Earl Simon de Montfort, Eleanor's son – how can he be less than glorious?'

Had it been any other man who so left himself out of the reckoning, I tell you, I would have been certain he did so only in the assurance that another would reprove and repair the omission. But with him that was not so, for he had always this rare humility that had no falsity in it, but, was experienced from the heart. And I felt no need to say to him what my own heart knew, that the son of Llewelyn ap Griffith would have the seeds of splendour in him even had his mother been much less than the jewel she was.

'You may yet find yourself nursing a daughter,' I said, to draw him a little nearer to the earth. But he only laughed silently.

'And I should be sorry for that? Then she will make some discerning king a most imperial queen. And she will have brothers to follow her.'

'One brother,' I said, thinking of those four of whom he was the second, and the great trouble and loss the other three had caused him between them. 'One will be enough, so he come lusty and strong into the world.' But at that, too, he only smiled.

'Ah, but her sons will be true brothers, and stand by the heir as extra arms for sword and shield. How could she bear small and envious children? Oh, Samson,' he said, 'we have waited three years for this sign from God, and neither of us ever said word about the waiting, never until now. And truth to tell, I have been so glad of her, and so greedy, I seldom thought of children, and might have felt some jealousy if I had, yet now that I know – something I never thought possible, and how to contain it I have still to learn! – now that I know, she is twice as dear even as before.'

It was wonderful how this promise of an heir put new life and heart into us all, from the highest to the lowest, how it made endurance seem easy, and the pinpricks of provocation light to bear. But Llewelyn did not let pass any occasion for just complaint, all the same, for now it was his future heir's prerogative that was slighted, and not merely his own. He wrote to Edward plainly concerning the frustration he had suffered at Montgomery, and the scandal of the loss of his writ, making it clear that he had no intention of countenancing an appearance in December, nor any faith in Master Ralph de Fremingham's ability to produce the writ, since there was no conceivable legal reason why it should be in his possession. He required, instead, that proper enquiry should be made for it, or for the record of its issue, where such records should be expected to be, in the royal chancery.

Early in November Edward replied at length to this letter, in a strain which was becoming familiar to us, so civil and anxious to please – though of course unable! – that I could see between the lines not only the droop of his left eyelid, but also the small, ironic curl of his lips that never quite became a smile. He opened as he always opened, by vowing fervently that he had faithfully considered the matters put to him, and would most happily do what Llewelyn asked of him, if he could do so without wronging anyone else, that he felt for the prince, and that his intent was, as it always had been, to observe the treaty of Aberconway faithfully, so far as he was able. But he could not, on that account, do less than justice to his barons and magnates, who also had rights.

'More, it seems,' said Llewelyn, 'than I have.' But he said it now with an even voice and an unfurrowed brow, even with disdain.

He had talked these matters over earnestly, said Edward, with his justices and council. Greatly as he longed to accede to the prince's wishes, he was advised that Griffith ap Gwenwynwyn had been perfectly correct in saying that as a baron of the king he was not obliged to answer without a writ. Another search of the rolls only confirmed this, and there was no way round it. For though they had hunted assiduously through all the records of writs issued, the original writ said to have been sworn out by the prince could not be found. And as the case could not proceed at all without the issue of a writ, without gross injustice to Griffith, there was nothing to be done but swear out a new writ and begin again. The prince, he said, with sad sympathy and mild reproach, must not resent the necessity.

To my way of thinking it was a cruel and insolent letter, meant to sting, but its point was blunted by Llewelyn's calming happiness, which strengthened his purpose and resolution rather than weakening them, but armoured him against humiliation and insult.

'He may bait me as he will,' he said, 'but he shall not gain anything by it, neither a step in retreat nor a spark to amuse him.' And for the Christmas season he let this matter lie, and we went with high hearts to Aber to keep the feast, and sent messengers to bid David and Elizabeth join us there.

They came riding in from Denbigh some days before the Nativity, having heard Eleanor's news, and Elizabeth flew to embrace the princess and give her joy, and thereafter hardly left her, being so full of good advice and sisterly confidences concerning childbirth and children that the days were not long enough to accommodate all she had to say. She was by five years the younger of the two, and yet had eight children of her own, and what she did not know of bearing and raising them was not worth knowing, but all was offered with such glowing and childlike goodwill and such visible reassurance and vigour and joy that Eleanor loved and bore with her, smiling. She was in serene health, the sickness she had suffered and hidden in the first days was gone, and her beauty was radiant, assured and glorious during all the time that she carried her child.

Elizabeth had brought with her only her youngest daughter, eleven months old, leaving the rest of that lovely tribe with their covey of nurses at Denbigh. It went against the grain with her to go anywhere without them, but in a hard winter it was something of an undertaking to transport so many little ones about the country. Therefore the only attendant she had with her was Cristin, and to complete my joy, Cristin without Godred. David had brought but a small company, and left all his knights at home. For this brief while I could brush sleeves with my love about the maenol as we went about our duties, and feel no need to look round for Godred's lurking, peering face. No need, either, to keep from looking round, for loathing of the bitter spark I should see flare in his eyes when they met mine. It was a good Christmas.

I said to her when we met in hall that first day that David, for all he had given his brother joy most affectionately, and kissed Eleanor's hand and cheek with reverent tenderness, was somewhat quiet and grave, liable to fall into deep thought, and thought that darkened his countenance.

'We've seen him moody before this,' said Cristin. 'He may well be weary, he's been in the saddle more than at home these last weeks, up and down into the south and the west, visiting his nephews in Iscennen, and Meredith ap Owen's sons in Cardigan, and I know not what others besides.'

'For what purpose?' I questioned, astonished, for though doubtless he felt some family affection for those young men in the south, his dead sister's sons, yet it was David's way to expect them to come to him, rather than go running after them.

'To compare his grievances with theirs, I suspect,' said Cristin with a shadowed smile, 'though I doubt if he'll get much comfort that way, or they, either. There isn't a chief in the Welsh lands who is not burning with his wrongs, and when they lay two fires together, who knows how far the blaze may spread? The sixteenth of this month he should have made an appearance in the Chester shire-court, where Venables is still encouraged to sue against him for Hope. Grey is justiciar there again, and all the Middle Country is taking that as a sign the noose will tighten from now on.'

'And he defaulted?' I said.

'He paid no heed whatever. He was somewhere in the west then, he got back only in time to ride with Elizabeth on this visit. And half of him he has left somewhere far distant, occupied with other matters than celebrating Christmas,' she said, and shook her head anxiously. 'And yet so quiet and so contained! We have not seen him in a fury but once in the past six weeks. Time was, he would rage over his mangled forests, and the many exactions he considered illegal, and being cited into Chester for this due and that, and a hundred things besides. Not all for himself!' she said, and her smile was wry and sweet, for she suffered, as I did, from an old and incurable affection for him. 'Lately I've heard him cry out but once. I think you will hear of it. I am sure Llewelyn will.'

I asked her: 'What was it happened?' And I chilled as I listened for her answer, for when had David been tolerant and patient, and withheld instant and fiery outcry when his prerogative was infringed by so much as the touch of a finger? And I saw him for myself sombre, withdrawn and mute.

'They have killed two of his men,' she said. 'A party went into Chester market for salt and honey, and to sell wool. There was some quarrelling there between them and some of the justiciar's people, but they kept their tempers and set out for home, and were over the border by Hope when the English waylaid and set on them. There was an English man-at-arms killed in the squabble. David's men drew off, but there were more of the English, and they cut out two of the Welsh and had them away into the shire, prisoners. Murder, they made it in the shire-court. They hanged them. By Welsh law it would not have been murder but homicide, and a blood-price would have salved it. But David's men are dead. And they were men he valued. And their widows cry to him.'

I was sick, for however the Welsh fall apart into warring clans, how-ever they fail of comprehending anything larger than their kinship and their tribe, within those bounds they cleave by their own, and every death cuts into the flesh of all. And David, as in my heart I knew, was Welsh in the old way, for all his English upbringing, and the many ways he had been tugged by his many affections.

'And he so still!' I said, seeing him even then at the high table, inclining to right and to left and making civil reply, with the sweet veiled smile upon his face.

'They are not the first,' she said, 'to be slain for offences we would have compounded rather to heal. And not all in his cantrefs. There are many with the same burning grievance. And he, I doubt he has them all by heart.' She watched him as I was watching him, with her great, iris-grey eyes that darkened so when most she was wrung. 'Samson, he may speak out to you, who does so now to none of us. If you can bring him to confession, do it for his sake. Not that he needs absolution, God knows he's been out of all nature virtuous and forbearing. But he does greatly need to shed whatever this load is upon his heart.'

'Does he not confide in his wife?' I asked. And Cristin smiled her pardonable scorn for such a question.

'He takes nothing to her but what is sweet, open and gay. He'd no more cast a shadow willingly upon her than he would upon his children. He may drag them all into the blackness of the pit with him yet, and they'd go, and never think twice. But that's another matter.'

I said that if he offered me any chance I would do what I could with him, but if he had it in mind to unburden himself to the prince, Llewelyn might well do more and better than I.

Howbeit, David kept his counsel and his ominous calm all through the Christmas feast, awaiting his best occasion, for he did not speak until the day, well into January, when Llewelyn got word from Reginald de Grey in Chester of a sudden and fresh distraint upon his property, in satisfaction of Robert of Leicester's long-discredited claim for his goods lost by wreck. If Llewelyn blazed up at this letter, he did so but briefly and hotly, and then recorded the new offence grimly among those matters he had still to take up, not with Grey, but with Grey's master. David, instead, burned into a fierce and corrosive silence, and made occasion, after we left the hall that night, to shut himself in with Llewelyn and me in the prince's private audience chamber. He had found the moment he sought, I knew then that he had come to speak, not to keep silence.

'This matter of your goods taken in Chester,' said David, standing tall and stiff over the glowing brazier, and himself burning almost as fiercely, 'is only the latest outrage of many, you know it as well as I. And do you believe Grey ever took up this persecution afresh, without direct orders from Edward? He would not dare, after such clear orders went to Chester earlier, to cease distraints and refer Robert to the Welsh court, where they admitted the case belonged. No, Edward has held this goad in abeyance for a while, until it suited him to use it again, and it is *his* hand that has acted against you now. And what will you do? How long will you go on enduring wrong after wrong? And watching us endure worse? You at least, within your own principality, are master of your own house, and cannot be arraigned or challenged, cannot see your rights and your lands taken from you, and your tenants robbed and ousted. They are not so lucky in the Middle Country. They have no such immunity in the south and in the west. We are worse treated than you, and we do nothing. Nothing!'

'If what I enjoy is immunity,' said Llewelyn drily, 'it is the strangest immunity ever I heard of. True, no one has yet crossed my borders to meddle within, but enough mischief can be done from without. Still, I grant you I can no longer do anything to help those cantrefs that have passed out of my hands. They are no longer my men in the Middle Country, nor in the south, nor in Cardigan, and I am no longer their lord.' He did not say that David, also, was no vassal of his, but David could not help but be reminded whose fault that was. 'If you think I do not feel for those who used to be mine,' said Llewelyn with warmth, 'you are foolish and mistaken. But I have no right now to speak for them or act in their name. Those grievances you have you must take to your own liege lord. I cannot help you.'

'You could,' said David, 'if you would. Where else can they look for help? Where else can we, all of us, look for leadership, if not to you? I tell you, there is not a chieftain in the whole of Wales outside your realm who is not groaning and raging under his wrongs, and burning to rise and avenge them. They come to me now with their complaints, as I am coming to you. Day after day new outrages, new exactions, new offences against the law and custom and order of our lives. And the treaty promised us we should enjoy our own manner of life unmolested! Now it has gone beyond oppression. Men of mine, men I valued, have been done to death, who by Welsh law would have been alive this day.'

That story he told, and after it, his tongue loosed and his thoughts racing, many another such story from many another cantref. 'I have been busy these last weeks,' said David passionately, 'putting together the grievances of all my own tenants and chiefs, yes, and all the men of Rhos and Tegaingl, too, who have no Welsh lord to whom they can go for help. And I've ridden the length and breadth of Wales and talked with the princes of Maelor and Cardigan, and our nephews in Iscennen. Do you want to hear what your sometime vassals cry against England?'

'Go on,' said Llewelyn. 'I am listening.'

David drew breath and began. It was a long recital, man by man, lawsuit by lawsuit, distraint by distraint, delay upon delay, offence piled on offence against the laws and customs of Wales that had been guaranteed to us by treaty, and were safe now only within Llewelyn's domain. Old allies of his brother now spoke through David's mouth, their young nephews cried out in David's voice, while that voice grew steadily larger and calmer and more princely in authority. And Llewelyn watched and listened with a still face and patient eyes as David spoke for the nation of

Wales, he who had been a dangerous obstacle to achieving that nationhood. For it was a national cause he argued, and he knew it, and knew the irony of his pleading, before the brother whose life-work he had helped to frustrate. His face burned to the brow, as if he heard within his own mind all those words Llewelyn forbore from uttering. But he would not turn back.

'And your wrongs,' he said at the end, and his voice shook for a moment. 'Those, too, I know. Do you need to be reminded?'

'No,' said Llewelyn, 'I need no reminders.'

'It is not only Arwystli. It is not only these robberies in Chester, nor the crude devices to delay justice, nor the border raids that are still countenanced, when you have paid the money due from you promptly every year, to the last mark. No, it is the manner and insolence of Edward's usage in all things. He has his officers order your men to appear before them wherever they choose, instead of meeting on the borders as was always done aforetime. He makes use of the most detestable of his Welsh renegades to visit your court and conduct his minor matters of business with you. Oh, saving the arch-renegade of all,' said David, turning crimson but with unflinching eyes, 'David ap Griffith – who is no longer available . . .'

'Hush!' said Llewelyn, stung and reproachful. 'This I will not hear!'

'No, I pray you pardon me, I had no right. Such things I should say only to myself, never to you who never have said them to me, and never will say them. But I do not forget, and I can feel the keenest pain when such a man as Rhys ap Griffith is sent into your court at Aberffraw with the king's authority, and feels free to insult you in your own house –'

'He paid for it,' said Llewelyn equably. For that bout of insolence had cost Rhys a hundred pounds sterling to quit him of the prince's prison.

'*He* paid,' said David. 'Edward has yet to pay. What manner of man would be so blockish and unfeeling as to send him to you? This is how he approaches us all. He tramples on every soreness and every bruise.' He drew breath, wearied and drained, and flung himself down in his chair. 'Well, I have done, I have told you.'

'And what,' said Llewelyn, 'do you want from me?'

'You are the prince of Wales. Where else should we go with our wrongs? Knowing that you also have yours? I want you to tell us, all of us, what we are to do, and what you mean to do.'

'I mean,' said Llewelyn, 'to go on pressing every issue with the king, resisting every encroachment at law as best I can, and bearing what I have no choice but to bear. There are realities by which you are bound, as well as I. There is not one of us but must sleep in the bed he made. I am the prince of what is left of Wales. I was the prince of a greater Wales, but when the testing came I had not done my work well enough. I failed Wales, and Wales failed me. These men who come to you now with their complaints, and bid you carry them to me for remedy, how many of them fell away from me then, to keep their own little plots of land safe? How many were willing to sue for Edward's peace rather than lose their small inheritance to preserve Wales? How many betrayed Wales? Now, because they do not like the rule they were glad to accept then, they send

683

you to urge on me an action that could only be a second and final ruin. What they want now is what they wanted then, to preserve their own small rights. David, never think this is a sudden, miraculous, united Wales you are offering me, the nation I wanted then and long for yet. These are still only a thousand little divided souls clinging desperately to their own privileges and their own lands, and seeing nothing beyond. As they turned from me to Edward, when he seemed best to promise them security, so now they will turn from Edward to me, now they are looking for another saviour. Oh, I do not hold them so much to blame. They are not yet ready to be a nation. But they are the reality with which we have to reckon. There is no salvation there. Not yet!'

'Nor ever,' said David, stiffening again in desperation, 'unless we deserve and fight for it.'

'Not yet, believe me, however well we deserve, however valiantly we fight. We have seen what Edward can do, even if he beggars himself in doing it. The same he could do again, and more. Never think Edward does not learn from experience. If Welshmen took arms now, Wales would be lost for ever. He would not halt for awe of a winter campaign, next time, nor waste six months on calling out his feudal muster. He would hire and buy, and bring ships and men from France, and take in archers and lancers at his wages. Welsh archers among them,' said Llewelyn, with sharp and sorrowful bitterness, and smiled ruefully at his brother, but David was mute. 'What I want for Wales,' said the prince, 'goes far beyond anything that could be gained now. That was my failure, that I tried to go too fast. The time for my vision is not now – not yet.'

He waited, and David had nothing to say, but sat steadily gazing at his brother, and his face as withdrawn and resigned as his brother's.

'But you are right,' said Llewelyn, answering what had not been said, 'that is not my reason for enduring still, and urging endurance upon you. All I have said is true, but as at this moment it is of small consequence. For the truth is, David, that this Wales that I long to see will never be won by my hand, unless time and God loose my hand. I am bound in honour and fealty to Edward, and to the terms of the treaty I made with him.'

'Which he has broken,' blazed David, 'by small means, like a mouse gnawing, a hundred times over, and laughs at you for keeping it.'

'No,' said Llewelyn immovably, 'for however I may overrate Edward, Edward knows and does not underrate me. If in the end I must despise him, as I pray God I never need, he will never be able to despise me. No, Edward may take every advantage, wring out every delay, he may well desire to laugh as he does it, smoothly parrying every letter I write to him, but he will not be able to enjoy his gains. He may discard his honour, if he so pleases. He will not be able to sever me from mine.'

'In the name of God!' said David, pale with passion but very still. 'Knowing Edward as you now know him, this giant of meanness, this great prince utterly without greatness, this monster who knows only one loyalty, to Edward, and acknowledges only one treason, against Edward – dear God, have I not reason to know it, who took my treason into his arms twice, and found a welcome for it there? – knowing all this, you hold fast to your oath and seal for *his* sake?'

'No,' said Llewelyn gently and patiently. 'No way for his sake. All for mine.'

I went out with David when he left his brother that night, so softly, with such a chastened face and quiet voice, after such submissive avowals of his own dues owed to Edward, and such resigned acceptance at last of the rightness of Llewelyn's stand. I followed at his shoulder by night along the corridors of Aber, and waited for him to speak. And he had nothing to say. He was out of words, having spent so many. Also he was very weary, much of his own strength also spent in the struggle he had lost. Since he did not at once go in towards his own apartment, but turned along the stone passage and went out into the darkness of the inner ward, I went with him, and he did not send me away, but slowed to bring me abreast of him, and laid his arm about my shoulders as we came out under the stars. A night of clear frost it was, we could see the glitter of rime along the crest of the wall, and hear the steely ring of the watchman's heels on the guardwalk above the postern gate. The sound drew David's gaze, and in the faint starlight I saw his face again sharp with remembrance.

'I see he keeps it guarded now, as well as barred,' he said, deliberately probing his old wounds and mine. 'God put a moat about it, that night. As well to be sure. There will never again be anything to fear from me, but who knows, there may be other Davids at large.' He turned his head suddenly, and stared into my face. 'You are still unsure of me, Samson, own it! You may, without penalty. I have not been notable for constancy. If you think I may still play him false or work to his harm, say it openly.'

Truth to tell, many a time I had asked myself that same question, and found no certain answer. Yet when it was he who asked, I found myself clear in mind, with no need to hesitate.

'No,' I said, 'I do not believe you will ever forsake him again. For better or worse, you said, he had won you. I never knew you to mean anything as solemnly as you meant that. But time and chance and a single moment of anger or folly may still work to his harm, even against your will.'

'And you do not trust my temper or my wisdom,' said David, without resentment. 'I think you trouble needlessly, seeing I am no vassal of his now, and nothing I do reflects on him – even though *you* may know, as I know, that at heart I am more his vassal now than ever in life I was before. My formal fealty is to Edward, and with Edward I have to deal, whether I keep it or break it. But if you need reassurance, I swear to you, Samson, I will not take one step before me, write one word, or so much as open my mouth, without weighing the consequences to Llewelyn and to Wales. Tongue and temper I'll watch, if you'll credit me I can, and for his sake above all. There, are you content?'

No question but he was in grave earnest, and I could not doubt him. On that note we parted and went to our beds. And from that night he made no more mention of the discontent that boiled through Wales, but came out of his abstraction and was very good company, merry without fever, even-tempered, resolute and amenable, as though he had put off a shadow. And when they left us to return to Denbigh, he kissed his brother and made his goodbyes with a bright, quiet, cloudless face, and a particular and solemn affection.

Cristin, carrying Elizabeth's youngest girl, warmly wrapped in woollen shawls, gave me her hand through the curtains of the litter, and drew eased and thankful breath as she watched him mount.

'He speaks now of taking up his men's case at law, since they were seized in land which is Welsh, even if it is not part of the principality of Wales. Not that a blood-price will bring them back, but at least it will provide for their families, and go some little way to vindicate and avenge them. And who knows, perhaps help to protect others who may get embroiled in the same way at Chester market. He may even consider appearing the next time he's called to the shire-court, if only to claim Welsh law and fling out again, as he did once before. By Welsh law he is not yet in default. And yet,' she said, drawing her slender black brows together in frowning wonder, 'does this sound like David to you?'

'He has promised,' I said, 'to do nothing without considering its prudence, for the prince's sake.'

'As a judge of what's prudent,' said Cristin, reluctantly smiling, 'David is likely to prove the most perilous justice on any bench. Yet it's something if he'll make the attempt.'

He was away out of the gates then, Elizabeth riding with him for the first few miles, and after them went the litter with its nest of furs, and the little rosy girl half-asleep in Cristin's lap. I watched until a hand waved from between the curtains at the gate, and then they were out of sight, and we were left to turn our attention once again to the long struggle, courtly in more senses than one, that showed now so urgent a face.

I think I had not fully realised how urgent, until I was at Llanfaes on Llewelyn's business, towards the end of January of that year twelve hundred and eighty-two, and Brother William de Merton spoke to me of his great disquiet at the way the prince was being treated, and told me, in confidence, that he had ventured to write directly to the king a strong protest and a stronger warning, urging the damage that must be done to relations between Wales and England if the injustices continued. For the prince, he said, had faithfully kept his side of the treaty, and had great occasion for complaint at the delays and obstacles impeding his lawsuit over Arwystli, since these clearly constituted a breach of the terms of the peace, just as the distraints made on behalf of Robert of Leicester infringed the prince's sovereignty in his own lands, the merchant never having brought suit in Wales, as he should have done. As Archbishop Peckham had brought his weight to the king's support, so Brother William came sturdily to the defence of Llewelyn's right, and that unasked, out of his concern for the peace, in part, but most of all for justice.

Llewelyn and Eleanor were at Nevin, in Lleyn, at that time, and thence the prince also sent a long, considered letter to Edward, protesting at the Chester distraint, and requesting the release of the detained goods.

Then he came to the matter of Arwystli, strongly contesting the latest device for delay, and demanding a just remedy.

'For your Grace may be assured,' said Llewelyn in conclusion, 'that in this matter we are far more concerned at the humiliation to ourselves than about any profit that can possibly accrue to us from the impleaded land.'

For all its force it was not a letter composed in anger or despair, but in stern dignity, and for all its admission that he recognised and resented the humiliation put upon him, it was a proud and princely letter, a reproof from one monarch who kept treaty strictly, to another who misused it. We did not then know it, but it was the last letter the prince of Wales ever wrote to the king of England. He thought of it then rather as a new beginning, setting out the ground on which he was prepared to fight with fresh heart for his son's inheritance, but certainly not to imperil it.

By the same courier Eleanor also wrote to her cousin. It was the second day of February, and she was in the fifth month of her pregnancy. But she still had time and thought for those unfortunates of her former household who remained prisoners after so long. One John Becard, as she had recently heard, had been pardoned and released at the entreaty of one of the king's magnates, and though she was glad he should have his freedom, it hurt her that her own frequent pleas for him should have been passed over, and his liberty restored only at someone else's instance. And so she told the king roundly. It was to me she dictated that letter, and though I do not recollect it word for word, after all this time, I have the gist of it by heart for ever. Somewhat thus it went:

'I should be glad to have some word from your Grace, and beg you to send me news of how you do. I have been surprised and grieved that your Grace allows my husband, the prince, to be annoyed by this merchant who still persecutes him, for as the prince is ready to show justice to every comer, according to the laws and customs of his land, I find it strange that credence should be given to such a complainant, before ever he has brought suit in the prince's own court, where this case by right belongs. I beg your Grace to give us a just remedy in this affair. I have also heard that certain of my men, captured with me, have been restored to your peace through the pleas of others, when I myself have often petitioned your Grace on their account, and have not been heard. I had not thought I was so estranged from you that you would turn a deaf ear to my prayers, and rather restore these men to your peace for the sake of others. Howbeit, by this writing I once again pray your Grace to receive to your peace Hugh de Pomfret, Hugh Cook, and Philip Taylor, for since these are poor men, and English, it will be easier for them to make a living here in England than elsewhere, and it would be cruel to send them into exile from their own land.

'Dated at Nevin, on the feast of the Purification of the Blessed Virgin.'

'Now take heart,' said Eleanor, when these letters had been despatched, 'for if Edward opens his prison at my urging, we may receive it as an omen of good. His grip is tight indeed, but one by one we have won my men out of his hold, and if he lets these go, then I'll press again for Amaury. They have suffered long enough, all of them, for the crime of escorting me to my marriage.'

It was in this spirit that they waited, so immovable in their resolve to hold station, and neither give way a step nor encroach a step, that I had to recall the grave and ominous face of Brother William de Merton before I could truly assess that point to which we were come. And within two weeks, as though heaven itself could not deny Eleanor her will, we received word that the three men she had prayed for had been granted their pardon and set free, at the instance of the princess of Wales.

'Now I believe,' said Llewelyn, clasping her gold head joyfully between his hands, 'that we shall make him into a feeling human creature yet, between us. Still a cheat and a manipulator at law, I don't doubt, but I can excuse a man for holding on tightly to what he hates to lose, provided there's a limit somewhere to the means he'll employ. And I mean to outstay every pretext he can raise against me. He shall wear out before I will.'

But still I could not forget Brother William, whose solemn view it was that Edward's means had already gone beyond all fair limits, and would not scruple to go further yet. So it came to this, that we might well lose Arwystli to Griffith, the arch-traitor, in defiance of all legal process whatsoever, the issue being decided in advance of law and outside law, in the king's mind and will. And though Gwynedd could stand without Arwystli, yet the omen was very evil even for all that remained. For where would legal contrivance end, if it succeeded here? So I was less happy than they, even in this one earnest of Edward's grudging good-will, though grateful even for that.

Thus we came back in March to Aber, to prepare for Easter. Some days before Palm Sunday we rode in, and it was early spring, very moist and mild and sparkling, and in such days, bright with the palest green of young leaves and the first butter-gold of flowers, there was no man living could resist the burgeoning hope that things must yet go well, that wrongs would be righted and enmities turned to friendships, and men and nations find a way of living in peace.

Tudor ap Ednyfed, the high steward of Wales, had a manor in Tegaingl. And that being one of the cantrefs of the Middle Country retained by King Edward in his own hands, Tudor now held his lands there of the king, and had all the vexations common to all those in that situation, wholly loyal to the prince but owing formal fealty also to Edward for one manor. Such were the complications that he was forced to pay frequent visits to his tenants there, and at this time he rode thence to join us for Easter.

He was not expected until the eve of Good Friday, but instead he rode into the maenol in the afternoon of Palm Sunday, and in great haste, flung his reins to a groom, and came striding into the high chamber where Llewelyn was.

'My lord,' he said, hoarse with long riding and the dust of spring, 'I pray your pardon, but this cannot wait. The word that came into my hall this morning I've ridden to bring you as fast as I could. There's battle and slaughter broke loose at Hawarden! In the night a Welsh force has stormed and sacked the castle. Clifford is prisoner, and all his garrison killed or captive.'

Llewelyn was on his feet by then, with a cry rather of impatience and exasperation than dismay. 'They are mad!' he said, and wrung his hands over such suicidal folly, seeing in this no more than a sudden ill-judged blaze of anger among the local tenants, unable any longer to endure submissively the exactions of Edward's bailiffs. 'The poor fools will pay for it heavily. What can they hope to do, a handful of half-armed men, without leaders and without plans?' He clenched his fists and shook them in despair at his own helplessness. 'And I can do nothing for them, to make their peace again after such a madness!'

'No,' said Tudor, 'it is not as you suppose! These are not half-armed farmers breaking out in rage, they are not without leaders, they have not struck without planning in advance. This has been very well planned, and very well done, but that it should not have been done at all. Hawarden fell like a felled tree, and they are marching on Flint, the town of Flint is rising to join them, the town of Rhuddlan is massing men to encircle the castle. I tell you, my lord, the whole of the Middle Country has risen in the night, at a planned hour, with a planned purpose. Villagers, tenants, lords, all are up together. My own people were left out of the secret to keep it from reaching my ears and yours too soon, but no question they're out with the rest by now. This is no border raid. It is war.'

Llewelyn stood braced and still, and looked upon him for a long moment without words. When he spoke again his face was set like stone, and his voice low, level and chill, for though he questioned, he already knew the answer. And so did I. 'Who made the plan?' he said. 'Who raised the cry that brought them out in arms, to their destruction and mine? Name him!'

'Who else,' said Tudor, 'but your brother, the Lord David?'

CHAPTER V

Within the hour I was in the saddle, with the prince's writ to commission fresh horses wherever I needed, and his orders to bring David to him as fast as we could ride. I rode alone. Tudor wondered at that, I think. If Llewelyn was to have his brother brought into his presence, it would have seemed to Tudor more reasonable to send a strong party. and bring him by force. Llewelyn thought otherwise. The night of reconciliation at Worcester he remembered, and every word of his last interview with his brother here in Aber, in January, only two months past, and there was a manner of doomed, disastrous sense in all.

'He has set himself up to speak for Wales,' he said, 'and now he has dared to strike for Wales. Very well, let him answer to Wales. I have no authority at law to drag him here in chains, he is no longer my man according to any known code, feudal or Welsh. But he has put his hand to a plough that is mine, and I will hold him answerable in the only manner he will acknowledge. Go and find him, at Flint or wherever he is, and bid him here to me on his fealty, not to me, but to Wales, unless his vaunted indignation for this land is a shabby lie like all the rest.'

Tudor said warily, for we trod through a legal marsh that sucked dangerously at our feet: 'There is no man has drawn sword yet within your principality. The Middle Country is no longer a part of Wales by law, whatever it may be by right.'

'And I can therefore abandon it?' said Llewelyn, with a brief and bitter smile. 'My brother by his act has declared that it is. He will stand by what he has done. And I cannot evade it.'

'And if he will not come?' said Tudor.

'He will come,' said Llewelyn with certainty.

I had no means of knowing, until I crossed the Conway, where I should find David, or how general was this call to arms. But as soon as I was out of the principality I saw for myself that not only David's two cantrefs, but also the two seaward ones which were retained in the king's own hands, had risen to the call, every hamlet was mustering men and weapons, and moving to encircle those points from which the royal bailiffs operated. And there was such exultation and such hope blazing across that countryside that I felt my own heart uplifted, against all reason, for dimly I knew, even as I rode, that by this headstrong and passionate act David had endangered and perhaps destroyed everything to which Llewelyn had devoted his life. Still, they cried greetings to me, and sped me on my way with directions and blessings, and the heat and ache of it got into my blood, and I exulted with them. How could I not, being Welsh?

David, they said, up to the last word they had of him, was at Flint, and the town there was his, and the English, such as were in the town and not the castle, dead or captive. But the castle, being so placed on that great plain of rock jutting out into the estuary, was strongly held, and could be supplied by sea from Chester, and they doubted if any attempt would be made to take it, for since it could be isolated and passed by at will it was not worth the men it would cost in the assault, or, above all, the time, where time was more precious than gold. For in the surprise of this rising lay its best strength. So it was possible, they said, that David had left force enough to hold down Flint from the landward side, and himself rushed on to Rhuddlan, where the Welsh of the surrounding trefs were penning the garrison into the castle, and picking off such of the defenders as they might, leaving the sea-way open, for they had no force as yet sufficient to block it. For Rhuddlan, then, I rode.

Other news I gleaned as I went, and could not choose but marvel how well he had done his work. It was no botched and misshapen rebellion he had offered Llewelyn at that last meeting, but the entire fruit of his able and fiery mind, and all those journeys of his had been threads in the web he had woven, and all held firm when the moment came. Not only here, they told me, but in the west, in Cardigan, in the vale of Towey, everywhere Wales was in arms. The men of Maelor were raiding Oswestry, in the west the Welsh of Llanbadarn had attacked the castle, and in the south David's nephews had raised their standards in Iscennen. And it was terribly sweet to me as I galloped to behold this red blaze sweeping across the whole face of my country, lighting up what had never been offered to Llewelyn before, a Wales entirely and passionately at one. And terribly bitter that it came at the wrong hour, called forth by the wrong man for the wrong reasons, and to what consummation I dared not guess. One half of me boiled like fevered blood, exulting in David's prowess, and one half raged and mourned that when Llewelyn, the true creator of this shadowy nation, cried out to it for fealty and heroism, then it fell short and played him false. For he asked that men should see beyond their own small boundaries, and they could not. And David cried out to them now that within those narrow fences their rights and interests were affronted, and they rose to him as one man to fight for them.

He had not lied to me, when he promised he would do nothing, utter nothing, write nothing, without due consideration of the consequences for Llewelyn and for Wales. He had considered, he had calculated, he had made his own judgment, and acted accordingly. Moreover, his tactics were right, for by striking the first blow at Hawarden, as close as possible to the borders and Chester, he ensured that no royal troops from Cheshire should be able to move west and interfere with whatever was toward in the rest of Wales. With Flint and Rhuddlan besieged, it would be all they could do to cling to the sea-ways and keep the garrisons fed, while David and his allies secured as much as possible of west Wales and the south, and – for I foresaw that this had all along been included in David's plans – gained time to raise also the levies of Gwynedd, which alone had been kept in the dark until the hour struck. After Christmas he had sounded out the prince's mind, and found it absolute against action, and therefore he had shut us out of the secret, and acted alone. Allies, yes, he had allies, enough, but there was but one mind and one will directing that insurrection, and one soul that must answer for it in the judgment.

I had thought to ride well into the night, take but a brief rest, and come to Rhuddlan in the dawn, for the soft days were lengthening, and the frosts were gone. But it was no more than deep of dusk, and I was still far from the valley of the Clwyd, when I saw a small knot of horsemen galloping towards me in purposeful haste, and made out one who led, and three who followed. It was then twilight, but with that gleam about it that draws light from every outline, so that flowers shine like faint lamps, and faces have the pure pallor of saints, and though the foremost rider showed under his blown cap of black hair only such an oval of light for a countenance, yet by his seat in the saddle, and the set of his shoulders and head, I knew him for David, and drew rein and waited in the middle of the way, for the man to whom I had been sent was coming to me of his own will.

I watched him come, and it was as if some years of happy and tamed living, wife and children and all, had been blown away by a wind out of time, and left him the David of my old remembrances, as bright and deadly as a lance, and miraculously young. The horse under him went as eagerly as if the two had been charmed into a centaur, and shared the same burning blood. He had been happy with his Elizabeth and her darling brood, but this was a different happiness that drove him at a gallop towards his judgment. I think he was never quite complete when he had not a battle on his hands, and the life he valued and delighted in was not at risk.

Even from the distance he knew me. I recognised it not by any change in him, but by the very omen that there was no change, that he drove on at the same speed, without even a tightening of his hand on the rein, until he was within twenty paces of where I sat in his path, and then checked his tall roan horse smoothly with hand and knee, and brought him to a stand almost within touch of me, so that we two sat side by side. He was light-armed, in a short tunic of mail, and his head bare, and the speed of his ride and the sharp evening wind had drawn back the blue-black locks from brow and cheek, and tangled them high on his crown. His face had a blazing, blanched brightness, half happiness, half desperation. He could have been angel or devil, but either of terrible beauty.

He smiled at me, distantly, as though I had come between him and a dream, and myself showed but like a shadow, and he said: 'Samson, here? Are you sent to me?'

'I am sent,' I said, 'to bid you come to the prince at Aber, upon your professed fealty not to him, for you owe him none and are no man of his, but to Wales. If your newfound devotion to Wales be not a lie like all the rest.'

'Then you call me where I am already bound,' said David, unmoved by any word or tone of mine, 'and never think but I've left all my fires well-fed behind me. And you'll need to ride hard to keep pace with me into Aber.'

I wheeled my horse and spurred after him, for he waited no longer, but galloped on. I fell into line beside him, and those three knights of his escort, mute and watchful, kept their station behind us as we rode.

Never a word more did we have to say to each other while that journey lasted, until we crossed again into Gwynedd, left the Conway behind, and changed horses on my authority in the dawn. For while the night lasted he set such a hazardous pace that we had no thought or care to spare for anything but the way. When we reached the first vil where Llewelyn's men kept guard I offered the prince's writ, and David was prompt to take advantage of it, as though he accepted, along with the fresh horses, the entire terms on which he was summoned. Then for the first time, as he tightened the girth and tried the length of the stirrup, he looked me in the eyes and said: 'Well, have you nothing to ask me? Nothing to say in praise or blame?'

I said there would be a time for that when we came to Aber, my part was simply to summon him, and that was done.

'As well!' said David. 'I will not make my defence twice over, I have urgent business waiting. Once must do both for you and for him.' And he was in the saddle again lightly, and away for Aber, with his back turned to the pale eastern sky where the sun just showed a golden rim. And as I rode after him I knew, from those few words, that he expected to have to defend what he had done, though he felt no guilt concerning it, and no doubt of its blazing rightness and wisdom. But I felt doubt, and could not get the weight of it off my heart. For this was the first time that David, three times false to Llewelyn and three times restored to grace, had turned traitor instead to Edward, who never forgot an injury, and never forgave, and who recognised, as David himself had said, only one loyalty, to Edward, and only one treason, against Edward. The king had twice embraced and sheltered Llewelyn's renegade, and seen no treason in him. He would not be so complacent now the same treachery had been used against his own head. For David, though not a principal party to the treaty of Aberconway, had sworn fealty and done homage to the king as Llewelyn had, and the breaking of that oath was unforgivable sin.

We eased our steaming horses as we approached Aber, and slowed to a walk when the outer wall of the maenol came in sight. It was a clear morning, not even cold, and the gulls were wheeling and spinning high over Lavan sands. So calm it was, the light breeze setting from the north-west, that I fancied I could hear all the little bells in the hermitage of Ynys Lanog chiming softly in the distance, across the strait. I remember no more peaceful morning than that, when all Wales outside Gwynedd was already at war.

'I hope to God,' I said, suddenly chilled, 'that you know what you are doing, and what you have done.'

'I do know,' said David. 'No man living, not even my brother, understands so well what I have done. I have burned down behind me all the bridges, holed all the boats, pitted all the fords, stopped every way and filled up every bolthole. I have made it certain that I can never go back. Now there is only one way to go, and that's forward. Now let's see if Llewelyn has learned as much.'

He had risen from his bed as soon as we were sighted in the distance, leaving the princess sleeping. When we had handed over our horses to the drowsy grooms and passed in through the hall, where the household was as yet but half-awake, he was waiting for us in the high chamber, alone. He rose from his great chair as we came in, but did not move to meet his brother, and at sight of his face David also stood, and fronted him from a clear space below the dais, offering neither his knee nor his kiss until they had spoken out what they had to say. He never took his eyes from Llewelyn's countenance, but when I would have withdrawn, seeing my errand was done, he reached out a hand to my arm and held me, and Llewelyn saw that gesture, and said:

'Yes, stay with us. There is no other witness either of us could bear, and who knows but we may need one faithful chronicler?' And then he said, staring upon David: 'I accuse you! I say to your face, David ap Griffith, that you are traitor and forsworn, and your hands are not worth any prince's enclosing within his own, and your oath not worth recording, and your seal not worth the wax it impresses. What you have owed in your time to King Edward you know better than any, and what you have pledged to him you know, and now you have broken fealty and shamed your homage. That is your own damnation. But you have also damned me! Everything I preserved, against you, *you*, Edward's ally, Edward's creature, at Aberconway, you have ruined for ever, and ruined me with it. No matter what I do now, my honour is lost.'

'No!' said David in a low, fierce cry, though until then he had moved no finger and made no sound. 'That is not true!'

'It is true. I am pledged to keep the treaty and the peace with England, and both lie in broken shards about my feet. But worse than what you have done to me is what you have done to Wales. This is too soon, and dishonourable, and disastrous, and it is you, *you* who have dashed Wales out of my hands and out of my son's hands. Do you not realise even now what it is you have done?'

'I know what I have done,' said David, his voice labouring in his throat, 'and you do not. I have done it with open eyes, and alone. I have listened to the wrongs and complaints of Welshmen all through the Middle Country, and borne them, as they have, until I cannot bear them any longer. Not only my own people, but the men of Rhos and Tegaingl have come running to me with their injuries. Where else could they go? To Badlesmere and Grey in Chester? As well to the devil himself! And to you, almost secure here in Gwynedd? What I have done is to travel this burdened land and seek out all the princes of like mind, and find bitter discontent and bitter wrong everywhere, justice delayed or denied, English law thrusting out Welsh law, and English custom Welsh custom. Until I was clear in heart and mind that Edward had broken treaty time after time after time, and there was no breach of treaty to be made now that had not already been made, except the last, the resort to arms. So then I had to weigh every care, every end that might arise from what I began. And that I have done, and I found no other way but this.'

'Having first,' said Llewelyn, with deep bitterness, 'sounded me out and found me determined to keep faith. And gone away from me like a secret thief, with a smooth, compliant face and a submissive voice, pretending honest patience, and carrying my honour away in your hands. You have lost me my honour, and you have lost me Wales!'

'No!' cried David, quivering. 'I have asked nothing of you! You have pledged nothing to me! I left you clear of what I did for this very reason, that you might not be touched. There is not a shadow or a stain upon your honour, all you have pledged you have kept, and so you may still. Am I asking you to break treaty? *I* have acted, and I shall continue to act, and on my head be it! You remain aloof and immune. What have you done? Nothing! You are innocent. *Mine* is the guilt! Hold your principality still, and leave me to end what I have begun. Whatever we can add to your realm we will add, and if we lose it will be our loss.'

There was a silence between them then, that came down upon all our hearts like the weight of a kingdom or a world, and I stood trembling where all my life I had stood, between those two and torn towards both. For though that love was not even, yet on both sides it went very deep, into my blood and my memory and my bowels, rending me. And for awe of the drawn-out anguish that bound and severed them, I could say no word. But at last Llewelyn stirred a little out of his stony stillness, and took up the struggle again, so low and gently that his voice was like the voice of prophecy that troubles the sleep of sinners and saints, but leaves common mankind alone.

'Fool!' he said, without heat. 'Do you think fate allows any neutrality to me? I have sworn fealty to Edward. My choice now is not between insurrection with you on the one hand, and cold neutrality on the other, hedging about what I have. Have you not understood what homage and oath mean? Or do they never mean anything to you?' Even this he said gently, as one explaining fidelity to some untutored alien soul unacquainted with the codes by which noble spirits live. 'My choice,' he said, 'is between insurrection with you, and taking arms to suppress your insurrection in the king's name. There is a vow binding us, and I owe him service. If he call me, what am I to answer? That is all my choice! And either way is dishonour! A manner of death! *This* is what you have done to me.'

I looked at David, and his face, all soiled and weary from the night ride, was drawn so pale and bright that the bones stood out like knives, and his eyes burned bluer than periwinkles in the sun at the edge of forests. He stood straight and held up his head, but all within he was wrung like a twisted clout. Still he put up his planned and foreshadowed fight, and never took his eyes from the ending he desired.

'If you come with us,' he said, hoarse with passion, 'you will have wronged no man. The treaty has been breached time and again, twisting words, loading legal scales, backing away from solemn oaths – Edward has trampled it underfoot long since, and you know it. You are absolved from it ten times over. If I have forced your hand, as you say I have, it was done because there is no other way open to us all, everyone who calls himself Welsh. Oh, cry out on me, as you have every right, that I of all men should be silent and bow my head when the cause of Wales is cried aloud, and the standard of Wales is raised, yet still God help me, I *am* Welsh, birth and blood urge me, the very air I breathe wrings my vitals, and tells me *I am Welsh*! I cannot get away! We can look for no justice now from Edward. We cannot hope to preserve, under him, our own laws, our own manner of life, our own ancient customs, not by patience and reason, not by law. *Edward is the law!* He moulds it in his hands, he interprets it at will. You know it, as well as I. He has practised it upon you as he has upon me. There is no way now but war, and every Welshman in the Middle Country, in the south, in the west – everywhere – cries out for justice and freedom by the only means that is left. Look!' he said in a hoarse cry, and flung himself forward on his knees under the dais where Llewelyn stood, and wreathed his hands about his brother's ankles. 'This is your call to arms, above all! Edward has given you what you have worked and prayed for, a Wales united at last! If you do not seize that weapon and strike with it now – *now*, when it is offered! – you will never have another chance. This – *this* is what I have done for you!'

He was so shaken that his fine, long hands were clasped close on the prince's feet, and even in the low candle-light his knuckles stood out white as frost. His face was uplifted, the tangle of black hair still erected by his ride strained back from his temples as though he had flown down to his abasement out of the skies. And still Llewelyn stood unmoving, if not unmoved, and looked down at him eye to eye, without remorse or compunction, but without anger, either, as though his eyes saw clean through flesh and bone and into his brother's mind, as it may well be they did at last.

'So you did know,' he said, 'what you were doing to me. And now you come with this talk of my standing apart in my innocence, knowing as well as I know that it is impossible. You are not even honest!'

'You would not listen,' cried David, his voice thick and laboured in his throat, 'you would not act! I saw the Wales of your vision offered to you at last, I, who had never before been able to see and desire it with a whole heart, far less believe in it! I heard it crying out to you. And all you would say was that you were bound! I could not bear it! I have cut your bonds. Now for God's sake rise up, take arms, be a prince again! It is too late to undo what I have done. By this Llanbadarn is in flames, like Flint, our nephews are out in the vale of Towey, the Middle Country is roused from Dee to Conway. If you choose to go with Edward, and keep the bondage of your seal, you could hold and kill me now, and doubtless Edward would bless you for it, but that would not put out the fire I have started.'

His voice by the end of this was loud and defiant and glad, that had begun choked and wild. He had no doubts and no regrets, and he was never going back, that he knew. But still he clung with wide, blazing blue eyes to Llewelyn's face, and could not look away, and even so fiercely his brother looked down upon him. Neither of them saw or heard anything outside their two selves. But I, for the sheer pain of watching them, turned my head aside to fix upon the dark, worn figures in the tapestry hangings behind the dais, the carving of the arm of the prince's chair, the blackened candle-sconce in the wall. And there, mute and still at the back of the room, where she had entered from the narrow door that led to their sleeping-chamber, Eleanor was standing.

I do not know how long she had been there, for the curtains cut off any draught from the door when it opened, and always she moved very surely and softly. Certainly she was incapable of stealth, and had entered in innocence, and the sight of those two locked in their death and life contention had halted her as soon as she came in, and held her unwilling to break the spell that bound them. She had come but two or three paces into the room, and the curtains still shadowed her, but silently and carefully she had closed the door behind her, that no one else might hear what passed between the brothers. And then she stood and waited, for had she tried to withdraw, that would have been as shattering a disturbance as if she had advanced to walk between them.

She was entering the seventh month of her pregnancy, and her body rounding, so that she stood with her hands lightly braced along her high girdle, and leaned a little backwards, and being so beautiful, she had that strange and royal grace that the Mother of God has in paintings and statues that show her in the time of the visitation. Her face was grave, considering and aware, and her eyes were on Llewelyn's face, and never left it but to look once full into mine, and though she gave me then no smile and made no sign, her glance acknowledged and was glad of me as one always and wholly, like her, a true lover of her lord. We stood apart, but we waited together, for those two to resolve the battle between them.

'There is no need to remind me,' said Llewelyn, staring down upon his brother with a darkened and shuttered face, 'that you have left me no choice but between two dishonours.' And he made one strong step back, and tore himself out of David's clasping hands. 'Now get out of my sight,' he said with terrible gentleness and more terrible despair, 'while I make that choice.'

David got up from his knees slowly, like a wounded man, and turned and went out from him reeling a little, as though exhausted, but still his face was bright and resolute as he passed me. When he was gone, Llewelyn sat down slowly in the great chair, and then Eleanor moved from her place and came to him out of the shadows. Released from his bitter concentration upon David's presence, he felt hers, and turned to her as plants turn to the sun, knowing who came before ever she stepped into the light.

Confronting this cataclysm that threatened her fortune, her peace and everything she loved, she looked as I saw her look once when she stood between the knights of her household and Edward's Bristol pirates, and addressed the chief of her captors with the fearless courtesy of queens, and the large, involuntary contempt of the noble for the base. Never did she protest at what was done and could not be undone, never turn her back on what must be faced and dealt with, never repine over what was past remedy. She looked the hour in the face, whether it smiled or frowned, and chose her course with a single-hearted gallantry, seldom in doubt, never in fear.

He watched her draw near, and when she was close he reached out and took her hand, and drew it into his breast. Always her approach reflected light over his face, but then it was a still and solemn light. He asked gently: 'How much have you heard?'

'Enough,' she said.

'I am glad. I would have told you, but now there is no need.'

'None,' she said. 'It is no choice at all. Between betraying Edward and betraying Wales there can be no choice.'

He drew breath long and deeply, eased of uttering what was inevitable, and had been from the moment David struck at Hawarden. 'They are two ways of dying,' he said, 'and both with dishonour. But he says truly, nothing I now do can undo what he has done. With me or without me, Wales is at war. Of all the things I cannot do, the furthest out of my scope is to take the field for Edward against my own people. And after that, hardly less impossible, to let them fall helpless into Edward's hands, and never draw sword to aid them.'

'There is no need to tell me so,' she said with resolute serenity. 'There is but one way to go, for you and for me. We go with Wales. Nor can we launch into this war with half our hearts and half our forces. Since we must go, let's go with our might, and triumph if we can.'

'Since I am throwing my honour into the scale,' he said with bitter resolve, 'I may well throw everything else in after it. The lot was cast for me without my will, but what I make of it now is on my own conscience. I had not thought, my heart,' he said, laying his cheek against the hand he held, 'to have dragged you into such a wilderness for love of me.'

'Never say so!' she said, and her green-gold eyes flared, and her long fingers curled and closed over his mouth, caressing him with passion. 'There is more in it than that! I go with you not only because I would go with you to the ends of the world, no matter how barren, and find there all the roses I want or need, and beyond that into hell, and think it a cool and pleasant place with you beside me – though so I would! No, this is my war no less than yours. I have a mind and a will, and honour to be staked and lost, like you, and in this matter I judge as you do. If you are Edward's liege-man, so am I his liege-woman. If you must bear the burden of a guilt you have not earned, then half that load is mine, and I claim it. Everything that is yours, whether it be glory or shame, is also mine. But your son whom I carry is guiltless. If you and I by staking our two souls can win for him a free Wales to be his inheritance, then I say let us submit our own dishonour gladly to the judgment of God, and pay whatever penalty is exacted with a high heart. So we sin together,' she said, 'and atone together! We can neither avert nor avoid this war. It only remains to fight it.'

'Fight it and win it!' he said, shaken half into laughter and half beyond into astonished grief, for there was never any of Earl Simon's sons, not even the eldest and best, looked and sounded so like his sire as did then this only daughter, this ivory dove among the eagles, with her world in peril, and the seed of kings and heroes quickening in her womb. He opened his arms and drew her down into his heart, circling all his dreams and labours and hopes within the compass of her rounding waist.

And I, who had held still for fear of troubling their immense solitude, slipped away out of the room unnoticed while they clung together in that three-fold embrace, and waited without, not far, until he should call me. For those two, having no comfort but in each other, and having accepted a war they had not sought and did not want, would not now be long inactive about it, even for love's sake. They would pursue it, rather, with all their gallantry and force, most of all for love's sake.

Nevertheless, for all the deeds he did thereafter, and all the pride and sovereignty of his leadership in the cause of Wales, I testify that a part of him died that day, when he tore himself free perforce from his plighted fealty and troth, and followed his brother and ill-demon into the last of his wars against England.

It was not ten minutes before he opened the door. And she was gone; and he was calm and hard as stone, and his eyes had deep fires burning in them, no passing sparkle, but the slow, enduring heart-red that burns through days and nights without failing or changing. His voice was low, brisk and mild. He said: 'Samson, call David back to me, and wait until he leaves. I need you here.'

So I called David, who was sitting with his head in his arms, asleep upon a trestle table in a corner of the hall, with the common bustle of life passing him by this way and that. At my touch on his shoulder he awoke and fell into a brief, strong shuddering, and started upright with a hand to his hilt and a wrung smile on his mouth, but his eyes still innocent and dazed and blue, a waking child's eyes. Then he knew me, and the frost of awareness clenched the blue into spearhead sharpness, and the lines of his face into sword-edges, and he was wide awake with a leap, as was usual with him, and laughed, for laughter was his armour.

'I thought you were Edward,' he said, 'and here's not my judge, but my confessor. Well, have I sped? God knows I left nothing to chance that I could ensure, to nail him to what he finds a cross. Oh, Samson, the first true gift ever I tried to bring him, and I throw that and myself at his feet, and look up at him, and his face, oh, God, is the face of a murdered man before he dies. Oh, Samson, must I be fatal still?' And by that he had left laughing, and his eyes were huge and veiled. But the next moment he laughed anew, for he, who derided most things, derided most of all himself. 'I should have stayed in Denbigh getting handsome daughters,' he said. 'It is what I am best at. At least a whole company of young men will have reason to praise me.'

I could not choose but note how he named Edward, and yet thereafter, meaning his brother, found no need to say other than 'he', for there was but one he who so occupied the whole ground of his heart and mind. So I said only: 'He bids you to him.' And he looked with unwonted earnestness in my face, to find what I had seen in his brother's face, and he came with me.

When we entered the high chamber Tudor was there before us, and the captain of the prince's household guard with him, and two clerks sat at a table below the dais. Llewelyn turned from them to meet us. I saw David's eyes noting these presences, and the parchments already strewn on the board among them, and the single brief glance they gave to him, such of them as looked up at all. He knew then that his cause had taken a great leap forward while he snatched his few minutes of exhausted sleep, and things were now gone far past any further argument or reproach. Never again would there be mention of what he had done. The blame for disaster would never be shaken off on to his shoulders, if the end was disaster, nor could he ever lay claim to the whole glory if the venture ended in glory. I think he knew with what deep anguish and shame Llewelyn accepted the destiny forced upon him, I do believe that in his rebellious and audacious heart he felt it almost as deeply that he was the cause, but his eyes were fixed upon the end he had set before him, and by comparison with that, no pain of his or his brother's was of any consequence.

'My writs go out within the hour,' said Llewelyn. 'I require from you an account of all your planned moves as they stand now, and the disposition of what forces you count on. But briefly!'

David dictated, and one of the clerks took down the list of those actions planned in secret, in various parts of Wales, to take place all in the same day, the eve of Palm Sunday. All these, he said, should now be under way. Also he told which princes and chiefs had committed their armies to the enterprise, and what numbers they represented.

'You did your work thoroughly,' said Llewelyn, without any word of blame but without any warmth, either. 'Very well!' he said. 'In two days my first levies shall be with your men at Rhuddlan. In three I myself shall join you. If you move your main base within that time, send me word where I shall find you. One of us may need to go south. Also there should now be consultation. Only a national council can speak for a nation.'

Thus he made it plain that the whole nobility of Wales ought at this crisis to stand as one, and utter with one authoritative voice its declaration of injury and its resort to the remedy of war. And David said at once, and submissively: 'If it please you to call your magnates to a parliament, and if it can be done quickly enough, I offer Denbigh. If they come there they will see for themselves what is in train already, and that we are at one in setting about it. There can be no factions.'

'As good a place as any,' said Llewelyn. 'They shall be called there. Six days from now? As much as possible must be done before Edward ever gets word of the rising.'

'He cannot have heard yet,' said David. 'We should have two or three days of grace, but we cannot hope for more.'

'Then you had best take what rest you need, and go back to your siege,' said Llewelyn, and would have turned from him without a word more, to get straight to the business of sending out his writs, at which the clerks were penning away busily. But David, with a face suddenly blanched beneath its dust, started forward so sharply as to halt the movement, and clashed to his knees again before his brother.

'As the lord prince orders,' he said, and lifted up his joined hands, palm to palm, towards Llewelyn, and so kept, unfaltering and unrelenting, though for what seemed a great while there was no move made to acknowledge or respond to his challenge. Deliberately he did it, before witnesses, remembering and reminding us how not an hour previously Llewelyn had told him that his hands were not worth any prince's while to enclose within his own, nor his oath of fealty worth recording. With those words still in his ears, and his sworn fealty to Edward but one day dead, nevertheless he kneeled and demanded, so motionless that it seemed he would grow into a praying stone monument there if he was refused.

There was a stillness and silence in the room, even the pens unmoving, while those two eyed each other long and hard, probing after a surer ground and a clearer understanding. So long it continued, and so remote and chill was the prince's face, that I thought he would end by turning away and leaving the petitioner to stay or go, live or die, as he saw fit. But the uplifted hands never quivered nor sank, but continued their silent clamour for admission to grace and subjection, and the fixed, passionate face implored and confided, and presently Llewelyn advanced his own hands slowly, and took his brother's between them, and held them hard. And David opened grey lips into which the red flowed back impetuously with the returning blood, and drew breath and began in a high, clear voice, like a priest exalted and translated by his office:

'I become your man from this time forth, and to you do homage, and shall be faithful and true during my life . . .'

Once before, very long ago after his first defection, he had offered this, and been plucked rashly from his knees and embraced with the words unspoken. This time he went on steadily to the end, and without pause or tremor passed over those phrases excepting the duty he owed and had promised to the king, for now at last he had but one sovereign lord, as the prince had none, but only God as overlord. And Llewelyn held him steadfastly to the end.

Thus David, who had pledged many fealties up to this time, and kept none, entered of his own will and at his own insistence into the last homage of his life, and having so entered, rose instantly from his knees and went out, taking no leave and no rest, chose himself a fresh horse from the stables, and rode out of Aber with a lighter heart than when he entered it, and went to begin the long labour of making good what he had sworn.

The prince's writs went out throughout the land that same day. With far happier hearts than their prince the men of Gwynedd rose. Only when the north was already ablaze, and all men could cry out their grievances and hatreds aloud, did I fully understand how bitterly deep went their sense of fellowship with their own kinsmen outside the principality, where no Llewelyn stood between Welshmen and their English bailiffs.

'There's nothing for bringing quarrelsome kin together,' said Eleanor ruefully to me, the day before we rode from Aber, 'like a common enemy whose arrows strike at them all. But it does not always last even through the battle. The longer I live, the more I see, Samson, that many men may have heroism in them, but few have constancy, and very few have it so at heart that when they feel it defaced, they may die of it. And for those very few, I think, this world has little use.'

It was not like her to sound disheartened or despairing, nor did she then, she was but measuring the possibilities of the future, and finding them bleak, and assessing also her own endurance, which did not fall short.

'I do not know,' she said, 'but David may be justified, and Edward has breached the treaty time and time again. But even if we are forsworn and recreant, as *he* believes, and our cause dishonoured, still the cause of Wales is not, and if a man can die for that and be proud, perhaps he can also offer up for it what is dearer than life, and not be ashamed. If we venture it, he and I, we shall discover how God looks upon it, shall we not? If he knows Llewelyn as I know him, he will not undervalue the sacrifice.'

In those days of preparation she took a full and active part. And when all was done that could be done before action, and we mustered to ride for Rhuddlan, she came out confident and serene, with her ladies at her back, and kissed her husband as if he were leaving for a day's hunting, and waved us away as long as we were in sight, in case he should look back at the last moment.

After we were gone, it may be she wept. I doubt it, but I do not know, I never saw her weep. If ever she did, it was in solitude.

CHAPTER VI

We joined forces with David south of Rhuddlan, where he was encamped to wait for us, having ringed the castle from every landward approach, secured the town, and done what damage he could to the Clwyd frontage and the little port where sea vessels put in. Time was then the most precious and effective ally we had, to waste it on winning such a castle as Rhuddlan would have lost us weeks, if not months, that we could not afford. There were other strongholds more vulnerable, and of greater use to us, and Llewelyn had already marked them down.

'Ruthin is not so firmly held, and they never look to see us there, the coast roads being their best approach and our greatest weakness. Now the men of Maelor are up, we have allies there to help us. We should do well to move up the Clwyd, and send ahead to them to meet us, you at Ruthin, me at Dinas Bran. If we move fast enough we may get both, and have a line of castles down the march.'

'Lestrange has newly garrisoned Dinas Bran,' said David.

'So much the better, he'll be over-confident.'

It proved as he said. The forces of both brothers, with the best-mounted levies of the Middle Country, swept south-east up the line of the Clwyd and while David surrounded Ruthin, the prince rushed onward to Dinas Bran, overhanging the valley of the Dee. A wild and rainy ride we had of it over the hills, with a gale blowing, but in such weather, even if he had yet heard of the rising, and considered his own situation, doubtless Lestrange thought us still far away, and unlikely to trouble him, so far south. We had scouts ahead, despatched before we set out, who brought us back word that the Welsh of Maelor to the east of us, and Edeyrnion and Cynllaith to the south, had risen joyfully to the prince's call, turning their backs even on the plunder of Oswestry, twice raided, to join in the assault, for Lestrange, who held the castle for the crown, was kin by marriage to Griffith ap Gwenwynwyn, and very well hated.

We closed in from three sides upon Dinas Bran, high on its great grassy ridge above the river valley. We from the north, approaching over the hills, had the best ground for attack, and came as the greatest shock to a garrison that thought us still busy with Rhuddlan and Flint. Moreover, I would not say the watch they kept was very competent, or we should not have got within striking distance of the main gatehouse before they gave the alarm. Speed, which had been our greatest asset in reaching them so soon, was also our strongest weapon in attack. They never had time to get the bars into their sockets before we stove in the doors, and were among them, and put our first parties up on to the walls to dispose of their archers, not only to have a commanding ring round the mêlée in the castle ward, but also to prevent them from shooting down upon our friends from Cynllaith as they stormed up the hill to join us. After that it was no great feat of arms, and cost us but a few men wounded, to get possession of the whole castle with most of the garrison, though Lestrange himself with a small, well-mounted party got out by a postern gate when he saw the castle was lost, and made clean away before we knew he was loose. But Dinas Bran was ours to garrison afresh for Wales, and the Welsh of those parts were eager and ready to man it in the prince's name.

Thus we held, within a few days, a strong line of castles running south-east from the sea almost to Oswestry, and guarding the whole of the northern march fronting Chester: from the north Denbigh, Ruthin and Dinas Bran, with Rhuddlan itself still in English hands but isolated at the northern extreme of the line, and Hope a somewhat vulnerable but as yet useful outpost, much nearer to Chester.

'They've tried hard enough to wrest it from me by law,' said David grimly, when we conferred with him again in captured Ruthin. 'Now let them come and try what they can do in arms.' He foresaw already that the time might come when he would be forced to abandon a position so exposed to the danger of being outflanked from Chester. 'As yet it's safe enough,' he said, eyeing the chances the future held, 'it takes time for Edward to get his lumbering muster into motion. But once he's launched, I may well have to relinquish Hope.' He grimaced at the double sound of that, and laughed. 'But it shall cost them dear and do them little service if I must abandon it.'

'This time,' warned Llewelyn, 'we should be fools to think Edward will hold his hand until the feudal host is ready. He knows as well as we how cumbersome the old way can be. He prefers paid men.'

At that time we had not and could not yet hope for any news from the court, and did not even know where Edward was at that moment, and whether he had yet heard of the sudden blaze of rebellion that was flaring through the west. For it was still no more than five days since David had stormed Hawarden, when we returned to Denbigh to prepare for the coming of the princes and the holding of the solemn parliament of Wales.

Denbigh was teeming with activity, armourers and fletchers hard at work, the first visitors riding in, and their grooms and men-at-arms loud and busy about stables and hall. The prince's couriers had reached every part of Wales that was open to us, and all the chiefs of the north came in person to the gathering, that it might have all possible authority. This time there was no question of dissent. There was barely a man who was not heart and soul committed to the struggle, for there was none whose own rights were not threatened.

From Cardigan, Griffith and Cynan, the sons and heirs of Meredith ap Owen, who had been a loyal ally of the prince lifelong, sent their seneschal, for they were still busy about securing the town of Llanbadarn and the country round, though their attempt upon the castle had been only partially and briefly successful. They could, nonetheless, prevent it from being relieved or receiving fresh supplies except by sea, and to send ships round to that western coast was by no means so quick and simple as to despatch food from Chester to Flint or Rhuddlan. Given a few weeks, they could starve out the royal garrison without cost to themselves.

From the vale of Towey came Griffith, the second of the prince's three nephews, together with envoys from his two brothers, to report that the combined forces of all three had risen in an onslaught on the castles of Llandovery and Carreg Cennen, both of which had formerly belonged to their house, and had been retained by the crown after the last war. With an old and strong royal enclave at Carmarthen, and Pembroke almost more English than Welsh, Edward had hopes of extending his hold by founding such another centre of administration at Dynevor and had also garrisoned the other castles along the Towey by way of outposts of this new royal region. Now, said Griffith, he stood to lose them, for though Carreg Cennen had not yet fallen, its fall was as good as certain, and Llandovery was already breached, and John Giffard, who held it from the king, had been forced to abandon it and withdraw into England.

Strange indeed were the shifting alliances and enmities of the border families of England and Wales, after so long of inter-marrying for land and policy. This same John Giffard, once an ardent follower of Earl Simon de Montfort, and later one of those young men who turned most violently against him, was married to Maud Clifford as her second husband, and that lady was cousin to Llewelyn and David, her mother being Margaret, daughter of Llewelyn Fawr. Giffard had been installed by Edward in Llandovery to the deprivation of his wife's young kinsmen, and now they in their turn had driven him out and regained their own by force of arms.

One more piece of news we gained at that conclave, and that was brought by the lord of Ial. 'Did you know, my lord,' he said, 'that your brother, the Lord Owen, came to spend Easter on the lands King Edward gave him, near the Cheshire borders? We made no approaches to his tenants, for fear it should get to his ears, and be betrayed.' Llewelyn looked at David, then, for that must have been by his orders. 'But when we rose, and they heard of it, they were up after us in a moment, and had hoped to carry him with them. It was a vain hope. Last night they brought word he's fled into Chester, to join de Grey.'

'It's no surprise,' said David indifferently, 'and he can do us no harm there now, Grey already knows only too well what we're up to, and by this time either he from Chester or Gilbert de Clare from Gloucester will surely have got word to Edward, wherever he may be. All Owen can offer them is his own single sword, and we have nothing to fear from that.'

It was a true but a cruel word, from the youngest to the eldest of those four brothers. For Owen Goch, who for some years in their youth had shared the rule in Gwynedd equally with Llewelyn, until he made war against him in the hope of gaining all, and so lost all, was certainly of little consequence by that time in the affairs of either England or Wales.

Edward had made his freedom and establishment in lands a condition of the treaty of Aberconway, and Llewelyn had given him the peninsula of Lleyn, and Edward added to his portion some manors bordering Cheshire, but I doubt if either of them had given a thought to him since that time, and all Owen had wanted, after so long of confinement, was to live comfortably and quietly on his own lands, and trouble no one. Now he was again cast, much against his will, into the turmoil of war, and found himself again landless, his eastern tenants having declared for Wales, and his western lands being just as surely lost to him, now that he had chosen to take refuge with his English protectors in Chester.

'I must send to his bailiff in Lleyn. At least his going solves one problem for us,' said the prince with compunction. 'I am glad he's safe out of our hands, for he never would have come in with us against the king, and as you say, he is no threat. He has taken no forces with him, and he can tell them nothing more than they already know.'

There was never to be a time when all those four brothers of Gwynedd stood side by side as one. Their fragmented fortunes contained within them all the history of Wales. But for the rest, there was no one missing from the muster but Rhys ap Meredith of Dryslwyn, always enemy to Llewelyn like his father before him, and the renegades of Pool, when the prince rose and put to the assembled parliament of Wales the issue that had brought them together, and with one voice, and a loud and passionate voice at that, they declared that the treaty of Aberconway had been breached time after time by England, until it had no further validity, but was null and void, and left to Wales no remedy but in arms. And formally they denounced the treaty, and gave their assent to the solemn acceptance of war.

Then it remained only to plan the next moves. And young Griffith begged, and the envoys from Cardigan supported his plea, that either Llewelyn or David would come south with them, and use his authority to direct their campaigns there.

'I will go,' said David, 'if the prince wills it.'

'It would be best,' said Llewelyn. 'While I complete the raising of Gwynedd. Take with you whatever part of your own forces you need, and I'll supply their place here as my levies come in.'

A hundred lances David took south with him, and a score of mounted archers, and among the lances was Godred. I was in the bailey that morning to watch them go, along with all the rest of the household, maidservants, menservants, grooms, falconers, pages, shepherds, armourers, cooks and scullions, every soul who could drop his burden and down his tools for a few minutes to see a gallant show and wish a great venture well. And I saw then, and heard, and felt, in all the tremor of movement and quiver of voices about me, how we had not so much taken a brave leap forward into an enlarged future, but harked back into a noble, turbulent, fruitless past, the heroic past of a Wales torn and self-tearing. It was like the old days, they said! But I would have had it like new days, days never before known, the beginning of an unbreakable unity and a new grandeur. And how many of us were ready for it, even then? Yet there was ardour enough in the courtyards of

Denbigh to make a nation, had a few more of us had any clear vision what a nation was.

Against my judgment I had hopes then. The trembling of the air with so many farewells and godspeeds set my heart shaking with it, and caused me to catch my breath like the rest. Both hope and despair were so native to Wales, they grew like weeds, and died like flowers in frost. And who could be sure that David had not judged his moment rightly, after all, and dealt his strokes wisely, and won a kingdom for us? It could have been so!

The troops massed and mounted, and I saw Godred among them, but if he saw me he said no word and made no sign. By his face I think he was glad to be turning his back upon Denbigh and his barren wife, and his face towards the loose skirmishes and casual plunder of war, in which he moved like a houseless vagabond, free of kin and kind, his bed and his food where he found it, and no questions asked. When I first met him, before ever I knew he was my father's son and my love's lost husband, in this fashion he was living, travelling light through a world in which there always had been and always would be room for him somewhere, a bed, a woman, food and a fire, and a lord to hire his agile body and ready sword. He owned nothing but the clothes he stood in, and his arms, and a horse, and to say truth even the horse was stolen from the earl of Gloucester's stables at Llangynwyd when it became clear that the castle must fall, and Godred deemed it wise to remove himself elsewhere. Other assets he had then, a comely face, a light, winning voice, and a heart givable and reclaimable as gaily as tossing a ball. All soiled and faded now, but still living, and keeping yet their colour and sap, like flowers pinched but not killed by frost. And often I thought that if I had not found him then, and restored him to princely service in Wales, and to the wife he had thought dead, and perhaps even mourned for a day or two with the surface of his shallow and sunlit mind, all we three might have gone through the world happy.

David came out from the great doorway of the hall with his wife on his arm, and Cristin walking behind with his two sons, one by either hand. David kissed them, kissed Elizabeth, and mounted, and wheeled away at the head of his column without a glance behind. There was no time for long farewells when he was already in arms, even his face bright and tempered for battle.

Elizabeth watched the cavalcade form and follow, until the gates closed after them, and the echo of their hooves had died away down the long, steep slope into the town. The little boys were bounding and shouting beside her, but she was still, narrowing her brown eyes to watch until the last glimpse of David's erect head was lost to her. He did not turn, and she had known he would not.

She had watched him go from her thus once before, after he had bestowed her and his children safely in England, and set his household troopers to prowl the middle march and harry the border cantrefs from Shrewsbury. But then it had been with all the might of England on his side, and now he rode against the same power, and his act was bitter and particular offence to the king who had maintained and protected him

707

then. And she was born English, daughter to the earl of Derby and kinswoman to Edward himself through her mother, and though she would have followed David without question wherever he chose to lead her, yet all her mind and heart stood in solemn awe of this terrible undertaking in which he now dared to engage, and it was with open eyes and conscious daring that she took her stand beside him, and blessed what he did. Married to him at eleven years old, she had borne her first child at fourteen, and motherhood had not put an end to her own childhood, but only prolonged and glorified it, so that she seemed but the gayest and most loving of older sisters to her own brood. But when David rode from Denbigh that morning to unite the Welsh of the south, in defiance of King Edward and all the power of England, I watched her face, the merry, good-natured face ever ready to kindle into laughter, and now so grave and so aware, and I saw her grow up before my eyes.

Denbigh being the best base from which to control and guard all that long eastern march, Llewelyn made it his headquarters until David's party should again come north, and though we were often out patrolling the line of fortresses, and sometimes withdrew to Conway and Aber and the western cantrefs to deploy the incoming levies as they mustered, it was always to Denbigh we returned. Such fighting as we had was limited to testing raids along the border. It seemed that all the barons of the march were putting their followings on a fighting footing, but not yet making any move to attack, rather merely holding their defences. We heard, but not with certainty, that a royal muster was expected in May at Worcester, but had heard no word of the usual summons going out for the assembly of the feudal host.

'He would rather by far raise his armies at his own wages,' said Llewelyn. 'I expected it. I wish we could get some word from Cynan. Wherever Edward is, there Burnell will be, and his clerks with him. Give him time, and he'll find a messenger.'

A week after he had left us, David sent word from the south that all was going well, the capture and partial dismantling of Llandovery and Carreg Cennen completed, and having left his nephews to keep a tight hold upon the vale of Towey, he himself was rushing with his own company to Llanbadarn, to help the sons of Meredith ap Owen finish what they had begun there. In mid-April a second courier brought news that the castle of Llanbadarn was taken and slighted, and all the English forces in the south and west had withdrawn into their strongholds of Cardigan and Dynevor, and were pinned down there so securely that they dared hardly venture out even on foraging raids. A week or two more to make certain of his dispositions, said David, and he would be able to bring his own force back to the Middle Country and stand shoulder to shoulder with his brother, to withstand the inevitable main thrust of Edward's revenge.

It was not until May, when the king's first army assembled at Worcester, that we got reliable news of Edward's counter-measures, for there Cynan found a trustworthy Welsh Franciscan on his way home to Bangor by way of Cwm Hir abbey, and confided to him a long letter for the prince. The friar delivered the letter faithfully to David, who sent it on to Llewelyn in advance of his own return. About the twentieth of May it reached us at Denbigh.

'Your thunderbolt,' wrote Cynan, 'struck us at Devizes some three days after it was launched, and shattered the Easter mood with a vengeance. No question but it was a thunderbolt. If any tells you the king had planned to provoke the storm, don't heed him. But he'll make use of it to the last drop of blood now it has fallen on him. If he had anything of the kind in mind, it was not expected to catch fire this year. Probably gradual encroachment was intended, as costing less in money, though more in patience. Take warning! One of his first measures, when he was able to speak and breathe for rage, has been to open negotiations with his Italian bankers, for loans so huge that he must intend to buy enough mercenaries to settle with Wales once for all. Put no faith this time in winter. His hate is such that neither frost nor snow will stop him, and the opportunity he has been offered he has already recognised, and will not lightly relinquish.

'I write in comparative safety at this time, and therefore at length, for God knows when I may next find the means. To present you all I know: At Devizes he enacted a number of furious orders and writs, giving instant command to his justiciars, but Gloucester has now been appointed to take command in the south. His Grace has not so far called out the feudal host. He sent instead to six earls and a number of crown tenants to raise their forces and meet him here at Worcester in the middle of May, as now they have done. These to be paid at his wages, mark. But the earl of Hereford is up in arms already, claiming his feudal right as constable, and I foresee the king will be forced to raise the host according to custom, much as he chafes at its carthorse paces. Further: he is calling out the whole fleet of the Cinque Ports at once to provision and fit out for sea, and he has sent out for supplies, horses and arms to Ireland, Gascony and Ponthieu, which province he now holds in right of the queen, as you know. He is asking in particular for Gascon crossbowmen. Every omen shows that he will spare nothing, drive every man but himself to death, and if need be himself after, to take his revenge, and in particular on the Lord David, the serpent he warmed in his bosom.

'That he has prevailed on his archbishop to send out letters ordering the excommunication of all the rebels, notably the lord prince and the Lord David, will be no surprise to you. Thus far I hear that our Welsh bishops have been in no haste to promulgate these letters. I pray their dullness of hearing may long continue, but they are also men, and subject to Canterbury and Rome.

'The best I have kept for last, that some good may show out of this much ill. Archbishop Peckham has urged the necessity for showing a front of justice and reason before the Holy Father, if his goodwill is to be invoked in this conflict, and has preached once again on his old text, that the detention of the Lord Amaury de Montfort is an offence and a scandal against the papacy, hardly likely to incline his Holiness to look with favour upon his captor, or any enterprise of his captor. And the king has at last agreed – it was like drawing a tooth! –that Amaury shall be free to sail from England when he will, and return to Rome, or to any place he pleases out of these islands. He is already loosed, and by the time this reaches you he may well be at sea, or even landed in France. Peckham has stood by him manfully.

'The king will certainly come himself to Chester, to confront the only enemies worthy of him. I may well be among those who follow him north, but in the expectation that I must be silent a while, until time again serve your ends and mine, I wish you a fair deliverance, and pledge you my service to the death.'

'I hope he may never have to make that good!' said Llewelyn when he had read this most helpful despatch. 'Well, thank God there is a least one good thing come out of it all. I have not thrown away my oath quite for nothing. Now Eleanor may take some comfort from her brother's release, if we have nothing more to offer her. And we know what we have to face. Edward will not wait for the feudal muster, even if he must call it now. He'll have them follow him north, and come north himself at once with what he already has.'

'He is quick enough to call for excommunication,' said Tudor bitterly, 'for treason to his own head, did ever you hear him even censure treason against you?'

But that was possibly the sanction Llewelyn, within his own country, had least reason to fear, and in balance against his Christian efforts for Amaury he held it against the archbishop not at all. The good news he sent at once to Eleanor at Aber. He could not then go himself, for we had much to do before David returned and Edward set out on his march to Chester, where by our reckoning Grey was already in command of some hundred and fifty lances, possibly more, and a great number of foot, of whom all too many were archers.

'He is arming half his footmen with bows – longbows or crossbows,' said Llewelyn, gnawing his lip as we made up the tale of our enemies. 'And according to the rumours from the south, they're bringing up crossbow quarrels by the thousand from Bristol. There's no relying on Edward to make war twice alike.'

'There are things that will not change,' said Tudor soberly. 'His best way in at us is still by the coast, and there he has his new roads, and so he has at a dozen places where he has hacked a way through the forests down the march. And he will still have an eye on the harvest in Anglesey, if he can come at it by any means, and we can neither hurry that forward and garner it now, nor bid it hold back until the winter. And he has the ships.'

'It is true!' said Llewelyn. 'I have been remiss in not providing more and better ships of our own. All those years of peace I could have done more, and saw no need.' And that was true, for those small craft that we used for shorewise traffic and for fishing were ample to our normal needs, and though he had been provident enough in the old days of constant vigilance and uncertainty, and done more to provide Gwynedd a navy than any prince before him, yet after the peace of Montgomery, during the years when he lived in amity with King Henry, he had not continued his precautions at sea, or more accurately, he had not extended them as he might have done. He had not planned for war then, nor foreseen what manner of war it would be when it came, never having faced Edward in the field until then. And after the harsh peace of Aberconway he had intended long endurance, endless patience, and honest labour to husband the peaceful resources of Wales, putting war far out of his mind. It was not a mistake Edward ever made. I could not choose but remember David's warning, how those forest roads would be Edward's last argument, after all his legal pleas were exhausted.

'At least,' said Llewelyn, 'we'll make the best use possible of what ships we have.' And he compiled a list of what was in service, and we made a rapid dash across into Lleyn and Anglesey, to set a coastal watch and commission our sea-captains, though we did not expect the Cinque Ports ships for some weeks yet, for they had to fit and provision, and had a long voyage to reach the Dee. And on our way back to Denbigh we stayed one night at Aber.

Once more those two lay the night through together, and when she came out on his arm in the dawn, to see us away again, she was as she always was, calm, resolute and kind, though pacing heavily now by reason of the child so near its entry into this turbulent but beautiful world. Never did Eleanor live upon the heart and courage of any other, or take from any other one particle of his strength, but always she gave, always she added, and her bounty was never exhausted. She was happy then because of her brother's restoration to liberty, seeing it was for her sake he had fallen into the king's hands, to be the scapegoat for all his hated race, six years a prisoner for no offence.

'You see, Amaury is already on his way to Rome,' she said, 'and only a month ago I would have said we might have to wait a decade yet to prise him out of our cousin's clutches. So may other matters resolve themselves before we look for the resolution, and more happily than we dare believe. It is not Edward alone who orders the future. Archbishop Peckham has played his part once, and may again.'

Llewelyn was troubled for her, and marked with anxious eyes every movement she made, her slower gait and careful balance, and he would have her remove to Llanfaes, which was certainly not threatened for some time to come, and would have been quieter for her. But she laughed at him and shook her head.

'I will not go one step further from you than here,' she said. 'I would rather come nearer, but that would only divide your mind when most it needs to be single, and you see there is no need, I am marvellously well. Go with a light heart, and never doubt me.' And she linked her hands behind his head and drew him down to her, and kissed him on the mouth. 'Nothing you do can wrong me,' she said. 'Nothing you do can be done without my hand joining its will and its weight to yours. For twenty years of peace I would not give up one day of my sharing with you, come war, or danger, or hardship, or whatever God send.'

He was never so ready with words as she, but he had his own eloquence. Silently he embraced her and kissed, and I think she had her reward in full, though she was never so concerned with getting as with giving.

Then we mounted and rode, and she stood to watch us go, with her women protectively about her on either side. Those two who came with her from France were always closest, feeling her belong to them in a particular way because they had been prisoners with her in Windsor. They were Englishwomen both, in her mother's service from the time when Eleanor was a child at Kenilworth, and exiled with her to the retirement of Montargis. Close at her shoulders they stood as she waved us away to the war. He looked back at the last, and so did I, and she shone erect and bright in her yellow gown, the colour of marsh marigolds, with one hand cradling the leaping child, and one raised high in salute to us, and the gay colours of her women like an embroidered hanging framing her. That is how I remember her best.

When we reached Denbigh David was there before us, the wards full of his troopers, and the children running hither and thither in excitement among them, tugging at the trophies they brought back with them, and demanding stories of their battles. Those were the late days of May, and quick with beauty to break the heart. From the walls of Denbigh on its lofty rock all that green countryside below looked new out of paradise, so fresh and vivid was the budding of the trees and the springing of the grasses, and the meadows so gold and purple with flowers and woollen white with lambs, and on the distant mountains the last fragile veils of snow against a sky blue as periwinkles.

David came striding out to kiss his brother, with that blinding brightness about him that came to its fullness only in stress and danger and the challenge of combat. He made report of his doings in the south with the ardour of success, but also as dutifully as ever did newly-fledged knight to his lord, such care he had to maintain before all men the vassalage he had wrested from Llewelyn almost against his will.

'I have left everything there in good order,' he said, 'but they will certainly be drafting in men as fast as they can, and the royal enclaves being sited as they are, with access from the south, they can reinforce Carmarthen without hindrance, and Cardigan they can provision from the sea. But Rhys Wyndod may be able to keep Dynevor isolated. He has it well surrounded, but they would have only a short way to cut a corridor if they get men enough. We shall be sent for if they need us there. And I got word as I came,' he said, 'of the feudal muster. It's called for Rhuddlan, in the first days of August. They say Edward has twenty-eight ships already in commission. But if the winds play our game, it may take them five or six weeks to make the circuit into the Dee. We have a little time yet.'

They rode the length of the front-line defences together. Llewelyn had his men strung in compact parties, each including some bowmen, along the edge of the forests, from close by Rhuddlan, overlooking the king's new coastal road, to Hawarden opposite Chester, thence southward by Hope and round the hills above the Dee to Dinas Bran, a line just within what we claimed as the border of Welsh land, but withdrawn only to the point where every company had safe cover at its back, either difficult hill country or deep forest, or indeed both together. South of the

712

upper Dee our command passed to the men of Maelor and Cynllaith, and south again to the rebellious tenants of Griffith ap Gwenwynwyn in Powys.

In all this planned line, the only salient was the castle of Hope, jutting well out into the lands securely held by English lords.

'We'll hold on to it as long as we may,' said David, who had fought so furiously for it at law, 'and make it cost them as high as we can, but it is not worth keeping it when it begins to cost us as dear. They'll not attack it on their march to Chester, but wait until they have all their army massed, and their communications secured. He'll want to come at you, brother, by Flint and Rhuddlan, as he did before, there's no other way. But I fancy he'll want to clip my wings here in Tegaingl before he dare turn his back on me. With me here he'll not find it so easy to guard his flank as last time.'

Never did he scruple to speak of that last time, or show any sign of shame in harking back to it, or, indeed, try to dissemble or forget that he had then fought on the side of the invaders. And never by word or look did Llewelyn remind him.

'The king is on the move by now,' said Llewelyn. 'The earliest we can hope to hinder him is after he's passed Oswestry. From Dinas Bran something might be done.' And for the first few days of June he took a small company of us south with him to that castle, and thence we pushed raiding parties as far to the east as we dared, and waited for King Edward's army on its way to Chester.

In a high summer once I watched Prince Edward's army closing in upon Evesham, where Earl Simon in the sprung trap waited with dignity for his death. Now in the early summer, from a hill-top above the winding Dee, I watched King Edward's army advancing upon my country with the same cold, confident discipline, learned from Earl Simon and turned against him then, bearing down now upon my lord. A strange, unearthly sight it was. We in our forests made our sudden assaults and rapid marches unseen and unheard, so quickly that we were come and gone before there was orderly sight of us or distinguishable sound. Edward with far greater numbers, too many for speed or stealth, made his slow, methodical way by full daylight and in the open, plodding inexorably like a great armoured beast, and surrounding his main body with a cloud of probing outriders, in restless, darting flight like the clouds of flies that accompany a drove of cattle. For miles before we had sight of man or horse we could detect their progress, for there hung over them in the air a faint, floating veil of bluish vapour and dust, hardly thick enough to be called a mist, for the season was not arid, but moist and mild. This serpent of vapour moved towards us over the green, rolling land, weaving as it came, and presently, before there was any colour or detail, came the sound of them, distant, rhythmic and continuous, a strange, murmuring, throbbing jingle, compounded of all manner of small sounds, but chiefly the tread of innumerable feet of men and horses drumming the earth. The light jangling of harness was there, too, the faint creak of the wheels of baggage carts, the chink of mail and clash of plate, the squeak of leather rubbing against leather, and the murmur of voices. Then, some time after this human river-music had reached us, came the first colours and lights, points of brightness scintillating through the cloud, lance-tips and pennants and the flashes of the sun fingering steel, then the whole dancing crest of the column in gleaming reds and blues and golds of flags and banneroles, the mane of the dragon, and at last the serried shapes of men and horses, the flesh and blood of the fabulous beast.

We kept pace with them northwards along the march, they below and we in the hills, and the rest of that journey we did them what damage we could, picking off any outrider who ventured too far west and let himself be encircled, in places favourable to us darting down upon their fringes in sudden raids, killing and looting, especially cutting out, where we could, one of the wagons, stripping its goods, and disabling it if we could not get it clean away. By night we tested the watch kept on their camp, and found it all too good, but made our way past it once or twice, and did them some hurt before we drew off again. There was not much we could do to so orderly and drilled an army, but every man and bow and horse, every morsel of food we could strip from them, counted as something gained. But never once did they break formation to follow us into the hills, where we should have had them at disadvantage. Edward's will ruled them all, and Edward was not to be trapped into any rash act, his plans were made and he adhered to them.

Thus we accompanied the royal army almost to Chester, where they arrived about the tenth day of June, and then we drew off and left them, rejoining David in Hope. He had had fighting, too, in advance of the king's coming, for Reginald de Grey had sent out a strong company under one of his bannerets to probe up the valley of the Dee and establish a forward post some miles south of the city, and though the Welsh had contested the attempt and cost them heavy losses, Grey had reinforced the camp, and David had not been able to dislodge him.

'He is already thinking he can cut me off here,' he said, 'and so he might, if I had any intention of staying here to fall into his hands. Hope has served its purpose. In a few days I think we must give it to him – what's left of it!'

Three days we spent dismantling the defences, breaching the walls, undermining the towers, and the broken masonry and rubble we emptied into the two castle wells until they were filled up and useless. What David did to his well-loved fortress cost the English two months' delay, and a great sum to repair. When it was done, and the whole site desolate, we drew off into the hills to westward. We were there keeping guard when Grey himself rode into the shattered shell, and appointed a constable with a strong garrison under him. By our count he left there more than thirty horse, and about the same number of crossbowmen, with a great number, we guessed at more than a thousand, longbowmen. We saw the reason for such immense numbers when they began to bring in scores of labourers, carpenters and foresters, and set to work frantically on trying to clear the first well, and fetch down a tower that had been left perilously leaning. The archers were deployed all round the site to protect the workmen.

'A pity,' said Llewelyn, 'if they should be disappointed since it seems they expect to be attacked. And a pity if they should begin to feel safe, and remove all those good bowmen to be used elsewhere.'

'Archers are useless by night,' said David, 'and there'll be no moon. And I have men here who know every way into Hope, and every way out, dark or light.'

Then some of his following proposed to test the new garrison that very night, and Llewelyn approved, for clearly if so many archers could be pinned down in this first capture, and prevent a further advance, or delay it for some weeks, it would be of the greatest service to us. There was ample cover in the hills around, small companies left to fend for themselves here and harry the repair work could easily lose any pursuit, even supposing the constable would countenance so rash a move, and could as easily be provisioned from the west, and rested at need. But he did not realise, until we missed David and looked for him in vain about the camp, that he had himself slipped away with his men to lead the foray.

He came back to us three hours later, smelling of smoke and leaving an ominous red glow far behind him in the ruins of Hope. His teeth gleamed like ivory in a soiled face and there was blood on him, but not his own. Every one of his men came back with him, none bearing more than a scratch to show for the venture, and David was brought up sharply by Llewelyn's furious reproach.

'Had you leave for any such folly, you who undertook this war in the name of Wales? It's easy to be daring, any fool boy can risk his head, but you are carrying the heads of all those you've committed to a life and death fight, and you may not indulge your vanity. Guard the life of every man who follows you, yes, as far as care can be carried, but guard your own for the sake of those who depend on you.'

I looked for a hot reply, or a haughty, dutiful, formal submission such as David had flaunted like an arrogant banner aforetime. But after a moment's shocked silence he stooped his head and kissed his brother's hand, so candidly and lightly that it passed for graceful penitence generously given, rather than a vassal's acknowledgement of rebuke.

'That was just,' he said. 'Very well, agreed, an end to childish games. I promise you I'll leave this to others now. But it was well worth the testing. That fire you see down there in the shell is their store of grain, and all the cords and some of the timber they've brought in for the work. And if they stop up the hole by which we got in undetected this time, there are some of us know of others. So spare to rend me!'

And he set to work, unchastened, to select a company of good, sound men, familiar with all the country round Hope as well as the castle itself, to remain behind when we withdrew to Denbigh, and by whatever means they found, to delay the repair of the defences, and so pin down all those archers in a constant alert. And an excellent job they made of it. Though Grey brought up as many as seven hundred woodmen, more than three hundred carpenters and forty stone-masons to the work, and kept about a thousand bowmen throughout to protect them, it took them until the end of August to clear out the wells and restore the walls, to

715

make Hope a habitable base for an army's next move.

The day following David's raid, the princes with their body-guards withdrew to Denbigh.

We had not been an hour inside the wards, barely time for David to kiss his wife and shed his mail, when there was a commotion of someone riding in at the gates in great haste, and clamouring for the prince of Wales. Llewelyn was just crossing the inner ward to the hall, and turned at the cry. A young page on a blown and trembling horse, and himself streaked with sweat and dust from a hard ride, fell rather than alighted from his saddle, and flung himself at the prince's feet.

'My lord, my lord, pardon the bringer of ill news! Pardon!' he said, panting, and began to sob, with the hem of the prince's tunic pressed to his face.

'Child!' said Llewelyn, startled and dismayed, and bent to take him by the arms and raise him, but the boy clung and wept. 'What is it?' demanded Llewelyn in quick alarm, and the mild wonder dashed from his face. 'Speak up! Tell truth, and you cannot be at fault. What has happened?'

'My lord, I'm sent from Aber to fetch you. Come, come as quickly as you can! The princess . . .' He choked and swallowed.

Llewelyn gripped and snatched him to his feet, and jerked up the boy's streaming face to stare into the drowned despair of his eyes. 'The princess! What has befallen her?' Such grief threatened the worst of terrors. '*She is not dead?*' he cried.

'No, no, not dead, but very sick . . . and growing weak . . . Two days in labour, and still no birth! Oh, my lord,' he wailed, 'they are afraid for her, we are all afraid!'

Llewelyn took his hands from him so abruptly that the child almost fell, and whirled towards the stables, and David, who had come out from the hall at the sound of the messenger galloping in, met and caught his brother in his arm, aghast at the sight of his face. 'What is it? What ails you?'

'Eleanor!' said the prince. 'You must manage here alone. I must go to my wife. Two days in labour, and no child – a bad birth . . . Let me go!'

'Oh, God!' said David, stricken, and followed him into the stables, and I went after. Even if my lord had bidden me to stay, I would not have let him ride alone. 'No, it cannot be so grave,' said David feverishly. 'She has been so well, she's so mistress of everything she touches, how can she fail even at this? It will be well, you'll see! It will end with a son in her arms, and she in yours. But take my Saracen, he's fresh and fast . . .'

It was David who shook and stammered, Llewelyn was steady and silent. He put aside, not roughly, the groom who fumbled in his agitation, and himself saddled the horse, David's tall English horse that was Edward's gift, with sure, rapid hands. When I also saddled up beside him, he met my eyes briefly, not refusing me though he had no part of him left then to welcome me, he was so far flown already on the road to her. We led out the horses, and he kissed David, and said he would come back when he could. And when the boy who had brought the news came

716

creeping, smudged with tears, to hold his stirrup, frantic for some look or touch of comfort, he looked down at him as though with astonished recognition, and then compunction, and laid his palm with brusque gentleness against the boy's cheek.

'Take your earned rest,' he said, 'and follow me home tomorrow. And leave grieving, rather pray.'

In this manner, in mourne silence and leaving mourne silence behind us, we galloped out of Denbigh to attend the birth of the prince's first and only child.

They were watching for us on both roads, by the coast and by the upland track over the hills from Caerhun, which is the shorter way. It was late afternoon when we left Denbigh, but barely dusk when we came over the last ridge by the old Roman road, and dropped into the head of the wooded valley that winds down to Aber. I doubt if that ten-league distance was ever covered faster. The watchman on the hills signalled our approach to the watchman on the wall below, there was sun enough yet to catch the red and white flutter of his pennant and the steel of his lance. When we passed at a gallop he saluted us and fell in at our heels, and thus heralded and escorted we came down to the long wall of the maenol and the village under it.

All that way he had not uttered one word to me, intent only on reaching her side as soon as he might. Nor had we any need of words, or, God knows, any matter for speech, being both in dread and doubt and hope so alike that I had nothing to offer him, and he nothing to ask of me. We rode towards her, and that was all we had mind or will for then. And prayed every mile of the way, as he had bidden the wretched boy to pray.

There was no comfort to be found in any face that met us, though in every one was a desperate, heartfelt welcome. The guards at the gates opened for us before we drew near, and their eyes strained for our approach and followed after our passing. The grooms in the outer ward ran to take our bridles, and they had the same look, fearful of a word, a sound, a breath, that might tip the balance between life and death. So we knew what awaited us, even before the castellan came running out of the hall to greet his lord, and Llewelyn cried out to him: 'The princess?' and all he could get out from a faltering throat was: 'Living!' There was nothing better than that to be said.

Llewelyn leaped from the saddle and went in through the hall, and I after him, and all the menservants and maidservants of the household, creeping wretchedly about their business, stood stock-still before him, and made their reverences as he passed with the same dazed and unbelieving eyes, many of the women smudging away tears. There had been little sound before we entered, only subdued voices and few words, but as we passed there was silence. Llewelyn clove through the midst as though he saw none of them, and had almost reached the door of the high chamber when it opened, and one of Eleanor's women came out. It was Alice, the older of those two who had been prisoners with the princess after their voyage from France, and felt her to be in a special way theirs. At sight of her Llewelyn halted abruptly at gaze, for she had a shawl-wrapped bundle in her arms.

'It is come, then?' he said in a whisper, drawing careful breath of hope. Her face was white and tired, and her hair awry, as though she had not

717

slept at all since her lady's labour began. She said tremulously: 'Four hours ago. The lord prince has a daughter. She is whole and fine . . .'

She leaned to hold out the child to him, and turn back the shawl from its face, but he never glanced down.

'Then the worst is past?' he said, hoping and dreading. 'Eleanor . . .?'

She turned her head aside, and the tears came slowly rolling from under her closed lids, and for the weight and burning of them she could not speak. But without words she turned and went before him to the tower stairway. By the time we had climbed to the level of the guard-walk on the wall she had her voice again, though it struggled through aching grief.

'We made the bed for her lying-in not in the great bedchamber, but in the room with a door on to the wall. It was so hot and dark and airless within, she was better there. She loves the sun.' Her tears fell on the child's shawl. 'Oh, my lord, it has been cruel! She is torn – she has lost so much blood . . .'

I think he knew then that Alice, at least, had no hope, that her tears were already tears of mourning. He put her aside gently at the door, and went in.

There were four of them about the bed, the prince's physician, the chaplain, and two of her women, and all of them turned their eyes upon him as he entered. In every face there was the same helplessness and resignation. They drew back from the bed as he drew near, and left her to him.

She lay under only a light linen cover, for it was indeed the height of a very hot summer. Her hands were spread upon the linen at her sides, transparent, bluish white, like broken lilies. Her hair was unbraided, for a braid might have caused her discomfort, and for the sake of coolness they had drawn it up from under her neck, and spread it back in a great aureole over a wide pillow. The very perfection of the halo, strand drawn out evenly by strand, showed that for some long time she had not moved her head. All that lustrous dark gold, darker than usual with the sweat of her anguish but radiant and vivid still, sprang aloft from a broad brow and smooth temples no longer of ivory, but alabaster, so crystal-clear that what blood she still had in her gleamed through in the softest of blues, like the tracery of veins in the petals of an anemone. Her closed eyelids – I had never before seen her so – had the same delicate texture, large, domed eyelids to cover great, candid eyes. Her mouth was folded firmly, like a budding rose, but a white rose, even the shadows that shaped it rather blue than rosy. Her cheeks were fallen and silver-white, her body under the linen cover lay straight and slight and frail, and so still that she might have been the carven woman she seemed, but for the dew of exhaustion and pain on her lips and her forehead, and the faint, slow rise and fall of her breast. If this was life, she still lived, and they had told us truth. But it was such life that to touch or breathe upon it would destroy it. Everyone in that room moved with slow and careful stealth, avoiding sound, for fear she should be startled through the doorway in which she hovered.

Llewelyn went on his knees beside the brychan, and leaned and gazed at her in silence, hardly breathing. The old doctor came creeping to his shoulder and whispered brokenly in his ear, as if he fended off blame for her condition.

'A bad birth, a difficult birth . . . The child lay awry. We have stopped the bleeding now, but it went on so long . . .'

'And such pain!' whispered Alice, crouched on a stool with the child in her lap. 'Day and night such pain, and never any respite, and hardly a moan out of her . . . But now she's worn out, she has no strength left.'

The chaplain said, as was his duty: 'She has received her saviour. I thought it needful.'

Llewelyn was still, watching the shallow rise and fall of her breast over the most gallant and generous heart that ever beat in a woman's body, and he never turned his head, though I think he heard all. Presently he said in a low voice: 'Leave us alone with her. If I need you – if she needs you – Samson shall call you.' And then for a moment, as in a distant dream, he bethought him of the child, and asked: 'There is a nurse? The little one is provided for?'

Alice said yes, the tears still coursing slowly from under her eyelids.

'Then leave us. One of you may sleep in the next room, in case of need. I shall watch with her through the night.'

They went away softly and closed the door after them. I asked if I, too, should wait without. He put his hands over his face for a moment, pressing hard as if to quicken tissues grown old, weary and stiff. 'No,' he said, 'stay with me. Stay with us! You knew her before ever I did, you first showed her to my soul's eyes. To no other but you can I uncover my heart now, and no other can I bear to have by, if she leaves me in the night without word or look. You need say nothing, but be with us. If God wants her, God will take her, but I can fight for her still. There were some in the old times, I have heard, wrestled with angels.'

On a table by the wall they had left a pitcher of red wine, and a bowl of cool, scented water, and soft cloths, and a little oil-lamp with a floating wick, that gave a dim, mellow light. He rose, and opened wide the door that gave upon the guard-walk, for even the night was hot. The sky was full of waking stars, and the air smelled fresh and sharp, of the salt marshes, and the sea. Then he came back to the bed, and remained on his knees beside her, looking earnestly into her face.

The trance in which she lay was not quite sleep, and not quite unconsciousness. Sometimes her lashes trembled, and seemed about to rise from the sunken cheeks, and then were still again. Once her lips quivered and curved, as though to speak, or smile, or kiss. But so white, so white, no blood in her, a spirit, not a body.

He took one of her wasted hands between his own, and caressed it. He bathed the sweat of weakness and fever from her lip and her brow as it formed, and drew back every strand of hair that seamed the smoothness of her neck. And time and again he spoke to her, laying his cheek beside her on the pillow, on the spread riches of her hair, whispering the endearments he kept for their bed. All night long he called her back to him from the perilous place where she stood hesitating whether to go or stay. But doubtless there was another voice calling her away.

Whether it was his caresses that reached her, or whether the change in the light penetrated her dreamless withdrawal, in the dove-grey of dawn before the sun rose I saw her lips move and part, and her brows draw together, and then she drew deeper breath, and when he leaned over her and said her name she opened her eyes, but so slowly, as if the weight of the world hung on her lids. In the dimness of the room her eyes looked dark, but as they clung to the face that bent so close to hers, they, summoned a gradual radiance from within, and the clear gold lights came back into them. She knew him. She had no strength to move or speak but even in its pallor her face grew marvellously bright, and when he stooped his head and kissed her with careful tenderness on the mouth, her lips answered him as best they could.

He bathed her face with the scented water, and with the tip of his finger moistened her lips with wine, but for wine she made no effort, all the life she had left she poured towards him with her eyes. And as he ministered he spoke to her, patient and soft, calling her by the secret names he had for her, telling her that her daughter was whole and perfect and well-cherished, and that she need trouble for nothing but to rest and grow strong, and think of nothing but that she was loved, and that while she needed him he would never again leave her. And all the ways in which he loved her, and all the beauties he loved in her, he told over one by one, he who was so inexpert with words. There was never any of his bards made so sweet and desperate a song as he did for her, to hold her spellbound from taking the last step away from him. But I think he knew then that she had only paused a moment for love of him, to listen from very far off, hanging back on the hand that led her.

Lying as it does in a cleft of the northern hills, with the great mountain mass of Penmaenmawr to the east, Moel Wnion to the west, and Foel-Fras to the south, the morning sun never enters Aber. But to look out at dawn to the north, over the narrow salt marshes to Lavan sands and the sea, that is wonderful. The deepening light, first tinted like the feathers of doves, then flushing into rose, then glowing like amber, comes sweeping westward from Conway over the sea, to strike in a glitter of foam and sand on the distant coast of Anglesey across the strait from us, as if a golden tide had surged across the sea-green tide, and flooded the visible world with light. That was such a morning. The only time that Eleanor's eyes left Llewelyn's face was to gaze at the morsel of sky seen through the open doorway, and he divined the last thirst that troubled her, she who loved the sun. If he could not take her where it would shine upon her, at least she might still look upon its beauty from the shadows.

He sat down beside her on the edge of the brychan, and lifted her against his shoulder, and carefully gathering the blankets of the bed about her, took her up in his arms. She made no sign or sound of pain, but only a soft sigh, and with his cheek pressed steadyingly against her hair he carried her out on to the guard-walk, and the few yards round the stony bulk of the tower to the northern parapet, and stood cradling her as the sun rose, their faces turned towards the sea.

There in the open the air was sweet and cool, and below us, beyond the shore road, the reeds and grasses of the marsh stood erect like small, bright lances, every one separate, going down in lush, tufted waves to where the sands began, with a great exultation of sea-birds filling the air above. The level sunrays made all the surface of the strait a dance of fireflies, but beneath the glitter the deeps shone green as emeralds, and darker blue in the centre, and the shallows where the sands showed through were the colour of ripening wheat. Along the horizon ran the purple line of the coast of Anglesey, and in the centre of that distant shore was the Franciscan friary of Llanfaes, the burying-place of the princesses of Gwynedd. In the morning light it appeared as the distant harbour of desire, absolute in beauty and peace.

She lay content in his arms and on his heart, her cheek against his cheek, and her eyes drew light from the picture on which she gazed, and grew so wide and wise in their hazel-gold that there was a moment when I believed he had won the battle. He knew better. Very still he stood, not to jar or hurt her, and softly still he spoke, of Wales, that she had taken to her heart and that loved her in return, and of a future when there would be no need of war, when this land would be free and united and honourable among the countries of Christendom, and kings and princes would pledge peace and keep it, and her child's children, the descendants of Earl Simon, would walk at large as heroes among their own people, and equals among the monarchs of the world.

Her lips moved, soundlessly, saying: 'Yes!' It was right that she should take her leave of the world, as she had greeted it in passing, with a cry of affirmation.

The sun was just clear of the horizon, and the sky to eastward the colour of primroses, and to westward of cornflowers, when the faintest of tremors passed through her body, and her head turned slightly upon his shoulder, her lips straining to his cheek. One word she said, and this time not silently shaping it, yet on so feeble a breath that neither he nor I could have caught it but for the great silence in which we stood. But hear it I did, and so did he. We never spoke of it, but I know.

'Cariad!' she said, and her breath caught and halted long, gently began again, and again sank into stillness.

He held her for a great while after that, but there was no more sound, and no more movement, and that was all her message to him. She did not leave him without saying farewell. Yes! Cariad!

When he was quite sure that it was a dead woman he held on his heart, he carried her in and laid her upon the bed, and with steady hands smoothed her hair again over the pillow, and crossed the frail hands on her breast. Gently he drew down the lace-veined eyelids over her eyes, and held them a while with reverent fingers. After he had kissed her brow, and signed her with a cross, he turned at last to me.

'Call the women,' he said. 'She has no more need of me.'

When he went out alone from the chamber where she lay, his face was a better likeness of death than hers.

CHAPTER VII

He made no outcry, abandoned no duty, himself directed all the sorrowful business of her funeral rites. He spoke with man and woman, high and low, as courteously and directly as always, was short with carelessness, patient with honest weakness, gentle with the timid. And all with that face of stone. He did not sleep until nightfall, but when he had done all that remained to do and fell to his lot, then he shut himself alone into the chapel, and there remained until darkness.

When he came forth, at least his face lived again, had eyes bruised and cavernous, but alive, and though he kept his grief withdrawn and apart, some portion of his senses and affections moved among us again, for he had accepted what could not be resisted. First he asked for the child, and Alice brought her and laid her beside him in her carved cradle, sleeping. A big infant she was, with long, fine bones, the crumpled face of all new human creatures, and a fuzz of russet-brown hair like her father's. But when Llewelyn edged a finger-tip into one tiny fist, and she gripped it firmly and opened her eyes, they were wide and hazel, flecked with green-gold, Eleanor's eyes. He looked upon her long and wonderingly, and could not love her yet, I think, not because he held her mother's death against her, but because so small and unfamiliar a being had no reality for him, and he had not David's easy gift of approaching even day-old infants with assurance. But he felt a heavy, protective tenderness at sight of such helplessness and smallness, and at the thought that she had lost as heavily as he had, for her mother was dead, and she had none but him left, as he had none but her. But at least for her he could be at rest, she slept and fed and thrived.

Having assured himself that all was well with the little one, and given orders for the morrow, he slept at last. And in the morning he called me to him, and had me stay at his side thereafter. I was with him when he went to look his last upon Eleanor in her coffin, before they covered her. With her hair braided and a golden gown upon her, she was beautiful still, but far beyond our reach. He kissed her brow and her lips, and I kissed the cold hands folded on her breast. There was none other with us.

'Thirteen years I waited for her,' he said, looking down upon her still face, 'and less than four years I have had her, and I suppose that was reward beyond my deserts. Now for me, as a man, there is nothing left to lose, what is there Edward or any other man can do to me that I cannot laugh to scorn? In the world's eyes my honour is gone, and now my love is gone, and there is no reason I should regard my life a day longer. That and all else I will throw into this war I never wanted. For now I want it! With all my soul and strength I will wage it to the end, and the kingdom I

722

could not lay at her feet I will build to be her memorial, God willing. And if I fail, another will succeed, building higher on what I have built. This child may bear the sons my dear love was not permitted to bear. Who am I to say when God's truth and justice will come to fruit? With what is left of my life I will fight for it, and leave the outcome to God.'

We buried Eleanor de Montfort, princess of Wales, in the friary of Llanfaes, in the heart of June, when all things were blossoming and ripening for fruit, and the days so fair the heart ached for their beauty, and more for the beauty that was rapt away in its Junetide. We carried her in solemn procession from Aber across the salt marshes, and rowed her from Lavan sands over the strait, and laid her beside Joan, lady of Wales aforetime, daughter to King John and wife to Llewelyn Fawr, my lord's grandsire. There her mortal part rests until the judgment, but surely her soul is gone like the flight of a lark, singing into the world of light. It is for ourselves we grieve.

At night in hall the bards made music in her honour, lamenting the rose of the world fallen untimely to a killing frost, praising her as the noble daughter of a noble sire, as indeed she was, and prophesying the gift of her beauty and goodness to her own child in the days to come. And he sat erect and grave through all, and did all that was required of him that day, taking pains to make all necessary dispositions for the care of his little daughter.

He named her Gwenllian, for it was a name in which Eleanor had found a pleasing music.

The next day we rode for Denbigh to rejoin David.

I knew, yet could not feel until we turned our faces again to the war, how changed was the world for Llewelyn and for me. When we had put Aber behind us, with all its denizens going about their daily business, and very properly so, then I understood how light my lord's life was now to him, and yet how precious it might be to the cause he championed. It was the only passion left to him, and since a live man must go on living for his honour's sake, what could he do better than cast the whole weight of his powers, his gallantry, his strength of will and quality of mind, into the battle for his sole remaining love?

As for all that great household we left behind, for them it was very different. Death comes and goes about the world, and plucks full-blown blossom and withered stalk and dewy bud indifferently, and those who remain mourn, yet even in mourning must be about the business of burial and worship and legal settlement, and by the time that is done the great rent in their lives is already partially stitched up, and soon quite healed, since the living have little choice but to live. So those good women in Aber wept for Eleanor, whom they had deeply loved, and wept longer than most mourners do, but they had also work to do, and the child to tend, and other affections of their own to cherish, and the great void that lady had left in dying must heal gradually until it vanished quite, but for a kind of sweet sadness that would now and again set one or other of the women saying: 'Do you remember . . .?' And remember they

723

would, every one. But time goes on, and memories have to wait for the leisure moments.

But for him nothing would ever again be the same, though life claimed its due, and he did not merely continue living, but lived at a fiercer heat than before, spent himself more vehemently, ventured his weal more rashly. The wound he bore would never be healed in this world, and the void in his heart never filled, and even Wales was to him from that day a changed worship, less reasoned, more devouring, a fire lit in her honour. There was no other way left for him to exalt her name and celebrate her memory, but in the exaltation and celebration of Wales.

We made almost as good speed back to Denbigh as we had on the way from it, the urgency of action beckoning us before, and too bitter and grievous memory galloping hard on our heels. If the prince could overtake the one, perhaps he could also outrun the other. From the day that she was taken from him he drove thus without pause, his eyes fixed always upon the war.

When we cantered up through the town at Denbigh, and walked our horses up the steep ascent to the castle gatehouse, word of our coming ran before us. By the time we entered the outer ward David was plunging out to meet us, with Tudor at his back, and a dozen more of his own captains and Llewelyn's hovering, and all with searching eyes and wary faces, peering for the omens in the prince's countenance. David waved the hurrying groom aside, and himself held his brother's bridle and stirrup. With drawn brows he peered up into Llewelyn's face, and waited for a voluntary word, but the prince lighted down in silence, and in silence kissed him. David held him by the shoulder, searching close.

'Well? What news? How is it with your wife?' Surely by then he knew, but there was no keeping the silence for ever. Elizabeth was out on the steps of the hall, anxiously watching them.

'She is dead,' said Llewelyn, ' and I have buried her.'

'Oh, God!' said David in a whisper, and clung hard when his brother would have put him by and walked on. 'The boy did warn us! But she was in such blossoming health, I could not believe it would go badly. Oh, brother, I am sorry!'

What is there to be said? Every day there is someone, somewhere, to whom the same words have to be offered, and I suppose they serve the same purpose as the words of the burial rites, a kind of incantation reconciling man to man, and man to his fate. It is hard to find any other form.

'She was beautiful and generous and brave!' said David in a sudden helpless rage. 'How can God justify it? Even men do not tear out flowers for sport! Oh, Llewelyn, I so grieve for you!'

'I know,' said Llewelyn, bearing with him at some cost, for with him all the words were spent, and even the best at little value. 'I know, you need say nothing. I take your grief as it is given, and am grateful. She is gone. It's over.'

Elizabeth was at his side then, the little thing so prolific and so joyous, teeming like the earth and with as slight effort. Great piteous eyes she fixed upon him, and said, true to her nature: 'And the child? The child lives, and is thriving?'

At her he looked with seeing eyes, and even smiled, for she had that singleness and innocence that spoke closely to his heart. 'I have a fine daughter,' he said, 'with eyes like her mother's eyes. Yes, she thrives, she will be beautiful.'

'Poor motherless babe!' said Elizabeth with starting tears. 'If ever it is needful, I would take her with mine, one more would be no burden, and here she has close and loving kin.'

He said that Gwenllian could have no better mother than the mother of all her cousins, wanting her own, but that he dared not for his life take her from Alice and Marion and their waiting-women, who had lost one princess and could not be robbed of a second. And Elizabeth wept, and embraced him, and said he was right to regard their grief, for it must be great indeed. And David looked upon her as she spoke, with eyes fixed and hungry, as though he had but now been taught that worshipped wives can die, and husbands can be left desolate.

Llewelyn, for his part, suffered them as then he suffered all, patient under sympathy which could change nothing, and indignation which could restore him nothing, but with his eyes for ever fixed upon the only passion he had left, and that consecrated to her memory. And as soon as he could he turned Elizabeth aside to her own cares, and shook all the womenfolk bustling in her train, and turned upon David and Tudor, and the captains and commanders who waited apart to know his will.

'I have been absent more than three days,' he said, 'and much may have happened without my knowledge. Call such of the council as we have at hand. I want full reports from every part. We have struck for a country, and we have a country to keep.'

Thus plainly but without emphasis he made clear to us all that he had returned to take upon himself the whole burden of his principality, that this war which had been forced upon him against his will was now irrevocably his war, a national war, and to him as the prince of this nation belonged the supreme command of it. And that 'we' he had uttered, though by it he meant to include his brother and all those like-minded in the fight, was nonetheless royal.

'At your orders, every man of us,' said David, and went with Tudor to do his bidding.

That afternoon he presided over the council, and David presented him the report of all that had happened in his absence.

'There is indeed news,' he said, 'of the greatest importance, brought in two days ago, and sent here to Denbigh, naturally, in the belief that it would find you here in person. If I was wrong in not sending it after you to Aber, pardon me the error. I knew it would keep, for it is good news, not bad. All through May and into this month, Gloucester has been building up his forces in the south, in Carmarthen and Dynevor, with orders to reconquer Llandovery and establish Giffard there again, and put the English settlers back into the country round Llanbadarn. They've had no success. A few raids, and some looting, but very little gained. Our people there have held off from pitched battle, rightly, and avoided losses, and struck back wherever they could, staying mainly in the hills and forests. So to the main matter. About the tenth of this month

Gloucester sent out a large force from Dynevor to raid towards Carreg Cennen, which they did for some days, and took a great deal of plunder along the valley, but on the way back to Dynevor our nephews on the one side and their allies on the other fell upon them unexpectedly at Llandeilo, and broke them utterly. A great victory, and a great slaughter, and all that booty regained. William of Valence has lost his son there, and a number of knights were killed with him. And if Gloucester has not lost his command, he has his reputation. We have good reason to be pleased, this clash has set him back two months or more.'

'How great,' asked Llewelyn, 'was this force?'

'Rhys Wyndod reckons at least fifteen hundred foot, and maybe a hundred horse, counting Gloucester's own retinue and that of Valence. They left a garrison of fifty or so and a gang of labourers in the shell of Carreg Cennen, as if they meant to repair it and occupy it as a fortress again, but now they'll be hard put to it even to get their men out, much less reinforce them. Rhys can pick them off at leisure.'

It was indeed a victory, and promised a respite of some weeks at least. Llewelyn burned, hearing it. 'That can also give us breathing space here. They'll not move a man from the south to add to the Chester army, far more likely to send some of the next levies into Ystrad Tywi, and try and hold the position there. Good! Rhys Wyndod and his brothers have done well by us. And what goes forward at Hope?'

'Very little, and very slowly. The companies we left there cannot delay the rebuilding indefinitely, but they are making it slow and costly. I have an eye,' said David, 'to Hawarden also, for I doubt if that can be held, once Edward gets into motion, but I'll hold it as long as I may. The king has made no move from Chester so far.'

'He will not move,' said the prince with certainty, 'until he gets his ships round Wales and lying off-shore in the Dee. In any case he needs the time. With the numbers he has to feed, and the distance he hopes to take them, he cannot yet have amassed half enough stores of food or arms, or made sure of his lines of transport. He'll be doubly careful of his organisation this time. There's no word yet of the ships being sighted at sea?'

'We may not sight them until they near Lleyn,' said Tudor, 'but there we shall certainly get news. I doubt if his first fleet is out of the Channel yet.'

'Edward will follow his old way,' said Llewelyn, 'by the new roads to Flint, and so to Rhuddlan. I doubt if we should put ourselves in his way before Flint, but we'll make him pay dear for the miles to Rhuddlan. But since he has the sea, in the end we cannot halt his advance, we can only pin him to the coast. How long have we? Five weeks – six? – before there'll be any action here in the north?'

David reasoned that it would take five weeks at least before the king was ready to attempt anything more than moving up to his two advanced bases, for it would take him all that time to ensure his commisariat and his supply lines, and have his ships at hand.

'And we have all our men in arms and ready,' said Llewelyn, 'and no prospect for that time of much work for them here. It is not good policy, once Welshmen are roused, to keep them waiting in idleness, their fires burn down if they are not fed. I think we may well make good use of those five or six weeks. If the south is in this disarray, Gloucester discredited, a new commander not yet appointed, and the troops disheartened after Llandeilo, we could do them further hurt while they're shaken, and make sure none of them can be spared to join Edward here. If we can force him to pour in more men in the south, so much the better. They cannot be in two places at once.'

'Would you have me go back there?' asked David readily.

'No, your men of the Middle Country know this region best, and can best hold it if the pressure does begin. Gwynedd beyond Conway he will not reach yet, and if he does – before he does – we can be back with you in three days whenever you call us. I am going myself,' said Llewelyn.

His dispositions were made the same day, and those levies of Gwynedd that he proposed to take with him detailed. He had with him then only his own household guard and a small company of horse, and with the rest we mustered two days later at Bala, on our way south.

Cristin came to me in the armoury, the evening before we marched, and wished me godspeed and a safe return. I had not realised until then, being too much concerned with Llewelyn's weal and woe, that I had not laid eyes on Godred since we returned to Denbigh. She moved and spoke and looked with that eased freedom she had when he was absent.

'He's gone with one of David's patrols to Dinas Bran,' she said. 'They'll be prowling the borders and the Dee valley, you may even run into them on your way south if they happen to be upstream just now. But they'll be back here in a week or two. Dinas Bran is well garrisoned, and the local men are jealous of their privileges. David well understands the border Welsh. He has made himself their pattern, his reputation stands high with them. But I wish to God,' she said, suddenly vehement, 'he had been content to be a good husband and father, and let go even of Hope in the shire-court if he had to. Oh, Samson, I dread the ending! I've seen Edward, as you have, and watched how he works. When we were in England, under his protection, I got to know that monumental face. Where his sovereignty is touched, his supremacy challenged, there is no compassion there at all, no human kindness. Whoever presumes to have rights level with his, is traitor and blasphemer. God knows he cannot help it, God made him so! But *why*?'

I said that doubtless God had his reasons, who balanced all and apportioned all, but I saw by her face that she questioned whether the balance was always just or the apportioning equitable.

'He has his own land,' she said, 'why must he also grasp at everything within his reach? Oh, he preferred law to the sword, while he was allowed the choice, it costs him less and is just as effective, if slower. But sooner or later, I tell you truly, he would have begun to devour us, by one means or another. He is a gluttonous appetite, and nothing enclosed in the same seas with him will be safe from him in the end. So I am wrong to blame David for striking first. It would have come, whether he had held his hand or no. He may even have done Wales good service by forcing the issue now, before Edward was quite ready.'

I had been thinking much the same, and admitted it. And now there was nothing for us but to fight to the end with everything we had, and deserve victory, and if we could, wrest it from Edward and from God himself at whatever cost in our lives and souls.

'Do you know, Samson,' said Cristin, drawing close to me and raising to my face great eyes purple almost to blackness in the dim light within the armoury, 'what I have been thinking? It may well be a cowardly thought that I should put away, but it will not leave my mind. It is there every time I look at Elizabeth, or watch the children playing. In the grief I feel for your princess it mingles always, like a voice overriding grief. If we fail, she at least is safe. There is nothing Edward can do now to hurt Eleanor. She is with God, and out of his reach.'

On the way south to Bala we made a single night camp after we had crossed the Dee, for the weather was still so hot and fine that it was pleasure to lie out in open woods, above the grassy bank of a tributary stream that offered cool bathing after the heat of the day. The water came down clear and fast from the Berwyns, and the bracken on the slopes above was full green and half-furled, and the gorse in the gullies deepest gold. In the dusk I went some way along the waterside to stretch my legs after riding, and left all the sounds of the camp behind me.

I was thinking, none too happily, of all that Cristin had said, for there was that about her at times that reminded me of my mother, who had strange insights, and knew things the rest of us were not permitted to know. And it was true, and in my heart I knew it, that Edward's power, once roused, was far greater than anything we could muster, at least in arms and men and ships and horses, and against these weapons truth and justice seemed to carry but little weight. And still I feared the ancient enemy, bred from old loyalties and old customs that took no count of the idea of a nation. For we knew only too well that Edward had already issued the usual orders to his bailiffs and officers everywhere, to receive such of the Welsh as would come to the king's peace, and show them grace. When the fight became bitter and the way hard, many might well heed that offer. But this time there was a sinister change, for the offer of clemency applied only to the common people. For their leaders there was to be no such mercy. And to me it seemed that this was more than a mere matter of policy, to sift the genuineness of those captains who sued for grace, before granting it. No, it was the king's warning to us that this time he meant to sever the Welsh from their own princes and barons, and take them bodily into his own administration.

And like Cristin, I could not but feel it as a kind of victory that the princess, at least, was safe for ever, that Edward had not and never again would have any power to touch or trouble her. But never could I face that thought without feeling like a traitor to her, for when had she ever turned her back upon any of the battles and agonies of living, or thought it better to be in quietude and hide from the storm? She would rather have been here at Llewelyn's side if she could, and shared every danger that threatened him. What right had I to be grateful for the safety she would have rejected with contempt? Yes, even knowing Edward as Cristin knew him, and having no illusions concerning the malignant extremes of which he was capable?

Her death was back with me in all its bitterness as I stood by the little river, peering down into the eddies that span about its pebbly bed under the overhanging turf of the bank. The drier grass on the uplands beyond was thick and spongy, and the little knot of riders that passed along the ridge at some distance made no sound. It was not until one of them wheeled out of line and began to wind his way down the slope, and the jingle of his harness reached me, that I looked up.

There were four of them, in David's livery, riding the crest above the Dee on patrol from Dinas Bran. Three had kept their station on the ridge, and were walking their horses easily eastward towards the castle, and the fourth, leaning lightly back in the saddle, was turning his mount with casual pressure of his knees down the slope, towards the river-bank opposite where I stood. And the fourth was Godred.

It was so long since he had approached me of his own will that I was curious, and stood to watch his approach warily enough, but without animosity. Whether we would or not, we were comrades in arms. His eyes were on me, and he was grinning in that private way he had, as if only he knew and could savour the sour joke the world presented to view. The rein lay easy in his hand, only his knees guided his thickset pony down the rough descent. Godred rode well, and knew it.

'Well, well!' he said, checking the pony on the level turf across the water from me. 'It *is* you! I thought I should know that priestly tilt of the head. So those were the prince's turfed fires we saw downstream. They show, Samson, my friend, you'd be at an enemy's disposal with no better care than that.'

'With you between us and the border,' I said, 'what need have we to fear an enemy? Five leagues at least to Oswestry and the Berwyns in between, besides your good sword. No prince was ever safer.'

'Pleasant,' he said, idling along the edge of the water and eyeing me with that small curl of his mouth that was barely a smile, 'pleasant indeed to know you have such faith in me. And how did you leave Cristin, when you rode from Denbigh? In good spirits?'

'As good as the rest of us,' I said. 'We're none of us making merry.'

'Shame,' he said, 'that her best and truest friend should be forced to leave her, just when her husband's away. She'll be quiet and solitary without the both of us.' And his light, sweet voice turned sharp as gall, yet soft as silk, as it always did when he was casting for me as for a fish. And I marvelled, for this he had not ventured of late, I had thought because his hatred had taken a more extreme turn that found no pleasure in baiting me, but perhaps, after all, rather because he had some qualms as to its safety. For now the river was between us, and he licked his lips, savouring the steps by which he tested how far he could go.

'Hardly quiet or solitary,' I said, 'with eight children round her skirts and another nurseling on the way.' For Elizabeth was also with child, her normal and happiest state. And the first and last fruit of love had been the death of Eleanor! I was thinking only of that sorrow, still so large and heavy on my heart, and did not consider how he might take what I said to himself, and count it as a stab in return for those he dealt out, seeing his own son had been still-born. It was perhaps the only grief he ever felt that was not all on his own account, and I had not meant to revive it.

'Some can breed, and some cannot,' he said, showing his even teeth in a snarling smile. 'Like the prince, poor soul! I hear he's lost his wife, and got him a daughter. Well, there's always a grain of good in every evil. Take heart, Samson, there's room again in his confidence for another favourite now, your nose may be back in joint soon enough. Even room in his bedchamber for a little sweet music at nights!' He laughed, seeing me stiffen, for though he never believed the foulness he invented, nor used it upon any but me, and therefore I could let it go by me with little feeling but contempt, yet there was a bound set to what my heart could endure at this time from him or from any.

'Keep your tongue within your teeth,' I said, 'and drink your own poison. I am not now in the mood to listen to frogs croaking.'

'Oh, you take me wrongly,' he protested, still grinning. 'Who is more concerned for my prince's consolation and my friend's than I? If I cannot rejoice in the advancement of one close to me as a brother, I am a poor-spirited creature.' And he made a smooth, round gesture with his bridle-hand, to let what light remained gleam for a moment on the silver ring by which I had first known him for my blood-kin. 'And what better promotion than to your old intimacy? A pity about the lady, but at least, if she could not give him a son, he has got a daughter. If indeed it was he who got her!' said Godred, and giggled, a bloodcurdling sound. 'After so many years of celibacy, I tell you, Samson, there were some of us had doubts of him, more ways than one! And she so loving and anxious to oblige him with an heir. Do you know of any who may have lent her a little help in the business? But there, they say *you* were the one closer in her secrets than any other.'

I heard him through a roaring in my ears, and saw him through a red blistering darkness, and went lunging towards him half-blind, through icy coldness. When my eyes cleared, he was away in a long traverse up the steep hillside, his malignant laughter drifting back to me like the clatter of small, cracked bells, and I was thigh-deep in the river with my dagger out, the deepest stony gully of the bed before me, and the sudden cold of mountain water gnawing my bones to the marrow, even in the summer night.

I watched him go, no help for it, he was away to his fellows, and among them no doubt circumspect and clean-mouthed. But if I could have got my hands on him then, I should have killed him.

I said no word to any other, then or ever, of what lay only between Godred and me, and to tell truth, I was half ashamed of having let him get under my guard, even with so gross and unexpected a profanation, for whatever weapon he clutched at, I was his mark and no other. If he spat his slime upon names dearer to me than my own, it was not because he believed one word of what he alleged, or had any malevolent intent against them, but only because he knew all too well where my armour was penetrable. And after we mustered at Bala the next day, and moved south at speed, I put him out of my mind and out of my hatred, for he was safely left behind in the Middle Country, and for many weeks I was to see no more of him.

It was the prince's intent to make rapid contact with his most effective allies rather than harry the marcher lands as we went, for once we were securely based in Ystrad Tywi, and knew what forces we had to contend with in the three royal bases ringing that region, then we could expand our action to strike outwards as chance offered. So we wasted no time in crossing eastward to the central march to probe Mortimer's defences on the upper Severn, or Lestrange's at Builth, but from Bala swept south-west through Merioneth, and crossed the Dovey to join hands with Griffith and Cynan ap Meredith in Llanbadarn.

Those two princes had had their hands full, until the battle of Llandeilo, in resisting constant English attacks, meant to re-establish the foreign settlers who had been ousted from the region, and by the detailed account they gave us of the large scale of this settlement it seemed clear that the king had intended to turn the castle of Llanbadarn into such another centre of royalist power as Carmarthen in the south. But since Llandeilo the attacks had ceased, and the remaining English troops been withdrawn into the castles, where they were safe, and there was hardly a skirmish to be hoped for on their side of the Teifi.

The same situation we found as we moved through the western lands. Everywhere the English were shut up within their castles, and came out only very cautiously and briefly to try how hot their reception still might be. But everywhere Llewelyn gave grim warning that this would not long continue, and meant nothing more than a temporary lull, which we would do well to use by strengthening our own resources of men and supplies, for it was only a matter of time before Edward's reserves came into play. The date fixed for the massing of the feudal host was still a month away, the second day of August, and once that was reached the king would have immensely greater numbers at his disposal for the statutory period of service, and would certainly retain most of them at his wages afterwards, besides what he might recruit at pay from the marches and from France. We were quick to muster and quick to move, and they were methodical, cumbersome and slow, but like a heavy-armoured horseman on a barded horse, once in motion they were desperately hard to halt or withstand. So the prince warned, and was hard upon all complacence.

From Llanbadarn, seeing they were alert and well-found there, we turned inland, still moving south, and crossed the watershed to reach Llandovery, where Rhys Wyndod, eldest of the prince's three nephews, was again installed since he had recovered it from Giffard. Rhys, like his uncles, had suffered the delays and humiliations of English law over this same Llandovery, to which Giffard laid claim through his wife, and that case, like the prince's, had dragged on through plea after plea for three years, and died at the outbreak of war, when the king handed over to Giffard the custody of the castle and the commote, though he did not hold it long. Rhys had fought as doughtily for Welsh law as had Llewelyn himself, and with the same lack of success. For him, at least, arms had proved more effective than words.

He was a man then thirty-three years old, fair and tall like his father before him, and a good fighter when he was roused, though in the previous war, hard-pressed and ill-prepared, he had surrendered to the English, while his younger brothers fled to the north and continued to fight for their uncle. This time, as Rhys himself bluntly said, he had not only seen sufficient cause to steel him to fight to the end, there being nothing to gain by compromise if the English were determined to put an end to Welsh law, but also he had burned his boats to settle the matter, and was committed for life and liberty and all. Of Edward's clemency to Welsh chiefs who had once resisted him he entertained no hope whatever.

From him we learned how those royal forces remaining in Ystrad Tywi were disposed.

'They are on the defensive now,' he said, 'and hardly stirring out, for they have enough supplies for the men they carry, and they are surely waiting for reinforcements, and expecting them soon. So far as we can determine, they have about seventy paid lances left, and have split them between Cardigan and Dynevor. Since Llandeilo we've seen nothing of the earl of Gloucester, but we heard that his own tenants in the march, all the Welsh among them, are up in revolt, and so are Hereford's, so he may well have been withdrawn and told to go and set his own house in order. The whisper is he's lost his command, but we've heard nothing of a successor yet. They're hanging on by their teeth and waiting. As soon as the feudal levies come in, they'll get the men they want. I doubt if the king will even wait for the day of his muster, but send them their orders in advance to report here in Carmarthen instead of Rhuddlan.'

'Then we'd better be about giving him even more reason to spread them over the whole country,' said Llewelyn briskly, 'and prevent him from getting the numbers he needs to break Gwynedd.'

And so we did, all through July and into August. We left the castle of Dryslwyn alone, with the traitor Rhys ap Meredith and his half-English garrison within it, for it was strong, and would have needed siege engines to break into it. But we left him little else. We kept a close watch on Dynevor and Carmarthen, on the alert for any sallies they might make to replenish supplies, and when they did venture out we did our best to lure them further from their bases by exposing some pitifully small party of our own, but they had their orders, and were seldom to be drawn. Very rarely did we get to grips with them, and then but briefly, for they stayed very close to home.

During this month of July we lived most of the time wild. We had Llandovery as a convenient rallying-point for the exchange of news and plans, and from there covered not only the vale of Towey, but also began to move out and rattle the teeth of Humphrey de Bohun, earl of Hereford and constable of England, at Brecon and the countryside round it, and to harass Lestrange at Builth, for there the Welsh of the region were always heartily glad to rise against their English masters. We kept in touch also with Griffith and Cynan ap Meredith, and sent a flying company to their aid whenever they required it. But for the most part we had little fighting. They dared not move from their castles, and we knew them too strongly positioned there to try storming them.

It was not long before we got word who was to replace Gloucester as commander in the south. Early in July Edward appointed his uncle, William of Valence, earl of Pembroke, the eldest of King Henry's Poitevin half-brothers, who had come over, years ago, to make their fortunes by marriages with English heiresses. I saw him once at Oxford, a lean, black-bearded, imperious person, hot-tempered and proud, bitter in his opposition to Earl Simon's Provisions, and unscrupulous in the means by which he fought them. But give him his due, he was not a bad soldier. With his own household guard Valence had sufficient troops to be able to move between Carmarthen and Cardigan, and once he took out a large force, some hundreds on foot besides lances to raid along the Cardigan coast against Griffith ap Meredith's lands, and tried to reach Llanbadarn, apparently with the hope of reoccupying the shell of the castle, but we closed in from the hills to eastward, and hunted them back towards Cardigan. He got them back in good disciplined order, or his losses would have been greater.

From the north David duly sent us word by courier when there was anything to report.

'The king has brought his army and headquarters to Rhuddlan,' he wrote late in July, 'and has got his first ships in the estuary, twenty-eight of them began their fifteen days of duty service on the tenth of this month. Twelve more have joined them since, and two great galleys from the Cinque Ports, besides some coastal boats got locally. We have kept close watch on the dock at Rhuddlan, and seen boats taking off men and arms to the ships off-shore, and returning empty. I believe Edward is putting aboard large numbers of archers and crossbowmen to be used at sea, if needed, but certainly in some planned landing. No move as yet to show what his plans are. Nothing will happen until after his August muster. He is busy now making his supply lines safe. There's little more to tell, except that I have withdrawn from Hawarden, as I was bound to do once they moved from Chester. I left them the shell. Hope is still rebuilding, and the wells still unserviceable. When my position is threatened, you shall hear of it.'

With the beginning of August, and the mustering of the feudal host, things changed with our warfare in the south. English reinforcements began to arrive in great numbers, our scouts brought us word of detachments of men being fed in through Carmarthen, to which the English had easy access from the southern marcher lordships, and distributed also to Dynevor and Cardigan, so many of them that it seemed clear Edward had ordered all the tenants-in-chief of some large region of his realm to do their feudal service under Valence, instead of joining the royal army at Rhuddlan.

'It is a tribute,' said Llewelyr, 'after its fashion. David's load will be lighter at least by these.'

It was what we had expected and intended, but it meant that we were now facing great odds, and had to base our movements, after the old Welsh fashion, on the high hills which we knew better than did the enemy, and on the speed of our sudden raids into the valleys, and as sudden withdrawals. If they came out in strength, and used that strength intelligently, we had nothing to match it, and could not and should not meet them in pitched battle or attempt to prevent them from occupying land. But what we could do was take back what they had occupied, as soon as they reduced the forces that held it, as they must in order to use them elsewhere. And as long as we were able to continue this system of reclamation and cession, and keep our own numbers intact, we could and did prevent them from moving away a single company to add to the main army in the north. And so we contrived all through August.

There were among these levies of foot, especially those from the march of Gwent and other baronial lands, large numbers of what they called Welsh friendlies, soldiers who served for pay and took their living as it came. During that month of August we got more than one recruit from their ranks, and gained not merely an archer or a spear-man, but also some useful information about Valence's resources and plans. In the middle of the month a deserter from a raiding party out of Dynevor told us that the king himself had laid down the campaign Valence should undertake. He was to furnish an expedition to conquer all the lands of Meredith's sons in Cardigan, and hand them over to the traitor Rhys of Dryslwyn, who naturally was expected to supply part of the army to carry out the assignment.

So we were prepared for the expedition when it came, and knew that its first aim was to bring us to battle, on the way to invade the lands of Griffith and Cynan. We were equally determined to avoid such action, and when the force issued from Carmarthen we had scouts trailing them all the way, and kept our main forces to the hills and forests, never far from the enemy but never confronting him. The English moved in a body up the Towey valley as far as Llangadoc, where Rhys's division joined them, and thence Valence crossed over the uplands to the river Ystwyth, and marched his men down that valley to Llanbadarn. We kept pace with him most of the way, but little enough did he see of us, only our traces where an outpost of his camp was found wiped out at dawn and stripped of its arms, or a group of stragglers cut off and killed. We struck often enough to let him know that we were still there, and he dared not allow his precautions to flag, or dispose of any of his men. But we never emerged from cover to stray within reach of his archers, and he was too cautious to come after us into the forests. We had sent on word to Griffith and Cynan, and they were prepared to use the like tactics, avoiding encounters, denying the enemy all possible supplies on the way, and waiting for his passing.

The shell of Llanbadarn was that and nothing more when Valence came to it. No defenders were there to be fought, the place was derelict, and having no workmen with them, and no prospect of bringing them in sufficient numbers until the whole cantref was pacified, they did not bother to occupy it, but marched by and left it as it was. So this great march ended none too gloriously down the coast, joining hands with Daubeny's garrison at Cardigan, by which time it was into the first days of September, and the forty days of feudal service was over. Most of the horse were certainly taken into pay and remained after that time, but some of the foot soldiers were discharged.

For that month's work they had gained little, though it is true that Rhys ap Meredith did get hold of a part of the lands belonging to his loyal kinsmen, and the English helped him to retain them. Still, Valence must have been cautious in his report to the king, for a very large and powerful garrison was still maintained at Dynevor. All the chief castles along the march were in similar case, Builth, Radnor, Montgomery, Oswestry, all anxious to secure a strong enough grip on their own region to spare lances and foot-men to send to the king at Rhuddlan, but all compelled to retain their garrisons undiminished. It was what we had set out to do, and for more than two months we had done it. But we knew, every man of us, that we, for our part, had raised by now every man we could raise, and stood only to see our forces dwindle, if some hard-pressed vils and commotes lost heart and lent an ear to the royal offers of grace, while Edward's numbers had not yet reached their maximum, but could be expanded steadily as long as he had or could borrow the money to pay his mercenaries. In the matter of numbers and resources time was not on our side. As regards the weather, it might be in the end, but we dared not reply on it. His hate is such, Cynan had said of Edward, that neither snow nor frost will stop him. Put no trust in winter!

When we got back to Llandovery, it was the youngest of the prince's nephews, his namesake, who came out to greet us, and kissed his uncle's hand.

'My brothers are out towards Dynevor,' he said, 'with a patrol. Giffard is back in Ystrad Tywi, so we've heard, and with a strong following. He has the king's leave to take back this castle, and all he can capture of Iscennen. He had not ours! We are planning a warm welcome for him.'

'You may find me some office in that welcome,' said the prince. 'We've had very little action in this circuit we've made with Valence.'

'Very gladly we would,' said the boy, 'but I think there may be graver calls upon you than ours, my lord. There's a courier here for you from David. Yesterday he rode in, but knowing you were on your way back I held him here rather than send out after you. I think, from what he says of movements in the north, you may be needed at home.'

Llewelyn went in with him from the bustle of the courtyard to the dimness of the hall, and there the messenger from Gwynedd came to salute him and present his letter. We knew him, he was a trooper of David's household at Hope, until that fortress was slighted and abandoned to Reginald de Grey. Llewelyn asked him, before he broke the seal: 'What goes forward in the Middle Country?'

'My lord, the Lord David sent me out the same day our outposts down the valley sighted King Edward's army advancing up the Clwyd. I thought he would have moved by the coast towards Conway. So he did in the last war. I think he has grasped that he dare not move further west while the Lord David holds the Middle Country. I think he is moving to break that hold, so that he may not be taken on the flank, and cut off from Chester.'

'I judge as you do,' said Llewelyn. 'The king keeps a measure of respect for my brother's prowess, however well he hates him.' And he broke the seal of David's letter, and read the message, brief enough and eloquent in its brevity:

'Luke de Tany, under Edward's commission, has landed an army in Anglesey, with all the fleet, more than forty ships, to cover him. The harvest is burned, garnered or lost, God knows in what measure. The king is marching up the Clwyd. Grey is crossing westwards from Hope, it seems aiming at Ruthin. Suddenly everything is on the move. It is time. Come!'

We made for Denbigh the next day, setting out at dawn, and beyond Bala Llewelyn took fresh horses and rode ahead with a small company of lances, leaving his household troops and the foot soldiers under Tudor to follow at their best pace. The town, when we reached it, was full of soldiery, and their bustle had a dourness and purpose about it that spoke loud in our ears, besides the relative absence of women and children about the streets. David had pickets out on the edge of the town, and a double guard on the gatehouse, the guard-walk on the wall was manned at every turret and angle, and the armoury was ringing with activity. There were all the indications of a garrison braced to siege conditions. Llewelyn looked about him sharply at all his brother's provisions, but could not fault them.

David was up on the tower, and when the watch signalled our coming he would have started down to us, but Llewelyn waved him back, and we went up to join him. He was unarmed, there in his own castle, but the stripped and austere state he kept spoke of pressures that might have him in mail and on the move at any moment. He came to meet us on the guard-walk, his face intent and grave.

'I'm glad you're come,' he said when they had embraced, and stood together staring out to eastward. 'Our situation here is not yet bad, but it is bad enough, I own it. I will not pretend I have done all things well.'

From that vantage point there was no warfare to be seen, and no enemy, only in the distance to the east, in the riverside plain, a few threads of smoke from sources hidden from us by the undulations of the land between. Llewelyn saw the thin blue drifts rising and dissolving, and knew what they meant.

'Yes, they are there,' said David. 'They have not struck at us yet, they passed us by, keeping close to the river, in the low ground. He is not yet ready, and Denbigh will not be easy to storm. But Ruthin is lost. De Grey moved west from Hope, at the same time as Edward set off with his own army up the Clwyd towards us. I could not send help to Ruthin for fear of an attack here, but he did not attempt it. What he has done is string the whole valley with outposts, and pass us by to join Grey, cutting off all the allies we have east of Clwyd. Now Ruthin is gone, and this advanced line of ours is breached, and the rest may have to go after Ruthin.'

'I never supposed,' said Llewelyn without passion, 'that we could have held it for long. You have held it for three months, I cannot see how you could have done much more. What do you know of his forces now? And how disposed?'

'By our count, he can command as many as eight thousand foot, and above seven hundred and fifty mounted, now he has the feudal levies up.

And besides the longbowmen and crossbowmen distributed among his flanking armies and his ships, there's a large body of archers encamped with his own command at Rhuddlan. And see, this is how he has parted his forces.' He drew in the stone of the parapet with the sheath of his dagger, the long north-south gash of the Clywd, and the level stroke of the coastline crossing its mouth. 'His own army, the main force, here at Rhuddlan, and now patrolling the river valley. Here to eastward, working from Hope and drawing his supplies from Chester, de Grey. He has Ruthin now, and Owen Goch is with him. And here, moving into the valley of the upper Dee from Oswestry, the earl of Surrey has yet a third army, and is aiming at Dinas Bran, and with Ruthin gone, even if I had men to spare here, I doubt if we could get them to Dinas safely. They feed one another with men,' said David, 'according to where the need is, for they can all join hands. Edward has three ways in to the west, none of them easy, and please God we'll make them hard for him indeed, but none impossible, given enough men and horses and arms. By the Dee, by Ruthin, and by the coast. But he has not moved a step further west than Rhuddlan yet. He's wary of extending his line while we are still here on his flank. He wants us rolled back into Eryri before he ventures.'

'Yes,' said Llewelyn, 'he has learned. And what of Anglesey? You say they're already established there. Oh, small blame to you, how could there be? *I* neglected the need for power by sea, not you. How did they mount their landing force, and how far has it gone?'

'Edward began loading great store of crossbow quarrels and arrows into ships before the end of July, and putting archers aboard, as many as thirty in some of the ships. No secret where they were bound, but there was nothing I could do to prevent. Forty ships in all he had, to carry and cover his landing force, and we dared not even get within range of their longbows. All I could do was make sure that coast was well manned, both the mainland and the island, they have not won it cheaply. And I sent orders as soon as we saw what was in the wind, that the islanders should reap whatever part of the grain was ripe enough, and get it ashore to us. The rest they were to let stand as long as possible, and reap it as it fell ready, and fire it if the enemy landed before it was all in. Or if they could garner any of it and hide it there for their own use, that they could do.'

'Did they get any part of it ashore in time?' asked the prince, mindful of all the soldiers he had to feed if this should continue into a winter war. 'After so hot a summer, it could be well forward.'

'Yes, a part they did get in, and have sent us some and hidden some, for they knew there'd be no escape for them once the English landed. But the greater part remained. No help for it! Edward can judge how far forward a western harvest will be in a good season,' said David bitterly, 'as well as we. Before the end of August he put Luke de Tany in command, he that was seneschal of Gascony, and sent them off from Rhuddlan. They had a hard fight of it to get ashore, and still have to beat off constant raids, but once they had a landing-place cleared they've been able to ferry more men in, until they have a considerable army there. They have a tight hold on the southern coast of the island now, and on two-thirds of our corn, though some our people did burn in time. My men saw fires there.'

'If he's poured so many men into Anglesey,' said Llewelyn frowning, 'it is not simply to hold down the islanders or take the harvest. That army he means to use again, to come at us from the west and north while he moves in from the east. What has Tany been up to this past month, besides reaping what's left of our grain?'

'There's more to tell,' David owned. 'Too much by far! Edward has the dock at Rhuddlan ringed with archers thicker than reeds, but we've raided there as chance offered, and slipped spies in once or twice by night, and we have some idea of what's happening there. Ever since de Tany got his force ashore the ships have been coming and going daily, not only with arrows and crossbow quarrels, but with stranger goods. Timber and iron and nails and cords, and small boats, and with them great numbers of men who carry no arms and are not soldiers, but carpenters and labourers. All this month past they've been building a bridge of boats across the narrows, between Porthaethwy on the island and Bangor on the main, with forty ships and any number of coastal boats to protect the work and bring the materials in, and archers enough to keep us at a distance. If they have not touched land yet, they will any day now, the thing is all but complete. Edward has even detached some of the Cinque Ports ships and sent them home. He cannot afford to turn the south coast traders against him by disrupting their traffic for too long, and he has plenty of ships left, with his small craft, and may get more yet from France. I have that coast manned as strongly as I can spare the men for it. Nothing has been attempted yet. But I see it as clearly as you, he is holding this fourth army in reserve until he feels the time ripe to draw a noose about Snowdon from both sides.'

He eyed his brother darkly and steadily, unafraid even of those memories that separated them. 'I have much to learn,' he said, 'but I, too, am learning. It was like this, the last time? It's fitting that I should be made to understand the realities of war with Edward. It is less just that you should be made to suffer it over again.'

'Justice has little to say in the matter,' said Llewelyn, with that distant, absent gentleness that marked his dealings with difficult men since Eleanor left him desolate. 'Little to do with Edward's law, and less with his warfare. I don't complain of him – *we* began it. But his warfare is the logical end of his law, an extension of the same discipline. And both are loaded upon one side.'

I marvelled to see David smiling at him. A tight and rueful smile it was, but it had its own warmth, all one man could spare to give to another at that pass. 'If that "we" is a royal one,' he said, 'it is too generous, and I denounce it. And if it means we, you and I, it is still generous indeed, for *I* began it, I alone. And if I ever was in doubt of the gravity of what I did, I'm in no doubt now. We are stretched to the end of our reach, so far as men and weapons go. And he is only just beginning to get his armies into motion, and has fresh men still to come. Did you know he has got his first Gascons? No question, we have one of them prisoner, he lost his way in the marshes of the Elwy, and we picked him off for what he could tell. Not a great company, this first one, forty or so foot and sixteen mounted crossbowmen. But there'll be more. We have no such reserve to draw on.'

'We have ourselves,' said Llewelyn, 'and no one else can let us fall. But you are right to look the truth in the face, we can fight no other way but face-forward. I never thought you had gone into this war lightly. Do you think,' he said with the faintest of smiles, 'I did not notice the quietness in the wards below? You have already sent the children away, have you not?'

'The day I sent to you,' said David. 'This is no place for them now. And Elizabeth and the women, too, though it was no easy matter to get her to go.'

'Where have you put them?' asked the prince.

'In Dolwyddelan, but I've sent word since to move them on to Dolbadarn. I can think of no better and safer place. If ever Edward penetrates so far into the mountains we're all lost. When you came, I was weighing in my mind the chances of holding Denbigh, and to be honest, I don't rate them high. Now that Ruthin's gone, we're in danger of being outflanked, and I don't intend to be shut up here like a rat in a trap, to be starved out in the end. I cannot afford to lose my army here, when Snowdon itself may need every man of us before the end. If I must abandon Denbigh to Edward, I cannot even afford to leave my castellan a strong garrison. It's either withdraw all, and destroy the place after us, or else withdraw all but a few, a skeleton force, and let them stand out the siege as long as they can, to give us more time. A sorry choice! I do not like asking any man of mine to stay and fight to the death here while I escape to fight on elsewhere. And even if he has my leave to surrender and get what terms he can, without fighting to the end, can we rely on any generosity from Edward?'

'Towards others, perhaps,' said Llewelyn. His voice was low and equable, implying nothing more than he said, but David heard no less clearly all that had not been said, that though the common spear-men and bowmen of Wales might look for clemency, being of little importance to the king once their resistance ceased, there would never again be mercy for the princes of Gwynedd. David had made his throw to win or lose all, and though for himself I think he had not changed his mind, his heart was shaken and racked for Llewelyn.

'I did this to you,' he said, 'and was certain I did well. Now I am stricken with doubts. What right had I to force your hand?'

'None,' said Llewelyn simply, 'but it is done, and the next step must be taken from here where we stand.' And seeing his brother's face desperately sombre, the eyes clinging upon him in hunger and thirst after some reassurance he could get from no other creature, the prince sighed, and did his best for him. 'Child,' he said patiently, as he might have reasoned with his youngest and most perilous brother long before, when he was indeed newly out of childhood and greedy for glory, 'you trouble needless. You did me no wrong. I am of your mind, it would have come to this, soon or late. I was for late, for making him show his hand, you saw it otherwise. But it's all one now, and your choice of time may well have been right, and mine wrong. I have no regrets, none. Nor need you have any. We are here together, and that is good. And what men can do, we shall do.'

CHAPTER VIII

What men could do, that they did. The prince held council briefly that same day with those of his own captains and David's as were at hand. The necessary work they parted among them, and agreed as to how much time and effort could reasonably be expended on holding the threatened eastern line, now that Ruthin was lost, and Dinas Bran under attack.

'I should be happier,' said David, 'if he would turn some of his forces on to me here, and ease the pressure on Dinas, but I fear he can see plainly enough that direct assault on Denbigh could lose him many men for little gain, and cost him weeks of work, no matter how many he threw into the siege. His aim is to isolate the garrison here as we used to do his garrisons at Degannwy and Diserth, in the past, and leave Denbigh helpless and useless while the war passes it by. But here we have no means of bringing relief and supplies by sea, as he had at Degannwy. No, he'll try to draw a noose about Denbigh while I'm still in it, and I cannot let him succeed. But I'll go when I must, and not before.'

Since Gray was in Ruthin, and the earl of Surrey closing in on Dinas Bran and the valley of the Dee, while Edward's base at Rhuddlan offered a northern approach, the move to outflank Denbigh might come from either side, or from both together, to join hands about him. Llewelyn warned him to take no risks by clinging to his castle a day too long, for he could not be spared, and the worst disaster that could now overtake Wales would be the separation of its two princes, one from the other. They were now not only the symbol, but the reality of the unity of Wales. At that David looked up quickly from the scrawled map he was drawing of the lines of Clwyd and Conway, and the highlands between, and withdrew his mind briefly from the consideration of Edward's next advance, to fix a glittering stare upon his brother's face. And in a moment he went back to his frowning study of his own imperilled position, and said, very low and deliberate of voice, that he would not make any mistake that might threaten that unity.

Very shortly after the council ended, Llewelyn took his own company and returned westward to meet his foot soldiers, leaving the defence of the Middle Country to his brother, while he deployed his own army along the northern coast from Conway to Carnarvon, keeping close contact along that line so that men could be moved quickly wherever need might arise. Another line he strung along the western bank of the Conway, in case the English made any attempt to penetrate by some inland route over the high watershed between the rivers, and left a number of outposts on the eastern side of Conway to keep touch with any moves David might make, and bring reinforcements to him quickly if he should be hard pressed.

This work we began, since the foot soldiers were more than a day behind us in their march from the south, at Ysbyty Ifan on the upper Conway, where they were appointed to meet with us. And as they were in need of rest, there we were all encamped overnight. It is no great way from there to the castle of Dolwyddelan, and in Dolwyddelan Elizabeth and all her children had now taken refuge, and with them was my Cristin. I was out on the first rise of the upland road in the early evening, looking towards the west and thinking of her, with the knot of longing drawn tight about my heart, when Llewelyn came quietly behind my shoulder and said: 'Will you ride there with me? We can be there by dark and leave with the dawn. I have a duty to see to the well-being of my sister and her children.'

So, perhaps, he had, and his affection for Elizabeth, who in her innocence had wrought so strongly on his brother, and deserved so well of them both, was deep and warm, and yet I knew he had rather my needs in mind then. When he laid his hand upon my arm I felt the touch pass into my flesh and blood like the comfort of a fire at the onset of a cold night. He had spoken but seldom and briefly since Eleanor died, always calmly, always to the point, always with consideration towards poor human creatures caught in this world's snares as he was, yet all his utterance lacking some part of him that we needed and missed, we who had known him when he was man alive. He touched me then, there above the Conway, and his hand was quick and kind, and his voice speaking into my ear was close instead of distant, and sounded to me strangely young, the voice of my eighteen-year-old star-brother when first I entered his service at Aber, long years before. So strong was that illusion that I was reluctant to turn my head and look at him, for grief at his silvered temples and lined brow, and more than all of his widowed eyes, that looked upon me with the awful compassion of those who have nothing to lose but through another's loss, and nothing to hope for but through another's gain.

I said: 'You ask foolishly. I will ride with you wherever you care to call me, whether it is towards my own weal or my own woe. And no one knows it so well as you.'

'God knows,' said Llewelyn, 'towards which of the two I am calling you in the end. But at least the woe should not have reached Dolwyddelan yet. Let's take the good where we find it.'

So we took horse gladly and rode together over the upland track to Penmachno, across the little river, and through the forested hills until we could see in the dusk the great angular tower rising on its ridge above us, and began the winding climb to the narrow inner ward, walled round every way. They kept a good guard, we were challenged before ever we got near the foot of the rock, and twice again on the way aloft. One of the men ran ahead as soon as the prince was known, and they came with flares to light us in, for the nights were drawing in fast then, though so far the clear weather held, and prolonged the daylight somewhat. Within the week the sky was to change, and autumn threaten with cloud and gales, but that night it was still and calm. Half the household came pouring out to greet us, the castellan leading them, and Elizabeth met us in the hall. She was within a month of her time then with her ninth child, and the balanced gait and careful step could not but remind him. David's heir, Owen, turned eight years old, stood close at her side, and was already as tall as her shoulder. The two eldest girls also came out after their mother, dark, glowing and beautiful, foreshadowing glorious women. The prince saw before him the blossoming shoots of his brother's tree, so lavish and so fair, while he was left barren but for one solitary bud, and never would love woman or get child again. And as I watched them, for all I could not question the will of God, I found his dispositions hard to understand and harder to bear, and it was all the more strange to me that what I saw in Llewelyn's face was a brooding, regretful tenderness that had no envy in it at all, but came terribly close to pity. It was made clear to me then, very sharply, that the more richly gifted she and David were in these radiant children, the more they had to lose, and the more to be feared were the weapons sharpened against them. And though David had the fire and challenge of his warfare to beguile and compensate him, she had no such distraction, but lived every day with the plain possibility of disaster.

She did not look afraid. Her face had lost its childish roundness of cheek and chin, and gained a clean-drawn firmness of line in the change. But though fear may be put away for oneself, she was surrounded by others at least as dear to her as her own life, and fear for such is infinitely more terrible, and with that fear, I think, she lived in close companionship night and day. Not that she doubted David's gallantry and skill. But now that childhood delightfully prolonged was at last put behind her, she knew that the gallant and the skilled can also die, can also fail.

She asked warmly how Llewelyn did, and only afterwards asked after David, with no show of haste or anxiety, and no protest at being sent away from him. Llewelyn told her that we had left him well, and Denbigh not so far threatened, and that he had orders not to take any risk of being cut off there. And he asked if she and the children had everything they needed, and if they were well, and whether there was any wish he could fulfil for them now that he was here. Thus with mutual courtesy, each grieved for the other, they went in to the high chamber together, and took the children with them. And in a moment Cristin came out to me.

'I knew you were here,' she said, 'before ever I saw it was the prince she was going out to meet. I felt you in the air of the evening, when you were drawing near.' She gave me her hand, and we stood close, hungrily gazing. I had not tasted to the full, until then, the three-months' fast without sight or sound of her, all that golden summer a desert, nor been pierced with so sharp an understanding of his loss, who could never again recover the presence and the radiance of his beloved in this world, nor clasp the hand she held out to him.

She had on a plain blue gown, and her black, silken hair was braided and coiled on her neck. Not even that summer, day after hot day out of doors with the children, had been able to burn the pure whiteness of her skin, that mates so seldom but so perfectly with pure black hair.

'There was not a day I did not miss you,' she said.

'And never a day,' I said, 'when I have not thought of you.'

'Was there fighting?' she asked, and her fingers closed and held me fast for a moment.

'Nothing heroic,' I said truthfully. 'As little fighting as we could contrive with the most mischief possible. The real battle will be here in the north.'

We went out from the noise and warmth of the hall into the night, and climbed to the wall, and looked out together over the rolling waste of heath and hill and furze and dimpling bog, bleached into black and white of crests and hollows under a half moon. The sky was immense and full of stars.

'He sent us here to be safe,' said Cristin, leaning her chin in her cupped hands on the parapet of the wall. 'But where is safety to be found? Now I hear we are to move again, further into the mountains, to Dolbadarn. What is safety? In time of peace women die in childbirth, cruelly, like the princess, and men stray into quaking ground in these uplands, and go under by inches with their feet held fast, until their mouths fill with peat-water and slime. And in war many survive, even many who never looked for survival. I think there is nothing to be done but go forward through each day as it comes, as straightly and honourably as a man may, and take a reasonable man's care, and after that not trouble overmuch. I see a kind of safety in that, live or die, soon or late. That cannot be the difference, since it comes to all. What matters is something else. Perhaps to live whole, and die whole. Whole? – erect? – I do not know the perfect word.'

I said that she had found two that were good enough for me. She might have been pondering how to describe Llewelyn.

'Tell me truly what we have to face,' she said, 'in the north and in the south. We see too close here, and see out of shape.'

I told her all that we had done in the south, and how we had left matters there, frozen into a wary deadlock, though that could not hold for long when the reinforcements came in sufficient numbers. And I told her how we had found things in the east, and what was to be expected there within the next one or two weeks, for I reckoned it could not be staved off much longer than that. She listened with grave attention. In the moonlight her tall, blanched forehead and huge dark lakes of eyes were more than half her face. And by that bone-white light, for all her forty-six years, there was never a line nor a furrow to mar her marble smoothness.

'In the end,' she said, 'it will be as it was the last time. I was not here then, but I do know. And if it all comes to grief, some of those who come after will blame him in their wisdom, and ask why he fell a second time into the same trap, hemmed about here in the mountains like a forsaken garrison in a castle without a moat. And he has no choice. No choice at all! He sees the danger as clearly as man may, and he cannot forestall it. In the end, Eryri is not large enough. God should have given us a coast three times as long, ripped apart with difficult inlets of the sea, wasting months either by water or land to reach us. Or blessed us with a harvest that ripens in May, and can be in the barns before Edward can get his muster into motion. One year is much like another in the same land, and what the king has learned in one he can use in any other, and there is nothing we can do to change it. Only ships, perhaps, as you say, ships might have altered the balance. But he thought himself at peace!'

I said: 'No neighbour of Edward's will ever be at peace.'

'No neighbour of Edward's,' she said, 'and no brother of David's.'

I said then what I strongly felt, and urgently desired to be true, and yet could not be quite sure I believed, that this time David would be true to his pledges, and stand by his brother to the end. And this was the one thing changed from the previous conflict, that those two were at one, and would remain one. That unity might well be worth an army to us.

'It is October already,' I said, 'the wind has changed and the weather will change, and still the king is held fast on the Clwyd, and dare not move on towards Degannwy. Even with Ruthin lost, even if David must let Denbigh go, still it will take some time to move on to the Conway. We may have cost him enough already to make him think hard about continuing into the winter, even with our corn to feed his thousands. It may be he'll think better of it, and be open to terms again.'

'But even so,' said Cristin shrewdly, 'will it not be all to do again very soon? I do not believe he can keep his hands and his hounds off Wales for long.'

I was of her mind, and could not but say so, for to offer her false comfort was impossible. So we knew and acknowledged together what it was we faced, and with us all those creatures we loved, and the land to which our blood belonged. We stood together on the wall under the moon as long as there was any stir about the wards, very loth to part. But at last she said that she must go, for there was only Nest with the younger children, and if any of them awoke it would be Cristin who was cried for. And since my lord and I were to leave at dawn to join the army on the Conway, I must also get my rest. So we said our goodnights, as always, without great to-do or many words, and yet, as she went from me towards the low, dark doorway in the tower wall, I felt the strings of my heart being drawn out to breaking with every step she took away from me.

She also felt it, for every step was slower than the last, and in the doorway she turned and came back no less slowly, and stood close, looking up into my face. Here were none but we, and tomorrow all the many hundreds of garrison and household would be seething about us.

'Kiss me!' she said. 'This once, kiss me. After the morning, who knows when I shall see you again?'

I took her by the shoulders, God knows as fearfully as if I had been handling windflowers that bruise and wither at a touch, though they are brave enough and strong enough to thrust their way through the snow into blossom. She made no move to touch me with her hands, but only raised her face to mine, and under my mouth her lips were cold and fresh and smooth, stirring only for an instant into frantic life before she withdrew hurriedly and went from me without looking back. I said after her, softly: 'I love you!' and her step checked once, and she said: 'I love you!' like a distant echo, never turning her head, and then the darkness of the doorway swallowed her up, and she was gone.

Only then did I begin to shake like a fevered man, as though I had been racked with a great storm of weeping that left all my body one bitter ache. For that was the first time that ever I kissed my love on the lips, in all those years we had known and sustained each other, and I could not but know that it might well also be the last.

I saw her in the morning, when we left, for she came out into the ward with Elizabeth to see us mount. She had the youngest girl in her arms, and the twins clinging to her skirts, and she was smiling as resolutely as Elizabeth smiled, sending the menfolk off to their war with a cheerful face and a good heart. Thus Llewelyn and I rode from Dolwyddelan towards the Conway to rejoin the army.

All along the river the prince strung his guard-posts against any crossing, with outposts on the eastern side to give due warning. We visited Aberconway and saw it well-manned, and thence, instead of the coastal road, which was always guarded, took to the uplands, the great rock highlands inland of Penmaenmawr, from the seaward crest of which we could scan all the expanse of the bay of Conway, from the peninsula of Creuddyn to the east to the distant point of Ynys Lanog and the shore of Anglesey on the west. Stormy we saw it then, all the miles of watery floor bright in a lurid sunlight but swept by strong winds, and the sky above heavy and bloated with cloud that drove before north-easterly gales in the upper air, and piled like toppling rocks on the western horizon.

'Autumn has remembered us,' said Llewelyn, 'I hope in time.'

We rode the whole circuit of the northern hills, and everywhere made our defences secure, concentrating strong companies the length of the coast fronting Anglesey, and especially above Bangor, where Edward's boatbridge was to touch land. We went down to the shore there, close in cover, and saw the bridge itself, a long snake of boats braced together, riding the water easily, though there was a strong swell there as the wind drove into the narrows. They had not brought the serpent fully to land, but anchored a separate long-boat ready on the more sheltered side, with a raised portion like a draw-bridge, having the whole thus ready for use but out of reach of attack from the mainland. Two coastal ships, teeming with men, most of them apparently archers, lay off on either side, and others along the Anglesey shore, and a small wooden turret on the end of the bridge itself was likewise manned by archers.

'A man has only to leave the trees here, and he's within their range,' said Tudor, scanning the heaving serpent, with the commander of the local company close at his elbow. 'But by that token, so are they within our range.'

'But better covered,' said the man ruefully, 'and bring up fresh ships if we show our faces. Twice we tried a raid, but lost too many men, and boats they can hole and sink as we approach, lying higher than our craft. By night we got a boat in, muffled, and boarded them, and killed the watch on the bridge, but had to draw off when one of them escaped us and gave the alarm. They keep even tighter guard now. Some damage we've done them by night, too, with fire-arrows, and picked off some of their men by the flames while they lasted, being in darkness ourselves. But they have so many workmen, the damage is soon repaired.'

'When they try to land troops,' said Llewelyn, 'they'll be open to archery, for they'll have this last gangway of theirs to get into place, and the first to come ashore will be within bowshot even from cover. Then it may well be worth risking men. Not now! We could lose more than we gain.' And he left a part of his own forces to strengthen the defences of Bangor, and having made the best disposition he could of the men at his command, he returned towards Conway by way of Aber.

All along that familiar shore road, his eyes were more often turned towards the coast of Anglesey, across the widening strait, to the friary of Llanfaes where Eleanor slept, than towards the royal maenol where his daughter was. It was for the child's sake he went at this time to Aber, but he did so from a sense of duty, and not from any consuming affection. He had seen her but once, after the birth that bereaved him of the creature he loved best in the world, and the child was still scarcely real to him. Even had she been a son, I do not think it would have changed things at all.

But when he saw her again, when heavily and out of duty he asked Alice to bring the baby to him, and her cradle was placed beside him in the high chamber, then it was another story. She was no longer so perilously tiny and new and fragile, but four months old and sturdy. The russet-brown feathers of her hair were a little lighter, almost approaching the dusky gold that was her mother's colour, and she stared up at him with large, golden-hazel eyes fringed with dark lashes, eyes that could already fix upon him and wonder, curious and unafraid. Perceiving a face watching her, and having as yet no reason to find any face unfriendly, she gazed and vaguely smiled. He felt for the first time, I think, the astonishment of this new life, and its close bond with the lost life it had replaced, and though she could never mean the same to him, she had a meaning of her own, as new as her being.

He called her softly by her name: 'Gwenllian!' savouring the sound that had given pleasure to Eleanor, and carefully he lifted the little one from her cradle, wrapping the blanket around her, and nursed her in his arms, and she leaned her head against his heart as infants do, for such heavy heads upon such tender necks will always nod to a support. But she was not all helpless, already she could reach out her hands to whatever took her attention and made her wonder. When he leaned to gather her to him, the medallion he wore round his neck, the enamelled image of Eleanor at twelve years old, Earl Simon's gift to him before Evesham, slipped from the open collar of his shirt, and lay visible on his breast. Towards that small, brightly-coloured picture Gwenllian reached her hands, and held and drew it to her, opening wide in wonder at it those green-golden eyes of his love.

He uttered a small, grievous sound, and with one hand shaded his face from view. And the child, finding him bent still nearer to her, held her toy with one hand, and with the other reached up to pat curiously at his chin, and his lips, and made her own contented, wordless song, as if she knew that with her own weapons she had won him.

'This one has kings, princes, dukes and saints in her ancestry,' he said, and lightly kissed the tiny palm with which she stroked him, 'and she has the noblest grandsire any princess could ever claim, and as illustrious a great-grandsire, and her mother was the loveliest and bravest and truest of women. If God wills, she will yet come into her rightful inheritance, and bear the princes who will finish my work, if I must leave it unfinished. We cannot say we have not a lady to fight for.'

From Aber we returned to the defence line of the Conway, and waited there for news from David, for we were uneasy in case he had misjudged Edward's speed when he moved, and perhaps been trapped into accepting battle, or worse, penned fast in Denbigh before he could break out of the threatening ring. But after three days more our outposts beyond the river reported the first companies of his army withdrawing in good order to Rhydcastell, and there the prince rode to see them safely into the grange the monks of Aberconway had there, where there was ample shelter and plentiful supplies. We did not expect David until all his men were safely withdrawn. In a few days more he came, riding in with the core of his body-guard, the last to draw back into Snowdonia. He came in armour, having had some mild brushes by the way, but he had brought off all his army intact.

'Surrey is in Dinas Bran,' he said, when he had shed his mail and broken his fast, and all his men were bestowed, and all his mounts watered and fed. 'The way I heard it, Edward has granted it to him, with Ial and other parts there, and Grey has been given Ruthin, with all my cantref of Duffryn Clwyd. Unworthily come and unworthily gone! Not county administrations, you'll mark, but marcher lordships these are to be. He must feel himself safer so. Better a marcher baron who has to mind his own, and can use his own brains to get the wheels turning, than chancery officials with parchments in one hand and pens in the other. He may very well be right, but he'll have a fight on his hands with his own marcher lords in the end, for it can't rest there.'

'Which of them moved?' asked Llewelyn, knee to knee with him by the fire.

'Edward and Grey both! But I think Grey's was a decoy, for he moved first, and not far. Clocaenog forest to his western front was full of Welsh, and he knew it, and so did I. I kept my best watch to the north, and was ready for Edward when he moved, too. Not along the coast, but inland from Rhuddlan, over the uplands, and in force. His ground was easier, and I had not such stout allies in his way, those parts were never mine.'

'How far has he come?' asked Llewelyn. 'He's still well north of you, it seems, you came out by the south.'

'He moved his headquarters as far as Llangernyw.' It was a vil due west of Denbigh, and dangerously far advanced. David saw the prince frown at the risk he seemed to have taken, and fended him off, smiling. 'I was out of Denbigh by then, and with my eye on every move he made. I knew I could outstrip him. We had much the same distance to cover to this place, but all that distance full of Welsh irregulars in arms. He has closed his ring round Denbigh, but I was out of the noose. I do not think he will even attempt to stay so far west, now I am clear of him. He'll creep in on Denbigh, and stay close to the Clwyd. It could still be dangerous in Llangernyw. The Middle Country will occupy him a week or two yet.'

'And what of Denbigh?' asked Llewelyn.

'I've left it intact,' said David, 'I could do no other. The garrison I've left there may hold it as long as they think advisable, and then let it go to him on the best terms they can get for themselves, now we've had time to draw clear. He will not know how few they are until they let him in, and the place will be little use to him but as a repository for stores or reserves of men, now that line's broken. But I was loth to leave it.'

As it turned out, David's castellan held out at Denbigh until past the middle of the month, giving us ample time to have our more westerly line well manned and guarded, with couriers keeping contact across the Conway with the free companies of Rhos and Rhufoniog. Then he surrendered, in time, as we hoped, to spare his garrison the worst extremes of the king's revenge.

Thus by mid-October Edward held all the line of castles which had formed our eastward defence, and could move freely along the Clwyd valley, though he still had not cleared all the land between the Clwyd and Conway, and seemed in no hurry to move against us until he had, for still de Tany waited in Anglesey and made no move, clearly having orders not to attempt the crossing until the king gave the word. The lull was hard on the nerves, but every day he delayed was a day nearer winter, and also encouraged us to believe it possible that he himself had similar thoughts.

From this time our headquarters was at Dolwyddelan, from which the women and children had already been withdrawn, but much of the time we were on the move, watching both the north coast and the strait, and also the Conway valley, for the attack, when it came, would come from both directions. From the south we had then little news. Certainly the Welsh in those parts were still in arms, but the weight of numbers had turned severely against them, all the castles of the crown were strongly garrisoned, and there were reserves to spare for penetrating again into Cardigan. The prince's nephews could not make headway against such forces, but they could and did prevent them from being depleted by sending further divisions to join the king.

So things stood on the twenty-third day of October, when two of our outposts at Rhydcastell rode into Dolwyddelan, bringing with them a Franciscan friar, a tall man of middle years and grave bearing, on a sturdy mountain pony. Their manner towards him was rather that of an honourable escort than of warders on a suspect interloper, and when they reached the gatehouse one of them spurred ahead to be his herald.

'This friar came alone into Rhydcastell, up the Dee valley from Dinas Bran, and asks for the lord prince. He says he bears letters from the archbishop of Canterbury, who is himself on his way to join the king at

Rhuddlan, by way of Chester. His messenger speaks good Welsh, and is of our blood. They call him John of Wales.'

The friar followed him in impassively, and dismounted, shaking down the gown he had worn kilted to the knee. He had a calm, fierce face, like a vessel of passion perfectly controlled, and his form was muscular and lean. He would as well have made a soldier as a friar, but his name I knew, for he had a high reputation among scholars of theology, and I had heard Brother William de Merton and others at Llanfaes speak of him, they being of the same order. A strange time it seemed for such a man to appear alone riding into Eryri, in the teeth of a roused and by then bitter war.

'I am come,' he said to the castellan, who hurried out to meet him, 'to present to the Lord Llewelyn, prince of Wales, the compliments of Archbishop Peckham, and my own credentials as his messenger. I have letters and articles for the lord prince. And the purpose of the archbishop's journey into Wales and my own is to try to put an end to this warfare, and bring about a just peace. If there is a welcome here for such an errand, I pray you bring me to Llewelyn.'

We brought him in with all ceremony, Tudor taking the guest in charge and offering him lodging and water and wine, after the old, honoured fashion, but he would take nothing until he had discharged his embassage to the prince. Llewelyn was in the armoury with his penteulu seeing certain minor damages to mail and weapons made good, and thither I went to tell him what manner of visitor we had. He reared his head sharply at the news, and opened his eyes wide, willing to go to meet every overture of peace, but putting as yet no great trust in this or any.

'So he has not altogether forgotten or discarded us,' he said, marvelling, and he was glad, whether good came of it or no, for he kept still, in spite of the archbishop's querulous strictures on Welsh law, a degree of respect and affection for that good, difficult man. 'And he sent us a Welshman! Well done! I do believe he has a genuine care for his wild western flock, however they plague him with their adherence to the old ways. Let's go in, then, by all means, and see what Brother John Peckham sends us by Brother John of Wales.'

He went in as he was, dun and plain in leather, to the high chamber, and sent for the friar to be brought in. And when he came, the prince rose and went to meet him, paying him the courtesy and reverence of one noble man saluting another. Brother John delivered the letters he carried, and their bulk caused a brief smile to pluck at Llewelyn's mouth. It was to be expected that the archbishop would use many and ardent words, for he was never one to go sparingly with his tongue or his pen, and it needed little wisdom to foresee that most of the words he had used in these scrolls would be of reproach, accusation and admonition. Yet if he had had nothing at all but these to offer he would not have sent his brother-Franciscan venturing into the mountains.

'You will understand,' said the prince, 'that we need time to weigh the archbishop's letters fairly, and also that I may consult my council, since I am acting not only for myself but for Wales. I trust you'll lodge with us and rest here in Dolwyddelan until we have our answer ready.'

'I am to wait for that answer,' said Brother John, 'as long as may be needful, though I urge haste. I am to carry your word on to meet the archbishop in the king's camp at Rhuddlan. And he prays you may be wisely guided, and provide him an answer that may end this warfare between kinsmen.'

'Justly,' said Llewelyn.

'Justly. So he has said, and so I say also.'

'Tell me,' said the prince, 'where is Archbishop Peckham now?'

'I left him the day before yesterday at Aldridge, on his way to Chester. By now he may have reached the city. I do not think he will yet have moved on.'

'Then what the archbishop has to propose to us in these letters is purely his own? The king does not know what he has written?'

'That is truth,' said Brother John. 'Indeed, he has taken this step very much against his Grace's will, and expects to incur his displeasure.'

'And if these letters provide a basis for further dealings, in the hope of a settlement, can we rely on truce while the argument goes forward?'

'For that I shall be able to answer only when I reach Rhuddlan with your reply, which is the chief reason for haste. At present this is but a sounding. But you know my archbishop, and you know that if he is once satisfied you mean to deal, and are in earnest, as he is, he can and will insist on truce being observed, so long as you and he continue to talk to each other like reasonable men.'

It was much to claim for any man, that he could venture into a deadly struggle without Edward's sanction, frustrate Edward's immediate plans, and hold him and all his army still while we bargained for a peace Edward did not want. Yet Llewelyn accepted that word without demur. Even Peckham might attempt it and fail, for all his valour, but he would not stop short of the ultimate effort, and if the truce he made was broken, he would not let even the king go unrebuked, whatever the consequences to himself. There was not much more could be asked of any man.

'I do not believe,' said David bluntly, when Brother John had withdrawn, 'in this displeasure of the king's. This friar may be honest in swearing his archbishop comes against Edward's will, Peckham himself may believe it, but I do not. November's on the doorsill, for all his new castles his plans have not gone forward so well as he must have hoped. I think this is Edward's way of sounding out the ground with us, without himself appearing to be bending from his purpose.'

'The better reason for taking advantage of it,' said Llewelyn drily. 'We dare not over-value our situation or under-value his. We are back where we began, David, in Gwynedd west of Conway, but for those outposts that must draw back to us as soon as Edward moves. We are not broken, nor near it, we have no reason to despair, we are not suing for peace. But by God, we had better not refuse it if it is offered on any reasonable terms. I have watched Edward come to this station once before, and judged him then, as you judge him now, to be weighing his chances and ready to welcome a move for peace. I know the peace I got was hard enough, but it was to my advantage and to his, rather than fight to the end, and we both knew it. This time he has proceeded differently, he is not beset as he was then. This time he began with a longer view than one summer. I do not think he means to stop short of victory. And since we will not tamely yield him everything he wants over a conference table, and I doubt he'll agree to any terms short of that, I advise you to be ready, as I am, to set your back against the rocks of Snowdon, and make him pay dearly for every stone.'

We called to Dolwyddelan for that council all the princes and captains and chief tenants of Gwynedd who could then leave their troops, and also had with us many councillors from the Middle Country and some from the south, for that castle had then become the court of Wales and its parliament. And there Llewelyn laid the archbishop's letters before his full council.

Most neatly and methodically they were laid out, the mark of the man in every line, and the very tone of his voice, voluble, hectoring, kindly-meant, sure of its own God-given rightness. In seventeen numbered articles he had drawn up his message to us, and thus they proceeded, though after so long a time I cannot answer for the exact wording. Yet the gist I remember very well:

1. That for the sake of our temporal and spiritual salvation, always dear to him, he was coming in person into our land.

2. That he came against the will of the king, who was said to be greatly displeased at his intervention.

3. That he begged and entreated us for the blood of Christ to return to our unity with the people of England and the king's peace, to which end he intended to do all that man could do.

4. That we should note that his stay in these parts could not be long.

5. That after his departure we should not find any other advocate to attempt the like for the sake of peace.

6. That if we spurned his overtures he intended to write to pope and curia with the grievous news of our obduracy, on account of the deadly sins that were multiplying every day through this discord.

7. That we should note that unless we accepted peace soon, the war would be waged against us with increased fury, beyond our bearing, since the royal power was every day growing greater.

8. That we should note that the realm of England was under the special protection of the apostolic see, exceeding all other lands.

9. That the Roman curia would in no wise allow the realm of England to be shaken, since that realm was particularly devoted to the faith.

10. That it caused him bitter grief to hear the Welsh described as crueller than the Saracens, since those take Christians prisoner for ransom, but as he had heard, the Welsh cut the throats of their prisoners on the spot, as if they delighted only in the shedding of blood, or, which was even worse, hand over the bodies of the murdered for ransom.

11. That nothing could excuse those who had launched a seditious, homicidal and destructive war at a time peculiarly sacred to the Redeemer.

12. That he begged us to return to true Christian penitence, since we could not long sustain this war we had begun.

13. That he begged us to inform him how we believed the disturbance of the king's peace, the public mischief and all other ills attendant, could be amended.

14. That he begged us to inform him how, at this stage, peace could be effectively re-established. Though it seemed vain indeed to believe in the establishment of peace, when it had been so assiduously violated.

15. Since the Welsh claimed that their laws and the terms of their treaty had not been honoured, let them state in detail the particulars complained of.

16. That we should note that even if it were true, as we alleged, though he had no knowledge of it, that the Welsh had been derogated to an inferior status, yet that in no way justified them in being judges of their own cause, that they should thus attack the king's majesty.

17. That unless some method of re-establishing peace were found, we should be proceeded against to the utmost by degree, military, ecclesiastical and parliamentary.

'He has learned nothing, understands nothing, and offers nothing,' said David with scorn, when we had all heard this reading. 'We should have known! He sees but one side throughout. And do you note any word there of a *just* peace?'

'He knows but one side because he has heard but one side,' said the prince. 'At least here he is asking us to put the other, and by my counsel, so we shall, and fully. He asks for our views on how the bitterness can be healed, the peace re-made. He asks us to enumerate our complaints, and say what clauses of the treaty have been broken. Those details we have by heart, for good reason, now let him hear every one, whether he can feel the smart of them as we have felt it, or no. It is our one opportunity.'

There were some among us more ready to be hopeful than he, and some who had less faith in the archbishop's sincerity, yet there was no man present who could afford to say other than yes to the invitation offered us. Late into the night and all the next day we clerks laboured with drafting and copying, answering one by one all the charges made against us, and setting out our own case for taking action in arms when all other redress was denied us, and compiling the huge list of wrongs done to us, and the treaty obligations spurned and broken to our damage since the peace of Aberconway. We had among our complainants the most trusted of Edward's Welsh judges, for Goronwy ap Heilyn, Hopton's colleague on the bench, had cast in his lot in angry despair of justice with David and the men of the Middle Country, and from this on acted as steward to David to the end. For more than four years he had done his best, both as justice and as bailiff of Rhos, to keep the balance between English and Welsh and do right to both, but when the breakage came he could do no other but go with Wales, for it was Wales that suffered wrong without remedy.

Eleven separate schedules of grievances we compiled among us, seven being from individual princes and chiefs, and four presenting the complaints of whole regions. These were from Rhos, Tegaingl, Penllyn and

Ystrad Alun. They varied in details as to forests thinned without leave, taxes exacted without right, arbitrary English law imposed where Welsh law applied, meadows misappropriated, vils occupied by force or extorted to add to the holdings of favoured hangers-on, but all cried out in grievous unison that an English tyranny had robbed them not only of their Welsh laws, which had been solemnly guaranteed by treaty, but even of their local customs which harmed none, and further, had proceeded against them with ever-increasing harshness and injustice, in many cases, even by the English law the administrators claimed to uphold. The men of the Middle Country denounced the exactions and cruelties of Reginald de Grey in Chester, those of Ystrad Alun the overbearing rule of Roger Clifford, those of Penllyn burned against the constable of Oswestry. From the prince to the cottager in the remote tref it was the same story, and that story was true.

Those who submitted schedules of their personal wrongs, apart from the prince himself, were David, all three of the nephews from Ystrad Tywi, Rhys Wyndod separately, and Griffith and Llewelyn together, all disinherited of lands rightfully theirs by the crown, the sons of Meredith ap Owen from Cardigan, Goronwy ap Heilyn, and Llewelyn ap Griffith ap Madoc of Maelor. Besides unjust disinheritance and expropriations, all complained of the interference of the king's officials within their lawful Welsh courts, of the arrogance of royal administrators who enforced attendance at their convenience wherever they chose, in defiance of old custom, of the exaction of illegal dues, interference with free movement and trade, and the infliction of English penalties, even to death, where a more humane Welsh law ought to have applied.

I think I myself had not fully realised, until we compounded all this formidable body of evidence in one great accusation, how universal was the attack upon all forms of Welsh life and usage, and how, when seen whole, it could no longer be regarded as the almost accidental product of high-handed and unfeeling officialdom, but emerged as purposeful and deliberate policy, using the resources of Edward's legal mind in pursuit of his ambition. His first object, so it seemed to me, was to extend, by all possible means, the lands on which he could impose English shire systems. His second was to rid all such lands of their Welsh customs and laws, and subject them to English common law and English organisation. His small bailiffs and tax-men were as they were, overbearing and harsh, because they divined, even if they did not fully understand, what was required of them. The shape their actions took, Edward gave them. They may, at times, have gone further than he would have wished them to go, but if so, it was but a difference of judgment due to limited intelligence. He had no quarrel with those excesses that were successful for his policies.

As for the prince, he and I drew up his schedule together, and it went directly to the question of what clauses of the treaty had been dishonoured by the English. Seven separate provisions he cited, in each case quoting the exact words of the treaty, in case the archbishop should need to have his memory of it refreshed, and then giving the instances in which it had been flouted, beginning with the clause under which he had sought to have Welsh law over Arwystli, and been denied it upon pretext after pretext. Other clauses concerned the promise that all transgressions committed during the war should be remitted from the treaty date, whereas de Grey, for one, had pursued many individuals for previous offences in the Middle Country. Also the article guaranteeing to various princes those lands they held at the time of the treaty, which afterwards were expropriated, and another assuring the tenants of the Middle Country that under the royal rule they should still enjoy all their traditional rights, which thereafter were gradually taken away from them. And sundry specific cases of incursion by royal officials into territory still indubitably Welsh, with the old grievance over Robert of Leicester and the wrongful distraints made in Chester on his behalf.

He added also one small but significant matter which I have not before mentioned, for at the time of his marriage at Worcester the king had presented him a document for agreement and seal, binding the prince not to harbour or maintain in his lands any persons contrary to the king's wish. Which he then sealed, partly unwilling to disturb the time, but also seeing no derogation in it, since the king's harbouring and maintaining the prince's Welsh traitors and assassins had been one of the main causes of the war, and he could not well resent agreement to the consideration he himself had so often urged in vain. But later at least one case arose where he found himself pressed to eject from his lands not an English fugitive or malefactor, but one of his own men, against whom the royal officers alleged some ill-supported offence. He therefore added this also to his list, referring drily to the use of such a clause to strip him of his loyal adherents at the king's will, and deprecated the grant of his seal in the common legal phrase used to object to an agreement obtained by duress or fraud.

'Therefore,' he wrote in concluding the tale of his wrongs, and further, the wrongs done to his people, 'it ought not to cause wonder to any man, if the aforesaid prince gave his assent to those who began the war.' And that was carefully said, for he himself had not begun it, but once begun it was his war whether he would or no, and he could not withhold his countenance from it.

In addition to this detailed schedule, meant to make one among the rest, he wrote also a long covering letter, personally answering the archbishop's seventeen articles.

That letter I remember so well that even now I can set it down, if not word for word, in its full sense and passion, and for the sake of those who will enquire into these things in time to come, when justice lives again, here I give it from beginning to end, that no man may be able to say Llewelyn wrote this, or this, falsely, but what he did indeed write shall endure to be set before the judgment. Thus the letter went:

'To the most reverend father in Christ, the Lord John, by the grace of God archbishop of Canterbury, primate of all England, from his humble and devoted son Llewelyn, prince of Wales, lord of Snowdon, salutation and filial affection, with all manner of reverence, submission and honour.

'For the heavy labours which your fatherly holiness has assumed at this time, out of the love you bear to us and our nation, we render you grateful thanks, all the more since, as you have intimated to us, you come against the king's will. You ask us to come to the king's peace. Your holiness should know that we are ready to do so, provided the lord king will truly observe that same peace as is due to us and ours. We rejoice that this interlude granted to Wales is at your instance, and you will find no impediments placed in the way of peace by us, for we would rather support your efforts than those of any other. We hope, God willing, there need be no occasion for you to write anything to the pope concerning our pertinacity, nor will you find us spurning your fatherly entreaties and strenuous endeavours, indeed we embrace them with all the warmth of our heart. Nor is it necessary for the king to weight his hand yet further against us, since we are fully prepared to render him obedience, always saving our rights and our laws, a reservation legally permitted to us.

'The realm of England may well be the special object of the Roman curia's affection, but the aforesaid curia has yet to learn, and must learn, and the lord pope likewise, what evils have been wrought upon us by the English, how the peace formerly made has been violated in all the clauses of the treaty, how churches have been fired and devastated, and ecclesiastical persons, priests, monks and nuns slaughtered, women slain with their children at the breast, hospitals and other houses of religion burned, Welsh people murdered in cemeteries, churches, yes, at the very altar, with other sacrilegious offences horrible to hear. All which are detailed in these *rotuli* we send in writing for your inspection.

'Now our best hope is that your fatherly piety may incline kindly towards us, and neither the Roman curia nor the realm of England need be shaken for our sake, provided it is understood in advance that the peace we seek be not only made, but observed. Those who do indeed delight in the shedding of blood are identified manifestly by their deeds, and thus far the English, in their usage of us, have spared none, whether for sex, or age, or weakness, nor passed by any church or sacred place. Such outrages the Welsh have not committed.

'It does, however, grieve us very deeply to acknowledge that it is true one ransomed prisoner was killed, but we have neither countenanced nor maintained the murderer, for he was wandering the forests as a freebooter.

'You speak of certain persons beginning the fighting at a holy season. We ourselves knew nothing of this until after the fact, when it was urged in their defence that if they had not struck then, death and rape threatened them, they dared neither dwell in their own houses at peace nor go about except in arms, and it was fear and despair that caused them to act when they did.

'As to the assertion that we are acting against God, and ought to repent as true Christians, seeking God's grace, if the war continues it shall not be set at our door, provided we can be indemnified as is our due. But while we are disinherited and slaughtered, it behoves us to defend ourselves to the utmost. Where any genuine injuries and damages come into consideration upon either side, we are prepared to make amends for those committed by our men, provided the like amends are made for damages inflicted upon us. In the making and preserving of peace we are similarly ready to assist to the limit of what is due from us. But when royal pacts and treaties made with us are of none effect, as thus far they have not been observed, it is impossible to establish peace, nor when new and unprecedented exactions against us and ours are daily being devised. In the accompanying *rotuli* we send to you the catalogue of our wrongs, and of the breaches of that treaty formerly made with us.

'We fight because we are forced to fight, for we, and all Wales, are oppressed, subjugated, despoiled, reduced to servitude by the royal officers and bailiffs, in defiance of the form of the peace and of all justice, more maliciously than if we were Saracens or Jews, so that we feel, and have often so protested to the king, that we are left without any remedy. Always the justiciars and bailiffs grow more savage and cruel, and if these become satiated with their unjust exactions, those in their turn apply themselves to fresh exasperations against the people. To such a pass are we come that they begin to prefer death to life. It is not fitting in such case to threaten greater armies, or move the Church against us. Let us but have peace, and observe it as due, as we have expressed above.

'You should not believe all the words of our enemies, holy father, the very people who by their deeds oppress and ill-use us, and in their words defame us by attributing to us whatever they choose. They are ever present with you, and we absent, they the oppressors, we the oppressed. In accordance with divine faith, instead of quoting their words in all things, you should rather examine their deeds.

'May your holiness long flourish, to the benefit and good order of the Church.'

'Enough!' said Llewelyn in revulsion and weariness, when we had finished. 'There is no more I can do, and no more to be said. I will neither beg nor bend. We have spoken out fully now, and they owe us truce at least until we come to terms, or break off the attempt.'

The next day we delivered all those *rotuli* to Brother John of Wales, and gave him an escort to see him on his way to Rhuddlan.

'Carry also,' said the prince in farewell, 'my thanks and reverences to Archbishop Peckham, for whether he speeds or not, it is great credit to him that he is willing to venture. And if he does not withhold his prayers from us, very surely we will not refuse them.'

'As soon as I can deliver these letters,' said the friar, 'I will beg him to confirm with the king the matter of truce. And I trust to visit you again, if God wills, in pursuit of peace.'

'It may serve,' said David looking after them as they rode down through the fold of the hills until the curve of the track and the deepening of the valley took them from our sight. 'If parliament rebels at extorting still more money for Edward's Gascons, if the king of France refuses them passage, if the clergy grudge him his twentieth, and his Italian usurers begin to bite, if the snow blocks the roads soon enough, and ice closes the port at Rhuddlan, *if* everything in God's earth conspires to hold Edward off from our throats and make him fear for his own, it *may* serve! If not, our swords must. We knew from the first there was no going back.'

Within three days we were reassured that we had truce, for nothing moved, we had gained a watchful quietness which we took care not to break. The weather was growing stormy, with strong winds from the north-east, though as yet the winter cold had not set in. In Anglesey the English garrison sat still, guarding their heaving bridge but not attempting to cross it, and the king, at Rhuddlan, uttered as yet no word, but launched no arrows either. I know that David had it in mind still that Edward was making a tool of the archbishop, however that worthy soul might preen himself on his bravery and initiative, and believe he was leading where in truth he was most subtly led. I cannot say, even now, whether he was right in this. He well may have been. Nevertheless, we began to believe that there was at least a manner of debate going on in the royal camp by the Clwyd.

But when the expected messenger came at last, on the first day of November, under a black and purple sky of towering, scudding cloud, it was not the lean, austere friar for whom we had kept watch. One of the prince's regular patrols escorted into Dolwyddelan, in a driving shower of rain, two horsemen of whom one was plainly groom and servant to the other, and held back obsequiously at his heels. The other sat solidly in the saddle, bedded down like a woolsack, but hopped down energetically enough in the courtyard, shook the rain from his cloak, and putting back the hood showed us the round, self-important, concerned face, not of Brother John of Wales, but of Brother John Peckham, archbishop of Canterbury.

CHAPTER IX

'I am come in person, my lord prince,' said the archbishop, when we had lodged and fed and served him in every point as well as a castle under war conditions could, 'because it seemed to me that those documents you sent me deserve that I should, and need every care I can bring to them. I have obtained his Grace's consent to a state of truce while we confer, and I assure you it will not be broken by his orders. I trust I may rely on you as far.'

'You may, my lord,' said Llewelyn. 'I, too, have given my orders.'

The archbishop stretched out his toes gratefully to the warmth of the brazier in the high chamber, for the nights were growing chill, and he had ridden far, and in very buffeting winds. I doubt if we had then the table to offer him that Edward could have mounted at Rhuddlan, for we went very sparsely fed ourselves, to husband what resources we had for the winter. But give him his due, this priest valued his appetite very little, and the offering of hospitality high, and our ceremonial heated water and towel for his weary feet had perhaps charmed him more than venison and wine. He looked round the private circle of us there, the prince, David, Tudor the high steward of Wales, the chaplain, Llewelyn, the prince's nephew, myself and Goronwy ap Heilyn as David's seneschal. 'I have only good remembrances of the lord prince's hospitality and kindness in Carnarvon, and I grieve all the more at this dissension with which we labour here today, that so severs us.'

'I, too,' said Llewelyn. 'But I do not think it severs us two. For my part, I feel no gulf between. I am too conscious of your former benefits and ever-present goodwill. Such other duties as I bear, however sacred, do not obscure these.'

'You greatly encourage me,' said Peckham. 'And now that we meet again, I beg you'll let me say how much it grieves me that we miss one face that graced our last meeting.' He was hesitant and soft of voice, the only time I ever saw or heard him so. 'I have sorrowed greatly,' he said, 'for your untimely loss in the death of your lady, the princess. God's purposes are sometimes cloudy to us, but doubtless he best knows his own way, and we see but with imperfect vision.'

'Doubtless,' said Llewelyn, courteous and patient as always when any tried to speak to him of her, and he gave thanks, but as always with a closed and forbidding face, so that the archbishop forbore from treading in further, but sighed and shook himself, and turned to business.

'I have studied all those *rotuli* you sent me, and I grant that these are very grave complaints. I brought them to the king's notice, and begged him to give them judicial remedy, and to hold them as sufficient excuse for the faults committed. I fear his Grace did not receive my intercession with any favour, for in his view the offence is inexcusable, since these grievances were not first referred to him as the head and fount of justice. If they had been so referred he would have been ready, as he always is, to give proper remedy where it is due, and no honest supplicant need fear rebuff, or resort to other and lawless means of redress.'

At that his fine delivery, which was by then assured and sonorous, was broken by the stir of indignation that rippled through all of us, and by David's gasp of unbelief.

'He dared say so?' he cried and drew in furious breath, but Llewelyn laid a hand on his arm, and he recoiled into angry silence.

'His Grace's memory,' said the prince hardly, 'is at fault. Every one of those matters of which I, personally, complain has been referred to him for redress time and time again, in his courts, yes, but also directly to his own hand and ear. In letter after letter I have informed him in every detail of my frustration over Arwystli, and let him know that I held it gross injustice, and required a remedy. Every one of those other wrongs I have brought to him, cited the treaty to him, demanded justice, but never obtained it. If now he claims I have passed him by, and makes that his reason for finding this insurrection inexcusable, then I say outright, he says what is not true. And since justice has been refused me at his hands a score of times already, if he expects me to put more trust in it the one-and-twentieth time, he insults both my wit and your credulity. As for my magnates, they will answer for themselves.'

And so they did, David first and most fiercely, recounting almost word for word the letters he had written to Edward, complaining of law that cited him to the Chester shire-court to answer for land purely Welsh. He spoke also for all the men of his two cantrefs, in whose name he had many times raised the issues that troubled them, but always without redress.

'To claim now that these have never been brought to him requires more effrontery than a king should use even towards his brother-kings, let alone those people over whom he has sovereign power, and towards whom he carries a sovereign's responsibility. It is unworthy to resort to lies,' he said in a steady, black blaze of rage, and his voice low, deliberate and sweet, as always when he was most deadly in his anger.

I must say of Peckham that he would listen as well as talk, even when his own indignation was rising. He did not then rebuke David for alleging that the king lied – it may be that his native honesty could not well deny it, and that he had encountered it himself in other connections – but invited those present to testify to the end on this point, and when both Tudor and young Llewelyn had had their say, Goronwy ap Heilyn ended those declarations with a very measured and reasoned recital of his own experiences as a judge of the Hopton bench and bailiff in Rhos. Many times he had witnessed miscarriages of justice and breaches of the rights guaranteed by treaty, and many times, sometimes to the king in person, he had pointed out the unwisdom of official procedures which were driving the Welsh to anger and despair. His moderation was as impressive as David's fury, and did our cause better service, besides sparing us all a long homily.

'This evidence,' said the archbishop earnestly, 'I accept as sincere, but

759

remember that you have spoken of many and diverse incidents and cases, scattered throughout the land and arising at different times. Those of such pleas are remembered which have been unsuccessful, while where redress has been granted the mind keeps no record. To say that his Grace has been informed on so many occasions of so many matters, minor when looked at singly though hurtful when regarded in the sum, is not the same as claiming that he has ever been presented with such a detailed and reasoned schedule of complaints as you have provided now, where the magnitude of the disquiet and grievance is made plain. I think his attitude natural enough, indeed justified, but I understand also the depth of your resentment and distrust. What needs to be done now is not to hurl further charges, but to bring about a reconciliation. I am doing my best to that end.'

'I acknowledge it and am grateful,' said Llewelyn, 'but I cannot relinquish my wrongs on that account. But I think you must have achieved some better hope than this, or you would not be here among us now.'

'I begged the king,' said the archbishop, 'to allow you to have free access to him at Rhuddlan, and freely return so that you could discuss your grievances with him face to face. I will not say that he gave me the answer I hoped for, all he would say was that you could come, and return without hindrance *if you earned that right*. It is not absolute refusal, but for the sake of swift reconciliation I resolved rather to come myself to talk with you, and try to bring you to a degree of reason and goodwill that may admit you again to the king's grace. For I am sure he is not fast shut against you.'

We were less sure, but this ardent busybody had a strong compulsion about him, and as long as he sat here with us arguing and preaching and scolding, there was hope that he would bring forth a minor miracle. So we settled to enjoy, enlighten and convince him, as he strove to comfort, chasten and pluck us from the burning.

Three days the archbishop stayed with us, and during that time had several conferences with Llewelyn, alone and in council, and with David also. And strange it was to see how, as that celibate innocent with his warm, intrusive kindness disarmed David, so did David's insinuating charm melt the archbishop, as it had many another. So that when they parted at the end it was with a wry grace and affection, David pretending a humility he did not feel, Peckham forgetfully blessing the foremost of those he had consigned to outer darkness with his general excommunication, issued from Devizes when the war first began.

At his last full conference with prince and council, the archbishop again exhorted us to humility, and a return to the fealty sworn at Westminster after the previous war, reminding Llewelyn that he had then consented to a form which entailed submitting himself without condition to the king's will – this for the sake of the king's relations with his own barons, which he dared not compromise – but on the tacit understanding that in fact the terms behind the phrase would be honourable and fair. And would he not, he said almost wistfully, again submit himself in the same form.

'The terms behind the phrase then,' said Llewelyn, 'were not merely promised as acceptable, but argued out through a whole month of bargaining, and known and agreed by both sides, so that I knew precisely how that clause of absolute submission was limited and conditioned by all the clauses that followed. So did all those who took part in the negotiations, there could be no withdrawal. I should require as clear an understanding of the limiting clauses this time, before I would consent to the form of unconditional submission. I am the sovereign prince of a free and sovereign state. I am willing to return to the homage and fealty of the treaty of Aberconway, provided its terms are observed, as heretofore they have not been. I am willing to make submission as I did then, the terms of that submission being understood and agreed by us both, and in that case I will keep them, as I kept the others. But always saving my right as prince of Wales, and my responsibility to my people.'

'But you do not refuse,' said Peckham, pleading and urgent, 'the same fealty you pledged before.'

'No, I do not refuse it,' said Llewelyn. 'I incurred it, and I was bound by it. I was not the first to break it then, and if it is renewed in good faith, I shall not be the first to break it now.'

It was not all the archbishop could have wished, but it was enough to encourage him, and send him back to Edward with word that the Welsh were not irreconcilable, if they were offered honourable terms. And he thanked Llewelyn, I am sure sincerely, for his hospitality and patience, and assured us he would return to Rhuddlan to do his best for us.

'I was so unused to these wild lands,' he said, 'and to venturing among men at war, that I thought myself gallant to set out from Rhuddlan, and held my life to be at risk. I even appointed Bishop Burnell, the king's chancellor, to be my vicar in my absence, for fear I might not return. But I find sons here in Snowdon as in Westminster, or Canterbury, and am confirmed in feeling myself bound to all the sheep of my flock.'

And he took leave of us kindly, and Llewelyn sent a princely escort to see him safely on his way as far as the Clwyd, as much to show his faith in the truce as to honour the archbishop.

David stood at the outer gate and watched them go, down through the furze and heath that skirted the pathway. 'Well, I have bleated my sweetest for him,' he said, mocking himself and Peckham both, but somewhat ruefully. 'Who would have thought that office could truly confer fatherhood upon one so childlike? And he barely my age.'

'He is a good man,' said Llewelyn, but in a manner detached and almost indifferent. 'Honest and kind.'

'By that measured and measuring voice,' said David, 'I read your mind. Honesty and kindness will hardly be enough.'

I do not know, but I think we prayed, all three, from that day, for Peckham's courage, perseverance and eloquence, for the pope's lightnings to strike through his uplifted forefinger, and God's through the pope, loosing angelic justice and truth upon the earth. But we kept all our armouries busy, none the less, fletching arrows and honing steel, hammering blades and repairing mail. And the quiet continued, and the weather wavered between calm and storm, smiling and frowning on our hopes by turns.

'One thing at least he brought us,' said David, 'he and his crusading into savage territory where men eat men, and even priests take their lives in their hands. Not that I underrate his bravery! This is a gallant little innocent as ever was. He told us Burnell is his vicar in his absence. And where the chancellor is – and plainly he's in Rhuddlan now – there Cynan is likely to be, also. We have an ally in the king's camp. We may get useful information yet, if this truce fails.'

As it fell out, the first news we got came back to us with the escort, when they returned from seeing the archbishop safely to within a few miles of Rhuddlan. For the captain who had borne him company sought out Llewelyn immediately on his return, to recount what had passed on the way.

'We were well beyond Conway, my lord,' he said, 'when suddenly the archbishop clicks his tongue and snaps his fingers, and says he, he has done ill to let it slip his mind, he should have offered you his sympathies on the death of your cousin Mortimer –'

'Mortimer dead?' said Llewelyn, astonished and dismayed. 'When? This must be new, or word would have reached us somehow.'

'The twenty-sixth of last month, my lord, at Wigmore. Gently in his bed, it seems, after a fever. I made bold to ask further, and he said he knew you two kinsmen had a respect and liking for each other, war or no war, and he was sorry he had failed to speak of it to you. I tried what I could get from the groom, privately, for if Mortimer's gone so unexpectedly there may well be disarray in the middle march. What with the court being at Rhuddlan and the king preoccupied, it seems nobody's paid much attention to young Edmund's claims. Sprenghose, the sheriff of Salop, has all the Mortimer lands in his charge meantime, and the heir can wait for his seisin until Edward pleases to have time for him, and that goes down very ill. You know both the sons better than I, but I know enough of them to know they're like their father, and think a Mortimer equal to a king, any day of the year. They say there was a good deal of sympathy for the Welsh cause round Wigmore and Radnor and Builth already, among the tenants, there may well be a measure of feeling even in the castles now.'

'There well may!' said Llewelyn, remembering his last meeting and compact with his cousin.

'And the groom let out that the king's been none too happy with the way the war was being conducted in those parts, what with the old lord ill, and very little being done to hunt the Welsh out of the hills. I don't say he suspects any man's loyalty, but he has no high opinion of their zeal, that's certain. Yes, and one more thing that will madden the Mortimers above all – Griffith ap Gwenwynwyn is already reviving his old claim to the thirteen vils against the heir, now the old lord's gone, and he thinks better of his chances.'

That was the very cause that Mortimer had successfully defended by Welsh law, when the same was denied to Llewelyn. By Roger's death these townships came formally back into the king's hand, along with all the other Mortimer lands, until seisin was granted to the heir, and doubtless Griffith thought this was his best chance to regain them, seeing they were now at Edward's disposal, at least on parchment. But even Edward would stop to think very carefully before withholding part of his inheritance from a Mortimer, even if he failed to comprehend the degree of offence he could give by delaying the grant of seisin, as though it was of little urgency, and could wait his leisure.

'Yes,' said the prince, pondering, 'there are interesting possibilities there to be exploited, if needs must. While the truce holds and we have hopes of agreement, there's nothing more we can do. But I am sorry,' he said, 'that Roger's gone. He was a rough, fair enemy and a sturdy friend.'

In this great but fragile quietness that had fallen upon us, we needed all the information we could garner, whether or not there was any immediate use we could make of it. If there was disaffection even among the greater tenants round Radnor, and Edward in his single-minded fury against Wales had failed to understand how easily inflamed the Mortimer pride could be, then the central march might be a fruitful field for recruitment if the fighting had to continue, and even the young lords, stung by the king's neglect and delay in establishing the right feudal relationship with them in their father's place, might at least turn a blind eye to what their Welsh tenants did, though it was hard to believe their own loyalty was assailable. But the niceties of feudal usage cut both ways. Until the king gave Edmund seisin of his inheritance, no fealty existed, and no treason was possible and, the boy might well claim, no loyalty either.

'I should be sorry to lure any man away from his faith,' said the prince, 'but what's offered I'll not refuse. Well, let it lie, we are at truce. We may yet have no need of such weapons.' But I knew by his tone, that was steady, equable but joyless, that he had no great faith in Peckham's valiant offices.

Howbeit, we waited, and nursed such resources as we had. And a day or so later one of our patrols brought in a solitary wretch, drenched and shivering, from the bleak hills the further side of Conway, and having heard his account of himself, delivered him to Tudor, who in turn brought him to Llewelyn.

'For he came gladly into their arms instead of running from them,' said Tudor, 'and he has a parchment he says is for the lord prince. We have fed him, for he was famished, he'd been on the run from Rhuddlan for two days, he says, and all but fell into the clutches of a patrol from the outpost at Llangernyw.'

The man was young, no more than thirty, and sturdy, though soiled and unkempt after his solitary travelling. He said he was a borderer from Cynllaith, Welsh by blood, but drafted for the king's work by the constable of Oswestry. He was a carpenter, one of many pressed to serve in the making of the boat-bridge across the strait, and he had left a young wife at home, and sought the first opportunity of getting back to her. Many of the hundreds of carpenters had been discharged now that the bridge was ready, but he as a skilled man had been one of those retained to maintain the work, for the seas were growing rough there, and several times there had been damages to repair. And as he could not swim at all, let alone well enough to risk that passage, he had stowed away on one of the coastal ships returning to Rhuddlan after unloading a cargo of crossbow quarrels. It was going back to the lion's den, but there was no help for it, and he had trusted to his wits and judgment to get clear undiscovered when the ship docked.

'And so I did, my lord,' he said, 'and would have made off upstream to where I could ford the Clwyd, but there was too much bustle about the dock, and I had to lie up among the stores until dark, and there, by what I thought then very ill-luck, I was spied by one of the clerks going back and forth with inventories of the arms and timber being loaded. But it turned out the best of luck for me, for he put a bland face on it, and gave me his scrip and schedules to carry for him, and so hid me until night by not hiding me at all. And by darkness he put me across the river with a bundle of food and this letter to the lord prince, and advised me to cut as briskly into Welsh-held land as I could. Which I have done, and gratefully. And here I deliver his letter, and keep my promise.'

The scroll was but a fragment of a leaf, and the hand not as precise or leisured as usual, but it was still recognisable. Llewelyn smiled as he unrolled it. 'You owe him your liberty, and I owe him many years of staunch service.'

'Did I not say,' said David, also knowing that hand, 'that we should hear from him?' And he leaned at Llewelyn's shoulder to read with him. That was the briefest letter we ever had from Cynan:

'Your advocate here labours hard for you, but against the grain. The truce holds fast, Tany in Anglesey has his orders not to stir unless the king gives the word. But hear what the bearer has to say, and be on guard accordingly. If I can find no further messenger, accept with this my fealty and valediction. God shield you, is the prayer of your servant.'

'What is this?' said David, startled and hushed. 'He is saying goodbye! He is watched! No, or he would not be going freely about Burnell's business checking the loading of ships. If he had lost the chancellor's confidence they would have a man at his heels every moment, he'd have had no chance to help a fugitive out of Rhuddlan.'

'He went about as having authority everywhere,' said the carpenter. 'I could not see that any man questioned it, or looked sidewise at him.'

'He is Welsh,' said Llewelyn dispassionately, 'and feels the day drawing in.' And he looked up calmly at the messenger, and said: 'Tell us what it is you have to tell, concerning Tany and Anglesey. That part of his news he has left to you.'

'My lord,' said the man, 'what the clerk says is true, every man in Anglesey knew that Luke de Tany has his orders not to move until the king bids him cross his bridge. But when the news came that the archbishop had come to Wales, and was going back and forth trying to make peace, Tany flew into a bitter rage, and swore his meddling should not prosper, for he would put an end to it if the king would not. He said the king had set out to annex Wales to his realm, and he should do it, in spite of Peckham and pope and all.'

'Did he so?' said Llewelyn, drawing slow and thoughtful breath. 'You heard this?'

'Not I, but the lads who were working at the end of the bridge, they heard it, for the despatches were carried to him there. My lord, I had friends among them I trust. They have not lied. If I did not hear his ravings, I saw his face not an hour later, and it was still black.'

'He was Edward's seneschal in Gascony,' said David. 'He sees another province within his grasp. I believe it.'

'I, too,' said Llewelyn, and re-rolled Cynan's letter in his hands. 'Take a day and a night of rest here,' he said to the carpenter, 'and then you shall have food and a cloak, and my safe-conduct to pass you south round-about, by the Berwyns, back to your home. You'll be safe enough on the way. But how will you fare in your own village, if you're within the English pale?'

The man grinned, stocky and resolute, no way intimidated at the prospect. 'Let me alone, my lord, to take care of that. My village is two men out of three Welsh, and a good reeve to fend for us, and no such tight hold now, I judge, as when I was pressed. God grant your Grace as hopeful a way before you.'

'Amen!' said Llewelyn, and smiled and dismissed him.

'Very well,' he said to David, leaning and quivering at his elbow, 'send at once to Bangor, let them know what's said of Tany and his grievance, and have them double the watch on the bridge. But not move until I so bid, or Tany brings it headlong on his own head by treachery. I will not be the one to break this truce. You hear me?'

'Nor I, believe me,' said David. 'I value my life too high to toss away the hope of keeping it. But if he strikes, so may we, and harder. But this half-Gascon courtier will never really venture?' he said, marvelling and rejecting. 'Against Edward's orders?'

'Who can tell,' said Llewelyn, 'what men will dare do? I see no limits to human rashness.' He looked into his brother's face, bent most earnestly, brow and eye, to search his heart and mind. He smiled, bewildered and rueful, as one who stakes nothing of value, and sees others dear to him hurl their souls away. 'I teach where I have learned,' he said. 'Go and set your snare, David, but leave Tany to spring it. Edward will not forgive that, and the guilt will not be yours. We have a mediator, and a truce. It is not time yet to think of how to die.'

Thus we manned our defences above Bangor, and held reserves ready in the hills behind the strait, and made no further move, bound by that autumnal silence that was heavy and still as the lull between storm-winds. While Brother John Peckham argued and sweated both for us and for England, and for his pope and his God, who hated, the one as the other, dissent among believing creatures, and the shedding of Christian blood. I do acquit him whom sometimes I have resented, reviled and damned, of any insincerity. He did as he saw right, he never lied, he never left grieving. It was not his fault if he could not see beyond the end of a very short nose, or stretch his academic mind into the bleak, bare summits of our mountains, and comprehend the love we had for our barren, beautiful land. He came from a softer soil and a narrower learning. He did his best.

In the afternoon of the sixth day of November, in that year twelve hundred and eighty-two, Brother John of Wales rode into our outposts from Rhuddlan, bearing the desperate and devoted fruit of his archbishop's labours on behalf of peace. In camp at Garthcefn, in the highlands of our Snowdon, Llewelyn received Archbishop Peckham's envoy, and the terms of peace he brought us.

Three letters Brother John brought with him on this occasion, and asked at once for private audience with the prince, which was at once granted.

Therefore until the council met, which was late in the same afternoon, none but the prince knew what was contained in those two scrolls committed to Llewelyn, or the third, which was for David. After the friar had withdrawn the prince sent for his brother, and those two were closeted together until they came forth into the assembly of the council. Because of the truce we had an unusually full gathering for time of war, as was right and proper when the whole fate of Wales hung upon our proceedings.

When the prince took his place, his countenance was stone-still but calm. The grey that had salted his temples was now a silver dust over the thick autumnal bracken- brown of his whole head, and this gradual frost had overtaken him since Eleanor died. He stood at the threshold of a double winter, of the year and of his own glory, unless God willed a miracle to Wales. I saw, as suddenly I was seeing for the first time clearly all the signs of his advancing age and mine, that he had lost flesh, and the bones of his face stood clear and hard and polished, rather bronze than stone. The chill winds of war and death had driven him past the bright summer of his prime. There was no way now to go but towards old age and the dark. What mattered was the manner of the going.

I looked at David, who sat close at his side, very pale and grim, and noted how from time to time he watched his brother with strained and passionate attention, as though he, too, was seeing the threat of ruin as great as the former glory. But he saw it as in part his own work, and was aghast and stricken mute before that knowledge.

'By favour of Archbishop Peckham and Brother John of Wales,' said the prince, 'we have received replies to those articles we sent in our defence, asking for justice. Before I put them before this council, I must tell you what Brother John reports of the reception our letters received in Rhuddlan. The archbishop presented to the king my reply that I am willing to submit myself to his will, saving always my sovereign dignity and my duty to my people. King Edward refuses to allow any conditions. We must submit to his will absolutely, without reserve. I am grateful to the archbishop for this, that he understood and said that unless we were offered honourable terms we would not surrender, and as Brother John reports, he persisted until he induced the king to agree that he might consult the magnates present at Rhuddlan, and with them try to draw up terms which should be mutually acceptable. For what the king's own magnates agreed to could hardly be derogatory to the king's sovereignty and honour. What I now hold is the fruit of those discussions, and to these terms the king has given his consent, though I am told not gladly.' He looked round about at all the intent faces, and said with slow emphasis: 'I make it clear – if this form is not accepted, we may very well ask the archbishop to continue his efforts. But whether he will again prevail upon the king to allow another form to be put forward, that I question. It is fair,' he said, 'that you should know what is at stake.'

Out of their great, expectant hush Tudor asked: 'Does Brother John report his archbishop as believing these terms to be fair and just? Does he expect us to find them so?'

'Brother John says it cost his archbishop long and hard labour to get agreement to them, and he is satisfied he could do no better for us. Yes, as I judge, he expects compliance,' said Llewelyn, and briefly and terribly smiled. 'There are three letters. The first and shorter of the two addressed to me I am free to lay before this council, the second is superscribed to be delivered to me in private, and so has been. I make no distinction. My fate and the fate of Wales march together, and Wales must know as fully as I everything that is proposed concerning this war and this peace.'

'Read them,' said Tudor. And David said in a low voice: 'For God's sake, put us all out of our pain! Peace or war I could bear, but this headlong falling in the cleft between the two is too much for me.'

'In the name of God, then,' said Llewelyn, and unrolled the first of the archbishop's two scrolls. 'This contains the open terms.' And he read aloud:

'These to be delivered to the prince in council:

'First: That the lord king will entertain no discussion or dealings concerning the Middle Country, and those lands already granted by him to his magnates, nor concerning the island of Anglesey.

'Item: As to the tenants of the aforesaid cantrefs, if they come to the king's peace they shall be treated as befits and is pleasing to the king's majesty. But we are confident that he will deal with them mercifully if they accept of peace, and with other friends we propose to do our utmost to achieve this end, and are confident of success.

'Item: As to the Lord Llewelyn, we have been able to get no other response but that he must submit simply and absolutely to the lord king's will, and we are convinced that the lord king will deal mercifully with him. To which end we promise to labour with all our might, together with other friends, and we are certain our efforts will be effective.'

'It is no offer of honourable terms at all,' cried young Llewelyn, burning indignantly for his uncle's sake, 'it is an ultimatum, and nothing more!'

'Wait!' said the prince, wryly smiling. 'It is the covering letter of an offer of sorts. The king cannot afford, or thinks he cannot, for the sake of his standing with his own magnates, who may also at some time offend him and be brought to submission – to cede the formula of absolute surrender to his will. The archbishop's intimations about the magnates and their undertakings to obtain mercy for us mean more than they say. He has already extorted King Edward's agreement, however grudging, to what is contained in this second roll – the private provisions which qualify this public declaration.'

He unrolled the second letter, which was but little longer and read in a voice deliberate and firm:

'These to be put to the prince in secret:

'First: This is the form of the royal grace drawn up by the king's magnates: The Lord Llewelyn having submitted himself to the king's will, the king will provide for him honourably, bestowing upon him an estate to the value of a thousand pounds sterling, with the rank of an earl, in some part of England. In accordance with which, the said Llewelyn shall cede to the lord king, absolutely, perpetually and peaceably, his seisin of Snowdonia.

And the king himself will provide for the prince's daughter, in accordance with his obligations to his own blood-kin. To this end the magnates are confident of being able to incline the king's mind to tenderness.

'Item: Should the said Llewelyn take a second wife, and by her have male issue, the magnates undertake to procure of the lord king that such heirs shall succeed in perpetuity to Llewelyn's inheritance, in his earldom of one thousand pounds' value.

'Item: Concerning those people presently subject to the prince, in Snowdonia or elsewhere, provision shall be made for them as God sanctions, and as is consistent with the safety, honour and wellbeing of such people. To which course the king's mind is already strongly inclined, since he desires to provide for all his people with conciliatory clemency.'

Round that table there were muted cries of disbelief and anger long before he reached the end, but all those who opened their mouths to exclaim aloud held their breath again and heard him out, not because his visage was wrung or his voice torn and jagged, but because his awesome calm rode over them, as a calm at sea takes the air out of a ship's sails, and lays it drifting and helpless.

When he was done he looked up at us all, and in his bleak but serene face his eyes had their old red brilliance, the fire that burned up out of the depths when he was most roused to contempt and disdain. Then indeed they began to cry out, many voices together.

'And we,' cried Tudor, half-choked with his own gall, half so incredulous he could hardly forbear from laughing, 'we are to be handed over with Snowdon, delivered to whatever overlord Edward pleases to set over us, to do homage to a stranger? It is infamous! They have run mad!'

'Say no word yet,' said Llewelyn, loudly and peremptorily. 'We have time for thought, and we have need of thought. After a fashion, make no mistake, this is intended generously by those who send it. We are all offered life – life of a kind, and the means of living. And I require,' he said, his eyes burning into gold flame, 'that no man here shall lightly cast his life away, or prejudice the judgment of another. I require, further, that your answer shall be made only after proper consideration of what you do, for your own future, and without regard to me. In that answer I have nothing to say, it is you who speak for Wales. It would be unworthy to act in haste, for there will be no more such offers.'

'But *your* answer?' cried his nephew, clinging in desperation to the prince's sleeve. 'How can we speak without you?'

'My answer I'll tell you willingly, when you have conferred without me, and not today. Tudor may call you together when he sees fit, and when you need me, send for me. But my answer need not compromise yours. I shall leave you now, and if you will you may continue this council, but I advise that no voice be taken yet, not until tomorrow, or the day after tomorrow. We have a truce. We have time.'

So he said, and in the face of their seething distress, confusion and anger, he rose to put an end to the meeting, but David laid a hand on his arm and checked him.

'Wait! There is one more letter to be made public – mine. I am a

Welshman, too, by the prince's grace I am even in fealty, but I hold no lands. I have still a word to say, and I have leave to answer for myself and myself only, having lost already my two cantrefs and all the Welsh who were my charge.'

He stood with the parchment unrolled, in his hands, and there was sweat on his brow and his lips, I saw the torchlight dewed into bright beads there, and saw the anguish of his face, and guessed at the deeper anguish of the mind within.

'Thus Archbishop Peckham writes to me,' he said, high and clear:

'These to be delivered to David:

'First: If, to God's honour and his own, he will take upon him the burden of the Cross, and journey to aid the crusade in the Holy Land, he shall be provided with an establishment suitable to his rank, on condition that he shall never return unless recalled by the king's mercy. We will ask, and we are sure successfully, that the lord king shall provide for his children.

'To all the Welsh, of our own initiative, we add these warnings, that dangers will threaten them ever more gravely as time passes, as we have already admonished them by word of mouth, and written to them most urgently, for it grows infinitely burdensome to continue in arms for a longer time, only in the end to be totally extirpated, for the perils menacing you will every day be aggravated.

'Item: After a longer time it grows ever more difficult to live in a state of war, in anguish of heart and body, for ever among malignant perils, and at last to die in mortal sin and anger.

'Item: Which grieves us sorely, if you do not come to peace to the best you may, we dread the necessity of urging ecclesiastical feeling against you to the last extreme, by reason of your excesses, for which there is no way you can be excused. But in which you shall find mercy, if you come to peace.

'Concerning the above, let me have written answer.'

The beauty of David's voice, whether in mirth, or malice, or ferocious disdain, was equal to the beauty of his face, and even then it kept its piercing sweetness. And most of those who listened, perhaps, heard first how savagely he mimicked Peckham's hectoring and caressing tone in the warning to the people. But I heard the ache of longing and temptation, and was wrung with him. And I saw, as he was seeing, Elizabeth among her darling brood in Dolbadarn, the little, merry brown English mouse bestowed on him in cold largesse by Edward, and charmed alive into limitless excess and delight of love by God's gift and David's, not Edward's, so that she poured out her hidden treasure upon him in lovely, vivid children. And I saw suddenly how little he had believed in deliverance from this, his last act of rebellion, and how immense a gift mere life could be, having his charm and persuasion, and years ahead in which to earn his recall from crusade to wife and children, and a future not all without lustre. He was not wedded to Wales, as Llewelyn was in his widowerhood, he exulted in his children and worshipped his wife, he was by upbringing almost as English as he was Welsh, he had suffered his dual allegiance lifelong, eternally torn, he could as well have chosen England once for all, as twice he had chosen it before, only to be torn anew.

Also, he was afraid of death, as once he had told me, reared up to confront it as he spoke, for fear, though it agonised him, never deflected him. And all this I remembered, watching him shattered and re-created before my eyes, there in the hall of Garthcefn, and loving him, as I did, only a little less than I loved his brother.

'Thus the archbishop writes,' said David, 'to me and to all men of Welsh blood, and now you understand that I had a need to let this council know of this last warning, for it concerns them as well as me.'

He turned his head and stared insatiably upon Llewelyn, as Llewelyn was also earnestly regarding him. Eye to eye they questioned and answered each other in silence, and there were no secrets between them then. The prince lifted a hand, and said quickly: 'Let it rest now! Say no word more till we meet again. This is not the moment.'

But indeed it was the moment, and that was why he spoke. It was the one moment on which David had never counted, the moment when he was offered escape from the consequences of his own act. He had life in his hands again, his submission depended upon no other man, and with compelling eye and compassionate face Llewelyn gave him leave in silence to deliver himself, without blame, fending him off from too impulsive self-committal while his blood was hot, before fear and self-interest had time to work upon him.

'But with your leave I will speak,' said David, deadly quiet, 'for I am the one man concerned, so Edward would say, only with my own personal fortunes, holding no land in Wales, and now none in the Middle Country, which is excluded from the argument. I am the one who has no legal right in the council of Wales, and none to speak for her, and what I say now is no prejudice to any but myself.'

He paused to moisten dry lips, and I saw how Tudor watched him with narrowed eyes, ready to condemn, for Tudor had never loved David or been beguiled by him, and now he thought he caught the drift of this exposition, and knew where it was leading, and where he had expected it to lead. And truly at that moment it could have been what he thought, a cautious withdrawal, the apology for submission.

'I am also,' said David, 'the one who began this war, and whether I owe fealty to the lord prince for lands or not, I have paid it for more than lands, and whether I have rights in Wales or not, I have a great debt to her. And I say now, that no matter what others may answer, my answer to King Edward is no! No, I will never forsake this land in which I hold no seisin. No, I will not be a party to these insulting terms. No, I will not go on crusade at any man's bidding, nor wait on any man's word before I dare enter my own country. I cast my lot here and now, rather for war to the death than for such a peace!'

And having reached this ending, with a loud, clear voice but a white and desperate countenance, he turned and went out from us, a little clumsily, as though he could not see very well before him.

Llewelyn rose in his chair with authority to close that session.

'As for my brother's decision,' he said, 'it cannot be accepted as binding until this council has had time to consider the terms without heat or haste.

I will not have the remaining door closed, by my brother's hand or any other, until we have heard all men's voices.'

When I was alone with him in the inner room, he sat for some moments mute and weary, a heavy sadness upon him, which God knows was no wonder. And when he spoke it was rather to himself than to me, for he said, in a tone of bitter and marvelling derision:

'Who would have believed it? That any man could be so crass and thick of wit!'

I was at a loss, for my mind had been full of David. 'Ah, no, not my brother!' he said, and smiled and took comfort for a moment. 'No, my brother you shall find for me presently. He did not tell me what he meant to do, or I might have contrived to dissuade him, at least for this time. But who knows? He might not have thanked me for it if I had. It is for him to answer as he chooses, and I have no right to ask of him either that he shall go with me or abandon me. I can only ensure that he stays or goes with my blessing. No, all is well between David and me.'

And again he was silent, and shook his head over the all but incredible, and wrung vainly at a stranger grief.

'And I have respected these men!' he said. 'I had an advocate I could almost have loved, for all his faults, to which, God knows, I never was blind. And here he sends me with pride and confidence this contemptible and affronting offer! I thought he had some understanding of me, and he has none. I thought the warmth he had in him could at least feel the reality of another man's warmth, but he is as blockish as a dead tree. And he will be angry and wounded, even amazed, when his service is cast back in his face! Has he no place on earth that means anything to him, that he should truly believe he does me a kindness by uprooting me from Wales, and bidding me strike root in an English shire? He should have known, if he was one-tenth part of the man I thought him; that I would not give Edward one boulder of all the rocks of Snowdon, or one man who was bred among them, for his thousand pounds a year and his earldom. Or is there still hope for Peckham? Did this come solely from Edward, and has Peckham only sent and urged it upon me with shame and reluctance, in despair of better? It does not show in his wording, but then, he might steel himself to banish it, if this was all he could offer. I would I knew! I should have liked to go on thinking well of him!'

I said never a word, for there was no man could ever again give him back the pleasure he had taken in liking and trusting the archbishop. Always he had been too easily given to affection, by nature seeing the best in men, and taking for granted that they would do as much for him. Yet I did remember and recall to him the genuine courage and perseverance with which Peckham had laboured for Amaury's release.

'A Christian obligation,' said Llewelyn, 'and his duty to his church, yes . . . But was there more heart and wisdom in that than in this blind, arrogant benevolence he now holds out to me? Did he ever feel anything for Amaury, the man and the prisoner? Or only for the papal chaplain over whose detention the pope so bitterly complained? Truly I wonder! Oh, Samson, bear with me,' he said, 'for this is the first pain I have felt since my love died in my arms! For besides this man I took to be my friend, I have lost the one I knew to be my enemy. I respected and esteemed him still! If he had been as large as his body I could well have loved him. And all that liking and emulation I have wasted on the dwarf lurking within the giant. Do you remember, it was she said that of him? He could have crushed me fairly in drawn-out war, and I should not have lost him thus, or felt myself so demeaned by having respected him. He could have stood stark now and refused me any quarter, and that I could have borne ungrudging. But that he should believe of me, or of any decent man, that I would surrender Wales into his hands, and take myself off to some soft English pasture as his broken hound! Sell him my home and my people for a safe earldom! Has he known so little of me, that he could suffer this savage insult to be offered me? Has he no love for his English earth, that he acquits me of love for my Wales?'

'He loves it,' I said, roused and certain of my ground, 'as belonging to him and conferring lustre upon him. He has never loved wife or child in any other way. As for his roots, they are almost all in southern France, where all his forebears on his mother's side come from, and half those on his father's. His roots are everywhere and his heart nowhere. No, he has no understanding of what you feel for this barren, lovely land.'

'Yet he has had pretensions to it from a child,' said Llewelyn, fretting at what was beyond his understanding. 'And he has learned nothing! He understands nothing! He feels nothing! Land is only an enlargement of his own magnificence. And if I can keep Wales from him with my blood and my body and my curse, he shall never have it. And if he wins it, those who come after him shall again lose it, for what he has is still not a right, only a pretension, a greed, a lust. I am delivered from the shadow and the weight of Edward. He is lighter than ash. There is nothing to be done with him but despise him. I never thought to see the day!'

'A good day,' I said, furious that he should so suffer over so unworthy a creature, however gifted of God as he was also maimed of God. 'A good day, when you are freed of the last illusion, and can do your worst against him, and be at peace. You have no obligations to him any longer, none. Even though he may destroy, he cannot match you. He is beneath your feet!'

'More to my purpose,' said Llewelyn grimly, 'that Wales should not end beneath his feet. As for me, I have a life I may throw away as I please, to the best advantage of Wales, and never grieve. Of what other value is it to me? I am a rampart, frail enough, between Edward and Wales. It matters not a whit if I am trampled into the earth, provided Wales outlives me.' He leaned his head into his hands a moment, and drew a great sigh, as though he were indeed lightened of all trivial and unworthy burdens, whether of love or hate. But he was never a hater. He could resent and burn up in flame, but he could not nurse grudges, and when he uncovered falsity and meanness he had no recourse but to heave them from him and draw clear, as swimmers heave off weed and slime to breathe clean air and get back safe to land.

'Well, we go forward,' he said, and shook his shoulders free of Peckham's crass incomprehension and Edward's cold, malignant

772

littleness. 'They'll not deny us the right to a few days of continued truce, and until we have all cooled from our first rage, and considered well what we are doing, I will not let any answer be made.'

'One has already been made,' I said, 'and I do not think it will be changed.'

He gave me a long look, and said: 'Neither do I. He reads me too well, he knows my mind without any word spoken – as Edward should have known it, and should for shame have refrained from so debasing himself and so insulting me. But until John of Wales sets out for Rhuddlan with written answers from us, what has been said can be given back as freely as it was offered. David may save himself if he chooses, with my forbearance and goodwill. I shall never hold it against him. Find him, Samson, and tell him so.'

I did find him, and I did tell him so. He had walked out of camp to the crest of a hill to westward, and was leaning in the shelter of the rocks that cropped out there in the lee of a copse, his shoulders braced in a cleft, and his head tilted back against the slate-blue stone. He was looking across the hills to the west, where level black clouds streaked a sinking sun, though there was yet an hour or two of daylight left. His face was still and calm and awed, as though he had accomplished something that both terrified and assuaged him, and gave him, if not joy, a strenuous satisfaction. When he heard me come, he did not look round.

'And very apt, too,' he said, 'to send me my confessor, when I have just nailed together my own coffin. And deliberately, mark you! I must be out of my wits.'

'There was no need,' I said, sitting down on a ledge of the rocks beside him, 'to be in such haste about it.' And at that he laughed loud and sweet and still a little short of desperation.

'Oh, yes, there was! For me there was dire need. If I had not done it then I might never have done it at all. You need not tell me, there were some there waiting for me to turn my coat again and buy my life at any cost. Now I am committed. However many times I must repeat it, I can do it, for I dare not for shame go back on it.'

'There's one,' I said, 'won't stand in your way or blame you for it if you do. I think he might even welcome it.'

'I do believe it,' said David, when I had told him what Llewelyn had said. 'But not even for him will I take back what I have sworn. I have pledged it once for all, and I am glad. Not that I look my death in the eyes with any great joy,' he said wryly, 'being flesh, and very self-indulgent flesh at that, and knowing Edward as I know him. Bear with me, Samson, if I preen myself a little on being the first to hurl the glove in Edward's face, who should be the last if I were in my right mind. I, the most hated, the furthest banished from any possibility of forgiveness! The orphan and exile he whines and prays about having taken in and succoured, when he knows, as I know, that what he did was to welcome a useful and unscrupulous traitor, worth an army to him in his war against Llewelyn. I used him openly, and he used me, but in his self-deceiving way, convinced he had bought me and made me his for all time. No, if ever I fall into Edward's

773

hands now it will be my death, and such a death as might well make me turn tail, even now, and rush to embrace his contemptible crusade. But does not!' he said, himself marvelling, and curled a lip in a brief smile, and shook his head helplessly over his own maniac audacity. 'I begin to think well of myself, I am braver than I thought.'

'You go to meet fate too soon,' I said. 'Even if this attempt at mediation fails –'

'It has already failed,' said David. 'You saw Llewelyn's face, you know as well as I he feels nothing but scorn and disgust. I came late to the under-standing of his love of Wales, and if I feel it now, I feel it only through him. I could live as merrily in London as here in the mountains, and I daresay I could make pretty good shift at making myself comfortable even in the Holy Land. But not he! We have a few days of truce left out of this great labour, until the replies go back to Peckham. And that is all we have.'

'Yet even so,' I said, 'the war is neither won nor lost, and nobody knows on which side the lot will fall in the end. Wales has fought off all the power of England in the past, and may again. It would be shame to us if we lost the battle before it was even fought.'

'In the past,' said David, 'we had not Edward to deal with, never until the last bout, and then he was but cutting his teeth on us, now he has all his fangs full-grown, and knows how to bite, and for all I will do my utmost, body and soul, against him, I cannot choose but see the scale inclining to his side, and I cannot lie about it to myself, and will not to you. A miracle or two would alter the balance, and prick up my heart very nicely. Do you suppose God is listening?'

He shook himself suddenly out of his mood, and came and flung an arm about my shoulders. 'Come, you've done your errand, and need not fret for me. If ever a man pulled the sky down upon himself, I am that man. And pulled it down upon Llewelyn, too, God forgive me, though I think in the end it would have toppled even without me. There's no way to go but forward! I've committed my life to Llewelyn's cause and the cause of Wales, and there's an end of it. And now, for God's sake, if you can spare an hour before the light goes, come and ride with me, I'm no fit company yet for less tolerant men.'

So I went with him, glad to hear the resolution and gaiety come back into his voice, even if both bore still the edged tone of desperation. We took horses, and rode together over the hill-track to the north-west, and rode further afield than we had intended, for pleasure of leaving thought behind and feeling nothing but the sting of the air and the buffeting of the wind. Earlier in the day great gales had swept the mountains from the north-east, but by that hour in the evening they were no more than boisterous winds, that whipped the blood into David's face and streamed cold and rough through his erected hair.

We had reined in on a crest, and were thinking it time to turn back when we sighted a rider coming towards us at a gallop from the direction of Bangor, and waited for his coming in some curiosity. No one whose business was not urgent would have been riding a hill-track at that speed and in that deepening twilight. He saw us from the distance and spurred to meet us with a shout, and recognising David as he drew nearer, raised a hand in salute, and cried to us that he brought news from Bangor for the prince.

'God make it good,' said David to me, 'for we need it.'

The man heard that as he pulled up glowing beside us, his horse blown and lathered. 'Good enough, my lord! To say all in a breath – a battle and a victory!'

'A breath of life!' said David heartily. 'Draw deep again and tell us more!'

'Why, my lord, at low water this morning de Tany crossed his bridge. A great company, Tany himself and any number of bannerets with him, and some hundreds of men-at-arms.'

David struck his hands together with a shout that made his horse start and sidle. 'Then he dared! He dared break truce, and against even Edward's ban. The fool! Go on, man, what followed? Were they stopped on the shore?'

'We did better than that. The wind was rising, and the sea rough, and our old men foretold north-east gales. You know how they drive in there, and pile the waters as the tide comes in. So we let the English land, all that company, and drew back a mile or so before them as they moved up into the hills, until the gale was at its worst. Then we loosed everything we had down the slopes at them, and drove them back to the strand. It was high water then, and what with the winds driving in, the waves were threshing up among the trees, and sweeping in tall as a man. They ripped the bridge from its moorings on our side, and set it lashing like a cat's tail, and two or three of the boats went plunging away loose down the strait. They had no way of getting back. If they had any eye or nose for weather they'd have known it! We rolled them into the sea, or killed them in the woods if they turned and fought. A slaughter, my lord! A few bold souls fought it out and are prisoners. A few rode their horses into the strait and swam for it, and perhaps one here and there got through, but with their heavy armour I doubt it. Most have drowned. All are dead, or skulking in the woods and being ferreted out now, or prisoner, or gone draggle-tailed back, the very few of them, to tell the tale.'

'And a noble tale!' crowed David, shivering and shaken between laughing and weeping. 'Go on, make this perfect! Tell me de Tany is taken!'

'Not by us,' said the messenger in vengeful glee. 'But taken, surely. The sea has taken him. Myself I saw him go down, his grand Gascon armour dragging him below. He will not again break truce!'

'And all's quiet there now?' pressed David. 'No threat left ashore, and everything in disarray on Anglesey? You do my heart good! Oh, dear heaven,' he said, shuddering, 'I never knew my prayers had such potency. Samson, have you heard? God was listening!'

I took him by the arm, leaning from my broad-beamed mountain pony, for he was shivering and tense like a sick man. I said to the messenger: 'Your horse is tired, friend, and ours are fresh. Let us take the word ahead of you into Garthcefn, and you come after at your own speed, and you shall be not the loser. We will report you faithfully, and have lodging and audience ready for you when you come.'

'With goodwill!' he said heartily, 'and speak me a bed and meat beforehand, and stabling. And this good brute can amble as he pleases now, it's not so far.'

We rode, David and I, at David's pace, that tried the light and the track hard. I kept at his side throughout, watching his face, so long as I could see it still by that failing light, the thrusting profile so beautifully drawn against the sky. He went as one gifted with such perfect assurance that even his mount trod blessedly, wafted on favouring winds into Garthcefn. Only once, short of the maenol, did he rein in, and turn to gaze at me, attentive beside him, and his face was blanched and bright, the last after-light of the sunset gilding it.

'God was listening,' he said. 'We have got our miracle.' And he looked fully at me, and his eyes were wide as moons, and his mouth smiling. 'No, it is not *that* makes me thus drunk,' he said, 'no sense of being spared. I am here to be spent like Edward's minted coin for my brother's dream. No, I am thanking God for something very different, my own honour, my own soul. Now we have a victory in hand that will send the king on the defensive into his castles of Rhuddlan and my Denbigh for five, six weeks, maybe longer. He has lost his bridge and half his Anglesey army. But when I pledged my fealty and spat in Edward's face, we had no such promise. Oh, Samson, this at least I have done in a state of innocence! This at least was pure!'

We brought the news into Garthcefn, and it fell like music on every man's ears, and lifted up every heart, as well it might. We had good reason to rejoice, for we had gained not only the several weeks it must take the king to repair his losses, but also our reputation was enhanced and our position strengthened, for they, not we, had broken truce, and they, not we, had received the sharp reward of treachery. Nor would Llewelyn allow free action against the English forces elsewhere, but maintained truce still upon his part, countenancing only defence against further bad faith, and stressing to Brother John of Wales that he expected the like from the king's side, holding de Tany's treachery to be the crime of one man, and not to be attributed to all his comrades-in-arms. What the friar thought or felt he never gave to view, being well schooled in diplomacy, and less garrulous than his archbishop.

I am certain that this victory, most welcome as it was, had no effect upon Llewelyn's response to the English terms. To him there was only one answer possible to such a suggestion. It did not influence David, either, for his heart was fixed, but it did sweeten the choice for him and fill him with fresh hope. Concerning the men of the council, for individual voices I cannot speak, but I am sure the general voice would have been the same whether or not de Tany had made his fatal onslaught and met his deserved death. Yet it was no wonder if we sat down to the slow and careful work of composing our replies with calmer minds and refreshed courage. There was no question but the situation was greatly changed in our favour, and if fighting must begin again the king would be held in his castles for some time, for want of the very advantage he had planned by the occupation in strength of Anglesey.

So by the eleventh day of November we had ready our letters to Archbishop Peckham, each party replying separately, though all had sat in conference several times together. And that day John of Wales departed for Rhuddlan with these documents, which I give here, David's letter in part, the rest complete.

'This is the reply of David, brother of the prince.

'That when he shall see fit to go to the Holy Land, he will do so of his own free will and in fulfilment of his own vow, for God, not for man. Not at any man's bidding will he go wandering into distant lands, for forced service is known to be displeasing to God. And should he chance indeed to go to the Holy Land of his own free will, out of devotion, it would hardly be fitting that on that account he and his heirs should incur perpetual disinheritance, on the contrary, they might rather look to be rewarded.

'The war which the prince and his people have waged was not motivated by hatred for any creature, nor by lust of gain or conquest, invading the territories of others, but only by the desire to defend their own rightful heritage, laws and liberties, while the king and his people wage their war out of inveterate hatred, with the aim of conquering our lands. Therefore we believe ours to be the just war, and place our hope and trust in God.'

Then he also repeated the accusations made against the English soldiery concerning their usage of churchmen and sacred places, repudiated utterly the suggestion that any Welsh chief should leave his own lands and go into virtual exile among his enemies, saying that if we could not have peace in the land which was ours by right, how much less could we expect to live at peace in a foreign land. And lastly, he complained of the difference made between himself and other barons holding of the king, who had likewise at times offended against him, and been forced to make reparation, but never by total disinheritance, or perpetual banishment.

And strange indeed did I find it that David should so fight for his own privilege to the last, as the old David, and in the same letter speak out so well for the Wales he had so often deserted, a new David borrowing his love and his light by reflection from Llewelyn, but freer far with words than ever was his brother.

The reply from the council of Wales was drawn up chiefly by Tudor, Master William and Goronwy ap Heilyn, but agreed and approved by all. And thus it ran:

'The reply of the council of Wales.

'Though it may please the king to say that he will allow no discussion concerning the Middle Country, or Anglesey, or the other lands bestowed upon his magnates, nevertheless the prince's council, if peace is to be made at all, will not countenance any departure from the premise that these cantrefs are a part of the unquestionable holding of the prince, lying within the bounds within which the prince and his predecessors have held right since the time of Camber, son of Brutus. Further, they belong to the principality renewed to the prince by confirmation, at the instance of Ottobuono of blessed memory, legate of the apostolic see in the realm of England, with the consent of the lord king and his magnates, as is manifest in the treaty. Moreover, it is more equitable that the true heirs should hold the said cantrefs, if need be from the lord king for fee and customary service, rather than they should be given over to strangers and newcomers, even though these may have been powerful supporters of the king's cause.

'Further, all the tenants of all the cantrefs of Wales declare with one voice that they dare not come to the king's will, to allow him to dispose of them according to his royal majesty, for these reasons: First, because the lord king has kept neither treaty nor oath nor charter towards their lord prince and themselves from the beginning. Second, because the king's men have used the most cruel tyranny against ecclesiastical establishments and persons. Third, that they cannot be bound by the offered terms, since they are the liege-men of the prince, who is prepared to hold the said lands of the king by customary service.

'As to the demand that the prince shall submit absolutely to the king's will, we reply that since not one man of all the aforesaid cantrefs would dare to submit himself to that will, neither will the community of Wales permit its prince to do so upon such terms.

'As to the king's magnates guaranteeing to procure an earldom for the prince, we say he need not and should not accept any such provision, procured by the very magnates who are striving to have him disinherited, so that they may possess his lands in Wales.

'Item: The prince is no way bound to forgo his heritage and that of his forebears from the time of Brutus, and again confirmed as his by the papal legate, as is suggested, and accept lands in England, where language, manners, laws and customs are foreign to him, and where, moreover, malicious mischiefs may be perpetrated against him, out of hatred, by English neighbours, from whom that land has been expropriated in perpetuity.

'Item: Since the king is proposing to deprive the prince of his original inheritance, it seems unbelievable that he will allow him to hold land in England, where he is seen to have no legal right. And similarly, if the prince is not to be allowed to hold the sterile and uncultivated land rightfully his by inheritance from old times, here in Wales, it is incredible to us that in England he will be allowed possession of lands cultivated, fertile and abundant.

'Item: That the prince should place the king in seisin of Snowdonia, absolutely, perpetually and peaceably. Since Snowdonia is a part of the principality of Wales, which he and his ancestors have held since the time of Brutus, as we have said, his council will not permit him to renounce the said lands and accept land less rightfully his in England.

'Item: The people of Snowdonia for their part state that even if the prince desired to give the king seisin of them, they themselves would not do homage to any stranger, of whose language, customs and laws they are utterly ignorant. For by so doing they could be brought into perpetual captivity and barbarously treated, as other cantrefs around them have been by the royal bailiffs and officers, more savagely than ever was wreaked upon Saracen enemies, as we have said above, reverend father, in the *rotuli* we sent to you.'

And last, I give my prince's letter, by contrast so brief, courteous, dignified and distant, for he was writing to a man who had been close to being loved,

778

and was now dead to him, and waited only his last retort to be buried.

'To the most reverend father in Christ, the Lord John, by the grace of God archbishop of Canterbury and primate of all England, from his devoted son in Christ, Llewelyn, prince of Wales and lord of Snowdon, greeting, with an earnest prayer for his benevolence towards his son, and all manner of reverences and respects.

'Holy father, as you have counselled, we are ready to come to the king's grace, if it be offered in a form safe and honourable for us. But the form contained in the articles submitted to us is in no particular either safe or honourable, in the judgment of our council and ourselves, indeed, so far from it that all who hear it are astonished, since it tends rather to the destruction and ruin of our people and our person than to our honour and safety. There is no way in which our council could be brought to permit us to agree to it, even should we so wish, for never would our nobles and subjects consent in the inevitable destruction and dissipation which would surely derive from it.

'Wherefore we beg your fatherly holiness, as you are bound to pursue that renewed peace, honourable and secure, for which you have exerted such heroic labours already, to devise some expedient bearing a just relation to those articles we have submitted to you in writing.

'It would surely be more honourable, and more consonant with reason, if we should hold from the king those lands in which we have right, rather than to disinherit us, and hand over our lands and our people to strangers.

'Dated at Garthcefn, on the feast of Saint Martin.'

So read my lord's last letter to Archbishop Peckham.

Archbishop Peckham's last letter to my lord was delivered some days later, combining in one long, voluble diatribe his rage and rejection against all the careful legal points we had urged. Now he had nothing to offer us but damnation, and the prospect of war to the death, and the distant spectacle of his own wounded vanity at having his efforts undervalued, so that all the first part of his letter was an almost incoherent outpouring in his own praise, how he had laboured for us, taken compassion on us when none other would, ventured his very life among great perils to rescue his strayed sheep, been the advocate of our necessity – though in the first place he had invited himself into that role – dealt with the majesty and magnates of England, made his frail body a bridge by which we might again cross into grace, all to have the fruit of his labours scorned. It had not fully appeared until then how he rated us as some manner of breed a little below humanity, so that he could not well understand our resentment of subjection, which seemed to him our fitting state, a kindness for which we ought to be grateful.

All the legal points we had made he dismissed as 'pernicious subterfuges', and went on to produce some surprising law of his own. We should not, he said, vaunt ourselves upon being descended from Brutus, fools that we were and worse than fools, since Brutus was one of those Trojans who were dispersed and scattered because they defended the adulterous Paris, and such a descent as we claimed no doubt accounted for our notorious looseness in morals, and the small regard we paid to legitimate

779

marriage, in that we did not bar children born out of wedlock from having a respected place in our kinships, and even inheriting property. He went further, and accused us of encouraging incest, but in the flood of words he could probably barely stop himself by then. And had not the Trojans, our ancestors, he said, invaded these islands and driven out the Scythian giants who then inhabited them?

'Why, therefore, we ask, are the Angles and Saxons of this generation doing you any injury, if in the process of time they are now disturbing your enjoyment of usurped dominions? It is written: Ye who despoil others, shall not you be despoiled? Fools that you are, it is not wise to glory in origins stemming from adultery, idolatry and the plunder of usurpation!'

Then he went on to dismiss our indubitable claim that in the treaty made by the papal legate Ottobuono all these Welsh territories had been confirmed to Llewelyn, with King Henry's consent. A frivolous allegation, said Peckham, for certainly Ottobuono had had no intention of thereby weakening the king's law, civil or canon, so as to render it invalid, and for the crime of lese-majeste of which we stood accused, all hereditary rights are forfeit and perish, so that even in Snowdonia, Llewelyn's by rightful inheritance, the prince was now stripped of all power, and we with him, having no rights at all still existent except the right to beg the king's clemency. And to this astonishing proposition he appended his legal references in full, verse and line, of *English law*! English law, to which Snowdon never had been subject, and was not subject now! English law, which with its encroaching claims where it had no right had begun this whole contention!

As to our statement that we could not rely on the king's word, since he had not kept it in the past, Peckham demanded, who says so? Only from us, the Welsh, did this charge stem, and that meant we were presuming to be judges in our own cause. *And he was not?* As for the legal code of Howel Dda, the only authority Howel had had for it had been delegated to him by the devil.

The whole would be wearisome, though I have not forgotten any of it. But thus the gentle prelate, with many threats of excommunication, damnation, and extirpation by total war, ended his favours to us:

'While other men are freely adorned with the gifts of God, in your remote fastnesses these are cast utterly to waste, inasmuch as you give no aid to the Church in contending against its enemies, and confer upon your clergy no wise learning, except in the meanest degree, and the majority of your people wallow in idleness and lechery, so that the world hardly knows that such a people exists, but for the few of you who are seen begging their bread in France.'

And with that he consigned us to our fate and turned his back upon Wales.

This letter Llewelyn read with a face of indifferent distaste, and by the end of it his already dead regard for this narrow and unperceptive priest was also buried deep, to be thought of no more. He himself read it to his assembled council, and dusted his hands and left it lying when he had done.

'I had expected to be cursed,' he said, 'but not in the language of the city kennels. Well, that is over. Back to the cleaner business of war!'

CHAPTER X

We held urgent council that same day how to proceed, for the next two or three weeks might be invaluable to us if well used. We knew already that great numbers of carpenters had again been shipped in haste to Anglesey, where the earl of Hereford was now in command, so plainly an attempt was to be made to repair the bridge of boats, but even that enterprise would take some time, and the great loss of men and armour and horses in the strait would not be easily replaced. The king remained at Rhuddlan, and had even withdrawn his advanced outposts, so that now none of his garrisons, apart from that in Anglesey, was further west than the Clwyd valley.

'By the number of foot soldiers he's dismissed,' Tudor said, 'he could be abandoning the fight for this season, but I doubt it. I think he's waiting for his Gascons, and meantime saving money and stores. Feeding such an army as his is no light matter, even with our corn harvest, and when he's ready, and some prospect of the Anglesey division being ready to move with him, he can easily send out fresh writs, and pay whatever numbers he can raise, if he thinks the period of service need not be long.'

Llewelyn heard them all out, and pondered the courses open to him. 'What we must not do,' he said, 'is to be shut up here with no way of linking hands with those allies we have to the south, and no channel by which we can move to help them, or they to help us. David, can you hold everything here for a while, if I go south?'

David grimaced, calculating the possible term of his security. 'I shall be safe enough for a while, and have nothing to do but keep watch. As long as four weeks, surely, perhaps longer. He cannot make good his losses earlier than that.'

The young Llewelyn said, earnestly watching his uncle's face: 'Are you coming to us? My brothers have gone to ground there. If you come, we might do much.'

'I am going into the waist of Wales,' said the prince, 'but you shall come with me, and go home to help your brothers. I shall be holding hands one way with you, and the other here with David, and keeping the ways open. I am going into Maelienydd and Builth, to see what recruiting Edward has done for me there in Mortimer country.'

'Good!' said David. 'It's a right choice. Of all things we need a highway north and south. Go with God, and leave the north to me for four weeks, and if the need arises, I'll send to you.'

So we made ready to march within two days, and the winds that had torn apart Edward's bridge sank submissively into stillness now that

Edward was embattled in Rhuddlan with his rage and his hatred and his temporary helplessness. Halfway through November the sun came through, as it does freakishly, gilding all the mountain tops and filling all the valleys with fine blue mist, like a meadow full of harebells. And in this hush we massed and marched.

The parting of those two brothers was as spare and brief that day as their dangers were great, their resolution unbending, and their need extreme. While we were gathering in the bailey they spoke but few words to each other, and those to the point, of arms and supplies, and how the forces each had could best be used. There were clouds massing again to the north, though the rest of the sky was fair, and David said that in two or three days there would be a change, and we might look for snow. And all the while they eyed each other steadily and hard, with great eyes, but never spoke one word from beneath the guarded surface of their minds. But when the prince went to mount, David himself stooped to hold the stirrup for him, and when he was in the saddle, kissed the hand that held the bridle, and Llewelyn leaned down and kissed him brotherly on the cheek. And then we rode, and did not look back.

We made south for Bala, crossing the upper Dee, to keep the great bleak ridge of the Berwyns between us and the forces from Oswestry. Not until we were well south of the river, and I was riding in my own place close at his left side, did Llewelyn say suddenly, as an honourable man grieving over his debts unpaid: 'I have missed telling him so many things! But doubtless he knows.' And no more did he say then of David, but I knew his mind was on the old days before ever discontent and treason came between them, when this youngest was by far the best loved of his brothers, who had after cost him the most loss, danger and grief, and in the end drew close again and made reparation for all, in this final union that not even the fear of death could dissolve. So his evil genius ended loved as he began, and those two were one as never before had they been one.

We kept long, hard marches, and broke into the lands of Griffith ap Gwenwynwyn along with the first snow, about the nineteenth day of November. There we came apparently unheralded, for we were able to help ourselves to the contents of several of Griffith's scattered barns and farms, and drive off a good many head of his cattle, to our great satisfaction, for by then we had cut our rations to the point where most of us were hungry.

Llewelyn had a little castle at Aberedw, south of Builth, that he had used formerly as a hunting lodge, and though it was on the eastern side of Wye, it was still secure, and as an intelligence base for an army, to be used and quitted as best served, it was excellent. There the prince took up his headquarters for a time, while we probed the state of feeling in the country round, and found friends enough, though they went in fear of the king's men, and reported Builth castle as impregnable, a judgment we accepted. When we came there, young Edmund Mortimer had still not received seisin of his father's lands, though it was granted at last about the twenty-fourth of November, and both the young men were said to be much affronted by the delay, and not at all unsympathetic to the Welsh among their tenants, even though they knew these men willed victory to the prince. In some degree, to be a marcher baron was to understand the passion of sovereign lordship in others, and respect it, as kings were unable to do, who lived by overlordship, and desired to suppress that identity with land that such as Mortimer truly felt, and reduce them to mere custodians for the crown.

Roger Lestrange had taken over the command at Montgomery after Mortimer died, and John Giffard had succeeded him in charge of the garrison of Builth, that same Giffard who had so long maintained lawsuit over Llandovery in right of his wife, Dame Maud Clifford. As soon as we were sure that both these crown officers knew we were in their territory, we used Aberedw but sparingly, as a base for receiving news and messages, and moved the army westward into Mynydd Eppynt and the hills beyond, and held aloof from the river valleys except when we had good information as to where the English forces were. It was the one thing we could do far better than they could, against such overwhelming odds, this living wild in the onset of winter, and moving on foot at the speed of horses, and double their agility.

In the last days of November the big snow came, the ally for which we waited. We saw it first glittering on the crests of the distant mountains, and then the heavy clouds came down and dimmed that shining, and all the sky was darkened, and in the night the fall began. It lasted fitfully into the first week of December, drifting strongly in the valleys, swept thin on the ridges, and driving the English back into their castles for shelter. A great snow it was, that buried unwary travellers and whole flocks of sheep, some of which we dug out before their shepherds ever got near them, and took for our own use. As for us, we were then encamped in the forests of the hills north-west of the river Irfon, perhaps three or four miles from the castle of Builth, close by which castle the Irfon empties into the Wye.

Those are wild hills with few inhabitants, but we had found all those who had their dwellings within that region were good friends to us, and would open their huts to us freely as shelter at need, and for the rest, we were used to providing our own roofs, and made dug-outs of firboughs and bracken in the drifts, and the forests gave us both warmth and covering. All the land on our side the river we held, and had a strong party guarding the only bridge at Orewin, for in these conditions they had little hope of crossing by any other means to get at us. The drifted snow made any attempt at fording most dangerous, every hazard being concealed, and when a partial thaw set in, about three days into December, the perils were no way lessened, for that river drains very mountainous land, and in the thaw the waters come down furiously, and boil out wide over the fields of the lowlands, and where normally the stream might be forded with care, then it runs deep and fast. For that reason we had given the guard at Orewin bridge more than their fair share of our best archers, to prevent close approach from the other side. And we, from the hills above, raided wherever we could sight a party of the

English in arms, harried such of their patrols and ambushed such of their stores as we could, and evaded any possibility of being brought to pitched battle in the valley.

Westward we had contact with the sons of Meredith ap Owen in Cardigan, though over some of the bleakest uplands in all Wales, and across the Irfon by night we could still get word back and forth to Aberedw. Many of the local Welshry had risen and joined the prince's banner, and there were others who hesitated whether to dare, of whom we had word from time to time, and encouraged such leanings every way we could, even taking risks in the matter. So it seemed but one more similar approach, from Welshmen tempted but afraid to take the plunge, when a messenger slipped through to us from Aberedw in the night of the eighth of December, to say that a furtive stranger had come urgently begging to get word to the prince of Wales, from some who willed him well but were close under Lestrange's eye, and must tread softly, and therefore wanted a secret meeting. Of whom this very uneasy visitor was only the envoy, and knew little, but could promise that those who sent him might be of the greatest help, for they were no common farmers or troopers. So far, apart from this mention of higher personages, it was much what we had been receiving for ten days or more, in some cases to good effect. But it took quite a new turn when our man produced from under his cotte a written roll, brought and left by the stranger. We had not expected a letter. Most people were afraid to write even if they knew how, or could get a clerk to do it for them.

Llewelyn held the roll to the light of our sheltered fire, but it bore no superscription, and the seal was deliberately mutilated, which was no wonder. The wonder was that anyone under Lestrange's eye would dare set quill to parchment at all. Nor did many of the troopers write, or have to do with clerks but very rarely.

'And, my lord,' said the messenger, 'this man hid his face as well as he might, and was in haste to be gone, but he stayed long enough to say what he'd been told to say, that here you'll find the time and place where they hope to come safely to meet with you, and that they entreat you to come if by any means you can. Also that you will understand that those matters there mentioned are but tokens, from which you may guess at truth where others might miss. Then he went, and was glad to have his errand done. But I know one thing more that he did not tell. For he went in a hooded cloak like a countryman, but when he mounted the wind blew the fronts of his cloak apart, and I saw he had a stout leather coat under it, and a badge on the coat. The Mortimer badge!'

'Mortimer!' said Llewelyn, arrested with the seal under his fingers. 'You are sure?'

'Sure, my lord. I know it well. And his horse was no country cob neither.'

'Is it possible?' said Llewelyn in a whisper, more to himself than to any other. And he broke the seal and read the letter, bending close to have the firelight on the leaf, and frowning in doubt and wonder.

'No date or place or salutation. I should expect none. But the rest! The cause of Wales, they tell me, has friends here, where tenant and lord alike may be burdened with fealties that try them hard, and cross the natural bent of their blood and affections, no less than their faith in justice. I am bidden remember a bond of mutual support, never yet called upon but never repudiated, and to think on a double tie through father and mother. And if I trust as they trust me, I am to come two miles north from here, to the track that runs above the bank of the Wye, to a barn at the edge of the forest where three paths meet, as soon as I may after noon on the eleventh day of this month, when by God's grace they will be free of watching eyes, and there wait for me. To come out of mail and plain, like a countryman, as they must, for there are eyes everywhere. And not in force, but alone or with but one companion. And they entreat me, if I am there first, to wait for them in hiding, for they will surely come.'

'It is much to ask,' said Tudor at his elbow, anxious and distrustful.

'It is what they might well be forced to ask, for their own safety,' said Llewelyn, 'if they are what they purport to be. Even a countryman may carry sword or dagger under his cloak, these days, but he would hardly be cased in mail. They ask but reasonably. Modest travellers do not go with armed escorts. And who else claims kinship with me on both sides his parentage? Who else is fast bound under Lestrange's eye on the one side, and Giffard's, according to report, on the other?'

For the Mortimer brothers, who might well recall their father's recent pact of mutual aid with Llewelyn – in peace or war, saving his duty to the king! –had a paternal grandmother who was Llewelyn Fawr's daughter, but also a mother who was sister to the wife of Llewelyn Fawr's son David, from whom my lord inherited. And the elder, Edmund, now newly in seisin of his lands, was attached to Lestrange's force working from Montgomery, and no doubt under close tutelage, since he had made plain his displeasure at the king's neglect of his right. And Roger, the younger, was said to be serving with Giffard from Builth. Moreover, the messenger had certainly worn the Mortimer badge.

Tudor in his turn asked: 'Is this possible?'

Llewelyn thought, and said: 'It is possible. I would not have said it of their father, however warmly he had pledged me support and aid, that he could ever have swerved from his fealty to Edward, for my sake or any other man's. But after Edward has kept this young man landless and owing no fealty and receiving no royal countenance for a month, I would not say but Edmund might consider his faith and service to be slighted and undervalued, and be more inclined to sting in return.'

'Now, when seisin has been granted, and he newly owes his homage for it?' said Tudor.

'But has not yet paid it,' said Llewelyn. And that was true, for homage could not be paid for the lands until Edward and Edmund Mortimer met face to face, and the king was in Rhuddlan, and Edmund here in the middle march.

They discussed it long, not blinking the possible dangers, but the upshot was that he would go. For the promise of reinforcements he thought the risks worth taking, and rated them no higher than many he had taken lightly enough in the past. No man rushes headlong into what may be an ambush, but in this affair he took what precautions were sensible, and then ventured boldly. I myself took the letter by daylight, and scrutinised the defaced seal with care, and I thought that by such traces as were left I was justified in believing it Mortimer's. And whatever we could credit of those two young men, we could not credit that they would lend themselves to personal treachery. A high-spirited young nobleman smarting at neglect and humiliation may take his sword over to the opposing side. We held him less likely to connive at deceit and murder.

'And if I go,' said Llewelyn, 'I go upon the terms held out. I will not put them in peril by any cheat, as I do not believe they would imperil me but in open battle, and fairly. I go alone.'

I said no. And then he looked at me as though he had awakened out of a short and troubled sleep, and stood at gaze. 'Or with one companion,' I said.

'True!' said Llewelyn, and smiled. 'I am allowed to have you with me, now as ever. So be it!'

On the tenth of December there was fresh snow, but moist and fitful, lying wetly over that already fallen, that was dimpling into holes like frayed cloth, and the grudging waters of the slow thaw dribbling down to swell the already swollen river. We rode the hills and surveyed our defences, and made due inspection of the guard at the bridge below, and all was dank and chill and still, not a soul stirring out of Builth. They said that the lady was there, Dame Maud, come hither with her husband when he took over this command, and now held there by the snows from returning to her more congenial Llandovery. A sad lady I think she was, widowed from her first husband, William Longspée, a son of the earl of Salisbury, whom she had loved, and married now to this greedy, ambitious creature whom I fear she loved not at all, and who used her and her royal descent and claims to further his own desires, as often as not against her will. She did not love litigation, and had to suffer his insistent use of her name beside his in case after case, since he had few pretensions but through her. She did not love war, but was trapped within it like so many women before her, her heart-strings drawn out upon both sides.

In the night it froze again, but not hard. We rose to a leaden sky, and made ready.

The prince had with him on this campaign, as always, the full trappings of his chapel, that with us were perhaps more modest than those of the English crown, and could be carried more easily. And let it not be thought that the general excommunication levelled against his person had deprived him of the consolations of his faith. There was never wanting priest or brother to sing his mass. The bishop of St Asaph, cited by Peckham to answer for his failure to issue the letters of excommunication against the prince, had risen in anger to demand the excommunication of the English soldiery who burned his cathedral. And the Cistercians, closest of all brotherhoods to the defiant austerity of Wales, followed, served, harboured him wherever he showed his face, loved him and all his to the last. We had with us then a Cistercian brother who sang mass for the prince that eleventh day of December, in the half-frozen snows in the forest above the Irfon, in the murk of a morning hovering between ice and tears.

Then, when the day was well advanced, with time and to spare for the distance we had to go, he and I rode, dun and plain in homespun cloaks and without armour, but keeping our swords. We had one stream to cross on the way, that drained down into the Wye in the town of Builth, like the Irfon, but here in the uplands it was but a swollen brook, and no stay to us. Some miles to the north there was a bridge over the Wye, too distant to be of value to them in approaching the present position of the prince's army, for we could withdraw long before they got near us, but we guessed that those who planned to meet us at the barn would come by that way, all the more certainly if, as we thought likely, they were coming from Radnor. We made for the track that kept the shoulder of the hills, overhanging the river valley, and rode openly until we judged we must be nearing the place. Woodlands skirted the way on the upland side, and on the river side the slope dipped steeply, and was open grass beneath the snow, but for occasional clumps of trees where the folded ground gave shelter. Here Llewelyn bade me take to the forest and keep pace with him there unseen, while he kept the open track.

'Let me seem to be coming alone, if that is what they want, and still have a friend in reserve to guard my back.'

So I wove my way in the trees, sufficiently withdrawn not to be seen from the road, and at a rise of the track Llewelyn checked, gazing before him, and I guessed that he could see, though without emerging I could not, the spot ahead of us where the three tracks met, and the barn to which we were bound. I drew somewhat nearer, and he turned his head and said clearly: 'It is the place. One track comes up from the Wye, by the valley of some small brook, I judge. There are trees in the cleft. One track moves off to the north-west, into the hills, and the forest swallows it. The barn is there on the edge of the level ground, between those two roads.'

'And no man stirring there?' I said.

'No. We are early. I shall be first at the meeting-place Stay in cover,' he said, 'but keep close. I doubt if I shall need your help, but I shall be right glad to know it's within call.'

So we held station as before, and went on at this soft pace, and soon I caught between the trees, where they thinned, glimpses of a large timber building, black against the fretted snow. Nothing moved about us as we drew near to it. Llewelyn sat his horse for some minutes, watching, and he and I might have been the only creatures in the world. The great door of the barn hung open, its heavy bar jutting. Within was only a darkness and a silence.

'I am going in,' he said, when he was satisfied. 'Keep within cover and keep watch for me, and do whatever seems best to you.'

I came as close as I could to where the forest path crossed me, and watched him ride up to the open door, and hitch his horse to a solitary sapling that grew from the foot of the wall. A moment he stood in the open doorway, and then, finding the place empty, passed within.

There was a long, judged moment of delay after he vanished, and then suddenly and silently a man broke out of the bushes, above the right-hand path that climbed obliquely from the Wye, and ran to the door and heaved it to, slamming the wooden bar into its socket and shutting the prince within. One man only, for no more followed, and this one was so intent on his task that I was upon him and riding him down before he heard me, and turned with a cry, plucking out a dagger from his belt. A second great shout he uttered, loud and defiant in warning, and flung towards the downhill track, before my sword took him in the hollow of neck and shoulder, and half-shore head from body, and he dropped into the snow, and jerked like a broken spider away from under my horse's hooves, leaving red smears behind him, and after a few crippled writhings, lay still.

I leaped down and dragged back the bar, and Llewelyn burst out into daylight, and grasping the need without words, raced to unhitch his horse, and was in the saddle beside me even before we heard the thudding of hooves and flurry of voices climbing out of the valley.

'He called them,' I said, 'as I struck him . . . God knows how many of them.'

The first rose into view, labouring furiously up the slope from the copse below, where they had lain hidden, and though they were not yet upon us, they were between us and the way by which we had come. Ten of them in view, perhaps even more behind them. There was but one way for us to go, if we were not to fight our way through them, and that was by the forest path and into the hills to westward, and there we headed, crouched low in expectation that they would have archers with them, but there were no shots, only the great shout they launched after us before we vanished into the darkness of the trees.

Llewelyn set the pace, and well for us we had hardly done more than walk our horses on the way, while the company pursuing us may well have ridden further than we, certainly if they came from Radnor. But there was no way of knowing, for they wore no distinguishing livery, and the man I had killed bore no badge. For some time we rode hard and kept to the track to increase our lead, but we knew they were no great way behind, though blessedly out of sight, when Llewelyn struck off to the left, hoping to make a circle in cover and come out upon the road again as soon as we dared. But they had spread out their forces, some to the right of the track, some to the left, the main body keeping to the open where speed was possible. We heard them crashing between the trees at no distance behind, and had the choice of turning again and running ahead of them, or continuing our course at dangerous speed and hoping to cross them undetected and draw clear. Llewelyn chose the former, rightly, for we should surely have run into the arms of the most widely deployed of them. We ran again, weaving and gained on them, and turned left again, and so gradually bore round across their flank by stages, as the hare runs, until in deep forest we were suddenly aware how the sounds of them were passing us by. Then Llewelyn reined in, and I beside him, and we sat like stone until we were sure. We had drawn clear by so short a distance, their out-stretched arms had almost brushed us as they passed. The clash and clamour of the hunt drew away, keeping its forward course. And we turned and bore left again, until we found a foot-track that eased our going, and must lead us back, certainly not to the road above the Wye, but by a much greater circle to reach our camp from the west.

'They meant no killing,' said Llewelyn, now that we could draw breath and talk again, 'or they would have had bowmen and used them. No, I was to be taken alive. Edward would be glad of such a triumph.' And he asked: 'Whose men were they? Did you see any trace?'

But they could have been any from among the ranks of our enemies, there was no way of knowing.

'I do not believe,' he said firmly, 'that my young cousins had any hand in this. It is not Mortimer fighting. What if the messenger at Aberedw wore Edmund's badge? It need not have been Edmund who sent him. Far more likely to be Giffard or Lestrange. Both have Mortimer troops with them. Both are in Edward's confidence, and not above using underhand ways to do his will and get his gratitude.'

As to this, I doubt if the truth will ever be known. It was a foul trick, and its dirt has clung to the name of Mortimer in the popular tale, but considering how Edmund showed later, I, too, doubt if the guilt was his. It may not even belong to Lestrange or Giffard or any of the king's captains, but to some ingenious regional officer of his who saw how the Mortimer dudgeon might be exploited to betray the prince and end the war. Of only one thing do I feel certain, that Edward knew of it and had sanctioned it. I do not believe any man of his would have dared, without that assurance of approval.

'Well, so may all treacheries fail,' said Llewelyn, and shook the ugliness of it from his shoulders, and pressed ahead, for we had lost the middle part of the day, and had many more miles to go than by the way we had come.

Nevertheless, he thought no further evil, nor did I, until we broke out of the forest into fields we recognised, and were back within a mile or two of our camp. The short day was drawing down into murk and mist an hour or more ahead of twilight, and out of the river valley drifting clouds of vapour coiled. And then, clear of the muffling trees, we heard in the distance the muffled echoes of voices bellowing and horses screaming, and the clash of weapons and stamping of flight and pursuit, fitful and far and terrible, the noises of battle, and battle already as good as lost and won.

He uttered a great cry of grief and understanding and loss, knowing at last for what purposes, besides his own capture, he had been lured away. 'Oh, God!' he said. 'They are here among us! But how have they crossed? They cannot have stormed the bridge. Oh, God, what have I done?' And he set spurs to his horse and rode headlong for those places, invisible in the murk of distance, where the lamentable sounds cried out for him. And I after him as hard as I could go, but even so he drew ahead of me, and for the coils of mist, that shifted and spun, sometimes I saw him clear, and sometimes he showed as a wraith of mist himself, and sometimes was lost.

So we came into those fields below the camp, and in the snow about us there were men lying scattered here and there, huddles of rags hardly swelling the drifts where they lay, and blood spattered along the soiled whiteness, and now and again a horse heaving and crying, or a broken lance. And still before us, but receding, the clamour of fighting, shrill and bitter with despair. Towards that he rode, seeing but twenty yards or so before him clear at any time, wild to get back to his own and live or die with them.

They had come at us two ways, for the sounds encircled the place where the camp had been, closing in both from the river valley and from the heights beyond. And in great force, or so we judged as best we could, for we came too late to serve or save. All we knew was that they had swept all this slope from Orewin bridge clear of life, and only the dead and the wounded and the stragglers remained, scattered round us in the soiled and bloody snow. Even the clash of arms receded before us, mocking his desperate pursuit.

Men, living men, rose out of the mist ahead of us, English lancers prowling the slopes after the main army had passed on, killing and looting. Three of them there were, bent over a tumbled body, when Llewelyn burst upon them hardly even aware when these puny creatures started up between him and his broken army. Two of them sprang clear and ran in terror before the galloping horse. The third, caught on his knees, half-rose too late, and then dropped again, according to his training, and braced his lance in the blood-stained earth, and leaned his body on to it to hold it fast. He closed his eyes and his mind, and made himself all dogged weight, seeing no other escape.

Llewelyn had not even drawn his sword, there was no mail upon him, he was naked to death as men come naked to life. He rode full upon the embedded lance, taking it under the breast-bone. It seemed to me that he sprang erect and stood in his stirrups, tall as the heavens, and the terrified horse raced on from under him, and he was left impaled, upright and motionless in the air a long moment, and then crashed like a great and splendid tree to earth, his fall shaking it so that all that hillside shuddered and shrank at the shock. The lance-head, that had passed clean through him and stood out a foot and more behind his shoulders, snapped off short in flying splinters as he fell. He lay on his back in deep snow, his arms cast wide on either side his body, and the lance shaft erect from under his breast. And the lancer who had pierced him scuttled on all fours away from the impact, and picked himself up and ran headlong after his fellows, seeing me burst out of the murk and bear down upon him.

I over-rode him by some yards before I could draw rein and fall, rather than climb, out of the saddle. I let my bridle go, and dropped into the snow beside Llewelyn. All the sounds of fighting dwindled away and were lost, and that slope from the river was narrowed into a little place of cold and quiet and loss. It was so still I could hear the Irfon bubbling along its bed below us, between the piled stones and under the melting floes.

He lay with his hands braced deep through the snow beside him, his fingers digging down to clutch at the bereaved and bloodied soil of Wales. Blood welled slowly round the haft of the lance with every breath he drew, and the shaft quivered and leaned to the same measure, counting his remaining moments in labour and pain. His face was like a bronze mask, fixed and motionless, with open, anguished eyes. When I leaned close to be seen, and laid fearful hands upon him, his lips moved, saying: 'Samson? I have spent what you saved for me . . . I am sorry!' And frantic tears sprang. 'Oh, God, I have failed!' he said in a whisper. 'Now *you* save!'

I felt about his body, and knew, as he knew, that he had his death-wound. Even for the breaking of the lance I thanked God, that he was not impaled in air, in indignity and worse agony, but lay like a king on his death-bed, though his pillows were the drifts of snow, thawed and again frozen into great cushions of white. I shrugged my cloak off me and wrapped it over him as well as I could for the jutting shaft, and all the time I wept like a madman who does not know he weeps. The blood spread gradually like a great, dark rose under him, in no haste, but there was life in him yet, and still he had a voice, soft, feeling and tranquil.

He said: 'Samson . . .' and after a long gathering of his darkened powers: 'I need you! Don't fail me now, you who never failed me.' And then he waited, his eyes fixed upon the sky that leaned in heavy dusk over him. 'A priest,' he said. 'Find me a priest. I have got my death, get me my peace with God.' And again, after long silence, faint as a sigh: 'I cannot go to her in my sins!'

I was loth to go even a pace away from him, all the more with those scavengers already prowling the field and despoiling the dead, but his wish was my law. Priests, like crows, come where battle has been, not to batten on the bodies but to salvage the souls. Where is there greater need of them? All our own people were scattered far, those who still lived, gone to ground in the deep forests until they could gather and form some ordered company once more. But from Builth there was free passage now across the Irfon, and Builth was not far, and here about this desolate hillside there must be English as well as Welsh at the point of most dire need, and they would not be left to die unshriven. Therefore I made a cast down towards the bridge, as close as I could without losing sight of my lord, and saw a small picket of four men keeping the crossing, stamping their chilled feet and pacing to keep their blood moving, and passing in, now and again, a handful of foot soldiers, or a mounted man. And at last what I waited for, a robed priest, distressed and in haste, with a little serving boy at his heels carrying cross and paten.

I let him get some way up the slope, away from the guards, before I stepped in his path and entreated him to come with me, where a man was dying. And he came, unquestioning. A young man he was, earnest and sad, and he said that he was in the service of the Lady Maud, and sent at her instance. When I brought him to the prince he knelt in the snow beside him, and looked long into the upturned face, and marvelled, though he said no word then but to do his office. He stooped low to take confession from Llewelyn's lips, for the prince's voice, though clear, was faint as a breath. I kneeled beside and covered my face. There is no man, not the best, is not better for unburdening his heart even of those matters no other would take for sins. And he was going to another and perpetual bridal, who had been unable to approach the first without first cleansing from his spirit the last shadow and the last bitterness.

But when he had ended and made his act of contrition, and the priest would have pronounced absolution, clearly and loud Llewelyn said: 'No, that you cannot. I do not ask it. I am excommunicate.' And at that the young man started up in wonder and dismay, and drew me a little aside to question.

'This man by his clothing is Welsh. He is unarmed, what was he doing here in battle without mail, to come by such a death? And excommunicate? All I can do for him I will do, and pray rest to his soul, for with God it makes no difference of what race he comes, or for what cause he fought. But to him it may, and to me, and to others. I must know, who is he?'

And I told him, for soon all men would know it, it would be cried from end to end of England with triumphant joy, and carried throughout Wales in terrible lamentation. 'He is Llewelyn ap Griffith, prince of Wales. Let your lady know of it, for she is his cousin, and give her his thanks for this last grace.'

'God sort all!' said the chaplain, awe-stricken. 'She shall know it, and she shall be the first to know it from me.' And he went back to pray with the prince, and courteously begged his forgiveness that he might not give to him the sacrament he carried to others. Yet he blessed him to God before he left us and went to all those other sad duties that waited for him. And then we two were left alone.

Llewelyn's eyes were closed, and from the effort of speech a few flecks of blood dewed his lips. I watched the great rose of blood, in the heart of which he lay, spread its wine-red petals and melt the snow until the soiled green of grass showed through. I took his hand between mine, that he might be assured, who could, as I thought, no longer see me, that I was still beside him. But at that touch he opened his eyes, and they were bright and fierce, and he gripped my hand hard.

'Samson!' he said, and I leaned down to hear. 'You can do better for me than grieve,' he said, reading my face. 'There is still a prince of Wales. Go to my brother, Samson. Be to him as you have been to me. It is not yet over, because I am out of the fight.'

'As long as you live,' I said, 'I will never leave you.'

'Yes,' he said, 'you will. I bid you, and you cannot refuse me. When did I ever ask anything of you in vain? Now I want three things of you, on your allegiance. No, on your love! The first . . . Her picture is round my neck. Let me have it in my hand!'

In terror of aggravating his pain, I raised his head enough to lift clear the medallion of the child Eleanor, and laid it in his right hand, closing the fingers over it. In all that bleak expanse of cold and darkness, this one small thing was warm from the great, failing fire of his heart.

'And the second and third are my last commission to you, and then I thank God for you, and take my leave. Pull out the lance –'

I cried aloud that I neither could nor would, for that was his death, and the end of a world for me.

'Dear fool Samson,' he said softly, 'I am a dead man already. I grow weary of this waiting. Pull out the lance, and go to David!'

He was my lord, and I did his bidding. First I kneeled and kissed him on the brow, and then I laid hold on the shaft of the lance, and dragged it out of his body, streaming tears like heavy rain. He was lifted from the ground with it, like a man starting up from sleep, but even then he never uttered cry or moan. Then the shaft came away, and his body fell back and lay still upon crimson, and crimson came boiling out of his riven breast and covered him royally, and still it seemed to me that he smiled.

They say he was still breathing, and lived some few minutes more, when Lestrange's men found him and knew him at last. If so, they must have come very soon after I left him. I let fall the broken shaft out of my hand, and turned and went stumbling and groping up the slope towards the forest, fleeing that field of Orewin bridge as once I fled the field of Evesham, and leaving, as then, a great piece of my own being dead beside the body of a man I loved and revered above all others. And I cried silently to God in the darkness of my spirit and the darkness of the night, as I had cried for Earl Simon, that in this world there was no justice, but the best were calumniated and betrayed and brought to nought, as God himself was when he ventured among the sons of men.

CHAPTER XI

Concerning Orewin bridge and what followed, I tell now, to make all plain, those things I learned only long afterwards, by laborious gleaning from many sources, for I could not rest until I knew to the last what had befallen even the poor body of my lord. To this day I do not know who sent the letter that drew him away from his army, but I do know it was written as part of the plan of attack that trapped the Welsh forces into pitched battle at last. For the English had found a local man who knew a secret and safe fording-place upstream from the bridge, and sheltered from view, and on the appointed day, aided by the drifting mist, they put a strong company across the Irfon there and took the outpost at the bridge from the rear, and killed every man. Then they brought all their force across by both routes, and sent one company of cavalry and men-at-arms by a great circuit to the rear of the Welsh position, and only when they had taken station, launched their frontal attack at speed up the slope. They had many archers, who held by the stirrup-leathers of the troopers and ran with them, and as they came within range, dropped aside and began to shoot at will. Without the prince, the Welsh fought savagely and well, but in disorder, being surrounded and greatly outnumbered. In the end they broke, and each man sought his own escape. Had Llewelyn been there, I do not believe it could ever have happened so. He could both plan, and work by instinct when plans fell apart. But he was not there. He came too late to save, only in time to die.

As for the forces that took part in that battle, certainly all Giffard's troops from Builth were there, and both the Mortimer brothers with their followings, and part of the Montgomery garrison, though I could never hear that Lestrange himself was present. In the evening certain of his men, as he reported to Edward, found and knew the body of the prince, some said they were there before he died. In the pouch he wore inside the belt of his chausses they found the letter that betrayed him, and his privy seal, and in his hand the little enamelled portrait of his wife, the gift of Earl Simon. These Edmund Mortimer took into his keeping. By the very fact that Edmund preserved the letter, and was not ashamed to show it, to notify the archbishop and have it copied for him, I am sure that he was not guilty of uttering it, and of that I am glad. There are also other proofs speaking for him.

It was not to be hoped that those enemies who came upon the prince at his death should respect his body, more than Earl Simon's body was respected after Evesham. Some man of Giffard's or Lestrange's struck off the head, and Lestrange sent it to Edward at Rhuddlan for his comfort and reassurance, and thence it was sent to be displayed at the Tower of London, the brow wreathed in ivy as a mocking crown. For a brow that could no longer bleed or feel pain, ivy served as well as thorns.

And for that dear body, it rests headless, like Earl Simon's body, felon and saint, yet it rests, in the unrelenting memories of men as in the gentle earth. The young chaplain kept his word, and reported faithfully to Dame Maud Giffard the news of her cousin's death, and before worse slight could be put upon his person she sent and had the corpse delivered with all reverence into the care of the Cistercian brothers of Cwm Hir abbey, and forthwith wrote to Archbishop Peckham, requesting absolution for Llewelyn, that he might be buried in consecrated ground. Peckham replied, and dutifully notified Edward that he had so replied, that he could not without sin do as she asked, unless she provided proof that the prince had shown sign of penitence before he died. Whereupon she showed that he had asked for a priest, and that her priest had indeed ministered to him. And further, Edmund Mortimer testified that his servants, present on the field, had also borne witness that the prince had made confession to a priest, while his brother Roger said that a Cistercian had sung mass for the prince the day he died, and the furnishings of his chapel, and the vestments, were in Roger's care, and could be seen.

So they spoke for him, and they prevailed, and he is buried in blessedness at Cwm Hir, in a spot so remote and fair and still, they who are laid there cannot but sleep well.

And for these reasons here set out, I absolve the Mortimers of that cruel treachery that slew Llewelyn and stripped Wales of its shield and sword. And I am glad, as he is glad, where he abides. For they were his kin, and he had a kindness for them.

As for us, the remnant, desolate, broken and bereaved, we crawled westward into the hills and forests as best we could, licking wounds that healed over vainly, since they covered one great wound that would never again be healed, for the heart was riven out of us with his going, however we might still fight for the shell of our hopes. Once we were out of reach of the huntsmen we paused to look for our fellows, and recovered with shame the discipline of an army, gathering in companies, even making war when the chance offered. I found such a party that night, Tudor among them, wounded, shattered and old in a day, and dealt him what I think was his death-blow, for though he lived to reach his northern lands again, he never bore arms more, and his hurts were never cured. The word went forth throughout Wales that the great prince was dead, and the laments the bards made for him cried to heaven that without him we were left orphaned and forsaken, robbed of our only shield and stay. And I could not but think how some of those who thus lamented had turned their coats nimbly enough in the past, and left him naked to the storm, and how, if they had been always as steadfast as he, Wales might have been a nation indeed, and Llewelyn might have lived to see his dream stay with him as the sun rose, instead of vanishing with the dark.

But we are men, faulty and weak and foolish, and we were back in the chaos of the past, and threatened by worse than all the past had ever done to us, and he was dead who was more than my prince to me, my star-brother born in the same night, with whom I should have died also.

So many of the best were dead, or left behind wounded on the field of Orewin bridge, or prisoner to Giffard in Builth, that we were but a remnant, unable to hold the centre of Wales to make a highroad north and south. Rhys Wyndod and his brothers in Ystrad Tywi, Meredith's sons in Cardigan, must fend for themselves. All we could do was with-draw into Gwynedd, for if that heartland was lost, all was lost. So we returned, limping and hungry, to rejoin David in Dolwyddelan, and I, having my lord's charge heavy upon me, took horse and rode ahead at speed, to carry the news to David that he was the heir to his brother's right and his brother's burden.

All was as we had left it when I rode in by the steep track, and climbed to the ward. They had had no fighting beyond occasional brushes between patrols. Edward had kept fast in Rhuddlan, grimly debating whether to force the fight through the winter or lie up and nurse his present gains until the spring. But I think he had made up his mind to press on at all costs, even before he heard of Llewelyn's death. Certainly he felt his load lightened as by a miracle, and his war as good as won, when Lestrange's letter and the envied, respected, hated head reached him together, which may well have been about the time that I went with the same word to David in the armoury of Dolwyddelan.

He was out of mail, for he had his watch well posted, and had not been called to arms since we left him. He was watching the careful tempering of his own sword, and turned from it to stare upon me when I came in. The shadow of my news was in my face, for he said: 'Come within!' and drew me in his arm into the high chamber, and shut us in together. And there I told him all I had to tell.

David sat with white and carven face, and never took his eyes from me. At the end he was silent a long moment, walled within himself, and then he said: 'And this charge he laid on me? Those are his words? There is still a prince in Wales. It is not over yet, because I am out of the fight. That is his message to me?'

I said that it was, word for word.

'God's pity!' said David very softly, as if to himself. And to me: 'What have they done with him?'

I said what I then believed, and after was justified in believing, that the lady in Builth would not suffer him to be misused, and her chaplain had tended him, and sworn to see right done to him.

'God himself has fallen short of that,' said David, 'with less excuse than man, who labours with very faulty tools.' His voice was low, burdened and bitter. 'I speak who know,' he said. 'Who has done more or worse to him? I have been his downfall and his death.'

'You are now,' I said, 'his hope and his heir. The talaith he wore comes down on your brows now. It is no heavier than when he wore it.'

'It has hammered him into the earth,' said David, and laughed, but with so curious and estranged a laughter that it did not jar. 'For God's sake,' he said, 'give me leave to weep a while, you who know me best. I am lost, like you. I loved him out of all measure, and I have been his bane. And he is dead!' But if he wept indeed, it was within. He said aloud: 'Lord, if it be possible, take away this cup from me. Nevertheless, not as I will but as thou wilt!' And he laughed again, very grimly, at his own blasphemy, for he was speaking not to his God, but to his brother.

'Who knows but it may still be possible?' I said. 'The king may be resolved on getting his way, but he may still be glad to get it without further killing or deeper debt. Llewelyn set you free once to buy your life at Edward's price, if you so chose. He would not blame you now. Send and try!'

'You know better than that,' said David. 'I might have been tempted to forsake him, living, to keep my own life. But neither for that nor for any other cause will I forsake him, dead. I am my brother now. I cannot disgrace him.'

So again we addressed ourselves to the war, as the year ended, at great disadvantage but not wholly without hope. Our losses in men and horses were great, and in our food resources still greater, but greater than all was the loss of Llewelyn, who alone could bind the Welsh together, and with whose death the heart was gone out of them. Edward, on the other hand, had had such huge expenses that he was then quite without money, besides owing some near thirty thousand marks to his Italian bankers. But kings have always some way of extorting money. His Gascons were then coming in in considerable numbers, probably as many as two thousand cavalry and foot, including large companies of crossbowmen, and soon we saw only too clearly that he was planning an immediate advance, without waiting for the snows to pass. He had sent his close friend Otto of Granson to reform the disorganised army in Anglesey, and was again amassing great numbers of woodmen and foresters, and putting his Gascons into the field as fast as they came, both in the garrisons of Rhuddlan and other castles, and also in Anglesey. In the first week of January he again moved up a strong force from Rhuddlan to establish an advanced post at Llangernyw, and though we sent out reinforcements for the troops already fighting there, and did our best to prevent, we had not the strength to hold them back for long. They paid heavily in men, but they set up their base. We could do nothing to cut the safe lines of communication they enjoyed with Chester, by which they brought up their newly raised English levies, and thus manned and overmanned Llangernyw became impregnable. We had expected an advance along the coast towards Aberconway but he chose instead to cross the uplands to these higher waters.

'He is coming here to uproot us,' said David. 'He wants me out of Dolwyddelan.'

Edward's next move proved him right, for the strike that followed was towards the river at Llanrwst, and thence to secure a closer base at Bettws. David took the field then with all the troopers he could raise, to hold off the enemy from his castle, and there was very bitter fighting and great slaughter all the way, but nevertheless, they advanced. Again great numbers of archers guarded the woodmen as they felled, opening a great road towards Dolwyddelan. Some of the Gascon companies lost as many as half their men, but still they came on, having many more in reserve. We could afford no such losses.

Then also began the inevitable since all those chiefs cut off from us in the Middle Country, and in Maelor and the south, found themselves facing impossible numbers, and had no choice but to fight to the death or come to the king's peace, and many surrendered on the promise of grace, only to find themselves under grave pressure to change their allegiance and fight for the English. Edward's grace was never freely given.

Worse than these, who were helpless once severed from David's leadership, were those who began, as of old, to calculate where their interests lay, and deliberately change their coats accordingly. Tudor's sickness and melancholy were aggravated when his own son Griffith deserted David, turned to the besiegers, and aided them with his knowledge of the tracks around Dolwyddelan. In acknowledgement of which service he was afterwards made constable of that castle, a traitor in command of the birthplace of Llewelyn Fawr! For before the end of January we could no longer sustain the siege, but were forced to withdraw and hold the mountain ways that protected Dolbadarn. Edward had got his way, and again froze into armed and powerful stillness while he garrisoned and repaired Dolwyddelan to use as a forward base, and waited for the weather to improve. For he now commanded all the left bank of the Conway, and could make his way up and down the valley at leisure.

I think that David had seen the end long before, but he did not waver in his undertaking. When we heard that Granson had crossed from Anglesey to Bangor, and there established a strong bridge-head, David sent to bring the royal child Gwenllian with her attendants to join Elizabeth at Dolbadarn, for once the English were on the northern coast, Aber would not long be safe. All that he could do, to make the best use of such forces as he had left, that he did, always with a calm and resolute face, but by then, God knows, there were some faces among us far from either calm or resolution, for not to put it more gravely, we were exhausted and half-starved, and living wild in the hills, in the wretched end of a cold winter, in continuing frosts. What wonder if a few deserted and made their way to more congenial places?

I shared the shelter of a crevice of rock once with another unfortunate patrolling in a late snow-storm and a howling wind, and found I was sitting beside Godred, my half-brother, shoulder huddled to shoulder for warmth. In the stress of the time I had not thought of him at all, had seen him now and then among the rest and felt nothing, not even a memory of old envies and malices, for we lived only for one thing, life itself, the continuance of a desperate hope and a sacred defiance. And all I felt for him then was startled pity, so wan and thin and soiled he was. So were we all, but I had not realised it until I looked thus closely at him. He knew me, he could not choose but know me, but so little attention had he to spare then from his own miseries that he could not resent me, and had no energy to plague me. He was too empty of food and too full of himself, and even I was an audience.

'We suffer here worse than hunted rats,' he said, shivering. 'Only an army of heroes could survive on meagre pay of a handful of grain and a drop of milk. Can you blame the ones who run? But that they're fools, all the same,' he said bitterly, 'for where is there to run? What use to scurry where there's food enough – and our food, at that! –if you're left no throat for swallowing?'

I had a hunk of bread in my pouch, and broke it with him. He took his share almost greedily, not greatly caring whence it came. I saw as he handled it that he still had the silver ring on his finger, but now it hung slack between his jutting joints, he was so shrunken. I saw in him how we were all grown older, soon to grow old indeed, if we lived on at all. And I was seized with such a grief for us all that it was hardly to be borne. For Godred embittered and disappointed, for Cristin childless and cheated of love, for David driven and trapped in a duty he had never sought, for myself grown old in two loves and fruitful at the end in neither, for Elizabeth who cast all she had without thought into the scale of her loving, and was doomed to be robbed of all, and for Llewelyn and Wales indivisibly, for they were one, harried, cheated, wronged and martyred, the dream and the dreamer hacked down together. I could no longer sit there with my half-brother, my valid image, my bright part grown thus dimmed and withered. For but for his fair colouring and my darkness, his comeliness and my plainness, it was my own face I looked upon. I rose and left him, and rode into the snow.

Yet strangest of all, we still had some who ran to us, and not away, and they were my justification and hope. And the least expected of them was a big, portly, ageing man in a fine, kilted gown and riding a tall, well-fed, stolen horse, who delivered himself into our camp above Llanberis the first day of March, St David's day. He had a sword girt about him, and seemed to know its use, at least enough to be of service, and the horse itself, having sometime been Edward's, was a huge satisfaction to us, for ours were gaunt enough, for want of feed after such a winter. He had a smooth, clerkly face, and the tonsure time had given him, and he spoke very good and forthright Welsh when he was challenged.

'If you want a guarantor for me,' he said, 'bring Master Samson and tell him Cynan is here to fulfil an old prophecy. I tire of the fleshpots. I have come to lay my bones in what is left of Wales.'

He was offhand with me when I questioned him concerning the occasion of his removal to us. He said that he had found himself full of tidings with no way of despatching them, and highly discontented with his isolation, and had worked his way with the commissariat and weaponry to Bettws, as being the nearest base to us, and there simply filched the noble horse he brought with him. To which asset we were welcome, since he had brought whatever he had to add to the common store. Though his wit, he dreaded, was little advantage at this stage, since he had just proved he had none. But even an unpractised hand might be of some worth. And if we were somewhat short of food, he had every hope he might benefit from the restriction, for unlike us, he was too fat for comfort.

I think of Cynan often. I was beside him when he died, he, the arch-clerk, with a sword in his hand. It was in late March, after Edward had moved on to Conway, and there established his new forward base. He had then more than three thousand men in his army, cavalry, footmen and archers, and Granson had enlarged his bridge-head at Bangor, and pushed westward to Carnarvon, and thence crossed the shoulder of Lleyn and reached as far south as Harlech. The great mass of Snowdon stood encircled from every side, at last reduced to that castle under siege that Edward had desired, and now he had only to close in and strangle it. They had ships at their disposal, and kept touch by sea. We were slowly being walled into our lovely, fated mountains.

If David did not find some means of breaking out of the circle, it was only a matter of time before it closed, and crushed him, and with him his wife and family, for they were still at Dolbadarn, and that fortress in the very womb of Snowdon no longer looked a safe refuge. David had a castle at Bere, in Merioneth, in the equally wild region round Cader Idris, and determined to move his family there and garrison the castle as his main base, and in the middle of March the move was made.

That was a most wearisome journey for the women and children, but they made never a murmur, and never owned to need of rest on the way, and certainly got none until they were well through the cordon, and made welcome at Cymer abbey. To cover their withdrawal, which was made at speed and with a picked escort, the main army following to guard the rear against detection and pursuit, David led a raid in the opposite direction, towards Carnarvon, from which base Dolbadarn was most threatened. He would take with him only volunteers, and Cynan claimed a place.

'You should not, you of all people,' said David, frowning. 'If you ever fall again into Edward's hands, you know what mercy to expect.'

'The better reason,' said Cynan, 'for inviting a different fate. Better a private blade than a public halter. By the same token, you should reason with yourself.'

'I twisted the halters that wait for all of us,' said David with his drear smile, but argued with him no more. So Cynan went with us.

For once we had luck that day, and broke through into the very outskirts of Carnarvon, and fired the outlying houses and barns. When they massed hastily to beat us off, in greater numbers than we could well stand and fight, David drew us away as though in headlong flight into the hills, and there waited for them in a wooded place, where we might pass for more than we were, and give them the impression that Dolbadarn was still strongly held, and dared take the offensive. The English approached confidently in the open, and we loosed our few archers at them, and then rode their first ranks down between the trees, and did disproportionate slaughter. And while they were in confusion we drew off and rode hard for the castle.

Cynan was beside me for more than half the homeward ride, but before we reached the lake he pitched suddenly sidewise over his horse's shoulder, and crashed to the ground. There was blood upon him, but we had not thought it his, and indeed most of it was not, for he had shown a very apt hand with a sword since he took to it. But when I lighted down

800

to him, and cut away the, matted folds of his gown at the left side, I saw that he had taken an arrow close under the heart, and part of the head had broken off in him. I do not believe he had even known, in the heat of fighting, that he was wounded, but the rough ride had shaken the steel into his heart, and he lived but a handful of minutes after. I never knew that man surprised, or at loss for a word. With barely time for a prayer, he said, knowing me and hoisting his brows as I bent over him: 'Write of me that my career in arms was glorious but brief!' And with that he choked on blood and died. And his bones are indeed laid in the land of Wales, as he chose, for we bore him on with us, and buried him at Llanberis. And what few possessions he had brought with him we took to Bere when we abandoned Dolbadarn, and gave to his nephew Morgan, who was among the garrison there.

In Castell-y-Bere we had certainly broken out of the iron ring into more remote mountains, within reach of Cardigan, where Meredith ap Owen's one remaining son at liberty, Griffith, was maintaining his outlaw warfare, but if he was close, he was fully as weak as we, and Valence was almost as close, installed in Llanbadarn castle with formidable forces, and Lestrange at Montgomery had so cleared his own region that he could be spared to come hunting us in the west. Though Bere was withdrawn into a narrow valley, on a shelf from which it covered all the passes, and could be approached in force by only one way, we had not the provisions to stock it for long siege, nor the men to operate at distance from it. There was no escape for us.

Lestrange with his Shropshire men was the first ordered to come and hunt us out, and him we held off successfully for two weeks, but by the middle of April Valence was moving up from the south with fourteen hundred reinforcements, and David, desperate for his family, resolved to take them with a protective force out of the castle, and maintain a roaming army in the mountains, from which he hoped he might yet help the garrison left in Bere by drawing off the attackers, or at least so hampering their movements that they could not effectively storm the place. David was so far Welsh on this point, at least, that he had a horror of being shut up in castles.

Again we took them secretly, all those beautiful, gallant children, still further into the recesses of Cader Idris, thanking God that at least spring was beginning, and the days not severely cold. Elizabeth never questioned, but what he required of her, that she did, and required as much of others, proud, capable, even-tempered, though God knows her heart was eaten hollow with fear for those chicks of hers, and for David. She rode a mountain pony nursing her youngest daughter in her arms, for the child was not yet a year old. Cristin carried the two-year-old. The rest were shared among us. The elder ones, who understood very well in what straits we laboured, bore themselves like royalty conscious of their rights and their wrongs. The little ones, who understood nothing, looked to their parents and trusted, and took these furtive flights and wanderings as great adventures, riding them buoyantly. I had David's second boy, Llewelyn, on the saddle before me, six years old, with eyes like the peat-pools of the mountain bogs in sunlight. He slept confidingly on my heart when he grew tired, and all my body warmed from the warmth of his leaning cheek and russet hair, and for a little while I believed in the future, I believed in truth again, and justice. David himself carried his heir, Owen, nearly nine years old, and too proud to ride double with anyone but his father. Somewhere among the body-guard, Godred also nursed one of the little girls. We had contrived but one litter, and that was given to Gwenllian, born princess of Wales, ten months old and fast asleep in Alice's arms. What could we do with her but take her with us wherever we were driven?

Cristin brought her pony close to mine, when we were clear and covered by twilight, and could speak. The child rode lightly in her arm, wound securely in her cloak. The hood had slipped back from her braided black hair, that showed no thread of grey, and her windflower face, only clearer and whiter and finer because she had gone so long hungry, like all of us. In that thin, translucent countenance her eyes had grown huge and deep. I never glimpsed her across courtyard or hall, even in these months when we passed speechlessly because there was all to be done and nothing to be said, without being enlarged and refreshed and agonised, never saw her but I saw her for the first time, young, solitary, voluntarily in peril for her lady and friend, and pleading for a dying man.

'For God's sake,' she said softly over the nestling child, 'stay close to David. I go in terror for him.'

I understood then that her compassion and her prayers were still for a dying man. She knew it, and I. And he knew it also.

'And what's to become of all these?' she said, grieving.

I said all those things that remained to be said by way of reassurance without lying, for it was impossible to lie to Cristin. I said that we were not yet at the end, nor near it, for the most difficult territory in all Wales still lay unconquered, and with the coming of spring and summer, we, light-moving and assured of stubborn support among the people, at least in Gwynedd, would have the advantage over troops hunting us in force. Time and endurance might, after all, fight on our side. And I said that even at the worst, the children were Edward's own kin, and guiltless even by his grim measure, and he did not eat children. But to say truth, I myself saw that this last attempt at comfort wiped out the first, for already I was contemplating the worst as though it had become the inevitable. I said in despair: 'I misuse words, and am of no comfort to you at all!'

'Ah, but you are!' said Cristin, flashing sudden fire from hollow grey eyes. 'It is my comfort that we ride here knee to knee, as we did that first time – do you remember? – on the way from the south to Llewelyn at Bala. That now I see you daily, even if we seldom speak and never touch, and now we shall be close until the end, and nevermore deprived of this unity. I tell you, I would not be anywhere on earth but where I am, with the remnant of Wales, with Elizabeth and these innocents, and with you. I would not change this honourable station for peaceful palaces, nor one stone of Snowdon for all the fat fields of England. So he said, and so I say. But above all, I lean on your nearness to sustain me, for without you even Wales would not be enough to keep up my heart.'

I had no words to answer her that did not sound too poor to be worth offering, so grievously I loved her, and had loved her from our first meeting. My life drew its last courage only from her, since my lord was lost to me. She was the one spring left me when all other wells had run dry. But I said never a word.

In a remote forest holding, difficult of approach, we bestowed the women and children, but such respite as they had there could not last long. The guard left to watch over them could be but small, and had to rely on secrecy rather than strength, but David with all the main part of his forces held ground between them and Castell-y-Bere, covering both as best he could. For ten days more he circled and raided, hindering all attacks upon the castle, picking off any unwary parties that ventured aside from the camps of the besiegers. He had lost none of his fire and audacity, but men he was losing with every exertion, as a wounded man loses blood, while Sprenghose was bringing up new levies to aid Valence, and the English had sufficient numbers to detach one army to link hands with Otto of Granson at Harlech, whence they could provision their camp by sea. There was no way we could get more food into Bere, and we knew they could not last long unless we broke through. On the twenty-fifth of April the starving garrison surrendered. They could do no more. We had left all our sick and wounded there, unable to keep pace of our movements. Only surrender could give them any chance of mercy. So our last castle was gone from us, and we were left a, homeless rabble hunted here and there in the mountains. And bitterest of all, the English appointed as constable of Bere the second son of Griffith ap Gwenwynwyn, Llewelyn's enemy, traitor and would-be assassin. Lewis de la Pole this young man called himself, after his family's new English style.

For a whole month following, both Valence and Lestrange remained on guard, repairing the defences of Bere and sending out search parties everywhere to hunt for David. By the end of April it was clear that the English grip on Merioneth was tighter than on Snowdon, and we could not hope to keep a way to the south open against so many. It was better to remove again, while we still had a shrunken but faithful army, into the north, to the heart of our land.

And so we did, bringing off Elizabeth and her household successfully, back to Llanberis, and thence, since the king's companies were everywhere probing cautiously along the valleys, and Dolbadarn, though still not occupied by the English, was too obvious a place of shelter, we took them up into the wilds of the mountains. Even the forests were too accessible. But there was a place we knew of, high in the bleak marshlands on the tree-line, withdrawn into cliffs behind, and covered by a mile of peat-bog in front, through which only those who knew the safe path could hope to pass without the risk of drowning or being sucked under. There were two huts there, where once hermits had chosen to live apart from the world, and one of these was but a wooden cell built directly on to the rock, but with a great and roomy cavern behind. Such places, utterly withdrawn from the world, the old saints of the Celtic church had loved, and now this hermitage made a primitive court for the last prince of Wales. So David had twice styled himself, in letters of credit he issued at Llanberis, though owning his right was irregular.

'It is only a pennant flown against the wind,' he said. 'For Llewelyn's sake I will not let them say there was no claimant after him, nor that he ever ceded what was his.'

Such treasure and valuables as he had he bestowed in hiding in the cave, and we made that and the two cabins habitable for the women and children, and left them a household guard under Godred and two other captains, and posted always a look-out at the outer end of the path, which was not marked out in any way for strangers, but had to be learned by heart. The remnant of the army kept aloof from this place, to avoid drawing attention to it, and was usually on the move, evading notice, striking where it could with secrecy, fighting now for little more than to remain at liberty. For Edward held all Snowdonia in his death-grip, and was piercing it at every point where penetration was possible. Scattered and isolated, Welshmen surrendered in despair everywhere, and the king made their pardon conditional on their joining in the hunt for his arch-enemy.

'He has almost everything he wanted,' said David, lying in the turf with me one night above the head-waters of one of Conway's western tributaries, at the rim of his camp. 'Only one thing he lacks – my heart to eat. He will be hungry until he gets it.'

Could I deny it? More vehemently even than with his soldiery, all the land and the air of Wales was filled and aching with Edward's hatred, all its rivers already poisoned by his venom.

'Oh, I know my fate before,' said David, staring unblinking upon his downfall and death. 'I knew it when I loosed this war upon Llewelyn, and when I refused the terms Peckham brought me – God knows how he got from Edward any offer that could bear to leave me alive! I cannot complain, I knew what I did. I do not repent! Of many things I repent, but not of this. And of one thing, Samson, I am so glad I thank God every hour. That Llewelyn is dead, safe for ever, cleanly slain with his war still in the balance, neither lost nor won. Edward cannot get at him in the grave. He will never be paraded in chains to satisfy that monstrous malice. As I shall,' he said, in the driest and grimmest of voices.

'It is not yet over,' I said, 'and he has first to get you into his hands.'

'No, not over yet. And we'll make him work for his triumph. But where is there left to run that his shadow does not fall? It is only a matter of time,' he said, 'and time is no longer on our side. I have done what I could, but I am not Llewelyn. To be killed in battle and never surrender is victory. My ending will not be like that.'

I cannot have meant it, but I said what men say to fend off certainty, that nothing is ever quite certain, that Edward had grown up in David's company, and time after time showed him favour . . .

'As a weapon aimed at Llewelyn,' said David, bitterly grinning.

. . . and that when he had his victory, and had his foe at his mercy, he might be appeased and relent. But there I stopped, for not only was that impossible, but in putting it forward as a thing to be hoped I was affronting David.

'You know better than that,' he said. 'This is a great man certainly – in all but three particulars, without which there can be no greatness. He lacks humility – oh, so do I, I know it! –but he is also insensible, as I am not, of other men except as objects for his own use. And he is utterly without magnanimity.'

He spoke as one having weighed and considered, and sure of his ground. And all his life long, David knew himself and other men through and through, and never blinked what he saw.

It was past the onset of twilight then, the glow of our camp-fires was turfed down to be invisible, but the sky above, a May sky of spring and blossom and promise, was clear and pure and full of soft light, untouched by our trouble. In that light I saw his face clear, honed to a finer edge by abstinence and exhaustion and the unflinching acceptance of the fear of death, his eyes bluer and larger within their fringed black of lashes and hollowed blue of sockets, his cheeks drawn smooth and gaunt beneath the jutting bone. And I ached for him then as I had never thought to ache again for any lord, since my own lord died. The one anguish I knew for an echo and reaffirmation of the other. Surely they were brothers, those two as far apart as the east from the west, and as close as two buds on the same branch.

'I am prepared for Edward,' said David, watching with some wonder the bowl of the sky that poured such distant lustre upon us, and would not darken in spite of the descending darkness. 'As for the children,' he said, feeling his way implacably along a planned course, 'they are his blood, and not through me, and therefore, I trust, sacred. Can Edward's blood err? They never chose their sire. And for Elizabeth, she is his close kin, he'll let her fret a while, and then make use of her, as he does of all who come within his grip. She is royal and valuable. He'll punish her some months, maybe as long as a year, for loving me, and then marry her to some prince or baron he needs for his own purposes, and proposes to buy, and be gracious at her marriage . . .'

He put up his hands suddenly and clutched his lean cheeks between them, and the wild black hair fell over his eyes, but even so I saw his face shattered as by a mailed blow, fallen apart in terrible grief, that had not quivered for his own doom. He said: 'Lisbet!' through his teeth, in a soft, whining moan, like a wild beast in pain, and then he folded forward into the thick turf, and wept like the breaking of the spring rains after long frost. And I held him, who had nothing else to give, hard on my heart, my head against his head. My mother's nurseling, my charge when he was five years old. God knows what I uttered into his ear. It can have had no mortal sense, I pray God it had some sense beyond mortal. One thing I know I said, like the voice of prophecy, for this I knew to be truth.

'Never fear for Elizabeth! You know her! That lady will never love any man but you to the day she dies, never regret anything done in loyalty to you, or anything suffered for your sake. And to her, if you are gone first out of this world, death will be only a leap into your arms.'

*　　*　　*

805

We came into June again, the height of the summer and the beginning of the end.

After many days of absence, David went again, with only myself to bear him company, to visit Elizabeth in her lonely hermitage. The guard in hiding at the outer end of the path passed us through, and returned to his place among the bushes, and we made the winding journey from rushes to heather clump, to the firm rim of a sullen pool, and so by those small marks of nature we had learned by heart, into the rising turf before the huts. The two little boys, brown and half-naked, came rushing out to fling themselves into David's arms, several of the girls like a flurry of butterflies after them, and Godred and his fellows, who had stood to alertly at the first sight of us in mid-passage, went back satisfied to their work. When he came to his family, David took pains to make himself fine and princely still, and wore jewellery, the great gold torque he most prized, and rings in his ears. The rest of his treasury, money, jewellery and plate, was hidden securely in the sand of the floor at the back of the cave.

We slept there the night over, the last night David ever lay with his Elizabeth. By night three guards kept the outer end of the path, ready to give warning at the first approach of any stranger, and all within could sleep in peace. For none but we and half a dozen, perhaps, of the men of those regions knew the place or the way in.

In the darkest of the night, before the dawn hours, we were startled awake by sudden alarms of steel clashing and voices shouting, and sprang up in confusion to reach for our weapons. We in the hut that covered the mouth of the cave were groping to our feet hastily when David burst out upon us from within, sword in hand, and behind him we heard one of the children crying, and the women's voices raised in comfort and reassurance, though God knows they themselves had little enough of either. We gathered to David, and would have fought it out there and then, as he may well have longed to do, but we waited on his order, and he never gave it.

They were there in the hut, blocking out the faint light at the doorway, two braced lances fronting us, and several bared swords, and behind them others, too many by far for us to kill and break loose through their ranks. And the little boys came crowding behind their father, and their sisters peered fearfully, clasped in the women's arms. He could have struck then, and forced them to give him a quick death, but he would not, with those beloved creatures watching. He laid a hand about the head of his heir, who bristled at his hip with his own small dagger in hand, and drew the boy close against his side, and said: 'Hush, now! Put up your bodkin, no need for that.' His voice was soft and even for reassurance.

He regarded the men before him, black against the paler space of sky, mere shapes to him, and said: 'You are looking for me, I think. Have the goodness not to alarm the women within, and my daughters.' And the hand that caressed and gentled his son pointed the exception he made for his menfolk, who were not of a mettle to give way to alarm.

'You are David ap Griffith, the king's rebel and felon?' said the foremost shadow, gravel-voiced.

'I am David ap Griffith, prince of Wales and lord of Snowdon,' said

David, and with a deliberate movement, made slowly to be seen and understood as well by us as by them, he reversed the sword in his hand and proffered the hilt in surrender.

They herded us out at lance-point, man, woman and child, to the half-circle of firm grassland, where the men of the body-guard were already overpowered and disarmed, two of them dead, others dripping blood from gashes got in the sudden onset, Godred among them. There must have been thirty at least of Edward's men in that hunting party, and others stationed at those points across the bog where the path turned, marking the way for the return journey. This was no chance discovery, someone who knew the track had taught them every step of the safe crossing.

They mounted us, the men with hands tied, the women free, of necessity, since they had to carry the babies in arms. Elizabeth, pale as death but mute and proud, never uttered complaint, and her sons did as she did. Some of the English troopers took up the other children to ride with them, and to their greater honour than their master, were gentle and soothing to them, even playful. But David they bound hand and foot with leather thongs, lashing his feet together under the horse's belly. Throughout that journey, Elizabeth never took her eyes from him, pouring towards him the whole force of the pride and courage and love that was in her, when she herself went in such dire need. Thus we set out on our dolorous ride into captivity.

We saw the three men of the outer guard as we passed, tossed bloodily among their hide of bushes, knifed down in the darkness by men who knew where to find them. The traitor had taught these English everything they needed to know. David marked the discarded bodies as he passed, and the frozen stillness of his face shook with grief and anger. And before we had gone far, the first rays of the sun broke clear of the peaks, and levelled like lances across the upland, glittering on David's golden torque, and gilding all the doomed beauty of his countenance, and all those hapless, lovely echoes of his grace that followed him, all those dark girls, fit brides for princes, and the two boys, heirs of the royal line of Gwynedd, themselves princes if there had been any justice left in the world. All of them passing through this mocking radiance of dawn into the darkness of Edward's shadow, and the stony coldness of his prisons.

CHAPTER XII

They made a savage show of us in Rhuddlan, parading our chains through the town and into the castle, with the whole garrison, menials, hangers-on and all, crowding to gaze at the arch-enemy in thrall. But there was one who did not come to feast his eyes, whether out of haughtiness or fear and guilt I cannot say, and that was Edward. Surely he savoured his poisoned joy in private, but from first to last he never showed his face.

In the wards of the castle, above the placid tidal waters of the Clwyd, we were torn apart, we men flung into tiny cells below ground, two by two where there was barely room for one, and the devil so contrived that I had Godred for partner. The women were also hustled away into close captivity, but above-ground, with the children to keep them living and believing in goodness, and with their needs supplied. It was but a veil of grace over an implacable purpose, but for all that we were glad of it then.

As for David, he vanished out of our knowledge and out of our sight, loaded down with chains. They say that he urgently prayed the king to give him audience face to face, but if he did, it can only have been for the sake of wife and children. Edward refused him. From the first he was resolved on killing, and memorably, and proceeded accordingly, sending out writs for a parliament to meet in Shrewsbury on the thirtieth day of September, to deal with 'the matter of Wales'. But no writs were sent to the bishops and abbots, for they, as is well-known, have no vote in cases of blood, and 'the matter of Wales' meant, first and last, the destruction of David.

The only one who did find her way into Edward's presence was Elizabeth, for at his peremptory summons she was brought before him in chains. She stood alone and small in face of that giant, and pleaded with dignity for husband and children, though never did she acknowledge, life-long, that David had ever done wrong, since for her he could do no wrong. All the king had to say to her was to upbraid her savagely for her treachery and ingratitude to him, and her guilt in countenancing David's rebellion, and not repudiating the sinner and blasphemer. And she reared her head and looked him in the eyes, that little brown mouse, once so demure and silent with others, and so loud and gay with David, and said in her mild, steely, deliberate voice:

'How have I offended against your Grace? You yourself gave me to my husband, with your own hand, when I was still a child, and taught me that my duty was to love and be serviceable to him all my days, to cleave to him loyally and be obedient to him. And so I have loved, according to your orders, and so will love him while I have breath. It was your gracious bidding I did throughout. How, then, have I been false to you?'

He did not strike her. No, not quite that, but he made her pay for her defiance, and dearest of all for the love she proclaimed and gloried in, even in her anguish. For he took away from her not only the children, but also Cristin and Alice, and every other soul who was familiar and dear to her. David she never saw again in this life. Edward knew how to punish. Her chains, after that public display of her servitude, were removed, but she remained solitary in close confinement.

Two months we lay thus out of the world, knowing nothing of what was happening outside our prison, not even whether David still lived, nor what had become of the children. And Godred and I, perforce, learned to sit side by side and exchange words without sickening or snarling, and I could feel at last nothing but grief and kindness for him, now we were both severed from Cristin and both prisoners. Sometimes he even sounded like the Godred I had first met, sharp-eyed for his own interests, wry in comment.

'God knows,' he said, 'I must have lost my gift for self-preservation, or I should have been off out of this long before it got to this pass. Why did I not take to my heels while the going was good?'

But he had not, and that was commendation enough. Truly I began to feel to him as to a brother, and even that was a possession to be valued, the awareness of another living creature. For there was nothing left after David was taken, nothing to hope for, nothing to fight for. In the south his three nephews, exhausted and forlorn, at last surrendered to the earl of Hereford, and were sent to imprisonment in the Tower of London. Everywhere the cause of Wales was lost, and in the bright summer the winter darkness fell upon us.

There was but one burning, bitter desire left in the heart of every true Welshman, and that was to hunt down the traitor who had betrayed the last prince of Gwynedd, and tear him apart. We even debated in our dungeon, sometimes, who it could have been, and could only suppose that it was some solitary countryman of those parts who had watched us come and go, and thought what he had learned worth a high price. Strange it is that the men of Wales were flighty and changeable, and turned their coats openly for security, or pique, or dudgeon, but never, or almost never, furtively for gain. And for that sin there was no forgiveness.

In early September we were haled forth and allowed to cleanse ourselves of the muck of our fetid cell, and brought out into dazzling light in the castle ward, again chained. And there for the first time we saw Cristin and Alice again, and the girl children, pale, mute and wary, all girded for travelling.

Last they brought out David, for we were bound into England, to Shrewsbury for his trial. He came forth emaciated and pale, but straight and immaculate as of old, with that gift he always had of emerging pure out of any contamination, but now so withdrawn that he seemed already to have abandoned this world. Only so could he pass through it for what was left of his course, unbroken. He wore the same golden jewellery he had on him at his capture, and his wrists were loaded with chains. Sixty archers were his escort through the town of Rhuddlan, no less, so high they prized him, and so greatly they still feared him. All we followed, the children with their nurses, the two knights and five troopers of the bodyguard, and I, his clerk and friend. I saw with my own eyes, and I say this was a more royal progress than many in which Edward played the chief part, and the bearing and grandeur of the prince excelled the mere overbearing bodily menace of the king. But of the ending there could be no question.

We went where we were driven, and we came where we were bound, into Shrewsbury, where all this history concerning Wales and England began. There David, five years old and handsome and clever, first confronted King Henry of England, and charmed him with his wit, and passed into his care, to become the companion and idol of the king's own son, three years younger. In the refectory of Shrewsbury abbey, where that meeting took place, Edward the king caused his sometime darling to be brought to trial of high treason, murder, and sundry other grave charges, before the lords of parliament assembled, and judges duly appointed by the king himself, presiding in his own cause, though in absence. They say he spent those days as guest of his chancellor, Robert Burnell, who had a princely mansion not far from the town. Certain it is that Edward never confronted David after his capture, never once encountered him eye to eye. He hung aloof at Acton Burnell, devouring his own gall and savouring the messages that brought him degree after degree of triumph over his enemy.

Yet what monarch who feels himself triumphant need exact what he exacted? I judge rather that he felt himself eternally bested, by what infernal arts only Llewelyn and David knew. How else to account for his malignant venom?

All we of David's train were shut in close hold within Shrewsbury castle, we saw nothing of that trial. Yet I see him behind my eyelids whenever I remember, still chained, and marked by his chains, still disdainful in his beauty, for what other resource had he but disdain? God knows where Elizabeth was then, not in Shrewsbury, at least he was spared that torture. He stood to be judged, knowing Edward had already decreed what the judgment should be. That he had done homage to Edward, and was in vassalage to him, that he would never be allowed to dispute. That he had revolted against that homage was plain to be seen. He had known, from long before, that he was a dead man. The means he had not known, but I doubt if even they astonished him. There was no barbarism invented by man and speciously justified by legal ingenuity that was enough to satisfy Edward's vengeance. He was forced to find something never before wreaked upon man by the courts of England, and to have his lawyers devise a formula by which it could be sanctioned. Thus for the first time, by awarding a separate part of sentence for every charge they alleged against the prisoner, they fashioned that frightful weapon Edward afterwards used freely against all who offended him, even boys barely grown, a death after his own heart.

And we who had served under David and been true to him were made to witness it. I speak of what I know. They brought us out of the castle prisons in our chains and made us line the open square about the gallows, that was set up at the high cross. The second day of October this befell, and all the town crowded and chattered there where the chief streets met, making a holiday of slaughter. Our part was to be displayed as the object of abhorrence and mockery, and to observe and report to others the reward of the only possible treason, treason against Edward. But I remember rather a great and awful silence when it came to the act, and whispers of pity and horror. The very sight of the tools of slaughter there assembled was terrible enough to sicken the mind, all the more as swordsman, stone slab, knives and burning brazier seemed then inexplicable and monstrous under the shadow of the gallows, itself the instrument of death.

What Edward had lusted after was done in full. They brought David out of his prison, and dragged him behind horses, bound hand and foot upon a hurdle, through the streets and lanes of the town to the high cross. I stood beside Godred, where we were posted, and for truth's sake and love's sake I would neither close my eyes nor turn them away. Everything he endured to suffer I endured to see, and if I still wake sweating and sobbing in the night after dreaming of it, he is at peace long since.

I looked upon him when they unbound and raised him, and for all the dust and dirt of the ways, I swear to you, he still shone, his gift had not left him. It was dry weather. Even for that I was grateful, that he was not utterly soiled and spoiled when he put them off and walked unaided to the foot of the ladder, and there put up his hands, joined by a short chain, and himself unloosed the gold torque from his neck, and handed it like unregarded largesse to the hangman's man who stood at the ladder's foot. He turned back the collar of his cotte and shirt, and looked round him once at earth and sky, and then I saw his face full, an alabaster face from a tomb, and the early autumn sun caught the blue of his eyes still vivid in their bruised hollows, frantic life looking through the submissive stillness of death. He saw neither me nor any other among all those frozen hundreds, his gaze was fixed only on light and air and colour, the brightness of the world. Then he turned and climbed the ladder without faltering, and leaned his head to the noose. He had said truly, he was Llewelyn now, and he did not disgrace him.

When he felt those below lay hand to the ladder to jerk it away, he did not wait to slip tamely into the strangling noose, but suddenly braced himself and sprang strongly out into air, and dropped with a great, shuddering shock that caused all those watching to gasp and groan. I pray, I pray God still, though it is all past, that he did what he willed to do, that he broke his neck in that leap, and all that passed after was contemptible to him and vain. They say it can be done, by a resolute man who has the heart, when he must go, to go quickly. Certainly he never uttered sound after. But I do not know! I do not know! I wish to God I did.

Whether with a living body or a dead, Edward had his way with all that was left of David. They cut him down after barely a minute, they stretched him on the slab, they slit that fine trunk open, tore out heart and bowels and cast them bubbling into the brazier. Godred beside me stood with head bent, barely able to stand at all, he shook and swayed so, and retched and swallowed vomit, his eyes tight shut. I watched to the end. I owed it to David to know and to remember, to remain with him to the last, and if ever vengeance came within my grasp, to avenge. And I owed it to Llewelyn, who had sent me to him with his dying breath, to be to the last brother as I had been all my life through to the second.

When the headsman at last struck off that raven head that had rested so often in half-mocking, half-jealous affection against my shoulder, and I knew that he was free, the rest, though unseemly butcher's work, mattered not at all. That was not David they quartered like meat to display as a dreadful warning in four of the cities of the realm. He heeded it no longer. He was far out of reach.

'You can open your eyes now,' I said to Godred, between comfort and contempt, 'it is all over.'

After that day, King Edward had no further use for the women who had cared for David's children, for good reason. The two boys, Owen and Llewelyn, had already been sent away to close confinement in Bristol castle, and there or in some similar fastness they surely lie to this day, for never, never must that dreaded and hated stock be left free to breed other princes to poison Edward's life. And the girls, it seemed, had also been disposed of in some way, for suddenly I was haled out of my cell and told that since I was but a clerk, and not a soldier, I was to be set free to return to Aber, and escort the royal nurses home to that maenol. The knights and troopers were held several weeks longer, until Edward was more secure in his administration of his newly conquered territories, and even we were required to take an oath of submission before we left. I was glad that Godred did not know why I was removed from him, but it would have been useless trying to win his release in my place, Cristin's husband though he might be, for Edward was very slow to set free any man who had borne arms against him. As I, indeed had, to the best I could, but a clerk should be a clerk, and so I was set down in his lists.

I was given a letter of safe-conduct, permitting me and my companions to travel only to Aber, and reside only in Aber, for he had not as yet extended his administration, and for the time being the Welsh castellans who had submitted continued in office, only the major fortresses were held and garrisoned by English forces. The king wanted a settled people, and where he could compel residence in a fixed place, that he did. It made the task of his bailiffs easier.

Joy we had none then, in any relief or any mitigation, yet there was an aching thankfulness in me when I took my safe-conduct on the appointed day, and waited for Cristin and Alice to come out to join me. And only Cristin came.

She was thin, pale and quiet, with huge, dark-rimmed eyes that devoured half her face, but in their depths there was still the purple flame that kindled when we two came together. We stood a long moment simply looking at each other, after long severance and silence.

'Alice has found a household to take her in,' she said, answering the first unasked question. 'She is English, and some of Hereford's Bohun kinsmen have offered her service. There is no one but me.'

So for us two it was like, and dolorously unlike, that first journey we made together, for we rode, as then, home to Gwynedd, to a royal seat, but now the home was ravaged, the princes dead, the mountains defiled, the land ravished. Yet we two rode together, and there was an anguished, elegiac sweetness in that. I asked her, as we mounted, what she had failed to answer without being questioned: 'What has he done with the children, that he has taken them from you?' And I longed for her to say that Edward had given them back, the girls at least, surely the little ones, to their mother. But Cristin's eyes filled with tears, and she was slow in answering, for the strangling pain that closed her throat.

'He has sent them by some of the queen's women,' she said at last, 'to be brought up in the Sempringham convents. Not even together! They are scattered, they will grow up solitary, not even knowing their sisters. The twins will die of it.'

But David's stock and Elizabeth's did not die easily, they were strong and splendid and sunlit. For such there is no escape into the grave.

'Gwenllian, too?' I asked.

'Gwenllian, too. She is gone to Sempringham in her cradle. They will none of them ever get out,' said Cristin with bitter certainty. 'He will see to it that none of his magnates ever look upon such beauty, to want them in marriage. They will be nuns before they are of age, and no choice offered them. Do you think he will ever let David's daughters, or Llewelyn's, bear children?'

I thought of all those bright beings, so apt for future courtship and love, shut up through long lives of silent rebellion, only to die in captivity at the end of it, and I thought that perhaps after all David had done well to die, even so barbarously. And I was sorriest of all for Elizabeth, who had possessed all possible joy and fulfilment for a time, and been robbed of all, and was barely twenty-six years old, with a life before her totally empty, a life I am sure she did not want. God knows what Edward has done or will do with her. I have not heard of her again. Yet she spoke her mind to her persecutor, and vaunted her love like a blow in his face, and for that I shall always love her, and always be glad.

Having the king's safe-conduct, we made no haste, and had no troubles on the way. Four days we rode leisurely together, my love and I, and there was no third with us, neither friend nor foe, and our tongues were loosened, and talked freely of all that had been, in a strange autumnal world all hush and afterglow, for October was soft, mellow and sad. We spoke also of Godred, a thing we had never done, for he was prisoner still, and we felt for him only pity and sorrow, for he was caught in this immense grief as we were, and with less means of surviving it. I told her how I had left him, not ill but in sorry enough condition. And she told me what David had not known, or he might have told me long before.

'I did not tell you,' she said, 'how I came to lose the child. Nor of the life he led me then, slavering over me, showing me off to the world, he who had never wanted a child for its own sake, but only as a weapon to strike at you and me. If he could have pretended the child was yours, he would have done it, while exulting that it was his. But he could not, it was conceived long after we were in England, and you were left behind in Wales. I suppose he began to value it, after his fashion, but mostly as a blow at you, and time and again he trailed your name before me, this way and that, tormenting me, until I was sick from containing the love I felt for you, and the loathing he gave me for what he had implanted in my womb.'

'That is not true,' I said. 'You could not feel loathing for any hapless child, however conceived. I know you, and I know.'

'That was my penance,' she said, 'if I could not help loving while I loathed. But in the end he went too far in his misuse of you, gloating that you were far away and left like a fool childless for your virtuous pains. And I turned on him, and went down to his level in my rage, and asked him how he knew, in his wisdom, that there were not other men even in England I might prefer to him, and men capable of getting a child. And he struck me,' she said, remembering without hatred or regret, 'a great blow with his fist, here in my breast. I was standing at the head of the steps going down from a gallery, and I fell all that flight, rolling and clutching and missing my hold. They picked me up in labour, and within two hours I miscarried. It was the only time he ever struck me, and he killed his son.'

That was his judgment. And she had told no one how she came to fall, not even Elizabeth.

'Why speak of it?' she said, turning upon me her wan and grieving smile. 'It was done and past. He blamed me, and in some measure I was to blame. He suffered, too. And I was free of him, for he troubled me no more. And now there's nothing left but pity and sorrow, now he is lost in this misery like the rest of us. How can I hate him now? And when he creeps home, how can I desert him if he needs me?'

'No,' I said, resigned, 'I see you cannot. Nor can I do him any injury. He held out to the end with the rest of us, I have shared his prison, and left him still buried alive now I am free. His rights are as safe with you and me as if he rode here between us.'

'I shall be still his dutiful wife,' she said implacably, 'if that is what he needs for healing and help. There is nothing else I can do. It does not touch, it never did, it never will, the love I bear to you.'

'So be it,' I said. 'But God has given us this respite in the time of our most need, a harvest to keep us alive through the winter to come, and it would be ungrateful not to use it.'

And use it we did, in such ways as were allowed to us, living out together in shared tenderness and devotion all the love that had no other means of living, like a soul without a body. For those few days, at least, there was no need to contain the words for which we hungered and thirsted. I said to her all the things I had ever wanted to say, I touched her, went hand in hand with her, and at night, where we lodged, I sat with her late over the fire, and kissed her without sin when we parted. And we were middle-aged, stubborn, abstinent in the face of great longing, she forty-seven years old, I well past fifty, and love was as painful and wonderful as ever it had been in youth, more painful, more wonderful, by reason of that long, fasting loyalty, a love more intimate than passion and infinitely larger than lust.

We came to Aber towards the end of October. It was like a household of ghosts, from old habit learned in life still moving about tasks that no longer had meaning, a headless household, bereft of lord, and lady, and family. Cristin was lady-in-waiting to none, nurse to none, and I clerk to none, and bereaved of my friend. All we did was simply wait to know Edward's mind for us, and to receive Edward's seneschal and officers. The very hall rang emptily to our tread. The sea moaned along Lavan sands, and I noticed as never before how the crying of the seagulls over the shallows was more than wild and sad, desperate in defiance, like the shrieking of beings driven mad with grief.

Late in November the two knights and five troopers of David's body-guard came home from their captivity, wretched, gaunt, half-starved, bearing the marks of their chains. Godred wept when he came into Cristin's presence, and went like a heartbroken child into her arms. Over his shoulder I saw her face, blanched and steadfast and without hope, her great eyes clinging to me as he clung to her, just as I had seen it in Dolwyddelan long before, when I brought her lost husband back to her, and watched the light of her face go out as he embraced her. And even as then, I turned and went away blindly, and left them together.

It was the second night after the guards came home that I awoke suddenly after midnight, and she was standing beside my bed, white, mute and strange. I started up and reached to take her hand, in terror that something evil had happened to her, that he, perhaps a little demented from his hardships, had done her some cruel harm. She was cold and stiff, but her hand gripped mine hard, and before I could do more than whisper her name in alarm and dismay, she laid her free palm over my mouth to hush me.

'Let me in to you,' she said, low and fiercely, 'this once let me in! Take me into your bed! No, say no word!' she pleaded, gripping my cheeks with finger-tips icy-cold. 'I entreat you, if you love me, ask me nothing, nothing, only take me in to you at last!'

She shook so, and was so strange, I could not believe she knew what she did, so to tempt me against all that she and I had understood and agreed long since. I held her, and drew her down to sit beside me, and asked her wildly: 'What is it? What has he done to you?'

'Nothing,' she said, and her white face smiled, but terribly, 'to me, nothing! No one has touched or harmed me. I know what I am doing! I am not mad, I forget nothing. Ask no more questions, only trust me and take me into your bed. This once take me!'

I understood nothing, except that she was frantic like a bird trapped in a narrow room, and crying to me for rescue, and even at this pass I could not believe anything she did was without reason and virtue. And I am as much a man as any other man, and what she begged of me was what I most starved for, so that only then did I know fully the magnitude of my hunger. Confounded between anguish and joy, I flung back the covers and drew her in beside me, and at the passion of her embrace I embraced her again with all my heart and soul, and was lost and drowned in agonising bliss. Dismay and wonder I forgot, there was nothing left in the world but the desperation and discovery of our coupling, and the delight of feeling her grow warm and supple and young in my arms, and the mutual, measureless tenderness of her caresses and mine, and our two breaths mingling in silken endearments and fathomless sighs. We loved like frenzied creatures, as though not only for the first, but also the last and only time. And when we were exhausted, we fell asleep in each other's arms.

When I awoke the first light was already turning from grey to pallid gold, and she was gone.

I rose hastily and did on my clothes, for the memory of her passion made me fear for her, and still I did not know what had happened to bring her to my bed. I went to the room where her own bed was, where Godred had joined her on his return, but the door stood half-open, and there was no one within. The brychan was tumbled, as though someone had lain there, and Godred's frayed and tattered leather jerkin lay tossed on the floor beside it. I saw that the stitching of one seam gaped, and a needle with waxed thread was stabbed into it, as though Cristin in resignation and compassion had taken up the coat to mend it, after he was asleep. Godred had drunk deep in his misery, as did so many of us then, and might well have slept while she was still wakeful.

I do not know why this should have disquieted me, but so it did, for surely Cristin had dropped this jerkin where it lay when she came in stark demand and desperate hunger to where I was sleeping. But what there could be in a half-mended coat to turn her away from all former resolves was dark to me, nor could I guess where she was gone now, or Godred either. I went back very uneasily to my own chamber, and looked about for any trace that she had ever been there, and beneath the pillow where her head had lain was a linen wimple which I knew belonged to her, folded small about some coiled object that slid and unfolded heavily within the cloth. I shook it out upon the bed, and stood staring uncomprehendingly at a broad collar of links of gold, twisted and fitted together like leaves, fine work and known to me. There were not two such. I had seen it about David's throat when the English came and seized us all in the cavern beyond the bog. I had seen it last when with his chained hands he unfastened it from about his neck and handed it to the hangman's apprentice at the foot of the ladder.

There was no other hand could have placed this thing under my pillow but Cristin's hand. There was no other place she could have found it, but hidden inside the padding of the leather jacket she had been mending, Godred's jacket. This was what sent her half-mad to my bed, and this she had left for me to decipher after she was gone. Having found it, how could she remain one moment with the man who had provided the goods for which this was payment? But neither could she speak out his eternal shame, only in this way, silently, after she was gone. Who but the betrayer is rewarded with the adornments of the betrayed?

Only for a moment, half-stunned as I was, did I reason stupidly that Godred had been taken with the rest of us, even wounded, though it was but a scratch, that he had rotted in prison beside me, been held like the rest of the troopers when I was released. So he had, and how better bargain to escape all suspicion? His confinement had been no more than tedious, doubtless after I was removed he fared reasonably well, but it was expedient that he should await his dismissal in meek submission like the rest of the household, for his protection. He was sure of his pay. Small chance the executioner's boy had ever had of keeping that princely largesse, it was already promised.

There was no other way this could have been. But now where was Cristin? Where was Godred? She left him sleeping there, snoring, perhaps, but not so drunk but that he awoke after she departed, to find the bed unpressed beside him, no Cristin there. With his conscience that would fetch him clean out of sleep and out of drink, fumbling for his secret and finding its hiding-place ravished of treasure. If David's torque was gone, Godred's security, Godred's very life, was gone after it. What could he do then but run? He had planned to walk humbly and innocently in Wales like the rest of us, until his advancement in the new administration could pass for acceptable, but now that road was stopped and his gains gone. He would run, yes, knowing his secret would not long be a secret, and only the English could now guarantee his safety. But empty-handed? Perhaps he also had David's ear-rings somewhere in hiding, but they were a small prize compared with this splendid collar from round my breast-brother's mangled throat.

I remembered everything, and understood everything, all his monstrous duplicity, how he had sat beside me in Edward's prison sourly mourning his failure to flee from his allegiance while there was time, and I like a fool had warmed to him for staying at his peril, how he had stood by me sick and shivering at the death, and had not had the hardihood to look on at the abomination he had not scrupled to bring about. I knew why he had chosen this devious way, sharing our captivity and returning with us to Aber, rather than taking service with one of Edward's captains and openly casting in his lot with England. And I knew where he was gone. All we were bereft of our treasure, our princes, our liberty, even our land, what were a few bits of gold and coin abandoned in the sand to us? But his treasure was of this world. He had come back to dig up the balance of his thirty pieces of silver, and he was off in haste now to secure it, before he fled to safety in some English garrison.

I knew then what I had to do. But first I had to find Cristin, and satisfy myself that no harm had come to her, that she would wait here for me and trust me. For I was still confused, and had not yet realised the meaning of her action in full. I understood only after I had hunted through Aber and failed to find her. She came of a long line of bards and warriors, the honour of Wales was her honour. And when I came to belt on sword and dagger, I found I had no dagger, it had been unclasped from the straps sheath and all, and no one but Cristin could have taken it. She had taken upon herself the vengeance of Wales. I had not mistaken that shattering union of ours in the night, it was indeed to be the first, last and only time.

Godred had a good grey horse, and it had been returned to him for the journey home. In trivial matters Edward was honest. There was but one of that colour among us, and it was gone from the stables. The sleepy boy who was just rolling out of the hay of the loft said that he had not heard anyone come or go in the night, but there had been someone saddling up below about an hour before I came. He had not come down to see, but he had looked out at the loft door, and seen a young fellow canter away towards the postern gate, no more than a boy by the cut of him, and his voice below when he gentled the horse was light and young. Then I knew that I was right.

I took the best horse I found, and saddled and rode, inland from the postern gate like Cristin before me, like Godred before Cristin. She had left him sleeping, and come to me to give and receive but once what was her due and mine, and before first light had risen softly from beside me, and taken my dagger, to awake him and do justice upon him face to face, and if need be die in doing it. I knew her. She would never have struck a sleeping man. But he had already fled, and like me, Cristin knew where he would go. She was his wife, a traitor's wife, and there was no way of cleansing herself of his shame but in his blood.

That was no very long ride, but a hard one, by the upland way that she had taken, and it was Cristin I had to overtake, rather than Godred. For I reasoned as I rode that if he reached the cave before full daylight, as he well might, he would lie up there in hiding until the darkness came down again, rather than risk being hunted by day, as he surely would be once the word went out that he was Judas. One more night ride, and he could be safe in Carnarvon, which was strongly garrisoned by the English. They might not countenance Welsh traitors as approvingly as Edward did, but they would not let Edward's lap-dog be handed over to Welsh vengeance. There was time, therefore, for Godred, but little time to forestall Cristin, since she had an hour's start of me. I pressed hard, but saw no horseman ahead. Cristin had been in no less haste.

If she had crossed the bog that protected the hermitage as often as I had, while Elizabeth kept her wild court there, I should never have overtaken her in time. But when I came to the broken tangled copse where our look-outs had been slain, there was a brown horse on a long tether grazing the thinning turf. Godred had crossed mounted. She was wary of attempting that, and had left her mount here and chosen to feel her way along the bog path on foot, to be a lighter burden on the quaking ground, and have a surer sense of the security of her footholds as she went. For a different reason I left my horse beside hers, for a man afoot could go partially screened half the way, but a man on horseback would be seen. I did not want her to hurry, but to go slowly. I knew my way here very well, and hoped to gain on her if she had not already reached firm ground.

I saw her when I was close to the halfway mark, slight and dark among the waist-high rushes and the tufted reeds, and blessedly she was so intent on picking her way with care that she never looked back. She had not given a thought to pursuit. I was able to overtake her unheard until I was close, and the the rustle of the reeds alarmed her, and she turned and knew me, and was alarmed no more. I laid my arms round her, and she let her head rest against my shoulder, and neither of us said a word. When I held out my hand for the dagger she turned it and offered me the hilt, surrendering into my hands her quarrel and the quarrel of Wales. And I led her in my arms the rest of the way to safe ground, and we came to the door of the cliff-hut together. There I kissed her and went in, and closed the door after me.

The sun, even on a brighter day, would not have shed much light under these rocks until afternoon, and it was dim and cold in the hut, but the entrance of the cave beyond was shaped in fitful, flickering light. He was there. He had kindled a fire, and lit two torches and wedged them among the rocks to give him light. The brychans that had served David's children for beds were still there, and a stone table, and some other desolate reminders. At the back of the cavern Godred was on his knees, raking with careful hands through the deep sand-pocket where David's valuables were buried, and bringing up coins, one by one, to lay in a pile beside the trinkets he had already raised. Some leathern pouch that held them had rotted or parted at the neck and spilled the money into the gravel.

I made no sound in the doorway, and the light was before me, I had a long moment to look upon him before he knew I was there. He had lost that curious, furtive look with which he had come home, there was no mask to hide his greed, and rage, and resolution. All his life his first charge had been to take good care of Godred. If he had lost his best piece of gold, he was determined to have all he could get of what was left, and above all his life. And this was my half-brother, my father's son. Gwynedd was beset with brothers, they were the cords of the rack that broke her joint from joint.

I took one step forward into the cave, and he leaped about and stood crouching and staring, the stone table between us. He knew me, and slowly he straightened up, wary and alert, and gradually a small, malicious smile curled his lips.

'You,' he said softly. 'I might have known! Where else would she go but to you? Have you come to make sure of your share even of this, now you've got the other? Oh, but I know my dear brother, my father's bastard, well enough to know he'll have always a noble motive for all he does! You're here to execute the justice of Wales? *You*, the by-blow of a passing guest and a witless maidservant?'

He was trying to provoke me into some rash onset, but it was strange, I felt no need to speak word to him, and never did so again. I drew my sword, and went in towards him, and he circled and kept the table of stone between us, and still taunted and sweated, watching for a false move.

'You really believe you've followed me here to avenge David? Fool, all you've done is seize on the first, best pretext you ever were offered to be rid of me! What you want is to possess your brother's wife – in purity, oh, in *purity*, naturally! Saint Samson, too chaste to stoop to adultery! Half-man, do you still not know what you are? A whole man would have taken her long ago!'

I was not moved, I came on still, and took care not to veer from between him and the doorway. I levelled the sword before me, and then he raised and showed his empty hands, and I saw by the firelight the sweat glistening on his forehead. Well I knew he must have a sword somewhere in that place, but it was not on him, and he did not offer to get it. And I, without a word, flung sword and scabbard from me into the corner where his little hoard lay, sending the coins rolling, and after the sword the dagger. I came on with my bare hands.

I should have known he would always have one more trick in him. He stood up straight and ceased to circle, coming slowly into the open rock floor facing me, his hands at shoulder-level and a little spread, as if to reach for a wrestling hold. But as I flung myself upon him his right hand flashed to the back of his neck where the hood of his capuchon hung in folds, and the blade of a long hunting-knife caught the torch-light and slashed down my sleeve and into my left thigh in a glancing wound. If I had not flinched away from the flash of light, that stroke would have come close to my heart. I had gone for his throat, and forced his head back with my right hand, but I had to use the left to grapple his wrist and hold the knife off from me as best I could. We fell together, the fine sand flying, and hearing the long blade clash flatly on rock I rolled sidewise over it to pin his arm down. He was taller than I, and with a longer reach. It did not matter. It did not matter that he had a weapon and I had none. He never heaved free from my weight to use his knife again, for I got both hands round his throat and clung, he flapping and threshing and choking under me, with his free hand clawing at my wrists. When I felt even the hand on which I lay loose its grip of the knife's haft, forgetting everything but the struggle for breath, I rolled over to the right, dragging him with me, and rolled him beneath me again in the scattered faggots and ashes of his fire. Even with two hands he was past doing more than claw the skin from my wrists and forearms, and when in his throes he again thought of the knife, and groped desperately about the floor for it, it was out of his reach. I think I kept my grip on his throat long after he died. I think I said to him over and over: 'Remember David! In hell remember David!' But by then he may already have been dead.

I got up from him slowly at last, with bloody, aching hands, and stood and looked at what I had done. I do not remember any remorse or any exultation. There could have been no other ending. I left him there, sprawled like a trampled spider by his fire, and left the coins and bits of gold finery beside him. Of what value were they now to any man? Wales was avenged on Godred, yes, but not on Edward. Never on Edward! Never until judgment day!

I went out, and Cristin was sitting on the doorstep with her hood drawn over her hair, and her arms round her knees. When she heard me come she rose and lifted her head, and her sad face became glorious. She came and held me in her arms, breast to breast, and I felt great breaths of thankfulness and ease drawn down deep, deep into her body. I came to her red-handed, stepping over her husband's corpse, and she did not turn from me. David had foretold it, long before.

She asked nothing, and I told her nothing then. There would be a time for that. I did not kiss her. The bitterness of rage and hatred was too rank on my mouth. But I led her back over the marsh in my arm, and there we sat by the horses and rested a while, and she bound up the gash in my thigh, and washed the blood from my wrists with water from one of the pools. Only then did I remember Godred's horse, that must be somewhere there about the hermitage. We sent to fetch him later. I could not go back then. I was so full of the deaths of princes and the imperative of vengeance, there was no more action left in me.

After a while a kind of peace came back to us, so strange at such a time that I could not at first account for it, grateful as I was, but then it came to me that it was the removal of Godred that made the world at its darkest endurable. Not only because there was no longer a malignant shadow barring Cristin from me, but because the air we breathed, however chill and sad, was cleansed of the venom that had sought to poison even honour itself, even chastity. In the great darkness there remained this small, clear light, and having lost the land that had been ours, we were given seisin of a free country once again, narrow and profound, the love we bore each other, love justified, married love. We grew aware of it at the same moment. She turned to me, and I to her, and we lay down in the turf together, in that bleak place that so well represented such future as was left to us and to Wales, and loved a second time for affirmation, not wildly as in the night, but with solemn tenderness and tears.

Together, afterwards, we rode home to Aber.

It is not less dark in Wales because we have a private light, a little marsh-light that leads faithfully and does not betray. In the night of Edward's shadow, it is still the gift of God that two may go hand in hand, and not be utterly desolate. If there is another hope, it is that no night, no winter, can last for ever. And when there is promise of another daybreak, there will still be Welshmen to awaken and arise. For I will not believe that my lord has lived and died to no purpose.

Now I have made an end of the chronicle of the Lord Llewelyn, son of Grfffith, son of Llewelyn, son of Iorwerth, lord of Gwynedd, the eagle of Snowdon, the shield of Eryri, first and only true Prince of Wales, and of David, his brother. All true men who read, pray for them and for us, that this darkness may pass.

GLOSSARY

ap: son of

brychan: plaid or blanket of homespurn, and by extension the truckle beds so furnished

cantref: hundred: regional division of land, literally 'hundred hamlets'

castellan: custodian of the castle

clas: monastic community of lay canons under an abbot, and including at least one other priest

commote: division of land, smaller than the cantref, on which the courts of justice are based

crwth: small stringed instrument, played with a bow

distain: steward, the chief official of a principality

edling: the official heir, nominated by a prince in his own lifetime and accepted by his people

fawr, mawr: great

fychan: lesser: attached to a name often distinguishes son from father

goch, coch: red

llyn: lake

llys: court: the royal seat in each region of a principality

maenol: manor; in particular the fortified dwelling of a chief

penteulu: the captain of the prince's permanent household army

saesneg: English: thus Maelor Saesneg is the commote of Maelor which thrusts into English territory

talaith: the gold diadem of royal office

teulu: the prince's household army

tref: homestead or hamlet

ynys: island

ystrad: valley: Ystrad Tywi is the Vale of Towy